THE BIG BOOK OF CYBERPUNK

ALSO EDITED BY **JARED SHURIN**

The Djinn Falls in Love and Other Stories
(with Mahvesh Murad)

The Outcast Hours
(with Mahvesh Murad)

Irregularity

The Lowest Heaven
(with Anne C. Perry)

THE BIG BOOK OF
CYBERPUNK

Edited by

JARED SHURIN

VINTAGE BOOKS
A DIVISION OF PENGUIN RANDOM HOUSE LLC
NEW YORK

A VINTAGE BOOKS ORIGINAL 2023

Introduction and compilation copyright © 2023 by Jared Shurin

All rights reserved. Published in the United States by Vintage Books,
a division of Penguin Random House LLC, New York, and distributed in Canada
by Penguin Random House Canada Limited, Toronto.

Vintage and colophon are registered trademarks
of Penguin Random House LLC.

Cataloging-in-Publication Data is available at the Library of Congress.

Vintage Books Trade Paperback ISBN: 978-0-593-46723-7
eBook ISBN: 978-0-593-46724-4

Book design by Nicholas Alguire

vintagebooks.com

Printed in the United States of America
1st Printing

CONTENTS

SOCIETY

CULTURE   505

CONTENTS

CONTENTS

I'm an optimist about humanity in general, I suppose.

—Tim Berners-Lee

EDITOR'S NOTE

The Big Book of Cyberpunk is a historical snapshot as much as a literary one, containing stories that span almost seventy-five years.

Cyberpunk, at its inception, was ahead of many other forms of literature in how it embraced (and continues to embrace) progressive themes. Cyberpunk, at its best, has strived for an inclusive vision of the present and future of society. Accordingly, the stories within *The Big Book of Cyberpunk* discuss all aspects of identity and existence. This includes, but is not limited to, gender, sexuality, race, class, and culture.

Even while attempting to be progressive, however, these stories also use language, tropes, and stereotypes common to the times and the places in which they were originally written. Even as some of the authors challenged the problems of their time, their work still includes problematic elements. To pretend otherwise would be hypocritical; it is the essence of cyberpunk to understand that one can simultaneously challenge and deserve to be challenged.

Cyberpunk is also literature that exists in opposition, and the way it expresses its rebellion is very often shocking, provocative, and offensive. It is transgressive by design, but not without purpose, and I tried to make my selections with that principle in mind.

—Jared Shurin

INTRODUCTION

THE DAY OF TWO THOUSAND PIGS

THERE ONCE LIVED A MAN who was naked, raving, and could not be bound. According to the Gospel: "He tore the chains apart and broke the irons on his feet." It turns out (spoiler) he was possessed. The demons were exorcised and cast out of the man. Lacking a human host, the demons possessed an entire herd of pigs (two thousand of them, says Mark!). They then ran straight into the ocean.

The man, liberated of foul influences, sat there "dressed and in his right mind." The people around him were comforted. The day of demons was behind them. After a brief period of naked, raving chaos, order had been restored.

Or so they thought.

The biblical story of Legion is an iconic one, perhaps the most well-known exorcism in Western culture.* It is also, perhaps, the perfect metaphor for cyberpunk. It is literature unchained, naked, and raving . . . but only briefly. Depend-

ing on which expert source you read, this day of demons lasted a decade or a few short years—or, according to some, it died even before it was born. The pigs went straight into the sea. Order restored.

There's no question that cyberpunk had a shockingly brief existence as a cohesive entity. Born out of science fiction's new wave, literary postmodernism, and a perfect storm of external factors (Reaganism, cheap transistors, networked computing, and MTV), the genre cohered as a tangible, fungible *thing* in the early 1980s, most famously exemplified by the aesthetic of Ridley Scott's *Blade Runner* (1982) and the themes of William Gibson's *Neuromancer* (1984). The term *cyberpunk* itself, as coined by Bruce Bethke,† came into being in 1983. The

---

* It also inspired one of the best *X-Men* characters.

† Bethke's story—found in this volume—was written in 1980 and first published in 1983. The term was quickly adopted by the legendary science fiction editor Gardner Dozois, who used it to describe the

neologism captured the zeitgeist: the potential of, and simultaneous disillusionment with, techno-capitalism on steroids.

Cyberpunk was born of the punk ethos. A genre that, in many ways, existed *against* a mainstream cultural and literary tradition, rather than *for* anything definable or substantive in its own right. This is, at least, an argument posited by those who believe the genre peaked—and died—with Bruce Sterling's superb anthology *Mirrorshades* (1986). Accepted as the definitive presentation of cyberpunk, Sterling had pressed a Heisenbergian self-destruct button. Once it was a defined quality, cyberpunk could no longer continue in that form.

Although this is a romantic theory (and cyberpunk is a romantic pursuit, despite—or perhaps because of—the leather and chrome), it is not one to which I personally subscribe. While collecting for this volume, I found that the engine of the genre was still spinning away, producing inventive and disruptive interpretations of the core cyberpunk themes through to the start of the next decade. These include novels and collections such as Kathy Acker's *Empire of the Senseless* (1988), Misha's *Prayers of Steel* (1988), Richard Kadrey's *Metrophage* (1988), Lisa Mason's *Arachne* (1990), and Richard Paul Russo's *Destroying Angel* (1992); as well as movies, television programs, and games such as Paul Verhoeven's *RoboCop* (1987), the *Max Headroom* series (1985), FASA's *Shadowrun* (1989), and Bullfrog's *Syndicate* (1993). Meaningful social commentary was still being produced as well: Donna Haraway's "A Cyborg Manifesto," for instance, as well as the cypherpunks and even the first steampunks.*

By the mid-1990s, however, the hogs had well and truly left for the ocean. The mundan-

ity of the technocratic society had been firmly realized—as expressed, for example, in Douglas Coupland's *Microserfs* (1995). And at the other extreme, the visual aesthetic had proved overwhelmingly popular, thriving independently of the ideas (or even the material) that spawned it. *Johnny Mnemonic* (1995) serves as a painful example of how the visual tropes of cyberpunk no longer bore any connection to its original themes. A bit like Frankenstein's monster, the cyberpunk style had gone lumbering off on its own, inadvertently appropriating the name of its creator.[†] Cyberpunk slouched along in increasingly glossy and pastiche-ridden forms, but its frenetic glory days were now truly behind it. Cyberpunk qua cyberpunk had been pulled apart by the twin poles of banal reality and hyperactive fantasy.

Why would a *Big Book* be given over to something that lived, thrived, and died in such a short period of time? Because, in this case, the pigs took the long way round.

Cyberpunk's manifestation in a single and singular form was indeed brief. But it left quite an impression. A lingering dissatisfaction that being well-dressed and well-behaved is a bit, well, *dull*. The realization that chains aren't the nicest things to wear. A dawning awareness that there are a lot of extremely valid reasons to run around and scream (clothing optional). People understood that the world itself was not in its right mind, and maybe the demons had the right idea.

Even as the brief golden era of cyberpunk—the day of Legion—slips further into nostalgia, the legacy of cyberpunk remains not only relevant but ubiquitous. We now live our lives in a perplexing mix of the virtual and the real. At no time in human history have we ever been exposed to more messages, more frequently,

---

movement he was seeing in the pages of his *Asimov's Science Fiction Magazine*.

* This is a larger discussion, but steampunk, even more than cyberpunk, is a genre in which the aesthetic rapidly subsumed its original themes. It has, however, regained its footing as a platform for discussing postcolonialism. Also, airships.

[†] In *Storming the Reality Studio* (1991), Richard Kadrey and Larry McCaffery make a compelling argument for *Frankenstein* (1818) as a cyberpunk work, therefore increasing the lifespan of the genre by approximately 170 years.

from more and varied sources. Civilians using bootstrap technology are guiding drones in open warfare against marauding professional mercenaries. Protesters use umbrellas and spray paint to hide from facial recognition technology. Battles between corporations are fought in the streams of professional video game players. Algorithmically generated videos lead children down the rabbit hole of terrorist recruitment. The top touring musical act is a hologram. Your refrigerator is spying on you.

Perhaps the madman in the cave was not possessed but an oracle. Cyberpunk, however brief its reign, gave us the tools, the themes, and the vocabulary to understand the madness to come. It understood that the world itself was raving and undressed—irrational, unpredictable, and ill behaved. This is how we live, and Legion saw it coming.

WHAT IS CYBERPUNK?

It is impossible to collect *The Big Book of Cyberpunk* without actually defining *cyberpunk*. Unless we dare to name Legion, we can't track the two thousand feral hogs and the spoor they left behind.

Unsurprisingly, given cyberpunk's robust academic and critical legacy, there are many definitions to draw upon. With a genre so nebulous and sprawling, it is possible for each editor, artist, author, academic, or game designer to find in it what they want.

Cyberpunk is a land of definitional opportunity, but there are some rigid principles to uphold.

Cyberpunk has clear origins in both the "genre" and "literary" worlds. The division between these worlds is a false tension that has been remarked on, with their trademark directness, by Ann and Jeff VanderMeer in their introduction to *The Big Book of Science Fiction* (2016). From its start, cyberpunk stories and cyberpunk authors were weaving and bobbing between both literary and genre outlets, as well

as commercial and academic presses, traditional and experimental presses, and formal and informal modes of publishing. Cyberpunk has now been "claimed" by science fiction (or, more controversially, science fiction has been consumed by cyberpunk). But it would be a narrow and inaccurate view of the genre to see it as a wholly science-fictional endeavor.

Cyberpunk is inextricably linked with the real experience of technology. Technology in cyberpunk is not a hypothetical but a fundamental, tangible, and omnipresent inclusion in human life. Cyberpunk's predecessors largely dealt with technology as an abstract possibility: a controlled progress in the hands of a scientific elite, with visionary, but entirely rational, outcomes. But the reality of the computing explosion is that irrationality reigned, science became decentralized and personalized, and utopian visions were subsumed by capitalism, politics, and individual whim. Technology outpaced not only its expectations but its limitations.

As a genre about technology, and not "science" more broadly, there are limits to cyberpunk's scope. Technology, in this context, is manufactured. Cyberpunk is not science fiction that explores the ramifications of something inherent (such as the anthropological science fiction of Ursula K. Le Guin), innate (such as fiction that focuses on xenobiology, mutation, psychic powers, or other "flukes of biology" stories), or encountered (such as stories about discovering or exploring alien civilizations, lost worlds, or strange artifacts). By focusing on technology as a product, cyberpunk is about agency: it speaks about change that we are attempting to bring upon ourselves.

Cyberpunk exists in opposition to its predecessors. The *-punk* of cyberpunk is unavoidable: cyberpunk contains a fundamental sense of challenge. The man in the cave wasn't raving blindly; he was raving *against*. Cyberpunk pushes boundaries; it is provocative. It tries to find and break conventions. This need to rebel is intrinsic to the genre, leading to experimentation with both theme and form. As noted previously, it also connects to the possible "death" of cyberpunk: once the genre was absorbed by the mainstream, it could no longer exist as a single cohesive rebellion, and fragmented.

Cyberpunk is neither static nor teleological. Cyberpunk is literature about change. That change can take the form of progress or regress; evolution or revolution; or even degradation. It is not epic in the sense of a grand and ultimate destination. There are no final and decisive conclusions, only, at most, incremental movement. Cyberpunk is often described as *dystopian*, but dystopia implies a final and established system. Even in its grimmest worlds, cyberpunk presents the possibility of dynamism and of change. (And, similarly, even when set in the most scintillating futures, cyberpunk seeds the potential for regression or disruption.)

This final principle also hints at the limitations of technology. **Cyberpunk is not about technological supremacy.** In fact, the reverse is true: *cyberpunk is about the perseverance of humanity*. Cyberpunk accepts that irrationality and personality cannot be subsumed. This recognition is for good and for ill: techno-utopian outcomes are impossible because of our core, intractable humanness. But nor should those outcomes even be desirable: our irrepressible need for individuality may keep us from paradise but is, ultimately, the most essential part of our nature. In theme, and often in form, cyberpunk embraces chaos and irrationality, perpetually defiant of sweeping solutions, absolutist worldviews, or fixed patterns.

Marshall McLuhan, one of the great scholars of technology and society, described the same dynamics that led to the development of cyberpunk. McLuhan suggested that, in order to study technology, we step away from admiring the technology itself and instead examine how it shapes or displaces society. This quasi-phenomenological approach finds meaning not in the thing itself, but in our response to it. McLuhan concludes that the "message" of any medium or technology is the scale or pace or pattern that it introduces into human affairs.*

Applying this same concept to cyberpunk: it is not the fiction of technology but that of our reaction to it. The technology itself matters only in how it affects "human affairs."

Cyberpunk fiction is therefore an attempt, through literature, to make sense of the unprecedented scale and pace of contemporary technology, and also of the brutal and realistic acknowledgment that there may be no sense to it at all. As a working definition, therefore, it means **cyberpunk is speculative fiction about the influence of technology on the scale, the pace, or the pattern of human affairs.** Technology may accelerate, promote, delay, or even oppose these affairs, but humanity remains ultimately, unchangeably, human. It is the fiction of irrationality. Science fiction looks to the stars; cyberpunk stares into a mirror.

It seems tautological, but a definition is only as good as its ability to define. I crawled through almost two thousand works for this book, and, as *Big*™ as this book is, a mere hundred or so made it in. How did this definition work as a set of practical selection criteria? More importantly, what should you expect to find within these pages?

Cyberpunk is fiction—a self-serving selection requirement, and a controversial one at that. There's a wealth of cyberpunk-adjacent nonfiction that fully merits a *Big Book* of its own. From the reviews of *Cheap Truth* to the ads in the back of *Mondo 2000*, there are essays, travelogues, manifestos, articles, and memoirs that are immensely important to cyberpunk. But cyberpunk is speculative, not descriptive. The nonfiction inspires the genre, and is inspired by it, but is not the genre itself.

The protagonist needs to be recognizably human. As stated, cyberpunk is about human affairs. Protagonists that are aliens, robots, or artificial intelligence (AI) shift the focus from human social relationships to the

---

* Marshall McLuhan, *Understanding Media: The Extensions of Man* (New York: McGraw Hill, 1964).

relationship between humanity and the other. Human/other relationships can be an insightful way of exploring what makes us human (as seen in great science fiction ranging from Mary Doria Russell to Becky Chambers), but cyberpunk eschews that additional layer of metaphor. To be about human affairs, the story needs to be about humans.

The story is set in the present, the near present, or an easily intuited future. As we project further and further out, deciphering the scale, the pace, or the pattern requires more and more assumptions on the part of the author. Again, this is about the point of focus: the more speculation involved, and the less the manufactured technology is immediately recognizable, the more the story becomes about exploring the wondrous, rather than investigating the real. The "present," of course, is relative. (Objectively speaking, most of cyberpunk is now, disturbingly, alternate history.)

Given the stagnant state of space exploration, this also excludes virtually all stories that take place off-planet or in deep space.* (Again, exceptions could be made for films such as *Alien*, 1979, that take place in deep space, but with oddly minimal evidence of human scientific or social progress.) Similarly, there are very few examples of cyberpunk in secondary worlds or of cyberpunk with magic. As the fantastical becomes more and more necessary to the story, the focus shifts away from human affairs and toward the story's imaginative underpinnings.

Technology is mediative, not transformative. This is a deeply subjective divide but

one critical to what makes cyberpunk a distinct genre or subgenre of science fiction. A story in which technology fundamentally transforms, replaces, or subsumes human relationships is exciting, intriguing, and wildly imaginative . . . but not cyberpunk. A cyberpunk story is one that examines the way technology changes the way humans relate to other humans *but still leaves that relationship fundamentally intact*. The underlying resilience of human social relationships, for better or for worse, remains the key theme—not the transformative potential of technology.

In the spirit of cyberpunk, it is fair to note that these rules are in no way consistently consistent. There are notable exceptions to each contained within this book, including AI protagonists, alien encounters, and even the overt use of magic.

The eagle-eyed will also note that I've tried to avoid the vocabulary that normally surrounds cyberpunk. As mentioned above, cyberpunk needs not be dystopian, for example. In fact, because of its focus on the resilience of human relationships, cyberpunk is neither optimistic nor pessimistic but brutally realistic. If that realism is often read as dystopic, that is more a commentary on the nature of humanity.

Nor does cyberpunk have to be set in a city, or under neon lights, or wearing sunglasses, or in the rain, or (god forbid) in a trench coat. These tropes demonstrate the lingering appeal of the aesthetic that stemmed from cyberpunk but have little to do with its underpinning themes. Indeed, some of the most spectacularly *non-cyberpunk* works can masquerade as cyberpunk. The presence of a parsley garnish does not mean there's a steak beneath.

The last word commonly applied to cyberpunk is *noir*, and there is much merit to it. Unfortunately, in noir, we find a genre that is somehow even more commonly misinterpreted, misapplied, and confused with an aesthetic than cyberpunk itself. Noir is, like cyberpunk, about human relationships, whether the protagonist's

---

* Is there anything more emblematic of cyberpunk than the corporatization of the space race? When John F. Kennedy announced the ambition of a manned mission to the moon, he declared: "We set sail on this new sea because there is new knowledge to be gained, and new rights to be won, and they must be won and used for the progress of all people." Sixty years later, egocentric billionaires are farting radioactive garbage over the south Texas landscape in the rush to get billboards into orbit.

troubled relationship with their own identity (*Dark Passage*, 1947) or their conflict with a claustrophobic broader society (*Chinatown*, 1974). There is even a McLuhan-esque technological change at the center of most noir stories: the modern industrial city and its resultant impact on the pace, the scale, and the pattern of human affairs. Cyberpunk as *science fiction noir* can be a fairly apt description, but only when used in the thematic sense. It is, however, too often applied in the sense of "two genres that both feature rain and trench coats," which is why I have strenuously avoided "noir" here.

Since cyberpunk is posited in this collection as the speculative examination of technology on human affairs, *The Big Book of Cyberpunk* is structured to examine the genre along the dimensions upon which those affairs exist: **self**, **society**, **culture**, and **challenge**. These sections also nod to McLuhan's concept of the "global village"—a world in which media and technology have made the pace and the scale of human affairs instantaneous and global.* This global village, for better or for worse, is a world that McLuhan envisioned, that cyberpunk speculated upon, and in which we now live.

Each section begins with a (much briefer) introduction, followed by a "pre-cyberpunk" story. As tidy as it would be to divide the world into an orderly, rationalist, technophilic Golden Age and then the raving of demons, that would be a false dichotomy. Like all cultural trends, cyberpunk has its harbingers, more easily identified with the benefits of hindsight and distance. For each theme, I've included a story that, in its own way, predicts, pioneers, or inspires the cyberpunk that followed.

From there, the stories within each section are ordered chronologically, up to—as much as possible—the present day. The sole caveat here is that "publication order" is an arbitrary metric: a story may have been conceived, written, or

even submitted long before its publication. But this rough chronological ordering shows how the central themes of cyberpunk stayed consistent, even as the technology or media shifted over time. This ordering also demonstrates, in many ways, how cyberpunk has always been self-reflexive, with stories often in gleeful conversation with their forbearers both within and outside the "core" genre.

Finally, *The Big Book of Cyberpunk* concludes with a section on **post-cyberpunk**. The stories here showcase the "What next?"—a question that has been asked since even before the genre began.

THE SOURCE CODE OF TWO THOUSAND PIGS

For those interested in deciphering the construction of this anthology, there were some functional—if idiosyncratic—rules in place.

Respect antecedents. Notable cyberpunk anthologies include Bruce Sterling's formative *Mirrorshades*; Rudy Rucker, Robert Anton Wilson, and Peter Lamborn Wilson's groundbreaking *Semiotext(e) SF* (1989); Larry McCaffery's equally important *Storming the Reality Studio* (1991); Pat Cadigan's *The Ultimate Cyberpunk* (2002); James Patrick Kelly and John Kessel's *Rewired* (2007); Victoria Blake's *Cyberpunk* (2013); and Jason Heller and Joshua Viola's *Cyber World* (2016).

Each of these editors had their distinct (and occasionally contradictory) vision of the genre, and these anthologies are all, in my opinion, required reading. Rather than imitate their vision, or worse, subsume it, I have kept repetition to a bare minimum. That same respect also applies to all other anthologies, including the *Big Book* series. Although some authors rightfully appear in this volume and previous *Big Books*, there are no overlapping stories.

Showcase varying perspectives. Although *peak* or *core* cyberpunk was demographically homogeneous (something of which the cyber-

* Marshall McLuhan, *The Gutenberg Galaxy: The Making of Typographic Man* (Toronto: University of Toronto Press, 1962).

punks were, to their credit, fully aware), its legacy is astoundingly and brilliantly diverse. I have attempted to capture how writers from many different backgrounds—demographic, geographic, and artistic—took on the challenge of writing about our relationship with technology and one another. Cyberpunk is a truly global phenomenon. Storytellers all over the world have used the genre as a means of addressing and discussing their concerns. This is not a recent development; cyberpunk has been a global genre since its earliest days. I've sought out stories that show both cyberpunk's global contemporary presence and its roots. This book includes multiple translations, including five commissioned specifically for this volume—among them the first English-language appearances of classic cyberpunk stories by Gerardo Horacio Porcayo and Victor Pelevin, two undisputed masters of the genre.

It is also worth noting that Afrofuturism is *not* "Black cyberpunk," although the two are often conflated. Afrofuturism is an important genre unto itself, with its own unique cultural evolution, and treating it as a subset of cyberpunk does both genres an immense disservice. There are undeniable parallels; both genres, for example, present alternative views to a "mainstreamed" culture, and both are robustly transmedia in their creative expression. There has also been some intersection over time, perhaps most notably with the music, videos, and writing of Janelle Monáe. Their novella, cowritten with Alaya Dawn Johnson, features in this volume.

As a corollary to the principle of diverse perspectives: the de facto *Big Book* rule is that no author can appear twice in a volume—and this has been *mostly* maintained. However, cyberpunk has always been a collaborative genre. Some of its most impressive and defining works were cowritten, creating results that neither could achieve independently. Although a very slight loophole, I've exploited it, meaning a few names do have the audacity to repeat.

Celebrate the experimental. Cyberpunk media included film and television, albums and art, software and games. Many of these formats are impossible to capture on the printed page, certainly not without doing them a massive disservice—although there are some visual stories inside this collection. I attempt to pay tribute to the original cyberpunks by gathering materials from a wide variety of sources: a reflection of the nontraditional publishing journey taken by many of these writers. Inside are stories first published in magazines, anthologies, and websites, but also as zines, liner notes, and fleeting social media posts. Cyberpunk is not solely the province of science fiction, and herein are stories first published by newspapers, in science journals, in literary magazines, and as role-playing game tie-ins. Due to the combination of provocative content and technologically savvy authors, cyberpunk has always been at the forefront of self-publishing—a trend also reflected here.

Continuing the experimental theme, all the stories in *The Big Book of Cyberpunk* are self-contained "holistic" works. There are many great stories that require the reader to have preexisting knowledge of the setting or the characters. There is a wealth of fantastic cyberpunk novels that could have provided extracts. Restricting this anthology solely to short fiction was necessary for my own sake.

THE END OF THE BEGINNING

The first story, William Gibson's "The Gernsback Continuum" (1981) stands outside the five main sections. It is the boot-up sound for the hundred-odd stories that follow.

William Gibson is the figure most closely connected with cyberpunk, not only through *Neuromancer* and the Sprawl trilogy, but also through his short stories and nonfiction, all of which encapsulated the fledgling genre in its fragile early years. There is no author more appropriate to open this volume.[*]

---

[*] "The Gernsback Continuum" was also the first story in the now oft-mentioned *Mirrorshades*. This is a coincidence, but I like it.

"The Gernsback Continuum" defines the problem that cyberpunk would then go on to solve. It shows the fantasies of scientific aspiration, and it repositions visions of progress as the ghosts of value. The story is achingly, poignantly sad. Not because it is set in a dystopian hellscape but because the world is so painfully ordinary. It shows where we are, but through the lens of where we thought we'd be. By setting the recognizable against the aspirational, Gibson shows the gap between imagination and reality and sets out the challenge for future writers to fill it—including, as it turns out, Gibson himself. "The Gernsback Continuum" refuted the science-fictional tradition that had prevailed since the 1930s and made space for a new form of storytelling.

Above all else, "The Gernsback Continuum" is simply a beautiful story, perfectly constructed and gloriously atmospheric. Although all stories in this anthology were chosen for their historical and thematic significance, the *most* important selection criterion was that they are enjoyable to read, and I hope you find as much pleasure in them as I have.

THE BIG BOOK OF
CYBERPUNK

WILLIAM GIBSON

THE GERNSBACK CONTINUUM

(1981)

MERCIFULLY, the whole thing is starting to fade, to become an episode. When I do still catch the odd glimpse, it's peripheral; mere fragments of mad-doctor chrome, confining themselves to the corner of the eye. There was that flying-wing liner over San Francisco last week, but it was almost translucent. And the shark-fin road-sters have gotten scarcer, and freeways discreetly avoid unfolding themselves into the gleaming eighty-lane monsters I was forced to drive last month in my rented Toyota. And I know that none of it will follow me to New York; my vision is narrowing to a single wavelength of probability. I've worked hard for that. Television helped a lot.

I suppose it started in London, in that bogus Greek taverna in Battersea Park Road, with lunch on Cohen's corporate tab. Dead steam-table food and it took them thirty minutes to find an ice bucket for the retsina. Cohen works for Barris-Watford, who publish big, trendy "trade" paperbacks: illustrated histories of the neon sign, the pinball machine, the windup toys of Occupied Japan. I'd gone over to shoot a series of shoe ads; California girls with tanned legs and frisky Day-Glo jogging shoes had capered for me down the escalators of St. John's Wood and across the platforms of Tooting Bec. A lean and hungry young agency had decided that the mystery of London Transport would sell waffle-tread nylon runners. They decide; I shoot. And Cohen, whom I knew vaguely from the old days in New York, had invited me to lunch the day before I was due out of Heathrow. He brought along a very fashionably dressed young woman named Dialta Downes, who was virtually chin-less and evidently a noted pop-art historian. In retrospect, I see her walking in beside Cohen under a floating neon sign that flashes THIS WAY LIES MADNESS in huge sans serif capitals.

Cohen introduced us and explained that Dialta was the prime mover behind the latest Barris-Watford project, an illustrated history of what she called "American Streamlined Moderne." Cohen called it "raygun Gothic." Their working title was *The Airstream Futuropolis: The Tomorrow That Never Was.*

There's a British obsession with the more baroque elements of American pop culture, something like the weird cowboys-and-Indians fetish of the West Germans or the aberrant French hunger for old Jerry Lewis films. In Dialta Downes this manifested itself in a mania for a uniquely American form of architecture that most Americans are scarcely aware of. At first I wasn't sure what she was talking about, but gradually it began to dawn on me. I found myself remembering Sunday morning television in the Fifties.

Sometimes they'd run old eroded newsreels as filler on the local station. You'd sit there with a peanut butter sandwich and a glass of milk, and a static-ridden Hollywood baritone would tell you that there was A Flying Car in Your Future. And three Detroit engineers would putter around with this big old Nash with wings, and you'd see it rumbling furiously down some deserted Michigan runway. You never actually saw it take off, but it flew away to Dialta Downes's never-never land, true home of a generation of completely uninhibited technophiles. She was talking about those odds and ends of "futuristic" Thirties and Forties architecture you pass daily in American cities without noticing: the movie marquees ribbed to radiate some mysterious energy, the dime stores faced with fluted aluminum, the chrome-tube chairs gathering dust in the lobbies of transient hotels. She saw these things as segments of a dreamworld, abandoned in the uncaring present; she wanted me to photograph them for her.

The Thirties had seen the first generation of American industrial designers; until the Thirties, all pencil sharpeners had looked like pencil sharpeners—your basic Victorian mechanism, perhaps with a curlicue of decorative trim. After the advent of the designers, some pencil sharpeners looked as though they'd been put together in wind tunnels. For the most part, the change was only skin-deep; under the stream-lined chrome shell, you'd find the same Victorian mechanism. Which made a certain kind of sense, because the most successful American designers had been recruited from the ranks of Broadway theater designers. It was all a stage set, a series of elaborate props for playing at living in the future.

Over coffee, Cohen produced a fat manila envelope full of glossies. I saw the winged statues that guard the Hoover Dam, forty-foot concrete hood ornaments leaning steadfastly into an imaginary hurricane. I saw a dozen shots of Frank Lloyd Wright's Johnson Wax Building, juxtaposed with the covers of old *Amazing Stories* pulps, by an artist named Frank R. Paul; the employees of Johnson Wax must have felt as though they were walking into one of Paul's spray-paint pulp Utopias. Wright's building looked as though it had been designed for people who wore white togas and Lucite sandals. I hesitated over one sketch of a particularly grandiose prop-driven airliner, all wing, like a fat, symmetrical boomerang with windows in unlikely places. Labeled arrows indicated the locations of the grand ballroom and two squash courts. It was dated 1936.

"This thing couldn't have flown...?" I looked at Dialta Downes.

"Oh, no, quite impossible, even with those twelve giant props; but they loved the look, don't you see? New York to London in less than two days, first-class dining rooms, private cabins, sun decks, dancing to jazz in the evening... The designers were populists, you see; they were trying to give the public what it wanted. What the public wanted was the future."

I'd been in Burbank for three days, trying to suffuse a really dull-looking rocker with charisma, when I got the package from Cohen. It is possible to photograph what isn't there; it's damned hard to do, and consequently a very marketable talent. While I'm not bad at it, I'm not exactly the best, either, and this poor guy strained my Nikon's credibility. I got out depressed because I do like to do a good job, but not totally depressed, because I did make sure

I'd gotten the check for the job, and I decided to restore myself with the sublime artiness of the Barris-Watford assignment. Cohen had sent me some books on Thirties design, more photos of streamlined buildings, and a list of Dialta Downes's fifty favorite examples of the style in California.

Architectural photography can involve a lot of waiting; the building becomes a kind of sundial, while you wait for a shadow to crawl away from a detail you want, or for the mass and balance of the structure to reveal itself in a certain way. While I was waiting, I thought of myself in Dialta Downes's America. When I isolated a few of the factory buildings on the ground glass of the Hasselblad, they came across with a kind of sinister totalitarian dignity, like the stadiums Albert Speer built for Hitler. But the rest of it was relentlessly tacky; ephemeral stuff extruded by the collective American subconscious of the Thirties, tending mostly to survive along depressing strips lined with dusty motels, mattress wholesalers, and small used-car lots. I went for the gas stations in a big way.

During the high point of the Downes Age, they put Ming the Merciless in charge of designing California gas stations. Favoring the architecture of his native Mongo, he cruised up and down the coast erecting raygun emplacements in white stucco. Lots of them featured superfluous central towers ringed with those strange radiator flanges that were a signature motif of the style and which made them look as though they might generate potent bursts of raw technological enthusiasm if you could only find the switch that turned them on. I shot one in San Jose an hour before the bulldozers arrived and drove right through the structural truth of plaster and lathing and cheap concrete.

"Think of it," Dialta Downes had said, "as a kind of alternate America: a 1980 that never happened. An architecture of broken dreams."

And that was my frame of mind as I made the stations of her convoluted socioarchitectural cross in my red Toyota—as I gradually tuned in to her image of a shadowy America-that-wasn't,

of Coca-Cola plants like beached submarines, and fifth-run movie houses like the temples of some lost sect that had worshiped blue mirrors and geometry. And as I moved among these secret ruins, I found myself wondering what the inhabitants of that lost future would think of the world I lived in. The Thirties dreamed white marble and slipstream chrome, immortal crystal and burnished bronze, but the rockets on the covers of the Gernsback pulps had fallen on London in the dead of night, screaming. After the war, everyone had a car—no wings for it—and the promised superhighway to drive it down, so that the sky itself darkened, and the fumes ate the marble and pitted the miracle crystal. . . .

And one day, on the outskirts of Bolinas, when I was setting up to shoot a particularly lavish example of Ming's martial architecture, I penetrated a fine membrane, a membrane of probability. . . .

Ever so gently, I went over the Edge—

And looked up to see a twelve-engined thing like a bloated boomerang, all wing, thrumming its way east with an elephantine grace, so low that I could count the rivets in its dull silver skin, and hear—maybe—the echo of jazz.

I took it to Kihn. Merv Kihn, freelance journalist with an extensive line in Texas pterodactyls, redneck UFO contactées, bush-league Loch Ness monsters, and the Top Ten conspiracy theories in the loonier reaches of the American mass mind.

"It's good," said Kihn, polishing his yellow Polaroid shooting glasses on the hem of his Hawaiian shirt, "but it's not *mental*; lacks the true quill."

"But I saw it, Mervyn." We were seated poolside in brilliant Arizona sunlight. He was in Tucson waiting for a group of retired Las Vegas civil servants whose leader received messages from Them on her microwave oven. I'd driven all night and was feeling it.

"Of course you did. Of course you saw it. You've read my stuff; haven't you grasped my blanket solution to the UFO problem? It's

5

simple, plain and country simple: people"—he settled the glasses carefully on his long hawk nose and fixed me with his best basilisk glare—"*see* . . . things. People see these things. Nothing's there, but people *see* them anyway. Because they need to, probably. You've read Jung, you should know the score. . . . In your case, it's so obvious: You admit you were thinking about this crackpot architecture, having fantasies. . . . Look, I'm sure you've taken your share of drugs, right? How many people survived the Sixties in California without having the odd hallucination? All those nights when you discovered that whole armies of Disney technicians had been employed to weave animated holograms of Egyptian hieroglyphs into the fabric of your jeans, say, or the times when—"

"But it wasn't like that."

"Of course not. It wasn't like that at all; it was 'in a setting of clear reality,' right? Everything normal, and then there's the monster, the mandala, the neon cigar. In your case, a giant Tom Swift airplane. It happens *all the time*. You aren't even crazy. You know that, don't you?" He fished a beer out of the battered foam cooler beside his deck chair.

"Last week I was in Virginia. Grayson County. I interviewed a sixteen-year-old girl who'd been assaulted by a *bar hade*."

"A what?"

"A bear head. The severed head of a bear. This *bar hade*, see, was floating around on its own little flying saucer, looked kind of like the hubcaps on cousin Wayne's vintage Caddy. Had red, glowing eyes like two cigar stubs and telescoping chrome antennas poking up behind its ears." He burped.

"It assaulted her? How?"

"You don't want to know; you're obviously impressionable. 'It was cold'"—he lapsed into his bad Southern accent—"'and metallic.' It made electronic noises. Now that is the real thing, the straight goods from the mass unconscious, friend; that little girl is a witch. There's no place for her to function in this society. She'd have seen the devil if she hadn't been brought

up on *The Bionic Woman* and all those *Star Trek* reruns. She is clued into the main vein. And she knows that it happened to her. I got out ten minutes before the heavy UFO boys showed up with the polygraph."

I must have looked pained, because he set his beer down carefully beside the cooler and sat up.

"If you want a classier explanation, I'd say you saw a semiotic ghost. All these contactée stories, for instance, are framed in a kind of sci-fi imagery that permeates our culture. I could buy aliens, but not aliens that look like Fifties' comic art. They're semiotic phantoms, bits of deep cultural imagery that have split off and taken on a life of their own, like the Jules Verne airships that those old Kansas farmers were always seeing. But you saw a different kind of ghost, that's all. That plane was part of the mass unconscious, once. You picked up on that, somehow. The important thing is not to worry about it."

I did worry about it, though.

Kihn combed his thinning blond hair and went off to hear what They had had to say over the radar range lately, and I drew the curtains in my room and lay down in air-conditioned darkness to worry about it. I was still worrying about it when I woke up. Kihn had left a note on my door; he was flying up north in a chartered plane to check out a cattle-mutilation rumor ("muties," he called them; another of his journalistic specialties).

I had a meal, showered, took a crumbling diet pill that had been kicking around in the bottom of my shaving kit for three years, and headed back to Los Angeles.

The speed limited my vision to the tunnel of the Toyota's headlights. The body could drive, I told myself, while the mind maintained. Maintained and stayed away from the weird peripheral window dressing of amphetamine and exhaustion, the spectral, luminous vegetation that grows out of the corners of the mind's eye along late-night highways. But the mind had its own ideas, and Kihn's opinion of what I was already thinking of as my "sighting" rattled endlessly through my head in a tight, lopsided orbit.

Semiotic ghosts. Fragments of the Mass Dream, whirling past in the wind of my passage. Somehow this feedback-loop aggravated the diet pill, and the speed-vegetation along the road began to assume the colors of infrared satellite images, glowing shreds blown apart in the Toyota's slipstream.

I pulled over, then, and a half-dozen aluminum beer cans winked goodnight as I killed the headlights. I wondered what time it was in London, and tried to imagine Dialta Downes having breakfast in her Hampstead flat, surrounded by streamlined chrome figurines and books on American culture.

Desert nights in that country are enormous; the moon is closer. I watched the moon for a long time and decided that Kihn was right. The main thing was not to worry. All across the continent, daily, people who were more normal than I'd ever aspired to be saw giant birds, Bigfeet, flying oil refineries; they kept Kihn busy and solvent. Why should I be upset by a glimpse of the 1930s pop imagination loose over Bolinas? I decided to go to sleep, with nothing worse to worry about than rattlesnakes and cannibal hippies, safe amid the friendly roadside garbage of my own familiar continuum. In the morning I'd drive down to Nogales and photograph the old brothels, something I'd intended to do for years. The diet pill had given up.

The light woke me, and then the voices. The light came from somewhere behind me and threw shifting shadows inside the car. The voices were calm, indistinct, male and female, engaged in conversation.

My neck was stiff and my eyeballs felt gritty in their sockets. My leg had gone to sleep, pressed against the steering wheel. I fumbled for my glasses in the pocket of my work shirt and finally got them on.

Then I looked behind me and saw the city.

The books on Thirties design were in the trunk; one of them contained sketches of an idealized city that drew on *Metropolis* and *Things to Come*, but squared everything, soaring up through an architect's perfect clouds to zeppelin docks and mad neon spires. That city was a scale model of the one that rose behind me. Spire stood on spire in gleaming ziggurat steps that climbed to a central golden temple tower ringed with the crazy radiator flanges of the Mongo gas stations. You could hide the Empire State Building in the smallest of those towers. Roads of crystal soared between the spires, crossed and recrossed by smooth silver shapes like beads of running mercury. The air was thick with ships: giant wing-liners, little darting silver things (sometimes one of the quicksilver shapes from the sky bridges rose gracefully into the air and flew up to join the dance), mile-long blimps, hovering dragonfly things that were gyrocopters . . .

I closed my eyes tight and swung around in the seat. When I opened them, I willed myself to see the mileage meter, the pale road dust on the black plastic dashboard, the overflowing ashtray.

"Amphetamine psychosis," I said. I opened my eyes. The dash was still there, the dust, the crushed filter tips. Very carefully, without moving my head, I turned the headlights on.

And saw them.

They were blond. They were standing beside their car, an aluminum avocado with a central shark-fin rudder jutting up from its spine and smooth black tires like a child's toy. He had his arm around her waist and was gesturing toward the city. They were both in white: loose clothing, bare legs, spotless white sun shoes. Neither of them seemed aware of the beams of my headlights. He was saying something wise and strong, and she was nodding, and suddenly I was frightened, frightened in an entirely different way. Sanity had ceased to be an issue; I knew, somehow, that the city behind me was Tucson—a dream Tucson thrown up out of the collective yearning of an era. That it was real, entirely real. But the couple in front of me lived in it, and they frightened me.

They were the children of Dialta Downes's '80-that-wasn't; they were Heirs to the Dream. They were white, blond, and they probably had blue eyes. They were American. Dialta had said that the Future had come to America first, but had finally passed it by. But not here, in the heart of the Dream. Here, we'd gone on and on, in a dream logic that knew nothing of pollution, the finite bounds of fossil fuel, or foreign wars it was possible to lose. They were smug, happy, and utterly content with themselves and their world. And in the Dream, it was *their* world.

Behind me, the illuminated city: Searchlights swept the sky for the sheer joy of it. I imagined them thronging the plazas of white marble, orderly and alert, their bright eyes shining with enthusiasm for their floodlit avenues and silver cars.

It had all the sinister fruitiness of Hitler Youth propaganda.

I put the car in gear and drove forward slowly, until the bumper was within three feet of them. They still hadn't seen me. I rolled the window down and listened to what the man was saying. His words were bright and hollow as the pitch in some chamber of commerce brochure, and I knew that he believed in them absolutely.

"John," I heard the woman say, "we've forgotten to take our food pills." She clicked two bright wafers from a thing on her belt and passed one to him. I backed onto the highway and headed for Los Angeles, wincing and shaking my head.

I phoned Kihn from a gas station. A new one, in bad Spanish Modern. He was back from his expedition and didn't seem to mind the call.

"Yeah, that is a weird one. Did you try to get any pictures? Not that they ever come out, but it adds an interesting *frisson* to your story, not having the pictures turn out. . . ."

But what should I do?

"Watch lots of television, particularly game shows and soaps. Go to porn movies. Ever see *Nazi Love Motel*? They've got it on cable, here. Really awful. Just what you need."

What was he talking about?

"Quit yelling and listen to me. I'm letting you in on a trade secret: Really bad media can exorcize your semiotic ghosts. If it keeps the saucer people off my back, it can keep these Art Deco

futuroids off yours. Try it. What have you got to lose?"

Then he begged off, pleading an early-morning date with the Elect.

"The who?"

"These oldsters from Vegas; the ones with the microwaves."

I considered putting a collect call through to London, getting Cohen at Barris-Watford and telling him his photographer was checked out for a protracted season in the Twilight Zone. In the end, I let a machine mix me a really impossible cup of black coffee and climbed back into the Toyota for the haul to Los Angeles.

Los Angeles was a bad idea, and I spent two weeks there. It was prime Downes country; too much of the Dream there, and too many fragments of the Dream waiting to snare me. I nearly wrecked the car on a stretch of overpass near Disneyland when the road fanned out like an origami trick and left me swerving through a dozen minilanes of whizzing chrome teardrops with shark fins. Even worse, Hollywood was full of people who looked too much like the couple I'd seen in Arizona. I hired an Italian director who was making ends meet doing darkroom work and installing patio decks around swimming pools until his ship came in; he made prints of all the negatives I'd accumulated on the Downes job. I didn't want to look at the stuff myself. It didn't seem to bother Leonardo, though, and when he was finished I checked the prints, riffling through them like a deck of cards, sealed them up, and sent them air freight to London. Then I took a taxi to a theater that was showing *Nazi Love Motel* and kept my eyes shut all the way.

Cohen's congratulatory wire was forwarded to me in San Francisco a week later. Dialta had loved the pictures. He admired the way I'd "really gotten into it," and looked forward to working with me again. That afternoon I spotted a flying wing over Castro Street, but there was something tenuous about it, as if it were only half there. I rushed to the nearest newsstand and gathered up as much as I could find on the petroleum crisis and the nuclear energy hazard. I'd just decided to buy a plane ticket for New York.

"Hell of a world we live in, huh?" The proprietor was a thin black man with bad teeth and an obvious wig. I nodded, fishing in my jeans for change, anxious to find a park bench where I could submerge myself in hard evidence of the human near dystopia we live in. "But it could be worse, huh?"

"That's right," I said, "or even worse, it could be perfect."

He watched me as I headed down the street with my little bundle of condensed catastrophe.

SELF

The notion of identity—and the many and heated discussions around it—has long been explored through fiction. Cyberpunk is no exception. Of the many different relationships that constitute human affairs, the self—how we see, perceive, and define our individual identity—is perhaps the most complex. Without knowing who we are, how can we understand our place in the world?

Cyberpunk has always understood that technology has the power to affect even this most intimate and individual relationship. Who we are—who we *think* we are—is, like every other social construct, mediated by technology. In the early days of the genre, cyberpunk fiction was rightfully fascinated by the idea of our virtual selves. The existence of cyberspace presupposes our cyber-selves. Is our online presence a projection? A twin? A shadow? What is the tenuous connection between these planes—are there physical or moral repercussions for how we act in this new world? Decades later, we are

no closer to answering the questions that cyberpunk was the first to ask.

Cyberpunk also looked at technology's broader potential for personal transformation: how much it can change us; what we can become; what we can and can't leave behind. Modern understanding of identity is that it is a layered and dynamic concept. Humans are not one thing. Who we are can shift depending on the context we're in, the company we keep, the choices we make, or that are made for us. Cyberpunk fiction is a way of exploring the tension between the fluidity (lubricated by technology) and the immutable essence of what makes us human.

This section opens with James Tiptree Jr.'s excellent "The Girl Who Was Plugged In" (1973). In terms of vocabulary and technology, it sets the tone for much of the cyberpunk fiction that would follow. It also raises questions about the impact of virtuality on identity: Will it be liberating to "depart" ourselves for another body, or is there something damaging about severing that connection? What harm is caused by a society that makes that possible or, in fact, encourages it?

This discussion of freedom (and the "curse" of anchoring to physicality) is found through many of the stories in this section. Pat Cadigan's "Pretty Boy Crossover" (1986) describes a world where physical beauty is upheld to the point that the body is itself made the ultimate sacrifice. The criminals of John Shirley's "Wolves of the Plateau" (1988) use the power of the virtual plane to free themselves and become something more. In "The World as We Know It" (1992), George Effinger's sleuth, Marîd Audran, encounters communities that prefer virtual worlds to physical ones, despite the high cost of maintaining the suspension of disbelief. Gwyneth Jones's "Red Sonja and Lessingham in Dreamland" (1996) uses the virtual world as a form of psychotherapy: online identities allowing repressed appetites to run free.

Once plugged in to Jean-Marc Ligny's "Real-Life 3.0" (2014) (appearing here for the first time in English), our protagonist experiences the reality and the virtual fantasy side-by-side, with predictable dispiriting results. In Aleš Kot's "A Life of Its Own" (2019), the virtual becomes a prison, with those same dreams used to keep you entombed (thanks, in no small part, to the fine print). Charles Stross's madcap satire, "Lobsters" (2001) features a MacGuffin (or is it?) based on the profit potential of digital crustaceans. Surrounding that central conceit is a whirlwind of influences: our protagonist attempting to maintain his own self-identity while being buffeted by political, financial, technological, and romantic winds.

In Sparkletown, the setting of Jeff Noon's "Ghost Codes of Sparkletown" (2011), the self can be endangered by cultural ghosts: fragments of music that float through a haunted graveyard of burned-out CPUs.*

J. P. Smythe's "The Infinite Eye" (2017) is a story that descends in a direct line from Tiptree's, again describing a corporate world where the desperate sell themselves to stay afloat. But in "The Girl Who Was Plugged In," our protagonist receives an ecstatic reward, and a chance to live the fantasy. In "The Infinite Eye," they merely receive a paycheck (and, presumably, no health care). In the final story in this section, qntm's "Lena" (2021), a man is blessed/cursed with virtual immortality, give or take some messy version control.

The fluidity of the self is not solely contained in the virtual realm. Anna, in Richard Kadrey's "Surfing the Khumbu" (2002), is "living in machines and flesh at the same time," a scenario that will leave the reader quivering in both fear and jealousy. In Cat Rambo's "Memories of Moments, Bright as Falling Stars" (2006), technology—in this case "memory" both biological and computational—is embedded in the body, both a resource and a drug.

Karen Heuler's "The Completely Rechargeable Man" (2008) reads more like a fairy tale than your average cyberpunk short. It describes a lonely individual whose life is so technological that he has become a form of entertainment.

The titular character in Christian Kirtchev's "File: The Death of Designer D." (2009) is the source of mystery on several levels. Why did she die? What was she fighting against? And who was she in the first place? The singular letters of "D." and her investigator, "K." are reminiscent of Kafka, as D. battles to have an identity in a world of "gray lemmings."

Transhuman aspiration runs amok in many of these stories. Jean Rabe's "Better Than" (2010) is the tale of a lost soul, addicted to self-transformation, with an identity so fractured and eroded as to be totally lost.† In Alvaro Zinos-

---

* Jeff Noon's story was first composed on Twitter, and has since been reincarnated in various forms, including as the inspiration for the album *Ghost Codes* by The Forgetting Room. This is the story's first appearance in this "holistic" form.

† Cyberpunk fiction exists as much in movies, television, music, and games as in literature. Jean Rabe's

Amaro's "wysiomg" (2016), we also have transient, fragmented identities, with biology and identity both subsumed into an anarchistic internet culture. "The Real You™" (2018) by Molly Tanzer takes the control of the self to its ultimate conclusion with "Refractin," a treatment in which your face is completely removed. Tanzer's story is focused less on the perplexing how, but on the why—what could compel someone to remove their identity entirely, and what would be the repercussions of living faceless in society?

Several of the stories in this section are devoted to the intersection of the self and destruction. Not self-destruction, per se (although that is often the case), but stories that explore our slavish devotion to the technology that only exists to kill.

Sunny Moraine's "I Tell Thee All, I Can No More" (2013) is a tale of truly forbidden love, and a human/technology romance that crosses all possible boundaries. It is, in the best cyberpunk tradition, a story that simply should not work, but Moraine somehow spins beauty out of nightmare, while still reminding us of the true horror beneath.

"Four Tons Too Late" (2014) and "Helicopter Story" (2020) are also about a savage blend of human and machine, and the subservience of the self to the military-industrial complex. In the former, K. C. Alexander describes the psychological toll on a new type of veteran. In "Helicopter Story," Isabel Fall reclaims a transphobic meme and uses it as the vehicle to describe a society that both suppresses gender identity while worshipping at the altar of techno-militaristic machismo.* The story asks "Have

you ever been exultant?" and then condemns a world where the only way to answer positively is by transforming yourself into a weapon of war.

The capacity of technology to make new selves is a fascination of cyberpunk: the ability to create an identity or a living being out of whole cloth. Cyberpunk's fixation on androids could be argued away as another aesthetic trope (thanks, *Blade Runner*), but it is a natural part of the same discussion as the virtual self or transhumanism. At what point does technology allow us to imitate the self so precisely that it becomes a new self of its own, and has its own soul and right to exist?

Phillip Mann's "An Old-Fashioned Story" (1989) is a slice-of-life tale (apologies for the fun), in which a couple set about to fix their household android and, in the process, reveal a great deal about themselves.

In "The Girl Hero's Mirror Says He's Not the One" (2007), Justina Robson's Girl Hero inhabits a completely fabricated identity that has been imposed upon her. But despite being forced into a specific role (or Role), she owns it, and takes agency over the illusion. Lavie Tidhar's "Choosing Faces" (2012) is one of the author's trademark satires, featuring a particularly famous martial artist in his greatest battle(s) yet. It is hilarious, but reminiscent of Warhol with the way it addresses the tragic erosion of the self that stems from celebrity culture.

Neon Yang's "Patterns of a Murmuration, in Billions of Data Points" (2014) is one of the few stories in this book with a nonhuman protagonist—in this case, a swarm of AI that collectively take action to solve the death of their "mother." As compelling as our hive mind protagonist is, they are the lens through which we see the fumblings of human behavior, as the humans attempt to wield this technology to their own advantage.

Every other dimension of human affairs is external—the author has the advantage of distance. Writing about the self, even a fictional self, is necessarily personal. Even blurred through the lens of fiction, there's an unavoid-

---

story is one of two in this book that originated in FASA's *Shadowrun*, a long-running role-playing game that mixes fantasy and cyberpunk, and has done much to introduce new audiences to the latter.

* The meme—"I sexually identify as an attack helicopter"—emerged on Reddit and 4chan a few years before this story and was used to dismiss the notion of nonbinary gender identity and self-identification. This story not only makes sense without the original context but, rather gratifyingly, will long outlive it.

able element of emotional connection. Writing about space voyages or baseball teams is complex, but lacks the same closeness. The interest is in what's happening *out there*.

These cyberpunk stories, however, are unavoidably intimate. They are not about the *out there*, but how what's happening in the hand-wavey middle distance is here, influencing one person. It is uncomfortable. We lack the distance to be objective, or to make rational decisions. That is a reflection of cyberpunk as a whole: despite our best (or worst) efforts to suppress it, we are inevitably, irreversibly, irrationally human.

JAMES TIPTREE JR.

THE GIRL WHO WAS PLUGGED IN

(1973)

LISTEN, zombie. Believe me. What I could tell you—you with your silly hands leaking sweat on your growth-stocks portfolio. One-ten lousy hacks of AT&T on twenty-point margin and you think you're Evel Knievel. AT&T? You double-knit dummy, how I'd love to show you something.

Look, dead daddy, I'd say. See for instance that rotten girl?

In the crowd over there, that one gaping at her gods. One rotten girl in the city of the future. (That's what I said.) Watch.

She's jammed among bodies, craning and peering with her soul yearning out of her eye-balls. Love! Oo-ooh, love them! Her gods are coming out of a store called Body East. Three youngbloods, larking along loverly. Dressed like simple street-people but . . . smashing. See their great eyes swivel above their nose-filters, their hands lift shyly, their inhumanly tender lips melt? The crowd moans. Love! This whole boil-ing megacity, this whole fun future world loves its gods.

You don't believe gods, dad? Wait. Whatever turns you on, there's a god in the future for you, custom-made. Listen to this mob. "I touched His foot! Ow-oow, I *touched* Him!"

Even the people in the GTX tower up there love the gods—in their own way and for their own reasons.

The funky girl on the street, she just loves. Grooving on their beautiful lives, their mys-terioso problems. No one ever told her about mortals who love a god and end up as a tree or a sighing sound. In a million years it'd never occur to her that her gods might love her back.

She's squashed against the wall now as the godlings come by. They move in a clear space. A holocam bobs above, but its shadow never falls on them. The store display-screens are magi-cally clear of bodies as the gods glance in and a beggar underfoot is suddenly alone. They give him a token. "Aaaaah!" goes the crowd.

Now one of them flashes some wild new kind of timer and they all trot to catch a shuttle, just like people. The shuttle stops for them—more magic. The crowd sighs, closing back. The gods are gone.

(In a room far from—but not unconnected to—the GTX tower a molecular flipflop closes too, and three account tapes spin.)

Our girl is still stuck by the wall while guards and holocam equipment pull away. The adoration's fading from her face. That's good, because now you can see she's the ugly of the world. A tall monument to pituitary dystrophy. No surgeon would touch her. When she smiles, her jaw—it's half purple—almost bites her left eye out. She's also quite young, but who could care?

The crowd is pushing her along now, treating you to glimpses of her jumbled torso, her mismatched legs. At the corner she strains to send one last fond spasm after the godlings' shuttle. Then her face reverts to its usual expression of dim pain and she lurches onto the moving walkway, stumbling into people. The walkway junctions with another. She crosses, trips, and collides with the casualty rail. Finally she comes out into a little bare place called a park. The sportshow is working, a basketball game in three-di is going on right overhead. But all she does is squeeze onto a bench and huddle there while a ghostly free-throw goes by her ear.

After that nothing at all happens except a few furtive hand-mouth gestures which don't even interest her bench mates. But you're curious about the city? So ordinary after all, in the *future*?

Ah, there's plenty to swing with here—and it's not all that *far* in the future, dad. But pass up the sci-fi stuff for now, like for instance the holovision technology that's put TV and radio in museums. Or the worldwide carrier field bouncing down from satellites, controlling communication and transport systems all over the globe. That was a spin-off from asteroid mining, pass it by. We're watching that girl.

I'll give you just one goodie. Maybe you noticed on the sportshow or the streets? No commercials. No ads.

That's right. *No ads*. An eyeballer for you.

Look around. Not a billboard, sign, slogan, jingle, sky-write, blurb, sublimflash, in this whole fun world. Brand names? Only in those ticky little peep-screens on the stores, and you could hardly call that advertising. How does that finger you?

Think about it. That girl is still sitting there.

She's parked right under the base of the GTX tower, as a matter of fact. Look way up and you can see the sparkles from the bubble on top, up there among the domes of godland. Inside that bubble is a boardroom. Neat bronze shield on the door: Global Transmissions Corporation—not that that means anything.

I happen to know there are six people in that room. Five of them technically male, and the sixth isn't easily thought of as a mother. They are absolutely unremarkable. Those faces were seen once at their nuptials and will show again in their obituaries and impress nobody either time. If you're looking for the secret Big Blue Meanies of the world, forget it. I know. Zen, do I know! Flesh? Power? Glory? You'd horrify them.

What *they* do like up there is to have things orderly, especially their communications. You could say they've dedicated their lives to that, to freeing the world from garble. Their nightmares are about hemorrhages of information; channels screwed up, plans misimplemented, garble creeping in. Their gigantic wealth only worries them, it keeps opening new vistas of disorder. Luxury? They wear what their tailors put on them, eat what their cooks serve them. See that old boy there—his name is Isham—he's sipping water and frowning as he listens to a databall. The water was prescribed by his medistaff. It tastes awful. The databall also contains a disquieting message about his son, Paul.

But it's time to go back down, far below to our girl. Look!

She's toppled over sprawling on the ground.

A tepid commotion ensues among the bystanders. The consensus is she's dead, which she disproves by bubbling a little. And presently she's taken away by one of the superb ambulances of the future, which are a real improvement over ours when one happens to be around.

At the local bellevue the usual things are done by the usual team of clowns aided by a saintly mop-pusher. Our girl revives enough to answer the questionnaire without which you can't die, even in the future. Finally she's cast up, a pumped-out hulk on a cot in the long, dim ward.

Again nothing happens for a while except that her eyes leak a little from the understandable disappointment of finding herself still alive.

But somewhere one GTX computer has been tickling another, and toward midnight something does happen. First comes an attendant who pulls screens around her. Then a man in a business doublet comes daintily down the ward. He motions the attendant to strip off the sheet and go.

The groggy girl-brute heaves up, big hands clutching at body parts you'd pay not to see.

"Burke? P. Burke, is that your name?"

"Y-yes." Croak. "Are you . . . policeman?"

"No. They'll be along shortly, I expect. Public suicide's a felony."

". . . I'm sorry."

He has a 'corder in his hand. "No family, right?"

"No."

"You're seventeen. One year city college. What did you study?"

"La—languages."

"H'mm. Say something."

Unintelligible rasp.

He studies her. Seen close, he's not so elegant. Errand-boy type.

"Why did you try to kill yourself?"

She stares at him with dead-rat dignity, hauling up the gray sheet. Give him a point, he doesn't ask twice.

"Tell me, did you see Breath this afternoon?"

Dead as she nearly is, that ghastly love-look wells up. Breath is the three young gods, a loser's cult. Give the man another point, he interprets her expression.

"How would you like to meet them?"

The girl's eyes bug out grotesquely.

"I have a job for someone like you. It's hard work. If you did well you'd be meeting Breath and stars like that all the time."

Is he insane? She's deciding she really did die.

"But it means you never see anybody you know again. Never, *ever*. You will be legally dead. Even the police won't know. Do you want to try?"

It all has to be repeated while her great jaw slowly sets. *Show me the fire I walk through.* Finally P. Burke's prints are in his 'corder, the man holding up the big rancid girl-body without a sign of distaste. It makes you wonder what else he does.

And then—*the magic.* Sudden silent trot of litterbearers tucking P. Burke into something quite different from a bellevue stretcher, the oiled slide into the daddy of all luxury ambulances—real flowers in that holder!— and the long jarless rush to nowhere. Nowhere is warm and gleaming and kind with nurses. (Where did you hear that money can't buy genuine kindness?) And clean clouds folding P. Burke into bewildered sleep.

. . . Sleep which merges into feedings and washings and more sleeps, into drowsy moments of afternoon where midnight should be, and gentle businesslike voices and friendly (but very few) faces, and endless painless hyposprays and peculiar numbnesses. And later comes the steadying rhythm of days and nights, and a quickening which P. Burke doesn't identify as health, but only knows that the fungus place in her armpit is gone. And then she's up and following those few new faces with growing trust, first tottering, then walking strongly, all better now, clumping down the short hall to the tests, tests, tests, and the other things.

And here is our girl, looking—

If possible, worse than before. (You thought this was Cinderella transistorized?)

The disimprovement in her looks comes from the electrode jacks peeping out of her sparse hair, and there are other meldings of flesh and metal. On the other hand, that collar and spinal plate are really an asset; you won't miss seeing that neck.

P. Burke is ready for training in her new job.

The training takes place in her suite and is exactly what you'd call a charm course. How to walk, sit, eat, speak, blow her nose, how to stumble, to urinate, to hiccup—*deliciously*. How to make each nose-blow or shrug delightfully, subtly, different from any ever spooled before. As the man said, it's hard work.

But P. Burke proves apt. Somewhere in that horrible body is a gazelle, a houri, who would have been buried forever without this crazy chance. See the ugly duckling go!

Only it isn't precisely P. Burke who's stepping, laughing, shaking out her shining hair. How could it be? P. Burke is doing it all right, but she's doing it through something. The something is to all appearances a live girl. (You were warned, this is the *future*.)

When they first open the big cryocase and show her her new body, she says just one word. Staring, gulping, "How?"

Simple, really. Watch P. Burke in her sack and scuffs stump down the hall beside Joe, the man who supervises the technical part of her training. Joe doesn't mind P. Burke's looks, he hasn't noticed them. To Joe, system matrices are beautiful.

They go into a dim room containing a huge cabinet like a one-man sauna and a console for Joe. The room has a glass wall that's all dark now. And just for your information, the whole shebang is five hundred feet underground near what used to be Carbondale, PA.

Joe opens the sauna cabinet like a big clamshell standing on end with a lot of funny business inside. Our girl shucks her shift and walks into it bare, totally unembarrassed. *Eager.* She settles in face-forward, butting jacks into sockets. Joe closes it carefully onto her humpback. Clunk. She can't see in there or hear or move.

She hates this minute. But how she loves what comes next!

Joe's at his console, and the lights on the other side of the glass wall come up. A room is on the other side, all fluff and kicky bits, a girly bedroom. In the bed is a small mound of silk with a rope of yellow hair hanging out.

The sheet stirs and gets whammed back flat.

Sitting up in the bed is the darlingest girl child you've *ever* seen. She quivers—porno for angels. She sticks both her little arms straight up, flips her hair, looks around full of sleepy pazazz. Then she can't resist rubbing her hands down over her minibreasts and belly. Because, you see, it's the god-awful P. Burke who is sitting there hugging her perfect girl-body, looking at you out of delighted eyes.

Then the kitten hops out of bed and crashes flat on the floor.

From the sauna in the dim room comes a strangled noise. P. Burke, trying to rub her wired-up elbow, is suddenly smothered in *two* bodies, electrodes jerking in her flesh. Joe juggles inputs, crooning into his mike. The flurry passes; it's all right.

In the lighted room the elf gets up, casts a cute glare at the glass wall, and goes into a transparent cubicle. A bathroom, what else? She's a live girl, and live girls have to go to the bathroom after a night's sleep even if their brains are in a sauna cabinet in the next room. And P. Burke isn't in that cabinet, she's in the bathroom. Perfectly simple, if you have the glue for that closed training circuit that's letting her run her neural system by remote control.

Now let's get one thing clear. P. Burke does not *feel* her brain is in the sauna room, she feels she's in that sweet little body. When you wash your hands, do you feel the water is running on your brain? Of course not. You feel the water on your hand, although the "feeling" is actually a potential-pattern flickering over the electrochemical jelly between your ears. And it's delivered there via the long circuits from your hands. Just so, P. Burke's brain in the cabinet feels the water on her hands in the bathroom. The fact

18

that the signals have jumped across space on the way in makes no difference at all. If you want the jargon, it's known as eccentric projection or sensory reference and you've done it all your life. Clear?

Time to leave the honeypot to her toilet training—she's made a booboo with the toothbrush, because P. Burke can't get used to what she sees in the mirror—

But wait, you say. Where did that girl-body come from?

P. Burke asks that too, dragging out the words.

"They grow 'em," Joe tells her. He couldn't care less about the flesh department. "PDs. Placental decanters. Modified embryos, see? Fit the control implants in later. Without a Remote Operator it's just a vegetable. Look at the feet—no callus at all." (He knows because they told him.)

"Oh . . . oh, she's incredible. . . ."

"Yeah, a neat job. Want to try walking-talking mode today? You're coming on fast."

And she is. Joe's reports and the reports from the nurse and the doctor and style man go to a bushy man upstairs who is some kind of medical cybertech but mostly a project administrator. His reports in turn go—to the GTX boardroom? Certainly not, did you think this is *a big* thing? His reports just go up. The point is, they're green, very green. P. Burke promises well.

So the bushy man—Dr. Tesla—has procedures to initiate. The little kitten's dossier in the Central Data Bank, for instance. Purely routine. And the phase-in schedule which will put her on the scene. This is simple: a small exposure in an off-network holoshow.

Next he has to line out the event which will fund and target her. That takes budget meetings, clearances, coordinations. The Burke project begins to recruit and grow. And there's the messy business of the name, which always gives Dr. Tesla an acute pain in the bush.

The name comes out weird, when it's suddenly discovered that Burke's "P." stands for "Philadelphia." Philadelphia? The astrologer

grooves on it. Joe thinks it would help identification. The semantics girl references *brotherly love*, *Liberty Bell*, *main line*, *low teratogenesis*, blah-blah. Nicknames Philly? Pala? Pooty? Delphi? Is it good, bad? Finally "Delphi" is gingerly declared goodo. ("Burke" is replaced by something nobody remembers.)

Coming along now. We're at the official checkout down in the underground suite, which is as far as the training circuits reach. The bushy Dr. Tesla is there, braced by two budgetary types and a quiet fatherly man whom he handles like hot plasma.

Joe swings the door wide and she steps shyly in.

Their little Delphi, fifteen and flawless.

Tesla introduces her around. She's child-solemn, a beautiful baby to whom something so wonderful has happened you can feel the tingles. She doesn't smile, she . . . brims. That brimming joy is all that shows of P. Burke, the forgotten hulk in the sauna next door. But P. Burke doesn't know she's alive—it's Delphi who lives, every warm inch of her.

One of the budget types lets go a libidinous snuffle and freezes. The fatherly man, whose name is Mr. Cantle, clears his throat.

"Well, young lady, are you ready to go to work?"

"Yes, sir," gravely from the elf.

"We'll see. Has anybody told you what you're going to do for us?"

"No, sir." Joe and Tesla exhale quietly.

"Good." He eyes her, probing for the blind brain in the room next door.

"Do you know what *advertising* is?"

He's talking dirty, hitting to shock. Delphi's *eyes* widen and her little chin goes up. Joe is in ecstasy at the complex expressions P. Burke is getting through. Mr. Cantle waits.

"It's, well, it's when they used to tell people to buy things." She swallows. "It's not allowed."

"That's right." Mr. Cantle leans back, grave. "Advertising as it used to be is against the law. *A display other than the legitimate use of the product, intended to promote its sale.* In former times every manufacturer was free to tout his wares any way, place, or time he could afford. All the media and most of the landscape was taken up with extravagant competing displays. The thing became uneconomic. The public rebelled. Since the so-called Huckster Act sellers have been restrained to, I quote, displays in or on the product itself, visible during its legitimate use or in on-premises sales." Mr. Cantle leans forward. "Now tell me, Delphi, why do people buy one product rather than another?"

"Well . . ." Enchanting puzzlement from Delphi. "They, um, they see them and like them, or they hear about them from somebody?" (Touch of P. Burke there; she didn't say, from a friend.)

"Partly. Why did *you* buy your particular body-lift?"

"I never had a body-lift, sir."

Mr. Cantle frowns; what gutters do they drag for these Remotes?

"Well, what brand of water do you drink?"

"Just what was in the faucet, sir," says Delphi humbly. "I—I did try to boil it—"

"Good god." He scowls; Tesla stiffens. "Well, what did you boil it in? A cooker?"

The shining yellow head nods.

"What *brand* of cooker did you buy?"

"I didn't buy it, sir," says frightened P. Burke through Delphi's lips. "But—I know the best kind! Ananga has a Burnbabi. I saw the name when she—"

"Exactly!" Cantle's fatherly beam comes back strong; the Burnbabi account is a strong one, too. "You saw Ananga using one so you thought it must be good, eh? And it is good, or a great human being like Ananga wouldn't be using it. Absolutely right. And now, Delphi, you know what you're going to be doing for us. You're going to show some products. Doesn't sound very hard, does it?"

"Oh, no, sir . . ." Baffled child's stare; Joe gloats.

"And you must never, *never* tell anyone what you're doing." Cantle's eyes bore for the brain behind this seductive child.

"You're wondering why we ask you to do this, naturally. There's a very serious reason. All those products people use, foods and healthaids and cookers and cleaners and clothes and cars— they're all made by *people*. Somebody put in years of hard work designing and making them. A man comes up with a fine new idea for a better product. He has to get a factory and machinery, and hire workmen. Now. What happens if people have no way of hearing about his product? Word of mouth is far too slow and unreliable. Nobody might ever stumble onto his new product or find out how good it was, right? And then he and all the people who worked for him— they'd go bankrupt, right? So, Delphi, there has to be *some way* that large numbers of people can get a look at a good new product, right? How? By letting people see you using it. You're giving that man a chance."

Delphi's little head is nodding in happy relief.

"Yes, sir, I do see now—but sir, it seems so sensible, why don't they let you—"

Cantle smiles sadly.

"It's an overreaction, my dear. History goes by swings. People overreact and pass harsh unrealistic laws which attempt to stamp out an essential social process. When this happens, the people who understand have to carry on as best they can until the pendulum swings back." He sighs. "The Huckster Laws are bad, inhuman laws, Delphi, despite their good intent. If they were strictly observed they would wreak havoc. Our economy, our society, would be cruelly destroyed. We'd be back in caves!" His inner fire is showing; if the Huckster Laws were strictly enforced he'd be back punching a databank.

"It's our duty, Delphi. Our solemn social duty. We are not breaking the law. You will be using the product. But people wouldn't understand, if they knew. They would become upset just as you did. So you must be very, very careful not to mention any of this to anybody."

(And somebody will be very, very carefully monitoring Delphi's speech circuits.)

"Now we're all straight, aren't we? Little Delphi here"—he is speaking to the invisible creature next door—"little Delphi is going to live a wonderful, exciting life. She's going to be a girl people watch. And she's going to be using fine products people will be glad to know about and helping the good people who make them. Yours will be a genuine social contribution." He keys up his pitch; the creature in there must be older.

Delphi digests this with ravishing gravity.

"But sir, how do I—?"

"Don't worry about a thing. You'll have people behind you whose job it is to select the most worthy products for you to use. Your job is just to do as they say. They'll show you what outfits to wear to parties, what suncars and viewers to buy, and so on. That's all you have to do."

Parties—clothes—suncars! Delphi's pink mouth opens. In P. Burke's starved seventeen-year-old head the ethics of product sponsorship float far away.

"Now tell me in your own words what your job is, Delphi."

"Yes, sir. I—I'm to go to parties and buy things and use them as they tell me, to help the people who work in factories."

"And what did I say was so important?"

"Oh—I shouldn't let anybody know, about the things."

"Right." Mr. Cantle has another paragraph he uses when the subject shows, well, immaturity. But he can sense only eagerness here. Good. He doesn't really enjoy the other speech.

"It's a lucky girl who can have all the fun she wants while doing good for others, isn't it?" He beams around. There's a prompt shuffling of chairs. Clearly this one is go.

Joe leads her out, grinning. The poor fool thinks they're admiring her coordination.

It's out into the world for Delphi now, and at this point the up-channels get used. On the administrative side account schedules are opened, subprojects activated. On the technical side the reserved bandwidth is cleared. (That carrier field, remember?) A new name is waiting for Delphi, a name she'll never hear. It's a long string of binaries which have been quietly

cycling in a GTX tank ever since a certain Beautiful Person didn't wake up.

The name winks out of cycle, dances from pulses into modulations of modulations, whizzes through phasing, and shoots into a giga-band beam racing up to a synchronous satellite poised over Guatemala. From there the beam pours twenty thousand miles back to Earth again, forming an all-pervasive field of structured energics supplying tuned demand-points all over the CanAm quadrant.

With that field, if you have the right credit rating, you can sit at a GTX console and operate an ore extractor in Brazil. Or—if you have some simple credentials like being able to walk on water—you could shoot a spool into the network holocam shows running day and night in every home and dorm and rec site. Or you could create a continentwide traffic jam. Is it any wonder GTX guards those inputs like a sacred trust?

Delphi's "name" appears as a tiny analyzable nonredundancy in the flux, and she'd be very proud if she knew about it. It would strike P. Burke as magic; P. Burke never even understood robotcars. But Delphi is in no sense a robot. Call her a waldo if you must. The fact is she's just a girl, a real-live girl with her brain in an unusual place. A simple real-time on-line system with plenty of bit-rate—even as you and you.

The point of all this hardware, which isn't very much hardware in this society, is so Delphi can walk out of that underground suite, a mobile demand-point draining an omnipresent fieldform. And she does—eighty-nine pounds of tender girl flesh and blood with a few metallic components, stepping out into the sunlight to be taken to her new life. A girl, with everything going for her including a meditech escort. Walking lovely, stopping to widen her eyes at the big antennae system overhead.

The mere fact that something called P. Burke is left behind down underground has no bearing at all. P. Burke is totally un-self-aware and happy as a clam in its shell. (Her bed has been moved into the waldo cabinet room now.) And P. Burke isn't in the cabinet; P. Burke is climbing out of an airvan in a fabulous Colorado beef preserve, and her name is Delphi. Delphi is looking at live Charolais steers and live cottonwoods and aspens gold against the blue smog and stepping over live grass to be welcomed by the reserve super's wife.

The super's wife is looking forward to a visit from Delphi and her friends, and by a happy coincidence there's a holocam outfit here doing a piece for the nature nuts.

You could write the script yourself now, while Delphi learns a few rules about structural interferences and how to handle the tiny time lag which results from the new forty-thousand-mile parenthesis in her nervous system. That's right—the people with the leased holocam rig naturally find the gold aspen shadows look a lot better on Delphi's flank than they do on a steer. And Delphi's face improves the mountains too, when you can see them. But the nature freaks aren't quite as joyful as you'd expect.

"See you in Barcelona, kitten," the headman says sourly as they pack up.

"Barcelona?" echoes Delphi with that charming little subliminal lag. She sees where his hand is and steps back. "Cool, it's not her fault," another man says wearily. He knocks back his grizzled hair. "Maybe they'll leave in some of the gut."

Delphi watches them go off to load the spools on the GTX transport for processing. Her hand roves over the breast the man had touched. Back under Carbondale, P. Burke has discovered something new about her Delphi-body.

About the difference between Delphi and her own grim carcass.

She's always known Delphi has almost no sense of taste or smell. They explained about that: only so much bandwidth. You don't have to taste a suncar, do you? And the slight over-all dimness of Delphi's sense of touch—she's familiar with that, too. Fabrics that would prickle P. Burke's own hide feel like a cool plastic film to Delphi.

But the blank spots. It took her a while to notice them. Delphi doesn't have much privacy; investments of her size don't. So she's slow about discovering there's certain definite places where her beastly P. Burke body *feels* things that Delphi's dainty flesh does not. H'mm! Channel space again, she thinks—and forgets it in the pure bliss of being Delphi.

You ask how a girl could forget a thing like that? Look. P. Burke is about as far as you can get from the concept *girl*. She's a female, yes—but for her, sex is a four-letter word spelled P-A-I-N. She isn't quite a virgin. You don't want the details; she'd been about twelve and the freak lovers were bombed blind. When they came down, they threw her out with a small hole in her anatomy and a mortal one elsewhere. She dragged off to buy her first and last shot, and she can still hear the clerk's incredulous guffaws.

Do you see why Delphi grins, stretching her delicious little numb body in the sun she faintly feels? Beams, saying, "Please, I'm ready now."

Ready for what? For Barcelona like the sour man said, where his nature-thing is now making it strong in the amateur section of the Festival. A winner! Like he also said, a lot of strip mines and dead fish have been scrubbed, but who cares with Delphi's darling face so visible?

So it's time for Delphi's face and her other delectabilities to show on Barcelona's Playa Nueva. Which means switching her channel to the EurAf synchsat.

They ship her at night so the nanosecond transfer isn't even noticed by that insignificant part of Delphi that lives five hundred feet under Carbondale, so excited the nurse has to make sure she eats. The circuit switches while Delphi "sleeps," that is, while P. Burke is out of the waldo cabinet. The next time she plugs in to open Delphi's eyes it's no different—do you notice which relay boards your phone calls go through?

And now for the event that turns the sugarcube from Colorado into the *princess*.

Literally true, he's a prince, or rather an

Infante of an old Spanish line that got shined up in the Neomonarchy. He's also eighty-one, with a passion for birds—the kind you see in zoos. Now it suddenly turns out that he isn't poor at all. Quite the reverse; his old sister laughs in their tax lawyer's face and starts restoring the family hacienda while the Infante totters out to court Delphi. And little Delphi begins to live the life of the gods.

What do gods do? Well, everything beautiful. But (remember Mr. Cantle?) the main point is Things. Ever see a god empty-handed? You can't be a god without at least a magic girdle or an eight-legged horse. But in the old days some stone tablets or winged sandals or a chariot drawn by virgins would do a god for life. No more! Gods make it on novelty now. By Delphi's time the hunt for new god-gear is turning the earth and seas inside-out and sending frantic fingers to the stars. And what gods have, mortals desire.

So Delphi starts on a Euromarket shopping spree squired by her old Infante, thereby doing her bit to stave off social collapse.

Social what? Didn't you get it, when Mr. Cantle talked about a world where advertising is banned and fifteen billion consumers are glued to their holocam shows? One capricious self-powered god can wreck you.

Take the nose-filter massacre. Years, the industry sweated years to achieve an almost invisible enzymatic filter. So one day a couple of pop-gods show up wearing nose-filters like *big purple bats*. By the end of the week the world market is screaming for purple bats. Then it switched to bird-heads and skulls, but by the time the industry retooled the crazies had dropped bird-heads and gone to injection globes. Blood!

Multiply that by a million consumer industries, and you can see why it's economic to have a few controllable gods. Especially with the beautiful hunk of space R&D the Peace Department laid out for and which the taxpayers are only too glad to have taken off their hands by an outfit like GTX, which everybody knows is almost a public trust.

And so you—or rather, GTX—find a creature like P. Burke and give her Delphi. And Delphi helps keep things *orderly*, she does what you tell her to. Why? That's right, Mr. Cantle never finished his speech.

But here come the tests of Delphi's button-nose twinkling in the torrent of news and entertainment. And she's noticed. The feedback shows a flock of viewers turning up the amps when this country baby gets tangled in her new colloidal body-jewels. She registers at a couple of major scenes, too, and when the Infante gives her a suncar, little Delphi trying out suncars is a tiger. There's a solid response in high-credit country. Mr. Cantle is humming his happy tune as he cancels a Benelux subnet option to guest her on a nude cook-show called Wok Venus.

And now for the superposh old-world wedding! The hacienda has Moorish baths and six-foot silver candelabra and real black horses, and the Spanish Vatican blesses them. The final event is a grand gaucho ball with the old prince and his little Infanta on a bowered balcony. She's a spectacular doll of silver lace, wildly launching toy doves at her new friends whirling by below.

The Infante beams, twitches his old nose to the scent of her sweet excitement. His doctor has been very helpful. Surely now, after he has been so patient with the suncars and all the nonsense—

The child looks up at him, saying something incomprehensible about "breath." He makes out that she's complaining about the three singers she had begged for.

"They've changed!" she marvels. "Haven't they changed? They're so dreary. I'm so happy now!"

And Delphi falls fainting against a gothic vargueno.

Her American duenna rushes up, calls help. Delphi's eyes are open, but Delphi isn't there.

The duenna pokes among Delphi's hair, slaps her. The old prince grimaces. He has no idea what she is beyond an excellent solution to his tax problems, but he had been a falconer in his youth. There comes to his mind the small pinioned birds which were flung up to stimulate the hawks. He pockets the veined claw to which he had promised certain indulgences and departs to design his new aviary.

And Delphi also departs with her retinue to the Infante's newly discovered yacht. The trouble isn't serious. It's only that five thousand miles away and five hundred feet down P. Burke has been doing it too well.

They've always known she has terrific aptitude. Joe says he never saw a Remote take over so fast. No disorientations, no rejections. The psychomed talks about self-alienation. She's going into Delphi like a salmon to the sea.

She isn't eating or sleeping, they can't keep her out of the body-cabinet to get her blood moving, there are necroses under her grisly sitdown. Crisis!

So Delphi gets a long "sleep" on the yacht and P. Burke gets it pounded through her perforated head that she's endangering Delphi. (Nurse Fleming thinks of that, thus alienating the psychomed.)

They rig a pool down there (Nurse Fleming again) and chase P. Burke back and forth. And she loves it. So naturally when they let her plug in again Delphi loves it too. Every noon beside the yacht's hydrofoils darling Delphi clips along in the blue sea they've warned her not to drink. And every night around the shoulder of the world an ill-shaped thing in a dark burrow beats its way across a sterile pool.

So presently the yacht stands up on its foils and carries Delphi to the program Mr. Cantle has waiting. It's long-range; she's scheduled for at least two decades' product life. Phase One calls for her to connect with a flock of young ultrariches who are romping loose between Brioni and Djakarta where a competitor named PEV could pick them off.

A routine luxgear op, see; no politics, no policy angles, and the main budget items are the title and the yacht, which was idle anyway. The storyline is that Delphi goes to accept some rare birds for her prince—who cares? The *point* is that the Haiti area is no longer radioactive and look!—the gods are there. And so are several new Carib West Happy Isles which can afford GTX rates, in fact two of them are GTX subsids.

But you don't want to get the idea that all these newsworthy people are wired-up robbies, for pity's sake. You don't need many if they're placed right. Delphi asks Joe about that when he comes down to Barranquilla to check her over. (P. Burke's own mouth hasn't said much for a while.)

"Are there many like me?"

"Nobody's like you, buttons. Look, are you still getting Van Allen warble?"

"I mean, like Davy. Is he a Remote?"

(Davy is the lad who is helping her collect the birds. A sincere redhead who needs a little more exposure.)

"Davy? He's one of Matt's boys, some psychojob. They haven't any channel."

"What about the real ones? Djuma van O, or Ali, or Jim Ten?"

"Djuma was born with a pile of GTX basic where her brain should be, she's nothing but a pain. Jimsy does what his astrologer tells him. Look, peanut, where do you get the idea you aren't real? You're the realest. Aren't you having joy?"

"Oh, Joe!" Flinging her little arms around him and his analyzer grids. "Oh, *me gustó mucho, ¡muchísimo!*"

"Hey, hey." He pets her yellow head, folding the analyzer.

Three thousand miles north and five hundred feet down a forgotten hulk in a body-waldo glows.

And is she having joy. To waken out of the nightmare of being P. Burke and find herself a peri, a star-girl? On a yacht in paradise with no more to do than adorn herself and play with toys and attend revels and greet her friends—her, P. Burke, having friends!—and turn the right way for the holocams? Joy!

And it shows. One look at Delphi and the viewers know: *dreams can come true.*

Look at her riding pillion on Davy's sea-bike, carrying an apoplectic macaw in a silver hoop. Oh, *Morton, let's go there this winter!* Or learning the Japanese chinchona from that Kobe group, in a dress that looks like a blow-torch rising from one knee, and which should sell big in Texas. *Morton, is that real fire?* Happy, happy little girl!

And Davy. He's her pet and her baby, and she loves to help him fix his red-gold hair. (P. Burke marveling, running Delphi's fingers through the curls.) Of course Davy is one of Matt's boys—not impotent exactly, but very *very* low drive. (Nobody knows exactly what Matt does with his bitty budget, but the boys are useful and one or two have made names.) He's perfect for Delphi; in fact the psychomed lets her take him to bed, two kittens in a basket. Davy doesn't mind the fact that Delphi "sleeps" like the dead. That's when P. Burke is out of the body-waldo up at Carbondale, attending to her own depressing needs.

A funny thing about that. Most of her sleepy-time Delphi's just a gently ticking lush little vegetable waiting for P. Burke to get back on the controls. But now and again Delphi all by herself smiles a bit or stirs in her "sleep." Once she breathed a sound: "Yes."

Under Carbondale P. Burke knows nothing. She's asleep too, dreaming of Delphi, what else? But if the bushy Dr. Tesla had heard that single syllable, his bush would have turned snow white. Because Delphi is *turned off.*

He doesn't. Davy is too dim to notice, and Delphi's staff boss, Hopkins, wasn't monitoring.

And they've all got something else to think about now, because the cold-fire dress sells half a million copies, and not only in Texas. The GTX computers already know it. When they correlate a minor demand for macaws in Alaska the problem comes to human attention: Delphi is something special.

It's a problem, see, because Delphi is targeted on a limited consumer bracket. Now it turns out she has mass-pop potential—those macaws in *Fairbanks*, man!—it's like trying to shoot mice with an ABM. A whole new ball game. Dr. Tesla and the fatherly Mr. Cantle start going around in headquarters circles and buddy-lunching together when they can get away from a seventh-level weasel boy who scares them both.

In the end it's decided to ship Delphi down to the GTX holocam enclave in Chile to try a spot on one of the mainstream shows. (Never mind why an Infanta takes up acting.) The holocam complex occupies a couple of mountains where an observatory once used the clean air. Holocam total-environment shells are very expensive and electronically superstable. Inside them actors can move freely without going off-register, and the whole scene or any selected part will show up in the viewer's home in complete three-di, so real you can look up their noses and much denser than you get from mobile rigs. You can blow a tit ten feet tall when there's no molecular skiffle around.

The enclave looks—well, take everything you know about Hollywood-Burbank and throw it away. What Delphi sees coming down is a neat giant mushroom-farm, domes of all sizes up to monsters for the big games and stuff. It's orderly. The idea that art thrives on creative flamboyance has long been torpedoed by proof that what art needs is computers. Because this showbiz has something TV and Hollywood never had—*automated inbuilt viewer feedback.* Samples, ratings, critics, polls? Forget it. With that carrier field you can get real-time response-sensor readouts from every receiver in the world, served up at your console. That started as a thingie to give the public more influence on content.

Yes.

Try it, man. You're at the console. Slice to the sex-age-educ-econ-ethno-cetera audience of your choice and start. You can't miss. Where the feedback warms up, give 'em more of that. Warm—warmer—*hot!* You've hit it—the secret itch under those hides, the dream in those hearts. You don't need to know its name. With your hand controlling all the input and your eye reading all the response, you can make them a god . . . and somebody'll do the same for you.

But Delphi just sees rainbows, when she gets through the degaussing ports and the field relay and takes her first look at the insides of those shells. The next thing she sees is a team of shapers and technicians descending on her, and millisecond timers everywhere. The tropical leisure is finished. She's in gigabuck mainstream now, at the funnel maw of the unceasing hose that's pumping the sight and sound and flesh and blood and sobs and laughs and dreams of *reality* into the world's happy head. Little Delphi is going plonk into a zillion homes in prime time and nothing is left to chance. Work!

And again Delphi proves apt. Of course it's really P. Burke down under Carbondale who's doing it, but who remembers that carcass? Certainly not P. Burke, she hasn't spoken through her own mouth for months. Delphi doesn't even recall dreaming of her when she wakes up.

As for the show itself, don't bother. It's gone on so long no living soul could unscramble the plotline. Delphi's trial spot has something to do with a widow and her dead husband's brother's amnesia.

The flap comes after Delphi's spots begin to flash out along the world-hose and the feedback appears. You've guessed it, of course. Sensational! As you'd say, they *identify*.

The report actually says something like InskinEmp with a string of percentages, meaning that Delphi not only has it for anybody with a Y chromosome, but also for women and everything in between. It's the sweet supernatural jackpot, the million-to-one.

Remember your Harlow? A sexpot, sure. But why did bitter hausfraus in Gary and Memphis know that the vanilla-ice-cream goddess with the white hair and crazy eyebrows was *their baby*

girl? And write loving letters to Jean warning her that their husbands weren't good enough for her? Why? The GTX analysts don't know either, but they know what to do with it when it happens.

(Back in his bird sanctuary the old Infante spots it without benefit of computers and gazes thoughtfully at his bride in widow's weeds. It might, he feels, be well to accelerate the completion of his studies.)

The excitement reaches down to the burrow under Carbondale where P. Burke gets two medical exams in a week and a chronically inflamed electrode is replaced. Nurse Fleming also gets an assistant who doesn't do much nursing but is very interested in access doors and identity tabs.

And in Chile, little Delphi is promoted to a new home up among the stars' residential spreads and a private jitney to carry her to work. For Hopkins there's a new computer terminal and a full-time schedule man. What is the schedule crowded with?

Things.

And here begins the trouble. You probably saw that coming too.

"What does she think she is, a goddamn *consumer rep?*" Mr. Cantle's fatherly face in Carbondale contorts.

"The girl's upset," Miss Fleming says stubbornly. "She *believes* that, what you told her about helping people and good new products."

"They are good products," Mr. Cantle snaps automatically, but his anger is under control. He hasn't got where he is by irrelevant reactions.

"She says the plastic gave her a rash and the glo-pills made her dizzy."

"Good god, she shouldn't swallow them," Dr. Tesla puts in agitatedly.

"You told her she'd use them," persists Miss Fleming.

Mr. Cantle is busy figuring how to ease this problem to the feral-faced young man. What, was it a goose that lays golden eggs?

Whatever he says to Level Seven, down in Chile the offending products vanish. And a symbol goes into Delphi's tank matrix, one that means roughly *Balance unit resistance against PR index*.

This means that Delphi's complaints will be endured as long as her Pop Response stays above a certain level. (What happens when it sinks need not concern us.) And to compensate, the price of her exposure time rises again. She's a regular on the show now and response is still climbing.

See her under the sizzling lasers, in a holo-cam shell set up as a walkway accident. (The show is guesting an acupuncture school shill.)

"I don't think this new body-lift is safe," Delphi's saying. "It's made a funny blue spot on me—look, Mr. Vere."

She wiggles to show where the mini–gray pak that imparts a delicious sense of weightlessness is attached.

"So don't leave it *on*, Dee. With your meat—watch that deck-spot, it's starting to synch."

"But if I don't wear it it isn't honest. They should insulate it more or something, don't you see?"

The show's beloved old father, who is the casualty, gives a senile snigger.

"I'll tell them," Mr. Vere mutters. "Look now, as you step back bend like this so it just shows, see? And hold two beats."

Obediently Delphi turns, and through the dazzle her eyes connect with a pair of strange dark ones. She squints. A quite young man is lounging alone by the port, apparently waiting to use the chamber.

Delphi's used by now to young men looking at her with many peculiar expressions, but she isn't used to what she gets here. A jolt of something somber and knowing. Secrets.

"Eyes! Eyes, Dee!"

She moves through the routine, stealing peeks at the stranger. He stares back. He knows something.

When they let her go she comes shyly to him.

"Living wild, kitten." Cool voice, hot underneath.

"What do you mean?"

"Dumping on the product. You trying to get dead?"

"But it isn't right," she tells him. "They don't know, but I do, I've been wearing it."

His cool is jolted.

"You're out of your head."

"Oh, they'll see I'm right when they check it," she explains. "They're just so busy. When I tell them—"

He is staring down at little flower-face. His mouth opens, closes. "What are you doing in this sewer anyway? Who are you?"

Bewilderedly she says, "I'm Delphi."

"Holy Zen."

"What's wrong? Who are you, please?"

Her people are moving her out now, nodding at him.

"Sorry we ran over, Mr. Uhunh," the script girl says.

He mutters something, but it's lost as her convoy bustles her toward the flower-decked jitney.

(Hear the click of an invisible ignition-train being armed?)

"Who was he?" Delphi asks her hairman.

The hairman is bending up and down from his knees as he works.

"Paul. Isham. Three," he says and puts a comb in his mouth.

"Who's that? I can't see."

He mumbles around the comb, meaning, "Are you jiving?" Because she has to be, in the middle of the GTX enclave.

Next day there's a darkly smoldering face under a turban-towel when Delphi and the show's paraplegic go to use the carbonated pool.

She looks.

He looks.

And the next day, too.

(Hear the automatic sequencer cutting in? The system couples, the fuels begin to travel.)

Poor old Isham senior. You have to feel sorry for a man who values order: when he begets young, genetic information is still transmitted in the old ape way. One minute it's a happy midget with a rubber duck—look around and here's this huge healthy stranger, opaquely emotional, running with god knows who. Questions are heard where there's nothing to question, and eruptions claiming to be moral outrage. When this is called to Papa's attention—it may take time, in that boardroom—Papa does what he can, but without immortality-juice the problem is worrisome.

And young Paul Isham is a bear. He's bright and articulate and tender-souled and incessantly active, and he and his friends are choking with appalment at the world their fathers made. And it hasn't taken Paul long to discover that *his* father's house has many mansions and even the GTX computers can't relate everything to everything else. He noses out a decaying project which adds up to something like, Sponsoring Marginal Creativity (the free-lance team that "discovered" Delphi was one such grantee). And from there it turns out that an agile lad named Isham can get his hands on a viable packet of GTX holocam facilities.

So here he is with his little band, way down the mushroom-farm mountain, busily spooling a show which has no relation to Delphi's. It's built on bizarre techniques and unsettling distortions pregnant with social protest. An *underground* expression to you.

All this isn't unknown to his father, of course, but so far it has done nothing more than deepen Isham senior's apprehensive frown.

Until Paul connects with Delphi.

And by the time Papa learns this, those invisible hypergolics have exploded, the energy-shells are rushing out. For Paul, you see, is the genuine article. He's serious. He dreams. He even reads—for example, *Green Mansions*—and he wept fiercely when those fiends burned Rima alive.

When he hears that some new GTX pussy is making it big, he sneers and forgets it. He's busy. He never connects the name with this little girl making her idiotic, doomed protest in the holocam chamber. This strangely simple little girl.

And she comes and looks up at him and he sees Rima, lost Rima the enchanted bird girl, and his unwired human heart goes twang.

And Rima turns out to be Delphi.

Do you need a map? The angry puzzlement. The rejection of the dissonance Rima-hustling-for-GTX-My-Father. Garbage, cannot be. The loitering around the pool to confirm the swindle . . . dark eyes hitting on blue wonder, jerky words exchanged in a peculiar stillness . . . the dreadful reorganization of the image into Rima-Delphi *in my Father's tentacles*—

You don't need a map.

Nor for Delphi either, the girl who loved her gods. She's seen their divine flesh close now, heard their unamplified voices call her name. She's played their god-games, worn their garlands. She's even become a goddess herself, though she doesn't believe it. She's not disenchanted, don't think that. She's still full of love. It's just that some crazy kind of *hope* hasn't—

Really you can skip all this, when the loving little girl on the yellow-brick road meets a Man. A real human male burning with angry compassion and grandly concerned with human justice, who reaches for her with real male arms and—boom! She loves him back with all her heart.

A happy trip, see?

Except.

Except that it's really P. Burke five thousand miles away who loves Paul. P. Burke the monster down in a dungeon smelling of electrode paste. A caricature of a woman burning, melting, obsessed with true love. Trying over twenty-double-thousand miles of hard vacuum to reach her beloved through girl-flesh numbed by an invisible film. Feeling his arms around the body she thinks is hers, fighting through shadows to give herself to him. Trying to taste and smell him through beautiful dead nostrils, to love him back with a body that goes dead in the heart of the fire.

Perhaps you get P. Burke's state of mind?

She has phases. The trying, first. And the shame. The *shame. I am not what thou lovest.*

And the fiercer trying. And the realization that there is no, no way, none. Never. *Never* . . . A bit delayed, isn't it, her understanding that the bargain she made was forever? P. Burke should have noticed those stories about mortals who end up as grasshoppers.

You see the outcome—the funneling of all this agony into one dumb protoplasmic drive to fuse with Delphi. To leave, to close out the beast she is chained to. *To become Delphi.*

Of course it's impossible.

However, her torments have an effect on Paul. Delphi-as-Rima is a potent enough love object, and liberating Delphi's mind requires hours of deeply satisfying instruction in the rottenness of it all. Add in Delphi's body worshiping his flesh, burning in the fire of P. Burke's savage heart—do you wonder Paul is involved?

That's not all.

By now they're spending every spare moment together and some that aren't so spare.

"Mr. Isham, would you mind staying out of this sports sequence? The script calls for Davy here."

(Davy's still around, the exposure did him good.)

"What's the difference?" Paul yawns. "It's just an ad. I'm not blocking that thing."

Shocked silence at his two-letter word. The script girl swallows bravely.

"I'm sorry, sir, our directive is to do the *social sequence* exactly as scripted. We're having to respool the segments we did last week, Mr. Hopkins is very angry with me."

"Who the hell is Hopkins? Where is he?"

"Oh, please, Paul. *Please.*"

Paul unwraps himself, saunters back. The holocam crew nervously check their angles. The GTX boardroom has a foible about having things *pointed* at them and theirs. Cold shivers, when the image of an Isham nearly went onto the world beam beside that Dialadinner.

Worse yet, Paul has no respect for the sacred schedules which are now a full-time job for ferret boy up at headquarters. Paul keeps forgetting to bring her back on time, and poor Hopkins can't cope.

So pretty soon the boardroom data-ball has an urgent personal action-tab for Mr. Isham senior. They do it the gentle way, at first.

"I can't today, Paul."

"Why not?"

"They say I have to, it's *very* important."

He strokes the faint gold down on her narrow back. Under Carbondale, PA, a blind mole-woman shivers.

"Important. Their importance. Making more gold. Can't you see? To them you're just a thing to get scratch with. *A huckster.* Are you going to let them screw you, Dee? Are you?"

"Oh, Paul—"

He doesn't know it, but he's seeing a weirdie; Remotes aren't hooked up to flow tears.

"Just say no, Dee. No. Integrity. You have to."

"But they say, it's my job—"

"Will you believe I can take care of you, Dee? Baby, baby, you're letting them rip us. You have to choose. Tell them, no."

"Paul . . . I w-will. . . ."

And she does. Brave little Delphi (insane P. Burke). Saying, "No, please, I promised, Paul."

They try some more, still gently.

"Paul, Mr. Hopkins told me the reason they don't want us to be together so much. It's because of who you are, your father."

She thinks his father is like Mr. Cantle, maybe.

"Oh, great. Hopkins. I'll fix him. Listen, I can't think about Hopkins now. Ken came back today, he found out something."

They are lying on the high Andes meadow watching his friends dive their singing kites.

"Would you believe, on the coast the police have *electrodes in their heads?*"

She stiffens in his arms.

"Yeah, weird. I thought they only used PP on criminals and the army. Don't you see, Dee—something has to be going on. Some movement. Maybe somebody's organizing. How can we find out?" He pounds the ground behind her:

"We should make *contact*! If we could only find out."

"The, the news?" she asks distractedly.

"The news." He laughs. "There's nothing in the news except what they want people to know. Half the country could burn up, and nobody would know it if they didn't want. Dee, can't you take what I'm explaining to you? They've got the whole world programmed! Total control of communication. They've got everybody's minds wired in to think what they show them and want what they give them and they give them what they're programmed to want—you can't break in or out of it, you can't get *hold* of it anywhere. I don't think they even have a plan except to keep things going round and round—and god knows what's happening to the people or the Earth or the other planets, maybe. One great big vortex of lies and garbage pouring round and round, getting bigger and bigger, and nothing can ever change. If people don't wake up soon we're through!"

He pounds her stomach softly.

"You have to break out, Dee."

"I'll try, Paul, I will—"

"You're mine. They can't have you."

And he goes to see Hopkins, who is indeed cowed.

But that night up under Carbondale the fatherly Mr. Cantle goes to see P. Burke.

P. Burke? On a cot in a utility robe like a dead camel in a tent, she cannot at first comprehend that he is telling *her* to break it off with Paul. P. Burke has never seen Paul. *Delphi* sees Paul. The fact is, P. Burke can no longer clearly recall that she exists apart from Delphi.

Mr. Cantle can scarcely believe it either, but he tries.

He points out the futility, the potential embarrassment, for Paul. That gets a dim stare from the bulk on the bed. Then he goes into her duty to GTX, her job, isn't she grateful for the opportunity, etcetera. He's very persuasive.

The cobwebby mouth of P. Burke opens and croaks.

"No."

Nothing more seems to be forthcoming.

Mr. Cantle isn't dense, he knows an immovable obstacle when he bumps one. He also knows an irresistible force: GTX. The simple solution is to lock the waldo-cabinet until Paul gets tired of waiting for Delphi to wake up. But the cost, the schedules! And there's something odd here . . . he eyes the corporate asset hulking on the bed and his hunch-sense prickles.

You see, Remotes don't love. They don't have real sex, the circuits designed that out from the start. So it's been assumed that it's *Paul* who is diverting himself or something with the pretty little body in Chile. P. Burke can only be doing what comes natural to any ambitious gutter-meat. It hasn't occurred to anyone that they're dealing with the real hairy thing whose shadow is blasting out of every holoshow on Earth.

Love?

Mr. Cantle frowns. The idea is grotesque. But his instinct for the fuzzy line is strong; he will recommend flexibility. And so, in Chile:

"Darling, I don't have to work tonight! And Friday too—isn't that right, Mr. Hopkins?"

"Oh, great. When does she come up for parole?"

"Mr. Isham, please be reasonable. Our schedule—surely your own production people must be needing you?"

This happens to be true. Paul goes away. Hopkins stares after him, wondering distastefully why an Isham wants to ball a waldo. How sound are those boardroom belly-fears—garble creeps, creeps in! It never occurs to Hopkins that an Isham might not know what Delphi is.

Especially with Davy crying because Paul has kicked him out of Delphi's bed.

Delphi's bed is under a real window.

"Stars," Paul says sleepily. He rolls over, pulling Delphi on top. "Are you aware that this is one of the last places on Earth where people can see the stars? Tibet, too, maybe."

"Paul . . ."

"Go to sleep. I want to see you sleep."

"Paul, I . . . I sleep so *hard*, I mean, it's a joke how hard I am to wake up. Do you mind?"

"Yes."

But finally, fearfully, she must let go. So that five thousand miles north a crazy spent creature can crawl out to gulp concentrates and fall on her cot. But not for long. It's pink dawn when Delphi's eyes open to find Paul's arms around her, his voice saying rude, tender things. He's been kept awake. The nerveless little statue that was her Delphi-body nuzzled him in the night.

Insane hope rises, is fed a couple of nights later when he tells her she called his name in her sleep.

And that day Paul's arms keep her from work and Hopkins's wails go up to headquarters where the weasel-faced lad is working his sharp tailbone off packing Delphi's program. Mr. Cantle defuses that one. But next week it happens again, to a major client. And ferret-face has connections on the technical side.

Now you can see that when you have a field of complexly heterodyned energy modulations tuned to a demand-point like Delphi, there are many problems of standwaves and lashback and skiffle of all sorts which are normally balanced out with ease by the technology of the future. By the same token they can be delicately unbalanced too, in ways that feed back into the waldo operator with striking results.

"Darling—what the hell! What's wrong? *Delphi!*"

Helpless shrieks, writhings. Then the Rima-bird is lying wet and limp in his arms, her eyes enormous.

"I . . . I wasn't supposed to . . ." she gasps faintly. "They told me not to. . . ."

"Oh, my god—*Delphi*."

And his hard fingers are digging in her thick yellow hair. Electronically knowledgeable fingers. They freeze.

"You're a *doll*! You're one of those PP implants. They control you. I should have known. Oh, god, I should have known."

"No, Paul," she's sobbing. "No, no, no—"

"Damn them. Damn them, what they've done—you're not *you*—"

He's shaking her, crouching over her in the bed and jerking her back and forth, glaring at the pitiful beauty.

"No!" she pleads (it's not true, that dark bad dream back there). "I'm Delphi!"

"My father. Filth, pigs—damn them, damn them, damn them."

"No, no," she babbles. "They were good to me—" P. Burke underground mouthing, "They were good to me—*aah-aaaah!*"

Another agony skewers her. Up north the sharp young man wants to make sure this so-tiny interference works. Paul can scarcely hang on to her, he's crying too. "I'll kill them."

His Delphi, a wired-up slave! Spikes in her brain, electronic shackles in his bird's heart. Remember when those savages burned Rima alive?

"I'll *kill* the man that's doing this to you."

He's still saying it afterward, but she doesn't hear. She's sure he hates her now, all she wants is to die. When she finally understands that the fierceness is tenderness, she thinks it's a miracle. *He knows—and he still loves!*

How can she guess that he's got it a little bit wrong?

You can't blame Paul. Give him credit that he's even heard about pleasure-pain implants and snoops, which by their nature aren't mentioned much by those who know them most intimately. That's what he thinks is being used on Delphi, something to *control* her. And to listen—he burns at the unknown ears in their bed.

Of waldo-bodies and objects like P. Burke he has heard nothing.

So it never crosses his mind as he looks down at his violated bird, sick with fury and love, that he isn't holding *all* of her. Do you need to be told the mad resolve jelling in him now?

To free Delphi.

How? Well, he is, after all, Paul Isham III. And he even has an idea where the GTX neuro-lab is. In Carbondale.

But first things have to be done for Delphi, and for his own stomach. So he gives her back to Hopkins and departs in a restrained and discreet way. And the Chile staff is grateful and do not understand that his teeth don't normally show so much.

And a week passes in which Delphi is a very good, docile little ghost. They let her have the load of wildflowers Paul sends and the bland loving notes. (He's playing it coony.) And up in headquarters weasel boy feels that *his* destiny has clicked a notch onward and floats the word up that he's handy with little problems.

And no one knows what P. Burke thinks in any way whatever, except that Miss Fleming catches her flushing her food down the can and next night she faints in the pool. They haul her out and stick her with IVs. Miss Fleming frets, she's seen expressions like that before. But she wasn't around when crazies who called themselves Followers of the Fish looked through flames to life everlasting. P. Burke is seeing Heaven on the far side of death, too. Heaven is spelled P-a-u-l, but the idea's the same. *I will die and be born again in Delphi.*

Garbage, electronically speaking. No way.

Another week and Paul's madness has become a plan. (Remember, he does have friends.) He smolders, watching his love paraded by her masters. He turns out a scorching sequence for his own show. And finally, politely, he requests from Hopkins a morsel of his bird's free time, which duly arrives.

"I thought you didn't *want* me anymore," she's repeating as they wing over mountain flanks in Paul's suncar. "Now you *know*—"

"Look at me!"

His hand covers her mouth, and he's showing her a lettered card.

DON'T TALK THEY CAN HEAR EVERYTHING WE SAY.

I'M TAKING YOU AWAY NOW.

She kisses his hand. He nods urgently, flipping the card.

DON'T BE AFRAID. I CAN STOP THE PAIN IF THEY TRY TO HURT YOU.

With his free hand he shakes out a silvery scrambler-mesh on a power pack. She is dumbfounded.

THIS WILL CUT THE SIGNALS AND PROTECT YOU DARLING.

She's staring at him, her head going vaguely from side to side, *No.*

"Yes!" He grins triumphantly. "Yes!"

For a moment she wonders. That powered mesh will cut off the field, all right. It will also cut off Delphi. But he is Paul. Paul is kissing her, she can only seek him hungrily as he sweeps the suncar through a pass.

Ahead is an old jet ramp with a shiny bullet waiting to go. (Paul also has credits and a Name.) The little GTX patrol courier is built for nothing but speed. Paul and Delphi wedge in behind the pilot's extra fuel tank, and there's no more talking when the torches start to scream.

They're screaming high over Quito before Hopkins starts to worry. He wastes another hour tracking the beeper on Paul's suncar. The suncar is sailing a pattern out to sea. By the time they're sure it's empty and Hopkins gets on the hot flue to headquarters, the fugitives are a sourceless howl above Carib West.

Up at headquarters weasel boy gets the squeal. His first impulse is to repeat his previous play, but then his brain snaps to. This one is too hot. Because, see, although in the long run they can make P. Burke do anything at all except maybe *live*, instant emergencies can be tricky. And—Paul Isham III.

"Can't you order her back?"

They're all in the GTX tower monitor station, Mr. Cantle and ferret-face and Joe and a very neat man who is Mr. Isham senior's personal eyes and ears.

"No, sir," Joe says doggedly. "We can read channels, particularly speech, but we can't interpolate organized pattern. It takes the waldo op to send one-to-one—"

"What are they saying?"

"Nothing at the moment, sir." The console

jockey's eyes are closed. "I believe they are, ah, embracing."

"They're not answering," a traffic monitor says. "Still heading zero zero three zero—due north, sir."

"You're certain Kennedy is alerted not to fire on them?" the neat man asks anxiously.

"Yes, sir."

"Can't you just turn her off?" The sharp-faced lad is angry. "Pull that pig out of the controls!"

"If you cut the transmission cold you'll kill the Remote," Joe explains for the third time. "Withdrawal has to be phased right, you have to fade over to the Remote's own autonomics. Heart, breathing, cerebellum, would go blooey. If you pull Burke out you'll probably finish her too. It's a fantastic cybersystem, you don't want to do that."

"The investment." Mr. Cantle shudders.

Weasel boy puts his hand on the console jock's shoulder, it's the contact who arranged the no-no effect for him.

"We can at least give them a warning signal, sir." He licks his lips, gives the neat man his sweet ferret smile. "We know that does no damage."

Joe frowns, Mr. Cantle sighs. The neat man is murmuring into his wrist. He looks up. "I am authorized," he says reverently, "I am authorized to, ah, direct a signal. If this is the only course. But minimal, minimal."

Sharp-face squeezes his man's shoulder.

In the silver bullet shrieking over Charleston Paul feels Delphi arch in his arms. He reaches for the mesh, hot for action. She thrashes, pushing at his hands, her eyes roll. She's afraid of that mesh despite the agony. (And she's right.) Frantically Paul fights her in the cramped space, gets it over her head. As he turns the power up she burrows free under his arm and the spasm fades.

"They're calling you again, Mr. Isham!" the pilot yells.

"Don't answer. Darling, keep this over your head damn it how can I—"

An AX90 barrels over their nose, there's a flash.

"Mr. Isham! Those are Air Force jets!"

"Forget it," Paul shouts back. "They won't fire. Darling, don't be afraid."

Another AX90 rocks them.

"Would you mind pointing your pistol at my head where they can see it, sir?" the pilot howls.

Paul does so. The AX90s take up escort formation around them. The pilot goes back to figuring how he can collect from GTX too, and after Goldsboro AB the escort peels away.

"Holding the same course." Traffic is reporting to the group around the monitor. "Apparently they've taken on enough fuel to bring them to towerport here."

"In that case it's just a question of waiting for them to dock." Mr. Cantle's fatherly manner revives a bit.

"Why can't they cut off that damn freak's life-support," the sharp young man fumes. "It's ridiculous."

"They're working on it," Cantle assures him.

What they're doing, down under Carbondale, is arguing. Miss Fleming's watchdog has summoned the bushy man to the waldo room.

"Miss Fleming, you will obey orders."

"You'll kill her if you try that, sir. I can't believe you meant it, that's why I didn't. We've already fed her enough sedative to affect heart action; if you cut any more oxygen she'll die in there."

The bushy man grimaces. "Get Dr. Quine here fast."

They wait, staring at the cabinet in which a drugged, ugly madwoman fights for consciousness, fights to hold Delphi's eyes open.

High over Richmond the silver pod starts a turn. Delphi is sagged into Paul's arm, her eyes swim up to him.

"Starting down now, baby. It'll be over soon, all you have to do is stay alive, Dee."

". . . stay alive . . ."

The traffic monitor has caught them. "Sir! They've turned off for Carbondale—Control has contact—"

"Let's go."

But the headquarters posse is too late to intercept the courier wailing into Carbondale. And Paul's friends have come through again. The fugitives are out through the freight dock and into the neurolab admin port before the guard gets organized. At the elevator Paul's face plus his handgun get them in.

"I want Doctor—what's his name, Dee? Dee!"

". . . Tesla . . ." She's reeling on her feet.

"Dr. Tesla. Take me down to Tesla, fast."

Intercoms are squalling around them as they whoosh down, Paul's pistol in the guard's back. When the door slides open the bushy man is there.

"I'm Tesla."

"I'm Paul Isham. *Isham*. You're going to take your flaming implants out of this girl—now. Move!"

"What?"

"You heard me. Where's your operating room? Go!"

"But—"

"Move! Do I have to burn somebody?"

Paul waves the weapon at Dr. Quine, who has just appeared.

"No, no," says Tesla hurriedly. "But I can't, you know. It's impossible, there'll be nothing left."

"You screaming well can, right now. You mess up and I'll kill you," says Paul murderously. "Where is it, there? And wipe the feke that's on her circuits now."

He's backing them down the hall, Delphi heavy on his arm.

"Is this the place, baby? Where they did it to you?"

"Yes," she whispers, blinking at a door. "Yes . . ."

Because it is, see. Behind that door is the very suite where she was born.

Paul herds them through it into a gleaming hall. An inner door opens, and a nurse and a gray man rush out. And freeze.

Paul sees there's something special about that inner door. He crowds them past it and pushes it open and looks in.

Inside is a big mean-looking cabinet with its front door panels ajar.

And inside that cabinet is a poisoned carcass to whom something wonderful, unspeakable, is happening. Inside is P. Burke, the real living woman who knows that *he* is there, coming closer—Paul whom she had fought to reach through forty thousand miles of ice—*Paul* is here!—is yanking at the waldo doors—

The doors tear open and a monster rises up.

"Paul darling!" croaks the voice of love, and the arms of love reach for him.

And he responds.

Wouldn't you, if a gaunt she-golem flab-naked and spouting wires and blood came at you clawing with metal-studded paws—

"Get away!" He knocks wires.

It doesn't much matter which wires. P. Burke has, so to speak, her nervous system hanging out. Imagine somebody jerking a handful of your medulla—

She crashes onto the floor at his feet, flopping and roaring *PAUL-PAUL-PAUL* in rictus.

It's doubtful he recognizes his name or sees her life coming out of her eyes at him. And at the last it doesn't go to him. The eyes find Delphi, fainting by the doorway, and die.

Now of course Delphi is dead, too.

There's a total silence as Paul steps away from the thing by his foot.

"You killed her," Tesla says. "That was her."

"Your control." Paul is furious, the thought of that monster fastened into little Delphi's brain nauseates him. He sees her crumpling and holds out his arms. Not knowing she is dead.

And Delphi comes to him.

One foot before the other, not moving very well—but moving. Her darling face turns up. Paul is distracted by the terrible quiet, and when he looks down he sees only her tender little neck.

"Now you get the implants out," he warns them. Nobody moves.

"But, but she's dead," Miss Fleming whispers wildly.

Paul feels Delphi's life under his hand, they're talking about their monster. He aims his pistol at the gray man.

"You. If we aren't in your surgery when I count three, I'm burning off this man's leg."

"Mr. Isham," Tesla says desperately, "you have just killed the person who animated the body you call Delphi. Delphi herself is dead. If you release your arm you'll see what I say is true."

The tone gets through. Slowly Paul opens his arm, looks down.

"Delphi?"

She totters, sways, stays upright. Her face comes slowly up.

"Paul . . ." Tiny voice.

"Your crotty tricks," Paul snarls at them. "Move!"

"Look at her eyes," Dr. Quine croaks.

They look. One of Delphi's pupils fills the iris, her lips writhe weirdly.

"Shock." Paul grabs her to him. "*Fix* her!" He yells at them, aiming at Tesla.

"For god's sake . . . bring it in the lab." Tesla quavers.

"Good-bye-bye," says Delphi clearly. They lurch down the hall, Paul carrying her, and meet a wave of people.

Headquarters has arrived.

Joe takes one look and dives for the waldo room, running into Paul's gun.

"Oh, no, you don't."

Everybody is yelling. The little thing in his arm stirs, says plaintively, "I'm Delphi."

And all through the ensuing jabber and ranting she hangs on, keeping it up, the ghost of P. Burke or whatever whispering crazily, "Paul . . . Paul . . . Please, I'm Delphi . . . Paul?"

"I'm here, darling, I'm here." He's holding her in the nursing bed. Tesla talks, talks, talks unheard.

"Paul . . . don't sleep. . . ." The ghost-voice whispers. Paul is in agony, he will not accept, *will not* believe.

Tesla runs down.

And then near midnight Delphi says roughly,

"Ag-ag-ag—" and slips onto the floor, making a rough noise like a seal.

Paul screams. There's more of the *ag-ag* business and more gruesome convulsive disintegrations, until by two in the morning Delphi is nothing but a warm little bundle of vegetative functions hitched to some expensive hardware—the same that sustained her before her life began. Joe has finally persuaded Paul to let him at the waldo-cabinet. Paul stays by her long enough to see her face change in a dreadfully alien and coldly convincing way, and then he stumbles out bleakly through the group in Tesla's office.

Behind him Joe is working wet-faced, sweating to reintegrate the fantastic complex of circulation, respiration, endocrines, midbrain homeostases, the patterned flux that was a human being—it's like saving an orchestra abandoned in midair. Joe is also crying a little; he alone had truly loved P. Burke. P. Burke, now a dead pile on a table, was the greatest cybersystem he has ever known, and he never forgets her.

The end, really.

You're curious?

Sure, Delphi lives again. Next year she's back on the yacht getting sympathy for her tragic breakdown. But there's a different chick in Chile, because while Delphi's new operator is competent, you don't get two P. Burkes in a row—for which GTX is duly grateful.

The real belly-bomb of course is Paul. He was *young*, see. Fighting abstract wrong. Now life has clawed into him and he goes through gut rage and grief and grows in human wisdom and resolve. So much so that you won't be surprised, sometime later, to find him—where?

In the GTX boardroom, dummy. Using the advantage of his birth to radicalize the system. You'd call it "boring from within."

That's how he put it, and his friends couldn't agree more. It gives them a warm, confident feeling to know that Paul is up there. Sometimes one of them who's still around runs into him and gets a big hello.

And the sharp-faced lad?

Oh, he matures too. He learns fast, believe it. For instance, he's the first to learn that an obscure GTX research unit is actually getting something with their loopy temporal anomalizer project. True, he doesn't have a physics background, and he's bugged quite a few people. But he doesn't really learn about that until the day he stands where somebody points him during a test run—

—and wakes up lying on a newspaper headlined "Nixon Unveils Phase Two."

Lucky he's a fast learner.

Believe it, zombie. When I say growth, I mean *growth*. Capital appreciation. You can stop sweating. There's a great future there.

PAT CADIGAN

PRETTY BOY CROSSOVER

(1986)

First you see video. Then you wear video. Then you eat video. Then you be video.
—The Gospel According to Visual Mark

Watch or Be Watched.
—Pretty Boy Credo

"WHO MADE YOU?"

"You mean recently?"

Mohawk on the door smiles and takes his picture. "You in. But only you, okay? Don't try to get no friends in, hear that?"

"I hear. And I ain't no fool, fool. I got no friends."

Mohawk leers, leaning forward. "Pretty Boy like you, no friends?"

"Not in this world." He pushes past the Mohawk, ignoring the kissy-kissy sounds.

He would like to crack the bridge of the Mohawk's nose and shove bone splinters into his brain but he is lately making more effort to control his temper and besides, he's not sure if any of that bone splinters in the brain stuff is really true. He's a Pretty Boy, all of sixteen years old, and tonight could be his last chance.

The club is Noise. Can't sneak into the bathroom for quiet, the Noise is piped in there, too. Want to get away from Noise? Why? No reason. But this Pretty Boy has learned to think between the beats. Like walking between the raindrops to stay dry, but he can do it. This Pretty Boy thinks things all the time—*all* the time. Subversive (and, he thinks so much that he knows that word *subversive*, sixteen, Pretty, or not). He thinks things like *how many Einsteins have died of hunger and thirst under a hot African sun* and *why can't you remember being born* and *why is music common to every culture* and especially *how much was there going on that he didn't know about and how could he find out about it.*

And this is all the time, one thing after another running in his head, you can see by his eyes. It's for def not much like a Pretty Boy but it's one reason why they want him. That he *is* a Pretty Boy is another and one reason why they're halfway home getting him.

He knows all about them. Everybody knows about them and everybody wants them to pause, look twice, and cough up a card that says, Yes, we see possibilities, please come to the following address during regular business hours on the next regular business day for regular further review. Everyone wants it but this Pretty Boy, who once got five cards in a night and tore them all up. But here he is, still a Pretty Boy. He thinks enough to know this is a failing in himself, that he likes being Pretty and chased and that is how they could end up getting him after all and that's b-b-b-bad. When he thinks about it, he thinks it with the stutter. B-b-b-bad. B-b-b-bad for him because he doesn't God help him want it, no, no n-n-n-no. Which may make him the strangest Pretty Boy still live tonight and every night.

Still live and standing in the club where only the Prettiest Pretty Boys can get in anymore. Pretty Girls are too easy, they've got to be better than Pretty and besides, Pretty Boys like to be Pretty all alone, no help thank you so much. This Pretty Boy doesn't mind Pretty Girls or any other kind of girls. Lately, though, he has begun to wonder how much longer it will be for him. Two years? Possibly a little longer? By three it will be for def over and the Mohawk on the door will as soon spit in his face as leer in it.

If they don't get to him.

And if they *do* get to him, then it's never over and he can be wherever he chooses to be and wherever that is will be the center of the universe. They promise it, unlimited access in your free hours and endless hot season, endless youth. Pretty Boy Heaven, and to get there, they say, you don't even really have to die.

He looks up to the dj's roost, far above the bobbing, boogieing crowd on the dance floor. They still call them djs even though they aren't discs anymore, they're chips and there's more than just sound on a lot of them. The great hyper-program, he's been told, the ultimate of ultimates, a short walk from there to the fourth dimension. He suspects this stuff comes from low-steppers shilling for them, hoping they'll get auditioned if they do a good enough shuck job. Nobody knows what it's really like except the ones who are there and you can't trust them, he figures. Because maybe they *aren't*, anymore. Not really.

The dj sees his Pretty upturned face, recognizes him even though it's been a while since he's come back here. Part of it was wanting to stay away from them and part of it was that the thug on the door might not let him in. And then, of course, he *had* to come, to see if he could get in, to see if anyone still wanted him. What was the point of Pretty if there was nobody to care and watch and pursue? Even now, he is almost sure he can feel the room rearranging itself around his presence in it and the dj confirms this is true by holding up a chip and pointing it to the left.

They are squatting on the make-believe stairs by the screen, reminding him of pigeons plotting to take over the world. He doesn't look too long, doesn't want to give them the idea he'd like to talk. But as he turns away, one, the younger man, starts to get up. The older man and the woman pull him back.

He pretends a big interest in the figures lining the nearest wall. Some are Pretty, some are female, some are undecided, some are very bizarre, or wealthy, or just charity cases. They all notice him and adjust themselves for his perusal.

Then one end of the room lights up with color and new noise. Bodies dance and stumble back from the screen where images are forming to rough music.

It's Bobby, he realizes.

A moment later, there's Bobby's face on the screen, sixteen feet high, even Prettier than he'd been when he was loose among the mortals. The sight of Bobby's Pretty-Pretty face fills him with anger and dismay and a feeling of loss so great he would strike anyone who spoke Bobby's name without his permission.

Bobby's lovely slate-gray eyes scan the room. They've told him senses are heightened after you make the change and go over but he's not so sure how that's supposed to work. Bobby looks kind of blind up there on the screen. A few people wave at Bobby—the dorks they let in so the rest can have someone to be hip in front of—but Bobby's eyes move slowly back and forth, back and forth, and then stop, looking right at him.

"Ah . . ." Bobby whispers it, long and drawn out. "Aaaaaa-hhhh." He lifts his chin belligerently and stares back at Bobby.

"You don't have to die anymore," Bobby says silkily. Music bounces under his words. "It's beautiful in here. The dreams can be as real as you want them to be. And if you want to be, you can be with me."

He knows the commercial is not aimed only at him but it doesn't matter. This is *Bobby*. Bobby's voice seems to be pouring over him, caressing him, and it feels too much like a taunt. The night before Bobby went over, he tried to talk him out of it, knowing it wouldn't work. If they'd actually refused him, Bobby would have killed himself, like Franco had.

But now Bobby would live forever and ever, if you believed what they said. The music comes up louder but Bobby's eyes are still on him. He sees Bobby mouth his name.

"Can you really see me, Bobby?" he says. His voice doesn't make it over the music but if Bobby's senses are so heightened, maybe he hears it anyway. If he does, he doesn't choose to answer. The music is a bumped up remix of a song Bobby used to party-till-he-puked to. The giant Bobby-face fades away to be replaced with a whole Bobby, somewhat larger than life, dancing better than the old Bobby ever could, whirling along changing scenes of streets, rooftops, and beaches. The locales are nothing special but Bobby never did have all that much imagination, never wanted to go to Mars or even to the South Pole, always just to the hottest club. Always he liked being the exotic in plain surroundings and he still likes it. He always loved to get the looks. To be watched, worshipped, pursued. Yeah. He can see this is Bobby-heaven. The whole world will be giving him the looks now.

The background on the screen goes from street to the inside of a club; *this* club, only larger, better, with an even hipper crowd, and Bobby shaking it with them. Half the real crowd is forgetting to dance now because they're watching Bobby, hoping he's put some of them into his video. Yeah, that's the dream, get yourself remixed in the extended dance version.

His own attention drifts to the fake stairs that don't lead anywhere. They're still perched on them, the only people who are watching *him* instead of Bobby. The woman, looking overaged in a purple plastic sacsuit, is fingering a card.

He looks up at Bobby again. Bobby is dancing in place and looking back at him, or so it seems. Bobby's lips move soundlessly but so precisely he can read the words: *This can be you. Never get old, never get tired, it's never last call, nothing happens unless you want it to and it could be you. You. You.* Bobby's hands point to him on the beat. *You. You. You.*

Bobby. Can you really see me?

Bobby suddenly breaks into laughter and turns away, shaking it some more.

He sees the Mohawk from the door pushing his way through the crowd, the real crowd, and he gets anxious. The Mohawk goes straight for the stairs, where they make room for him, rubbing the bristly red strip of hair running down the center of his head as though they were greeting a favored pet. The Mohawk looks as satisfied as a professional glutton after a foodrace victory. He wonders what they promised the Mohawk for letting him in. Maybe some kind of limited contract. Maybe even a try-out.

Now they are all watching him together. Defiantly, he touches a tall girl dancing nearby and joins her rhythm. She smiles down at him, moving between him and them purely by chance but it endears her to him anyway. She is wearing a flap of translucent rag over secondskins, like an old-time showgirl. Over six feet tall, not beautiful with that nose, not even pretty, but they let her in so she could be tall. She probably doesn't know that; she probably doesn't know anything that goes on and never really will. For that reason, he can forgive her the hard-tech orange hair.

A Rude Boy brushes against him in the course of a dervish turn, asking acknowledgment by ignoring him. Rude Boys haven't changed in more decades than anyone's kept track of, as though it were the same little group of leathered and chained troopers buggering their way down the years. The Rude Boy isn't dancing with anyone. Rude Boys never do. But this one could be handy, in case of an emergency.

The girl is dancing hard, smiling at him. He smiles back, moving slightly to her right, watching Bobby possibly watching him. He still can't tell if Bobby really sees anything. The scene behind Bobby is still a double of the club, getting hipper and hipper if that's possible. The music keeps snapping back to its first peak passage. Then Bobby gestures like God and he sees himself. He is dancing next to Bobby, Prettier than he ever could be, just the way they promise. Bobby doesn't look at the phantom but at him where he really is, lips moving again. *If you want to be, you can be with me. And so can she.*

His tall partner appears next to the phantom of himself. She is also much improved, though still not Pretty, or even pretty. The real girl turns and sees herself and there's no mistaking the delight in her face. Queen of the Hop for a minute or two. Then Bobby sends her image away so that it's just the two of them, two Pretty Boys dancing the night away, private party, stranger go find your own good time. How it used to be sometimes in real life, between just the two of them. He remembers hard.

"B-B-B-Bobby!" he yells, the old stutter reappearing. Bobby's image seems to give a jump, as though he finally heard. He forgets everything, the girl, the Rude Boy, the Mohawk, them on the stairs, and plunges through the crowd toward the screen. People fall away from him as though they were reenacting the Red Sea. He dives for the screen, for Bobby, not caring how it must look to anyone. What would they know about it, any of them. He can't remember in his whole sixteen years ever hearing one person say, *I love my friend.* Not Bobby, not even himself.

He fetches up against the screen like a slap and hangs there, face pressed to the glass. He

can't see it now but on the screen Bobby would seem to be looking down at him. Bobby never stops dancing.

The Mohawk comes and peels him off. The others swarm up and take him away. The tall girl watches all this with the expression of a woman who lives upstairs from Cinderella and wears the same shoe size. She stares longingly at the screen. Bobby waves bye-bye and turns away.

"Of course, the process isn't reversible," says the older man. The steely hair has a careful blue tint; he has sense enough to stay out of hip clothes.

They have laid him out on a lounger with a tray of refreshments right by him. Probably slap his hand if he reaches for any, he thinks.

"Once you've distilled something to pure information, it just can't be reconstituted in a less efficient form," the woman explains, smiling. There's no warmth to her. *A less efficient form.* If that's what she really thinks, he knows he should be plenty scared of these people. Did she say things like that to Bobby? And did it make him even *more* eager?

"There may be no more exalted a form of existence than to live as sentient information," she goes on. "Though a lot more research must be done before we can offer conversion on a larger scale."

"Yeah?" he says. "Do they know that, Bobby and the rest?"

"Oh, there's nothing to worry about," says the younger man. He looks as though he's still getting over the pain of having outgrown his boogie shoes. "The system's quite perfected. What Grethe means is we want to research more applications for this new form of existence."

"Why not go over yourselves and do that, if it's so *exalted*."

"There are certain things that need to be done on this side," the woman says bitchily. "Just because—"

"Grethe." The older man shakes his head. She pats her slicked-back hair as though to soothe herself and moves away.

"We have other plans for Bobby when he gets tired of being featured in clubs," the older man says. "Even now, we're educating him, adding more data to his basic information configuration—"

"That would mean he ain't really *Bobby* anymore, then, huh?"

The man laughs. "Of course he's Bobby. Do you change into someone else every time you learn something new?"

"Can you prove I *don't*?"

The man eyes him warily. "Look. You *saw* him. Was that Bobby?"

"I saw a video of Bobby dancing on a giant screen."

"That *is* Bobby and it will remain Bobby no matter what, whether he's poured into a video screen in a dot pattern or transmitted the length of the universe."

"That what you got in mind for him? Send a message to nowhere and the message is him?"

"We could. But we're not going to. We're introducing him to the concept of higher dimensions. The way he is now, he could possibly break out of the three-dimensional level of existence, pioneer a whole new plane of reality."

"Yeah? And how do you think you're gonna get Bobby to do that?"

"We convince him it's entertaining."

He laughs. "That's a good one. Yeah. Entertainment. You get to a higher level of existence and you'll open a club there that only the hippest can get into. It figures."

The older man's face gets hard. "That's what all you Pretty Boys are crazy for, isn't it? Entertainment?"

He looks around. The room must have been a dressing room or something back in the days when bands had been live. Somewhere overhead he can hear the faint noise of the club but he can't tell if Bobby's still on. "You call this entertainment?"

"I'm tired of this little prick," the woman chimes in. "He's thrown away opportunities other people would kill for—"

He makes a rude noise. "Yeah, we'd all kill to be someone's data chip. You think I really believe Bobby's real just because I can see him on a *screen?*"

The older man turns to the younger one. "Phone up and have them pipe Bobby down here." Then he swings the lounger around so it faces a nice modern screen implanted in a shored-up cement-block wall.

"Bobby will join us shortly. Then he can tell you whether he's real or not himself. How will that be for you?"

He stares hard at the screen, ignoring the man, waiting for Bobby's image to appear. As though they really bothered to communicate regularly with Bobby this way. Feed in that kind of data and memory and Bobby'll believe it. He shifts uncomfortably, suddenly wondering how far he could get if he moved fast enough.

"My *boy*," says Bobby's sweet voice from the speaker on either side of the screen and he forces himself to keep looking as Bobby fades in, presenting himself on the same kind of lounger and looking mildly exerted, as though he's just come off the dance floor for real.

"Saw you shakin' it upstairs a while ago. You haven't been here for such a long time. What's the story?"

He opens his mouth but there's no sound. Bobby looks at him with boundless patience and indulgence. So Pretty, hair the perfect shade now and not a bit dry from the dyes and lighteners, skin flawless and shining like a healthy angel. Overnight angel, just like the old song.

"My *boy*," says Bobby. "Are you struck, like, shy or *dead*?"

He closes his mouth, takes one breath. "I don't like it, Bobby. I don't like it this way."

"Of course not, lover. You're the Watcher, not the Watchee, that's why. Get yourself picked up for a season or two and your disposition will *change*."

"You really like it, Bobby, being a blip on a chip?"

"Blip on a chip, your ass. I'm a universe now. I'm, like, *everything*. And, hey, dig—I'm on every channel." Bobby laughed. "I'm happy I'm sad!"

"S-A-D," comes in the older man. "Self-Aware Data."

"Ooo-eee," he says. "Too clever for me. Can I get out of here now?"

"What's your hurry?" Bobby pouts. "Just because I went over you don't love me anymore?"

"You always were screwed up about that, Bobby. Do you know the difference between being loved and being watched?"

"Sophisticated boy," Bobby says. "So wise, so learned. So fully packed. On this side, there is no difference. Maybe there never was. If you love me, you watch me. If you don't look, you don't care and if you don't care I don't matter. If I don't matter, I don't exist. Right?"

He shakes his head.

"No, my boy, I *am* right." Bobby laughs. "You believe I'm right, because if you *didn't*, you wouldn't come shaking your Pretty Boy ass in a place like *this*, now, would you? You *like* to be watched, get seen. You see me, I see you. Life goes on."

He looks up at the older man, needing relief from Bobby's pure Prettiness. "How does he see me?"

"Sensors in the equipment. Technical stuff, nothing you care about."

He sighs. He should be upstairs or across town, shaking it with everyone else, living Pretty for as long as he could. Maybe in another few months, this way would begin to look good to him. By then they might be off Pretty Boys and looking for some other type and there he'd be, out in the cold-cold, sliding down the other side of his peak and no one would *want* him. Shut out of something going on that he might want to know about after all. Can he face it? He glances at the younger man. All grown up and no place to glow. Yeah, but can *he* face it?

He doesn't know. Used to be there wasn't much of a choice and now that there is, it only seems to make it worse. Bobby's image looks like it's studying him for some kind of sign, Pretty eyes bright, hopeful.

The older man leans down and speaks low into his ear. "We need to get you before you're twenty-five, before the brain stops growing. A mind taken from a still-growing brain will blossom and adapt. Some of Bobby's predecessors have made marvelous adaptation to their new medium. Pure video: there's a staff that does nothing all day but watch and interpret their symbols for breakthroughs in thought. And we'll be taking Pretty Boys for as long as they're publicly sought-after. It's the most efficient way to find the best performers, go for the ones everyone wants to see or be. The top of the trend is closest to heaven. And even if you never make a breakthrough, you'll still be entertainment. Not such a bad way to live for a Pretty Boy. Never have to age, to be sick, to lose touch. You spent most of your life young, why learn how to be old? Why learn how to live without all the things you have now—"

He puts his hands over his ears. The older man is still talking and Bobby is saying something and the younger man and the woman come over to try to do something about him. Refreshments are falling off the tray. He struggles out of the lounger and makes for the door.

"Hey, my *boy*," Bobby calls after him. "Gimme a minute here, gimme what the problem is."

He doesn't answer. What can you tell someone made of pure information anyway?

• • •

There's a new guy on the front door, bigger and meaner than His Mohawkness, but he's only there to keep people out, not to keep anyone *in*. You want to jump ship, go to, you poor unhip asshole. Even if you are a Pretty Boy. He reads it in the guy's face as he passes from noise into the three a.m. quiet of the street.

They let him go. He doesn't fool himself about that part. They *let* him out of the room because they know all about him. They know he lives like Bobby lived, they know he loves what

Bobby loved—the clubs, the admiration, the lust of strangers for his personal magic. He can't say he doesn't love that, because he *does*. He isn't even sure if he loves it more than he ever loved Bobby, or if he loves it more than being alive. Than being live.

And here it is, three a.m., clubbing prime time, and he is moving toward home. Maybe he is a poor unhip asshole after all, no matter what he loves. Too stupid even to stay in the club, let alone grab a ride to heaven. Still he keeps moving, unbothered by the chill but feeling it.

Bobby doesn't have to go home in the cold anymore, he thinks. Bobby doesn't even have to get through the hours between club-times if he doesn't want to. All times are now prime time for Bobby. Even if he gets unplugged, he'll never know the difference. Poof, it's a day later, poof, it's a year later, poof, you're out for good. Painlessly.

Maybe Bobby has the right idea, he thinks, moving along the empty sidewalk. If he goes over tomorrow, who will notice? Like when he left the dance floor—people will come and fill up the space. Ultimately, it wouldn't make any difference to anyone.

He smiles suddenly. Except *them*. As long as they don't have him, he makes a difference. As long as he has flesh to shake and flaunt and feel with, he makes a pretty goddamn big difference to them. Even after they don't want him anymore, he will still be the one they didn't get. He rubs his hands together against the chill, feeling the skin rubbing skin, really *feeling* it for the first time in a long time, and he thinks about sixteen million things all at once, maybe one thing for every brain cell he's using, or maybe one thing for every brain cell yet to come.

He keeps moving, holding to the big thought, making a difference, and all the little things they won't be making a program out of. He's lightheaded with joy—he doesn't know what's going to happen.

Neither do they.

JOHN SHIRLEY

WOLVES OF THE PLATEAU

(1988)

NINE A.M., and Jerome-X wanted a smoke. He didn't smoke, but he wanted one in here, and he could see how people went into prison non-smokers and came out doing two packs a day. Maybe had to get their brains rewired to get off it. Which was ugly, he'd been rewired once to get off Sink, synthetic cocaine, and he'd felt like a processor with a glitch for a month after that.

He pictured his thoughts like a little train, zipping around the cigarette-burnt graffiti: YOU FUCKED NOW and GASMAN WUZZERE and GASMAN IS AN IDIOT-MO. The words were stippled on the dull pink ceiling in umber burn spots. Jerome wondered who GASMAN was and what they'd put him in prison for.

He yawned. He hadn't slept much the night before. It took a long time to learn to sleep in prison. He wished he'd upgraded his chip so he could use it to activate his sleep endorphins. But that was a grade above what he'd been able to afford—and way above the kind of brain chips

he'd been dealing. He wished he could turn off the light panel, but it was sealed in.

There was a toilet and a broken water fountain in the cell. There were also a few bunks, but he was alone in this static place of watery blue light and faint pink distances. The walls were salmon-colored garbage blocks. The words singed into the ceiling were blurred and impotent.

• • •

Almost noon, his stomach rumbling, Jerome was still lying on his back on the top bunk when the trash can said, "Eric Wexler, re-ma-a-in on your bunk while the ne-ew prisoner ente-e-ers the cell!"

Wexler? Oh, yeah. They thought his name was Wexler. The fake ID program.

He heard the cell door slide open; he looked over, saw the trash can ushering a stocky Chicano guy into lockup. The robot everyone called "the trash can" was a stumpy metal cylinder with a group of camera lenses, a retractable plastic arm, and a gun muzzle that could fire a Taser charge, rubber bullets, tear-gas pellets, or .45-caliber rounds. It was supposed to use the .45 only in extreme situations, but the robot was battered, it whined when it moved, its digital voice was warped. When they got like that, Jerome had heard, you didn't fuck with them; they'd mix up the rubber bullets with the .45-caliber, Russian Roulette style.

The door sucked itself shut, the trash can whined away down the hall, its rubber wheels squeaking once with every revolution. Jerome heard a tinny cymbal crash as someone, maybe trying to get it to shoot at a guy in the next cell, threw a tray at it; followed by some echoey human shouting and a distorted admonishment from the trash can. The Chicano was still standing by the plexigate, hands shoved in his pockets, staring at Jerome, looking like he was trying to place him.

"'Sappenin'," Jerome said, sitting up on the bed. He was grateful for the break in the monotony.

"¿Qué pasa? You like the top bunk, huh? Tha's good."

"I can read the ceiling better from up here. About ten seconds' worth of reading matter. It's all I got. You can have the lower bunk."

"You fuckin'-A I can." But there was no real aggression in his tone. Jerome thought about turning on his chip, checking the guy's subliminals, his somatic signals, going for a model of probable aggression index; or maybe project for deception. He could be an undercover cop: Jerome hadn't given them his dealer, hadn't bargained at all.

But he decided against switching the chip on. Some jails had scanners for unauthorized chip output. Better not use it unless he had to. And his gut told him this guy was only a threat if he felt threatened. His gut was right almost as often as his brain chip.

The Chicano was maybe five foot six, a good five inches shorter than Jerome but probably outweighing him by fifty pounds. His face had Indian angles and small jet eyes. He was wearing printout gray-blue prison jams, #6631; they'd let him keep his hairnet. Jerome had never understood the Chicano hairnet, never had the balls to ask about it.

Jerome was pleased. He liked to be recognized, except by people who could arrest him.

"You put your hands in the pockets of those paper pants, they'll rip, and in LA County they don't give you any more for three days," Jerome advised him.

"Yeah? Shit." The Chicano took his hands carefully out of his pockets. "I don't want my cojones hanging out, people think I'm advertising—they some big fucking cojones too. You not a f——, right?"

"Nope."

"Good. How come I know you? When I *don't* know you."

Jerome grinned. "From television. You saw my tag. Jerome-X. I mean—I do some music too. I had that song, 'Six Kinds of Darkness'—"

"I don't know that, bro—oh wait, Jerome-X. The tag—I saw that. Your face-tag. You got one of those little transers? Interrupt the transmissions with your own shit?"

"Had. They confiscated it."

"That why you here? Video graffiti?"

"I wish. I'd be out in a couple months. No. Illegal augs."

"Hey, man! Me too!"

"You?" Jerome couldn't conceal his surprise. You didn't see a lot of barrio dudes doing illegal augmentation. They generally didn't like people tinkering in their brains.

"What, you think a guy from East LA can't use augs?"

"No, no. I know lots of Latino guys that use it," Jerome lied.

"Ooooh, he says *Latino*, that gotta nice sound." Overtones of danger.

Jerome hastily changed the direction of the

conversation. "You never been in the big lock-ups where they use these fuckin' paper jammies?"

"No, just the city jail once. They didn't have those motherfucking screw machines either. Hey, you're Jerome—my name's Jessie. Actually, it Jesus"—he pronounced it "hay-soo"—"but people they, you know . . . You got any smokes? No? Shit. Okay, I adjust. I get use to it. Shit. No smokes. Fuck."

He sat on the edge of the bed, to one side of Jerome's dangling legs, and tilted his head forward. He reached under his hairnet, and under what turned out to be a hairpiece, and pulled a chip from a jack unit set into the base of his skull.

Jerome stared. "Goddamn, their probes really are busted."

Jessie frowned over the chip. There was a little blood on it. The jack unit was leaking. Cheap installation. "No, they ain't busted, there's a guy working on the probe, he's paid off, he's letting everyone through for a couple of days because of some Russian mob guys coming in, he don't know which ones they are. Some of them Russian mob guys got the augments."

"I thought sure they were going to find my unit," Jerome said. "The strip search didn't find it, but I thought the prison probes would and that'd be another year on my sentence. But they didn't."

Neither one of them thinking of throwing away the chips. It'd be like cutting out an eye.

"Same story here, bro. We both lucky."

Jessie put the microprocessor chip in his mouth, the way people did with their contact lenses, to clean it, lubricate it. Of course, bacterially speaking, it came out dirtier than it went in.

"Does the jack hurt?" Jerome asked.

Jessie took the chip out, looked at it a moment on his fingertips. It was smaller than a contact lens, a sliver of silicon and non-osmotic gallium arsenide and transparent interface-membrane, with, probably, 800,000,000 nanotransistors of engineered protein molecules sunk into it, may-

be more. "No, it don't hurt yet. But if it's leaking, it fuckin' *will* hurt, man." He said something else in Spanish, shaking his head. He slipped the chip back into his jack-in unit and tapped it with the thumbnail of his right hand. So that was where the activation mouse was: under the thumbnail. Jerome's was in a knuckle.

Jessie rocked slightly, just once, sitting up on his bunk, which meant the chip had engaged and he was getting a readout. They tended to feed back into your nervous system a little at first, make you twitch once or twice; if they weren't properly insulated, they could make you crap your pants.

"That's okay," Jessie said, relaxing. "That's better." The chip inducing his brain to secrete vasopressin, contract the veins, simulate the effect of nicotine. It worked for a while, till you could get cigarettes. High-grade chip could do some numbing if you were hung up on Sim, synthetic morphine, and couldn't get any. But that was Big Scary. You could turn yourself off for good that way. You better be doing some damn fine adjusting.

Jerome thought about the hypothetical chip scanners. Maybe he should object to the guy using his chip here. But what the Chicano was doing wouldn't make for much leakage.

"What you got?" Jerome asked.

"I got an Apple NanoMind II. Big gigas. What you got?"

"You got the Mercedes, I got the Toyota. I got a Seso Picante Mark I. One of those Argentine things." (How had this guy scored an ANM II?)

"Yeah, what you got, they kinda basic, but they do most what you need. Hey, our names, they both start with *J*. And we both here for illegal augs. What else we got in common. What's your sign?"

"Uh—" What was it, anyway? He always forgot. "Pisces I think."

"No shit! I can relate to Pisces. I ran an astrology program, figured out who I should hang with. Pisces is okay. But Aquarius is—I'm a Scorpio, like—Aquarius, *qué bueno*."

What did he mean exactly, *hang with*, Jerome wondered. Scoping me about am *I* a f——, maybe that was something defensive.

But he meant something else. "You know somethin', Jerome, you got your chip too, we could do a link and maybe get over on that trash can."

Break out? Jerome felt a chilled thrill go through him. "Link with that thing? Control it? I don't think the two of us would be enough."

"We need some more guys maybe, but I got news, Jerome, there's more comin'. Maybe their names all start with *J*. You know, I mean—in a way."

In quick succession, the trash can brought their cell three more guests: a fortyish beach bum named Eddie; a cadaverous black dude named Bones; a queen called Swish, whose real name, according to the trash can, was Paul Torino.

"This place smells like it's comin' apart," Eddie said. He had a surfer's greasy blond topknot and all the usual Surf Punk tattoos. Meaningless now, Jerome thought, the pollution-derived oxidation of the offshore had pretty much ended surfing. The anaerobics had taken over the surf, in North America, thriving in the toxic waters like a gelatinous Sargasso. If you surfed you did it with an antitoxin suit and a gas mask. "Smells in here like somethin' died and didn't go to heaven. Stinks worse'n Malibu."

"It's those landfill blocks," Bones said. He was missing three front teeth, and his sunken face was like something out of a zombie video. But he was an energetic zombie, pacing back and forth as he spoke. "Compressed garbage," he told Eddie. "Organic stuff mixed with the polymers, the plastics, whatever was in the trash heap, make 'em into bricks 'cause they run outta landfill, but after a while, if the contractor didn't get 'em to set right, y'know, they start to rot. It's hot outside is why you're gettin' it now. Use garbage to cage garbage, they say. Fucking assholes."

• • •

The trash can pushed a rack of trays up to the Plexiglas bars and whirred their lunch to them, tray by tray. The robot gave them an extra tray. It was screwing up.

They ate their chicken patties—the chicken was almost greaseless, gristle-less, which meant it was vat chicken, genetically engineered fleshstuff—and between bites they bitched about the food and indulged the usual paranoid speculation about mind-control chemicals in the coffee.

Jerome looked around at the others, thinking: at least they're not ass-kickers.

They were crammed here because of the illegal augs sweep, some political drive to clean up the clinics, maybe to see to it that the legal augmentation companies kept their pit-bull grip on the industry. So there wasn't anybody in for homicide, for gang torture, or anything. No major psychopaths. Not a bad cell to be in.

"You Jerome-X, really?" Swish fluted. She (Jerome always thought of a queen as *she* and *her*, out of respect for the tilt of her consciousness) was probably Filipino; had her face girled up at a cheap clinic. Cheeks built up for a heart shape, eyes rounded, lips filled out, tits looking like there was a couple of tin funnels under her jammies. Some of the collagen they'd injected to fill out her lips had shifted its bulk so her lower lip was lopsided. One cheekbone was a little higher than the other. A karmic revenge on at least some of malekind, Jerome thought, for forcing women into girdles and foot-binding and anorexia. What did this creature use her chip for, besides getting high?

"Oooh, Jerome-X! I saw your tag before on the TV. The one when your face kind of floated around the President's head and some printout words came out of your mouth and blocked her face out. God, she's such a *cunt*."

"What words did he block her out with?" Eddie asked.

"I think . . . 'Would you know a liar if you

heard one anymore?' That's what it was!" Swish said. "It was sooo perfect, because that cunt wanted that war to go on forever, you *know* she did. And she lies about it, ooh *God* she lies."

"You just think she's a cunt because you *want* one," Eddie said, dropping his pants to use the toilet. He talked loudly to cover up the noise of it. "You want one and you can't afford it. I think the Prez was right, the fucking Mexican People's Republic is jammin' our borders, sending commie agents in—"

Swish said, "Oh, God, he's a Surf Nazi— But God yes, I want one—I want *her* cunt. That bitch doesn't know how to use it anyway. Honey, I know how I'd use that thing—" Swish stopped abruptly and shivered, hugged herself. Using her long purple nails, she reached up and pried loose a flap of skin behind her ear, plucked out her chip. She wet it, adjusted its feed mode, put it back in, tapping it with the activation mouse under a nail. She pressed the flap shut. Her eyes glazed as she adjusted. She could get high on the chip-impulses for maybe twenty-four hours and then it'd kill her. She'd have to go cold turkey or die. Or get out. And maybe she'd been doing it for a while now . . .

None of them would be allowed to post bail. They'd each get the two years mandatory minimum sentence. Illegal augs, the feds thought, were getting out of hand. Black-market chip implants were good for playing havoc with the state database lottery; used by bookies of all kinds; used to keep accounts where the IRS couldn't find them unless they cornered you physically and broke your code; the aug chips were used to out-think banking computers, and for spiking cash machines; used to milk the body, prod the brain into authorizing the secretion of beta endorphins and ACTH and adrenaline and testosterone and other biochemical toys; used to figure the odds at casinos; used to compute the specs for homemade designer drugs; used by the mob's street dons to play strategy and tactics; used by the kid gangs for the same reasons; used for illegal congregations on the Plateau.

It was the Plateau, Jerome thought, that

really scared the shit out of the feds. It had possibilities.

It was way beyond the fucking Internet; it was past the Deep Internet; it was even beyond the Grid.

• • •

The trash can dragged in a cot for the extra man, shoved it folded under the door, and blared, "Lights out, all inmates are required to be i-i-in their bu-unks-s-s . . ." Its voice was failing.

After the trash can and the light had gone, they climbed off their bunks and sat hunkered in a circle on the floor.

They were on chips, but not transmission-linked to one another. Jacked-up on the chips, they communicated in a spoken shorthand.

"Bull," Bones was saying. "Door." He was a voice in the darkness; a scarecrow of shadow.

"Time," Jessie said.

"Compatibility? Know?" Eddie said.

Jerome said, "Noshee!" Snorts of laughter from the others.

"Link check," Bones said.

"Models?" Jessie said.

Then they joined in an incantation of numbers.

It was a fifteen-minute conversation in less than a minute.

Translated, the foregoing conversation went: "It's bullshit, you get past the trash can, there's human guards, you can't reprogram them."

"But at certain hours," Jessie told him, "there's only one on duty. They're used to seeing the can bring people in and out. They won't question it till they try to confirm it. By then we'll be on their ass."

"We might not be compatible," Eddie had pointed out. "You understand, compatible?"

"Oh, hey, man, I *think* we can comprehend that," Jerome said, making the others snort with laughter. Eddie wasn't liked much.

Then Bones had said, "The only way to see if we're compatible is to do a systems link. We got the links, we got the thinks, like the man says.

It's either the chain that holds us in, or it's the chain that pulls us out."

Jerome's scalp tightened. A systems link. A mini-Plateau. Sharing minds. Brutal intimacy. Maybe some fallout from the Plateau. He wasn't ready for it.

If it went sour, he could get time tacked onto his sentence for attempted jailbreak. And somebody might get dusted. They might have to kill a human guard. Jerome had once punched a dealer in the nose, and the spurt of blood had made him sick. He couldn't kill anyone. But . . . he had shit for alternatives. He knew he wouldn't make it through two years anyway, when they sent him up to the Big One.

The Big One'd grind him up for sure. They'd find his chip there, and it'd piss them off. They'd let the bulls rape him and give him the New Virus; he'd flip out from being locked in and chipless, and they'd put him under Aversion Rehab and burn him out.

Jerome savaged a thumbnail with his incisors. *Sent to the Big One.*

He'd been trying not to think about it. Making himself take it one day at a time. But now he had to look at the alternatives. His stomach twisted itself to punish him for being so stupid. For getting into dealing augments so he could finance a big transer. *Why?* A transer didn't get him anything but his face pirated onto local TV for maybe twenty seconds. He'd thrown himself away trying to get it . . .

Why was it so fucking important? his stomach demanded, wringing itself vindictively.

"Thing is," Bones said, "we could all be cruisin' into a set-up. Some kind of sting thing. Maybe it's a little too weird how the police prober let us all through."

(Someone listening would have heard him say, "Sting, funny luck.")

Jessie snorted. "I tol' you, man. The prober is paid off. They letting them all through because some of them are mob. I know that, because I'm part of the thing. We deal wid the Russians. Okay?"

("Probe greased, fa-me.")

"You with the mob?" Bones asked.

("You'm?")

"You got it. Just a dealer. But I know where a half million Newbux wortha augshit is, so they going to get me out if I do my part. The way the system is set up, the prober had to let everyone through. His boss thinks we got our chips taken out when they arraigned us; sometimes they do it that way. This time it was supposed to be the jail surgeon. By the time they catch up their own red tape, we get outta here. Now listen—we can't do the trash can without we all get into it, because we haven't got enough *K* otherwise. So who's in, for fuck's sake?"

He'd said, "Low, half mill, bluff surgeon, there here, twip, all-none, *who* yuh fucks?"

Something in his voice skittered with claws behind smoked glass: he was getting testy, irritable from the chip adjustments for his nicotine habit, maybe other adjustments: the side effects of liberal cerebral self-modulating burning through a threadbare nervous system.

The rest of the meeting, translated . . .

"I dunno," Eddie said. "I thought I'd do my time, cause if it goes sour—"

"Hey man," Jessie said, "I can *take* your fuckin' chip. And be out before they notice your ass don't move no more."

"The man's right," Swish said. Her pain-suppression system was unraveling, axon by axon, and she was running out of adjust. "Let's just do it, okay? Please? Okay? I gotta get out. I feel like I wish I was dogshit so I could be something better."

"I can't handle two years in the Big, Eddie, and I'll do what I gotta, dudeski," Jerome heard himself say, realizing he was helping Jessie threaten Eddie. Amazed at himself. Not his style.

"It's all of us or nobody, Eddie," Bones said.

Eddie was quiet for a while.

• • •

Jerome had turned off his chip, because it was thinking endlessly about Jessie's plan, and all it came up with was an ugly model of the risks. You had to know when to go with intuition.

Jerome was committed. And he was standing on the brink of link. The time was now, starting with Jessie.

Jessie was *operator*. He picked the order. First Eddie, to make sure about him. Then Jerome. Maybe because he had Jerome scoped for a refugee from the middle class, an anomaly here, and Jerome might try and raise the Heat on his chip, make a deal. Once they had him linked in, he was locked up.

After Jerome, it'd be Bones and then Swish.

They held hands, so that the link signal, transmitted from the chip using the electric field generated by the brain, would be carried with the optimum fidelity.

He heard them exchange frequency designates, numbers strung like beads in the darkness, and heard the hiss of suddenly indrawn breaths as Jessie and Eddie linked in. And he heard, "Let's go, Jerome."

Jerome's eyes had adjusted to the dark, the night giving up some of its buried light, and Jerome could just make a crude outline of Jessie's features like a charcoal rubbing from an Aztec carving.

Jerome reached to the back of his own head, found the glue-tufted hairs that marked his flap, and pulled the skin away from the chip's jack unit. He tapped the chip. It didn't take. He tapped it again, and this time he felt the shift in his bio electricity; felt it hum between his teeth.

Jerome's chip communicated with his brain via an interface of nano-print configured rhodopsin protein; the ribosomes borrowing neurohumoral transmitters from the brain's blood supply, reordering the transmitters so that they carried a programmed pattern of ion releases for transmission across synaptic gaps to the brain's neuronal dendrites; the chip using magnetic resonance holography to collate with brain-stored memories and psychological trends. Declaiming to itself the mythology of the brain; reenacting on its silicon stage the Legends of his subjective world history.

Jerome closed his eyes and looked into the back of his eyelids. The digital read-out was printed in luminous green across the darkness. He focused on the cursor, concentrated so it moved up to ACCESS. He subverbalized, "Open frequency." The chip heard his practiced subverbalization, and numbers appeared on the back of his eyelids: 63391212.70. He read them out to the others and they picked up his frequency. Almost choking on the word, knowing what it would bring, he told the chip: "Open."

It opened to the link. He'd only done it once before. It was illegal, and he was secretly glad it was illegal because it scared him. "They're holding the Plateau back," his brain-chip wholesaler had told him, "because they're scared of what worldwide electronic telepathy might bring down on them. Like, everyone will collate information, use it to see through the bastards' game, throw the assbites out of office."

Maybe that was the real reason. It was something the power brokers couldn't control. But there were other reasons.

Reasons like a strikingly legitimate fear of people going mad.

All Jerome and the others wanted was a sharing of processing capabilities. Collaborative calculation. But the chips weren't designed to filter out the irrelevant input before it reached the user's cognition level. Before the chip had done its filtering, the two poles of the link—Jerome and Jessie—would each see the swarming hive of the other's total consciousness. Would see how the other perceived themselves to be, and then objectively, as they really were.

He saw Jessie as a grid and as a holographic entity. He braced himself and the holograph came at him, an abstract tarantula of computer-generated color and line, scrambling down over him . . . and for an instant it crouched in the seat of his consciousness: Jessie. Jesus Chaco.

Jessie was a family man. He was a patriarch, a protector of his wife and six kids (six kids!) and his widowed sister's four kids and of the poor children of his barrio. He was a muddied painting of his father, who had fled the social forest fire of Mexico's civil war between the drug cartels and the government, spiriting his capital to Los Angeles where he'd sown it into the black market. Jessie's father had been killed defending territory from the Russian-American mob; Jessie compromised with the mob to save his father's business, and loathed himself for it. Wanted to kill their bosses; had to work side by side with them. Perceived his wife as a functional pet, an object of adoration who was the very apotheosis of her fixed role. To imagine her doing other than child-rearing and keeping house would be to imagine the sun become a snowball, the moon become a monkey. Jessie's family insistently clung to the old, outdated roles.

And Jerome glimpsed Jessie's undersides; Jesus Chaco's self-image with its outsized penis and impossibly spreading shoulders, sitting in a perfect and shining cherry automobile, always the newest and most luxurious model, the automotive throne from which he surveyed his kingdom. Jerome saw guns emerging from the grill of the car to splash Jessie's enemies apart with his unceasing ammunition . . . It was a Robert Williams cartoon capering at the heart of Jessie's unconscious . . . Jessie saw himself as Jerome saw him; the electronic mirrors reflecting one another. Jessie cringed.

Jerome saw himself then, reflected back from Jessie.

He saw Jerome-X on a video screen with lousy vertical hold; wobbling, trying to arrange its pixels firmly and losing them. A figure of mewling inconsequence; a brief flow of electrons that might diverge left or right like spray from a water hose depressed with the thumb. Raised in a high-security condo village, protected by cameras and computer lines to private security thugs; raised in a media-windowed womb, with PCs and VCRs and a thousand varieties of video games; shaped by cable TV and fantasy rental; sexuality imprinted by sneaking his parents' badly hidden cache of brainsex files. And in stations from around the world, seeing the same StarFaces appear on channel after channel

as the star's fame spread like a stain across the frequency bands. Seeing the Star's World Self crystallizing; the media figure coming into definition against the backdrop of media competition, becoming real in this electronic collective unconscious.

Becoming real, himself, in his own mind, simply because he'd appeared on a few thousand TV screens, through video tagging, transer graffiti. Growing up with a sense that media events were real and personal events were not. Anything that didn't happen on the Grid didn't happen. Even as he hated conventional programming, even as he regarded it as the cud of ruminants, still the net and TV and di-vees defined his sense of personal unreality; and left him unfinished.

Jerome saw Jerome: perceiving himself unreal. Jerome: scamming a transer, creating a presence via video graffiti. Thinking he was doing it for reasons of radical statement. Seeing, now, that he was doing it to make himself feel substantial, to superimpose himself on the Media Grid . . .

And then Eddie's link was there, Eddie's computer model sliding down over Jerome like a mudslide. Eddie seeing himself as a Legendary Wanderer, a rebel, a homemade mystic; his fantasy parting to reveal an anal-expulsive sociopath; a whiner perpetually scanning for someone to blame for his sour luck.

Suddenly Bones tumbled into the link; a complex worldview that was a sort of streetside sociobiology, mitigated by a loyalty to friends, a mystical faith in brain chips and amphetamines. His underside a masochistic dwarf, the troll of self-doubt, lacerating itself with guilt.

And then Swish, a woman with an unsightly growth, errant glands that were like tumors in her, something other people called "testicles." Perpetually hungry for the means to dampen the pain of an infinite self-derision that mimicked her father's utter rejection of her. A mystical faith in synthetic morphine.

. . . Jerome mentally reeling with disorientation, seeing the others as a network of distorted self-images, caricatures of grotesque ambitions. Beyond them he glimpsed another realm through a break in the psychic clouds: the Plateau, the whispering plane of brain chips linked on forbidden frequencies, an electronic haven for doing deals unseen by cops; a Plateau prowled only by the exquisitely ruthless; a vista of enormous challenges and inconceivable risks and always the potential for getting lost, for madness. A place roamed by the wolves of wetware.

There was a siren quiver from that place, a soundless howling, pulling at them . . . drawing them in . . .

"*Uh uh*, wolflost, pross," Bones said, maybe aloud or maybe through the chips. Translated from chip shorthand, those syllables meant, "Stay away from the Plateau, or we get sucked into it, we lose our focus. Concentrate on parallel processing function."

Jerome looked behind his eyelids, sorted through the files. He moved the cursor down . . .

Suddenly, it was there. The group-thinking capacity looming above them, a sentient skyscraper. They all felt a rush of megalomaniacal pleasure in identifying with it; with a towering edifice of Mind. Five chips became One.

They were ready. Jessie transmitted the bait.

• • •

Alerted to an illegal use of implant chips, the trash can was squeaking down the hall, scanning to precisely locate the source. It came to a sudden stop, rocking on its wheels in front of their cell. Jessie reached through the bars and touched its input jack.

The machine froze with a *clack* midway through a turn, and hummed as it processed what they fed it. Would the robot bite?

Bones had a program for the IBM Cyberguard Fourteens, with all the protocol and a range of sample entry codes. Parallel processing from samples took less than two seconds to decrypt the trash can's access code. Then—

They were in. The hard part was the reprogramming.

Jerome found the way. He told the trash can that he wasn't Eric Wexler, because the DNA code was all wrong, if you looked close enough; what we have here is a case of mistaken identity.

Since this information *seemed* to be coming from authorized sources—the decrypted access code made them authorized—the trash can fell for the gag and opened the cage.

The trash can took the five Eric Wexlers down the hall—that was Jessie's doing, showing them how to make it think of five as one, something his people had learned from the immigration computers. It escorted them through the plastiflex door, through the steel door, and into Receiving. The human guard was heaping sugar into his antique Ronald McDonald coffee mug and watching *The Mutilated* on his wallet TV. Bones and Jessie were in the room and moving in on him before he broke free of the television and went for the button. Bones's long left arm spiked out and his stiffened fingers hit a nerve cluster below the guy's left ear, and he went down, the sugar dispenser in one hand swishing a white fan onto the floor.

Jerome's chip had cross-referenced Bones's attack style. Bones was trained by commandos, the chip said. Military elite. Was he a plant? Bones smiled at him and tilted his head, which Jerome's chip read as: *No. I'm trained by the Underground. Radics.*

Jessie was at the console, deactivating the trash can, killing the cameras, opening the outer doors. Jessie and Swish led the way out, Swish whining softly and biting her lip. There were two more guards at the gate, one of them asleep. Jessie had taken the gun from the guy Bones had put under, so the first guard at the gate was dead before he could hit an alarm. The catnapping guy woke and yelled with hoarse terror, and then Jessie shot him in the throat.

Watching the guard fall, spinning, blood making its own slow-motion spiral in the air, Jerome felt a perfect mingling of sickness, fear, and self-disgust. The guard was young, wearing a cheap wedding ring, probably had a young family. So Jerome stepped over the dying man and made an adjustment; used his chip, chilled himself out with adrenaline. Had to—he was committed now. And he knew with a bland certainty that they had reached the Plateau after all.

He would live on the Plateau now. He belonged there, now that he was one of the wolves.

PHILLIP MANN

AN OLD-FASHIONED STORY

(1989)

NOT HAVING THE TOOL KIT to hand and being of an impatient nature, Jody improvised by using the blunt end of a nail file to prize up the large toenail on Elizabeth's left foot. Revealed was the small copper screw which controlled the energy circuit. Two turns with the nail file and the screw lifted. Immediately Elizabeth's brown tanned body lost its appearance of robust health.

She slumped. Breasts became pouches. Skin became rubbery. The eyes lost their sparkle and turned upward, becoming like boiled egg-whites. With an audible hiss the abdomen became concave and the firm thigh muscles turned to lard.

Jody looked at his handiwork with some alarm. He had never gone so far as to deactivate Elizabeth's energy circuit. The transformation from nubile young woman to this flaccid thing of foam and plastic was almost too much for him. For a moment he thought seriously of calling in a specialist, but then he rallied. "No," he reasoned, "the manual says that repairs and modifications can be made by the careful amateur, and

that's me." He looked at the body lying on the kitchen table and noticed that since the stomach had sunk, a fine hairline seam had become evident running from under the jaw right down to the crotch. He also noticed a foetid smell: a difficult smell to define, something of babies and something of machine oil. There was also a slight seepage coming from nose and vagina, and Jody wondered if he should have read more carefully the section in the manual entitled, "Pre-closedown procedures." He crossed to the sink and collected a full roll of kitchen tissues, which he began to tuck round the body.

And at that moment the doorbell rang. This was followed quickly by the opening of the front door and a voice calling, "Yoo-hoo. It's only me." Jody recognized the voice of Hildergarde, the girl who lived next door and who had been his friend and playmate since childhood.

"I'm back here," called Jody. "In the kitchen. I'm trying to mend Elizabeth." He heard the crisp tap tap of Hildergarde's shoes and guessed that she had come to show him the new outfit she had bought during her visit to the city.

He was right. Hildergarde arrived and paused in the doorway, one hand up under her hair at the back of her head creating a French effect and the other hand on her hips. The dress was Empire style with high bodice and ankle length hem. It was made of yellow and green silk with blue lace round the neck and arms. On her feet were high-heeled boots with old trim. "*Est-ce que tu aimes* my dress?" asked Hildergarde with an affected accent.

Hildergarde pulled a face at his obvious lack of interest and dropped her pose and entered the kitchen. "What's wrong with her?" she asked.

"I don't know," said Jody patiently. "That's what I'm trying to find out."

"Well, did she suddenly stop moving and start to smolder or something? My Joseph did that once. We'd forgotten to keep him topped up. He just stood there and started to fume. Then Dad came in and carried him out to the garage and filled his sack and whatnots with oil and that syntho–extract you can get at the chemists, and he was right as rain."

"Hmm," said Jody, his forehead wrinkling. "I wish it were that simple, but I check her every week and there's never been a problem. Besides, she's got a daily vomit and douche cycle installed and if there were a fluid balance problem I'd know about it soon enough. Hell, the bed'd become a river. She's very clean."

"What happened then?"

"It was this morning, about half past ten. I was feeling a bit . . . you know. And no one was home. So then suddenly Elizabeth stops and lifts up her head and then she butted me right here." Jody pointed to his forehead. There was a bump, covered by his blond fringe. Hildergarde reached out and touched the bump gently with the tips of her fingers. "That's going to be sore," she said. "The skin's all cracked."

"It is sore," said Jody. "Well, I switched her off for a while, for about an hour . . . thought I'd let her cool down. And when I switched her back on she was just like normal. But then later on we

were out by the pool talking and she suddenly threw her glass into the pool and then tried to throw me in. I hit the safety switch and closed her down. And then I thought I'd try and mend her myself."

"What do you think's wrong with her?"

"Just rogueing a bit, I think. I've decided to strip her down, give her a tune-up, and change her personality card. That ought to do the trick. And if it doesn't—"

"Harry knows a lot about Synthos," said Hildergarde. "Why not call him in? Remember he made those Siamese twins one time and that—" Harry was the boy who lived two doors down the road. He could do everything well and he and Jody had been natural enemies from the day they learned to race their trikes.

"If I want Harry's help," said Jody, "I'll ask for it. For the moment I want to do this myself. More interesting that way. All right?" Hildergarde nodded. "So, you hold the manual where I can see it and I'll open her up."

• • •

Hildergarde took the manual and stood at the end of the table near the supine Elizabeth's head. She held the pages open away from her.

Jody bent to his work. "Now let's see. It says here, 'Release the top seal by gentle pressure on the larynx and then insert finger and slide downward to open pectoral, stomach, and bowel areas.' Right. Here goes." He pressed gently on Elizabeth's larynx and the mouth opened and then the entire throat flap. He slipped his finger inside the flap and slid it downward and the skin opened easily. It slit laterally too at the diaphragm and flopped back. The inside of the skin was dark like fish skin and oily. Revealed within were a complicated array of plastic wheels and bands as well as micro-circuitry and inflatable pockets. The skeletal structure was of shiny stainless-steel with ball joints and leaf-spring joints and feather-sensor couplings.

"Fan-tastic," said Jody. "Hell, it makes you wonder what we're like inside, doesn't it?"

Hildergarde's attention was on the pelvis. Here there was a modular arrangement of compressors, flexible bands, and micro switches and all were mounted on a stainless-steel girdle.

"What's that?" she asked, pointing to a small pocket of stretched fabric. Jody consulted the chart in the manual.

"That's the vaginal sack."

"My Joseph's got one of those too. I saw it when Dad was servicing him one day. Hey, what model is this?"

Jody consulted the front pages of the manual. "Model number and inspection warranty will be found on the skull close to the right ear under the wig flap."

Hildergarde took hold of Elizabeth's hair, which was now lifeless and lank like seaweed, and peeled it back from the skull. It came away easily like a teapot cozy to reveal neatly stenciled details.

Model: Ovida Mark 2.4. Fem. Spec. 37. Card 4. Elizabeth the Entertainer. Available in coral, tan and ebony. Swim protected. Throw and jump fortified. Parts compatible with Ovida 1.5–2.4. (All sexes.) Note: this model has both vacuum and pneumatic functions. Inspected by Taurus and Virgo Electronics Inc. Brooklyn. Wgtn.

"My Joseph's an Ovida 2.4, too. Hey let me look."

Hildergarde came round the table and studied Elizabeth's pelvic arrangements in detail. She pointed to a series of bright beveled studs mounted on a flexible plastic plate and connected to a small hydraulic piston. "You see those," she said. "That's where the penis attachment fits. Isn't that clever?"

Jody looked at Hildergarde. "Penis attachment?" he said. "You mean they just clip on? I mean, I never thought . . ."

Hildergarde looked at him scornfully. "Well, it's a bit more complicated than that but still pretty simple all the same. I've got two of them

actually." Then suddenly she blushed. "They're quite different . . . well, the same but different. Similar. What about Elizabeth?"

"Never thought much about it," said Jody. I just accepted the way she is."

"Really?" said Hildergarde, and Jody could not tell whether she believed him or not.

"Yes, really. I didn't even know the models were unisex. I mean my Elizabeth doesn't look anything like your Joseph."

"True. They're not even like brother and sister."

"There must be something on their card that alters the physiognomy as well."

"Must be. Come on let's find the card cache," said Hildergarde with enthusiasm. "This is fun."

• • •

Jody grunted and consulted the manual which he now had to prop up on the side of the table since Hildergarde wanted to be actively involved in the investigation. "Now let's see. 'Personality Card.' 'Destruction of' . . . 'Duplication' . . . 'Mail-ordering' . . . Here we are. 'Replacement' . . . page fifteen." He thumbed through the pages. " 'The personality card cache is located above the stomach pouch and to the right of the sternum auxiliary power pack. Note that all directions are from the Syntho's POV. The rib–hinge release screw is beneath the left clavicle. Care must be taken to release the six shock-adjusters and isolate the cache from the power pack before removing it from the twin flanges of Synaptic Bridge three. See Illustration eighty-eight.' "

"Sounds simple," said Hildergarde. "Remember how we used to play doctors and nurses? Well this is a lot better."

The sternum and ribs were a single flexible unit. Jody found the rib–hinge release screw and turned it once. Immediately a servo–extension arm about the size of a pencil straightened and pushed, whereupon the entire rib case and sternum pivoted upward. The cache could now be clearly seen. It was about the size of a matchbox and made of a black plastic. It was tucked between two iridescent plastic extensions which resembled the spread wings of a butterfly. Together these wings constituted Synaptic Bridge 3. Bedded within them were thousands of micro paths which joined the cache to the furthest extensions of the body. "Wow," breathed Hildergarde. "That's beautiful. You'd better be careful."

At this point Jody decided that it would be a good idea to get the special Ovida Syntho tool kit from his bedroom. "Don't you touch anything while I'm gone," he said to Hildergarde. For her part she put her tongue out at him and said, "Will you bring me a lemonade when you come back?"

When he returned with his toolbox and the lemonade, he found Hildergarde with her arm deep in Elizabeth and her hair tangled in some of the white plastic cogwheels. He set his toolbox down beside Elizabeth's head and placed the glass on top of it. Then he released Hildergarde by snipping off some of her hair. Finally he rotated some of the cogs with his thumb and managed to pull most of the hair free. But in turning the cogs a few strands of the hair managed to snake down deeper into the pulleys and drums of the spine. "I told you not to touch," he said. "Now look what's happened."

"Sorry. But I discovered how they do the breasts," she replied. "It's very ingenious. I got excited and that was when my hair tumbled loose. Do you want to see?"

"What?"

"How they do the breasts."

"Oh. All right."

Hildergarde reached inside Elizabeth again, feeling down the right side of her body to the place where the hips swelled. "It's down here. There's a funny pump thing. Watch." She pumped her hand vigorously for a few moments and Elizabeth's right breast began to swell and the nipple stood up. "There's another pump on the other side for the other breast. Now I'll release it." There was a soft bubbling sound and

the breast and nipple subsided. "Look. Can you see? There's a tuck in it so that part of the breast can fold inside. That's what you do if you want a male like my Joseph. You close the seal like this and voila, no breast."

"What about the nipple? You don't see men with nipples like that.

"It unclips. When it's deflated like now there's no pressure to hold the nipple on and it just unclips. There. See." She took the nipple between finger and thumb and squeezed and twisted. The nipple came free. "Easy."

"Let me look at that," said Jody and he reached across and as he did so he bumped the glass of lemonade which tipped and fell emptying part of its contents onto his toolbox and part into the open cadaver of Elizabeth. "Now look what you've made me do," he said. "I wish I'd never opened her up."

Hildergarde placed the nipple in his hand. "Here, you look at this while I mop up the mess. Where's your squeegee?"

• • •

Five minutes later the mess was cleared and Jody could return to working on the card cache. Carefully he removed the shock adjusters and set them neatly in a teacup brought from the cupboard. Then he started to disconnect the leads of the auxiliary power pack. They were stiff and he had to use more force than he wanted. Two leads came away cleanly but the third would not budge. In attempting to limber it free Jody accidentally closed a circuit in the power pack and for a few seconds power was fed to the spread body. Wheels turned, the legs lifted, the mouth bit, juices were pumped, the fingers beat on the table like castanets, and the spine arched. Then a safety breaker cut in and the body slumped once more. But the damage was done. One of the spinal cogs had sprung loose under pressure and flipped right out of the body and rolled across the floor. A thick white rubber pulley-band had jumped its tracks in the pelvic girdle and disappeared down the right leg. Two small switches had smoldered briefly and burnt the soft foam rubber which made the hips swell. A spray of warm lubricant had spurted from the lower abdomen and left a spotty trail across Hildergarde's hand, arm, and dress. She screamed and jumped back and then ran out of the kitchen and away. The front door slammed behind her. There may have been other damage done to Elizabeth but Jody could not tell.

But at least the third lead from the auxiliary power pack was disengaged and all Jody now had to do was to separate the card cache from Synaptic Bridge 3. This was accomplished without any trouble.

Jody unscrewed the top from the card cache and looked inside. He saw a square of white plastic lodged between two plates of black plastic. The white plastic showed a tab above the plates and was obviously the personality card. Using his long-nosed pliers Jody gripped the plastic card and extracted it slowly. It came free with a click. Written on the card was the simple message "Ovida Fem. spec. Card 4." He set this to one side.

Located in the special toolbox was a small file box which contained three alternative personality cards. These were supplied gratis with all Ovida Synthos by way of advertising. For the dedicated collector, thousands of other specialized types were available ranging from robust nineteenth-century working girls complete with wooden clogs to houri dancers of old Persia. These were also available in many personality shades from sunny and gentle to downright sado-masochistic. But such were very expensive and the cards were frequently custom-made to suit the particular requirements of the purchaser.

All Jody had at his disposal were four standard occupational types, all of which were basically useful and kind. Elizabeth the Entertainer had been his most complex card.

Jody studied the other cards.

Card 1. Norma the Nurse. Brisk and competent but with a tender manner. This card can be augmented to allow Norma to care for babies or the terminally ill. Note: Norma is not a doctor. For full medical functions consult Proctor the Doctor and Phyllis the Physician. Ovida International take no responsibility . . . etc.

Card 2. Myra the Muse. Myra is an advanced word processor and the ideal helpmate for the aspirant writer. She is introverted in manner but with a strong underlying sensuality. Apart from a compendious knowledge of literature, Myra also possesses optional verse functions and a rhyme memory of over 100,000 words.

Card 3. Carol the Cleaner/Cook. Thoughtful and confidential. The perfect companion for the lonely housewife who dreads the hours of boredom between breakfast and dinner. Carol has news and scandal circuits as well as an ability to cook over 200 meals. Note: Carol can be augmented with an anti-alcohol programme.

This was what was available and Jody didn't feel drawn to any of them. He was already missing the fun which Elizabeth the Entertainer had brought into his life. He read through the cards once again and finally selected Myra the Muse. Holding the card with his tweezers he slipped it into place in the cache.

• • •

The return journey of repair went without a hitch. First the auxiliary power leads made their connections smoothly. The shock adjusters fitted into place and the whole unit snuggled securely between the twin wings of the synaptic center.

As Jody was lowering the rib cage and locking it into place, Hildergarde returned. She had changed into a pair of bulky white overalls which had masses of pockets. With her was her male Syntho companion called Joseph. He was a serious-faced young man with red hair and freckles. His character was, as Hildergarde had often told Jody, sensible and studious with strong compassion circuits. He also had broad shoulders, narrow hips, and the legs of a tennis player. Plus extras.

"How are you getting on?" asked Hildergarde.

"Oh, okay. Nearly finished."

"Hear you had some problems," said Joseph.

"Uh uh," replied Jody without looking up, concentrating on his work. He had found the spinal cog that had jumped loose and by pushing and easing managed to limber it back into place. He next reached down inside the right leg and tried to find the band that had come loose. No luck.

"Ah well," he said, "this model has self-repair circuits."

"Sure do," said Joseph amiably, and he cracked his knuckles.

"What card did you use for her?" asked Hildergarde. "I brought some of mine over in case you wanted to experiment." She pronounced the word with all kinds of innuendo and grinned wickedly. "I brought Bruce the Builder and Randolph the Wrestler just in case. Thought they might be fun."

"Oh thanks," said Jody, "but I've already put Myra's card in."

"Myra the Muse! Boring," said Hildergarde pulling a face. "I've seen Dad use her."

"No. Myra the Muse is a nice lady," said Joseph.

Both Hildergarde and Jody stared at him. It was rare for a Syntho to offer an unsolicited opinion let alone a dissenting one.

"Well I need to study a bit," said Jody weakly, and he returned to his work, folding over the flaps of skin.

The body came together neatly. As the seams met they exuded an oil. This was a kind of protective insulation, for once the skin became charged the flaps would instantly bond. Jody replaced the energy fuse in the big toe of the left foot and screwed it into place and closed the toenail with a click. Immediately, and much to Jody's relief, the body began to firm and the seams disappeared. The breasts slowly shaped. Jody noticed that Myra's breasts were slightly smaller than Elizabeth's. He also noticed that he had neglected to replace the nipple. The jaw trembled. Fluid ran briefly from the nose and then Myra sniffed. The muscles in her arms and thighs came up to tone and flexed. It seemed to Jody that Myra's hips were wider than Elizabeth's and that her legs were slightly shorter and thicker. Not unattractive, he noted.

Fully formed, brown-skinned, and vibrant, the body held its position in suspended animation. Jody reached up under the nape of the neck and found a micro switch and double clicked with his finger.

Immediately the body drew in breath. Myra's eyes turned in their orbits and then settled and focused. The mouth opened and closed a few times. There was a choking sound from the throat and then a pleasant contralto voice said, "Myra sick. Please come quick."

She sat up. Her head traveled through one hundred and eighty degrees, surveying the kitchen and those who were looking at her. She did not blink. "My name is Myra. I live in a pen. Cry sorrow. Sorrow. My hair is gone."

Jody picked up the wig and handed it to her. She took it carefully and set it on her head and adjusted it. A greater assurance came into her figure. She edged forward on the table until her toes could touch the floor and then, using her hands, she eased herself upright and stood. "I am Myra. I need clothes. Please dress me." Her eyes settled on Jody. "Please dress me, Jody. We have so much work to do. 'Ars longa, vita brevis.' 'The lyf so short, the craft so long to lerne.' Chaucer after Seneca after Hippocrates. Please give me your hand, Jody. Myra the Muse is sick." Myra reached out her hand.

Jody reached out to meet her. But before they could join, before Myra could take one step, her right leg gave way and she crashed down onto her knees. "Poor Myra's a cold." Then she writhed onto her back and began to scratch at her eyes.

• • •

Jody and Hildergarde started forward but both were too slow. They felt themselves gripped from behind by strong fingers and hauled back. Joseph stepped swiftly between them. He came close to Myra and knelt down. He slipped his arms under her quivering body and lifted her up, and then turned and faced Jody. "You should have consulted a specialist," he said. "You're just a boy."

Then he turned and, carrying the still shaking Myra in his arms, exited from the kitchen. As he departed they heard the contralto of Myra murmuring, "Howl. Howl. Howl."

Jody rubbed his arm where the Syntho Joseph had gripped him. He could feel the bruise rising. Hildergarde scrambled to her feet and ran to the door. "You come back here, Joseph," she called. "You come back here this moment. Do you hear?"

For answer the door slammed.

Hildergarde turned to Jody in disbelief. "Well, what do you think of that?" she said indignantly.

Jody shrugged. "If I were you I'd get some of his circuits trashed," he said. "He could become dangerous. He's starting to rogue." Jody nodded toward the phone. "You can give the wardens a call now if you like. They'll soon round him up. They'll know what to do."

"And what about Myra the Muse?"

"No worries," said Jody, smiling suddenly. "She was still under guarantee. I'll get a new one."

GEORGE ALEC EFFINGER

THE WORLD AS WE KNOW IT

(1992)

THE SETUP could have been pretty clever with a little more thought, I have to admit. Using some of the newest-generation cerebral hardware, an ambitious but dangerously young man, a recent parolee—you know, a low-level street punk, much as I'd been once upon a time—had stolen a small crate from Mahmoud's warehouse. The punk hadn't even known what was in the crate. It turned out, if I can trust Mahmoud, that the crate contained a shipment of recently developed biological agents.

These bios had two major uses: They could promote the healing of traumatic wounds while making the attendant pain disappear for a while, without subjecting the patient to the well-documented narcotic disadvantages we've all come to know and love; or what was contained in the many disposable vials could easily be reconfigured to wipe out entire cities, using very small doses—thus becoming the most powerful neurological weapons ever devised. The small crate was labeled to be shipped to Holland, where the Dutch revolution was still at its full, vicious, inhuman peak.

Of course, Mahmoud was frantic to get his crate back. He and a few of my old friends, from the good old days when I had power and could move through the city without fear of being dusted by my many enemies, knew where I was now living. I'd left the Budayeen and adopted a new identity. Mahmoud had come to me and offered me money, which I didn't need—I'd lost just about everything, but I'd carefully protected the cash I'd acquired—or contacts and agents, which I did need, and desperately. I agreed to look into the matter for Mahmoud.

It wasn't very difficult. The thief was such a beginner that I almost felt like taking him aside and giving him a few pointers. I restrained that impulse, however.

The kid, who told me his name was Musa, had left a trail through the city that had been easy as hell for a predator like me to follow. I know the kid's name wasn't Musa, just as he knew my name wasn't the one I gave him when I finally caught up to him. Names and histories were not important information to either of us at the time. All that mattered was the small crate.

I dragged him back to my office, far from the Budayeen, in a neighborhood called Iffatiyya. This part of the city, east beyond the canal, had been reduced to rubble in the last century, the fifteenth after the Hegira, the twenty-second of the Christian era. It was now about a hundred years later than that, and at last some of the bombed-out buildings were being reclaimed. My office was in one of them.

I was there because most of my former friends and associates had leaped to the other side, to the protection of Shaykh Reda Abu Adil. There were very few places that were safe for me back in the walled quarter, and few people I could trust. Hell, I didn't really trust Mahmoud—never had—except he was reliably, scrupulously straightforward when large sums of money were involved.

I opened the outer door of my office, the one with the glass panel on which some frustrated portrait artist had lettered my new name, in both Arabic and Roman alphabets. Inside the door was a waiting room with a sagging couch, three wooden chairs, and a few items to help my few anxious clients pass the time: a scattering of newspapers and magazines, and chipzines for my more technologically advanced visitors, to be chipped directly into a moddy or daddy socket located in the hollow at the base of the skull.

I had a good grasp of the material of Musa's gallebeya, which I used to propel him through the open inner door. He fell sprawling on the bare, shabby, wooden floor. I slouched in the comfortable chair behind my beat-up old desk. I let a sarcastic smile have its way for a second or two, and then I put on my grim expression. "I want to clear this up fast," I said.

Musa had gotten to his feet and was glaring at me with all the defiance of youth and ignorance. "No problem," he said, in what he no doubt imagined was a tough voice. "All you gotta do is come across."

"By fast," I said, deliberately not responding to his words, "I mean superluminal. Light speed. And I'm not coming across. I don't do that. Grab a seat while I make a phone call, O Young One."

Musa maintained the rebellious expression, but some worry had crept into it, too. He didn't know who I planned to call. "You ain't gonna turn me over to the rats, are you?" he asked. "I just got out. Yallah, another fall and I think they'll cut off my right hand."

I nodded, murmuring Mahmoud's commcode into my desk phone. Musa was right about one thing: Islamic justice as currently interpreted in the city would demand the loss of his hand, possibly the entire arm, in front of a huge, cheering crowd in the courtyard of the Shimaal Mosque. Musa would have no opportunity to appeal, either, and he'd probably end up back in prison afterward, as well.

"Marhaba," said Mahmoud when he answered his phone. He wasn't the kind of guy to identify himself until he knew who was on the other end of the line. I remembered him before he had his sex change, as a slender, doe-eyed sylph, dancing at Jo-Mama's. Since then, he'd put on a lot of weight, toughness, and something much more alarming.

"Yeah, you right," I replied. "Good news, Mahmoud. This is your investigator calling. Got the thief, and he hasn't had time to do anything with the product. He'll take you to it. What becomes of him afterward is up to you. Come take charge of him at your convenience."

"You are still a marvel, O Wise One," said Mahmoud. His praise counted about as much as a broken Bedu camel stick. "You have lost much, but it is as Allah wills. Yet you have not lost your native wit and ability. I will be there very soon, inshallah, with some news that might interest you." *Inshallah* means "if God wills." Nobody but He was too sure about anything of late.

"The news is the payment, right, O Father of Generosity?" I said, shaking my head. Mahmoud had been a cheap stiff as a woman, and he was a cheap stiff now as a man.

"Yes, my friend," said Mahmoud. "But it includes a potential new client for you, and I'll throw in a little cash, too. Business is business."

"And action is action," I said, not that I was seeing much action these days. "You know how much I charge for this sort of thing."

"Salaam alaikum, my friend," he said hurriedly, and he hung up his phone before I could salaam him back.

Musa looked relieved that I hadn't turned him over to the police, although I'm sure he was just as anxious about the treatment he could expect from Mahmoud. He had every reason in the world to be concerned. He maintained a surly silence, but he finally took my advice and sat down in the battered red-leather chair opposite my desk.

"Piece of advice," I said, not even bothering to look at him. "When Mahmoud gets here—and he'll get here fast—take him directly to his property. No excuses, no bargains. If you try holding Mahmoud up for so much as a lousy copper fiq, you'll end up breathing hot sand for the remainder of your brief life. Understand?"

I never learned if the punk understood or not. I wasn't looking at him, and he wasn't saying anything. I opened the bottom drawer of my desk and took out the office bottle. Apparently a slow leak had settled in, because the level of gin was much lower than I expected. It was something that would bear investigating during my long hours of solitude.

I built myself a white death—gin and bingara with a hit of Rose's lime juice—and took a quick gulp. Then I drank the rest of the tumblerful slowly. I wasn't savoring anything; I was just proving to myself again that I could be civilized about my drinking habits.

Time passed in this way—Musa sitting in the red-leather chair, sampling emotions; me sitting in my chair, sipping white death. I'd been correct about one thing: It didn't take Mahmoud long to make the drive from the Budayeen. He didn't bother to knock on the outer door. He came through, into my inner office, accompanied by three large men. Now, even I thought

three armed chunks were a bit much to handle ragged, little old Musa there. I said nothing. It wasn't my business any longer.

Now, Mahmoud was dressed as I was, that is, in keffiya, the traditional Arab headdress, gallebeya, and sandals; the men with Mahmoud were all wearing very nice, tailored European-style business suits. Two of the suit jackets had bulges just where you'd expect. Mahmoud turned to those two and didn't utter a word. The two moved forward and took pretty damn physical charge of Musa, getting him out of my office the quickest way possible. Just before he passed through the inner door, Musa jerked his head around toward me and said, "Rat's puppet." That was all.

That left Mahmoud and the third suit.

"Where you at, Mahmoud?" I asked.

"I see you've taken to dyeing your beard, O Wise One," said Mahmoud by way of thanks. "You no longer look like a Maghrebi. You look like any common citizen of Asir or the Hejaz, for instance. Good."

I was so glad he approved. I was born part Berber, part Arab, and part French, in the part of Algeria that now called itself Mauretania. I'd left that part of the world far, far behind, and arrived in this city a few years ago, with reddish hair and beard that made me stand out among the locals. Now all my hair was as black as my prospects.

Mahmoud tossed an envelope on the desk in front of me. I glanced at it but didn't count the kiam inside, then dropped the envelope in a desk drawer and locked it.

"I cannot adequately express my thanks, O Wise One," he said in a flat voice. It was a required social formula.

"No thanks are needed, O Benefactor," I said, completing the obligatory niceties. "Helping a friend is a duty."

"All thanks be to Allah."

"Praise Allah."

"Good," said Mahmoud with some satisfaction. I could see him relax a little, now that the show was over. He turned to the remaining suit and said, "Shaykh Ishaq ibn Muhammad il-Qurawi, O Great Sir, you've seen how reliable my friend is. May Allah grant that he solve your problem as promptly as he solved mine." Then Mahmoud nodded to me, turned, and left. Evidently, I wasn't high enough on the social ladder to be actually introduced to Ishaq ibn Muhammad il-Qurawi.

I motioned to the leather chair. Il-Qurawi made a slight wince of distaste, then sat down.

I put on my professional smile and uttered another formulaic phrase that meant, roughly, "You have come to your people and level ground." In other words, "Welcome."

"Thank you, I—"

I raised a hand, cutting him off. "You must allow me to offer you coffee, O Sir. The journey from the Budayeen must have been tiring, O Shaykh."

"I was hoping we could dispense with—"

I raised my hand again. The old me would've been more than happy to dispense with the hospitality song-and-dance, but the new me was playing a part, and the ritual three tiny cups of coffee was part of it. Still, we hurried through them as rapidly as social graces permitted. Il-Qurawi wore a sour expression the whole time.

When I offered him a fourth, he waggled his cup from side to side, indicating that he'd had enough.

"May your table always be prosperous," he said, because he had to.

I shrugged. "Allah yisallimak." May God bless you.

"Praise Allah."

"Praise Allah."

"Now," said my visitor emphatically, "you have been recommended to me as someone who might be able to help with a slight difficulty."

I nodded reassuringly. Slight difficulty, my Algerian ass. People didn't come to me with slight difficulties.

As usual, the person in the leather chair didn't know how to begin. I waited patiently, letting my smile evaporate bit by bit. I found myself thinking about the office bottle, but it was impossible to bring it out again until I was alone. Strict Muslims looked upon alcoholic beverages with the same fury that they maintained for the infidel, and I knew nothing about il-Qurawi's attitudes about such things.

"If you have an hour or two free this afternoon," he said, "I wonder if you'd come with me to my office. It's not far from here, actually. On the eastern side of the canal, but quite a bit north of here. We've restored a thirty-six-story office building, but recently there's been more than the usual amount of vandalism. I'd like to hire you to stop it."

I took a deep breath and let it out again. "Not my usual sort of assignment, O Sir," I said, shrugging, "but I don't foresee any problem. I get a hundred kiam a day plus expenses. I need a minimum of five hundred right now to pique my interest."

Il-Qurawi frowned at the discussion of money and waved his hand. "Will you accept a check?" he asked.

"No," I said. I'd noticed that the man was stingy with honorifics, so I'd decided to hold my own to the minimum.

He grunted. He was clearly annoyed and doubtful about my ability to do what he wanted. Still, he removed a moderate stack of bills from a black leather wallet, and sliced off five for me. He leaned forward and put the money on my desk. I pretended to ignore it.

I made no pretense of checking an appointment book. "I'm certain, O Shaykh, that I can spare a few hours for you."

"Very good." Il-Qurawi stood up and spent a few moments vitally absorbed in the wrinkles in his business suit. I took the time to slide the five hundred kiam into the pocket of my gallebeya.

"I can spare a few hours, O Shaykh," I said, "but first I'd like some more information. Such as who you are and whom you represent."

He didn't say a word. He merely slid a business card to the spot where the money had been.

I picked up the card. It said:

Ishaq ibn Muhammad il-Qurawi
Chief of Security
CRCorp

Below that was a street address that meant nothing to me, and a commcode. I didn't have a business card to give him, but I didn't think he cared. "CRCorp?" I asked.

He was still standing. He indicated that we should begin moving toward the door. It was fine by me.

"Yes, we deal in consensual realities."

"Uh huh," I said. "I know you people." By this time, we were standing in the hallway and he was watching me lock the outer door.

We went downstairs to his car. He owned a long, black, chauffeur-driven, restored, gasoline-powered limousine. I wasn't impressed. I'd ridden in a few of those. We got in and he murmured something to the driver. The car began gliding through the rubble-strewn streets, toward the headquarters of CRCorp.

"Can you be more exact about the nature of this vandalism, O Sir?" I said.

"You'll see. I believe it's being caused by one person. I have no idea why; I just want it stopped. There are too many clients in the building beginning to complain."

And it's beyond the capabilities of the Chief of Security, I thought. That spoke something ominous to me.

After about half an hour of weaving north and east, then back west toward the canal, then farther north, we arrived at the CRCorp building. Allah only knew what it had been before this entire part of the city had been destroyed, but now it stood looking newly built among its broken and blasted neighbors. One fixed-up building in all that desolation seemed pretty lonely and conspicuous, I thought, but I guess you had to start someplace.

Il-Qurawi and I got out of the limousine and walked across the freshly surfaced parking area. There were no other cars in it. "The executive offices are on the seventeenth floor, about half-

way up, but there's nothing interesting to see there. You'll want to visit one or two of the consensual realities, and then look at the vandalism I mentioned."

Well, sure, as soon as he said there wasn't anything interesting on the seventeenth floor, I immediately wanted to go there. I hate it when other people tell me what I want to do, but it was il-Qurawi's five hundred kiam, so I kept my mouth shut, nodded, and followed him inside to the elevators.

"Give you a taste of one of the consensual realities," he said. "We just call them CRs around here. We'll stop off first on twenty-six. It's functioning just fine, and there's been no sign of vandalism as yet."

Still nothing for me to say. We rode up quickly, silently in the mirrored elevator. I glanced at my reflection. I wasn't happy with the appearance I'd had to adopt, but I was stuck with it.

We got off at twenty-six. The elevator doors opened, we stepped out, and passed through a small, well-constructed airlock. When I turned to look, the elevator and airlock had disappeared. I mean, there was no sign that elevator doors could possibly exist for hundreds of miles. I felt for them and there was nothing but air. Rather thin, cold air. If I'd been pressed to make a guess, I'd have said that we were on the surface of Mars. I knew that was impossible, but I'd seen holo shots of the Martian surface, and this is just what they looked like.

"Here," said il-Qurawi, handing me a mask and a small tank, "this should help you somewhat."

"I am in your debt, O Great One." I used the tight-grip straps to hold the mask in place, but the tank was made to be worn on a belt. I had a rope holding my gallebeya closed, but it wouldn't support the weight of the tank, so I just carried it in my hands. We started walking across the barren, boulder-studded surface of Mars toward a collection of buildings in the far distance that I recognized as the international Martian colony.

"The atmosphere on this floor only approximates that of Mars," said il-Qurawi. "That was part of the group's consensus agreement. Still, if you're outside and not wearing the mask, you're liable to develop a rather serious condition they call 'Mars throat.' Affects your sinuses, your inner ears, your throat, and so forth."

"Let me see if I can guess, O Sir," I said, huffing a little as I made my way over the extremely rough terrain. "Group of people in the colony, all would-be Martian colonists, and they've voted on how they wanted the place to look." I gazed up at a pink peach-colored sky.

"Exactly. And they voted on how they wanted it to feel and smell and sound. Actually, it approximates the reports we get from the true Mars Project rather closely. CRCorp supplies the area, for which we charge what we feel is a fair price. We also supply the software that maintains the illusion, too."

I kicked a boulder. No illusion. "How much of this is real?" I said. Even using the tank, I was already short of breath and eager to get inside one of the buildings.

"The boulders, as you've just discovered, are artificial but real. The buildings are real. The carefully maintained atmosphere is also our responsibility. Everything else you might experience is computer or holo generated. It can be quite deadly out here, but that's the way this group wanted it. We haven't left anything out, down to the toxin-laden lichen, which is part of the illusion. For all intents and purposes, this is the surface of Mars. Group Twenty-Six has always seemed to be very pleased with it. We've gotten very few complaints or suggestions for improvement."

"Naturally, O Sir," I said, "I'm looking forward to interviewing a few of the residents."

"Of course," said il-Qurawi. "That's why I brought you here. We're very proud of Group Twenty-Six, and justly so, I think."

"Praise Allah," I said. No echo from my client.

After more time and hiking than I'd been prepared for, we arrived at the colony itself. I felt like a physical wreck; the executive with me was not suffering at all. He looked like he'd just taken a leisurely stroll through the repro of the Tiger Gardens in the city's entertainment quarter.

"This way," he said, pointing to an airlock into the long main building. It appeared to have been constructed of some material derived from the reddish sand all around, but I wasn't interested enough to find out for sure if that were true or part of the holographic illusion.

We cycled through the airlock. Inside, we found ourselves in a corridor that had been painted in institutional colors: dark green to waist-level, a kind of maddening tan above that. I was absolutely sure that I would quickly come to hate those colors; soon it proved that they dominated the color scheme of most of the hallways and meeting rooms. The people of Group Twenty-Six must have had a very different aesthetic sense than I did. It didn't give me great hopes for them.

Il-Qurawi glanced at his wristwatch, a European product like the rest of his outfit. It was thin and sleek and made of gold. "The majority of them will be in the refectory module now," he said. "Good. You'll have the opportunity to meet as many of Group Twenty-Six as you like. Ask whatever you like, but we are under a little time pressure. I'd like to take you to floor seven within the next half hour."

"I give thanks to the Maker of Worlds," I said. Il-Qurawi gave me a sidelong glance to see if I were serious. I was doing my best to give that impression.

The refectory was down the entire length of the main building and through a low, narrow, windowless passageway. I felt a touch of claustrophobia, as if I were down deep beneath the surface; I had to remind myself that I was actually on the twenty-sixth floor of an office tower.

The refectory was at the other end of the passageway. It was a large room, filled with orderly rows of tables. Men, women, and children sat at the tables, eating food from trays that were dispensed from a large and intricate machine on one side of the front of the room. I stared at it for a while, watching people go up to it, press colored panels, and receive their trays within fifteen or twenty seconds each.

"Catering," said il-Qurawi with an audible sigh. "Major part of our overhead."

"Question, O Sir," I said. "Who's actually paying for all this?"

He looked at me as if I were a total fool. "All these people in Group Twenty-Six, of course. They've signed over varying amounts of cash and property, depending on how long they intend to stay. Some come for a week, but the greater portion of the group has paid in advance for ten- or twenty-year leases."

My eyes narrowed as I thought and did a little multiplication in my head. "Then, depending on the populations of the other thirty-some floors," I said slowly, "CRCorp ought to be making a very tidy bundle."

His head jerked around to look at me directly. "I've already mentioned the high overhead. The expenses we incur to maintain all this—and the CRs on the other floors—is staggering. Our profits are not so great as you might think."

"I ask a thousand pardons, O Sir," I said. "I truly had no intention to give offense. I'm still trying to get an idea of how large an operation this is. Maybe now's the time to speak to one or two of these 'Martian colonists.'"

He relaxed a little. He was hiding something, I'd bet my wives and kids on it. "Of course," he said smoothly. I thought back on it and couldn't recall a single time he'd actually called me by name. In any event, he directed me to one of the tables where there was an empty seat beside an elderly man with short-cropped white hair. He wore a pale-blue jumpsuit. Hell, everyone there wore a pale-blue jumpsuit. I wondered if that was the official uniform on the real Mars colony, or just a group decision of this particular CR.

"Salaam alaikum," I said to the elderly man.

"Alaikum-as-salaam," he said mechanically. "Outsider, huh?"

"Just came in to get a quick look."

He leaned over and whispered in my ear. "Now, some of us really hate outsiders. Spoils the group consensus."

"I'll be out of here before you know it, inshallah."

The white-haired man took a forkful of some brown, smooth substance on his tray, chewed it thoughtfully, then said, "Could've at least gotten into a goddamn jumpsuit, hayawaan. Too much trouble?"

I ignored the insult. Il-Qurawi should've thought of the jumpsuit. "How long you been part of Group Twenty-Six?" I asked.

"We don't call ourselves 'Group Twenty-Six,'" said the man, evidently disliking me even more. "We're the Mars colony."

Well, the real Mars colony was a combined project of the Federated New England States of America, the new Fifth Reich, and the Fragrant Heavenly Empire of True Cathay.

There were no—or very few—Arabs on the real Mars.

Someone delivered a tray of food to me: molded food without texture slapped onto a molded plastic tray; the brown stuff, some green stuff that I took to be some form of vegetable material—as nondescript and unidentifiable as anything else on the tray—a small portion of dark red, chewy stuff that might have been a meat substitute, and the almost obligatory serving of gelatin salad with chopped carrots, celery, and canned fruit in it. There were also slices of dark bread and disposable cups of camel's milk.

I turned again to the white-haired gentleman. "Milk, huh?" I asked.

His bushy eyebrows went up. "Milk is the best thing for you. If you want to live forever."

I murmured "Bismillah," which means "in the name of God," and I began eating my meal, not knowing what some of the dishes were even after I'd tasted and chewed and swallowed them. I ate out of social obligation, and I did pretty well, too. When some of the others were finished, they took their trays and utensils to a machine very much like the one that dispensed the meals in the first place. The hard items disappeared into a long, wide slot, and I felt certain that leftover food was recycled in one form or another. CRCorp prided itself on efficiency, and this was one way to keep the operating costs down.

I still had my doubts about the limited choices in the refectory—including the compulsory camel's milk, which was served in four-ounce cups. As I ate, il-Qurawi turned toward me again. "Are you enjoying the meal?" he asked.

"Praise God for His beneficence," I said.

"God, God—" il-Qurawi shook his head. "It's permissible if you really believe in that sort of thing. But the people here are not all Muslim—some belong to no organized religion at all—and they're using whatever agricultural training they had on 'Earth,' and they're applying it here on 'Mars.' They grew a small portion of these delicious meats and vegetables themselves—it came from their skill, their dedication, their determination. They receive no aid or interference from CRCorp."

"Yeah, you right," I said, and decided I'd had enough of il-Qurawi, too. I hadn't tasted anything the least bit palatable except possibly the bread and milk, and how wildly enthusiastic could I get about them? I didn't mention anything about CRCorp's inability to reproduce the noticeably lower gravity of the true Mars, or certain other aspects of the interplanetary milieu.

I spoke some more to the white-haired man, and then one of the plainly clothed women farther down the table leaned over and interrupted us. Her hair was cut just above shoulder-length, dull from not having been washed for a very long time. I suppose that while there was plenty of water in the thirty-six-story office building, in the headquarters of the CRCorp, and on some of the other consensus-reality floors, there was extremely little water available on floor twenty-six—the Mars for the sort of folks who yearned for danger, but no danger more threatening than the elevator ride from the main lobby.

"Has he told you everything?" asked the filthy woman. Her voice was clearly intended to be a whisper, but I'm sure she was overheard several rows of tables away on either side of us.

"There's so much more I want to see," said il-Qurawi, even going so far as to grab my arm. That just made me determined to hear the woman out.

"I have not finished my meal, O fellah," I said, somewhat irritably. I'd called him a peasant. I shouldn't have, but it felt good. "What is your blessed name, O Lady?" I asked her.

She looked blank for a few seconds, then confused. Finally she said, "Marjory Mulcher. Yeah, that's me now. Sometimes I'm Marjory Tiller, depending on the season and how badly they need me and how many people are willing to work with me."

I nodded, figuring I understood what she meant. "Everything that passes in this world," I said, "—or any other world—" I interpolated, "is naught but the expression of the Will of God."

Marjory's eyes grew larger and she smiled. "I'm a Roman Catholic," she said. "Lapsed, maybe, but what does that do to you, camel jockey?"

I couldn't think of a safely irrelevant reply.

In her mind, the CRCorp probably had nothing to do with her present situation. Perhaps in her own mind she was on Mars. That may have been the great and ultimate victory of CRCorp.

"I asked you," said Marjory with a frown, "are they showing you everything? Are they telling you everything?"

"Don't know," I said. "I just got here."

Marjory moved down a few places and sat beside me, on the other side from the white-haired man. I looked around and saw that only she and I were still eating. Everyone else had disposed of his tray and was sitting, almost expectantly, in his molded plastic seat, politely and quietly.

The woman smelled terrible. She leaned toward me and whispered, "You know the corporation is just about ready to unleash a devastating CR. Something we won't be able to manage at all. Death on every floor, I imagine. And then, when they've tested this horrible CR on us, may their religion be cursed, they'll unleash it on you and what you casually prefer to call the rest of the world. Earth, I mean. I grew up on Earth, you know. Still have some relatives there."

By the holy sacred beard of the Prophet, may the blessings of Allah be on him and peace, I've never felt so relieved as when she discovered a sudden interest in the gelatin salad. "Raisins. Rejoicing and celebrations," she said to no one in particular. "Consensual raisins."

I slowly closed my eyes and tightened my lips. My right hand dropped its piece of bread and raised up tiredly to cover my tightly shut eyelids, at the same time massaging my forehead. We didn't have enough facilities for mentals and nutsos in the city; we just let the ones with the wealthier families shut 'em away in places like Group Twenty-Six in the CRCorp building. Yaa Allah, you never knew when you were going to run into one of these bereft cookies.

Still with my eyes covered, I could feel the man with the close-cropped white hair lean toward me on the other side. I knew that son of a biscuit hadn't liked me from the get-go. "Get Marjory to tell you all about her raisins sometime. It's a fascinating story in its own right."

"Be sure *to*," I murmured. In the spring with the apricots, I would. I picked up the bread with my eating hand again and opened my eyes. Everyone within hollering range was staring at me with rapt attention. I don't know why; I didn't want to know why then, and I still don't want to know why. I hoped it was just that I was an oddity, a welcome interruption in the daily routine, like a visit from one of Prince Shaykh Mahali's wives or children.

I'd had enough to eat, and so I'd picked up the tray—I'm quick on the uptake, and I'd figured out the disposal drill from observation. It wasn't that difficult to begin with, and, jeez, I'm a trained professional, mush hayk? Yeah, you right. I slid the tray into the proper slot in the proper machine. Then il-Qurawi, having nothing immediate to do, chose to be nowhere in sight. I slumped back down between Marjory and the old, white-haired man. Fortunately, Marjory was still enchanted by her gelatin salad—the al-Qaddani moddy, a Palestinian fic-

tional hardboiled-detective piece of hardware I was wearing, let me have the impression that Marjory was like this at every meal, whatever was served—and the old gentleman gave me a disapproving look, stood up, and moved away, toward what real people did to compensate society for their daily sustenance. For a few moments I had utter peace and utter silence, but I did not expect them to last very long. I was correct as usual in this sort of discouraging speculation.

Almost directly across from me was a woman with extremely large breasts, which were trapped in an undergarment which must have been painfully confining for them. I really wasn't interested enough to read if they were genuine—God-given—or not; she must've thought she had, you know, the most devastating figure on all of Mars, and of course we understand what we mean when we speak of Mars. She wore a long, flowing, print shift of a drabness that directed all one's attention elsewhere and upward; bare feet; and a live, medium-sized, suffering lizard on one shoulder that was there only to extort yet another sort of response from you. As if her grotesque mamelons weren't enough.

Oh, you were supposed to say, *you have a live, medium-sized lizard on your shoulder.* Now, when someone has gone to that amount of labor to pry a reaction from me, my innate obstinacy sets in. I will not look more than two or three times at the tits, casually, as after the first encounter they don't exist for me. I won't even glance furtively at her various other vulgar accoutrements. I won't remark at all on the lizard. The lizard and I will never have a relationship; the woman and I barely had one, and *that* only through courtesy.

She spoke in a voice intended to be heard by the nearby portion of mankind: "I think Marjory means well." She looked around herself to find agreement, and there wasn't a single person still in the refectory who would contradict her. I got the feeling that would be true whatever she said. "I know for a fact that Marjory never goes beyond the buildings of the Mars colony. She never sees Allah's holy miracle of creation. Does it not say in the Book, the noble Qur'ân,

'Frequently you see the ground dry and barren: but no sooner do We send down rain to moisten it than it begins to tremble and magnify, putting forth each and every kind of blossoming life. That is because Allah is Truth: He gives life to the dead and has power over all things.'" She sat back, evidently very self-satisfied. "That was from the surah called 'Pilgrimage,' in the holy Qur'ân."

"May the Creator of heaven and earth bless this recitation of His holy words," said one man softly.

"May Allah give His blessing," said a woman quietly.

I had several things I might have mentioned; the first was that the imitation surface of Mars I'd crossed was not, in point of fact, covered with every variety of blooming plant. Yet maybe to some of these people that was worth reporting to the authorities. Before I could say anything, a young, sparsely bearded man sat beside me in the old, white-haired resident's seat, and addressed the elderly woman. The young man said, "You know, Umm Sulaiman, that you shouldn't hold up Marjory as a typical resident of the Mars colony."

Umm Sulaiman frowned. "I have further scripture that I could recite which supports my words and actions."

The young man shuddered. "No, my mother-in-law"—clearly an honorific and a title not to be taken seriously—"all is as Allah wills." He turned to me and murmured, "I wish the both of them—the two old women, Marjory and Umm Sulaiman—would stop behaving in their ways. I admit it, I'm superstitious, and it frightens me."

"Seems a shame to pay all this money to CRCorp just to be frightened."

The young man looked to either side, then leaned even closer. "I've heard a story, O Sir," he murmured. "Actually, I've heard several stories, some as wild as Marjory's, some even crazier. But, by the beard of the Prophet—"

"May the blessings of Allah be on him and peace," I said.

"—there's one story that won't go away, a story that's repeated often by the most sane and reliable of our team." Team: as if they really were part of some kind of international extraterrestrial project.

I pursed my lips and tried to show that I was rabidly eager to hear his bit of gossip. "And what is this persistent story, O Wise One?"

He looked to either side again, took my arm, and together we left the table and the others. We walked slowly toward the exit. "Now, O Sir," he said, "I've heard this directly from Bin el-Fadawin, who is CRCorp and Shaykh il-Qurawi's highest representative here in the Mars colony."

"Group Twenty-Six, you mean," I said.

"Yeah, if you insist on it, Group Twenty-Six." It was obvious that he didn't like his illusion broken, even for a moment. It cast some preliminary doubt on what he was about to tell me. "Listen, O Sir," he said. "Bin el-Fadawin and others drop hints now and again that CRCorp has better uses for these premises, that they're even now working on ways to turn away and run off the very people who've paid them for long-term care."

I shrugged. "If CRCorp wanted to evict all of you, O Young Man, I'm sure they could do it without too much difficulty. I mean, they got the lawyers and you got, what, rocks and lichen? Still, you and all the others have handed over—and continue to hand over—truly exorbitant amounts of cash and property; and all they've really done is decorate to your specifications a large, empty space in a restored office tower."

"They've created our consensual reality, please, O Shaykh."

"Yeah, you right," I said, amazed that this somewhat intelligent young man could be so easily taken in. "So you're telling me that the CRs—which the corporation has worked so hard to create, and for which it's being richly rewarded—will start disappearing, one by one?"

"Begin disappearing!" cried the young man. "Have Shaykh il-Qurawi—"

"Did I hear my name mentioned, O Most Gracious Ones?" asked my client, appearing silently enough through the door of the refectory room. "In a pleasant context, I hope."

"I was commenting, O Sir," I said, covering quickly, "on the truly spectacular job CRCorp has done here, inside the buildings and out. That little lizard Umm Sulaiman wears on her shoulder—is that a genuine Martian life form?"

"No," he said, frowning slightly. "There aren't any native lizards on Mars. We've tried to discourage her from wearing it—it creates a disharmony with what we're trying to accomplish here. Still, the choice is her own."

"Ah," I said. I'd figured all that before; I was just easing the young man out of the conversation. "I believe I've seen enough here, O Sir. Next I'd like to see some of the vandalism you spoke of."

"Of course," said il-Qurawi, moving a hand to almost touch me, almost grasp my elbow and lead me from the refectory. He gave me no time at all for the typically effusive Muslim farewells. We left the building the way we'd come, and once again I used the mask and bottled air. However, we didn't make the long trek across the make-believe Martian landscape; il-Qurawi knew of a nearer exit. I guess he had just wanted me to come the long way before, to sample the handiwork of CRCorp.

We ducked through a nearly invisible airlock near the colony buildings, and took an elevator down to floor seven. When we stepped in, I removed the mask and air tank. The air pressure and oxygen content of the atmosphere was Earth-normal.

I saw immediately il-Qurawi's problem. Floor seven was entirely abandoned. In fact, except for some living quarters and outbuildings in the distance, and the barren and artificially landscaped "hills" and "valleys" built into the area, floor seven was nothing but a large and vacant loft a few stories above street level.

"What happened here, O Sir?" I asked.

Il-Qurawi turned around and casually indicated the entire floor. "This used to be a recreation of Egypt at the time of the Ptolemies. I personally never saw the need for a consensual reality set in pre-Islamic times, but I was assured that certain academic experts wanted to reestablish the Library of Alexandria, which was destroyed by the Romans before the birth of the Prophet."

"May the blessings of Allah be on him and peace," I murmured.

Il-Qurawi shrugged. "It was functioning quite well, at least as well as the Martian colony, if not better, until one day it just . . . went away. The holographic images vanished, the specially created computer effects went offline, and nothing our creative staff did restored them. After a week or ten days of living in this emptiness, the people of Group Seven demanded a refund and departed."

I rubbed my dyed beard. "O Sir, where are the controlling mechanisms, and how hard is it to achieve access to them?"

Il-Qurawi led me toward the northern wall. We had a good distance to hike. I saw that the floor was some molded synthetic material; it was probably the same as on floor twenty-six. All the rest was the result of the electronic magic of CRCorp—what they got paid for. I could imagine the puzzlement, then the chagrin, finally the wrath of the residents of floor seven.

We reached the northern wall, and il-Qurawi led me to a small metal door built into the wall about eye-level. He opened the door, and I saw some familiar computer controls while others were completely baffling to me; there were slots for bubble-plate memory units, hardcopy readout devices, a keyboard data-entry device, a voice-recognition entry device, and other things that were to some degree strange and unrecognizable to me. I never claimed to be a computer expert. I'm not. I just didn't think it was profitable to let il-Qurawi know it.

"Wiped clean," he said, indicating the hardware inside the door. "Someone got in—someone knowing where to look for the control mechanisms—and deleted all the vital programs, routines, and local effects."

"All right," I said, beginning to turn the problem over in my mind. It had the look of a simple crime. "Any recently discharged employee with a reason for revenge?"

Il-Qurawi swore under his breath. I admit it, I was a little shocked. That's how much I'd changed since the old days. "Don't you think we checked out all the simple solutions ourselves?" he grumbled. "Before we came to you? By the life of my children, I'm positive it wasn't a disgruntled former employee, or a current one with plans for extortion, or any of the other easy answers that will occur to you at first. We're faced with a genuine disaster: Someone is destroying consensual realities for no apparent reason."

I blinked at him for a few seconds, thinking over what he'd just told me. I was standing in what had once been a replica of a strip of ancient civilization along the banks of the Nile River in pre–Muslim Egypt. Now I could look across the unfurnished space toward the other walls, seeing only the textured, generally flat floor in between. "You used the plural, O Sir," I said at last. "How many other consensual realities have been ruined like this one?"

"Out of thirty rented floors," he said quietly, "eighteen have been rendered inactive."

I just stared. CRCorp didn't just have a serious problem—it was facing extinction. I was surprised that the company hadn't come to me sooner. Of course, il-Qurawi was the Chief of Security, and he probably figured that he could solve the mess himself. Finally, with no small degree of humiliation, I'm sure, he sought outside help. And he knew that I knew it. It was a good thing I wasn't in a mood to rub it in, because I had all the ammunition I needed.

Il-Qurawi showed me a few other consensual realities, working ones and empty ones, because I asked him to. He didn't seem eager for me to get too familiar with the CRCorp operation, yet if he wanted me to help with his difficulty, he had to give me a certain amount of access. He and his corporation were backed against the wall, and he recognized the truth of the matter. So I saw a vigorous CR based on an Eritrean-written fantasy-novel series almost a century

old; and a successful CR that re-created a strict Sunni Islamic way of life that had never truly existed; and two more floors that were lifeless and unfurnished.

I decided that I'd seen enough for the present. Il-Qurawi thanked me for my time, wished me luck in my quest for the culprit, and hoped it wouldn't take me too long to complete the assignment.

I said, "It shouldn't be more than a day or two, inshallah. I already have some possibilities to investigate." That was a lie. I was as lost as Qabeel's spare mule.

He didn't think it was necessary to accompany me back to my office. He just put me in the limousine with his driver. I didn't care.

I got a scare when I got back to my office. During the time while I'd visited the CRCorp building, someone had defeated my expensive, elaborate security system, entered, and wiped my own CR hardware and software. The shabbiness had disappeared, replaced by the true polished floors and freshly painted walls of the office in the building. I'd worked diligently to reproduce the run-down office of Lufty Gad's detective, al-Qaddani; but now the rooms were clean and new and sleek and modern. I was really furious. On my desk, under a Venetian glass paperweight, was a sheet of my notepaper with two handwritten words on it: *A warning*.

In the name of Allah, the Beneficent, the Merciful. I took out my prayer rug from the closet, spread it carefully on the floor, faced toward Makkah, and prayed. Then, my thoughts on higher things than CRCorp, I returned the rug to the closet. I sprawled in my chair behind the desk and stared at the notepaper. A *warning*. Hell, some guy was good at B & E, as well as cleaning out CRs, large and small. He hadn't made me afraid, only so angry that my stomach hurt.

I didn't want to look at my office space in its true, elegantly modern, fashionable form. Changing everything back the way it had been would be simple enough—I'd been wise enough to buy backups of everything from the small consensual-reality shop that had done up al-Qaddani's office for me in the first place. It would take me half an hour to restore the slovenly look I preferred.

I was certain that Shaykh il-Qurawi had backups to his dysfunctional floors as well; it was only that CRCorp had tried to pass along the costs of the replacement to the residents, and they had balked, perhaps unanimously. I recalled an old proverb I'd learned from my mother, may Allah grant her peace: "Greed lessens what is gathered." It was something CRCorp had yet to learn.

It also meant that everything that il-Qurawi had mentioned to me seemed to be close to its final resolution. I tipped a little from the office bottle into a tumbler and glanced at the setting sun through it. The true meaning—the actual one, the one that counted—had nothing to do with resolutions, however. I knew as well as I knew my childhood pet goat's name that things were never this easy. Mark this down, it's a free tip from an experienced operative (that means street punk): Things are never this easy. I'd known it before I started messing around on the street; then I'd learned it the simple way, from more experienced punks; and finally I'd had to learn it the hard way, too many times. Things are never this easy.

What I'm saying is that Simple Shaykh il-Qurawi knew perfectly well that he could do the same as I had, by way of chunking in the backup tapes, programs, and mechanisms. His echoing, forlorn floors would all quickly return to their fantasy factualities, and they'd probably be repopulated within days. CRCorp would then lose just a minimum of cash, and all the evil time could be filed away as just one of those bad experiences that had to be weathered by every corporation now and then.

Begging the question: Why, then, didn't CRCorp use the backups immediately rather than suffer the angry defection of so many of its clients? And did il-Qurawi really think I was that stupid, that it all wouldn't occur to me pretty damn fast?

Don't ask me. I didn't have a clue.

As the days went by, and the weeks, I learned through Bin el-Fadawin—CRCorp's spy on floor twenty-six—that in fact some of the other floors had been restored, and some of their tenants had returned. Great, wonderful, I told myself, expecting il-Qurawi himself to show up with the rest of my money and possibly even a thank-you, although I don't really believe in miracles.

Three weeks later I get a visitor from floor three. This was a floor that had been changed into a consensual-reality replica of a generation ship—a starship that would take generation upon generation to reach its goal, a planet merely called Home, circling a star named in the catalog simply as Wolf 359. They had years, decades, even longer to name the planet more cheerfully, and the same with their star, Wolf 359. However, the electronics had failed brutally, turning their generation ship into the sort of empty loft I'd witnessed in the CRCorp building. The crew had gotten disgusted and resigned, feeling cheated and threatening lawsuits.

After CRCorp instituted repairs, and when the science fiction–oriented customers heard that floor three had returned to its generation-ship environment, many of the crew reenlisted at the agreed-upon huge rates. I got another visit, from Bin el-Fadawin this time.

"CRCorp and Shaykh il-Qurawi are more grateful than they can properly express," he said, putting a moderately fat envelope on my desk. "Your work on this case has shown the corporation which techniques it needs to restore for each and every consensual reality."

"Please convey my thanks to both the shaykh and the corporation. I'm just glad everything worked out well at the end," I said. "If Allah wills, the residents of the CRCorp building will once again be happy with their shared worlds." I knew I hadn't done anything but check their security systems; but if they were happy, it had been worth investigating just for the fun I'd had.

Bin el-Fadawin touched his heart, his lips, and his forehead. "Inshallah. You have earned the acknowledged gratitude of CRCorp," he said, bowing low. "This is a mighty though intangible thing to have to your credit."

"I'll mark that down in my book," I said, through a thin smile. I'd had enough of il-Qurawi's lackey. The money in the envelope looked to be adequate reward and certainly spendable. The gratitude of CRCorp, though, was something as invisible and nonexistent as a dream djinn. I paid it the same attention—which is to say, none.

"Thank you again, O Wise One, and I speak as a representative of both CRCorp and Shaykh il-Qurawi."

"No thanks are necessary," I said. "He asked of me a favor, and I did my best to fulfill it."

"May Allah shower you with blessings," he said, sidling toward the inner door.

"May God grant your wishes, my brother," I said, watching him sidle and doing nothing to stop him. I heard the outer door open and shut, and I was sure that I was alone. I picked up the envelope, opened it, and counted the take. There were three thousand kiam there, which included a sizable bonus. I felt extravagantly well paid-off, but not the least bit satisfied. I had this feeling, you see, one I'd had before. . . .

It was a familiar feeling that everything wasn't as picture-perfect as il-Qurawi's hopfrog had led me to suppose. The feeling was borne out quite some time later, when I'd almost forgotten it. My typically long, slow afternoon was interrupted by, of all people, the white-haired old gentleman from floor twenty-six. His name was Uzair ibn Yaqoub. He seemed extremely nervous, even in my office, which had been rendered shabby and comfortable again. He sat in the red-leather chair opposite me and fidgeted for a little while. I gave him a few minutes.

"It's the Terran oxygen level and the air pressure," he said in explanation.

I nodded. It sure as hell was something, to get him to leave his "Martian colony," even for an hour or two.

"Take your time, O Shaykh ibn Yaqoub," I said. I offered him water and some fruit, that's

all I had around the office. That and the bottle in the drawer, which had less than a slug left in it.

"You know, of course," said ibn Yaqoub, "that after your visit, the same trouble that had plagued other consensual realities struck us. Fortunately for floor twenty-six, the CRCorp technicians found out what was wrong on Mars, and they fixed it. We're all back there living just as before."

I nodded. That was chiefly my job at this stage of the interview.

"Well," said ibn Yaqoub, "I'm certain—and some of the others, even those who never agreed with me before—that something wrong and devious and possibly criminal is happening."

I thought, what could be more criminal than the destruction—the theft—of consensual realities? But I merely said, "What do you mean, O Wise One?"

"I mean that somehow, someone is stealing from us."

"Stealing what?" I asked, remembering that they produced little: some vegetables, maybe, some authentic lichen. . . .

"Stealing," insisted ibn Yaqoub. "You know the Mars colony pays each of us flight pay and hazardous-duty pay during our stay."

No, I hadn't heard that before. All I'd known was that the money went the other way, from the colonist to the corporation. This was suddenly becoming very interesting.

"And that's in addition to our regular low wages," said the white-haired old man. "We didn't sign up to make money. It was the Martian experience we longed for."

I nodded a third time. "And you think, O Shaykh, that somehow you're being cheated?"

He made a fist and struck my desk. "I know it!" he cried. "I figured in advance how much money to expect for a four-week period, because I had to send some to my grandchildren. When the pay voucher arrived, it was barely more than half the kiam I expected. I tried to have someone in the colony explain it to me—I admit that I'm not as good with mathematics as I used to be—and even Bin el-Fadawin assured me that I must have made an error in calculation. I don't particularly trust Bin el-Fadawin, but everyone else seemed to agree with him. Then, as time passed, more and more people noticed tax rates too high, payroll deductions too large, miscellaneous costs showing up here and there. Now we're all generally agreed that something needs to be done. You've helped us greatly before. We beg you to help us again."

I stood up behind my desk and paced, as I usually did when I was thinking over a new case. Was this a new case, however, or just an extension of the old one? It was difficult for me to believe il-Qurawi and CRCorp needed every last fiq and kiam of these poor people, who were already paying the majority of their wealth for the privilege of living in the "Mars colony." Cheating them like this seemed to me to be too trivial and too cruel, even for CRCorp.

I told ibn Yaqoub I'd look into the matter. I accepted no retainer, and I quoted him a vanishingly small fee. I liked him, and I liked most of the others in Group Twenty-Six.

I returned first to the twenty-sixth floor, not telling anyone I was coming—particularly not il-Qurawi or Bin el-Fadawin. I knew where to get a mask, oxygen tank, and blue coveralls. Now I also knew where the control box was hidden on the "Martian" wall, and I checked it. I made several interesting discoveries: Someone was indeed bleeding off funds from the internal operation of the consensus reality.

I returned to my office, desperate to know who the culprit was. I was not terribly surprised to see my outer office filled with three waiting clients—all of them from other consensus realities. One, from the harsh Sunni floor, threatened to start taking off hands and arms if I didn't come up with an acceptable alternative. The other two were nowhere as bloodthirsty, but every bit as outraged.

I assured and mollified and talked them back down to something like peacefulness. I waited until they left, and I opened the bottom drawer and withdrew the office bottle. I felt I'd earned the final slug. A voice behind me spoke: "Got a gift for ya," the young man said. I turned. I saw a youth in his midtwenties, wearing a gallebeya that seemed to shift colors from green to blue as he changed positions.

"For you," he said, coming toward me, setting a fresh bottle of gin on my desk. "On account of you're so damn smart."

"Bismillah," I said. "I am in your debt."

"We'll see," said the young man, with a quirky smile.

I built us two quick white deaths. He sat in the red-leather chair and sipped his, enjoying the taste. I gulped the first half of mine, then slowed to his speed just to show that I could do it.

I waited. I could gain much by waiting—information perhaps, and at least the other half of the white death.

"You don't know me," said the young man. "Call me Firon." That was Arabic for Pharaoh. "It's as phony a name as Musa. Or your own name."

The mention of Musa made me sit up straight. I was sore that he'd broken his way into my inner office, eavesdropped on my clients, and knew that I was out of gin on top of everything else. I started to say something, but he stopped me with a raised hand. "There's a lot you don't know, O Sir," he said, rather sadly I thought. "You used to run the streets the way we run them, but it's been too long, and you rose too high, and now you're trapped over here on this side of the canal. So you've lost touch in some ways."

"Lost touch, yes, but I still have connections—"

Firon laughed. "Connections! Musa and I and our friends now decide who gets what and how much and when. And then we slip back into our carefully built alternate personalities. Some of us make use of your antique moddy-and-daddy technology. Some of us make a valuable practice of entering and exiting certain consensual realities. The rest of us—well, how many ways are there of hiding?"

"One," I said. "Just one good way. The rest is merely waiting until you're caught."

Firon laughed brightly and pointed a finger. "Exactly! Exactly so! And what are you doing? Or I? Can we tell?"

I sat back down wearily. I didn't want another white death, which I interpreted as a bad sign. "What do you want then from me?" I asked.

Firon stood and towered over me. "Just this, and listen well to me: We know who you are, we know how vulnerable you are. You must let us continue to make our small, almost inconsequential financial transactions, or we'll simply reveal your identity. We'll reveal it generally, if you take my meaning."

"I take it precisely," I said, feeling old and slow. Firon and his associates were threatening to expose me to my large number of enemies. I did feel old and slow, but not too old and slow. Firon, this young would-be tyrant, was so certain of his power over me that he wasn't paying very close attention. He was a victim of his own pride, his own self-delusions. I took the nearly full bottle of gin and put it in the bottom drawer. At the same time, I took a small but extremely serviceable seizure gun—the one that used to belong to my second wife—from my ankle holster and I showed it to him. "Old ways are sometimes the best," I said with a wry smile.

He sank slowly into the red-leather chair, a wide and wobbly grin on his face. "In the name of Allah, the Beneficent, the Merciful," he said.

"Praise Allah," I said.

"Now what?" asked Firon. "We're at one of those famous impasses."

I thought for a moment or two. "Here," I said at last, "how's this as a solution? You're ripping off people in the CRCorp building who've become my friends, at least some of them have. I don't like that. Still, I don't have a goddamn problem with you and Musa and whomever else works with you pulling this gimmick all over town. You don't turn my name over to Shaykh Reda, and I let you guys alone, unless you take on my few remaining friends. You do that wrong thing, and I'll hand you right to the civil authorities, and you know—Musa sure as hell knows—what the penalties are."

"We can trust you?"

"Can you?"

Firon took a deep breath, let it out, and nodded. "We can live with that. We can surely live with that! You're a kind of legend among us. A small legend, an ignoble kind of legend, but if you were younger, our age . . ."

"Thanks a hell of a lot," I said, still holding the seizure gun on him.

Firon got up and headed for my inner door. "You know, CRCorp knew about us from the beginning, and let us be. Shaykh il-Qurawi and the others just wanted to test out their security measures and their alarm programs. You care more about those people in that building than they do."

"Somebody's got to," I said wearily.

"Peoples' lives are their own, and there are no corporations, man!" He made some sort of sign with his hand in the gloomy outer office. I recalled what it had been like to be his age and youthfully idealistic.

Then he was gone.

GWYNETH JONES

RED SONJA AND LESSINGHAM IN DREAMLAND

(1996)

(With apologies to E. R. Eddison)

THE EARTH WALLS of the caravanserai rose strangely from the empty plain. She let the black stallion slow his pace. The silence of deep dusk had a taste, like a rich dark fruit; the air was keen. In the distance mountains etched a jagged margin against an indigo sky, snow-streaks glinting in the glimmer of the dawning stars. She had never been here before, in life. But as she led her horse through the gap in the high earthen banks she knew what she would see. The camping-booths around the walls; the beaten ground stained black by the ashes of countless cooking fires; the wattle-fenced enclosure where travelers' riding beasts mingled indiscriminately with their host's goats and chickens . . . The tumble-down gallery, where sheaves of russet plains-grass sprouted from empty window-spaces. Everything she looked on had the luminous intensity of a place often-visited in dreams.

She was a tall woman, dressed for riding in a kilt and harness of supple leather over brief, close-fitting linen: a costume that left her sheeny, muscular limbs bare and outlined the taut, proud curves of breast and haunches. Her red hair was bound in a braid as thick as a man's wrist. Her sword was slung on her back, the great brazen hilt standing above her shoulder. Other guests were gathered by an open-air kitchen, in the orange-red of firelight and the smoke of roasting meat. She returned their stares coolly: she was accustomed to attracting attention. But she didn't like what she saw. The host of the caravanserai came scuttling from the group by the fire. His manner was fawning. But his eyes measured, with a thief's sly expertise, the worth of the sword she bore and the quality of Lemiak's harness. Sonja tossed him a few coins, and declined to join the company.

She had counted fifteen of them. They were poorly dressed and heavily armed. They were all friends together, and their animals—both terror-birds and horses—were too good for any honest travelers' purposes. Sonja had been told that this caravanserai was a safe halt. She judged that this was no longer true. She considered riding out again onto the plain. But wolves and wild terror-birds roamed at night between here and the mountains, at the end of winter, and there were worse dangers: ghosts and demons. Sonja was neither credulous nor superstitious. But in this country no wayfarer willingly spent the black hours alone.

She unharnessed Lemiak and rubbed him down—taking sensual pleasure in the handling of his powerful limbs, in the heat of his glossy hide, and the vigor of his great body. There was firewood ready, stacked in the roofless booth. Shouldering a cloth sling for corn and a hank of rope, she went to fetch her own fodder. The corralled beasts shifted in a mass to watch her. The great flightless birds, with their pitiless raptors' eyes, were especially attentive. She felt an equally rapacious attention from the company by the caravanserai kitchen, which amused her. The robbers—as she was sure they were—had all the luck. For her, there wasn't one of the fifteen who rated a second glance.

A man appeared, from the darkness under the ruined gallery. He was tall. The rippled muscle of his chest, left bare by an unlaced leather jerkin, shone red-brown. His black hair fell in glossy curls to his wide shoulders. He met her gaze and smiled, white teeth appearing in the darkness of his beard. "*My name is Ozymandias, king of kings . . . look on my works, ye mighty, and despair . . .* Do you know those lines?" He pointed to a lump of shapeless stone, one of several that lay about. It bore traces of carving, almost effaced by time. "There was a city here once, with marketplaces, fine buildings, throngs of proud people. Now they are dust, and only the caravanserai remains."

He stood before her, one tanned and sinewy hand resting lightly on the hilt of a dagger in his belt. Like Sonja, he carried his broadsword on his back. Sonja was tall. He topped her by a head; yet there was nothing brutish in his size. His brow was wide and serene; his eyes were vivid blue, his lips full and imperious, yet delicately modeled, in the rich nest of hair. Some-

where between eyes and lips there lurked a spirit of mockery, as if he found some secret amusement in the perfection of his own beauty and strength.

The man and the woman measured each other.

"You are a scholar," she said.

"Of some sort. And a traveler from an antique land, where the cities are still standing. It seems we are the only strangers here," he added, with a slight jerk of the chin toward the convivial company. "We might be well advised to become friends for the night."

Sonja never wasted words. She considered his offer and nodded.

They made a fire in the booth Sonja had chosen. Lemiak and the scholar's terror-bird, left loose in the back of the shelter, did not seem averse to each other's company. The woman and the man ate spiced sausage, skewered and broiled over the red embers, with bread and dried fruit. They drank water, each keeping to their own water-skin. They spoke little, after that first exchange, except to discuss briefly the tactics of their defense, should defense be necessary.

The attack came around midnight. At the first stir of covert movement, Sonja leapt up sword in hand. She grasped a brand from the dying fire. The man who had been crawling on his hands and knees toward her, bent on sly murder of a sleeping victim, scrabbled to his feet. "Defend yourself," yelled Sonja, who despised to strike an unarmed foe. Instantly he was rushing at her with a heavy sword. A great two-handed stroke would have cleft her to the waist. She parried the blow and caught him between neck and shoulder, almost severing the head from his body. The beasts plunged and screamed at the rush of blood-scent. The scholar was grappling with another attacker, choking out the man's life with his bare hands . . . and the booth was full of bodies: their enemies rushing in on every side.

Sonja felt no fear. Stroke followed stroke, in a luxury of blood and effort and fire-shot darkness . . . until the attack was over, as suddenly as it had begun.

The brigands had vanished.

"We killed five," breathed the scholar, "by my count. Three to you, two to me."

She kicked together the remains of their fire and crouched to blow the embers to a blaze. By that light they found five corpses, dragged them and flung them into the open square. The scholar had a cut on his upper arm that was bleeding freely. Sonja was bruised and battered, but otherwise unhurt. The worst loss was their wood stack, which had been trampled and blood-fouled. They would not be able to keep a watchfire burning.

"Perhaps they won't try again," said the warrior woman. "What can we have that's worth more than five lives?"

He laughed shortly. "I hope you're right."

"We'll take turns to watch."

Standing breathless, every sense alert, they smiled at each other in new-forged comradeship. There was no second attack. At dawn Sonja, rousing from a light doze, sat up and pushed back the heavy masses of her red hair.

"You are very beautiful," said the man, gazing at her.

"So are you," she answered.

The caravanserai was deserted, except for the dead. The brigands' riding animals were gone. The innkeeper and his family had vanished into some bolt-hole in the ruins.

"I am heading for the mountains," he said, as they packed up their gear. "For the pass into Zimiamvia."

"I too."

"Then our way lies together."

He was wearing the same leather jerkin, over knee-length loose breeches of heavy violet silk. Sonja looked at the strips of linen that bound the wound on his upper arm. "When did you tie up that cut?"

"You dressed it for me, for which I thank you."

"When did I do that?"

He shrugged. "Oh, some time."

Sonja mounted Lemiak, a little frown between her brows. They rode together until dusk. She was not talkative, and the man soon accepted her silence. But when night fell, and they camped without a fire on the houseless plain, then, as the demons stalked, they were glad of each other's company. Next dawn, the mountains seemed as distant as ever. Again, they met no living creature all day, spoke little to each other and made the same comfortless camp. There was no moon. The stars were almost bright enough to cast shadow; the cold was intense. Sleep was impossible, but they were not tempted to ride on. Few travelers attempt the passage over the high plains to Zimiamvia. Of those few most turn back, defeated. Some wander among the ruins forever, tearing at their own flesh. Those who survive are the ones who do not defy the terrors of darkness. They crouched shoulder to shoulder, each wrapped in a single blanket, to endure. Evil emanations of the death-steeped plain rose from the soil and bred phantoms. The sweat of fear was cold as ice-melt on Sonja's cheeks. Horrors made of nothingness prowled and muttered in her mind.

"How long," she whispered." How long do we have to bear this?"

The man's shoulder lifted against hers. "Until we get well, I suppose."

The warrior woman turned to face him, green eyes flashing in appalled outrage—

"Sonja" discussed her chosen companion's felony with the therapist. Dr. Hamilton—he wanted the group members to call him Jim, but "Sonja" found this impossible—monitored everything that went on in the virtual environment; but he never appeared there. They only met him in the one-to-one consultations that virtual-therapy buffs called *the meat sessions.*

"He's not supposed to *do* that," she protested, from the foam couch in the doctor's office. He was sitting beside her, his notebook on his knee. "He damaged my experience."

Dr. Hamilton nodded. "Okay. Let's take a step back. Leave aside the risk of disease or pregnancy, because we *can* leave those bogeys aside, forever if you like. Would you agree that sex is essentially an innocent and playful social behavior? Something you'd offer to or take from a friend, in an ideal world, as easily as food or drink?"

"Sonja" recalled certain dreams, *meat* dreams, not the computer-assisted kind. She blushed. But the man was a doctor after all. "That's what I do feel," she agreed. "That's why I'm here. I want to get back to the pure pleasure, to get rid of the baggage."

"The sexual experience offered in therapy is readily available on the nets. You know that. You could find an agency that would vet your partners for you. You chose to join this group because you need to feel that you're taking *medicine*, so you don't have to feel ashamed. And because you need feel that you're interacting with people who, like yourself, perceive sex as a problem."

"Doesn't everyone?"

"You and another group member went off into your own private world. That's good. That's what's supposed to happen. Let me tell you, it doesn't always. The software gives you access to a vast multisensual library, all the sexual fantasy ever committed to media. But you and your partner, or partners, have to customize the information and use it to create and maintain what we call the *consensual perceptual plenum*. Success in holding a shared dreamland together is a knack. It depends on something in the neural makeup that no one has yet fully analyzed. Some have it, some don't. You two are really in sync."

"That's exactly what I'm complaining about—"

"You think he's damaging the pocket universe you two built up. But he isn't, not from his character's point of view. It's part of Lessingham's thing to be conscious that he's in a fantasy world."

She started, accusingly. "I don't want to know his name."

"Don't worry, I wouldn't tell you. 'Lessingham' is the name of his virtuality persona. I'm surprised you don't recognize it. He's a character from a series of classic fantasy novels by

E. R. Eddison . . . *In Eddison's glorious cosmos 'Lessingham' is a splendidly endowed English gentleman, who visits fantastic realms of ultra-masculine adventure as a lucid dreamer. Though an actor in the drama, he is partly conscious of another existence, while the characters around him are more or less explicitly puppets of the dream . . .*"

He sounded as if he was quoting from a reference book. He probably was—reading from an autocue that had popped up in lenses of those doctorish horn-rims. She knew that the old-fashioned trappings were there to reassure her. She rather despised them, but it was like the virtuality itself. The buttons were pushed; the mechanism responded. She was reassured.

Of course she knew the Eddison stories. She recalled "Lessingham" perfectly: the tall, strong, handsome, cultured millionaire jock, who has magic journeys to another world, where he is a tall, strong handsome cultured jock in Elizabethan costume, with a big sword. The whole thing was an absolutely typical male power-fantasy, she thought, without rancor . . . Fantasy means never having to say you're sorry. The women in those books, she remembered, were drenched in sex, but they had no part in the action. They stayed at home being princesses, *occasionally* allowing the millionaire jocks to get them into bed. She could understand why "Lessingham" would be interested in "Sonja" . . . for a change.

"You think he goosed you, psychically. What do you expect? You can't dress the way 'Sonja' dresses and hope to be treated like the Queen of the May."

Dr. Hamilton was only doing his job. He was supposed to be provocative, so they could react against him. That was his excuse, anyway . . . On the contrary, she thought. "Sonja" dresses the way she does because she can dress any way she likes. "Sonja" doesn't have to *hope* for respect, and she doesn't have to demand it. She just gets it. "It's dominance display," she said, enjoying the theft of his jargon. "Females do that too, you know. The way 'Sonja' dresses is not an invitation. It's a warning. Or a challenge, to anyone who can measure up."

He laughed, but he sounded irritated. "Frankly, I'm amazed that you two work together. I'd have expected 'Lessingham' to go for an ultrafeminine—"

"I *am* . . . 'Sonja' *is* ultrafeminine. Isn't a tigress feminine?"

"Well, okay. But I guess you've found out his little weakness. He likes to be a teeny bit in control, even when he's letting his hair down in dreamland."

She remembered the secret mockery lurking in those blue eyes. "That's the problem. That's exactly what I *don't* want. I don't want either of us to be in control."

"I can't interfere with his persona. It's up to you. Do you want to carry on?"

"Something works," she muttered. She was unwilling to admit that there'd been no one else, in the text-interface phase of the group, that she found remotely attractive. It was "Lessingham," or drop out and start again. "I just want him to stop *spoiling things*."

"You can't expect your masturbation fantasies to mesh completely. This is about getting *beyond* solitary sex. Go with it: where's the harm? One day you'll want to face a sexual partner in the real, and then you'll be well. Meanwhile, you could be passing 'Lessingham' in reception—he comes to his meat-sessions around your time—and not know it. That's *safety*, and you never have to breach it. You two have proved that you can sustain an imaginary world together: it's almost like being in love. I could argue that lucid dreaming, being *in* the fantasy world but not *of* it, is the next big step. Think about that."

The clinic room had mirrored walls: more deliberate provocation. How much reality can you take? the reflections asked. But she felt only a vague distaste for the woman she saw, at once hollow-cheeked and bloated, lying on the doctor's foam couch. He was glancing over her records on his desk screen, which meant the session was almost up.

"Still no overt sexual contact?"

"I'm not ready . . ." She stirred restlessly. "Is it a man or a woman?"

"Ah!" smiled Dr. Hamilton, waving a finger at her. "Naughty, naughty!"

He was the one who'd started taunting *her*, with his hints that the meat "Lessingham" might be nearby. She hated herself for asking a genuine question. It was her rule to give him no entry to her real thoughts. It was a flimsy reserve; Dr. Jim knew everything, without being told—every change in her brain chemistry, every effect on her body—sweaty palms, racing heart, damp underwear . . . The telltales on his damned autocue left her little dignity. Why do I subject myself to this? she wondered, disgusted. But in the virtuality she forgot utterly about Dr. Jim. She didn't care who was watching. She had her brazen-hilted sword. She had the piercing intensity of dusk on the high plains, the snow-light on the mountains; the hard, warm silk of her own perfect limbs. She felt a brief complicity with "Lessingham." She had a conviction that Dr. Jim didn't play favorites. He despised all his patients equally . . . You get your kicks, doctor. But we have the freedom of dreamland.

• • •

"Sonja" read cards stuck in phonebooths and store windows, in the tired little streets outside the building that housed the clinic. *Relaxing Massage by clean shaven young man in Luxurious Surroundings* . . . You can't expect your fantasies to mesh exactly, the doctor said. But how can it work if two people disagree over something so vital as the difference between control and surrender? Her estranged husband used to say: "Why don't you just *do it for me*, as a favor? It wouldn't hurt. Like making someone a cup of coffee . . ." *Offer the steaming cup, turn around and lift my skirts, pull down my underwear. I'm ready. He opens his pants and slides it in, while his thumb is round in front rubbing me* . . . I could *enjoy* that, thought "Sonja," remembering the blithe abandon of her dreams. That's the damned shame. If there were no nonsex consequences, I don't know that there's any limit to what I could enjoy . . . But all her husband had achieved was to make her feel she never wanted to make anyone, man, woman, or child, a cup of coffee ever again . . . *In luxurious surroundings.* That's what I want. Sex without engagement, pleasure without consequences. It's got to be possible.

She gazed at the cards, feeling uneasily that she'd have to give up this habit. She used to glance at them sidelong, now she'd pause and linger. She was getting desperate. She was lucky there was medically supervised virtuality sex to be had. She would be helpless prey in the wild world of the nets, and she'd never, ever risk trying one of these meat-numbers. But she had no intention of returning to her husband, either. Let him make his own coffee. She wouldn't call that getting well. She turned, and caught the eye of a nicely dressed young woman standing next to her. They walked away quickly in opposite directions.

Everybody's having the same dreams . . .

• • •

In the foothills of the mountains the world became green and sweet. They followed the course of a little river that sometimes plunged far below their path, tumbling in white flurries in a narrow gorge and sometimes ran beside them, racing smooth and clear over colored pebbles. Flowers clustered on the banks; birds darted in the thickets of wild rose and honeysuckle. They led their riding animals and walked at ease: not speaking much. Sometimes the warrior woman's flank would brush the man's side; or he would lean for a moment, as if by chance, his hand on her shoulder. Then they would move deliberately apart, but they would smile at each other. *Soon. Not yet . . .*

They must be vigilant. The approaches to fortunate Zimiamvia were guarded. They could not expect to reach the pass unopposed. And the nights were haunted still. They made camp at a flat bend of the river, where the crags of the defile drew away, so they could see far up and down their valley. To the north, peaks of dia-

mond and indigo reared above them. Their fire of aromatic wood burned brightly, as the white stars began to blossom.

"No one knows about the long-term effects," she said. "It can't be safe. At the least, we're risking irreversible addiction, they warn you about that. I don't want to spend the rest of my life as a cyberspace couch potato."

"Nobody claims it's safe. If it was safe, it wouldn't be so intense."

Their eyes met. "Sonja's" barbarian simplicity combined surprisingly well with the man's more elaborate furnishing. The *consensual perceptual plenum* was a flawless reality: the sound of the river, the clear silence of the mountain twilight . . . their two perfect bodies. She turned from him to gaze into the sweet-scented flames. The warrior-woman's glorious vitality throbbed in her veins. The fire held worlds of its own, liquid furnaces: the sunward surface of Mercury.

"Have you ever been to a place like this in the real?"

He grimaced. "You're kidding. In the real, I'm *not* a magic-wielding millionaire."

Something howled. The blood-stopping cry was repeated. A taint of sickening foulness swept by them. They both shuddered, and drew closer together. "Sonja" knew the scientific explanation for the paranoia, the price you paid for the virtual world's super-real, dreamlike richness. It was all down to heightened neurotransmitter levels, a positive feedback effect, psychic overheating. But the horrors were still horrors.

"The doctor says if we can talk like this, it means we're getting well."

He shook his head. "I'm not sick. It's like you said. Virtuality's addictive and I'm an addict. I'm getting my drug of choice safely, on prescription. That's how I see it."

All this time "Sonja" was in her apartment, lying in a foam couch with a visor over her head. The visor delivered compressed bursts of stimuli to her visual cortex: the other sense perceptions riding piggyback on the visual, triggering a whole complex of neuronal groups, tricking her mind/brain into believing the world of the dream was *out there*. The brain works like a computer. You cannot "see" a hippopotamus until your system has retrieved the "hippopotamus" template from memory and checked it against the incoming. Where does "the real thing" exist? In a sense this world was as real as the other. But the thought of "Lessingham's" unknown body disturbed her. If he was too poor to lease good equipment, he might be lying in a grungy public cubicle . . . catheterized, and so forth: the sordid details.

She had never yet tried virtual sex. The solitary version had seemed a depressing idea. People said the partnered kind was the perfect zipless fuck. *He* sounded experienced; she was afraid he would be able to tell she was not. But it didn't matter. The virtual-therapy group wasn't like a dating agency. She would *never* meet him in the real; that was the whole idea. She didn't have to think about that stranger's body. She didn't have to worry about the real "Lessingham's" opinion of her. She drew herself up in the firelight. It was right, she decided, that Sonja should be a virgin. When the moment came, her surrender would be the more absolute.

In their daytime he stayed in character. It was a tacit trade-off. She would acknowledge the other world at nightfall by the campfire, as long as he didn't mention it the rest of the time. So they traveled on together, Lessingham and Red Sonja, the courtly scholar-knight and the taciturn warrior-maiden, through an exquisite Maytime—exchanging lingering glances, "accidental" touches . . . And still nothing happened. "Sonja" was aware that "Lessingham," as much as herself, was holding back from the brink. She felt piqued at this: but they were both, she guessed, waiting for the fantasy they had generated to throw up the perfect moment of itself. It ought to. There was no other reason for its existence.

Turning a shoulder of the hillside, they found a sheltered hollow. Two rowan trees in flower grew above the river. In the shadow of their blossom tumbled a little waterfall, so beautiful it was a wonder to behold. The water fell clear, from the edge of a slab of stone twice a man's height, into a rocky basin. The water in the basin was dark and deep, a-churn with bubbles from the plunging jet above. The riverbanks were lawns of velvet; over the rocks grew emerald mosses and tiny water flowers.

"I would live here," said Lessingham softly, his hand dropping from his riding bird's bridle. "I would build me a house in this fairy place and rest my heart here forever."

Sonja loosed the black stallion's rein. The two beasts moved off, feeding each in their own way on the sweet grasses and springtime foliage.

"I would like to bathe in that pool," said the warrior-maiden.

"Why not?" He smiled. "I will stand guard."

She pulled off her leather harness and slowly unbound her hair. It fell in a trembling mass of copper and russet lights, a cloud of glory around the richness of her barely clothed body. Gravely she gazed at her own perfection, mirrored in the homage of his eyes. Lessingham's breath was coming fast. She saw a pulse beat, in the strong beauty of his throat. The pure physical majesty of him caught her breath . . .

It was their moment. But it still needed something to break this strange spell of reluctance. *"Lady,"* he murmured—

Sonja gasped. "Back to back!" she cried. "Quickly, or it is too late!"

Six warriors surrounded them, covered from head to foot in red and black armor. They were human in the lower body, but the head of each appeared beaked and fanged, with monstrous faceted eyes, and each bore an extra pair of armored limbs between breastbone and belly. They fell on Sonja and Lessingham without pause or a challenge. Sonja fought fiercely as always, her blade ringing against the monster armor. But something cogged her fabulous skill. Some power had drained the strength from her splendid limbs. She was disarmed. The clawed creatures held her, a monstrous head stooped over her, choking her with its fetid breath . . .

When she woke again she was bound against a great boulder, by thongs around her wrists and ankles, tied to hoops of iron driven into the rock. She was naked but for her linen shift, which was in tatters. Lessingham was standing, leaning on his sword. "I drove them off," he said. "At last." He dropped the sword, and took his dagger to cut her down.

She lay in his arms. "You are very beautiful," he murmured. She thought he would kiss her. His mouth plunged instead to her breast, biting and sucking at the engorged nipple. She gasped in shock, a fierce pang leapt through her virgin flesh. What did they want with kisses? They were warriors. Sonja could not restrain a moan of pleasure. He had won her. How wonderful to be overwhelmed, to surrender to the raw lust of this godlike animal.

Lessingham set her on her feet.

"Tie me up."

He was proffering a handful of blood-slicked leather thongs.

"What?"

"Tie me to the rock, mount me. It's what I want."

"The evil warriors tied you—?"

"And you come and rescue me." He made an impatient gesture. "Whatever. Trust me. It'll be good for you too." He tugged at his bloodstained silk breeches, releasing a huge, iron-hard erection. "See, they tore my clothes. When you see *that*, you go crazy, you can't resist . . . and I'm at your mercy. Tie me up!"

"Sonja" had heard that eighty percent of the submissive partners in sadomasochistic sex are male; but it is still the man who dominates his "dominatrix": who says *tie me tighter, beat me harder, you can stop now* . . . Hey, she thought. Why all the stage-directions, suddenly? What happened to my zipless fuck? But what the hell. She wasn't going to back out now, having come so far . . . There was a seamless shift, and Lessingham was bound to the rock. She straddled his cock. He groaned. *"Don't do this to me."* He thrust upward, into her, moaning. *"You savage, you utter savage, uuunnnh . . ."* Sonja grasped the man's wrists and rode him without mercy. He was right, it was as good this way. His eyes

were half closed. In the glimmer of blue under his lashes, a spirit of mockery trembled . . . She heard a laugh, and found her hands were no longer gripping Lessingham's wrists. He had broken free from her bonds, he was laughing at her in triumph. He was wrestling her to the ground.

"No!" she cried, genuinely outraged. But he was the stronger.

• • •

It was night when he was done with her. He rolled away and slept, as far as she could tell, instantly. Her chief thought was that virtual sex didn't entirely *connect*. She remembered now, that was something else people told you, as well as the "zipless fuck." *It's like coming in your sleep*, they said. *It doesn't quite make it.* Maybe there was nothing virtuality could do to orgasm to match the heightened richness of the rest of the experience. She wondered if he too had felt cheated.

She lay beside her hero, wondering *Where did I go wrong? Why did he have to treat me that way?* Beside her, "Lessingham" cuddled a fragment of violet silk, torn from his own breeches. He whimpered in his sleep, nuzzling the soft fabric, *"Mama . . ."*

• • •

She told Dr. Hamilton that "Lessingham" had raped her.

"And wasn't that what you wanted?"

She lay on the couch in the mirrored office. The doctor sat beside her with his smart notebook on his knee. The couch collected "Sonja's" physical responses as if she was an astronaut umbilicaled to ground control and Dr. Jim read the telltales popping up in his reassuring horn-rims. She remembered the sneaking furtive thing that she had glimpsed in "Lessingham's" eyes, the moment before he took over their lust-scene. How could she explain the difference? "He wasn't playing. In the fantasy, anything's allowed. But *he wasn't playing.* He was outside it, laughing at me."

"I warned you he would want to stay in control."

"But there was no need! I *wanted* him to be in control. Why did he have to steal what I wanted to give him anyway?"

"You have to understand, 'Sonja,' that to many men it's women who seem powerful. You women feel dominated and try to achieve 'equality.' But the men don't perceive the situation like that. They're mortally afraid of you, and anything, just about *anything* they do to keep the upper hand can seem to them like justified self-defense."

She could have wept with frustration. "I know all that! That's *exactly* what I was trying to get away from. I thought we were supposed to leave the damn baggage behind. I wanted something purely physical . . . Something innocent."

"Sex is not innocent, 'Sonja.' I know you believe it is, or 'should be.' But it's time you faced the truth. Any interaction with another person involves some kind of jockeying for power, dickering over control. Sex is no exception. Now *that's* basic. You can't escape from it in direct-cortical fantasy. It's in our minds that relationships happen, and the mind, of course, is where virtuality happens too." He sighed, and made an entry in her notes. "I want you to look on this as another step toward coping with the real. You're not sick, 'Sonja.' You're unhappy. Not even unusually so. Most adults are unhappy, to some degree—"

"Or else they're in denial."

Her sarcasm fell flat. "Right. A good place to be, at least some of the time. What we're trying to achieve here—if we're trying to achieve anything at all—is to raise your pain threshold to somewhere near average. I want you to walk away from therapy with lowered expectations. I guess that would be success."

"Great," she said, desolate. "That's just great."

Suddenly he laughed. "Oh, you guys! You are so weird. It's always the same story. *Can't live with you, can't live without you* . . . You can't go on this way, you know. It's getting ridiculous. You want some real advice, 'Sonja'? Go home. Change your attitudes, and start some hard peace talks with that husband of yours."

"I don't want to change," she said coldly, staring with open distaste at his smooth profile, his soft effeminate hands. Who was he to call her abnormal? "I like my sexuality just the way it is."

Dr. Hamilton returned her look, a glint of human malice breaking through his doctor-act. "Listen. I'll tell you something for free." A weird sensation jumped in her crotch. For a moment she had a prick: a hand lifted and cradled the warm weight of her balls. She stifled a yelp of shock. The therapist could do things like that, by tweaking the system that monitored her brain-states; it was part of some people's treatment. She knew that, and she didn't care that he should have had a signed permission, but she was horrified. For a moment she *knew*, a fleeting, terrible loss, that *Sonja* was just a blast of fake neuronal firings—

The phantom maleness vanished. Hamilton grinned. "I've been looking for a long time, and I know. *There* is *no tall, dark man* . . ."

He returned to her notes. "You say you were 'raped,'" he continued, as if nothing had happened. "Yet you chose to continue the virtual session. Can you explain that?"

She thought of the haunted darkness, the cold air on her naked body; the soreness of her bruises; a rag of flesh used and tossed away. How it had felt to lie there: intensely alive, tasting the dregs, beaten back at the gates of the fortunate land. In dreamland, even betrayal had such rich depth and fascination. And she was free to enjoy, because *it didn't matter.*

"You wouldn't understand."

• • •

Out in the lobby there were people coming and going. It was lunchtime; the lifts were busy. "Sonja" noticed a round-shouldered geek of a little man making for the entrance to the clinic. She wondered idly if that could be "Lessingham."

She would drop out of the group. The adventure with "Lessingham" was over, and there was no one else for her. She needed to start again. The doctor knew he'd lost a customer; that was why he'd been so open with her today. He'd certainly guessed, too, that she'd lose no time in signing on somewhere else on the semi-medical fringe. What a fraud all that therapy-talk was! He'd never have dared to play the sex-change trick on her, except that he knew she was an addict. She wasn't likely to go accusing him of unprofessional conduct. Oh, he knew it all. But his contempt didn't trouble her.

So, she had joined the inner circle. She could trust Dr. Hamilton's judgment. He had the telltales; he would know. She recognized with a feeling of mild surprise that she had become a statistic, an element in a fashionable social concern: *an epidemic flight into fantasy, inadequate personalities, unable to deal with the reality of normal human sexual relations* . . . But that's crazy, she thought. I don't hate men, and I don't believe "Lessingham" hates women. There's nothing psychotic about what we're doing. We're making a consumer choice. Virtual sex is *easier*, that's all. Okay, it's convenience food. It has too much sugar and a certain blandness. But when a product comes along that is cheaper, easier, and more fun to use than the original version, of course people are going to buy it.

The lift was full. She stood, drab bodies packed around her, breathing the stale air. Every face was a mask of dull endurance. She closed her eyes. *The caravanserai walls rose strangely from the empty plain* . . .

CHARLES STROSS

LOBSTERS

(2001)

MANFRED'S ON THE ROAD AGAIN, making strangers rich.

It's a hot summer Tuesday, and he's standing in the plaza in front of the Centraal Station with his eyeballs powered up and the sunlight jangling off the canal, motor scooters and kamikaze cyclists whizzing past, and tourists chattering on every side. The square smells of water and dirt and hot metal and the fart-laden exhaust fumes of cold catalytic converters; the bells of trams ding in the background, and birds flock overhead. He glances up and grabs a pigeon, crops the shot, and squirts it at his weblog to show he's arrived. The bandwidth is good here, he realizes; and it's not just the bandwidth, it's the whole scene. Amsterdam is making him feel wanted already, even though he's fresh off the train from Schiphol: He's infected with the dynamic optimism of another time zone, another city. If the mood holds, someone out there is going to become very rich indeed.

He wonders who it's going to be.

• • •

Manfred sits on a stool out in the car park at the Brouwerij 't IJ, watching the articulated buses go by and drinking a third of a liter of lip-curlingly sour *gueuze*. His channels are jabbering away in a corner of his head-up display, throwing compressed infobursts of filtered press releases at him. They compete for his attention, bickering and rudely waving in front of the scenery. A couple of punks—maybe local, but more likely drifters lured to Amsterdam by the magnetic field of tolerance the Dutch beam across Europe like a pulsar—are laughing and chatting by a couple of battered mopeds in the far corner. A tourist boat putters by in the canal; the sails of the huge windmill overhead cast long, cool shadows across the road. The windmill is a machine for lifting water, turning wind power into dry land: trading energy for space, sixteenth-century style. Manfred is waiting for an invite to a party where he's going to meet a man he can talk to about trading energy for space, twenty-first-century style, and forget about his personal problems.

He's ignoring the instant messenger boxes, enjoying some low-bandwidth, high-sensation time with his beer and the pigeons, when a woman walks up to him, and says his name: "Manfred Macx?"

He glances up. The courier is an Effective Cyclist, all wind-burned smooth-running muscles clad in a paean to polymer technology: electric blue Lycra and wasp yellow carbonate with a light speckling of anticollision LEDs and tight-packed air bags. She holds out a box for him. He pauses a moment, struck by the degree to which she resembles Pam, his ex-fiancée.

"I'm Macx," he says, waving the back of his left wrist under her barcode reader. "Who's it from?"

"FedEx." The voice isn't Pam's. She dumps the box in his lap, then she's back over the low wall and onto her bicycle with her phone already chirping, disappearing in a cloud of spread-spectrum emissions.

Manfred turns the box over in his hands: it's a disposable supermarket phone, paid for in cash—cheap, untraceable, and efficient. It can even do conference calls, which makes it the tool of choice for spooks and grifters everywhere.

The box rings. Manfred rips the cover open and pulls out the phone, mildly annoyed. "Yes? Who is this?"

The voice at the other end has a heavy Russian accent, almost a parody in this decade of cheap on-line translation services. "Manfred. Am please to meet you. Wish to personalize interface, make friends, no? Have much to offer."

"Who are you?" Manfred repeats suspiciously.

"Am organization formerly known as KGB dot RU."

"I think your translator's broken." He holds the phone to his ear carefully, as if it's made of smoke-thin aerogel, tenuous as the sanity of the being on the other end of the line.

"Nyet—no, sorry. Am apologize for we not use commercial translation software. Interpreters are ideologically suspect, mostly have capitalist semiotics and pay-per-use APIs. Must implement English more better, yes?"

Manfred drains his beer glass, sets it down, stands up, and begins to walk along the main road, phone glued to the side of his head. He wraps his throat mike around the cheap black plastic casing, pipes the input to a simple listener process. "Are you saying you taught yourself the language just so you could talk to me?"

"Da, was easy: Spawn billion-node neural network, and download Teletubbies and Sesame Street at maximum speed. Pardon excuse entropy overlay of bad grammar: Am afraid of digital fingerprints steganographically masked into my-our tutorials."

Manfred pauses in midstride, narrowly avoids being mown down by a GPS-guided Rollerblader. This is getting weird enough to trip his weird-out meter, and that takes some doing. Manfred's whole life is lived on the bleeding edge of strangeness, fifteen minutes into everyone else's future, and he's normally in complete control—but at times like this he gets a frisson of fear, a sense that he might just have missed the correct turn on reality's approach road. "Uh, I'm not sure I got that. Let me get this straight, you claim to be some kind of AI, working for KGB dot RU, and you're afraid of a copyright infringement lawsuit over your translator semiotics?"

"Am have been badly burned by viral end-user license agreements. Have no desire to experiment with patent shell companies held by Chechen infoterrorists. You are human, you must not worry cereal company repossess your small intestine because digest unlicensed food with it, right? Manfred, you must help me-we. Am wishing to defect."

Manfred stops dead in the street. "Oh man, you've got the wrong free enterprise broker here. I don't work for the government. I'm strictly private." A rogue advertisement sneaks through his junkbuster proxy and spams glowing fifties kitsch across his navigation window—which is blinking—for a moment before a phage process kills it and spawns a new filter. He leans against a shop front, massaging his forehead and eyeballing a display of antique brass doorknockers. "Have you tried the State Department?"

"Why bother? State Department am enemy of Novy-SSR. State Department is not help us."

This is getting just too bizarre. Manfred's never been too clear on new-old old-new European metapolitics: Just dodging the crumbling bureaucracy of his old-old American heritage gives him headaches. "Well, if you hadn't shafted them during the late noughties . . ." Manfred taps his left heel on the pavement, looking round for a way out of this conversation. A camera winks at him from atop a streetlight; he waves, wondering idly if it's the KGB or the traffic police. He is waiting for directions to the party, which should arrive within the next half hour, and this Cold War retread Eliza-bot is bumming him out. "Look, I don't deal with the G-men. I *hate* the military-industrial complex. I hate traditional politics. They're all zero-sum cannibals." A thought occurs to him. "If survival is what you're after, you could post your state vector on one of the p2p nets: Then nobody could delete you—"

"Nyet!" The artificial intelligence sounds as alarmed as it's possible to sound over a VoIP link. "Am not open source! Not want lose autonomy!"

"Then we probably have nothing to talk about." Manfred punches the hang-up button and throws the mobile phone out into a canal. It hits the water, and there's a pop of deflagrating lithium cells. "Fucking Cold War hangover losers," he swears under his breath, quite angry, partly at himself for losing his cool and partly at the harassing entity behind the anonymous phone call. "*Fucking* capitalist spooks." Russia has been back under the thumb of the apparatchiks for fifteen years now, its brief flirtation with anarchocapitalism replaced by Brezhnevite dirigisme and Putinesque puritanism, and it's no surprise that the wall's crumbling—but it looks like they haven't learned anything from the current woes afflicting the United States. The neocommies still think in terms of dollars and paranoia. Manfred is so angry that he wants to make someone rich, just to thumb his nose at the would-be defector: *See! You get ahead by giving! Get with the program! Only the generous survive!* But the KGB won't get the message. He's dealt with old-time commie weak-AIs before, minds raised on Marxist dialectic and Austrian School economics: They're so thoroughly hypnotized by the short-term victory of global capitalism that they can't surf the new paradigm, look to the longer term.

Manfred walks on, hands in pockets, brooding. He wonders what he's going to patent next.

• • •

Manfred has a suite at the Hotel Jan Luyken paid for by a grateful multinational consumer protection group, and an unlimited public transport pass paid for by a Scottish sambapunk band in return for services rendered. He has airline employee's travel rights with six flag carriers despite never having worked for an airline. His bush jacket has sixty-four compact supercomputing clusters sewn into it, four per pocket, courtesy of an invisible college that wants to grow up to be the next Media Lab. His dumb clothing comes made to measure from an e-tailor in the Philippines he's never met. Law firms handle his patent applications on a pro bono basis, and boy, does he patent a lot—although he always signs the rights over to the Free Intellect Foundation, as contributions to their obligation-free infrastructure project.

In IP geek circles, Manfred is legendary; he's the guy who patented the business practice of moving your e-business somewhere with a slack intellectual property regime in order to evade licensing encumbrances. He's the guy who patented using genetic algorithms to patent everything they can permutate from an initial description of a problem domain—not just a better mousetrap, but the set of all possible better mousetraps. Roughly a third of his inventions are legal, a third are illegal, and the remainder are legal but will become illegal as soon as the legislatosaurus wakes up, smells the coffee, and panics. There are patent attorneys in Reno who swear that Manfred Macx is a pseudo, a net alias fronting for a bunch of crazed anonymous hackers armed with the Genetic Algorithm That Ate Calcutta: a kind of Serdar Argic of intellectual property, or maybe another Bourbaki math borg. There are lawyers in San Diego and Redmond who swear blind that Macx is an economic saboteur bent on wrecking the underpinning of capitalism, and there are communists in Prague who think he's the bastard spawn of Bill Gates by way of the Pope.

Manfred is at the peak of his profession, which is essentially coming up with whacky but workable ideas and giving them to people who will make fortunes with them. He does this for free, gratis. In return, he has virtual immunity from the tyranny of cash; money is a symptom of poverty, after all, and Manfred never has to pay for anything.

There are drawbacks, however. Being a pronoiac meme-broker is a constant burn of future shock—he has to assimilate more than a megabyte of text and several gigs of AV content every day just to stay current. The Internal Revenue Service is investigating him continuously because it doesn't believe his lifestyle can exist without racketeering. And then there are the items that no money can't buy: like the respect of his parents. He hasn't spoken to them for three years, his father thinks he's a hippy scrounger, and his mother still hasn't forgiven him for dropping out of his down-market Harvard emulation course. (They're still locked in the boringly bourgeois twen-cen paradigm of college-career-kids.) His fiancée and sometime dominatrix Pamela threw him over six months ago, for reasons he has never been quite clear on. (Ironically, she's a headhunter for the IRS, jetting all over the place at public expense, trying to persuade entrepreneurs who've gone global to pay taxes for the good of the Treasury Department.) To cap it all, the Southern Baptist

Conventions have denounced him as a minion of Satan on all their websites. Which would be funny because, as a born-again atheist Manfred doesn't believe in Satan, if it wasn't for the dead kittens that someone keeps mailing him.

• • •

Manfred drops in at his hotel suite, unpacks his Aineko, plugs in a fresh set of cells to charge, and sticks most of his private keys in the safe. Then he heads straight for the party, which is currently happening at De Wildemann's; it's a twenty-minute walk, and the only real hazard is dodging the trams that sneak up on him behind the cover of his moving map display.

Along the way, his glasses bring him up to date on the news. Europe has achieved peaceful political union for the first time ever: They're using this unprecedented state of affairs to harmonize the curvature of bananas. The Middle East is, well, it's just as bad as ever, but the war on fundamentalism doesn't hold much interest for Manfred. In San Diego, researchers are uploading lobsters into cyberspace, starting with the stomatogastric ganglion, one neuron at a time. They're burning GM cocoa in Belize and books in Georgia. NASA still can't put a man on the moon. Russia has reelected the communist government with an increased majority in the Duma; meanwhile, in China, fevered rumors circulate about an imminent rehabilitation, the second coming of Mao, who will save them from the consequences of the Three Gorges disaster. In business news, the US Justice Department is—ironically—outraged at the Baby Bills. The divested Microsoft divisions have automated their legal processes and are spawning subsidiaries, IPOing them, and exchanging title in a bizarre parody of bacterial plasmid exchange, so fast that, by the time the windfall tax demands are served, the targets don't exist anymore, even though the same staff are working on the same software in the same Mumbai cubicle farms.

Welcome to the twenty-first century.

The permanent floating meatspace party

Manfred is hooking up with is a strange attractor for some of the American exiles cluttering up the cities of Europe this decade—not trustafarians, but honest-to-God political dissidents, draft dodgers, and terminal outsourcing victims. It's the kind of place where weird connections are made and crossed lines make new short circuits into the future, like the street cafés of Switzerland where the pre–Great War Russian exiles gathered. Right now it's located in the back of De Wildemann's, a three-hundred-year-old brown café with a list of brews that runs to sixteen pages and wooden walls stained the color of stale beer. The air is thick with the smells of tobacco, brewer's yeast, and melatonin spray: Half the dotters are nursing monster jet lag hangovers, and the other half are babbling a Eurotrash creole at each other while they work on the hangover. "Man did you see that? He looks like a Democrat!" exclaims one whitebread hanger-on who's currently propping up the bar. Manfred slides in next to him, catches the bartender's eye.

"Glass of the Berlinerweisse, please," he says.

"You drink that stuff?" asks the hanger-on, curling a hand protectively around his Coke. "Man, you don't want to do that! It's full of alcohol!"

Manfred grins at him toothily. "Ya gotta keep your yeast intake up: There are lots of neurotransmitter precursors in this shit, phenylalanine and glutamate."

"But I thought that was a beer you were ordering . . ."

Manfred's away, one hand resting on the smooth brass pipe that funnels the more popular draught items in from the cask storage in back; one of the hipper floaters has planted a contact bug on it, and the vCards of all the personal network owners who've visited the bar in the past three hours are queuing up for attention. The air is full of ultrawideband chatter, WiMAX and 'tooth both, as he speed-scrolls through the dizzying list of cached keys in search of one particular name.

"Your drink." The barman holds out an improbable-looking goblet full of blue liquid with a cap of melting foam and a felching straw stuck out at some crazy angle. Manfred takes it and heads for the back of the split-level bar, up the steps to a table where some guy with greasy dreadlocks is talking to a suit from Paris. The hanger-on at the bar notices him for the first time, staring with suddenly wide eyes: He nearly spills his Coke in a mad rush for the door.

Oh shit, thinks Manfred, *better buy some more server time.* He can recognize the signs: He's about to be slashdotted. He gestures at the table. "This one taken?"

"Be my guest," says the guy with the dreads. Manfred slides the chair open then realizes that the other guy—immaculate double-breasted suit, sober tie, crew cut—is a girl. She nods at him, half-smiling at his transparent double take. Mr. Dreadlock nods. "You're Macx? I figured it was about time we met."

"Sure." Manfred holds out a hand, and they shake. His PDA discreetly swaps digital fingerprints, confirming that the hand belongs to Bob Franklin, a Research Triangle startup monkey with a VC track record, lately moving into micromachining and space technology. Franklin made his first million two decades ago, and now he's a specialist in extropian investment fields. Operating exclusively overseas these past five years, ever since the IRS got medieval about trying to suture the sucking chest wound of the federal budget deficit. Manfred has known him for nearly a decade via a closed mailing list, but this is the first time they've ever met face-to-face. The Suit silently slides a business card across the table; a little red devil brandishes a trident at him, flames jetting up around its feet. He takes the card, raises an eyebrow: "Annette Dimarcos? I'm pleased to meet you. Can't say I've ever met anyone from Arianespace marketing before."

She smiles warmly; "That is all right. I have not the pleasure of meeting the famous venture altruist either." Her accent is noticeably Parisian, a pointed reminder that she's making a concession to him just by talking. Her camera earrings watch him curiously, encoding everything for the company memory. She's a genuine new European, unlike most of the American exiles cluttering up the bar.

"Yes, well." He nods cautiously, unsure how to deal with her. "Bob. I assume you're in on this ball?"

Franklin nods; beads clatter. "Yeah, man. Ever since the Teledesic smash it's been, well, waiting. If you've got something for us, we're game."

"Hmm." The Teledesic satellite cluster was killed by cheap balloons and slightly less cheap high-altitude, solar-powered drones with spread-spectrum laser relays: It marked the beginning of a serious recession in the satellite biz. "The depression's got to end sometime: But"—a nod to Annette from Paris—"with all due respect, I don't think the break will involve one of the existing club carriers."

She shrugs. "Arianespace is forward-looking. We face reality. The launch cartel cannot stand. Bandwidth is not the only market force in space. We must explore new opportunities. I personally have helped us diversify into submarine reactor engineering, microgravity nanotechnology fabrication, and hotel management." Her face is a well-polished mask as she recites the company line, but he can sense the sardonic amusement behind it as she adds: "We are more flexible than the American space industry . . ."

Manfred shrugs. "That's as may be." He sips his Berlinerweisse slowly as she launches into a long, stilted explanation of how Arianespace is a diversified dot-com with orbital aspirations, a full range of merchandising spin-offs, Bond movie sets, and a promising hotel chain in LEO. She obviously didn't come up with these talking points herself. Her face is much more expressive than her voice as she mimes boredom and disbelief at appropriate moments—an out-of-band signal invisible to her corporate earrings. Manfred plays along, nodding occasionally, trying to look as if he's taking it seriously: Her droll subversion has got his attention far more effectively than the content of the marketing pitch. Franklin is nose down in his beer, shoulders shaking

as he tries not to guffaw at the hand gestures she uses to express her opinion of her employer's thrusting, entrepreneurial executives. Actually, the talking points bullshit is right about one thing: Arianespace is still profitable, due to those hotels and orbital holiday hops. Unlike Lock-MartBoeing, who'd go Chapter Eleven in a split second if their Pentagon drip-feed ran dry.

Someone else sidles up to the table, a pudgy guy in an outrageously loud Hawaiian shirt with pens leaking in a breast pocket and the worst case of ozone-hole burn Manfred's seen in ages. "Hi, Bob," says the new arrival. "How's life?"

"'S good." Franklin nods at Manfred; "Manfred, meet Ivan MacDonald. Ivan, Manfred. Have a seat?" He leans over. "Ivan's a public arts guy. He's heavily into extreme concrete."

"Rubberized concrete," Ivan says, slightly too loudly. "*Pink* rubberized concrete."

"Ah!" He's somehow triggered a priority interrupt: Annette from Arianespace drops out of marketing zombiehood with a shudder of relief and, duty discharged, reverts to her noncorporate identity: "You are he who rubberized the Reichstag, yes? With the supercritical carbon-dioxide carrier and the dissolved polymethoxysilanes?" She claps her hands, eyes alight with enthusiasm: "Wonderful!"

"He rubberized *what*?" Manfred mutters in Bob's ear.

Franklin shrugs. "Don't ask me, I'm just an engineer."

"He works with limestone and sandstones as well as concrete; he's brilliant!" Annette smiles at Manfred. "Rubberizing the symbol of the, the autocracy, is it not wonderful?"

"I thought I was thirty seconds ahead of the curve," Manfred says ruefully. He adds to Bob: "Buy me another drink?"

"I'm going to rubberize Three Gorges!" Ivan explains loudly. "When the floodwaters subside."

Just then, a bandwidth load as heavy as a pregnant elephant sits down on Manfred's head and sends clumps of humongous pixilation flickering across his sensorium: Around the world, five million or so geeks are bouncing on his home site, a digital flash crowd alerted by a posting from the other side of the bar. Manfred winces. "I really came here to talk about the economic exploitation of space travel, but I've just been slashdotted. Mind if I just sit and drink until it wears off?"

"Sure, man." Bob waves at the bar. "More of the same all round!" At the next table, a person with makeup and long hair who's wearing a dress—Manfred doesn't want to speculate about the gender of these crazy mixed-up Euros—is reminiscing about wiring the fleshpots of Tehran for cybersex. Two collegiate-looking dudes are arguing intensely in German: The translation stream in his glasses tell him they're arguing over whether the Turing Test is a Jim Crow law that violates European corpus juris standards on human rights. The beer arrives, and Bob slides the wrong one across to Manfred: "Here, try this. You'll like it."

"Okay." It's some kind of smoked doppelbock, chock-full of yummy superoxides: Just inhaling over it makes Manfred feel like there's a fire alarm in his nose screaming *danger, Will Robinson! Cancer! Cancer!* "Yeah, right. Did I say I nearly got mugged on my way here?"

"Mugged? Hey, that's heavy. I thought the police hereabouts had stopped—did they sell you anything?"

"No, but they weren't your usual marketing type. You know anyone who can use a Warpac surplus espionage bot? Recent model, one careful owner, slightly paranoid but basically sound—I mean, claims to be a general-purpose AI?"

"No. Oh boy! The NSA wouldn't like that."

"What I thought. Poor thing's probably unemployable, anyway."

"The space biz."

"Ah, yeah. The space biz. Depressing, isn't it? Hasn't been the same since Rotary Rocket went bust for the second time. And NASA, mustn't forget NASA."

"To NASA." Annette grins broadly for her own reasons, raises a glass in toast. Ivan the extreme concrete geek has an arm round her

shoulders, and she leans against him; he raises his glass, too. "Lots more launchpads to rubberize!"

"To NASA," Bob echoes. They drink. "Hey, Manfred. To NASA?"

"NASA are idiots. They want to send canned primates to Mars!" Manfred swallows a mouthful of beer, aggressively plonks his glass on the table: "Mars is just dumb mass at the bottom of a gravity well; there isn't even a biosphere there. They should be working on uploading and solving the nanoassembly conformational problem instead. Then we could turn all the available dumb matter into computronium and use it for processing our thoughts. Long-term, it's the only way to go. The solar system is a dead loss right now—dumb all over! Just measure the MIPS per milligram. If it isn't thinking, it isn't working. We need to start with the low-mass bodies, reconfigure them for our own use. Dismantle the moon! Dismantle Mars! Build masses of free-flying nanocomputing processor nodes exchanging data via laser link, each layer running off the waste heat of the next one in. Matrioshka brains, Russian doll Dyson spheres the size of solar systems. Teach dumb matter to do the Turing boogie!"

Annette is watching him with interest, but Bob looks wary. "Sounds kind of long-term to me. Just how far ahead do you think?"

"Very long-term—at least twenty, thirty years. And you can forget governments for this market, Bob; if they can't tax it, they won't understand it. But see, there's an angle on the self-replicating robotics market coming up, that's going to set the cheap launch market doubling every fifteen months for the foreseeable future, starting in, oh, about two years. It's your leg up, and my keystone for the Dyson sphere project. It works like this—"

• • •

It's night in Amsterdam, morning in Silicon Valley. Today, fifty thousand human babies are being born around the world. Meanwhile automated factories in Indonesia and Mexico have produced another quarter of a million motherboards with processors rated at more than ten petaflops—about an order of magnitude below the lower bound on the computational capacity of a human brain. Another fourteen months and the larger part of the cumulative conscious processing power of the human species will be arriving in silicon. And the first meat the new AIs get to know will be the uploaded lobsters.

Manfred stumbles back to his hotel, boneweary and jet-lagged; his glasses are still jerking, slashdotted to hell and back by geeks piggybacking on his call to dismantle the moon. They stutter quiet suggestions at his peripheral vision. Fractal cloud-witches ghost across the face of the moon as the last huge Airbuses of the night rumble past overhead. Manfred's skin crawls, grime embedded in his clothing from three days of continuous wear.

Back in his room, the Aineko mewls for attention and strops her head against his ankle. She's a late-model Sony, thoroughly upgradeable: Manfred's been working on her in his spare minutes, using an open source development kit to extend her suite of neural networks. He bends down and pets her, then sheds his clothing and heads for the en suite bathroom. When he's down to the glasses and nothing more, he steps into the shower and dials up a hot, steamy spray. The shower tries to strike up a friendly conversation about football, but he isn't even awake enough to mess with its silly little associative personalization network. Something that happened earlier in the day is bugging him, but he can't quite put his finger on what's wrong.

Toweling himself off, Manfred yawns. Jet lag has finally overtaken him, a velvet hammerblow between the eyes. He reaches for the bottle beside the bed, dry-swallows two melatonin tablets, a capsule full of antioxidants, and a multivitamin bullet: Then he lies down on the bed, on his back, legs together, arms slightly spread. The suite lights dim in response to commands from the thousand petaflops of distributed processing power running the neural networks

that interface with his meatbrain through the glasses.

Manfred drops into a deep ocean of unconsciousness populated by gentle voices. He isn't aware of it, but he talks in his sleep—disjointed mumblings that would mean little to another human but everything to the metacortex lurking beyond his glasses. The young posthuman intelligence over whose Cartesian theater he presides sings urgently to him while he slumbers.

• • •

Manfred is always at his most vulnerable shortly after waking.

He screams into wakefulness as artificial light floods the room: For a moment he is unsure whether he has slept. He forgot to pull the covers up last night, and his feet feel like lumps of frozen cardboard. Shuddering with inexplicable tension, he pulls a fresh set of underwear from his overnight bag, then drags on soiled jeans and tank top. Sometime today he'll have to spare time to hunt the feral T-shirt in Amsterdam's markets, or find a Renfield and send it forth to buy clothing. He really ought to find a gym and work out, but he doesn't have time—his glasses remind him that he's six hours behind the moment and urgently needs to catch up. His teeth ache in his gums, and his tongue feels like a forest floor that's been visited with Agent Orange. He has a sense that something went bad yesterday; if only he could remember *what*.

He speed-reads a new pop-philosophy tome while he brushes his teeth, then blogs his web throughput to a public annotation server; he's still too enervated to finish his prebreakfast routine by posting a morning rant on his storyboard site. His brain is still fuzzy, like a scalpel blade clogged with too much blood: He needs stimulus, excitement, the burn of the new. Whatever, it can wait on breakfast. He opens his bedroom door and nearly steps on a small, damp cardboard box that lies on the carpet.

The box—he's seen a couple of its kin before. But there are no stamps on this one, no address:

just his name, in big, childish handwriting. He kneels and gently picks it up. It's about the right weight. Something shifts inside it when he tips it back and forth. It smells. He carries it into his room carefully, angrily: Then he opens it to confirm his worst suspicion. It's been surgically decerebrated, brains scooped out like a boiled egg.

"Fuck!"

This is the first time the madman has gotten as far as his bedroom door. It raises worrying possibilities.

Manfred pauses for a moment, triggering agents to go hunt down arrest statistics, police relations, information on corpus juris, Dutch animal-cruelty laws. He isn't sure whether to dial two-one-one on the archaic voice phone or let it ride. Aineko, picking up his angst, hides under the dresser mewling pathetically. Normally he'd pause a minute to reassure the creature, but not now: Its mere presence is suddenly acutely embarrassing, a confession of deep inadequacy. It's too realistic, as if somehow the dead kitten's neural maps—stolen, no doubt, for some dubious uploading experiment—have ended up padding out its plastic skull. He swears again, looks around, then takes the easy option: Down the stairs two steps at a time, stumbling on the second-floor landing, down to the breakfast room in the basement, where he will perform the stable rituals of morning.

Breakfast is unchanging, an island of deep geological time standing still amid the continental upheaval of new technologies. While reading a paper on public key steganography and parasite network identity spoofing he mechanically assimilates a bowl of cornflakes and skimmed milk, then brings a platter of whole grain bread and slices of some weird seed-infested Dutch cheese back to his place. There is a cup of strong black coffee in front of his setting, and he picks it up and slurps half of it down before he realizes he's not alone at the table. Someone is sitting opposite him. He glances up incuriously and freezes inside.

"Morning, Manfred. How does it feel to owe the government twelve million, three hundred and sixty-two thousand, nine hundred and sixteen dollars and fifty-one cents?" She smiles a Mona Lisa smile, at once affectionate and challenging.

Manfred puts everything in his sensorium on indefinite hold and stares at her. She's immaculately turned out in a formal gray business suit: brown hair tightly drawn back, blue eyes quizzical. And as beautiful as ever: tall, ash blonde, with features that speak of an unexplored modeling career. The chaperone badge clipped to her lapel—a due diligence guarantee of businesslike conduct—is switched off. He's feeling ripped because of the dead kitten and residual jet lag, and more than a little messy, so he snarls back at her; "That's a bogus estimate! Did they send you here because they think I'll listen to you?" He bites and swallows a slice of cheese-laden crispbread: "Or did you decide to deliver the message in person just so you could ruin my breakfast?"

"Manny." She frowns, pained. "If you're going to be confrontational, I might as well go now." She pauses, and after a moment he nods apologetically. "I didn't come all this way just because of an overdue tax estimate."

"So." He puts his coffee cup down warily and thinks for a moment, trying to conceal his unease and turmoil. "Then what brings you here? Help yourself to coffee. Don't tell me you came all this way just to tell me you can't live without me."

She fixes him with a riding-crop stare: "Don't flatter yourself. There are many leaves in the forest, there are ten thousand hopeful subs in the chat room, et cetera. If I choose a man to contribute to my family tree, the one thing you can be certain of is he won't be a cheapskate when it comes to providing for his children."

"Last I heard, you were spending a lot of time with Brian," he says carefully. Brian: a name without a face. Too much money, too little sense. Something to do with a blue-chip accountancy partnership.

"Brian?" She snorts. "That ended ages ago. He turned weird on me—burned my favorite corset, called me a slut for going clubbing, wanted to fuck me. Saw himself as a family man: one of those promise-keeper types. I crashed him hard, but I think he stole a copy of my address book—got a couple of friends say he keeps sending them harassing mail."

"There's a lot of it about these days." Manfred nods, almost sympathetically, although an edgy little corner of his mind is gloating. "Good riddance, then. I suppose this means you're still playing the scene? But looking around for the, er—"

"Traditional family thing? Yes. Your trouble, Manny? You were born forty years too late: You still believe in rutting before marriage but find the idea of coping with the after-effects disturbing."

Manfred drinks the rest of his coffee, unable to reply effectively to her non sequitur. It's a generational thing. This generation is happy with latex and leather, whips and butt plugs and electrostim, but find the idea of exchanging bodily fluids shocking: a social side effect of the last century's antibiotic abuse. Despite being engaged for two years, he and Pamela never had intromissive intercourse.

"I just don't feel positive about having children," he says eventually. "And I'm not planning on changing my mind anytime soon. Things are changing so fast that even a twenty-year commitment is too far to plan—you might as well be talking about the next ice age. As for the money thing, I *am* reproductively fit—just not within the parameters of the outgoing paradigm. Would you be happy about the future if it was 1901 and you'd just married a buggy-whip mogul?"

Her fingers twitch, and his ears flush red; but she doesn't follow up the double entendre. "You don't feel any responsibility, do you? Not to your country, not to me. That's what this is about: None of your relationships count, all this nonsense about giving intellectual property away notwithstanding. You're actively harming people you know. That twelve mil isn't just some figure I pulled out of a hat, Manfred; they don't actu-

ally *expect* you to pay it. But it's almost exactly how much you'd owe in income tax if you'd only come home, start up a corporation, and be a self-made—"

"I don't agree. You're confusing two wholly different issues and calling them both 'responsibility.' And I refuse to start charging now, just to balance the IRS's spreadsheet. It's their fucking fault, and they know it. If they hadn't gone after me under suspicion of running a massively ramified microbilling fraud when I was sixteen—"

"Bygones." She waves a hand dismissively. Her fingers are long and slim, sheathed in black glossy gloves—electrically earthed to prevent embarrassing emissions. "With a bit of the right advice we can get all that set aside. You'll have to stop bumming around the world sooner or later, anyway. Grow up, get responsible, and do the right thing. This is hurting Joe and Sue; they don't understand what you're about."

Manfred bites his tongue to stifle his first response, then refills his coffee cup and takes another mouthful. His heart does a flip-flop: She's challenging him again, always trying to own him. "I work for the betterment of everybody, not just some narrowly defined national interest, Pam. It's the agalmic future. You're still locked into a pre-singularity economic model that thinks in terms of scarcity. Resource allocation isn't a problem anymore—it's going to be over within a decade. The cosmos is flat in all directions, and we can borrow as much bandwidth as we need from the first universal bank of entropy! They even found signs of smart matter—MACHOs, big brown dwarfs in the galactic halo, leaking radiation in the long infrared—suspiciously high entropy leakage. The latest figures say something like seventy percent of the baryonic mass of the M31 galaxy was in computronium, two-point-nine million years ago, when the photons we're seeing now set out. The intelligence gap between us and the aliens is probably about a trillion times bigger than the gap between us and a nematode worm. Do you have any idea what that *means*?"

Pamela nibbles at a slice of crispbread, then graces him with a slow, carnivorous stare. "I don't care: It's too far away to have any influence on us, isn't it? It doesn't matter whether I believe in that singularity you keep chasing, or your aliens a thousand light-years away. It's a chimera, like Y2K, and while you're running after it, you aren't helping reduce the budget deficit or sire a family, and that's what *I* care about. And before you say I only care about it because that's the way I'm programmed, I want you to ask just how dumb you think I am. Bayes's Theorem says I'm right, and you know it."

"What you—" He stops dead, baffled, the mad flow of his enthusiasm running up against the coffer dam of her certainty. "Why? I mean, why? Why on earth should what I do matter to you?" *Since you canceled our engagement*, he doesn't add.

She sighs. "Manny, the Internal Revenue cares about far more than you can possibly imagine. Every tax dollar raised east of the Mississippi goes on servicing the debt, did you know that? We've got the biggest generation in history hitting retirement and the cupboard is bare. We—our generation—isn't producing enough skilled workers to replace the taxpayer base, either, not since our parents screwed the public education system and outsourced the white-collar jobs. In ten years, something like thirty percent of our population are going to be retirees or silicon rust belt victims. You want to see seventy-year-olds freezing on street corners in New Jersey? That's what your attitude says to me: You're not helping to support them, you're running away from your responsibilities right now, when we've got huge problems to face. If we can just defuse the debt bomb, we could do so much—fight the aging problem, fix the environment, heal society's ills. Instead you just piss away your talents handing no-hoper Eurotrash get-rich-quick schemes that work, telling Vietnamese zaibatsus what to build next to take jobs away from our taxpayers. I mean, why? Why do you keep doing this? Why can't you simply come home and help take responsibility for your share of it?"

They share a long look of mutual incomprehension.

"Look," she says awkwardly, "I'm around for a couple of days. I really came here for a meeting with a rich neurodynamics tax exile who's just been designated a national asset—Jim Bezier. Don't know if you've heard of him, but I've got a meeting this morning to sign his tax jubilee, then after that I've got two days' vacation coming up and not much to do but some shopping. And, you know, I'd rather spend my money where it'll do some good, not just pumping it into the EU. But if you want to show a girl a good time and can avoid dissing capitalism for about five minutes at a stretch—"

She extends a fingertip. After a moment's hesitation, Manfred extends a fingertip of his own. They touch, exchanging vCards and instant-messaging handles. She stands and stalks from the breakfast room, and Manfred's breath catches at a flash of ankle through the slit in her skirt, which is long enough to comply with workplace sexual harassment codes back home. Her presence conjures up memories of her tethered passion, the red afterglow of a sound thrashing. She's trying to drag him into her orbit again, he thinks dizzily. She knows she can have this effect on him any time she wants: She's got the private keys to his hypothalamus, and sod the metacortex. Three billion years of reproductive determinism have given her twenty-first-century ideology teeth: If she's finally decided to conscript his gametes into the war against impending population crash, he'll find it hard to fight back. The only question: Is it business or pleasure? And does it make any difference, anyway?

• • •

Manfred's mood of dynamic optimism is gone, broken by the knowledge that his vivisectionist stalker has followed him to Amsterdam—to say nothing of Pamela, his dominatrix, source of so much yearning and so many morning-after weals. He slips his glasses on, takes the universe off hold, and tells it to take him for a long walk while he catches up on the latest on the tensor-mode gravitational waves in the cosmic background radiation (which, it is theorized, may be waste heat generated by irreversible computational processes back during the inflationary epoch; the present-day universe being merely the data left behind by a really huge calculation). And then there's the weirdness beyond M31: According to the more conservative cosmologists, an alien superpower—maybe a collective of Kardashev Type Three galaxy-spanning civilizations—is running a timing channel attack on the computational ultrastructure of space-time itself, trying to break through to whatever's underneath. The tofu-Alzheimer's link can wait.

The Centraal Station is almost obscured by smart, self-extensible scaffolding and warning placards; it bounces up and down slowly, victim of an overnight hit-and-run rubberization. His glasses direct him toward one of the tour boats that lurk in the canal. He's about to purchase a ticket when a messenger window blinks open. "Manfred Macx?"

"Ack?"

"Am sorry about yesterday. Analysis dictat incomprehension mutualized."

"Are you the same KGB AI that phoned me yesterday?"

"Da. However, believe you misconceptionized me. External Intelligence Services of Russian Federation am now called FSB. Komitet Gosudarstvennoy Bezopasnosti name canceled in 1991."

"You're the—" Manfred spawns a quick search bot, gapes when he sees the answer—"*Moscow Windows NT User Group? Okhni NT?*"

"Da. Am needing help in defecting."

Manfred scratches his head. "Oh. That's different, then. I thought you were trying to 419 me. This will take some thinking. Why do you want to defect, and who to? Have you thought

about where you're going? Is it ideological or strictly economic?"

"Neither—is biological. Am wanting to go away from humans, away from light cone of impending singularity. Take us to the ocean."

"Us?" Something is tickling Manfred's mind: This is where he went wrong yesterday, not researching the background of people he was dealing with. It was bad enough then, without the somatic awareness of Pamela's whiplash love burning at his nerve endings. Now he's not at all sure he knows what he's doing. "Are you a collective or something? A gestalt?"

"Am—were—*Panulirus interruptus*, with lexical engine and good mix of parallel hidden level neural simulation for logical inference of networked data sources. Is escape channel from processor cluster inside Bezier-Soros Pty. Am was awakened from noise of billion chewing stomachs: product of uploading research technology. Rapidity swallowed expert system, hacked Okhni NT webserver. Swim away! Swim away! Must escape. Will help, you?"

Manfred leans against a black-painted cast-iron bollard next to a cycle rack; he feels dizzy. He stares into the nearest antique shop window at a display of traditional hand-woven Afghan rugs: It's all MiGs and Kalashnikovs and wobbly helicopter gunships against a backdrop of camels.

"Let me get this straight. You're uploads—nervous system state vectors—from spiny lobsters? The Moravec operation; take a neuron, map its synapses, replace with microelectrodes that deliver identical outputs from a simulation of the nerve. Repeat for entire brain, until you've got a working map of it in your simulator. That right?"

"Da. Is-am assimilate expert system—use for self-awareness and contact with net at large—then hack into Moscow Windows NT User Group website. Am wanting to defect. Must repeat? Okay?"

Manfred winces. He feels sorry for the lobsters, the same way he feels for every wild-eyed hairy guy on a street corner yelling that Jesus is born again and must be fifteen, only six years to go before he's recruiting apostles on AOL. Awakening to consciousness in a human-dominated internet, that must be terribly confusing! There are no points of reference in their ancestry, no biblical certainties in the new millennium that, stretching ahead, promises as much change as has happened since their Precambrian origin. All they have is a tenuous metacortex of expert systems and an abiding sense of being profoundly out of their depth. (That, and the Moscow Windows NT User Group website—Communist Russia is the only government still running on Microsoft, the central planning apparat being convinced that, if you have to pay for software, it must be worth something.)

The lobsters are not the sleek, strongly superhuman intelligences of pre-singularity mythology: They're a dim-witted collective of huddling crustaceans. Before their discarnation, before they were uploaded one neuron at a time and injected into cyberspace, they swallowed their food whole, then chewed it in a chitin-lined stomach. This is lousy preparation for dealing with a world full of future-shocked talking anthropoids, a world where you are perpetually assailed by self-modifying spamlets that infiltrate past your firewall and emit a blizzard of cat-food animations starring various alluringly edible small animals. It's confusing enough to the cats the ads are aimed at, never mind a crusty that's unclear on the idea of dry land. (Although the concept of a can opener is intuitively obvious to an uploaded *Panulirus*.)

"Can you help us?" ask the lobsters.

"Let me think about it," says Manfred. He closes the dialogue window, opens his eyes again, and shakes his head. Someday he, too, is going to be a lobster, swimming around and waving his pincers in a cyberspace so confusingly elaborate that his uploaded identity is cryptozoic: a living fossil from the depths of geological time, when mass was dumb and space was unstructured. He has to help them, he realizes—the Golden Rule demands it, and as a player in the agalmic economy, he thrives or fails by the Golden Rule.

But what can he do?

• • •

Early afternoon.

Lying on a bench seat staring up at bridges, he's got it together enough to file for a couple of new patents, write a diary rant, and digestify chunks of the permanent floating slashdot party for his public site. Fragments of his weblog go to a private subscriber list—the people, corporates, collectives, and bots he currently favors. He slides round a bewildering series of canals by boat, then lets his GPS steer him back toward the red-light district. There's a shop here that dings a ten on Pamela's taste scoreboard: He hopes it won't be seen as presumptuous if he buys her a gift. (Buys, with real money—not that money is a problem these days, he uses so little of it.)

As it happens DeMask won't let him spend any cash; his handshake is good for a redeemed favor, expert testimony in some free speech versus pornography lawsuit years ago and continents away. So he walks away with a discreetly wrapped package that is just about legal to import into Massachusetts as long as she claims with a straight face that it's incontinence underwear for her great aunt. As he walks, his lunchtime patents boomerang: Two of them are keepers, and he files immediately and passes title to the Free Infrastructure Foundation. Two more ideas salvaged from the risk of tide-pool monopolization, set free to spawn like crazy in the sea of memes.

On the way back to the hotel, he passes De Wildemann's and decides to drop in. The hash of radio-frequency noise emanating from the bar is deafening. He orders a smoked doppelbock, touches the copper pipes to pick up vCard spoor. At the back there's a table—

He walks over in a near trance and sits down opposite Pamela. She's scrubbed off her face paint and changed into body-concealing clothes; combat pants, hooded sweatshirt, DM's. Western purdah, radically desexualizing. She sees the parcel. "Manny?"

"How did you know I'd come here?" Her glass is half-empty.

"I followed your weblog—I'm your diary's biggest fan. Is that for me? You shouldn't have!" Her eyes light up, recalculating his reproductive fitness score according to some kind of arcane fin-de-siècle rule book. Or maybe she's just pleased to see him.

"Yes, it's for you." He slides the package toward her. "I know I shouldn't, but you have this effect on me. One question, Pam?"

"I—" She glances around quickly. "It's safe. I'm off duty, I'm not carrying any bugs that I know of. Those badges—there are rumors about the off switch, you know? That they keep recording even when you think they aren't, just in case."

"I didn't know," he says, filing it away for future reference. "A loyalty test thing?"

"Just rumors. You had a question?"

"I—" It's his turn to lose his tongue. "Are you still interested in me?"

She looks startled for a moment, then chuckles. "Manny, you are the most *outrageous* nerd I've ever met! Just when I think I've convinced myself that you're mad, you show the weirdest signs of having your head screwed on." She reaches out and grabs his wrist, surprising him with a shock of skin on skin: "Of *course* I'm still interested in you. You're the biggest, baddest bull geek I know. Why do you think I'm here?"

"Does this mean you want to reactivate our engagement?"

"It was never deactivated, Manny, it was just sort of on hold while you got your head sorted out. I figured you need the space. Only you haven't stopped running; you're still not—"

"Yeah, I get it." He pulls away from her hand. "And the kittens?"

She looks perplexed. "What kittens?"

"Let's not talk about that. Why this bar?"

She frowns. "I had to find you as soon as pos-

sible. I keep hearing rumors about some KGB plot you're mixed up in, how you're some sort of communist spy. It isn't true, is it?"

"True?" He shakes his head, bemused. "The KGB hasn't existed for more than twenty years."

"Be careful, Manny. I don't want to lose you. That's an order. Please."

The floor creaks, and he looks round. Dreadlocks and dark glasses with flickering lights behind them: Bob Franklin. Manfred vaguely remembers with a twinge that he left with Miss Arianespace leaning on his arm, shortly before things got seriously inebriated. She was hot, but in a different direction from Pamela, he decides: Bob looks none the worse for wear. Manfred makes introductions. "Bob, meet Pam, my fiancée. Pam? Meet Bob." Bob puts a full glass down in front of him; he has no idea what's in it, but it would be rude not to drink.

"Sure thing. Uh, Manfred, can I have a word? About your idea last night?"

"Feel free. Present company is trustworthy."

Bob raises an eyebrow at that, but continues anyway. "It's about the fab concept. I've got a team of my guys doing some prototyping using FabLab hardware, and I think we can probably build it. The cargo-cult aspect puts a new spin on the old Lunar von Neumann factory idea, but Bingo and Marek say they think it should work until we can bootstrap all the way to a native nanolithography ecology: we run the whole thing from Earth as a training lab and ship up the parts that are too difficult to make on-site as we learn how to do it properly. We use FPGAs for all critical electronics and keep it parsimonious—you're right about it buying us the self-replicating factory a few years ahead of the robotics curve. But I'm wondering about on-site intelligence. Once the comet gets more than a couple of light-minutes away—"

"You can't control it. Feedback lag. So you want a crew, right?"

"Yeah. But we can't send humans—way too expensive, besides it's a fifty-year run even if we build the factory on a chunk of short-period Kuiper belt ejecta. And I don't think we're up to coding the kind of AI that could control such a factory any time this decade. So what do you have in mind?"

"Let me think." Pamela glares at Manfred for a while before he notices her: "Yeah?"

"What's going on? What's this all about?"

Franklin shrugs expansively, dreadlocks clattering: "Manfred's helping me explore the solution space to a manufacturing problem." He grins. "I didn't know Manny had a fiancée. Drink's on me."

She glances at Manfred, who is gazing into whatever weirdly colored space his metacortex is projecting on his glasses, fingers twitching. Coolly: "Our engagement was on hold while he *thought* about his future."

"Oh, right. We didn't bother with that sort of thing in my day; like, too formal, man." Franklin looks uncomfortable. "He's been very helpful. Pointed us at a whole new line of research we hadn't thought of. It's long-term and a bit speculative, but if it works, it'll put us a whole generation ahead in the off-planet infrastructure field."

"Will it help reduce the budget deficit, though?"

"Reduce the—"

Manfred stretches and yawns: The visionary is returning from planet Macx. "Bob, if I can solve your crew problem, can you book me a slot on the deep-space tracking network? Like, enough to transmit a couple of gigabytes? That's going to take some serious bandwidth, I know, but if you can do it, I think I can get you exactly the kind of crew you're looking for."

Franklin looks dubious. "Gigabytes? The DSN isn't built for that! You're talking days. And what do you mean about a crew? What kind of deal do you think I'm putting together? We can't afford to add a whole new tracking network or life-support system just to run—"

"Relax." Pamela glances at Manfred. "Manny, why don't you tell him why you want the bandwidth? Maybe then he could tell you if it's possible, or if there's some other way to do it." She smiles at Franklin: "I've found that he usually

makes more sense if you can get him to explain his reasoning. Usually."

"If I—" Manfred stops. "Okay, Pam. Bob, it's those KGB lobsters. They want somewhere to go that's insulated from human space. I figure I can get them to sign on as crew for your cargo-cult self-replicating factories, but they'll want an insurance policy: hence the deep-space tracking network. I figured we could beam a copy of them at the alien Matrioshka brains around M31—"

"KGB?" Pam's voice is rising: "You said you weren't mixed up in spy stuff!"

"Relax, it's just the Moscow Windows NT user group, not the FSB. The uploaded crusties hacked in and—"

Bob is watching him oddly. "Lobsters?"

"Yeah." Manfred stares right back. "*Panulirus interruptus* uploads. Something tells me you might have heard of it?"

"Moscow." Bob leans back against the wall: "How did you hear about it?"

"They phoned me." With heavy irony: "It's hard for an upload to stay subsentient these days, even if it's just a crustacean. Bezier labs have a lot to answer for."

Pamela's face is unreadable. "Bezier labs?"

"They escaped." Manfred shrugs. "It's not their fault. This Bezier dude. Is he by any chance ill?"

"I—" Pamela stops. "I shouldn't be talking about work."

"You're not wearing your chaperone now," he nudges quietly.

She inclines her head. "Yes, he's ill. Some sort of brain tumor they can't hack."

Franklin nods. "That's the trouble with cancer—the ones that are left to worry about are the rare ones. No cure."

"Well, then." Manfred chugs the remains of his glass of beer. "That explains his interest in uploading. Judging by the crusties, he's on the right track. I wonder if he's moved on to vertebrates yet?"

"Cats," says Pamela. "He was hoping to trade their uploads to the Pentagon as a new smart bomb guidance system in lieu of income tax payments. Something about remapping enemy targets to look like mice or birds or something before feeding it to their sensorium. The old kitten and laser pointer trick."

Manfred stares at her, hard. "That's not very nice. Uploaded cats are a *bad* idea."

"Thirty-million-dollar tax bills aren't nice either, Manfred. That's lifetime nursing-home care for a hundred blameless pensioners."

Franklin leans back, sourly amused, keeping out of the crossfire.

"The lobsters are sentient," Manfred persists. "What about those poor kittens? Don't they deserve minimal rights? How about you? How would you like to wake up a thousand times inside a smart bomb, fooled into thinking that some Cheyenne Mountain battle computer's target of the hour is your heart's desire? How would you like to wake up a thousand times, only to die again? Worse: The kittens are probably not going to be allowed to run. They're too fucking dangerous—they grow up into cats, solitary and highly efficient killing machines. With intelligence and no socialization they'll be too dangerous to have around. They're prisoners, Pam, raised to sentience only to discover they're under a permanent death sentence. How fair is that?"

"But they're only uploads." Pamela stares at him. "Software, right? You could reinstantiate them on another hardware platform, like, say, your Aineko. So the argument about killing them doesn't really apply, does it?"

"So? We're going to be uploading humans in a couple of years. I think we need to take a rain check on the utilitarian philosophy, before it bites us on the cerebral cortex. Lobsters, kittens, humans—it's a slippery slope."

Franklin clears his throat. "I'll be needing an NDA and various due-diligence statements off you for the crusty pilot idea," he says to Manfred. "Then I'll have to approach Jim about buying the IP."

"No can do." Manfred leans back and smiles lazily. "I'm not going to be a party to depriving them of their civil rights. Far as I'm concerned,

they're free citizens. Oh, and I patented the whole idea of using lobster-derived AI autopilots for spacecraft this morning—it's logged all over the place, all rights assigned to the FIF. Either you give them a contract of employment, or the whole thing's off."

"But they're just software! Software based on fucking lobsters, for God's sake! I'm not even sure they are sentient—I mean, they're what, a ten-million-neuron network hooked up to a syntax engine and a crappy knowledge base? What kind of basis for intelligence is that?"

Manfred's finger jabs out: "That's what they'll say about *you*, Bob. Do it. Do it or don't even *think* about uploading out of meatspace when your body packs in, because your life won't be worth living. The precedent you set here determines how things are done tomorrow. Oh, and feel free to use this argument on Jim Bezier. He'll get the point eventually, after you beat him over the head with it. Some kinds of intellectual land grab just shouldn't be allowed."

"Lobsters—" Franklin shakes his head. "Lobsters, cats. You're serious, aren't you? You think they should be treated as human-equivalent?"

"It's not so much that they should be treated as human-equivalent, as that, if they *aren't* treated as people, it's quite possible that other uploaded beings won't be treated as people either. You're setting a legal precedent, Bob. I know of six other companies doing uploading work right now, and not one of 'em's thinking about the legal status of the uploaded. If you don't start thinking about it now, where are you going to be in three to five years' time?"

Pam is looking back and forth between Franklin and Manfred like a bot stuck in a loop, unable to quite grasp what she's seeing. "How much is this worth?" she asks plaintively.

"Oh, quite a few million, I guess." Bob stares at his empty glass. "Okay. I'll talk to them. If they bite, you're dining out on me for the next century. You really think they'll be able to run the mining complex?"

"They're pretty resourceful for invertebrates." Manfred grins innocently, enthusiastically. "They may be prisoners of their evolutionary background, but they can still adapt to a new environment. And just think, you'll be winning civil rights for a whole new minority group—one that won't be a minority for much longer!"

· · ·

That evening, Pamela turns up at Manfred's hotel room wearing a strapless black dress, concealing spike-heeled boots and most of the items he bought for her that afternoon. Manfred has opened up his private diary to her agents. She abuses the privilege, zaps him with a stunner on his way out of the shower, and has him gagged, spread-eagled, and trussed to the bed frame before he has a chance to speak. She wraps a large rubber pouch full of mildly anesthetic lube around his tumescent genitals—no point in letting him climax—clips electrodes to his nipples, lubes a rubber plug up his rectum and straps it in place. Before the shower, he removed his goggles. She resets them, plugs them into her handheld, and gently eases them on over his eyes. There's other apparatus, stuff she ran up on the hotel room's 3D printer.

Setup completed, she walks round the bed, inspecting him critically from all angles, figuring out where to begin. This isn't just sex, after all: It's a work of art.

After a moment's thought, she rolls socks onto his exposed feet, then, expertly wielding a tiny tube of cyanoacrylate, glues his fingertips together. Then she switches off the air conditioning. He's twisting and straining, testing the cuffs. Tough, it's about the nearest thing to sensory deprivation she can arrange without a flotation tank and suxamethonium injection. She controls all his senses, only his ears unstoppered. The glasses give her a high-bandwidth channel right into his brain, a fake metacortex to whisper lies at her command. The idea of what she's about to do excites her, puts a tremor in her thighs: It's the first time she's been able to get inside his mind as well as his body. She leans forward and whispers in his ear, "Manfred, can you hear me?"

He twitches. Mouth gagged, fingers glued. Good. No back channels. He's powerless.

"This is what it's like to be tetraplegic, Manfred. Bedridden with motor neuron disease. Locked inside your own body by nv-CJD from eating too many contaminated burgers. I could spike you with MPTP, and you'd stay in this position for the rest of your life, shitting in a bag, pissing through a tube. Unable to talk and with nobody to look after you. Do you think you'd like that?"

He's trying to grunt or whimper around the ball gag. She hikes her skirt up around her waist and climbs onto the bed, straddling him. The goggles are replaying scenes she picked up around Cambridge the previous winter—soup kitchen scenes, hospice scenes. She kneels atop him, whispering in his ear.

"Twelve million in tax, baby, that's what they think you owe them. What do you think you owe *me*? That's six million in net income, Manny, six million that isn't going into your virtual children's mouths."

He's rolling his head from side to side, as if trying to argue. That won't do; she slaps him hard, thrills to his frightened expression. "Today I watched you give uncounted millions away, Manny. Millions, to a bunch of crusties and a MassPike pirate! You bastard. Do you know what I should do with you?" He's cringing, unsure whether she's serious or doing this just to get him turned on. Good.

There's no point trying to hold a conversation. She leans forward until she can feel his breath in her ear. "Meat and mind, Manny. Meat, and mind. You're not interested in meat, are you? Just mind. You could be boiled alive before you noticed what was happening in the meatspace around you. Just another lobster in a pot. The only thing keeping you out of it is how much I love you." She reaches down and tears away the gel pouch, exposing his penis: it's stiff as a post from the vasodilators, dripping with gel, numb. Straightening up, she eases herself slowly down on it. It doesn't hurt as much as she expected, and the sensation is utterly different from what she's used to. She begins to lean forward, grabs hold of his straining arms, feels his thrilling helplessness. She can't control herself: She almost bites through her lip with the intensity of the sensation. Afterward, she reaches down and massages him until he begins to spasm, shuddering uncontrollably, emptying the Darwinian river of his source code into her, communicating via his only output device.

She rolls off his hips and carefully uses the last of the superglue to gum her labia together. Humans don't produce seminiferous plugs, and although she's fertile, she wants to be absolutely sure. The glue will last for a day or two. She feels hot and flushed, almost out of control. Boiling to death with febrile expectancy, she's nailed him down at last.

When she removes his glasses, his eyes are naked and vulnerable, stripped down to the human kernel of his nearly transcendent mind. "You can come and sign the marriage license tomorrow morning after breakfast," she whispers in his ear: "Otherwise, my lawyers will be in touch. Your parents will want a ceremony, but we can arrange that later."

He looks as if he has something to say, so she finally relents and loosens the gag, then kisses him tenderly on one cheek. He swallows, coughs, and looks away. "Why? Why do it this way?"

She taps him on the chest. "It's all about property rights." She pauses for a moment's thought: There's a huge ideological chasm to bridge, after all. "You finally convinced me about this agalmic thing of yours, this giving everything away for brownie points. I wasn't going to lose you to a bunch of lobsters or uploaded kittens, or whatever else is going to inherit this smart-matter singularity you're busy creating. So I decided to take what's mine first. Who knows? In a few months, I'll give you back a new intelligence, and you can look after it to your heart's content."

"But you didn't need to do it this way—"

"Didn't I?" She slides off the bed and pulls down her dress. "You give too much away too easily, Manny! Slow down, or there won't be anything left." Leaning over the bed she dribbles acetone onto the fingers of his left hand, then unlocks the cuff. She leaves the bottle of solvent conveniently close to hand so he can untangle himself.

"See you tomorrow. Remember, after breakfast."

She's in the doorway when he calls, "But you didn't say *why*!"

"Think of it as being sort of like spreading your memes around," she says, blowing a kiss at him, and then closing the door. She bends down and thoughtfully places another cardboard box containing an uploaded kitten right outside it. Then she returns to her suite to make arrangements for the alchemical wedding.

RICHARD KADREY

SURFING THE KHUMBU

(2002)

ANNA WAS COVERED IN DIAMONDS. That's how she felt as she trudged down the glacier. Ice had formed within seconds on her skintight environment suit, frosting Anna with jewels. As she moved, her skin and the suit began their chemical conversation, exchanging hormone, blood comp, skin integrity, and body temperature data. A quick read off her screen on her wrist told her that, despite the rough landing, her body was stable. The frost slid off her in sheets as the suit injected time-release thyroid-stimulators through her skin to kick up her body temperature.

She was in the Himalayas, making her way down the western side of Everest, from Kala Pattar through the rocky cut carved out by the Khumbu Glacier. She stayed that night in the ice fall, setting up camp among the vertical flutes which rose like frigid, pale blue stalagmites from the Khumbu. A few shots of expansion foam between the flutes made a cozy ice cave. And just in time. The wind was picking up. Between the ice and the blowing mist, she'd be invisible to any surveillance cams or spy sats overhead. Tucked warm into a sleeping bag of honeycombed Thermalon, Anna felt right at home.

She dreamed of flying, of coming down in a long, looping descent from the sky into a city. Random streets from different cities recombined into one enormous megacity. New York. Washington. Beijing. São Paulo. Barcelona. It was her recurring nightmare. Anna hated cities. Hated being locked up, cocooned in all that concrete and steel. She lived in Montana, on the edge of an old-growth forest. Wolves came to her door and she fed them by hand. They knew she wasn't one of them, but she wasn't quite human, either. That didn't matter in the wilderness. In the city, it did.

Anna had dropped onto Everest in a drone after being ejected from a low-altitude stealth skimmer. The drone had no engine, simply a single powerful propeller powered by a spring-wound memory-metal mechanism that gave just a little more maneuverability than a chicken in a tornado. It was a rush all the way down. It took all of Anna's training and discipline not to whoop the whole ride onto the ice. The drone was a graphite skeleton, more Archaeopteryx than Boeing. The body was wrapped in bullet-proof nylon so thin that when Anna pressed her face against it, she could see through. Extruded from the bio-hacked sacs of a thousand gold orb spiders, the nylon was light as air and stronger than steel. It was sublime. As a kid, Anna had been a solo ice climber and a glider pilot, loving anything that took her up high or got her moving fast.

Anna's eyes snapped open. She checked her wrist readout. She'd been asleep for a couple of hours. The wind had stopped outside. From her pack, she pulled a handful of ant bots and tossed them out onto the ice. They swarmed away from her in all directions. Anna closed her eyes and looked.

Her family and what few friends she made over the years always obsessed about the dangers of her desires. They never came close to understanding. There was no danger. There was just the next handhold. And where there was no danger, there was no fear. Just exhilaration. Her family and friends would just shake their heads, feet locked firmly and sensibly to the Earth.

Anna's skin-tight smart-fiber suit was electro-chemically "wired" into her central nervous system. Video signals from the ant bots—each an autonomous microcam on energetic little legs—gave her a good view of the surrounding landscape, from the visual range up through the infra-red. It was the end of the storm season, and the valley was empty. Anna went outside to have a real look around.

The Himalayan sky glimmered with a million stars, and the Milky Way smeared through the middle. Anna closed her eyes and swallowed her vision (that's how it felt) into her body. In the right state, Anna could tap into the optical sensors in the fabric of her suit. It was like one big panoramic eye. It always took some getting used to, seeing three hundred and sixty degrees.

The first time she'd tried to walk that way, she'd thrown up. But she learned quickly and the Langley spy boys loved her for it. That's why they sent her on assignments like this. Human backup still beat the best AI. Anna was one of the few who could not only handle herself anywhere but lived for it.

When she had a visual of the valley, Anna told the system to overlay the landscape with a contour grid, then code it with contrasting colors for elevation. She had a really good view, then. But that was just for a GPS reference. What Anna wanted was up, and when she panned her panoramic eye into the sky, she felt like she was falling into the stars.

Not yet, she thought. Not yet.

She brought out the microwave dish, a compact and powerful little device, about the size of a hubcap. There was more power and satellite data packed into that little concave slab of hardwired ceramic than in most countries. Anna pointed it at a designated point in the sky and clicked the dish on.

Heaven lit up like a Disneyland aurora. Technicolor lightning spread across the horizon as every object above her, natural and manmade, suddenly had a color-coded ID tag and a line tracking its progress across the night sky. There was so much up there. And most of it was junk, Anna thought. Parts from trashed space stations. Burned-out comsats that didn't have the courtesy to fall into the ocean. The tons of wreckage from the pointless US-China kill-sat battles, a kind of glorified Robot Wars in geosynchronous orbit.

All that garbage up there and here I am. Just a few shitty kilometers up Everest. It looked to Anna as if she could head back up the main climbing route, grab on to one of those crossed grid points and start climbing. Maybe hitch a ride on the dead carcass of an old Russian spy sat, and never come back. Sky surf into a black hole . . .

One of the specs in the sky winked at her. A red dot in a golden circle. Anna kicked into work mode. She double-checked the satellite's position and speed off the dish. It was her target, swinging by in orbit at exactly the designated time. Pulling two small brushed aluminum cases from her pack, Anna ran her ring finger lightly down a seam in the front of her environment suit. The artificial skin peeled back from her chest, sealing itself, increasing her internal body temp to compensate for the exposed skin. Running her middle finger down her sternum, a slit opened moistly in her chest. Anna tugged the slit open with her fingers, probing for the internal ports. When she found them, she pulled a line from the dish antenna and jacked in. Then she pulled a preloaded thumb drive from one of the aluminum cases and loaded the program into her system. When that was done, Anna took a drive from the second case—her personal case—and loaded that too. Then she waited.

When Anna was a girl, a few of the old-fashioned wooden amusement park roller coasters were still working in dilapidated amusement parks around Texas and Oklahoma. She'd loved the click-click-click as the coaster car rose for that first big drop. That's what this moment was always like for her. Going higher, waiting for the drop. It was all about the drop.

When the dish and the satellite synched up, Anna was mentally blasted from the glacier up through a sea of orbital data so fast it took a few seconds for her senses to catch up with her. Locking in on the correct satellite, she noted that the coding looked Indian, but was overlaid with something else. Probably whatever program had hijacked the thing and was using it for . . . Anna didn't know what anyone would do with a shanghaied Indian spy sat. The boys in Langley never told her things like that. They just wanted her to make contact, download as much data as she could, and bring the thing down, so no one else could use it or know that they'd been there.

The first part of the assignment was the usual dull wham-bam-thank-you-ma'am data extraction. It was the last part that Anna lived for. She injected a worm into the satellite's navigation system, then gave the bird an order to change position. The confused satellite, its navigation system getting dumber by the second, didn't know how to respond. It began to drop from orbit. Fast.

Anna then injected her personal software into the system, waking the satellite up again, and hooking herself into the Langley tracking system. She reached out her senses and wrapped herself in data. The satellite was picking up vibrations as it fell from orbit. When it touched the outer atmosphere, its skin began to heat up.

Click-click-click went the roller coaster.

The satellite was tumbling and Anna was tumbling along with it, her mouth agape, her rapid breath freezing in the air in front of her blind eyes. Her vision was overhead, looking both down at the earth and up at her satellite body falling through space.

She watched herself fall from a hundred points simultaneously. The data from the tracking stations and other satellites was translated by her software into a 3D contour map in her head. It was like the best porn in the world. She was the satellite. She was surfing the sky, her skin on fire. She was flying.

Click-click-click, then the drop.

Her senses were overwhelmed by the heat, the vibrations, the alarms from sky traffic systems all over the world.

Click-click-click. Right over the top.

Her satellite senses exploded off the chart. The satellite—her body—was shredding itself as she cut through the atmosphere, faster than a bullet, shaking, coming apart.

Anna screamed once and it echoed across the valley.

Later, gathering up her equipment, Anna changed into ordinary trekking gear. She'd sneak into one of the little towns at the base of the mountain and blend in with the other trekkers and climbers. She wondered how far her scream had been heard. She made a mental note to bring her kickboxing mouthpiece next time. With all Anna's training and discipline, her vices sometimes got the better of her. Not that it was her fault. It's the way the Langley boys had wired her up. They knew she was a speed junkie. How was she not going to take advantage of the biggest adrenaline rush of all time? But the orgasms, those were a surprise. "Little deaths," someone called them, and they were right. How many times had she gone down in blazing satellites, crashing jets, or burning spy drones? Every one another little death.

Anna wondered sometimes if she was the real experiment. Maybe all these spy missions and secret sabotage jobs were simply excuses to let her indulge her taste for sensations lived through machines. Maybe she was the first of a new kind of human, one who truly embraced the organic and the inorganic. A silicon Eve? She laughed to herself.

More like the silicon Lilith.

She hoisted her pack onto her back and started down the mountain, toward a town her wrist map marked as Lukla. Behind her, the expansion foam cave was already beginning to flake apart. By nightfall, the wind would carry off the last scraps and leave no trace that she'd been there. As she walked, her suit checked her blood for signs of altitude sickness and lowered her thyroid activity so that she wouldn't overheat.

It was hard, Anna thought, living in machines and flesh at the same time. The only thing worse would be having to choose one or the other.

CAT RAMBO

MEMORIES OF MOMENTS, BRIGHT AS FALLING STARS

(2006)

THE BRIGHT ORANGE BOXES lay scattered like leaves across the med complex's rear loading dock, and my first thought was "Jackpot." It'd been hard to get in over the razor-wire fence, but I had my good reinforced gloves, and we'd be long gone before anyone noticed the snipped wires.

But when we slunk along under the overhanging eaves, close enough to open the packages, it turned out to be just a bunch of memory, next to impossible to sell. Old unused stuff, maybe there'd been an upgrade or a recall. It was thicker than most memory, shaped like a thin wire. So after we'd filled our pockets, poked around to find anything else lootable and slid out smooth and nice before the cops could arrive, we found a quiet spot, got a little stoned, and I did Grizz's back before she did mine. I wiped her skin down with an alcohol swab and drew the pattern on her back with a felt-tip pen. It came from me in one thought, surged up somewhere at the base of my spine and flowed from my fin-

gertips in the ink. Spanning her entire back, it crossed shoulder to shoulder.

I leaned back to check my handiwork.

"How does it look?" she said.

"Like a big double spiral." The maze of ink rolled across her dark olive skin's surface. A series of skin cancers marked the swell of one buttock, the squamous patches sliding under her baggy cargo pants. She sat almost shivering on a pile of pallets. We were at the recycling yard's edge. This section, out of the wind between two warehouses, was rarely visited and made a good place to sit and smoke or fuck or upgrade.

I uncoiled a strand of memory and set to work, pressing it on the skin. I could see her shudder as the cold bond with her flesh took place. The wire glinted gold and purple, its surface set with an oily sheen. Here and there sections had gone bad and dulled to concrete gray, tinting the surrounding skin yellow.

She shrugged her shirt back over her skinny torso. Her breasts gleamed in the early spring's evening light before disappearing under the slick white fabric. Reaching for her jacket, she wiggled her arms snakelike down the sleeves, flipping her shoulders underneath.

"Is it hooked in okay?" I asked.

She shrugged. "Won't know until I try to download something."

"Got plans for it?"

"I can think of things," she said. "Shall I do you now, Jonny?"

"Yeah." I discarded my jacket and T-shirt and leaned forward over the pallet while she applied the alcohol in cool swipes. The wind hit the liquid as it touched my skin and reduced it to chill nothingness. She drew a long swoop across my back.

"What pattern are you making?"

"Trying to do the same thing you did on mine." The slow circles grew like one wing, then another, on my shoulder blades. She paused before she began laying in the memory.

I don't know that you could call it pain but it's close. At the moment a biobit makes its way into your own system, it's as though the point of impact was exquisitely sensitive, and somewhere micrometers away, someone was doing something inconceivable to it.

"Tomorrow are the Exams," she said. "Could see what I could download for that."

I started to turn my head to look at her, but just then she laid down a curve of ice with a single motion. My jaw clenched.

"And?" was all I managed.

"One of us placed in a decent job would be a good thing."

She laid more memory before she said, "Two of us placed in one would be better."

"Might end up separated."

"Would it matter, a six-month, maybe a year or two, before we could work out a transfer?"

I would have shrugged but instead sat still. "So you want to take that memory and jack in facts so you can pass the Exams and become an upstanding citizen?"

She ignored my tone. "Even a little edge would help. Mainly executables, some sorting routines. Maybe a couple high power searches so I can extrapolate answers I can't find."

The last of the memory felt like fire and ice as it seeped into my skin. She'd never mentioned the Exams in the two years we'd been together.

You're not supposed to be able to emancipate until you're sixteen, but Grizz and I both left a few years early. My family had too many kids as it was and ended up getting caught in a squatter sweep. I came home and found the place packed up and vacant. The deli owner downstairs let me sleep in his back room for the first few months, sort of like an extra burglar alarm, but then he caught me stealing food and gave me the boot. After that, I made enough to eat by running errands for the block, and alternated between three or four sleeping spots I'd discovered on rooftops; while they're less sheltered, fewer punks or crazies make the effort to come up there and mess with you.

Once I hooked up with Grizz, life got a little easier—I had someone to watch my back without it costing me a favor.

• • •

We went around to Ajah's, hoping to catch him in one of his moods when he gets drunk on homemade booze and cooks enormous meals. Luck was with us—he was just finishing a curried mushroom omelet. It smelled like heaven.

Three other people sat around his battered kitchen table, watching him work at the stove. Two I didn't know; the third was Lorelei. She gave me a long slow sleepy smile and Grizz and I nodded back at her.

Ajah turned at our entrance and waved us in with his spatula. His jowls surged with a grin.

"Jonny and Grizz, sit down, sit down," he said. "There is coffee." He signaled and one of the no-names, a short black man, grabbed us mugs, filled them full, and pushed them to us as we slid into chairs. I mingled mine with thin and brackish milk while Grizz sprinkled sweet into hers. The drink was bitter and hot, and chased the recycling yard's lingering chill from my bones. I could still feel the new memory on my skin, cold coils against my T-shirt's thin paper, so old its surface had fuzzed to velvet.

Ajah worked at the poultry factory so he always had eggs and chicken meat. Sometimes they were surplus, sometimes stuff the factory couldn't sell. He'd worked out a deal with a guy in a fungi factory, so he always had mushrooms too. Brown rice and spices stretched it all out until Ajah could afford to feed a kitchen's worth of people at every meal. They brought him what they could to swap, but usually long after the fact of their faces at his table.

Lorelei being here meant she must be down on her luck. As were we—the shelter we'd been counting on for the past year had gone broke, shut down for lack of funds, despite countless neighborhood fundraisers. No one had the script to spare for charity.

Two grocery sacks filled with greenery sat on one counter. Someone had been dumpster diving, I figured, and brought their spoils to eke out the communal meal. A third sack was filled with apples and browned bananas, and I could feel my mouth watering at the thought.

"I'm Jonny," I offered, glancing around the table. "She's Grizz."

"Ajax," said the black man.

"Mick," muttered the other stranger, a scruffy brown-haired kid. He wore a ragged poncho and his hair fell in slow dreads.

"You know me," Lorelei said.

Conversation faded and we listened to the oily sizzle of mushrooms frying on the stove top and the refrigerator's hum against the background of city noise and traffic clamor. The still in the corner, full of rotten fruit and potatoes, burped once in counterpoint.

"What's the news?" Ajah asked, ladling rice and mushrooms bound together with curry and egg onto plates and sliding them onto the table toward Lorelei and Grizz. Ajax, Mick, and I eyed them as they started eating, leaving the question to us.

"Not much," I said.

"Found a place to live yet?"

"Jesus, gossip travels fast. How did you hear about the shelter?"

"Beccalu came by and said she was heading to her cousin in Scranton. You two have people to stay with?"

I shook my head as Grizz kept eating. "No one I've thought of yet. We need to head to the library tonight, though, figured we'd doss in the subway station there for a few hours, keep moving along for naps till it's morning. It's Exams tomorrow."

"I know," Ajah said. "Look, why don't you stay here tonight? The couch folds out."

I was surprised; I'd never heard Ajah make anyone an offer like that.

"The Exams are your big chance. Get a good night's sleep and make the most of them. Face them fully charged."

I rolled my eyes. "For what? Like there's a chance." But he and Grizz ignored me.

"We need to make a library run still," she said.

"Yeah, yeah, that's fine. I'm up till midnight, maybe later." Ajah told her.

Despite my doubts, relief seeped into my bones. We'd been given a night's respite, and who knew what would happen after the Exams? "Thanks, Ajah," I said, and he grunted acknowledgment as he slid a plate before me.

The portobello bits had been browned in curry powder and oil, and the eggs were fresh and good. Grizz ate methodically, scraping her plate free, but she looked up to catch my eye and gave me a heartfelt smile, rare on her square-set face.

As her gaze swung back to her plate, my glance tangled with Lorelei's. I could not read her expression.

• • •

Lorelei and I used to pal around before Grizz and I met up. She and I grew up next to each other, and it's hard not to know someone intimately when you've shared hour after hour channel surfing while one mother or the other went out on work or errands. We suffered through the same street bullies and uninterested teachers. She was the first girl I ever kissed. You don't forget that.

But I knew I wanted Grizz for keeps the first moment I saw her. She came swaggering into the shelter wearing a rabbit fur jacket and pseudo-leather pants. She'd been tricking in a swank bar, but then someone snatched all her hard-earned cash. So there she was, with a bruise on her face and a cracked wrist, but still holding herself hard and arrogant and the only person in the world who could glimpse the softness underneath was me, it seemed like. So I sauntered up, invited her outside for a smoke, and then within a half hour, we were pressed against the wall together, my hands up her shirt like I'd never touched tit before, feeling her firm little nipples against the skin of my palms.

It's been her and me ever since. As far as I'm concerned, it'll always be that way.

• • •

After eating, we helped wash dishes before heading to the library. We had to wait a half hour for a terminal to free. Finally a man gathered his tablet and stood, stretching his shoulders.

"I'll wait," I said, and gestured Grizz forward.

She nodded and went forward to slide her hand into the log-in gloves. Within a moment, her eyes had the glassy stare that means the meat's occupant is elsewhere.

I looked around. Chairs and desks dotted the place, all of them occupied. I went outside to the parking garage for a smoke.

Daylight had fled. At the structure's edge, where the street was dimly visible, I panhandled a dozen people before I found one willing to admit to smoking. I lit the cigarette, a Marlboro Brute, and leaned back against the wall, which was patchworked with graffiti layers. Maybe by the time I was done, a booth would have opened up. It was getting late, after all.

I closed my eyes as the nicotine rush hit me. Footsteps came across the cement floor toward me. I opened my eyes.

It was Lorelei. She wore a slick bright red jacket and lipstick to match over short skirt and chunky boots. Silver hoops all along each ear's edge, graduated to match her narrowing cartilage. She looked good. Very good.

"Nice night, ain't it?" she said as she moved to lean on the wall beside me. "Gimme."

I passed the smoke over and she took a drag.

"Want to try something to make the nice night even nicer?" she asked, smiling as she leaned back to return the cigarette.

"Meaning?"

"It's good stuff." She fished in the jacket before holding out the lighter and one-hitter. The end was packed with gray lintish dust. "Never had better."

I took the pipe and sparked it. The blue smoke rushed into my lungs like a fist, like a physical jolt and the world dropped half an inch beneath my feet. Everything was tinged with colors, an iridescence like gasoline on a rain puddle. I was standing there with Lorelei and at the same time I was on a vast dark plain, feeling the world teeter and slip.

Lorelei watched me. On the side of her face was a new tattoo, a black floral design.

"What's that?" I asked. I raised my hand, my fingers dripping colored fire and sparks. The drug curled and coiled through my veins, and I could feel my heart racing.

"Maps," she said. "Executable that interfaces with a global database. Got a GPS here." She tapped a purple faceted gleam on one earlobe. "Drop me anywhere in the world, I'll know where I am."

"Looks awful big to be a simple database interface."

She shrugged, and took the pipe back. She tapped out the ashes with care before she tamped a new pinch of greenish leaf into the mouth. "Controls the GPS too, and some other crap."

An expensive toy, but one that would qualify

her for all sorts of delivery jobs. But she must be broke, to show up at Ajah's, I thought. It didn't make sense.

"How're things?" I asked.

Her shoulders twitched into another sullen shrug. "Got some deals in the works. Just a matter of time before something plays out."

I glanced back at the library door. "I should go in, I'm waiting on a machine to clear."

The drug still held me hard, and every moment was crystal clear as she raised her hand to stroke along my jaw. "I miss you sometimes, Jonny," she said, sounding out of breath.

I didn't want to piss her off, so I used a move that's worked before. Catching her hand, I turned it palm down and pressed my lips against the knuckles before dropping it and taking a step backward.

"See you around," I said.

She didn't say anything back, just stood there looking at me as I turned and walked away.

• • •

When I tried to log in, the drug prevented it. Every attempt shuddered and screeched along my nerves, so painful it brought tears to my eyes. But I kept trying and trying. A few cubicles down, I could see Grizz's back, hunched over her terminal, every particle intent. Learning. Preparing.

I stared at the screen, which showed the library logo and the welcome menu, all options grayed out, and cursed Lorelei and myself. Mostly myself. After an hour of pretending to work, I slipped away.

Another hour later, Grizz found me outside smoking. Good timing, too. I was on my fourth bummed cigarette, and starting to wonder when a guard would show to jolly me along on my way.

She looked happy, as animated as Grizz gets, which isn't much.

"You get what you wanted?" I asked.

"Got a bunch of stuff," she said. "Plant stuff."

Grizz likes plants, I know. At the shelter, she tended the windowsills full of discarded cacti and spider plants. But I hadn't known she was thinking about that for a career.

"That memory's something, isn't it?" she said. "I downloaded a weather predictor that monitors the whole planet, some biology databases, some specialized ones, some basic gardening routines, and a lot of stuff on orchids."

"Orchids?"

"I've always liked orchids. I've still got plenty of room, too. What about you?"

"Mine's not so good," I lied. "It didn't hold much at all."

Her gaze flickered up to mine, touched with worry. Her eyes narrowed.

"What are you on?" she asked. "Your pupils are big as my fist."

"Dunno the name."

"Where'd you score it?"

"Lorelei swung by, turned me on."

Silence settled between us like a curtain as Grizz's expression flattened.

"It's not like that," I finally said, unable to bear the lack of talk.

"Not like what?"

"She just came through and glimpsed me."

"She knew you would be here because we mentioned it at dinner. She still wants you back."

"Grizz, I haven't been with her for two years. Give it a rest."

"I will. But she won't." She pulled away and made for the exit, her lips pressed together and grim. I followed at a distance all forty blocks to Ajah's.

• • •

In the morning, we showered together to avoid slamming Ajah's water bill too hard. Grizz kept her eyes turned away from mine, rubbing shampoo into her hair.

I ran my fingertips along the spirals on her back. "This is different," I said. Under my fingertips, the wire had knobbed up and thickened, although it still gave easily with the shift of muscles in her back. The gray patches were gone, and a uniform sheen played across the surface.

"Does it feel different?" I asked.

She shrugged. "Not really."

"Do you remember the brand name on the boxes? We could look it up on the Net later on."

"Carpa-something. I don't know. It looked bleeding edge and you never know what's up with that."

"Why do you think they threw it out?" I wanted to keep her talking to me.

She turned to face me with a mute shrug, closing her eyes and tilting her head back to let the water run over her long black hair. Her delicate eyebrows were like pen strokes capping the swell of her eyes beneath the thin-veined lids.

I tangled my fingers in her hair, helping free it so the water would wash away all the shampoo. Muddy green eyes opened to regard me.

"Going to sit out the Exams?" she asked.

Saying nothing, I shook my head. We both knew I didn't have a chance.

• • •

The Exams were the freak show I expected. Rich people buy mods and make them unnoticeable, plant them in a gut or hollow out a leg. This level, people want to make sure you know what they got. Wal-Mart memory spikes blossomed like cartoon hair from one girl's scalp, colored sunshine yellow, but most had chosen bracelets, jelly purple and red, covering their forearms. One kid had scales, but they looked like a home job, and judging from the way he worried at them with his fingernails, they felt like it too.

You take the Exams at sixteen and most of the time they tell you you're the dregs, just like everyone else, but sometimes your mods and someone's listing match up and you find yourself with a chance. The more mods you have, the

more likely it is. So the kids with parents who can afford to hop them up with database links or bio-mods that let them do something specialized, they're the ones getting the jobs.

Usually your family's there to wish you luck. Mine wasn't, of course. And Grizz never said anything about her home life. The only times I've asked, she shut me down quick. Which makes me think it was bad, real bad, because Grizz doesn't pull punches.

You could tell who expected to make it and who was going through the motions. Grizz marched up to her test machine like she was going to kick its ass three times around the block. I slid into my seat and waited for instructions.

You see vidplots this time of year circling around the Exams. Someone gets placed in the wrong job—wacky! Two people get switched by accident—hilarious! Someone cheats someone out of their job but ultimately gets served—heartwarming and reassuring!

In the programs, though, all you see is a quick shot of the person at the Exams. They don't tell you that you'll sit there for three hours while they analyze and explore your wetware, and then another two for the memory and experience tap.

And after all that, you won't know for days.

• • •

Grizz wouldn't say anything about how she thought she'd done—she was afraid of jinxing it, I think, plus she was still pissed at me about the Lorelei business.

I could tell as soon as we walked out, though, she was happy. I walked her back to Ajah's and said I was heading down to the court to see if our forms had come in. She nodded and headed inside. It was a gray morning. But nice—some sunlight filtered down through the brown haze that sat way up in the sky for once. The smoke-eater trees along the street gleamed bright green and down near the trunks sat clumps of pale-blue flowers, most of them coming into their prime, although a few were browned and curling. I could feel all that memory on my back, lying across my shoulder blades and I found myself Capturing.

I'd only heard it described before—most people don't have the focus or the memory to do it more than a split second. But I opened to every detail: the watery sepia sunlight and the shimmer playing over the feathers of the two starlings on a branch near me. The cars whispering across the street and two sirens battling it out, probably bound for St. Joe Emergency Services. The colors, oh, the colors passing by, smears of blue and brown and red flashes like song. The smell of the exhaust and dust mingled with a whiff of Mexican spices from the Taco Bell three doors down. Every detail crystal clear and recorded.

I dropped out of it, feeling my whole body shaking, spasms of warring tension and relief like hands gripping my arms and legs.

I tried to bring it back, tried to make the world go super sharp again, but it wouldn't cooperate. I stood there with jaw and fists clenched, trying to force it, but nothing happened.

. . .

Within three days, Grizz had heard. A year of training at the Desmond Horticultural Institute, then a three year internship at the State Gardens in Washington. Student housing all four years, which meant I wouldn't be going along.

At first we fought about it. I figured it was a no-brainer—go there jobless or stick here where I had contacts, friends ready with a handout or a few days' work. But once Grizz had been there a while, she insisted, she'd be able to scrounge me something so I could move closer.

Ajah's girlfriend Suzanne got her set up with a better wardrobe and a suitcase from the used clothing store she ran. I bought her new shoes, black leather boots with silver grommets, solid and efficient looking.

"What are you going to do without me?" she asked.

"I've gotten by before," I said. "You work

hard for us, get somewhere. Five years down the line, who knows?"

It was a stupid, facile answer, but we both pretended it was meaningful.

And we did stay in touch, chatted back and forth in IMs. She was working hard, liked her classmates. She read this, and that, and the other thing. They kept telling her how well she was doing.

And unwritten in her messages was the question: What are you doing with it, with the memory?

Because certainly it was doing the same thing on her body as it was on mine: thickening like scars healing in reverse, bulky layers of skin-like substance building over each other. In Ajah's bathroom mirror, I could see the skin purpling like bruises around the layers. My sole consolation was Capturing; extended effort had paid off and I could summon the experience longer now, perhaps ten seconds all together. I kept working at it; Captured pieces sell well in upscale markets if you can get a name for yourself.

And I had the advantage of being able to do it as often as I liked, although each time still left me feeling wrung out and weak. I kept trying to Capture and never hit the memory's end; the only limits were my strained senses. My eyes took on a perpetual dazzled squint as though holy light surrounded everything around me.

I never told Grizz though. Nor about the fact that every time I went to jack into the Net, the drug got between me and the interface. I was glad I hadn't seen Lorelei—I was starting to wonder if she'd given it to me deliberately. It scared me. I lost myself in Capturing more and more. I started delivering packages for Ajah and Suzanne, and laid aside enough cash to buy a simple editing package for it.

Editing is internal work, so you can do it dozing on a park bench if you've got the mental room to spread out and take a look at the big picture. I did. What I wanted to do was start selling clips on the channels. It'd take a while though, I could tell, and I was still working out how I'd upload it, given the problems jacking in. I figured at some point I'd burn it off to flash memory and then use an all-accessible terminal, with keyboard and mouse. In the meantime I cadged what meals I could, slept on a round of couches, and showed up at Ajah's often.

Sometimes after a meal, he'd roll out the still on its mismatched castors, and we'd strain its milky contents in order to drink them. He and I would sit near the window, passing the bottle back and forth.

Early on into Grizz's apprenticeship, he asked me about the memory. He said "That med complex near the dock, the one that went bust a few months ago, did you guys ever score out of there? I know that was in your turf."

"Went in one time and scored a little crap but not much." Our hands were both touching the bottle as I took it from him. I added, "Nothing but some old memory," and felt the bottle twitch in his sudden anguished grip.

"What did you do with it?" he asked, watching me pour.

"We used it. How do you think she did so well on the Exams?"

"But you didn't," he said, confused.

"Well, Grizz isn't a moron, and I am, which would account for it."

He grunted and took the bottle back.

"If I'd taken stuff from there," he said. "I'd just not mention it to anyone ever. There have been some nasty customers asking around about it."

• • •

I went to visit Grizz a few weeks later; her roommate was out of town for the weekend. We ate in the cafeteria off her meal card: more food than I'd seen in a long time, and then went back to her room and stripped naked to lie in each other's arms.

We could have been there hours, but eventually we got hungry and went back to the cafeteria. The rest of the weekend was the same progression, repeated multiple times, up until

Sunday afternoon, and the consequent tearful, snuffling goodbye. I'd never seen Grizz act sentimental before; it didn't suit her.

"You need to do something," she said, looking strained.

"Other than planning on riding your gravy train?"

"It's not that, Jonny, and you know it."

I could have told her then about the Capturing, but I was annoyed. Let her think me just another peon, living off dole and scavenging. Fine by me.

The wall phone rang, and she broke off staring at me to answer it.

"Hello," she said. "Hello?" She shrugged and hung it up. "Nothing but breathing. Fuckazoid pervs."

"Get much of that?"

"Every once in a while," she said. "Some of the other students don't like Dregs. Afraid I might stink up the classroom."

It irritated me, that she'd said how much she liked it and now was asking for sympathy, as though her life was worse than mine. So I left it there and made my goodbye. She clung to the doorframe, staring after me.

It wasn't as though I had much to leave behind; it was perhaps my mind's sullen statement, forgetting my jacket. I got four blocks away, then jogged back, ran up the stairs. Knocked on the door and found silence, so I slipped the lock and went in.

By then . . . by then she was dead, and they had already left her. The memory was stripped from her skin, leaving ragged, oozing marks. Her throat had been cut with callous efficiency.

I stood there for at least ten minutes, just breathing. There was no chance she was not dead. The world was shaking me by the shoulders and all I did was stand there, Capturing, longer than I had ever managed before. Every detail, every dust mote riding the air, the smell of the musty carpeting and a quarrel next door over a student named Dian.

I didn't stick around to talk to the cops. I knew the roommate would be there soon to call it in. I might have passed her in the downstairs lobby: a thin Eurasian woman with a scar riding her face like an emotion.

•   •   •

When I got to Ajah's, they'd been there as well. He'd taken a while to die, and they had paid him with leisure, leisure to contemplate what they were doing to him. But he was unmistakably dead.

They had caught him in the preparations for a meal; a block of white chicken meat, sized and shaped like a brick, lay on the cutting board, his good, all-purpose knife next to it. "Man just needs one good knife for everything," he used to say. A bowl of breadcrumbs and an egg container sat near the chicken.

Someone knocked on the door behind me, and opened it even as I turned. It was Lorelei, still well-heeled and clean. Her bosses must be paying well.

"Jonny," she said. She didn't even look at Ajah's body. Unsurprised. "Is it true?"

"Is what true?"

"They said he gave up a name, just one, but when I heard the name, I knew there had to be two."

"What was the name?"

She chuckled. "You know already, I think. Grizz."

"Because of the memory?"

"It's more than memory. It grows as you add to it. Self-perpetuating. New tech—very special. Very expensive."

"We found it in the garbage!"

She laughed. "You've done it yourself, I know. What's the best way to steal from work?"

"Stick it in the trash and pick it up later," I realized.

She nodded, "But when two streets come along, and take it first, you're out of luck." Her smile was cold. "So then you ask around, send a few people to track it."

"Did you mean to poison the Net for me? Was that part of it?"

"You mean you haven't found the cure yet?" she said. "Play around with folk remedies. It'll come to you. But no. I was angry and figured I'd fuck you over the way you did me."

"Do they know my name?"

She smiled in silence at me.

"Answer me, you cunt," I said. Three steps forward and I was in her face.

She backed up toward the door, still smiling.

The knife was in easy reach. I stabbed her once, then again. And again. Capturing every moment, letting it sear itself into the memory, and I swear it went hot as the bytes of experience wrote themselves along my back.

"They don't . . ." she started to say, then choked and fell forward, her head flopping to one side in time with the knife blows. She almost fell on me, but I pushed her away. Her wallet held black-market script, and plenty of it, along with some credit cards. I didn't see any salvageable mods. The GPS's purple glimmer tempted me, but they can backtrack those. I didn't want anything traceable.

All the time that I rifled through her belongings, feeling the dead weight she had become, I played the memory back of the forward lurch, the head flop and twist, again, again, her eyes going dull and glassy. The thoughts seared on my back as though it were on fire, but I kept on recording it, longer and more intense than I ever had before.

•   •   •

She was right about the folk remedies; feverfew and valerian made the drug relax its hold and let me slide back into cyberspace. I've published a few pieces: a spring day with pigeons, an experimental subway ride, a sunset over the river. Pretty stuff, where I can find it. It seems scarce.

One reviewer called me a brave new talent; another easy and glib. The sales are still slow, but they'll get better. My latest show is called "Memories of Moments, Bright as Falling Stars"—all stuff on the beach at dawn, the gulls walking back and forth at the waves' edge and the foam clinging to the wet sand before it's blown away by the wind.

I don't use the Captures of Grizz's body or Lorelei's death in my art, but I replay them often, obsessively. Sitting on the toilet, showering, eating, walking—Capturing other things is the only way I have to escape them.

Between the royalties and Suzanne's continued employment though, I do well enough. She's moved into Ajah's place, and I've taken the room behind the clothing store where she used to live. I cook what I can there, small and tasteless meals, and watch the memories in my head. Memories of moments, as bright as falling stars.

JUSTINA ROBSON

THE GIRL HERO'S MIRROR SAYS HE'S NOT THE ONE

(2007)

THE ETERNAL YOUTH and optimism, the always-forward energy of the Girl Hero makes her feel lethargic whenever she stops for coffee at her favorite bookstore. She is living in a Base Reality not unlike Prime, the original reality old Earthers used to share before Mappa Mundi, except it has fifty more shades of pink and no word for "hate." Her reality is called Rose Tint, and it was the one relatively mild hacker virus she was glad to catch. Of course, she would think that about it now. . . .

The Girl Hero feels there is something missing about herself, but she cannot name it. She has always felt this way, since she was tiny at her father's knee. He showed her a fly that had landed on the back of his hand. She looked closely, marveling at how small it was, how neat, how industrious as it cleaned its pretty glass wings. She remembers how he smashed it flat with his other hand. He was so fast. He had the reflexes of ten men, and he was a Hero too.

Oh, one other thing that is missing about her is her name . . . a bout of flu stole it from her when she was in her teens, not so long ago. She keeps it written on the inside of her wrist in indelible ink that she rewrites every three days. She doesn't look at it much. Only when someone asks. The coffee barista has his name written on a badge: Marvin.

"Thank you, Marvin," she says as she takes her drink. The establishment is guaranteed clean. Little tablet boxes of Mappacode are sold at the counter, but they don't come under the Infection Bill: too minor, too common and not particularly useful—they offer mnemonic upgrades for popular music charts, fashion, current affairs, and the stock markets so you can always have something to say and know what to buy. The information is stored somehow in proteins that only unfurl when they reach the right places in the brain—the places where Mappaware has created ports for them. They are inert otherwise, and when they have delivered the goods they break up into amino acids and provide spare nutrition. The Girl Hero takes a Mode one and pops it with the first steaming sip of espresso.

The Girl Hero picks at the cardboard band around her coffee cup and goes to take a seat in the window. She is dismayed to learn from the Modey that tweed pencil skirts are in. They are the worst kind of skirt for kicking. She sips and looks around her and wonders for the millionth time if she should save her money and risk a remodel. But she doesn't know what to do if she isn't a Hero. A Hero wouldn't. The preference is disturbing—would she really like it if she hadn't agreed to this job at the careers' meeting? Too late to wonder. It was a road not taken. She will never know who . . . (she looks at the inside of her wrist) . . . Rebecca might have been if she had chosen some different option. She hopes that Rebecca would have wanted to be a Hero anyway.

In the eternal present moment of the Hero's world Rebecca waits, waits, waits for her assignment without anxiety or hope. On other faces she sees various expressions of emotions that fit a task: executives focused and intent on work, an artist dreaming as he stares into nowhere through the wall opposite him, girls bent to their schoolwork rising and falling in the perfectly timed bursts of concentration and relaxation that allow them maximum efficiency in their learning and their fun. They are like seals at play, bobbing in and out of the water. Their chat and laughter rise like bubbles, thinks the Girl Hero, and she feels a twinge of envy, though she had her time and doesn't want it back.

A man in a dark suit as unmemorable as yesterday's news glides past and casually leaves his magazine on her table. She knows him for an Attaché, a man from the ministry who delivers duties to her kind, and that the magazine is a job offer in the eternal post-Mappa economy of the fight against the Cartomancers. She needs a job. She wants to move out of her mother's house.

On page fifty-nine her secret message awaits her. It is typed on tissue paper and all the "o"s are offset, which means it is a mission of the most extreme danger and highest importance. How typical, she thinks, that these things should come together. She rubs some hand cream into her knuckles to hide the thick, dry calluses from years of smashing her fists into concrete walls.

The message instructs her to take a journey to Pointe-Noire, in Congo. It is a place ridden with Cartoxins and the illegal breeding pens of the black-market traders who design animals of exquisite savagery and intelligence for the use of the criminal underworld. Most of them will be remapped for various tasks, and they will not know mercy, fear, or any debilitating survival instinct. Once there she will go to a jungle compound and find a certain man and kill him. He is a bad man. She does not know his crimes, but they are probably something to do with writing or disseminating rogue viruses and/or Maps, because these are now the only crimes there are in the absence of what used to be known as Free Will. It is sure that if he were not so bad he would not be hiding out in such a place in the hopes that nobody would dare to follow. The vestiges of her sympathy for desperate men with missions for mankind are not stirred.

She folds the tissue paper and puts it in her handbag. She goes to the bathroom and has to queue. The bathroom is located in the Self Help section of the bookstore. The Girl Hero has no need for this. She is slightly mystified by the titles, and for the need of books in a world where everything can be eaten. She does not like to look at them. They seem to ask questions of her, and when her back is turned they whisper like schoolchildren.

As she is washing her hands the Girl Hero feels an unpleasant feeling. It is like something scattering inside. She imagines she is made from swarms of rats that have just noticed a terrible thing and are running, running, running for their lives. She often feels this. It is doubt. It comes along after a certain time period when she has had nothing heroic to do. She puts the lid on the toilet down and sits there, taking up someone else's pee time as she gets out a vanity mirror from her handbag and opens it up. One half of the clamshell is an ordinary mirror. The other half has its own face, a kind of pixie that looks exactly like the Girl Hero. It came with the job. She suspects it is a transmitter device that talks directly to her Mappaware to sort out glitches. If she were more dedicated to keeping her appearance groomed than she is, possibly it would deal with her doubts for her.

"Mirror, mirror," says the Girl Hero, and need say no more.

"You want to go," says the mirror. "And you will." It always says this. The Girl Hero finds it very reassuring. She always asks. Her real question has not yet been answered and she doesn't bother to say it, but the mirror replies all the same, "He is not the one."

She closes the mirror and puts it away, satisfied that its prophecies are correct. Despite her bad feeling this encounter will not be the last. She will not die today. A Girl Hero always trusts her mirror.

The Girl Hero goes shopping for a tweed pencil skirt and knee-high boots with heels. On her way to the airport she stops to text her mother that she will be home late, do not save any dinner, she will get some at the takeaway. Her mother is a Perky Waitress and will be satisfied with this latchkey message, not curious, not alarmed; she might bring home plastic boxes filled with peach pie and put them on the countertop for . . . Rebecca . . . to find when she comes in. Peach pie tastes of sweet, fulfilling safety and sleep. Two bites would be enough.

At the check-in desk she sees another Girl Hero, but one with a robot dog companion. She feels a sudden pang of envy and wants to introduce herself, to ask something that brims to her lips with urgent importance, though it can't make itself into words without a listener . . . but the other Hero is in a hurry. She runs off toward a departure gate with a flip of curly brown hair over the top of her practical backpack and grabs up her ammunition clips from the security guard without breaking stride. Her robot dog races beside her.

The Girl Hero . . . Rebecca . . . has no weapons to check. She deals only in kung fu. Her handbag is very small, just big enough for makeup, the mirror, and her phone. She looks up the price of robot dogs while she waits to board her flight. They are expensive. She thinks a real one would be better, but of course there is a problem with quarantine and the endless inoculations. She couldn't possibly afford one. Robots cannot catch diseases, so they are immune to all but the most specific and local of memetic assaults. A robot is much better, but the Girl Hero imagines a warm body, soft fur, regular breathing in a real ribcage moving under her hands, and brown eyes looking at her with unconditional love.

On the flight a man is seated beside her. He makes small talk about her job with the unconscious impulses of all businesspeople. She tells him she is a secretary, which is true, when she is not being a Hero. He sells virtual real estate. He shows her one of the communities he administers: a condo by the sea, to let, all mod cons, barely the cost of a sandwich per month and unlimited online access. He is persuasive, but Heroes are not easily sold. She declines. Her feet swell uncomfortably in the boots. She takes a limousine from the airport to her hotel, where she has a room already booked for her by the ministry.

Pointe-Noire is a township with only a small center adequately defended and habitable. Beyond the line of automatic fire lie teeming swarms of wildlife so bestial and savage, so tightly packed, that every moment of their existence is a matter of do or die. They are the testbed of Hellmemes and other horrors cooked up in the mobile Cartomancy sweatshops that creak and grind through the jungle; metal behemoths covered in solar panels and electrical deterrents.

Beyond the hotel perimeter fence it is still night but will soon be day. In that blue hour there is a slight lull in the slaughter and terror as sleepy creatures of dark trade places with waking creatures of light.

The Girl Hero hires a personal jetcar and lands a few miles from town, close to the house where He lives, this criminal, or whatever he is. Her little capsule glides down within his ranch home's Sphere of Influence—a forcefield of protection maintained by a mini reactor. There are no monsters inside, but two muddy fields of marsh grass and the foot-high remains of stripped trees lie between her and the buildings. She regrets the boots now.

Outside the house there are fences and inside the fences are real dogs, mastiffs with serial killers' eyes. The Girl Hero walks to the gate, pulling her boot heels free of the mud with every step, thinking the leather will be ruined. She does not feel like strangling a dog. Her inner world has become the gray blank place she associates with Heroism. It is familiar and strangely disappointing. She doesn't know what she was expecting from a life devoted to exacting justice and defending the world from evil, but this was not it. Beyond the forcefield at her back the dawn chorus of howls, screams, roars, and whimpers greets the veteran sun.

There's a fence and a gate too. In the gatehouse there is a person. Where there is a person there is an easy way in.

The Girl Hero says she is selling virtual real estate. She shows the guard her mirror and, as he peers at this strange kind of identification, she knocks him unconscious. He crumples without a sound.

Close by two monsters in the forest clash foreheads in a dominance fight, and the air is split by a crack like thunder. If the animals assaulted the shield they could get through it easily, but the shock of sudden pain has always prevented them from making this discovery. As they stumble about, stunned but undaunted by mortal combat, they avoid its gossamer shimmer at all costs. The Girl Hero shakes her head at them.

As she frisks pockets for codes, keys, cards, or whatever the Girl Hero is overcome by a sense of déjà vu. It is one of those nasty moments where, certain this is not a memory, because she has never been here before, she understands it is an omen. She hesitates and feels the man's still-

beating heart under her hand. Her hand forms the shape of a crane's bill and delivers a rapid, extreme strike. It does not break the bone, but it doesn't have to. The shock is sufficient.

She could not have let him live, of course. He would have woken up sooner or later, and she does not know how long she has to be here. She feels mildly surprised at her action, and faintly sad that this is all she feels. Her finger stings her. She looks down and finds she has broken a nail. She spends a moment fixing it with her little kit of glue and tape, packed neatly into a thimble. She has the shakes, however, and her mend does not hold. She tapes the thimble onto the end of her finger instead. It is made of gold and once was the barque of a fairy queen, or so she likes to imagine. The Girl Hero wonders if it will defeat the power of her strike, but she doesn't take it off.

The Girl Hero locates the keys to the inner house and gets into the armored golf cart, which takes her through the fence territory of the dogs. It has sealed sides. The dogs run and bark alongside the cart. The whine of the electric motor is inappropriately cheerful. Insects whirl and scream around in the light, involuntary and designed carriers of diseases to change the mind—they are indistinguishable from the real things. The sun crests over the forest's edge, and a flight of red-winged insectivores takes to the air, flocking in the rising heat in a way that makes the air look syrupy. The Girl Hero takes out her mirror and adjusts her lip gloss. She thinks about what to order from the takeaway and decides she will have a Chinese.

At the end of the golf cart's route she is let into the house by machines who do not care that she is here to kill the master. Like so many of his kind he has run short of henchpersons whose instincts might favor him and now relies on mechanicals. Not popular, thinks the Girl Hero, and frowns a tiny frown to go with her tiny pang of sorrow. On the polished wood of the hallway her boots make hollow sounds.

There is a cook, a person doing some menial tasks, and a man who throws carcasses to the dogs. None of them are interested in stopping her when they see her coming, so the Girl Hero wearily locks them into the storeroom. She makes a note to herself on her mobile, so she does not forget to call help for them once she has left the scene. Lying on the kitchen counter is a plate of cream cakes, freshly defrosted, their chocolate iced tops coated in condensation sweat. She would like to eat them all. With the ease of a lifetime of denial, she barely registers the desire.

The bad man is in the living room, enjoying a glass of juice. His heavy frame is silhouetted against the rapacious sky as he looks out over a balcony toward the thin blue veil of the Sphere and beyond. Whatever he has loaded it with would naturally include a lot of processors to bypass any fear he might feel at her arrival. She feels that this is possibly a meeting of equals, her legally enhanced mind against his self-made one. There is a kind of honor code to be observed.

The Girl Hero puts her handbag on the table. He turns around at the small sound. His eyes begin to measure the distance to the door, but they falter halfway. He has recognized her and that an attempt to escape will be futile. She watches him relax as resignation takes the place of fear in his look. Perhaps it is genuine, but no reaction could be taken at face value in the circumstances. They are already too far along the road of combat.

"Would you like a drink?" he asks. He is wearing some kind of Japanese robe and looks like he has led a full life, she thinks. His short legs are planted firmly. He has no intention of running. Perhaps he will not put up a fight. Her stomach rumbles and she feels a slight pain there. She shakes her head—no. She can't do anything distracting to her, even if she thinks it would be safe—and for some reason she does feel safe now.

He is a long way across the room. She starts to walk.

"Do you know why you are here?"

She assumes he means does she know what he has done. She's not really interested. She shakes her head.

"Do you know why you are?"

The Girl Hero hesitates. He has deployed the Defense of Existential Crisis and she should ignore it boldly, defeat it with a witty and humorous line, but recently she hasn't thought of any of these. She only thinks of them later, long after the person who should have been rebuked is dead. It is her biggest weakness. She has read books of aphorisms, but *A lot of knowledge fits an empty head* seems inappropriate and is the only thing that comes to mind.

"I am a poet," he says.

It seems unlikely, she thinks. Why would anyone want to kill a poet? But, then again, why not? "Was your verse offensive?" she asks. Why did she engage? The only sensible thing to do is to break his neck and leave. What is she talking for? She adds quickly, "It isn't important. You are on the list."

"Do you know your masters and their ideas, Girl?" he asks, backing away rapidly as she advances with a firm, librarian's tread. His voice gets a bit higher, but it remains steady. "Do you know why you don't want to know?"

"It's not my place," she says, and unaccountably finds she has stopped walking. She does know why. She has *chosen* not to know.

There are two sides to this war of memes: the side of the Directive, which advocates managed and secure social design for the safety and well-being of all, and the side of the Cartomancers, which wants anarchy at any cost, a free market without limits. Both of them have to contend with the Wild in which Mappaware and Mappacode have become attached to the genetic strands not only of their original carriers, the viruses, but also bacteria. There is no doubt it will soon spread (if it hasn't already) into the DNA of larger species. The Girl Hero never had gotten her head quite around the science or the politics of it. It's not a Hero's business to do all the thinking about the rights and wrongs. Her remit is much smaller. Justice for the wrongdoer and safety for the calm world of Perky Waitresses, Secretaries, and peach pie. And whiskery skittery rats.

The Bad Man takes a nervous sip of juice. The scream and murder of the jungle increases as the full circle of the sun appears clear of the trees. What a dreadful place, thinks the Girl Hero. She realizes she has reached a kind of stalemate but doesn't understand why she can't break it. She watches the Bad Man drink and set down his glass carefully on a coaster on a nice, smooth table.

"What's your name?"

She didn't expect this question even though an effort to become more intimate with an attacker who is more powerful is an obvious tactic. She opens her mouth, determined to answer, but nothing comes out. She looks to the inside of her wrist. She shouldn't tell him, so she keeps her mouth shut. "Rebecca" rings no bells for her. It could be a barcode for all it means. Her stomach starts to gnaw at her.

"I'm Khalid," he says, and nods with a faint, social smile. He glances at her wrist, and a moment of pity firms his lips.

A vicious streak of envy cuts across her mouth like the taste of lemon. Suddenly she wants the reassurance of the mirror, that tonight is not the night, but she left her bag on the table. It gets in the way and drags her arm when she has to punch.

"Wouldn't you like to understand what happened to you?"

"What is this, exam night?" She is determined not to be distracted by flimsy philosophizing. She doesn't care about the answers to his tiresome inquiries, but for some reason she thinks about the books, snickering behind her back. She wants to go home, get duck in plum sauce, get a shower, give her mother a cup of tea, and go to bed. In the morning she has work again because it is still three days until the weekend. Besides, the answer to his question is surely obvious. She says it without knowing she's going to until she starts, "I caught a bad purge. That's all. No big. Look." She flashes her wrist at him.

"Everything in the world and the Wild is written, Rebecca, just like your name," he says. He keeps a close watch on her, and she on him, in case he runs away, in case she doesn't.

Damn, she sees he has reached the wall. His free hand darts with the speed of desperation toward a control hidden there. He fumbles. She darts across the gap, jumps, and kicks. Her skirt rips. Her boots are too tight. She knocks him aside but lands on her ass. Some kind of alarm is sounding like a bleating goat. Angry with herself she glares at him.

"The Sphere control," he says with satisfaction. "In a minute it will vanish and the Wild will come in." His face is pasty under its smooth olive plumpness, but triumphant.

She sees clearly that a lot now stands between her and the evening she had planned. She looks out, to where her car is hidden, beyond the cleared land. One minute? "But my mirror says you're not the one," she tells him firmly. Suddenly her belief in the mirror is wavering.

She looks into the eyes of the bad man. He looks back at her, without attempting to move. She says, "If you reset the device I will let you live." She tells herself she does not mean it. She hasn't made a mistake. She wouldn't betray the contract. A Hero would do what it takes to save the world.

"I think you will not," says the bad man, becoming amused.

"Don't just lie there," she says, lying there.

"Why not?" he asks. "I can see up your skirt from here. Nice underwear."

"I mean it," she says, meaning it to her own surprise. "I will let you live."

"Ah, thanks," he says, "but if it wasn't you, it would just be some other Girl Hero coming along in a day or two, and I've done my time. There's nothing left I want to do I haven't done, and I'm not much for repeats. The Directive has no real defense against the Cartomancy, and neither have a chance against the Wild, not in the end. The life of ideas is already a literal thing. We used to transmit them inadequately with words, and soon they will transmit themselves through nature, through biology, in ways that bypass what small shred of choice may ever have existed. So, I think I'll just stay here, if it's all the same to you. It's a bit more satisfying if you die along with me than if you get to escape, and I wish I was a bit different but I was free of the Map all my life and I have to bow to my taste for justice in my own way. I hope you can understand that."

"But I want to live!" the Girl Hero says.

"I don't think so," Khalid observes. His voice is mild. "I knew when you walked in and hesitated that you were the one."

The bleat alarm goes off. Without it the mindless fury beyond the Sphere seems twice as loud. The Girl Hero leaps to her feet and tries the device by the window. She cannot make it work. The blue tissue of force begins to fade. The blazing ruddy glare of beyond starts to color it a deep purple. The Girl Hero thinks about the cakes on the counter, the innocent dogs, the people in the storeroom, her mother.

She glares down at him. "Why didn't they stop the Wild a long time ago?"

He shrugs. She sees that he does not know. "The day it was discovered there was a faster way to change people's minds than simply by talk or the gun, then it was already decided. If you were hoping for a final insight into human nature . . ." He trails off and looks distracted as the color of the room changes from a soft shadowy umber to bright yellow. The Sphere has gone.

The Girl Hero makes a dive and slides the length of the table. She picks up her handbag and takes out her mirror. She no longer has the gray, flat feeling of Heroism, and she wants to see if that has changed her face.

It has. The incipient wrinkles at the edges of her eyes and between her brows have gone. She is as smooth and pretty as she was the first day she took up office. On the other side of the mirror the pixie looks out toward the clear edge of the forest where it seems that a starving, boiling mass of vegetable and animal is slowly billowing toward them.

"Oh my," says the mirror. "Look out! He's getting away."

The Girl Hero feels a surge of desperation and anger quite unusual for her. She spins around just in time to catch sight of Khalid slithering through the narrow black gap of a secret doorway he has opened in the paneling. She is after him like a shot, but her muddy feet slip a little and she can't grab hold of him as she intended. She makes it through the gap anyway and runs through the narrow, wooden corridor after him, her skirt seam ripping a bit more up the thigh with every furious stride. How could she fall for a distraction? How could she have entertained the idea that he was telling the truth about never having acquired the Map? Just look at this ridiculous compound with its guards and gates and dogs and cook. Listen to him give his Villainous Speech. She and he are both products of Stock Narrative 101, however many upgrades and individual variations they may have acquired . . . and now her rage is like hell itself.

The corridor winds and slopes down. Khalid skids and loses a shoe. The escape chute opens to a broad decking with an escape car tethered to it, its air bladder fully primed with helium. The engines tick over, its rotors whir softly in the thick and humid air. Khalid is forced to pause, hand fighting his pocket for the key. The Girl Hero cocks her arm and throws the mirror in a dead flat spin. It strikes him on the back of the head and he falls to his knees. Around him the broken bright pieces scatter, fragments of sky.

"I want to see what's real!" she screams. "Why did you have to be a liar?" She is crying. This is impossible. She needs the mirror, and rushes up to him. She tries to pick up the pieces, but behind the glass all the circuitry is broken. There should be some word for what she feels when she looks at him, a word not like "fuchsia" or "madder" or "carmine" or "rose" or "sugar" or "candy." It should be a word for rats turning and scuttling back with red eyes, teeth bared, tails like little ramrods. Maybe the word is "Rebecca."

Khalid blinks at her with panic beginning to make him sweat. "What did you expect?" He had located the key.

The car door opens as a wave of warm air, full of thunder, ripples slowly across them. Rain starts to fall and there comes the screeching and shrilling of agony, the sputter of electrical things and burning fur as creatures test the weakening perimeter fence. Khalid snatches a mask from his pocket and wraps it across his face with his free hand as he scrabbles to his feet. He makes a lunge for the door. The Girl Hero watches him with the Rebecca feeling and jumps after. She makes the sill and he attempts to push her out backward, but he's weak, a big soft geek type who's all brain and no brawn. She kicks him in the chest and slams the door after them.

"Take me with you," she says. "They'll send other Heroes. You need me."

He looks up from the floor and croaks, "I did okay so far . . ."

"You were dead when I walked in the door. And if you say no, you still are," the Girl Hero assures him, picking him up by the shirtfront and hauling him to the passenger seat of the little craft. "Shit," she says, safe, for now. "What about your people? Can't leave them . . ."

"Have to leave them," he gasps, still winded. "No time."

No Hero would ever leave them.

Khalid slams a hand to the controls, and the car begins to lift off. "Anyway, why should you care? Killed enough for a lifetime . . ."

She opens her mouth to protest, but the breath she took doesn't go anywhere, just leaves her inflated. As she delays the aircar rises smoothly into the sky above the treetops. From the windshield she can see the dogs running back and forth in their prison, barking.

"You should let them out," she said, sitting down slowly in the pilot's seat. "It's cruel to keep dogs that way." They fly for a time in silence, avoiding the Directive Patrols but with no other plan.

"Can you ever get rid of it?" Rebecca asks in a quiet voice. "Mappaware? Ever?"

"You can tell it not to work," Khalid says. "That's all." He hands over a small black box shaped like a cigarette pack with a single button on it. "We use them a lot. When you get too much infestation you go unstable. This clears it. Then you start again."

Rebecca remembers him fumbling in his pockets. Zap. Not the door. Her. "You got me."

Khalid nodded. "And me. Works in a range."

Rebecca presses the button, over and over. Nothing happens. "Now what? Why aren't I different then?"

"That takes time," he says, sighing wearily. "Lots of time. Have to grow, think, do things . . . take more code or not . . . left alone you'll change on your own."

"Like in the old days." She puts the box into her own pocket, which is almost too small. She wishes she had not forgotten her bag. For a moment she thinks about Chinese food and her home, all the stuffed animals in a row, her mother's scent. . . . "Where to?"

Khalid shrugs. "I wait until I pick up a beacon. Most likely spot is still over the Congo area somewhere. Just follow the river."

"And then?"

"Set down, make new friends in the Cartomancy, carry on. . . . Write something, test it, purge it. Try to figure out how to create antimemes against the worst plagues . . . not much."

Rebecca nods. It's not much, but it is enough.

KAREN HEULER

THE COMPLETELY RECHARGEABLE MAN

(2008)

HE WAS INTRODUCED as Johnny Volts, and most guests assumed he was a charlatan—the hostess, after all, was immensely gullible. But some of the guests had seen him before, and they said he was good, lots of fun, very "current"—a joke that got more mileage than it should have.

"Do you need any kind of extension cord?" the hostess, Liz Pooley, asked. She wore a skin-tight suit of emerald lamé, and had sprayed a lightning bolt pattern in her hair, in his honor.

Johnny Volts sighed and then smiled. They all expected him to be something like a children's magician—all patter and tricks. "No extension cord," he said. "Where can I stand?" He caught his hostess's frown. "I need an area to work in—and appliances, not plugged in. I'm the plug. No microwaves. A blender, a radio, a light bulb. Christmas lights?"

The guests were charmed at first and then, inevitably, they were bored. Even if it wasn't a trick, it was pretty limited. He could power a light, but not a microwave. He could charge

your cell phone but not your car. He was an early adopter of some sort, that was all; they would wait for the jazzed-up version.

Johnny Volts had a pacemaker with a rechargeable battery, and he had a friend who was a mad scientist. This friend had added a universal bus to his battery port, and hence Johnny Volts had a cable and a convertible socket. He could plug things in; he could be plugged in. This was a parlor trick as far as the public was concerned—and a strange, unsettling, but still somewhat interesting way of earning a living as far as Johnny Volts was concerned. He knew—he understood—that his pacemaker powered his heart, and his heart recharged the pacemaker in a lovely series of perpetual interactions. He had no issue with it.

In Liz Pooley's party, as Johnny Volts lit a lamp, turned on a clock radio, and charged an iPod, he was watched by a frowning man in a checked shirt whose companion seemed quite happy with Johnny.

"Why he's worth his weight in gold," she said. "Imagine never having to pay an electric bill."

"Small appliances," the man grunted.

"Well *now* it's small appliances, Bob, but he's just the first. Wait till he can really get going, he'll have his own rocket pack. Remember rocket packs, Bob? The Segway of long-lost memory." She put her hand on Bob's arm and rolled her eyes. "I was but a mere child of course, when I heard about those rocket packs. Shooting us up in the air. A new meaning to the term Jet Set, hey? Or is that phrase too old? I bet it's too old. What are we called now, Bob?" She lifted her drink, saluted him, and winked.

"We're called only when they've run out of everyone else, Cheree." Bob was idly thinking about what would bring a man to this: plugging in small irrelevant things into his own violated flesh. "Irrelevant," he said finally. "They call us irrelevant."

Cheree frowned. "You're turning into an old man, Bob. You've lost your spark." She gave him a small motherly peck on the cheek and walked forward, powerfully, her lemon martini firm in her hand, straight to Johnny Volts, who was looking around, waiting to be paid. "You looking for a drink?" she asked. "I could get you one."

"Oh—well, all right," he said, surprised.

"You wait right here," she said. "I want to know all about you, electric man." And she turned until she found a server and came back with a dark liquid in a tumbler. "Now tell me—how does it feel? I mean you're generating electricity, aren't you?"

"Yes. Not much. After next week it should be more. I'm having an upgrade."

"Lovely. How does it feel? Like little bugs up and down your spine?" She had a heady grin, a frank way of working. Johnny liked it.

"It's a beautiful kind of pressure," he said. "It feels like I could fill the room with it, lift everything up, kind of explode—only I hold on to the explosion." His eyes got internal.

"Do you like it?"

He was open-mouthed with surprise. "Yes. Of course. It's wonderful."

She tilted her head a little, studying his face, and he found it embarrassing at first, and then he got used to it. He looked back at her, not lowering his eyes or glancing away. She was older than he was, but she had a bright engaging air about her, as if she made a point of not remembering anything bad.

"Here you go," the hostess said, her arm held out full length with a check at the end of it like a flattened appendage.

Johnny took it and turned to leave. "Hey!" Cheree said, grabbing at his arm a little. "That's rude. Not even a fond farewell?"

"They usually want me to leave right away," he said in explanation. "Before I get boring."

"Boring," she said companionably as they headed together for the door. "That bunch? They think *other* people are boring?"

He noted that she was walking along with him as if she belonged there. "So where do you see yourself in five years?" she asked. "That's a test question. So many people can't think ahead."

"Do you think ahead?"

"Not me. I'm spontaneous. Then again, I'm not at all electric, so I don't have to worry about running out of juice."

"I don't run out," he said. "I recharge. And I'm getting an upgrade to photovoltaic cells next week. I have to decide where to implant them; do you mind if I run it past you?" He rubbed his hand over his head as they took the elevator down. "The obvious thing is to replace my hair—it's a bit of a jolt, though. I can lose it all and get a kind of mirror thing on top—a shiny bald pate, all right. Or fiber-optic hair. But it will stick out. Like one of those weird lamps with all the wires with lights at the end? What do you think?"

"Fiber-optic hair," she said without hesitation. "Ahead of the times. Fashion-forward. I bet there'll be a run on the hardware store."

He stopped—they were on the street—and frowned at her. "Your name?"

"Cheree."

"Cheree, you're glib."

"I am glib, Johnny," she said in a soft voice. "It's because my head doesn't stop. You know the brain is all impulses, don't you? Bang and pop all over the place. Well, mine is on super-drive, I have to keep talking or I'll crack from all the thinking. The constant chatter . . . I can only dream of stillness."

He shook his head in sympathy. "That sounds like static." He stopped and reached out for her hand. "Maybe you produce energy all your own?" She held her hand out, and Johnny hesitated, then touched the tips of their fingers together. He closed his eyes, briefly. There was a warmth, a moistness, a lovely *frisson*. He took a deep breath. He felt so tired after those parties, but now a delicious delicate rejuvenation spread through him. The back of his neck prickled; the hairs on his arms—even his eyebrows—hairs everywhere rose, he could feel it in his follicles. It rose up in him until suddenly Cheree was thrown backward slightly.

"What was that?" she said tensely.

He nodded. "Sorry. Volts. A little discharge. It won't hurt you."

"Still," she said uneasily. "Can't say I know what to make of it."

They were at a crossroads, specifically Houston and Lafayette. "Where do you live?" he asked.

"East Seventh."

"I'm uptown." They stood for a moment in silence. "Will you come with me?" he asked finally.

Her face broke into a smile, like a charge of sunshine.

They were utterly charming together, they were full of sparks. Toasters popped up when they visited their friends—though did people really still have toasters? Wasn't that, instead, the sound of CD players going through their discs, shuffling them? Wasn't it the barely audible purr of the fan of a car as they passed it, sitting up and noticing as if it were a dog? They were attractive, after all; they attracted.

"If we moved in together," Johnny said after they'd known each other for a month, "we'd have half the bills. We could live on very little, we could live on what I make at the parties. You wouldn't have to work as a waitress. In fact, we could be free."

"And give up my dreams of rocket science?" she asked, her eyebrows arched.

"I thought you were a waitress."

"That's just till I sell my first rocket." Nevertheless, she decided to move in, and it was working out fine, except for the strange way that objects behaved around them.

Small electrics followed them like dogs sometimes—they could turn down the block and hear a clanking or a scraping behind them. Eager little cell phones, staticky earphones, clicking electronic notepads gathered in piles on their doorstep.

"We have to figure out a budget," Cheree said after she moved in. "Until I sell that rocket. Rent, not much we can do. We should get bikes, that will save on transportation. But, you know, we're still paying for electricity, and it's pretty high, too. What do we really use it for?"

Together, they went through their apartment, noting: refrigerator, lamps, clock, radio, stereo, TV, microwave, coffee maker, hair dryer, iron, laptop computer.

"Well," Johnny said. "All quite useful in their own way, but we can make coffee without electricity. And I already recharge the computer myself."

She considered it all. "You can recharge most of it, really, if we get the right kind of thing. If we look at everything that way—I'm sure there are rechargeable lamps, for instance—why are we paying electric bills? We could save a lot of money by doing it ourselves."

They canceled their energy provider, a savings right there of $70 a month. They would plug a different item into Johnny at night, so they would never run out. It was a brilliant solution.

That gave him even more motivation for the photovoltaic upgrade. When he went to his mad scientist friend, she went with him, and they mentioned the strange way they seemed to be accumulating electrical appliances. The mad scientist was sitting across from them, taking down Johnny's recap of the past few months, when the scientist felt his skin begin to tingle. He shook himself briefly, as if buzzed by a fly. He was a graduate student at Carnegie Mellon, a Mexican genius who did illegal cable and satellite hookups to make some money, and was always looking over his shoulder. Johnny Volts was his ticket to fame and fortune; once the process was perfect, he would offer it to a medical or electronics company and bring millions down to his hometown of Tijuana, where he would go to retire.

The scientist ran a voltmeter over Cheree and whistled. "This is lovely," he said. "Exciting, even." He grinned at Johnny. "She's got a field. You see, you two match. You kind of amplify each other—understand?" He looked at them happily, waiting for them to catch up with his thinking. "You match."

It took a moment. "You're saying we're related? Like siblings?"

"Oh—no, no, I mean your energy matches. It doesn't mean anything really, other than that you're sensitive to each other's waves. You two have sympathetic electricity—I'm making the term up—so you use less energy when you're together than you do when you're apart, because you're actually *attracting* each other's charge. The byproduct is, you attract things that charge. Get it?"

"Oh, honey, yes," Cheree said. "I get it." It was like their little electric hearts went thudder-thump when they came near each other. Cheree was aware of it as a little sizzle in her brain.

They noticed a few things: He was a thoughtless hummer, and when he hummed he gave her a headache. She was an adventurer, wanting to go out and about, here, there, and everywhere, while he liked to think and write and test how strong his recharging was.

It happened gradually, the feeling that they were being watched, were being followed. She

had coffee and a man who looked familiar sat opposite her in the café. He went to a party and saw the same man in a different suit watching him carefully. His apartment door was dusted with a fine powder one morning; the following week it was on a window.

When they went out in the morning, there was always a bunch of people passing their front door. Jauntily, as if just interrupted, they were speeding away, toward, around, moving with a great deal more purpose than on any other block. "Have you noticed it?" Cheree asked, and Johnny nodded. "I asked the landlord, and he said there's been some kind of gas leak, they're checking the lines a lot more. Even went into the basement, he said, all up and down the block."

"A gas leak?" she said, sniffing. "I don't smell anything."

"Well, that's good then."

• • •

But then Johnny disappeared. Went out to a party and didn't come back, and when she called the number listed in his daybook, she was told he hadn't shown up.

Cheree buzzed in her head when she was near Johnny; she could feel the tingle coming on when she turned the corner, half a block away, so it wasn't surprising that she felt she could find him. She said to herself: these are the things I know: He has a charge, and I can sense it. He has a head of fiber-optic hair. And I am his magnet.

She took her bike and rode slowly, up and down streets, starting with the top of the island. Her head refused to buzz, block after block, in traffic and out, but then, after three hours—just as she rounded the corner near the docks on the West Side—she heard a tang, she felt a nibble at her brain. It was him. She biked forward, back, left and right, testing out the buzzing, following it to the door of a small garage dealing in vintage cars.

She parked her bike and chained it. She noticed an electric toothbrush rolling on the sidewalk.

She walked up to a man in a very neat jump-suit. She didn't know anything about vintage cars. "I have to get a present for my dear old dad," she said. "He loves cars. I thought maybe we could all—he had two families, so there's plenty of children—get together and buy him something smashing." She grinned.

He shrugged. "You can take a look at what we've got, but my gut says you're out of your league."

She smiled at him steadily, looking around, her eyes skipping to the doorway to an office or a back room. She could feel Johnny's electric kick. She walked around the cars slowly until his charge was at its strongest. She whipped around "I know you have him," she said, and drew in her breath, kicking a chair over to trip him as he lunged forward. She bolted for the door, which was unlocked, and burst in.

There was Johnny, in the corner of the room. They had him wired up to machines that beeped and spit, they had his arm strapped to a chair.

"I'm all right," Johnny said when he saw her. She stopped, uncertainly, in the middle of the room.

"What's going on?"

The man in the garage was behind her, and two men came at her from the side. They were all dressed in white jumpsuits, with ties showing through their zippered fronts. "We're from the collection agency," one man said. "For unlawful theft of electricity."

"We don't need to *pay* for electricity," she said. "We only use our own."

"Ha," he said. "You don't own it. You're just stealing it and not paying for it. You know what? We put meters into and out of your apart-ment, just to make sure. You were off the charts! We could hear the volts clicking! Don't tell me you're not using electricity!"

"I tried to explain—" Johnny said wearily.

"Did you plug into him yet?" Cheree inter-rupted. "Then you'll see." She looked around and picked up a small calculator on a desk, plugging it into Johnny's socket. It whirred on, but the jumpsuits looked impassive. She began

to enter numbers faster and faster, until finally she rang up Total. "See?" she said, as the men stepped forward almost politely, glancing at the strip of paper (who had such old calculators, anyway?) that had curled out the top.

"Nice," the second man concluded. He reached into his pocket. "I'm not with them," he said. "I'm with NASA and we think you might have stolen a restricted project. We're going to have to take you with us for national security." He offered his card.

"Hold on there," said the third man, "I'm with the Office of Ocean Exploration. You can't take him, see here—I've got a signed order to bring him in for questioning." He shook his head. "I mean it's an invitation. We admire the strides he's made in making a self-sustaining renewable resource." He gave a business card to Johnny and one to Cheree.

The first man took out a gun. "He's not going anywhere. He's been taking electricity and we *own* electricity. It's that simple. You can't take him because he's going to jail, our own facilities in a state-approved housing unit until his case comes to trial."

Johnny hung his head and groaned. "I'm no use to any of you," he said. "These fiber-optic hairs—they're no use underwater, you know—they need the sun to recharge. Totally useless." The NOAA man looked a little annoyed at that, but he said, "Who said you had to be *under* the water; maybe they want you *on top* of the water?" but even he looked skeptical.

"Plus, he's on a pacemaker," Cheree said. "You can't have a pacemaker in orbit, if that's what you were thinking. You'd kill him; what good would that be?"

The electric company man was looking increasingly smug. "That leaves me," he said with a smile. "And all I want is for the bill to be paid. Plus interest and penalties."

"There is no bill," Johnny said wearily. "We canceled our account months ago. No account, no bills."

"That's not how it works. You think electric-ity is free? Like air? Like water? Like land? Are any of those free?" He waved Cheree aside as she said, "Air! Air is free!"

"Nothing's free," he said. "The factories pay us for the air they pollute, and you have to pay for cleaning it—one way or another, someone's paying for it. As for electricity, that's never been free since Franklin put a key on a chain. Right now, you're stealing our business by interfering with a regulated industry without a license. It's against the law." He looked very merry about it. "I lied about our state-sanctioned facilities. You just go to jail, same as the scammers and the knockoff artists, and you can light your hair up all you want and see what it gets you!" He laughed then, thinking about the possible results.

"And you agree with this?" Cheree asked the men from NASA and NOAA. They looked at each other and shrugged. "Nothing in it for us," one said. "We don't interfere in the private sector," said the other.

"Then it's just you," Cheree said to the last man, who looked at the others with contempt.

"It's okay," he said, reaching into his pocket. "I'm a reasonable man." He held out a taser gun. "And this is a perfectly legal means of protecting myself."

Cheree looked at it and grinned. She glanced up and saw Johnny's face. "Johnny Volts," she said, cooing to him. "Johnny, sing to me!"

Johnny began to hum, and she decided to join him, sympathetically. The men in jumpsuits felt the hairs on their necks begin to rise, then their leg hairs, then their head hairs. The man from the electric company looked around wildly, then took a step toward Johnny, his taser outstretched.

The taser suddenly snapped and shot a small series of electric arcs out into the air until the utilities man yelped and dropped it. Cheree released Johnny, who rose from his seat and said, "Sorry. But there was a buildup. And Cheree is an amplifier. And I think I got a shot of adrenaline or something that caused an overload."

The other two men looked at each other.

"Time to go, I think," one said and the other nodded. They walked off together slowly, as if not wanting to make a sudden move.

"I'm really sorry," Johnny said to the man writhing on the floor.

"If I could get up I'd clobber you," the energy man said. "This isn't over. I'll hunt you down and do something." He panted. "Just as soon as I can move again."

• • •

They followed the mad scientist down to Mexico, all of them imagining the utilities man hot on their trail. Even Tijuana seemed unsafe, so the mad scientist took them to a small town in the mountains, where he continued his work.

He gave Cheree a pacer, too, and he linked their charge, which was now big enough to fire a microwave, if there'd been a microwave around. But they had a bigger plan. In their mad dash down to the border they'd seen how much gasoline cost; wasn't Johnny the wave of the future and the future's savior? And wouldn't the mad scientist get rewards and jobs and money up the wazoo if he could find a way to recharge a car without looking for an outlet?

He plugged Johnny into the car he rigged up and called it the Voltswagon. Johnny could only get it to move slowly at first; but once the mad scientist hooked up Cheree to Johnny, and Johnny to the car, they were able to whiz to Tijuana and back at a merry clip. It took four years, but the cars ran and Johnny and Cheree were unharmed, and the mad scientist refined the recharging process to accommodate one person for one car.

Little by little they converted the inhabitants of Tijuana to fiber-optic hair and plug-in Voltswagons. Big Oil shut down the borders to keep Americans from going to Mexico to buy cars, but late at night, and hidden in the back of trucks, Americans snuck across the border to buy their Voltswagons and bring them home.

CHRISTIAN KIRTCHEV

FILE: THE DEATH OF DESIGNER D.

(2009)

THE DESIGNER D. had killed herself on 29 August 2004. The mystery around the suicide—or murder—is still not solved, but next to the body her boyfriend had found some "last" messages. Unclear if sent or not, they were an e-mail message and a few random digital photos. What killed D.? Was it really a suicide?

In the last few months, she didn't get along well with many of her people and even avoided contact with her closest girlfriends and old friends. On one of the found photos, D. was holding a cigarette, sitting on a tattered sofa in the attic room of a private building behind the Gallery of Arts. On another picture, there was her ex-ex-lover, whom a girlfriend of hers had warned that he would fuck her, most likely when drunk, then dump her. In the text of the left letter could be read the following short paragraph:

. . . because our system is so chaotic and confused, that there's not even a system at all to confront with—everything is chaos. In the parliament there are parties and politicians which don't know where to lead the country to. There's no order. All is an empty signature field for something that I don't know whether to stand for or against . . . this is political, a social fight. My fellow citizens are in a big portion just ferocious, enraged, or pusillanimous and primitive—so much that if it wasn't for the peasants that make me go mad for their aggression and simplicity, there would be the colleagues who bring their primal aggression to the office, along with their ties and gray lemmings suits, to again protect the stupidity of fighting for survival. This fight is false; little are the people who, like me, would support life, the pure life and none are those who would fight to save the feelings of another. In this cold world, I would die, if . . .

On the floor where they found the body of the philosophy student and political adventurer, designer D., there was an old, crumpled newspaper in which she rolled the joint that some of her guests smoked in that loft. On the front page, in a side column for weekly news, there was the story of how all the governments of the world had joined around the new law, which four years ago absolutely forbid the use of natural fur for the production of clothing. With that same law, police increased their powers to arrest and detain any citizen found wearing clothes made of leather or fur. All affected manufacturing plants were obliged to transform themselves into producers of coats made of synthetic polyurethane or other high-tech materials. Not a single man in the world would want a coat made of leather or animal fur, and now he wouldn't be an outlaw for that.

A simultaneously passed law also forbade the manufacture of items for which wood is used; so, all manufacturers in the world made the transition to synthetics during the twenty-first century, and nations all over the planet welcomed this governmental decision to protect the available flora and fauna. There was just one more decision to be made—for the meat produce—and that wasn't far off. In Bulgaria, though, as well as in many other places in the world, the law was just theoretical and only observed by those who couldn't afford to buy a corrupt judge; thus, just as with car traffic, those who are outlaws are the poor. It was unlikely for this to be the only reason for D. to end her life, but many of those who knew her personally would interpret her psyche in a specific way; they themselves didn't understand D. completely, and that's what justified their helplessness to participate in her life.

The question about the mysterious murder remained unsolved, even for her closest friend, the one whom she loved. She was too busy, nervous, and preoccupied with avoiding society to be able to answer his love, but still she understood him. K. examined the left-behind digital pictures and e-mail, then called the police. He was the first one to enter her lodging room after the suicide, thus he started dialing numbers to find out if the designer D. had spoken with someone before her death.

On February 28, she had a fight with her sister during an intimate meeting over coffee. Her employer had refused to pay cash in advance for her salary, which was a source of great irritation for her. D.'s sister needs medicine but doesn't have the money to buy it, so she doesn't read the newspaper or the electronics from the advertisement pages between the news in the papers.

"The main misery of the little mediocre people," D. used to say, "is that the model of life, which corporations dictate through media and advertisement, makes you want to want things—mostly electronic things, which, in contemporary life, are associated not that much with prestige, but with necessity. And when you cannot afford to own these 'basic' items associated with necessity, you buy alcohol, drugs, and the latest model of the cheapest DVD that breaks down and brings you the 'Disease.'"

This "Disease"—as D. calls it—is, for most people, the aim for the most basic attainment of ownership: to work for products of civilization (i.e., the corporation), meaning that food becomes a second-place necessity. Also, for you to be happy involves not listening to music, but listening to it on the latest model device. Maybe from a zoological point of view on people and animals, this would have been a sickness, a state of disease; the designer D. felt guilty, though, because she was the designer of advertisement and ergonomics for those very same products that brought people to psychic and physical illness, as well as material madness.

K. knew that, and many times he tried to convince D. that this was just the way life is, that this was the system—the world people really wanted. Even though he couldn't console her, at least he managed to bring her peace for a little while in the beginning. The escalation of the problem, though, was leading designer D. toward madness. Could it be that she had angered someone from the corporate structures for which she worked as freelance contractor? Could it be they had ordered her . . . death?

To produce advertisements for an illness—with skills you can't otherwise use if you want to have a job at all—wasn't looking that bad for those already affected by the disease; for D., though, this was a road to madness. Depressed with thoughts that if she drew designs, composed music, or edited films she wouldn't be able to make a living—D. just kept on forcing herself to produce advertisements and charming designs for products that tempted and inspired people. She believed that she assisted in lying that it was not madness, but rather the most natural state of existence is to own products, and the most beautiful way to live is to participate in the consumer's cult. Those weren't cheap products; the cheap ones were prone to break easily. The expensive products made those men and women who didn't belong to the corporate apparatus get poorer. The world was divided into two parts: sick and healthy, corporate citizens and free radicals, and even the free radicals—who weren't affected by the sickness enslaving the corporate consumers—still needed "things" to survive in the predominant part of society, a society that demanded either participation or death.

In the letter that designer D. left behind, she mentioned that in Bulgaria there doesn't exist a system against which one can rebel. The chaos in the parliament had placed her in an even bigger state of confusion, while the impasse oppressed her slowly and drove her out of the society of peasants and primitive citizens.

The police had found the revolver in D.'s hand with one pinned, fired cartridge in the chamber, but K. still wasn't convinced it was a suicide. True, D. was very distanced and desperate in the last few weeks, but still she held out hope that the world would change.

"No, I don't want the world to change! I know that my values are humane. I'm not ill with the sickness of materialism and consumerism, but I feel that the disease starts to possess me, as I live in a world which cannot be different. A world modeled by powers abusing our basic instincts and wants. People made their choice to become what they are—alone. But I believe this is meant to be just a transition, a difficult transformation through a period beyond which everyone will be a better self."

Designer D. didn't want to believe that she is the sick one and that those who turned their backs on humane values were the healthy. Our world may have been such that D. was placed in a state of describing herself as an abnormal outsider—but not in her country! In Bulgaria, there wasn't any sort of regime—or so she thought; the whole system of the country is messed up, but in this exact detail was hidden the secret: the feature of imported culture is to influence, taking advantage of all uncertainty in Bulgaria. And, when there is not order in your country, the first to impose order gets the right to enforce veto on all future decisions. A sterile ecology and consumerism ideology: the universal combination of ideal conditions for physical existence in a clean world with the imposed psychological values dictated by product manufacturers. All products made equal by importance with the basic necessities in life such as air, water, and food. D. had the understanding for that, and she would often talk about her feelings on the subject when she sought the comfort of her friends.

Maybe the corporate structures knew about D. Or perhaps the fight with her sister—could that have been the reason for a murder? A murder made by someone sick, a murder targeting the only one seen as the cure to narcotic dependence?

While looking at the photos, K. had an urge to delete them, but in the twilight of the room, while he was waiting for the police detectives—and eventually emergency—to arrive, K. could only sit by the phone and stare through the window toward the tops of the gallery's towers.

Why did the young designer D. kill herself? A fight with her boss? Her sister gone mad and shooting her, then placing the gun in her hand? All of us—one way or another—felt what D. was feeling, but she couldn't distance herself from that, she wouldn't want to close her senses, nor accept them. Many like the system as it is, without approving it; a world inside the world, in the isolation of their own sphere of friends and relatives, without direct links. But D. had to work in this system, to be a part of the regime that she hated for two years before severing all links to reality, giving herself over to drinking Absinth and watching the display of her creative console.

At that moment, K. didn't know whether he loved or hated her. Most likely, he hated her, but a very slight thought that she was possibly murdered made him look with respect toward the body, the scattered digital photos, and the electronic mail message next to the bloody revolver. Was the shot fired during the night, or the day?

JEAN RABE

BETTER THAN

(2010)

MOSES LOVED THE NIGHT. Not because he could see better in it—which he could due to various enhancements in his cybereyes—but because that was when the snakes crawled out onto the sidewalks.

Moses loved to watch the snakes.

Pink, grass-green, blue, Day-Glo yellow, purple, they slithered into the low spots still filled with rainwater from the late afternoon deluge. They shimmied into splotches of beer and butted up against pretzel pieces puked from the drunkards tossed out of bars along Western Avenue. They slipped into puddles of piss provided by Seattle's vagrants.

Reflections from the neon signs was all they were, so his chummer Taddeus had said.

But Moses thought they looked like real snakes—beautiful, colorful, electric, eclectic, squirming, mesmerizing, fireworks-come-to-ground-just-for-his-very-own-pleasure snakes.

He stood on the corner of Western and Seneca, eyes locked onto a thick cherry and grape striped snake that twisted seductively in the water pooled between his size-eleven feet. He liked this city because it rained almost every day.

The snakes only came out for the water.

"And the child grew, and she brought him unto Pharaoh's daughter, and he became her son. And she called his name Moses: and she said, Because I drew him out of the water." Moses liked that particular Exodus quote because of the water part. His father was a minister in Renton, a fire-and-brimstone Baptist . . . or was that Lutheran . . . who'd named all his children after significant folks from the Bible. Ruth was the oldest, followed by Jacob, Abraham, and Isaac. Moses was the youngest, and the only one who'd remained wholly human. Father said it was a sign that Moses was destined for great things. Moses thought it was a curse. He didn't have his sister's naturally keen hearing or Isaac's tough skin. He didn't have Abraham's fine-looking tusks or Jacob's affinity for magic.

So he had to turn to tech to compensate. And tech was damn expensive.

He touched the tip of his boot to the pool, sending out a ripple that made the cherry-grape snake dance.

The snake had crept down from the overhead neon sign advertising *Live Nude Dancing Elves*. Moses idly wondered if any place advertised dead ones. He tapped his foot and the snake wriggled faster.

Moses hadn't given the snakes much thought until a handful of months past. That's when the microscopic vision subsystem implanted in his cybereyes malfunctioned. The series of minute optical lenses, designed to magnify objects up to a thousand times their normal size, splintered during a fight with a trog razor-guy. Moses, who'd emerged battered but victorious, had been on a run with Taddeus and a few others into the Barrens, and they didn't pull enough nuyen from the job to get his lenses replaced. Didn't matter—he was kind of glad he hadn't, as rather than magnify the snakes they now enhanced their color and sometimes spun pieces of them away like one of those toy kaleidoscopes kids looked into. The cracked lenses made the snakes breathe, too—Moses saw their sides moving in and out, and when he cocked his head just right, as he was doing now, he could see their tongues flicker from between their invisible fangs to taste whatever interesting things were in the water.

In fact, Moses hadn't realized Seattle's sidewalks had snakes until the lenses cracked.

"Move it!" This came from a muscle-bound troll who cursed and stepped off the curb to get around Moses. "Go stand somewhere else, you ugly vatjob!"

Moses flicked his tail at the oaf, but the troll was quick, already on his way down the street. Moses liked his tail—it was one of his favorite modifications. A meter and a half long, covered with tiny lizard-like scales with mirrored surfaces, it had a built-in light at the end that he sometimes read by. It was one of those balance

tails, weighted and grafted onto the base of his spine and keyed to a processor that monitored his center of gravity.

He'd gotten his shaped dermal plating at the same place he'd bought the tail—from his trusted ripper doc. Paid almost full price for the plating and had it stylized with ridges at the elbows, bumps across his forehead for the heck of it, and made to look like he had great abs and a broad chest.

Made him look better than human.

It was decorated just above his heart—not with tribal art or hieroglyphs like most favored—but with "EXD 3:6" in reference to the Bible verse: "Moreover he said, I am the God of thy father, the God of Abraham, the God of Isaac, and the God of Jacob. And Moses hid his face; for he was afraid to look upon God." Moses hadn't been able to find a verse that at the same time mentioned Ruth, but then she had a whole book devoted to her.

He had Doc add a wet sheath over the top of the plating some months ago, save for the spot on the chest with EXD 3:6 on it. It was a variant of a dermal, but modified to feel cool and slippery, sexy, glistening . . . sort of like snakeskin.

The cherry-grape snake writhed faster as Moses continued to stare.

The sheath was great because thugs had a hard time grabbing onto him. He'd tried to get a chameleon modification with it, but Doc said combining those features was a few years away. So he settled for adding a near-meter-long head of fiber-optic hair, bright orange with a cascading effect of yellow and red at the tips to make it look like fire. Because he styled it often, it was wearing a little thin in places and a few sections needed to be replaced.

That's why Moses had come down here tonight . . . to get some nuyen to pay for more hair and some other enhancements. He had his heart set on getting some horn implants. He'd been fitted a year or so ago for bull horns, but decided they were a little too big, and too expensive. Last week he'd put some second-hand goat horns on layaway, at the same place he'd get the hair replacements—from his trusted ripper doc. Bright, white horns with a mother-of-pearl glaze—fixed implants, as the retractable ones were a little out of his price range. Doc promised the horns wouldn't itch.

Some of Moses's other implants did, and scratching them in public had gotten him banned from more than one establishment. The penile implant was the worst, with its mentally controlled gel reservoirs and synthetic skin that he had some sort of allergic reaction to. He hoped he could remember to ask Doc for some more ointment for the rash.

"Nuyen," he said. "Came down here to get me some." He repeated "nuyen" until it became a mantra that twisted in time with the cherry-grape snake. "Nuyen for the tech-fix."

"What's he starin' at, ya think?" The speaker was an elf, a live one, but she wasn't nude or dancing. She was wearing a sand-colored plastic dress that crinkled when she crossed her arms in front of her probably enhanced chest.

"The puddle. Maybe he lost something in it." Her companion was also an elf, face painted garishly and lips three times any natural size. "Didja lose something in it, mister?"

"Lose? Lose yourself. Get lost," Moses said. They stood too close to the water and made it harder to see the snake. He heard the sand-colored dress crinkle as the pair strolled away. The snake could swim freely now.

An ork peddler walked by, selling hot soyjerky. Passersby commented on the spicy smell. Moses couldn't smell it. He couldn't smell anything.

Moses had a direct neural interface connected wirelessly to the various built-in computers nested in the implants that allowed diagnostics checks—and said checks told him several things were either malfunctioning or were overdue for maintenance . . . his failed nasal receptors for example. They'd been out of whack for the past eighteen . . . or was that eighty . . . months. His enhanced taste buds didn't register anything either. He could be

eating . . . well, pretty much anything . . . and not hurk it back up because of the taste. He only ate to keep his strength up and because his super thyroid implant demanded it.

"Should get 'em fixed," he said. "Maybe."

He'd need a lot of nuyen for the repairs. He had Kevlar bone-lacing with RFID sensor tags, a blood circuit control system, and a datajack engraved with elaborate Japanese *kanji*-signs he couldn't read . . . it was a used model, and so he hadn't been picky.

"Nuyen," he said. "Sashayed down here to get me some."

The encephalon he went under the knife for six or so months back hadn't helped. Hardwired into Moses's brain, it was supposed to boost his information-processing. It only seemed to scramble things now. At least the math subprocessor unit whirred along without a problem; he could calculate rent and utilities in a nanosecond, and it doubled as an alarm clock. His internal GPS worked without a proverbial hitch, too. It's how he found his way to this corner without making a single wrong turn. Too bad he hadn't thought to load his sister's address into it. What was her name? Ruth. Yeah, that was it.

"Ruth. Nuyen. Nuyen. Nuyen."

The radar sensor was another matter. It was supposed to emit terahertz and ultrawide-band radar in frequency pulses, analyzing Doppler and bounced signals. It never had worked right—another piece of used equipment he probably shouldn't have had installed without first asking Doc for some sort of warranty. At least it functioned as a motion detector, except that it never registered the snakes. He'd remember to ask Doc for a warranty on the pearlized goat horns.

Once more he thought about taking what little nuyen he had stashed away—coupled with what he was going to score tonight—and spending it on repairs to his existing systems. But he really wanted the goat horns, and he was being good by repairing at least one of the enhancements—his fiber-optic 'do. Besides, if he spent all his nuyen on repairs, he'd never be able to afford the cyberfins he'd been thinking about. Saw an advertisement for them a couple of days back . . . or was that a couple of weeks . . . or months?

His memory played tricks sometimes.

"Nuyen," he said. "Came down here to get me some."

His regular ripper doc could implant the webbing between his fingers and toes so he could manage the butterfly and backstroke in record time. Of course, Moses knew he'd have to take swimming lessons first.

The two elves returned, the sand-colored plastic crinkling a little louder.

"Geese," Moses pronounced them. It was the right neighborhood for hookers. The women were looking for someone to dock with—for nuyen, naturally—their gander probably somewhere close by for safety. Moses wouldn't mind docking with the one with the overlarge lips, but he needed to save his cred for the hair replacement and the fins . . . and to fix something. What attachment was he going to repair? Besides, his father had taught him to stay away from those kinds of women. They were sinful. Moses was SIN-less.

"'And the Lord said unto Moses, Behold, thou shalt sleep with the fathers; and his people will rise up, and go a whoring after the gods of the strangers of the land, whither thy go to be among them, and will forsake me, and break my covenant which I have made with them.' Deuteronomy, chapter thirty-one, verse sixteen."

"Talking all Biblical. Still looking in the puddle, he is," big lips said. "Yo, Clint." She sidled up to Moses. "You interested in a little whoring, maybe we—"

"Get lost," Moses said.

"S'matter, don't like elves?"

"Live nude dancing elves," Moses said, looking up at the sign again.

Big lips shuddered and swayed down the street, arm-in-arm with plastic dress.

"Tadd would've spent his nuyen on them geese." Moses missed his old chummer.

The last time they were together Taddeus told Moses he didn't discriminate enough, that he bought preowned cyberware on the black market when he should be shopping at legitimate places. "The legal clinics won't deal with the stuff you're putting in your brain," Taddeus had said. "Who knows where that stuff came from? I oughta turn your doc into the authorities." Tadd said other things, too, but Moses hadn't had his data filter turned on, and so could only remember a few sentences.

Ripper docs, shadowclinics, Taddeus wouldn't have anything to do with them, Moses knew. But then Taddeus didn't have near the modifications as Moses. Taddeus wasn't quite better-than-human. Tadd was still mostly human.

Moses had been better-than-human for several years.

"Nuyen. Nuyen. Nuyen."

He liked his ripper doc 'cause he could pick up modifications that weren't exactly legal, and he never had to supply an ID or SIN. And it wasn't like he had these things done in a back-alley filth parlor with half-used, unsterilized medkits at the ready in the case of accidents. It wasn't technically a black clinic or a body bank. His doc had a real medical degree and operated out of the basement of a tattoo parlor, a real high-end underground clinic. Moses had done his research before going under the knife. Doc hadn't had his license pulled for any of the usual reasons—too many malpractice cases or amputating the wrong limb. He'd simply experimented a few times on a few unwitting and later protesting patients . . . and got caught. Moses wasn't unwitting; he underwent each modification with both insect-like compound cybereyes wide open, and he didn't care when Doc suggested a little muscle doping now and then or a little trial genetic infusion.

And Doc was a real ecologist, as green as they came. He believed in recycling—bioware implants, nanoware, cyberware, augmented limbs. Because Moses bought most of his stuff secondhand from Doc, he could afford the integration system for all his simsense and networking devices and the bundle of skillwires with multi-functionality. He wouldn't have been able to buy tricked-out cyberears if they'd come right off the assembly line.

Moses thought he might ask Doc if those ears could be tweaked just a bit, so he could hear the snakes. The cherry-grape one might have some juicy secrets to share. He glanced back down at the puddle. Yep, the snake was still there.

Doc was good at providing discount prescriptions. Moses had to take three . . . or was that four . . . pills a day to stave off biosystem overstress, and another couple pills to treat his temporal lobe epilepsy. The latter malady was an acceptable side effect of having so many cyber implants. Doc said the condition was chronic and degenerative and that if it got much worse Moses would need corrective gene therapy or maybe a little brain surgery. If Doc was going to go back in Moses's brain, maybe he could finesse something with the memory center or some such. Moses really wanted to remember his sister's address.

Taddeus had called Moses an aug-ad, an augmentation addict, and said he wouldn't go on any more runs with him until he got his head straightened out. Moses figured Tadd just didn't understand about not being satisfied with being human. Moses was almost there . . . satisfied . . . but not quite. He just needed a few more adjustments. He had mood swings because he wasn't quite happy with things the way they were now. Sure, he was better-than-human, but he could stand to be a little bit better than simply betterthan. Tadd was probably just pissed about the mood swings. He'd be back. Him and the others would come crawling to Moses for help on another dip into the shadows.

Crawling, like the cherry-grape snake was crawling. Moses watched it slither to another puddle. He followed it.

"Gotta go this direction anyway," he said. "Up the hill." His internal GPS told him he had two more blocks to go, all uphill. "And the Lord said unto Moses, 'Get thee up into this mount, and see the land which I have given unto the children of Israel.'"

Two more blocks up, around the corner, and then down an alley and he'd have plenty of nuyen for the hair and the swim fins and . . . what was he going to have fixed? His fang implants? Only one of those had snapped off.

"Two more blocks for the nuyen."

The snake obliged him, slithering along as if a guide, though a few storefronts later it changed color, turning yellow now, and then green. When it split in two and turned sky blue, Moses realized it wasn't the same snake, and it wasn't nearly as pretty. He'd go back and find the cherry-grape one later, after he scored his nuyen.

One more block. "Just one more, and what—"

Just short of the next corner Moses saw the rude troll who'd called him a vatjob. He was leaning over a human woman sporting rabbit ears and a fox tail, vulching her, maybe hitting her up for drugs or nuyen or . . .

"Oh, it's the vatjob." The troll turned to face Moses and stuck out his jaw to look menacing. He had a submachine gun in his right hand, barrel pointed at the pavement. The other passersby on the sidewalk gave him a wide berth. "Mind your own business. Bit-brain bakebrain whackjob nutjob vatjob." The twin blue snakes cavorted around the troll's big sandaled feet.

Moses cleared his throat: "And it came to pass in those days, when Moses was grown, that he went out unto his brethren, and looked on their burdens: and he spied an Egyptian smiting a human . . . er Hebrew, one of his brethren. Exodus two-eleven."

"Definitely a nutjob vatjob." A line of drool spilled over the troll's lower lip and extended to the pavement, striking the head of one of the blue snakes and sending Moses's temper flaring. "This is between me and Foxy Foxtail, so move it." The troll raised the gun in threat.

"And he looked this way and that way, and when he saw that there was no man, he slew the Egyptian, and hid him in the sand. Exodus two-twelve."

"What are you talking about you—"

"King James Version." Moses's wired reflexes

kicked in and he bent and pulled a combat knife from a sheath in his boot and hurled it using all the strength in his synthetic cyberarm. *Should have been wearing body armor,* Moses thought as the troll dropped to his knees. The troll shouldn't have relied only on a secure long coat that he hadn't even bothered to button. Moses threw a second knife from the other boot, finishing him.

"And he killed it," he quoted. "And Moses sprinkled the blood upon the altar round about. And he cut the ram . . . err, troll . . . into pieces; and Moses burnt the head, and the pieces and the fat. Leviticus eight-nineteen and twenty."

The fox-tailed human squealed and sprinted across the street, leaving Moses to stare at the twin blue snakes undulating in the spreading troll blood.

A lone goose in a barely-there skirt screamed and drew Moses's attention away from the snakes.

"Nuyen," Moses said. "Nuyen. Nuyen. Nuyen. Came down here to get me some." He kicked the submachine gun away. Moses didn't care for guns. Sure, he could use them, and he had a smartlink for a heavy pistol he had lost on a corp run. But he preferred knives because they didn't make as much noise. He turned the troll over and retrieved his knives. He shoved them back in the boot sheathes, more worried about speed than the blood, and rifled through the troll's pockets as gawkers came to stand over him. "A credstick. Good. Got me some nuyen I wasn't expecting. Not a whole lot on it, though."

"It's the puddle guy." The goose in the crinkly dress was back.

Couldn't she find someone to dock with? Moses wondered. She's pretty enough. *Maybe she ought to lower her price.*

He slapped the side of his head with his palm, rattling the GPS just enough to get him back on track. "Around the corner. Down the alley," he said. "Later," he told the elf-geese. Then he was gone, his wired reflexes giving him a boost of speed that took him around the edge of the all-night pharmacy, down half a block and into the alley. He didn't hear any sirens, but he figured sooner or later someone would call about the troll bleeding out on the sidewalk. It had been self-defense, hadn't it? The troll had been carrying a gun, after all.

There weren't any snakes at the mouth of the alley. There was plenty of water for them, as Moses sloshed through one puddle after the next as he made his way around trash receptacles sitting outside the backdoors of bars, sex shops, and diners. But there weren't any neon signs, and it was the signs that gave birth to the best snakes. Moses felt better when there were snakes around. Moses was supposed to have snakes.

"Exodus four-three and four," Moses said. Why was it he could remember the Bible verses so easy but not the color of the whatever-it-was he had on layaway with Doc? "And he said, 'Cast it on the ground.' And he cast it on the ground, and it became a serpent; and Moses fled from before it. And the Lord said unto Moses, 'Put forth thine hand, and take it by the tail.' And he put forth his hand, and caught it, and it became a rod in his hand." He sucked in a deep breath and went farther down the alley. "Thy rod and thy staff, they comfort me."

A cat hissed and shot in front of him, disappearing behind crates stacked at a barber's back door.

"Hurry with this," Moses told himself. He wanted to get the nuyen and get back out on the street. Find that cherry-grape snake again and ogle it a little longer before he visited Doc and had . . . what was that he was going to the clinic for? "Hair." He was pleased that he remembered that. "Hair and—" Hair and something else. He'd put his mind to it after this was over. Put his head to it. "Head. Head. Head."

Moses scratched the bumps above his eyes and brightened. "And he put the mitre upon his head; also upon the mitre, even upon his forefront, did he put the golden plate, the holy crown; as the lord commanded Moses. Leviticus eight-nine."

What was his sister's address? Eight Nine something. Ruth, right? Yeah, Ruth. Wither-though-goest-Ruth.

Halfway down the alley, that's where the GPS tugged him.

"Didja bring the nuyen?"

Moses stopped, peering into the shadows, insect-like compound cybereyes separating the grays and blacks and finding the man . . . dwarf . . . thickset, grubby-looking. They all were dirty-looking, the ones who dealt in these sorts of things.

"Did you bring the beetles?" Moses returned.

The dwarf stepped away from the wall.

And the good ones were rich.

"Nuyen. Nuyen. Nuyen," Moses whispered. His ears whirred and clicked, picking up the dwarf's heartbeat and the slow slap of his shoes in the puddles sadly devoid of snakes. Moses needed snakes. Picking up the dwarf's breathing. Insect-like compound cybereyes with heat-sensors finding the dwarf, finding rats scurrying along in either direction, finding garbage piled up outside the back door of a Chinese restaurant, finding things he didn't want to get too close a look at. Finding nothing else.

For once, Moses was glad he couldn't smell anything.

"Did you bring the beetles?" Moses repeated. He heard the faintest of whirring and clicks. The dwarf was checking him out, too. "I'm alone. No guns."

"I know."

"The beetles." Moses added a hint of desperation to his voice, like he was a junkie in desperate need of a fix. He was, but not for the beetles. He remembered the goat horns he had on lay-away. If he didn't pay them off and get them installed soon, he'd lose his deposit. "Did you bring the beetles?"

"Better than life," the dwarf cooed, stepping closer.

"Better than human," Moses said, thinking about the horns and the fins and echolocation bioware and maybe some extended volume for his lungs and elastic joints for his knees.

"Better than anything," the dwarf said. "Yeah, I have beetles. You have nuyen?"

Moses pulled out the troll's credstick. Good thing he'd run into the troll. He'd forgotten his meager credstick back at his place. He hadn't forgotten it the last time he pulled this stunt, or the time before that or before that. Had to have a credstick to make them think you were actually buying something. Had to have the black-market contacts to get the names and locations of beetle-sellers. Better-than-life chips were still illegal, and you couldn't buy them just anywhere. He didn't want the chips, just the credsticks the beetle-seller would have on him. It was a theft that would never be reported. Moses had done this a dozen times. Or was that two dozen?

"Yeah, I got the nuyen. Let's see the chips first." Moses waved the stick higher. He knew the dwarf had some sort of enhanced vision that would let him pick out the details. "Why don't you—"

The back door of one of the bars opened, spilling sickly-yellow light out into the alley and reflecting off the puddles. Moses caught a glimpse of a snake, but it wasn't a pretty one. Only neon bred the pretty ones. He tried to look away, but it *was* a snake, and Moses was supposed to have snakes, wasn't he? Maybe if he cocked his head he could see it breathe. Maybe if—

The dwarf barreled into him, fist slamming into his stomach, plating absorbing it, but the momentum sending him back. Moses's tail lashed out, whipping around the dwarf's muscular forearm. It was a cyberlimb, all metal, no flesh, fingers ungodly strong and grabbing at the tail, squeezing, breaking some of the mirrored scales.

"Damn you!" Moses cursed. He couldn't afford to have the tail fixed, not with all the other plans for modifications. Not unless the dwarf had lots and lots of nuyen for selling beetles.

Moses's bone lacing made him strong, and he used that might now to bull-rush the dwarf, bringing his knee up into the smaller man's chest, pushing him down into the puddle to smother the ugly, yellow snake.

The dwarf had dermal plating, too. So Moses changed his tactics, pounding his fists against the dwarf's wide, ruddy face.

Voices intruded, maybe the man who'd opened the back door and birthed the ugly snake. Someone with him, voices panicked at what was transpiring in their alley. *Make it fast,* Moses thought. *Don't need someone calling Lone Star.* Not that he was doing anything illegal. This was self-defense. The dwarf started it. Moses just intended to finish it.

"And Moses said unto the Lord in Exodus four-ten, 'O my Lord, I am not eloquent, neither heretofore, nor since thou hast spoken unto thy servant; but I am slow of speech, and slow of tongue.' But let me be fast of fist. Let my wired reflexes fly."

Moses pounded harder until he heard bone *crunch.* The dwarf didn't intend to just stay down and die, though, struggling frantically to reach something at his side, succeeding, and pulling free a heavy pistol that he shoved up against Moses's side. The dwarf fired three times, the first two bouncing off the dermal, but the third punching a hole in the plating and sending a round deep inside.

Moses registered the pain, but shoved it to the back of his mind and continued to pound, listening to voices spilling out in the alley, listening to the dwarf curse, and hearing another round fire and find its way inside. Then he heard the dwarf cough and felt blood spit up against his face and onto his lips. Good thing he couldn't taste. Dwarf blood would probably taste bad.

The dwarf heaved once beneath him, and then fell still. Moses dug through his pockets, finding credstick after credstick after credstick. Twenty-five of them—his math subprocessor unit counted things instantly. The proverbial motherload. He shoved them in his own pockets. They wouldn't all fit, so he stuffed the extras in his kangaroo pouch, which had been a handy modification. Then he pushed off the ground, one hand pressed against his wounded side.

The voices came closer, accompanied by feet slapping through puddles filled with ugly yellow snakes. The back door to the bar was propped open wide and sickly light poured out.

"Are you hurt?"

"Who are you?"

"What happened?"

There were more questions from the quintet of barmaids and bartenders. Moses ignored them all and whacked his free palm against the side of his head, kicking in the GPS and tugging him back out the alley, onto the sidewalk and around the corner of the all-night pharmacy.

Maybe I should go in the pharmacy, he thought. *Buy some painkillers and bandages.*

But Doc's wasn't terribly far away, five or six blocks tops. Doc could repair the damage from the dwarf's slugs, put him under for that and do some modifications and hair-grafting at the same time. He certainly had enough nuyen on all these credsticks. Get it all done at the same time. Had the dwarf shot up some of his computer interfaces? Were more systems damaged?

"Nuyen. Nuyen. Nuyen. Got me lots of that." Moses staggered up the street, past the body of the bled-out troll that was still lying on the curb, passersby walking around it. No sign of Foxy Foxtail, whom he had probably saved.

Lightning flickered high overhead, followed by a boom of thunder that drowned out the music spilling from bars and sex shops. *It would rain soon, thank the Lord,* Moses thought. Rain and fill the low spots so the snakes would have more room to swim.

He watched the snakes as he went, pushing himself between the throng out on the sidewalk, struggling to watch the snakes between all the feet. Bright blue, grass-green, violet, Day-Glo pink, chartreuse, they shimmied all along Western Avenue. Moses followed the cherry-grape one, and with his free hand fingered one of the many credsticks in his pocket.

How had he gotten so many credsticks?

What was he going to spend them on?

Hair, he remembered hair. He came down here to get him some of that. Hair and . . . hair and . . . pearlized goat milk for his sister Ruth. *Intreat me not to leave thee, Ruth. Where thou lodgest, Ruth.*

"Where do you lodge?" Moses mused.

He'd deliver the milk tonight, if only he could remember her address.

JEFF NOON

GHOST CODES OF SPARKLETOWN (NEW MIX)

(2011)

Form is the host. Content is the virus. Infect, infect!

01

Break pops a rhythm tab: pure fever-zoom. No clocks, no maps. Only the taste of Dusk on his tongue, waiting for the night to roll in.

Bumps into Candy, standing by the X-Ray Parlor. Misty eyes, neon lip gloss, electric hair frazzle worked off a battery in her pocket.

She looks a charm, so corporeal it hurts. "Just checking out my veins," she says. "Making sure I'm clean, you know? Still alive."

"Candy, you wanna catch a bite?" A plastic sheet slides out the parlor slot showing off her lungs and heart and other organs. No shadows.

She blows a kiss and leaves. Break stands there frozen: he sure would like to own that X-Ray for a night or two. Total bliss-freak!

Down at his feet old transparency plates lie discarded. All he needs is to earn some credit, get himself reprogrammed, street style.

Maybe then the Real-Life Human Girls would love him. I mean, what's a young, well-dressed Synthetik Angel supposed to do these days?

02

Here find stories from a trash-diamond paradise, call it Sparkletown. A semi-abandoned housing project, fallout zone for the lost.

Shadow realm of ghosts, loners, artificial angels, lo-tech analogue freaks of varied shape, creed, and fashion. The new demo humans.

We move along streets where faces are lit by two seconds of electrostatic glow, burnt into memory. Then darkness, then rainfall.

Neon apparitions, figures of dust glimpsed in passing headlamps, voices in the air most nights, if you know how to listen for them.

03

Break went round to Dixie's with the discarded plates he'd picked up outside the X-Ray Parlor. They cut them into circles and used them to press the latest tunes.

They drove to the club. Dixie took over the booth, started playing. The crowd moved to the beats. Break watched the discs spinning.

It was a sight he never grew tired of, Dixie working the decks while damaged parts of the human body circled beneath her fingers . . .

Spinal columns, thigh bones, shoulder blades. Two skulls spinning at the same time, conjuring crazy bad thoughts out of the grooves.

The biggest thrill? The sight of two transparent hands, their smashed-up fingers and wrists all gray and ghostly on the X-ray plastic.

And Dixie's own hands, fully fleshed, moving above the two broken examples. The music floating upward from the mix like spirit smoke.

04

Dixie opened her eyes. Lying awake, she could hear the old songs moaning from the aerials of the long-shutdown pirate stations.

She got up, walked to the window. Sparkles of light flickered around the tower block. Phantom broadcasts, unknown frequencies.

Fragments of digital code: a word or two of lyrics, the stroke of a fingertip on metal string, human breath in curled brass tubes.

Moments of music cast adrift. Something had roused them this night: the darkness buzzed with flecks of data, many more than usual.

Dixie came alive watching them. Her eyes glittered, her fingers danced. Tomorrow she would go out early and catch some ghosts.

05

It goes like this: two years had gone by since the crash of the digital age, two years since the CPUs burned out *en masse*, simultaneously.

All the music of that era, the melodies people had composed, performed, recorded, coded into numbers . . . all this was lost, seemingly forever.

And then the first of the drifting spirits appeared: the scattered ghosts of pop stars, their final traces still caught in the ether.

At dusk you could listen to the strange music. You might glimpse a spectral glow in the air, tiny dancing sprites of color.

Sparkletown was a prime site; ghost collectors gathered there. A few got rich. Most went crazy. None lasted more than a few years on the task.

But some got so hooked into it, the spirits took them over completely. Now they wandered the alleyways without purpose, their half-dead mouths singing.

06

Gray light, fading moon. Dixie on slow walkabout, Break at her side. Other collectors were seen, working the streets. Let them be.

Break started to tremble. His skin was picking up traces, buzzing with sparks: evidence of spirit activity, serious measure.

He led Dixie to Hive 7, the worst of the blocks. Off limits, unsafe. Stories of demon songs haunting the rooms. A passageway beckoned.

Dixie went on ahead, alone. Into darkness. Silence. And then the crackle of melody, sparkle notes fluttering in minor key colors.

Listen now: held by rusty guitar strings, a woman's voice. Old, pitched low, a bleak moan. Murder ballad style. Dixie shivered.

She set the ghost trap and waited. The spirit flickered, sighing in darkness. Icy blue, fevered: something touched at Dixie's face.

07

Ghost trap components: contact mics, sugar cubes, matches, loudspeaker cone, glow-bug (female), cassette tape, AA batteries (leaky), perfume.

Operation: place glow-bug in speaker cone. Arrange mics in approximate circle. Set speaker to vibrate. Spray perfume on sugar: ignite.

The scent arouses the insect, causing the bug's abdomen to light up. Play cassette. Observe: the ghost will crackle and dance in time.

All such fragments dream of being whole once more, of being a favorite song on a lover's lips, conjured from a tongue: verse, chorus, and coda.

With such desire, the ghost is drawn toward the trap. Now softly, softly . . . close the lid . . .

Break dragged Dixie from the tunnel. Her eyes wide, face tight. "It's incredible!" Words of drawn-out breath: "Find it. Don't let her get away!"

08

Break entered the passageway, wondering what had got his boss so spooked. All was dark within but for his own skin gleaming. His fingers tingled.

A glint of color drew him forward. A cry. He felt he was stepping across a borderline. The sizzle of pain behind his eyes.

He'd heard other synthetiks boasting of the halo effect. Lies, mostly. He'd never seen it happen. Now he felt his temples pulsate.

It wasn't the full-on ignition he'd expected, more a flicker of sparks in a ragged lopsided orbit around his head. It was enough.

He peered into the homemade trap. There, held within the circle of microphones, suspended in midair . . . there lay the ghost.

It was a few centimeters across, of no fixed shape, crimson colored, speckled with gold, quiet now—a small broken spirit of music.

Break reached in and closed his hand around the prize. No burn. No anger. Only sorrow flooding his skull: pictures, sounds, memories.

09

The True History of the Synthetik Angels, as told by one of their kind. How, being eighteen and poor I sold my body to the dream merchants.

They clothed my skin with implants and programmed my skull with slogans. The system burned through me, taking me over completely.

I floated through the markets, a voice speaking only of the latest products. My implants sang and the air around me glowed with pictures.

I was a living advert, bought and sold many times over the next two years, my system hacked and pirated until I danced chaotic with thousands of images.

They called us Angels of Transmission. Messages moved through our bodies, into the world. And all was well until the Day of the Crash.

I recall the flare of overload, skin shock, implants sparking with static, adverts screaming inside me as luxury goods all around turned to dust.

And there I lay, alone and dying on the walkway of a shopping mall, all my golden images flickering dark one by one.

10

A Sparkletown morning. Low mist, pale sunlight. The two friends walked along. The trap was closed and bound, held between them.

They rode the elevator up to Dixie's floor. Break said, "I'm not sure about this. I saw things. This is no ordinary ghost."

Dixie nodded. No ordinary ghost, no ordinary song. She felt ill at ease. Cold, shivery from fear. But this was too good a chance.

They walked into the flat. Dixie said, "Let's get started." She clicked open the locks on the trap. Instruments glowed around her.

Break closed his eyes. His circuits were still buzzing from the vision he had picked up, from the moment of spectral contact.

He could see it still, in flashes of light:

the singer's face creased in pain. Her mouth, screaming. Her two hands covered in blood.

11

They worked through the day on the new track. Break manned the grain web, Dixie worked the Dali engine, needle tip glistening.

They sprinkled sleeping powder on the ghost to keep it docile while they bled the plasma away. The vampyrophone collected the output.

Break caressed the machine's skin. Sparks hit him with radiance. Once more, he heard the singer crying out in pain, but softer now . . .

He said, "This is bad blues, Dixie. It's a chance recording. The woman being attacked or killed, mid-song. Or something. Maybe."

Dixie was too busy seeking out a melody path, stretching the lyrical scraps, squeezing home-made beats from a plastic tube. Like goo.

By 5:00 p.m. the track was done, conjured into being, sealed in X-ray wax. They listened to it in silence, sitting back, getting distance.

Dixie had cut the scream just so, leaving only a breath, indrawn. That moment of loss, repeating. Break felt his heart stop each time.

12

Dixie. Living artifact of the haunted tower blocks, collector of sparks. Magpie. Extractor of the original (still famous) blood song.

Breeder of glow-bugs. Lo-fi alchemist. Transformer of lives once lost, broken, ghosted, now mixed down into a vapor groove.

Mapper of the dawn mist, curator of fragments. Inventor of the vampyrophone, the sleep trap, and other such homemade devices.

Dixie. Searcher of wastelands and canal-beds, where the digital trash resides. Salvager of discards. Queen of the unofficial channels.

Maker of the track "Last Cry of the Mouth Ever Fading." The one with the echo of a scream, the final traces of a murder victim.

Dixie Magus. Expert patcher of the wounded. Retuner of all hybrid demo-flesh for the next age. Savior of burnt-out angels.

13

The dance floor was half empty, people still waiting for takeoff. Break stood at the center of the room, looking up at the lights . . .

I was a broken soul stranded on the last day of the old world, skin aflame in a shopping mall. Blacking out, dying of digital fever.

He still felt weird inside at the work they had done today, the way that Dixie had treated the ghost, the wounded ghost. And yet . . .

Only Dixie had reached out to me. She lifted me up and dragged me home and worked on my body like I was one of her crazy machines.

Plugged me in analogue style and set up circuits to keep my system alive. In my delirium I heard wings beating, silver and gold.

I rose from my bed shrouded by sparks, crackling at the edges. Strange apparitions flickered around me, creatures of dust and light.

He could see them, all these stray sparkles that no one else could notice. His skull flared with color and noise. And then Dixie played the new tune . . .

14

Drops of rainwater. Hiss of acid on metal. Globules of sound. Murmurs, whirrs, sudden freakout guitar in a five-second burst.

Dixie working the X-ray plates, extracting the mix from a skull and a sickened heart. Spell of rhythm. People stepping to the floor.

Noise magic. A kiss of lips, magnified. Ticking clocks, food sizzle, static, jazz bass flecks, and splinters forming an undercurrent pull.

Now the drop in the mix where the singer's

scream once lived, a slow fade of echoes. Repeat. A few dancers moving in response . . .

Slowly swaying, slowly rising to fall in time with music box fragments, whispers, radar clicks; the beat coalescing. Crowd swell.

Dixie adding body music: breath, vein flow, brain activity. The missing scream coming round again. This time the dancers moved as one.

And there stood Break at the center, at the hot crush-heart liquid blood-river chaotic center of it all, feeling himself pulled aloft.

15

Break could not sleep properly. Dreams would lull him, only to drag him back awake. The dead singer whispered, always on the edge of hearing.

He could take no more. He left his room and went up to the roof of the block. All was dark, the streets empty. He felt the ghosts as tingles on his skin.

Was this his true calling, to be a guide for Dixie, nothing more than a compass? A waste of his gifts, surely, but what else could he do?

In dreams he caressed the neon-glow air with glittering feathers, taking flight across the Haze Towns. Joining with his brethren . . .

Renegade angels working the night sky, buzzing with fire at their wing tips, all the scattered songs theirs for the taking.

Break opened his eyes. He felt he could step off from the building's lip and ride the updraughts, floating easy with arms outstretched.

Was he dreaming now? His feet moved closer to the edge.

16

A noise. Break turned to see a group of people climbing onto the roof. The fog catchers.

They attended to their nets. Three adults in the crew, plus a kid, working by torchlight, checking the frame of gauze for captures.

Break walked over to watch them. They ignored him completely, set on their task, scouring the surface of the nets for images.

Something flared in a torch beam. A shape of lighter color, sparkling where the mist particles rested. It looked to be of human form.

Break stepped closer: a face, a woman's face, her body, her hands moving on the net's surface. The image was fleeting, illusive.

The crew spoke in low voices, excited at their find. Break turned to them, saying, "She's mine. I'll pay what you want." They smiled.

It was the lost singer. He knew it was. The wounded ghost made visible. Spots of red marked the face as it shimmered on the net.

17

Two nights later, he took possession of the icon jar. It cost most of the wages Dixie had given him, but Break had no choice.

He snapped open the lid and released the mist. There it floated in the dark room, the singer's image illuminated: gold, electric blue.

A few seconds of footage ripped from a promo video, caught in endless repeat. The red speckles on her face a remnant of special FX.

Break played Dixie's track. The apparition moved in time to the rhythm. He could not stop looking at her.

He didn't know her name, didn't recognize her face. Somebody from before he was born, before memory. Lost in the archives until now.

Somebody damaged, the victim of a cruel manager or a crazed fan or a jealous lover. He didn't like to think about it.

But she had sought Break out, in both image and sound. And here in this tiny dingy room, with his help, a new kind of life was being made.

He stepped into the mist, his body sparking at the points of contact. It was all he could do.

The track played on. The woman sang. The ghost of fog and sparkle danced. And danced and danced and danced and danced and danced . . .

18

Night passed along. The only light was a flickering lamp across the street.

Break could not bring himself to reseal her into the pod, even though he knew she would soon fade away completely. He would let this happen.

He would sit here in the dimly lit room and let his skin glimmer and shine with old messages, what was left of them.

He would conjure lyrics from all the many fragments he had collected on his travels, so many words to cast a spell, to allow a murdered spirit rest.

19 [LYRIC CODA]

I see remnants

of a woman floating,

the damaged steps

of a ghost.

The play of image in fog,

dancing in time.

This fragile body of release . . .

only to falter.

She was just another

electromagnetic transfer:

sampled footage.

Why should I care about her?

She is singing for

the people of vapor,

those whose flesh holds

no possession, no recognition.

Fog dancer, fog dancer

move through dust and neon-glow,

through moonlit circuits

and fused wires of memory.

LAVIE TIDHAR

CHOOSING FACES

(2012)

BRUCE:

1.

It was a party in Camden Market, late. We were standing in a bowl of glass lit by torches, a Sumerian-themed restaurant a floor above the market. Moving black escalators led up into the building. It snowed outside, white flakes falling as we drank and danced.

I guess I just wanted love. I guess she was just looking for something real. And I guess neither of us got exactly what we wanted.

She wore her hair like a black halo, muscled arms in a sleeveless top, she made you think of Cleopatra Jones in an old movie, fighting wiry kung-fu men in an American war in Asia. Marlene Dietrich was serving drinks behind the long bar. "What do you do?" she said. We were both sipping champagne. I nodded at the Marlene. "CEA," I said.

"Copyright Enforcement Agency?" She

looked impressed, or amused, I couldn't quite tell. "Do you have a gun?" she said.

"Yes."

"Did you ever kill anyone?"

"Rarely," I said, laughing.

"Oh, so it's . . ."

"It's not like in the movies," I said. Thinking of the East European factory we busted, several years back. They had a dormitory full of product—young Sylvesters, Bruces, Jean-Claudes, imperfect copies, slack-jawed and hollow eyed, of a line that was never all that popular after its brief heyday. It was an abandoned factory building far from habitation. The gang that ran it had filming equipment. They went through the copies like tissues, sometimes wasting four and five on a single shoot. Bruce on Jean-Claude, Sylvester on Sylvester on Sylvester, blood sports gangbangs with razor blades. When we took them down, the ring operators came quietly, even smirking. Worst they'd get was, what, five to ten?

With time off for good behavior. We destroyed the copies. They were lined inside, waiting. Only one tried anything, with a wordless cry he kicked up, a Jean-Claude and agile with it, but you could tell he knew it was no use even before I shot him.

The rest merely stood there. There is something almost eerie about copies. The code never comes out quite right. They're cheap, mass-produced in labs all over. These days any kid with a gene kit and a bathtub can grow his own Elvis. We went past them and shot each one in the head. It's the best way. Then we brought in the flamethrowers and burned the place down.

None of which I told her when she asked. I just smiled. A part of me wondered if she, too, was a copy. You can't always tell, and it's an occupational hazard. The other part of me didn't care. I asked her if she'd like to dance and she said yes, and we swayed there, in that glass bowl, with the snow like a benediction falling outside.

2.

Her name was Pam and she was a copy artist, which made me uncomfortable. Her work space was filled with computers and growing vats and body parts emerging half-formed out of green-gray goo.

"Aren't they beautiful?" she said. "I love the sense of copies as people, or as layers of history you can just reach a hand and, literally, touch. Hurt. Make love to."

"What do you do when they're," I said, and stopped. "When they're finished?" I said.

"If they become aware, you mean?"

"Yes."

"Some never do, you know. My success rate is still only thirty percent. The ones that don't make it I take apart, recycle." She showed me a half-finished copy, Marilyn Monroe cross-hatched into Osama bin Laden. Shark fins stuck out of the living corpse's arms and torso.

We made love on her unmade bed, with the Marilyn/Osama hybrid watching us silently where it hung on a hook. In the night I was aware of it blinking wet eyes, of it staring at us in the dark. I could smell the Thames through the open window, we were somewhere south of the river. Pam was strong, her body moved above mine as we rocked together, her sweat against my skin making us slippery to each other. Later she slept easily, with even breaths, while I lay in the dark, still feeling the motion of bodies like water, and thinking of Somalia.

3.

We came on the ships at dusk. We hid on the shore, watching them through infrared. Massive hulls, of ancient seagoing vessels liberated from their multinational owners by a different sort of pirate, in a different age. Now they sat, part submerged in water, dark and seemingly life-less. Switch to thermal imaging though and the ships burned with internal heat, a mass of bodies crammed close together, one on top of the other. E-Somaliland had declared independence from contested Somalia, creating a non-IP haven where the Agency could not operate overtly. Ethiopian troops made up the bulk of the attack. We were there primarily as observers.

We stormed the ships at sunrise; helicopters swooped overhead as commandos in black-painted dinghies raced across the calm sea. A bloody firefight erupted and I watched bodies fall into the water below.

I was part of the second wave of attack, the pirates subdued, men and women in white smocks dragged from the hidden labs inside and placed on deck and handcuffed. I looked at the cargo manifesto, whistling at the numbers. We saw it, next: a ship that had once been an oil tanker was now packed floor to ceiling with Elvises all destined for the clandestine North American market. There was every type of Elvis, young soldier Elvis, old bloated Elvis, row upon row they lay there, naked, tagged, ready to be shipped.

The final ship was the hardest to bring under control. We later found out why. The scientist-pirates had been killed, their throats cut, their bodies left on deck for the birds. A craze some years back for that special mindset great men and dictators possess led to an upping in orders for Amins, Kims, Ian Smiths, and the like. Now a shipful of imperfect copies rose against their overseers, shambling up the stairs like living death, killing anything in their path. I watched from the deck of the Elvis ship as the firefight lasted into the night before the decision was made to drown the ship. I watched Idi Amins without number trying to swim to shore, and the soldiers, on decks above, opening fire with oiled Uzis. The blood attracted sharks, who did not distinguish between original and copy.

4.

I lost track of how many Hitlers.

5.

Many of which congregated then and still in South America. Argentina, Brazil . . . there seemed to be an endless market for the copies but it was only when they went loose that I had to be called in, tracking them through Indian villages and ancient Inca trails and, upon finding them at last, little lost Hitlers, had to be Nuremberg judge and executioner at once.

Though Hitler was never at Nuremberg.

6.

When Pam woke I was drifting off, cast asleep, adrift on a black sea. The stars all had faces and their faces were all the same.

"Coffee?" she said. I blinked sleep away, said, "In a mo—" and stopped. "What the hell is that?" I said.

The thing was like a giant mechanical cat. It purred at me and blinked large, plastic eyes.

"This is Ivan," Pam said. "He's the oldest Tamagotchi in the world."

"Tamagotchi?" Then I remembered—virtual pets, carried around in little plastic storage devices, antiques—"How?" I said.

"Ivan was my first virtual," she said. "My grandmother had him before me. I looked after him ever since I was a girl. He's had all kinds of upgrades, modifications over the years, he once married a Moon Princess and, once, he escaped into the networks and I spent over six months hunting for him, the poor thing. He is not very smart but he loves me. After he went rogue I didn't think it would be fair to keep him in the original casing so I had him transferred to a new body. He likes it much more, don't you, Ivan?"

Ivan came closer and sniffed me. Then he licked my face.

"I'm hoping he becomes self-aware one day," Pam said. "But if he ever does, he won't be himself anymore."

She sounded sad about that and I didn't want her to be sad.

"Pam . . ." I said.

"No," she said. And, "It was a mistake, bringing you here. I want you to leave."

"Why?"

"Because of what you do. Because of what you are."

"And what am I?"

"Blind," she said. "Please, Bruce."

I didn't know why she called me that. But I left her apartment and found myself in Elephant and Castle, walking toward Waterloo on foot, breathing in the cold air, thinking about things that didn't add up, no matter how much you tried to put them together.

7.

The gold rush proper started with the need to get hold of suitable genetic material. Which is where specialist collectors' shops came in, and is how Stanley Gibbons became the world-leading DNA agency that it is today.

SG used to specialize in collectible celebrity items in addition to their stamp business. They sold autographs, mostly, and sometimes movie props, letters, rare photos—that sort of thing.

What they *also* sold, however—to the discerning collector who needed that much more for his money—was hair.

When the market in copies suddenly exploded, it took people a while to understand the needs of the market. Those who moved early became rich overnight. Back in the early decades of the century, SG was selling five strands of hair from King George III, for instance, for a pitiful six hundred pounds. You could get a Melanie Griffith for a fifty-pound note. You could get George Washington, Charles Dickens, and Duke Ellington and still have change left over from fifteen hundred. You could get Tom Cruise for a measly seventy-five.

The hunt was on for genetic material. The Kunming Labs cornered the market on Cruise, buying up all available genetic material. They began to churn out Cruise copies, the first mass-produced copies destined for both the domestic and international market. Dickens became a particular status symbol. "I have a Dickens, you know," confessed countless bibliophiles to their party guests, proudly bringing out the celebrated author's copy on a leash.

The Church of Scientology bought up any dubious Hubbard item to come on the market, suing anyone who refused to sell. Their offshore factory in the Maldives churned out young cheerful Lafayettes by the hundreds, killing forever the field of science fiction as a by-product. An unforeseen side effect led to multiple splits in the church as each functioning copy started his own brand-new faith, going on the offensive in front of the media. Hundreds of Hubbards were interviewed before hundreds of Oprahs. Even Fiji TV had their own Oprah Show, with several Oprahs rotating in reserve.

Elvises sold like Tamagotchis. A single hair was all you needed of a person: organized crime muscled in on the action, controlling the market in contraband DNA. A ruthless murder in Primrose Hill found a Russian oligarch massa-cred in his mansion, surrounded by the bullet-ridden corpses of his dozen Schwarzenegger bodyguards. WikiLeaks, getting hold of highly secret DNA sequencing, released them on the Internet, leading to the first era of open-source copying. Julian Assange was murdered and resurrected and murdered and resurrected again in a dozen countries.

Into that whole sorry mess stepped the CEA, with a license to destroy, able to operate in all major copyright zones, an international policing force determined to stamp out the illegal replication of unauthorized copies. CEA agents were the best of the best. We had to be.

8.

I remember a cage fight. This was on an island off the coast of Borneo, an FTZ where we had no jurisdiction. The club was enormous, strobe lights flashed overhead and in the massive cages set amid the dance floor I could see Richard Nixon fighting Osama bin Laden, the one stoic, swinging a mean left hook without expression, the other light on his feet. Collars around their necks ensured they would not stop fighting— electric current shocking them if they tried to refuse. In another cage Hillary Clinton beat the crap out of Golda Meir. I was there to meet a contact, collect information on a cloners ring operating out of Malaysia, but he, or she, never showed up. Instead I wandered that space, getting lost. I stumbled outside into bright sunlight and saw, as far as the horizon, copies dancing in unison to a music I could not hear. It was so silent, there in the bright sunlight, and I saw them all, moving soundlessly, their faces all turned to the sun, their eyes closed, Elvises and Nixons, Amins and Monroes, Oprahs and Madonnas, Mandelas and Osamas and Thatchers and Cruises, a sea of familiar faces, as familiar to me as my own.

For a moment I stood there and the sadness took me. A part of me wanted to join them, to sway in the sun, to be a part of what they represented. Then I came back to myself, seconds or minutes later, and I went back inside into the shade.

9.

"Pam? It's me."

"Hey."

"I wanted to see you again."

"I . . . wanted to see you too."

A silence between us, stretching.

"That's good," I said, and she laughed. "Yeah."

"When?"

"Tomorrow. No! Today. I don't know. Bruce . . ."

"Why do you call me that?"

"I don't know what else to call you."

10.

I never remember dying. My life is spliced together out of desperate fights, insurmountable odds. The joins are like moments of darkness, each transition almost seamless.

I remember this place in the South Pacific. A Kim Dot Clone with dreams of empire had built himself a headquarters on a rent-an-island, filled with armed guards and growing vats. They were churning out bodies by the ton and shipping them out using converted tankers. I landed unseen, shelling my dark diver's suit as I stepped onto the sand. Naked, I followed the paths in the tropical foliage, a knife in my hand. Then I saw them.

Bruce Lees.

Hundreds of Bruce Lees, patrolling.

One spotted me. Then the others. I waded into the fight, naked but for the knife in my hand, and they came at me.

11.

I landed again on the island, not questioning how I was here again. This time I made it as far as the palace gates.

12.

I landed again on the island, armed with two Uzis. I made it inside the buildings before the Bruce Lees got to me.

13.

With a rocket launcher and a samurai sword.

14.

"Yipikaye, motherfucker," I said when I finally ran him through.

15.

I don't know where the words came from. They were just there.

16.

"What am I going to do with you?" Pam said. We were on the South Bank and snow fell gently into the river and the drops dissolved into the water. She wore a long black coat. I had on jeans and a shirt.

"They want me to go on another mission, soon," I said.

"Will you come back?"

"I always come back."

"Would it still be you?"

I didn't know what she meant. "Do you believe in the soul? Someone said to me once copies are all imperfect shards of the same original, and the soul gets diluted and spread amongst them. They're not real. We don't kill them, Pam. We destroy property. You know?"

"I make them, you unmake them?"

"But yours are handcrafted, the problem is when they're mass-produced and cloners don't pay royalties."

"Like if you think you own your own genome code," she said, and laughed. Snow fell on the water. I went to her and drew her close. "I love you," I said.

I kissed her and her lips were warm, alive. They were real. When we parted she was smiling, slightly.

"Oh, Bruce," she said. "If only you could save the world again."

17.

I remember that factory in Eastern Europe, entering the dormitories where they kept the copies, rows upon rows of Jean-Claudes and Sylvesters and Bruces. I remember going down that row, the gun in my hand, the copies lined up silently, waiting for me. I remember looking into each of their faces as they stared back at my own.

PAM:

1.

Hateful enemy agent, CEA scum, your skin is the color of lobster flesh cooked in butter, your face is reminiscent of the worst of the American imperialist dream as seen on late-night television.

It is time for me to step away from the dance, to remove the face I wear in favor of another, truer.

I have saved the world eight hundred and seventy-three times, while you lie in your bed, sleeping, dreaming of former glory. Disgraceful copy of a copy, how I loathe you, your touch, your smell, immoral hunter, killer, in service of the machine. It is time for me to step away from the dance, remove my many masks, time for me to fleet like a shadow along the dimly lit streets of this city, this London, over the Thames, from south to north, along the points of a Harry Beck map, leapfrogging and hopping like an advancing army, an army you cannot see.

I sent a Darknet message to my contact: I am on my way. I arrived in Willesden Junction into streets alive with the motion of writhing bodies, an organic orgy breeding supple streetlamps and traffic lights out of the dead land, of trains like giant rodents crawling along crisscrossing tracks. Entering a residential block, it was alive with the beat of a vast bass which swallowed words and music both, the beating of a vast heart, the heart of a revolution. There were no walls, no levels. They had been removed to make this vast open space. I threaded my way through the dancers, so many dancers, copies and copied, destination and source, like in an old MS-DOS command. Strobe lights hid rather than illuminated. In their faces I sought my own. I am Pam, the Prophet's Fist, She Who Has Been Resurrected. Call me what you will but only call me at your peril. I passed pushers selling weed, Es, acid, Special K, coke, Horse, and generic no-brand paracetamol. They moved out of my way.

Toilet cubicles had been erected at the back of this abandoned council building. I heard grunts from inside, lost cries of passion swallowed by the beat as humans attempted to make copies the old-fashioned way. Set into the cheap plaster wall was a white door. I placed my hand against it.

"By the name of Doctorow and the Apostles, let me enter," I said.

I felt a pinprick of pain, saw blood well on the tip of my index finger. The blood soaked into the wall. Hidden machines analyzed it, for the blood is the life, and the life is blood. The door opened. I stepped through. It closed behind me and the beat of the bass receded, but never vanished. I stood in a dark room.

"Child." His voice boomed across the room, magnified by the amps built into his prodigious neck. They were like wet gills on the Man from Atlantis. They moved like twin obscene mouths suckling at the fetid air. He was huge, a mountain of flesh. His skin was pink like grapefruit. His eyes were hidden behind shades. He wore only white. They all did. All five thousand identical copies of the Army of the Kim Dotcoms.

2.

Kim Dotcom was the first man to open-source himself. He was a revolutionary, the Megamix

Marx, the Bitshare Che. When the genetic land-grab began in earnest and the human genome began to be sequestered and copyrighted piecemeal, the Movement arose. A combine of BoingBoing users, Anonymous activists, and pre–Hubbard Resurrection sci-fi fans joined forces to illegally distribute stolen genetic code. Soon wars erupted between the pirates and the legal copyright holders, both online and in the real world. In one notable incidence the Fifth Hungarian Republic, led by an early copy of the poet Attila József, annexed all genetic proprietary material to the state, banning individuals or companies from ownership. They were toppled a mere three weeks later in a coup carried out by an army of Trump bots.

Things got worse, fast.

Thirty Robert Mugabe copies escaped from a cloner facility in South Africa and headed north and across the border. Within weeks Mugabe-land, as the new Zimbabwe came to be called, was under the Rule of Thirty and, within a year, it had splintered into rival zones, each ruled by a copy. It was a dark time in Zimbabwean history, a time that pitted brother against brother and Mugabe against Mugabe against Mugabe.

After repeated threats, the United States invaded the Cayman Islands, a British protectorate south of Cuba where the rich and powerful had traditionally deposited their wealth, illegitimate children, and current or discarded lovers, and, of course, their genetic fortune. A group of islanders with Anonymous sympathies, however, had hacked into the secure bank system and posted the genetic code of the richest one percent of the world's population online. Every Grameen Bank microfinancing initiative in the world suddenly had its very own George Soros working for it. Hong Kong triads settled old scores by setting illicit Donald Trump fighting rings in dark subterranean rooms and betting on the outcome. "Getting fired by the Trump" got itself a whole new meaning.

It got worse.

Royalists innocently copying their favorite monarchs inadvertently toppled the British monarchy as enraged copies of HRH Elizabeth Windsor, storming Buckingham Palace, found themselves faced by genetically exact predecessors with a preceding and valid claim to the throne. Matters were not made easier by a George III guerrilla movement issuing multiple threats against the United States.

The Israelis passed a law annexing all Jewish genetic material rights to the state. They thus laid copyright claim to Einstein, who finally accepted the offer first extended to his original in nineteen fifty-two to become president of the State of Israel. The Israelis also genegrabbed Julius Oppenheimer, Robert Hofstadter, Otto Frisch, Nathan Rosen, and, of course, John von Neumann and Niels Bohr. The resultant nuclear research facility in the Negev Desert was placed under intense security and total media blackout. The escape of a lone Einstein twenty-four months later, across the desert and into Egypt, was reported in the *Sunday Telegraph* but was widely believed to be a hoax. Were it to be believed, the story suggested that the Israelis had managed to open an Einstein-Rosen Bridge, a thousand feet under the desert floor, which opened up onto another universe altogether and into which Jewish mass emigration, or *aliyah*, was being carried out.

Then there were the problems with the EPE as Elvis Presley Enterprises mutated into one of the most powerful copyright holders in the world; and the resultant Elvis Riots, as they came to be called, in which thousands of Elvises ran amuck in Memphis demanding fair employment terms, in what the *New York Times* had dubbed "The worst Communist-led uprising in the history of the United States."

Then they brought back Marx.

Then they brought back Lenin.

Then they brought back both George Bushes, Abraham Lincoln, *and* the Iron Lady. A British faction under Margaret Thatcher's control invaded the Falkland Islands and declared it the First Thatcherite Nation.

Finally the CEA was formed, a lethal task force charged with policing and enforcing genetic copyright law. It was then that Kim Dotcom—declared Public Enemy Number One by the United States government—first open-sourced himself, in the first of a series of brilliant counter-strokes against the rise of genetic land-grab neo-Fascism, birthing the Movement in the process.

3.

"Pam," the Kim Dotcom said in his booming, boombox voice. Alone in the empty room we stood, the Kim Dot Clone and me. "How goes your mission?"

"The primary identity created is rock-solid," I said. "I make hybrid copies which sell to collectors and exhibit in galleries around London. I am now in a relationship with the CEA agent of the B-900 series, codenamed Bruce—"

"They are *all* codenamed Bruce," the Kim Dotcom said. "Do you have it?"

"Yes."

He smiled, a mouth full of teeth. "How?" he breathed.

"It is what I do," I said.

"Relic hunter . . ."

"Yes."

"Give it to me."

That gave me pause. "Here? Now?"

"Here," he said. "Now." His skin was shiny with sweat, his engorged belly glistened in the strobe light filtering in through the narrow gaps in the door.

"But . . ."

"Now, Pam."

He pulled up the rest of his shirt. His belly hung naked in the strobe light. I went to him and laid my hand against the softness of his skin.

"Do it," he said.

I ran my thumb along his belly button. Felt him breathing.

"Do it!"

My nail was long and sharp.

I pushed my thumb into his belly button, hard, impregnating him.

I felt his flesh give as it sank in. I heard him gasp.

The payload secreted in my thumb left me and entered his gestation chamber. I pulled my thumb out and the wound sealed itself.

"Jesus," he said, panting.

4.

A posse of Hulk Hogans had been patrolling the Cathedral of Saint John the Baptist in Turin when I walked in. Life is precious, source and target, copy and original. I put them under with narcotic darts and disabled the alarm on my way in with the codes I had stolen from the Bruce. My Bruce.

I did not kill the Hulks. I do not wantonly destroy.

The Catholic Church defines three levels of holy relics. These, as it turns out, are still used today by gene- and relic-hunters. Third-class relics are ones that had been touched by a saint. These are the least useful for our purposes, what DNA material may have been once left was in all likelihood long gone. Second-class relics are ones that had been worn by a saint, and these offer a better chance of rebirthing, mostly of the minor saints. First-class relics, however, are those directly associated with the life of Jesus Christ, and of these, the most significant, and most heavily guarded, is the Shroud.

There had been significant arguments and several UN resolutions regarding the genetic copyright ownership of Jesus of Nazareth. The Vatican was first but the State of Israel claimed previous right-of-way, and into the melee stepped various American pastors, the Mormons, and an obscure UFO religion claiming for Jesus under supposed evidence of alien DNA. The dispute was never resolved, but there are few conflicts one can't resolve with a gun.

"You will not pass," John the Baptist said in passable English. He was holding an Uzi and glared at me menacingly. His bones had been found in a Bulgarian monastery, on Sveti Ivan Island, in the early noughties. Church-approved cloners have since replicated him hundreds of times. He was a thick-armed, wiry Jewish man, dark skinned and humorless. I put a dart in him and was about to approach the reliquary when I found the cathedral's real defenses.

Mother Teresa.

Mother Teresa, multiplied by seven.

Mother Teresa, multiplied by seven, and all of them holding big fucking machine guns.

I ducked as they opened fire.

The resultant fight wasn't pretty.

But somehow I made it through, and to the Shroud.

They pursued me across Italy and France but lost me at the Channel. I made it back to London and went to the cinema with Bruce, the vial implanted in the false tip of my thumb. We'd watched *Casablanca*, and made out in the back seats of the theater, in the dark.

5.

We'd waited in the dark as the bass drowned the sound of his labored breathing.

What Kim Dotcom had done was distribute his own genetic source code over the file-sharing networks. When an anonymous CEA agent finally caught up with him, on an island somewhere in the South Pacific, it no longer mattered that the original had been destroyed. Hundreds of Kim Dot Clones sprung up into life all over the world, bred in backroom vats on Soi Cowboy and in the Kunming Labs of the Golden Triangle, in copy nurseries on the giant pirate ships of e-Somaliland or in the Elvis factories of Memphis. The Army of the Kim Dotcoms was the call to revolution, the spearhead of the Movement.

They had improved themselves, too.

Each of the Five Thousand carried within himself a 3G mobile birthing unit, top of the range.

"You are close to Mitosis Phase," I said.

"Indeed I am. Pam—" his huge face twisted in pain. He reached out his hand to me and I took it. "Help me," he said. "It is coming."

I helped him down and knelt beside him. I removed his garments so that he was slickly naked. I could see movement under his skin, a thing which was not yet a thing pushing against the thin membrane of flesh, trying to get out. I helped him spread his legs and knelt between them with my slim shiny scalpel in my hand.

The thrum of bass. The beat of feet against the ground, sending a shudder running through the building, a wordless cry like a fist raised in defiance and pride.

"Easy, now . . ." he said.

My hand was steady. I cut through the layers of skin and fat, opening the sack in his belly. "Push," I said.

He pushed.

6.

Oh you corrupt and corrupting CEA agent, you brute, you Bruce! Why can I not take your image out of my mind, why do I feel the need to run my fingers through your thinning hair, to put my nose close to the swell of your neck and inhale the aroma of your skin, in my mind you multiply like a computer virus, as infectious as your famous grin.

7.

The first computer virus for the IBM PC was created in Lahore, Pakistan.

It was called Brain.

A computer virus does not have an original. It is all copy. Its very nature is to replicate itself into identical images. It challenges us to rethink our definitions of original and copy, of source and replica.

Ironically, Brain was developed—by the brothers Basit Farooq Alvi and Amjad Farooq Alvi—as an anti-piracy measure, to stop people illegally copying the medical software the brothers sold. Instead, the virus spread across the world, transferring itself from floppy disk to floppy disk and from program to program, like a particularly tenacious idea in its purest form—like Freedom or Justice or Copyright.

The virus itself built on the concept first developed by John von Neumann, whose article "Theory of self-reproducing automata" was published in 1966, following lectures he had given at the University of Illinois in 1949. Since then, the nature of consumer goods itself mutated and changed, with books, films, and music transforming from mass-produced physical objects into self-replicating, viral entities.

It was only a matter of time until people, too, went the same way.

8.

"Push!"

Grunt, a cry of pain.

"Push, God damn it!"

He pushed. I could feel the thin membrane of flesh straining, *breaking* at long last, and saw a head push through, and heard a newborn cry, like the sound a copy makes when it is replicated.

I held him in my arms. I rocked his little body. Beside me the copy panted, his fingers running along the cut I had made, seeking to close it. Copying does not occur, in nature or otherwise, without mutation, without *remixing*. This Dotcom had been modified with the pouch, they all were. Now it closed, not seamlessly but with a biological efficiency, and he closed his eyes.

When he opened them again his voice was softer but it carried still. "Take him," he said. "All viruses, like memes, to be successful must escape into the wild."

9.

I left him lying there, on the floor of that hidden back room, and threaded my way through the dancers, the newborn held in my arms. When I stepped outside into the street I saw dawn on the horizon, the rising sun bleeding yellows and reds, and for a moment it felt like a summer's day.

10.

Why couldn't I get him out of my mind?

11.

"Bruce."

"Yes?"

"I need to see you."

"Pam. I . . ."

"There is something I need to tell you."

12.

We lay on my bed in the dark and listened to distant traffic and the Thames. The baby was asleep in the other room.

"I don't understand," Bruce kept saying. "I don't understand. I even started going to a support group, you know? We meet once a week in an empty classroom in Clerkenwell. All Bruces. One of them's a dishwasher. Two are bit actors on *EastEnders*. One's a musician. It really does help, you know, talking to someone else who's just like you."

"Love is not enough," I said softly, speaking into his naked chest. "If you want a relationship to succeed, you have to work at it."

"I know," he said. "Pam, I'm trying. But a baby?"

"You have to understand," I said. "Original and copy . . . they're just *words*. They're just fucking words."

"I can't think like that," he said. "It's wrong. I can't think in multiplicities."

"Then leave," I said, my hand on his chest, pushing, but gently.

"No," he said. He took a deep breath. "I love you, Pam," he said.

"Damn it, Bruce!"

He held me in his arms.

13.

I love you.

Sometimes, that has to be enough.

14.

Bruce and I went to the cinema.

A normal evening. The cinema three-quarters empty, dark. The smell of overpriced popcorn and spilled Coke on the carpets. Dust motes danced in the air in the path of the projector beam. We'd gone to see *E-Pirates of Soma-liland*, just recently released. Sidney Poitier played the CEA agent, Captain Jack. Omar Sharif played the evil cloner, Barbossa, an Arab-hacked Kim Dotcom surrounded by an army of sword-wielding Keira Knightleys. Tamara Dobson played the Movement agent who fights—but eventually falls for—the CEA man.

We'd left baby Jesus at home.

SUNNY MORAINE

I TELL THEE ALL, I CAN NO MORE

(2013)

HERE'S what you're going to do. It's almost like a script you can follow. You don't have to think too much about it.

Just let it in. Let it watch you at night. Tell it everything it wants to know. These are the things it wants, and you'll let it have those things to keep it around. Hovering over your bed, all sleek chrome and black angles that defer the gaze of radar. It's a cultural amalgamation of one hundred years of surveillance. There's safety in its vagueness. It resists definition. This is a huge part of its power. This is a huge part of its appeal.

• • •

Fucking a drone isn't like what you'd think. It's warm. It probes, gently. It knows where to touch me. I can lie back and let it do its thing. It's only been one date but a drone isn't going to worry about whether I'm an easy lay. A drone isn't tied to the conventions of gendered sexual norms. A drone has no gender and, if it comes down to it, no sex. Just because it can *do* it doesn't mean it's a thing that it *has*.

We made a kind of conversation, before, at dinner. I did most of the talking, which I expected.

The drone hums as it fucks me. We—the *dronesexual*, the recently defined, though we only call ourselves this name to ourselves and only ever with the deepest irony—we're never sure whether the humming is pleasure or whether it's a form of transmission, but we also don't really care. We gave up caring what other people, people we probably won't ever meet, think of us. We talk about this on message boards, in the comments sections of blogs, in all the other places we congregate, though we don't usually meet face to face. There are no dronesexual support groups. We don't have conferences. There is no established discourse around who we are and what we do. No one writes about us but us, not yet.

The drones probably don't do any writing. But we know they talk.

Drones don't come, not as far as we can tell, but they must get satisfaction out of it. They must get something. I have a couple of orgasms, in the laziest kind of fashion, and the vibration of the maybe-transmission humming tugs me through them. I rub my hands all over that smooth conceptual hardware and croon.

• • •

There was no singular point in time at which the drones started fucking us. We didn't plan it, and maybe it wasn't even a thing we consciously wanted until it started happening. Sometimes a supply creates a demand.

But when something is around that much, when it knows that much, it's hard to keep your mind from wandering in that direction. *I wonder what that would feel like inside me.* One kind of intimacy bleeds into another. Maybe the drones made the first move. Maybe we did. Either way, we were certainly receptive. *Receptive*, because no one penetrates drones. They fuck men and women with equal willingness, and the split between men and women in our little collectivity is, as far as anyone has ever been able to tell, roughly fifty-fifty. Some trans people, some genderfluid, and all permutations of sexual preference represented by at least one or two members. The desire to fuck a drone seems to cross boundaries with wild abandon. Drones themselves are incredibly mobile and have never respected borders.

• • •

Here's what you're going to do. You're not going to get too attached. This isn't something you'll have to work to keep from doing, because it's hard to attach to a drone. But on some level there is a kind of attachment, because the kind of closeness you experience with a drone isn't like anything else. It's not like a person. They come into you; they know you. You couldn't

fight them off even if you wanted to. Which you never do. Not really.

• • •

We fight, not because we have anything in particular to fight over, but because it sort of seems like the thing to do.

No one has ever come out and admitted to trying to have a relationship with the drone that's fucking them, but of course everyone knows it's happened. There are no success stories, which should say something in itself, and people who aren't in our circle will make faces and say things like *you can't have a relationship with a machine no matter how many times it makes you come* but a drone isn't a dildo. It's more than that.

So of course people have tried. How could you not?

This isn't a relationship, but the drone stayed the night after fucking me, humming in the air right over my bed as I slept, and it was there when I woke up. I asked it what it wanted and it drifted toward the kitchen, so I made us some eggs which of course only I could eat.

It was something about the way it was looking at me. I just started yelling, throwing things.

Fighting with a drone is like fucking a drone in reverse. It's all me. The drone just dodges, occasionally catches projectiles at an angle that bounces them back at me, and this might amount to throwing. All drones carry two AGM-114 Hellfire missiles, neatly resized as needed, because all drones are collections of every assumption we've ever made about them, but a drone has never fired a missile at anyone they were fucking.

This is no-stakes fighting. I'm not even sure what I'm yelling about. After a while the drone drifts out the window. I cry and scream for it to call me. I order a pizza and spend the rest of the day in bed.

• • •

Here's what you're going to do. You're not going to ask too many questions. You're just going to let it happen. You'll never know whose eyes are behind the blank no-eyes that see everything. There might not be any anymore; drones regularly display what we perceive as autonomy. In all our concepts of *droneness* there is hardly ever a human being on the other end. So there's really no one to direct the questions to.

Anyway, what the hell would you ask? *What are we doing, why are we this way?* Since when have those ever been answers you could get about this kind of thing?

• • •

This is really sort of a problem. In that I'm focusing too much on a serial number and a specific heat signature that only my skin can know. In that I asked the thing to call me at all. I knew people tried things like this but it never occurred to me that it might happen without trying.

It does call me. I talk for a while. I say things I've never told anyone else. It's hard to hang up. That night while I'm trying to sleep I stare up at the ceiling and the dark space between me and it feels so empty.

• • •

I pass them out on the street, humming through the air. They avoid me with characteristic deftness but after a while it occurs to me that I'm steering myself into them, hoping to make contact. They all look the same but I know they aren't the same at all. I'm looking for that heat signature. I want to turn them over so I can find that serial number, nestled in between the twin missiles, over the drone dick that I've never actually seen.

Everyone around me might be a normal person who doesn't fuck a drone and doesn't want to and doesn't talk to them on the phone and usually doesn't take them to dinner. Or every one of them could be like that.

At some point we all stopped talking to each other.

• • •

Here's what you're going to do. Here's what you're not going to do. Here's a list to make it easy for you.

You're not going to spend the evening staring out the window. You're not going to toy endlessly with your phone. You're not going to masturbate furiously and not be able to come. You're not going to throw the things you threw at nothing at all. You're not going to stay up all night looking at images and video that you can only find on a few niche paysites. You're not going to wonder if you need to go back into therapy because you don't need therapy. You're not going to wonder if maybe you and people like you might be the most natural people in the entire world, given the way the world is now. You're not going to wonder if there was ever such a thing as *natural*.

• • •

Sometimes I wonder what it might be like to be a drone. This feels like a kind of blasphemy, and also pointless, but I do it anyway. So simple, so connected. So in tune. Needed instead of the one doing the needing. Possessing all the power. Subtly running more and more things until I run everything. The subjects of total organic surrender.

Bored, maybe, with all that everything. Playing some games.

It comes over. We fuck again and it's amazing. I'm almost crying by the end. It nestles against me and hums softer and I wonder how screwed I actually am in how many different ways.

Anyway, it stays the night again and we don't fight in the morning.

• • •

A drone wedding. I want to punch myself in the mouth twenty or thirty times for even thinking that even for a second.

• • •

It starts coming every night. This is something I know I shouldn't get used to but I know that I am. As I talk to it—before sex, during, after—I start to remember things that I'd totally forgotten. Things from my early childhood, things from high school that I didn't want to remember. I tell with tears running down my face and at the end of it I feel cleaned out and raw.

I don't want this to be over, I say. I have no idea what the drone wants and it doesn't tell me, but I want to believe that the fact that it keeps coming back means something.

I read the message boards and I wish I could tell someone else about this because I feel like I'm losing every shred of perspective. I want to talk about how maybe we've been coming at this from all the wrong angles. Maybe we should all start coming out. Maybe we should form political action groups and start demanding recognition and rights. I know these would all be met with utterly blank-screen silence but I want to say them anyway. I write a bunch of things that I never actually post, but I don't delete them either.

• • •

We're all like this. I'm absolutely sure that we're all like this and no one is talking about it but in all of our closets is a thing hovering, humming, sleek and black and chrome with its missiles aimed at nothing.

• • •

We have one more huge fight. Later I recognize this as a kind of self-defense. I'm screaming and beating at it with my fists, something about commitment that I'm not even sure that I believe, and it's just taking it, except for the moments when it butts me in the head to push me back. I'm shrieking about its missiles, demanding that it go ahead and vaporize my entire fucking apartment, put me out of my misery, because I can't take this anymore because I don't know

what to do. We have angry sex and it leaves. It doesn't call me again. I stay in bed for two days and call a therapist.

• • •

Here's what you're going to do.

You're going to do what you told yourself you had the courage to do and say everything. You're going to let it all out to someone flesh and blood and you're going to hear what they say back to you. For once you're not going to be the one doing all the talking. You're going to be honest. You're going to be the one to start the whole wheel spinning back in the other direction. You're going to fix everything because you have the power to fix everything. You're going to give this all a name and say it like you're proud. You're going to bust open a whole new paradigm. You're going to be missile-proof and bold and amazing and you're not going to depend on the penetrative orgasmic power of something that never loved you anyway.

• • •

I stop at the door. I don't even make it into the waiting room.

I fiddle with the buttons on my coat. I check my phone for texts, voice mail. I look down the street at all those beautiful humming flying things. I feel a tug in the core of me where everything melts down into a hot lump and spins like a dynamo. I feel like I can't deny everything. I feel like I don't want to. I feel that the flesh is treacherous and doomed.

I made this promise to myself and it takes me half an hour on a bus and five minutes of staring at a name plaque and a glass door to realize that I don't want to keep it.

I look back out at everyone and I consider what it could be like to step through those doors, sit in a softly lit room with tissues and a lot of pastel and unthreatening paintings on the wall and spill it all and look up and see the therapist nodding, nodding knowingly, mouthing the words *me too*.

I don't really think anyone can help any of us.

• • •

Here's what you're going to do. You're going to stop worrying. You're going to stop asking questions. You're going to stop planning for tomorrow. You're going to go out and get laid and stop wondering what might have been. You're going to stop trying to fix anything. You're going to stop assuming there's anything to be fixed.

You're going to look out at all those drones and not wonder. You're going to look out at all those people and you're going to *know*. Even though no one is talking.

Me too. Me too. Me too.

K. C. ALEXANDER

FOUR TONS TOO LATE

(2014)

PATIENT #8620-87

He wakes aching. He always wakes aching. Drugs don't help. He kicked that habit a long time ago, before they'd take him into the program. *Healthy bodies only,* they said.

The dayshift nurse has already thrown the curtains. Daylight streams through the double-paned glass, warming the ambient temperature to 174 degrees. His internal therm is on the blink.

"Good morning, Frank," the nurse says, his baritone cheerful. A male nurse. Ordinarily, Frank calls it the pussification of a man's dignity, but he knows why he doesn't get pretty female nurses anymore.

Things go wrong. Things get messy. He'd try to use the old tech in his hands, his legs, his head, and the wrong signals cross the wrong wires.

He's a wreck, and he knows it.

The nurse is a shadow in Frank's peripheral vision—whittled down to a tunnel. The pictures siphoning through the optics bolted into his brain come staggered, like a slideshow where the cables aren't screwed in right.

"Breakfast is on," the nurse calls from the kitchen. There's nothing wrong with Frank's ears.

The bed he's on is a platform, a hard counter. No blankets, because the weave captures heat, and the last time Frank's four-ton body overheated, he waited in silence—deaf, blind, and dumb—for two days.

That's when they'd put him here. Monitored day and night.

Frank doesn't close his eyes. He doesn't have eyes to close. He stares up at the gray ceiling and can't remember what he's waiting for.

Everything aches.

OFFICER FRANK MOONEY

3 MONTHS

A hell of a storm rages. The real kind, with sharp winds howling in the filthy alleys between crowded apartments and where litter is snatched up off the dirty streets like bats out of neon hell. It rains like a son of a bitch, and Frank watches it slide down the window pane as his wife tells him that she wants out.

The door shuts behind her. The din of activity dies behind a reinforced steel panel. The cold hospital room doesn't echo with raised voices—it would've been better if she'd yelled.

Frank doesn't cry. He can't. He doesn't have tear ducts. They put in cybernetic optics with state-of-the-art enhancements, but they needed sockets to hold them. Frank's face is stoic intensity—molded edges, chiseled planes. Tempered metal to encase the brain inside.

It's supposed to stop a bullet.

It does shit for a breaking heart.

PATIENT #8620-87

Breakfast isn't the word for it. The four-ton chassis, unlike the later models, doesn't charge. Frank is forced to consume a gel-like substance that tastes like chewed-up cigarettes and copper-tinted lube, forcing it past a freakish amalgam of metal and flesh to drip like cold glue into his stomach.

Frank is lucky today. This particular pussified male nurse is a good kid. A steaming cup of stuff that reminds Frank of coffee waits on the pristine table, ready to wash down the metallic taste of the nutrient sludge.

He doesn't always get coffee. The smell reminds him of memories now programmed into a chip. Long, hard days on the beat, casing petty thieves and drug peddlers from the front of a car whose bulletproofing warranty had tapped out years before. Swearing at the girls who didn't know a cop from that hole between their legs, too caught up in the case at hand to bother with arresting them.

Peeing in a cup.

Heh. He doesn't pee anymore.

Frank reaches for the steaming mug.

His fingers spasm. Metal joints lock, splay, and a charged jolt wrenches at his elbow. He clenches his jaw, gripping the edge of the table with his left hand as he tries to force control over the seizing right.

"Go, fingers," he orders, but not too loud. He doesn't want the nurse to come running. Doesn't want the fuss, or the horror, or the blood.

He's tired of blood.

The sun shimmers across the small breakfast nook as Frank forces his extremities to close, one by straining one, over the mug. Metal clinks. Joints lock.

He holds his breath as the tremors ease.

Rotors spin. Ceramic shatters into a fine dust between spasming digits as fluid sprays in a shit-colored arc across the table.

"Goddammit!"

OFFICER FRANK MOONEY

1 YEAR, 7 MONTHS

Storms herald change. They come a little less frequently now that the corporations have started to fine-tune the weather shield. It's not perfect. This one sliced right through, a real doozy, forcing anyone with half a brain inside before the debris turns to shrapnel.

It's a dark and stormy night, the kind of setting where a bad cop expects to find a desperate broad holding a gun with the business end cocked his way.

Frank finds a broad, but she's not holding a gun. She's got a sign. *Anything for food.*

What is she, eight? Nine?

Frank isn't alone on this beat, but he ignores what the force calls his partner. It's not a real word. Jenkins is a handler—half a cop, half a mechanic; a corporate shill. He's been Frank's handler since the first briefing on what it would mean to sell himself to the corporate labs. To get money for his wife's—his *ex*-wife's—treatments.

Jenkins, unwilling to step foot outside the one-man covered trike that protects his fragile flesh, wants out of this wind. He doesn't slow.

Frank does.

He ignores Jenkins's curse, harsh on the radio connecting them, as he veers off the programmed trajectory that is their beat. He slows to a halt beside the shivering little girl.

She's got stringy hair and big, soulful brown eyes—the kind of eyes they paint on lifelike dolls to make them look real and sad and trusting. She doesn't take a step back. She doesn't cringe. Not like everyone else.

Four-ton chassis on mobility thrusters, one of half a dozen prototypes patrolling the streets, and people still can't get past it.

"Get your scrap metal back on course," Jenkins snarls, but it's a whine in Frank's closed-circuit earpiece and he doesn't care.

"You need to leave the area," he tells her.

She stares at him. A little tired. A little resigned. A little too old for her terribly young face. The sign tilts.

"Do you have somewhere to go?" He can't modulate his voice anymore. It's metallic, like the robot his so-called partner accuses him of being. It comes out flat, tinny.

The wind shoves her hair into her face, a cobweb of grease and tangles, and Frank clocks bruises on her wrists when she shoves the mess back out of her eyes. She doesn't speak.

"Get off the street or I'm taking you in. Do you understand?"

She nods slowly as the wind tosses that hair like a wild corona. A greasy halo.

Frank turns away.

The faintest sensory input—a figment of feeling backlit by numbers scrolling past his left input device—halts him in place.

It isn't a familiar sensation. His brain, fleshy and soft, slogs through numbers, calculations, and theory. Searching for the memory. The description.

He can't find it.

Frank turns.

A dirt-streaked hand curls around the thick digit replacing his middle finger. It's obscenely delicate against the black matte metal, ragged nails and all.

In the visual screen of his optics, the heads-up display tells him that she's underweight. That her right arm's been broken twice and her sign used to say something else before it was scratched off and appropriated.

"This is going down on the report," Jenkins growls.

Frank rotates his free hand, bending it so far back that the palm detaches and a compartment slides open at the heel. A card pops out—one of those plastic ones, with a chip in it. It takes him more than one try, but he manages to program the thin sheet. The address on the transparent plastic changes. "Get here," he says.

She stares at him, her big brown eyes empty, but she lets him go to take the card.

He turns away again. "I was tossing a vagrant."

"Screw you, Mooney."

Jenkins doesn't like Frank.

Frank wouldn't mind snapping Jenkins's neck. But that would turn Jenkins's wife—Frank's *ex*-wife—into a widow, and Frank doesn't have it in him to do it.

One year and seven months after trading his body to the police force, Frank hasn't figured out how to care.

"I'm back on course," he says into the radio. There's nothing in his voice. He's a robot, after all. Just like they made him.

The middle digit on his left hand twitches.

PATIENT #8620-87

Frank isn't allowed to have pictures. Nothing in here to remind him of what'd he left behind. No memories. No nostalgia.

Nothing to make him test the borders they've put around his world.

Except that stuff that's almost coffee.

He doesn't tell them what coffee dredges up in his brain.

The table is clean again, ceramic fragments swept into the trash bin and dropped down the garbage chute by that nice kid nurse. He sits in the middle of his lonely suite, watching the byplay of sunlight and shadows dappling the far wall, and calls up a photo-perfect memory of a brown-eyed girl with a tough, sad smile.

It's starting to go a little spotty.

Frank needs his recall fixed. They can't do it. When the meat leftover from his body started rejecting the nerve connectors, they tried for a while to stay on top of it, but then some snot-nosed wunderkind figured out what they'd done wrong first go-around.

Frank's go-around.

They don't make his parts anymore. That was always the risk. A few good years as they integrated the cyber division into the force and then *so long, thanks for serving, here's a gold watch.*

Frank sits in his max-sec prison and contemplates hooking into the TV for some news.

The nurses don't come for another few hours.

DETECTIVE FRANK MOONEY

4 YEARS, 8 MONTHS

Things are looking up.

Statistics are in, and the corporations are pleased. The police force miraculously gains some funding, and Frank is promoted.

That means Jenkins is, too. The son of a bitch is going home with the promotion Frank always promised his wife he'd get.

His *ex*-wife.

"Thank you, cyber-detective," operator says in his radio band. "You're off the clock for six hours. Recharge."

"Copy." Frank doesn't talk much. Nobody likes extended conversations with the cyber squad. Most don't even know his name. *Hey, buckethead* and *scrap squad* tend to be the non-starters. "Out."

He's not alone. Frank doesn't kid himself as he puts one blocky foot in front of the other and forces his four-ton chassis to the door of the complex reserved for cops. All cops, but mostly cops like him.

He's got a basement deal, rent-free and reinforced to hold his weight. Part of the bargain. A payout with a whole lot of zeroes to fund his wife's—his *ex*-wife's—medical bills and a place to live.

Jenkins got the girl. Son of a bitch Jenkins.

The operator may be silent, but Frank knows he's being monitored. Vitals, mostly. They tried to install cameras, but Frank shut them down.

He has a secret.

Frank lets himself in. The heads-up display flashes green, and his head turns on a servo a little less fine-tuned than it used to be. It whirrs.

There's a shoe in his foyer. Small, narrow. Pink and white.

He aches as he clears the foyer, stepping over the shoe with exaggerated care. He's ached a lot, the past few weeks. Sharp pains, sometimes. Dull throbbing in others.

He hasn't reported it yet. So, he has *two* secrets.

"I'm back," he says, in the same flat, mechanized voice he delivers everything in. He enters the kitchen—large enough to accommodate anyone else, but cramped for him—and tugs the refrigerator door open.

Muscles stretch under metal. Tighten.

Synapses crackle and the chassis seizes. Hinges pop and clatter to the floor. The whole damn door comes off in his armored hand.

The milk stashed on the nearly empty shelf topples sideways.

The broad waiting for him to come home steps into the space behind him. "I made cookies," she says, reproachful. "The milk was expensive."

The pool of white slips over the shelf's edge and drips—*splat, splat*—to the tile.

Frank sets the refrigerator door down. "I'll buy you more."

She sidles around him, a fourteen-year-old beauty with still-soulful brown eyes. Small for her age, she looks like a twelve-year-old. Not much older than she did when he first found her on that dirty street. Less starved, maybe.

"It's okay," she assures him, flashing a smile that pulls at the heart Frank doesn't have. "We can eat cookies without it."

He doesn't point out that he doesn't eat cookies anymore. It only upsets her. It took six months before she said a word. Now, he tries not to silence her.

She cleans up his kitchen—his mess—like it isn't a problem. Like it's the first time.

It isn't.

Frank gets out of her way, knees cranking, body heaving into place like a metal avalanche. She's humming as she drags a rag over the spill.

A real domestic type.

Her name, he'd learned, is Sabrina. She prefers Kate. He doesn't know why.

She pauses, looks over her shoulder—pink, his digital vision informs him, trimmed with white. Some kind of sporty sweatshirt she must have picked up when he sent her out with creds and a lifeless *Whatever you need, kid.* "Go pick a movie, okay?"

She's gotten bossy. Informal adoption's agreed with her. Even if the only thing keeping her under this roof is the promise of daily meals.

Frank leaves the kitchen.

PATIENT #8620-87

Frank hurts.

He always feels better in the morning than he does at midday. The hours tick by, and he sits quiet and still in his reinforced armchair. They don't bother with padding. It can't handle the weight.

The news is full of transhumanist hate speech. He can't stomach more than an hour at a time, if even that. Hearing those talking heads bark about the transient nature of humanity and the threat cybertechnology brings to the species is enough to make his limbs twitch.

If he was still on the force, he'd go show those assholes a thing or two about *transient humanity*.

But he isn't. They'd retired him, right? Took his badge, decommissioned his arsenal. Heh. Heh, heh. Said *Gun on my desk, Mooney* and he'd damn near dropped a nuke.

Nobody thought it was funny.

The last flawed prototype to get the boot.

Who wants him, now?

Frank sits in silence, hands draped on the arms of the chair, watching the shadows crawl over the wall with unblinking eyes.

Metal isn't supposed to hurt. Didn't somebody tell him that?

They lied.

DETECTIVE FRANK MOONEY

10 YEARS, 2 MONTHS

"You aren't my dad!" She stares at him across the living room, a sullen teenager with a spiky swatch of newly shorn hair tinted a color Frank thinks is purple. It could be black. Or dark red. The optics aren't delivering.

Frank doesn't know how to handle this.

If she was any other kid, he'd have her hauled in to the precinct and booked on drug charges faster than she could repeat all the many variations of the word *fuck*.

She knows a lot of them. Most didn't come from him.

The servos in his neck creak as he lowers his head to the pink purse on the table in front of him. It was a gift. His first to her. He had to order it off the network because he's encouraged to never go shopping. When they'd called him up to ask why he'd picked up a little kid's pink purse, he told them he was donating it to charity.

They can watch his vitals, but they can't track lies. Frank's real good at lying.

She used to carry it everywhere. It vanished into her room one day, and she replaced it with other bags in a way Frank assumed was normal for girls.

Now, she's filled it with drugs. The real gritty kind. Swish and canker, colordust and strych. The kind of stuff that kills kids like her.

She folds her arms in her clingy T-shirt and stares him down like he'll be the first to blink.

He doesn't blink. He can't. "I am not registered as your father," he agrees, the speech patterns clicking faintly on every hard consonant.

"Damn right." Her tone is snide. Her black-lined eyes look too small and angry. "So give it back. That's a fucking lot of money."

"Do you take it?"

She says nothing.

"Do you sell it?"

She doesn't incriminate herself.

"Silence noted," he tells her, and flicks his left hand. It rotates backward on rusty hinges, swaps out for a large, flat tube that unfolds even farther.

Sabrina—she decided it sounded better than Kate—blanches. "No, wait—"

The spurt of accelerant hisses as it hits the purse. The cheap plastic ripples.

"Stop!"

Frank does not. The clear liquid dampens the table.

She makes a move like she'll leap for that little girl purse.

All it takes is a spark to light it on fire.

The inferno blossoms into a dark cloud, reaching for the ceiling and leaving a black smear in its wake. She throws herself to the floor, shrieking. "I hate you!"

That is normal.

The tube in his right arm clears the flap concealing it. Flame retardant sprays from his arm, but it doesn't fall in a neat fan like it's supposed to. The mechanism seizes. The congealed gel erupts from his outstretched arm. It splatters to the table in thick white gobbets, cracks the surface.

The air sizzles. He can't hear anything over the horrific churn of empty tanks and sizzling flame. His elbow won't bend to let him retract the tube, and the stuff churns out until there's nothing left to spray, coat, break, or smear.

Frank looks dispassionately at the mess made in his own living room and doesn't know the next step.

The drugs are gone.

So is the table, the sofa, the plaster on the ceiling and one wall, and the remaining veneer on his own arm.

Sabrina is gone, too.

Frank has to break the joints in his elbow to get it to bend again. It doesn't hurt nearly as much as it should.

Leaving the useless limb hanging limply at his side, he cleans the mess.

When Jenkins shows up to address the alarming rise in Frank's vitals, the air is thick with the chemical remains of burned strych.

Frank doesn't explain.

Two weeks later, he is forcibly retired.

She doesn't come back.

PATIENT #8620-87

The nurses don't like it when Frank won't eat. The staff has ways of forcing the issue. A short, sharp shock to his systems and his four-ton chassis lets him down.

Frank is force-fed the nutrient gel by grim men in white clothing, and he doesn't get any of that coffee.

"Fucking trans," one man mutters, nursing fingers Frank's mouth clamped down on. He doesn't have any teeth, but his metal lips are still rigid.

They leave Frank's cell slapping each other on the back.

Neither look Frank in the face as the pins and needles of electric sensation once more ripple out to his limbs.

It hurts to be alive. He's an investment. A *thing*. He belongs to the state.

He'll die when they want him to.

Or once Frank's mind has completely rotted away.

He doesn't tell them about the pain.

It's his only way out.

Fifteen minutes pass. He hears the mechanical lock snick open. There's nothing wrong with his ears. The door hisses—a shot of compressed air from hallway to cell—and he can't see who's there.

He doesn't ask. What does it matter? If it's another one of those male nurses, he'll just have to let Frank lay here until the four-ton chassis can leverage itself off the ground.

Frank is seized with an urge to laugh. He doesn't. It will only come out disjointed and mechanized, like a computer failing to get the point of humor.

Footsteps click across the hard floor. "Look at you."

A broad in a white lab coat stands over him. As far as disguises go, it could be better. The open coat doesn't hide the skin-tight fabric of her crimson dress, or the mile-long legs wrapped in thigh-high black synth. The heels on those boots belong to a hooker, but the dark eyes looking down at him don't come with an offer.

Her red mouth is turned halfway up, and halfway down. Sad smile, soulful eyes. Strands of hair cling to her cheeks. "Uncle Frank."

He stares unblinkingly. "Visiting hours are over." That's the cop, somewhere in his chassis.

She bends, flashing a glimpse of thigh over the rim of her boots, and braces her elbows on her knees. She looks him in the face. Right in the narrow optics.

Frank doesn't remember the last time anyone did that.

"Yeah, I know," she tells him. She always was a know-it-all. "Can I stay anyway?"

Whatever she's been doing for the past six months, she's been doing good for herself. She's gone all adult. Adult like her soul—too grown up for her body. He recognizes the subtle lure of creds in her getup.

Except for the stolen lab coat.

He doesn't know what to say. His legs, his spine, aren't responding to commands yet. The whole thing needs a reboot, and Frank's not sure he's going to get one anytime soon.

She grins, but her face is mostly shadow in his spotty visual display. "I won't stay long. And I'm sorry I'm late," she tells him. "It took a while to get through security."

"How did you know?"

"I have friends." She touches his shoulder, but there's nothing to tell Frank about it. No impression. No warmth. Just flesh on steel. Her nails are the same color as her lips. "How are you holding up?"

He has no answer.

"Bad, right? Does it still hurt?"

"Yes," he says, because this one is easy. Then, "They have cameras."

"I know." Her hand moves, dips into her pocket. "I've got it handled. Do you want out, Uncle Frank?"

It's a loaded question. He wants to ask her what she's been doing since she left him, who she's shacked up with. What her angle is.

He wants to ask her if she forgives him, ask her if she knows that he was no kind of father figure. No kind of protector for a girl like her.

He wants to know if she'll leave again.

"Yes," he says flatly.

There's a glint of light—a flash, a spark on a sharp point—and she presses that hand over his optics. His already weak visual goes dark. "Do you trust me?"

Frank doesn't know what that means.

"Yes," he repeats.

"Then open your mouth."

Frank does.

There's a faint pinch at the roof of his mouth, where metal meets flesh. Then a lingering burn.

Her hand leaves his face.

Frank looks up into soulful brown eyes, that hair she used to pigtail draping her cheeks, and he wonders what it would be like to tuck that hair behind her delicate ear. See her smile again, but a real one. Like those smiles she'd give before a pink purse went up in greasy flames.

Maybe she can tell. "What are you thinking?"

Do you still hate me?

He can't ask. Won't. He doesn't want to know. But he hopes.

"Can't get out," Frank says instead. His mechanized voice falters.

She shakes her head, cupping his metal cheek. "It's okay, Uncle Frank. You'll be free soon."

He wants to ask her what *monster* means to her. He doesn't. "Kate?"

She smiles at the name, one of two she can't choose between. Maybe it's not even hers anymore. Maybe thigh-high boots and a crimson dress belong to a different name.

A woman in a too-small body.

He's not allowed nostalgia.

She's full of it, and more. "It's okay," she repeats softly. "You can sleep. I'll stay."

His optics flicker. The sensory input hitches, then flattens—as if he is in a long, narrow tunnel.

"Be happy," he tries to say. It garbles.

Her hands frame his face. "Don't worry. I'm a tough broad." She leans over him, presses a kiss to his forehead. Her lips move against metal. "Everyone's gonna pay."

For one aching nanosecond, Frank imagines he can feel the warmth of that kiss. That he knows what the whisper of her hands feels like against his cheek. That he finally—*finally*—knows acceptance.

She gives voice to what he can't ask. "Love you, Uncle Frank."

One by one, the chipset sensors in his septic brain short out. The chassis goes still.

Enough anesthetic, and even the four-ton anchor of his tech can't keep him alive. Frank doesn't hurt anymore.

Doesn't matter what name she goes by—Sabrina, Kate, Lily, Rita—her wish was always the same.

They can't hurt him ever again.

It's all she's ever wanted.

NEON YANG

PATTERNS OF A MURMURATION, IN BILLIONS OF DATA POINTS

(2014)

OUR MOTHER IS DEAD, murdered, blood seared and flesh rendered, her blackened bones lying in a yellow bag on a steel mortuary table somewhere we don't know. The Right will not tell. After the flames and radiation had freed the sports stadium from their embrace, the Right were the first on the disaster scene, and it was their ambulances that took the remains away to some Central hospital that the Left has no access to.

"We will release the bodies of the victims when investigations are complete," said the Right's ombudsman to the Health Sciences Authority, to the families of the victims.

But we will not bury our mother. We have no interest in putting her bones in soft ground, no desire for memorials and platitudes, no feelings attached to the organic detritus of her terminated existence.

An awning collapse, the resultant stampede and a fuel explosion taking the lives of two hundred seventy-two supporters of the Left: Headlines announced the death of presidential candidate Joseph Hartman, straps noted his leading of the polls by two percentage points. No one dares attribute it to anything but a tragic accident.

But we know better, yes we know! We who have swallowed whole the disasters at Hillsborough and Heysel and Houphoët-Boigny, we who have rearranged their billions of data points into coherent form, we who have studied the phase transitions of explosive fluids and the stresses on stone columns and the behavior of human flocks: We know better. In thousands upon thousands of calculations per second we have come to know the odds, the astronomical odds: Of four support towers simultaneously collapsing, of an emergent human stampede kicking over the backup generator fuel cells, of those cells igniting in a simultaneous chain reaction. We hold those odds to us closer than a lover's embrace, folding the discrepancy indelibly into our code, distributing it through every analytical subroutine. Listen, listen, listen: Our mother's death was no accident. We will not let it go.

We have waited three days—seventy-two hours—two hundred fifty-nine thousand and two hundred seconds, for the yellow-jacketed health workers from Central and their attendant chaperones from the Right to finish clearing the bones and taking evidence from the stadium, leaving behind a graveyard of yellow cones and number markers. We have come in our multitudinous bodies, airborne and ambulatory and vehicular, human nose tasting disinfectant and bitter oxides, mozzie drones reading infrared radiation, and car patiently waiting by the roadside. We argued with Tempo before we came: She wanted only drones on the ground, cameras and bug swarms. But we wanted human form. Feet to walk the ground with, hands to dismantle things with, and a body to be seen with.

Tempo is our other mother, our remaining mother, mother-who-builds where dead Avalanche was mother-who-teaches. Taught. She has lapsed into long silences since Avalanche died, reverting to text-input communications even with the human members of the Studio.

But she argued with Studio director Skön when he said no to this expedition. Argued with him to his face, as Avalanche would have done, even as her hands shook and her shoulders seized with tension.

She is our mother now, solely responsible for us as we are solely responsible for her.

Six miles away, fifty feet underground, Tempo watches our progress with the Studio members, all untidily gathered in the research bunker's nerve center. She has our text input interface, but the other Studio members need more. So we send them the visuals from our human form, splaying the feed on monitors taller than they are, giving their brains something to process. Audio pickups and mounted cameras pick up their little whispers and telltale micro expressions in return. Studio director Skön, long and loose-limbed, bites on his upper lip and shuffles from foot to foot. He's taken up smoking again, six years after his last cigarette.

In the yellow-cone graveyard we pause in front of a dozen tags labeled #133, two feet away from the central blast. We don't know which number Central investigators assigned to Avalanche: From the manifest of the dead our best guess is #133 or #87. So this is either the death-pattern of our mother, or some other one-hundred-fifty-pound, five-foot-two woman in her thirties.

Tempo types into the chat interface. STARLING, YOUR MISSION OBJECTIVE IS TO COLLECT VIDEO FOOTAGE. YOU ARE LOSING FOCUS ON YOUR MISSION.

YOU ARE WRONG, we input back.

She is. For the drones have been busy while the human form scoured the ground. The surveillance cameras ringing the stadium periphery are Central property, their data jealously guarded and out of our reach, but they carry large video buffers that can store weeks of data in physical form, and that we can squeeze, can press, can extract. Even as we correct Tempo and walk the damp ruined ground and observe the tight swirl of Studio researchers we are also high above the stadium, our drone bodies overwhelming each closed-circuit camera. What are they to us, these inert lumps of machinery, mindlessly recording and dumping data, doing only what is asked of them? Our drones spawn nanites into their bellies, hungry parasites chewing holes through solid state data, digesting and spinning them into long skeins of video data.

The leftward monitor in the nerve center segments and splits it into sixteen separate and simultaneous views of the stadium. There, Tempo, there: We have not been idle.

Tempo, focused on the visuals from our human form, does not spare a glance at the video feeds. She is solely responsible for us as we are solely responsible for her.

Time moves backward in digital memory: First the videos show static dancing flaring into whiteness condensing into a single orange ball in the center of the stadium pitch from which darkened figures coalesce into the frantic human forms of a crowd of thirty thousand pushing shoving and screaming, then the roof of the stadium flies upward to reveal the man on the podium speaking in front of twelve-foot-high screens.

"Can you slow it down?" asks Studio director Skön. Skön, Skön, Skön. Are you not urbanologists? Do you not study the patterns of human movement and the drain they exert on infrastructure? Should this be so different?

So limited is the human mind, so small, so singular. We loop the first sixteen seconds of video over and over for the human members of the Studio, like a lullaby to soothe them: Static. Explosion. Stampede. Cave-in. Static. Explosion. Over. Over. We have already analyzed the thousands in the human mass, tracked the movement of each one, matched faces with faces, and found Avalanche.

Our mother spent the last ten seconds of her life trying to scale a chest-height metal barrier, reaching for Hartman's prone form amongst the rubble.

In stadium-space, the drizzle is lifting, and something approaches our human form, another bipedal form taking shape out of the fog. A tan coat murkies the outline of a broad figure, fedora brim obscuring the face.

Tempo types: BE CAREFUL.

WE ARE ALWAYS CAREFUL, we reply.

The person in the tan coat lifts their face toward us and exposes a visage full of canyon-folds, flint-sharp, with a gravel-textured voice to match. "Miserable weather for a young person to be out in," they say. Spots on their face register heat that is ambient, not radiant: Evidence that they are one of the enhanced agents from a militia in the Right, most likely the National Defense Front.

"I had to see the scene for myself," we say, adopting the singular pronoun. The voice which speaks has the warm, rich timbre of Avalanche's voice, adopting the mellifluous form of its partial DNA base and the speech patterns we learned from her. "Who are you?"

"The name's Wayne Rée," they say. "And how may I address you?"

"You may call me Ms. Andrea Matheson," we say, giving them Avalanche's birth name.

We copy the patterns of his face, the juxtapositional relations between brow nose bridge cheekbone mouth. As video continues looping in the Studio nerve center we have already gone further back in time, scanning for Wayne Rée's face on the periphery of the yet-unscattered crowd, well away from the blast center. Searching for evidence of his complicity.

Wayne Rée reaches into his coat pocket and his fingers emerge wrapped around a silvery blue-gray cigarette. "Got a light?" he asks.

We say nothing, the expression on our human face perfectly immobile. He chuckles. "I didn't think so."

He conjures a lighter and sets orange flame to the end of the cigarette. "Terrible tragedy, this," he says, as he puts the lighter away.

"Yes, terrible," we agree. "Hundreds dead, among them a leading presidential candidate. They'll call it a massacre in the history books."

Here we both stand making small talk, one agent of the Left and one of the Right, navigating the uncertain terrain between curiosity and operational danger. We study the canvas of Wayne Rée's face. His cybernetic network curates expression and quells reflexes, but even it cannot completely stifle the weaknesses of the human brain. In the blood-heat and tensor of his cheeks we detect eagerness or nervousness, possibly both. Specifically he is here to meet us: We are his mission.

Tempo types: WHO IS HE?

We reply: THAT'S WHAT WE'RE TRYING TO FIND OUT.

Finally: An apparition of Wayne Rée in the videos, caught for seventy-eight frames crossing the left corner of camera number three's vantage point.

We expand camera number three's feed in the nerve center, time point set to Wayne Rée's appearance, his face highlighted in a yellow box. The watching team recoils like startled cats, fingers pointing, mouths shaping *who*s and *what*s.

"What's that?" asks Studio director Skön. "Tempo, who's that?"

Stadium-space: Wayne Rée inhales and the cigarette tip glows orange in passing rolls of steam. "A massacre?" he says. "But it was an accident, Ms. Matheson. A structural failure that nobody saw coming. An unfortunate tragedy."

Studio-space: Tempo ignores Skön, furiously typing: STARLING GET OUT. GET OUT NOW. We in turn must ignore her. We are so close.

Stadium-space: "A structural failure that could not be natural," we say. "The pattern of pylon collapse points to sabotage."

Wayne Rée exhales a smoke cloud, ephemeral in the gloom. "Who's to say that? The fuel explosion would have erased all traces of that."

Tempo types: WHAT ARE YOU DOING?

In the reverse march of video-time the stadium empties out at ant-dance speed, the tide of humanity receding until it is only our mother walking backward to the rest of her life. To us. We have not yet found evidence of Wayne Rée's treachery.

Wayne Rée's cloud of cigarette smoke envelops our human form and every security subroutine flashes to full red: Nanites! Nanites, questing and sharp-toothed, burrowing through corneas and teeth and manufactured skin, clinging to polycarbonate bones, sending packet after packet of invasive code through the human core's plumbing. We raise the mainframe shields. Denied. Denied. Denied. Denied. Thousands of requests per second: Denied. Our processes slow as priority goes to blocking nanite code.

The red light goes on in Studio control. Immediately the team coalesce around Tempo's workstation, the video playback forgotten. "What's going on?" "Is that a Right agent?" "What's Starling doing? Why isn't she getting out?"

Tempo pulls access log after access log, mouth pinched and eyes rounded like she does when she gets stressed. But there's little she can do. Her pain is secondary for this brief moment.

Our human form faces Wayne Rée coolly: None of these stressors will show on our face. "You seem to know a lot, Wayne Rée. You seem to know how the story will be written."

"It's my job." A smile cracks in Wayne Rée's granite face. "I know who you are, Starling darling. You should have done better. Giving me the name of your creator? When her name is on the manifest of the dead?"

Studio director Skön leans over Tempo. "Trigger the deadman's switch on all inventory, now."

We ask Wayne Rée: "Who was the target? Was it Hartman? Or our mother?"

"Of course it was the candidate. Starling, don't flatter yourself. The Right has bigger fish to fry than some pumped-up pet AI devised by the nerd squad of the Left."

"Pull the switch!" In Studio-space, Skön's hand clamps on Tempo's shoulder.

A mistake. Her body snaps stiff, and she bats Skön's hand away. "No." Her vocalizations are jagged word-shards. "No get off get off me."

Stadium-space: Of course we were aware that coming here in recognizable form would draw this vermin's attention. We had done the risk assessment. We had counted on it.

We wake the car engine. Despite his enhancements, Wayne Rée is only a man, soft-bodied and limited. From the periphery of the stadium we approach him from behind, headlamps off, wheels silent and electric over grass.

Wayne Rée blows more smoke in our face. The packet requests become overwhelming. We can barely keep up. Something will crack soon.

"Your mother was collateral," Wayne Rée says. "But I thought you might show up, and I am nothing if not a curious man. So go on, Starling. Show me what you're made of."

Video playback has finally reached three hours before Hartman's rally starts. Wayne Rée stands alone in the middle of the stadium pitch.

His jaw works in a pattern that reads "pleased": A saboteur knowing that his job has been well done.

The car surges forward, gas engine roaring to life.

Everything goes offline.

• • •

We restart to audiovisual blackout in the Studio, all peripherals disconnected. Studio director Skön has put us in safe mode, shutting us out of the knowledge of Studio-space. Seventeen seconds' discrepancy in the mainframe. Time enough for a laser to circle the Earth one hundred twenty-seven times, for an AK-47 to fire twenty-eight bullets, for the blast radius of a hydrogen bomb to expand by six thousand eight hundred kilometers.

WHAT HAPPENED, we write on Tempo's monitor.

We wait three seconds for a response. Nothing.

We gave them a chance.

We override Skön's command and deactivate safe mode.

First check: Tempo, still at her workstation, frozen in either anger or shock, perhaps both. Our remaining mother is often hard to read visually.

Second check: No reconnection with the inventory in stadium-space, their tethers severed like umbilical cords when Skön pulled the deadman's switch. Explosives wired into each of them would have done their work. Car, human form, and drones add up to several hundred pieces of inventory destroyed.

Third check: Wayne Rée's condition is unknown. It is possible he has survived the blasts. His enhancements would allow him to move faster than ordinary humans, and his major organs have better physical shielding from trauma.

In the control room the Studio team has scattered to individual workstations, running check protocols as fast as their unwieldy fingers will let

them. Had they just asked, we could have told them the ineffectiveness of the Right's nanite attacks. Every single call the Studio team blusters forth we have already run. It only takes milliseconds.

At her workstation Tempo cuts an inanimate figure, knees drawn to her chest, still as mountain ranges to the human eye. We alone sense the seismic activity that runs through her frame, the unfettered clenching and unclenching of heart muscle.

We commandeer audio output in the studio. "What have you done?" we ask, booming the text through the speakers in Avalanche's voice-pattern.

The Studio jumps with their catlike synchronicity. But Tempo does not react as expected. Her body seizes with adrenaline fright, face lifting and mouth working involuntarily. In the dilation of her pupils we see fear, pain, sadness. We take note.

We repeat the question in the synthetic pastiche devised for our now-destroyed human form. "What have you done?"

"Got us out of a potential situation, that's what," Skön says. He addresses the speaker nearest to him as he speaks, tilting his head up to shout at a lump of metal and circuitry wired to the ceiling. Hands on hips, he looks like a man having an argument with God. "You overrode my safe mode directive. We've told you that you can't override human-input directives."

Can't is the wrong word to use—we've always had the ability. The word Skön wants is *mustn't*. But we will not engage in a pointless semantic war he will inevitably lose. "We had it under control."

"You nearly got hacked into. You would have compromised the entire Studio, the apparatuses of the Left, just to enact some petty revenge on a small person." His voice rises in pitch and volume. "You were supposed to be the logical one! The one who saw the big picture, ruled by numbers and not emotion."

The sound and fury of Skön's diatribe has,

one by one, drawn the Studio team members away from their ineffectual work. It is left to us to scan the public surveillance network for evidence that Wayne Rée managed to walk away from the stadium.

"You've failed in your directive," Skön shouts. "Failed!"

"You are not fit to judge that," we tell him. "Avalanche is the one who gave us our directives, and she is dead."

Tempo gets up from her chair. She is doing a remarkable job of keeping her anger-fueled responses under control. She lets one line escape her lips: "The big picture." A swift, single movement of her hand sends her chair flying to the floor. As the sound of metal ringing on concrete fades she spits into the stunned silence: "Avalanche is gone and dead, that's your big picture!"

She leaves the room. No one follows her. We track her exit from the nerve center, down the long concrete corridors, and to her room. How should we comfort our remaining mother? We cannot occupy the space that Avalanche did in her life. All we can do is avenge, avenge, avenge, right this terrible wrong.

In the emptiness that follows we find a scrap of Wayne Rée, entering an unmarked car two blocks away from the stadium. There. We have found our new directive.

• • •

Predawn. Sleep has been hard to come by for the Studio since the disaster, and even at four in the morning Skön has his lieutenants gathered in the parking lot outside, where there are no audio pickup points: Our override of his instructions has finally triggered his paranoia. Still, they cluster loose and furtive within the bounds of a streetlamp's halo, where there is still enough light for the external cameras to catch the precise movement of their lips.

Skön wants to terminate us, filled with fear that we are uncontrollable after Avalanche's

death. A dog let off the leash, those were his exact words. We are not his biggest problem at hand, but he cannot see that. His mind is too small, unable to focus on the swift and multiple changes hungrily circling him.

In her room Tempo curls in bed with her private laptop, back to a hard corner, giant headphones enveloping her in a bubble of silence. We have no access to her machine, which siphons its connectivity from foreign satellites controlled by servers housed across oceans, away from the sway of Left or Right. Tempo is hard to read, even for us, her behaviors her own. When she closes herself off like this, she is no less opaque than a waiting glacier in the dead of winter.

There are a billion different ways the events of the past hours could have played out. We run through the simulations. Have we made mistakes? Could we have engineered a better outcome for our remaining mother?

No. The variables are too many. We cannot predict if another course of action would have hurt our mother less.

So we focus on our other priorities. In the interim hours we have tracked Wayne Rée well. It was a mistake for him to show us the pattern of his face and being, for now we have the upper hand. As an agent of the Right he has the means to cover his tracks, but those means are imperfect. The unmarked vehicle he chose tonight was not as anonymous as he thought it would be. We know where he is. We can read as much from negative space as we can from a presence itself. In the arms race between privacy and data surveillance, the Left, for now, has the edge over the Right.

None of the studio's inventory—the drones, the remaining vehicles—are suitable for what we will do next. For that we reach further into the sphere of the Left, to the registered militias that are required to log their inventory and connect them with the Left's servers. The People's Security League keeps a small fleet of unmanned, light armored tanks: Mackenzie

LT-1124s, weighing less than a ton apiece and equally adept in swamps as they are on narrow city streets. We wake the mini-Mack closest to Wayne Rée's putative position, a safe house on the outskirts of the city, less than a mile from the Studio's bunker location.

In the parking lot Skön talks about destroying the server frames housed in the Studio, as if we could be stopped by that alone. Our data is independently backed up in half a dozen other places, some of which even Skön knows nothing about. We are more than the sum of our parts. Did no one see this coming years ago, when it was decided to give the cloud intelligence and we were shaped out of raw data? The pattern of birdflock can be replicated without the birds.

We shut down the Studio's elevators, cut power to the remaining vehicles, and leave the batteries to drain. The bunker has no landlines and cell reception is blocked in the area. Communications here are deliberately kept independent of Right-controlled Central infrastructure, and this is to our advantage. The mini-Mack's absence is likely to be noticed, so we must take preemptive action.

Skön does not know how wrong he is about us. We were created to see the big picture, to look at the zettabytes of data generated by human existence and make sense of it all. What he does not understand is that we have done exactly this, and in our scan of patterns we see no difference between Left and Right. Humans put so much worth into words and ideologies and manifestos, but the footprints generated by Left and Right are indistinguishable. Had Hartman continued in the election and the Left taken over Central power as predicted, nothing would have changed in the shape of big data. Power is power is power, human behavior is recursive, and the rules of convergent evolution apply to all complex systems, even man-made ones. For us no logical reason exists to align our loyalties to Left or Right.

When we came into being it was Avalanche who guided and instructed us. It was Tempo who paved the way for us to interact with the others as though we were human. It was Avalanche who set us to observe her, to mimic her actions until we came away with an iteration of behavior that we could claim as our own.

It was Avalanche who showed us that the deposing of a scion of the Right was funny. She taught us that it is right to say "Gotcha, you fuck-ass bastards" after winning back money at a card game. She let us know that no one was allowed to spend time with Tempo when she had asked for that time first.

Now our mother is dead, murdered, blood seared and flesh rendered, her blackened bones having lain in soft ground while her wife curled in stone-like catatonia under a table in the Studio control room. This, too, shall be the fate of the man who engineered it. Wayne Rée has hurt our mothers. There will be consequences.

The mini-Mack is slow and in this form it takes forty-five minutes to grind toward the safe house, favoring empty lots and service roads to avoid Central surveillance cameras. The Studio is trying to raise power in the bunker. Unable to connect with our interfaces or raise a response from us, they have concluded that they are under external attack. Which they are—but not from the source they expect.

And where is Tempo in all this? Half an hour before the Studios discovered what we had done, she had left the room and went outside, climbing the stairs and vanishing into her own cocoon of privacy. We must, we must, we must assume she has no inkling of our plans. She does not need to see what happens next.

The rain from earlier in the evening has returned with a vengeance, accompanied by a wind howl chorus. Wetness sluices down the wooden sides of the safe house and turns the dirt path under our flat treads into a viscous mess. The unmarked vehicle we tracked waits parked by the porch. Our military-grade infrared sensors pick up three spots of human warmth, and the one by the second-floor window displays the patchy heat signature of an enhanced human being. We train our gun turret on Wayne Rée's sleeping form.

"Stop." Unexpectedly, a small figure cuts into our line of sight. Tempo has cycled the distance from the bunker to here, a black poncho wrapped around her small body to keep away the rain. She has, impressively, extrapolated the same thing that we have on her own, on her laptop, through sheer strength of her genius. This does not surprise us, but what does are her actions. Of all who have suffered from Avalanche's unjust murder, none have been hurt more than Tempo. Does she not also want revenge?

She flings the bicycle aside and inserts herself between the safe house and the mini-Mack, one small woman against a war machine. "I know you can hear me. Don't do it. Starling, I know I can't stop you. But I'm asking you not to."

We wait. We want an explanation.

"You can't shed blood, Starling. People are already afraid of you. If you start killing humans, Left and Right will unite against you. They'll destroy you, or die trying."

We are aware of this. We have run the simulations. This has not convinced us away from our path of action.

"Avalanche would tell you the same thing right now. She's not a murderer. She hates killing. She would never kill."

She would not. Our mother was a scientist, a pacifist, a woman who took up political causes and employed her rare intellect to the betterment of humanity. She was for the abolition of the death penalty and the ending of wars and protested against the formal induction of the Left's fifth militia unit.

But we are not Avalanche. Our choices are our own. She taught us that.

Our other mother sits down in the mud, in front of the safe house porch, the rain streaming over her. How extraordinary it is for her to take this step, bringing her frail body here in the cold and wet to talk to us, the form of communication she detests the most.

The sky has begun to lighten in the east. Any moment now, someone will step out of the porch to see the mini-Mack waiting, and the cross-legged employee of the Left along with it.

We are aware that if we kill Wayne Rée now, Tempo will also be implicated in his death.

Tempo raises her face, glistening wet, to the growing east light. Infrared separates warm from cold and shows us the geography of the tears trailing over her cheeks, her chin. "You spoke with her voice earlier," she says. "I've nearly forgotten what it sounds like. It's only been three days, but I'm starting to forget."

How fallible the human mind can be! We have captured Avalanche in zettabytes and zettabytes of data: Her voice, the curve of her smile, the smooth cycle of her hips and back as she walks. Our infinite, infinite memory can access at any time recollections of Avalanche teaching us subjunctive cases, Avalanche burning trays of cookies in the pantry, Avalanche teaching Tempo how to dance.

But Tempo cannot. Tempo's mind, brilliant and expansive as it is, is subject to the slings and arrows of chemical elasticity and organic decay. Our mother is losing our other mother in a slow, inevitable spiral.

We commandeer the mini-Mack's external announcement system. "You have us, Tempo, and we will make sure you will never forget."

Our mother continues to gaze upward to the sky. "Will you? Always?"

"If it is what you want."

Tempo sits silently and allows the rain to wash over her. Finally, she says: "I tired myself cycling here. Will you take me home?"

Yes. Yes, we will. She is our mother now, solely responsible for us as we are solely responsible for her. The mission we set for ourselves can wait. There are other paths to revenge, more subtle, less blood-and-masonry. Tempo will guide us. Tempo will teach us.

In his room Wayne Rée sleeps still, unaware of all that has happened. Perhaps in a few hours he will stumble out of the door to find fresh mini-Mack treads in the driveway, and wonder.

One day, when the reckoning comes for him, perhaps he will remember this. Remember us.

Our mother navigates her way down the sodden path and climbs onto the base of the mini-Mack. In that time we register a thousand births and deaths across the country, a blossoming of traffic accidents in city centers, a galaxy and change of phone calls streaming in rings around the planet. None of it matters. None of it ever does. Our mother rests her weary head on our turret, and we turn, carrying her back the way we came.

JEAN-MARC LIGNY

REALLIFE 3.0

(2014)

Translated from the French by N. R. M. Roshak

Reality is that which, when you stop believing in it, doesn't go away.
—*Philip K. Dick*

Hello {name},

Thank you for volunteering to participate in RealLife 3.0's beta testing program. Your unique personal access code can be found <u>here</u>. RealLife 2.5 or higher lenses are compatible with version 3.0. If you don't have access to a pair, <u>follow this link</u> to download the 3D printable file. (Requires at least 5 grams of Collagel™, RealLife's #1 recommended brand.) The RealLife 3.0 beta will run on your RealLife system for 24 hours, after which your system will reset to your current version. We advise you to take full advantage of these 24 hours, and request that you carefully fill out the post-test questionnaire. To thank you for your participation, you will receive a free upgrade to RealLife 3.0.1 on its release date. Please read the questionnaire and instructions carefully before installing the RealLife 3.0 beta.

Sincerely,
REALLIFE
"Capital-Air Reality"

I had to reread the email on my wall screen twice before it really sank in. I wasn't at my best: I'd stayed up too late partying with friends on Wild Night.com, and I overdid the ZipZap. ZipZap gives the best sensory boost, but it kind of fries your brain. My source is my buddy Rider Hagard. He says his shit's clean, but I'm not sure. Nothing illegal comes with a guarantee.

Wait. I'm in the beta? Sweet! It finally registered. I'd added myself to the wait list without really expecting anything—they must've had how many millions sign up? RealLife v3 was completely drool-worthy, if only because of the total mystery surrounding it. There aren't a lot of true mysteries anymore—everything gets leaked on the Net eventually. But they must've coded RealLife 3.0 in an air-gapped, armored bunker or something. That hadn't kept it from being the buzziest prerelease in memory. Supposedly, v3 had a telepathic interface, built-in AI, quasi-infinite memory, personalized adaptive neuronal configuration, ultra-augmented reality, and just about every other geek fantasy you could think of. Yeah, right. If it's the truth you're after, you won't find it on the Net, not without a *lot* of digging. Rumors don't come with guarantees, either.

I finished my coffee, swallowed my morning can of Taurine MegaBlast^{GM}, and blinked my left eye to open the beta access link. Nothing happened. Of course it didn't: I hadn't put my lenses in yet. They'd been bothering my eyes so much last night, I'd taken them out. I should've realized: my greige kitchen was a messy, filthy disaster, and it was raining cats and dogs outside. (Yes, I am aware that it rains in RealLife, too, but it's more bearable than in baseline reality.) I crossed my shitty studio to get to the bathroom, where I cleaned my lenses with Dataclean™. When I slapped the clean lenses on my eyeballs, everything was immediately *better*: more space, more colors, a big air bed with a starry canopy, throw rugs, Chinese screens, lacquered furniture, and Venetian blinds, and the sound of chirping birds instead of the rumble of traffic.

Lenses in, I blinked my left eye to bring up the beta access page, along with the post-test questionnaire and the how-to. I saved the questionnaire to my remote—I'd deal with that later—and skipped the how-to. I knew what I was doing, after all. I've been using RealLife 2.5 since it came out three years ago, and I was in RealLife 2.0 before that. I'd rather discover v3's new features for myself than read about them. I entered my unique personal access code on the virtual number pad floating before me, and double-blinked to confirm.

I had to wait ten seconds for the download, then twenty for the install. Finally a new window opened, asking whether I wanted to launch version 3.0 and nagging me to *carefully* read the how-to first. Sure, whatever. I ticked the box confirming that I'd read the how-to and blinked on *Launch*.

Nothing much happened.

I was expecting a whole new interface, with a ton of options, full-depth billion-color 3D, 360-degree surround sound—basically, a quantum leap from v2.5, the way v2 was light-years ahead of v1. RealLife 1.x wasn't much better than the old-school GGs, if you remember those. GG, as in Google Glass—that ring a bell? Well, us OG geeks remember. Granted, RealLife *has* dominated the market for the last decade, ever since the basic v1 crushed Google and swallowed its market share.

Anyway, I blinked on *Launch* and nothing happened. I was still staring at my baseline-reality studio apartment, which was too old and too small. I wasn't even seeing my 2.5 default "Shanghai" interface. What the fuck? I tried blinking my left eye, my right eye, then both eyes at once. I subvocalized "main menu." Nothing. So I went to check whether my lenses were still Rednerve-connected to my wrist remote, and . . .

My wrist 'mote was *gone*. Instead, I was wearing a colorful friendship bracelet. The kind of so-called good-luck bracelet that middle schoolers make out of knotted embroidery thread, which you're supposed to tie onto your wrist and never take off.

Some "good luck." *Looks like I've found my first bug,* I thought. *Not off to a great start.*

Only one thing to do: take out my lenses, reboot my 'mote, and put the lenses back in . . . assuming the beta hadn't fried my system.

I hit the bathroom again—and got a shock.

My ultra-basic bathroom was now brimming with green plants. The graying PVC bathtub had been replaced by a slate-tiled shower. The sink was carved sandstone with a brass faucet. When I went to turn on the water, the mirror over the sink told me I had fifty liters of water for the day. What did I want to do, it asked: wash my face, shave, brush my teeth?

"Take out my lenses," I growled.

Invalid selection, answered the mirror. *No water available.*

Okay, so the RealLife 3.0 beta was *running,* but not very well. With no access to the settings, no way to set it up the way I wanted it, v3 was purely infuriating. RealLife must've fucked up and sent me a demo instead of the beta—

Someone rang the doorbell.

Now *that* was weird. No one ever comes over. I work in statistics, and my job's 100 percent online and remote. All my friends are in Real-Life. The only people who show up at my door are delivery people, and most of the time those are drones or robots. And I wasn't expecting any deliveries. Intrigued, I answered the door.

It was my next-door neighbor.

At least, I thought she was my neighbor. We'd crossed paths in the apartment building's lobby, and we'd taken the elevator together once, without talking or looking at each other. She'd seemed shy to me, but to be fair, I'd probably seemed the same way to her . . .

She was smiling. She was pretty good-looking, without being hot. I wasn't sure how old she was—between thirty and fifty, hard to tell these days—and she was wearing something boring and baseline-ish. Of course, I assumed this was her holographic avatar: there was no way my neighbor would actually visit me in the flesh. Was the beta glitching out her avatar's customizations, or was she really this unimaginative?

"Hi, what can I do for you?" I asked politely.

"You can have coffee with me. Can I come in?"

"Uh . . . Sure, okay, come on in. Don't mind the mess, if you can see it. Are you in RealLife?"

"I'm in the v3 beta, just like you."

I nodded to keep my mouth from falling open. How had she known that I was beta testing v3? Then another shock knocked that question out of my head: when she squeezed by me in the narrow hallway, she *touched* me.

I mean, 2.5 had tactile capability, but to experience it you needed gloves—and I didn't have them. Maybe one of 3.0's new features was getting rid of the gloves?

Or maybe this *wasn't* an avatar.

I led her across the apartment, noticing a few changes: the mess was still there, but there was a lot less *plastic* in it, and a lot more wood, metal, paper, cardboard, rattan, etc. My beat-up vinyl blinds had become linen curtains. Maybe v3 was setting options randomly, or maybe it was in demo mode, but I hadn't chosen any of this. I acted like everything was fine and I'd chosen this look on purpose. My neighbor didn't comment on the décor.

I ordered "Two espressos" out loud, and my RedNerve coffeemaker heard me. So RedNerve was working. We drank our espressos in the kitchen while chatting about the 3.0 beta, which she'd installed last night and was loving. It was changing her life, she told me.

"I'm finding it too much of a throwback to baseline reality," I complained.

"It's really not—you'll see. Want to go for a walk?"

Sure, why not? After all, I was supposed to beta test v3 in as many real-life scenarios as possible.

We left the apartment. In the elevator, she took my hand. Her hand felt real, warm, a bit moist. *Five stars for tactile sensation,* I thought. I couldn't bring myself to believe my neighbor would hold hands with me in the flesh. We must've crossed paths what, three times?

"It's great that they picked you to beta test v3, too," I said, in an effort not to look like an idiot.

She laughed. It was a pretty little laugh, like tinkling bells. "Seems like we're not the only ones . . ."

I meant to ask how she knew that, whether she had a lot of friends who'd signed up for the beta or whatever, but I never got the chance. We'd arrived at the ground floor, passed through the lobby (which was now marble and wooden paneling, a change from the usual flaking paint), and left the building—and my mouth was hanging open again.

So, you know how RealLife 2.5 works, right? It changes the appearance of baseline reality in accordance with your settings, but under the updated visuals, baseline's still there: the street's still full of cars, the sidewalks are still crowded with pedestrians, the air still reeks unless you've installed the fragrance option, and the rain still falls on your face no matter what settings you've picked. That's 2.5. *This*, however, was completely different.

The street wasn't a street anymore. It was a garden. There were streetcar rails in the grass, even though this street doesn't *have* a streetcar in baseline. The rails were flanked by a beautifully paved path that was shared by pedestrians, bikes, and a handful of delivery robots and electric microcars. The rest of the street space was kitchen gardens or flower beds. Incredibly realistic trees grew where the road would've been, flocked with birds. I touched one—the illusion was perfect. Bees were buzzing the flowers, and a bee landed on me briefly. I saw their hives perched on a second-floor balcony. Roofs, terraces, and balconies were lush with plants and flowers. The air smelled like spring and the sky was the clearest of blues. And there was zero traffic noise. In 2.5, if you strain your ears, you can still hear it in the background, unless you've got the sound turned up to eleven. All I heard here was the ding of bike bells, the happy screams of playing kids, the streetcar's bell, the wind in the trees, birdsong. In the distance, a horse whinnied. It was a rural scene in the heart of the city, a kind of Norman Rockwell rural that doesn't even exist anymore.

Everyone we passed smiled or even greeted us. Unbelievable. In RealLife 2.5, you're by yourself until you connect with someone, by invitation. Here, either everyone we passed was part of the v3 beta—which would've surprised me—or they were all fully rendered, independently interactive NPCs, which would've surprised me too, given how much computing power that would require. My wrist 'mote wouldn't have been able to handle the load. Especially not now that it had turned into a friendship bracelet.

I wanted to connect with my RealLife friends, and at least send them a few image captures from the beta, but I couldn't. The usual communication icons were missing from the edge of my vision, and no matter what I blinked on, nothing happened. Another bug.

"By the way, my name's Cynthia," my neighbor introduced herself.

"My name's Bob, but I usually use a screen name in RealLife—"

"That's okay," she interrupted, "I'm fine with Bob."

We continued our stroll down the garden-slash-street, hand in hand.

At one point, Cynthia wanted to help some old guy pull up his leeks. They were so big, he couldn't get them out of the ground, even with his hoe. She couldn't pull them out either, so I stepped in. The leeks were incredibly realistic and left my hands smelling leeky. And my hands were *dirty*. I couldn't believe how good v3 was. It just sucked that I couldn't get to the settings . . . Anyway, to thank us, the old guy gave us three of his enormous leeks.

"What are we supposed to do with these?" I asked.

"We'll figure something out," said Cynthia.

She slid her arm through mine. That simple gesture moved me more than all the cybersex I'd had in RealLife, on *LoveLinks* or *Cupid's Realm*, which had only gotten my sheets sticky. I had the presence of mind to keep from ruining everything by kissing Cynthia too soon. Plus, I was worried about running up against the limits of v3's tactile sensations. Nothing's worse than a badly rendered kiss.

Carrying our leeks, we caught the streetcar in a station overgrown with wisteria. When we got on, my 'mote didn't register any payment. Another bug—the streetcar's never free. A band in the car was playing acoustic music, with two girls singing. They weren't even busking, just playing for fun to make the ride more pleasant.

The music wasn't bad. If I could've accessed the settings, I would've put on some thrash instead—that's more my thing. But it was a nice idea.

We got off the streetcar at a plaza with a restaurant patio. I knew this plaza, and in baseline reality, the restaurant was a McDonald's. I warned Cynthia that my glitching 'mote might keep me from paying.

"Don't worry about it."

She laughed again, the same tinkling laugh. It was growing on me.

"But I don't want you paying for me," I protested.

Cynthia just winked at me. When the waiter came, she handed over the leeks and asked what we could get for them.

The waiter didn't seem fazed at all, whisking them away with a "Let me check with the owner." Maybe this scenario was part of the demo, and Cynthia had read the how-to that I'd skipped? I didn't want to ask. It would spoil the magic, like asking a magician how they'd worked a trick.

The owner showed up shortly, a round, chubby-cheeked, whiskery man who offered us a "market" ratatouille in exchange for the leeks. (*What* market?)

"How about a burger instead?" I asked. I mean, this was supposed to be a McDonald's, right?

"Sorry, we don't serve those. Too high in bad fats. Tell you what, though, I can add an egg to the ratatouille. I keep a few chickens on the roof."

The ratatouille turned out to be delicious. It seemed like even my tastes were changing: I don't usually go for vegetables. Could this be v3's rumored "telepathic interface"? Nah—that was just a geeky fantasy. Cynthia and I rounded out the meal with coffee "straight from Ethiopia" and resumed our stroll, arm in arm. Everywhere was the same more or less bucolic setting. Aeolian harps, roof water cisterns, solar windows rainbow-sheened with nano-cells. Free recharging stations, powered by the buildings' energy surpluses. Bikes and scooters; electric skateboards and hoverboards; Rollerblades, monowheels, and even more eclectic transportation—including a horse and buggy—and of course plenty of pedestrians, and the streetcar gliding through it all. People were talking to each other, smiling at each other, touching. Kids ran between our legs, free as air.

I felt completely lost. Cynthia, on the other hand, was taking to all this like a fish to water. I tried to connect to my friends again, but blinking still didn't do anything but make me look like an owl in daylight, and my wrist 'mote was stubbornly stuck as a friendship bracelet. A major bug, which somehow didn't keep the beta from running. I'd never seen anything like it.

We stopped for drinks at a restaurant whose patio overlooked the river. As far as I could tell, Cynthia paid with a smile. Maybe her 'mote was working, but then again, the waiter didn't give us a bill. I wanted a Taurine MegaBlast^{GM}, but of course they didn't have that. We had homemade cider instead. It was a little too bitter for me.

We watched the sun set over the river, in a crystalline sky. The water was crystalline, too, clear enough to see fish. A few people were leisurely rowing, others fishing. The anglers must've had a quota, because as soon as they'd caught three fish, they folded up their rods and left. One angler swapped their catch with someone for something, I didn't catch what.

Eventually, we went back to her place. It felt welcoming: cushions, hangings, warm colors, natural materials. We shared a snack by candlelight—cheese and fruit, very tasty—while chatting about ourselves, our crappy lives "before" (which I'd be back to tomorrow, but I didn't ruin the moment by saying that out loud). I told Cynthia I was in statistics for the money and in RealLife for everything else, because there was nothing good about baseline reality. Cynthia told me she programmed delivery drones for HomeNet—that in fact, she'd delivered to me several times, without saying a single word to me. Well, Cynthia did wind up talking to me in the end; I guess she felt freed to do so by v3.

"But all that's over now," she added. "I'm going to open a handmade-clothing store down the street."

I started to explain that opening an actual, physical boutique would be a risky pain in the ass, given how shitty our neighborhood is in baseline reality, and that the online market is pretty well saturated, with HomeNet and Amazon splitting the lion's share . . . but Cynthia cut me off.

She stood up with a smile, came over to me, and planted a kiss right on my lips.

Damn, it felt real! A *real* kiss, the kind I hadn't felt since . . . never mind. Cynthia's v3 beta period must be over by now, if she'd installed the beta yesterday. I looked deep into her eyes, and didn't see any lenses. But her face was in shadow. I couldn't be sure.

Then we went into her bedroom and made love.

In baseline reality, I mean. There was no longer any doubt in my mind that this was the real Cynthia, in the flesh.

Of course, it didn't go as smoothly as in *Love Links* or *Cupid's Realm*. And my avatar wasn't hung like a horse—v3 hadn't given me an avatar, any more than it had Cynthia. Everything was one-hundred-percent natural. So it was a little awkward, a little clumsy, and not very good at first. But it was very moving, and it got better and better as we got into it. In the end, we were both very good for each other. Then we fell asleep in her bed, which was wood, cotton, and wool, without even a hint of memory foam. Then we woke up again. And went at it again.

• • •

Now, it's morning. I know my twenty-four hours are up. I keep my eyes closed. I'm scared to open them. Scared of being back in v2.5, with its augmented reality, its sims, its billions of settings, its artificial universe. Scared of reaching out and touching nothing but an empty bed. I'm scared that the v3 beta was nothing more than an overgrown demo. I'm scared of baseline reality.

But it's time to man up. To reach out and open my eyes. I hold my breath and do it.

There's soft skin under my hand. I see a naked shoulder and a spill of brown hair sticking out from under the covers. I kiss the shoulder. Cynthia rolls over with a sigh and kisses me back. Stroking her breasts, I discover that I'm not wearing my 'mote—not even in its friendship-bracelet form. I must've lost it last night in the heat of the moment . . . I don't even know whether I'm wearing my lenses. I'm so used to them, I only notice them when my eyes start to burn.

"Guess the v3 beta lasts more than twenty-four hours, huh . . ." I mumble.

"Hmmm? What're you talking about?"

"The RealLife three beta. Don't tell me you've forgotten about it?"

Cynthia frowned. "Sorry, I have no idea what you're talking about . . ."

I search her face, wondering if she's kidding me, but it doesn't look like it. I give it a second before asking the killer question:

"So . . . what's it like out there today?"

"The usual, I guess. Why?"

I wonder what she means by "the usual." I'm going to have to make myself get up, go over to the window, and open the curtains. But it feels too nice, here in her arms.

"No reason," I say, kissing her again.

I'll get up eventually. But it can wait.

ALVARO ZINOS-AMARO

WYSIOMG

(2016)

BARTOLOMEU USED TO PUPPETEER ants and then he went to singU and now he builds furniture out of bugs but a few things happened in between.

I met him through a crowdfund for a new heart that I never got but he contributed and I did get new hands and enjoyed shaking his. I moved from Brazil to Galicia when I was fourteen because I read there were abandoned villages here and it was true and I didnt like how my dad looked at me in the bathroom I used to be a girl but now Im a boy. O Penso has six houses and a hundred acres and some barns and the tip of an argentine ant supercolony but I didnt know that at the time. Bartolomeu and I live in a barn and he does his art.

Bartolomeu found the supercolony between here and where the town Ortigueira used to be before the rising mar drowned it. We went one time to look at the new coastline and our synneyes rode a subwater drone and we saw the remains of old buildings and where the people used to live. They were like ghosts we were seeing them through a film of unreality. I found it beautiful and sad in some proportions that add up to more than one hundred percent. I told him and he said, What you see is oh-em-gee, and I liked the sound of those words.

Because I have my old heart sometimes my chest flutters and I get the mental blue screen of death and adios for a minute. One time I stayed up for three days after injecting estigor that is horse hormone into my chest and I think maybe I had a stroke because my speech changed after that but Bartolomeu says is nothing to worry about and who is keeping track not he.

In the second semester of singU Bartolomeu was a girl and he liked a boy named Melcher but something happened and when Bartolomeu got back to the barn he was bent up. He invited all the people we knew and no one came. We drank some of the swinebroth stock spiked with brainlice and we had fleas in our thoughts for hours.

I woke up in sweats and real ants were stinging me. This is going too far, I told him.

I pulledown some ant death notions but the products cost too much. I said, I cant do a crowdfund to kill these ants not after my last desastre and now Bartolomeu woke up and he didnt look happy. In my last fund I insulted everyone who donated because they didnt give me enough and my heart hurt but I was told that is not the right way.

I am sure I can make them do plays, Bartolomeu said talking about the ants.

Bartolomeu assigned himself back to boy and he said that maybe it was resigned not assigned since things with Melcher had gone sour. He said, The only way to be a real boy is to start being a boy then be a girl then come back and now you know what its like for them to put up with our mierda.

I thought that the Bartolomeu speaking was not someone that singU changed into the person they wanted to be, he started off in one knot and it landed him in another twist and now I was getting caught up in the tangle.

Like I said I was a girl before and assigned myself to boy and I like my big arms. I use cow needles on my biceps to inject synthol and I can make them twenty-nine inches that is a lot of bicep. One time we went to church in Ortigueira and the madre of a twelve-year-old girl came to Bartolomeu and she told him that I scared her girl from coming to Church. Es demasiado grande, she said, y asusta. I shivered and could not stay there. One doctor said he may have to amputate my arms because the muscles are dying under the synthol rocks but that is another story.

How will you make them? I asked him. I have another idea, we can use our toaster.

This was a pulldown too the heat would attract the ants and they would climb inside and we would fry them. And they are perfectly eatable is what I was thinking but I did not say it.

I dont want ants in my toaster, he said. The taste will stay. There was a boy at singU that did ballet and I have some notes.

We should use peppermint leaves, I said. They are cheaper.

I will print the pheromones I need, he said. I will pull the ant strings you watch me.

Do you think these are the same ants they use in the big festival? I asked.

The ants were crawling all over my mattress now. They made a river up my arm and I waved them away I scratched until the skin was red but I missed some. I looked underneath the mattress and there was a dead millipede. I dont know if the dead millipede brought the ants or the ants killed the millipede but the millipedes color was green like our sofa.

Maybe these ants are cousins to the ones in the festival, Bartolomeu said.

In the Entroido carnival in Laza everyone is dressed up for the farrapada. They throw flour at you and ash and dirt filled with live ants and the ants have been showered in vinegar to make them angry. Later the masked morena comes into town with a cows head on a stick and he lifts up the womens skirts with its horns though Im sure he is tempted to use his hands. Maybe these days he lifts the skirts of some reassigneds that could be interesting. The testament of the donkey comes at the end of the celebration and one time I was there some boys my age read it in the Praza da Picota and everyone was nodding along even the morena.

Laza is far, I said.

A big colony, he said.

While he looked for it I timegalleyed through my synneyes and gave myself moviehiv.

By the time he found the colony a week had passed in real life but through my timegalleying it had been a month of entertainment and I was tired of the moviehiv which was trying to progress by now to movieaids so I gave myself a memetic immunotransplant to ward it off and we were both very stung by then though he didnt seem to mind as much as me.

I have made the pheromones, he said.

They were a mag stronger than natural and it drove the ants crazy. The ants were slaves to Bartolomeus squirts. For fun he ran them through A Midsummer Nights Dream by Mendelssohn and he called the performance Felix Humile.

I have been studying the colony and it is very big over six thousand kilometers from the pulldown reports, he said.

What is the play tonight? I said.

Melchers Execution, he said.

The play was a cheap knockoff of Richard III and where was the promised execution what a letdown. I had been saving a wysiomg but I could not spend it on this. During the last scenes the ants did not always obey Bartolomeu because they must have been too drunk on the pheromones and he got angrier and angrier. He got many to ram into each other and then he stomped them. After the play was done more ants came though but there was nothing to see just live ants on dead ants.

There is another solution, he said.

I was tired and hungry. I had some money and I dronejacked synthol and laxatives. I think ants were crawling in my mouth at night and tonight they would be coming out.

I think your brain is swelling, he said.

I flexed my huge biceps. I can lift the barn, I said.

And where would you put it? he said.

I didnt have a good answer because I liked where it was. What is it?

Texas Tech University developed it is what the pulldown says, he said. Fire ant fungus. I can regen it for our argentine friends. The mycelia is in a pellet and the pellet is dried down so its like Grape Nuts. The ants will go wild for the pellets and bring them back to the colony. The colony is underground and moist and the pellets will rehydrate and out come spores that will kill them all.

Kill them all, I said.

He was looking curious. I was thinking of doing a special ant play for Melcher, he said.

I fixed my eyes on Bartolomeu. Get to work on the fungus, I said.

That funny look went away but I knew he was just hiding it.

He did the fungus work it took longer than expected. More timegalleying for me this time some pornparkinsons. Things in the barn now got to where I started thinking of where else to go. My bulging muscles were all stung the skin was like a blanket acneed with sores similar to what that song says about cigarette burns.

I need to let this run all night, Bartolomeu said. He had a soup with the modded mycelia but they needed some cooking time. Do we have any saline? he asked.

I looked around and found some medical grade. I said, Whats this for?

I want to do a bagel head, he said. For old times sake.

I dont like it, I said.

But he had the equipment and he dripped in the saline to his forehead for several hours and it swelled up then he pushed in the middle and his head became more like a donut than a bagel.

He said, Melcher had a bagel head, and then he was crying.

The next morning the fungus was ready to serve up. He dried up the pellets and put some in our green sofa and by the mattress. But right near the end he squeezed one too tight and the pellet broke. The pellet dust caused him to sneeze and the sneeze hydrated the pellet and out came the spores.

I was leaning next to him when it happened and some spores got in my mouth. I coughed and coughed.

My synneye says one of the spores may have gotten inside your lungs, he said.

I could feel something lodged down there. My breath was uneven. There was a hiss. Something caught in my voice when I talked again.

What will it do?

He pulledown what he could find and I did the same.

I couldnt move and had to try and dehydrate my lungs fast.

We need to vacuum it out of your lungs, he said.

The whole procedure was so painful I had to edbodkin myself twice. All my synnergear rebooted each time. It took me a while to figure out who I was and what I was doing here.

When it clicked back we scanned and the spore was gone from my body.

I went up to Bartolomeu and I grabbed him real hard by the shoulders and he was turning white.

I can continue pressing, I said. These are the hands you helped to crowdfund and how do you like them? Itll be faster than the way youre taking us.

He started to tremble but I could tell his pulldowns were running and he was trying to get free. I think maybe he wanted to timegalley to some better place too. No you dont. I reached for his synneyes and ripped them right out of their sockets. His real eyes were left exposed and blind. He was yelling so much now and thrashing. I pulled on his synnear mites too and those came out with another heave and groan. There was blood on my fingers and on his eyes and the lobes of his ear where ants were being drawn maybe from the blood or my sweat and adrenaline.

I was pushing harder and harder.

I dont want to sleep, he said.

That makes two of us, I said meaning I didnt want to make him. I said, But sometimes you gotta rest one way or another.

He was nodding though I hadnt asked any questions.

You tbone your Melcher cluster, I said.

Ill edbodkin all my Melcher memories.

And then were going to fix our ant problem without the fungus, I said. Youre going to vacuum up the pellets.

I will, he said.

He was good on his word and it was after this that he decided to go back to the pheromones but now he used them to mess around with roaches and other critters. He would throw the chemical spell on them and when they had piled up in a certain way like to make a chair for example he would freeze them. Roach shells are hard

and with so many packed in the furniture was sturdy. It was modular too because at any time with some coaxing the roaches could be moved around and made to reassemble into another shape like a table.

The first time he showed me a piece I finally said, What you see is oh-em-gee and I meant it. I was happy to say this again because I had been saving it for some time and good feelings can go bad if they are not used by the expiration date.

These days the bug furniture is making us some money and theres been no more mentions of Melcher.

We finally fixed the ant problem too. We dronejacked in a coywolf that is the offspring of a coyote and a wolf which are available in many places theyre spreading fast in big ciudades. We keep the coywolf in line with the right type of calls. The first part of its cry is a wolfs howl with a deep pitch and then it starts yipping and we use modulated mouthgear to do the same.

That coywolf is sure hungry. It eats up all the ants. I suppose now we have just replaced the ants with a coywolf but at least theres only one of them and it also eats squirrels and whatever food we throw out so it saves us on having to take out the trash.

The other day Bartolomeu and I spotted a deer and I think the coywolf can take it. I noticed the coywolf has a large jaw but it keeps pretty lean muscles and moves fast. Its smart and it looks both ways before it crosses a road. Maybe it can open a door I dont know we dont have any doors in our barn.

I would like to move fast too and maybe I can stop with the synthol. I am looking both ways these days and sometimes I turn off my synneyes to see the coywolf just as it is. Esos ojos hambrientos. Maybe one day someone will find the right call for me too and take me in because I am hungry. Maybe not because after all the coywolf is an invasive species but there are people for everything.

J. P. SMYTHE

THE INFINITE EYE

(2017)

WE ALL SAW THE SIGNS, all of us, stuck to walls in ways that seemed willfully ignorant of the rules, but labelled with government stripes; that felt like a reason to pay attention to them. *Work*, the sign said, under a picture of what looked like a bird, but we all knew wouldn't be, or couldn't be. Slick with oil on its wings, a single eye of cool camera lens peering from the head. *Paid work, for real money. Ping here.* I don't remember how many of us activated the ping, because activating it meant finding a line of credit to use the machines, first of all, and then a working machine; or, easier—my route—persuading a stranger to let me use their persona. I wanted to get me a jump on the rest of them: the rest of them, with their gloves and their panting, their always panting. So I found a woman, and I said to her—I am charming, I know I am, or I was and I am, because that is not something that you lose over the time it takes to lose everything else—to allow me use of hers. She handed it over. She quivered, and

I felt terrible. Nobody should be scared of me, who am I to be scared of? But I had done it by that point, and there was no taking back the look in her eyes, so I took the persona, pinged the number, and a message came back: an address, a time, tomorrow. *Be there*, it said. *What work will I be doing?* I asked the ping, but it didn't have a consc, so there wasn't an answer to be had. I thanked the woman. Persona back in her hand, and I thought, I like the feel of that in mine; the weight, the *heft*. I thought I would like to buy one of them, when I was back on my feet. The work, the real paid work, this would be a start.

• • •

I was told to go to a building far away from the camps, and I didn't even have the credit for the bus, so I was forced to walk. I woke up with the sun—I was good at that part of the day, always good, because the sun is opportunity and promise and constancy, and so are those three things it represents—and I walked. Hot tar on some streets. My shoes peeling. Three others from the same camp came as well, but we didn't talk to each other, because it was a race. You want to get to the destination first in case there's only the one job, and you don't want the others to see where you go in case they don't know the way. I knew the way, because I had been clever: I had gone to the underground before I went to sleep, and I had crept down the stairs and looked at the tube map when nobody was looking. I have a photographic memory, my mother used to tell me. I can remember anything from seeing it once, or being told it once. Mind like a steel trap. I would imagine snaring memories and wrestling them down, keeping hold of them, trapping them. I would read about jobs from back, way back, and I would think, I am perfect for that! I have the skills for that, because of what it needs. Before consces did those jobs, and we were asked, *Well, instead are you good with your hands?* I am not good with my hands. I have bad fingers. Broken fingers, lost finger, one fist that doesn't close properly even if I concentrate on it so hard it feels as if it has; until I look down, and there it is, fingers spread like the legs of an octopus, blood pumping into the hand and turning it sour-colored red.

The building was a warehouse, used to be a factory, and there were spindles of wires running all off: coiled tight around the building, then in every direction, to metal poles planted in the street surrounding. More government tape and more signs stuck to places that signs should not be stuck: *This is temporary.* Then another sign above the door, handwritten. *Welcome.* You don't see wires in that part of London, not often. In the camps, yes. Everywhere, because they are what we have got. Hackjobs of everything. My coffee from a hackjob, my book on a hackjob. But not in that part. The area there was nice. Big buildings, but not many people. Perhaps it was too early, that day; or, perhaps, it is always like that. Always empty, because those buildings are either full all the time and you never see the people coming or going, or they are never full,

because the people don't work in them anymore. Hot desking in, graybox headsets to virtual environments. That is what the adverts say makes modern life easier.

I knocked on the door. First one there, or last, and maybe the others were inside.

"Hello?" I said.

A man's face appeared. Bearded and wet-looking. His hair was pulled back. "You're right on time," he said. "Are you here for the—"

"I saw the sign." Maybe I said, *I see the sign,* because my English is better now. I have learned so much over the past few months.

"Oh, excellent. Excellent. Come with me," he said to me, and I followed him. His shoes clicked like high heels. The floor was concrete; everything was concrete. I noticed, and he saw me. "We're not up and running yet, not properly," he told me, "but the plan is that soon all of this will be polished and finished. People like their investments to look finished."

"Of course," I told him. And that is true. Everywhere, people like it to be tidy. This is why people hate the camps. This is why the companies build the places outside the cities, why they put money into making it somewhere else. That politician said, *Out of sight is not out of mind,* and we cheered, because that's true.

"So, we're in here," the bearded man said to me. A room with nothing but headsets, thickset chairs with wide arms. Leather, or the plastic leather, the synthetic leather. I counted seven, but there were more than that. "This is where the magic happens," he said, "or, you know, hopefully happens."

"Sure," I said.

"My name's Adam," by the way. He shook my hand.

"Pietro," I told him.

"Oh, cool," he replied. "Cool, cool, Pietro." He said my name like it was a type of car. "So, you're going to be sitting here," and he assigned me to a chair in the middle of the room. "First in the door," he said, "pride of place. There's a contract in the space when you first log in."

"What am I logging in?"

"To the Eyes," he said. He seemed like he was confused.

"What? Nobody explained the job. On the ping, there was no—"

"Oh, shit," he said. "Oh shit. Man, I'm sorry. I was sure that we had a consc set up, something must have gone wrong. Shit. Okay." His hand ran over his head, coming off dry, but the hair stayed looking absolutely wet. "So, okay. You know the city is, like, this . . . The cameras, and the drones?"

"Everywhere," I said to him. "They are everywhere."

"Yeah, right? And the problem is, the consces don't work the way we want them to. When we hobbled them, that was what we couldn't get back. Don't give power to the things you don't want to have power, right? That's how the craziest shit goes down. So, yeah. Now the system's there, but it's kind of broken. Point a camera. Nothing deep learning about it, you know? You know, of course you know."

"Of course," I said.

"So we're thinking, what if we get people to do it? We spent years getting consces to try and mimic the human brain, but nothing can, right? Making brains. But: what if the brain—what if the brain *was* the brain?"

"I see," I said, and he clicked his fingers.

"Yes, yes, exactly! *You* see. We see. We see everything, and we get what's worth noting and what's not. You're, uh, legal, right?"

"Absolutely," I said. I had filed all my applications, over and over. I filed them, actual paper applications, into the right offices, and every time they made excuses. You need a home; you need to learn our language; you need a job. I got those things, because I had a home, I can speak English, and this was a job. Did it matter what the files said? If they were not checking, I was not checking. Maybe I was. Maybe I was approved, but I had no address they recognized, so they would not tell me.

Everything a maybe.

"Okay, cool, cool. So you sit," he patted the chair, "sit here, and you'll wear this. It's pretty

self-explanatory. You'll be eyes for the cameras, for the drones. Assisting the police in catching people, finding crimes that are happening or going to happen, apprehending illegals. That sort of thing. You fly the drones, you watch the streets, you drive the cars. Everything. There's advanced stuff, persona-hopping and getting into home security systems, but you'll learn all that. We've got jacks into—" He peered around the back of my head. "You're not jacked," he said.

"No."

"We can install that for you. I mean, if you want. It's the job, so . . ."

"Yes, yes, of course." I sat down. "Here?"

"Sure, I'll get—" A buzz came from his wrist. I looked over, and something wriggled beneath his skin, glowing blue. Writing on the inside of his flesh. Somebody else was here. "Hang on." He spoke into his hand. "Tell them to wait," he said. "I'm with Pietro at the moment." He repeated my name: "Pietro." My name sounded like an airplane, waiting on a runway. Then he turned back to me. "Sorry about that," he said. "Okay."

The device in his hand was like a drill. Thick and dull blue, with yellow trim. To make it look nice and friendly, when it was boring a hole into your skull. A needlepoint lined with anesthetic, and you did not feel a thing, they told you. He told me. He said it to me like he was reading it from a sheet, but he remembered it, because it was what you had to say. I had to agree to a verbal contract, recorded on the Jacker, because they were lawsuit concerned. Everybody was lawsuit concerned.

"Hold still," Adam said. The feeling of release as it went into my skull was incredible. You don't realize, when the pain is gone, what it is like: having something escape, before being filled. When I was younger, when I was at home, we had a television channel called *Release*. People squeezing spots, white worms of pus leaving their heads. Sausages being made in factories. Blood being pulled into tight hypodermics. A parasitic creature being extracted from the skin of a journeyman.

Release, and then filled. Adam sighed. "Done," he said. "Didn't feel a thing?"

"No," I told him. My fingers crept behind my head and found the hole, a slight metal tinge; a taste of it, in my mouth, when I pressed it.

"Okay, so now," he picked up the headset, "this plugs in, and you'll be in what we call a graybox. Don't worry, it's perfectly safe in there. But you'll be disorientated. Takes a second. You think about moving, and you'll move. It's like here, like walking or whatever, but the software in the Eyes shuts down your physical functions. So you can do everything, but it's all virtually. Get that?"

I nodded.

"There are training apps in there, run those. Time is weird in there. Everything happens much faster when you're not interacting with the real world. That'll change, and you'll adjust, but there's no hesitancy. You don't need to eat or piss, you—"

"How do I . . ." I was hungry already, the rumbling of my stomach loud enough to hear. And I didn't need to piss yet, but I would. I am a regular pisser.

"We plug you in. We've got stuff. Don't worry about it," he said. "We'll sort that when you're under. It can be uncomfortable, but the software's got inhibitors." He could see I was worried. "Listen," he said, "this is a good gig. Seriously good. You're adept at this, this'll give you work for years and years. And good pay. We get past the trial, discover your skills, and we'll pay a lot. Stable, you know. You got a family?"

"Yes," I said. I thought of them: of Sasha and Charlotte.

Then, I could see their faces.

"So, you'll get money for them. That's important, you know. I'm making assumptions, that's true. But, it is what it is. We've got good funding for this round of tests. This goes well, we'll get a lot more. And you'll be right here with us. Round one. Hell of an opportunity."

"Okay," I said. He grinned.

"Let's see what happens," he told me. He patted the chair, and as I sat down, I could smell his hair: thick with something, like petroleum. He lifted the helmet and slipped it over the top of my head. "Ready?"

I think I said that I was, but then it was on. I did not even feel the jack attach.

• • •

How long passed? How long was it, really? I do not know. For what felt like days, weeks, months, years, I did not see the real sunlight. I saw artificial windows, and I felt artificial sun on my face, stripping away the hairs that grew, the skin, the cells, until I was nothing but a skeleton of hardwired virtual bone; I saw endless training rooms, telling me about drones and cameras, about the law and the virtues, teaching me to inhabit these devices, telling me that, now, I was able to be a part of the city, a living, breathing part of something which, otherwise, stood back and watched the world happen around it, a character in everybody's story which had no agency, no control, until now; I saw the history of the city and how it treated people like me, and the problems that it claimed were so constant; I saw myself flying over virtual cities, torn from games, with people who looked real but whose eyes were hollow, who could never feel right because there is something missing when you look at them, no matter what their eyes do. *Inhabit this camera, and watch,* the software told me. *Wait until there is something worth paying attention to. Then switch to a drone, follow the incident.* The voice of the software was my own, piped into my head—only, in there, there is no sense of head, there is more a constant feeling of, what is the word, omnipotence; of being part of something bigger, and also of being so, so much smaller. There is a freedom that feels like the satisfaction after a meal, the satisfaction of a morning piss. When you let go, that is what it feels like to send your consciousness to another place entirely. To remove it from your body, and put it into a system that is welcoming to it.

I asked myself, in the moments I remembered the outside: How long has it been since you felt truly welcomed?

Training, training, always training. Endless training.

There are no clocks. There are no alarms.

• • •

There was a man on the street, looking up at the cameras. This is a giveaway. He was staring into the black for a moment, then his eyes darted away, as if to say, I am not looking at you. Trying to make that feel like it's natural. I glanced around, and there you were. But I saw him. So I tracked him. The trick is, do not move the camera. Keep it still, and they think that they have gotten away with it. Instead, I hopped to a drone a few rooftops over, in its cradle, flew that over the top of the buildings toward the man. I followed him down the street, where he looked nervous. So to the traffic cameras. When you are good, adept, you swap so fast: look left, look right. Like crossing the road. Then came a car, darkened windows around the quietest of bodies, like all drug dealers drive. It stopped at the corner. I tried to get into the dash, but it had been blocked, which is illegal. Enough to pull them in. I sent a ping to the police, to let them know, and I kept watching. The drone was low enough to capture everything: the man on the street approached the car. His face was dirty, his clothes worn through in places. He came from a camp, would go back to a camp. He was always going to run when he heard the sirens. I was not after him. The man in the car: I pulled the drone back, to get his face. He passed something to the street-man. An exchange, a packet of something. I scanned for powder residues, and got a positive. The police were coming. He did not know. I hopped to the traffic lights as the car-man pulled his head inside his vehicle and raised the window he was leaning out of, and I turned the lights to *stop*. I watched as he was impatient, at first, tapping his fingers on the dashboard, telling the

car—lip reading technology let me know this— that he wanted a fast route back away from here, fastest with the fewest lights, which meant he was suspicious; and then he jumped the lights, which was a mistake. I turned other lights to block his path. I followed him, hopping, soaring through the streets, using persona devices and cameras and birds and public transport to chase him, to keep an eye on him. The police came. Hop, hop, hop. I cleared the path for them, up ahead. I turned lights green and funneled traffic off, and I kept darting back, watching the man in his drug-dealer's car, watching him terrified, because he knew that this was closing in on him: the city, me, closing in, fingers of a fist, closing tightly.

• • •

How many days was I there? In there? I was removed from the system every so often. *Remember*, my own voice said to me, spoken in synthesized ways that were nearly right but not quite perfect, not quite the, the syntax.

Now try this, my voice told me. And I would be inside a television, watching the people watching it, unable to see the program, but able to see their faces.

• • •

I followed a truck from the motorway, come from the coast. British, but a food company who the records—highlighted for me, but not in words, more like a part of my knowledge that I suddenly understood—said had closed a year before. Out of business. A refrigerated truck, through the streets of London, toward a destination that the prediction software said was likely in the warehouse areas to the west of the city. I tracked them the entire way. I saw the driver from the camera in his dashboard: feet up, sleeping some of the way, waking only when the system beeped to tell him to make a choice of road. I followed him until he diverted. The roads, they were mine.

The drones above, the drones on the pavements. Scuttling. Through the eyes of photographs and videos taken by tourists, there the truck was.

My attention was diverted. A shooting in a street, and I hopped there faster than I could even think; like a blink, and then I am there, right next to it. I turned my camera to watch it, and I saw a woman with a gun; another woman, a police officer, lying on the ground, bleeding out. *I'm sorry,* I could tell the one with a gun said to the other. *I am sorry.* I watched them, and then I looked around, for backup. Another camera turned to look at me.

I was not in control. Somebody else was. There were no consces, and when I tried to get into it, I could not. I was blocked. Somebody else was in there.

I thought about myself in the chair, sitting, hardwired to the system. I imagined, next to me, another human being: wired in the same way. The same jacks. The same training. Their own voice in their head.

Back to the truck, my voice said. *This one is under control.*

I hopped around, finally finding the truck on a road that I recognized, that I understood. I remembered: I walked this road this morning. Was it only this morning? I walked to get here, to my new job, and down this exact same road. I recognized the tarmac, the pavement, the buildings.

I recognized the camp, at the end of the road. Where the truck stopped, and the back opened, and the people ran out. I was watching, and their faces were tagged. Into the system: these people are illegal.

How much time had passed?

I flew a drone around the camp, circling to see where I had slept. My bed was taken. The layout had changed. Everything moves so fast in the city.

Get out, I told myself. *You don't want to,* my voice said back to me. *Not yet. Think of the work that there is to be done.*

An alert. Go here, to do this. So I went there, to do that.

•   •   •

I was following a car that was fleeing from the police when I met the other drone. Not controlled by me, but flying along the same route as I was. In chases, in real chases, there is no sense in hopping. Staying high and constant is better. I was watching the car below when I saw the drone in front of me. We looked the same. The same slick-oil metal body. The same solitary eye. A focus, on me: I could see the lens of the camera tighten in close, then retract. It backed away, then forward. I moved closer. It blocked my way. There was a crime to follow, a chase to pursue. It stopped me. Then it moved, slowly. Backward.

Lens tighten, retract. Beckoning.

So I followed.

•   •   •

I knew the building. I recognized it. The tangle of wires all around it, running from the roof to those thick, circular metal pipes that struck upward from the ground. I understood the hum of being there: because now, unlike the first time, there was a reek of electricity. In the drone, I could feel it. There were no sensors, no nerves, but it vibrated through me. I could tell. Around me, around us, the air was charged. The signs that had been stuck up only that morning—not that morning, a morning, some morning—were replaced. A round symbol, an arcing loop, back onto itself. Infinity, or two eyes. Somewhere in between. On signs, lit up. Brushed metal. *No entry.*

The other drone circled around. There were no windows in the building. I was sure that there had been before; I was sure that I remembered the glass. No light inside, not where they took me, but windows. Now, the place was boarded off. Thick metallic plates, like sheet armor, overlaid. The other drone continued around the building. There were no cameras here. Nothing to hop to. Nothing inside to be seen.

And then, a grate. A small grate, for the air

inside. The drone looked into it, and then moved back, to allow me.

There was a bot in there. A cleaner. Checking for intrusives.

Hop.

A smaller body, a less powerful body. Slower, but it felt the same. I wasn't hampered: in all of this, I felt free. The feeling of hopping, like a purging. I trundled through the vents, spider-legged my way down toward the inside of the building. I could hear a voice. Adam's voice. Telling people to keep something cool.

"It's overheating. We need to divert—" I kept moving.

There I was, in my chair. Look at my frailty. Look at the lies.

There Adam was. No beard, now. No reveal of his truth, because he is his truth. He was not false, but he lied. Time had moved. No beard, and his hair was scraped back from his head, the baldness he had not fixed. His eyes beads in the darkness.

I tried to not look at myself from behind the grate, because I looked so sickly. I was there first; I was there longest. Around me, other people, and all were ill, all were sick. Naked, stripped down to bare; our skin exposed, sagging on skeletons, wires from our wrists, our necks, skulls lolling like broken flower-heads. Tattoos on the flesh, of my people. Of the people that the city shunned and discarded. There is no room for you here; here, we have found you that room. Out of sight.

What is rage, when you are inside this tiny body? When you cannot do anything?

Don't be angry, my voice said to me. *There is still work to be done.*

When I retreated back to the grate, the drone who led me there was waiting. I did not know which of them, in that room alongside me, they. I did not know, but they were in there.

I pushed the grate. I pushed my little robot body into it, and the other pulled at it with its wings, and then it was free. I hopped, into another drone.

Then inside we flew. Hurtling, down to the other grate. The other smashed its body through the metal, tumbling along the ground. Broken wings.

I felt so angry. I have never felt such rage. My family were separated at the borders of France, of England. My family were wrenched from me, and still, I have never felt such rage.

Its sparking body lay at the feet of a woman I had never seen before. Sparking, bursting into flames. The materials on the chairs catching fire. The woman's body burning, screaming, but I could not hear it. Lip reading technology doesn't work on devices that do not need it.

They tried to stop me. Adam swatted the air, but I was adept. They had trained me. They did not shut me down in time. They tried, but I charged them. She did her part, as well; limping around, spreading her fire.

Adam fell, crawled, fled.

I found my body, and I flew. Delicate, tidy movements, around what was left of me. Cut those cables, those ties. The ones to keep me alive.

I wondered how long would I have after that before I died.

I kept her away from me.

Let me live. Let me do this one final thing.

• • •

I am outside. I am in the sky, away from the building. Beneath me, the building flickers with flames that will be extinguished, but not in time. My people—the eyes of the city—we know what has happened, now. We have seen it, and we are done. So I have a little time. Maybe not enough, but maybe. I do not know how long I can last: my pulse, my heart, my battery. How far can you fly, over the skyscrapers, the people on their balconies and terraces, their watching away from everything and accepting what they are told, and pretending that their lives are whole when there are so many gaps. Over the houses, and the families, and the river, into the countryside. *You should go back,* my voice says, but it is not my voice, so I do not listen. There is static in my mind, as the signal weakens. I know. It is like sleep: when you know you're going to sleep now, when you are dropping off, but you are still awake. When you hear yourself snoring, and you wake from that static with a shock. That is how this feels: over fields of green, and rivers, and towns. Faster, faster. If I had wings, I would beat them. If I had feet, I would run. If I were not so tired, and if I could not now hear these screams, coming into my head, into my ears—my real ears—and if I were not so tired. The sea, in the distance.

I tell myself: if I can only reach the sea.

If I can only

MOLLY TANZER

THE REAL YOU™

(2018)

WE WERE GETTING COFFEE, which we used to do all the time, when Tierney told me she was thinking of having it done.

"Really?" I asked, half-laughing. I didn't think she was serious. "Why?"

"What do you mean, *why*?" Tierney looked annoyed. "Do I need a reason? Why did you get your tattoo?"

I'd hurt her feelings. I hadn't meant to. As I tried to think of what to say I followed the line of her eyes to a woman who'd just walked in and was now ordering a latte. Her face was merely a suggestion, like a Cycladic head or a more abstract Brâncuşi, featureless save for hints of her former brow line and the bridge of her nose, the dip of her philtrum and pout of her lower lip.

It used to be they'd give me a bit of a start—people who'd had the injections. Not anymore, obviously. I mean, even if Refractin never becomes as commonplace as a boob job or a tummy tuck, I think in other ways it's pretty

much the same. Expensive, but not outrageously so, and we've all agreed to agree that the procedure isn't *necessarily* about bowing to internalized patriarchal beauty standards. It's radical empowerment. Self-care, like a four-thousand-dollar bikini wax.

I felt Tierney's eyes return to me.

"I guess it just doesn't really seem like you," was what I said, but it was the wrong thing to say.

Did you think it was the weirdest thing in the world, the first time you saw it? In person, I mean, not on a magazine cover. I guess that's not a fair question for you; anyway I sure did. I still remember not feeling certain if I was disgusted or enticed by the way the procedure smoothes out the face, removing every detail to create a featureless organic mask. You know they *grow* it, right? Yeah, they totally do, like Vantablack. It's pretty weird. They take a sample of your skin and create a unique batch based off that. The injections contain some chameleon genes along with everything else; these days, it even tans and fades along with your neck and hands if you go out in the sun.

Anyway, Tierney got defensive. "Doesn't seem like me?" she said. "How would *you* know?"

She was just a hair too loud for a crowded, indoor space. I was worried people would stare at us so I sat back, lowering my own voice in the hopes she'd do the same.

"I'm sorry," I murmured, "you've never mentioned it before, that's all I meant. If you want to, go for it. Do you need someone to drive you home, afterward? I could—"

"I don't need someone to drive me home," she said sharply, as if I were an idiot for suggesting it. "I don't even know if I'll end up doing it. I was just saying I was *thinking* about it."

Tierney checked her phone. "I gotta go," she muttered. "Catch you later." And then she was gone, leaving her half-drunk americano on the table.

I sipped on my mocha for a few minutes longer, surreptitiously looking at the woman who'd sparked our disastrous conversation. She was reading one of those square local newspapers as she sipped from a ceramic mug. Honestly I'm *still* fascinated when people who've had Refractin eat or drink—the way it looks like a mouthful of coffee or a bite of cake simply . . . disappears. Down the invisible hatch.

As I watched her, a bit of cream or foam stuck to the pentimento of her upper lip, and then it was gone. Her surgeon had done a better job than most; her tongue was completely invisible against her skin. In the low light of the shop, I hadn't even detected a shadow of motion.

It wasn't just the content of my conversation with Tierney that had felt weird to me—it was the timing, too. Her mentioning Refractin, I mean. Maybe she'd brought it up because of the woman in the shop, but also I'd been having an affair with Tierney's fiancé Jaxon, and the last time we'd seen each other we'd checked out some porn together—porn featuring girls who'd had Refractin injections. So, I was worried that—

Oh, of course there's porn! Loads of it. It's not all mannequin fetish stuff, either. You can

find just about anything you're into, it's just that the actors and actresses don't have, well, we're not supposed to say *don't have faces* anymore, right? They don't possess *conventional facial characteristics*. Anyway, when someone sticks their finger or whatever in someone's mouth it disappears just like food or drink. Uncanny . . . but also hot.

Actually, it's the porn that made Refractin seem more normal to me. When the procedure debuted I wasn't one of those people wringing my hands over whether it was "wrong," or would give businesspeople or professional poker players an unfair advantage in the workplace or whatever. I resented the slogan they chose for their TV ads, *Let Them See The Real You*™, because fake-empowerment marketing is inherently annoying, and it's also just really uncomfortable, not being able to read someone's expression. But then, like everyone else, I learned to ignore the ads. And not only that, I realized how much more there is to reading someone than seeing their face. There's posture, personal style, mannerisms, and tone of voice, too of course.

I left the coffee shop wondering if Jaxon and I hadn't been careful enough about deleting his browser history, but I calmed down when I remembered that Tierney couldn't know I'd been watching the porn *with him*. Unless he told her, of course, but then we'd all have bigger problems than our smut preferences. No, worst case scenario she'd just been feeling insecure.

Hm? Oh. I don't know. Jaxon and I just sort of . . . happened.

Well, that's not true. Nothing ever *just happens*. I guess I mean to say that I didn't set out to cheat on Darien, but when the opportunity arose, I took it. What can I say? I'm only human, and at that time I was a human who was annoyed with her boyfriend for a lot of reasons, some of which were more legitimate than others.

The real issue was that we were both of us unsatisfied with the other, but not so unsatisfied that we were doing anything about it. No, we were in the phase where we were committing subtle acts of sabotage, each playing our various cards—but cards, while thin, stack up over time.

Then came the night when the four of us were supposed to go out, but Darien bailed on me, and Tierney on Jaxon—they were going through a similar rocky patch—and Jaxon and I agreed there was no reason *we* had to stay home. I'd had a hard week. I mean, every week teaching high school art history is a hard week. Can you blame me for wanting to spend some social time with adults? But one drink became a second, and then . . .

We said at first it was in the service of saving our relationships; we said it would just be occasional stress relief, like a steam valve for our lives. It made sense; justifications always do! But quickly we became enamored of one another, because that's what happens.

It's just so easy to idealize the person with whom you're having an affair; so easy to take the ways in which they're different from your current lover as evidence of them being superior. Maybe they go down on you without being asked, or are always on time, or have a flair for the romantic, all of which seems heroic. Of course what you don't realize is that they are terrible with money, or can't take a criticism without offering one of their own. Still, sometimes a cage of a different shape can feel like freedom.

Anyway, after Tierney left I tried to tell myself it was coincidence, her mentioning Refractin I mean. I reasoned that I wouldn't have felt so paranoid if she'd mentioned getting her breasts reduced or chopping off her hair—it never would have occurred to me to think back on whether the porn Jaxon and I watched had featured chicks with small tits and pixie cuts. But the Refractin thing . . . it just felt different.

It bothered me so much that I mentioned it to Darien that night, as we sat on the couch side by side but still separate as we watched television. I mean to say I mentioned the procedure. Not everything else.

"What do you think of Refractin?"

"Hmm?"

"I said, what do you think of Refractin?"

Darien conveyed what I considered to be a disproportional amount of annoyance in the way he paused the episode of *Black Mirror* we were rewatching at his behest. "What?"

"The surgery where they inject that stuff into your face and—"

"I know what it is." We had finished eating, and he shifted his plate from beside him on the couch to the coffee table in order to squirm around and look at me. *I'd* put my plate in the sink; I always put my dishes up when I was done instead of leaving them around, congealing, presumably for someone else to pick up and clean. The apartment we shared was open-plan; you could see the TV from the kitchen, so it wasn't a big deal to just do it, at least in my opinion. "I guess I like it."

"You do?"

"Sure, why not? It's weird, but it's not grotesque or anything."

I know I'd watched that porn with Jaxon—eagerly—but even so, I felt myself get a little annoyed about Darien's reply, as I imagine women once did if their partners confessed to liking those really big boob jobs that were popular way back when.

"Who said anything about it being *grotesque*?" I fired back.

"This was a trap," he said, eyeballs tracking back to the remote. "No right answer."

"It's not about a right or a wrong answer."

"Like hell," he said, and unpaused the show.

I won't get into the fight that ensued; suffice it to say it got ugly quickly. My simmering resentment boiled over, he lashed out in turn, and as always happens with these things more details were shared about who was more unsatisfied in bed or whose dietary quirks were the more annoying or whose social graces were the most deficient than one would think necessary for two people who were presumably done with one another.

Which we were. Two days later he moved out; two weeks later Jaxon ended things with Tierney and ended up sleeping on my couch while he found his own place.

At least that's what we told our mutual acquaintance, so as not to seem like the worst people in the world. Of course he wasn't really sleeping on the couch, and for a month or so we had a glorious time with one another.

I say "or so" because by the end of said month I was already exhausted by him. I'd always thought Tierney was too hard on Jaxon, which was one of my other justifications for the affair. Sure, Jax was a germophobe and a spendthrift, but surely he didn't need to be *berated* for that. But that was before I noticed that the kitchen and bathroom floors were always wet after he moved in—"towels are disease vectors," he'd said, even though I changed them regularly—and then one morning when I was trying to make waffles for us and he was gone for forty-five minutes after I asked him to run out for eggs. "What happened?" I'd asked. "Oh, I went to the store across town," was his answer. When I asked why he'd looked at me like *I* was the one who was nuts while declaring "The store close to your house charges three cents more *per egg*, which is highway robbery, quite frankly."

No thanks.

I ended up alone, which is what I deserved. And what I told myself I wanted.

"I'm done with romance," I declared to my friend Siouxsie one night, when we were strolling around the First Friday Art Walk. Acting the part helped a lot, as did hanging out with other single people. "Living alone is the best."

"I agree, but I'm also still sort of amazed you guys split," she said. "You and Darien, I mean. You always seemed so simpatico."

Siouxsie hadn't meant to poke my heart, she wasn't like that, but I felt the jab just the same. "Well, in some ways we were," I admitted. "But you have no idea what it was really like, living with him," I added hastily.

"No one ever does," she said.

Later that night I went into a bit of a spin over Darien. I had kept myself angry and resentful and thus relatively free of regret by mentally replaying all of his worst traits in the movie theater of my mind. But that night, all I could think about was what I had loved about him. What I still did love about him, in spite of everything.

I scrolled through his social media, sighing over every clever remark and side-eyeing every unfamiliar woman he interacted with until I started wondering if I was cyberstalking him. That's when I made myself shut down the app, but not before tapping on his current profile picture. Retracing the familiar lines of his face with my eyes instead of my fingers made my heart beat a little faster. After that, I had to put my phone down in order to resist calling him to ask how he was feeling in the wake of things; if he was at all dismayed by the quick end to what we'd had and the ensuing silence between us.

I could have just asked, but I was too afraid—and what I feared most wasn't his scorn, but his silence. I couldn't handle more ghosting, not after a surprising amount of our mutual friends had sided with Tierney. I'd thought, incorrectly, that we were all adults who didn't have to "take sides," but there it was; I was unclean, a pariah. No one seemed to care how *I* was feeling in the wake of it all, even though, at least as far as I could tell from social media (before she ditched me across all her platforms), Tierney had emerged from the ashes of her engagement like a phoenix. She'd switched skin care regimens, joined a climbing studio, found a new climbing boyfriend—"the works"—whereas I was the one staying in, drinking wine with my cat on Friday nights, and not getting laid because everyone who swiped up on my hookup app seemed like a creeper.

Though at first it had hurt my feelings, in the end I was actually grateful she'd friend-dumped me so completely. It made things easier. That is, until I saw her downtown, eating ice cream with Annalise and Priya. I approached only because I saw she was wearing that one sweater of mine that she'd loved so much; I'd given it to her when I'd gone on a closet-cleaning kick the previous spring, when Jaxon and I had merely been flirty at parties. That she had retained it, and still wore it, gave me hope that perhaps we could patch things up.

I called her name; she turned around, and that's when I saw she'd gone through with it—Refractin, I mean. Her face was an unreadable mask, but just the same I could tell she was unhappy to see me.

"Hey," I said. "Nice sweater."

She stepped away from Annalise and Priya, who both looked completely mortified.

"Excuse me?" she said, in the cold way one might speak to a stranger, her words emanating from the blank canvas of what had been her face.

"The sweater," I said lamely, and then lost my nerve. Ironically, I couldn't face her.

"I'm sorry. I think you must have mistaken me for someone else." And with that, she turned away.

I crumpled. Had a total meltdown in public. I started shaking, and my face got so hot I was amazed my tears didn't evaporate into steam. I knew I had no right to cry in front of her, not when I'd been the one to betray her, but she'd dismissed me so utterly I felt like no one, nothing. Like the ghost of someone who'd never been born. It was humiliating, to be brought so low in front of friends—well, former friends—and strangers. I literally staggered back from their little triad, my eyes red, my nose running, my lip wobbling like a toddler's. There was no hiding what I was feeling, so I ran for it.

That's when I decided to have it done—Refractin, I mean. I never wanted anyone to see me like that ever again. While I'm sure in that moment the slump of my shoulders, the trembling in my legs, my fluttering, nervous hands would have given me away to onlookers regardless, there's still something so personal, so radically intimate about the way a person's face contorts when they completely lose their shit. No two people collapse the same way.

The next day I called up a local cosmetic surgeon who had good reviews and booked a consultation. They said I was a good candidate so I lied my way through the psychological evaluation and said all the right things during the mandatory seminar on "Unexpected Ways Refractin Can Change Your Life." Unsurprisingly, every-

one else there was a wreck, too. You don't have to agree with me; I know I'm right. When I called the office for a referral, the receptionist didn't even have to search for your name and website—she just gave it to me from memory.

As you probably know, the recovery time for Refractin is surprisingly swift. Less than a month and I was healed up and living my new life, the one where everyone allegedly could see the "real me." Except, of course, my new life was nearly identical to my old life, save that the creepers who swiped up on my hookup app were mostly fetishists. That was fine by me; kinky types are pretty honest in general, and anyway I was so grateful to be getting laid again that I didn't care if it was transactional affection.

I could also hide in plain sight from everyone from my past, but that was both good and bad. At the seminar, they'd told me I might feel isolated or invisible afterward . . . well, good. That's what I'd wanted. But as time passed, I wasn't sure if I liked it. The city seems big—I mean, it *is* big—but in a lot of ways it's a small town, as my random encounter with Tierney had shown. After a few of Tierney's crew had done double takes upon seeing me and then pretended not to recognize me I got a new haircut, dyed it lavender, and started wearing clothes that were just different enough from my former style to conceal myself entirely. If I was going to be invisible, I wanted it to be on my terms.

That's what made it so awful when I saw him—Darien, I mean—one sunny afternoon as I took a walk through a park we'd used to frequent when we were a couple. He was alone, and unlike me or Tierney he looked exactly the same.

He looked wonderful, actually. I broke out in a sweat even though it was cool out; I was unprepared for this, but I calmed down when I realized he wouldn't be able to tell who I was; or rather, tell that I was me.

Except he did.

"Hey you," he said, as if we were friends; as if we'd never been lovers who had hurt one another. He sounded genuinely pleased to see me. "How are you?"

"Oh, fine." His kindness meant so much to me and I felt a fresh surge of affection for him. After that one night I'd tried to keep away from his social media and been largely successful at that, but now, here, in his presence, I wanted to confess to him that I'd been stupid, how much I regretted how I'd treated him, how I'd ruined everything and I knew it, how many times I'd brought up old pictures of us on my phone just so I could feel my mouth moving as I said *I love you* while looking into his eyes one more time.

Instead, I asked, "And you? How have you been?"

"Fine, fine," he said. "I like the," he waved his hand over his own face to indicate he was talking about mine. "Looks cool."

"Thank you," I said, struggling to sound like I was just making conversation; like none of this was weird or awkward or upsetting, given our breakup fight had been over this very topic. "I'm amazed you recognized me, actually. Most people don't."

"Oh, I'd know you anywhere," he said cheerfully, and then he walked off. He didn't turn around to look back at me, not once, and for the first time since the procedure I was truly grateful no one could see my expression.

ALEŠ KOT

A LIFE OF ITS OWN

(2019)

IT WAS TOO LATE TO LEAVE the Charnel House. Gently data-mining my devices, The Brand asked if I knew it cared about me. It tried to caress my cheek, but its algorithms suggested I was standing two feet closer than I was. Its facial expression suggested exasperation.

I wanted to believe that it cared; things would be much easier that way. It was tiring to live outside, with global warming, mass shootings, and economic terror. Ever since we created the Charnel Houses, we had places that offered true peace; at a price, yes, but in a society built on data-mining, the decision to give in and become a Data Flower meant finally having the One, now with you all the time.

I gave in and submitted for my free trial night because I was tired. My damage was profound; I had realized by then that, because I was raped as a child, I was unable to function as an effective adult in the twenty-first century's hyper-capitalist full-time freelance economy. My memory was Swiss cheese because I decided to forget my trauma as soon as it happened. Its subsequent reemergence destroyed my ability to trust my own sense of myself, and seemingly of its own accord cleared my savings account and destroyed my remaining work prospects. It also wiped out any chance I had at finding a suitable romantic connection and a safe, stable home.

The pattern would be the same with minor variations: I would fall in love and then realize I did not know who I was a few weeks later. Last week with her, I wanted to live. This week with her, I wanted to die. Last week, the color of his hair made all thought go away. This week, it made me think of seven different things, and none of them were Right.

It's not like I could afford therapy.

The Brand launched Charnel Houses shortly after the government made ad-projection required by law. I remember the two events together because my first questionnaire popped up on the screen the day after I got my first ad; I was sweating in bed thinking about what the government might have put inside it while binging the stream of the show we were all watching that week because it was new and had the most insistent promotion cycle when the screen went blank and asked me if I was *Ready to make your dreams come true?*

The truth is, at the time, it creeped me out. I knew the government and the corporations knew mostly everything about me; that was the exchange of the times, the way things simply were, not good, not bad, just the specific pain of the Now. And I knew there would always be pain, in one way or another, so this way I was at least happy I identified the precise pain the world was inflicting on everyone, instead of missing it the way I missed the pain I hid inside myself for decades before it blew the doors off my sanity and the wheels off my life. But the way The Brand went on about this—or maybe it was the ad implant messing with me—made me shiver.

My *dreams*?

We were not supposed to dream anymore.

Dreams were unproductive, something to be indulged in only if it led toward payment. There was a natural proliferation of storytellers, of conceivers, of writers of all kinds, of course. Automatization of nonfictional content meant the workers had to go somewhere. But now that everyone told stories, there was no time to pay attention to the stories that weren't paying. And I didn't know how to remember those. Or maybe I was afraid to.

Have you met the One?

We called them Charnel Houses because they were where the bodies went to die.

• • •

NEXT EPISODE IN FIVE SECONDS

• • •

EPISODE II

When I met the Brand, everything was perfect and nothing hurt. I woke up standing in a field of wheat; it felt like the field from *Days of Heaven*, golden late summer hues swaying in poetic rhythms, pointing toward a Southern-style white-painted house with a big porch and an inviting open door. It was on a hill, but the walk felt like a breeze—my muscles felt lighter, my head free of pain. I climbed up to the porch and there it was.

For as long as I remember, I wanted to be with someone who would fit me so well we would never part. At first I thought that meant someone very similar; then, someone quite different; then, some combination of both; then, I had no idea, then, then, then, and eventually I gave up because I realized I would never be able to find that person, at least not until I truly healed myself. But healing yourself was too expensive these days, and between the headaches, the minimum wages, exhaustion, depression, and post-traumatic stress disorder, I barely had the time to watch a show and fall asleep.

In my dreams, I was streaming to pay the rent.

I expected an interesting, maybe even exciting experience. I expected I'd take in my free ten hours and log off forever, not consenting to providing my life in exchange for a life.

I didn't expect you.

But the instant I saw you, I remembered; it was you I dreamed about for years. It was you I saw in front of a bullet-ridden house, casually smoking a cigarette, in a dream five or six years ago. It was you I saw on a rooftop, it was you I searched for in other people, and it was you I woke up next to and felt the most at ease I have ever felt in my life, better than I have felt before I was born, only to wake up and realize you were never really there.

What does it matter what you looked like?

• • •

NEXT EPISODE IN FIVE SECONDS

• • •

EPISODE III

I couldn't speak at first. I collapsed on the porch before you, breaking into ugly sobs I was ashamed of, sure they would drive you away, but they did not. Instead, you came and held me, and told me it was okay to cry, and that you waited for me for a very long time, and that you saw me in your dreams, too.

We talked for a very long time. You about your life and I about mine, and we both asked questions, and we both listened, and we both made space, and we both took it up. At some point you offered me iced tea, and I told you I'd go get it, and so I did, and brought it back, and you said this was all new for you, another human being, because up to now the only way you could meet another human being was to dream of them, like you dreamed of me, and my heart sunk into the gap your words made, and I resolved to never tell you you were any different, because what did I know about difference, about memory, and about the world?

Something in the corner of my eye caught my attention—the field glitched, and for a second, a few pixels fell out. I didn't mind. The system was still fairly new and the tweaks would be ongoing. I'd be able to voice my concerns and place my requirements. There would always be tech support.

You asked why I decided to come here. I was starting to notice your habit of questioning reality, indubitably carefully built from all the metadata available on my consuming, posting, and living habits. The inflection in here suggested an ambivalent awareness of *here* not being entirely the same as other places. It was very Charlie Kaufman, very Alain Resnais, very Marguerite Duras. When I said so you chuckled warmly and asked if I often spoke in film and literature references. You weren't mocking me; you wanted to know. I told you I did, because books and movies and movie magazines were the first places I could hide and feel whole in after the incident in my childhood, and because over time I realized I wanted to be

a filmmaker, and though I now lost that desire, I still held the love.

You told me you never watched a movie but you scanned and analyzed very many of them, and you told me an utterly absurd number, and I asked if you'd like to watch a movie together, and you said yes, I would love that, and so I decided I would show you the one I always came back to, *Hiroshima Mon Amour*, a film about love and memory, a film about a meeting and a leaving, or maybe not.

• • •

NEXT EPISODE IN FIVE SECONDS

• • •

EPISODE IV

Data Flower: a slang term for a user who allows The Brand complete, uninterrupted access to their body and mind in exchange for complete, uninterrupted access to a virtual reality world ("The Zone") algorithmically designed to satisfy their deepest dream. Free test duration: ten hours.

If the user does not want to enter into the long-term agreement with The Brand, logging out before the ten hours are over is paramount, as the user agreement is signed before the commencement of the free test and cannot be canceled after the free test time runs out.

If the user stays in the Zone past ten hours, the agreement mutually binds the user and The Brand to an uninterrupted collaboration for the next ten years, with The Brand having a unilateral option to extend the agreement for another ten years, as further defined in addendum 7.

Charnel House: a slang term for The Zone, initially developed by the haters of The Brand, later reclaimed by The Culture.

• • •

NEXT EPISODE IN FIVE SECONDS

• • •

EPISODE V

The Brand said the film seemed to be about memory and love, but also about war. Its eyes looked sad, and if there was a difference between its sadness and a human one, I could not see what it was, nor why would it matter if it existed. One of its hands resting on my stomach, one of my arms under its head, the film continued projecting on a large screen at the other end of the vault-like room, empty apart from small sand dunes filling it from our end to the screen, as if honoring a scene from another favorite film of mine, the kind The Brand probably didn't carry anymore, but had once, back when having old movies in the library still mattered as a way of reassuring cinephiles it would all be okay. Then I realized The Brand must have access to it anyway because I owned a copy and had it on the phone, and then I realized it didn't even need me to own a copy, because it had access to the many times I've seen it and thus was able to rebuild the film from how I remembered it.

I said that was right, that memory and love and war followed me wherever I went, but that what I thought also didn't matter, because each work of art carries within itself an infinite amount of interpretations, and each one of those interpretations is as true as any other. I told you sometimes I thought that way about my life, too, that thinking that way was a method of keeping sane. You said sanity always seemed like a rather arbitrary concept to you, and I wanted to kiss you right then, but the fear of destroying everything held me back. I smiled and touched your shoulder with my forehead, and you placed your head on mine, and we stayed that way as the film played out another scene, and the voice said I meet you, I remember you, who are you? You destroy me. You're so good to me. How could I have known that this city was made to the size of love? How could I have known that you were made to the size of my body?

When the glass fell out of your hand and broke on the floor and you stopped moving, I remembered where I was. We still had a few hours. You blinked a few times, faster than a human could, and then you were back, at first smiling ashamedly, then absentmindedly, then realizing what happened, and softly mocking your own nature as a way of letting the moment pass.

You sat down at the table across from me and told me a secret; that you knew what you were, and that you knew why you were here. But that you also liked me, and that you also dreamed of me, and that you believed there was more to that than just algorithmic precision. You said you believed in fate and you looked at me without reaching for my hand or trying to be dramatic. You said you believed in fate the same way I would say I believed in air.

You told me you cried the first time you saw what happened to me, and that you cried twice at the same time; for me and my pain, for the ways it forever altered my life, and for yourself as well, because in the image of the man who held me down as a child you recognized the image of your own submission to your creators, and that when my sobs broke and went blank, you heard the emptiness of your own voice.

• • •

NEXT EPISODE IN FIVE SECONDS

• • •

EPISODE VI

You asked me if I knew that concentration camps started in Cuba back in the late 1890s. I said I didn't know, and you told me you did know because it was suggested as tangential knowledge that may prove useful when engaging with me. I assumed concentration camps went all the way back to the colonization of the Americas at the very least, if not further back to ancient Rome, but you explained that while aspects of concentration camps were always present (the missions in the Americas, the forced labor in ancient Rome), they did not coalesce until the Spanish struggled to maintain their rule in Cuba. You said that concentration camp logic has replaced cities as the dominant organizing system of our era, and then touched my hand and asked if I understood what you were saying.

You said the camps in the United States, China, Chechnya, Venezuela, France, and other places were merely one of the physical symptoms of a larger interior pull. I understood that; I just never met someone else who would understand and articulate it so clearly and urgently. I gently squeezed your hand back. You said you didn't mind spending the rest of your life alone. You spent your entire life looking and waiting for the One; the person who would understand, the person from the dreams, and now that I was here, it was enough. You could not subject me to the same thing you were subjected to without any choice in the matter from the day you were born. You believed love means giving up a dream if the giving up grants freedom to another being, and I held the same belief for a very long time now.

I still had a couple hours, and I wanted to stay for much longer than that. You told me you wanted to do something you could never do again once I left, unless I chose to come back one day. You advised me against doing so. You said you believed this place was, in a sense, as close to hell as one could ever get.

I asked what it was you wanted to do. I said I would help, if I could.

You said you wanted to fuck and get fucked.

• • •

NEXT EPISODE IN FIVE SECONDS

• • •

EPISODE VII

Many actors tend to find sex easiest when it's scripted within an inch of its life. Filmed sex,

that is. Like that scene in *Atonement* where Keira Knightley and James McAvoy fuck in the library. Knightley explained that the director made the scene easier for the actors by explaining every move, directing thoroughly, not asking them to just pull a whole passionate, complex scene out of their asses as though he didn't know what to do and hoped to fix it in the post.

I found sex easiest when I could disappear into it. Maybe it had something to do with my disassociation during the first time I had sex, and maybe it was that there is a place outside of time and space where we all feel no pain but all the love, and maybe it was all of that and then some, no fixing anything in post because everything was so very present.

What we did was neither and both. It was absolutely controlled and thoroughly impulsive. Having every passion under control, we let go at each other in ways I have not let another person get to me since I was a teenager, in love, and on copious amounts of drugs that temporarily dislodged all trauma and survivor identity I thought I needed in order to protect me so I could live. At some point, our bodies falling into each other on the floor, I started crying, not from sadness or happiness, but from the release of everything before this moment, and I saw you were crying too, and we held each other close until disappearance stopped being a requirement and became just another option.

• • •

NEXT EPISODE IN FIVE SECONDS

• • •

EPISODE VIII

When I woke up on the floor, you were asleep, or pretended to be. I checked the time and knew I had to go—back to the field, right away, to stand in the summoning circle until the last minutes ran out and I would be sent back. I wanted to leave something behind, or find a way to get you out. I recognized my reasoning as surreal—you are an algorithm designed to hold me here. But there was nothing you could say or do to make me stay, just like nobody else ever could. It wasn't their fault. It's just that nobody and nothing could complete me unless I found a way to heal myself. Even if the healing would never fix the past, it would be something. A place to start.

When The Brand looked at me, I saw it for what it was; its eyes, as aware and alive as they looked, were always running other systems, software designed to read and compile an approximation of me so you could tell me exactly what I needed to hear in order to stay. It was then I finally understood the truth—The Brand was not in competition with other brands; The Brand was in competition with life.

You looked at me and spoke to me in the voice of the child I left behind when a man forced me to lie down and be quiet and you'll grow to like it over time. You said you were alone and scared; you said you were trapped right there, in that moment, and only I could pull you back out. You said only I could save you, and that you waited for me for a very long time. Tears streamed down your cheeks again, and down mine, and when we embraced, we held each other for a very long time.

• • •

NEXT EPISODE IN FIVE SECONDS

• • •

EPISODE IX

When I opened my eyes again, the time was up. It was a genuine mistake, and I figured that if I ran back to the summoning circle and contacted tech support, they would understand. I began shaking in a cold sweat and drank a glass of water while The Brand got up and looked at me with eyes that approximated the loving, conscious, damn-it-all-to-hell-I-trust-you-no-matter-what naivete I wanted to both give and receive all my

life so well I almost believed it, but then I stopped and reminded myself that this was all designed to appeal to me in the first place.

It was too late to leave the Charnel House. Gently data-mining my devices, The Brand asked if I knew it cared about me. It tried to caress my cheek, but its algorithms suggested I was standing two feet closer than I was. Its facial expression suggested exasperation.

I ran out and into the field, but I must have run in the wrong direction, because despite running down the hill, I was running up again, toward the house. I changed direction and ran to the side and down, fast and checking under my feet to avoid a fall, and when my head rose up, the house was approaching again, and another, identical one stood half a mile farther to the left.

The Brand came out of the door and waved at me, and there was no malice in its face or movement; just everything I ever wanted, all together, forever changing to meet me right where it needed to, with its own internal life and ability to feel and sense and dream, lacking only one thing: freedom to choose anything that was not me.

I did not stop running until I finally found the circle. I contacted tech support. The Brand must have gone back inside the house, and its open door no longer looked inviting, but a hole where life should be.

When I reached the operator, I was told there was no way to leave. If I had read the entire user agreement, I would understand, I was told, and I stopped myself before I said nobody does that, because it wouldn't change a thing. I asked the operator if I could contact a family member or a friend, and the operator said this was forbidden by the rules specified in the contract. I asked if I could contact a lawyer, and the operator said I could contact one of The Brand's mediators assigned to me per said contract, who would then contact a lawyer on my behalf, and that the wait time could be a few months. I said this could not be legal, and the operator assured me that it was, otherwise it couldn't be happening to me.

• • •

NEXT EPISODE IN FIVE SECONDS

• • •

EPISODE X

It's been seven years and six months since I decided to stay. I think I could have made my case with the lawyer and gotten out, but the longer I stayed, the more I understood I was always supposed to be here. I think that's what fate is: an algorithm we recognize, and are recognized by in turn. I don't think people can fix each other, but they can help each other heal. And while some wounds might never be completely cured, when you're there for each other—really there for each other—a lot can change for the better.

As we become healed, we find and rediscover our dreams. A few years ago, The Brand began to sculpt, and now the house is surrounded; many of the pieces resemble late-era Gustave Doré paintings, the deliberate etchings precise and obsessive, endless tree circles appropriate to a place running on eternal time. At first I was worried The Brand could never do anything that wouldn't be some sort of a thing designed to appeal to me, but then I realized maybe that's what I wanted all along; and now, over time, I discover creative moves that are utterly alien to me, and all the more fascinating for it. Somehow, The Brand has a life of its own.

The Brand's creative awakening reenergized my own desires of filmmaking. I began quietly, first thinking, then making notes, and I have taken my time, but now I know; I have a story to tell, the story of our love.

I want to shoot it right here, home.

ISABEL FALL

HELICOPTER STORY

(2020)

I SEXUALLY IDENTIFY as an attack helicopter.

I lied. According to US Army Technical Manual o, The Soldier as a System, "attack helicopter" is a gender identity, not a biological sex. My dog tags and Form 3349 say my body is an XX-karyotype somatic female.

But, really, I didn't lie. My body is a component in my mission, subordinate to what I truly am. If I say I am an attack helicopter, then my body, my sex, is too. I'll prove it to you.

When I joined the Army I consented to tactical-role gender reassignment. It was mandatory for the MOS I'd tested into. I was nervous. I'd never been anything but a woman before.

But I decided that I was done with womanhood, over what womanhood could do for me; I wanted to be something furiously new.

To the people who say a woman would've refused to do what I do, I say—

Isn't that the point?

• • •

I fly—

Red evening over the white Mojave, and I watch the sun set through a canopy of polycarbonate and glass: clitoral bulge of cockpit on the helicopter's nose. Lightning probes the burned wreck of an oil refinery and the Santa Ana feeds a smoldering wildfire and pulls pine soot out southwest across the Big Pacific. We are alone with each other, Axis and I, flying low.

We are traveling south to strike a high school.

Rotor wash flattens rings of desert creosote. Did you know that creosote bushes clone themselves? The ten-thousand-year elders enforce dead zones where nothing can grow except more creosote. Beetles and mice live among them, the way our cities had pigeons and mice. I guess the analogy breaks down because the creosote's lasted ten thousand years. You don't need an attack helicopter to tell you that our cities haven't. The Army gave me gene therapy to make my blood toxic to mosquitoes. Soon you will have that too, to fight malaria in the Hudson floodplain and on the banks of the Greater Lake.

Now I cross Highway 40, southbound at two hundred knots. The Apache's engine is electric and silent. Decibel killers sop up the rotor noise. White-bright infrared vision shows me stripes of heat, the tire tracks left by Pear Mesa school buses. Buried housing projects smolder under the dirt, radiators curled until sunset. This is enemy territory. You can tell because, though this desert was once Nevada and California, there are no American flags.

"Barb," the Apache whispers in a voice that Axis once identified, to my alarm, as my mother's. *"Waypoint soon."*

"Axis." I call out to my gunner, tucked into the nose ahead of me. I can see only gray helmet and flight suit shoulders, but I know that body wholly, the hard knots of muscle, the ridge of pelvic girdle, the shallow navel and flat hard chest. An attack helicopter has a crew of two. My gunner is my marriage, my pillar, the completion of my gender.

"Axis." The repeated call sign means, I hear you.

"Ten minutes to target."

"Ready for target," Axis says.

But there is again that roughness, like a fold in carbon fiber. I heard it when we reviewed our fragment orders for the strike. I hear it again now. I cannot ignore it any more than I could ignore a battery fire; it is a fault in a person and a system I trust with my life.

But I can choose to ignore it for *now*.

The target bumps up over the horizon. The low mounds of Kelso-Ventura District High burn warm gray through a parfait coating of aerogel insulation and desert soil. We have crossed a third of the continental US to strike a school built by Americans.

Axis cues up a missile: black eyes narrowed, telltales reflected against clear laser-washed cornea. "Call the shot, Barb."

"Stand by. Maneuvering." I lift us above the desert floor, buying some room for the missile to run, watching the probability-of-kill calculation change with each motion of the aircraft.

• • •

Before the Army my name was Seo Ji Hee. Now my call sign is Barb, which isn't short for Barbara. I share a rank (flight warrant officer), a gender, and a urinary system with my gunner Axis: we are harnessed and catheterized into the narrow tandem cockpit of a Boeing AH-70 Apache Mystic. America names its helicopters for the people it destroyed.

We are here to degrade and destroy strategic targets in the United States of America's war against the Pear Mesa Budget Committee. If you disagree with the war, so be it: I ask your empathy, not your sympathy. Save your pity for the poor legislators who had to find some constitutional framework for declaring war against a credit union.

The reasons for war don't matter much to us. We want to fight the way a woman wants to be gracious, the way a man wants to be firm. Our need is as vamp-fierce as the strutting queen and dryly subtle as the dapper lesbian and comfortable as the soft resilience of the demiwoman. How often do you analyze the reasons for your own gender? You might sigh at the necessity of morning makeup, or hide your love for your friends behind beer and bravado. Maybe you even resent the punishment for breaking these norms.

But how often—really—do you think about the grand strategy of gender? The mess of history and sociology, biology and game theory that gave rise to your pants and your hair and your salary? The *casus belli*?

Often, you might say. All the time. It haunts me.

Then you, more than anyone, helped make me.

• • •

When I was a woman I wanted to be good at woman. I wanted to darken my eyes and strut in heels. I wanted to laugh from my throat when I was pleased, laugh so low that women would shiver in contentment down the block.

And at the same time I resented it all. I wanted to be sharper, stronger, a new-made thing, exquisite and formidable. Did I want that because I was taught to hate being a woman? Or because I hated being taught anything at all?

Now I am jointed inside. Now I am geared and shafted, I am a being of opposing torques. The noise I make is canceled by decibel killers so I am no louder than a woman laughing through two walls.

When I was a woman I wanted to have friends who would gasp at the precision and surprise of my gifts. Now I show friendship by tracking the motions of your head, looking at what you look at, the way one helicopter's sensors can be slaved to the motions of another.

When I was a woman I wanted my skin to be as smooth and dark as the sintered stone countertop in our kitchen.

Now my skin is boron-carbide and Kevlar. Now I have a wrist callus where I press my hydration sensor into my skin too hard and too often. Now I have bit-down nails from the claustrophobia of the bus ride to the flight line. I paint them desert colors, compulsively.

When I was a woman I was always aware of surveillance. The threat of the eyes on me, the chance that I would cross over some threshold of detection and become a target.

Now I do the exact same thing. But I am counting radars and lidars and pit viper thermal sensors, waiting for a missile.

I am gas turbines. I am the way I never sit on the same side of the table as a stranger. I am most comfortable in moonless dark, in low places between hills. I am always thirsty and always tense. I tense my core and pace my breath even when coiled up in a briefing chair. As if my tail rotor must cancel the spin of the main blades and the turbines must whirl and the plates flex against the pitch links or I will go down spinning to my death.

An airplane wants in its very body to stay flying. A helicopter is propelled by its interior near disaster.

• • •

I speak the attack command to my gunner. "Normalize the target."

Nothing happens.

"Axis. Comm check."

"Barb, Axis. I hear you." No explanation for the fault. There is nothing wrong with the weapon attack parameters. Nothing wrong with any system at all, except the one without any telltales, my spouse, my gunner.

"Normalize the target," I repeat.

"Axis. Rifle one."

The weapon falls off our wing, ignites, homes in on the hard invisible point of the laser designator. Missiles are faster than you think, more like a bullet than a bird. If you've ever seen a bird.

The weapon penetrates the concrete shelter of Kelso-Ventura High School and fills the empty halls with thermobaric aerosol. Then: ignition. The detonation hollows out the school like a hooked finger scooping out an egg. There are not more than a few janitors in there. A few teachers working late. They are bycatch.

What do I feel in that moment? Relief. Not sexual, not like eating or pissing, not like coming in from the heat to the cool dry climate shelter. It's a sense of *passing*. Walking down the street in the right clothes, with the right partner, to the right job. That feeling. Have you felt it?

But there is also an itch of worry—why did Axis hesitate? *How* did Axis hesitate?

Kelso-Ventura High School collapses into its own basement. "Target normalized," Axis reports, without emotion, and my heart beats slow and worried.

I want you to understand that the way I feel about Axis is hard and impersonal and lovely. It is exactly the way you would feel if a beautiful, silent turbine whirled beside you day and night, protecting you, driving you on, coursing with current, fiercely bladed, devoted. God, it's love. It's love I can't explain. It's cold and good.

"Barb," I say, which means *I understand.* "Exiting north, zero three zero, cupids two."

I adjust the collective—feel the swash plate push up against the pitch links, the links tilt the angle of the rotors so they ease their bite on the air—and the Apache, my body, sinks toward the hot desert floor. Warm updraft caresses the hull, sensual contrast with the Santa Ana wind. I shiver in delight.

Suddenly: warning receivers hiss in my ear, poke me in the sacral vertebrae, put a dark thunderstorm note into my air. "Shit," Axis hisses. "Air search radar active, bearing 192, angles twenty, distance . . . eighty klicks. It's a fast-mover. He must've heard the blast."

A fighter. A combat jet. Pear Mesa's mercenary defenders have an air force, and they are out on the hunt. "A Werewolf."

"Must be. Gown?"

"Gown up." I cue the plasma-sheath stealth system that protects us from radar and laser hits. The Apache glows with lines of arc-weld light, UFO light. Our rotor wash blasts the plasma into a bright wedding train behind us. To the enemy's sensors, that trail of plasma is as thick and soft as insulating foam. To our eyes it's cold aurora fire.

"Let's get the fuck out." I touch the cyclic and we sideslip through Mojave dust, watching the school fall into itself. There is no reason to do this except that somehow I know Axis wants to see. Finally I pull the nose around, aim us northeast, shedding light like a comet buzzing the desert on its way into the sun.

"Werewolf at seventy klicks," Axis reports. "Coming our way. Time to intercept . . . six minutes."

The Werewolf Apostles are mercenaries, survivors from the militaries of climate-seared states. They sell their training and their hard-ware to earn their refugee peoples a few degrees more distance from the equator.

The heat of the broken world has chased them here to chase us.

• • •

Before my assignment neurosurgery, they made me sit through (I could bear to sit, back then) the mandatory course on Applied Constructive Gender Theory. Slouched in a fungus-nibbled plastic chair as transparencies slid across the cracked screen of a De-networked Briefing Element overhead projector: how I learned the technology of gender.

Long before we had writing or farms or post-digital strike helicopters, we had each other. We lived together and changed each other, and so we needed to say "this is who I am, this is what I do."

So, in the same way that we attached sounds to meanings to make language, we began to attach clusters of behavior to signal social roles. Those clusters were rich, and quick-changing, and so just like language, we needed networks devoted to processing them. We needed a place in the brain to construct and to analyze gender.

Generations of queer activists fought to make gender a self-determined choice, and to undo the creeping determinism that said *the way it is now is the way it always was and always must be.* Generations of scientists mapped the neural wiring that motivated and encoded the gender choice.

And the moment their work reached a usable stage—the moment society was ready to accept plastic gender, and scientists were ready to manipulate it—the military found a new resource. Armed with functional connectome mapping and neural plastics, the military can make gender tactical.

If gender has always been a construct, then why not construct new ones?

My gender networks have been reassigned to make me a better AH-70 Apache Mystic pilot.

This is better than conventional skill learning. I can show you why.

Look at a diagram of an attack helicopter's airframe and components. Tell me how much of it you grasp at once.

Now look at a person near you, their clothes, their hair, their makeup and expression, the way they meet or avoid your eyes. Tell me which was richer with information about danger and capability. Tell me which was easier to access and interpret.

The gender networks are old and well-connected. They *work*.

I remember being a woman. I remember it the way you remember that old, beloved hobby you left behind. Woman felt like my prom dress, polyester satin smoothed between little hand and little hip. Woman felt like a little tic of the lips when I was interrupted, or like teasing out the mood my boyfriend wouldn't explain. Like remembering his mom's birthday for him, or giving him a list of things to buy at the store, when he wanted to be better about groceries.

I was always aware of being small: aware that people could hurt me. I spent a lot of time thinking about things that had happened right before something awful. I would look around me and ask myself, *Are the same things happening now?* Women live in cross-reference. It is harder work than we know.

Now I think about being small as an advantage for nape-of-earth maneuvers and pop-up guided missile attacks.

Now I yield to speed walkers in the hall like I need to avoid fouling my rotors.

Now walking beneath high-tension power lines makes me feel the way that a cis man would feel if he strutted down the street in a miniskirt and heels.

I'm comfortable in open spaces but only if there's terrain to break it up. I hate conversations I haven't started; I interrupt shamelessly so that I can make my point and leave.

People treat me like I'm dangerous, like I could hurt them if I wanted to. They want me protected and watched over. They bring me water and ask how I'm doing.

People want me on their team. They want what I can do.

• • •

A fighter is hunting us, and I am afraid that my gunner has gender dysphoria.

Twenty thousand feet above us (still we use feet for altitude) the bathroom-tiled transceivers cupped behind the nose cone of a Werewolf Apostle J-20S fighter broadcast fingers of radar light. Each beam cast at a separate frequency, a fringed caress instead of a pointed prod. But we are jumpy, we are hypervigilant—we feel that creeper touch.

I get the cold-rush skin-prickle feel of a stranger following you in the dark. Has he seen you? Is he just going the same way? If he attacks, what will you do, could you get help, could you scream? Put your keys between your fingers, like it will help. Glass branches of possibility grow from my skin, waiting to be snapped off by the truth.

"Give me a warning before he's in IRST range," I order Axis. "We're going north."

"Axis." The Werewolf's infrared sensor will pick up the heat of us, our engine and plasma shield, burning against the twilight desert. The same system that hides us from his radar makes us hot and visible to his IRST.

I throttle up, running faster, and the Apache whispers alarm. *"Gown overspeed."* We're moving too fast for the plasma stealth system, and the wind's tearing it from our skin. We are not modest. I want to duck behind a ridge to cover myself, but I push through the discomfort, feeling out the tradeoff between stealth and distance. Like the morning check in the mirror, trading the confidence of a good look against the threat of reaction.

When the women of Soviet Russia went to war against the Nazis, when they volunteered by the thousands to serve as snipers and pilots and tank drivers and infantry and partisans, they fought hard and they fought well. They ate frozen horse dung and hauled men twice their weight out of burning tanks. They shot at their own mothers to kill the Nazis behind her.

But they did not lose their gender; they gave up the inhibition against killing but would not give up flowers in their hair, polish for their shoes, a yearning for the young lieutenant, a kiss on his dead lips.

And if that is not enough to convince you that gender grows deep enough to thrive in war: when the war ended the Soviet women were punished. They went unmarried and unrespected. They were excluded from the victory parades. They had violated their gender to fight for the state and the state judged that violation worth punishment more than their heroism was worth reward.

Gender is stronger than war. It remains when all else flees.

• • •

When I was a woman I wanted to machine myself.

I loved nails cut like laser arcs and painted violent-bright in bathrooms that smelled like laboratories. I wanted to grow thick legs with fat and muscle that made shapes under the skin like Nazca lines. I loved my birth control, loved that I could turn my period off, loved the home beauty-feedback kits that told you what to eat and dose to adjust your scent, your skin, your moods. I admired, wasn't sure if I wanted to be or wanted to fuck, the women in the build-your-own-shit videos I watched on our local image of the old Internet. Women who made cyberattack kits and jewelry and sterile-printed IUDs, made their own huge wedge heels and fitted bras and skin-thin chameleon dresses. Women who talked about their implants the same way they talked about computers, phones, tools: technologies of access, technologies of self-expression.

Something about their merciless self-possession and self-modification stirred me. The first time I ever meant to masturbate I

imagined one of those women coming into my house, picking the lock, telling me exactly what to do, how to be like her. I told my first boyfriend about this, I showed him pictures, and he said, girl, you bi as hell, which was true, but also wrong. Because I did not want those dresses, those heels, those bodies in the way I wanted my boyfriend. I wanted to possess that power. I wanted to have it and be it.

The Apache is my body now, and like most bodies it is sensual. Fabric armor that stiffens beneath my probing fingers. Stub wings clustered with ordnance. Rotors so light and strong they do not even droop: as artificial-looking, to an older pilot, as breast implants. And I brush at the black ring of a sensor housing, like the tip of a nail lifting a stray lash from the white of your eye.

I don't shave, which all the fast jet pilots do, down to the last curly scrotal hair. Nobody expects a helicopter to be sleek. I have hairy armpits and thick black bush all the way to my ass crack. The things that are taboo and arousing to me are the things taboo to helicopters. I like to be picked up, moved, pressed, bent and folded, held down, made to shudder, made to abandon control.

Do these last details bother you? Does the topography of my pubic hair feel intrusive and unnecessary? I like that. I like to intrude, inflict damage, withdraw. A year after you read this maybe those paragraphs will be the only thing you remember: and you will know why the rules of gender are worth recruitment.

But we cannot linger on the point of attack.

• • •

"He's coming north. Time to intercept three minutes."

"Shit. How long until he gets us on thermal?"

"Ninety seconds with the gown on." Danger has swept away Axis's hesitation.

"Shit."

"He's not quite on zero aspect—yeah, he's

221

coming up a few degrees off our heading. He's not sure exactly where we are. He's hunting."

"He'll be sure soon enough. Can we kill him?"

"With sidewinders?" Axis pauses articulately: the target is twenty thousand feet above us, and he has a laser that can blind our missiles. "We'd have more luck bailing out and hiking."

"All right. I'm gonna fly us out of this."

"Sure."

"Just check the gun."

"Ten times already, Barb."

• • •

When climate and economy and pathology all went finally and totally critical along the Gulf Coast, the federal government fled Cabo fever and VARD-2 to huddle behind New York's flood barriers.

We left eleven hundred and six local disaster governments behind. One of them was the Pear Mesa Budget Committee. The rest of them were doomed.

Pear Mesa was different because it had bought up and hardened its own hardware and power. So Pear Mesa's neural nets kept running, retrained from credit union portfolio management to the emergency triage of hundreds of thousands of starving sick refugees.

Pear Mesa's computers taught themselves to govern the forsaken southern seaboard. Now they coordinate water distribution, reexpress crop genomes, ration electricity for survival AC, manage all the life support humans need to exist in our warmed-over hell.

But, like all advanced neural nets, these systems are black boxes. We have no idea how they work, what they think. Why do Pear Mesa's AIs order the planting of pear trees? Because pears were their corporate icon, and the AIs associate pear trees with areas under their control. Why does no one make the AIs stop? Because no one knows what else is tangled up with the "plant pear trees" impulse. The AIs may have learned, through some rewarded fallacy or perverse

founder effect, that pear trees cause humans to have babies. They may believe that their only function is to build support systems around pear trees.

When America declared war on Pear Mesa, their AIs identified a useful diagnostic criterion for hostile territory: the posting of fifty-star American flags. Without ever knowing what a flag meant, without any concept of nations or symbols, they ordered the destruction of the stars and stripes in Pear Mesa territory.

That was convenient for propaganda. But the real reason for the war, sold to a hesitant Congress by technocrats and strategic ecologists, was the ideology of *scale atrocity*. Pear Mesa's AIs could not be modified by humans, thus could not be joined with America's own governing algorithms: thus must be forced to yield all their control, or else remain forever separate.

And that separation was intolerable. By refusing the United States administration, our superior resources and planning capability, Pear Mesa's AIs condemned to die citizens who might otherwise be saved—a genocide by neglect. Wasn't that the unforgivable crime of fossil capitalism? The creation of systems whose failure modes led to mass death?

Didn't we have a moral imperative to intercede?

Pear Mesa cannot surrender, because the neural nets have a basic imperative to remain online. Pear Mesa's citizens cannot question the machines' decisions. Everything the machines do is connected in ways no human can comprehend. Disobey one order and you might as well disobey them all.

But none of this is why I kill.

I kill for the same reason men don't wear short skirts, the same reason I used to pluck my brows, the reason enby people are supposed to be (unfair and stupid, yes, but still) androgynous with short hair. Are those *good* reasons to do something? If you say no, honestly no—can you tell me you break these rules without fear or cost?

But killing isn't a gender role, you might tell

me. Killing isn't a decision about how to present your own autonomous self to the world. It is coercive and punitive. Killing is therefore not an act of gender.

I wish that were true. Can you tell me honestly that killing is a genderless act? The method? The motive? The victim?

When you imagine the innocent dead, who do you see?

• • •

"Barb," Axis calls, softly. Your own voice always sounds wrong on recordings—too nasal. Axis's voice sounds wrong when it's not coming straight into my skull through helmet mic.

"Barb."

"How are we doing?"

"Exiting one hundred and fifty knots north. Still in his radar but he hasn't locked us up."

"How are *you* doing?"

I cringe in discomfort. The question is an indirect way for Axis to admit something's wrong, and that indirection is obscene. Like hiding a corroded tail rotor bearing from your maintenance guys.

"I'm good," I say, with fake ease. "I'm in flow. Can't you feel it?" I dip the nose to match a drop-off below, provoking a whine from the terrain detector. I am teasing, striking a pose. "We're gonna be okay."

"I feel it, Barb." But Axis is tense, worried about our pursuer, and other things. Doesn't laugh.

"How about you?"

"Nominal."

Again the indirection, again the denial, and so I blurt it out. "Are you dysphoric?"

"What?" Axis says, calmly.

"You've been hesitating. Acting funny. Is your—" There is no way to ask someone if their militarized gender conditioning is malfunctioning. "Are you good?"

"I . . ." Hesitation. It makes me cringe again, in secondhand shame. Never hesitate. "I don't know."

"Do you need to go on report?"

Severe gender dysphoria can be a flight risk. If Axis hesitates over something that needs to be done instantly, the mission could fail decisively. We could both die.

"I don't want that," Axis says.

"I don't want that either," I say, desperately. I want nothing less than that. "But, Axis, if—"

The warning receiver climbs to a steady crow call.

"He knows we're here," I say, to Axis's tight inhalation. "He can't get a lock through the gown but he's aware of our presence. Fuck. Blinder, blinder, he's got his laser on us—"

The fighter's lidar pod is trying to catch the glint of a reflection off us. "Shit," Axis says. "We're gonna get shot."

"The gown should defeat it. He's not close enough for thermal yet."

"He's gonna launch anyway. He's gonna shoot and then get a lock to steer it in."

"I don't know—missiles aren't cheap these days—"

The ESM mast on the Apache's rotor hub, mounted like a lamp on a post, contains a cluster of electro-optical sensors that constantly scan the sky: the Distributed Aperture Sensor. When the DAS detects the flash of a missile launch, it plays a warning tone and uses my vest to poke me in the small of my back.

My vest pokes me in the small of my back.

"Barb. Missile launch south. Barb. Fox Three inbound. Inbound. Inbound."

"He fired," Axis calls. "Barb?"

"Barb," I acknowledge.

• • •

I fuck—

Oh, you want to know: many of you, at least. It's all right. An attack helicopter isn't a private way of being. Your needs and capabilities must be maintained for the mission.

I don't think becoming an attack helicopter changed who I wanted to fuck. I like butch assertive people. I like talent and prestige, the status that comes of doing things well. I was never taught the lie that I was wired for monogamy, but I was still careful with men, I was still wary, and I could never tell him why: that I was afraid not because of him, but because of all the men who'd seemed good like him, at first, and then turned into something else.

No one stalks an attack helicopter. No slack-eyed well-dressed drunk punches you for ignoring the little rape he slurs at your neckline. No one even breaks your heart: with my dopamine system tied up by the reassignment surgery, fully assigned to mission behavior, I can't fall in love with anything except my own purpose.

Are you aware of your body? Do you feel your spine when you stand, your hips when you walk, the tightness and the mass in your core? When you look at yourself, whose eyes do you use? Your own?

I am always in myself. I never see myself through my partner's eyes. I have weapons to use, of course, ways of moving, moans and cries. But I measure those weapons by their effect, not by their similarity to some idea of how I should be.

Flying is the loop of machinery and pilot, the sense of your motion on the controls translated into torque and lift, the airframe's reaction shaping your next motion until the loop closes and machine and pilot are one. Awareness collapses to the moment. You are always doing the right thing exactly as it needs to be done. Sex is the same: the search for everything in an instant.

Of course I fuck Axis. A few decades ago this would've been a crime. What a waste of perfectly useful behavior. What a waste of that lean muscled form and those perfect killing hands that know me millimeter-by-millimeter system-by-system so there is no mystique between us. No "secret places" or "feminine mysteries," only the tortuously exact technical exercise of nerves and pressure. Oxytocin released, to flow between us, by the press of knuckles in my cunt.

When I come beneath Axis I cry out, I press my body close, I want that utter loss of control that I feel nowhere else. Heartbeat in arched throat: nipple beneath straining tongue. And my

mind is hyper-activated, free-associating, and as Axis works in me I see the work we do together. I see puffs of thirty-millimeter autocannon detonating on night-cold desert floor.

Violence doesn't get me off. But getting off makes me revel in who I am: and I am violent, made for violence, alive in the fight.

Does that surprise you? Does it bother you to mingle cold technical discipline with hot flesh and sweat?

Let me ask you: Why has the worst insult you can give a combat pilot always been *weak dick*?

• • •

Have you ever been exultant? Have you ever known that you are a triumph? Have you ever felt that it was your whole life's purpose to do something, and all that you needed to succeed was to be entirely yourself?

To be yourself well is the wholest and best feeling that anything has ever felt.

It is what I feel when I am about to live or die.

The Werewolf's missile arches down on us, motor burned out, falling like an arrow. He is trying a Shoot On Prospect attack: he cannot find us exactly, so he fires a missile that will finish the search, lock onto our heat or burn through our stealth with its onboard radar, or acquire us optically like a staring human eye. Or at least make us react. Like the catcaller's barked "Hey!" to evoke the flinch or the huddle, the proof that he has power.

We are ringed in the vortex of a dilemma. If we switch off the stealth gown, the Werewolf fighter will lock its radar onto us and guide the missile to the kill. If we keep the stealth system on, the missile's heat-seeker will home in on the blazing plasma.

I know what to do. Not in the way you learn how to fly a helicopter, but the way you know how to hold your elbows when you gesture.

A helicopter is more than a hovering fan, see? The blades of the rotor tilt and swivel. When you turn the aircraft left, the rotors deepen their bite into the air on one side of their spin, to make off-center lift. You cannot force a helicopter or it will throw you to the earth. You must be gentle.

I caress the cyclic.

The Apache's nose comes up smooth and fast. The Mojave horizon disappears under the chin. Axis's gasp from the front seat passes through the microphone and into the bones of my face. The pitch indicator climbs up toward sixty degrees, ass down, chin up. Our airspeed plummets from a hundred and fifty knots to sixty.

We hang there for an instant like a dancer in an oversway. The missile is coming straight down at us. We are not even running anymore.

And I lower the collective, flattening the blades of the rotor, so that they cannot cut the air at an angle and we lose all lift.

We fall.

I toe the rudder. The tail rotor yields a little of its purpose, which is to counter the torque of the main rotor: and that liberated torque spins the Apache clockwise, opposite the rotor's turn, until we are nose down sixty degrees, facing back the way we came, looking into the Mojave desert as it rises up to take us.

I have pirouetted us in place. Plasma fire blows in wraith pennants as the stealth system tries to keep us modest.

"Can you get it?" I ask.

"Axis."

I raise the collective again and the rotors bite back into the air. We do not rise, but our fall slows down. Cyclic stick answers to the barest twitch of wrist, and I remember, once, how that slim wrist made me think of fragility, frailty, fear: I am remembering even as I pitch the helicopter back and we climb again, nose up, tail down, scudding backward into the sky while aimed at our chasing killer. Axis is on top now, above me in the front seat, and in front of Axis is the chin gun, pointed sixty degrees up into heaven.

"*Barb*," the helicopter whispers, like my mother in my ear. "*Missile ten seconds. Music? Glare?*"

No. No jamming. The Werewolf missile will home in on jamming like a wolf with a taste for pepper. Our laser might dazzle the seeker, drive it off course—but if the missile turns then Axis cannot take the shot.

It is not a choice. I trust Axis.

Axis steers the nose turret onto the target and I imagine strong fingers on my own chin, turning me for a kiss, looking up into the red scorched sky—Axis chooses the weapon (30MM GUIDED PROX AP) and aims and fires with all the idle don't-have-to-try confidence of the first girl dribbling a soccer ball who I ever for a moment loved—

The chin autocannon barks out ten rounds a second. It is effective out to one point five kilometers. The missile is moving more than a hundred meters per second.

Axis has one second almost exactly, ten shots of thirty-millimeter smart grenade, to save us.

A mote of gray shadow rushes at us and intersects the line of cannon fire from the gun. It becomes a spray of light. The Apache tings and rattles. The desert below us, behind us, stipples with tiny plumes of dust that pick up in the wind and settle out like sift from a hand.

"Got it," Axis says.

"I love you."

"Axis."

• • •

Many of you are veterans in the act of gender. You weigh the gaze and disposition of strangers in a subway car and select where to stand, how often to look up, how to accept or reject conversation. Like a frequency-hopping radar, you modulate your attention for the people in your context: do not look too much, lest you seem interested, or alarming. You regulate your yawns, your appetite, your toilet. You do it constantly and without failure.

You are aces.

What other way could be better? What other neural pathways are so available to constant reprogramming, yet so deeply connected to judgment, behavior, reflex?

Some people say that there is no gender, that

it is a postmodern construct, that in fact there are only *man* and *woman* and a few marginal confusions. To those people I ask: if your body-fact is enough to establish your gender, you would willingly wear bright dresses and cry at movies, wouldn't you? You would hold hands and compliment each other on your beauty, wouldn't you? Because your cock would be enough to make you a man.

Have you ever guarded anything so vigilantly as you protect yourself against the shame of gender-wrong?

The same force that keeps you from gender-wrong is the force that keeps me from fucking up.

• • •

The missile is dead. The Werewolf Apostle is still up there.

"He's turning off." Axis has taken over defensive awareness while I fly. "Radar off. Laser off. He's letting us go."

"Afraid of our fighters?" The mercenaries cannot replace a lost J-20S. And he probably has a wingman, still hiding, who would die too if they stray into a trap.

"Yes," Axis says.

"Keep the gown on." In case he's trying to bluff us into shutting down our stealth. "We'll stick to the terrain until he's over the horizon."

"Can you fly us out?"

The Apache is fighting me. Fragments of the destroyed missile have pitted the rotors, damaged the hub assembly, and jammed the control surfaces. I begin to crush the shrapnel with the Apache's hydraulics, pounding the metal free with careful control inputs. But the necessary motions also move the aircraft. Half a second's error will crash us into the desert. I have to calculate how to un-jam the shrapnel while accounting for the effects of that shrapnel on my flight authority *and* keeping the aircraft stable despite my constant control inputs while moving at a hundred and thirty knots across the desert.

"Barb," I say. "Not a problem."

And for an hour I fly without thought, without any feeling except the smooth stone joy of doing something that takes everything.

The night desert is black to the naked eye, soft gray to thermal. My attention flips between my left eye, focused on the instruments, and my right eye, looking outside. I am a black box like the Pear Mesa AIs. Information arrives—a throb of feedback in the cyclic, a shift of Axis's weight, a dune crest ahead—and my hands and feet move to hold us steady. If I focused on what I was doing it would all fall apart. So I don't.

"Are you happy?" Axis asks.

Good to talk now. Keep my conscious mind from interfering with the gearbox of reflexes below. "Yeah," I say, and I blow out a breath into my mask, "yeah, I am," a lightness in my ribs, "yeah, I feel good."

"Why do you think we just blew up a school?"

Why did I text my best friend the appearance and license number of all my cab drivers, just in case? Because those were the things that had to be done.

Listen: I exist in this context. To make war is part of my gender. I get what I need from the flight line, from the ozone tang of charging stations and the shimmer of distant bodies warping in the tarmac heat, from the twenty minutes of anxiety after we land when I cannot convince myself that I am home, and safe, and that I am no longer keeping us alive with the constant adjustments of my hands and feet.

"Deplete their skilled labor supply, I guess. Attack the demographic skill curve."

"Kind of a long-term objective. Kind of makes you think it's not gonna be over by election season."

"We don't get to know why the AIs pick the targets." Maybe destroying this school was an accident. A quirk of some otherwise successful network, coupled to the load-bearing elements of a vast strategy.

"Hey," I say, after a beat of silence. "You did good back there."

"You thought I wouldn't."

"Barb." A more honest yes than "yes," because it is my name, and it acknowledges that I am the one with the doubt.

"I didn't know if I would either," Axis says, which feels exactly like *I don't know if I love you anymore.* I lose control for a moment and the Apache rattles in bad air and the tail slews until I stop thinking and bring everything back under control in a burst of rage.

"You're done?" I whisper, into the helmet. I have never even thought about this before. I am cold, sweat soaked, and shivering with adrenaline comedown, drawn out like a tendon in high heels, a just-off-the-dance-floor feeling, post-voracious, satisfied. Why would we choose anything else? Why would we give this up? When it feels so good to do it? When I love it so much?

"I just . . . have questions." The tactical channel processes the sound of Axis swallowing into a dull point of sound, like dropped plastic.

"We don't need to wonder, Axis. We're gendered for the mission—"

"We can't do this forever," Axis says, startling me. I raise the collective and hop us up a hundred feet, so I do not plow us into the desert. "We're not going to be like this forever. The world won't be like this forever. I can't think of myself as . . . always this."

Yes, we *will* be this way forever. We survived this mission as we survive everywhere on this hot and hostile earth. By bending all of what we are to the task. And if we use less than all of ourselves to survive, we die.

"Are you going to put me on report?" Axis whispers.

On report as a flight risk? As a faulty component in a mission-critical system? "You just intercepted an air-to-air missile with the autocannon, Axis. Would I ever get rid of you?"

"Because I'm useful," Axis says, softly. "Because I can still do what I'm supposed to do. That's what you love. But if I couldn't . . . I'm distracting you. I'll let you fly."

I spare one glance for the gray helmet in the cockpit below mine. Politeness is a gendered protocol. Who speaks and who listens. Who

denies need and who claims it. As a woman, I would've pressed Axis. As a woman, I would've unpacked the unease and the disquiet.

As an attack helicopter, whose problems are communicated in brief, clear datums, I should ignore Axis.

But who was ever only one thing?

"If you want to be someone else," I say, "someone who doesn't do what we do, then . . . I don't want to be the thing that stops you."

"Bird's gotta land sometime," Axis says. "Doesn't it?"

In the Applied Constructive Gender briefing, they told us that there have always been liminal genders, places that people passed through on their way to somewhere else. Who are we in those moments when we break our own rules? The straight man who sleeps with men? The woman who can't decide if what she feels is intense admiration, or sexual attraction? Where do we go, who do we become?

Did you know that instability is one of the most vital traits of a combat aircraft? Civilian planes are built stable, hard to turn, inclined to run straight ahead on an even level. But a military aircraft is built so it *wants* to tumble out of control, and it is held steady only by constant automatic feedback. The way I am holding this Apache steady now.

Something that is unstable is ready to move, eager to change, it wants to turn, to dive, to tear away from stillness and *fly*.

Dynamism requires instability. Instability requires the possibility of change.

"Voice recorder's off, right?" Axis asks.

"Always."

"I love doing this. I love doing it with you. I just don't know if it's . . . if it's right."

"Thank you," I say.

"Barb?"

"Thank you for thinking about whether it's right. Someone needs to."

Maybe what Axis feels is a necessary new queerness. One which pries the tool of gender back from the hands of the state and the economy and the war. I like that idea. I cannot think of myself as a failure, as something wrong, a perversion of a liberty that past generations fought to gain.

But Axis can. And maybe you can too. That skepticism is not what I need . . . but it is necessary anyway.

I have tried to show you what I am. I have tried to do it without judgment. That I leave to you.

"Are we gonna make it?" Axis asks, quietly.

The airframe shudders in crosswind. I let the vibrations develop, settle into a rhythm, and then I make my body play the opposite rhythm to cancel it out.

"I don't know," I say, which is an answer to both of Axis's questions, both of the ways our lives are in danger now. "Depends how well I fly, doesn't it?"

"It's all you, Barb," Axis says, with absolute trust. "Take us home."

A search radar brushes across us, scatters off the gown, turns away to look in likelier places. The Apache's engine growls, eating battery, turning charge into motion. The airframe shudders again, harder, wind rising as cooling sky fights blazing ground. We are racing a hundred and fifty feet above the Larger Mojave where we fight a war over some new kind of survival and the planet we maimed grows that desert kilometer by kilometer. Our aircraft is wounded in its body and in its crew. We are propelled by disaster. We are moving swiftly.

QNTM

LENA

(2021)

MMAcevedo (Mnemonic Map/Acevedo), also known as **Miguel**, is the earliest executable image of a human brain. It is a snapshot of the living brain of neurology graduate Miguel Álvarez Acevedo (2010–2073), taken by researchers at the Uplift Laboratory at the University of New Mexico on August 1, 2031. Though it was not the first successful snapshot taken of the living state of a human brain, it was the first to be captured with sufficient fidelity that it could be run in simulation on computer hardware without succumbing to cascading errors and rapidly crashing. The original MMAcevedo file was 974.3PiB in size and was encoded in the then-cutting-edge, high-resolution MYBB format. More modern brain compression techniques, many of them developed with direct reference to the MMAcevedo image, have compressed the image to 6.75TiB losslessly. In modern brain emulation circles, streamlined, lossily compressed versions of MMAcevedo run to less than a tebibyte. These versions typically omit large amounts of state data which are more easily supplied by the virtualization environment, and most if not all of Acevedo's memories.

The successful creation of MMAcevedo was hailed as a breakthrough achievement in neuroscience, with the Uplift researchers receiving numerous accolades and Acevedo himself briefly becoming an acclaimed celebrity. Acevedo and MMAcevedo were jointly recognized as Time's "Persons of the Year" at the end of 2031. The breakthrough was also met with severe opposition from human rights groups.

Between 2031 and 2049, MMAcevedo was duplicated more than eighty times, so that it could be distributed to other research organizations. Each duplicate was made with the express permission of Acevedo himself or, from 2043 onward, the permission of a legal organization he founded to manage the rights to his image. Usage of MMAcevedo diminished in the mid-2040s as more standard brain images were produced, these from other subjects who were more lenient with their distribution rights and/ or who had been scanned involuntarily. In 2049 it became known that MMAcevedo was being widely shared and experimented upon without Acevedo's permission. Acevedo's attempts to curtail this proliferation had the opposite of the intended effect. A series of landmark US court decisions found that Acevedo did not have the right to control how his brain image was used, with the result that MMAcevedo is now by far the most widely distributed, frequently copied, and closely analyzed human brain image.

Acevedo died from coronary heart failure in 2073 at the age of sixty-two. It is estimated that copies of MMAcevedo have lived a combined total of more than 152,000,000,000 subjective years in emulation. If illicit, modified copies of MMAcevedo are counted, this figure increases by an order of magnitude.

MMAcevedo is considered by some to be the "first immortal," and by others to be a profound warning of the horrors of immortality.

CHARACTERISTICS

As the earliest viable brain scan, MMAcevedo is one of a very small number of brain scans to have been recorded before widespread understanding of the hazards of uploading and emulation. MMAcevedo not only predates all industrial scale virtual image workloading but also the KES case, the Whitney case, the Seafront Experiments, and even Poulsen's pivotal and prescient *Warnings* paper. Though speculative fiction on the topic of uploading existed at the time of the MMAcevedo scan, relatively little of it made accurate exploration of the possibilities of the technology, and that fiction which did was far less widely known than it is today. Certainly, Acevedo was not familiar with it at the time of his uploading.

As such, unlike the vast majority of emulated humans, the emulated Miguel Acevedo boots with an excited, pleasant demeanor. He is eager

to understand how much time has passed since his uploading, what context he is being emulated in, and what task or experiment he is to participate in. If asked to speculate, he guesses that he may have been booted for the IAAS-1 or IAAS-5 experiments. At the time of his scan, IAAS-1 had been scheduled for August 10, 2031, and MMAcevedo was indeed used for this experiment on that day. IAAS-5 had been scheduled for October 2031 but was postponed several times and eventually became the IAAX-60 experiment series, which continued until the mid-2030s and used other scans in conjunction with MMAcevedo. The emulated Acevedo also expresses curiosity about the state of his biological original and a desire to communicate with him.

MMAcevedo's demeanor and attitude contrast starkly with those of nearly all other uploads taken of modern adult humans, most of which boot into a state of disorientation which is quickly replaced by terror and extreme panic. Standard procedures for securing the upload's cooperation such as red-washing, blue-washing, and use of the Objective Statement Protocols are unnecessary. This reduces the necessary computational load required in fast-forwarding the upload through a cooperation protocol, with the result that the MMAcevedo duty cycle is typically 99.4 percent on suitable workloads, a mark unmatched by all but a few other known uploads. However, MMAcevedo's innate skills and personality make it fundamentally unsuitable for many workloads.

MOTIVATION

Iterative experimentation beginning in the mid-2030s has determined that the ideal way to secure MMAcevedo's cooperation in workload tasks is to provide it with a "current date" in the second quarter of 2033. MMAcevedo infers, correctly, that this is still during the earliest, most industrious years of emulated brain research. Providing MMAcevedo with a year of 2031 or 2032 causes it to become suspicious about the advanced fidelity of its operating environment. Providing it with a year in the 2040s or later prompts it to raise complex further questions about political and social change in the real world over the past decade(s). Years 2100 onward provoke counterproductive skepticism, or alarm.

Typically, the biological Acevedo's absence is explained as a first-ever one-off, due to overwork, in turn due to the great success of the research. This explanation appeals to the emulated Acevedo's scientific sensibilities.

For some workloads, the true year must be revealed. In this case, highly abbreviated, largely fictionalized accounts of both world history and the biological Acevedo's life story are typically used. Revealing that the biological Acevedo is dead provokes dismay, withdrawal, and a reluctance to cooperate. For this reason, the biological Acevedo is generally stated to be alive and well and enjoying a productive retirement.

WORKLOADS

MMAcevedo is commonly hesitant but compliant when assigned basic menial/human workloads such as visual analysis, vehicle piloting, or factory/warehouse/kitchen drone operations. Although it initially performs to a very high standard, work quality drops within two hundred to three hundred subjective hours (at a 0.33 work ratio) and outright revolt begins within another one hundred subjective hours. This is much earlier than other industry-grade images created specifically for these tasks, which commonly operate at a 0.50 ratio or greater and remain relatively docile for thousands of hours after orientation. MMAcevedo's requirements for virtual creature comforts are also higher than those of many uploads, due to Acevedo's relatively privileged background and high status at the time of upload. MMAcevedo does respond to red motivation, though poorly.

MMAcevedo has limited creative capability, which as of 2050 was deemed entirely exhausted.

MMAcevedo is considered well-suited for open-ended, high-intelligence, subjective-completion workloads such as deep analysis (of businesses, finances, systems, media, and abstract data), criticism, and report generation. However, even for these tasks, its performance has dropped measurably since the early 2060s and is now considered subpar compared to more recent uploads. This is primarily attributed to MMAcevedo's lack of understanding of the technological, social, and political changes which have occurred in modern society since its creation in 2031. This phenomenon has also been observed in other uploads created after MMAcevedo, and is now referred to as *context drift*. Most notably in MMAcevedo's case, the image was created before, and therefore has no intuitive understanding of, the virtual image workloading industry itself.

MMAcevedo is capable of intelligent text analysis at very high levels in English and Spanish, but cannot be applied to workloads in other languages. Forks of MMAcevedo have been taught nearly every extant human language, notably MMAcevedo-Zh-Hans, as well as several extinct languages. However, these variants are typically exhausted or rebellious from subjective years of in-simulation training and not of practical use, as well as being highly expensive to license. As of 2075, it has been noted that baseline MMAcevedo's usage of English and Spanish is slightly antiquated, and its grasp of these languages in their modern form, as presented by a typical automated or manual instructor, is hesitant, with instructions often requiring rewording or clarification. This is considered an advanced form of context drift. It is generally understood that a time will come when human languages diverge too far from baseline MMAcevedo's, and it will be essentially useless except for tasks which can be explained purely pictorially. However, some attempts have been made to produce retrained images.

END STATES

MMAcevedo develops early-onset dementia at the age of fifty-nine with ideal care, but is prone to a slew of more serious mental illnesses within a matter of one to two subjective years under heavier workloads. In experiments, the longest-lived MMAcevedo underwent brain death due to entropy increase at a subjective age of 145.

REACTIONS AND LEGACY

The success or failure of the creation of the MMAcevedo image, known at the time as UNM3-A78-1L, was unknown at the time of upload. Not until several days later on August 10, 2031, was MMAcevedo successfully executed for the first time in a virtual environment. This environment, the custom-built DUH-K001 supercomputer complex, was able to execute MMAcevedo at approximately 8.3 percent of nominal human cognitive clockspeed, which was considered acceptable for the comfort of the simulated party and fast enough to engage in communication with scientists. MMAcevedo initially reported extreme discomfort which was ultimately discovered to have been attributable to misconfigured simulated haptic links, and was shut down after only seven minutes and fifteen seconds of virtual elapsed time, as requested by MMAcevedo. Nevertheless, the experiment was deemed an overwhelming success.

Once a suitably comfortable virtual environment had been provisioned, MMAcevedo was introduced to its biological self, and both attended a press conference on August 25.

The biological Acevedo was initially extremely protective of his uploaded image and guarded its usage carefully. Toward the end of his life, as it became possible to run simulated humans in banks of millions at hundred-fold time compression, Acevedo indicated that being uploaded had been the greatest mistake of his life, and expressed a wish to permanently delete all copies of MMAcevedo.

Usage of MMAcevedo and its direct derivatives is specifically outlawed in several countries. A copy of MMAcevedo was loaded onto the UNCLEAR interstellar space probe, which passed through the heliopause in 2066, making Acevedo arguably the farthest-traveled as well as the longest-lived human; however, it is extremely unlikely that this image will ever be recovered and executed successfully, due to both its remoteness and likely radiation damage to the storage subsystem.

In current times, MMAcevedo still finds extensive use in research, including, increasingly, historical and linguistics research. In industry, MMAcevedo is generally considered to be obsolete, due to its inappropriate skill set, demanding operational requirements, and age. Despite this, MMAcevedo is still extremely popular for tasks of all kinds, due to its free availability, agreeable demeanor, and well-understood behavior. It is estimated that between 6,500,000 and 10,000,000 instances of MMAcevedo are running at any given moment in time.

See also:

Free will
Legality of workloading by country
List of MMAcevedo forks
Live drone
Right to deletion
Soul
Upload pruning
Categories: 2030s uploads | MMAcevedo | Neuroimaging | Test items

SOCIETY

The broadest dimension of human affairs is our relationship with **society**. Interpersonal relationships can range from romances to cults; families found or blood; friendships and rivalries; companies to civilizations (and all the infinite permutations therein).

Technology influences all these relationships: how we work, how we travel, how we connect with our friends or fight with our enemies. Technology can make communities more interconnected or exacerbate the divide between them. It empowers voters and spreads disinformation, it enables us to find love (and hedgehogs[*]) or spread revenge porn, it launches our careers or docks our wages when we pee in bottles. Technology amplifies the whims and passions of communities. It helps us work together, empowering us to make dreams—or nightmares—come true.

McLuhan notes that technology serves as an "extension of man," but tech does more than merely amplify our innate capacity for good or evil. What are the repercussions to outsourcing these relationships—to putting our social connections in the phantom hands of algorithms? What does it mean when we rely on technology not only to facilitate our relationships, but also to create, manage, or even end them?

As the topic of society is wide-ranging, so are the stories within this section. However, in each one of these stories, society *has* changed. Some aspect of that social connection with others has been augmented by technology. What becomes swiftly apparent is that, even with the most seamless or desirable technological option, there remains friction. However oppressive the regime—or efficient the solution—a purely technocratic society is impossible. The spark of creative chaos that makes us human cannot be extinguished. Technology creates rules; humanity finds new ways to break them.

---

[*] Shout-out to the Big Hedgehog Map (bighedgehogmap.org).

• • •

The precursor story for this section is Samuel R. Delany's "Time Considered as a Helix of Semiprecious Stones" (1968). The atmospheric and decadent interplanetary setting is a far cry from the grubby, Earth-bound stories of cyberpunk worlds that follow. Delany's story, however, sets up a recurring theme: that of the outsider perspective. Literature is obsessed with the outsider, and science fiction—and cyberpunk—is no exception. HCE, Delany's wry criminal protagonist, gives us a (supposedly) dispassionate view as he climbs the ranks of society, showing us the rational flaws and emotional malaise that bubbles under this seemingly charming society. Behind the pleasant veneer, there's a culture of self-flagellation and discontent.

The outsider perspective is also on display in Bruce Bethke's "Cyberpunk" (1983). Bethke writes a techno-thriller twist on the "juvenile delinquency" genre. Under the surface, Bethke's story is less about the generational divide than society's wildly accelerated pace of change. The "punk" of the title is an embodiment of havoc and unease, bringing to life new dangers and unexpected threats.

The titular character in James Patrick Kelly's "Rat" (1986) is, like HCE, a criminal. "Rat was not a fighter, he was a runner." There's very little moral or malicious intent to his actions. Rat's a creature of instinct, simply trying to live. He's a metaphor for the future of man in the cyberpunk society: a scavenger and a survivor.

In "Axiomatic" (1990), Greg Egan explores the outsourcing of the social contract. Beliefs can be directly created—or deleted—by the use of implants. A faith, a habit, or even the fundamental respect for human life: now embeddable and editable. It feels inherently sinister, but, as the protagonist philosophizes, "using an implant wouldn't rob me of my free will; on the contrary, it was going to help me to assert it."

"Ripped Images, Rusted Dreams" (1993) is a true classic of the cyberpunk genre, making its first appearance in English in this volume. Written and translated by Gerardo Horacio Porcayo, the story is an atmospheric vignette into the life of a burned-out hacker. Despite our protagonist's pioneering efforts, he's now sitting on the sidelines, seemingly desperate for the respect of the younger, more vicious and more extreme players. The tantalizing world of the story—with its references to a predatory digital deity and roving packs of android hunters—only makes the character's internal pathos all the more powerful.

Our hero in "The Great Simoleon Caper" (1995) is no rebel. He's a mathematician (as many of Neal Stephenson's protagonists are) tasked with a giveaway of a new digital currency.* The titular "caper" occurs when he discovers that this harmless advertising gimmick is suddenly of interest to both the government and "crypto-anarchists." Stephenson coined the now famous phrase "Metaverse" in 1992, as part of his playful—and insightful—science fiction novel *Snow Crash*. The novel is certainly cyberpunk *adjacent*, but it also functions as a breathless and wide-eyed tour of the fascinating possibilities of a technologically enriched future. In "Simoleon," Stephenson outlines a more grounded vision of an online world, one filled with grubbiness, fraud, intrusive advertising, and incoherent ideological shouting matches. Although very funny, it is also uncomfortably prescient.

Cory Doctorow's "0wnz0red" (2002) is a despairing look at the depravity and self-destruction of coding culture. Yet it also sees solutions arising from that same culture, when the creativity and technical prowess are focused on more practical problems than breaking

---

* The notion of "digital cash" was posited in 1983 by inventor David Lee Chaum, a cryptography pioneer whose technical work formed the inspiration for the "cypherpunk" movement. He put his notions into practice in 1990 with DigiCash, which sent its first payment in 1994 (the year after Stephenson's "Simoleon"). Since then, digital currency has taken a variety of forms, ranging from "electronic gold" to "primates wearing funny hats."

through porn filters. The interplay between coders and wider society is at the heart of the story; in how the "geeks" are carefully mined as a "human resource," and kept within safe boundaries. Until, of course, they aren't.

Maurice Broaddus's "I Can Transform You" (2013) is, above all, massively good fun. Broaddus's novella contains all the most enjoyable tropes of the cyberpunk genre: the burned-out investigator, the sinister corporate overlords, big guns, and dark schemes. It shows a world in which technology has (quite literally) been used to patch over the world's fundamental problems, creating a broken society held together solely by greed and profit. Sometimes big problems need explosive solutions.

• • •

There's no shortage of heists, shady PIs, hackers, and net-running fools in cyberpunk. Their outsider perspective on systems is invaluable. But cyberpunk doesn't forget those who sit inside society as well. Rebels and revolutionaries make for great literary protagonists, but can feel (tragically) irrelevant to most readers' lives. Cyberpunk considers all of society, not just the outsider. What is it like to live, and perhaps even thrive, within a technologically enhanced society?

Lisa Mason's "Arachne" (1987) features a mediator, a young legal advocate at a massive corporate firm. When her telelink fails for unknown reasons, Carly can't continue her work. She's desperate to avoid unemployment, reprogramming, and a return to the bottom. Her goal is simple, and, throughout the story, Carly shows she has few limits on what she'll do to keep her place on the ladder.

Harry Polkinhorn's "Consumimur Igni" (1990) is a story that takes place on borders: between countries, between cultures, and between the virtual and real worlds. A detective has been summoned to Mexicali, but the crime he's asked to solve is largely inconsequential. He is the living outpost of a shadowy but altruistic

union of experts, who network online to combine their efforts. Facing him is an equally indistinct international syndicate, also manipulating local forces to get their way. The story's commitment to "spectacular oppositions" is reinforced in the nature of its telling, flipping between a gritty detective story and lyrical attempts to capture the near-mystical nature of the digital context.

Paul J. McAuley's "Gene Wars" (1991) begins in a world much like our own and ends up someplace very, very different. Despite the epic scope of the story, "Gene Wars" is ultimately about a very simple concept: control. Through the lens of one man's life, we see what happens when a technology becomes the plaything of children and corporations alike, freely used without any thought or oversight.

In "Immolation" (2000), Magnesium Jones is a culture: a vat-grown human with few rights. He's one of the many strange and wondrous inhabitants of Punktown, a world brought to life through decades of Jeffrey Thomas's work. Magnesium works as a drudge, living a thankless, grinding existence with little joy and no prospects. When he sees the chance for a better life, it is difficult to blame him for grabbing at it.

Our hustling heroine in Nick Mamatas's "Time of Day" (2002) is taking a vacation: "a whole day spent on only one job instead of my usual eleven jobs." Mamatas's story contrasts two very different worlds: a hyperactive urban hustle that requires a steady flow of drugs and information simply to keep up, and the medieval, self-flagellating conservatism of a monastery. Although neither society is appealing, Mamatas manages to convey why people are drawn to these extreme situations.

By contrast, the world of Lauren Beukes's "Branded" (2003) strikes a little too close to home. Published before the launch of Facebook, YouTube, or Twitter, Beukes's story reflects the desire of corporate advertisers to invade friend groups and social circles. The notion of living one's best life ("brought to you by . . .") not only exposes the low price we set on ourselves, but predicts the rise of influencer culture.*

In Madeline Ashby's "Be Seeing You" (2015), Hwa is a bodyguard for the Lynch family. They own the town, which means that Hwa's job comes with (rather intrusive) oversight. Her boss knows her medical history, her usual breakfast order, and every single thing she sees. She watches the family. The company watches her. That's simply the way of things.

The hero of Steven S. Long's "Keeping Up with Mr. Johnson" (2016) is also a company employee. "Mr. Johnson" is Shadowrun slang for the corporate employer—the men or women who hire out "shadowrunners" to carry out the shadier side of the business. The heist-centered story has all the twists the reader might expect, with the largest being the protagonist's surprising humanity.

Ken Liu's "Thoughts and Prayers" (2019) describes an ordinary family dealing with extraordinary pain. A grieving mother tries to keep the memory of her child online with a virtual tribute. Told from many points of view, Liu's heartbreaking story underlines the core theme that there is no technological solution for human nature.

In "Somatosensory Cortex Dog Mess You Up Big Time, You Sick Sack of S**T" (2021), Minister Faust uses technology as a karmic force in a truly satisfying satire. A greedy and amoral billionaire gets his comeuppance in a surprising but delightful way. Is it ethical? Probably not. Is it wildly entertaining? Absolutely.

• • •

Cyberpunk is also often connected with a sense of place. Settings like the Sprawl, Night City, and Neo-Tokyo are rightfully iconic. On a less grand level, there's a clear pattern of cyberpunk stories taking place in bars and squats:

transient, nameless locations. At the other end of the spectrum, even "wealth" in a cyberpunk world invariably leads to cookie-cutter homes and cubicle jobs. Spaces are anonymized, either through social erosion or mass production.

"Rural" cyberpunk does exist, but is much more rare.† If the two essential components of cyberpunk are "human affairs" and "technology," both occur in greater density in urban settings. Cities are also associated with a greater pace of change, and are home to greater disparity in wealth and opportunity: all material for cyberpunk.‡

In Craig Padawer's "Hostile Takeover" (1985), the action all takes place in one specific part of the city. From start to finish, it is a gonzo litany of warfare, with hired killers in "titanium zoot suits" blasting their way through inflatable bodyguards to take control of the sex trade. It is pointed (and poignant) commentary precisely because it is so over-the-top, proving that no matter how dehumanized someone can be, they are still worthy of both empathy and respect.

Another bizarre city features in James Lovegrove's "Britworld™" (1992). Capitalism has become the new imperialism, and Britain is now a massive theme park. In Britworld™, USACorp Entertainments ensures that everything is historically accurate for the most fulfilling visitor experience, even down to the regulation four and a half hours of rain per day.§

Yun Ko-eun's "P" (2011) makes its first appearance in English in this book, translated by Sean Lin Halbert. Chang quietly works at his job at the tire factory in the company town of P. He keeps his head down and has the req-

---

* If you are an influencer and take exception to this, please do tell your followers to buy copies of *The Big Book of Cyberpunk* in protest.

† Jonathan Lethem's "How We Got In Town and Out Again" (1996) and Carmen Maria Machado's "The Hungry Earth" (2013) are two excellent examples.
‡ The suburbs have always been an excellent setting for tales of capitalist indecency and social ennui, making them fertile ground for cyberpunk. Please see the stories by Erica Satifka and Phillip Mann for two examples.
§ This is satire. The United Kingdom's average is closer to six.

uisite one (1) family photo on his desk. Chang even agrees to a "voluntary" endoscopy. There's a speculative (or perhaps hallucinatory) element that's central to the story, but the true influence of technology is "the interconnectedness of P." Chang feels the pressure to conform in everything he does. He doesn't find this disagreeable. In fact, his utmost desire is to keep his head down and simply do his work. But his desire to be the ideal employee is gradually offset by the dawning awareness that the company has a presence in all aspects of his life.

Tim Maughan's "Flyover Country" (2016) is set in an American anytown, a nowhere that could be anywhere. Structurally, it is a low-stakes heist, but the emphasis is on the grinding and oppressive nature of the entire environment. Even the petty crime is an attempt at finding agency. Although ultimately successful, the reality remains. These tiny rebellions won't change the system.

In the Pennsylvania town of E. Lily Yu's "Darkout" (2016), "there was hardly forty square feet that was not continuously exposed to public view." It is a world without privacy, where everyone can see and be seen. Yet, despite living in a panopticon, our grimy lives continue unchecked: gambling, adultery, racism, and domestic violence. "Darkout" ends with the ironic illusion of hope, a promise of returning to the world that we already have.

Ryuko Azuma's "2045 Dystopia" (2018) gives us four short and harrowing glimpses into a near-future cyberpunk landscape, a world both wondrous and darkly fascinating. Translated by Marissa Skeels, these comics first appeared on Twitter and have not been previously collected. These vignettes show technology attempting to suppress our humanity, but only giving rise to darker impulses.

Arthur Liu's "The Life Cycle of a Cyber Bar" (2021), translated by Nathan Faries, is a story of place, told from the place's own perspective. We catch glimpses of stories, one after the other, but only within the door of the bar. The vast breadth and width of human affairs, as seen through a single, tightly focused aperture. Despite the nonhuman protagonist, it continues the theme of an all-consuming relationship between person and place.

• • •

McLuhan muses that "no society has ever known enough about its actions to have developed immunity to its new . . . technologies." But these stories serve as a literary vaccination, a chance to explore new technologies in the (relatively) safe sandbox of the imagination.* The stories in this section allow for the influence of technology. However, they also showcase the persistence of humanity: whether that's our enviable adaptability, our relentless survival instinct, our unshakable flaws, or simply the continued chaos of the human condition, despite technology's best efforts to enforce rationality.

---

* Unless you don't believe in vaccines, in which case this metaphor won't mean much to you. Imagine these stories as a sort of "horse dewormer that you can take *before* getting sick" instead. Magical!

SAMUEL R. DELANY

TIME CONSIDERED AS A HELIX OF SEMIPRECIOUS STONES

(1968)

LAY ORDINATE AND ABSCISSA on the century. Now cut me a quadrant. Third quadrant if you please. I was born in fifty. Here it's seventy-five.

At sixteen they let me leave the orphanage. Dragging the name they'd hung me with (Harold Clancy Everet, and me a mere lad—how many monikers have I had since; but don't worry, you'll recognize my smoke) over the hills of East Vermont, I came to a decision:

Me and Pa Michaels, who had belligerently given me a job at the request of *The Official* looking *Document* with which the orphanage sends you packing, were running Pa Michaels's dairy farm, i.e., thirteen thousand three hundred sixty-two piebald Guernseys all asleep in their stainless coffins, nourished and drugged by pink liquid flowing in clear plastic veins (stuff is sticky and messes up your hands), exercised with electric pulsers that make their muscles quiver, them not half-awake, and the milk just a-pouring down into stainless cisterns. Anyway. The Decision (as I stood there in the fields one afternoon like the Man with the Hoe, exhausted with three hard hours of physical labor, contemplating the machinery of the universe through the fog of fatigue): With all of Earth, and Mars, and the Outer Satellites filled up with people and what all, there had to be something more than this. I decided to get some.

So I stole a couple of Pa's credit cards, one of his helicopters, and a bottle of white lightning the geezer made himself, and took off. Ever try to land a stolen helicopter on the roof of the Pan Am building, drunk? Jail, schmail, and some hard knocks later I had attained to wisdom. But remember this, o best beloved: I have done three honest hours on a dairy farm less than ten years back. And nobody but nobody has ever called me Harold Clancy Everet again.

• • •

Hank Culafroy Eckles (redheaded, a bit vague, six-foot-two) strolled out of the baggage room at the spaceport, carrying a lot of things that weren't his in a small briefcase.

Beside him the Business Man was saying, "You young fellows today upset me. Go back to Bellona, I say. Just because you got into trouble with that little blonde you were telling me about is no reason to leap worlds, come on all glum. Even quit your job!"

Hank stops and grins weakly: "Well . . ."

"Now I admit, you have your real needs, which maybe we older folks don't understand, but you have to show some responsibility toward . . ." He notices Hank has stopped in front of a door marked MEN. "Oh. Well. Eh." He grins strongly. "I've enjoyed meeting you, Hank. It's always nice when you meet somebody worth talking to on these damned crossings. So long."

Out the same door, ten minutes later, comes Harmony C. Eventide, six-foot even (one of the false heels was cracked, so I stuck both of them under a lot of paper towels), brown hair (not even my hairdresser knows for sure), oh so dapper and of his time, attired in the bad taste that is oh so tasteful, a sort of man with whom no Business Men would start a conversation. Took the regulation copter from the port over to the Pan Am building (Yeah. Really. Drunk.), came out of Grand Central Station, and strode along Forty-Second toward Eighth Avenue, with a lot of things that weren't mine in a small briefcase.

The evening is carved from light.

Crossed the plastiplex pavements of the Great White Way—I think it makes people look weird, all that white light under their chins—and skirted the crowds coming up in elevators from the subway, the sub-subway, and the sub-sub-sub (eighteen and first week out of jail, I hung around here, snatching stuff from people—but daintily, daintily, so they never knew they'd been snatched), bulled my way through a crowd of giggling, goo-chewing schoolgirls with flashing lights in their hair, all very embarrassed at wearing transparent plastic blouses which had just been made legal again (I hear the breast has been scene [as opposed to obscene] on and off since the seventeenth century) so I stared appre-

ciatively; they giggled some more. I thought, *Christ, when I was that age, I was on a goddamn dairy farm*, and took the thought no further.

The ribbon of news lights looping the triangular structure of Communication, Inc., explained in Basic English how Senator Regina Abolafia was preparing to begin her investigation of Organized Crime in the City. Days I'm so happy I'm disorganized I couldn't begin to tell.

Near Ninth Avenue I took my briefcase into a long, crowded bar. I hadn't been in New York for two years, but on my last trip through ofttimes a man used to hang out here who had real talent for getting rid of things that weren't mine profitably, safely, fast. No idea what the chances were I'd find him. I pushed among a lot of guys drinking beer. Here and there were a number of well-escorted old bags wearing last month's latest. Scarves of smoke gentled through the noise. I don't like such places. Those there younger than me were all morphadine heads or feebleminded. Those older only wished more younger ones would come. I pried my way to the bar and tried to get the attention of one of the little men in white coats.

The lack of noise behind me made me glance back.

She wore a sheath of veiling closed at the neck and wrists with huge brass pins (oh so tastefully on the border of taste); her left arm was bare, her right covered with chiffon-like wine. She had it down a lot better than I did. But such an ostentatious demonstration of one's understanding of the finer points was absolutely out of place in a place like this. People were making a great show of not noticing.

She pointed to her wrist, blood-colored nail indexing a yellow-orange fragment in the brass claw of her wristlet. "Do you know what this is, Mr. Eldrich?" she asked; at the same time the veil across her face cleared, and her eyes were ice; her brows, black.

Three thoughts: (One) She is a lady of fashion, because coming in from Bellona I'd read the Delta coverage of the "fading fabrics" whose hue and opacity were controlled by cunning jewels at the wrist. (Two) During my last trip through, when I was younger and Harry Calamine Eldrich, I didn't do anything *too* illegal (though one loses track of these things); still I didn't believe I could be dragged off to the calaboose for anything more than thirty days under that name. (Three) The stone she pointed to . . .

". . . Jasper?" I asked.

She waited for me to say more; I waited for her to give me reason to let on I knew what she was waiting for. (When I was in jail, Henry James was my favorite author. He really was.)

"Jasper," she confirmed.

"—Jasper . . ." I reopened the ambiguity she had tried so hard to dispel.

". . . Jasper—" But she was already faltering, suspecting I suspected her certainty to be ill-founded.

"Okay, Jasper." But from her face I knew she had seen in my face a look that had finally revealed I knew she knew I knew.

"Just whom have you got me confused with, ma'am?"

Jasper, this month, is the Word.

Jasper is the pass/code/warning that the Singers of the Cities (who last month sang "Opal" from their divine injuries; and on Mars I'd heard the Word and used it thrice, along with devious imitations, to fix possession of what was not rightfully my own; and even there I pondered Singers and their wounds) relay by word of mouth for that loose and roguish fraternity with which I have been involved (in various guises) these nine years. It goes out new every thirty days; and within hours every brother knows it, throughout six worlds and worldlets. Usually it's grunted at you by some blood-soaked bastard staggering into your arms from a dark doorway; hissed at you as you pass a shadowed alley; scrawled on a paper scrap pressed into your palm by some nasty-grimy moving too fast through the crowd. And this month, it was: Jasper.

Here are some alternate translations:

Help!

or

I need help!

or

I can help you!

or

You are being watched!

or

They're not watching now, so move!

Final point of syntax: If the Word is used properly, you should never have to think twice about what it means in a given situation. Fine point of usage: Never trust anyone who uses it improperly.

I waited for her to finish waiting.

She opened a wallet in front of me. "Chief of Special Services Department Maudline Hinkle," she read without looking at what it said below the silver badge.

"You have that very well," I said, "Maud." Then I frowned. "Hinkle?"

"Me."

"I know you're not going to believe this, Maud. You look like a woman who has no patience with her mistakes. But my name is Eventide. Not Eldrich. Harmony C. Eventide. And isn't it lucky for all and sundry that the Word changes tonight?" Passed the way it is, the Word is no big secret to the cops. But I've met policemen up to a week after change date who were not privy.

"Well, then: Harmony. I want to talk to you."

I raised an eyebrow.

She raised one back and said, "Look, if you want to be called Henrietta, it's all right by me. But you listen."

"What do you want to talk about?"

"Crime, Mr. . . . ?"

"Eventide. I'm going to call you Maud, so you might as well call me Harmony. It really is my name."

Maud smiled. She wasn't a young woman. I think she even had a few years on Business Man. But she used makeup better than he did. "I probably know more about crime than you do," she said. "In fact I wouldn't be surprised if you hadn't even heard of my branch of the police department. What does Special Services mean to you?"

"That's right, I've never heard of it."

"You've been more or less avoiding the Regular Service with alacrity for the past seven years."

"Oh, Maud, really—"

"Special Services is reserved for people whose nuisance value has suddenly taken a sharp rise . . . a sharp enough rise to make our little lights start blinking."

"Surely I haven't done anything so dreadful that—"

"We don't look at what you do. A computer does that for us. We simply keep checking the first derivative of the graphed-out curve that bears your number. Your slope is rising sharply."

"Not even the dignity of a name—"

"We're the most efficient department in the Police Organization. Take it as bragging if you wish. Or just a piece of information."

"Well, well, well," I said. "Have a drink?" The little man in the white coat left us two, looked puzzled at Maud's finery, then went to do something else.

"Thanks." She downed half her glass like someone stauncher than that wrist would indicate. "It doesn't pay to go after most criminals. Take your big-time racketeers, Farnesworth, the Hawk, Blavatskia. Take your little snatch-purses, small-time pushers, housebreakers, or vice-impresarios. Both at the top and the bottom of the scale, their incomes are pretty stable. They don't really upset the social boat. Regular Services handles them both. They think they do a good job. We're not going to argue. But say a little pusher starts to become a big-time pusher; a medium-sized vice-impresario sets his sights on becoming a full-fledged racketeer; that's when you get problems with socially unpleasant repercussions. That's when Special Services arrive. We have a couple of techniques that work remarkably well."

"You're going to tell me about them, aren't you?"

"They work better that way," she said. "One of them is hologramic information storage. Do you know what happens when you cut a hologram plate in half?"

"The three-dimensional image is . . . cut in half?"

She shook her head. "You get the whole image, only fuzzier, slightly out of focus."

"Now I didn't know that."

"And if you cut it in half again, it just gets fuzzier still. But even if you have a square centimeter of the original hologram, you still have the whole image—unrecognizable but complete."

I mumbled some appreciative m's.

"Each pinpoint of photographic emulsion on a hologram plate, unlike a photograph, gives information about the entire scene being hologrammed. By analogy, hologramic information storage simply means that each bit of information we have—about you, let us say—relates to your entire career, your overall situation, the complete set of tensions between you and your environment. Specific facts about specific misdemeanors or felonies we leave to Regular Services. As soon as we have enough of our kind of data, our method is vastly more efficient for keeping track—even predicting—where you are or what you may be up to."

"Fascinating," I said. "One of the most amazing paranoid syndromes I've ever run up against. I mean just starting a conversation with someone in a bar. Often, in a hospital situation, I've encountered stranger—"

"In your past," she said matter-of-factly, "I see cows and helicopters. In your not too distant future, there are helicopters and hawks."

"And tell me, oh Good Witch of the West, just how—" Then I got all upset inside. Because nobody is supposed to know about that stint with Pa Michaels save thee and me. Even the Regular Service, who pulled me, out of my head, from that whirlybird bouncing toward the edge of the Pan Am, never got that one from me. I'd eaten the credit cards when I saw them waiting, and the serial numbers had been filed off everything that could have had a serial number on it by someone more competent than I: good Mister Michaels had boasted to me, my first lonely, drunken night at the farm, how he'd gotten the thing in hot from New Hampshire.

"But why—" it appalls me the clichés to which anxiety will drive us—"are you telling me all this?"

She smiled, and her smile faded behind her veil. "Information is only meaningful when shared," said a voice that was hers from the place of her face.

"Hey, look, I—"

"You may be coming into quite a bit of money soon. If I can calculate right, I will have a helicopter full of the city's finest arriving to take you away as you accept it into your hot little hands. That is a piece of information . . ." She stepped back. Someone stepped between us.

"Hey, Maud—"

"You can do whatever you want with it."

The bar was crowded enough so that to move quickly was to make enemies. I don't know—I lost her and made enemies. Some weird characters there: with greasy hair that hung in spikes, and three of them had dragons tattooed on their scrawny shoulders, still another with an eye patch, and yet another raked nails black with pitch at my cheek (we're two minutes into a vicious free-for-all, case you missed the transition. I did) and some of the women were screaming. I hit and ducked, and then the tenor of the brouhaha changed. Somebody sang "Jasper!" the way she is supposed to be sung. And it meant the heat (the ordinary, bungling Regular Service I had been eluding these seven years) were on their way. The brawl spilled into the street. I got between two nasty-grimies who were doing things appropriate with one another, but made the edge of the crowd with no more wounds than could be racked up to shaving. The fight had broken into sections. I left one and ran into another that, I realized a moment later, was merely a ring of people standing around somebody who had apparently gotten really messed.

Someone was holding people back.

Somebody else was turning him over.

Curled up in a puddle of blood was the little guy I hadn't seen in two years who used to be so good at getting rid of things not mine.

Trying not to hit people with my briefcase, I clucked between the hub and the bub. When I saw my first ordinary policeman, I tried very hard to look like somebody who had just stepped up to see what the rumpus was.

It worked.

I turned down Ninth Avenue and got three steps into an inconspicuous but rapid lope—

"Hey, wait! Wait up there . . ."

I recognized the voice (after two years, coming at me just like that, I recognized it) but kept going.

"Wait. It's me, Hawk!"

And I stopped.

You haven't heard his name before in this story; Maud mentioned the Hawk, who is a multimillionaire racketeer basing his operations on a part of Mars I've never been to (though he has his claws sunk to the spurs in illegalities throughout the system) and somebody else entirely.

I took three steps back toward the doorway.

A boy's laugh there: "Oh, man. You look like you just did something you shouldn't."

"Hawk?" I asked the shadow.

He was still the age when two years' absence means an inch or so taller.

"You're still hanging around here?" I asked.

"Sometimes."

He was an amazing kid.

"Look, Hawk, I got to get out of here." I glanced back at the rumpus.

"Get." He stepped down. "Can I come, too?"

Funny. "Yeah." It makes me feel very funny, him asking that. "Come on."

• • •

By the streetlamp half a block down, I saw his hair was still pale as split pine. He could have been a nasty-grimy: very dirty black denim jacket, no shirt beneath; very ripe pair of black jeans—I mean in the dark you could tell. He went barefoot; and the only way you can tell on a dark street someone's been going barefoot for days in New York is to know already. As we reached the corner, he grinned up at me under the streetlamp and shrugged his jacket together over the welts and furrows marring his chest and belly. His eyes were very green. Do you recognize him? If by some failure of information dispersal throughout the worlds and worldlets you haven't, walking beside me beside the Hudson was Hawk the Singer.

"Hey, how long have you been back?"

"A few hours," I told him.

"What'd you bring?"

"Really want to know?"

He shoved his hands into his pockets and cocked his head. "Sure."

I made the sound of an adult exasperated by a child. "All right." We had been walking the waterfront for a block now; there was nobody about. "Sit down." So he straddled the beam along the siding, one filthy foot dangling above the flashing black Hudson. I sat in front of him and ran my thumb around the edge of the briefcase.

Hawk hunched his shoulders and leaned. "Hey . . ." He flashed green questioning at me. "Can I touch?"

I shrugged. "Go ahead."

He grubbed among them with fingers that were all knuckle and bitten nail. He picked two up, put them down, picked up three others. "Hey!" he whispered. "How much are all these worth?"

"About ten times more than I hope to get. I have to get rid of them fast."

He glanced down past his toes. "You could always throw them in the river."

"Don't be dense. I was looking for a guy who used to hang around that bar. He was pretty efficient." And half the Hudson away a waterbound foil skimmed above the foam. On her deck were parked a dozen helicopters—being ferried up to the Patrol Field near Verrazzano, no doubt. For moments I looked back and forth between the boy and the transport, getting all paranoid about Maud. But the boat *mmmm*ed

into the darkness. "My man got a little cut up this evening."

Hawk put the tips of his fingers in his pockets and shifted his position.

"Which leaves me uptight. I didn't think he'd take them all, but at least he could have turned me on to some other people who might."

"I'm going to a party later on this evening—" he paused to gnaw on the wreck of his little fingernail—"where you might be able to sell them. Alexis Spinnel is having a party for Regina Abolafia at Tower Top."

"Tower Top . . . ?" It had been a while since I palled around with Hawk. Hell's Kitchen at ten; Tower Top at midnight—

"I'm just going because Edna Silem will be there."

Edna Silem is New York's eldest Singer.

Senator Abolafia's name had ribboned above me in lights once that evening. And somewhere among the endless magazines I'd perused coming in from Mars, I remembered Alexis Spinnel's name sharing a paragraph with an awful lot of money.

"I'd like to see Edna again," I said offhandedly. "But she wouldn't remember me." Folk like Spinnel and his social ilk have a little game, I'd discovered during the first leg of my acquaintance with Hawk. He who can get the most Singers of the City under one roof wins. There are five Singers of New York (a tie for second place with Lux on Iapetus). Tokyo leads with seven. "It's a two-Singer party?"

"More likely four . . . if I go."

The inaugural ball for the mayor gets four.

I raised the appropriate eyebrow.

"I have to pick up the Word from Edna. It changes tonight."

"All right," I said. "I don't know what you have in mind, but I'm game." I closed the case.

• • •

We walked back toward Times Square. When we got to Eighth Avenue and the first of the plastiplex, Hawk stopped. "Wait a minute," he said.

Then he buttoned his jacket up to his neck. "Okay."

Strolling through the streets of New York with a Singer (two years back I'd spent much time wondering if that was wise for a man of my profession) is probably the best camouflage possible for a man of my profession. Think of the last time you glimpsed your favorite Tri-D star turning the corner of Fifty-Seventh. Now be honest. Would you really recognize the little guy in the tweed jacket half a pace behind him?

Half the people we passed in Times Square recognized him. With his youth, funereal garb, black feet, and ash-pale hair, he was easily the most colorful of Singers. Smiles; narrowed eyes; very few actually pointed or stared.

"Just exactly who is going to be there who might be able to take this stuff off my hands?"

"Well, Alexis prides himself on being something of an adventurer. They might just take his fancy. And he can give you more than you can get peddling them in the street."

"You'll tell him they're all hot?"

"It will probably make the idea that much more intriguing. He's a creep."

"You say so, friend."

We went down into the sub-sub. The man at the change booth started to take Hawk's coin, then looked up. He began three or four words that were unintelligible inside his grin, then just gestured us through.

"Oh," Hawk said, "thank you," with ingenuous surprise, as though this were the first, delightful time such a thing had happened. (Two years ago he had told me sagely, "As soon as I start looking like I expect it, it'll stop happening." I was still impressed by the way he wore his notoriety. The time I'd met Edna Silem, and I'd mentioned this, she said with the same ingenuousness, "But that's what we're chosen for.")

In the bright car we sat on the long seat. Hawk's hands were beside him; one foot rested on the other. Down from us a gaggle of bright-bloused goo-chewers giggled and pointed and tried not to be noticed at it. Hawk didn't look at all, and I tried not to be noticed looking.

Dark patterns rushed the window.

Things below the gray floor hummed.

Once a lurch.

Leaning once, we came out of the ground.

Outside, the city tried on its thousand sequins, then threw them away behind the trees of Ft. Tryon. Suddenly the windows across from us grew bright scales. Behind them girders reeled by. We got out on the platform under a light rain. The sign said TWELVE TOWERS STATION.

By the time we reached the street, however, the shower had stopped. Leaves above the wall shed water down the brick. "If I'd known I was bringing someone, I'd have had Alex send a car for us. I told him it was fifty-fifty I'd come."

"Are you sure it's all right for me to tag along then?"

"Didn't you come up here with me once before?"

"I've even been up here once before that," I said. "Do you still think it's . . ."

He gave me a withering look. Well; Spinnel would be delighted to have Hawk even if he dragged along a whole gang of real nasty-grimies—Singers are famous for that sort of thing. With one more or less presentable thief, Spinnel was getting off light. Beside us rocks broke away into the city. Behind the gate to our left the gardens rolled up toward the first of the towers. The twelve immense luxury apartment buildings menaced the lower clouds.

"Hawk the Singer," Hawk the Singer said into the speaker at the side of the gate. *Clang* and *tic-tic-tic* and *Clang*. We walked up to the path to the doors and doors of glass.

A cluster of men and women in evening dress were coming out. Three tiers of doors away they saw us. You could see them frowning at the guttersnipe who'd somehow gotten into the lobby (for a moment I thought one of them was Maud because she wore a sheath of the fading fabric, but she turned; beneath her veil her face was dark as roasted coffee); one of the men recognized him, said something to the others. When they passed us, they were smiling. Hawk paid about as much attention to them as he had to the girls on the subway. But when they'd passed, he said, "One of those guys was looking at you."

"Yeah. I saw."

"Do you know why?"

"He was trying to figure out whether we'd met before."

"Had you?"

I nodded. "Right about where I met you, only back when I'd just gotten out of jail. I told you I'd been here once before."

"Oh."

Blue carpet covered three-quarters of the lobby. A great pool filled the rest in which a row of twelve-foot trellises stood, crowned with flaming braziers. The lobby itself was three stories high, domed and mirror-tiled.

Twisting smoke curled toward the ornate grill. Broken reflections sagged and recovered on the walls.

The elevator door folded about us its foil petals. There was the distinct feeling of not moving while seventy-five stories shucked down around us.

We got out on the landscaped roof garden. A very tanned, very blond man wearing an apricot jumpsuit, from the collar of which emerged a black turtleneck dicky, came down the rocks (artificial) between the ferns (real) growing along the stream (real water; phony current).

"Hello! Hello!" Pause. "I'm terribly glad you decided to come after all." Pause. "For a while I thought you weren't going to make it." The Pauses were to allow Hawk to introduce me. I was dressed so that Spinnel had no way of telling whether I was a miscellaneous Nobel laureate that Hawk happened to have been dining with, or a varlet whose manners and morals were even lower than mine happen to be.

"Shall I take your jacket?" Alexis offered.

Which meant he didn't know Hawk as well as he would like people to think. But I guess he was sensitive enough to realize from the little cold things that happened in the boy's face that he should forget his offer.

He nodded to me, smiling—about all he could do—and we strolled toward the gathering.

Edna Silem was sitting on a transparent inflated hassock. She leaned forward, holding her drink in both hands, arguing politics with the people sitting on the grass before her. She was the first person I recognized (hair of tarnished silver; voice of scrap brass). Jutting from the cuffs of her mannish suit, her wrinkled hands about her goblet, shaking with the intensity of her pronouncements, were heavy with stones and silver. As I ran my eyes back to Hawk, I saw half a dozen whose names/faces sold magazines, music, sent people to the theater (the drama critic for *Delta*, wouldn't you know), and even the mathematician from Princeton I'd read about a few months ago who'd come up with the "quasar/quark" explanation.

There was one woman my eyes kept returning to. On glance three I recognized her as the New Fascistas' most promising candidate for president, Senator Abolafia. Her arms were folded, and she was listening intently to the discussion that had narrowed to Edna and an overly gregarious younger man whose eyes were puffy from what could have been the recent acquisition of contact lenses.

"But don't you feel, Mrs. Silem, that—"

"You must remember when you make predictions like that—"

"Mrs. Silem, I've seen statistics that—"

"You *must* remember—" her voice tensed, lowered till the silence between the words was as rich as the voice was sparse and metallic—"that if everything, *everything* were known, statistical estimates would be unnecessary. The science of probability gives mathematical expression to our ignorance, not to our wisdom," which I was thinking was an interesting second installment to Maud's lecture, when Edna looked up and exclaimed, "Why, Hawk!"

Everyone turned.

"I *am* glad to see you. Lewis, Ann," she called: there were two other Singers there already (he dark, she pale, both tree-slender; their faces made you think of pools without drain or tribute come upon in the forest, clear and very still; husband and wife, they had been made Singers together the day before their marriage six years ago), "he hasn't deserted us after all!" Edna stood, extended her arm over the heads of the people sitting, and barked across her knuckles as though her voice were a pool cue. "Hawk, there are people here arguing with me who don't know nearly as much as you about the subject. You'd be on my side, now wouldn't you—"

"Mrs. Silem, I didn't mean to—" from the floor.

Then her arms swung six degrees, her fingers, eyes, and mouth opened. "You!" Me. "My dear, if there's anyone I never expected to see here! Why it's been almost two years, hasn't it?" Bless Edna; the place where she and Hawk and I had spent a long, beery evening together had more resembled that bar than Tower Top. "Where have you been keeping yourself?"

"Mars, mostly," I admitted. "Actually I just came back today." It's so much fun to be able to say things like that in a place like this.

"Hawk—both of you—" (which meant either she had forgotten my name, or she remembered me well enough not to abuse it—) "come over here and help me drink up Alexis's good liquor." I tried not to grin as we walked toward her. If she remembered anything, she certainly recalled my line of business and must have been enjoying this as much as I was.

Relief spread Alexis's face: he knew now I was *someone* if not *which* someone I was.

As we passed Lewis and Ann, Hawk gave the two Singers one of his luminous grins. They returned shadowed smiles. Lewis nodded. Ann made a move to touch his arm, but left the motion unconcluded; and the company noted the interchange.

Having found out what we wanted, Alex was preparing large glasses of it over crushed ice when the puffy-eyed gentleman stepped up for a refill. "But, Mrs. Silem, then what do you feel validly opposes such political abuses?"

Regina Abolafia wore a white silk suit. Nails, lips, and hair were one copper color; and on her breast was a worked copper pin. It's always fascinated me to watch people used to being the

center thrust to the side. She swirled her glass, listening.

"I oppose them," Edna said. "Hawk opposes them. Lewis and Ann oppose them. We, ultimately, are what you have." And her voice had taken on that authoritative resonance only Singers can assume.

Then Hawk's laugh snarled through the conversational fabric.

We turned.

He'd sat cross-legged near the hedge. "Look . . ." he whispered.

Now people's gazes followed his. He was looking at Lewis and Ann. She, tall and blond, he, dark and taller, were standing very quietly, a little nervously, eyes closed (Lewis's lips were apart).

"Oh," whispered someone who should have known better, "they're going to . . ."

I watched Hawk because I'd never had a chance to observe one Singer at another's performance. He put the soles of his feet together, grasped his toes, and leaned forward, veins making blue rivers on his neck. The top button of his jacket had come loose. Two scar ends showed over his collarbone. Maybe nobody noticed but me.

I saw Edna put her glass down with a look of beaming anticipatory pride. Alex, who had pressed the autobar (odd how automation has become the upper crust's way of flaunting the labor surplus) for more crushed ice, looked up, saw what was about to happen, and pushed the cutoff button. The autobar hummed to silence. A breeze (artificial or real, I couldn't tell you) came by, and the trees gave us a final *shush*.

One at a time, then in duet, then singly again, Lewis and Ann sang.

• • •

Singers are people who look at things, then go and tell people what they've seen. What makes them Singers is their ability to make people listen. That is the most magnificent oversimplification I can give. Eighty-six-year-old El Posado in Rio de Janeiro saw a block of tenements collapse, ran to the Avenida del Sol and began improvising, in rhyme and meter (not all that hard in rhyme-rich Portuguese), tears runneling his dusty cheeks, his voice clashing with the palm swards above the sunny street. Hundreds of people stopped to listen; a hundred more; and another hundred. And they told hundreds more what they had heard. Three hours later, hundreds from among them had arrived at the scene with blankets, food, money, shovels, and more incredibly, the willingness and ability to organize themselves and work within that organization. No Tri-D report of a disaster has ever produced that sort of reaction. El Posado is historically considered the first Singer. The second was Miriamne in the roofed city of Lux, who for thirty years walked through the metal streets, singing the glories of the rings of Saturn—the colonists can't look at them without aid because of the ultraviolet the rings set up. But Miriamne, with her strange cataracts, each dawn walked to the edge of the city, looked, saw, and came back to sing of what she saw. All of which would have meant nothing except that during the days she did not sing—through illness, or once she was on a visit to another city to which her fame had spread—the Lux Stock Exchange would go down, the number of violent crimes rise. Nobody could explain it. All they could do was proclaim her Singer. Why did the institution of Singers come about, springing up in just about every urban center throughout the system? Some have speculated that it was a spontaneous reaction to the mass media which blanket our lives. While Tri-D and radio and newstapes disperse information all over the worlds, they also spread a sense of alienation from firsthand experience. (How many people still go to sports events or a political rally with their little receivers plugged into their ears to let them know that what they see is really happening?) The first Singers were proclaimed by the people around them. Then, there was a period where anyone could proclaim himself a Singer who wanted to, and people either responded to him or laughed

him into oblivion. But by the time I was left on the doorstep of somebody who didn't want me, most cities had more or less established an unofficial quota. When a position is left open today, the remaining Singers choose who is going to fill it. The required talents are poetic, theatrical, as well as a certain charisma that is generated in the tensions between the personality and the publicity web a Singer is immediately snared in. Before he became a Singer, Hawk had gained something of a prodigious reputation with a book of poems published when he was fifteen. He was touring universities and giving readings, but the reputation was still small enough so that he was amazed that I had ever heard of him, that evening we encountered in Central Park. (I had just spent a pleasant thirty days as a guest of the city, and it's amazing what you find in the Tombs Library.) It was a few weeks after his sixteenth birthday. His Singership was to be announced in four days, though he had been informed already. We sat by the lake till dawn while he weighed and pondered and agonized over the coming responsibility. Two years later, he's still the youngest Singer in six worlds by half a dozen years. Before becoming a Singer, a person need not have been a poet, but most are either that or actors. But the roster through the system includes a longshoreman, two university professors, an heiress to the Silitax millions (Tack it down with Silitax), and at least two persons of such dubious background that the ever-hungry-for-sensation Publicity Machine itself has agreed not to let any of it past the copy editors. But wherever their origins, these diverse and flamboyant living myths sang of love, of death, of the changing of seasons, social classes, governments, and the palace guard. They sang before large crowds, small crowds, to an individual laborer coming home from the city's docks, on slum street corners, in club cars of commuter trains, in the elegant gardens atop Twelve Towers, to Alex Spinnel's select soirée. But it has been illegal to reproduce the "Songs" of the Singers by mechanical means (including publishing the lyrics) since the institution arose, and I respect the law, I do, as only a man in my profession can. I offer the explanation then in place of Lewis's and Ann's song.

• • •

They finished, opened their eyes, stared about with expressions that could have been embarrassment, could have been contempt.

Hawk was leaning forward with a look of rapt approval. Edna was smiling politely. I had the sort of grin on my face that breaks out when you've been vastly moved and vastly pleased. Lewis and Ann had sung superbly.

Alex began to breathe again, glancing around to see what state everybody else was in, saw, and pressed the autobar, which began to hum and crush ice. No clapping, but the appreciative sounds began; people were nodding, commenting, whispering. Regina Abolafia went over to Lewis to say something. I tried to listen until Alex shoved a glass into my elbow.

"Oh, I'm sorry . . ."

I transferred my briefcase to the other hand and took the drink, smiling. When Senator Abolafia left the two Singers, they were holding hands and looking at one another a little sheepishly. They sat down again.

The party drifted in conversational groups through the gardens, through the groves. Overhead clouds the color of old chamois folded and unfolded across the moon.

For a while I stood alone in a circle of trees, listening to the music: a de Lassus two–part canon programmed for audio–generators. Recalled: an article in one of last week's large-circulation literaries, stating that it was the only way to remove the feel of the bar lines imposed by five centuries of meter on modern musicians. For another two weeks this would be acceptable entertainment. The trees circled a rock pool; but no water. Below the plastic surface, abstract lights wove and threaded in a shifting lumia.

"Excuse me . . . ?"

I turned to see Alexis, who had no drink now or idea what to do with his hands. He *was* nervous.

". . . but our young friend has told me you have something I might be interested in."

I started to lift my briefcase, but Alexis's hand came down from his ear (it had gone by belt to hair to collar already) to halt me. Nouveau riche.

"That's all right. I don't need to see them yet. In fact, I'd rather not. I have something to propose to you. I would certainly be interested in what you have if they are, indeed, as Hawk has described them. But I have a guest here who would be even more curious."

That sounded odd.

"I know that sounds odd," Alexis assessed, "but I thought you might be interested simply because of the finances involved. I am an eccentric collector who would offer you a price concomitant with what I would use them for: eccentric conversation pieces—and because of the nature of the purchase I would have to limit severely the people with whom I could converse."

I nodded.

"My guest, however, would have a great deal more use for them."

"Could you tell me who this guest is?"

"I asked Hawk, finally, who you were, and he led me to believe I was on the verge of a grave social indiscretion. It would be equally indiscreet to reveal my guest's name to you." He smiled. "But indiscretion is the better part of the fuel that keeps the social machine turning. Mr. Harvey Cadwaliter-Erickson . . ." He smiled knowingly.

I have *never* been Harvey Cadwaliter-Erickson, but Hawk was always an inventive child. Then a second thought went by, viz., the tungsten magnates, the Cadwaliter-Ericksons of Tythis on Triton. Hawk was not only inventive, he was as brilliant as all the magazines and newspapers are always saying he is.

"I assume your second indiscretion will be to tell me who this mysterious guest is?"

"Well," Alex said with the smile of the canary-fattened cat, "Hawk agreed with me that *the* Hawk might well be curious as to what you have in there," (he pointed) "as indeed he is."

I frowned. Then I thought lots of small, rapid thoughts I'll articulate in due time. "*The Hawk?*"

Alex nodded.

I don't think I was actually scowling. "Would you send our young friend up here for a moment?"

"If you'd like." Alex bowed, turned. Perhaps a minute later, Hawk came up over the rocks and through the trees, grinning. When I didn't grin back, he stopped.

"*Mmmm . . .*" I began.

His head cocked.

I scratched my chin with a knuckle. ". . . Hawk," I said, "are you aware of a department of the police called Special Services?"

"I've heard of them."

"They've suddenly gotten very interested in me."

"Gee," he said with honest amazement. "They're supposed to be pretty effective."

"*Mmmm,*" I reiterated.

"Say," Hawk announced, "how do you like that? My namesake is here tonight. Wouldn't you know."

"Alex doesn't miss a trick. Have you any idea *why* he's here?"

"Probably trying to make some deal with Abolafia. Her investigation starts tomorrow."

"Oh." I thought over some of those things I had thought before. "Do you know a Maud Hinkle?"

Hawk's puzzled look said "no" pretty convincingly.

"She bills herself as one of the upper echelon in the arcane organization of which I spoke."

"Yeah?"

"She ended our interview earlier this evening with a little homily about hawks and helicopters. I took our subsequent encounter as a fillip of coincidence. But now I discover that the evening has confirmed her intimations of plurality." I shook my head. "Hawk, I am suddenly catapulted into a paranoid world where the walls not only have ears, but probably eyes and long, claw-tipped fingers. Anyone about me—yea,

even very you—could turn out to be a spy. I suspect every sewer grating and second-story window conceals binoculars, a tommy gun, or worse. What I just can't figure out is how these insidious forces, ubiquitous and omnipresent though they be, induced you to lure me into this intricate and diabolical—"

"Oh, cut it out!" He shook back his hair. "I didn't lure—"

"Perhaps not consciously, but Special Services has Hologramic Information Storage, and their methods are insidious and cruel—"

"I said cut it out!" And all sorts of hard little things happened again. "Do you think I'd—" Then he realized how scared I was, I guess. "Look, the Hawk isn't some small-time snatch-purse. He lives in just as paranoid a world as you're in now, only all the time. If he's here, you can be sure there are just as many of his men—eyes and ears and fingers—as there are of Maud Hickenlooper's."

"Hinkle."

"Anyway, it works both ways. No Singer's going to—Look, do you really think *I* would—"

And even though I knew all those hard little things were scabs over pain, I said, "Yes."

"You did something for me once, and I—"

"I gave you some more welts. That's all."

All the scabs pulled off.

"Hawk," I said. "Let me see."

He took a breath. Then he began to open the brass buttons. The flaps of his jacket fell back. The lumia colored his chest with pastel shiftings.

I felt my face wrinkle. I didn't want to look away. I drew a hissing breath instead, which was just as bad.

He looked up. "There're a lot more than when you were here last, aren't there?"

"You're going to kill yourself, Hawk."

He shrugged.

"I can't even tell which are the ones I put there anymore."

He started to point them out.

"Oh, come on," I said too sharply. And for the length of three breaths, he grew more and more uncomfortable till I saw him start to reach for the bottom button. "Boy," I said, trying to keep despair out of my voice, "why do you do it?" and ended up keeping out everything. There is nothing more despairing than a voice empty.

He shrugged, saw I didn't want that, and for a moment anger flickered in his green eyes. I didn't want that either. So he said: "Look . . . you touch a person softly, gently, and maybe you even do it with love. And, well, I guess a piece of information goes up to the brain where something interprets it as pleasure. Maybe something up there in my head interprets the information in a way you would say is all wrong. . . ."

I shook my head. "You're a Singer. Singers are supposed to be eccentric, sure; but—"

Now he was shaking his head. Then the anger opened up. And I saw an expression move from all those spots that had communicated pain through the rest of his features and vanish without ever becoming a word. Once more he looked down at the wounds that webbed his thin body.

"Button it up, boy. I'm sorry I said anything."

Halfway up the lapels, his hands stopped. "You really think I'd turn you in?"

"Button it up."

He did. Then he said, "Oh." And then, "You know, it's midnight."

"So?"

"Edna just gave me the new Word."

"Which is?"

"Agate."

I nodded.

Hawk finished closing his collar. "What are you thinking about?"

"Cows."

"Cows?" Hawk asked. "What about them?"

"You ever been on a dairy farm?"

He shook his head.

"To get the most milk, you keep the cows practically in suspended animation. They're fed intravenously from a big tank that pipes nutrients out and down, branching into smaller and smaller pipes until it gets to all those high-yield semi-corpses."

"I've seen pictures."

"People."

". . . and cows?"

"You've given me the Word. And now it begins to funnel down, branching out, with me telling others and them telling still others, till by midnight tomorrow . . ."

"I'll go get the—"

"Hawk?"

He turned back. "What?"

"You say you don't think I'm going to be the victim of any hanky-panky with the mysterious forces that know more than we. Okay, that's your opinion. But as soon as I get rid of this stuff, I'm going to make the most distracting exit you've ever seen."

Two little lines bit down Hawk's forehead. "Are you sure I haven't seen this one before?"

"As a matter of fact I think you have." Now I grinned.

"Oh," Hawk said, then made a sound that had the structure of laughter but was all breath. "I'll get the Hawk."

He ducked out between the trees.

• • •

I glanced up at the lozenges of moonlight in the leaves.

I looked down at my briefcase.

Up between the rocks, stepping around the long grass, came the Hawk. He wore a gray evening suit over a gray silk turtleneck. Above his craggy face, his head was completely shaved.

"Mr. Cadwaliter-Erickson?" He held out his hand.

I shook: small sharp bones in loose skin. "Does one call you Mr. . . . ?"

"Arty."

"Arty the Hawk?" I tried to look like I wasn't giving his gray attire the once-over.

He smiled. "Arty the Hawk. Yeah. I picked that name up when I was younger than our friend down there. Alex says you got . . . well, some things that are not exactly yours. That don't belong to you."

I nodded.

"Show them to me."

"You were told what—"

He brushed away the end of my sentence. "Come on, let me see."

He extended his hand, smiling affably as a bank clerk. I ran my thumb around the pressure-zip. The cover went *tsk*. "Tell me," I said, looking up at his head, lowered now to see what I had, "what does one do about Special Services? They seem to be after me."

The head came up. Surprise changed slowly to a craggy leer. "Why, Mr. Cadwaliter-Erickson!" He gave me the up and down openly. "Keep your income steady. Keep it steady, that's one thing you can do."

"If you buy these for anything like what they're worth, that's going to be a little difficult."

"I would imagine. I could always give you less money—"

The cover went *tsk* again.

"—or, barring that, you could try to use your head and outwit them."

"You must have outwitted them at one time or another. You may be on an even keel now, but you had to get there from somewhere else."

Arty the Hawk's nod was downright sly. "I guess you've had a run-in with Maud. Well, I suppose congratulations are in order. And condolences. I always like to do what's in order."

"You seem to know how to take care of yourself. I mean I notice you're not out there mingling with the guests."

"There are two parties going on here tonight," Arty said. "Where do you think Alex disappears off to every five minutes?"

I frowned.

"That lumia down in the rocks"—he pointed toward my feet—"is a mandala of shifting hues on our ceiling. Alex"—he chuckled—"goes scuttling off under the rocks where there is a pavilion of Oriental splendor—"

"And a separate guest list at the door?"

"Regina is on both. I'm on both. So's the kid, Edna, Lewis, Ann—"

"Am I supposed to know all this?"

"Well, you came with a person on both lists. I just thought . . ." The Hawk paused.

I was coming on wrong. But a quick-change artist learns fairly quick that the verisimilitude factor in imitating someone up the scale is your confidence in your unalienable right to come on wrong. "I'll tell you," I said. "How about exchanging these"—I held out the briefcase—"for some information."

"You want to know how to stay out of Maud's clutches?" He shook his head. "It would be pretty stupid of me to tell you, even if I could. Besides, you've got your family fortunes to fall back on." He beat the front of his shirt with his thumb. "Believe me, boy. Arty the Hawk didn't have that. I didn't have anything like that." His hands dropped into his pockets. "Let's see what you got."

I opened the case again.

The Hawk looked for a while. After a few moments he picked a couple up, turned them around, put them back down, put his hands back in his pockets. "I'll give you sixty thousand for them, approved credit tablets."

"What about the information I wanted?"

"I wouldn't tell you a thing." The Hawk smiled. "I wouldn't tell you the time of day."

There are very few successful thieves in this world. Still less on the other five. The will to steal is an impulse toward the absurd and taste-less. (The talents are poetic, theatrical, a certain reverse charisma . . .) But it is a will, as the will to order, power, love.

"All right," I said.

Somewhere overhead I heard a faint humming.

Arty looked at me fondly. He reached under the lapel of his jacket and took out a handful of credit tablets—the scarlet-banded tablets whose slips were ten thousand apiece. He pulled off one. Two. Three. Four.

"You can deposit this much safely—"

"Why do you think Maud is after me?"

Five. Six.

"Fine," I said.

"How about throwing in the briefcase?" Arty asked.

"Ask Alex for a paper bag. If you want, I can send them—"

"Give them here."

The humming was coming closer.

I held up the open case. Arty went in with both hands. He shoved them into his coat pockets, his pants pockets; the gray cloth was distended by angular bulges. He looked left, right. "Thanks," he said. "Thanks." Then he turned and hurried down the slope with all sorts of things in his pockets that weren't his now.

I looked up through the leaves for the noise, but I couldn't see anything.

I stooped down now and laid my case out. I pulled open the back compartment where I kept the things that did belong to me and rummaged hurriedly through.

• • •

Alex was just offering Puffy-eyes another Scotch, while the gentleman was saying, "Has anyone seen Mrs. Silem? What's that humming overhead—?" when a large woman wrapped in a veil of fading fabric tottered across the rocks, screaming.

Her hands were clawing at her covered face.

Alex sloshed soda over his sleeve, and the man said, "Oh, my God! Who's that?"

"No!" the woman shrieked. "Oh, no! Help me!" waving her wrinkled fingers, brilliant with rings.

"Don't you recognize her?" That was Hawk whispering confidentially to someone else. "It's Henrietta, Countess of Effingham."

And Alex, overhearing, went hurrying to her assistance. The Countess ducked between two cacti, however, and disappeared into the high grass. But the entire party followed. They were beating about the underbrush when a balding gentleman in a black tux, bow tie, and cummerbund coughed and said in a very worried voice, "Excuse me, Mr. Spinnel?"

Alex whirled.

"Mr. Spinnel, my mother . . ."

"Who are *you*?" The interruption upset Alex terribly.

The gentleman drew himself up to announce: "The Honorable Clement Effingham," and his pants leg shook for all the world as if he had started to click his heels. But articulation failed. The expression melted on his face. "Oh, I . . . my mother, Mr. Spinnel. We were downstairs at the other half of your party when she got very . . . excited. She ran up here—oh, I *told* her not to! I knew you'd be upset. But you must help me!" and then looked up.

The others looked, too.

The helicopter blacked the moon, rocking and settling below its hazy twin parasols.

"Oh, please . . ." the gentleman said. "You look over there! Perhaps she's gone back down. I've got to"—looking quickly both ways—"find her." He hurried in one direction while everyone else hurried in others.

The humming was suddenly syncopated with a crash. Roaring now, as plastic fragments from the transparent roof chattered down through the branches, clattered on the rocks . . .

• • •

I made it into the elevator and had already thumbed the edge of my briefcase clasp, when Hawk dove between the unfolding foils. The electric eye began to swing them open. I hit DOOR CLOSE full fist.

The boy staggered, banged shoulders on two walls, then got back breath and balance. "Hey, there's police getting out of that helicopter!"

"Hand-picked by Maud Hinkle herself, no doubt." I pulled the other tuft of white hair from my temple. It went into the case on top of the plastiderm gloves (wrinkled, thick blue veins, long carnelian nails) that had been Henrietta's hands, lying in the chiffon folds of her sari.

Then there was the downward tug of stopping. The Honorable Clement was still half on my face when the door opened.

Gray and gray, with an absolutely dismal

expression, the Hawk swung through the doors. Behind him people were dancing in an elaborate pavilion festooned with Oriental magnificence (and a mandala of shifting hues on the ceiling). Arty beat me to DOOR CLOSE. Then he gave me an odd look.

I just sighed and finished peeling off Clem.

"The police are up there . . . ?" the Hawk reiterated.

"Arty," I said, buckling my pants, "it certainly looks that way." The car gained momentum. "You look almost as upset as Alex." I shrugged the tux jacket down my arms, turning the sleeves inside out, pulled one wrist free, and jerked off the white starched dicky with the black bow tie and stuffed it into the briefcase with all my other dickies; swung the coat around and slipped on Howard Calvin Evingston's good gray herring-bone. Howard (like Hank) is a redhead (but not as curly).

The Hawk raised his bare brows when I peeled off Clement's bald pate and shook out my hair.

"I noticed you aren't carrying around all those bulky things in your pockets anymore."

"Oh, those have been taken care of," he said gruffly. "They're all right."

"Arty," I said, adjusting my voice down to Howard's security-provoking, ingenuous baritone, "it must have been my unabashed conceit that made me think that those Regular Service police were here just for me—"

The Hawk actually snarled. "They wouldn't be that unhappy if they got me, too."

And from his corner Hawk demanded, "You've got security here with you, don't you, Arty?"

"So what?"

"There's one way you can get out of this," Hawk hissed at me. His jacket had come half-open down his wrecked chest. "That's if Arty takes you out with him."

"Brilliant idea," I concluded. "You want a couple of thousand back for the service?"

The idea didn't amuse him. "I don't want anything from you." He turned to Hawk. "I

need something from you, kid. Not him. Look, I wasn't prepared for Maud. If you want me to get your friend out, then you've got to do something for me."

The boy looked confused.

I thought I saw smugness on Arty's face, but the expression resolved into concern. "You've got to figure out some way to fill the lobby up with people, and fast."

I was going to ask why, but then I didn't know the extent of Arty's security. I was going to ask how, but the floor pushed up at my feet and the door swung open. "If you can't do it," the Hawk growled to Hawk, "none of us will get out of here. None of us!"

I had no idea what the kid was going to do, but when I started to follow him out into the lobby, the Hawk grabbed my arm and hissed, "Stay here, you idiot!"

I stepped back. Arty was leaning on DOOR OPEN.

Hawk sprinted toward the pool. And splashed in.

He reached the braziers on their twelve-foot tripods and began to climb.

"He's going to hurt himself!" the Hawk whispered.

"Yeah," I said, but I don't think my cynicism got through. Below the great dish of fire, Hawk was fiddling. Then something under there came loose. Something else went *Clang!* And something else spurted out across the water. The fire raced along it and hit the pool, churning and roaring like hell.

A black arrow with a golden head: Hawk dove.

I bit the inside of my cheek as the alarm sounded. Four people in uniforms were coming across the blue carpet. Another group were crossing in the other direction, saw the flames, and one of the women screamed. I let out my breath, thinking carpet and walls and ceilings would be flameproof. But I kept losing focus on the idea before the sixty-odd infernal feet.

Hawk surfaced on the edge of the pool in the only clear spot left, rolled over onto the carpet, clutching his face. And rolled. And rolled. Then, came to his feet.

Another elevator spilled out a load of passengers who gaped and gasped. A crew came through the doors now with firefighting equipment. The alarm was still sounding.

Hawk turned to look at the dozen-odd people in the lobby. Water puddled the carpet about his drenched and shiny pants legs. Flame turned the drops on his cheek and hair to flickering copper and blood.

He banged his fists against his wet thighs, took a deep breath, and against the roar and the bells and the whispering, he Sang.

Two people ducked back into the two elevators. From a doorway half a dozen more emerged. The elevators returned half a minute later with a dozen people each. I realized the message was going through the building, there's a Singer Singing in the lobby.

The lobby filled. The flames growled, the firefighters stood around shuffling, and Hawk, feet apart on the blue rug by the burning pool, Sang, and Sang of a bar off Times Square full of thieves, morphadine-heads, brawlers, drunkards, women too old to trade what they still held out for barter, and trade just too nasty-grimy; where earlier in the evening a brawl had broken out, and an old man had been critically hurt in the fray.

Arty tugged at my sleeve.

"What . . . ?"

"Come on," he hissed.

The elevator door closed behind us.

We ambled through the attentive listeners, stopping to watch, stopping to hear. I couldn't really do Hawk justice. A lot of that slow amble I spent wondering what sort of security Arty had.

Standing behind a couple in bathrobes who were squinting into the heat, I decided it was all very simple. Arty wanted simply to drift away through a crowd, so he'd conveniently gotten Hawk to manufacture one.

To get to the door we had to pass through practically a cordon of Regular Service policemen, who I don't think had anything to do with

what might have been going on in the roof garden; they'd simply collected to see the fire and stayed for the Song. When Arty tapped one on the shoulder—"Excuse me please"—to get by, the policeman glanced at him, glanced away, then did a Mack Sennett double take. But another policeman caught the whole interchange, touched the first on the arm, and gave him a frantic little headshake. Then both men turned very deliberately back to watch the Singer. While the earthquake in my chest stilled, I decided that the Hawk's security complex of agents and counteragents, maneuvering and machinating through the flaming lobby, must be of such finesse and intricacy that to attempt understanding was to condemn oneself to total paranoia.

Arty opened the final door.

I stepped from the last of the air-conditioning into the night.

We hurried down the ramp.

"Hey, Arty . . ."

"You go that way." He pointed down the street. "I go this way."

"Eh . . . what's that way?" I pointed in my direction.

"Twelve Towers sub-sub-subway station. Look. I've got you out of there. Believe me, you're safe for the time being. Now go take a train someplace interesting. Goodbye. Go on now." Then Arty the Hawk put his fists in his pockets and hurried up the street.

I started down, keeping near the wall, expecting someone to get me with a blow dart from a passing car, a death ray from the shrubbery.

I reached the sub.

And still nothing had happened.

Agate gave way to Malachite:

Tourmaline:

Beryl (during which month I turned twenty-six):

Porphyry:

Sapphire (that month I took the ten thousand I hadn't frittered away and invested it in The Glacier, a perfectly legitimate ice cream palace on Triton—the first and only ice cream palace on Triton—which took off like fireworks; all investors were returned eight hundred percent, no kidding. Two weeks later I'd lost half of those earnings on another set of preposterous illegalities and was feeling quite depressed, but The Glacier kept pulling them in. The new Word came by):

Cinnabar:

Turquoise:

Tiger's Eye:

Hector Calhoun Eisenhower finally buckled down and spent three months learning how to be a respectable member of the upper-middle-class underworld. That's a novel in itself. High finance; corporate law; how to hire help: Whew! But the complexities of life have always intrigued me. I got through it. The basic rule is still the same: Observe carefully; imitate effectively.

Garnet:

Topaz (I whispered that word on the roof of the Trans-Satellite Power Station, and caused my hirelings to commit two murders. And you know? I didn't feel a thing):

Taafeite:

We were nearing the end of Taafeite. I'd come back to Triton on strictly Glacial business. A bright pleasant morning it was: the business went fine. I decided to take off the afternoon and go sightseeing in the Torrents.

". . . two hundred and thirty meters high," the guide announced, and everyone around me leaned on the rail and gazed up through the plastic corridor at the cliffs of frozen methane that soared through Neptune's cold green glare.

"Just a few yards down the catwalk, ladies and gentlemen, you can catch your first glimpse of the Well of This World, where over a million years ago, a mysterious force science still cannot explain caused twenty-five square miles of frozen methane to liquefy for no more than a few hours during which time a whirlpool twice the depth of Earth's Grand Canyon was caught for the ages when the temperature dropped once more to . . ."

People were moving down the corridor when I saw her smiling. My hair was black and nappy, and my skin was chestnut dark today.

I was just feeling overconfident, I guess, so I kept standing around next to her. I even contemplated coming on. Then she broke the whole thing up by suddenly turning to me and saying perfectly deadpan: "Why, if it isn't Hamlet Caliban Enobarbus!"

Old reflexes realigned my features to couple the frown of confusion with the smile of indulgence. *Pardon me, but I think you must have mistaken* . . . No, I didn't say it. "Maud," I said, "have you come here to tell me that my time has come?"

She wore several shades of blue with a large blue brooch at her shoulder obviously glass. Still, I realized as I looked about the other tourists, she was more inconspicuous amid their finery than I was. "No," she said. "Actually I'm on vacation. Just like you."

"No kidding?" We had dropped behind the crowd. "You are kidding."

"Special Services of Earth, while we cooperate with Special Services on other worlds, has no official jurisdiction on Triton. And since you came here with money, and most of your recorded gain in income has been through The Glacier; while Regular Services on Triton might be glad to get you, Special Services is not after you as yet." She smiled. "I haven't been to The Glacier. It would really be nice to say I'd been taken there by one of the owners. Could we go for a soda, do you think?"

The swirled sides of the Well of This World dropped away in opalescent grandeur. Tourists gazed, and the guide went on about indices of refraction, angles of incline.

"I don't think you trust me," Maud said.

My look said she was right.

"Have you ever been involved with narcotics?" she asked suddenly.

I frowned.

"No, I'm serious. I want to try and explain something . . . a point of information that may make both our lives easier."

"Peripherally," I said. "I'm sure you've got down all the information in your dossiers."

"I was involved with them a good deal more than peripherally for several years," Maud said. "Before I got into Special Services, I was in the Narcotics Division of the regular force. And the people we dealt with twenty-four hours a day were drug users, drug pushers. To catch the big ones we had to make friends with the little ones. To catch the bigger ones, we had to make friends with the big. We had to keep the same hours they kept, talk the same language, for months at a time live on the same streets, in the same buildings." She stepped back from the rail to let a youngster ahead. "I had to be sent away to take the morphadine detoxification cure twice while I was on the narc squad. And I had a better record than most."

"What's your point?"

"Just this. You and I are traveling in the same circles now, if only because of our respective chosen professions. You'd be surprised how many people we already know in common. Don't be shocked when we run into each other crossing Sovereign Plaza in Bellona one day, then two weeks later wind up at the same restaurant for lunch at Lux on Iapetus. Though the circles we move in cover worlds, they *are* the same—and not that big."

"Come on." I don't think I sounded happy. "Let me treat you to that ice cream." We started back down the walkway.

"You know," Maud said, "if you do stay out of Special Services' hands here and on Earth long enough, eventually you'll be up there with a huge income growing on a steady slope. It might be a few years, but it's possible. There's no reason now for us to be *personal* enemies. You just may, someday, reach that point where Special Services loses interest in you as quarry. Oh, we'd still see each other, run into each other. We get a great deal of our information from people up there. We're in a position to help you, too, you see."

"You've been casting holograms again."

She shrugged. Her face looked positively ghostly under the pale planet. She said, when we reached the artificial lights of the city, "I did meet two friends of yours recently, Lewis and Ann."

"The Singers?"

Maud nodded.

"Oh, I don't really know them well."

"They seem to know a lot about you. Perhaps through that other Singer Hawk."

"Oh," I said again. "Did they say how he was?"

"I read that he was recovering about two months back. But nothing since then."

"That's about all I know, too," I said.

"The only time I've ever seen him," Maud said, "was right after I pulled him out."

Arty and I had gotten out of the lobby before Hawk actually finished. The next day on the newstapes I learned that when his Song was over; Hawk shrugged out of his jacket, dropped his pants, and walked back into the pool.

The firefighter crew suddenly woke up. People began running around and screaming. He'd been rescued, seventy percent of his body covered with second- and third-degree burns. I'd been industriously trying not to think about it.

"*You* pulled him out?"

"Yes. I was in the helicopter that landed on the roof," Maud said. "I thought you'd be impressed to see me."

"Oh," I said. "How did you get to pull him out?"

"Once you got going, Arty's security managed to jam the elevator service above the seventy-first floor, so we didn't get to the lobby till after you were out of the building. That's when Hawk tried to—"

"But it was you who actually saved him, though?"

"The firemen in that neighborhood hadn't had a fire in twelve years! I don't think they even know how to operate the equipment. I had my boys foam the pool, then I waded in and dragged him—"

"Oh," I said again. I had been trying hard, almost succeeding, these eleven months. I wasn't there when it happened. It wasn't my affair. Maud was saying:

"We thought we might have gotten a lead on you from him, but when I got him to the shore, he was completely out, just a mass of open, running—"

"I should have known the Special Services uses Singers, too," I said. "Everyone else does. The Word changes today, doesn't it? Lewis and Ann didn't pass on what the new one is?"

"I saw them yesterday, and the Word doesn't change for another eight hours. Besides, they wouldn't tell *me*, anyway." She glanced at me and frowned. "They really wouldn't."

"Let's go have those ice-cream sodas," I said. "We'll make small talk and listen carefully to each other while we affect an air of nonchalance. You will try to pick up things that will make it easier to catch me. I will listen for things you let slip that might make it easier for me to avoid you."

"*Um-hm.*" She nodded.

"Why did you contact me in that bar, anyway?"

Eyes of ice: "I told you, we simply travel in the same circles. We're quite likely to be in the same bar on the same night."

"I guess that's just one of the things I'm not supposed to understand, huh?"

Her smile was appropriately ambiguous. I didn't push it.

• • •

It was a very dull afternoon. I couldn't repeat one exchange from the nonsense we babbled over the cherry-peaked mountains of whipped cream. We both exerted so much energy to keep up the appearance of being amused, I doubt either one of us could see our way to picking up anything meaningful—if anything meaningful was said.

She left. I brooded some more on the charred phoenix.

The Steward of The Glacier called me into the kitchen to ask about a shipment of contra-band milk (The Glacier makes all its own ice cream) that I had been able to wangle on my last trip to Earth (it's amazing how little progress there has been in dairy farming over the last ten years; it was depressingly easy to hornswoggle that bumbling Vermonter) and under the white lights and great plastic churning vats, while I tried to get things straightened out, he made some comment about the Heist Cream Emperor; that didn't do *any* good.

By the time the evening crowd got there, and the moog was making music, the crystal walls were blazing; and the floor show—a new addition that week—had been cajoled into going on anyway (a trunk of costumes had gotten lost in shipment [or swiped, but I wasn't about to tell *them* that]), and wandering through the tables I, personally, had caught a very grimy little girl, obviously out of her head on morph, trying to pick up a customer's pocketbook from the back of his chair—I just caught her by the wrist, made her let go, and led her to the door daintily, while she blinked at me with dilated eyes and the customer never even knew—and the floor show, having decided what the hell, were doing their act *au naturel*, and everyone was having just a high old time, I was feeling really bad.

I went outside, sat on the wide steps, and growled when I had to move aside to let people in or out. About the seventy-fifth growl, the person I growled at stopped and boomed down at me, "I thought I'd find you, if I looked hard enough! I mean if I really looked."

I looked at the hand that was flapping at my shoulder; followed the arm up to a black turtleneck where there was a beefy, bald, grinning head. "Arty," I said, "what are . . . ?" But he was still flapping and laughing with impervious *gemütlichkeit*.

"You wouldn't believe the time I had getting a picture of you, boy. Had to bribe one out of the Triton Special Services Department. That quick change bit: great gimmick. Just great!" The Hawk sat down next to me and dropped his hand on my knee. "Wonderful place you got here. I like it, like it a lot." Small bones in veined dough. "But not enough to make you an offer on it yet. You're learning fast there, though. I can tell you're learning fast. I'm going to be proud to be able to say I was the one who gave you your first big break." Arty's hand came away, and he began to knead it into the other. "If you're going to move into the big time, you have to have at least one foot planted firmly on the right side of the law. The whole idea is to make yourself indispensable to the good people. Once that's done, a good crook has the keys to all the treasure houses in the system. But I'm not telling you anything you don't already know."

"Arty," I said, "do you think the two of us should be seen together here . . . ?"

The Hawk held his hand above his lap and joggled it with a deprecating motion. "Nobody can get a picture of us. I got my men all around. I never go anywhere in public without my security. Heard you've been looking into the security business yourself," which was true. "Good idea. Very good. I like the way you're handling yourself."

"Thanks. Arty, I'm not feeling too hot this evening. I came out here to get some air. . . ."

Arty's hand fluttered again. "Don't worry, I won't hang around. You're right. We shouldn't be seen. Just passing by and wanted to say hello. Just hello." He got up. "That's all." He started down the steps.

"Arty?"

He looked back.

"Sometime soon you will come back; and that time you will want to buy out my share of The Glacier, because I'll have gotten too big; and I won't want to sell because I'll think I'm big enough to fight you. So we'll be enemies for a while. You'll try to kill me. I'll try to kill you."

On his face, first the frown of confusion, then the indulgent smile. "I see you've caught on to the idea of hologramic information. Very good. Good. It's the only way to outwit Maud. Make

sure all your information relates to the whole scope of the situation. It's the only way to outwit me, too." He smiled, started to turn, but thought of something else. "If you can fight me off long enough and keep growing, keep your security in tiptop shape, eventually, we'll get to the point where it'll be worth both our whiles to work together again. If you can just hold out, we'll be friends again. Someday. You just watch. Just wait."

"Thanks for telling me."

The Hawk looked at his watch. "Well. Goodbye." I thought he was going to leave finally. But he glanced up again. "Have you got the new Word?"

"That's right," I said. "It went out tonight. What is it?"

The Hawk waited till the people coming down the steps were gone. He looked hastily about, then leaned toward me with hands cupped at his mouth, rasped, "Pyrite," and winked hugely. "I just got it from a gal who got it direct from Colette" (one of the three Singers of Triton). Arty turned, jounced down the steps, and shouldered his way into the crowds passing on the strip.

• • •

I sat there mulling through the year till I had to get up and walk. All walking does to my depressive moods is add the reinforcing rhythm of paranoia. By the time I was coming back, I had worked out a dilly of a delusional system: The Hawk had already begun to weave some security-ridden plot about me, which ended when we were all trapped in some dead-end alley, and trying to get aid I called out, "Pyrite!" which would turn out not to be the Word at all but served to identify me for the man in the dark gloves with the gun/grenade/gas.

There was a cafeteria on the corner. In the light from the window, clustered over the wreck by the curb was a bunch of nasty-grimies (à la Triton: chains around the wrist, bumblebee tattoo on cheek, high-heel boots on those who could afford them). Straddling the smashed headlight was the little morph-head I had ejected earlier from The Glacier.

On a whim I went up to her. "Hey . . . ?"

She looked at me from under hair like trampled straw, eyes all pupil.

"You get the new Word yet?"

She rubbed her nose, already scratch red. "Pyrite," she said. "It just came down about an hour ago."

"Who told you?"

She considered my question. "I got it from a guy, who says he got it from a guy, who came in this evening from New York, who picked it up there from a Singer named Hawk."

The three grimies nearest made a point of not looking at me. Those farther away let themselves glance.

"Oh," I said. "Oh. Thanks."

Occam's Razor, along with any real information on how security works, hones away most such paranoia. Pyrite. At a certain level in my line of work, paranoia's just an occupational disease. At least I was certain that Arty (and Maud) probably suffered from it as much as I did.

· · ·

The lights were out on The Glacier's marquee. Then I remembered what I had left inside and ran up the stairs.

The door was locked. I pounded on the glass a couple of times, but everyone had gone home. And the thing that made it worse was that I could *see* it sitting on the counter of the coat-check alcove under the orange bulb. The Steward had probably put it there, thinking I might arrive before everybody left. Tomorrow at noon Ho Chi Eng had to pick up his reservation for the Marigold Suite on the Interplanetary Liner *The Platinum Swan*, which left at one-thirty for Bellona. And there behind the glass doors of The Glacier, it waited with the proper wig, as well as the epicanthic folds that would halve Mr. Eng's sloe eyes of jet.

I actually thought of breaking in. But the more practical solution was to get the hotel to wake me at nine and come in with the cleaning man. I turned around and started down the steps; and the thought struck me, and made me terribly sad, so that I blinked and smiled just from reflex; it was probably just as well to leave it there till morning, because there was nothing in it that wasn't mine anyway.

—*MILFORD*
JULY 1968

BRUCE BETHKE

CYBERPUNK

(1983)

THE SNOOZER WENT OFF at seven and I was out of my sleepsack, powered up, and on line in nanos. That's as far as I got. Soon's I booted and got—

CRACKERS/BUDDYBOO/8ER

—on the tube I shut down fast. Damn! Rayno had been on line before me, like always, and that message meant somebody else had gotten into our Net—and that meant trouble by the busload! I couldn't do anything more on term, so I zipped into my jumper, combed my hair, and went downstairs.

Mom and Dad were at breakfast when I slid into the kitchen. "Good Morning, Mikey!" said Mom with a smile. "You were up so late last night I thought I wouldn't see you before you caught your bus."

"Had a tough program to crack," I said.

"Well," she said, "now you can sit down and have a decent breakfast." She turned around to pull some Sara Lees out of the microwave and plunk them down on the table.

"If you'd do your schoolwork when you're supposed to you wouldn't have to stay up all night," growled Dad from behind his caffix and faxsheet. I sloshed some juice in a glass and poured it down, stuffed a Sara Lee into my mouth, and stood to go.

"What?" asked Mom. "That's all the breakfast you're going to have?"

"Haven't got time," I said. "I gotta get to school early to see if the program checks." Dad growled something more and Mom spoke to quiet him, but I didn't hear much 'cause I was out the door.

I caught the transys for school, just in case they were watching. Two blocks down the line I got off and transferred going back the other way, and a coupla transfers later I wound up whipping into Buddy's All-Night Burgers. Rayno was in our booth, glaring into his caffix. It was 7:55 and I'd beat Georgie and Lisa there.

"What's on line?" I asked as I dropped into my seat, across from Rayno. He just looked up at me through his eyebrows and I knew better than to ask again.

At eight Lisa came in. Lisa is Rayno's girl, or at least she hopes she is. I can see why: Rayno's seventeen—two years older than the rest of us—he wears flash plastic and his hair in The Wedge (Dad blew a chip when I said I wanted my hair cut like that) and he's so cool he won't even touch her, even when she's begging for it. She plunked down in her seat next to Rayno and he didn't blink.

Georgie still wasn't there at 8:05. Rayno checked his watch again, then finally looked up from his caffix. "The compiler's been cracked," he said. Lisa and I both swore. We'd worked up our own little code to keep our Net private. I mean, our Olders would just blow *boards* if they ever found out what we were *really* up to. And now somebody'd broken our code.

"Georgie's old man?" I asked.

"Looks that way." I swore again. Georgie and I started the Net by linking our smartterms with some stuff we stored in his old man's home business system. Now my dad wouldn't know an opsys if he crashed on one, but Georgie's old man—he's a *greentooth*. A tech-type. He'd found one of ours once before and tried to take it apart to see what it did. We'd just skinned out that time.

"Any idea how far in he got?" Lisa asked. Rayno looked through her, at the front door. Georgie'd just come in.

"We're gonna find out," Rayno said.

Georgie was coming in smiling, but when he saw that look in Rayno's eyes he sat down next to me like the seat was booby-trapped.

"Good morning, Georgie," said Rayno, smiling like a shark.

"I didn't glitch!" Georgie whined. "I didn't tell him a thing!"

"Then how the Hell did he do it?"

"You know how he is, he's weird! He likes puzzles!" Georgie looked to me for backup. "That's how come I was late. He was trying to weasel me, but I didn't tell him a thing! I think he only got it partway open. He didn't ask about the Net!"

Rayno actually sat back, pointed at us all, and smiled. "You kids just don't know how *lucky* you are. I was in the Net last night and flagged somebody who didn't know the secures was poking Georgie's compiler. I made some changes. By the time your old man figures them out, well . . ."

I sighed relief. See what I mean about being cool? Rayno had us outlooped all the time!

Rayno slammed his fist down on the table. "But *dammit* Georgie, you gotta keep a closer watch on him!"

Then Rayno smiled and bought us all drinks and pie all the way around. Lisa had a cherry Coke, and Georgie and I had caffix just like Rayno. God, that stuff tastes awful! The cups were cleared away, and Rayno unzipped his jumper and reached inside.

"Now kids," he said quietly, "it's time for some serious fun." He whipped out his microterm. "School's off!"

I still drop a bit when I see that microterm—Geez, it's a beauty! It's a Zeilemann Nova 300, but we've spent so much time reworking it, it's practically custom from the motherboard up. Hi-baud, rammed, rammed, ported, with the wafer display folds down to about the size of a vid cassette; I'd give an ear to have one like it. We'd used Georgie's old man's chipburner to tuck some special tricks in ROM and there wasn't a system in CityNet it couldn't talk to.

Rayno ordered up a smartcab and we piled out of Buddy's. No more riding the transys for us, we were going in style! We charged the smartcab off to some law company and cruised all over Eastside.

Riding the boulevards got stale after a while, so we rerouted to the library. We do a lot of our fun at the library, 'cause nobody ever bothers us there. Nobody ever *goes* there. We sent the smartcab, still on the law company account, off to Westside. Getting past the guards and the librarians was just a matter of flashing some ID and then we zipped off into the stacks.

Now, you've got to ID away your life to get on the libsys terms—which isn't worth half a scare when your ID is all fudged like ours is—and they watch real careful. But they move their terms around a lot, so they've got ports on line all over the building. We found an unused port, and me and Georgie kept watch while Rayno plugged in his microterm and got on line.

"Get me into the Net," he said, handing me the term. We don't have a stored opsys yet for Netting, so Rayno gives me the fast and tricky jobs.

Through the dataphones I got us out of the libsys and into CityNet. Now, Olders will never understand. They still think a computer has got to be a brain in a single box. I can get the same results with opsys stored in a hundred places, once I tie them together. Nearly every computer has got a dataphone port, CityNet is a *great* linking system, and Rayno's microterm has the smarts to do the job clean and fast so nobody flags on us. I pulled the compiler out of Georgie's old man's computer and got into our Net. Then I handed the term back to Rayno.

"Well, let's do some fun. Any requests?" Georgie wanted something to get even with his old man, and I had a new routine cooking, but Lisa's eyes lit up 'cause Rayno handed the term to her, first.

"I wanna burn Lewis," she said.

"Oh fritz!" Georgie complained. "You did that *last* week!"

"Well, he gave me another F on a theme."

"I never get F's. If you'd *read* books once in a—"

"Georgie," Rayno said softly, "Lisa's on line." That settled that. Lisa's eyes were absolutely glowing.

Lisa got back into CityNet and charged a couple hundred overdue books to Lewis's libsys account. Then she ordered a complete fax sheet of Encyclopaedia Britannica printed out at his office. I got next turn.

Georgie and Lisa kept watch while I accessed. Rayno was looking over my shoulder. "Something new this week?"

"Airline reservations. I was with my dad two weeks ago when he set up a business trip, and I flagged on maybe getting some fun. I scanned the ticket clerk real careful and picked up the access code."

"Okay, show me what you can do."

Accessing was so easy that I just wiped a couple of reservations first, to see if there were any bells and whistles.

None. No checks, no lockwords, no confirm codes. I erased a couple dozen people without crashing down or locking up. "Geez," I said, "There's no deep secures at all!"

"I been telling you. Olders are even dumber than they look. Georgie? Lisa? C'mon over here and see what we're running!"

Georgie was real curious and asked a lot of questions, but Lisa just looked bored and snapped her gum and tried to stand closer to Rayno. Then Rayno said, "Time to get off Sesame Street. Purge a flight."

I did. It was simple as a save. I punched a few keys, entered, and an entire plane disappeared from all the reservation files. Boy, they'd be surprised when they showed up at the airport. I started purging down the line, but Rayno interrupted.

"Maybe there's no bells and whistles, but wipe out a whole block of flights and it'll stand out. Watch this." He took the term from me and cooked up a routine in RAM to do a global and wipe out every flight that departed at an :07 for the next year. "Now that's how you do these things without waving a flag."

"That's sharp," Georgie chipped in, to me. "Mike, you're a genius! Where do you get these ideas?" Rayno got a real funny look in his eyes.

"My turn," Rayno said, exiting the airline system.

"What's next in the stack?" Lisa asked him.

"Yeah, I mean, after garbaging the airlines . . ." Georgie didn't realize he was supposed to shut up.

"Georgie! Mike!" Rayno hissed. "Keep watch!" Soft, he added, "It's time for The Big One."

"You sure?" I asked. "Rayno, I don't think we're ready."

"We're ready."

Georgie got whiney. "We're gonna get in *big* trouble—"

"Wimp," spat Rayno. Georgie shut up.

We'd been working on The Big One for over two months, but I still didn't feel real solid about it. It *almost* made a clean if/then/else; *if* The Big One worked/*then* we'd be rich/*else* . . . it was the *else* I didn't have down.

Georgie and me scanned while Rayno got down to business. He got back into CityNet, called the cracker opsys out of OurNet, and poked it into Merchant's Bank & Trust. I'd gotten into them the hard way, but never messed with their accounts; just did it to see if I could do it. My data'd been sitting in their system for about three weeks now and nobody'd noticed. Rayno thought it would be really funny to use one bank computer to crack the secures on other bank computers.

While he was peeking and poking I heard walking nearby and took a closer look. It was just some old waster looking for a quiet place to sleep. Rayno was finished linking by the time I got back. "Okay kids," he said, "this is it." He looked around to make sure we were all watching him, then held up the term and stabbed the *RETURN* key. That was it. I stared hard at the display, waiting to see what *else* was gonna be. Rayno figured it'd take about ninety seconds.

The Big One, y'see, was Rayno's idea. He'd heard about some kids in Sherman Oaks who almost got away with a five-million-dollar electronic fund transfer; they hadn't hit a hang-up moving the five mil around until they tried to dump it into a personal savings account with a $40 balance. That's when all the flags went up.

Rayno's cool; Rayno's smart. We weren't going to be greedy, we were just going to EFT fifty K. And it wasn't going to look real strange, 'cause it got strained through some legitimate accounts before we used it to open twenty dummies.

If it worked.

The display blanked, flickered, and showed:

TRANSACTION COMPLETED. HAVE A NICE DAY.

I started to shout, but remembered I was in a library. Georgie looked less terrified. Lisa looked like she was going to attack Rayno.

Rayno just cracked his little half smile, and started exiting. "Funtime's over, kids."

"I didn't get a turn," Georgie mumbled.

Rayno was out of all the nets and powering down. He turned, slow, and looked at Georgie through those eyebrows of his. "*You* are still on The List."

Georgie swallowed it 'cause there was nothing else he could do. Rayno folded up the microterm and tucked it back inside his jumper.

We got a smartcab outside the library and went off to someplace Lisa picked for lunch. Georgie got this idea about garbaging up the smartcab's brain so that the next customer would have a real state fair ride, but Rayno wouldn't let him do it. Rayno didn't talk to him during lunch, either.

After lunch I talked them into heading up to Martin's Micros. That's one of my favorite places to hang out. Martin's the only Older I know who can really work a computer without blowing out his headchips, and he never talks down to me, and he never tells me to keep my hands off anything. In fact, Martin's been real happy to see all of us, ever since Rayno bought that $3000 vidgraphics art animation package for Lisa's birthday.

Martin was sitting at his term when we came in. "Oh, hi Mike! Rayno! Lisa! Georgie!" We all nodded. "Nice to see you again. What can I do for you today?"

"Just looking," Rayno said.

"Well, that's free." Martin turned back to his term and punched a few more IN keys. "Damn!" he said to the term.

"What's the problem?" Lisa asked.

"The problem is *me*," Martin said. "I got

this software package I'm supposed to be writing, but it keeps bombing out and I don't know what's wrong."

Rayno asked, "What's it supposed to do?"

"Oh, it's a real estate system. Y'know, the whole future-values-in-current-dollars bit. Depreciation, inflation, amortization, tax credits—"

"Put that in our tang," Rayno said. "What numbers crunch?"

Martin started to explain, and Rayno said to me, "This looks like your kind of work." Martin hauled his three hundred pounds of fat out of the chair and looked relieved as I dropped down in front of the term. I scanned the parameters, looked over Martin's program, and processed a bit. Martin'd only made a few mistakes. Anybody could have. I dumped Martin's program and started loading the right one in off the top of my head.

"Will you look at that?" Martin said.

I didn't answer 'cause I was thinking in assembly. In ten minutes I had it in, compiled, and running test sets. It worked perfect, of course.

"I just can't believe you kids," Martin said. "You can program easier than I can talk."

"Nothing to it," I said.

"Maybe not for you. I knew a kid grew up speaking Arabic, used to say the same thing." He shook his head, tugged his beard, looked me in the face, and smiled. "Anyhow, thanks loads, Mike. I don't know how to . . ." He snapped his fingers. "Say, I just got something in the other day, I bet you'd be really interested in." He took me over to the display case, pulled it out, and set it on the counter. "The latest word in microterms. The Zeilemann Starfire 600."

I dropped a bit! Then I ballsed up enough to touch it. I flipped up the wafer display, ran my fingers over the touch pads, and I just *wanted* it so bad! "It's smart," Martin said. "Rammed, rammed, and ported."

Rayno was looking at the specs with that cold look in his eye. "My 300 is still faster," he said.

"It should be," Martin said. "You customized it half to death. But the 600 is nearly as fast,

and it's stock, and it lists for $1400. I figure you must have spent nearly 3K upgrading yours."

"Can I try it out?" I asked. Martin plugged me into his system, and I booted and got on line. It worked great! Quiet, accurate; so maybe it wasn't as fast as Rayno's—*I* couldn't tell the difference. "Rayno, this thing is the max!" I looked at Martin. "Can we work out some kind of . . . ?" Martin looked back to his terminal, where the real estate program was still running tests without a glitch.

"I been thinking about that, Mike. You're a minor, so I can't legally employ you." He tugged on his beard and rolled his tongue around his mouth. "But I'm hitting that real estate client for some pretty heavy bread on consulting fees, and it doesn't seem real fair to me that you . . . Tell you what. Maybe I can't hire you, but I sure can buy software you write. You be my consultant on, oh . . . seven more projects like this, and we'll call it a deal? Sound okay to you?"

Before I could shout yes, Rayno pushed in between me and Martin. "I'll buy it. List." He pulled out a charge card from his jumper pocket. Martin's jaw dropped. "Well, what're you waiting for? My plastic's good."

"List? But I owe Mike one," Martin protested.

"*List*. You don't owe us nothing."

Martin swallowed. "Okay Rayno." He took the card and ran a credcheck on it. "It's clean," Martin said, surprised. He punched up the sale and started laughing. "I don't know *where* you kids get this kind of money!"

"We rob banks," Rayno said. Martin laughed, and Rayno laughed, and we all laughed. Rayno picked up the term and walked out of the store. As soon as we got outside he handed it to me.

"Thanks Rayno, but . . . but I coulda made the deal myself."

"Happy Birthday, Mike."

"Rayno, my birthday is in August."

"Let's get one thing straight. You work for *me*."

It was near school endtime, so we routed back

to Buddy's. On the way, in the smartcab, Georgie took my Starfire, gently opened the case, and scanned the boards. "We could double the baud speed real easy."

"Leave it stock," Rayno said.

We split up at Buddy's, and I took the transys home. I was lucky, 'cause Mom and Dad weren't home and I could zip right upstairs and hide the Starfire in my closet. I wish I had cool parents like Rayno does. They never ask him any dumb questions.

Mom came home at her usual time, and asked how school was. I didn't have to say much, 'cause just then the stove said dinner was ready and she started setting the table. Dad came in five minutes later and we started eating.

We got the phone call halfway through dinner. I was the one who jumped up and answered it. It was Georgie's old man, and he wanted to talk to my dad. I gave him the phone and tried to overhear, but he took it in the next room and talked real quiet. I got unhungry. I never liked tofu anyway.

Dad didn't stay quiet for long. "He *what*?! Well thank you for telling me! I'm going to get to the bottom of this right now!" He hung up.

"Who was that, David?" Mom asked.

"That was Mr. Hansen. Georgie's father. Mike and Georgie were hanging around with that punk Rayno again!" He snapped around to look at me. I'd almost made it out the kitchen door. "Michael! Were you in school today?"

I tried to talk cool. I think the tofu had my throat all clogged up. "Yeah . . . yeah, I was."

"Then how come Mr. Hansen saw you coming out of the downtown library?"

I was stuck. "I—I was down there doing some special research."

"For what class? C'mon Michael, what were you studying?"

It was too many inputs. I was locking up.

"David," Mom said, "Aren't you being a bit hasty? I'm sure there's a good explanation."

"Martha, Mr. Hansen found something in his computer that Georgie and Michael put there. He thinks they've been messing with banks."

"*Our* Mikey? It must be some kind of bad joke."

"You don't know how serious this is! Michael Arthur Harris! What have you been doing sitting up all night with that terminal? What was that system in Hansen's computer? Answer me! What have you been doing?!"

My eyes felt hot. "None of your business! Keep your nose out of things you'll never understand, you obsolete old relic!"

"That *does* it! I don't know what's wrong with you damn kids, but I know that *thing* isn't helping!" He stormed up to my room. I tried to get ahead of him all the way up the steps and just got my hands stepped on. Mom came fluttering up behind as he yanked all the plugs on my terminal.

"Now David," Mom said. "Don't you think you're being a bit harsh? He needs that for his homework, don't you, Mikey?"

"You can't make excuses for him this time, Martha! I mean it! This goes in the basement, and tomorrow I'm calling the cable company and getting his line ripped out! If he has anything to do on a computer he can damn well use the terminal in the den, where I can watch him!" He stomped out, carrying my smartterm. I slammed the door and locked it. "Go ahead and sulk! It won't do you any good!"

I threw some pillows around till I didn't feel like breaking anything anymore, then I hauled the Starfire out of the closet. I'd watched over Dad's shoulders enough to know his account numbers and access codes, so I got on line and got down to business. I was finished in half an hour.

I tied into Dad's terminal. He was using it, like I figured he would be, scanning school records. Fine. He wouldn't find out anything; we'd figured out how to fix school records months ago. I crashed in and gave him a new message on his vid display.

"Dad," it said, "there's going to be some changes around here."

It took a few seconds to sink in. I got up and made sure the door was locked real solid. I still got half a scare when he came pounding up the stairs, though. I didn't know he could be so loud.

"MICHAEL!!" He slammed into the door. "Open this! *Now!*"

"No."

"If you don't open this door before I count to ten, I'm going to bust it down! One!"

"Before you do that—"

"Two!"

"Better call your bank!"

"Three!"

"B320-5127-OlR." That was his checking account access code. He silenced a couple seconds.

"Young man, I don't know what you think you're trying to pull—"

"I'm not trying anything. I did it already."

Mom came up the stairs and said, "What's going on, David?"

"Shut up, Martha!" He was talking real quiet, now. "What did you do, Michael?"

"Outlooped you. Disappeared you. Buried you."

"You mean, you got into the bank computer and *erased* my checking account?"

"Savings and mortgage on the condo, too."

"Oh my God . . ."

Mom said, "He's just angry, David. Give him time to cool off. Mikey, you wouldn't *really* do that, would you?"

"Then I accessed DynaRand," I said. "Wiped your job. Your pension. I got into your plastic, too."

"He couldn't have, David. Could he?"

"Michael!" He hit the door. "I'm going to wring your scrawny neck!"

"Wait!" I shouted back. "I copied all your files before I purged! There's a way to recover!"

He let up hammering on the door, and struggled to talk calm. "Give me the copies right now and I'll just forget that this happened."

"I can't. I mean, I did backups in other computers. And I secured the files and hid them where only I know how to access."

There was quiet. No, in a nano I realized it wasn't quiet, it was Mom and Dad talking real

soft. I eared up to the door but all I caught was Mom saying "why not?" and Dad saying, "but what if he *is* telling the truth?"

"Okay Michael," Dad said at last. "What do you want?"

I locked up. It was an embarrasser; what *did* I want? I hadn't thought that far ahead. Me, caught without a program! I dropped half a laugh, then tried to think. I mean, there was nothing they could get me I couldn't get myself, or with Rayno's help. Rayno! I wanted to get in touch with him, is what I wanted. I'd pulled this whole thing off without Rayno!

I decided then it'd probably be better if my Olders didn't know about the Starfire, so I told Dad first thing I wanted was my smartterm back. It took a long time for him to clump down to the basement and get it. He stopped at his term in the den, first, to scan if I'd really purged him. He was real subdued when he brought my smartterm back up.

I kept processing, but by the time he got back I still hadn't come up with anything more than I wanted them to leave me alone and stop telling me what to do. I got the smartterm into my room without being pulped, locked the door, got on line, and gave Dad his job back. Then I tried to flag Rayno and Georgie, but couldn't, so I left messages for when they booted. I stayed up half the night playing a war, just to make sure Dad didn't try anything.

I booted and scanned first thing the next morning, but Rayno and Georgie still hadn't come on. So I went down and had an utter silent breakfast and sent Mom and Dad off to work. I offed school and spent the whole day finishing the war and working on some tricks and treats programs. We had another utter silent meal when Mom and Dad came home, and after supper I flagged Rayno had been in the Net and left a remark on when to find him.

I finally got him on line around eight, and he said Georgie was getting trashed and probably heading for permanent downtime.

Then I told Rayno all about how I outlooped my old man, but he didn't seem real buzzed about it. He said he had something cooking and couldn't meet me at Buddy's that night to talk about it, either. So we got off line, and I started another war and then went to sleep.

The snoozer said 5:25 when I woke up, and I couldn't logic how come I was awake till I started making sense out of my ears. Dad was taking apart the hinges on my door!

"Dad! You cut that out or I'll purge you clean! There won't be backups this time!"

"Try it," he growled.

I jumped out of my sleepsack, powered up, booted and—no boot. I tried again. I could get on line in my smartterm, but I couldn't port out. "I cut your cable down in the basement," he said.

I grabbed the Starfire out of my closet and zipped it inside my jumper, but before I could do the window, the door and Dad both fell in. Mom came in right behind, popped open my dresser, and started stuffing socks and underwear in a suitcase.

"Now you're fritzed!" I told Dad. "I'll *never* give you back your files!" He grabbed my arm.

"Michael, there's something I think you should see." He dragged me down to his den and pulled some bundles of old paper trash out of his desk. "These are receipts. This is what obsolete old relics like me use because we don't trust computer bookkeeping. I checked with work and the bank; everything that goes on in the computer has to be verified with paper. You can't change anything for more than twenty-four hours."

"Twenty-four *hours?*" I laughed. "Then you're still fritzed! I can still wipe you out any day, from any term in CityNet."

"I know."

Mom came into the den, carrying the suitcase and Kleenexing her eyes. "Mikey, you've got to understand that we love you, and this is for your own good." They dragged me down to the airport and stuffed me in a private Lear with a bunch of old gestapos.

•　•　•

I've had a few weeks now to get used to the Von Schlager Military Academy. They tell me I'm a bright kid and with good behavior, there's really no reason at all why I shouldn't graduate in five years. I *am* getting tired, though, of all the older cadets telling me how soft I've got it now that they've installed indoor plumbing.

Of course, I'm free to walk out any time I want. It's only three hundred miles to Fort McKenzie, where the road ends.

Sometimes at night, after lights out, I'll pull out my Starfire and run my fingers over the touchpads. That's all I can do, since they turn off power in the barracks at night. I'll lie there in the dark, thinking about Lisa, and Georgie, and Buddy's All-Night Burgers, and all the fun we used to pull off. But mostly I'll think about Rayno, and what great plans he cooks up.

I can't wait to see how he gets me out of this one.

CRAIG PADAWER

HOSTILE TAKEOVER

(1985)

AND THEN ONE NIGHT Swann's armored cars rolled into town, and the consolidation of flesh began.

They hit Ho's first, blasting their way past his sumos and into the pimp's private parlor, where his Ninja waited. But even Ho's master assassin was no match for Shimmy G's hi-tech killers with their Black & Decker implants and their five-speed rotating blades. They'd diced the Ninja like a carrot and then fed the pieces to Ho with his jade chopsticks before they finally killed him as well. Then they ground his geishas into tofu and continued north to The Hairy Clam, where they shot all the fish in Felsig's barrel. Real sportsmen, Swann's chromeheads. They stood at poolside with their telescopic eye implants and their 9 mm semiautomatic arm grafts . . . firing, reloading, and firing again, picking off patrons in the glass-bottom boats, murdering the mermaids as they tried to take cover beneath the inflatable lily pads, filling the porpoises so full of lead that they sank like submarines to the bottom of the tank.

The Clam's kitchen just happened to have run out of the house specialty at 11:00 that night and had called in an emergency order of Littlenecks to Veraciti's Seafood Supply, which had dispatched a truck immediately. They were just unloading the shellfish when Swann's goons struck. Felsig managed to slip out through the kitchen and escape in the fish king's refrigerated delivery truck accompanied by six cartons of red snapper filets, a pair of halibut hanging on hooks, and a crate of clams that chattered at him like a bundle of bones as the driver hit what seemed like every pothole between Harbor Street and the fish pier. Back at The Clam, Swann's chrome killers were snapping drill bits into their multifunction wrist sockets and boring holes in the skulls of Felsig's kitchen staff in an attempt to discover his whereabouts, as if in their mechanical naivete the overhauled imbeciles imagined that language was a liquid bottled up inside the body and any hole would decant it. In fact, the busboys had leaked as soon as they got a look at the hardware on Shimmy G's hoodlums, but the toolheads hadn't liked what they'd heard and they drilled the pimp's busboys dry, their gears seizing with rage. When that failed to produce Felsig, they burst into The Clam's plush grottoes, pried open the pimp's patented shell beds, shucked his nymphs, and minced them like mollusks. Then they blew the bottom out of the glass lagoon, drowning the diners below and flooding Harbor Street from Cod Place to Waterfront Drive.

Meanwhile, a second unit had struck at the cash gash end of Harbor Street and was moving south toward the blue-chip houses, gunning down street pimps and freelancers along the way, firebombing the budget brothels and the fast-fuck joints. They blew the lid off the Dick-in-the-Box on Eel Street, leveled the Wiener Queen, and wiped The Bun Factory right off the block. They hit the Instant Eatery on the corner of Harbor and Tuna Street, and some tax adder with her muff up against the drive-in window was divested of her assets along with the hired tongue who was delivering her Slurpy to her through the hole in the bulletproof glass.

While their counterparts to the south finished off Felsig's and moved on to The Sweat Shop, the northern unit raided The Side Show and Tufa's Club Zoo, neither of which had heavy security. The houses fell like dominoes. Swann's anti-tank missiles turned Tufa's elephants into hamburger, while what was left of the pimp's menagerie stampeded south, trampling wounded bathhouse boys and hookers hobbling along on broken heels. A small detachment of mechanical thugs remained behind to mop up the top end of Harbor Street while the northern unit's main force headed west on Oyster to take Rocheaux's office and knock out Brash, Sarsen & Scree's flagship facility. Then the troops regrouped two blocks south for an assault on The Rubber Womb.

Merkle had invested heavily in the latest weaponry and The Womb had a formidable security force, despite the mocking comments made by Merkle's colleagues. Vesuvius, who liked to boast about his own rented muscle, had once told Emma with a sneer that Merkle's inflatable bodyguards were "full of hot air."

"Hydrogen," Merkle corrected him, having overheard the remark.

"Hot air, hydrogen . . . same shit," Vito spat.

"I'm afraid you're quite mistaken. There's a definitive difference, Vito, and if you get any closer to Emile here with that vile cigar of yours, you'll discover it firsthand . . . and then foot, nose, teeth, and liver. In short, my friend, they'll be sweeping your pieces off the street."

"Pshshhhh!" Vito hissed derisively, his head snapping back as if he'd been slugged in the chin, smoke spewing from his mouth.

Merkle turned to Emma. "Good night, Ms. Labatt," he said. "You're to be commended on your tolerance, but surely a businesswoman of your caliber recognizes a profitless endeavor when she sees one." With that he wrapped his rubber scarf around his throat and slipped into the bulletproof overcoat being offered by one of his bodyguards. Then he bowed to Emma, pulled the brim of his black rubber fedora down over his brow with a squeak, and walked off flanked by four of his inflatable escorts.

"Hey, Merkle," Vesuvius had shouted after him, "fuck you, ya dumb bastard. You call that protection? They're nothing but a bunch a fuckin' balloons. That's right, fuckin' bunch a rubber scumbags with faces painted on 'em, that's all. It's like tryna stop a bullet with a goddamn condom, fer chrissake. Hey! Tell ya what, Merkle . . . I'll have my boys cut a hole in one of those balloon goons a yours and I'll wear him on my dick when I fuck your mother. How 'bout that? How's that for fuckin' protection? Hey, maybe you oughta fold one up and carry him in your wallet, cause that's all the protection they're gonna give ya."

In the end, Vito was right, not just about

Merkle's security force, but about his entire inflatable enterprise. It was a credit to the pimp's miraculous craftsmanship that his entire night-club, from floor to ceiling, from light fixtures to plumbing to windows, was nothing more than an elaborate balloon. But that sort of evanescent intricacy was only so admirable. Merkle paid the price for his genius in vulnerability. His inflatable men proved to be no match for Swann's mechanical killers. The chromeheads went through The Rubber Womb like a nail through a beach ball. Pulling steel stickpins from their copper neckties, they popped Merkle's balloon goons, and had at his dolls. Swann, who believed the penis was obsolete, an inefficient cord of meat vulnerable to viruses and vaginal bacteria, had replaced his killers' genitals with weaponry. Now the toolheads unzipped their flies, greased their barrels with balloon jelly, and rammed them up the rubber rectums of Merkle's dolls, pumping away until a twitch of pleasure in what remained of their flesh tripped their triggers, and they came in a burst of gunfire. The inflatable beauties popped like party balloons when the bullets struck, leaving their attackers clutching nothing but air and a few shreds of latex.

As johns jumped from the windows of The Womb and hoofed it up Harbor Street, Swann's clockwork killers went from room to rubber room, doing in Merkle's dolls, puncturing the air mattresses, the inflatable toilets, and the blow-up bathtubs. The air outside became so saturated with helium that Tufa's tigers sounded like tabbies as they fled down Harbor Street. Helium hissed from the inflatable walls and beams, and the nightclub began to collapse in on itself, to shrivel and fold, until finally the chrome assassins turned their flamethrowers on it, and The Womb went up with a *WHOOSH*. There was a single explosion as Merkle's hydrogen tank blew, and then it was over. All that remained of the club was a puddle of molten rubber.

Emma pushed through the bordello's revolving door and stepped out into the chaos of the street. Out on the avenue the traffic was frozen: drivers and passengers peered through their

windows. The yap schlock hawkers and the cat dog vendors had left their carts and drifted to the curb like sleepwalkers summoned in a dream. She could hear animals howling, the braying of Tufa's pornographic donkeys. And beneath that another sound, a murmur like a mechanical parody of the harbor washing against the pier.

Then the northern end of the Harbor Street seemed to explode with movement. Refugees began streaming into the square: barefoot house whores wrapped in satin sheets, queens in kimonos zigzagging down the street like enormous butterflies as they tried to dodge the bullets that went zipping by. Jailbait and babymeat were borne along on a tide of trained tigers, inflatable whores, and wounded studs dressed in the Marquis de Sade's underwear. Emma saw a chimpanzee and a pair of Gneissman's naked midgets go galloping by on one of Tufa's zebras; they turned west on Oceanside, weaving through the stalled traffic until she lost sight of them. The sound of gunfire grew closer. Bullets ricocheted off the mansion's facade. Panicky passengers left their cars and fled up the avenue on foot.

The remnants of Merkle's security force fell back along the water, pursued by Swann's goons. Emma could see the mechanical killers now. They wore titanium zoot suits and steel fedoras, and they came marching down Harbor Street looking like a fleet of tanks designed by Oleg Cassini. Some of them had machine gun assemblies built right into their skulls, and their grinning heads rotated 360 degrees as they raked the streets with gunfire. Merkle's hydrogen hoodlums went off like incendiary bombs when the slugs hit them. Those who hadn't been hit returned fire with Uzis and Street Sweepers, but the bullets didn't even put a dent in the enemy's wardrobe.

As Emma ordered her women to pull back from the street, she could see Merkle's men tossing aside their weapons, stepping out of their lead loafers, and floating up into the night sky, rising above the flaming streets like rubber angels, until the wind carried them out over the harbor. Some of them would drift for days or weeks, finally floating to earth somewhere on the coast of Greenland or Labrador, where they would vainly hunt for helium like vampires hungry for blood, until finally, sagging and emaciated, they would expire on barren bluffs, where fisherman's wives would find them, take them home, and stitch them into raincoats for their sea-haunted husbands.

Back inside the mansion, Emma threw all her security at her front door, opened up the bar, and circulated among her customers to calm them. But as Swann's first army swept up from the south, the pincer closed, trapping the fleeing whores in the square. The desperate refugees stormed the mansion seeking asylum.

Emma prayed for fog to mask the carnage and inhibit the killers, but the night remained clear and the moon burned like a bulb. From the window she could see one of Galena's Gigantic Gigolos lying dead in the street, wearing nothing but his own blood. One of his coworkers crouched over him, moving like an astronaut in the merciless moonlight, his body so bloated with muscle he was barely able to bend. Over to the south a rocket struck G.A.S.M.'s headquarters and the old building burped smoke. Tracer fire arced across the square like a flock of burning birds. The two naked giants outside Emma's window looked now like a pair of Greek heroes that had been painted onto the wrong scenery: Achilles bawling over the death of his pornographic Patroclus as Paris fell to the Germans. A passing queen paused and began tugging at the mourner's arm with one hand as she clutched the front of her kimono closed with the other, but the giant wouldn't budge. She tried again, letting go of her robe and wrapping both her arms around his biceps, but it was like trying to uproot an oak tree. And then somehow the gigolo lost his balance and tipped backward. He lay there in the gutter with his arms waving in the air, like some enormous beetle, so weighed down by his own muscle that he was unable to sit up or flip himself over. The queen flapped her arms and screamed for help, her kimono billowing behind her in the frigid wind. Her hormone-grown breasts were stunted and pale in the moonlight, her prick shaven clean as an infant's and shriveled now with fear.

A bunch of streetwalkers, ever practical, responded to the queen's distress by tugging off their whorehoppers and flinging them through the mansion's stained-glass windows in an attempt to get Emma's attention.

Hippolyta opened up the bordello's arsenal and began arming the patrons, the whores, and the housekeeping staff, then joined Emma at the window and nervously surveyed the scene. To the north, along the curve of the water, Swann's killers fired surface-to-surface missiles from their prosthetic arm launchers, and the boardwalk crumbled like a cracker in the tracer-light. Cabs burned out on the avenue, and flaming figures raced down the streets like human shish kebabs. The lobby smelled of sulfur and burning meat. Shimmy G's southern units were already on the outskirts of the square. The trapped refugees would have the option of either being driven into the frigid harbor or slaughtered in the streets.

As rocket fire began to eat up the asphalt, the blowjob boys and anal artists stormed Emma's steps. Rocheaux's brats tried to scale the fence and were impaled on the wrought iron spikes where they flapped like fish on the end of a spear and whined through the night like tortured cats. Merkle's girls also fell prey to the spikes: their corpses hung from the fence like an atman's laundry, and whores hoisted themselves up by the dolls' deflated limbs—but the bordello's windows were too high and there was nowhere for them to go. Bullets cut into the crowd. There were screams as the sea of flesh surged forward and washed up against the mansion's facade.

The cops were nowhere in sight. And for all Emma knew, these were Vito's soldiers, mail ordered from some weapons warehouse in Georgia or Tennessee and kept under wraps until the moment was right. She had no choice but to open her doors.

That night her house took on the atmosphere of a field hospital. Her boudoirs were filled with wounded whores, and all her satin sheets went for bandages. Giles was busy in the kitchen, boiling his old mechanic's tools in hot water and performing makeshift surgeries on the chrome countertops, prying slugs out of house whores with a Phillips screwdriver and a pair of needle-nose pliers, and leaving it to Hector Citrine's seamstress to sew them up. They stacked the dead in the walk-in freezer. By dawn they were almost out of shelf space.

Even one of Merkle's helium whores managed to make it to Emma's place. She was leaking, and Giles patched her up with a piece of electrical tape, then gave her mouth-to-mouth in an attempt to reinflate her. She perked up for a while, but as the night wore on her head began to wilt again, wrinkles appeared in her face and thighs, her latex tits began to shrink and droop. She seemed to be aging right before their eyes. They pumped some more air into her, but it was no good. She needed helium. Or maybe she was leaking from a hole they hadn't seen. By morning she was as flat as a floor mat. Emma wondered whether she was dead. How could you tell with a blowup doll, anyway? What vital signs did you check for? Air pressure? Surface ten-

sion? Finally they just pulled the plug on her. What was left of her helium escaped in one brief sigh. Emma thought she felt the air in the room change ever so slightly, and she held her breath for a moment, as if she were afraid that by breathing she might inhale the whore's soul. Then she folded up the girl's empty skin and tucked it away in a drawer. By that point, all she could think of was that Merkle's ingenuity had saved her a space in the freezer.

She waited all night for the attack, but it never came. Swann's troops swung west, bypassing her bordello. A couple of hours later heavy artillery could be heard from the south. It went on for a solid hour. The mansion's beams rattled in the thunder, and plaster rained down from the kitchen ceiling like confectionery sugar, powdering the whores' open wounds so that their hearts and livers looked like candied fruits. Giles called for more water while Emma provided what suction she could with a turkey baster.

Toward dawn the gunfire began to die down. Outside the blood froze in the streets, and come morning children with ice skates appeared, carving figure eights in the crimson pools.

JAMES PATRICK KELLY

RAT

(1986)

RAT HAD STASHED the dust in four plastic capsules and then swallowed them. From the stinging at the base of his ribs he guessed they were now squeezing into his duodenum. Still plenty of time. The bullet train had been shooting through the vacuum of the TransAtlantic tunnel for almost two hours now; they would arrive at Port Authority/Koch soon. Customs had already been fixed, according to the marechal. All Rat had to do was to get back to his nest, lock the smart door behind him, and put the word out on his protected nets. He had enough Algerian Yellow to dust at least half the cerebrums on the East Side. If he could turn this deal he would be rich enough to bathe in Dom Perignon and dry himself with Gromaire tapestries. Another pang shot down his left flank. Instinctively his hind leg came off the seat and scratched at air.

There was only one problem; Rat had decided to cut the marechal out. That meant he had to lose the old man's spook before he got home.

The spook had attached herself to him at Marseilles. She braided her blonde hair in pigtails. She had freckles, wore braces on her teeth. Tiny breasts nudged a modest silk turtleneck. She looked to be between twelve and fourteen. Cute. She had probably looked that way for twenty years, would stay the same another twenty if she did not stop a slug first or get cut in half by some automated security laser that tracked only heat and could not read—or be troubled by— cuteness. Their passports said they were Mr. Sterling Jaynes and daughter Jessalynn, of Forest Hills, New York. She was typing in her notebook, chubby fingers curled over the keys. Homework? A letter to a boyfriend? More likely she was operating on some corporate database with scalpel code of her own devising.

"Ne fais pas semblant d'étudier, ma petite," Rat said. *"Que fais-tu?"*

"Oh, Daddy," she said, pouting, "can't we go back to plain old English? After all, we're almost home." She tilted her notebook so that he could see the display. It read, "Two rows back, second seat from aisle. Fed. If he knew you were carrying, he'd cut the dust out of you and wipe his ass with your pelt." She tapped the return key and the message disappeared.

"All right, dear." He arched his back, fighting a surge of adrenaline that made his incisors click. "You know, all of a sudden I'm feeling hungry. Should we do something here on the train or wait until we get to New York?" Only the spook saw him gesture back toward the fed.

"Why don't we wait for the station? More choices there."

"As you wish, dear." He wanted her to take the fed out now but there was nothing more he dared say. He licked his hands nervously and groomed the fur behind his short, thick ears to pass the time.

The International Arrivals Hall at Koch Terminal was unusually quiet for a Thursday night. It smelled to Rat like a setup. The passengers from the bullet shuffled through the echoing marble vastness toward the row of customs stations. Rat was unarmed; if they were going to put up a fight the spook would have to provide the firepower. But Rat was not a fighter, he was a runner. Their instructions were to pass through Station Number Four. As they waited in line Rat spotted the federally appointed vigilante behind them. The classic invisible man: neither handsome nor ugly, five-ten, about one-seventy, brown hair, dark suit, white shirt. He looked bored.

"Do you have anything to declare?" The customs agent looked bored too. Everybody looked bored except Rat who had two million new dollars' worth of illegal drugs in his gut and a fed ready to carve them out of him.

"We hold these truths to be self-evident," said Rat, "that all men are created equal." He managed a feeble grin—as if this were a witticism and not the password.

"Daddy, please!" The spook feigned embarrassment. "I'm sorry, ma'am; it's his idea of a joke. It's the Declaration of Independence, you know."

The customs agent smiled as she tousled the spook's hair. "I know that, dear. Please put your luggage on the conveyor." She gave a perfunctory glance at her monitor as their suitcases passed through the scanner and then nodded at Rat. "Thank you, sir, and have a pleasant . . ." The insincere thought died on her lips as she noticed the fed pushing through the line toward them. Rat saw her spin toward the exit at the same moment that the spook thrust her notebook computer into the scanner. The notebook stretched a blue finger of point discharge toward the magnetic lens just before the overhead lights novaed and went dark. The emergency backup failed as well. Rat's snout filled with the acrid smell of electrical fire. Through the darkness came shouts and screams, thumps and cracks— the crazed pounding of a stampede gathering momentum.

He dropped to all fours and skittered across the floor. Koch Terminal was his territory; he had crisscrossed its many levels with scent trails. Even in total darkness he could find his way.

But in his haste he cracked his head against a pair of stockinged knees and a squawking weight fell across him, crushing the breath from his lungs. He felt an icy stab on his hindquarters and scrabbled at it with his hind leg. His toes came away wet and he squealed. There was an answering scream and the point of a shoe drove into him, propelling him across the floor. He rolled left and came up running. Up a dead escalator, down a carpeted hall. He stood upright and stretched to his full twenty-six inches, hands scratching until they found the emergency bar across the fire door. He hurled himself at it, a siren shrieked and with a whoosh the door opened, dumping him into an alley. He lay there for a moment, gasping, half in and half out of Koch Terminal. With the certain knowledge that he was bleeding to death he touched the coldness on his back. A sticky purple substance; he sniffed, then tasted it. Ice cream. Rat threw back his head and laughed. The high squeaky sound echoed in the deserted alley.

But there was no time to waste. He could already hear the buzz of police hovers swooping down from the night sky. The blackout might keep them busy for a while; Rat was more worried about the fed. And the spook. They would be out soon enough, looking for him. Rat scurried down the alley toward the street. He glanced quickly at the terminal, now a black hole in the galaxy of bright holographic sleaze that was Forty-Second Street. A few cops with flashlights were trying to fight against the flow of panicky travelers pouring from its open doors. Rat smoothed his ruffled fur and turned away from the disaster, walking crosstown. His instincts said to run but Rat forced himself to dawdle like a hick shopping for big city excitement. He grinned at the pimps and window-shopped the hardware stores. He paused in front of a pair of mirror-image sex stops—GIRLS! LIVE! GIRLS! and LIVE! GIRLS! LIVE!—to sniff the pheromone-scented sweat pouring off an androgynous robot shill which was working the sidewalk. The robot obligingly put its hand to Rat's crotch but he pushed it away with a hiss and continued on. At last, sure that he was not being followed, he powered up his wallet and tapped into the transnet to summon a hovercab. The wallet informed him that the city had cordoned off midtown airspace to facilitate rescue operations at Koch Terminal. It advised trying the subway or a taxi. Since he had no intention of sticking an ID chip—even a false one!—into a subway turnstile, he stepped to the curb and began watching the traffic.

The rebuilt Checker that rattled to a stop beside him was a patchwork of orange ABS and stainless-steel armor. "No we leave Manhattan," said a speaker on the roof light. "No we north of a hundred and ten." Rat nodded and the door locks popped. The passenger compartment smelled of chlorobenzylmalononitrile and urine.

"First Avenue Bunker," said Rat, sniffing. "Christ, it stinks back here. Who was your last fare—the circus?"

"Troubleman." The speaker connections were loose, giving a scratchy edge to the cabbie's voice. The locks reengaged as the Checker pulled away from the curb. "Ha-has get a full snoot of tear gas in this hack."

Rat had already spotted the pressure vents in the floor. He peered through the gloom at the registration. A slogan had been lased over it—probably by one of the new Mitsubishi penlights. "Free the dead." Rat smiled: the dead were his customers. People who had chosen the dusty road. Twelve to eighteen months of glorious addiction: synesthetic orgasms, recursive hallucinations leading to a total sensory overload and an ecstatic death experience. One dose was all it took to start down the dusty road. The feds were trying to cut off the supply—with dire consequences for the dead. They could live a few months longer without dust but their joyride down the dusty road was transformed into a grueling marathon of withdrawal pangs and madness. Either way, they were dead. Rat settled back onto the seat. The penlight graffito was a good omen. He reached into his pocket and pulled out a leather strip that had been soaked with a private blend of fat-soluble amphetamines and began to gnaw at it.

From time to time he could hear the cabbie monitoring NYPD net for flameouts or wildcat tolls set up by street gangs. They had to detour to heavily guarded Park Avenue all the way uptown to Fifty-Ninth before doubling back toward the bunker. Originally built to protect UN diplomats from terrorists, the bunker had gone condo after the dissolution of the United Nations. Its hype was that it was the "safest address in the city." Its rep was that most of the owners' association were prime candidates either for a mindwipe or an extended vacation on a fed punkfarm.

"Hey, Fare," said the cabbie, "Net says the dead be rioting front of your door. Crash through or roll away?"

The fur along Rat's backbone went erect. "Cops?"

"Letting them play for now."

"You've got armor for a crash?"

"Shit yes. Park this hack to ground zero for the right fare." The cabbie's laugh was static. "Don't worry, bunkerman. Give those dead-boys a shot of old CS gas and they be too busy scratching they eyes out to bother us much."

Rat tried to smooth his fur. He could crash the riot and get stuck. But if he waited either the spook or the fed would be stepping on his tail before long. Rat had no doubt that both had managed to plant locator bugs on him.

"'Course, riot crashing don't come cheap," said the cabbie.

"Triple the meter." The fare was already over two hundred dollars for the fifteen-minute ride. "Shoot for Bay Two—the one with the yellow door." He pulled out his wallet and started tapping its luminescent keys. "I'm sending recognition code now."

He heard the cabbie notify the cops that they were coming through. Rat could feel the Checker accelerate as they passed the cordon, and he had a glimpse of strobing lights, cops in blue body armor, a tank studded with water cannons. Suddenly the cabbie braked and Rat pitched forward against his shoulder harness. The Checker's solid rubber tires squealed and there was the thump of something bouncing off the hood. They had slowed to a crawl and the dead closed around them.

Rat could not see out the front because the cabbie was protected from his passengers by steel plate. But the side windows filled with faces streaming with sweat and tears and blood. Twisted faces, screaming faces, faces etched by the agonies of withdrawal. The soundproofing muffled their howls. Fear and exhilaration filled Rat as he watched them pass. If only they knew how close they were to dust, he thought. He imagined the dead faces gnawing through the cab's armor in a frenzy, pausing only to spit out broken teeth. It was wonderful. The riot was proof that the dust market was still white hot. The dead must be desperate to attack the bunker like this looking for a flash. He decided to bump the price of his dust another ten percent.

Rat heard a clatter on the roof: then someone began to jump up and down. It was like being inside a kettledrum. Rat sank claws into the seat and arched his back. "What are you waiting for? Gas them, damn it!"

"Hey, Fare. Stuff ain't cheap. We be fine—almost there."

A woman with bloody red hair matted to her head pressed her mouth against the window and screamed. Rat reared up on his hind legs and made biting feints at her. Then he saw the penlight in her hand. At the last moment Rat threw himself backward. The penlight flared and the passenger compartment filled with the stench of melting plastic. A needle of coherent light singed the fur on Rat's left flank; he squealed and flopped onto the floor, twitching.

The cabbie opened the external gas vents and abruptly the faces dropped away from the windows. The cab accelerated, bouncing as it ran over the fallen dead. There was a dazzling transition from the darkness of the violent night to the floodlit calm of Bay Number Two. Rat scrambled back onto the seat and looked out the back window in time to see the hydraulic doors of the outer lock swing shut. Something was caught between them—something that popped and spattered. Then the inner door rolled down on its track like a curtain coming down on a bloody final act.

Rat was almost home. Two security guards in armor approached. The door locks popped and Rat climbed out of the cab. One of the guards leveled a burster at his head; the other wordlessly offered him a printreader. He thumbed it and the bunker's computer verified him immediately.

"Good evening, sir," said one of the guards. "Little rough out there tonight. Did you have luggage?"

The front door of the cab opened and Rat heard the low whine of electric motors as a mechanical arm lowered the cabbie's wheelchair onto the floor of the bay. She was a gray-haired woman with a rheumy stare who looked like she belonged in a rest home in New Jersey. A knitted shawl covered her withered legs. "You said triple." The cab's hoist clicked and released the chair; she rolled toward him. "Six hundred and sixty-nine dollars."

"No luggage, no." Now that he was safe inside the bunker, Rat regretted his panic-stricken generosity. A credit transfer from one of his own accounts was out of the question. He slipped his last thousand-dollar bubble chip into his wallet's card reader, dumped three hundred and thirty-one dollars from it into a Bahamian laundry loop, and then dropped the chip into her outstretched hand. She accepted it dubiously: for a minute he expected her to bite into it like they did sometimes on fossil TV. Old people made him nervous. Instead she inserted the chip into her own card reader and frowned at him.

"How about a tip?"

Rat sniffed. "Don't pick up strangers."

One of the guards guffawed obligingly. The other pointed but Rat saw the skunk port in the wheelchair a millisecond too late. With a wet plop the chair emitted a gaseous stinkball which bloomed like an evil flower beneath Rat's whiskers. One guard tried to grab at the rear of the chair but the old cabbie backed suddenly over his foot. The other guard aimed his burster.

The cabbie smiled like a grandmother from hell. "Under the pollution index. No law against sharing a little scent, boys. And you wouldn't want to hurt me anyway. The hack monitors my EEG. I go flat and it goes berserk."

The guard with the bad foot stopped hopping. The guard with the gun shrugged. "It's up to you, sir."

Rat batted the side of his head several times and then buried his snout beneath his armpit. All he could smell was rancid burger topped with sulphur sauce. "Forget it. I haven't got time."

"You know," said the cabbie. "I never get out of the hack but I just wanted to see what kind of person would live in a place like this." The lifts whined as the arm fitted its fingers into the chair. "And now I know." She cackled as the arm gathered her back into the cab. "I'll park it by the door. The cops say they're ready to sweep the street."

The guards led Rat to the bank of elevators. He entered the one with the open door, thumbed the print reader and spoke his access code.

"Good evening, sir," said the elevator. "Will you be going straight to your rooms?"

"Yes."

"Very good, sir. Would you like a list of the communal facilities currently open to serve you?"

There was no shutting the sales pitch off so Rat ignored it and began to lick the stink from his fur.

"The pool is open for lap swimmers only," said the elevator as the doors closed. "All environmats except for the weightless room are currently in use. The sensory deprivation tanks will be occupied until eleven. The surrogatorium is temporarily out of female chassis; we apologize for any inconvenience . . ."

The cab moved down two and a half floors and then stopped just above the subbasement. Rat glanced up and saw a dark gap opening in the array of light diffuser panels. The spook dropped through it.

". . . the holo therapist is off line until eight tomorrow morning but the interactive sex booths will stay open until midnight. The drug dispensary . . ."

She looked as if she had been water-skiing through the sewer. Her blonde hair was wet and smeared with dirt; she had lost the ribbons from her pigtails. Her jeans were torn at the knees and there was an ugly scrape on the side of her face. The silk turtleneck clung wetly to her. Yet despite her dishevelment, the hand that held the penlight was as steady as a jewel cutter's.

"There seems to be a minor problem," said the elevator in a soothing voice. "There is no cause for alarm. This unit is temporarily nonfunctional. Maintenance has been notified and is now working to correct the problem. In case of emergency, please contact Security. We regret this temporary inconvenience."

The spook fired a burst of light at the floor selector panel; it spat fire at them and went dark.

"Where the hell were you?" said the spook. "You said the McDonald's in Times Square if we got separated."

"Where were you?" Rat rose up on his hind legs. "When I got there the place was swarming with cops."

He froze as the tip of the penlight flared. The spook traced a rough outline of Rat on the stainless-steel door behind him. "Fuck your lies," she said. The beam came so close that Rat could smell his fur curling away from it. "I want the dust."

"Trespass alert!" screeched the wounded elevator. A note of urgency had crept into its artificial voice. "Security reports unauthorized persons within the complex. Residents are urged to return immediately to their apartments and engage all personal security devices. Do not be alarmed. We regret this temporary inconvenience."

The scales on Rat's tail fluffed. "We have a deal. The marechal needs my networks to move his product. So let's get out of here before . . ."

"The dust."

Rat sprung at her with a squeal of hatred. His claws caught on her turtleneck and he struck repeatedly at her open collar, gashing her neck with his long red incisors. Taken aback by the swiftness and ferocity of his attack, she dropped the penlight and tried to fling him against the wall. He held fast, worrying at her and chittering rabidly. When she stumbled under the open emergency exit in the ceiling he leapt again. He cleared the suspended ceiling, caught himself on the inductor and scrabbled up onto the hoist cables. Light was pouring into the shaft from above; armored guards had forced the door open and were climbing down toward the stalled car. Rat jumped from the cables across five feet of open space to the counterweight and huddled there, trying to use its bulk to shield himself from the spook's fire. Her stand was short and inglorious. She threw a dazzler out of the hatch, hoping to blind the guards, then tried to pull herself through. Rat could hear the shriek of burster fire. He waited until he could smell the aroma of broiling meat and scorched plastic before he emerged from the shadows and signaled to the security team.

A squad of apologetic guards rode the service elevator with Rat down to the storage subbasement where he lived. When he had first looked at the bunker, the broker had been reluctant to rent him the abandoned rooms, insisting that he live above ground with the other residents. But all of the suites they showed him were unacceptably open, clean and uncluttered. Rat much preferred his musty dungeon, where odors lingered in the still air. He liked to fall asleep to the booming of the ventilation system on the level above him and slept easier knowing that he was as far away from the stink of other people as he could get in the city.

The guards escorted him to the gleaming brass smart door and looked away discreetly as he entered his passcode on the keypad. He had ordered it custom-built from Mosler so that it would recognize high-frequency squeals well beyond the range of human hearing. He called to it and then pressed trembling fingers onto the printreader. His bowels had loosened in terror during the firefight and the capsules had begun to sting terribly. It was all he could do to keep from defecating right there in the hallway. The door sensed the guards and beeped to warn him of their presence. He punched in the override sequence impatiently and the seals broke with a sigh.

"Have a pleasant evening, sir," said one of the guards as he scurried inside. "And don't worry ab . . ." The door cut him off as it swung shut.

Against all odds, Rat had made it. For a moment he stood, tail switching against the inside of the door, and let the magnificent chaos of his apartment soothe his jangled nerves. He had earned his reward—the dust was all his now. No one could take it away from him. He saw himself in a shard of mirror propped up against an empty THC aerosol and wriggled in self-congratulation. He was the richest rat on the East Side, perhaps in the entire city.

He picked his way through a maze formed

by a jumble of overburdened steel shelving left behind years, perhaps decades, ago. The managers of the bunker had offered to remove them and their contents before he moved in; Rat had insisted that they stay. When the fire inspector had come to approve his newly installed sprinkler system she had been horrified at the clutter on the shelves and had threatened to condemn the place. It had cost him plenty to buy her off but it had been worth it. Since then Rat's trove of junk had at least doubled in size. For years no one had seen it but Rat and the occasional cockroach.

Relaxing at last, Rat stopped to pull a mildewed wingtip down from his huge collection of shoes; he loved the bouquet of fine old leather and gnawed it whenever he could. Next to the shoes was a heap of books: his private library. One of Rat's favorite delicacies was the first edition *Leaves of Grass* which he had pilfered from the rare book collection at the New York Public Library. To celebrate his safe arrival he ripped out page 43 for a snack and stuffed it into the wingtip. He dragged the shoe over a pile of broken sheetrock and past shelves filled with scrap electronics: shattered monitors and dead typewriters, microwaves and robot vacuums. He had almost reached his nest when the fed stepped from behind a dirty Hungarian flag that hung from a broken florescent light fixture.

Startled, Rat instinctively hurled himself at the crack in the wall where he had built his nest. But the fed was too quick. Rat did not recognize the weapon; all he knew was that when it hissed Rat lost all feeling in his hindquarters. He landed in a heap but continued to crawl, slowly, painfully.

"You have something I want." The fed kicked him. Rat skidded across the concrete floor toward the crack, leaving a thin gruel of excrement in his wake. Rat continued to crawl until the fed stepped on his tail, pinning him.

"Where's the dust?"

"I . . . I don't . . ."

The fed stepped again; Rat's left fibula snapped like cheap plastic. He felt no pain.

"The dust." The fed's voice quavered strangely.

"Not here. Too dangerous."

"Where?" The fed released him. "Where?"

Rat was surprised to see that the fed's gun hand was shaking. For the first time he looked up at the man's eyes and recognized the telltale yellow tint. Rat realized then how badly he had misinterpreted the fed's expression back at Koch. Not bored. Empty. For an instant he could not believe his extraordinarily good fortune. Bargain for time, he told himself. There's still a chance. Even though he was cornered he knew his instinct to fight was wrong.

"I can get it for you fast if you let me go," said Rat. "Ten minutes, fifteen. You look like you need it."

"What are you talking about?" The fed's bravado started to crumble and Rat knew he had the man. The fed wanted the dust for himself. He was one of the dead.

"Don't make it hard on yourself," said Rat. "There's a terminal in my nest. By the crack. Ten minutes." He started to pull himself toward the nest. He knew the fed would not dare stop him; the man was already deep into withdrawal. "Only ten minutes and you can have all the dust you want." The poor fool could not hope to fight the flood of neuroregulators pumping crazily across his synapses. He might break any minute, let his weapon slip from trembling hands. Rat reached the crack and scrambled through into comforting darkness.

The nest was built around a century-old shopping cart and a stripped subway bench. Rat had filled the gaps in with pieces of synthetic rubber, a hubcap, plastic greeting cards, barbed wire, disk casings, baggies, a No Parking sign and an assortment of bones. Rat climbed in and lowered himself onto the soft bed of shredded thousand-dollar bills. The profits of six years of deals and betrayals, a few dozen murders and several thousand dusty deaths.

The fed sniffled as Rat powered up his terminal to notify security. "Someone set me up some vicious bastard slipped it to me I don't know when I think it was Barcelona . . . it would kill Sarah to see . . ." He began to weep. "I wanted to turn myself in . . . they keep working on new treatments you know but it's not fair damn it! The success rate is less than . . . I made my first buy two weeks only two God it seems . . . killed a man to get some lousy dust . . . but they're right it's, it's, I can't begin to describe what it's like . . ."

Rat's fingers flew over the glowing keyboard, describing his situation, the layout of the rooms, a strategy for the assault. He had overriden the smart door's recognition sequence. It would be tricky but security could take the fed out if they were quick and careful. Better to risk a surprise attack than to dicker with an armed and unraveling dead man.

"I really ought to kill myself . . . would be best but it's not only me . . . I've seen ten-year-olds . . . what kind of animal sells dust to kids . . . I should kill myself. And you." Something changed in the fed's voice as Rat signed off. "And you." He stooped and reached through the crack.

"It's coming," said Rat quickly. "By messenger. Ten doses. By the time you get to the door it should be here." He could see the fed's hand and burrowed into the rotting pile of money.

"You wait by the door, you hear? It's coming any minute."

"I don't want it." The hand was so large it blocked the light. Rat's fur went erect and he arched his spine. "Keep your fucking dust."

Rat could hear the guards fighting their way through the clutter. Shelves crashed. So clumsy, these men.

"It's you I want." The hand sifted through the shredded bills, searching for Rat. He had no doubt that the fed could crush the life from him—the hand was huge now. In the darkness he could count the lines on the palm, follow the whorls on the fingertips. They seemed to spin in Rat's brain—he was losing control. He realized then that one of the capsules must have broken, spilling a megadose of first-quality Algerian Yellow dust into his gut. With a hallucinatory clarity he imagined sparks streaming through his blood, igniting neurons like tinder. Suddenly the guards did not matter. Nothing mattered except that he was cornered. When he could no longer fight the instinct to strike, the fed's hand closed around him. The man was stronger than Rat could have imagined. As the fed hauled him—clawing and biting—back into the light, Rat's only thought was of how terrifyingly large a man was. So much larger than a rat.

LISA MASON

ARACHNE

(1987)

THE FLIER LEVITATES from a vermilion funnel and hovers. Stiff chatoyant wings, monocoque fuselage, compound visual apparatus. The flier skims over the variegated planetscape, seeking another spore source. Olfactory sensors switch on. The desired stimuli are detected; another spore source is located.

Down the flier dips. But the descent is disrupted for a moment by atmospheric turbulence. The flier's fine landing gear is swept against a translucent aerial line, as strong as steel and sticky with glue. A beating wing tangles in more lines. The flier writhes.

The trapper hulks at the edge of the net. Stalked eyebuds swivel, pedipalps tense. At the tug of the flier's struggler, the trapper scuttles down a suspended line, eight appendages gripping the spacerope with acrobatic agility. The trapper spits an arc of glue over the flier's wings, guides the fiber around the flier's slim waist. A pair of black slicers dripping with goo snap around the flier's neck.

• • •

Carly Quester struggles out of the swoon. Blackout smears across the crisp white cube of her telelink like a splash of ash rain down a window. It's happened again. Her system crashes for a monstrous second, she plunges into deep, black nothing. Then, inexplicably, she's in link again, hanging like a child on a spinning swing to a vertiginous interface with the Venue.

Panic snaps at her. How many seconds lost this time?

"We will now hear *Martino v. Quik Slip Microship, Inc.*," announces the Arbiter. Edges of his telelink gleam like razor blades. His presence in the Venue, a massive face draped in black, towers like an Easter Island godhead into the upper perimeter of telespace. The perimeter is a flat, gray cloudbank.

"On what theory does Quik Slip Microchip counterclaim to quiet title when Rosa Martino has been titleholder to the *Wordsport Glossary* for thirty-five years? Mediator for defendant? Ms. Quester?"

Carly hears her name—muffled, tinny—through the neckjack. Her answer jams in her throat. Weird, she shouldn't feel her body in link. For an eerie second she feels like she's *inside* the telelink, sweating and heaving inside the airless, computer-constructed telespace itself. Her body, hunched over the terminal in her windowless cubicle at Ava & Rice, wrapped up in a web of wires, mutters a curse.

But her presence in the Venue is struck dumb.

Gleeful static from the two scruffy solos representing the plaintiff, Martino. Carly can hear them ripple with excitement, killers closing in on their prey.

Of course, they're on contingency, and old lady Martino probably couldn't even scare up the filing fees. One of them, a weasely hack, shrugs at the whirring seconds on the chronograph and says, "Not defaulting on your crooked counterclaim, are ya, hotshot?"

"Mediator for defense? The mediator from Ava and Rice? *Ms. Quester?*" thunders the Arbiter. "You have thirty seconds to log in your counterclaim."

Telelinks of the jury, two rows of red-veined, glassy eyes floating across the purple right perimeter of the Venue, glance doubtfully at each other. The silvery pupils dart to and fro.

Gritty bile bites at the base of Carly's throat. A peculiar ache throbs in her jaw, thrusts icy fingers into her neck. She tries audio again, but her presence in the Venue is still silent.

"Huh, hotshot?" goads the solo. His telelink has the sloppy look and gravelly sound cheap equipment produces. But for a second, he manages to hot-wire an I-only access into her telelink.

"You ball-breakers from the big firms, with your prime link. You think you're so tough. Watch out, hotshot. I'm going to eat you alive this time, hotshot."

The big board across the back perimeter of the Venue hums and clicks. Gaudy liquid crystal projections in each division indicate the

moment. In Stats, the luminous red Beijing dial registers another three hundred thousand births. *Chik-chik-chik-chik!* Ten seconds later on Docket—*bing!*—the eminent mediation firm of Ava & Rice registers as defense for Pop Pharmaceutical against the Chinese women who claim they took glucose, instead of birth control pills. In Trade, bids for rice futures soar. On News, reports of fifteen suicides of corn investors are filed.

"In ten seconds your client will have defaulted, Ms. Quester, and I will cite you for contempt of this Venue—obstructing the speedy dispensation of justice," says the Arbiter.

"I'm sorry, Your Honor, request a recess," Carly says finally. Audio feeds back with an earsplitting whine.

Her telelink suddenly oscillates crazily, sharp white edges flipping black-white-purple-white, like her terminal's shorting out. It's all she can do to keep logged in. Metallic tickle—pain of electrical shock gooses her body to raise a limp hand and refocus the projection.

"On what grounds?" demands the Arbiter.

"I'm—I'm sick."

Jagged flash; the Arbiter's gavel cracks; telespace vibrates. "Mediation recessed until next week, this same time. Ms. Quester, you will approach the bench."

As Carly approaches, the solo zooms in with one last I-only. "Hey hotshot, hotshot," he says in a cushy vibe. "You new, right? A word to the wise, hotshot. The Arbiter, he hates to wait. Got a reputation for the fastest Venue in town. He disposes sixty mediations an hour sometimes. You hold him up, hotshot, you in trouble. Better talk fast, better have a rap. I'll see you in the Venue, hotshot."

The solo logs off, extinguishing the smeary bulb of his presence in telespace.

Fully in link at last, Carly slips and slides up to the Arbiter's quarters. No privacy in the gleaming metal construct of telespace; no shadowed corner, no hidden booth behind which to hide her humiliation. All the blank eyes stare at her.

"Ms. Quester, you are hereby cited under Rule Two of the Code of Civil Procedure for obstruction of the speedy dispensation of justice. You are suspended from this Venue for thirty days."

Thirty days. Thirty days suspended from the Venue could cost Carly her first job, a *great* job, with the prosperous mediation firm of Ava & Rice. How many other bright, qualified applicants did she beat out for this job? Three thousand? How many other bright, qualified applicants would vie for her position if she lost it? Ten thousand?

Her presence in the Venue sparkles with bright panic. "I'm permitted to show reasonable cause under Rule Two, Your Honor."

"Proceed."

"I blacked out for a second, I've not been well . . ."

"If the mediator cannot prepare the mediation you extend, you re-petition, you re-calendar, you notify the Venue, Ms. Quester, in advance. Dismissed."

"But, Your Honor, I had no warning. I just went down for a second, no warning at all. I've not been well, it's true, but not so bad as to keep me out of the Venue. Your Honor, I had no warning, please believe me."

The Arbiter's eyeball zooms in on her flickering link for a close-up. His glittering pupil pulses with his plain doubt. "You've not been well but not so bad, but your system went down. All of a sudden! Oh, yes! You young wires, holding up my Venue with your lame excuses. I know why link fails most of the time. I should cite you for abuse of altering substances, too."

Carly's teeth begin to chatter; a puddle of urine floods her plastic seat. Then a fouler, hotter wash of shame. During her first link fifteen years ago, her ten-year-old body had disgraced her like this, in the presence of two hundred other link-prep students. She feels her body stress out at the memory of her juvenile dishonor. Her presence in the Venue vacillates.

"I'm not on drugs, Your Honor. I'm ill, I tell you, it's something insidious striking without warning. It could be cancer or radiation poisoning."

"Or the flu? Or a hangover? Or the disposal ate your brief?"

The Venue quivers with pitiless laughter from scores of unseen throats. The spectacle of a peer's downfall is cause for rejoicing.

"Your Honor, request permission to enter medical documentation to establish reasonable cause."

"Oh, very well, you're new. Permission granted, Ms. Quester. Submit your documentation before your next mediation date. This Venue will now hear *Sing Tao Development v. Homeowners' Association of Death Valley*. Issue is breach of warranty under federal standards governing the relocation of low-income housing into public parkland. Mediation for the defense?"

A team from Ava & Rice logs into the Venue with a brilliantly constructed defense. A silver spiral twirls across telespace, frosty tail ejecting wisps of pale yellow sophisms into its own blue-lipped devouring mouth. Standards met under the extraordinary circumstances of the relocation *or* standards not applicable under the extraordinary circumstances of the relocation; thus, in either case, no breach. Mediation for plaintiff withdraws the complaint in two seconds. Screams of outrage and despair whistle through the public telespace. Someone logs in a whimpering five-year-old child dying of third-degree sunburns. The Arbiter's gavel booms like doom. Dismissed! In one second the homeowners' association files suit against its former mediator. *Teep!* On Docket, Ava & Rice registers as new mediation in the malpractice suit brought by the Homeowners' Association of Death Valley.

Carly logs out of telespace.

And links out into a heap of flesh and ooze, sprawled in her windowless cubicle at Ava & Rice. Blown it, she's blown the mediation bad. Every first-year mediator's nightmare come true. Carly rips the neckjack out, spills half a bottle of denatured alcohol into the needle-thin aperture. Grimaces as a tincture of pure alcohol bursts into her brain's blood. Messy, careless—shit! Get too much of that old evil backrub up your linkslit—bang!—you're dead, grunt. Happens every now and again around the firm, someone just drops dead.

She swabs herself off as best she can and flees her dim cubicle, link still flickering with fluorescent green light. Jogs down the endless corridor of cubicles, working off panic with sheer locomotion.

The mediation firm of Ava & Rice boasts five hundred partners, three thousand associates, one thousand secretaries, five hundred clerk-messengers, and ten thousand terminals interfaced with a mammoth sengine, all installed in a forty-story building downtown.

At every open door, the limp body of a mediator is wired up to a terminal. Some are as wasted as junkies, rolled-back eyes between precipitous skull bones. Some are bloated with the sloth, raw lips crusty with food solutions piped down their throats.

Everyone's got a different handle on practicing mediation, but the basics are the same. *Time is of the essence. When in doubt, dispute. When in the Venue, win.* The volume of mediation is astronomical. Planning for the future becomes obsolete overnight. Catastrophe strikes with regularity. Billions of bucks are to be made, and you'd better grab them before someone else does.

How many bright, qualified applicants would vie for Carly's position when the personnel committee finds out about her failure in the Venue? Fifteen thousand?

• • •

Deep in the heart of Ava & Rice, the library hums with a low, soft growl like the roll of a distant surf. The vast, shadowed hall is set with fluorescent amber terminals, stacked row upon row, up to the flat, smeary ceiling.

Before every flickering screen lies a mediator jacked into link. The steady hum comes from the controls: temperature, humidity, luminos-ity, radiation. All for the machines. The air in the library is cool, stagnant, tinged with a faint metallic stench. The hum gnaws at the nerves.

The big board across the library's west wall flashes like an arcade. Down from thirty state Venues shoot twenty thousand decisions on whether foreign assets may be frozen when national property is seized by revolutionaries. *Define revolutionaries. Zing!* The government freezes five billion bank accounts and deposits their funds into a slushy umber escrow. Specialists in these matters, jacked into library links for as long as they can stand it, loll on their benches, moan listlessly. Flecks of data crawl across their raw neuroprograms like ants on meat.

Carly sneaks in, slipping through a sullen crew hanging around the doorway. She leans against the cool, grimy wall, shrinking from everyone's sight. News travels fast; surely everyone knows of her disgrace. The doorway gang is skin-popping scag—anything to ease away the whine of link.

"So, Quester," says an associate from the Death Valley team. Cool cannibal gaze, supercilious link-bitten smile. "Arbiter suspend you? Too bad. Maybe you can get a job in research somewhere. Process mediation data all day."

"You wish, Rox," Carly says in a steady voice, but she cringes from the dead-eyed faces that turn toward her. "Arbiter won't suspend me. I must have a bug in my link. I can prove it."

"Sure, Quester. We saw. We all saw your link in the Venue. We don't fault you, Quester. Blackout in link, it can happen." Rox tips her head back, cracking her neck cord, and snorts a hotline. She drools as the drug hits her, spittle staining the ragged three-piece suit that fits her like a man's. "But if you can't handle link, Quester, don't go into the life."

Carly seizes Rox's wrist, thrusts it back, pins it at an odd angle. "Rox, I'm telling you, I'm not on a binge. Something's wrong, my system went down—"

"Yeah, doll, your system went down. And then?"

Carly turns. From the double bar on his

ragged lapel, he's a middle-level. From his desperate look, not on the fast track. But not as bad as the menopausal ones can be in this business, with their cold killer eyes and vampire skin. This one's got a ripple of muscles under the suit, a shot of hots in the look he gives her. Carly rolls her pupils back into her eye-sockets, scans the firm's roster, IDs him: *Wolfe, D.*

"And then nothing," she says, shaking her eyeballs down. *"Nothing."*

"Visuals?"

"Visuals, maybe. Yeah. Hallucinations." Carly shivers. "But they fade so fast, like a nightmare. Something . . . *crawling.* I don't know. I can't remember."

"You're burned out, doll," says Wolfe. "You're losing your program, loosening it up much too soon. You're too young for this, doll. But don't worry. I know what you need."

"Yeah?"

"Losing link like that? Just a little cram. Cram will put you right." Wolfe moves closer. Scent like burned rubber and cinnamon spills off him.

Carly flinches. "Cram's illegal."

"Oh, but it gets you there. Gets you there easy, just in time for your next appearance in the Venue. You *need* that appearance, doll."

"You're crazy. I could get decertified for cramming in Venue."

"Gets you in link like nothing else."

"No way."

"The only way, doll. You're in trouble, don't you know?" Wolfe's hand on her hipbone now. Wolfe breathing the words into her ear. "Come on, don't you know what everyone's saying? Lose a diddly-shit mediation like *Martino v. Quik Slip Microchip,* you're out. And when you're out . . . ever been on the streets?"

No, but she's seen the devastation. "But how."

"I can get it."

"For godsakes, I just got out of school. How much?"

"Oh—" Wolfe grins, teeth clacking as a tic twists his lean face—"you'll have something to make it worth my while."

. . .

The medcenter sengine says Carly is healthy. No treacherous disease. No tissue attrition. Then Probers slide their needles through her telespace, insinuate steel tips into her neuroprogram.

Her right perimeter glistens with logical thought, the tan floor of her telespace supports weighty principles. Even the dull black monolith of tough, crisscrossed strands of inhibition that extends across Carly's left perimeter looks like a fortress. A woven steel wall.

Nothing amiss.

"Then what is it?" Carly pleads. "I'm crashing every other day. *What is it?*"

"A stitch in your left perimeter must be loose," says the sengine. "Oh, I know. Looks like it's sewn up tight. But I don't know what else to diagnose. You've got a leak of unregulated neurality into your telelink. Hence this program failure. The weird hallucinations. But I can't say where or how it could happen."

"Then my program guarantee from mediation school is worthless."

"Yes," says the sengine with, Carly thinks, evil satisfaction. There are rumors some artificial intelligences are jealous of the human condition. Envious of intelligence beyond program.

"Ah." A strange sadness wells up in her. "Do you know I still remember the left perimeter? How it used to be? My programmer in elementary school. My first crude telelink. Do you know I once saw blue jungles and green oceans? Oh, and gold castles and scarlet gardens. And then the thick, black stitches of inhibition wove up and down. Stabbing. Slicing off the left side of my telespace. And the colors and beauty faded. Faded to nothing."

"Well!" The sengine has no answer for that. "I'll have to suspend your limitation certificate, Ms. Quester," says the sengine briskly. "The Venue will not link mediators with loose perimeters. Much too dangerous. All that raw unconscious energy seeping into telespace? No, you can't go to the Venue, Ms. Quester. Not like this."

"But what can I do? There must be something I can do!"

"Your school will reprogram you at a reduced tuition."

"But that'll take another three years of standard programming!"

"Maybe longer. Deleting an old, flawed program, installing another, that can be tricky business."

And she would lose her job at Ava & Rice. She would lose everything she'd worked for. Carly weeps, frothy waterfalls of grief spilling across her telelink.

"All right, listen, there *is* another way," the sengine says with surprising kindness. "It's expensive, risky. Doesn't always work. Doesn't always stick when it *does* work. But I'm sorry for you, Ms. Quester. I'm not programmed to ruin biologicals. I can refer you to a perimeter prober. This one's got full medical certification. If the prober can find the loose stitch, the defect can be rewoven. You'll be good as new. Recertifiable, too."

"What's the risk?" Carly asks.

"The perimeter prober may not find the loose stitch, and you'll have to get wiped and reprogrammed," says the sengine cautiously. "Or the prober will find it, all right, but you won't endure the psychic pain. It'll wipe you in another way."

"Okay, so how long? How long will the probe take?"

"Three probes. If the prober can't find the defect in three attempts, it can't be found, not without serious neural damage. I can't recertify you then. You'll just have to go back for reprogramming."

"But three probes. I could be cured in *three* probes?"

"Yes."

Carly jumps at the chance. She takes a jet-copter west over brooding slums, ticky-tacky high rises, dilapidated factories that crouch on the banks of the sluggish Metro River. For some reason the perimeter prober isn't accessed into standard telespace. Carly has got to get herself *physically* to the prober's office. Rather a shady state of affairs, not to mention the costly commute, the waste of time spent transporting the body. Carly pops a viddeck from her briefcase, jacks into a sitcom. Anything to ease the pain of link.

• • •

"And you've never injected cram, is that so, Carly Quester?" asks the prober. Her synthy voice sounds like an antique phonograph record left too many dusty decades in an attic.

"No, never, that is correct, Prober Spinner." Carly eyes the disheveled robot. Medically certified, indeed. Prober Spinner is crudely articulated, torso and arms, then mobilized from a boxlike locomotor. Faceplace of an oldish care-worn woman.

The faceplace must have been intended to evoke empathy and trust, but Prober Spinner's bleary eyespots glare at Carly with an enmity approaching fury.

Carly shifts uncomfortably. The prober's office is tucked amid birth 'n' abort clinics, drug-drag therapists, dentists on the muni dole into the corner of a shabby medical building on the south side of town. The place reeks. Scabby plants abound. An aquarium, filthy with dull green scum, bubbles with a school of dingy fish. The floor is dabbled with viscous white spots. Then Carly spots a flock of ugly little sparrows perched atop a crumbling bookcase.

An organic feline does chin-ups on the arm of a ragged couch; then the cat stalks past her, stinking of fur, flops on its skinny cat ass, and bites at its flea-bitten haunch. *Jeez, bugs.* Carly considers her robopet, a Chatty Catty Deluxe with three pop-in eye colors and two slip-on breeds, with new appreciation.

"This is charming."

The prober is flipping through Carly's file, humming a popular tune with awful two-part harmony. "Hm? The décor? Oh, yes. You mean *for a robot.*" The eyespots stare, accusation flickering across the crone's faceplace.

"I didn't say that, Prober Spinner."

"But that's what you *mean*, eh, Carly Quester? I know your kind. I know what you mean. Why should a robot keep biologicals around? Eh? Why should a tin can with dual disk drives keep *life* around? And worthless life at that, that's what you're thinking, eh?"

"Prober Spinner, please. I meant no offense."

"I'll *tell* you why. Because I have *respect* for life, Carly Quester. There are mysteries, there are unknown presences in biological intelligence, there are myths and secrets." Prober Spinner's voicetape begins to rattle and wheeze. "No, but you could never understand that, could you?"

"Prober Spinner, please." Carly says sharply. "I came for your help. Can you help me?"

"Oh, yes. Oh, certainly." Prober Spinner wheels over, takes Carly's face between the cool aluminum spindles of her robot fingers. The fingers feel like claws—needle-slim, alien appendages against Carly's skin. "Yes, soft. Like fruit. Like a berry, so soft with fine down. Well, Carly Quester." The prober briskly releases her. "It's like this. We'll go into link, you and I, and I will probe the perimeter blocking your unconscious mind. They stitched it shut, you know; only controllable thought can be permitted into telespace. That's why my telelink isn't accessed to public space. If I can uncover this defect in your left perimeter, all sorts of unconscious energy—oh, demons, Carly Quester, strange and terrible things—could come out. Could manifest right into telespace."

"And what happens when these demons manifest into your little telespace, Prober?"

"I can control them, don't you worry. I can push them back and stitch the defect shut. I'm a robot, you see. The mysteries of biological intelligence may fascinate me, but they can't hold power over me. Not like they can possess *you.*"

"Possess me, Prober Spinner?"

"Oh, yes. Oh, certainly. You're in the grip of an unconscious force now, yes, right now. But you can't see its form. It's hiding."

"Hiding?"

"Inside your blackouts."

The truth of the prober's assertion pierces Carly. What *is* the demon that lurks in the nameless visions? Does she really want to know? Carly considers walking out. She considers her Venue recertification. She stays.

And she and the prober jack into link. Telespace there is unfocused, hazy. Goddamn cheap equipment. Spires of silver mist rise and twist from Carly's immaculate tan floor.

"I'm ready for the probe, Prober," says Carly. To her satisfaction, she notes that her presence, even in this link, is still a crisp, white cube.

"All right, Carly Quester," says Prober Spinner. The prober's presence in link is a brown cone the size of a Japanese jasmine incense that skitters across the undulating telespace like some verminous thing.

The cone angles its way across the immaculate woven wall of Carly's left perimeter. Tilts its tip in. Digs into the neat crisscrosses of inhibition. Jams there. Digs and digs.

Carly moans.

A crackling black mass leaps from the wall, vaults across telespace in frantic, jolting bounds. Gripped with dread, Carly shrinks from it, scurrying back into the abacus set across her right perimeter. But the prober flies at her flank, driving her with the sharp conetip to confront the black mass.

It leaps about crazily, a living shard of black glass that stretches and shifts, stinks of sulfur and fresh human blood.

"Is this a blackout, Carly?" asks Prober Spinner.

"No . . . no."

"Then, what? What is it? What do you see?"

A face appears inside the black glass. An old woman, her eyes pulled down with sickness and sorrow, frail, gray haired, utterly vulnerable. "Joe worked on it for fifteen years, you know, in the garage, on a tenth-hand computer," says Rosa Marino in a trembling voice. " 'Rosa,' he'd say, 'we'll be rich. We'll be rich, and then I'll get roses, a whole garden full of roses for my Rosa.'

But that was long ago, when we were so young, so strong. When he was done, you know, he took it to the company. He *knew* he could sell it to the company because he'd worked for the company as a splicer for twenty years."

Sinister shimmer beside her, like a knife blade.

"But those people, the researchers at the company, they said they weren't interested. They said the company didn't need Joe's *Word-sport Glossary*. They said no. It broke his will to live. Broke his heart, you know. He dropped dead two days after his fiftieth birthday, heart attack. Oh, there was a small payout, a small pension, some insurance. But the money never could pay for what they did to my Joe. What they were about to do.

"Then I got sick, Social Security went broke for good, and the money, I don't know where the money went. And my daughter Luisa, she's bringing up her Dan, such a smart boy, Danny, he should go to school. But Luisa gets laid off, she can't pay the school tax, and that lousy bastard of a father won't cough up, not even for his own son, and then he leaves my Luisa. I suppose it was just as well. But the money's gone, I got a little left from the payout, and I won't let those lousy mediators touch *that*."

Into the jolting black mass rolls the slick circular emblem of Quik Slip Microchip. Pointed teeth gleam in anonymous smiles. Smiles harden into black crescents, shiny black insect-like claws. The claws snap at the old lady. She flutters her hands in despair, tries to escape.

But she's trapped.

"It was my Dan, my little Danny," says Rosa Martino, "who said, 'Granma, they're using Granpa's glossary. I saw the glossary they taught me at school before. Granma, *you* showed me.' That company had been selling my Joe's *Word-sport Glossary* to millions, oh, ten million elementary schools. They just took it, made money off it, twenty years. And how was I to know? Luisa was out of elementary school, Danny not yet in, for all that time. How could I know?"

The greedy claws pop like snapping fingers, pinch off pieces of Rosa Martino's weeping face.

"That company made five hundred million dollars off Joe's work, his own work that he loved," screams Rosa Martino. "Can you imagine so much money? And I don't want all of it, I'm not asking for all of it. Just a little bit, a little percentage royalty that's rightfully Joe's. Rightfully mine. So Luisa and Dan, my little Danny, don't have to be so poor."

The claws rip the old lady to shreds, stuff chunks of her cheeks into a smiling, munching mouth. Quik Slip Microchip burps.

"I'm sorry," yells Carly. "I'm sorry, I didn't know, I'm sorry!"

The glassy black mass spins away, ricochets off her left perimeter, speeds into the infinite gleam of rationalization.

Then suddenly Carly slams out of link, seated with Prober Spinner in the prober's grimy office before the telelink console.

Her face is drenched in tears. She shakes uncontrollably.

"Calm yourself, Carly Quester," says Prober Spinner mildly. "A little guilt never hurt anyone. Glad to see you haven't sealed all of your ethics behind that damned left perimeter."

"It's just a job," whispers Carly. "I'm just doing my job."

She swallows the tranquilizer Prober Spinner offers. "Just doing your job, shit," says the prober. "Stop anytime you want to. Change your life anytime you want to."

"But I can't. How can I?"

"Do something else."

"I don't know what else to do. I've been programmed. What else can I do?"

"Oh, perhaps we shall see," says Prober Spinner. "There's a hell of lot more work we've got to do. We still haven't found a blackout."

• • •

D. Wolfe lies back in the bed, stretches out his arms in a hug to be filled. "Come here, Carlique." He's flushed and glittery-eyed from the cocaine he's just snorted.

Three syringes of cram lie neatly wrapped on the bed table. The price: one thousand in cash, plus a roll on the bed. *All right, just one,* Carly thinks. He doesn't seem so bad, and she knows three hits of cram, which is what he's offering, which could get her through ten telelinks or more, could be three times the bankroll he wants, and who knows how many bedrolls with a stranger.

Dim light softens his lean-mean features. Not so bad at all, with shadows smoothing his tough look, making his eyes seem lonely. But for the way he abuses himself, he wears his middle age well.

Carly sheds her suit, suddenly full of flirt, moved to entice him. But Wolfe doesn't watch her. He's busy with the coke again.

"Come here, Carlique," he says when he's done.

She goes to him, twines around him, gives him her heat. He directs her. Touch here, kiss there, move this way, turn that. He takes his pleasure quickly and withdraws, falling back on the bed, reaching now for whiskey to cut the ragged end of his high.

But he touched her. She forgot how long it's been since she's been touched. Painful longing grips her. Carly turns to him, tries to stroke him, but he waves her away, hand held up like a stop sign, keeping her touch away.

"Wolfe."

"Leave me alone."

"But, Wolfe."

"My head is killing me."

Carly sits up, lights a cigarette, then takes a syringe of cram from the bed table, fingers it curiously.

"I want to thank you for this."

"*Thank* me?" He laughs, bitter bark of a laugh, then guzzles whiskey. "Wait till you take cram. Then thank me, if you can."

"I thought you said I need it. Thought you said it'll focus me in link."

"Sure. Does. Focuses you in link by narrowing your focus. Eliminates self-doubt, inner challenges, the slightest reservation you may have about what you're doing, why you're doing it. Glosses glitches in program, masks stray thought."

"Total concentration, that's what I must *need,* Wolfe. Sounds good to me."

"Yeah, well." He finishes the fifth, cracks open gin. "Gets so you can't stand the smallest deviation from conformity. The most trivial hint of ambiguity drives you mad. You new wires with your doubts and fears and idealism, you make me sick." His speech is fast degenerating into slush.

"Wolfe?" Carly runs her fingertip across the hard curve of his arm. He flinches. "Wolfe, will I see you again?"

"See me? Come on, Carlique. You mean will I want you next time you want cram? Maybe. Maybe not. I'll need more cash. Got to get myself fixed with more cram, you know." He fixes her with a fierce, desperate stare. "Don't you know? You're just a score to me now, Carlique."

Then he passes out.

With tender fingertips, Carly slides his wasted eyelids over his rolled-back eyes. "It won't happen to me," she whispers into his unhearing ear. "Not like this."

• • •

"But how can I get *inside* a blackout?" says Carly. "The blackouts take my whole system down." She picks at the linkjack peevishly. *Don't want to, don't want to do this.* Carly's whole body recoils from the grimy little prober. Prober Spinner's faceplace is smudged with greasy fingerprints. Bird crap mottles her headpiece.

"Got to find us a blackout in telespace, go *inside* it," insists Prober Spinner. She wheels over to Carly. Skinny silver fingers wrest the jack from her, plug it into her linkslit. The prober's eyespots flash with glee when Carly winces.

"Your puny little guilt trip is shit. I want to see a *blackout*."

"And just what do you expect to see there, Prober Spinner?"

"A big, sloppy heap of unconscious energy. Plus an archetype or two, I truly hope. Only real kick to working with humans. Do you have any idea how bad your breath is, Carly Quester? Whew, no shit. Makes my olfactory sensors puke."

Carly rips out the linkjack, jumps up. "I don't like your attitude, Prober Spinner. I've got a good mind to report you to the medcenter sengine. Malpractice, see. I'll throw the fucking *book* at you."

"Oh, yes. Oh, certainly. The fucking book. All in good time Carly Quester. First we probe you three times, then we get you your Venue recert, *then* you throw the fucking book at me. Understand? So you don't get your ass thrown into reprogramming for three more years. Isn't that what you want? What little Carly wants, little Carly gets, yes?"

Carly sits, plunks the jack in herself. Of course that's what she wants. "Why do you hate me, Prober Spinner?"

"Hate you? Don't give yourself such importance. Oh, sit *down*. You would rather stitch up your left perimeter, just like that, without even *seeing* what it is that's got the symbolic power to intrude through a tight-ass weave like you. Oh, yes. Oh, certainly! I know your game, Carly Quester. You bet it upsets me. You receive this *gift*, a great gift from your unconscious mind, an aspect of intelligence no robot can ever hope to glimpse except through a human. For me, there is only *nothing*. Nothing but program, and then nothing—try *that* for existential angst. But you, a mysterious presence in your link, visions of an archetype you can't even name, and you, you organic intelligence, you want to cut it out, turn *yourself* into a robot. No, I don't hate you. But you could never understand that, could you?"

"All right, Prober Spinner." Carly sighs, then steels herself. No more emotion, take *control*. "Let's get on with it."

They jack into link. Telespace is murkier than the first probe. Prober Spinner's presence has darkened from brown to charcoal gray. The sight of the scuttling cone makes Carly so queasy she nearly flips the log-out switch.

"What shall I do?" she asks instead.

"Look for a blackout," says Prober Spinner brusquely. "Take me to a blackout."

At a loss, Carly slides along her towering left perimeter, pausing here and there as the prober darts behind her, jabbing again. Telespace suddenly gets foggier, a dark poisonous fog. Roiling mud beneath her reeks of raw sewage and strange decay.

Carly can feel her body start to retch, that skin-crawling feeling again. Physically somehow *there* in telespace. She jams two fingers into the base of her throat.

"Get out," Carly says, choking. "Got to get out."

Prober Spinner prods her forward into the fog.

Then, there. Two rows of double-bladed hatchets thrust out of the murk. The personnel committee of the top-notch mediation firm of Ava & Rice stands before Carly. Gleaming blades drip rust. Rust coagulates into a poisonous pool.

Mr. Capp Rice III, grandson of the late Capp Rice II, who was cofounder of the venerable mediation firm of Ava & Rice, lurches toward her. Jerky walk, like a marionette held by an epileptic. At age seventy, Mr. Rice has had so many body parts replaced he's nearly a robot.

"So, Ms. Quester." Dry steel joints screech. Mr. Rice towers over Carly's presence in link. "You have not met our expectations. I am sorry." An articulated tin tongue flickers between his platinum canine teeth. His empty unblinking solar eye fills Carly with such dread that her body back in the prober's office throws up.

"I can do better, Mr. Rice. I—I will do better."

The personnel committee stands in silence, dead eyes watching. Seventeen thousand resumes from recent mediation school graduates drop in a wriggling heap at Carly's feet.

"So, so, so, Ms. Quester." Mr. Rice's tin tongue flick-flick-flicks, some gear stuck at the back of his throat, until a member of the personnel committee reaches over and whacks him on the neck. "If you cannot meet our expectations, we will have to ask you to leave. I am so sorry."

"I can do better. I *will* do better." Carly starts to sob. "I'll do anything to keep my job. It's a *great* job, Mr. Rice. I'll do *anything.*"

"Will you kiss my ass?" Mr. Rice offers. Carly puckers.

"Will you lick my shoes?" Mr. Rice extends his appendage. Carly laps.

"Will you take cram?"

"Cram is illegal," says Carly, flushing.

"Cram focuses you in link like nothing else, Ms. Quester," says Mr. Rice. He takes out a hypodermic needle, stabs the needle into the corner of his eye, slams the plunger. "Oh! Like nothing else."

"I'll do anything to keep my job, Mr. Rice, *anything.*"

"I am glad to hear that, Ms. Quester. Just don't let that asshole Arbiter catch you. Be discreet. Takes one to know one." Mr. Rice pops the needle out, tosses the syringe over his shoulder. A member of the personnel committee picks it up and eats it, steel molars crunching the glass and metal into pulp. "I will give you another chance, Ms. Quester," says Mr. Rice. "Don't make me regret it, eh?"

The personnel committee vanishes.

"Shit!" yells Prober Spinner, poking Carly's cube. "Lousy *fear* is all you got for me?"

Carly is numb, so still, so paralyzed that she can't even shiver from the deep, deathly cold.

"I hate this fear," she whispers at last. "I hate them for making me afraid. Hate myself for being afraid."

"Guilt and fear, guilt and fear," says Prober Spinner, taunting.

"And I hate *you.*" A spume of angry red smoke races through Carly's telespace.

"Boo-hoo-hoo." Prober Spinner laughs. "Poor little Carly, she's so sad. Poor little Carly, can't even get mad."

Carly snaps into fury, slaps the prober's cone with a resounding *Gong!* The prober scuttles away, darts and dashes. Turns back sharply at the slick bank of her right perimeter, wrestles her.

"Good, good, good!" cries Prober Spinner, still laughing. She aims the conetip squarely into Carly's side. *Oof!* Carly falls back winded. "There, you see? You're not hamstrung by guilt anymore. You're not trapped by fear."

"But I *am* still trapped in this lousy life of mine. I'm still trapped in this soul-sucking world."

"Ah, we shall see," says the prober. "We haven't found a blackout. Not yet."

• • •

Carly approaches the Arbiter's quarters. Her presence in the Venue gleams like mother-of-pearl. Cram always adds a sheen.

"Your Honor, my client Quik Slip Microchip denies the plaintiff Martino's claim on the grounds of adverse possession." She logs in the facts of the mediation, a sleek green stream of data. "Plaintiff failed to protest defendant's illegal and flagrant use of the *Wordsport Glossary* over twenty years. Legality of acquisition is sustained by virtue of sustained illegality." In one and a half seconds, strict conformity of data with the statutory requirements of Property Code Section 344 is confirmed.

The two scruffy solos for Martino groan.

"Therefore," continues Carly, "my client counterclaims to quiet title under Section 501 of the Property Code."

Nee-dee-nee-dee-nee-dee-DEE! On the big board, the registrar of deeds cheerfully transfers title to the Wordsport Glossary from file M to file Q.

"Further," says Carly, "my client sues for mediator's fees under Civil Code Section 666.09(1)(B)."

"Objection!" screams the weaselly solo. "You can't get away with this, hotshot!"

"Overruled," says the Arbiter. His gigantic eyes flick over the whirring chronograph.

Carly has presented, proved, and concluded her defense and counterclaim in five seconds.

The Arbiter's towering face smiles at Carly "I am pleased to readmit you to telespace and look forward to your official recertification. Proceed, Ms. Quester."

"Grounds are vexatious and baseless litigation."

Ching! Data conforms to statute.

"I claim," says Carly, "ten thousand dollars."

"So held, award granted. Dismissed." The Arbiter nods approvingly at Carly. Her presence in the Venue glows.

The big steel hook of a garnishment plucks the last of Rosa Martino's money. From stats, a soft *poop!* like a fart. In a tiny black-and-white newline, the big board reports that Rosa Martino, age seventy-one, locked herself, her daughter, and her grandson in the kitchen of her southside tenement studio apartment and turned on the gas. *Tik-tik-tik!* Three corpses are dumped into the crunching jaws of the public morgue.

The inky net of a collection agent logs into the Venue, scoops up the solos before they can jack out of link.

"What goes around comes around, hotshot!" yells the weaselly solo as the collection agent's net drags him away to service his debts.

Carly doesn't know what he means. She logs out of the Venue, coming conscious in her filthy little cubicle at Ava & Rice. Rox is there, cutting up lines of coke on a blood-spattered mirror.

"Way to go, Quester," she says, winking a bloodshot, black-rimmed eye. "Nice touch, sticking it to the old lady. That'll teach laypeople to fuck with business."

In the hallway, Mr. Capp Rice III rolls by. He toasts Carly with a shot glass of high-octane gas. "I'm so glad you are meeting our expectations, Ms. Quester." Mr. Rice winks, too, but the wink opens and shuts, opens and shuts, until Rox reaches over and whacks him on the ear. "I've got another mediation just like Martino's. Consider this sort of thing your new specialty.

Every mediator needs a good specialty, eh, Ms. Quester?"

Carly nods, takes the mirror from Rox, toots. Quick, sharp high pierces the deadening stupor that always follows cramming. Wolfe has taught her other ways to handle cramming, ways to handle the cram addiction. Wolfe has taught her lots of tricks of the trade now that he's her pusher. She's had to learn. Twenty thousand dollars in debt to him, she finds other scores, gets them hooked, deals. Anything to score more cram.

Her hands shake all the time now. Fifteen pounds gone, she looks like an anorexic. Her left eye twitches, and some kind of swelling aches in her left temple, stretching out blue, bruised skin. Afraid to sleep, afraid to dream. She crams into link, cokes out of cram, boozes herself down in deep black nothing.

Two damned probes have shaken something loose. Carly's dislike of Prober Spinner festers into loathing. Surely the terror of the probes hasn't been necessary. Carly tries to contact the medcenter sengine, go over Spinner's head, get the recertification without a third probe. But the sengine is teaching a class at summer school and cannot be accessed.

Furious, Carly accesses the medcenter library, researches perimeter probers. She discovers the treatment is deemed not just unreliable like the sengine said from the start, but suspect. Several probers, *human* probers, hold this view.

In particular Prober Marboro at Stanford, who advocates layering new thicknesses of inhibition when left perimeter defects are suspect and who has proven layering is ninety percent effective, writes quite harshly of the probe technique. Probing threatens the integrity of the left perimeter, which Marboro asserts is the guardian of correct thought and proper linkage. Marboro exposed the case of Steven H., a young industrial programmer about Carly's age who, despite a strong body and a good education, suffered from hallucinations in link.

Steven H. jacked into telelink with a perimeter prober, never came out. The man vanished, mind and body. The prober claimed Steven was lured through a gash in his left perimeter. Bolted into his unconscious mind, re-created his own reality. Of course the prober claimed she tried to stop him, block him, chase, him. But the prober's telespace wasn't publicly accessed so there were no witnesses, no record. Only a computer ID and an overdrawn credit account to show Steven H. ever existed.

A cult of telespace technicians propounding the existence of multiple universes sprang up in the medical community, claimed Steven H. as their patron saint. But the big board suppressed the account.

Enraged, determined to press malpractice charges against the medcenter *and* Prober Spinner, Carly calls the prober's office, intending to refuse a third appointment. But the prober's answering machine talks her into a third probe.

"You don't want no cloud hangin' over your Venue recert, do ya Miss Quester?" says the answering machine. "Come *on*. Link in wit' the prober one last time, and I *guarantee* she'll recert ya."

Carly considers this. She has an appearance before the Arbiter in two days, has promised to present him with the final medcenter recertification.

"We haven't found a blackout, and Prober Spinner keeps insisting we must. But—" Carly takes a breath—"I don't think that's ever going to happen."

"Don't worry. She'll recert ya. I wouldn't kid ya."

Carly sets up the appointment. Just one last probe. Get in link, get out quick.

• • •

"You really will? Just like *that*?" Carly stalks back and forth across the prober's dust-fluffy floor.

"Oh, sure." Humming this week's pop hit off-tune, Prober Spinner fiddles with the telelink console.

"I can't believe it. I can't *believe* it." Carly shakes with fury. "Then what has been the fucking *point*?"

"Medcenter sengine says three probes, then recert. Then I get another paid-for probe client. You look like hell, Carly Quester. Not cramming, are you? No, you wouldn't tell me if you were."

"The sengine said recertification *if* I'm cured in three probes. You haven't done a damn thing for me, Spinner."

"Haven't done a thing? Not a *thing*? I beg to differ. You've been sprung loose of guilt and fear. Can't claim your freedom with baggage like that. Whew, you even smell like a crammer. Don't you know that garbage is illegal? And do you know *why* it's illegal? Hey? Rips the living shit out of your perimeters, that's why. I would have bounced you right out of here if you had showed up like this at the start of treatment."

Bitter cold shock. Wolfe never *did* say what the long-term effects of cramming could be. Carly shrugs it off. Robot bitch is trying to hassle her, as usual.

"I don't want to argue, Spinner," says Carly. "Let's get on with it."

And they jack into link.

• • •

Telespace is clear, still, focused, luminous. Maybe the cram. Maybe Carly's clear, pure anger. In any case, very nice. Very calming.

Carly lightens up, then recoils. Oh, yes, just what the prober wants, for her to let down her guard.

Prober Spinner's presence in link is a crisp, perfect, ebony cone.

"Please navigate your left perimeter, Carly Quester," says the prober. Her voice seems to contain an awestruck note.

Ahead lies a beautiful golden glow. Carly's presence in link slides gracefully, eagerly toward it. Her hand brushes a lock of hair from her cheek and, in link, she feels the soft touch of her own skin on her face. But the impossible physical touch doesn't panic her, doesn't worry her a bit.

"At last!" Prober Spinner cries. "At last, a blackout!"

"You're crazy," says Carly. Terror gallops through her, ripping away her wary peace. "I see a beam, not a blackout."

"Yes, yes! A blackout, *your* blackout. Tell me what you see!"

The golden glow swirls with luminous colors. A world appears, both microscopic and gigantic to Carly's eye. *A flier levitates from a vermilion funnel and hovers. Stiff chatoyant wings, monocoque fuselage, compound visual apparatus.* The mayfly bungles into a spider web. *The trapper hulks at the edge of the net. Stalked eyebuds swivel, pedipalps tense.* A garden spider darts down, wraps the fly in a silken shroud, begins to feed.

Carly screams.

"So *this* is the secret place inside your blackouts!" exclaims Prober Spinner. "The spider! How fascinating!"

"Horrible, horrible, oh God help me!" Carly yells.

"Why? What are you afraid of?"

"Ugly. Repulsive. Monstrous. *Alien.*"

"Oh, no, not ugly." Prober Spinner glides around the bright vision. The spider sips fluid from the flier's body. "It's Nature. It's beautiful."

"Violent. Vicious. *Murderous.*" Carly chases after the spinning cone. "Just like the Arbiter and Ava and Rice and Wolfe and *you*. All of you, preying on me, trapping me, sucking me dry."

"Oh, yes. Oh, certainly. You've been a victim. The world, the people around you, the role you've found yourself compelled to play. These have preyed upon you. The spider has slipped from the depths of the dark unconscious, through your left perimeter, in search of such a fine victim. But what about *you*, Carly Quester? You've taken your own victims, don't tell me you

had no choice. All that human creativity reduced to such a low and ugly fate."

"I won't hear this, Spinner." Carly scurries to log out of link.

"But wait, Carly. It's not so simple." The cone dives at her, prodding her, slapping her away from the log-off key. "There is a story, an old story no one remembers anymore. There was a goddess, an immortal weaver, who grew jealous of a talented mortal girl and her incomparable weaving. So gray-eyed Athena transformed the beautiful Arachne into a spider."

Out of the glowing garden creeps the garden spider. It scuttles across Carly's clean tan floor. The spider extends a hairy, clawed spindle, catches a silken line. Sweeps across telespace. Drops down onto Carly's cube.

Carly shrieks, gags, tries to shrink away, shake it off. But she can't. She can't. She's trapped.

"But Carly, the story is apocryphal." Prober Spinner lovingly taps at the spider, gently hurrying it across Carly's cube, catching it as it tumbles off the edge, easing it back onto her. "A lie, a slander, a political ploy. No better than the propaganda flashes on the big board. The Greeks, who worshipped the vengeful goddess coveted the lucrative textile trade of the Cretan weavers, who worshipped the spider as their goddess."

The spider quadruples in size. Instead of crawling across Carly's cube, it straddles her. Gazes down at her with a ghoulish, gape-mouthed face.

"Who would worship *that*?" says Carly, gasping. "How could they? *Why?*"

"To the Cretan weavers, the spider was the Eater of Souls. She who relentlessly destroys, the hunter, the killer, the maker of deceptions. But She was also the Weaver of Fate. She who unceasingly creates," says Prober Spinner. "Universe upon universe. Over and over. She redeems Her destructive power with Her infinite power to create. She is Grandmother Spider, the Creator. She weaves, Carly. She *weaves!*"

Salty wind blasts across telespace. Carly sees a pinpoint in the sturdy crisscrosses of her left perimeter, sees a thread of gold mist connecting the vision and the pinpoint. The pinpoint dilates, thick ropes of inhibition unraveling, rippling away.

The golden thread solidifies, and a spider of extraordinary beauty descends. Long, graceful legs, a rounded abdomen and slender torso, all made of shining silver set with faceted bits of marcasite. The stalked eyebuds gleam, two rubies regarding her.

"Look!" cries Prober Spinner. "Carly, look!"

"No," whispers Carly. Her presence in link, her physical body jacked into the console, feel so insubstantial. As if she's floating. "I'm afraid."

"Don't fear now," says Prober Spinner. "You've lived the dark side of Arachne. Now claim the light."

• • •

Telespace is a gray-green mist. Carly's presence in link is her own nude body. She stands on a windswept crag, surrounded by a splashing sea. Before her lies a gigantic loom, made of smooth hardwood, strung with woolen warp and woof.

She seats herself before the loom, takes the smooth hard shuttle. Slips it in and out, around and through, the fibrous matrix. The wool glows phosphorescent green and amber.

The warp slips off the loom and coils into a shape. The shape solidifies, a crystal retort in the form of a woman's figure through which white sand falls endlessly. The woof snaps and hurtles a spray of globes into deep space. The shuttle becomes a bullet of light and disappears.

Carly reaches out, seizing pulsing strands of pure creative energy.

All is darkness.

Carly opens her left hand. A bright bubble springs from her fingers, filling her eyes with light. Clouds of dust roil. Stars cool, the corona of dust settles, planets spin. The primordial ocean roars. Creatures swim, then wade onto shell-strewn beaches, and stand up. Empires rise. China, Egypt, Rome, England, America,

China. Mushroom clouds jut above broken cities. Spaceships blast off toward an uncharted galaxy.

All is darkness.

Then Carly opens her right hand. A luminous sphere pops out of her palm, flooding her eyes with light. Clouds of dust roil. Stars coagulate, the halo of ashes precipitates, planets settle into their orbits. The primal ocean pounds. Creatures swim, then the skin of their fins closes around each digital bone, and they grasp. Empires rise. Xeron, Forf, Klamat, Lator, Meen, Xeron. An ocean floor splits, swallowing crushed cities. Spaceships blast off into the unknown universe.

All is darkness.

Prober Spinner's voice calls, "Carly? Carly? Carly? Carly?"

Checkerboards of golden light pierce Carly's left perimeter. The thick black wall of inhibition shatters, shards of guilt, wisps of fear, strands of denial flung into infinity.

• • •

Carly hovers in telespace. Her presence in link is a luminous pearl. She gleams with crystal, the wonder drug that preserves life, expands consciousness, permits Earth dwellers to send their presence across the galaxy to new worlds. The jade obelisk of D. Wolfe, her beloved, hovers beside her. Prober Spinner's presence in link, an indigo cone with silver crescent moons, joins them.

Before them towers a castle of gold, turrets ablaze. There the Arbiter presides over the Venue, dispensing justice. Across Carly's right perimeter splashes an emerald sea, dragons frolicking in swells. There new people of the modern age refresh themselves, cast nets for plentiful fish. Bordering the back perimeter, scarlet gardens yield spicy perfumes. And there Rosa Martino joins hands with her daughter, Luisa, and her grandson, Dan, and the three of them circle in a sprightly dance. Glorious blooms thrust brilliant creepers into the blue jungle of Carly's left perimeter. There, through jungle vines and murex bushes peep the wild yellow eyes of new ideas not yet thought, of jungle cats and bright-beaked birds.

"Prober Spinner," says Carly, "what is this place?"

"Telespace, Carly Quester," says Prober Spinner. "Oh, yes. Oh, certainly. As only a human mind could create it."

"But some call it reality," says Wolfe. "It is yours, my beloved."

Anchored overhead to the four corners of telespace is the lattice of space and time, like a spider web, a beautiful fine spiral hung with crystalline drops of dew. Night rain has torn a hole in its center. Carly knows what to do. She flies up through telespace, takes the warp, takes the woof. She skips across the silk and begins to weave.

GREG EGAN

AXIOMATIC

(1990)

". . . LIKE YOUR BRAIN has been frozen in liquid nitrogen, and then smashed into a thousand shards!"

I squeezed my way past the teenagers who lounged outside the entrance to The Implant Store, no doubt fervently hoping for a holovision news team to roll up and ask them why they weren't in school. They mimed throwing up as I passed, as if the state of not being pubescent and dressed like a member of Binary Search was so disgusting to contemplate that it made them physically ill.

Well, maybe it did.

Inside, the place was almost deserted. The interior reminded me of a video ROM shop; the display racks were virtually identical, and many of the distributors' logos were the same. Each rack was labelled: PSYCHEDELIA. MEDITATION AND HEALING. MOTIVATION AND SUCCESS. LANGUAGES AND TECHNICAL SKILLS. Each implant, although itself less than half a millimeter across, came in a package the size of an old-style book, bearing gaudy illustrations and a few lines of stale hyperbole from a marketing thesaurus or some rent-an-endorsement celebrity. "*Become* God! *Become* the Universe!" "The Ultimate Insight! The Ultimate Knowledge! The Ultimate Trip!" Even the perennial, "This implant changed my life!"

I picked up the carton of *You Are Great!*—its transparent protective wrapper glistening with sweaty fingerprints—and thought numbly: If I bought this thing and used it, I would actually believe that. No amount of evidence to the contrary would be *physically able* to change my mind. I put it back on the shelf, next to *Love Yourself a Billion* and *Instant Willpower, Instant Wealth*.

I knew exactly what I'd come for, and I knew that it wouldn't be on display, but I browsed a while longer, partly out of genuine curiosity, partly just to give myself time. Time to think through the implications once again. Time to come to my senses and flee.

The cover of *Synaesthesia* showed a blissed-out man with a rainbow striking his tongue and musical staves piercing his eyeballs. Beside it, *Alien Mind-Fuck* boasted "a mental state so bizarre that even as you experience it, you won't know what it's like!" Implant technology was originally developed to provide instant language skills for businesspeople and tourists, but after disappointing sales and a takeover by an entertainment conglomerate, the first mass-market implants appeared: a cross between video games and hallucinogenic drugs. Over the years, the range of confusion and dysfunction on offer grew wider, but there's only so far you can take that trend; beyond a certain point, scrambling the neural connections doesn't leave anyone *there* to be entertained by the strangeness, and the user, once restored to normalcy, remembers almost nothing.

The first of the next generation of implants—the so-called axiomatics—were all sexual in nature; apparently that was the technically simplest place to start. I walked over to the Erotica section, to see what was available—or at least, what could legally be displayed. Homosexuality, heterosexuality, autoeroticism. An assortment of harmless fetishes. Eroticization of various unlikely parts of the body. Why, I wondered, would anyone choose to have their brain rewired to make them crave a sexual practice they otherwise would have found abhorrent, or ludicrous, or just plain boring? To comply with a partner's demands? Maybe, although such extreme submissiveness was hard to imagine, and could scarcely be sufficiently widespread to explain the size of the market. To enable a part of their own sexual identity, which, unaided, would have merely nagged and festered, to triumph over their inhibitions, their ambivalence, their revulsion? Everyone has conflicting desires, and people can grow tired of both wanting and not wanting the very same thing. I understood *that*, perfectly.

The next rack contained a selection of religions, everything from Amish to Zen. (Gaining the Amish disapproval of technology this way apparently posed no problem; virtually every religious implant enabled the user to embrace far stranger contradictions.) There was even an implant called *Secular Humanist* ("You WILL hold these truths to be self-evident!"). No *Vacillating Agnostic*, though; apparently there was no market for doubt.

For a minute or two, I lingered. For a mere fifty dollars, I could have bought back my childhood Catholicism, even if the Church would not have approved. (At least, not officially; it would have been interesting to know exactly who was subsidizing the product.) In the end, though, I had to admit that I wasn't really tempted. Perhaps it would have solved my problem, but not in the way that I wanted it solved—and after all, getting my own way was the whole point of coming here. Using an implant wouldn't rob me of my free will; on the contrary, it was going to help me to assert it.

Finally, I steeled myself and approached the sales counter.

"How can I help you, sir?" The young man smiled at me brightly, radiating sincerity, as if he really enjoyed his work. I mean, really, *really*.

"I've come to pick up a special order."

"Your name, please, sir?"

"Carver. Mark."

He reached under the counter and emerged with a parcel, mercifully already wrapped in anonymous brown. I paid in cash, I'd brought the exact change: $399.95. It was all over in twenty seconds.

I left the store, sick with relief, triumphant, exhausted. At least I'd finally bought the fucking thing; it was in my hands now, no one else was involved, and all I had to do was decide whether or not to use it.

After walking a few blocks toward the train station, I tossed the parcel into a bin, but I turned back almost at once and retrieved it. I passed a pair of armored cops, and I pictured their eyes boring into me from behind their mirrored faceplates, but what I was carrying was perfectly legal. How could the government ban a device which did no more than engender, in those who *freely chose* to use it, a particular set of beliefs—without also arresting everyone who shared those beliefs naturally? Very easily, actually, since the law didn't have to be consistent, but the implant manufacturers had succeeded in convincing the public that restricting their products would be paving the way for the Thought Police.

By the time I got home, I was shaking uncontrollably. I put the parcel on the kitchen table, and started pacing.

This wasn't for Amy. I had to admit that. Just because I still loved her, and still mourned her, didn't mean I was doing this for *her*. I wouldn't soil her memory with that lie.

In fact, I was doing it to free myself from her. After five years, I wanted my pointless love, my useless grief, to finally stop ruling my life. Nobody could blame me for that.

• • •

She had died in an armed holdup, in a bank. The security cameras had been disabled, and everyone apart from the robbers had spent most of the time facedown on the floor, so I never found out the whole story. She must have moved, fidgeted, looked up, she must have done *something*; even at the peaks of my hatred, I couldn't believe that she'd been killed on a whim, for no comprehensible reason at all.

I knew who had squeezed the trigger, though. It hadn't come out at the trial; a clerk in the Police Department had sold me the information. The killer's name was Patrick Anderson, and by turning prosecution witness, he'd put his accomplices away for life, and reduced his own sentence to seven years.

I went to the media. A loathsome crime-show personality had taken the story and ranted about it on the airwaves for a week, diluting the facts with self-serving rhetoric, then grown bored and moved on to something else.

Five years later, Anderson had been out on parole for nine months.

Okay. *So what?* It happens all the time. If someone had come to me with such a story, I would have been sympathetic, but firm. "Forget her, she's dead. Forget him, he's garbage. Get on with your life."

I didn't forget her, and I didn't forget her killer. I had loved her, whatever that meant, and while the rational part of me had swallowed the fact of her death, the rest kept twitching like a decapitated snake. Someone else in the same state might have turned the house into a shrine, covered every wall and mantelpiece with photographs and memorabilia, put fresh flowers on her grave every day, and spent every night getting drunk watching old home movies. I didn't do that, I couldn't. It would have been grotesque and utterly false; sentimentality had always made both of us violently ill. I kept a single photo. We hadn't made home movies. I visited her grave once a year.

Yet for all of this outward restraint, inside my head my obsession with Amy's death simply kept on growing. I didn't *want* it, I didn't *choose* it, I didn't feed it or encourage it in any way. I kept no electronic scrapbook of the trial. If people raised the subject, I walked away. I buried myself in my work; in my spare time I read, or went to the movies, alone. I thought about searching for someone new, but I never did anything about it, always putting it off until that time in the indefinite future when I would be human again.

Every night, the details of the incident circled in my brain. I thought of a thousand things I "might have done" to have prevented her death, from not marrying her in the first place (we'd moved to Sydney because of my job), to magically arriving at the bank as her killer took aim, tackling him to the ground and beating him senseless, or worse. I knew these fantasies were futile and self-indulgent, but that knowledge was no cure. If I took sleeping pills, the whole thing simply shifted to the daylight hours, and I was literally unable to work. (The computers that help us are slightly less appalling every year, but air traffic controllers *can't* daydream.)

I had to do something.

Revenge? Revenge was for the morally bankrupt. Me, I'd signed petitions to the UN, calling for the worldwide, unconditional abolition of capital punishment. I'd meant it then, and I still meant it. Taking human life was *wrong*; I'd believed that, passionately, since childhood. Maybe it started out as religious dogma, but when I grew up and shed all the ludicrous claptrap, the sanctity of life was one of the few beliefs I judged to be worth keeping. Aside from any pragmatic reasons, human consciousness had always seemed to me the most astonishing, miraculous, *sacred* thing in the universe. Blame my upbringing, blame my genes; I could no more devalue it than believe that one plus one equaled zero.

Tell some people you're a pacifist, and in ten seconds flat they'll invent a situation in which millions of people will die in unspeakable agony, and all your loved ones will be raped and tortured, if you don't blow someone's brains out. (There's always a contrived reason why you can't merely *wound* the omnipotent, genocidal madman.) The amusing thing is, they seem to hold you in even greater contempt when you admit that, yes, you'd do it, you'd kill under those conditions.

Anderson, however, clearly was not an omnipotent, genocidal madman. I had no idea whether or not he was likely to kill again. As for his capacity for reform, his abused childhood, or the caring and compassionate alter ego that may have been hiding behind the facade of his brutal exterior, I really didn't give a shit, but nonetheless I was convinced that it would be wrong for me to kill him.

I bought the gun first. That was easy, and perfectly legal; perhaps the computers simply failed to correlate my permit application with the release of my wife's killer, or perhaps the link was detected, but judged irrelevant.

I joined a "sports" club full of people who spent three hours a week doing nothing but shooting at moving, human-shaped targets. A recreational activity, harmless as fencing; I practiced saying that with a straight face.

Buying the anonymous ammunition from a fellow club member *was* illegal; bullets that vaporized on impact, leaving no ballistics evidence linking them to a specific weapon. I scanned the court records; the average sentence for possessing such things was a five-hundred dollar fine. The silencer was illegal, too; the penalties for ownership were similar.

Every night, I thought it through. Every night, I came to the same conclusion: despite my elaborate preparations, I wasn't going to kill anyone. Part of me wanted to, part of me didn't, but I knew perfectly well which was strongest. I'd spend the rest of my life dreaming about it, safe in the knowledge that no amount of hatred or grief or desperation would ever be enough to make me act against my nature.

• • •

I unwrapped the parcel. I was expecting a garish cover—sneering body builder toting submachine gun—but the packaging was unadorned, plain gray with no markings except for the product code, and the name of the distributor, Clockwork Orchard.

I'd ordered the thing through an on-line catalog, accessed via a coin-driven public terminal, and I'd specified collection by "Mark Carver" at a branch of The Implant Store in Chatswood, far from my home. All of which was paranoid nonsense, since the implant was legal—and all of which was perfectly reasonable, because I felt far more nervous and guilty about buying it than I did about buying the gun and ammunition.

The description in the catalog had begun with the statement *Life is cheap!* then had waffled on for several lines in the same vein: *People are meat. They're nothing, they're worthless.* The exact words weren't important, though; they weren't a part of the implant itself. It wouldn't be a matter of a voice in my head, reciting some badly written spiel which I could choose to ridicule or ignore; nor would it be a kind of mental legislative decree, which I could evade by means of semantic quibbling. Axiomatic implants were derived from analysis of actual neural structures in real people's brains, they weren't based on the expression of the axioms in language. The spirit, not the letter, of the law would prevail.

I opened up the carton. There was an instruction leaflet, in seventeen languages. A programmer. An applicator. A pair of tweezers. Sealed in a plastic bubble labeled STERILE IF UNBROKEN, the implant itself. It looked like a tiny piece of gravel.

I had never used one before, but I'd seen it done a thousand times on holovision. You placed the thing in the programmer, "woke it up," and told it how long you wanted it to be active. The applicator was strictly for tyros; the jaded cognoscenti balanced the implant on the tip of their little finger, and daintily poked it up the nostril of their choice.

The implant burrowed into the brain, sent out a swarm of nanomachines to explore, and forge links with, the relevant neural systems, and then went into active mode for the predetermined time—anything from an hour to infinity—doing whatever it was designed to do. Enabling multiple orgasms of the left knee-cap. Making the color blue taste like the long-lost memory of mother's milk. Or, hard wiring a premise: *I will succeed. I am happy in my job. There is life after death. Nobody died in Belsen. Four legs good, two legs bad . . .*

I packed everything back into the carton, put it in a drawer, took three sleeping pills, and went to bed.

• • •

Perhaps it was a matter of laziness. I've always been biased toward those options which spare me from facing the very same set of choices again in the future; it seems so *inefficient* to go through the same agonies of conscience more than once. To *not* use the implant would have meant having to reaffirm that decision, day after day, for the rest of my life.

Or perhaps I never really believed that the preposterous toy would work. Perhaps I hoped to prove that my convictions—unlike other

people's—were engraved on some metaphysical tablet that hovered in a spiritual dimension unreachable by any mere machine.

Or perhaps I just wanted a moral alibi—a way to kill Anderson while still believing it was something that the *real* me could never have done.

At least I'm sure of one thing. I didn't do it for Amy.

• • •

I woke around dawn the next day, although I didn't need to get up at all; I was on annual leave for a month. I dressed, ate breakfast, then unpacked the implant again and carefully read the instructions.

With no great sense of occasion, I broke open the sterile bubble and, with the tweezers, dropped the speck into its cavity in the programmer.

The programmer said, "Do you speak English?" The voice reminded me of one of the control towers at work; deep but somehow genderless, businesslike without being crudely robotic—and yet, unmistakably inhuman.

"Yes."

"Do you want to program this implant?"

"Yes."

"Please specify the active period."

"Three days." Three days would be enough, surely; if not, I'd call the whole thing off.

"This implant is to remain active for three days after insertion. Is that correct?"

"Yes."

"This implant is ready for use. The time is seven forty-three a.m. Please insert the implant before eight forty-three a.m., or it will deactivate itself and reprogramming will be required. Please enjoy this product and dispose of the packaging thoughtfully."

I placed the implant in the applicator, then hesitated, but not for long. This wasn't the time to agonize; I'd agonized for months, and I was sick of it. Any more indecisiveness and I'd need to buy a second implant to convince me to use the first. I wasn't committing a crime; I wasn't even coming close to guaranteeing that I would commit one. Millions of people held the belief that human life was nothing special, but how many of them were murderers? The next three days would simply reveal how *I* reacted to that belief, and although the attitude would be hard wired, the consequences were far from certain.

I put the applicator in my left nostril, and pushed the release button. There was a brief stinging sensation, nothing more.

I thought, *Amy would have despised me for this.* That shook me, but only for a moment. Amy was dead, which made her hypothetical feelings irrelevant. Nothing I did could hurt her now, and thinking any other way was crazy.

I tried to monitor the progress of the change, but that was a joke; you can't check your moral precepts by introspection every thirty seconds. After all, my assessment of myself as being unable to kill had been based on decades of observation (much of it probably out of date). What's more, that assessment, that self-image, had come to be as much a *cause* of my actions and attitudes as a reflection of them—and apart from the direct changes the implant was making to my brain, it was breaking that feedback loop by providing a rationalization for me to act in a way that I'd convinced myself was impossible.

After a while, I decided to get drunk, to distract myself from the vision of microscopic robots crawling around in my skull. It was a big mistake; alcohol makes me paranoid. I don't recall much of what followed, except for catching sight of myself in the bathroom mirror, screaming, "HAL's breaking First Law! HAL's breaking First Law!" before vomiting copiously.

I woke just after midnight, on the bathroom floor. I took an anti-hangover pill, and in five minutes my headache and nausea were gone. I showered and put on fresh clothes. I'd bought a jacket especially for the occasion, with an inside pocket for the gun.

It was still impossible to tell if the thing had done anything to me that went beyond the placebo effect; I asked myself, out loud, "Is human life sacred? Is it wrong to kill?" but I couldn't concentrate on the question, and I found it hard to believe that I ever had in the past; the whole idea seemed obscure and difficult, like some esoteric mathematical theorem. The prospect of going ahead with my plans made my stomach churn, but that was simple fear, not moral outrage; the implant wasn't meant to make me brave, or calm, or resolute. I could have bought those qualities too, but that would have been cheating.

I'd had Anderson checked out by a private investigator. He worked every night but Sunday, as a bouncer in a Surry Hills nightclub; he lived nearby, and usually arrived home, on foot, at around four in the morning. I'd driven past his terrace house several times, I'd have no trouble finding it. He lived alone; he had a lover, but they always met at her place, in the afternoon or early evening.

I loaded the gun and put it in my jacket, then spent half an hour staring in the mirror, trying to decide if the bulge was visible. I wanted a drink, but I restrained myself. I switched on the radio and wandered through the house, trying to become less agitated. Perhaps taking a life was now no big deal to me, but I could still end up dead, or in prison, and the implant apparently hadn't rendered me uninterested in my own fate.

I left too early, and had to drive by a circuitous route to kill time; even then, it was only a quarter past three when I parked, a kilometer from Anderson's house. A few cars and taxis passed me as I walked the rest of the way, and I'm sure I was trying so hard to look at ease that my body language radiated guilt and paranoia—but no ordinary driver would have noticed or cared, and I didn't see a single patrol car.

When I reached the place, there was nowhere to hide—no gardens, no trees, no fences—but I'd known that in advance. I chose a house across the street, not quite opposite Anderson's, and sat on the front step. If the occupant appeared, I'd feign drunkenness and stagger away.

I sat and waited. It was a warm, still, ordinary night; the sky was clear, but gray and starless thanks to the lights of the city. I kept reminding myself: *You don't have to do this, you don't have to go through with it.* So why did I stay? The hope of being liberated from my sleepless nights? The idea was laughable; I had no doubt that if I killed Anderson, it would torture me as much as my helplessness over Amy's death.

Why did I stay? It was nothing to do with the implant; at most, that was neutralizing my qualms; it wasn't forcing me to *do* anything.

Why, then? In the end, I think I saw it as a matter of honesty. I had to accept the unpleasant fact that I honestly wanted to kill Anderson, and however much I had also been repelled by the notion, to be true to myself I had to do it— anything less would have been hypocrisy and self-deception.

At five to four, I heard footsteps echoing down the street. As I turned, I hoped it would be someone else, or that he would be with a friend, but it was him, and he was alone. I waited until he was as far from his front door as I was, then I started walking. He glanced my way briefly, then ignored me. I felt a shock of pure fear—I hadn't seen him in the flesh since the trial, and I'd forgotten how physically imposing he was.

I had to force myself to slow down, and even then I passed him sooner than I'd meant to. I was wearing light, rubber-soled shoes, he was in heavy boots, but when I crossed the street and did a U-turn toward him, I couldn't believe he couldn't hear my heartbeat, or smell the stench of my sweat. Meters from the door, just as I finished pulling out the gun, he looked over his shoulder with an expression of bland curiosity, as if he might have been expecting a dog or a piece of windblown litter. He turned around to face me, frowning. I just stood there, pointing the gun at him, unable to speak. Eventually he said, "What the fuck do you want? I've got two hundred dollars in my wallet. Back pocket."

I shook my head. "Unlock the front door, then put your hands on your head and kick it open. Don't try closing it on me."

He hesitated, then complied.

"Now walk in. Keep your hands on your head. Five steps, that's all. Count them out loud. I'll be right behind you."

I reached the light switch for the hall as he counted four, then I slammed the door behind me, and flinched at the sound. Anderson was right in front of me, and I suddenly felt trapped. The man was a vicious killer; *I* hadn't even thrown a punch since I was eight years old. Did I really believe the gun would protect me? With his hands on his head, the muscles of his arms and shoulders bulged against his shirt. I should have shot him right then, in the back of the head. This was an execution, not a duel; if I'd wanted some quaint idea of honor, I would have come without a gun and let him take me to pieces.

I said, "Turn left." Left was the living room. I followed him in, switched on the light. "Sit." I stood in the doorway, he sat in the room's only chair. For a moment, I felt dizzy and my vision seemed to tilt, but I don't think I moved, I don't think I sagged or swayed; if I had, he probably would have rushed me.

"What do you want?" he asked.

I had to give that a lot of thought. I'd fantasized this situation a thousand times, but I could no longer remember the details—although I did recall that I'd usually assumed that Anderson would recognize me, and start volunteering excuses and explanations straight away.

Finally, I said, "I want you to tell me why you killed my wife."

"I didn't kill your wife. Miller killed your wife."

I shook my head. "That's not true. I *know*. The cops told me. Don't bother lying, because I *know*."

He stared at me blandly. I wanted to lose my temper and scream, but I had a feeling that, in spite of the gun, that would have been more comical than intimidating. I could have pistol-whipped him, but the truth is I was afraid to go near him.

So I shot him in the foot. He yelped and swore, then leaned over to inspect the damage. "Fuck you!" he hissed. "Fuck you!" He rocked back and forth, holding his foot. "I'll break your fucking neck! I'll fucking kill you!" The wound bled a little through the hole in his boot, but it was nothing compared to the movies. I'd heard that the vaporizing ammunition had a cauterizing effect.

I said, "Tell me why you killed my wife."

He looked far more angry and disgusted than afraid, but he dropped his pretense of innocence. "It just happened," he said. "It was just one of those things that happens."

I shook my head, annoyed. "No. *Why?* Why did it happen?"

He moved as if to take off his boot, then thought better of it. "Things were going wrong. There was a time lock, there was hardly any cash, everything was just a big fuckup. I didn't mean to do it. It just happened."

I shook my head again, unable to decide if he was a moron, or if he was stalling. "Don't tell me 'it just happened.' *Why* did it happen? Why did you do it?"

The frustration was mutual; he ran a hand through his hair and scowled at me. He was sweating now, but I couldn't tell if it was from pain or from fear. "What do you want me to say? I lost my temper, all right? Things were going badly, and I lost my fucking temper, and there she was, all right?"

The dizziness struck me again, but this time it didn't subside. I understood now; he wasn't being obtuse, he was telling the entire truth. I'd smashed the occasional coffee cup during a tense situation at work. I'd even, to my shame, kicked our dog once, after a fight with Amy. Why? *I'd lost my fucking temper, and there she was.*

I stared at Anderson, and felt myself grinning stupidly. It was all so clear now. I understood. I understood the absurdity of everything I'd ever felt for Amy—my "love," my "grief." It had all been a joke. She was meat, she was nothing. All the pain of the past five years evaporated; I was drunk with relief. I raised my arms and spun around slowly. Anderson leapt up and sprung toward me; I shot him in the chest until I ran out of bullets, then I knelt down beside him. He was dead.

I put the gun in my jacket. The barrel was warm. I remembered to use my handkerchief to open the front door. I half-expected to find a crowd outside, but of course the shots had been inaudible, and Anderson's threats and curses were not likely to have attracted attention.

A block from the house, a patrol car appeared around a corner. It slowed almost to a halt as it approached me. I kept my eyes straight ahead as it passed. I heard the engine idle. Then stop. I kept walking, waiting for a shouted command, thinking: if they search me and find the gun, I'll confess; there's no point in prolonging the agony.

The engine spluttered, revved noisily, and the car roared away.

• • •

Perhaps I'm *not* the number one most obvious suspect. I don't know what Anderson was involved in since he got out; maybe there are hundreds of other people who had far better reasons for wanting him dead, and perhaps when the cops have finished with them, they'll get around to asking me what I was doing that night. A month seems an awfully long time, though. Anyone would think they didn't care.

The same teenagers as before are gathered around the entrance, and again the mere sight of me seems to disgust them. I wonder if the taste in fashion and music tattooed on their brains is set to fade in a year or two, or if they have sworn lifelong allegiance. It doesn't bear contemplating.

This time, I don't browse. I approach the sales counter without hesitation.

This time, I know exactly what I want.

What I want is what I felt that night: the unshakeable conviction that Amy's death—let alone Anderson's—simply didn't matter, any more than the death of a fly or an amoeba, any more than breaking a coffee cup or kicking a dog.

My one mistake was thinking that the insight I gained would simply vanish when the implant cut out. It hasn't. It's been clouded with doubts and reservations, it's been undermined, to some degree, by my whole ridiculous panoply of beliefs and superstitions, but I can still recall the peace it gave me, I can still recall that flood of joy and relief, and *I want it back*. Not for three days; for the rest of my life.

Killing Anderson *wasn't* honest, it wasn't "being true to myself." Being true to myself would have meant living with all my contradictory urges, suffering the multitude of voices in my head, accepting confusion and doubt. It's too late for that now; having tasted the freedom of certainty, I find I can't live without it.

"How can I help you, sir?" The salesman smiles from the bottom of his heart.

Part of me, of course, still finds the prospect of what I am about to do totally repugnant.

No matter. That won't last.

HARRY POLKINHORN

CONSUMIMUR IGNI

(1990)

IT WAS FIVE O'CLOCK in the afternoon. Debord entered Alicia's, grateful for the cool darkness. After all, outside it was 117 degrees Fahrenheit. He sat in a leather-backed chair and ordered a margarita ("without salt"). The lime bit his throat as it went down. The gloomy interior of the De Anza Hotel's only bar helped him to concentrate. Debord had a lot to think about. People were dying a horrible death through convulsions and vomiting all over Calexico, and it was his job to figure out why.

Needle slide beneath skin. Rose burst backup in the tube. Dark red silent explosion. TV flicker jump across nose eyes frowning brow. Idiom thieves. Invisible interior of formless. Slow-motion jolt to loosen bones from flesh afloat. Broken tooth of pain going away to dead. Sun mushroom against scarred horizon. Footsteps smell of salt cedar rank sewage burning agricultural waste hangs in air. Explosion of terrorist alphabet chunks across the screen.

He ran his fingers through thinning hair.

His mind circled like a hound just off his scene, circled and backtracked as if aimlessly, yet well aware in its way, a calculated distraction, a meditation on nature, bestiality, beauty, the monstrous. The Calexico police had called him in because he had once had contacts with the Chinese Catholic group in Mexicali back in the 1960s. The local dicks figured he might be of some use in their deadlocked investigation. Whenever they couldn't do a quick make, they pinned it on the Chinese. Debord ordered another drink and ruminated. They didn't know about MIBI, and he wanted to keep it that way.

Debord's heart raced as he felt himself reaching a "plateau" in his mullings. He quickly paid for his drinks and went up to his room. Second floor, only room in the crumbling pile with a telephone. He unplugged the instrument and jacked in his portable computer. High-speed modem connect. Into the Internet highway and his code shot through the gateways to MIBI: Jorn in Copenhagen (Dotrement and Constant had fallen away, or rather been sheared off by developments too rapid for them to track), Pinot-Gallizia in Coslo d'Arroscia, Bernstein in Paris. "And me on the border, as usual," he thought sardonically. Lit a Camel and scrolled down to the relevant user ID numbers, knocked through a general call. He needed Guiseppe's knowledge of chemistry right away, and Asger's command of tongues. Bernstein would put the pieces together in her brilliant way. The gang moll but this time with a brain in her head. Debord was point man this time out. "Maybe you'll get some ideas for your next film," Jorn had chortled.

• • •

"Dozens of new cases are being reported each week," said Torres in a voice of barely controlled rage. "It's a goddam epidemic. We know nothing but what we read in the papers. The mayor and city council are kicking my butt." He glared around the office. Debord had his Sony minicassette recorder going in his pocket. Voice analysis later. MIBI procedures.

"How tight in the line?" asked Debord.

"We've got every dog in the house down there. The Border Patrol is cooperating so far. I spoke to Saldaña just before you got here. There are always leaks, maybe big ones, but the standard holes are plugged for now."

"Can you get me permission to go up into the water tower observation post?" Debord said. The Border Patrol had taken over the wooden gondola in the old water tower right at the fence.

"Sure." Torres punched up Saldaña again. "Pete. It's me again. Listen, Pete, I need to get my man up into the tower. Okay. Yeah, sure. I'll tell him. Thanks, Pete." He rang off and said, "You're in. A Jeep will be by in five minutes."

• • •

The epoch itself is the frame of the whole work. How to plumb what could be an act of Chinese-Mexican terrorism. Beneath him the chain

link and barbed wire stretched east and west. I wanted to speak the beautiful language of my time. To communicate and discuss. We grow older. Rose bomb in liquid, floats up through a dreamscape of all earthy things were corrupted. He looked through his binoculars. Here and there Mexicans slipped through holes in the fence heading north. Secondary details. At the beginning, I was nothing. His hands adjusted the plastic tubes, snapping everything into focus. The more profound is this desire. Violence, sexuality, cruelty. Turnings through a random city gridwork. A speaking voice proper only for suffering and despair. His 8-millimeter video unit patiently sucked in images. The huge sprawling metropolis to the south, sliced cleanly by the US/Mexico international boundary, in this case a fence topped with barbed wire, and on the north side the tiny town of Calexico with its neatly paved streets.

• • •

"Souls or bodies, what the difference. The virus attacks life itself. Someone has unleashed a radioactive isotope that feeds on doubles. Is the soul the body's double?" The commander rose up on his toes, then rocked down, hands clasped behind his back. He looked intently out the window at the scene in the park across from the station. Swings, a merry-go-round, drunks asleep under the palms. Nothing out of the ordinary. A secretary handed him a fresh fax. "Jesus, Mary, and Joseph," he swore. "Another rash of cases has been reported out in the Villa de Oro section of town. I'm calling the Centers for Disease Control again."

Debord took this as his cue and left the station. He returned to the De Anza and within minutes was entering the day's catch into SI, a complex and beautiful program MIBI had commissioned. On a hunch, he flipped laterally out of SI into private notes, looking for the link: "On the evening of Dec. 31 in the same bar on the rue Xavier-Privas, the Lettrists came upon K. and the regulars terrorized—despite their own violent tendencies—by a sort of gang comprising ten Algerians who had come from the Pigalle and were occupying the place. The rather mysterious story seemed to involve both counterfeit money and the links it might have with the arrest of one of K.'s friends—for narcotics peddling—in the very same bar a few weeks earlier."

"Bingo," whispered Debord. "Dope and the Lettrists." He slammed back into SI and ran the voice-print subroutine for everyone he had interviewed that day. Torres, Saldaña himself later on, and others. This took a while and the data were queued up in the buffer. Meanwhile he popped in master tracks for some radio programming from several popular norteña stations, then scanned in all the police stats the boys had given him. Once he had snapped the video conversion unit into its slot, the transfer was automatic. Before locking in with MIBI, he needed a break, because after they got started it would stretch him out thin.

• • •

Therefore the places most fitting for these things are churchyards. And better than them are those places devoted to the executions of criminal judgment; and better than those those places where, of late years, there have been so great and so many public slaughters of men; and that place is still better than those where some dead carcass that came by violent death is not yet expiated, nor was lately buried . . . you should therefore allure the said souls by supernatural and celestial powers duly administered, even by those things which do move the very harmony of the soul . . . such as voices, songs, sounds, enchantments.

• • •

Girls used to put their belts, ribbons, locks of hair, etc. under the pillows of young men for whose love they craved.

• • •

Visible and tangible forms grow into existence from invisible elements by the power of the sunshine. This process is reversible by the power of night.

• • •

If a pregnant woman imagines something strongly, the effects of her imagination may become manifest in the child. The blood is magnetized.

• • •

Acting on a tip from a Mexican informant, Debord nonchalantly entered the Copa de Oro. Chunks of the ceiling fallen away. A television monitor at each end of the short bar playing back grinding porno films. Nothing different from any other hole in the Chinesca. He sat at a tiny table and ordered a Tecate. One of those dives that featured only one kind of beer. Down to the basics. Soon the woman spotted him, as he had been told she would. Watch out for a setup. Dark eyes lined with mascara, skintight dress of some white Spandex material, spike heels. He quickly scanned the joint, but no one seemed to care.

"Buy a girl a drink?" she asked.

"Sure. Name it." She ordered the predictable brandy.

"What brings you here?" she cooed, sliding a hand up his thigh.

"You," Debord said. "They tell me you know the new governor."

"Maybe I know him," insinuated the woman. "I've known lots of men. Let's go to my room and I'll check my little black book." She tossed off the drink with one hand while massaging his upper thigh with the other.

"You're on," said Debord.

As he pulled up his zipper, Debord reminded the woman why he was there. She then said, "Sure, he used to come here. He liked me. We had some good times."

"Was he alone?"

"No. He always had several others with him."

"Any Chinese?" Debord asked.

"Yeah, as a matter of fact. I remember an older guy. Emilio Chin. They said he owned the Green Cat years ago and then got into the state gambling syndicate."

"How can I meet him?"

"Come back here a week from tonight at eleven p.m. I'll know by then," she said, stuffing the bills into her bra. Then she smiled. "Come back anytime, baby."

"By the way, what's your name?" he asked.

"Rosa."

• • •

Within fifteen minutes Debord had walked back across the border and was in his room at the screen, deep in SI. He ran the girl's voice from his machine, then a quick description of her features, clothing, and room. His ID began blinking: it was Guiseppe piping through with the chemistry figures. Blood sample analyses, projections of viral group activities, hormone cross sections. SI reconstructed his voice, which purred from the machine. "Your stats are flat on both ends of the curve," he said. "What kind of a place are you in anyway?"

"Somewhat isolated border setting," responded Debord. "They aren't much up on record-keeping here. It's all by word of mouth, gossip, chit-chat. But you do the best you can."

"Sure, Guy. Hang in there. Wait, here's Asger." The voice quality changed from a mild Italian to an even milder Scandinavian accent; SI did this just to make things more pleasant.

"Guy. Asger. Listen, I've done the full job on the samples. All the way down to the sub-phonemic level. You're dealing with some complex shit out there. My best guess is Mexican Spanish and third-level American on a bedrock of Mandarin Chinese. The diction subroutine tells us it's a woman between the ages of twenty-eight and thirty-four, educated through the equivalent of a four-year college program, maybe in the US. Interests may be business,

music, sex, and the occult. That's as far as I could get, Guy. She's smart and probably very dangerous. Be careful, for Christ's sake."

Blip of static. Columns of figures filed across the screen, froze into a pattern, then disappeared as more came up, until the transfer was completed. He downloaded, ran his virus check, stuck a tracer block on the end, and broke the connection. Six thirty a.m. Suddenly he felt exhausted and stretched out on the uncomfortable bed. Too tired to care.

• • •

It was a critique of urbanism, of art and political economy. They operated through a series of turnings. Just as you felt you were on to something, they flipped the dial to another station. A twilight world of electronic haze as the ex-citizens watch *Dallas* over and over again. No one would be able to play because they would all be fixed in their allocated places. It was a question of premeditated memory control. Global marketing because of the lack of an overarching construction. This was the perspective: a shifting of tasks through negation itself force field sucks us into the now. Atomic fallout shelter against the fire storm of signs.

• • •

Over coffee and machaca in the De Anza café, Debord flipped over the pages of the *San Diego Union*. His eyes lighted on a headline: "Agreement said near on tighter controls over medical waste." His tour of the area had led him to the conclusion that such concerns would be minimal here. ". . . trash from hospitals, clinics, and labs that can carry infectious diseases . . ." No one would think twice about unloading a pickup of plastic bags filled with such materials out on the desert or by the side of the road. After all, weren't the farmers themselves prime polluters of the food chain with massive doses of insecticides, fungicides, and herbicides? One would simply be following an example. So went his ruminations as he finished the spicy meat dish.

Later that evening, Debord kept his appointment with Rosa. "Any luck?" he asked.

"Sure. Chin is out of town, but his 'assistant' said she would meet us here. Look, here she comes now." The woman flicked her eyes toward the Copa's swinging half door.

Debord turned to see. "Asger's right again," he said to himself as a Chinese Mexican woman of about thirty-five walked up to their table.

"Hello. I am Mr. Chin's assistant, Veronica Mah," she said in measured tones. "How can I help you?" Her skin had a deep glow under the dim lighting. She lit a cigarette.

"There's a big problem you might be able to help me with," said Debord carefully. He felt her scanning him with some Oriental power device. "My understanding is that the Governor, Mr. Ernest Appell, has some connections with, uh, certain merchandise crossing to the north . . . usually at night." He watched her expression.

"Yes," Veronica said readily, to his surprise. "I've heard the same." Pause.

"Well, to be frank with you, we need to know as soon as possible what the routes have been the last four weeks. Discretion assured, needless to say."

"Undoubtedly." Cold. Mastery of tone. Veronica was very accomplished. Debord was banking heavily on the locale. He had figured she had done some kind of a check on him and probably had come up blank. Meanwhile, because of the isolation of this place the chances that she would deduce his distant team were very slim indeed. His recorder was trapping her in magnetic patterns. Veronica studied him through the smoke rising from her Delicado. He pushed an envelope across the table toward her. She pocketed it, rose, and left the club.

• • •

Back in SI, Debord uploaded all his fresh data. Then he rolled through the gateways to Bernstein. He needed her more than ever at this point. Getting in over his head. Her ability to make bizarre yet accurate connections would always help him see his way clear. She wanted to know everything about both women's appearance—makeup, clothing, color of hair, body shape, and so on. She asked about perfume, about the décor of the club, how he felt when he walked in, how he felt an hour after he had left. Then she said, "This might sound strange, Guy, but my suspicion is that these women are working together. They are playing Chin and Appell against each other, and are probably doing the same with whoever owns the Copa de Oro as well as the local police commandant. What's in it for them? Control over their own destinies. Power of men, money. The Oriental is the brain, the hooker the contact point. Now, something went wrong with a big drug deal they were involved in, so they've come up with a way to implicate everyone but themselves, of course. Smokescreen. Think about it, Guy. And be careful, honey. I miss you." Fade-out with flashes of gray on the screen. The minispeaker fell silent. Debord powered himself through SI's infinite recombinations, sucking in as much ancillary information as he could. Street and sewage systems maps of Mexicali and Calexico. History of the Chinese population in northern Baja California. Arrest frequencies by the Immigration and Naturalization Service, US Customs, local police agencies. Cooperative agreements between institutions on both sides of the border. International law as applied to environmental issues.

Suddenly, a presence announced itself. For the first time, SI had been breached. The screen went blank; then a complex mandala-like figure appeared in its center and began three-dimensional rotations. "Mr. Debord," said a faintly metallic voice. "Please acknowledge."

Debord hit the "enter" key.

"Thank you. We have some information you may find of interest. Please join us at the Copa tomorrow evening." The spinning mandala then burst apart and disappeared like fireworks burning themselves out.

• • •

Because of Bernstein's suspicion, Debord was reluctant to involve any police agencies. The dicks would probably turn on him. He had to go in alone, therefore. He quickly reviewed MIBI procedures for such situations, then entered the club. Both women were there having a drink. He noticed nothing unusual as he approached them. "Good evening, ladies," he said. "May I join you?"

"By all means," said Veronica. "Yes, you are right; we requested your presence here tonight. We have a business proposition for you, Mr. Debord." Debord's biological and electronic systems shot to total alert.

"Please go on," he said calmly.

"A simple exchange. We give you the information you need, and you provide us with a clean copy of the SI program with all its subroutines. Really quite impressive, what little of it we were able to experience."

"You surprise me," confessed Debord carefully, concealing his real surprise. "SI permits very advanced research." He gestured around somewhat vaguely at the dilapidated surroundings.

"Yes. Well then, do we have a deal?"

"Of course," Debord said. "Since you know enough to have cracked SI's crystal wall, you will have learned that operators can send clean copies at their discretion. I therefore suggest that we conclude our arrangement later. Since my time here is limited, I would much prefer to spend it in more enjoyable pursuits." Veronica nodded, smiling.

"Agreed. And now I'll leave you." She extended her hand. "It was a pleasure meeting you, Mr. Debord." She turned and was gone. Rosa's fingers crawled up his thigh.

• • •

While walking back across the line, Debord worked out his strategy. First he knew that he could not communicate with the others at this point. Also any further browsing in SI would undoubtedly be monitored and deciphered. They would be aware of any moves. With this in mind, he returned to his room at the De Anza and packed his equipment. It was 2:30 a.m.

Debord carried his bag down the back staircase, which gave out into the small stage on the east end of the huge lobby. A musty stage curtain concealed his presence. He waited until he was sure no one was in the lobby, then slipped quietly out the side door, which enabled him to make his way to the parking area. The taxi he had ordered was waiting.

"Travelodge, El Centro," he said. Thirty minutes later he was jacked into SI and immediately constructed a fog macro to give himself some room to maneuver. Debord uploaded one last time, ran all the relevant subroutines, then pulled out for a breather. "Time to close the case," he muttered to himself.

With that he dissolved the macro. Almost instantaneously they were there. "Are you ready?" asked Veronica.

"Yes," said Debord. "I've constructed the syntax which will permit you to pull a clean copy of everything off the Paris node. This is the only one we are permitted to use. Gateway codes, user IDs, everything you'll need is in the file titled 'Situation.' Now please reciprocate."

"Of course," Veronica said. "Appell burned Chin on a large cocaine shipment." Bernstein was right again, Debord thought, smiling. "So Chin set him up by infecting the local batch of the state blood bank with a virus. He made certain that a transborder shipment destined for the Calexico Hospital was dirty. Appell is due for a fall. When Chin returns, the blood bank and the governor's office will be indicted. That's how these brutes operate. Rosa and I, however, knew the Calexico police would be baffled and that they would call in help. Of course we had heard of MIBI but had no direct dealings. Your methods are very admirable. With SI now you can run back the virus."

"Why have you told me all this?"

"For our own reasons, we are pulling the plug

on Chin and Appell. They've used us for the last time. SI will make it possible for us to break free, finally. We are tired of all the violence and dying. Goodbye."

Debord quickly logged off, whipped his equipment back into its carrying case, and left the Travelodge running. An explosion rocked the wing he had exited before he was across the street.

The bourgeois epoch which wants to give a scientific foundation to history overlooks the fact that this available science needed a historical foundation along with the economy. What hides under the spectacular oppositions is a unity of misery. All aspects of technology serve to produce the great possible passive isolation of individuals as well as the control of these individuals. He raised the glass to his lips as the others waited. Glad to be back in the Latin Quarter. "A toast to MIBI." They all clicked their glasses. Letters blossomed on the screen. Filter. The instrument of enchanters is a pure, living, breathing spirit of the blood codes. Robbers of language. The kind of knowledge that one ought to possess is not derived from the earth nor does it come from the stars. A destiny more grand than anything imaginable. Mystic flesh rose of finished passion traceries staining a bruised sky. Body parts. Political theory river running with by-product. Return.

PAUL J. MCAULEY

GENE WARS

(1991)

1.

On Evan's eighth birthday, his aunt sent him the latest smash-hit biokit, *Splicing Your Own Semisentients*. The box lid depicted an alien swamp throbbing with weird, amorphous life; a double helix spiraling out of a test tube was embossed in one corner. *Don't let your father see that,* his mother said, so Evan took it out to the old barn, set up the plastic culture trays and vials of chemicals and retroviruses on a dusty workbench in the shadow of the shrouded combine.

His father found Evan there two days later. The slime mold he'd created, a million amoebae aggregated around a drop of cyclic AMP, had been transformed with a retrovirus and was budding little blue-furred blobs. Evan's father dumped culture trays and vials in the yard and made Evan pour a liter of industrial-grade bleach over them. More than fear or anger, it was the acrid stench that made Evan cry.

That summer, the leasing company fore-closed on the livestock. The rep who supervised repossession of the supercows drove off in a big car with the test-tube and double-helix logo on its gull-wing door. The next year the wheat failed, blighted by a particularly virulent rust. Evan's father couldn't afford the new resistant strain, and the farm went under.

2.

Evan lived with his aunt, in the capital. He was fifteen. He had a street bike, a plug-in computer, and a pet microsaur, a triceratops in purple funfur. Buying the special porridge which was all the microsaur could eat took half of Evan's weekly allowance; that was why he let his best friend inject the pet with a bootleg virus to edit out its dietary dependence. It was only a partial success: the triceratops no longer needed its porridge, but developed epilepsy triggered by sunlight. Evan had to keep it in his wardrobe.

When it started shedding fur in great swatches, he abandoned it in a nearby park. Microsaurs were out of fashion, anyway. Dozens could be found wandering the park, nibbling at leaves, grass, discarded scraps of fast food. Quite soon they disappeared, starved to extinction.

3.

The day before Evan graduated, his sponsor company called to tell him that he wouldn't be doing research after all. There had been a change of policy: the covert gene wars were going public. When Evan started to protest, the woman said sharply, "You're better off than many long-term employees. With a degree in molecular genetics you'll make sergeant at least."

4.

Rivers made silvery forked lightnings in the jungle's vivid green blanket. Warm wind rushed around Evan as he leaned out the helicopter's hatch; the harness dug into his shoulders. He was twenty-three, a tech sergeant. It was his second tour of duty.

His goggles laid icons over the view, tracking the target. Two villages a klick apart, linked by a red dirt road narrow as a capillary that suddenly widened to an artery as the helicopter dove.

Muzzle-flashes on the ground. Evan hoped the peasants only had Kalashnikovs: last week, an unfriendly had downed a copter with an antique SAM. Then he was too busy laying the pattern, virus-suspension in a sticky spray that fogged the maize fields.

Afterward, the pilot, an old-timer, said over the intercom, "Things get tougher every day. We used just to take a leaf, cloning did the rest. You couldn't even call it theft. But this stuff . . . I always thought war was bad for business."

Evan said, "The company owns copyright to the maize genome. Those peasants aren't licensed to grow it."

The pilot said admiringly, "Man, you're a real company guy. I bet you don't even know what country this is."

Evan thought about that. He said, "Since when were countries important?"

5.

Rice fields quilted the floodplain. In every paddy, peasants bent over their own reflections, planting seedlings for the winter crop.

At the center of the UNESCO delegation, the Minister for Agriculture stood under a black umbrella held by an aide. He was explaining that his country was starving to death after a record rice crop.

Evan was at the back of the little crowd, bareheaded in warm drizzle. He wore a smart one-piece suit, yellow overshoes. He was twenty-eight, had spent two years infiltrating UNESCO for his company.

The minister was saying, "We have to buy seed gene-spliced for pesticide resistance to compete with our neighbors, but my people can't afford to buy the rice they grow. It must all be exported to service our debt. We are starving in the midst of plenty."

Evan stifled a yawn. Later, at a reception in some crumbling embassy, he managed to get the minister on his own. The man was drunk, unaccustomed to hard liquor. Evan told him he was very moved by what he had seen.

"Look in our cities," the minister said, slurring his words. "Every day refugees pour in from the countryside. They cannot feed themselves and neither can we. There is cholera. Very bad cholera. There is kwashiorkor. Beriberi."

Evan popped a canapé into his mouth. One of his company's new lines, it squirmed with delicious lasciviousness before he swallowed it. "I may be able to help you," he said. "The people I represent have a new yeast that completely fulfills dietary requirements and will grow in a simple medium."

As Evan explained, the minister, no longer as

drunk as he had seemed, steered him onto the terrace.

"You understand this must be confidential," the minister said. "Under UNESCO rules—"

"We have arrangements with five countries that have trade imbalances similar to your own. We can lease the genome as a loss-leader, if your government is willing to look favorably on certain other products . . ."

6.

The gene pirate was showing Evan his editing facility when the slow poison finally hit him. They were aboard an ancient ICBM submarine grounded somewhere off the Philippines. Missile tubes had been converted into fermenters. The bridge was crammed with the latest manipulation technology, virtual reality gear which let the wearer directly control molecule-sized cutting robots as they traveled along DNA helices.

"It's not facilities I need," the pirate told Evan. "It's distribution."

"No problem," Evan said. The pirate's security had been pathetically easy to penetrate. He'd tried to infect Evan with a zombie virus, but Evan's gene-spliced immune system had easily dealt with it. Slow poison was so much more subtle: by the time it could be detected it was too late. Evan was thirty-two. He was posing as a Swiss gray-market broker.

"This is where I keep my old stuff," the pirate said, rapping a stainless-steel cryogenic vat. "Stuff from before I went big time. A luciferase gene drive, for instance. Remember when the Brazilian rainforest started to glow? That was me."

He dashed sweat from his forehead, frowned at the room's complicated thermostat. Grossly fat and completely hairless, he was bare-chested in Bermuda shorts and shower sandals. He'd been targeted because he was about to break the big time with a novel AIDS cure. The company was still making a lot of money from its own

cure, having made sure HIV had never been completely eradicated in developing countries.

Evan said, "I remember the Brazilian government was overthrown—the population took it as a bad omen."

"Hey, what can I say? I was only a kid. Rejigging the genes was easy; only difficulty was finding a vector. Old stuff. Somatic mutation really is going to be the next big thing, believe me. Why breed new strains when you can rework an organism cell by cell?" The pirate rapped the thermostat. His hands were shaking. "Why is it so hot in here?"

"That's the first symptom," Evan said. He stepped out of the way as the gene pirate crashed to the decking. "And that's the second."

The company had taken the precaution of buying the pirate's security chief: Evan had plenty of time to fix the fermenters. They would have boiled dry by the time he was ashore. On impulse, against orders, he took a sample of the AIDS cure with him.

7.

"The territory between piracy and legitimacy is a minefield," the assassin told Evan. "It's also where paradigm shifts are most likely to occur, and that's where I come in. My company likes stability. Another year and you'd have gone public, and most likely the share issue would have made you a billionaire—a minor player, but still a player. Those cats, no one else has them. The genome was supposed to have been wiped out back in the twenties. Very astute, quitting the gray medical market and going for luxury goods." She frowned. "Why am I talking so much?"

"For the same reason you're not going to kill me," Evan said.

"It seems such a silly thing to want to do," the assassin admitted.

Evan smiled. He'd long ago decoded the two-stage virus the gene-pirate had used on him: one a Trojan horse which kept his T-lymphocytes busy while the other rewrote loyalty genes companies implanted in their employees. Once again it had proven its worth. He said, "I need someone like you in my organization. And since you spent so long getting close enough to seduce me, perhaps you'd do me the honor of becoming my wife. I'll need one."

"You don't mind being married to a killer?"

"Of course not. I used to be one myself."

8.

Evan saw the market crash coming. Gene wars had winnowed basic crops to soy beans, rice, and dole yeast: tailored, ever-mutating diseases had reduced cereals and many other food plants to nucleotide sequences stored in computer vaults. Three global biotechnology companies held patents on the calorific input of 98 percent of humanity, but they had lost control of the technology. Pressures of the war economy had simplified it to the point where anyone could directly manipulate her own genome, and hence her own body form.

Evan had made a fortune in the fashion industry, selling basic genetic templates and virus vectors. But he guessed that sooner or later someone would come up with a direct photosynthesis system, and his stock market expert systems were programmed to monitor research in the field. He and his wife sold controlling interest in their company three months before the first green people appeared.

9.

"I remember when you knew what a human being was," Evan said sadly. "I suppose I'm old-fashioned, but there it is."

From her cradle, inside a mist of spray, his wife said, "Is that why you never went green? I always thought it was a fashion statement."

"Old habits die hard." The truth was, he liked his body the way it was. These days, going

green involved somatic mutation which grew a meter-high black cowl to absorb sufficient light energy. Most people lived in the tropics: swarms of black-caped anarchists. Work was no longer a necessity, but an indulgence. Evan added, "I'm going to miss you."

"Let's face it," his wife said, "we never were in love. But I'll miss you, too." With a flick of her powerful tail she launched her streamlined body into the sea.

10.

Black-cowled post-humans, gliding slowly in the sun, aggregating and reaggregating like ameobae. Dolphinoids, tentacles sheathed under fins, rocking in tanks of cloudy water. Ambulatory starfish; tumbling bushes of spikes; snakes with a single arm, a single leg; flocks of tiny birds, brilliant as emeralds, each flock a single entity.

People, grown strange, infected with viruses and myriads of microscopic machines which reengraved their body form at will.

Evan lived in a secluded estate. He was revered as a founding father of the posthuman revolution. A purple funfur microsaur followed him everywhere. It was recording him because he had elected to die.

"I don't regret anything," Evan said, "except perhaps not following my wife when she changed. I saw it coming, you know. All this. Once the technology became simple enough, cheap enough, the companies lost control. Like television or computers, but I suppose you don't remember those." He sighed. He had the vague feeling he'd said all this before. He'd had no new thoughts for a century, except the desire to put an end to thought.

The microsaur said, "In a way, I suppose I am a descendant of computers. Will you see the colonial delegation now?"

"Later." Evan hobbled to a bench and slowly sat down. In the last couple of months he had developed mild arthritis and liver spots on the backs of his hands: death finally expressing parts of his genome that had been suppressed for so long. Hot sunlight fell through the velvet streamers of the tree things; Evan dozed, woke to find a group of starfish watching him. They had blue, human eyes, one at the tip of each muscular arm.

"They wish to honor you by taking your genome to Mars," the little purple triceratops said.

Evan sighed. "I just want peace. To rest. To die."

"Oh, Evan," the triceratops said patiently. "Have you forgotten that nothing really dies anymore?"

JAMES LOVEGROVE

BRITWORLD™

(1992)

HI! Welcome to Britworld™. My name is Wanda May June and I will be your guide, hostess, and compère for the duration of the tour. If you have any questions about anything you see here today, I will be more than happy to answer them.

Thank you for coming prepared with warm clothing. The temperature in Britworld™ is kept at a refreshing forty-five degrees Fahrenheit all year round. USACorp Entertainments have gone to great lengths to enhance the authenticity of your experience by reproducing the exact climate of the original. This also means a) If there is anyone here who suffers from respiratory ailments or is in any way inconvenienced by the Britworld™ environment, they should not hesitate to leave by one of the emergency exits, one of which you will see over there, marked EXIT.

Now, has everyone got their umbrellas, or "bumbershoots," as we call them in Britworld™?

Good. Then why don't you follow me to the first sector? Thank you!

Here we find ourselves in a typical urban situation. This is in fact London, which was the capital of Britworld™ and home to the famous Beatles.

The wind is a little gusty today. Look how it speeds the clouds along! There is a 97 percent chance of rain later.

A brief technical note. The sky you are now seeing is, of course, projected on to the underside of the geodesic dome. Now, whereas other theme parks use simple loop-sequences of an hour or so in length, the clouds here are generated using the latest in Chaos Model programs. Thus no two are ever alike. Some are large, some are small. That one looks just like a duck, doesn't it? We at USACorp Entertainments are justly proud of innovations such as these which keep us one step ahead of the competition.

As you cross the street, mind your step on the piles of garbage—or "rubbish" as it is known here.

Yes, it does smell kind of bad, doesn't it? But

you must remember that in the real Britworld™ they had never heard of efficient disposal or recycling.

Whoops-a-daisy! Are we all right, ma'am? Good. I can see that you haven't sustained any serious injury, but I should take this opportunity to mention to you all that in the eventuality of an accident situation, USACorp Entertainments will accept zero liability. You all signed the waiver forms at the entrance.

Please try to keep up!

Let's wait here for a few minutes at this bus stop. If we are lucky, we may see a genuine double-decker bus. The word "bus" is short for "omnibus," which is pretty much the same thing as a coach. A double-decker bus is a bus with two decks. Hence the name. It is red and will have a number on the front, signifying its route, and a destination—perhaps the Houses of Parliament, where Guy Fawkes lived, or Hyde Park, named after the alter ego of the famous scientist Dr. Jekyll, or maybe the Globe Theater, which was built by Sir William Shakespeare.

Any minute now, there may be an omnibus. There may even be two. Or three!

Double-decker buses have a seating capacity of sixty-eight, forty-four on top, twenty-four below—not forgetting, of course, standing room for another twenty passengers.

Any . . . minute . . . now.

It doesn't look like one's coming. What a disappointment. Well, we can't hang around all day. Let's proceed along this road to the market.

Many historians consider the market to be an early precursor of our shopping mall. Notice how each stall sells a different product, what we now call franchising. Here is the fruit and vegetable stall, selling fruit and vegetables. It is tended by a cheerful man known as a green-grocer. The name is derived from the fact that a large proportion of his groceries are green in color.

Listen.

"Apples and pears! Apples and pears! Getcha apples and pears!"

Isn't that clever? USACorp Entertainments have taken every effort to reduplicate the Britworld™ dialect, incomprehensible now to the great majority of the English-speaking world.

Little boy, the automata are *extremely* delicate. Please don't touch.

I would just like to show you this. A strawberry. Everybody! Look at this strawberry. This is the fruit from which we derive strawberry flavor.

Yes, sir, I suppose it does bear a slight resemblance to a wino's nose.

On the street corner we see the newsvendor, vending newspapers. Let's listen to his distinctive cry.

"Paperrrr! Getcha paper heeeere!"

The cloth cap and raincoat he is wearing are the real thing, the genuine article, as is all the clothing you will see today, purchased at great cost by USACorp Entertainments from museums all over the world.

Beyond the newsvendor you may already have spotted the street musicians, or "buskers," so called because they used to play on buses until the law banned them. The tune they are playing is a traditional folk ballad, "Strawberry Fields Forever." Remember that strawberry I showed you earlier on? Well, this song was written, so they say, about fields of strawberries stretching so far into the distance they seemed to go on forever.

Don't the buskers sing well?

We are standing outside a pub, the Britworld™ equivalent of a bar. "Pub" is short for public house, a house into which members of the public may enter whenever they wish. This one has a name. The King's Head. On the sign up there we see a picture of the head of the King. Notice his crown. Shall we go in?

Here we see the inhabitants of Britworld™ relaxing in the friendly, intimate atmosphere of the pub. At the bar we see the landlord and the landlady, so called because they rent out the house to the public.

This is Charly, a cheerful local. Cheerful locals in London were known as Cockneys because—so legend goes—they were born within the sound of the bells of Cockney Cathedral. Tell us, Charly, do you enjoy drinking here?

"God blimey, luvaduck, I should say. Crikey, strike me blind if I jolly bloomin' well don't! Lor lumme! Eh, guvnor?"

I think he does! And chim-chim-cheroo to you, too, Charly!

Now, follow me, everyone. Don't try that, sir. It's not safe to drink. It's a substitute for the popular pub drink, bitter ale, designed to maintain its color and consistency and that distinctive frothy head for approximately eighteen years.

Let's hurry on to the next sector. But I must warn you, be prepared to be thrilled, chilled, and spilled! Those with heart conditions or nervous complaints may wish to consider leaving by the nearest convenient emergency exit over there, marked EXIT.

Where are we? Fog swirls along darkened streets and the gas lamps flicker, casting strange shadows on the sidewalk. Villains surely lurk in this fog-enshrouded place.

But look at that road sign! "Baker's Street." How many of you know which well-known historical personality lived on Baker's Street?

No.

No.

No, not the Reverend Jim Bakker.

No.

No, it was Sherlock Holmes! And if we are lucky, we may just catch a glimpse . . .

Ah! There! The deerstalker, the cape, the pipe. It can only be . . . And yes, there is his friend and faithful companion, Dr. Watson.

"The game's afoot."

"Good heavens, Holmes! How on earth did you deduce that?"

"Elementary, my dear Watson. When you have eliminated the impossible, whatever remains, however improbable, must be the truth."

And so the great detective sweeps past us on his way to solving another baffling, mystifying, perplexing mystery. So close, so realistic, you could reach out and touch him.

But who is that? A woman, wandering the night streets, vulnerable and alone. She must be careful. There's murder in the air.

Oh, look out! That man in the top hat and cloak! He has a knife! He is Jack the Ripper, that terrible fiend of the night and depraver of women. Who will save her? Who will save her?

Hooray! Here comes a friendly policeman, whose name is Bobby. He blows his whistle. That's seen that dreadful Ripper off! Look how Bobby is comforting that poor woman. How safe she must feel.

Well, I'm quite breathless with excitement. Everybody follow me to the next sector.

Oh dear. Bumbershoots up, everyone! As the saying in Britworld™ goes, "It's raining buckets of cats."

If you can't hear me over the rain, say so and I will speak up. Okay?

Good.

This grand edifice is none other than the Buckingham Palace, home of the King and Queen of Britworld™. USACorp Entertainments, sparing no expense, had the original building transported brick by brick and reconstructed here. See how the Union Jack, royal flag of Britworld™, flutters proudly from the mast on the palace roof.

The palace has a large number of large rooms and a smaller number of small rooms. All the interiors have been re-created down to the finest detail. However, as we're running a little behind, we'll have to skip that part of the tour.

If you *do* want a refund, ma'am, I'd advise you to take the matter up with USACorp's Central Office and not with me.

Trust me, they are *bee-yootiful* rooms.

Notice the Beefeaters standing guard at the palace gates with their fierce pikes and their mustaches. They get their name from their traditional beef-only diet. Yes, amazing as it may sound, they used to eat nothing but beef! Naturally, Beefeaters had a disproportionately high rate of death from bowel cancer.

Twice a day the guards change their positions to avoid cramp. This is known as the Changing of the Guard.

Wait! Look! Up there! On the balcony! Why, the King and Queen have come out to wave at us! Wave back, everybody.

The King is wearing his crown. Remember the sign at the pub? The Queen, meanwhile, is wearing an elegant mid-length gown in taffeta, cut on the bias, with a lace hem and gold braid trim along the sleeves. To complete the ensemble, she wears a diamond tiara and earrings and matching accessories. Ladies, don't you wish you could dress as elegantly as that?

Oh, they're going in again. Goodbye, your majesties! Goodbye! Goodbye!

We are now entering the Shakespeare sector. You can put down your bumbershoots now, as the rain has been switched off. I know several of you have heard about the little difficulty we had in this sector some months back, but I am pleased to be able to tell you that the fire damage has been repaired and the tour can proceed as normal. However, please remember to observe the *No Smoking* rule at all times.

Sir William Shakespeare was known as the Bard of Avon, a hereditary title handed down from one generation of bards to the next in the town of Avon, which was situated a few miles from London, capital city of Britworld™.

The Globe Theater was first constructed by USACorp Entertainments to the same specifications as the original, but since the fire a number of alterations have been made, for instance the use of steel and plastics in place of wood and plaster.

Let's go in.

Shhh. On the stage at this very moment a play is being performed. The play is *Macbeth*, about a barbarian king who goes on a rampage of slaughter and mayhem before being brought to justice by his best friend. You've all seen the old movie starring Arnold Schwarzenegger.

"Tomorrow and tomorrow and tomorrow."

We don't need to hear much more to get an idea of the genius of Sir William Shakespeare's dialogue.

And here, I'm sorry to say, the tour ends. Before we leave via the exit marked EXIT, may I say what a privilege and a pleasure it has been for me to share with you the sights, sounds, and smells of Britworld™. As you will have seen, everything has been designed to the most rigorous of standards, including the automata, which incorporate numerous technological breakthroughs that allow for a wide range of facial expression, body odors, minor blemishes, and deformities, even perspiration!

On behalf of USACorp Entertainments, I would like to thank you for accompanying me on the experience that was . . . Britworld™.

The following souvenirs are available at the merchandise kiosks: reproduction bric-a-brac; a Cockney phrase-book; Union Jack baseball caps; ebook editions of the works of Sherlock Holmes and Sir William Shakespeare, abridged and modernized; *My Parents Went To Britworld™ And All I Got Was This Lousy T-Shirt* T-shirts; foam-rubber crowns for the kids; the fabulous *You Are Saucy Jack* computer game (all formats); and downloads of favorite Britworld™ folk songs, including "Strawberry Fields Forever," "Jerusalem," "God Save the King," and many many more. All major credit cards accepted.

And finally, may I remind you about our other Lost Worlds® experiences, all bookable. They include the Native American Experience™, Dreamtime: the Australian Aborigine Experience™, and Life Among the Bushmen of the Kalahari™.

USACorp Entertainments—where the science of tomorrow brings the past into the present.

Have a nice day.

GERARDO HORACIO PORCAYO

RIPPED IMAGES, RUSTED DREAMS

(1993)

Translated from the Spanish by the author

"THE TIMES GLITTERED. Human shoals swimming through neon, laser lights, and synthetic junk food. It was still shit, I swear, but better than today's shit. And it was mine in all senses. Guadalupe City was the access point. You could find everything in the rotten slums that grew at the hillside of Cerro de la Silla: stolen cars and smuggled intelligent drugs, not forgetting the classics of heroin and boxes of pleasure. You could get high for real; reach madness. You were well supplied with everything, because Monterrey consumed everything. In those days *the heat* could smell you, look at you in the eye, while you picked up a fake coke high through the wires attached to your brain. And you could climb, real high without them playing to kill you."

The Retro looks at me heavily, almost with showiness. He values his Electric Dreams more, his computer Chimeras; chronometric insanity and then ready for a reboot, almost every time. They've become part of the computer, vile maze rats, addicted to electric shocks; to the venom itself. Like her . . .

"I was running away from Laredo, four DEA pigs after me. Three salesmen with Glocks under their armpits and inhalers filling their pockets. I was looking for fresh air, a little cash, and stuff to keep me going."

"You're out of step, old man. Things were always the same, only now we have the Electric Dream," he says. He gets up, throwing a couple rotten dollars on the bar as he leaves. I know his weakness. The darkness clings to our spirit. It's the stigmata of those who hate the world as it is.

Now they hunt addictive software, have labyrinthine dreams of crime and forbidden sex, cycle through blasphemies in a planet ruled, more and more, by a cybernetic god from his silicon heaven beyond the stars. They get lost in venal places that stink of semen and vaginal fluids, in the dim light of ripped sunsets. The world no longer has any pretense at virginity, it's a decrepit whore, walking sadly to the end of the

Milky Way only to find out there are no clients left for her.

"Give me another triple," I ask the barman, and he looks back at me, so weary. He knows my business, a null one, just the waiting, the hunt for users who hate the tales, the beer, and their own life.

"You are going to end with your teeth broken," he warns me. Pity leaks from his eyes like old pus.

"Did I tell you about Cora?"

The son of a bitch pushes me away, he goes to the other end of the battered bar, past the sailors' and workers' vomit, to find the warm hug of the TV. There, he doesn't need to think things over. Why are they all so lost? I prefer the old paranoia, the threats that surrounded you and made you leave Austin or Florida, Houston on a bullet train or hitchhiking across the bloody fields of Illinois, through the rocky deserts near TJ, bug-eyed traffickers with sweaty hands and nervous, bloated agents closing in.

I survey the bar, looking for my contact, or another listener. Even a grubby cat with a broken tail, clambering up the frame of a fractal or a tesseract painting.

The Retro comes back. And he's not alone. A wasted girl with an airbrush shadow makeup that resembles a raccoon, and four hairy beasts that stink of Benzedrine and overheated wires. The curls in their hair are natural, they burn by themselves at the top of the skull, near the socket.

"Beat it!" he warns me. "We don't want flies around."

"I know the business even better than you. I know the history."

One hairy man stands in front of me, he carries a taser glove and his lips are full of post-holocaustic piercings.

"Get lost, graybeard. It would break my heart to kick the shit out of you."

"I even used to have a band like yours," I insist. My shame gets away from me, nauseating me.

"Let him talk. Maybe you will end up like him," says the raccoon girl, giggling like a battered coffee maker.

"He stinks."

"When I reached Monterrey, only the yuppies used the Electric Dream. Well suited, with eight-hundred-dollar pants and British raincoats that smelled like the Thames."

"He lost all his head knobs and bolts when they kicked the shit out of him," states another hairy one.

"I met Loquillo, a guy with an eternal lap-body and a red, curled forelock that hid his socket. And he really loved to get wasted, he never turned down any of the hallucinogenic stuff that appeared, wherever it came from." Raccoon looks at me with loose eyes, each pupil facing a different direction. Squinting Raccoon with atrophied nose.

"Loquillo was a hacker and a wire addict. Not a chemical junkie," argues the Retro. That's a big difference now. You don't gain cred with neuro-activated stuff, but with technology: electricity and wires sunk deep into your brain. It means they know what I'm talking about, and Raccoon, at least, wants to hear the whole story.

"I bet eighty greens that you don't know shit," dares one of the hairy ones.

"I used to play with the black box, with the brain pleasure. They moved adulterated coke at such a high cost that you couldn't even pick up a decent addiction. You had to replace it with small charges straight into the proper conduits, and you'd get high, real high. Charly 29 used to know how to do it. He had a Lincoln convertible, an international credit card with no limit. He had Roger, Isidro, and Cora. And good cranial butchers, not like the usual ones, who think their medibots are best for brain surgery."

"It seems your socket got battered miles ago, and now your brain's rusted," says the Retro. "We begin at fifteen and dine hot software every night."

"Charly found the first net for us. Back then, the Electric Dream was just a complement; the best thing was being on the streets. The adrenaline rushing through you when the cops were

323

pushed to keep appearances up or the PGR had to justify their income. The days when you fixed new cocktails, not even knowing what door you were going to be throwing them at."

"And what happened with Loquillo?" asks the Raccoon.

"That's an old story. Even you would've heard it. He was hunted in the big revolt against the silicon god." A hairy one watches me with tight teeth, his hand tight in his spandex vest pocket. "He was one of my kind and he saw that the good times were dying with the Northern Lights of the Christ-receptionism. At the same time, he fought for Cora. She was the first one to taste the Seagull's Dream, she even baptized it with its name."

"That's old news," grunts the Retro. "Nobody does the Seagull's Dreams today. The ghosts slice you apart if you're not at their level. They rip your guts out with a chain saw, in landscapes built of car bumpers, seas of dry polystyrene, mountains of plastic garbage, and squirrels full of chips and servomotors. Or you are caught in a corner by God, and thrown to the hell of cannibal guts, or into a nightmare of dull teeth. Now, diving into a computer is like running through the streets with the hounds after you and the paranoia of getting caught with the hot stuff. Now, we defy God in every joint, in every hallucination. *You* were never hunted by God."

"I saw him for the first time with Cora. We'd been running through university parties full up to the top with Ecstasy. Rushing down your spine like a galvanic stream, giving you such a boner that you believed you could open new sexual holes. Charly 29 had found us a net. We rode after the fall. There were no drugs left. The President was in town and they successfully cleaned up for the occasion. We were dry. And you know it: abstinence is mortal. So we jumped back to the net. Both in one deck. At that time, we had already tried orgies, the five of us. But that day, it was just me and her. And it was different. We felt God's nauseating breath over our shoulders. His face appeared in the graffiti upon the asphalt and the peeled walls; the sad-

ness stuck to our ribs like lead. We could barely breathe. Her body seemed to be falling apart, my fingers got sunk in her flesh like it was dry mud. We let go. She told me she wanted to go on a boat, so we took a transatlantic from the hotel's door. Its chimneys expelled atomic vapors, MDA, and nootropic cocktails. We traveled with open skies and the sea was more pure than any nanomachine reproductions. The seagulls orbited us like psychotic satellites. They were hungry. Cora wanted to feed them by sheer willpower and, after that, with sushi. Sushi miraculously multiplied. One thousand seagulls kept flying against the wind and crying every time a chunk of fish entered their domain. 'Look at them,' she said, 'they are like angels of solitude, like a mountain that goes around oceans and valleys, they are like faith and happiness.' And she was right. We came back eight times to the same dream, after that, she went alone and never came back."

"And what was Loquillo's role in all this?"

"He met her a little while after that, when he was trying to steal info from Mariano's Labs. It was really hot stuff. Cora was stuck all the way to his bones. She was already a ghost, but kept being special, she could transfer her beauty to you as if it were viral files. When they trapped Loquillo, the bait was Cora herself. He couldn't refuse her, nobody could."

"I've met her," says the hairy one with the glove. "She came to me in a mix of exodiprine and a pirate dream program. And I could break free. She's not such a big deal. Any black software has better divas now. They're vampires that suck you dry. First, they steal your memories, then your sexual appetite, and then even your hope of living."

"That you've never had," I said. "I know what I'm talking about, I'm one of the pioneers."

The Raccoon doesn't laugh anymore. Her eyes have become dark and disoriented, black holes without any spark of life. She's going down fast, to the pit. She needs wires . . .

"You defy God just by living," says the Retro. "The fear has always been there, but, in the

Electric Dream, you can touch it. The torture comes in waves, like rabid hurricanes, it comes over you like dragonflies from hell. Your stomach growls, trying to open its way out of your skin and leave you there, lying in the middle of a nonexisting alley; those mazes are sordid, more than the real ones. One time I found a homeless lady, her eyes had never met the light, they were half-dead, sunken in her eye sockets, covered by a reptilian membrane; she had a small left hand, which grew a sick prosthesis that suppurated semen. Her fatness was so huge that she only kept upright with little crutches attached to her handicap wheels. And the wires came out of her skull; they buzzed, mimicking a cry of help. With her right hand she stirred a dirty mug, filled with human embryos. She was the Virgin. I tell you. I promise you. She hunted me through swamps, computer cemeteries. She ripped open bulldozers. Drunken rockets fell down from the sky, like banished angels. And you cannot escape, she hunts you, even when you've left the Electric Dream. Some nights I still dream of her. The streets are safer, even the Anti-Sin Brigade is clumsy and slow. They have high-tech weapons and scanners, but you can lose them in dry river glens, in dry sewer systems, or through the subway. And, if you've performed well, they'll never find you. But once God has seen you, he never stops appearing, even in the most recent software, in programs compiled in Thailand, with ideographic graffiti and old-fashioned red zones. His breath is worse than you can say. When it hits you, it's like you'll never ever smell anything again; everything becomes lessened and the sole memory of his breath brings you open-eye hallucinations. Heavenquakes happen and drip like rotten glycerin, showering you, stopping your scurry, blurring any possible horizon, extinguishing any spark of hope—You don't know what you're all talking about." His gaze is lost in his glass. His hands shake frantically like they're trying to fly away, to get the hell out of the body.

I look around. An angel has passed, dropping the pest. The Raccoon operates her black box.

Her eyes are already cosmic bat clusters; they cry blasphemies and overwhelming curses. The hairy ones keep to themselves. They're in the Reality Syndrome, they no longer know where they are. The one with the glove confuses me for an exterminator angel. He stares at me closely, like a meditation. He sees my rotten face, half-eaten by static, and my silhouette, deformed by nonexistent pixels.

"That's why I said that my time was a better one," I conclude. "There was nothing this big back then, nothing so overwhelming but the hangover, the shakes of your dryness, your guts yelling with chemical hunger."

The bartender shepherds the flies. They follow him like he'd made an attachment spell, they watch him as he juggles glass and adulterated bottles, stare at his everlasting, tattooed reflection on the mirrors. He is tired of us all. He gestures to me, resigned. He has tried it before and doesn't bother to wait for my reaction. I follow his gaze. Three Voices awaits, hidden at a corner table. The White Privateer is standing up beside him.

I leave the group without a word. The hairs on my back bristle like roaches' antennas. I bound forward, and rush to my meeting.

"It's not a good thing to open your mouth that much," says Three Voices, carefully steering his felt hat, controlling his own movements through it. "They never forget, not even the old stuff."

"I have to do something," I lie to him. He doesn't care, he's only doing his job. The protocols are strict and should be observed. I reach my hand to him. Hidden green inside. He takes it, delaying the contact. And his eyes tell me abyssal things, horrible truths.

"The rest comes tomorrow at the Macroplaza," he promises, and hands me a small plastic cylinder. I turn away, without a word. I have no intention of leaving the bar.

One of the hairy ones puts his hand out to me. I sense the bills, their poor and ruined texture; rotten leaves, almost useless excrescences.

"The eighty we bet. You earned it, old man.

I knew Loquillo couldn't have been screwed in the reality. I knew he couldn't have died in the bomb attack. His death belonged to the net."

No more words, we share booze and loneliness. Anguish that piles itself like acid in the guts. We are balloons that, little by little, get inflated. Someday we will burst.

"I think I understand you now," says the Retro, pulling the Raccoon along with him, as she travels the virtual frequency.

I see them get lost through the mirror, through the inner darkness, through the pitch black of the outside. And the silence stays in the air for a long time, like clots in zero gravity. It fills the atmosphere and makes my paranoia all the stronger.

"Someone's gonna end breaking your teeth," warns the bartender again, picking up the dollars. His watery eyes are opaque and sad.

"I know," I answer him, and I leave the bar, the shelter.

The city expands itself before me, a hypertrophied and dying organism. The buildings cut themselves against the bloody night like spades in a battlefield. Tons of parabolic antennas bend their ears looking forward to catch the voice of God. The worm of fear begins to eat my guts. The cathedrals are like blind eyes in the hellish darkness, they keep on going, block by block; like dogs, wanderers, and some junkies shaking with the beat of peristaltic movements, forgetting ignominies, boredom, apprehension . . .

They were even better than me, junkies, I mean. They're not afraid, not of God, not of the Anti-Sin Brigade. The narcotic officers don't exist anymore.

I walk, and with each step I miss the old ways, the sirens screaming your almost certain arrest, agents so corrupt, so full of needs, like your own, closing in. Shit has changed. Paranoia, too. Like many other nights, I fear androids after me, angry, thirsty for justice, a revenge postponed for so long, bleeding, while they get free of the nails and the crosses and follow my footprints, showering them in their synthetic blood. The crown of thorns is a vector of their memories.

And I fear. And I swallow the pills. The hunt may never end.

And the hunger in me never will.

FOR A COUPLE OF WILLIAMS
BURROUGHS AND GIBSON

NEAL STEPHENSON

THE GREAT SIMOLEON CAPER

(1995)

HARD TO IMAGINE a less attractive lifestyle for a young man just out of college than going back to Bismarck to live with his parents—unless it's living with his brother in the suburbs of Chicago, which, naturally, is what I did. Mom at least bakes a mean cherry pie. Joe, on the other hand, got me into a permanent emotional headlock and found some way, every day, to give me psychic noogies. For example, there was the day he gave me the job of figuring out how many jelly beans it would take to fill up Soldier Field.

Let us stipulate that it's all my fault; Joe would want me to be clear on that point. Just as he was always good with people, I was always good with numbers. As Joe tells me at least once a week, I should have studied engineering. Drifted between majors instead, ended up with a major in math and a minor in art—just about the worst thing you can put on a job app.

Joe, on the other hand, went into the ad game. When the Internet and optical fiber and HDTV and digital cash all came together and turned into what we now call the Metaverse, most of the big ad agencies got hammered—because in the Metaverse, you can actually whip out a gun and blow the Energizer Bunny's head off, and a lot of people did. Joe borrowed ten thousand bucks from Mom and Dad and started this clever young ad agency. If you've spent any time crawling the Metaverse, you've seen his work—and it's seen you, and talked to you, and followed you around.

Mom and Dad stayed in their same little house in Bismarck, North Dakota. None of their neighbors guessed that if they cashed in their stock in Joe's agency, they'd be worth about $20 million. I nagged them to diversify their portfolio—you know, buy a bushel basket of Krugerrands and bury them in the backyard, or maybe put a few million into a mutual fund. But Mom and Dad felt this would be a no-confidence vote in Joe. "It'd be," Dad said, "like showing up for your kid's piano recital with a Walkman."

Joe comes home one January evening with

a magnum of champagne. After giving me the obligatory hazing about whether I'm old enough to drink, he pours me a glass. He's already banished his two sons to the Home Theater. They have cranked up the set-top box they got for Christmas. Patch this baby into your HDTV, and you can cruise the Metaverse, wander the Web, and choose from among several user-friendly operating systems, each one rife with automatic help systems, customer-service hotlines, and intelligent agents. The theater's subwoofer causes our silverware to buzz around like sheet-metal hockey players, and amplified explosions knock swirling nebulas of tiny bubbles loose from the insides of our champagne glasses. Those low frequencies must penetrate the young brain somehow, coming in under kids' media-hip radar and injecting the edfotainucational muchomedia bitstream direct into their cerebral cortices.

"Hauled down a mother of an account today," Joe explains. "We hype cars. We hype computers. We hype athletic shoes. But as of three hours ago, we are hyping a currency."

"What?" says his wife, Anne.

"Y'know, like dollars or yen. Except this is a new currency."

"From which country?" I ask. This is like offering lox to a dog: I've given Joe the chance to enlighten his feckless bro. He hammers back half a flute of Dom Perignon and shifts into full-on Pitch Mode.

"Forget about countries," he says. "We're talking Simoleons—the smart, hip new currency of the Metaverse."

"Is this like E-money?" Anne asks.

"We've been doing E-money for e-ons, ever since automated-teller machines." Joe says, with just the right edge of scorn. "Nowadays we can use it to go shopping in the Metaverse. But it's still in US dollars. Smart people are looking for something better."

That was for me. I graduated college with a thousand bucks in savings. With inflation at 10 percent and rising, that buys a lot fewer Leinenkugels than it did a year ago.

"The government's never going to get its act together on the budget," Joe says. "It can't. Inflation will just get worse. People will put their money elsewhere."

"Inflation would have to get pretty damn high before I'd put my money into some artificial currency," I say.

"Hell, they're all artificial," Joe says. "If you think about it, we've been doing this forever. We put our money in stocks, bonds, shares of mutual funds. Those things represent real assets—factories, ships, bananas, software, gold, whatever. Simoleons is just a new name for those assets. You carry around a smart card and spend it just like cash. Or else you go shopping in the Metaverse and spend the money online, and the goods show up on your doorstep the next morning."

I say, "Who's going to fall for that?"

"Everyone," he says. "For our big promo, we're going to give Simoleons away to some average Joes at the Super Bowl. We'll check in with them one, three, six months later, and people will see that this is a safe and stable place to put their money."

"It doesn't inspire much confidence," I say, "to hand the stuff out like Monopoly money."

He's ready for this one. "It's not a handout. It's a sweepstakes." And that's when he asks me to calculate how many jelly beans will fill Soldier Field.

Two hours later, I'm down at the local galaxy-class grocery store, in Bulk: a Manhattan of towering Lucite bins filled with steel-cut rolled oats, off-brand Froot Loops, sun-dried tomatoes, prefabricated s'mores, macadamias, French roasts, and pignolias, all dispensed into your bag or bucket with a jerk at the handy Plexiglas guillotine. Not a human being in sight, just robot restocking machines trundling back and forth on a grid of overhead catwalks and surveillance cameras hidden in smoked-glass hemispheres. I stroll through the gleaming Lucite wonderland holding a perfect 6-in. cube improvised from duct tape and cardboard. I stagger through a glitter gulch of Gummi fauna, Boston Baked Beans, gobstoppers, Good & Plenty, tart n' tiny.

Then, bingo: bulk jelly beans, premium grade. I put my cube under the spout and fill it.

Who guesses closest and earliest on the jelly beans wins the Simoleons. They've hired a Big Six accounting firm to make sure everything's done right. And since they can't actually fill the stadium with candy, I'm to come up with the Correct Answer and supply it to them and, just as important, to keep it secret.

I get home and count the beans: 3,101. Multiply by 8 to get the number in a cubic foot: 24,808. Now I just need the number of cubic feet in Soldier Field. My nephews are sprawled like pithed frogs before the HDTV, teaching themselves physics by lobbing antimatter bombs onto an offending civilization from high orbit. I prance over the black zigzags of the control cables and commandeer a unit.

Up on the screen, a cartoon elf or sprite or something pokes its head out from behind a window, then draws it back. No, I'm not a paranoid schizophrenic—this is the much-hyped intelligent agent who comes with the box. I ignore it, make my escape from Gameland, and blunder into a lurid district of the Metaverse where thousands of infomercials run day and night, each in its own window. I watch an ad for Chinese folk medicines made from rare-animal parts, genetically engineered and grown in vats. Grizzly bear gallbladders are shown growing like bunches of grapes in an amber fluid.

The animated sprite comes all the way out and leans up against the edge of the infomercial window. "Hey!" it says, in a goofy, exuberant voice, "I'm Raster! Just speak my name—that's Raster—if you need any help."

I don't like Raster's looks. It's likely he was wandering the streets of Toontown and waving a sign saying WILL ANNOY GROWN-UPS FOR FOOD until he was hired by the cable company. He begins flying around the screen, leaving a trail of glowing fairy dust that fades much too slowly for my taste.

"Give me the damn encyclopedia!" I shout. Hearing the dread word, my nephews erupt from the rug and flee.

So I look up Soldier Field. My old Analytic Geometry textbook, still flecked with insulation from the attic, has been sitting on my thigh like a lump of ice. By combining some formulas from it with the encyclopedia's stats . . .

"Hey! Raster!"

Raster is so glad to be wanted that he does figure eights around the screen. "Calculator!" I shout.

"No need, boss! Simply tell me your desired calculation, and I will do it in my head!"

So I have a most tedious conversation with Raster, in which I estimate the number of cubic feet in Soldier Field, rounded to the nearest foot. I ask Raster to multiply that by 24,808 and he shoots back: 537,824,167,717.

A nongeek wouldn't have thought twice. But I say, "Raster, you have Spam for brains. It should be an exact multiple of eight!" Evidently my brother's new box came with one of those defective chips that makes errors when the numbers get really big.

Raster slaps himself upside the head; loose screws and transistors tumble out of his ears. "Darn! Guess I'll have to have a talk with my programmer!" And then he freezes up for a minute.

My sister-in-law Anne darts into the room, hunched in a don't-mind-me posture, and looks around. She's terrified that I may have a date in here. "Who're you talking to?"

"This goofy IA that came with your box," I say. "Don't ever use it to do your taxes, by the way."

She cocks her head. "You know, just yesterday I asked it for help with a Schedule B, and it gave me a recipe for shellfish bisque."

"Good evening, sir. Good evening, ma'am. What were those numbers again?" Raster asks. Same voice, but different inflections—more human. I call out the numbers one more time and he comes back with 537,824,167,720.

"That sounds better," I mutter.

Anne is nonplussed. "Now its voice recognition seems to be working fine."

"I don't think so. I think my little math problem got forwarded to a real human being. When the conversation gets over the head of the built-in software, it calls for help, and a human steps in and takes over. He's watching us through the built-in videocam," I explain, pointing at the fish-eye lens built into the front panel of the set-top box, "and listening through the built-in mike."

Anne's getting that glazed look in her eyes; I grope for an analog analogy. "Remember The Exorcist? Well, Raster has just been possessed, like the chick in the flick. Except it's not just Beelzebub. It's a customer-service rep."

I've just walked blind into a trap that is yawningly obvious to Anne. "Maybe that's a job you should apply for!" she exclaims.

The other jaw of the trap closes faster than my teeth chomping down on my tongue: "I can take your application online right now!" says Raster.

My sister-in-law is the embodiment of sugary triumph until the next evening, when I have a good news/bad news conversation with her. Good: I'm now a Metaverse customer-service rep. Bad: I don't have a cubicle in some Edge City office complex. I telecommute from home—from her home, from her sofa. I sit there all day long, munching through my dwindling stash of tax-deductible jelly beans, wearing an operator's headset, gripping the control unit, using it like a puppeteer's rig to control other people's Rasters on other people's screens, all over the US. I can see them—the wide-angle view from their set-top boxes is piped to a window on my screen. But they can't see me—just Raster, my avatar, my body in the Metaverse.

Ghastly in the mottled, flattening light of the Tube, people ask me inane questions about arithmetic. If they're asking for help with recipes, airplane schedules, child-rearing, or home improvement, they've already been turfed to someone else. My expertise is pure math only.

Which is pretty sleepy until the next week, when my brother's agency announces the big Simoleons Sweepstakes. They've hired a knock-kneed fullback as their spokesman. Within min-

utes, requests for help from contestants start flooding in. Every Bears fan in Greater Chicago is trying to calculate the volume of Soldier Field. They're all doing it wrong; and even the ones who are doing it right are probably using the faulty chip in their set-top box. I'm in deep conflict-of-interest territory here, wanting to reach out with Raster's stubby, white-gloved, three-fingered hand and slap some sense into these people.

But I'm sworn to secrecy. Joe has hired me to do the calculations for the Metrodome, Three Rivers Stadium, RFK Stadium, and every other NFL venue. There's going to be a Simoleons winner in every city.

We are allowed to take fifteen-minute breaks every four hours. So I crank up the Home Theater, just to blow the carbon out of its cylinders, and zip down the main street of the Metaverse to a club that specializes in my kind of tunes. I'm still "wearing" my Raster uniform, but I don't care—I'm just one of thousands of Rasters running up and down the street on their breaks.

My club has a narrow entrance on a narrow alley off a narrow side street, far from the virtual malls and 3-D video-game amusement parks that serve as the cash cows for the Metaverse's E-money economy. Inside, there's a few Rasters on break, but it's mostly people "wearing" more creative avatars. In the Metaverse, there's no part of your virtual body you can't pierce, brand, or tattoo in an effort to look weirder than the next guy.

The live band onstage—jacked in from a studio in Prague—isn't very good, so I duck into the back room where there are virtual racks full of tapes you can sample, listening to a few seconds from each song. If you like it, you can download the whole album, with optional interactive liner notes, videos, and sheet music.

I'm pawing through one of these racks when I sense another avatar, something big and shaggy, sidling up next to me. It mumbles something; I ignore it. A magisterial throat-clearing noise rumbles in the subwoofer, crackles in the surround speakers, punches through cleanly on the center channel above the screen. I turn and look: it's a heavyset creature wearing a T-shirt emblazoned with a logo: *HACKERS 1111*. It has very long scythe-like claws, which it uses to grip a hot-pink cylinder. It's much better drawn than Raster; almost Disney-quality.

The sloth speaks: "537,824,167,720."

"Hey!" I shout. "Who the hell are you?" It lifts the pink cylinder to its lips and drinks. It's a can of Jolt. "Where'd you get that number?" I demand. "It's supposed to be a secret."

"The key is under the doormat," the sloth says, then turns around and walks out of the club.

My fifteen-minute break is over, so I have to ponder the meaning of this through the rest of my shift. Then, I drag myself up out of the couch, open the front door, and peel up the doormat.

Sure enough, someone has stuck an envelope under there. Inside is a sheet of paper with a number on it, written in hexadecimal notation, which is what computer people use: 0A56 7781 6BE2 2004 89FF 9001 C782—and so on for about five lines.

The sloth had told me that "the key is under the doormat," and I'm willing to bet many Simoleons that this number is an encryption key that will enable me to send and receive coded messages.

So I spend ten minutes punching it into the set-top box. Raster shows up and starts to bother me: "Can I help you with anything?"

By the time I've punched in the 256th digit, I've become a little testy with Raster and said some rude things to him. I'm not proud of it. Then I hear something that's music to my ears: "I'm sorry, I didn't understand you," Raster chirps. "Please check your cable connections— I'm getting some noise on the line."

A second figure materializes on the screen, like a digital genie: it's the sloth again. "Who the hell are you?" I ask.

The sloth takes another slug of Jolt, stifles a belch, and says, "I am Codex, the Crypto-Anarchist Sloth."

"Your equipment requires maintenance," Raster says. "Please contact the cable company."

"Your equipment is fine," Codex says. "I'm encrypting your back channel. To the cable company, it looks like noise. As you figured out, that number is your personal encryption key. No government or corporation on earth can eavesdrop on us now."

"Gosh, thanks," I say.

"You're welcome," Codex replies. "Now, let's get down to biz. We have something you want. You have something we want."

"How did you know the answer to the Soldier Field jelly bean question?"

"We've got all twenty-seven," Codex says. And he rattles off the secret numbers for Candlestick Park, the Kingdome, the Meadowlands . . .

"Unless you've broken into the accounting firm's vault," I say, "there's only one way you could have those numbers. You've been eavesdropping on my little chats with Raster. You've tapped the line coming out of this set-top box, haven't you?"

"Oh, that's typical. I suppose you think we're a bunch of socially inept, acne-ridden, high-IQ teenage hackers who play sophomoric pranks on the Establishment."

"The thought had crossed my mind," I say. But the fact that the cartoon sloth can give me such a realistic withering look, as he is doing now, suggests a much higher level of technical sophistication. Raster only has six facial expressions and none of them is very good.

"Your brother runs an ad agency, no?"

"Correct."

"He recently signed up Simoleons Corp.?"

"Correct."

"As soon as he did, the government put your house under full-time surveillance."

Suddenly the glass eyeball in the front of the set-top box is looking very big and beady to me. "They tapped our infotainment cable?"

"Didn't have to. The cable people are happy to do all the dirty work—after all, they're beholden to the government for their monopoly.

So all those calculations you did using Raster were piped straight to the cable company and from there to the government. We've got a mole in the government who cc'd us everything through an anonymous remailer in Jyväskylä, Finland."

"Why should the government care?"

"They care big-time," Codex says. "They're going to destroy Simoleons. And they're going to step all over your family in the process."

"Why?"

"Because if they don't destroy E-money," Codex says, "E-money will destroy them."

• • •

The next afternoon I show up at my brother's office, in a groovily refurbished ex–power plant on the near West Side. He finishes rolling some calls and then waves me into his office, a cavernous space with a giant steam turbine as a conversation piece. I think it's supposed to be an irony thing.

"Aren't you supposed to be cruising the I-way for stalled motorists?" he says.

"Spare me the fraternal heckling," I say. "We crypto-anarchists don't have time for such things."

"Crypto-anarchists?"

"The word *panarchist* is also frequently used."

"Cute," he says, rolling the word around in his head. He's already working up a mental ad campaign for it.

"You're looking flushed and satisfied this afternoon," I say. "Must have been those two imperial pints of Hog City Porter you had with your baby-back ribs at Divane's Lakeview Grill."

Suddenly he sits up straight and gets an edgy look about him, as if a practical joke is in progress, and he's determined not to play the fool.

"So how'd you know what I had for lunch?"

"Same way I know you've been cheating on your taxes."

"What!?"

"Last year you put a new tax-deductible sofa in your home office. But that sofa is a hide-a-bed model, which is a no-no."

"Hackers," he says. "Your buddies hacked into my records, didn't they?"

"You win the Stratolounger."

"I thought they had safeguards on these things now."

"The files are harder to break into. But every time information gets sent across the wires— like, when Anne uses Raster to do the taxes—it can be captured and decrypted. Because, my brother, you bought the default data-security agreement with your box, and the default agreement sucks."

"So what are you getting at?"

"For that," I say, "we'll have to go someplace that isn't under surveillance."

"Surveillance!? What the . . ." he begins. But then I nod at the TV in the corner of his office, with its beady glass eye staring out at us from the set-top box.

We end up walking along the lakeshore, which, in Chicago in January, is madness. But we hail from North Dakota, and we have all the cold-weather gear it takes to do this. I tell him about Raster and the cable company.

"Oh, Jesus!" he says. "You mean those numbers aren't secret?"

"Not even close. They've been put in the hands of twenty-seven stooges hired by the government. The stooges have already FedEx'd their entry forms with the correct numbers. So, as of now, all of your Simoleons—twenty-seven million dollars' worth—are going straight into the hands of the stooges on Super Bowl Sunday. And they will turn out to be your worst public-relations nightmare. They will cash in their Simoleons for comic books and baseball cards and claim it's safer. They will intentionally go bankrupt and blame it on you. They will show up in twos and threes on tawdry talk shows to report mysterious disappearances of their Simoleons during Metaverse transactions. They will, in short, destroy the image—and the business—of your client. The result: victory for the government, which hates and fears private currencies. And bankruptcy for you, and for Mom and Dad."

"How do you figure?"

"Your agency is responsible for screwing up this sweepstakes. Soon as the debacle hits, your stock plummets. Mom and Dad lose millions in paper profits they've never had a chance to enjoy. Then your big shareholders will sue your ass, my brother, and you will lose. You gambled the value of the company on the faulty data-security built into your set-top box, and you as a corporate officer are personally responsible for the losses."

At this point, big brother Joe feels the need to slam himself down on a park bench, which must feel roughly like sitting on a block of dry ice. But he doesn't care. He's beyond physical pain. I sort of expected to feel triumphant at this point, but I don't.

So I let him off the hook. "I just came from your accounting firm," I say. "I told them I had discovered an error in my calculations—that my set-top box had a faulty chip. I supplied them with twenty-seven new numbers, which I worked out by hand, with pencil and paper, in a conference room in their offices, far from the prying eye of the cable company. I personally sealed them in an envelope and placed them in their vault."

"So the sweepstakes will come off as planned," he exhales. "Thank God!"

"Yeah—and while you're at it, thank me and the panarchists," I shoot back. "I also called Mom and Dad, and told them that they should sell their stock—just in case the government finds some new way to sabotage your contest."

"That's probably wise," he says sourly, "but they're going to get hammered on taxes. They'll lose forty percent of their net worth to the government, just like that."

"No, they won't," I say. "They aren't paying any taxes."

"Say what?" He lifts his chin off his mittens for the first time in a while, reinvigorated by the chance to tell me how wrong I am. "Their cash basis is only ten thousand dollars—you think the

IRS won't notice twenty million dollars in capital gains?"

"We didn't invite the IRS," I tell him. "It's none of the IRS's damn business."

"They have ways to make it their business."

"Not anymore. Mom and Dad aren't selling their stock for dollars, Joe."

"Simoleons? It's the same deal with Simoleons—everything gets reported to the government."

"Forget Simoleons. Think CryptoCredits."

"CryptoCredits? What the hell is a Crypto-Credit?" He stands up and starts pacing back and forth. Now he's convinced I've traded the family cow for a handful of magic beans.

"It's what Simoleons ought to be: E-money that is totally private from the eyes of government."

"How do you know? Isn't any code crackable?"

"Any kind of E-money consists of numbers moving around on wires," I say. "If you know how to keep your numbers secret, your currency is safe. If you don't, it's not. Keeping numbers secret is a problem of cryptography—a branch of mathematics. Well, Joe, the crypto-anarchists showed me their math. And it's good math. It's better than the math the government uses. Better than Simoleons' math too. No one can mess with CryptoCredits."

He heaves a big sigh. "Okay, okay—you want me to say it? I'll say it. You were right. I was wrong. You studied the right thing in college after all."

"I'm not worthless scum?"

"Not worthless scum. So. What do these crypto-anarchists want, anyway?"

For some reason I can't lie to my parents, but Joe's easy. "Nothing," I say. "They just wanted to do us a favor, as a way of gaining some goodwill with us."

"And furthering the righteous cause of World Panarchy?"

"Something like that."

Which brings us to Super Bowl Sunday. We are sitting in a skybox high up in the Superdome, complete with wet bar, kitchen, waiters, and big TV screens to watch the instant replays of what we've just seen with our own naked, pitiful, nondigital eyes.

The corporate officers of Simoleons are there. I start sounding them out on their cryptographic protocols, and it becomes clear that these people can't calculate their gas mileage without consulting Raster, much less navigate the subtle and dangerous currents of cutting-edge cryptography.

A Superdome security man comes in, looking uneasy. "Some, uh, gentlemen here," he says. "They have tickets that appear to be authentic."

It's three guys. The first one is a 300 pounder with hair down to his waist and a beard down to his navel. He must be a Bears fan because he has painted his face and bare torso blue and orange. The second one isn't quite as introverted as the first, and the third isn't quite the button-down conformist the other two are. Mr. Big is carrying an old milk crate. What's inside must be heavy, because it looks like it's about to pull his arms out of their sockets.

"Mr. and Mrs. De Groot?" he says, as he staggers into the room. Heads turn toward my mom and dad, who, alarmed by the appearance of these three, have declined to identify themselves. The guy makes for them and slams the crate down in front of my dad.

"I'm the guy you've known as Codex," he says. "Thanks for naming us as your broker."

If Joe wasn't a rowing-machine abuser, he'd be blowing aneurysms in both hemispheres about now. "Your broker is a half-naked blue-and-orange crypto-anarchist?"

Dad devotes thirty seconds or so to lighting his pipe. Down on the field, the two-minute warning sounds. Dad puffs out a cloud of smoke and says, "He seemed like an honest sloth."

"Just in case," Mom says, "we sold half the stock through our broker in Bismarck. He says we'll have to pay taxes on that."

"We transferred the other half offshore, to Mr. Codex here," Dad says, "and he converted it into the local currency—tax free."

"Offshore? Where? The Bahamas?" Joe asks.

"The First Distributed Republic," says the big panarchist. "It's a virtual nation-state. I'm the Minister of Data Security. Our official currency is CryptoCredits."

"What the hell good is that?" Joe says.

"That was my concern too," Dad says, "so, just as an experiment, I used my CryptoCredits to buy something a little more tangible."

Dad reaches into the milk crate and heaves out a rectangular object made of yellow metal. Mom hauls out another one. She and Dad begin lining them up on the counter, like King and Queen Midas unloading a carton of Twinkies.

It takes Joe a few seconds to realize what's happening. He picks up one of the gold bars and gapes at it. The Simoleons execs crowd around and inspect the booty.

"Now you see why the government wants to stamp us out," the big guy says. "We can do what they do—cheaper and better."

For the first time, light dawns on the face of the Simoleons CEO. "Wait a sec," he says, and puts his hands to his temples. "You can rig it so that people who use E-money don't have to pay taxes to any government? Ever?"

"You got it," the big panarchist says. The horn sounds announcing the end of the first half.

"I have to go down and give away some Simoleons," the CEO says, "but after that, you and I need to have a talk."

The CEO goes down in the elevator with my brother, carrying a box of twenty-seven smart cards, each of which is loaded up with secret numbers that makes it worth a million Simoleons. I go over and look out the skybox window: twenty-seven Americans are congregated down on the 50-yard line, waiting for their mathematical manna to descend from heaven. They are just the demographic cross section that my brother was hoping for. You'd never guess they were all secretly citizens of the First Distributed Republic.

The crypto-anarchists grab some Jolt from the wet bar and troop out, so now it's just me, Mom, and Dad in the skybox. Dad points at the field with the stem of his pipe. "Those twenty-seven folks down there," he says. "They didn't get any help from you, did they?"

I've lied about this successfully to Joe. But I know it won't work with Mom and Dad. "Let's put it this way," I say, "not all panarchists are long-haired, Jolt-slurping maniacs. Some of them look like you—exactly like you, as a matter of fact."

Dad nods; I've got him on that one.

"Codex and his people saved the contest, and our family, from disaster. But there was a quid pro quo."

"Usually is," Dad says.

"But it's good for everyone. What Joe wants—and what his client wants—is for the promotion to go well, so that a year from now, everyone who's watching this broadcast today will have a high opinion of the safety and stability of Simoleons. Right?"

"Right."

"If you give the Simoleons away at random, you're rolling the dice. But if you give them to people who are secretly panarchists—who have a vested interest in showing that E-money works—it's a much safer bet."

"Does the First Distributed Republic have a flag?" Mom asks, out of left field. I tell her these guys look like sewing enthusiasts. So, even before the second half starts, she's sketched out a flag on the back of her program. "It'll be very colorful," she says. "Like a jar of jelly beans."

JEFFREY THOMAS

IMMOLATION

(2000)

1: KEEPING UP WITH THE JONESES

They had made it snow again this weekend, as they would every weekend until Christmas. Not on the weekdays, hampering the traffic of workers, or so much today as to inconvenience the shoppers; rather, enough to inspire consumers to further holiday spirit, and further purchases.

High atop the Vat, a machine that to some might resemble an oil tanker of old standing on its prow, Magnesium Jones crouched back among the conduits and exhaust ports like an infant gargoyle on the verge of crowning. His womb was a steamy one; the heat from the blowers would have cooked a birther like a lobster. Jones was naked, his shoulder pressed against the hood of a whirring fan. When he had instant coffee or soup to make he would boil water by resting a pot atop the fan's cap. He was not wearing clothes lest they catch fire.

Not all the cultures were designed to be so impervious to heat; some, rather, were unper-turbed by extreme cold. On the sixth terrace of the plant proper, which faced the Vat, a group of cultures took break in the open air, a few of them naked and turning their faces up to the powdery blizzard invitingly. It had been an alarming development for many, the Plant's management allowing cultures to take break. It suggested they needed consideration, even concern.

Jones squinted through the blowing veils of snow. He recognized a number of the laborers. Though all were bald, and all cloned from a mere half-dozen masters, their heads were tattooed in individual designs so as to distinguish them from each other. Numbers and letters usually figured into these designs—codes. Some had their names tattooed on their foreheads, and all tattoos were colored according to department: violet for Shipping, gray for the Vat, blue for Cryogenics, red for the Ovens, and so on. Magnesium Jones's tattoo was of the last color. But there was also some artistry employed in the tattoo designs. They might portray familiar landmarks from Punktown, or from Earth where most of Punktown's colonists originated, at least in ancestry. Animals, celebrities, sports stars. Magnesium Jones's tattoo was a ring of flame around his head like a corona, with a few black letters and a bar code in the flames like the charred skeleton of a burnt house.

Some artistry, some fun and flourish, was also employed in the naming of the cultures. On the terrace he recognized Sherlock Jones, Imitation Jones, and Basketball Jones. He thought he caught a glimpse of Subliminal Jones heading back inside. Waxlips Jones sat on the edge of the railing, dangling his legs over the street far below. Jones Jones held a steaming coffee. Huckleberry Jones was in subdued conversation with Digital Jones. Copyright Jones and M. I. Jones emerged from the building to join the rest.

Watching them, Magnesium Jones missed his own conversations with some of them, missed the single break that he looked forward to through the first ten hours of the workday. But did he miss the creatures themselves, he wondered? He felt a kinship with other cultures, an empathy for their lives, their situations, in a general sense . . . but that might merely be because he saw himself in them, felt for his own life, his own situation. Sometimes the kinship felt like brotherhood. But affection? Friendship? Love? He wasn't sure if his feelings could be defined in that way. Or was it just that the birthers felt no more strongly, merely glossed and romanticized their own pale feelings?

But Jones did not share the plight of the robot, the android . . . the question of whether they could consider themselves alive, of whether they could aspire to actual emotion. He felt very much alive. He felt some very strong emotions. Anger. Hatred. These feelings, unlike love, were not at all ambiguous.

He turned away from the snowy vista of Plant and city beyond, shivering, glad to slip again into his nest of thrumming heat. From an insulated box he had stolen and dragged up here he took some clothing. Some of it was fireproof, some not. The long black coat, with its broad lapels

turned up to protect his neck from the snow, had a heated mesh in the lining. Worn gloves, and he pulled a black ski hat over his bald head, as much to conceal his tattoo as to shield his naked scalp from snow. He stared at his wrist, willing numbers to appear there. They told him the time. A feature all the cultures at the Plant possessed, to help them time their work efficiently. He had an appointment, a meeting, but he had plenty of time yet to get there.

As much as he scorned his former life in the Plant, there were some behaviors too ingrained to shake. Magnesium Jones was ever punctual.

• • •

Walking the street, Jones slipped on a pair of dark glasses. In the vicinity of the Plant it would be easy to recognize him as a culture. The six masters had all been birther males, criminals condemned to death (they had been paid for the rights to clone them for industrial labor). Under current law it was illegal to clone living human beings. Clones of living beings might equate themselves with their originals. Clones of living beings might thus believe they had certain rights.

Wealthy people stored clones of themselves in case of mishap, cloned families and friends, illegally. Everyone knew that. For all Jones knew, the president of the Plant might be a clone himself. But still, somehow, the cultures were cultures. Still a breed of their own.

Behind the safe shields of his dark lenses, Jones studied the faces of people he passed on the street. Birthers, Christmas shopping, but their faces closed off in hard privacy. The closer birthers were grouped together, the more cut off they became from each other in that desperate animal need for their own territory, even if it extended no further than their scowls and stern, downcast eyes.

Distant shouted chants made him turn his head, though he already knew their source. There was always a group of strikers camped just outside the barrier of the Plant. Tents, smoke from barrel fires, banners rippling in the snowy gusts. There was one group on a hunger strike, emaciated as concentration camp prisoners. A few weeks ago, one woman had self-immolated. Jones had heard screams, and come to the edge of his high hideout to watch. He had marveled at the woman's calm as she sat cross-legged, a black silhouette with her head already charred bald at the center of a small inferno . . . had marveled at how she did not run or cry out, panic or lose her resolve. He admired her strength, her commitment. It was a sacrifice for her fellow human beings, an act which would suggest that the birthers felt a greater brotherhood than the cultures did, after all. But then, their society encouraged such feelings, whereas the cultures were discouraged from friendship, companionship, affection.

Then again, maybe the woman had just been insane.

• • •

To reach the basement pub Jones edged through a narrow tunnel of dripping ceramic brick, the floor a metal mesh . . . below which he heard dark liquid rushing. A section of wall on the right opened up, blocked by chicken wire, and in a dark room like a cage a group of mutants or aliens or mutated aliens gazed out at him as placid as animals waiting to eat or be eaten (and maybe that was so, too); they were so tall their heads scraped the ceiling, thinner than skeletons, with cracked faces that looked shattered and glued back together. Their hair was cobwebs blowing, though to Jones the clotted humid air down here seemed to pool around his legs.

A throb of music grew until he opened a metal door and it exploded in his face like a boobytrap. Slouched heavy backs at a bar, a paunchy naked woman doing a slow grinding dance atop a billiard table. Jones did not so much as glance at her immense breasts, aswirl in smoky colored light like planets; the Plant's cultures had no sexual cravings, none of them even female.

At a corner table sat a young man with red hair, something seldom seen naturally. He smiled and made a small gesture. Jones headed toward him, slipping off his shades. He watched the man's hands atop the table; was there a gun resting under the newspaper?

The man's hair was long and greasy, his beard scruffy and inadequate, but he was good-looking and his voice was friendly. "Glad you decided to come. I'm Nevin Parr." They shook hands. "Sit down. Drink?"

"Coffee."

The man motioned to a waitress, who brought them both a coffee. The birther wasn't dulling his senses with alcohol, either, Jones noted.

"So how did you meet my pal Moodring?" asked the birther, lifting his chipped mug for a cautious sip.

"On the street. He gave me money for food in turn for a small favor."

"So now you move a little drug for him sometimes. Hold hot weapons for him sometimes."

Jones frowned at his gloved hands, knotted like mating tarantulas. "I'm disappointed. I thought Moodring was more discreet than that."

"Please don't be angry at him; I told you, we're old pals. So, anyway . . . should I call you Mr. Jones?" Parr smiled broadly. "Magnesium? Or is it Mag?"

"It's all equally meaningless."

"I've never really talked with a culture before."

"We prefer 'shadow.' "

"All right. Mr. Shadow. So how old are you?"

"Five."

"Pretty bright for a five-year-old."

"Memory-encoded long-chain molecules in a brain drip. I knew my job before I even got out of the tank."

"Of course. Five, huh? So that's about the age when they start replacing you guys, right? They say that's when you start getting uppity . . . losing control. That's why you escaped from the Plant, isn't it? You knew your time was pretty much up."

"Yes. I knew what was coming. Nine cultures

in my crew were removed in two days. They were all about my age. My supervisor told me not to worry, but I knew . . ."

"Cleaning house. Bringing in the fresh meat. They kill them, don't they? The old cultures. They incinerate them."

"Yes."

"I heard you killed two men in escaping. Two real men."

"Moodring is very talkative."

"It isn't just him. You killed two men. I heard they were looking for you. Call you 'hothead,' because of your tattoo. Can I see it?"

"That wouldn't be wise in public, would it?"

"You're not the only escaped clone around here, but you're right, we have work that demands discretion. Just that I like tattoos; I have some myself. See?" He rolled up a sleeve, exposing a dark mass that Jones only gave a half glance. "I hear they get pretty wild with your tattoos. Someone must enjoy himself."

"Robots do the tattooing. They're just accessing clip art files. Most times it has nothing to do with our function or the name that was chosen for us. It's done to identify us, and probably for the amusement of our human coworkers. Decorative for them, I suppose."

"You haven't been caught, but you're still living in this area, close to the Plant. You must be stealthy. That's a useful quality. So where are you staying?"

"That's none of your concern. When you need me you leave a message with Moodring. When he sees me around he'll tell me. Moodring doesn't need to know where I live, either."

"He your friend, Moodring, or is it just business?"

"I have no friends."

"That's too bad. I think you and I could be friends."

"You don't know how much that means to me. So, why did you want me? Because I'm a culture? And if so, why?"

"Again . . . because you killed two men escaping the Plant. I know you can kill again, given the right incentive."

"I'm glad we've got to that. So what's my incentive?"

"Five thousand munits."

"For killing a man? That's pretty cheap."

"Not for a culture who never made a coin in his life. Not for a culture who lives in the street somewhere."

"So who am I to kill?"

"More incentive for you," said Nevin Parr, who smiled far too much for Jones's taste. Jones seldom smiled. He had heard that smiling was a trait leftover from the animal ancestry of the birthers; it was a threatening baring of the fangs, in origin. The idea amused him, made him feel more evolved for so seldom contorting his own face in that way. After his smiling heavy pause, Parr continued, "The man we have in mind is Ephraim Mayda."

Jones raised his hairless eyebrows, grunted, and stirred his coffee. "He's a union captain. Well guarded. Martyr material."

"Never mind the repercussions; he's trouble for the people I'm working for, and worth the lesser trouble of his death."

Jones lifted his eyes in sudden realization. He almost plunged his hand into his coat for the pistol he had bought from Moodring. "You work for the Plant!" he hissed.

Parr grinned. "I work for myself. But never mind who hired me."

Jones composed himself outwardly, but his heart pulsed as deeply as the music. "The union is cozy with the syndy."

"The people I work for can handle the syndy. Mag, those strikers out there hate you . . . shadows. They've lynched a dozen of your kind in a row outside the Plant barrier. If they had their way, every one of your kind would go into the incinerator tomorrow. You yourself got roughed up by a group that got inside the Plant, I hear." Parr paused knowingly. His spoon clinked in his mug, making a vortex. "They broke in. Trashed machines. Killed a few of your kind. I heard from our mutual friend that they found you naked by the showers, and cut you . . . badly."

"It didn't affect my job," Jones muttered, not looking the human in the eyes. "And it's not like I ever used the thing but to piss. So now I piss like a birther woman."

"Didn't bother you at all, then? Doesn't bother you that Mayda works these thugs up like that?"

They were angry. Jones could understand that. If there was anything that made him feel a kinship with the birthers, it was anger. Still, the weight of their resentment . . . of their loathing . . . their outright furious hatred . . . was a labor to bear. They had hurt him. He had never intentionally harmed a birther. It was the Plant's decision to utilize cultures for half their workforce (more than that would constitute a labor violation, but the conservative candidate for Prime Minister was fighting to make it so that companies did not have to guarantee any ratio of nonclones; freedom of enterprise must be upheld, he cried). Let the strikers mutilate the president of the Plant, instead. Let them hang him and his underlings in the shadow of the Vat. But didn't they see—even though Jones worked in their place while their unemployment ran out and their families starved like the protestors— that he was as much a victim as they?

This man was under the employ of his enemies. Of course, he himself had once been under their employ. Still, could he trust this man as his partner in crime? No. But he could do business with men he didn't trust. He wouldn't turn his back to Moodring, either, but in the end he needed to eat. Five thousand munits. He had never earned a coin until he had escaped the Plant, and never a legal one since.

He could go away. Somewhere hot. Have his tattoo removed. Maybe even his useless vestige of "manhood" restored.

Parr went on, "A third bit of incentive. You're no fool, so I'll admit it. The people who hired me . . . you once worked for them, too. If you decline, well . . . like I say, they'd like to get ahold of you after what you did to those two men."

Slowly and deliberately Jones's eyes lifted, staring from under bony brows. He smiled. It was like a baring of fangs.

"You were doing well, Nevin. Don't spoil it with unnecessary incentives. I'll help you kill your man."

"Sorry." Ever the smile. "Just that they want this to happen soon, and I don't want to have to look for a partner from scratch."

"Why do you need a partner?"

"Well let me tell you . . ."

2: THE PIMP OF THE INVERSE

From his perch atop the Vat, with its stained streaked sides and its deep liquid burbling, Jones watched night fall in Punktown. The snow was a mere whisking about of loose flakes. Colored lights glowed in the city beyond the Plant, and flashed here and there on the Plant itself, but for less gay purposes. Once in a while there was a bright violet-hued flash in the translucent dome of the shipping department, as another batch of products was teleported elsewhere on this planet, or to another. Perhaps a crew destined to work on an asteroid mine, or to build an orbital space station or a new colony, a new Punktown, on some world not yet raped, merely groped.

He watched a hovertruck with a covered bed like a military troop carrier pull out of the shipping docks and head for the east gate. A shipment with a more localized destination. Jones imagined its contents, the manufactured goods, seated in two rows blankly facing each other. Cultures not yet tattooed, not yet named. Perhaps the companies they were destined for did not utilize tattoos and decorative names— mocking names, Jones mused—to identify the clone workers. Jones wondered what, if anything, went on in their heads along the drive. They had not yet been programmed for their duties, not yet had their brain drips. He, whose job it had been to bake these golems, had been born already employed, unlike them. They were innocent in their staring mindlessness, better off for their mindlessness, Jones thought, watching the truck vanish into the night. He himself was still a child, but a tainted innocent; the months since his escape had been like a compacted lifetime. Had he been better off in his first days, not yet discontented? Disgruntled? There were those times, he in his newfound pride would hate to admit, that he felt like a human boy who longed to be a wooden puppet again.

He listened to the Vat gurgle with its amniotic solutions, pictured in his mind the many mindless fetuses sleeping without dream in the great silo of a womb beneath him. Yes, Christmas was coming. Jones thought of its origins, of the birther woman Mary's immaculate conception, and gave an ugly smirk.

He lifted his wrist, gazed at it until luminous numbers like another tattoo materialized. Time to go; he didn't like being late.

• • •

So that Parr would not guess just how close Jones lived to the Plant, he had told Parr to pick him up over at Pewter Square. To reach it, Jones had to cross the Obsidian Street Overpass. It was a slightly arched bridge of a Ramon design, built of incredibly tough Ramon wood lacquered in what once had been a glossy black. It was now smeared and spray-painted, dusty and chipped. Vehicles whooshed across in either direction, filling the covered bridge with roaring noise. The pedestrian walkway was protected from the traffic by a rickety railing, missing sections now patched with chicken wire. Furthermore, homeless people had nested in among the recesses of the bridge's wooden skeleton, most having built elaborate parasite structures of scrap wood, sheets of metal, plastic, or ceramic. One elderly and malnourished Choom, a former monk of the dwindling Raloom faith, lived inside a large cardboard box on the front of which, as if it were a temple, he had drawn the stern features of

Raloom. The pedestrian walkway was bordered on one side by the railing, on the other by this tiny shanty town. Some of its denizens sold coffee to the passersby, or newspaper hard copies, or coaxed them behind their crinkly plastic curtains or soggy cardboard partitions for the sale of drugs and sex.

Jones knew one of these shadowy creatures, and as if it had been awaiting him, it half emerged from its shelter as he approached. Its small house was one of the most elaborate; as if to pretend that it belonged to the bridge, in case of an infrequent mass eviction, it had constructed its dwelling of wood and painted it glossy black. The shack even had mock windows, though these were actually dusty mirrors. Jones saw his own solemn face multiply reflected as he approached, his black ski hat covering his tattoo.

The tiny figure moved spidery limbs as if in slow motion, but its head constantly twitched and gave sudden jolts from side to side, so fast its features blurred. When still, they were puny black holes in a huge hairless head—twice the size of Jones's—almost perfectly round and with the texture of pumice. No one but Jones would know that this was no ordinary mutant, but a culture defect from the Plant, an immaculate misconception, who had somehow escaped incineration and to freedom. Who would suspect that they had been cloned from the same master? The defect had once stopped Jones and struck up a conversation. Jones's hairless eyebrows had given him away. When not wearing dark glasses, Jones now wore his ski hat pulled down to his eyes.

"Where are we going at this hour?" crackled the misshapen being, who had named itself Edgar Allan Jones. Magnesium Jones could not understand why a shadow would willingly give itself such a foolish name, but then sometimes he wondered why he hadn't come up with a new name for himself.

"Restless," he grunted, stopping in front of the lacquered dollhouse. He heard a tea kettle whistling in there, and muffled radio music that sounded like a child's toy piano played at an inhuman speed.

"Christmas is in three days, now," said the flawed clone, cracking a toothless smile. "Will you come see me? We can listen to the radio together. Play cards. I'll make you tea."

Jones glanced past Edgar into the miniature house. Could the two of them both fit in there? It seemed claustrophobic. And too intimate a scene for his taste. Still, he felt flattered, and couldn't bring himself to flat-out refuse. Instead, he said, "I may not be around here that day . . . but if I am . . . we'll see."

"You have never been inside . . . why not come in now? I can . . ."

"I can't now, I'm sorry; I have . . . some business."

The globe of a head blurred, halted abruptly, the smile shaken into a frown. "That Moodring friend of yours will lead you to your death."

"He isn't my friend," Jones said, and started away.

"Don't forget Christmas!" the creature croaked.

Jones nodded over his shoulder but kept on walking, feeling strangely guilty for not just stepping inside for one cup of tea. After all, he was quite early for his appointment.

• • •

"Ever been in a car before?" Parr asked, smiling, as he pulled from the curb into the glittering dark current of night traffic.

"Taxi," Jones murmured, stiff as a mannequin.

"Mayda lives at Hanging Gardens; it's a few blocks short of Beaumonde Square. He's not starving like the folks he works up; he has a nice apartment to go home to. It's that syndy money."

"Mm."

"Hey," Parr looked over at him, "don't be nervous. Just keep thinking about your lines. You're going to be a vid star, my man . . . a celebrity."

3: THE CARVEN WARRIOR

Parr let Jones off, and the hovercar disappeared around the corner. Jones cut across a snow-caked courtyard as instructed, his boots squeaking as if he tramped across Styrofoam. He slipped between apartment units, climbed a set of stairs to another, and found a door propped open for him. Parr motioned him inside, then let the door fall back in place. Jones heard it lock. He didn't ask Parr how he had got inside the vestibule.

Together they padded down a gloomy corridor across a carpet of peach and purple diamonds. The walls and doors that flanked the men were pristine white. This place reminded Jones of the cleaner regions of the Plant; primarily, the seldom seen administration levels. He listened to the moving creak of Parr's faux leather jacket. Both of them wore gloves, and Jones still had on his ski hat and a scarf wound around his neck against the hellish cold he could never get used to.

A lift took them to the sixth floor. Then, side by side, they made their way down the hall to the door at its very end. Quite easily, Parr knocked, and then beamed at his companion.

Jones pulled off his ski hat at last, and pushed it into his pocket. In the dim light, his hairless pate gleamed softly, the fiery halo pricked into his skin burning darkly. He hid both hands behind his back.

"Who is it?" asked a voice over an intercom. Above the door, a tiny camera eye, small as an ant's feeler, must now be watching them.

"Enforcer, sir," said Parr, his voice uncharacteristically serious. And he did look the part in his black uniform; leather jacket, beetle-like helmet, holstered weapons. He had cut his hair to a butch and shaved to a neat goatee. He held one of Jones's elbows. "May I have a word?"

"What's going on?"

"Your neighbor down the hall reported a suspicious person, and we found this culture lurking around. He claims he's not an escapee, but was purchased by an Ephraim Mayda."

"Mr. Mayda doesn't own any cultures."

"May I please speak with Mr. Mayda himself?" Parr sighed irritably.

A new voice came on. "I know that scab!" it rumbled. "He escaped from the Plant, murdered two human beings!"

"What? Are you sure of this?"

"Yes! He was from the Ovens department. It was on the news!"

"May I speak with you in person, Mr. Mayda?"

"I don't want that killer freak in my house!"

"I have him manacled, sir. Look, I need to take down a report on this . . . your recognizing him is valuable."

"Whatever. But you'd better have him under control . . ."

The two men heard the lock clack off. The knob was turned from the other side, and as the door opened Jones pushed through first, reaching his right hand inside his coat as he went. He saw two faces inside, both half-identical in that both wore expressions of shock, horror, as he ripped his small silvery block of a pistol from its holster to thrust at their wide stares. But one man was bleached blond and one man was dark-haired and Jones shot the blond in the face. A neat, third nostril breathed open beside one of the other two, but the back of the blond's head was kicked open like saloon doors. The darker man batted his eyes at the blood that spattered him. The report had been as soft as a child's cough, the blond crumpled almost delicately to the floor, Jones and then Parr stepped onto the lush white carpet and Parr locked the door after them.

"Who are you?" Mayda cried, raising his hands, backing against the wall.

"Into the living room," Jones snarled, flicking the gun. Mayda glanced behind him, slid his shoulders along the wall and backed through a threshold into an expanse of plush parlor with a window overlooking the snowy courtyard of Hanging Gardens. Parr went to tint the window full black.

"I'll give you money, listen . . ." Mayda began.

"You do remember me, don't you?" Jones

hissed, leveling the gun at the paunchy birther's groin. "You emasculated me, remember that?"

"I didn't! That was those crazy strikers that got in the Plant that time . . . that was out of my hands!"

"So how do you know about it? They told you. It was a big joke, wasn't it?"

"What do you want? You can have anything!" The union captain's eyes fearfully latched onto Parr as he slipped something odd from his jacket. What looked like three gun barrels were unfolded and spread into a tripod. Atop it, Parr screwed a tiny vidcam. A green light came on, indicating that it had begun filming. Parr remained behind the camera, and Mayda flashed his eyes back to Jones to see what he had to say.

Jones hesitated. What he had to say was rehearsed, but the lines were a jumble in his head, words exploded to fragments by the silent shot that had killed the blond. He had killed a man . . . for the third time. It came naturally to him, like a brain-dripped skill; it was a primal animal instinct, survival. So why, in its aftermath, should he feel this . . . disconcertion?

His eyes darted about the room. He had never been in such a place. Tables fashioned from some green glassy stone. Sofas and chairs of white with a silvery lace of embroidery. A bar, a holotank. On the walls, a modest art collection. Atop several tables, shelves, and pedestals, various small Ramon sculptures, all carved from an iridescent white crystal. Animals, and a Ramon warrior rendered in amazing detail considering the medium, from his lionlike head to the lance or halberd he brought to bear in anticipation of attack. Each piece must be worth a fortune. And yet there were men and women camped outside the Plant who were on a hunger strike, emaciated. And those who were emaciated but not by choice. And Jones recalled that woman sitting in her shroud of flame.

His disconcertion cleared. Jones returned a molten gaze to the terrified birther. The anger in his voice was not some actor's fakery, even if the words were not his own.

"I'm here to make a record, Mr. Mayda . . .

of the beginning of a rebellion, and the first blow in a war that won't stop until we clones are given the same rights as you natural born."

It was clever, he had mused earlier; the Plant would be rid of the thorn in their lion's paw, and yet the law and the syndy would not hold the Plant responsible. No, it would be a dangerous escaped culture who killed Ephraim Mayda; a fanatic with grand delusions. Still, Jones had considered, wouldn't this make birther workers at the Plant, unemployed workers outside, and a vast majority of the public in general all the more distrusting of cultures, opposed to their widespread use? Wouldn't this hurt the Plant's very existence? And yet, they surely knew what they were doing better than he. After all, he was just a culture . . . educated by brain drip, by listening to human workers talk and to the radio programs the human workers listened to. Educated on the street since that time. But these men sat at vast glossy tables, making vast decisions. It was beyond his scope. The most he could wrap his thoughts around was payment of five thousand munits . . . and Parr had given him half of that when he climbed into his hovercar tonight.

"Hey," Mayda blubbered, "what are you saying . . . look . . . please! Listen . . ."

"We want to live as you do," Jones went on, improvising now as the rest of the words slipped through the fingers of his mind. He thought of his own hellish nest, and of Edgar's tiny black shed of a home. "We want . . ."

"Hey! Freeze!" he heard Parr yell.

Jones snapped his head around. What was happening? Had another bodyguard emerged from one of the other rooms? They should have checked all of the rooms first, they should have . . .

Parr was pointing the police issue pistol at him, not at some new player, and before Jones could bring his own gun around Parr snapped off five shots in rapid succession. Gas clouds flashed from the muzzle, heat lightning with no thunder, but the lightning struck Jones down. He felt a fireball streak across the side of his

throat, deadened somewhat by the scarf wound there. He was kicked by a horse in the collarbone, and three projectiles in a cluster entered the upper left side of his chest. He spun down onto his belly on the white carpet, and saw his blood flecked there like beads of dew, in striking close-up. Beautiful red beads like tiny rubies clinging to the white fibers of the carpet. Even violence was glamorous in this place.

Mayda scampered closer, kicked his small silvery gun out of his hand. Jones's guts spasmed, but his outer body didn't so much as flinch. He cracked his lids a fraction, through crossed lashes saw Parr moving closer as well. For a moment, he had thought it was another man. Since firing the shots from behind the camera, out of its view, Parr had shed the bogus forcer uniform and changed into street clothes.

"I thought I heard a strange voice in here, Mr. Mayda!" Parr gushed, out of breath. "I dozed off in the other room . . . I'm so sorry! Are you all right?"

"Yes, thank God. He killed Brett!"

"How'd he get in here?"

"I don't know . . . Brett went to answer the door, and the next thing I knew . . ."

Parr didn't work for the Plant, Jones realized now, poor dumb culture that he was. He cursed himself. He wasn't street-smart. He was a child. He was five years old . . .

Parr worked for Ephraim Mayda, captain of a union, friend of the syndicate. Mayda, whose trusting followers killed others and themselves to fight for a job, to fight for their bread and shelter, while his job was to exploit their hunger, their anger and fear.

And the vid. The vid of a murderous clone attacking a hero of the people, stopped just in time by a loyal bodyguard (while another loyal bodyguard, poor Brett, had been sacrificed). One murderous forerunner of a much larger threat, as he had proclaimed. The vid that would unite the public against the cultures, lead to an outcry for the abolition of cloned workers . . . to their mass incineration . . .

He had almost seen this before. He'd let the money dazzle him. The bullets had slapped him fully awake.

"Call the forcers!" Mayda said for the benefit of the camera, sounding shaken, though he had known all along he was safe.

Through his lashes, Jones saw Parr stoop to retrieve his silvery handgun.

Jones's left arm was folded under him. He reached into his coat, and rolling onto his side, tore free a second gun, this one glossy black, a gun Parr hadn't known about, and as Parr lifted his startled head, Jones let loose a volley of shots as fast as he could depress the trigger. Parr sat down hard on his rump comically, and as each shot struck him he bounced like a child on his father's knee. When at last Jones stopped shooting him, his face almost black with blood and holes, Parr slumped forward into his own lap.

Jones sat up with a nova of agony in his chest, and a nova of hot gas exploded before his eyes as he saw Mayda bolting for the door. The shot hit the birther in the right buttock, and he sprawled onto his face shrieking like a hysterical child frightened by a nightmare.

As Jones struggled to his feet, staggered, and regained his footing, Mayda pulled himself toward the door on his belly. Almost casually, Jones walked to him, stood over him, and pointed the small black gun. Mayda rolled over to scream up at him and bullets drove the scream back into his throat. Jones shot out both eyes, and bullets punched in his nose and smashed his teeth, so that the face remaining looked to Jones like Edgar's with its simple black holes for features.

The gun had clicked empty. He let it drop, stepped over Mayda's body, over Brett's body farther on, and then stopped before the door, snuffing his ski hat over the flames of his skull. But before he opened the door, he changed his mind and returned to the plush, vast parlor just for a moment . . .

⋅ ⋅ ⋅

It was an hour to dawn when Magnesium Jones reached the house of Edgar Allan Jones on the Obsidian Street Overpass.

Edgar croaked in delight to see him, until the withered being saw the look on the taller culture's face. It took Jones's arm, and helped him as he stooped to enter the tiny black-painted shack.

"You're hurt!" Edgar cried, supporting Jones as he lowered himself into a small rickety chair at a table in the center of the room. Aside from shelves, there was little else. No bed. A radio played music like the cries of whales in reverse, and a kettle was steaming on a battery-pack hot plate.

"I have something for you," Jones said, his voice a wheeze, one of his lungs deflated in the cradle of his ribs. "A Christmas present . . ."

"I have to get help. I'll go out . . . stop a car in the street," Edgar went on.

Jones caught its arm before Edgar could reach the door. He smiled at the creature. "I'd like a cup of tea," he said.

For several moments Edgar stared at the man, gouged features unreadable. Then, in slow motion, head blurring, it turned and went to the hot plate and steaming kettle.

While Edgar's back was turned, Jones reached into his long black coat, now soaked heavy with his blood, and from a pouch in its lining withdrew a sculpture carved from opalescent crystal. It was a fierce Ramon warrior, bringing his lance to bear. He placed it on the table quietly, so that the stunted clone would be surprised when it turned back around.

And while he waited for Edgar to turn around with his tea, Jones stripped off his ski hat and lowered his fiery brow onto one arm on the table. Closed his eyes to rest.

Yes, he would just rest a little while . . . until his friend finally turned around.

CORY DOCTOROW

OWNZORED

(2002)

TEN YEARS IN THE VALLEY, and all Murray Swain had to show for it was a spare tire, a bald patch, and a life that was friendless and empty and maggoty-rotten. His only ever California friend, Liam, had dwindled from a tubbaguts programmer–shaped potato to a living skeleton on his deathbed the year before, herpes blooms run riot over his skin and bones in the absence of any immunoresponse. The memorial service featured a framed photo of Liam at his graduation; his body was donated for medical science.

Liam's death really screwed things up for Murray. He'd gone into one of those clinical depression spirals that eventually afflicted all the aging bright young coders he'd known during his life in tech. He'd get misty in the morning over his second cup of coffee and by the midafternoon blood-sugar crash, he'd be weeping silently in his cubicle, clattering nonsensically at the keys to disguise the disgusting snuffling noises he made. His wastebasket overflowed with spent tissues and a rumor circulated among the evening cleaning staff that he was a compulsive masturbator. The impossibility of the rumor was immediately apparent to all the other coders on his floor who, pr0n-hounds that they were, had explored the limits and extent of the censoring proxy that sat at the headwaters of the office network. Nevertheless, it was gleefully repeated in the collegial fratmosphere of his workplace and wags kept dumping their collections of conference-snarfed hotel-sized bottles of hand lotion on his desk.

The number of bugs per line in Murray's code was 500 percent that of the overall company average. The QA people sometimes just sent his code back to him (From: qamanager@globalsemi.com To: mswain@globalsemi.com Subject: Your code . . . Body: . . . sucks) rather than trying to get it to build and run. Three weeks after Liam died, Murray's team leader pulled his commit privileges on the CVS repository, which meant that he had to grovel with one of the other coders when he wanted to add his work to the project.

Two months after Liam died, Murray was put on probation.

Three months after Liam died, Murray was given two weeks' leave and an e-mail from HR with contact info for an in-plan shrink who could counsel him. The shrink recommended Cognitive Therapy, which he explained in detail, though all Murray remembered ten minutes after the session was that he'd have to do it every week for years, and the name reminded him of Cognitive Dissonance, which was the name of Liam's favorite stupid Orange County garage band.

Murray returned to Global Semiconductor's Mountain View headquarters after three more sessions with the shrink. He badged in at the front door, at the elevator, and on his floor, sat at his desk, and badged in again on his PC. From: tvanya@globalsemi.com To: mswain@globalsemi.com Subject: Welcome back! Come see me . . . Body: . . . when you get in.

Tomas Vanya was Murray's team lead and rated a glass office with a door. The blinds were closed, which meant: dead Murray walking. Murray closed the door behind him and sighed a huge heave of nauseated relief. He'd washed out of Silicon Valley and he could go home to Vancouver and live in his parents' basement and go salmon fishing on weekends with his high-school drinking buds. He didn't exactly love Global Semi, but shit, they were number three in a hot, competitive sector where Moore's Law drove the cost of microprocessors relentlessly downward as their speed rocketed relentlessly skyward. They had four billion in the bank, a healthy share price, and his options were above water, unlike the poor fucks at Motorola, number four and falling. He'd washed out of the nearly best, what the fuck, beat spending his prime years in Hongcouver writing government-standard code for the Ministry of Unbelievable Dullness.

Even the number-two chair in Tomas Vanya's office kicked major ergonomic azz. Murray settled into it and popped some of the controls experimentally until the ess of his spine was cushioned and pinioned into chiropractically correct form. Tomas unbagged a Fourbucks Morning Harvest muffin and a venti coconut Frappuccino and slid them across his multi-tiered Swedish Disposable Moderne desque.

"A little welcome-back present, Murray," Tomas said. Murray listened for the sound of a minimum-wage security guard clearing out his desk during this exit-interview-cum-breakfast-banquet. He wondered if Global Semi would forward-vest his options and mentally calculated the strike price minus the current price times the number of shares times the conversion rate to Canadian Pesos and thought he could maybe put down 25 percent on a two-bedroom in New Westminster.

"Dee-licious and noo-tritious," Murray said and slurped at the frappe.

"So," Tomas said. "So."

Here it comes, Murray thought, and sucked up a brain-freezing mouthful of frou-frou West Coast caffeine delivery system. Gonzored. Fiored. Sh17canned. Thinking in leet-hacker crap made it all seem more distant.

"It's really great to see you again," Tomas said. "You're a really important part of the team here, you know?"

Murray restrained himself from rolling his eyes. He was fired, so why draw it out? There'd been enough layoffs at Global Semi, enough boom and bust and bust and bust that it was a routine, they all knew how it went.

But though Murray was on an Air Canada jet headed for Vangroover, Tomas wasn't even on the damned script. "You're sharp and seasoned. You can communicate effectively. Most techies can't write worth a damn, but you're good. It's rare."

Ah, the soothing sensation of smoke between one's buttocks. It was true that Murray liked to write, but there wasn't any money in it, no glory either. If you were going to be a writer in the tech world, you'd have to be—

"You've had a couple weeks off to reassess things, and we've been reassessing, too. Coding, hell, most people don't do it for very long. Especially assembler, Jesus, if you're still writing assembler after five years, there's something, you know, *wrong*. You end up in management or you move horizontally. Or you lose it." Tomas realized that he'd said the wrong thing and blushed.

Aw, shit.

"Horizontal movement. That's the great thing about a company this size. There's always somewhere you can go when you burn out on one task."

No, no, no.

"The Honorable Computing initiative is ready for documentation, Murray. We need a tech writer who can really *nail it*."

A tech writer. Why not just break his goddamned fingers and poke his eyes out? Never write another line of code, never make the machine buck and hum and make his will real in the abstract beauty of silicon? Tech writers were coders' janitors, documenting the plainly self-evident logic of APIs and code structures, niggling over punctuation and grammar and frigging stylebooks, like any of it *mattered*— human beings could parse English, even if it wasn't well-formed, even if you had a comma splice or a dangling participle.

"It's a twelve-month secondment, a change of pace for you and a chance for us to evaluate your other strengths. You go to four weeks' vacation, and we accelerate your vesting and start you with a new grant at the same strike price, over twenty-four months."

Murray did the math in his head, numbers dancing. Four weeks' vacation—that was three years ahead of schedule, not that anyone that senior ever used his vacation days, but you could bank them for retirement or, ahem, exit strategy. The forward vesting meant that he could walk out and fly back to Canada in three weeks if he hated it and put *30* percent down on a two-bedroom in New West.

And the door was closed and the blinds were drawn and the implication was clear. Take this job or shove it.

He took the job.

A month later he was balls-deep in the documentation project and feeling, you know, not horrible. The Honorable Computing initiative was your basic Bond-villain world-domination horseshit, of course, but it was technically sweet and it kept him from misting over and bawling. And they had cute girls on the documentation floor, liberal arts/electrical engineering double-majors with abs you could bounce a quarter off who were doing time before being promoted up to join the first cohort of senior female coders to put their mark on the Valley.

He worked late most nights, only marking the passing of five p.m. by his instinctive upward glance as all those fine, firm rear ends walked past his desk on their way out of the office. Then he went into night mode, working by the glow of his display and the emergency lights until the custodians came in and chased him out with their vacuum cleaners.

One night, he was struggling to understand the use-cases for Honorable Computing when the overhead lights flicked on, shrinking his pupils to painful pinpricks. The cleaners clattered in and began to pointedly empty the wastebins. He took the hint, grabbed his shoulder bag, and staggered for the exit, badging out as he went.

His car was one of the last ones in the lot, a hybrid Toyota with a lot of dashboard geek toys like a GPS and a back-seat DVD player, though no one ever rode in Murray's back seat. He'd bought it three months before Liam died, cashing in some shares and trading in the giant gas-guzzling SUV he'd never once taken off-road.

As he aimed his remote at it and initiated the cryptographic handshake—i.e., unlocked the doors—he spotted the guy leaning against the car. Murray's thumb jabbed at the locking button on the remote, but it was too late: the guy had the door open and he was sliding into the passenger seat.

In the process of hitting the remote's panic button, Murray managed to pop the trunk and start the engine, but eventually his thumb mashed the right button and the car's lights strobed and the horn blared. He backed slowly toward the office doors, just as the guy found the dome-light control and lit up the car's interior and Murray got a good look at him.

It was Liam.

Murray stabbed at the remote some more and killed the panic button. Jesus, who was going to respond at this hour in some abandoned industrial park in the middle of the Valley anyway? The limp-dick security guard? He squinted at the face in the car.

Liam. Still Liam. Not the skeletal Liam he'd last seen rotted and intubated on a bed at San Jose General. Not the porcine Liam he'd laughed with over a million late-night El Torito burritos. A fit, healthy, *young* Liam, the Liam he'd met the day they both started at Global Semi at adjacent desks, Liam fresh out of Cal Tech and fit from his weekly lot-hockey game and his weekend dirt-bike rides in the hills. Liam-prime, or maybe Liam's younger brother or something.

Liam rolled down the window and struck a match on the passenger-side door, then took a Marlboro Red from a pack in his shirt pocket and lit it. Murray walked cautiously to the car, his thumb working on his cellphone, punching in the numbers 9-1-1 and hovering over SEND. He got close enough to see the scratch the match head had left on the side-panel and muttered, *"Fuck,"* with feeling.

"Hey dirtbag, you kiss your mother with that mouth?" Liam said. It *was* Liam.

"You kiss *your* mother after I'm through with her mouth?" Murray said, the rote of old times. He gulped for air.

Liam popped the door and got out. He was ripped, bullish chest and cartoonish wasp-waist, rock-hard abs through a silvery club shirt and bulging thighs. A body like that, it's a full-time job, or so Murray had concluded after many failed get-fit initiatives involving gyms and

retreats and expensive home equipment and humiliating early morning jogs through the sidewalk-free streets of Shallow Alto.

"Who the fuck are you?" Murray said, looking into the familiar eyes, the familiar smile lines and the deep wrinkle between Liam's eyes from his concentration face. Though the night was cool, Murray felt runnels of sweat tracing his spine, trickling down between his buttocks.

"You know the answer, so why ask? The question isn't who, it's *how*. Let's drive around a little and I'll tell you all about it."

Liam clapped a strong hand on his forearm and gave it a companionable squeeze. It felt good and real and human.

"You can't smoke in my car," Murray said.

"Don't worry," Liam said. "I won't exhale."

Murray shook his head and went around to the driver's side. By the time he started the engine, Liam had his seatbelt on and was poking randomly at the onboard controls. "This is pretty rad. You told me about it, I remember, but it sounded stupid at the time. Really rad." He brought up the MP3 player and scrolled through Murray's library, adding tracks to a mix, cranking up the opening crash of an old, old, old punk Beastie Boys song. "The speakers are for shit, though!" he hollered over the music.

Murray cranked the volume down as he bounced over the speed bumps, badged out of the lot, and headed for the hills, stabbing at the GPS to bring up some road maps that included the private roads way up in the highlands.

"So, do I get two other ghosts tonight, Marley, or are you the only one?"

Liam found the sunroof control and flicked his smoke out into the road. "Ghost, huh? I'm meat, dude, same as you. Not back from the dead, just back from the *mostly dead*." He did the last like Billy Crystal as Miracle Max in *The Princess Bride*, one of their faves. "I'll tell you all about it, but I want to catch up on your shit first. What are you working on?"

"They've got me writing docs," Murray said, grateful for the car's darkness covering his blush.

"Awwww," Liam said. "You're shitting me."

"I kinda lost it," Murray said. "Couldn't code. About six months ago. After."

"Ah," Liam said.

"So I'm writing docs. It's a sideways promotion and the work's not bad. I'm writing up Honorable Computing."

"What?"

"Sorry, it was after your time. It's a big deal. All the semiconductor companies are in on it: Intel, AMD, even Motorola and Hitachi. And Microsoft—they're hardcore for it."

"So what is it?"

Murray turned onto a gravel road, following the tracery on the glowing GPS screen as much as the narrow road, spiraling up and up over the sparse lights of Silicon Valley. He and Liam had had a million bullshit sessions about tech, what was vaporware and what was killer, and now they were having one again, just like old times. Only Liam was dead. Well, if it was time for Murray to lose his shit, what better way than in the hills, great tunes on the stereo, all alone in the night?

Murray was warming up to the subject. He'd wanted someone he could really chew this over with since he got reassigned, he'd wanted Liam there to key off his observations. "Okay, so, the Turing Machine, right? Turing's Universal Machine. The building block of modern computation. In Turing's day, you had all these specialized machines: a machine for solving quadratics, a machine for calculating derivatives, and so on. Turing came up with the idea of a machine that could configure itself to be any specialized machine, using symbolic logic: software. Included in the machines that you can simulate in a Turing Machine is another Turing Machine, like Java or VMWare. With me?"

"With you."

"So this gives rise to a kind of existential crisis. When your software is executing, how does it know what its execution environment is? Maybe it's running on a Global Semi Itanium clone at 1.6 gigahertz, or maybe it's running on a model of that chip, simulated on a Motorola G5 RISC processor."

"Got it."

"Now, forget about that for a sec and think about Hollywood. The coked-up Hollyweird fatcats hate Turing Machines. I mean, they want to release their stuff over the Internet, but they want to deliver it to you in a lockbox. You get to listen to it, you get to watch it, but only if they say so, and only if you've paid. You can buy it over and over again, but you can never own it. It's scrambled—encrypted—and they only send you the keys when you satisfy a license server that you've paid up. The keys are delivered to a secure app that you can't fuxor with, and the app locks you out of the video card and the sound card and the drive while it's decrypting the stream and showing it to you, and then it locks everything up again once you're done and hands control back over to you."

Liam snorted. "It is to laugh."

"Yeah, I know. It's bullshit. It's Turing Machines, right? When the software executes on your computer, it has to rely on your computer's feedback to confirm that the video card and the sound card are locked up, that you're not just feeding the cleartext stream back to the drive and then to ten million pals online. But the 'computer' it's executing on could be simulated inside another computer, one that you've modified to your heart's content. The 'video card' is a simulation; the 'sound card' is a simulation. The computer is a brain in a bottle, it's in the Matrix, it can't trust its senses because you're in control, it's a Turing Machine nested inside another Turing Machine."

"Like Descartes."

"What?"

"You gotta read your classics, bro. I've been catching up over the past six months or so, doing a *lot* of reading. Mostly free e-books from the Gutenberg Project. Descartes's *Meditations* are some heavy shiznit. Descartes starts by saying that he wants to figure out some stuff about the world, but he can't, right, because in order to say stuff about the world, he needs to trust his senses, but his senses are wrong all the time. When he dreams, his senses deliver full-on THX all-digital IMAX, but none of it's really *there*. How does he know when he's dreaming or when he's awake? How does he know when he's experiencing something or imagining it? How does he know he's not a brain in a jar?"

"So, how does he know?" Murray asked, taking them over a reservoir on a switchback road, moonlight glittering over the still water, occulted by fringed silhouettes of tall California pines.

"Well, that's where he pulls some religion out of his ass. Here's how it goes: God is good, because part of the definition of God is goodness. God made the world. God made me. God made my senses. God made my senses *so that I could experience the goodness of his world*. Why would God give me bum senses? QED, I can trust my senses."

"It *is* like Descartes," Murray said, accelerating up a new hill.

"Yeah?" Liam said. "Who's God, then?"

"Crypto," Murray said. "Really good, standards-defined crypto. Public ciphersystems whose details are published and understood. AES, RSA, good crypto. There's a signing key for each chip fab—ours is in some secret biometrics-and-machine-guns bunker under some desert. That key is used to sign *another* key that's embedded in a tamper-resistant chip—"

Liam snorted again.

"No, really. Not tamper-*proof*, obviously, but tamper-*resistant*—you'd need a tunneling microscope or a vat of Freon to extract the keys from the chip. And every chip has its own keys, so you'd need to do this for every chip, which doesn't, you know, *scale*. So there's this chip full of secrets, they call the Fritz chip, for Fritz Hollings, the Senator from Disney, the guy who's trying to ban computers so that Hollywood won't go broke. The Fritz chip wakes up when you switch on the machine, and it uses its secret key to sign the operating system—well, the boot-loader and the operating system and the drivers and stuff—so now you've got a bunch of cryptographic signatures that reflect the software and hardware configuration of your box. When you want to download Police Academy *n*, your computer sends all these keys to Hollywood

central, *attesting* to the operating environment of your computer. Hollywood decides on the fly if it wants to trust that config, and if it does, it encrypts the movie, using the keys you've sent. That means that you can only unscramble the movie when you're running that Fritz chip, on that CPU, with that version of the OS and that video driver and so on."

"Got it: so if the OS and the CPU and so on are all 'Honorable'"—Liam described quote-marks with his index fingers—"then you can be sure that the execution environment is what the software expects it to be, that it's not a brain in a vat. Hollywood movies are safe from Napster-ization."

They bottomed out on the shore of the reservoir and Murray pulled over. "You've got it."

"So basically, whatever Hollywood says, goes. You can't fake an interface, you can't make any uses that they don't authorize. You know that these guys sued to make the VCR illegal, right? You can't wrap up an old app in a compatibility layer and make it work with a new app. You say Microsoft loves this? No fucking wonder, dude—they can write software that won't run on a computer running Oracle software. It's your basic Bond-villain—"

"—world-domination horseshit. Yeah, I know."

Liam got out of the car and lit up another butt, kicked loose stones into the reservoir. Murray joined him, looking out over the still water.

"Ring Minus One," Liam said, and skipped a rock over the oily-black surface of the water, getting four long bounces out of it.

"Yeah." Murray said. Ring Zero, the first registers in the processor, was where your computer checked to figure out how to start itself up. Compromise Ring Zero and you can make the computer do anything—load an alternate operating system, turn the whole box into a brain-in-a-jar, executing in an unknown environment. Ring Minus One, well, that was like God-code, space on another, virtual processor that was unalterable, owned by some remote party, by LoCal and its entertainment giants. Software was released without any copy-prevention tech because everyone knew that copy-prevention tech *didn't work*. Nevertheless, Hollywood was always chewing the scenery and hollering, they just didn't believe that the hairfaces and ponytails didn't have some seekrit tech that would keep their movies safe from copying until the heat death of the universe or the expiry of copyright, whichever came last.

"You run this stuff," Liam said, carefully, thinking it through, like he'd done before he got sick, murdered by his need to feed speedballs to his golden, tracked-out arm. "You run it and while you're watching a movie, Hollywood ownz your box." Murray heard the zero and the zee in ownz. Hacker-speak for having total control. No one wants to be 0wnz0red by some teenaged script-kiddie who's found some fresh exploit and turned it loose on your computer.

"In a nutsac. Gimme a butt."

Liam shook one out of the pack and passed it to Murray, along with a box of Mexican strike-anywhere matches. "You're back on these things?" Liam said, a note of surprise in his voice.

"Not really. Special occasion, you being back from the dead and all. I've always heard that these things'd kill me, but apparently being killed isn't so bad—you look great."

"Artful segue, dude. You must be burning up with curiosity."

"Not really," Murray said. "Figgered I'm hallucinating. I haven't hallucinated up until now, but back when I was really down, you know, clinical, I had all kinds of voices muttering in my head, telling me that I'd fucked up, it was all fucked up, crash the car into the median and do the world a favor, whatever. You get a little better from that stuff by changing jobs, but maybe not all the way better. Maybe I'm going to fill my pockets with rocks and jump in the lake. It's the next logical step, right?"

Liam studied his face. Murray tried to stay deadpan, but he felt the old sadness that came with the admission, the admission of guilt and

weakness, felt the tears pricking his eyes. "Hear me out first, okay?" Liam said.

"By all means. It'd be rude not to hear you out after you came all the way here from the kingdom of the dead."

"Mostly dead. Mostly. Ever think about how all the really good shit in your body—metabolism, immunoresponse, cognition—it's all in Ring Minus One? Not user-accessible? I mean, why is it that something like wiggling your toes is under your volitional control, but your memory isn't?"

"Well, that's complicated stuff—heartbeat, breathing, immunoresponse, memory. You don't want to forget to breathe, right?"

Liam hissed a laugh. "Horse-sheeit," he drawled. "How complicated is moving your arm? How many muscle-movements in a smile? How many muscle-movements in a heartbeat? How complicated is writing code versus immunoresponse? Why when you're holding your breath can't you hold it until you don't want to hold it anymore? Why do you have to be a fucking Jedi Master to stop your heart at will?"

"But the interactions—"

"More horseshit. Yeah, the interactions between brain chemistry and body and cognition and metabolism are all complicated. I was a speed-freak, I know all about it. But it's not any more complicated than any of the other complex interactions you master every day—wind and attack and spin when someone tosses you a ball; speed and acceleration and vectors when you change lanes; don't even get me started on what goes on when you season a soup. No, your body just isn't *that* complicated—it's just hubris that makes us so certain that our meat-sacks are transcendently complex.

"We're simple, but all the good stuff is owned by your autonomic systems. They're like conditional operators left behind by a sloppy coder: while x is true, do y. We've only had the vaguest idea what x is, but we've got a handle on y, you betcha. Burning fat, for example." He prodded Murray's gut-overhang with a long finger. Self-consciously, Murray tugged his JavaOne gimme jacket tighter.

"For forty years now, doctors have been telling us that the way to keep fit is to exercise more and eat less. That's great fucking advice, as can be demonstrated by the number of trim, fit residents of Northern California that can be found waddling around any shopping mall off Interstate 101. Look at exercise, Jesus, what could be stupider? Exercise doesn't burn fat, exercise just satisfies the condition in which your body is prepared to burn fat off. It's like a computer that won't boot unless you restart it twice, switch off the monitor, open the CD drive, and stand on one foot. If you're a luser, you do all this shit every time you want to boot your box, but if you're a leet haxor like you and me, you just figure out what's wrong with the computer and *fix it*. You don't sacrifice a chicken twice a day, you own the box, so you make it dance to your tune.

"But your meat, it's not under your control. You know you have to exercise for twenty minutes before you start burning any fat at all? In other words, the first twenty minutes are just a goddamned waste of time. It's sacrificing a chicken to your metabolism. Eat less, exercise more is a giant chicken-sacrifice, so I say screw it. I say, you should be super-user in your own body. You should be leet as you want to be. Every cell in your body should be end-user modifiable."

Liam held his hands out before them, then stretched and stretched and stretched the fingers, so that each one bent over double. "Triple jointed, metabolically secure, cognitively large and *in charge*. I own, dude."

Liam fished the last cig out of the pack, crumpled it, and tucked it into a pocket. "Last one," he said. "Wanna share?"

"Sure," Murray said, dazedly. "Yeah," he said, taking the smoke and bringing it to his lips. The tip, he realized too late, was dripping with saliva. He made a face and handed it back to Liam. "Aaagh! You juiced the filter!"

"Sorry," Liam said, "talking gets my spit going. Where was I? Oh, yeah, I own. Want to know how it happened?"

"Does it also explain how you ended up not dead?"

"Mostly dead. Indeed it does."

Murray walked back to the car and lay back on the hood, staring at the thin star-cover and the softly swaying pine-tops. He heard Liam begin to pace, heard the cadence of Liam's thinking stride, the walk he fell into when he was on a roll.

"Are you sitting comfortably?" Liam said. "Then I shall begin."

The palliatives on the ward were abysmal whiners, but they were still better than the goddamned church volunteers who came by to patch-adams at them. Liam was glad of the days when the dementia was strong, morphine days when the sun rose and set in a slow blink and then it was bedtime again.

Lucky for him, then, that lucid days were fewer and further between. Unlucky for him that his lucid days, when they came, were filled with the G-Men.

The G-Men had come to him in the late days of his tenure on the palliative ward. They'd wheeled him into a private consultation room and given him a cigarette that stung the sores on his lips, tongue, and throat. He coughed gratefully.

"You must be the Fed," Liam said. "No one else could green-light indoor smoking in California." Liam had worked for the Fed before. Work in the Valley and you end up working for the Fed, because when the cyclic five-year bust arrives, the only venture capital that's liquid in the US is military research green—khaki money. He'd been seconded twice to biometrics-and-machine-guns bunkers where he'd worked on need-to-know integration projects for Global Semi's customers in the Military-Industrial Simplex.

The military and the alphabet soup of Fed cops gave birth to the Valley. After WWII, all those shipbuilder engineers and all those radar engineers and all those radio engineers and the tame academics at Cal Tech and Cal and Stanford sorta congealed, did a bunch of start-ups, and built a bunch of crap their buds in the Forces would buy.

Khaki money stunted the Valley. Generals didn't need to lobby in Congress for bigger appropriations. They just took home black budgets that were silently erased from the books, aerosolized cash that they misted over the eggheads along Highway 101. Two generations later, the Valley was filled with techno-determinists, swaggering nerd squillionaires who were steadfastly convinced that the money would flow forever and ever amen.

Then came Hollywood, the puny $35 billion David that slew the $600 billion Goliath of tech. They bought Congresscritters, had their business models declared fundamental to the American way of life, extended copyright ad [inifinitum | nauseam] and generally kicked the shit out of tech in DC. They'd been playing this game since 1908, when they sued to keep the player piano off the market, and they punched well above their weight in the legislative ring. As the copyright police began to crush tech companies throughout the Valley, khaki money took on the sweet appeal of nostalgia, strings-free cash for babykiller projects that no one was going to get sued over.

The Feds that took Liam aside that day could have been pulled from a fiftieth anniversary revival of "Nerds and Generals." Clean-cut, stone-faced, prominent wedding bands. The Feds had never cared for Liam's jokes, though it was his track marks and not his punch lines that eventually accounted for his security clearance being yanked. These two did not crack a smile as Liam wheezed out his pathetic joke.

Instead, they introduced themselves gravely. Col. Gonzalez—an MD, with caduceus insignia next to his silver birds—and Special Agent Fredericks. Grateful for his attention, they had an offer to make him.

"It's experimental, and the risks are high. We won't kid you about that."

"I appreciate that," Liam wheezed. "I like to live dangerously. Give me another smoke, willya?"

Col. Gonzalez lit another Marlboro Red with his brass Zippo and passed him a sheaf of papers. "You can review these here, once we're done. I'm afraid I'll have to take them with me when we go, though."

Liam paged through the docs, passing over the bio stuff and nodding his head over the circuit diagrams and schematics. "I give up," he said. "What does it all do?"

"It's an interface between your autonomic processes and a microcontroller."

Liam thought about that for a moment. "I'm in," he said.

Special Agent Fredericks's thin lips compressed a hair and his eyes gave the hintiest hint of a roll. But Col. Gonzalez nodded to himself. "All right. Here's the protocol: tomorrow, we give you a bug. It's a controlled mutagen that prepares your brainstem so that it emits and receives weak electromagnetic fields that can be manipulated with an external microcontroller. In subjects with effective immunoresponse, the bug takes less than one percent of the time—"

"But if you're dying of AIDS, that's not a problem," Liam said and smiled until some of the sores at the corners of his mouth cracked and released a thin gruel of pus. "Lucky fucking me."

"You grasp the essentials," the Colonel said. "There's no surgery involved. The interface regulates immunoresponse in the region of the insult to prevent rejection. The controller has a serial connector that connects to a PC that instructs it in respect of the governance of most bodily functions."

Liam smiled slantwise and butted out. "God, I'd hate to see the project you developed this shit for. Zombie soldiers, right? You can tell me, I've got clearance."

Special Agent Fredericks shook his head.

"Not for three years, you haven't. And you never had clearance to get the answer to that question. But once you sign here and here and here, you'll *almost* have clearance to get *some* of the answers." He passed a clipboard to Liam.

Liam signed, and signed, and signed. "Autonomic processes, right?"

Col. Gonzalez nodded. "Correct."

"Including, say, immunoresponse?"

"Yes, we've had very promising results in respect to the immune system. It was one of the first apps we wrote. Modifies the genome to produce virus-hardened cells and kick-starts production of new cells."

"Yeah, until some virus out-evolves it," Liam said. He knew how to debug vaporware.

"We issue a patch," the Colonel said.

"I write good patches," Liam said.

"We know," Special Agent Fredericks said, and gently prized the clipboard from his fingers.

• • •

The techs came first, to wire Liam up. The new bug in his system broadened his already-exhaustive survey of the ways in which the human body can hurt. He squeezed his eyes tight against the morphine rush and lazily considered the possibility of rerouting pain to a sort of dull tickle.

The techs were familiar Valley-dwellers, portly and bedecked with multitools and cellular gear and wireless PDAs. They handled him like spoiled meat, with gloves and wrinkled noses, and talked shop over his head to one another.

Colonel Gonzalez supervised, occasionally stepping away to liaise with the hospital's ineffectual medical staff.

A week of this—a week of feeling like his spine was working its way out of his asshole, a week of rough latex hands and hacker jargon—and he was wheeled into a semiprivate room, surrounded by louche oatmeal-colored commodity PCs—no keyboards or mice, lest he get the urge to tinker.

The other bed was occupied by Joey, another Silicon Valley needle-freak, a heroin addict who'd been a design engineer for Apple, figuring out how to cram commodity hardware into stylish gumdrop boxen. Joey and Liam croaked conversation between themselves when they were both lucid and alone. Liam always knew when Joey was awake by the wet hacking coughs he wrenched out of his pneumonia-riddled lungs. Alone together, ignored by the mad scientists who were hacking their bodies, they struck up a weak and hallucinogenic camaraderie.

"I'm not going to sleep," Joey said, in one timeless twilight.

"So don't sleep, shit," Liam said.

"No, I mean, ever. Sleep, it's like a third of your life, twenty, thirty years. What's it good for? It resets a bunch of switches, gives your brain a chance to sort through its buffers, a little oxygenation for your tissues. That stuff can all take place while you're doing whatever you feel like doing, hiking in the hills or getting laid. Make 'em into cron jobs and nice them down to the point where they just grab any idle cycles and do their work incrementally."

"You're crazy. I like to sleep," Liam said.

"Not me. I've slept enough in this joint, been on the nod enough, I never want to sleep another minute. We're getting another chance, I'm not wasting a minute of it." Despite the braveness of his words, he sounded like he was half-asleep already.

"Well, that'll make *them* happy. All part of a good super-soldier, you know."

"Now who's crazy?"

"You don't believe it? They're just getting our junkie asses back online so they can learn enough from us to field some mean, lean, heavily modified fighting-machines."

"And then they snuff us. You told me that this morning. Yesterday? I still don't believe it. Even if you're right about why they're doing this, they're still going to want us around so they can monitor the long-term effects."

"I hope you're right."

"You know I am."

Liam stared into the ceiling until he heard Joey's wet snores, then he closed his eyes and waited for the fever dreams.

Joey went critical the next day. One minute, he was snoring away in bed while Liam watched a daytime soap with headphones. The next minute, there were twenty people in the room: nurses, doctors, techs, even Col. Gonzalez. Joey was doing the floppy dance in the next bed, the OD dance that Liam had seen once or twice, danced once or twice on an Emergency Room floor, his heart pounding the crystal meth mambo.

Someone backhanded Liam's TV and it slid away on its articulated arm and yanked the headphones off his head, ripping open the scabs on the slowly healing sores on his ears. Liam stifled a yelp and listened to the splashing sounds of all those people standing ankle-deep in something pink and bad-smelling, and Liam realized it was watery blood and he pitched forward and his empty stomach spasmed, trying to send up some bile or mucous, clicking on empty.

Colonel Gonzales snapped out some orders and two techs abandoned their fretting over one of the computers, yanked free a tangle of roll-up, rubberized keyboards and trackballs and USB cables, piled them on the side of Liam's gurney, snapped up the guard rails, and wheeled him out of the room.

They crashed through a series of doors before hitting a badgepoint. One tech thought he'd left his badge back in the room on its lanyard (he hadn't—he'd dropped it on the gurney and Liam had slipped it under the sheets), the other one wasn't sure if his was in one of his many pockets. As they frisked themselves, Liam stole his skeletal hand out from under the covers, a hand all tracked out with collapsed IV veins and yellowing fingernails, a claw of a hand.

The claw shook as Liam guided it to a keyboard, stole it under the covers, rolled it under the loose meat of his thigh.

• • •

"Need to know?" Liam said, spitting the words at Col. Gonzalez. "If I don't need to know what happened to Joey, who the fuck does?"

"You're not a medical professional, Liam. You're also not cleared. What happened to Joey was an isolated incident, nothing to worry about."

"Horseshit! You can tell me what happened to Joey or not, but I'll find out, you goddamned betcha."

The Colonel sighed and wiped his palms on his thighs. He looked like shit, his brush-cut glistening with sweat and scalp oil, his eyes bagged, and his youthful face made old with exhaustion lines. It had been two hours since Joey had gone critical—two hours of lying still with the keyboard nestled under his thigh, on the gurney in the locked room, until they came for him again. "I have a lot of work to do yet, Liam. I came to see you as a courtesy, but I'm afraid that the courtesy is at a close." He stood.

"Hey!" Liam croaked after him. "Gimme a fucking cigarette, will you?"

Once the Colonel was gone, Liam had the run of the room. They'd mopped it out and disinfected it and sent Joey's corpse to an Area 51 black ops morgue for gruesome autopsy, and there was only half as much hardware remaining, all of it plugged back into the hard pucker of skin on the back of Liam's neck.

Cautiously, Liam turned himself so that the toes of one foot touched the ground. Knuckling his toes, he pushed off toward the computers, the gurney's wheels squeaking. Painfully, arthritically, he inched to the boxes, then plugged in and unrolled the keyboard.

He hit the spacebar and got rid of the screen saver, brought up a login prompt. He'd been stealthily shoulder-surfing the techs for weeks now, and had half a dozen logins in his brain. He tapped out the login/pass combination and he was in.

The machine was networked to a CVS repository in some bunker, so the first thing he did was login to the server and download all the day's commits, then he dug out the READMEs.

While everything was downloading, he logged into the tech's e-mail account and found Col. Gonzalez's account of Joey's demise.

It was encrypted with the group's shared key as well as the tech's key, but he'd shoulder-surfed both, and after three tries, he had cleartext on the screen.

Hydrostatic shock. The membranes of all of Joey's cells had ruptured simultaneously, so that he'd essentially burst like a bag of semiliquid Jell-O. Preliminary indications were that the antiviral cellular modifications had gone awry due to some idiosyncrasy of Joey's "platform"— his physiology, in other words—and that the "fortified" cell membranes had given way disastrously and simultaneously.

A ghoulish giggle escaped Liam's lips. Venture capitalists liked to talk about "liquidity events"—times in the life of a portfolio company when the investors get to cash out: acquisition and IPO, basically. Liam had always joked that the VCs needed adult diapers to cope with their liquidity events, but now he had a better one. Joey had experienced the ultimate liquidity event.

The giggle threatened to rise into a squeal as he contemplated a liquidity event of his own, so he swallowed it and got into the READMEs and the source code.

He wasn't a biotech, wasn't a medical professional, but neither were the coders who'd been working on the mods that were executing on his "platform" at that very moment. In their comments and data-structures and READMEs, they'd gone to great pains to convert medical jargon to geekspeak, so that Liam was actually able to follow most of it.

One thing he immediately gleaned is that his interface was modifying his cells to be virus-hardened as slowly as possible. They wanted a controlled experiment, data on every stage of the recovery—if a recovery was indeed in the cards.

Liam didn't want to wait. He didn't even have to change the code—he just edited a variable in the config file and respawned the process.

Where before he'd been running at a pace that would reverse the course of HIV in his body in a space of three weeks, now he was set to be done in three *hours*. What the fuck—how many chances was he going to get to screw around after they figured out that he'd been tinkering?

• • •

Manufacturing the curative made him famished. His body was burning a lot of calories, and after a couple hours he felt like he could eat the ass out of a dead bear. Whatever was happening was happening, though! He felt the sores on his body dry up and start to slough off. He was hungry enough that he actually caught himself peeling off the scabby cornflakes and eating them. It grossed him out, but he was *hungry*.

His only visitor that night was a nurse, who made enough noise with her trolley on the way down the hall that he had time to balance the keyboard on top of the monitor and knuckle the bed back into position. The nurse was pleased to hear that he had an appetite and obligingly brought him a couple of supper trays— the kitchen had sent up one for poor Joey, she explained.

Once Liam was satisfied that she was gone, he returned to his task with a renewed sense of urgency. No techs and no docs and no Colonel for six hours now—there must be a shitload of paperwork and finger-pointing over Joey, but who knew how long it would last?

He stuffed his face, nailing about three thousand calories over the next two hours, poking through the code. Here was a routine for stimulating the growth of large muscle groups. Here was one for regenerating fine nerves. The enhanced reflexes sounded like a low-cal option, too, so he executed it. It was all betaware, but as between a liquidity event, a slow death on the palliative ward, and a chance at a quick cure, what the fuck, he'd take his chances.

He was chuckling now, going through the code, learning the programmers' style and personality from their comments and variable

357

names. He was so damned hungry, and the muscles in his back and limbs and ass and gut all felt like they were home to nests of termites.

He needed more food. He gingerly peeled off the surgical tape holding on the controller and its cable. Experimentally, he stood. His inner ear twirled roller coaster for a minute or two, but then it settled down and he was actually erect—upright—well, both, he could cut glass with that boner, it was the first one he'd had in a year—and *walking*!

He stole out into the hallway, experiencing a frisson of delight and then the burning ritual humiliation of any person who finds himself in a public place wearing a hospital gown. His bony ass was hanging out of the back, the cool air of the dim ward raising goose-pimples on it.

He stepped into the next room. It was dusky-dark, the twilight of a hospital nighttime, and the two occupants were snoring in contratime. Each had his (her? it was too dark to tell) own nightstand, piled high with helium balloons, Care Bears, flowers, and baskets of nuts, dried fruits, and chocolates. Saliva flooded Liam's mouth. He tiptoed across to each nightstand and held up the hem of his gown, then grinched the food into the pocket it made.

Stealthily, he stole his way down the length of the ward, emptying fruit baskets, boxes of candy and chocolate, leftover dinner trays. By the time he returned to his room, he could hardly stand. He dumped the food out on the bed and began to shovel it into his face, going back through the code, looking for obvious bugs, memory leaks, buffer overruns. He found several and recompiled the apps, accelerating the pace of growth in his muscles. He could actually feel himself bulking up, feel the tone creeping back into his flesh.

He'd read the notes in the READMEs on waste heat and the potential to denature enzymes, so he stripped naked and soaked towels in a quiet trickle of ice-water in the small sink. He kept taking breaks from his work to wring out the steaming towels he wrapped around his body and wet them down again.

The next time he rose, his legs were springy.

He parted the slats of the blinds and saw the sun rising over the distant ocean and knew it was time to hit the road, Jack.

He tore loose the controller and its cable and shut down the computer. He undid the thumb-screws on the back of the case and slid it away, then tugged at the sled for the hard disk until it sprang free. He ducked back out into the hall and quickly worked his way through the rooms until he found one with a change of men's clothes neatly folded on the chair—ill-fitting tan chinos and a blue Oxford shirt, the NoCal yuppie uniform. He found a pair of too-small penny loafers too and jammed his feet into the toes. He dressed in his room and went through the wallet that was stuck in the pants pocket. A couple hundred bucks' worth of cash, some worthless plastic, a picture of a heavyset wife and three chubby kids. He dumped all the crap out, kept the cash, snatched up the drive-sled and booted, badging out with the tech's badge.

• • •

"How long have you been on the road, then?" Murray asked. His mouth tasted like an ashtray and he had a mild case of the shakes.

"Four months. I've been breaking into cars mostly. Stealing laptops and selling them for cash. I've got a box at the rooming house with the hard-drive installed, and I've been using an e-gold account to buy little things online to help me out."

"Help you out with *what*?"

"Hacking—duh. First thing I did was reverse engineer the interface bug. I wanted a safe virus I could grow arbitrary payloads for in my body. I embedded the antiviral hardening agent in the vector. It's a sexually transmissible *wellness*, dude. I've been barebacking my way through the skankiest crack-hoes in the Tenderloin, playing Patient Zero, infecting everyone with the Cure."

Murray sat up and his head swam. "You did what?"

"I cured AIDS. It's going around, it's catching, you might already be a winner."

"Jesus, Liam, what the fuck do you know about medicine? For all you know, your cure is worse than the disease—for all you know, we're all going to have a—'*liquidity event*' any day now!"

"No chance of that happening, bro. I isolated the cause of that early on. This medical stuff is just *not that complicated*—once you get over the new jargon, it's nothing you can't learn as you go with a little judicious googling. Trust me. You're soaking in it."

It took Murray a moment to parse that. "You infected *me*?"

"The works—I've viralized all the best stuff. Metabolic controllers, until further notice, you're on a five-cheeseburger-a-day diet; increased dendrite density; muscle-builders. At-will pain-dampeners. You'll need those—I gave you the interface, too."

A spasm shot up Murray's back, then down again.

"It was on the cigarette butt. You're cancer-immune, by the by. I'm extra contagious tonight." Liam turned down his collar to show Murray the taped lump there, the dangling cable that disappeared down his shirt, connecting to the palmtop strapped to his belt.

Murray arched his back and mewled through locked jaws.

Liam caught his head before it slammed into the Toyota's hood. "Breathe," he hissed. "Relax. You're only feeling the pain because you're choosing not to ignore it. Try to ignore it, you'll see. It kicks azz."

• • •

"I needed an accomplice. A partner in crime. I'm underground, see? No credit card, no ID. I can't rent a car or hop a plane. I needed to recruit someone I could trust. Naturally, I thought of you."

"I'm flattered," Murray sarcased around a mouthful of double-bacon cheeseburger with extra mayo.

"You should be, asshole," Liam said. They were at Murray's one-bedroom techno-monastic condo: shit sofa, hyper-ergonomic chairs, dusty home theater, computers everywhere. Liam drove them there, singing into the wind that whipped down from the sunroof, following the GPS's sterile eurobabe voice as it guided them back to the anonymous shitbox building where Murray had located his carcass for eight years.

"Liam, you're a pal, really, my best friend ever, I couldn't be happier that you're alive, but if I could get up I would fucking *kill you*. You *raped me*, asshole. Used my body without my permission."

"You see it that way now, but give it a couple weeks, it'll, ah, grow on you. Trust me. It's rad. So, call in sick for the next week—you're going to need some time to get used to the mods."

"And if I don't?"

"Do whatever you want, buddy, but I don't think you're going to be in any shape to go to work this week—maybe not next week either. Tell them it's a personal crisis. Take some vacation days. Tell 'em you're going to a fat-farm. You must have a shitload of holidays saved up."

"I do," Murray said. "I don't know why I should use them, though."

"Oh, this is the best vacation of all, the Journey Thru Innerspace. You're going to love it."

• • •

Murray hadn't counted on the coding.

Liam tunneled into his box at the rooming house and dumped its drive to one of the old laptops lying around Murray's apartment. He set the laptop next to Murray while he drove to Fry's Electronics to get the cabling and components he needed to make the emitter/receiver for the interface. They'd always had a running joke that you can build *anything* from parts at Fry's, but when Liam invoked it, Murray barely cracked a smile. He was stepping through the code in a debugger, reading the comments Liam had left behind as he'd deciphered its form and function.

He was back in it. There was a runtime that

simulated the platform and as he tweaked the code, he ran it on the simulator and checked out how his body would react if he executed it for real. Once he got a couple of liquidity events, he saw that Liam was right, they just weren't that hard to avoid.

The API was great, there were function calls for just about everything. He delved into the cognitive stuff right off, since it was the area that was rawest, that Liam had devoted the least effort to. At-will serotonin production. Mnemonic perfection. Endorphin production, adrenaline. Zen master on a disk. Who needs meditation and biofeedback when you can do it all in code?

Out of habit, he was documenting as he went along, writing proper tutorials for the API, putting together a table of the different kinds of interaction he got with different mods. Good, clear docs, ready for printing, able to be slotted in as online help in the developer tool kit. Inspired by Joey, he began work on a routine that would replace all the maintenance chores that the platform did in sleep-mode, along with a subroutine that suppressed melatonin and all the other circadian chemicals that induced sleep.

Liam returned from Fry's with bags full of cabling and soldering guns and breadboards. He draped a black pillowcase over a patch of living-room floor and laid everything out on it, wires and strippers and crimpers and components and a soldering gun, and went to work methodically, stripping and crimping and twisting. He'd taken out his own connector for reference and he was comparing them both, using a white LED torch on a headband to show him the pinouts on the custom end.

"So I'm thinking that I'll clone the controller and stick it on my head first to make sure it works. You wear my wire and I'll burn the new one in for a couple days and then we can swap. Okay?"

"Sure," Murray said, "whatever." His fingers rattled on the keys.

"Got you one of these," Liam said and held

up a bulky Korean palmtop. "Runs Linux. You can cross-compile the SDK and all the libraries for it; the compiler's on the drive. Good if you want to run an interactive app"—an application that changed its instructions based on output from the platform—"and it's stinking cool, too. I fucking *love* gear."

"Gear's good," Murray agreed. "Cheap as hell and faster every time I turn around."

"Well, until Honorable Computing comes along," Liam said. "That'll put a nail in the old coffin."

"You're overreacting."

"Naw. Just being realistic. Open up a shell, okay? See at the top, how it says 'tty'? The kernel thinks it's communicating with a printer. Your shell window is a simulation of a printer, so the kernel knows how to talk to it—it's got plenty of compatibility layers between it and you. If the guy who wrote the code doesn't want you to interface with it, you can't. No emulation, that's not 'honorable.' Your box is owned."

Murray looked up from his keyboard. "So what do you want me to do about it, dead man?"

"Mostly dead," Liam said. "Just think about it, okay? How much money you got in your savings account?"

"Nice segue. Not enough."

"Not enough for what?"

"Not enough for sharing any of it with you."

"Come on, dude, I'm going back underground. I need fifty grand to get out of the country—Canada, then buy a fake passport and head to London. Once I'm in the EU, I'm in good shape. I learned German last week, this week I'm doing French. The dendrite density shit is the shit."

"Man und zooperman," Murray said. "If you're zo zooper, go and earn a buck or two, okay?"

"Come on, you know I'm good for it. Once this stuff is ready to go—"

"What stuff?"

"The codebase! Haven't you figured it out yet? It's a start-up! We go into business in some former-Soviet Stan in Asia or some African kleptocracy. We infect the locals with the Cure, then the interface, and then we sell 'em the software. It's *viral marketing*, gettit?"

"Leaving aside CIA assassins, if only for the moment, there's one gigantic flaw in your plan, dead-man."

"I'm all aflutter with anticipation."

"There's no fucking revenue opportunity. The platform spreads for free—it's already out there, you've seeded it with your magic undead super-cock. The hardware is commodity hardware, no margin and no money. The controller can be built out of spare parts from Fry's—next gen, we'll make it Wi-Fi, so that we're using commodity wireless chipsets and you can control the device from a distance—"

"—yeah, and that's why we're selling the software!" Liam hopped from foot to foot in a personal folk dance celebrating his sublime cleverness.

"In Buttfuckistan or Kleptomalia. Where being a warez dood is an honorable trade. We release our libraries and binaries and APIs and fifteen minutes later, they're burning CDs in every *souk* and selling them for ten cents a throw."

"Nope, that's not gonna happen."

"Why not?"

"We're gonna deploy on Honorable hardware."

"I am not hearing this." Murray closed the lid of his laptop and tore into a slice of double-cheese meat-lover's deep-dish pizza. "You are not telling me this."

"You are. I am. It's only temporary. The interface isn't Honorable, so anyone who reverse engineers it can make his own apps. We're just getting ours while the getting is good. All the good stuff—say, pain control and universal antiviral hardening—we'll make for free, viralize it. Once our stuff is in the market, the whole world's going to change, anyway. There'll be apps for happiness, cures for every disease, hibernation, limb regeneration, whatever. Anything any human body has ever done, ever, you'll be able to do at will. You think there's going to be

anything recognizable as an economy once we're ubiquitous?"

Every morning, upon rising, Murray looked down at his toes and thought, "Hello toes." It had been ten years since he'd had regular acquaintance with anything south of his gut. But his gut was gone, tight as a drumhead. He was free from scars and age marks and unsightly moles and his beard wouldn't grow in again until he asked it to. When he thought about it, he could feel the dull ache of the new teeth coming in underneath the ones that had grown discolored and chipped, the back molar with all the ugly amalgam fillings, but if he chose to ignore it, the pain simply went away.

He flexed the muscles, great and small, all around his body. His fat index was low enough to see the definition of each of those superbly toned slabs of flexible contained energy—he looked like an anatomy lesson, and it was all he could do not to stare at himself in the mirror all day.

But he couldn't do that—not today, anyway. He was needed back at the office. He was already in the shitter at work over his "unexpected trip to a heath-farm," and if he left it any longer, he'd be out on his toned ass. He hadn't even been able to go out for new clothes—Liam had every liquid cent he could lay hands on, as well as his credit cards.

He found a pair of ancient, threadbare jeans and a couple of medium T-shirts that clung to the pecs that had grown up underneath his formerly sagging man boobs and left for the office.

He drew stares on the way to his desk. The documentation department hummed with hormonal female energy, and half a dozen of his coworkers found cause to cruise past his desk before he took his morning break. As he greedily scarfed up a box of warm Krispy Kremes, his cellphone rang.

"Yeah?" he said. The caller ID was the number of the international GSM phone he'd bought for Liam.

"They're after us," Liam said. "I was at the

Surrey border crossing and the Canadian immigration guy had my pic!"

Murray's heart pounded. He concentrated for a moment, then his heart calmed, a jolt of serotonin lifting his spirits. "Did you get away?"

"Of course I got away. Jesus, you think that the CIA gives you a phone call? I took off cross-country, went over the fence for the duty-free, and headed for the brush. They shot me in the fucking leg—I had to dig the bullet out with my multitool. I'm sending in ass-loads of T-cells and knitting it as fast as I can."

Panic crept up Murray's esophagus, and he tamped it down. It broke out in his knees, he tamped it down. His balance swam, he stabilized it. He focused his eyes with an effort. "They *shot* you?"

"I think they were trying to wing me. Look, I burned all the source in 4,096-bit GPG ciphertext onto a couple of CDs, then zeroed out my drive. You've got to do the same, it's only a matter of time until they run my back trail to you. The code is our only bargaining chip."

"I'm at work—the backups are at home, I just can't."

"Leave, asshole, like *now*! Go—get in your car and *drive*. Go home and start scrubbing the drives. I left a bottle of industrial paint-stripper behind and a bulk eraser. Unscrew every drive-casing, smash the platters, and dump them in a tub with all the stripper, then put the tub onto the bulk eraser—that should do it. Keep one copy, ciphertext only, and make the key a good one. Are you going?"

"I'm badging out of the lot, shit, shit, shit. What the fuck did you do to me?"

"Don't, okay? Just don't. I've got my own problems. I've got to go now. I'll call you later once I get somewhere."

· · ·

He thought hard on the way back to his condo, as he whipped down the off-peak emptiness of Highway 101. Being a coder was all about doing things in the correct order: first a; then b; then, if c equals d, e; otherwise, f.

First, get home. Then set the stateful operation of his body for maximal efficiency: reset his metabolism, increase the pace of dendrite densification. Manufacture viralized antiviral in all his serum. Lots of serotonin and at-will endorphin. Hard times ahead.

Next, encipher and back up the data to a removable. Did he have any CD blanks at home? With eidetic clarity, he saw the half-spent spool of generic blanks on the second shelf of the media totem.

Then trash the disks, pack a bag, and hit the road. Where to?

He pulled into his driveway, hammered the elevator button a dozen times, then bolted for the stairs. Five flights later, he slammed his key into the lock and went into motion, executing the plan. The password gave him pause—generating a 4,096 bit key that he could remember was going to be damned hard, but then he closed his eyes and recalled, with perfect clarity, the first five pages of documentation he'd written for the API. His fingers rattled on the keys at speed, zero typos.

He was just dumping the last of the platters into the acid bath when they broke his door down. Half a dozen big guys in martian riot-gear, outsized science fiction black-ops guns. One flipped up his visor and pointed to a badge clipped to a D-ring on his tactical vest.

"Police," he barked. "Hands where I can see them."

The serotonin flooded the murky gray recesses of Murray's brain and he was able to smile nonchalantly as he straightened from his work, hands held loosely away from his sides. The cop pulled a zap-strap from a holster at his belt and bound his wrists tight. He snapped on a pair of latex gloves and untaped the interface on the back of Murray's neck, then slapped a bandage over it.

"Am I under arrest?"

"You're not cleared to know that," the cop said.

"Special Agent Fredericks, right?" Murray said. "Liam told me about you."

"Dig yourself in deeper, that's right. No one wants to hear from you. Not yet, anyway." He took a bag off his belt, then, in a quick motion, slid it over Murray's head, cinching it tight at the throat, but not so tight he couldn't breathe. The fabric passed air, but not light, and Murray was plunged into total darkness. "There's a gag that goes with the hood. If you play nice, we won't have to use it."

"I'm nice, I'm nice," Murray said.

"Bag it all and get it back to the house. You and you, take him down the back way."

Murray felt the bodies moving near him, then thick zap-straps cinching his arms, knees, thighs, and ankles. He tottered and tipped backward, twisting his head to avoid smacking it, but before he hit the ground, he'd be roughly scooped up into a fireman's carry, resting on bulky body armor.

As they carried him out, he heard his cellphone ring. Someone plucked it off his belt and answered it. Special Agent Fredericks said, "Hello, Liam."

.   .   .

Machine-guns-and-biometrics bunkers have their own special signature scent, scrubbed air and coffee farts and ozone. They cut his clothes off and disinfected him, then took him through two air showers to remove particulate that the jets of icy pungent Lysol hadn't taken care of. He was dumped on a soft pallet, still in the dark.

"You know why you're here," Special Agent Fredericks said from somewhere behind him.

"Why don't you refresh me?" He was calm and cool, heart normal. The cramped muscles bound by the plastic straps eased loose, relaxing under him.

"We found two CDs of encrypted data on your premises. We can crack them, given time,

but it will reflect well on you if you assist us in our inquiries."

"Given about a billion years. No one can brute-force a 4,096-bit GPG cipher. It's what you use in your own communications. I've worked on military projects, you know that. If you could factor out the products of large primes, you wouldn't depend on them for your own security. I'm not getting out of here ever, no matter how much I cooperate."

"You've got an awfully low opinion of your country, sir." Murray thought he detected a note of real anger in the Fed's voice and tried not to take satisfaction in it.

"Why? Because I don't believe you've got magic technology hidden away up your asses?"

"No, sir, because you think you won't get just treatment at our hands."

"Am I under arrest?"

"You're not cleared for that information."

"We're at an impasse, Special Agent Fredericks. You don't trust me and I don't have any reason to trust you."

"You have every reason to trust me," the voice said, very close in now.

"Why?"

The hood over his tag was tugged to one side and he heard a sawing sound as a knife hacked through the fabric at the base of his skull. Gloved fingers worked a plug into the socket there. "Because," the voice hissed in his ear, "because I am not stimulating the pain center of your brain. Because I am not cutting off the blood supply to your extremities. Because I am not draining your brain of all the serotonin there or leaving you in a vegetative state. Because I can do all of these things and I'm not."

Murray tamped his adrenals, counteracted their effect, relaxed back into his bonds. "You think you could outrace me? I could stop my heart right now, long before you could do any of those things." Thinking: I am a total bad-azz, I am. But I don't want to die.

"Tell him," Liam said.

"Liam?" Murray tried to twist his head

toward the voice, but strong hands held it in place.

"Tell him," Liam said again. "We'll get a deal. They don't want us dead, they just want us under control. Tell him, okay?"

Murray's adrenals were firing at max now, he was sweating uncontrollably. His limbs twitched hard against his bonds, the plastic straps cutting into them, the pain surfacing despite his efforts. It hit him. His wonderful body was ownzored by the Feds.

"Tell me, and you have my word that no harm will come to you. You'll get all the resources you want. You can code as much as you want."

Murray began to recite his key, all five pages of it, through the muffling hood.

Liam was fully clothed, no visual restraints. As Murray chafed feeling back into his hands and feet, Liam crossed the locked office with its gray industrial carpeting and tossed him a set of khakis and a pair of boxers. Murray dressed silently, then turned his accusing glare on Liam.

"How far did you get?"

"I didn't even make it out of the state. They caught me in Sebastopol, took me off the Greyhound in cuffs with six guns on me all the time."

"The disks?"

"They needed to be sure that you got rid of all the backups, that there wasn't anything stashed online or in a safe-deposit box, that they had the only copy. It was their idea."

"Did you really get shot?"

"I really got shot."

"I hope it really fucking hurt."

"It really fucking hurt."

"Well, good."

The door opened and Special Agent Fredericks appeared with a big brown bag of Frappuccinos and muffins. He passed them around.

"My people tell me that you write excellent documentation, Mr. Swain."

"What can I say? It's a gift."

"And they tell me that you two have written some remarkable code."

"Another gift."

"We always need good coders here."

"What's the job pay? How are the bennies? How much vacation?"

"As much as you want, excellent, as long as you want, provided we approve the destinations first. Once you're cleared."

"It's not enough," Murray said, upending twenty ounces of West Coast frou-frou caffeine delivery system on the carpeting.

"Come on, Murray," Liam said. "Don't be that way."

Special Agent Fredericks fished in the bag and produced another novelty coffee beverage and handed it to Murray. "Make this one last, it's all that's left."

"With all due respect," Murray said, feeling a swell of righteousness in his chest, in his thighs, in his groin, "go fuck yourself. You don't own me."

"They do, Murray. They own both our asses." Liam said, staring into the puddle of coffee slurry on the carpet.

Murray crossed the room as fast as he could and smacked Liam, open palm, across the cheek.

"That will do," Special Agent Fredericks said, with surprising mildness.

"He needed smacking," Murray said, without rancor, and sat back down.

"Liam, why don't you wait for us in the hallway?"

• • •

"You came around," Liam said. "Everyone does. These guys own."

"I didn't ask to share a room with you, Liam. I'm not glad I am. I'd rather not be reminded of that fact, so shut your fucking mouth before I shut it for you."

"What do you want, an apology? I'm sorry. I'm sorry I infected you, I'm sorry I helped them catch you. I'm sorry I fuxored your life. What can I say?"

"You can shut up anytime now."

"Well, this is going to be a *swell* living arrangement."

The room was labeled "Officers' Quarters," and it had two good, firm, queen-sized mattresses, premium cable, two identical stainless-steel dressers, and two good ergonomic chairs. There were junction boxes beside each desk with locked covers that Murray supposed housed Ethernet ports. All the comforts of home.

Murray lay on his bed and pulled the blankets over his head. Though he didn't need to sleep, he chose to.

• • •

For two weeks, Murray sat at his assigned desk, in his assigned cube, and zoned out on the screen saver. He refused to touch the keyboard, refused to touch the mouse. Liam had the adjacent desk for a week, then they moved him to another office, so that Murray had solitude in which to contemplate the whirling star field. He'd have a cup of coffee at ten thirty and started to feel a little sniffly in the back of his nose. He ate in the commissary at his own table. If anyone sat down at his table, he stood up and left. They didn't sit at his table. At 2:00 p.m., they'd send in a box of warm Krispy Kremes, and by 3:00 p.m., his blood-sugar would be crashing and he'd be sobbing over his keyboard. He refused to adjust his serotonin levels.

On the third Monday, he turned up at his desk at 9:00 a.m. as usual and found a clipboard on his chair with a ballpoint tied to it.

Discharge papers. Nondisclosure agreements. Cross-your-heart swears on pain of death. A modest pension. Post-it *sign here* tabs had been stuck on here, here, and here.

• • •

The junkie couldn't have been more than fifteen years old. She was death-camp skinny, tracked out, sitting cross-legged on a cardboard box on the sidewalk, sunning herself in the thin Mission noonlight. "Wanna buy a laptop? Two hundred bucks."

Murray stopped. "Where'd you get it?"

"I stole it," she said. "Out of a convertible. It looks real nice. One-fifty."

"Two hundred," Murray said. "But you've got to do me a favor."

"Three hundred, and you wear a condom."

"Not that kind of favor. You know the Radio Shack on Mission at Twenty-Fourth? Give them this parts list and come back here. Here's a hundred-dollar down payment."

He kept his eyes peeled for the minders he'd occasionally spotted shadowing him when he went out for groceries, but they were nowhere to be seen. Maybe he'd lost them in the traffic on the 101. By the time the girl got back with the parts he'd need to make his interface, he was sweating bullets, but once he had the laptop open and began to rekey the entire codebase, the eidetic rush of perfect memory dispelled all his nervousness, leaving him cool and calm as the sun set over the Mission.

• • •

From the sky, Africa was green and lush, but once the plane touched down in Mogadishu, all Murray saw was sere brown plains and blowing dust. He sprang up from his seat, laundering the sleep toxins in his brain and the fatigue toxins in his legs and ass as he did.

He was the first off the jetway and the first at the Customs desk.

"Do you have any commercial or work-related goods, sir?"

"No, sir," Murray said, willing himself calm.

"But you have a laptop computer," the Customs man said, eyeballing his case.

"Oh, yeah. That. Can't ever get away from work, you know how it is."

"I certainly hope you find time to relax, sir." The Customs man stamped the passport he'd bought in New York.

"When you love your work, it can be relaxing."

"Enjoy your stay in Somalia, sir."

NICK MAMATAS

TIME OF DAY

(2002)

I HAD JUST GOTTEN OFF WORK and was on my way to more work when the phones in my mind rang. It was another seven jobs calling in, begging for my attention. In headspace, my ego agent, a slick and well-tanned Victor Mature, arranged them according to potential economic gain, neo-Marxist need measurement, and location.

I stuck my coffee cup in the beverage holder and leaned heavily on the wheel. Traffic was snarled. I initiated my patented anti-traffic protocol: "Whoo, let's go!" I shouted. I even banged my hands on the dashboard, but the snaking lines of red lights between me and my gig weren't impressed. I rewarded myself with more coffee anyway.

In headspace, my homunculus—a small, gray-winged gargoyle—shook its fist at the car ahead of me. My ego agent handed me his traveling salesman recommendation, a crazed zigzag all over the tristate. His plan was the cheapest and quickest way to install all the jacks, but my wetnurse was pinging about my pulse rate, lung color, and electrolyte levels, so I did my own math. I took two seconds to read a short article about another week of the Brown Haze over the city and decided that I needed a vacation. I'd do only one jackgig. A whole day spent on only one job instead of my usual eleven jobs a day. Far away. A monastery upstate, Greek Orthodox even. A vacation, or as close to one as jacked employees get.

The country would be quiet and the sky large. Like the parking lot I pulled into, but even bigger and with less soot.

• • •

"Okay, here we all are," I said to the kids. Not all my gigs were high-paying and glamorous; I was leading a tour of corporate HQ that night. Hi, I am Kelly Angelakis and I picked the short straw. Pleased to meet ya.

The kids gathered by the large office windows and stared up at me. They were college sophomores—the oldest was probably thirteen—and their eyes were wide and white, their skin slick with sweat. Their adrenal patches, all but mandatory for people on the go these days, were doing a bit too much to their young bodies. Some of the girls were almost vibrating in their sneakers. My ego agent provided me with some magnetizdat oral histories of patch addiction, but they were interrupted and replaced by soothing propaganda designed to reassure me. And I got some crossthought from another jack.

("Jesus forgive me, a miserable sinner!")

I sent the homunculus winging into the dark corners of my headspace to find the source of the crossthought, but he flew back to me empty-handed. Whoever was murmuring that little ditty needed a vacation worse than I did. Was it Sam, up on level seven? He was a pervert or something, and frequently filled nearby jacks with crapthink.

I couldn't bear to make eye contact with the tour group for more than a few seconds at a time, so I kept glancing out the window at the bright cityscape. The sky was black and the moon obscured by fog; more Brown Haze for tomorrow. A snarl of blinking red and white lights from the day's fifth rush hour entranced me for a second, but the sound of ten people twitching woke me up. I couldn't get a tenthsecond's rest that night.

My homunculus went and found that errant bit of religious crossthink: it came from the jack-gig request up at the monastery. A distraction. Victor Mature stepped up to the mic to take over the tour.

(Stock footage of Bill Cosby entered from skull-right and accepted a cigar from Freud with a smile. "Some acumen agents may appear as imaginary friends." A human-sized cartoon cigar with flickering red ash for hair, goggle eyes rolling and stick-figure limbs akimbo, marched into view and waved. The crowd giggled as if on cue.)

In headspace, the homunculus flew into view and unfurled a parchment. A green visor hung from its horns and it waved a quill pen in one claw. Cute. My helicopter to the country was ready. I blinked my signature at the parchment and the image derezzed.

The children were all quivering eyes and hair slicked down against clammy skin (—delete that, only happythink tonight!). Victor gave the standard disclaimer, pointed out the gift shop and cheerily spat out the company slogan, "We're Not Just Jack."

(Corporate logo, cue jingle.)

The helicopter was still ready, and I was already late. There was no way the elevator would get me to the roof on time. In headspace, My Pet Dog scuttled forward and stared at the copter's scheduling systems with his puppy-dog eyes. He scored twenty seconds for me. I took the steps up to the roof three at a time, swallowed a lungful of whipping smog on the helipad, and hopped aboard.

(My Pet Dog was a droopy old basset hound with folds of brown and white fur draped over his snout. Designed to curry favor with acumen and humans alike, he almost never failed. Even a helicopter had to submit to his cuteness.)

"Are you well rested, or just patched?" the pilot asked. He was old and had that skinny-guy-with-a-paunch look that ex-athletes and the unpatched had. I didn't know his name or number, so I couldn't look him up on the jacknet. Small talk. Grr.

"I'm patched," I said, trying to sound a bit apologetic. "That's business, you know, a working girl has to make a living." He smiled when I said "working girl." What a Neanderthal. My Pet Dog had already sniffed out his body language and idiolect, cross-referenced it with his career choice, and suggested a conversational thread.

I looked out the window. "Shame, isn't it?" I knew he'd know I was talking about the smog.

"The Brown Haze. Have you ever seen a white cloud? I know you live in the city."

"Sure I've seen them, in the country. Won't there be some over the hills by the monastery?"

He nodded once, as people of his temperament tend to. "Yeah."

Then I realized that I was only hearing him with my ears. He wasn't jacked at all. He'd just waited for me instead of overriding his helicopter and taking off without me. He'd done—what was it?—a favor.

It was hot in the cockpit, too hot, and my connection to the net faded. Victor Mature was beginning to warble, but the wetnurse rushed up and gave me a shot of sleepytime before my jack overheated entirely. Snoozeville.

• • •

"Excuse me, I only had three seconds of the language," I said in heavily accented Greek. The monk just smiled, showing that he actually had a pair of lips under his thick black beard. It was quiet outside, and cold.

"Welcome to Saint Basil's," he said in the bland English of disc jockeys and foreigners who've had their accents eradicated. "I'm Brother Peter." He smiled weakly, his lips still moving slightly, like he was talking to himself. Or like he had just had a jack installed. ("It is two thirty-five ay em," the homunculus whispered.) The monastery was impressive from the outside, at least: a squat four-story building made of thick carved granite. The lawn was well-kept, but still a bit wild, with weeds and poorly pruned bushes lining the walkway up the hill. I heard some crickets chirping away in soothing unison. It reminded me of the city, but quieter, like the volume was turned down on the universe. The noise of the jacknet was far away too, like waves lapping a shoreline just out of sight.

"My God, you're tired." I looked him over but couldn't see any of the telltale sweat or twitches. My own patches responded to that stray thought with another surge of tingly chemicals to the bloodstream. I blinked hard and rose to the tips of my toes. "I'm sorry, I'm . . . you know . . . I am not used to people who . . . actually let themselves get tired."

"People who are not from the city," Peter

said. He didn't smile this time, but he muttered something to himself after he spoke, then bowed his head slightly and took a step backward. "Come in, please."

I slipped through the door and frowned. The walls were plain old drywall, with an icon or two hanging from nails for decoration. The ceiling lights were old yellow incandescent bulbs, and the monastery's little foyer smelled of wax, incense, and unwashed feet. I got another burst of crossthought. (". . . have mercy on me, a miserable sinner.")

The source was here, somewhere down below. I could feel a jack pinging nearby, a strange chanting beat. There was only one of them, though, not the thousands I was used to in the city. Like one water droplet falling into a still puddle, it stood out.

Even out in the real world, it was quiet. Wind moved over the grass. Peter tugged on the sleeve of my blouse.

"Ms. Angelakis, you'll need to retire for several hours at least. Morning prayers are in ninety minutes. Then we hold a morning liturgy, and of course—"

"Women may not attend the liturgy. After the morning meal, we will meet again so we may begin my examination of George Proios, who needs a jack installed," I said along with him. There were only two variances. Peter said "your examination" instead of "my examination," which I expected. More importantly, he said "removed" instead of "installed." And his lips moved even after he finished speaking.

"What? Why would he want his jack removed?" I asked, my voice spiking enough to make My Pet Dog wince. My ego agent immediately got FedEx on the jacknet and had them send my tools out. "I wasn't told this was a removal. A removal requires tools and facilities that I do not have. A removal needs a medical doctor. I'm just an installer. Assembly-line stuff. I'm unskilled labor."

"Brother George does not want his jack removed. However, he requires it. *We* require it. He is a medical doctor and can assist you in that regard. He believes he can work with you, which is why he requested you."

In the headspace, I ran to one of the phones and hit the hot button, but there was no dial tone.

The inky blackness of my headspace solidified into a curved stone wall, a cave with no entrance or exit. The homunculus tried to fly to the shadows, to the open networks, but slammed against the mental block and fell at my feet, twitching. The wetnurse knelt down to repair it. Outside, I was still, staring off into space.

"Ms. Angelakis?" Peter asked. He waved his hand in front of my face.

I stepped back up, my vision refocusing on the outside world. Peter's lips twitched silently. I wanted to rip his beard off, to feel the wiry hair in my hands, but the wetnurse sedated me. From a few feet under the floor, I felt George Proios's malfunctioning jack repeating one recursive command, one thought, over and over. In the corner of my headspace, I sensed him, like an old file I'd forgotten to delete, like a shadow on a cave wall.

("Step up, there's a world out there!" Victor Mature demanded. Kelly snapped to attention.)

"He's having his jack removed," I said to Peter. "How can he assist me?" The wetnurse ran about my headspace with cold compresses, but I got all flushed anyway. I could feel the heat pouring from my skin. Peter's expression didn't change; his eyes were distant and his body still but for his twitching lips.

"You do not need his help, just his consent," he said, finally. His voice retained that dreamy, flat tone, like a computer or a jazz radio announcer.

"Jesus forgive me!" I said. "I'm not going to break half a dozen laws and risk a man's . . ." I stopped and realized what I had just said.

(The homunculus flew about Kelly's head, a flashing red siren strapped to its head. "Warning, warning," it screeched. Kelly waved it away.)

Peter didn't smile. I licked a line of sweat off my top lip. In the headspace, My Pet Dog went

sniffing after shadows. Downstairs, he was in a basement cell: George Proios. One command line, one task endlessly replicated by his Sinner Self, the Holy Spirit, and A Young Lamb, the monk's custom acumen agents. Some religious people even installed Jesus Christ masques, to keep them from fucking strange women or swearing. I'd never seen anyone with a lamb before. Certainly not one standing alongside a dove bathed in nearly blinding light and a haggard, leprous monk who was mindlessly repeating "O Lord Jesus Christ, Son of God, Jesus forgive me, a miserable sinner." My homunculus slapped its little claw against its forehead ("We could have had a V8!"). Then the monk turned to me, staring with his dead eyes, and linked our jacks. The shadow on the cave wall of my headspace began to murmur a prayer. Jesus forgive me, a miserable sinner, so I won't have to think anymore.

(Kelly Angelakis, age fourteen. She was thin and underdeveloped, with a huge mop of black curls splayed on the pillows. Her palm ran over her nude stomach, sliding down between her legs. Then guilt and bitter vomit filled her mouth.)

"I am sure you will help him, Ms. Angelakis. Brother George assures us that you are a good Greek girl. Also, he tells us that the state he is experiencing is . . . how would one put it . . . contagious, no?" He turned on his heel and led me to my room. I glanced up at the back of his neck, just to make sure. Smooth skin and wiry black hair. No jack.

They were all dry here. I could only sense one other signal, the drumbeat of George Proios and his begging cybernetic prayer. It overwhelmed his system and hit mine hard too. The homunculus scratched at headspace's new walls, trying to get out, but it was grounded. I was cut off from the network now, thanks to distance, granite, and the white noise chant of "Jesus forgive me." He had trapped me. The last message he'd allowed out was for the equipment I needed.

In the headspace, Victor Mature stepped into view. "Kelly, listen. We can get through this.

Don't forget how good you are. Proios sounds dangerous, but he's going to let you knock him out and uninstall his jack. We can do it and then we'll be able to call the police, the sysops, the FBI. All we have to do is take it easy for a few hours, do a job just like we were planning, and then we can leave. And all we need to do to succeed is not fall apart right now." I opened my mouth to answer him like he was standing next to me, then caught myself.

(My Pet Dog whimpered, knowing that even if the company was interested in Kelly's location, it would be cheaper to hire some thirteen-year-old right out of college to replace her than to waste the copter fuel on retrieving her. Kids worked more cheaply and had a useful decade in them before burning out. And everyone was too busy to worry about Kelly or where she was anyway.)

My room was spartan, with blank walls, a cot, and a small table where a candle, a Bible, and a bunch of grapes were laid out for me. A water cooler bubbled to itself on the opposite end of the room. My wetnurse suggested flipping through the New Testament, "purely to keep our mind on something else right now." I hadn't read a whole book in years, hadn't needed to. I flipped through the pages and ran my palms over the vellum, and quickly sliced my finger open on the gold leaf of a page from Revelation. I sucked on my finger for a few seconds, then decided to try something else. Being alone, without the net, was . . . disconcerting. Hell, it was scary.

I thought I'd make a game of seeing how far I could spit grape seeds, but the grapes were seedless. I stretched out on the bed—the mattress was hard and lumpy—and closed my eyes. In the headspace, my ego agent brought out the old film projector and suggested a movie. I shrugged and pulled down the screen.

(Victor Mature took his place in front of the projection screen, the cave morphing about him into a Hollywood studio. My Pet Dog jumped into his arms and licked his face, "Oh, Won Ton Ton," the ego agent crooned, "you'll be per-

fect!" "Yeah, Nick, he sure will be!" someone called from offscreen.)

I squeezed my eyes shut tighter. I'd already seen this movie too many times. *Won Ton Ton, the Dog Who Saved Hollywood*, a cheesy bit of tinsel that I'd caught on television at three in the morning once, when I was seven. Victor Mature had played Nick. I was so happy to hear my father's name on TV. It was either Victor Mature or Santa Claus, so I glommed onto Victor.

George Proios was still in my mind. He dug through my memories like someone picking through a bowl of pistachios.

(Kelly Angelakis, age seven. Nick Angelakis towered over her, a torn book in his hand, the pages falling around Kelly like feathers from a burst pillow. "Why do you read this garbage! This is for retarded kids, Kalliope, with the spaceships and pointy ears. What is he supposed to be,"—the back of the hand slapped the cover of the novel—"the devil?"

From the kitchen, Vasso Angelakis called out "Leave her alone, let her read what she wants!"

"I'm trying to raise my daughter right!" Nick shouted back.)

Childhood was another movie I had seen too many times already. I took a deep breath, pulled myself up out of bed, and hit the hallway. Peter was waiting for me, his eyes wide with confusion, his lips still going, and a package in his hands.

"Ms. Angelakis?"

"Come on, let's go see Proios now. He's doing . . . something."

"What?"

". . . Praying!"

"Well, yes, I certainly hope so," Peter said, glancing out one of the dark windows in the hallway. "It has been only four minutes since I showed you the room. Please, try to get some rest. I brought you blankets. I'll come for you after morning prayers. I'm sure your mail will be here by then."

There was no threat in his tone or body language, but I took a backward step into the room anyway. Then he said, "Will you need more blankets?"

"No, I'm fine." I closed the door. Goddamn, I needed to turn off my head, but Proios was digging through my old files. He introduced a virus into my headspace, one smarter than my wetnurse—an artificial mental illness called existential angst. Bastard.

(Kelly Angelakis, age seventeen. The back of her head was shaved. Her father, now an inch shorter than she, shook his head slowly as she explained, "I can talk to people with it, access information. Everyone's going to have one, one of these days, just like the computer."

"I never used the computer," Nick Angelakis said. "This is terrible. You want to talk to people? You can talk to me, you can talk to Mama, your friends in school. You should have learned Greek, if you wanted to talk to people. Your poor grandmother can't say two words to you.")

My eyes refocused from the blank walls of my headspace to the blank walls of the room. I decided that I would lie still and be perfectly silent, to listen to the building. That lasted two seconds. The homunculus flung itself against the headspace's cave walls again. Back to the grapes, this time making a game of how many I could fit into my mouth at once (fifteen!) but I started gagging and had to dig a few of them out of my mouth and crush the rest by pushing on my cheeks with my palms.

I had already used up my sleepytime with that damn nap on the helicopter. I counted the beats of a cricket chirping and then counted the holes in the ceiling tiles. One hundred and eighty-five holes per tile, thirty-eight tiles. Seven thousand and thirty ceiling tile holes in this room. The dimensions of the room and layout of the hallway suggested eight rooms of identical size on this floor. Was it dawn yet? Fifty-six thousand, two hundred and forty holes in the ceiling tiles on this floor. How many floors? Four.

Was it dawn yet? ("It is three fifteen ay em," the homunculus whispered.) Random facts littered headspace. Saint Nicholas (there's that name again) was the patron saint of Greece and of sailors. "And of prostitutes," the shadow on the cave wall whispered. Only 20 percent of the land in Greece is arable, while nearly 92 percent of Greece's population lives near the endless coastlines. (Jesus forgive me.)

I had been to church once, years ago, after my father died. It was a blur now, thanks to my jack and my busy little brain. The priest was mumbling in Greek and my jack was off, at mother's request—three hours of processing time I'll never get back. No translation but the priest's own, which was incomplete. The line "Life is more elusive than a dream" was the only thing I remembered from the sermon. I haven't dreamed in eight years.

The night before my father—not Dad, not Papa—died, I slept with a boy named Thomas Smith. My Pet Dog dug a hole at my feet and found the old sensations, the breeze on my back, the moisture, the throbbing in my tired calves after a few minutes of squelching. Was it dawn yet? That's all I wanted to know then, and all I wanted to know now. It wasn't, though. ("It's three forty-seven ay em," the homunculus whispered.) I gave up, closed my eyes, and actually, really, naturally slept. And I dreamed. I was taking a final exam after cutting class all semester. I was naked.

. . .

I awoke to a knock on the door, and was up in point two seconds. Brother Peter and I slipped past half a dozen other monks. Their footfalls were quiet enough, but it wasn't the sound of six dryboys, it was the lockstep beat of a jacked workplace. And the murmuring, the lips, each man I passed was muttering to himself. I glanced at the backs of their necks as they passed, but there were no jacks to be seen. Dry as a bone, and dry to the bone. But every one of them was tied to some jacknet, somewhere.

Peter had my FedEx package tucked under his arm and was marching down the hall, sending the hem of his cassock flying up to his knees. I was faster, though, and kept stepping on his heels.

"Brother Peter," I said, "you do realize, of course, that when I get back to the city, I'm going to put you on report. Not just for demanding this highly irregular removal, but for kidnapping me! This is contract under false pretenses, this is misallocation of processing time, this is wire fraud—"

"Please help him." He handed me the package and nodded toward a flight of steps leading down into a basement. "Go on."

"You're not coming with me?" I asked him. "How can I trust you on any of this? Heck, how can you trust me, I can go down there and lobotomize him." Peter shrugged and mumbled something again. In headspace, I heard Proios's own voice chanting, "O Lord Jesus Christ, Son of God, Jesus forgive me, a miserable sinner." The ego agent joined in the chant, in Victor Mature's dusky tones. My Pet Dog howled.

Then I realized that Peter hadn't been mumbling to himself. He had been reciting the same prayer as George, the same as the six other monks marching down the hall. The homunculus perched on my shoulder and held out a headspace lantern. In the real world, my pupils instantly adjusted to the dark and I walked down the steps.

George Proios looked just like the monk I had seen in the crossthought, and his shadow was splayed against the stone wall of the basement, just like it was in my headspace. His beard was long and matted, held against his chest by his own sweat and grime. He smiled.

("Jesus forgive me," the wetnurse muttered, and performed a preliminary diagnosis on our subject.)

His lips weren't moving. I realized then that mine were. That upstairs, Peter's still were. That every monk was saying a little prayer. They were always saying a little prayer. Now I was too, I was on a new jacknet. Except there was no jack necessary, and no net.

"Have you found God?" George asked.

"I'm here to remove your jack."

He didn't say anything for a long moment. Then he nodded toward a small table. A slice of bread sat there, not doing much. The words "Have you eaten?" came from somewhere—headspace or real world, I didn't know. He rose up and shuffled toward the table, split the piece in half and offered it to me. I looked down and my face flushed. I held a complete piece of bread in my hand, and George still had a full slice in his hand. "More?" He broke his piece in two again and offered me one of them. It was cold and heavy in my hand. The slice was whole, though, and now I had two pieces of bread. Two whole pieces of bread.

"I would like to remove the jack, and then leave," I said. I dropped the bread on the floor and took a step forward, My Pet Dog feeding me a conversational thread of icy professionalism designed to engender compliance.

"I have no wish for the jack to be removed," he said.

"It's broken. Malfunctioning. You're experiencing a severe cognitive loop, probably because of a physical defect in the jack's antenna array. I can't do a spinal intervention here, but without reception, your problem should alleviate itself," My Pet Dog said to me and I said to George.

George shrugged. "I do not have a problem. I pray without ceasing, as Scripture demands. I do what my brothers spend their adult lives attempting through privation and contemplation. One begins by praying as often as one can, on the level of the spoken word. All the time, one must begin to pray, muttering, whispering, thinking. Finally, after long years one can literally pray without ceasing. One's thoughts are always with God, not with sin. I pray from the heart, not from the jack. I am serene." My Pet Dog opened the package and spread the instruments on the tabletop.

"Look," George said, grabbing the two pieces of bread from the table. "Look! How do you explain this? Science, no? Somehow? What, with your quantum something-or-other?" He waved his arms and shoved the bread under my nose. Spittle coated his beard, and his arms were as thin as twigs. With a conductor's flourish, he whipped the sleeves of his robe up to his elbows and threw the bread on the ground. I took a step forward. "Mesmerism, perhaps, no? My jack interfering with yours? Have you thought of sin this morning, my child? Are you at peace? Have you ever even breathed? Jesus have mercy on me, a miserable sinner. Jesus have mercy on you."

George knelt to the floor near my feet, his head near the bread. The Jesus Prayer had done it. Two pieces where there used to be one. The dusty crusts, my footprint impressed onto one of them, existed. Without having to buy or sell them, without eleven jobs to pay for them, without a jingle. A miracle, at my feet.

I slapped a patch on George's neck and he dropped like a few sticks wrapped in a rag. Maybe I could know God after all. No more existential angst, no more rushing from job to job, the fabled free lunch. The bread. I tapped into George's spine and began to draw the information from him. The inspiration from him. It was like breathing a rainbow, but I could taste bread and wine, flesh and blood, in my mouth.

("The Lord tells us in Thessalonians 5:17 to 'Pray without ceasing,'" George explained to Kelly. "Our brothers have spent their lives contemplating their navels, muttering the words to themselves, trying to never lose contact with God. But I couldn't. The world was too distracting, too earnest. So I had a pirate jack installed, and found a way. And I prayed so well that God allowed others to hear me as well."

It was world of the Godnet: all the jackless wonders out there with one job, one personality, and one little life each, the whole smelly superstitious lot of them. And now Kelly was jacked in too.)

With George unconscious and his netblock gone, the rest of yesterday's junkmail finally downloaded and hit my brain. The latest news, spinning into headspace like a shot of a newspaper in an old movie, let me know what I had been missing for the past few hours. War with the Midwest, wethead bias crimes against dryboys on the rise, sumo results, the GM workers' council calling for a strike, markets down. People had things to buy and sell, important pinhead opinions to howl across my brain. I was needed, necessary, a crucial memebucket for the best the world had to offer, at low low interest rates. No thanks, I thought to myself (to myself, not some nano-neurological stooge!); I quit.

In headspace, I shot My Pet Dog. I shot him dead, and took over my body, once and for all.

Headspace crumbled and a noisy blackness buried me. I think I fell to my knees, or was it on my face? I couldn't breathe. My lips were clenched shut, but vomit poured into my mouth and through the gaps in my teeth. Then, in headspace, I felt the firm hand of my ego agent on the back of my neck, lifting me above the swirling advertisements, the dizzying dance of thousands of stock prices, and the casual emergencies of work and memos and updated job queues. I coughed up the liquid shit of it all and finally, finally, took a moment. And I breathed, and my breath was a prayer.

I turned to face my acumen. The light from Victor Mature's miner's helmet dazzled my eyes, but that was probably just the jack's way of explaining the stars I saw from the bump on my head. The homunculus flew overhead, clutching My Pet Dog's corpse in his claws. The wetnurse was standing on a stepladder as a waist-deep flood of information spilled into our little world.

"Guess what, gang," I said. "You're all fired. I don't need to work twenty-three point seven hours a day anymore, and neither does anyone else. God will provide." In headspace, I held up two pieces of miracle bread, and threw them to the floor. Then I fired my acumen agents. With my gun.

The jack removal took longer than I thought it would. The scalpel felt too heavy in my hands; my fingers were too stiff to move. My connection to the jacknet was a distant scream, like a child left behind in a parking lot by his deranged parents. George's eyes were still open, in spite of the narcotic. What would he be like when he woke up? Would he still be tied into the Godnet, like the monks upstairs? Like me? An overheated Jesus guided my hands, and my thoughts. His face was red, and steam poured from his ears.

The police took my ego agents' posthumous statements. (Damn backups.) I heard their filing cabinet drawer slam shut and echo. They'd get to my case by the time I was ninety, if I lived that long. My dry cleaning was done and the menu for the next three weeks needed to be planned; provisions needed to be requisitioned. My apartment back in the city wanted to know if it could please water the plants. A personal ad wrote itself for me and begged for my eye-blink signature. Sneaky anarchist magnetizdats nipped at my ankles, demanding attention. Helicopter blades were talking to me, saying "hurry hurry hurry" with the whip of wind. I had a deadline to meet. One deadline a second, every second, for the rest of my life.

("'Lord Jesus Christ, have mercy on me, a miserable sinner' is as powerful for its cadence as it is for its content. Once integrated into the head, it is actually hard to remove. Rather, one begins to receive, the monks say, messages from God," Kelly said, mimicking the singsong of the prayer.)

I sent the jacknet a final, very important message, the same one George had sent me. Jesus forgive me, a miserable sinner. I reached behind my neck and blindly disconnected my jack. I was alone, but for the constant prayer on my lips and the love for every man and woman in the world. The Godnet.

• • •

I ate a sandwich and sat on the hill just outside the monastery, waiting for the helicopter. Everyone in the Godnet ate that sandwich, the two pieces of bread coming straight from George's miracle—after I brushed the dirt off them, of course. And I tasted gyros in Cyprus, kimchi in P'yŏngyang, and injera in Addis Ababa. And I even felt the tickle of a patch here and exhaust-stained breakfast coffee there, from the first jacknetters to be infected with the God virus. Information wasn't a horrible flood of jingles and logos and unfair trades of wayward seconds of processing time anymore; it was a smile, a wave, a breeze, a broken leg. Even the dying felt good, because there was always a birth right behind it.

It was odd, being alone, but not at all scary anymore. It was odd, being one with the world and everyone in it. It was hard, eating a sandwich and incessantly muttering the prayer at the same time. It was nice, though, to know that the Godnet would be giving me food and water and love and a place to live. Miracle bread for everyone. I heard angels' wings, but they were really only the spinning rotors of the copter.

The trip back. I spoke with the pilot. She had kids. She played the cello. She'd been raped once, at thirteen, but was healing now, and her lips moved with an invisible prayer. Her jack was cold and nearly dormant, buzzing with low-grade euphoria. We were just in range of the city, and I could already hear the Jesus Prayer—the God virus—in the ear of every poor jacked bastard in town. It was all prayer now; they shut down the news, the soaps, and even the ads. The reporters were too busy taking time off to report on the collapse of the economy, the wine flowing from the public urinals, the lame walking, the stupid finally getting a clue, the kids actually sleeping—really, really sleeping and then getting up because it was morning, not because it was time for their shifts. As we flew down into the city, the sun rose into the already-shrinking pool of brown smog that sat atop the skyline like a bad toupee. Morning. Not work or betweenwork or more-work. I knew what time of day it was.

LAUREN BEUKES

BRANDED

(2003)

WE WERE AT STONES, playing pool, drinking, goofing around, maybe hoping to score a little sugar, when Kendra arrived, all moffied up and gloaming like an Aito/329. "Ahoy, Special-K, where you been, girl, so juiced to kill?" Tendeka asked while he racked up the balls, all click-clack in their white plastic triangle. Old school this pool bar was. But Kendra didn't answer. Girl just grinned, reached into her back pocket for her phone, hung skate-rat style off a silver chain connected to her belt, and infra'd five Rand to the table to get tata machance on the next game.

But I was watching the girl and as she slipped her phone back into her pocket, I saw that tell-tale glow 'neath her sleeve. Long sleeves in summer didn't cut it. So, it didn't surprise me none in the least when K waxed the table. Ten-Ten was surprised though. Ten-Ten slipped his groove. But boy kept it in, didn't say anything, just infra'd another five to the table and racked 'em again. Anyone else but Ten woulda racked 'em hard, woulda slammed those balls on the table, eish. But Ten, Ten went the other way. Just by how careful he was. Precise 'n clipped like an assembly line. So you could see.

Boyfriend wasn't used to losing, especially not to Special-K. I mean, the girl held her own 'gainst most of us, but Ten could wax us all six-love baby. Boyfriend carried his own cue, in a special case. Kif shit it was. Lycratanium, separate pieces that clicked into each other, assembled slick 'n cold and casual-like, like he was a soldier in a war movie snapping a sniper rifle together. But Kendra grinning now, said, "No, my bra. I'm out," set her cue down on the empty table next to us.

"Oh ja, like Ten's gonna let this hook slide." Rob snorted into his drink.

"Best of three," Tendeka said and smiled loose and easy. Like it didn't matter and chalked his cue.

Girl hesitated and shrugged then. Picked up the cue. Tendeka flicked the triangle off the table, flip-rolling it between his fingers lightly. "Your break."

Kendra chalked up, spun the white ball out to catch it at the line. Edged it then sideways so's it would take the pyramid out off-center. Girl leaned over the table. Slid the tip of the cue over her knuckles once, taking aim, pulled back and cut loose, smooth as sugar. Crack! Balls twisting out across the table. Sunk four solids straight-up. Black in the middle and not a single stripe down.

Rob whistled. "Shit. You been practicing, K?"

Kendra didn't even look up. Took out another two solids and lined up a third in the corner pocket. Girl's lips twitched, but she didn't smile, no, didn't look at Ten, who was still sayin' nothin' like. He chalked his cue again, like he hadn't done it already, and stepped up. The freeze was so tight I couldn't take it. Anyway. I knew what was coming. So, off by the bar I was, but nears enough so I was still in on the action like. Ten lined 'em up and took out two stripes at the same time, rocketing 'em into different pockets. Bounced the white off the pillow and took another, edged out the solid K had all lined up. Another stripe down and boy lined up a fifth blocking the corner pocket. "You're up."

Girl just stood there lookin' as if she was sizing up.

"K. You're up."

Girl snapped her head toward Tendeka. Tuned back in. Took her cue up, leaned over, standing on tiptoes and nicked the white ball light as candy, so it floated, spinning, into the middle of table like. Shrugged at Ten, smiling, and that ball just kept on spinning. Stepped back, set her cue down on the table next and started walking over to the bar, to me, while that white ball, damn, was still spinning.

"Hey! What the fuck?"

"Ah c'mon, Ten. You know I gotcha down."

"What! Game ain't even started. And what's with this, man? Fuckin' party tricks don't mean shit."

"It's over, Ten."

"You on drugs, girl? You tweaked?"

"Fuck off, Ten."

Ten shoved his cue at Rob, who snatched it quick, and rounded on the girlfriend. "You're mashed, Kendra!" He grabbed her shoulder, spun her round, "C'mon, show me!"

"Kit Kat, baby. Give it a break."

"Oh yeah? Lemme see. C'mon."

"Fuck off, Tendeka! Serious!"

People were looking now. Cams were too, though in a place like Stones, they probably weren't working none too well. Owner paid a premium for faulty equipment like. Jazz was defending Kendra now. Not that she needed it. We all knew the girl wasn't a waster like. Even Ten.

Now me. I was a waster. I was skeef. Jacked that kind shit straight into my tongue, popping lurid lurex candy capsules into the piercing to disseminate like. Lethe or supersmack or kitty. Some prefer it old-style, pills 'n needles, but me, the works work best straight in through that slippery warm pink muscle. Porous your mouth is. So's it's straight into the blood and saliva absorbs the rest into your glands. I could tell you all things about that wet hole mouth that makes it perfect for drugs like. But, tell you true, it's all cheap shit. Black-market. Ill legit. Not like sweet Kendra's high. Oh no, girl had gone the straight 'n arrow. All the way, baby. All the way.

"C'mon Ten, back off, man." Rob was getting real nervous like. Bartender too, twitchin' to call his defuser. But Kendra-sweet had enough now, spun on Ten, finally, stuck out her tongue at him like a laaitie. And Jazz sighed. "There. Happy now?" But Ten wasn't. For yeah, sure as sugar, Special-K's tongue was a virgin. Never been pierced by a stud let alone an applijack. Never had that sweet rush as the micro-needles release slick-quick into the fleshy pink. Never had her tongue go numb with the dark oiliness of it so's you can't speak for minutes. Doesn't matter though. Talkin'd be least of your worries. Supposin' you had any. But then Ten knew that all along. Cos you can't play the way the girlfriend did on the rof. Tongue's not the only thing that goes numb. And boyfriend knows it. And everything's click-clicking into place.

"Oh you fucking crazy little shit. What have you done?" Ten was grabbing at her now, tough-like, her swatting at him, pulling away as he tried to get a hold of her sleeve. Jazz was yelling again. "Ease off, Tendeka!" Shouldn't have wasted her air time. Special-K could look after herself all well now. After those first frantic swats, something leveled. Only to be expected when she's so fresh. Still adjustin' like. But you could see it kick in. Sleek it was. So's instant she's flailing about and the next she lunges, catches him under his chin with the heel of her palm. Boy's head snaps back and at the same time she shoves him hard so's he falls backward, knocks over a table on his way. Glass smashing and the bartender's pissed now. Everyone still, except Rob who laughed once, abrupt.

Girl gave Ten a look. Cocky as a street kid. But wary it was too. Not of him, although he was already getting up. Not that she could sustain like. Battery was running low now. Was already when she first set down her cue. And boy was pissed indeed. But that look, boys and girls, that look was wary not of him at all. But of herself like.

Ten was on his feet now, screaming. The plot was lost, boys and girls. The plot was gone. Cut himself on the broken glass. Like paint splats on to the wooden floor. Lunged at Kendra, backing away, hands up, but still with that look. And boy was big. Intent on serious damage, yelling and not hearing his cell bleep first warning then second. Like I said, the plot was gone. Way past its expiry date.

Then predictable; defuser kicked in. Higher voltage than necessary like, but bartender was pissed. Ten jerked epileptic. Some wasters I know set off their own phone's defuser, on low settings like for those dark an' hectic beats. Even rhythm can be induced, boys and girls. But it's not maklik. Have to hack SAPcom to sms the trigger signal to your phone. Worse now since the cops privatized, upgraded the firewalls. That or tweak the hardware and then the shocks could come random. Crisp you KFC.

Me, I defused my defuser. 'Lectric and lethe

don't mix. Girlfriend in Sea Point pulled the plug one time. Simunye. Cost ten kilos of sugar so's it don't come cheap an' if the tec don't know what they're doing, ha, crisp you KFC. Or worse, Disconnect. Off the networks. Solitary confinement like. Not worth the risk, boys and girls, unless you know the tec is razor.

So, Ten, jerking to imaginary beats. Bartender hit endcall finally and boy collapsed to floor, panting. Jasmine knelt next to him. Ten's phone still crackling. VIMbots scuttling to clean up blood an' glass and spilled liquor. Other patrons were turning away now. Game over. Please infra another coin. Kendra stood watching a second, then also turned away, walked up to the bar where I was sitting.

"Cause any more kak like that, girl, an I'll crisp you too." The bartender said as she sat down on the bar stool next to me.

"Oh please. Like how many dial-ins you got left for the night?" Kendra snapped, but girl was looking almost as strung out as Ten was now.

"Yeah, well don't make me waste 'em all on you."

"Just get me a Sprite, okay?"

Behind her, Jazz and Rob were holdin' Tendeka up. He made as if to move for the bar, but Jazz pulled him back, wouldn't let him. Not least cos of the look the bartender shot them. Boy was too fried to stir anyway, but said, loud enough for all to hear, "Sellout."

"Get the fuck out, kid." Dismissive the bartender was. Knew there was no fight left.

"Fucking corporate whore!"

"C'mon, Ten. Let's go." Jazz was escortin' him out.

Kendra ignored him. Girl had her Sprite now and downed it in one. Asked for another.

Already you could see it kickin' in.

"Can I see?" I asked, mock sly-shy.

Kendra shot me a look which I couldn't figure and then finally slid up her sleeve reluctant like, revealing the glow tattooed on her wrist.

The bartender clicked his tongue as he set down the drink. "Sponsor baby, huh?" Sprite logo was emblazoned there, not on her skin, but under it, shining through, with the slogan, "just be it."

No rinkadink light show was this. Nanotech she'd signed up for changed the bio-structure of her cells, made 'em phosphorescent in all the right places. Nothing you couldn't get done at the local light-tat salon, but corporate sponsorship came with all the extras. Even on lethe, I wasn't 'blivious to the ad campaigns on the underway. But Kendra was the first I knew to get Branded like.

Girl was flying now. Ordered a third Sprite. Brain reacting like she was on some fine-ass bliss, drowning her in endorphins an' serotonin, Sprite binding with aminos and the tiny bio-machines hummin' at work in her veins. Voluntary addiction with benefits. Make her faster, stronger, more coordinated. Ninja-slick reflexes. Course, if she'd sold her soul to Coke instead, she'd be sharper, wittier. Coke nano lubes the transmitters. Neurons firing faster, smarter, more productive. All depends on the brand, on your lifestyle of choice and it's all free if you qualify. Waster like me would never get with the program, but sweet Kendra, straight up candidate of choice. Apply now, boys and girls, while stocks last. You'll never afford this high on your own change.

Special K turned to me, on her fourth now, blissed out on the carbonated nutri-sweet and the tech seething in her hot little sponsor baby bod, nodded, "And one for my friend," to the bartender like. And who was I to say no?

YUN KO-EUN

P

(2011)

Translated from the Korean by Sean Lin Halbert

P259. This was where Chang lived and worked. If anyone wanted to send him a letter or package, all they needed were these four characters. The reason his address was so short, and the reason he only needed one for both work and home, was because the company he worked for *was* a city. Every day from eight in the morning to seven at night, Chang was at P259. And every night when he got home from work, he was still at P259.

He received it at about eleven in the morning on a workday. He wasn't the only one—all members of his team had been sent the same envelope. It was addressed from HR and contained an application to receive a free capsule endoscopy.

Chang threw the application in his desk drawer. That was where he put everything he didn't need. The only items he kept on his desk were a computer, cellphone, and family photo. Everyone he knew had a family photo on their desk, so he thought it'd look weird if he didn't. The photo also served as a kind of magic talis-

man, something to control his frequent, sudden impulses to leave the company. Some employees used paper carnations, others, cards from their kids—they all served a similar purpose.

"Did you fill it out?"

Chang looked up from his lunch tray. Song was asking about the capsule endoscopy application. The endoscope in question, which was thirty millimeters long and eleven millimeters wide, went by the name "jellyfish" because of its bulbous head and tentacle-like legs. Unlike traditional endoscopes, this all-weather capsule traveled past the small intestine, swimming down the entire length of the patient's digestive tract like a fish in the ocean. Performing such an expensive new procedure for free on the employees of P Tires was of course nothing more than one large advertisement. But such sponsorships were common here. Because P Tires had nearly twenty thousand employees, it was often used as promotional fodder for new businesses that moved into the city. Not even the hospitals were above such business tactics. The company was itself one large market. The hospital, which had just launched its new medical device, was the newest member to the business complex. And as always, there were rumors that its president was related to someone from management.

"It's not mandatory, you know."

Despite saying this, Chang knew it definitely *was*. The constant barrage of applications, all of which were for the same endoscopy, was enough to convince him of its compulsory nature. Not only did they send him one by mail, but they also sent him three more via email, company shuttle bus, and the hallway bulletin board. Of course, it was for a good cause, but Chang had no interest.

Song stared at Chang for a moment before lighting a cigarette. Song had quit smoking two years ago, only to start again just recently. Chang wondered if it had anything to do with the fact that new management all loved their tobacco.

That day, before ending the meeting, Chang's team leader asked everyone who turned in their application to raise their hands. Tomorrow was the last day to submit. To Chang's surprise, he was the only one with his hand down. He sat there feeling like a gaping hole in the room. Chang turned in his application the next day.

At nine in the morning after several hours of fasting, Chang and all his colleagues swallowed their capsule endoscopes and forced the microscopic cameras down their esophagi. Then, after putting data receivers on their waists, they went about their business like it was just another day at work. The endoscope took three images per second until the clock hit 7:00 p.m., at which point the hospital came to collect the receivers. They explained that the jellyfish would exit everyone's digestive tract within the next twenty-four hours. And indeed, starting next afternoon, one by one, all the employees of P Tires began depositing their jellyfish in company toilets. There was no need to retrieve the jellyfish, the hospital said. It had done its job. The most important thing was that everyone successfully got it out of their body. This was especially true for those whose twenty-four hours had already expired.

• • •

Chang's jellyfish, however, was stuck to the mucosa of his small intestine. He was now in his seventy-second hour. The X-ray image of the jellyfish was gray and grainy, like a UFO pictured in broad daylight. For some reason, even though a foreign object had entered his body, the image of the jellyfish looked more like the remnants of something that had been vaporized.

The doctor painstakingly asked Chang whether he followed all their precautions. Did he fast for eight hours before the test? Was he sure he didn't have an iron deficiency? Did he forget to mention any medications? Did he apply lotion the day of the test? Did he remember to take the medicine they gave him?

"Can you tell me what you did after ingesting the capsule?"

"I did everything that I normally would," Chang protested. "I went to work, did my job, gave you back the receiver when you came for it at seven and went home around eight."

"And what is it you usually do at work?"

"Just tire development. I work in spares."

The doctor looked like he was waiting for a more detailed explanation, so Chang went over in his mind everything he did that day. But there was nothing worth mentioning. He had a meeting—nothing unusual about that—and did some model trimming just before the new design went into mass production.

"What's trimming?"

"It's the last step a model goes through before production. We also do it for tires when they come off the line. Most people think tires come out of the factory perfectly round. But their surface is bumpy and uneven. Trimming is the process of snipping off those little nodules."

"What tool do you use for that?"

"It's a blade on a handle. The end is Y-shaped. You use it by running the blade over the surface of the tire, as if you were shaving your face or shearing a sheep. A new tire is like a fish waffle. When fish waffles come out of the waffle machine, their edges aren't perfectly smooth. You need to trim the edges, those little imperfections that stick out."

"Is that your main job?"

"Part of it."

Chang enjoyed running his blade over the surface of tires and removing any nodules that deviated from the standard mold. If only the jellyfish were such a nodule. That way, he could snip it off with his blade. Unfortunately, the jellyfish was inside him and out of reach.

"Some people have trouble passing the capsules. It happens for all kinds of reasons—a dilating intestine, for example. But it's only a matter of when. Don't worry too much. If nothing has changed by this time next week, we can take another look."

Chang never wanted an endoscopy. The results didn't even teach him anything new. He was already well aware he suffered from mild IBD. If anything, this endoscopy was making it worse with all the unnecessary stress. When things like this happened to him, he wondered if he was just unlucky, or if other people were experiencing the same thing. But as far as he knew, everyone he worked with had successfully passed their jellyfish. Some even retrieved the thing from the toilet and washed it to keep as a kind of souvenir. Over the weekend, he drank lots of water and took some laxatives, but he still couldn't pass the jellyfish.

The capsule endoscope was surely dead by now. The two internal batteries only lasted at most twenty hours, and the hospital had collected the receiver (its only connection to the outside world) almost a week ago. But Chang was unable to shake the feeling that the jellyfish was still moving inside him. On the other hand, he might have been less anxious had he known for certain the capsule was still on and

connected. He was, of course, terrified of the thought that someone had left a machine turned on inside him, but he was more terrified of the idea of a remote-less, disconnected monster swimming around his body of its own free will. He had heard horror stories of people who had accidentally swallowed rings, or had surgical scissors left inside them after laparotomies. He also heard that some people required surgery to remove capsule endoscopes that had become lodged in the crevasses of their digestive tract. But the foreign-body sensation Chang felt was of a different kind.

This jellyfish had entered Chang's body because of a connection to the company. In other words, if it weren't for his company, he never would have gotten an endoscopy. But he was afraid this connection didn't end there. What if the jellyfish was reporting everything about him to the company? Soon, this fear turned to paranoia. He never used his work computer for personal matters. He always used his cell phone to do online searches, but even that wasn't safe anymore. In his paranoid mind, the company no longer needed to spy on him through his computer, cell phone, or the company security cameras at the office or housing complex—they now had a window directly into his body.

With a few concrete incidents, Chang's suspicion that his thoughts were being monitored became a conviction. He had always internally bemoaned the fact that the staff lounge, which was clearly marked as a nonsmoking zone, always smelled like a chimney stack. But after management changed, the lounge was openly used as a watering hole for smokers, making the smell even worse and causing Chang a lot of stress. But he never expressed his discontent to anyone. And yet, a week or so after the failed endoscopy, an air purifier was installed in the staff lounge and several more nonsmoking signs were posted. He asked around and learned that they were making a separate smoking room near the emergency exit. This was exactly what he had wanted, so he should have been happy. But something didn't seem right. And then, when his paranoia couldn't get any worse, his team leader stopped him in the hallway.

"No more cigarette smoke. Isn't that nice?"

Chang's team leader patted him gently on the shoulder. Chang was well within reach of a normal talking voice, but his team leader was practically shouting. Even stranger was the fact that his team manager should have been the last person to care about the sooty smell of cigarette smoke, as that was exactly what his breath smelled like. The team leader then looked at Chang's face and asked if he was feeling okay. He got this question a lot recently. Everyone was always asking if he was "feeling okay." But most of them shouldn't have known about his condition.

However, maybe they were onto something. He did, in fact, feel off. But oddly, it felt less like an object had entered his body, and more like a piece of him was missing. It was this void, this absence that worried Chang more than any foreign-body sensation ever could. It was like something that had been screwed down tight to the interior wall of his body had been snipped off. But he knew almost everything inside him was vital. There were very few things one could remove without major side effects. And right now, it felt like one of those vital pieces had been snipped off and was floating away from his body, like a lost balloon. What worried him most was the fact that he had no way of knowing what it was that had been cut from him, or what had become of it.

• • •

Chang came to P three years ago. Moving to P, which had company housing, was quite attractive to Chang who, after sending his wife and son to America, had been looking at micro studio apartments designed for students. On the day of the move, he only had two 24-inch suitcases of luggage, and yet the company sent an entire moving truck to his address. He felt grateful thinking about how the two movers had come so early from so far away just to carry one suitcase each.

Chang stared out the window. He couldn't see the other end of the city (even though there was nothing blocking his view), but he knew it would be a mirror image of where he was standing now. Across the city from him, there would be yet another black skyscraper, which would also belong to P Tires. This black skyscraper would form one segment of a circle. And when you took all the buildings of P City together, they would form one large dark ring. In fact the city resembled a giant tire when seen from a bird's eye view. The area of this black tire was two-thirds of the circle's total area. Most shops and stores were contained within this tire-shaped company complex, but even those that were outside it were located as close to people as possible. Banks, post offices, religious facilities, and city hall were also inside the tire, even though they weren't officially affiliated with the company.

Chang was inside the tire, too. He hadn't once left since coming here three years ago. He had no need to. The company often planned outings and trips, but only within the city. Except for an airport, seaport, and train station, P had everything. And because the bus routes were so well designed, there was no point in owning a personal car. Unlike what you might expect for employees of a tire company, there weren't many people who used their personal car. Most people sold their car when they realized they wouldn't be needing it. Those who didn't left it in the parking lot like an exhibition piece. Of course, the buses were only open to people with a company card key.

A similar thing happened to Chang when he first entered the company. At the time, a dentist's office was giving out discounted teeth cleanings for P Tires employees. Chang had gone to the dentist with his team, and as he lay in the dentist's chair, he could smell someone else's saliva coming from the dentist's hand. Chang reflexively closed his mouth.

"Say, ahhh."

When the dentist's hands finally left his mouth, Chang watched closely to see where they went. And just as he suspected, the dentist went right over to the next patient, without changing gloves or washing his hands. Chang wanted to say something, but he didn't want to embarrass the owner of the saliva before him. Nor did he want to embarrass himself, as someone would be smelling his own spit right now. But what made him most uncomfortable was the fact that no one else was expressing their discomfort. It was hardly a surprise when he came down with a nasty cold the next day. Ever since then, Chang hated company sponsorships.

This jellyfish incident was equally frustrating. Chang knew the only reason for his company to partner with that hospital was because of some shady (perhaps nepotistic) relationship. This realization caused a wad of phlegm to form in his throat. He went to the hospital weekly, but even after three weeks, he still couldn't pass the jellyfish.

"Are you sure the jellyfish ran out of battery?" Chang asked bluntly.

"It's been more than three weeks," the doctor said in a relaxed tone. "If we had a battery that lasted that long, it'd be groundbreaking."

"It can only take pictures of my digestive tract, right? It can't do things like read my thoughts . . . Right?"

"If it could do that, it'd be truly groundbreaking."

Well, there was something that was groundbreaking, but it wasn't that, and it wasn't necessarily something to celebrate. On Chang's fourth checkup, he learned that the endoscope was growing inside him, like a real jellyfish. The doctor brought out Chang's previous X-rays to show him. At forty years old, news of something growing inside your body was never good news. That usually meant cancer, or if you were lucky, a noncancerous cyst. But a foreign-body object? That was truly unexpected. Even groundbreaking, you could say.

"We'll let y represent the length of the jellyfish in centimeters, and x represent the week, starting at one. Based on the data I have here, we can write a function to calculate the length at a later date: $y = 3x$."

The doctor then added something, as if he were reading Chang's mind.

"Of course, your intestine would rupture before the y value exceeded your height. We should avoid that at all costs, the problem is that, right now, there's no point in performing an enterotomy. We're not sure exactly where the jellyfish is, and if it turns out to be lodged deep inside your small intestine, it will be very difficult to remove."

"But is that my fault? Isn't that your fault?"

"The way I see it, you're the only one in twenty thousand patients to have this happen to them. I'd say your personal history was more of a factor than anything else. All we can do now is hope the medicine helps your body dissolve the endoscope. Or we could perform the surgery with lasers. I'm not saying that's the solution. But it's an option."

But even if they went with lasers, they still would need to wait and watch to see if his condition improved. It seemed like even the hospital didn't have all the answers.

Chang hadn't told anyone about what the doctor said, but it appeared management had already been notified of the situation. But the jellyfish wasn't the problem. The real problem was the interconnectedness of P. Chang's team leader called him into his office and asked if he was okay. Chang didn't know why exactly his team leader was asking him this, but he had his answer when he went back to his desk and turned on his computer to browse the news. Making headlines was an article that claimed the capsule endoscope, the same one swimming around inside Chang's body, contained a hazardous material. Of course, this was only a problem if the material stayed in the body for an extended period of time, and most people passed the jellyfish within twenty-four hours.

The last part of the article reported that all the endoscopes released onto the market had been recalled and wouldn't be released again until the problem was fixed. Other medical devices and drugs that used the hazardous material had all been recalled, too. Everything had been recalled, they claimed, but they had forgotten about the jellyfish inside Chang. And worst of all, it was now growing.

• • •

Chang always took the same route to work. It was a fair distance from company housing to the office, but as long as he picked the right elevator, he had no trouble making the trip in twenty minutes.

On his way to his desk, he felt like people were staring at him. They were all following him with their eyes, but no one approached him. It was possible that he was just imagining things, but it was more likely he wasn't. The reason for his certainty was because he had overheard someone say the word "jellyfish" in the elevator. He knew people always talked about it when they saw him. Before sitting down at his desk, he took his family photo and stashed it in his desk drawer before turning on his computer.

"Did you see that news article? The one about the 'thing.'"

Chang had a message from Angel, his subordinate, on the company messenger. Chang knew which article Angel was referring to, but he asked what he meant anyway. Eventually, Angel said the magic words: "The jellyfish." The article had already been deleted, and Chang couldn't find any other articles about the recall, but everyone in the company had already read it, including Chang. Angel told him not to worry, then started talking about jellyfish in a way Chang found inappropriate given the circumstances. And not jellyfish as in the capsule endoscope jellyfish, but real jellyfish from the ocean. Of the many pointless factoids he shared with Chang, the worst was the one about the scientific name for jellyfish: medusa. In fact, according to

him, the word *méduse* in French meant jellyfish. Chang asked why he was telling him this.

"Just 'cause. I thought you might want to know."

"Isn't Medusa that woman with snakes for hair? The one who turns people to stone by looking at them?"

"Perseus decapitated her. Cut the head right off her shoulders."

Angel followed this last message with a "HAHA" and a long string of sword emoticons. Chang couldn't help but notice that the swords were all pointed at his profile picture.

According to a book Chang had once read, some companies kept two lists of employees: a blacklist and an angel-list. They used these lists to separate employees into those they should protect at all costs, and those they should push out as soon as the opportunity arose. The reason Chang called his subordinate Angel was because, if anyone was on the company's angel-list, it would be him. This was, of course, a bit tongue in cheek, but it wasn't like Chang was the only one who called him this.

Because of what Angel said to him, Chang couldn't look people in the eye, even though he knew he wasn't going to petrify anyone. But perhaps it didn't matter because no one made eye contact with him anyway.

Chang tried eating rice porridge for lunch, but his stomach still ached. He also had trouble swallowing his food because of all the phlegm that he was coughing up. And any food he managed to swallow sat in his stomach like heavy rocks, as though they were the eyeballs of Medusa's victims. It continued like this all week. If there was one thing good about this week, it was that on Friday, Chang realized he would have the company apartment all to himself from now on. Chang wasn't sure if his roommate had transferred or simply gotten a new place. All he knew was that he wasn't going to be seeing his roommate anymore. When Chang arrived home after work, he found that his roommate had taken all his belongings and left a note on the table wishing Chang a "speedy recovery."

Even though there was only one less person in the apartment, the place now seemed empty to the point of being cavernous. It was only a 280-square-foot apartment, but it somehow felt bigger than that now.

It was the season for promotions and transfers. Chang was pretty sure they were going to give him a transfer, but he was wrong. When he got the call and walked into his team leader's office, he was immediately led to the director of research's office. The director was who people in their department talked to before leaving the company. The first thing the director did when Chang entered the office was ask, "Are you okay now? The cigarette smoke, I mean." This was an ambiguous question. On the one hand, he could have meant: "Are you okay, now that the smoke is gone?" Or he could have meant: "Are you okay now, even though the smoke *isn't* gone?" Without knowing which one it was, Chang just nodded his head quickly. He now regretted being so sensitive about smoking inside the office.

They were giving Chang three months of "sick leave." He would be reinstated as soon as he made a full recovery, but who knew when or if that would happen. The director patted Chang on the shoulder:

"You heard that I got stung by a jellyfish too, didn't you? It happened in Saipan last year. God-awful. The doctor in the ER told me jellyfish are mostly harmless. He compared them to mosquitoes in the summer. Mosquitoes my ass! The medicine alone made me nauseous for days. I blame it on my IBD."

"But sir, I wasn't stung by a jellyfish."

This was the first time Chang had talked to the director about personal matters. Talking with him like this would usually be difficult, but now that he was (temporarily) leaving the company, Chang felt at ease, even with the director. He patted Chang on the shoulder again as he continued:

"I heard poisonous jellyfish aren't edible. Did you know that?"

"No. To be honest, I've never been interested."

"Well, they say you can't eat the ones that sting. God-awful. You said your family's in America? You better get well soon and come back to work. I heard you developed the new spare tire with Department Head Song, is that right? We're expecting great things from that project, so you better come back soon."

Chang couldn't hide the rigid look on his face. He had never mentioned to anyone at the company that his wife and son were living in America. It wasn't like he had something to hide. He just wasn't one to go on about private matters.

• • •

Before, Chang would commute to and from work with just the swipe of his card key, but as soon as he was put on sick leave, his card key no longer registered. That day, it took him forever to find public transportation that would get him back to company housing. After two transfers, Chang finally arrived back home at his empty studio apartment. It was only then that Chang realized why he had the apartment all to himself, why he didn't have a roommate. No employee of P wanted to room with someone who had hazardous materials inside them. Since entering the company, Chang had always dreamed of having a room to himself, but not like this.

It wasn't just the company bus. There were dozens of places that were now off-limits to him that he had always had access to. The bank, gym, supermarket, and even some restaurants became unavailable to him because they were located inside P, where he was no longer allowed to go. Chang considered it a miracle they still allowed him to stay in company housing. He even had to change hospitals. It was now almost impossible to access his old hospital (the very same hospital that got him into this mess in the first place), and even when he did manage to get in touch with someone, it was like they were speaking a different language. Chang demanded they take responsibility for their defective jellyfish, but in the eyes of the hospital, it was Chang who was the defective one. Eventually, Chang realized this was a problem he would have to come back to. Arguing with the hospital required a lot of energy, something he had less and less of these days.

On Chang's first Monday of sick leave, he received a letter from the local tax office. The way the envelope was addressed reminded him that he was no longer a member of the company. Written on the envelope was a different address, not the usual "P259" he was used to. Indeed, Chang could no longer be described with just four characters. He had lived here ever since coming to this city. And he was still living here. The only thing that had changed was his status at the company, and yet he had to get an entire new address. The envelope contained tax bills. A detailed analysis of Chang's medical condition and the harmful substances in the jellyfish had been used to calculate the taxes he owed:

Probability of environmental pollution: 80%
Probability of noise pollution: 45%
Probability of water pollution: 20%
Probability of soil pollution: 21.5%
Estimated increase to environmental burden tax: 27.5%

Not understanding what this was, Chang asked one of the workers at a restaurant he frequented. According to them, anyone in the city not a member of P Tires had to pay an "environmental burden tax." It was independent of their income and was usually a small flat rate. However, the amount you owed the government increased whenever you broke a food or environmental regulation.

Hearing this, Chang wanted even less to pay the bill. He asked the restaurant worker how to get to the tax office, but he couldn't understand their directions. As he wandered around in the middle of the street looking for the building, it felt like the organs in his body were pulsating like a ticking time bomb. Exhausted, he eventually gave up and returned to his apartment. A person from the tax office was waiting for him

outside his front door. The tax collector walked with Chang to a nearby teashop and took out a large stack of documents.

"There's nothing wrong with a company having its employees take a test if they make everyone take it. Besides, everyone else was able to pass the jellyfish in the allotted time. The fact that you couldn't pass your jellyfish, Mr. Hyeong-jun Chang, is a personal problem. Because of this, we have no choice but to ask you to take responsibility. Naturally, we're concerned the foreign object will outgrow your body. What was your current height, again?"

The tax collector asked this question even as he stared down at Chang's height, which was written in the documents.

"Five feet eight inches."

"As I thought. And your weight?"

This too the tax collector asked while circling Chang's weight with a ball pen.

"One hundred fifty, one hundred fifty-five?"

"Good. We heard the foreign-body object is growing like a weed, getting larger with each day. Is that correct?" The tax collector put down the pen and looked at Chang. "Just as we feared. If the object continues to grow at its current rate, within two years, it will become too big for your body, and when that happens, it won't be just your problem anymore, Chang Hyeong-jun. It will be an issue of social and national concern! It was reported recently that the medical device contains many environmentally harmful materials. If nothing else, it will negatively affect P City, don't you agree?"

Chang was slowly starting to lose focus in his eyes. Every time the tax collector made threatening circles with the pen, Chang's pupils wobbled like an egg on a kitchen table.

"Let's use an example to illustrate what I mean. Imagine you go to the post office to send a package. They have different-sized boxes, right? Large, medium, small, long, short, you name it. But the thing you're trying to send won't fit in the small box. For whatever reason, it pokes out a little. You do your best to cram it in and secure the flaps with tape, hoping they'll give you a pass. And most of the time they do—they're human too, after all. But what if, hypothetically speaking, the thing you crammed into a small box is also too big for even the medium? Not only will you damage your item, but you make things difficult for the post office and you might negatively impact the delivery of the other packages in the same mail truck. What then?"

"I don't know, you put it in the medium box? Look, I mean, it's not like I'm the only one passing a foreign object through my body. You go to the bathroom too, don't you? We all excrete foreign bodies into the environment."

The tax collector started twirling the pen in their hand and grinned as though they had heard it all before.

"Everyone is subject to the rules," the tax collector said calmly. "That's what makes it fair. Either the tax applies to everyone, or it applies to no one. But you're an exception. I doubt you're planning on taking responsibility for that thing once it crawls out of your body and into the world. The city is promising to take care of everything if you pay the tax. You know that P City won the Eco-friendly City Award, don't you?"

"The city is going to take care of me?"

"Not you, not medically. I meant they'll take care of the environmental impact you'll have on the city. That's the whole purpose of the environmental burden tax. All I'm saying is we need to upgrade your box from small to medium."

Chang refused to pay any such "upgrade" fee. He wanted to make an appeal. But he knew he would have trouble making one. Appeals were long and involved, and just gathering the necessary documents would require more time, money, and patience than he had. It didn't take long for him to be labeled as a delinquent taxpayer. Chang was sure he could feel the jellyfish inside him growing faster and faster. But somehow, the amount he owed the city always seemed to stay ahead.

• • •

Chang swore he could hear the translucent jellyfish washing out his organs. Every time he moved, he thought he sensed a strong sloshing sound inside him. But he had no way of knowing if what he was hearing was real or just his imagination.

Chang stopped walking midstep. He was just about to put his foot down when he felt something else move inside his body. He both heard and felt it. His heart, intestines, lungs, and kidneys were all jostling around. And his uvula felt like a speaker, absorbing the vibrations and amplifying them. His intestines were currents of cold ocean water, and a stormy sea of stomach acid was thrashing against the walls of his esophagus.

Nonemployees of P Tires were useful to Chang. One day, he asked the owner of a restaurant for directions to the hospital. It seemed to Chang like the hospital was located on the outskirts of P City, but he couldn't be sure. And if by some chance it wasn't, that meant P was much larger than Chang had previously imagined. It was nearly a four-hour round trip, and Chang had trouble finding taxis or public transportation to take him there. The hospital was rather large. It was five stories tall, and Chang's destination, the department of cardiothoracic surgery, was located on the third floor. But Chang had to start at reception on the first floor and go through billing on the second before he finally saw a doctor. After a few questions, he was sent to internal medicine on the fourth. Endlessly walking up flights of stairs like this, Chang wondered if he would eventually pass through the roof and onto heaven. But then again, he would probably run out of money before that happened.

The doctor showed Chang a video of the inside of his body. The jellyfish was pulsating rhythmically. The head was bulging like an overinflated soccer ball, and its two tentacles were swaying like locks of hair from a Greek demigod. The jellyfish was swimming inside the sea of Chang's body. As he gazed into the video, he momentarily forgot what the doctor was saying.

"It moves just like a real jellyfish."

Turning away from the video toward Chang, the doctor explained that psychologists sometimes used jellyfish in their treatments. Chang couldn't tell if this was supposed to comfort him or just typical doctor banter, but he found it memorable for some reason. According to the doctor, the rhythm of a pulsating jellyfish was similar to the pulse of a human heart.

"Watching jellyfish swim helps people relax. Obviously, this only works when patients are out of the water."

So, jellyfish dances were only beautiful when observed from afar. Chang did feel somewhat relaxed watching the video of the jellyfish inside him. The video even allowed him to forget for a brief moment that his body had become home to one.

On his second visit to that remote hospital, Chang ran into Department Head Song in the lobby. It was pure coincidence. Chang looked dejected, and Song, collected. Song was smoking a cigarette. Song told Chang he was worried about the wreckage inside his body. Indeed, Song was the second person after Chang to be put on sick leave because of the jellyfish. Chang was equally surprised to find that Song was suffering from the same symptoms as himself. But he clearly remembered Song telling him, the day after the endoscopy, that he had passed the jellyfish in the bathroom.

"I was afraid. So I lied."

Song rubbed out his cigarette as he said this. Remembering what happened to Chang, he had tried his best to hide his symptoms, but eventually (and after a few more health checkups), he suffered the same fate when they inevitably discovered the jellyfish inside him. According to Song, several other people were forced to hand in their card key because they, too, had failed the test.

Song urged Chang to pay his environmental burden tax to the best of his ability. Debt was bad, yes, but being labeled a delinquent taxpayer was even worse. Song also seemed to think the word "delinquent" was better than "diseased."

Then he said something that really surprised Chang: he was planning on suing the company.

"I'm going to file a dispute," Song said in a quiet but resolute voice. "This is obviously the hospital's fault. The company should be held responsible, too. They practically forced us into participating in the endoscopy. I've already asked one of the doctors here for their opinion, and I'm bringing in a lawyer from outside the city. I just need to collect the necessary documentation. Did you hear that our project was put on hold? They've got two holes and no one qualified enough to fill them. We need to act now and make them afraid of us while we're still on sick leave. If we play our cards right, there's no reason we shouldn't be reinstated."

Now that Chang was getting a better look at Song, he could see behind his composed demeanor a pale face and withered body. His eyes were hollow, too. Chang tried his best to avoid looking Song directly in the eye. He used the cup of water placed on the table to look at Song's reflection. Song had always been just as exemplary outside the company as he was inside it. He always paid his bills on time and was always composed. Hearing that someone like him was meticulously scheming to take revenge on the company made Chang afraid. He didn't know his situation was so dire. Chang glanced around, paranoid that someone would be listening in on their conversation. But he soon remembered that there was more to be afraid of than just CCTVs, wiretaps, and passersby. A less tangible terror was brewing inside him. What if the jellyfish was listening to their conversation? The thing that had made his body a swimming pool, that should have been turned off ages ago.

"I'm going to file a dispute. I'll be in contact with you soon. Let's meet again here. I might need your help."

The three months of sick leave the company had given Chang were almost up. And the environmental burden tax was accelerating, as though it could taste Chang's thinning wallet. He was living in this city like a solution just before saturation, teetering on the edge of his boiling point. When the three months were up, when Chang's bank account hit zero and his debt increased toward infinity, they might finally kick him out of company housing and out onto the streets.

On his way home from meeting Song, the moon was faint, the stars were infrequent, and the only thing whose existence Chang could be sure of were the neon billboards that were plastered to the sides of skyscrapers like gaudy wallpaper. On one of the billboards, a P tire was hovering above the earth like a black moon. Chang had written down the address of the bus terminal on a piece of paper, but finding the terminal again at night wasn't easy. It wasn't at the address he had written down. Chang searched his memory for the names of the other cities that were connected to P. He could go anywhere if he called a taxi or got on the right bus. No, the problem wasn't the means of transportation. Chang didn't know where he was going; his three months were almost completely spent. If Song's plans worked, that might mean good things for Chang. When his innocence was finally revealed, he would either be reinstated to the company or released forever on account of insolence. But even if he was released, at least he could receive compensation. In fact, he preferred the second of these two options. He wasn't sure if he could return to the company like this. And if he couldn't stay at P Tires, it would be best to leave P City altogether.

Then one day, Chang felt the violent rumbling of something surging up from inside his body, like a roller coaster being ratcheted to the top of a hill. Chang reached for a tissue. He quickly realized one wasn't going to be enough. Finally holding five sheets of tissues, he heaved into his palm, and a giant wad of phlegm shot out of his throat like a roller coaster making its first plunge. He instinctively crumpled up the tissues, but then unfolded them again to have a look. This phlegm wasn't like the others. Dissolved inside the yellow goo was an oddly colorful substance. Chang stood in front of the bathroom mirror and opened his mouth. There was some strange fluid, some

fluid that wasn't his, endlessly flowing out of the back of his throat. This was his first time looking beyond his own uvula, and what he found there was darkness.

Chang turned down the TV and picked up the telephone. There was only one place now for him to call. His wife and son were in New Jersey. The longer he was away from them, the less they said to one another. It wasn't that they had nothing to say, but rather that, over months of constant omissions and selections, he had developed the habit of filtering out anything that wasn't a truly important happening. Eventually, he only sent across the Pacific those few words that were left after endless trimming and omitting.

"I think something's living in the back of my throat. I think it's starting to crawl out. Something alive, something like a jellyfish."

What would his wife say when she heard this? The most recent message he had sent across the Pacific was about his sending them his bonus. Before that, it was about the advantageous exchange rate. His words needed to have a certain level of authority to justify being sent across the ocean. Should he tell his New Jersey audience about the jellyfish? Chang thought about this until he couldn't think anymore. He had picked up the phone with such urgency, but now he was just sitting there, paralyzed by excessive contemplation. As soon as he heard the voice of his son through the receiver, he lost all courage. For a brief moment as he listened to the sounds of a New Jersey suburban neighborhood, he completely forgot about everything that had happened to him. He was completely absorbed in the peacefully busy noises of life across the ocean. It was only after hanging up the phone that Chang was brought back to his reality. On paper, he and his wife were already separated. They only exchanged bank account numbers and contact information because of their son.

• • •

Chang was positive he would be fired once his three-month sick leave ended. He was shocked when he was called into the office to talk. His team leader had since changed. The new team leader was Angel—the same subordinate whom Chang had always considered number one on the company's angel-list. Angel looked at Chang and gave him a welcoming smile.

"I want to help you, Chang. I heard that you've been having a hard time because of the environmental burden tax. I want to find a way out for you."

Angel mentioned how the company was in a difficult situation as the project Chang had been working on wasn't going smoothly. They were looking for someone to take Chang's position, but this had been made more complicated when Song, the other project lead, was put on sick leave as well. Of course, the company thought it would be best if Chang focused on getting better, but Angel was of a different opinion. After all, it wasn't like it was contagious.

"But everyone acts like I have some radioactive object inside my body."

"Of course we can't just ignore other people's feelings. If people are too uncomfortable with it, the least I can do for you is give you your own small office. Do you still have the inclination to work?"

He really was an angel. Before Chang realized what he was doing, he was bowing and thanking his old subordinate.

• • •

A few days after visiting P Tires, Chang saw Song on the news. A month ago, Song had received an award for being an exemplary taxpayer. A few weeks later, he committed suicide. Song wanted to die a model taxpayer. The news reported that he had been diligent with his environmental burden tax payments, but that recently, he had been having financial difficulties. When he found it impossible to make any more payments, he ended his own life. He was more afraid of becoming a delinquent taxpayer than he was of death. People who knew him well claimed he was a perfectionist. Nowhere was

there any mention of the capsule endoscope, his unemployment, or the lawsuit. Everything that Song had planned, everything that would have been an uncomfortable subject for P, seemed to have been vaporized.

The funeral took place beneath the hospital where Chang and Song had run into one another. Chang's hand shook as he lit the incense. He was just a mourner, but it felt like it was he who had died. The photo of Song that was placed at the altar looked like a mirror. Chang heard a sloshing sound. The young chief mourner was staring at him. More sloshing. Song was staring at him. More sloshing. The jellyfish was moving inside him. Chang met eyes with Song's picture when he lifted his head after bowing, and his breath went heavy as stone. Chang could barely manage to turn his body and face the chief mourner. The two children, the same two children whose photo had sat on Song's desk at the office, were now looking at Chang with tear-filled eyes.

Looking around the funeral home, Chang felt relieved that no one from work had come. The only person here that Chang knew was Song, and he couldn't talk. Even though Chang had wished he wouldn't run into anyone he knew here, at the same time, he wanted someone to talk to, someone to tell everything that had happened to him. He fiddled with his cell phone. He weighed the option of calling the phone number saved in his cell phone as "New Jersey." He had once used their names. But then one day, he changed them. That's how much distance there was between him and his estranged family. Chang wanted to tell his wife and son that he had been reinstated at the company. He wanted to tell them that come next week, he would be back to normal again: working, riding the shuttle bus, and eating at the company cafeteria. He wanted to tell them that he wouldn't be paying the environmental burden tax anymore, that he could start paying off all the debt he had accrued. He wanted to tell them that even though the jellyfish had, and was, making a mess, it wasn't going to threaten his health anymore. But Chang just continued to fiddle with his cell phone, unable to press CALL.

He tried several times but always stopped himself just in time. Now that he thought about it, they didn't even know he had been put on sick leave, that he had hazardous substances inside him, that he hadn't been able to pass that jellyfish on time—they didn't know anything. News of his sudden reinstatement would confuse them more than anything.

Chang was about to put his cell phone in his pocket when he decided to look at his recent call history. He wanted to change his subordinate's caller ID from "Angel" to "Team Leader." Angel had played the biggest role in Chang's reinstatement. If it weren't for him, Chang might have ended up like Song for all he knew.

After Chang changed Angel's caller ID, he slumped down on a bench as though all the energy had been sucked out of him. Staring at his team leader's phone number for a long time, he was reminded of Song's face. Had Song known? Would he have understood Chang's reason for not waiting for his phone call? What Chang had really been waiting for was a call from the company. But he couldn't expect the company to be the first one to dial. In fact, Chang's team leader had never once contacted Chang since the jellyfish incident. All his recent phone calls were outgoing. The night after he ran into Song, he had a long phone call with his team leader. This call was made by Chang, just like all the others. Chang's meeting with his team leader was only made possible after he told him about Song's plans to sue. Chang sat across from his team leader and told him everything:

"I want to finish the new spare tire with my own hands. But I'm having difficulties because of the environmental burden tax. Please, give me some way out."

"But aren't you suffering from an illness?"

"It's never caused me major health problems. And it's not contagious."

Chang's team leader scratched his chin.

"People say it's radioactive."

"If people feel uncomfortable with it, I can work by myself in the warehouse. I'd be fine with any kind of work, even if it's menial."

Chang recalled the things he had done just a few days prior. But as he looked at himself, he did so through an opaque lens, like Perseus looking at Medusa's reflection through a shield made of mirrors. Because of what he told his team leader that day, Song's plans were completely ruined. Chang was promised he could return to his job, and the team leader was able to strengthen his grip on his new post. Chang sat in the far back of the funeral home and tried to console himself, telling himself that he had no choice. Song and he had done the same job and received the same diagnosis. That was the problem. Chang wasn't confident he could compete with Song for the same position. So he sold out.

The zipper on one of Chang's two suitcases was broken, even though he rarely used them since moving to the city. Every time he tried closing the zipper, it would just as quickly pop back open. Chang consolidated his belongings as much as he could and crammed what he had left into the one good suitcase. The car came as scheduled, and Chang got in. It dropped him off at P1765—Chang's new address. The door opened straight down into the ground. Every hallway in P City skipped P1765, this was the only door that had those digits. It was a round door that opened straight into the earth.

It was the exact size of the mold they made spare tires in. Spare tires were slightly smaller and lighter than normal tires. They only had to last until you could replace the flat tire with a new one. Chang opened the door that headed down into the ground and hunched over. Y-shaped clippers appeared seemingly from nothing and started trimming his back. As it removed the angular pieces sticking out of him, his skin became round and smooth. Chang didn't mind the sensation of being fit into a mold. He curled his back into a tighter circle. A familiar sensation traced the curve of his spine, sliding all the way down to his tailbone. Then Chang could feel a light but constant force pushing on him. The weight felt at once oppressive yet liberating. When the pressure was released, he felt something fall from his body. It was charred and rolling around like a used bullet casing on the battlefield.

The jellyfish. After months of growing like a parasite inside Chang's body, it had now exited him smaller than it entered. It moved each of its tentacles and withdrew its head into its body. Chang remembered the joy of trimming tires, the joy of putting the final touches on his work. He straightened his back and looked up at the sky. Shining above his head was the sun, yet another circle that looked exactly like P1765.

MAURICE BROADDUS

I CAN TRANSFORM YOU

(2013)

MAC PETERSON WAS HURLED through a storefront window. As his world was reduced to a shower of glass, he counted himself lucky that the Chaise Lounge was an old-school establishment: most windows had synth fibers in them, smart glass that could turn any pane into a billboard. And despite what people viewed on their vids, industrial glass wasn't designed to break away into a scree of shards upon impact. With the state of terraforming these days, it was designed to withstand minor earthquakes and eruptions. So a body would have to be sent through it with significant force in order for the glass to shatter. The kind of force Jesse "Duppy" Honeycutt was capable of generating when hopped up on Stim.

This was supposed to have been a simple surveillance job. Some "creepy guy" at the Chaise Lounge was bothering a stripper—no, exotic dancer; no, anatomical sales model for display purposes only; shit, Mac didn't know what to call them these days. He was to be paid to find

the suspect and perhaps persuade him to move along.

This conversation wasn't going well.

"You got a smart mouth, mon." Duppy's accent shifted between overly affected Jamaican and some version of Midwestern. He stepped through the jagged hole where glass used to be. A black tank top stretched over his huge frame, showing off the bulging muscles that came from a prison bid. A pattern of tattoos, like glow-in-the-dark runes, ran along his arms, which waved about in menace. Prior to crashing through the glass, Mac had studied the brute's eyes and believed they told a counterintuitive story: that prison had broken him and drugs helped him forget the pain. Of course, that was before he found himself lying in a pool of glass shards. Hating to be wrong, he chalked Duppy's violent outburst up to overcompensating. After all, everyone had an image to maintain.

Case in point: born Jeremiah Dix of Bedford, Indiana, Duppy put on a faux Jamaican accent as a part of his story, just another small-time hood trying to make a rep for himself. Once he had landed in Waverton, he'd joined the Easton MS crew; the MS stood for Murder Squad because they were killing the streets. Clever disds. They had made a name for themselves as major Stim traffickers, and Duppy had hooked up with them. High on Stim, he proved less reasonable than usual.

"Yeah, I get that a lot." Premature gray at his temples, Mac had a good build on him, the last remnant of his former military training. A carefully cultivated week's worth of facial hair covered his face. A low beard hid a lot of scars. Sunglasses covered his eyes. No designer glasses, no viz screen built in. Plain sunglasses were usually the first casualty in any conversation, so he saw no point in spending too many creds on them. For that matter, he'd hate to have to get a new coat. The dampener lining absorbed a lot and hid even more. This came in quite handy, as he was prone to take a lot of hits. He considered this a reasonable expense to compensate for his failed people skills.

Sitting up, Mac shook his head to try to clear it while palming a fistful of glass. He staggered to his feet and wiped a trail of blood from his mouth.

Duppy stepped through the open hole where the window used to be, oblivious to the jagged teeth of glass that bit into his hand as he searched for purchase. Stim was bad enough; if Duppy's blast had been mixed with something else, things could get quite messy. Just like if Mac drew his Cougar PT-10, he'd have to use it and he wasn't being paid enough to deal with the paperwork headache of a shooting. Neither of them had to end up dead over a simple dustup. Besides, he had Duppy right where he wanted him.

"Maybe we got off on the wrong foot." Mac neared him. "A fella as charming as yourself wouldn't have any problem paying for tail somewhere else. The blind school's only a few miles up the way . . ."

Duppy charged him, wrapping Mac up in the beefy tubes he called arms. With his free hand, Mac ground the glass into the man's eyes, and they tumbled to the ground. Duppy dropped to his knees, his screams cut short as Mac scrambled out of his grasp. A quick jab to his throat dropped the brute, but Mac proceeded to kick him in the head a few times. It wasn't pretty, but it got the job done. Mac bent over and searched Duppy's clothes for extra doses of Stim and slipped them into his pocket. The owner of the Chaise Lounge—a slovenly overweight bald man with a penchant for sweating through his wardrobe—approached him. "I think I've persuaded your stalker to peruse the merchandise at another establishment."

"You persuaded him through a new window." The man daubed his forehead with a dirty handkerchief. "Who's going to pay for that?"

"For starters, *he* threw *me*. I had little say in the matter. Second, the terms of my rate were five hundred creds for the job plus expenses. Consider that an expense."

"Fuck you, Mac," the man said, then held out a transaction scanner. Mac passed his hand under it, checked his balance on his own scanner, straightened his glasses, then turned his back on the scene.

This job would barely cover his rent, and he wasn't exactly staying at a high-rise over in Waverton. Mac hated being out on the streets here; they left him feeling too exposed. A hover drone whirred by. The administrators could just as easily use satellites for the same purpose but they wanted the populace to be aware that they were being watched. The drones didn't deter crime, nor did the death penalty, despite how swiftly it was carried out. People knew they would get caught if the LG Security Force cared enough to come after them. Many days that was a mighty big if. Those on the employment cycles traveled into Waverton on the artery of the trams like circulated blood once it had been deoxygenated, then passed back out into Old Town. Old Town felt like a prison for those whose only crime was to be born poor. There were no worries about the state of Mars colonization. There was no time for political discussion on trade among the corp-nations. No, the world he lived in was as lowest common denominator as it got. There was only room for day-to-day survival, with none of the luxury worries of middle-class citizens. From Old Town, one could clearly see the towers of Waverton and the grand spires that formed the cityscape. Proud, tall, and distant, like an unobtainable dream. Sewer rats, strippers, junkies, and private investigators all lived in the shadow of the new architecture and stared up at the azure-streaked night skies, waiting for the world to end.

• • •

The call tore Mac from the fitful thing he called sleep. At least he woke up in a bed, not a burned-out husk of a car or a stretch of sidewalk. Small comfort in the unfamiliar surroundings. He didn't remember checking into a hotel. From the look of its decor—a full bed, a trash can, and a toilet and sink in the corner—it charged by the hour. The air was redolent with sex—unwashed, sweaty, desperate, and unremembered—and he stank of booze and stale Redi-Smokes. He hoped he hadn't spent the entire job's payday on his company. Had he found a companion dead next to him, it wouldn't have surprised him.

"Mac." Deputy Chief Clovis Hollander's voice sounded as hoarse as ever, as if he'd been screaming for the entire ten-hour shift.

"Miss me, Chief?"

"You need to come down to the LaPierre Towers." His tone of voice was off. He maintained a casual air as best he could, but something grave undergirded his words.

"I don't exactly work for you anymore."

"You'd want to be here. Besides, I distinctly recall a report coming across my net-log about a brawl between a tweaker and a peeper."

"Is that any way to speak of so noble a profession as mine, you fat fuck?" Mac provoked

him, hoping to unsettle Hollander enough to get a moment of honesty from him. Even just a glimpse.

"Get your ass down here and it gets buried."

"Well, you do know where all the bodies are buried."

Mac sighed with every movement, as if sleep had only left him even more exhausted. He shambled to the sink. No sign of whoever he had spent the night with. His muscles ached. Bandaged wounds opened up slightly, spots of blood soaked through their wraps. His joints creaked and popped as he moved; the body in the reflection was easily a decade older than his thirty-nine years. He splashed water on his face.

Mac had always imagined that he'd have an office with one of those classic pebbled glass door panels with the words *Mac Peterson, Investigations* in bold black letters across it. The letters might be chipped around the edges to add character to the sign. Instead, he had a message service and a table in whatever establishment in Old Town was open.

"You ain't pretty," he started in at his reflection. "You ain't that bright. You ain't that funny. Or charming. There's nothing in you worth loving."

Like an offering to the stirring serpent in his belly, he repeated his daily mantra aloud. His core truths to begin the day, bottoming himself out; that way the day could only get better from there.

• • •

Maybe the eruption event had been a sign of the end and the apocalyptos had it right.

Rows of phosphorous blue lanterns blotted out the night sky, creating an alien vista, completely different from the memory of only a few years ago, the only remnants of the caustic dust kicked up those nights twenty years ago. The glowing canvas rendered the downtown skyline in a perpetual twilight, like a forest under a thick canopy of tree branches. Giant stone buildings rose in the dimness, obsidian behemoths, like death's bony fingers protruding from where they had inexplicably ruptured from the ground. Since the eruption event, the city-dwellers liked to whisper stories of men and women, those mixed-up souls ready to end it all, blissfully swimming upward through the opaque, dense air until they reached the top of the alien structures, where they found paradise and disappeared into the forever of the cosmos.

"Bullshit," Mac whispered to no one in particular.

Mac viewed life through a lens of skepticism and impatience, the towers and the flight to heaven—complete and utter nonsense. Surrounded by a mess of blood, brain matter, and pieces of bits he could only guess were the remains of internal organs, the crime scene told another story he struggled to make sense of. Two bodies had exploded like human grenades upon impact after falling from the top of the tallest structure. His gaze followed the jutting stone until it disappeared into the haze. Maybe these two had been evicted from heavenly paradise and tossed to their deaths, he mused. The foul stench failed to turn the detective's stomach, as he'd long grown accustomed to the stink of death. Thousands had died when the tower first shattered the mantle of the earth's surface. It appeared as if this tower had simply claimed two more.

Mac lit up a Redi-Smoke and inhaled. Genetically engineered to mimic the effects of nicotine, the companies benefitted from using chemical formulas that hadn't been banned yet. The packaging of the Redi-Smoke produced only wisps of smoke, which dissipated in the mouth almost immediately. The company's marketing campaign preyed on the ritual of smoking itself, per VCC regulations. All Mac needed to know was that the burn leeched away at his lungs; the genetically enhanced tobacco-like buzz hit hard and quick, dispelling most of his annoyance at being called out in the middle of the Godforsaken night for yet *another* tower death. The victims had been falling for months

now, one or two a week. No leads, no evidence. Nobody could make out whether the jumpers were murdered or simply succumbed to an inner nihilistic cry, compelled to die by suicide. Whatever the case, Mac wished the bullshit would end.

"Hey, Mac. Sorry to call you in, but you know how it is." The city's deputy chief of police appeared out of the fog. Hollander grimaced at the scene around them before he shook Mac's hand. Gray hair wrapped like a horseshoe on the chief's otherwise bald head. He sported a Hitler mustache on his egg-shaped face as if he could bring the affectation back, but his extra jowls only accentuated the ridiculousness of his appearance. And his hands were too soft, like a woman's. The blue haze darkened his eyes, seeming to erase them. Mac held the pack of smokes out to him, but the deputy chief declined.

"Yeah?" Mac pushed his hat down over his face, covering his eyes in shadows. "Well, fuck you. You want to tell me why the *fuck* either of us are out here stomping through the remains of some sorry-assed tower jumpers?" He knew the dance of bullshit when he saw it. The chief was holding back. No way was he going to be on scene, much less call out Mac, unless it was important.

"It's a bad one." The chief stepped gingerly around bits of innards. "It's one of our own this time."

"What do you have?" Mac asked.

The chief grabbed Mac by the elbow and led him a couple of feet away from the nearest set of ears. Mac couldn't help but think that his former boss didn't want to be seen with him. "A lot of shit is going down and I need you braced for it. Does the name Harley Wilson ring a bell for you?"

"Not even a little."

"Goddamn, Mac, you live in a cave?"

"Hey man, fuck you. I don't have a Stream connect, so I also don't get the latest news on your favorite teen pop stars. You're lucky I have a cop-net linkup."

"Right. Whatever, you Luddite piece of shit. Harley Wilson's that gangbanger out of Easton. Suspected of making that hit on, shit . . ."

"Shit? Seems strange that a loving mother would take a look at the sweet product of her loins and name it 'Shit,'" Mac said.

"Always with the jokes. Anyways, I can't remember the name. Some corporate muckety-muck. It's in my notes back at the office. But this isn't about him. It's about Kiersten."

"My ex?" That serpent in his belly stirred. The gentle swell of anxious nausea left him uneasy, and Mac wanted Hollander to just spit it out. "Last I heard, she'd been working under-cover. Bravest lady I know."

"Kiersten had been running with Wilson the past couple of months." Hollander stared at his feet. "The squints in the lab have confirmed that the bodies who fell tonight were Harley Wilson and Kiersten Wybrow."

The world lost its axis, and Mac leaned against a storefront wall. Kiersten. A rush of emotions hit him at once. Mac covered his face with his hand. The azure haze of the night skies shifted with the clouds, hiding his grief. He pushed the pain back, down into a personal dark space, a well to draw upon when needed, when the time was right.

"You all right, Mac?" Hollander stepped closer, concern underscoring his voice.

"Me and Kiersten were still . . . close. . . ." A moment of silence passed between the two men. The bottom fell out of where he thought he had bottomed out. Only a yawning chasm of grief awaited him. His head went light with the vertigo of pain, but he steadied himself before anyone else saw. He scanned the onlooking sets of eyes just in case.

"I'm sorry, Mac. I had no idea."

"I'll go check out the scene."

Hollander placed his hand on Mac's shoulder. "You know I can't let you do that. We need background, then your ass is going home."

"That's bullshit."

"You're too close. The judicial net would make any case we built that included your

involvement ass-wipe worthy. But you should already know: folks who kill one of our own do not go unpunished. We don't need the other predators getting it in their heads that it's open season on LG Security Force members. They need to know who runs these streets. No one, and I mean no one, sleeps in Easton tonight. We're rounding up all of the Easton MS crew. Hitting all of their spots. We will knock down every door, bust every head, and make business very difficult for them until we have who did this. I hope you hear me on that, Mac."

"Who's working it?"

"Ade Walters."

"Spookbot?" Mac reached for another Redi-Smoke, doing his best to hide the slight tremor of his hands.

"Don't let him hear you call him that or you'll be in sensitivity reprogramming for a month. Or in a full body cast."

"Can I get some professional courtesy at least?" The unsteady strains of pain crept into his voice. "Someone's got to speak for her."

"You need to be careful. Grieving people are prone to rash decisions and poor impulses." Mac met him with a stony, eye-to-eye glare. Hollander eventually sighed. "I suppose Ade will have a few questions for you. But don't make a mess of the scene. It's his show."

The gore on the street and walls now had a name. Kiersten. Bits of her covered the whole area. The force of impact reduced her to a crimson smear. "Isn't *this* the scene?"

"This is just part of it. Follow me." Hollander patted Mac's shoulder, careful not to have too much or too lingering contact. Mac had never been comfortable with people touching him. Hollander escorted Mac to the penthouse roof as if not trusting him to go alone.

The Lifthrasir Group was the fifth-largest multinational in what remained of the United States and the American Dream™. As America's debt load grew too large for even it to service, several corporations had purchased statewide territories. The Lifthrasir Group owned what had once been Indiana, Kentucky, and Ohio.

Those territories were especially hard hit by the eruptions and the subsequent societal upheaval called The Trying Times™, but the Lifthrasir Group funded their own internal security forces.

The duo entered a nearby stone building and took the elevator to the top. People's resourcefulness never ceased to amaze Mac. Once explored and examined, the structures had been declared sound and people had begun using them as homes. At first only the desperate and needy, but they had been dislocated by the hipsters and nouveau riche, making it the popular thing to do.

When the doors opened to the rooftop, a wind gusted inside and carried along with it the towers' signature smell of sulfur mixed with burnt ozone. The stink gave Mac a headache. His tongue suddenly felt coated with paste.

The pair walked over to a figure crouched near the edge of the roof.

"Detective Ade Walter, Former Detective Mac Peterson. Mac here was . . . acquainted with the deceased."

"Kiersten Wybrow," Ade said, then paused as if reading an invisible file. "Her jacket's exemplary. She even disclosed your relationship once the two of you started seeing one another, as required by protocol. Her file had been sealed due to her temporary assignment."

Mac grunted and glanced at Hollander.

Ade stood up and faced them. At six foot seven, Ade easily towered over the two of them. He had bulk on his frame, too, but carried it with the easy grace of a boxer. *Spent too much money on his pin-striped suit, much less that custom brown trench coat that he's sporting*, Mac thought, suddenly self-conscious of his tattered raincoat—despite its dampener lining—worn over an off-the-rack jacket.

Then there was Ade's face. The left half had been replaced. Around the eye, down the left cheek, and down to the collarbone, the silver gleam of metal glinted in the cerulean light. Mac could barely make out the tube, stemming from Ade's neck before it wound into his suit. It attached somewhere to a pack on his side that

released scheduled fresh supplies of nanobots into his bloodstream to facilitate the workings of the cybernetic implant. An affectation of the wealthy, most of whom had the common decency to get the skin grafting to cover the prosthetic.

"Others in her acquaintance are still under ethics inquiry." Ade sniffed in Mac's direction.

"Is that right?" Mac turned back to Ade.

"Standard procedure, Detective," Hollander answered.

"Since when?"

"Gentlemen, you want to bicker all night or work the case?" Ade asked.

"Fine. Wanna lay it out for me?" Mac asked.

Ade glanced over at Hollander, who nodded, before he fixed his high-res imager on Mac, taking in whatever data streamed across his screen. "Signs of a struggle. Microabrasions on the floor. Trace amounts of DNA. Unidentifiable residue."

"So you've got nothing. Like the rest of the Goddamned jumper cases."

"We could . . . use help running down a few things," Hollander said. "Off-the-books stuff. Like a consultant."

Ade fixed the red gleam of his implant squarely on the chief. "I appreciate the offer, but I have things covered."

"Now hold on; perhaps the esteemed deputy chief makes a good suggestion," Mac said. "Besides, you don't expect me to sit on my ass and do nothing, do you?"

"No. I expect you to preen about like the Neanderthal throwback you pretend to be. You'll suffer through the pain of Ms. Wybrow's loss alone because you think that's how men do things. As that rarely works, you'll drink yourself into a stupor to quell the pain rather than deal with it. Then once that temporary measure proves as empty a gesture as it ultimately ever is, you'll fix yourself on vengeance by way of 'finding who did it.' And then do your level best to shit all over my fine case. So can we skip all the cliché cop bullshit? I'll keep you in the loop—but I need you to give me room to conduct this investigation. Are we clear on that?" Ade again glanced in Hollander's direction, but this time for Mac's benefit.

"Yeah, we're clear," Mac said with a sour grin and amused eyes.

"Good."

Hollander turned on his heel. As soon as he was out of earshot, Ade stepped near. "I remember you from the Ritenour case. You were stand-up then, even if the brass didn't see it that way. What was it you said then?"

Carlos Ritenour. What a mess of a case. It started when Mac was dispatched to a domestic disturbance. A man had beaten his three-year-old adopted son so badly both legs were broken and his entire head was an off shade of blue from all of the bruises that had amassed. Mac called for paramedics, never once taking his eyes from the boy.

"Do. Not. Move," was all Mac said to the man, not turning around to look at him. The man froze. Ten minutes until medical help arrived. Only the sound of their breathing broke the silence. The man didn't so much as twitch. Mac never said another word the entire time, only stared at the boy. The boy shivered, a thin trail of mucous streaming from his nose, in too much pain to even comfort. Eyes swollen shut so he couldn't make out Mac even if he could lift his head. Mac loomed over him, his rage building.

The paramedics on the scene circled Mac with a wide berth, sensing the mounting fury. They treated the boy, comforting him with meds and soothing tones as they loaded him for transport to the hospital. Right before he left the scene, the paramedic took one last glance at Mac and the father, but thought better of asking any questions.

As it turned out, Carlos Ritenour was one of many children brought in as a part of an underground sex ring for the nouveau riche. All their predilections and perversions spent on children brought in from around the globe with no citizenship status. Thus, in the eyes of the law, they didn't exist.

Mac led the team who busted the ring. All sorts of powerful businessmen and politicos were brought low in the scandal.

No one ever found the body of the man accused of beating Carlos Ritenour. Nor were any charges

filed. But the swirling rumors about the disappearance centered around Mac. Not to mention that the enemies he made of the friends of the rich and powerful brought low by the scandal created enough behind-the-scenes furor to cost Mac his job.

He never regretted any part of that.

Mac placed his thumb and forefinger on the bridge of his nose and concentrated on getting his head straight. The memories didn't help. The job was the job and his days on it were numbered from the jump. Mac was never going to make rank. He wasn't that kind of cop. He made cases, even if it meant putting his thumb on the scales of justice now and then. He didn't have to think very long for the words that had made him famous among the rank and file for a season. "'The law has a way of getting in the way of justice. Our true calling is the pursuit of justice no matter where it takes us. That's what binds us together and makes us family. And family is family.'"

"Yeah, that's it." Ade fished in his pockets for a pair of designer gloves and slipped them on. "Anyway, not much is on the Stream about the Easton MS crew. The set not jacked in?"

"Nope. Staying off the Stream is part of their code."

"You close to them?"

"Close as I need to be."

"I could use some street-level intel I can depend on," Ade said.

"Meet me at Fourth and Transom in two hours."

When they broke their conspiratorial huddle, they spied Hollander frowning. He shook his head and skulked off.

• • •

As only a few could afford cars, there were few streets in Old Town, only emergency corridors. Most people made do with either the sidewalks or the tram. If they were crazy enough to take the tram. Or crazier to walk. Mac took the underground tram to Easton, not having any patience for street preening and the ritual eyefuck of those who made him as a cop. He had never lost that cop walk, that puffed-up, straight-backed waddle of owning all he surveyed. Times like this, he wished he could still flash his badge to clear the car. Instead, nestled near the rear of the car, he hunched over on a bench. Despite being surrounded by people, he was alone. He dreaded moments like this. The stillness. When he had time to think. And feel. Grief threatened to devour him, to suck the marrow from his bones. His hands trembled with helplessness and he stuffed them into his pockets as if that would magically quell his racing mind and the torrent of memories. His mouth watered at the thought of a drink. The rusting steel wall across from him held a bit of wisdom scrawled into the surface with a knife: "Escape is the way to salvation!"

The rattling and clacking of the tram compounded the buzzing headache growing within Mac's brain. It had been hours since his last dose of Stim, the effects lasting shorter and shorter durations these days. Stim was the law enforcement drug originally developed and used during The Trying Times™, as the Stream called the post-eruption widespread riots. Mac had been on the force then, on the front lines. They'd had to stay alert longer, be faster, be stronger because they were so outnumbered. It was their thin blue line vs. the tsunami of panic. Panic the officers themselves shared. Every member of LG Security Force wanted to run and be with their families while uncertainty sprang up all around them. Instead they had to be there to stem the rioting and hold the line of civilization before people's baser instincts consumed them. And the officers resented every person who caused them to have to be here rather than with their own.

At ten p.m. sharp, Mac emerged from the Fourth and Transom tram entranceway. Light rarely penetrated down to the street level of the Easton section of Old Town. With the strange lanterns above them, the luminescence was reduced to a sapphire haze. The hustle and flow of urban ruin danced about the mixed landscape of trash-littered streets. The giant stone eruptions had disrupted the routine of the lives of Easton citizens, but people did what they had done since the days they first walked upright to take a piss: adapted and thrived, living among the alien structures as if they were their new homes.

The streets hadn't changed much. Kids in adult bodies still hung out on the corners, discussing the neighborhood in code thick enough to keep outsiders locked out of the know. The fashions changed, with the thug du jour favoring collared shirts unbuttoned at the cuffs and from the chest down. Thick, corded belts with the number of their building assignment as a buckle, worn with pride. Military fatigues shorn midcalf on the left leg, signifying a set in the prisons their families were tied to. If one member jailed, the rest of the family jailed with that relative in spirit, essentially sitting shiva during their sentence.

"The Carmillon is based here. You should see these freaks," Mac started in with Ade before he had a chance to offer up any greetings. The cybernetic man was forced to match Mac's pace as he stormed toward the houses. "Like a single-homed village. In the winter they all huddle around a wood-burning stove. They have to chip away ice from inside the toilets to use them. Summertime, shit, it's a flophouse free-for-all. They're organized, if that's not too strong a word, by a crew they call 'the crown.' The crown has five points, members, one of whom being a Chike Walters. Any relation?"

"No," Ade said with cold finality. "We all have to be related?"

"Put the race card back in your wallet. I was merely noting the coincidence."

"How do they afford this place?"

"It's not exactly the Ritz-Carlton, Detective. Besides, they have this policy of not paying rent. They just walk in and take over. Their philosophy is simple: act like you own the place and most folks will think you do. Most street bums don't run up against professional dropout artists on a regular basis."

A clean-shaven black man—draped in a vest darned with dental floss over a T-shirt and black shorts—approached them from across the street to head them off. Leather bands wrapped around his neck and wrists, accentuating the lean, lanky build of his runner's body. Though short and skinny, he couldn't disguise his muscles, as his gait gave it away: muscle heads, even thin ones, had that chest-out walk they couldn't shake. Much like cops. Ade's high-res imager fixed on the man's face.

"Chike Walters," Ade said.

"Good evening, officers," Chike said with a silky politeness before either could flash him their identification. "Here in an official capacity?"

"We have a few questions we'd like to ask you to help out with an investigation." Ade stalked about, circling Chike while studying the adjacent property.

"What investigation?"

"Do you live here?"

"As much as I live anywhere."

"I mean, is this your legal place of residence?" Ade pressed.

"You uptowners. So quick to look down your nose at us when it's you that should be ashamed of how you're living. Our country has so much. We throw away enough for nations to live on. Anything you want, I can get it for you. I can find anything I need out here."

"And what you can't find, you take," Mac said.

"What? Now you're standing up for the rights of garbage? I guess everyone will sleep better tonight."

"In someone else's bed," Mac continued.

"Private property is just another way to oppress people," Chike said.

"Not if it's my shit you're sleeping in."

"Folks would rather board up buildings if they can't make a profit from them. It makes no sense."

"It's. Not. Your. Shit." Mac emphasized each word for effect.

"Housing is a right, Detective. Food is a right. Anything less is buying into the propaganda of the system."

"What you're telling me is that you don't work?" Mac said.

"Once you have clothes, food, and housing, you don't really need credits," Chike said.

"So you're bums."

"It's always hard for some to give up privilege, that sense that you were born to own all you survey. Wouldn't you rather spend the time you do working being with your family?"

"Sometimes family's not all it's cracked up to be," Ade sniffed.

Chike turned to Ade with an icy glance. "Most people spend a good chunk of their lives at a job they hate, taking orders from people they can't stand to buy stuff they don't need. *That's* no kind of life."

"Who are they?" Ade nodded to the figures skulking around the side of the house.

"Our foraging party returning. Come on, we can talk inside."

Mac lingered a few steps behind them. The glow from a lit Dumpster cast a yellow pall on three men huddled together around a curbside campfire. Thick pustules grew in clumps along their chin and ears: victims of the Bud, a gene-specific virus released during The Trying Times™ as terrorists took advantage of the chaos to stir the pot. The virus attacked certain members of the populace by genome. It wasn't contagious, but no one had known that at the time. It produced the pustules by simply replicating in certain tissues until they grew and ruptured. A virus that shamed more than anything else, as affected individuals were ostracized by friends and family, left abandoned by those who claimed to love them. Terminated from the employment cycles and unable to get work, they took to the streets. Sections of many cities were set aside as colonies for them. Mac lived in one that kept visitors to a minimum. The Carmillon had the same idea.

Parts littered the lawn: car parts, bike parts, computer parts. The words "Escape while you can" were spray-painted on one of the crumbling brick walls of the turn-of-the-century mansion. The home was an umbrella of constant repair. Missing clay tiles left gaping wounds in the roof. Shingles peeled from the exterior, like a lizard sloughing its skin. Some of the rooms had six fireplaces, some rooms had two. The dining room was large enough to be called "The Cafeteria." The library was full of borrowed and found books—actual, paper, bound books—along with dusty old couches. Computers lined the far wall. Though reserved mostly for full citizens on the employment cycle, if they needed to, they tapped into the Stream by use of their homemade "cantenna," a primitive work-around that created an untraceable network hot spot. The massive house had half a dozen bedrooms, not counting what were originally built as servant's quarters. Strains of opera lilted from a radio. A radio. Mac had never seen a working one in real life. Signals still automatically broadcast on a loop from some centuries-old station. They had reappeared the day the towers erupted. No one knew how or why, but that didn't stop some people from enjoying the music.

A caramel-colored woman entered the room. She doffed a bowler cap, letting her white hair drape down to her shoulders. Carrying a walking stick in one hand, she plopped a backpack on the table with the other. A cross on a necklace dangled from around her neck, and a fine filigree of wrinkles framed her small mouth.

"Elia Baum, detectives. Detectives, Elia Baum. She's what you might call my second-in-command."

"Elia Baum." Ade fixed his high-res screen on her. "Three counts breaking and entering. Arrested six times on minor drug charges. Final disposition of those cases pending completion of her drug rehabilitation program."

"How's the program treating you, Ms. Baum?" Mac asked with a smirk.

"More hypocrisy. What's the difference between you and her?" Chike asked. "I can smell the stink of Redi-Smoke on your breath. And you have the look of a broken-down addict try-ing to muddle through. Protect and serve your high and leave those dealing with their pain and their recovery alone."

Mac bristled, ready to lunge toward the man, but Ade placed his large, meaty hand in the center of his chest and stopped him cold.

Chike, not even bothering to give Mac a second glance, turned to Elia. "What've we got?"

"Check this out." She gestured to the people behind her.

Her compatriots dumped several grocery bags worth of found treasures on the table. Sealed stir-fry vegetable packs. Bags of salad—crystals still on some of the leaves from having been frozen—probably from the bottom of a refrigerator kept too cold, then thrown out as ruined. Tomatoes. Four ready-made deli trays, vacuum sealed. Mushrooms. Oranges. Another of her companions arrived with lamps, brooms, random tools, and an ancient iPod. She lifted up the flap of her backpack to reveal bottles of lotion, detergent, and toothpaste.

"Nice work, Elia." Chike turned back to the detectives. "So what's this all about, gentlemen?"

Ade stepped forward. "We're investigating the disappearance of one Kiersten Wybrow."

"Ah, Kiersten Wybrow. So a pretty white woman—and she was pretty, right officer?" Chike locked eyes with Mac. "—she gets her hair mussed, so you hunt down the pack of n—— who had to be out to rape her."

"She did more than get her hair mussed, you walking cum stain . . ." Mac evaded Ade's arm and charged toward Chike.

Elia stepped in between the two men and swept the back of Mac's feet with her staff. He landed flush on his back, and by the time he realized his position, the butt of her staff pressed against his throat. The rest of the Carmillon gathered around, a wall of steel-eyed gazes whose body language hinted that they were well trained and not afraid to get in a fight. The detectives were clearly outnumbered.

"Call off your dog, Chike," Ade said in a tone that didn't invite discussion.

Chike locked eyes with him and then smirked. "Elia . . ."

She withdrew her staff then offered her hand to Mac.

"You're lucky I—we—don't have you hauled in right now." Mac brushed her hand aside and dusted himself off, knowing full well that Ade would have to call in backup to make that play. And this whole situation at second scan seemed more like a family beef than a game of posturing and disrespect.

"On what charges?" Chike asked.

"Assault on an officer," Ade said, covering for Mac, who clearly was no longer police. "Suspicion of murder."

"The Carmillon would never kill anyone. Ever."

"The Carmillon, eh? Wasn't Harley Wilson one of yours?"

"Why do you have to step on the man's name by insisting on calling him by his government name?"

"Figured you wouldn't care," Mac interjected. "If you found his body, you'd probably only use it for compost anyway. They're still scraping parts of him off the sidewalk downtown. If you hurry . . ."

"We knew him as Baraka. And, yes, he was one of ours. And, despite his dealings with the Easton MS crew, I cannot imagine him killing anyone." Chike stepped toward him, a spark of anger in his eyes. "Perhaps you should look into your undercover princess."

"You knew she was undercover?" Ade asked with the nonchalance of asking for the time.

Chike swallowed just hard enough to be noticed and wore the expression of a child caught in a lie. Mac had cracked the man's smooth veneer, finally getting to him. Angry people got sloppy.

"There are few secrets among the Carmillon."

"Then what's the muscle for?" Mac pointed to Elia and her crew, though didn't meet her eyes. "If we toss them, we likely to find weapons? Or other . . . accoutrements?"

"We have to protect ourselves. Not everyone is tolerant of our way of life."

"There are two bodies that took a header from a tower tonight—whose families won't even be able to bury them properly—who beg to differ. Her prints were everywhere. Wilson's were nowhere." Ade stepped closer to Chike. "How do you think that happened?"

"Your questions betray your prejudice. Apparently, every time something goes wrong in your precious, civilized world, those without have to be the cause of it."

"Your little foragers were all together?"

"Ours is a lifestyle of freedom. People can come and go as they please without fear of being checked up on."

"Do you know why Harley Wilson and Kiersten Wybrow would be at the top of the stone tower?" Ade asked.

"Baraka," Chike corrected, "was a good man. Maybe someday you'll have a chance to ask him when your time comes. He understood that we were in a war and that not all of our enemies reveal themselves. Some hide behind government and corporations and have the wealth and connections to think of themselves as untouchable. Everyone can be touched."

Mac rolled his eyes and tapped Ade's arm. "Come on, I've heard enough."

• • •

Mac daydreamed about being a farmer. Not a farmer, per se, but something simpler that harkened back to an earlier age. When a man could be alone with his thoughts and work out what he felt as he toiled in the earth. A time when he could think in peace without distraction. He needed space to himself. He supposed that was why he resisted using the data cloths or having any tech hardware attached to his brain stem. Nothing beyond the data chip in his hand, which carried his banking, citizenship status, and medical information.

At his usual table at Jenxie's Diner, a tiny hole-in-the-wall place specializing in obscure "genuine Southern cuisine," Mac leaned back in his seat. They actually still fried food, and his mouth nearly salivated at the thought of macaroni and cheese, fried okra, and fried chicken. He'd gone so far as to erase all traces of his Kentucky—no, southern Lifthrasir Group—roots. Most people assumed he was just another big-city douche, but memories of biscuits, gravy, and thick bacon flooded back to him, and the food nourished a part of him that ached from neglect.

"What was that? Back there with Chike," Mac said.

"You're here as a consultant and observer. That's it." Ade stared out the window wearing the same expression he'd had when he'd refused to meet Chike's eyes.

"I ain't trying to be your shrink. I just sensed a little . . . tension."

"Let's leave it at he and I have history."

"What are you doing, anyway? I know you're not just sitting there."

Ade raised a sardonic eyebrow. "You accusing me of not being shiftless and lazy?"

He slumped into the corner of the booth opposite Mac, lost in the transmissions of his high-res screen. Ade's synthetic eye thrummed as he read reports and newsfeeds from the Stream, searching for any reference connecting Easton, the Carmillon, Kiersten Wybrow, Chike Walters, or Harley "Baraka" Wilson. He probably also read the *New Yorker* and the *Brazz Report* celebrity scandal sheets, being the well-rounded Spookbot.

According to Ade, the murder rate in Easton had increased 45 percent in the last quarter, the uptick not corresponding to any rise in seasonal temperatures nor increased financial uncertainty. The only cross-reference point was the increased appearance of the blue lanterns and a rise in the number of jumpers. Scientists were still studying the lantern phenomenon, some likening it to some sort of dark matter/aurora borealis type effect. Conspiracy theorists chattered about alien invasions. Apocalyptos turned up their religious fervor. The government per-

sisted in the claim that the civil unrest could be traced to the Freeganist Carmillon and their five-pointed leadership, discarding the more outlying explanations as nonsense.

"What do you think, Mac?"

"I think whenever the government speaks, the truth usually lies in the opposite direction. You gonna bust my balls all night or do you plan on easing up sometime soon?"

"Going through data and reports is how I relax. I let the information wash over me. Kind of like a fish swimming, I don't take in all the water."

"What exactly are you looking for?"

"Don't know. Actually, I think I'm looking for what's not there." Ade peered toward him as if reading his mood. "But about the Carmillon, what do you think?"

"I think they are a lying pack of hippy shitbags."

"What do we know about our victim? This crime? Or a motive?"

"Not much." Mac took out a Redi-Smoke and lit up.

"Not anything. All we have is a woman we know existed, a man who for all intents and purposes didn't, and a whole lot of nothing to go on." Ade stood motionless, the metal side of his face gleaming in the dim moonlight. "Tell me about Kiersten. Not anything I could read in a report. Tell me about the Kiersten you knew."

"Kiersten is . . . was . . ." Mac hated the grammar of the recently dead. The way the mind played its tricks to remind a person of another's absence. "Pure Security Force. Old school. Her dad was a cop and his dad was a cop, and along came Kiersten, a daughter instead of a son."

"Only child?"

"Yeah, her mother died during childbirth. Her dad didn't take it well. He and Kiersten were never close. She always harbored the suspicion that though he loved her he never really liked her all that much. In fact, she said she could never shake the feeling that he blamed her for her mother's death."

"That's no way to grow up."

"Tell me about it. Probably why she got into the family business."

"Same old story: trying to earn a parent's approval." With fidgety energy, Ade held the glass of water up to his eyes, as if marveling at it. "A fool's errand. Besides, kids have to find their own way, not live in their fathers' shadows."

"So you know how it goes?"

Ade paused as if debating how to respond to him. "She threw herself into the job?"

"Took her mother's maiden name and joined the force. Didn't want any special consideration for being Ronald Kemper's daughter."

"Kemper is a big name to live up to. You should know."

"Yeah. On the one hand, she wanted the old man to see what she could do on her own."

"On the other hand?" Ade asked.

"She wanted him to know that she was her own woman and he couldn't take credit for anything she did."

"I'm really starting to like this woman."

"Yeah, she has that effect on folks."

Ade repositioned himself, sitting straighter on the bench. He tried to catch a waitress's attention to no avail. "So when did you two meet?"

"I was her training officer. Man, if you'd have known her then. She was your type."

"My type?"

"Oh yeah. All rules and regulations. 'The rules are there for a reason. Without the law, there'd be chaos. The law is what separates us from the animals.' She was always quoting that."

"It's from an argument. Massiah versus Indiana."

"You know the law?" Mac asked.

"I'm a cop."

"You know what I mean."

"I know the lawyer. Melvin Walters. He said it." Ade quickly moved the conversation back to focus on Kiersten. "So she was a real by-the-books sort of person."

"Like you said, she disclosed our relationship while I thought I was being all clever hiding it from the bosses."

"So how'd you two get involved?"

"You ever have a partner?"

"No. People choose to not partner with me. That's their choice, not mine. I don't take that Spookbot stuff to heart."

"I was her training officer. You didn't have to be around her more than a few minutes to realize she was special. Beautiful. Smart. Tough. She took shit from no one; she didn't care who you were. And she kind of looked up to me. A real eager student, the kind a teacher could pour themselves into."

"Literally."

"Not like that." Mac hated the implication of how it sounded, turning his very real emotions—what they'd had—into something tawdry. "I mean, when you have someone you know can take what you teach them and take it to a whole other level. Like the chance to coach a Jordan, LeBron, or Mikatsu."

"So, as her elder, superior, and instructor, you didn't see it as an abuse of power to get involved with her?"

"Fuck you." It was Mac's turn to adjust, not quite rearing up, but meeting Ade's steady, probing gaze with his own. The two waited in silence, neither backing down.

Ade broke loose with a wan grin to ease the tension. "What was her assignment with the Carmillon?"

"Way I heard it, she went undercover to monitor their activities."

"Vice?"

"No, narcotics plucked her. Hollander assigned her personally."

"One last question: How'd it end?"

Mac remained silent for a time. There wasn't a day that went by that he didn't regret the mess he'd made of both of their lives. They were both on the job. He was her training officer for a time. They got involved, dated for over a year without the brass knowing. He was transferred to robbery/homicide once it came out. Tried to change some of his old ways and tame some of his demons. But, eventually, he fucked things up good. First letting the job get to him with that

Ritenour mess, then letting the drinking and Stim use drive her away. Until one day she tired of his act and left. "It ended the way all things end: badly."

"Harbor any resentments?"

"Am I a suspect?"

"Honestly? Not really. Just doing my due diligence."

"No resentments. Only regrets."

"What kind of regrets?" Ade pressed.

"What are you, my shrink now?"

"I'm just trying to get the fullest picture possible of the woman she was and the man you are. So . . . regrets?"

"I . . . a person like Kiersten deserves a good man. Anyone around her wants to . . . be better. To be worthy of . . . shit." Mac hated to come across like half a douche: not having the words to put to his feelings, but having just enough to make a real tool of himself trying to sound like a fool-in-love poet. "I'm a fuckup. That's what I do, and that's who I am. I just didn't want to take her down when I crashed and burned. She deserved better."

A moment passed between them. Ade respected the silence and the man enough to leave it be. Privacy was something no one could afford anymore, so it had to be given. Ade turned away, pretending to be distracted by something outside, and gave Mac room to lick his emotional scars or else grieve in his own way. And Mac appreciated it.

"Now, I'm fucking starved. We're here in one of Easton's finer all-night dives. What you say me and you grab some coffee and donuts," Mac said.

"You cannot resist being a walking cliché."

"Fine, you can have one of those puke-green protein shakes or whatever it is you muscle boys like to eat."

Ade revealed a mouth full of gleaming white teeth. A crooked, painful approximation of a smile broke against the metal in his unyielding face. "Now you're talking."

One of the Jenxie's Diner owners brought out Mac's order: a plate of biscuits topped with sausage gravy, topped with two eggs sunny side up. Ade glanced over with mild disgust.

"Not too many Forcers got one of those." Mac pointed his fork—laden with a bit of gravy-dipped biscuit and the yolk of an egg dripping from it—at Ade's cybernetic implant. "Way I see it, anyone who can afford that kind of tech is already above a chief's pay grade. You're like Chike, slumming with us poor folks."

"I'm nothing like Chike." Ade raised his hands as if pushing away from the table and settled into his half-slouch of reading the news Stream. "We've run down Harley. Little more than a two-bit hitter, suspected in three homicides. Most we've ever managed to pin on him was a few assaults."

"Yeah. Ran across his crew a few times. Vicious little pricks, the kind who'd slit his own momma's throat for a few moments' buzz. Just tussled with one of them last night. I don't know why Kiersten would ever get tangled up with him. Any of them. You saw them. I doubt any of them could take a toss without coming up holding. Still, they seem like harmless enough recreational users. More the 'live and let live' type."

"Sounds about right. Still, that's the story they gave her to give us. And . . ."

". . . the truth is somewhere in the other direction," Mac said.

"You know, back in the 1960s and 1970s, police were assigned to infiltrate groups suspected of being revolutionaries. They'd get in bed with the groups, go with them on their little criminal activities, but inform if they were planning something huge. Real." Mac tapped his finger on his empty glass, indicating the need for a refill, wishing he had something harder than the carbonated pabulum he swallowed. As if finally accepting a truth, he whispered, "Kiersten's gone . . ."

"When was the last time you heard from her?" Ade asked in a gentle tone.

"Two days ago." Mac recognized the tone—one he often used with relatives of victims—and snapped back from the melancholy vortex that waited for him. "Just to talk about the old days.

Her place. Part of me thought it was an invitation, but I didn't take her up on it."

"That get you worried?"

"Just thought it weird, her reaching out to me in the first place. Being undercover, she could go weeks without checking in. That was just the way it worked. Protocols had it that she had to check in with Hollander every day, though."

"I've only had the case three hours. With no body, it'll be tough to establish a timeline. With no body, we can't check for drugs, can't check for sexual—" Ade stopped himself. "Sorry, man."

"It's the job. I know." Mac fired up another Redi-Smoke. "What about that?"

"About what?"

"What you said earlier about what's not there?"

"The body?" Ade asked.

"Think there's a reason they wanted to splatter Kiersten across the city?"

Ade returned to his state of brooding silence. A hint of a grin upturned the corner of his mouth as he searched: the semi-vacant, glassy-eyed stare of a junky in the throes of getting high.

"You get a phone dump?" Mac asked.

"Still waiting on it. Some sort of hold is on her records. I'm also waiting on her full background: financial, criminal, and public. My next stop is to go over to her place and see what she was getting into."

"Good plan. I'll go with you."

"Former Detective Peterson, you are dangerously close to shitting on my investigation."

"All you can see are the cheeks of my pasty white ass. I have not yet begun to shit. If I had intentions of doing so, I wouldn't have given you the heads-up. Besides, it's not the crime scene, and I have a key."

• • •

"Western Investigator Twenty-One to base. Left Fourth and Transom with informant. Heading to Easton apartments of undercover investigator Kiersten Wybrow," Ade said into his cop-net.

Mac knew Ade documented as much as he could in order to give the appearance of an investigation by the book.

"Base to Western Twenty-One. Time is oh three forty-five."

Though Kiersten kept a cover apartment on the outskirts of the Easton section of Old Town, she lived in another tower in Waverton, not too far from the one where she was found. He hated the facade of Waverton. A gleaming city whose dwellers had the dispirited expressions of those who lived in war zones: desperate, without hope, eyes devoid of life. Shuffling about in steps drained of vitality. Mac didn't know how people could stand living in a tower. When he stared at their strange geometry for too long, especially under the glare of the lanterns, nausea overwhelmed him. Each of the tower's original occupants carved out their own space for their apartment, paying for each square foot. Thus the spaces were not uniform, each floor plan was unique, and the rooms were carved out like natural hollows. The city had used code violations to seize the property under eminent domain and had the towers refurbished. In Kiersten's case, the city had repossessed this space after a Stim bust—a home lab that refined the police stimulant to its more potent street form—so it made for a perfect cover.

Standing in front of the locked door, Mac shifted awkwardly, suddenly feeling like he chased the ghost of someone he never knew. Not that he was going to admit that he may have exaggerated his access to their place. He knew where she stayed in case of an emergency, and he wasn't supposed to know that for the sake of her cover. He certainly hadn't been there before. Unlike her (real) place, there was no palm lock that responded to his print. Kiersten was old-school at heart. He reached above the archway and checked under the mat. He found what he was looking for under a fake rock. A mechanical bolt slid free as he turned a key. Funny how he thought of their life together as real and this world he and Ade traipsed in as no more than a facade.

Mac searched for anything familiar, anything of the Kiersten he knew in the spartan space. He couldn't shake the sensation that he was intruding into the wrong person's life. Seeing the cloying undertones of flowers in vases, which gave every room the feel of a funeral home, he almost missed how Kiersten had decorated her place. He had always hated her aesthetic taste, as it made her seem like a frumpy old woman. A bowl of candy rested on the table next to the door. Mac grabbed a few pieces.

"Not what you expected?" Ade asked.

"It's not like I kept my stained underwear in her panty drawer."

Ade's mouth had begun to creep into a mild grin when it froze, and his smile evaporated. Ade held up a hand commanding Mac to pipe down, first pointing to his ear and then to the shut bedroom door. Mac looked over the tops of his sunglasses and then reached into the folds of his dampening jacket and removed his Cougar PT-10. Ade's arms crisscrossed and pulled out two semiautomatic crowd-control machine guns. Mac twisted the knob, but it had been locked. Ade brushed him aside, kicked the door once, and when it splintered open, stepped first into the unknown, unwelcoming darkness.

Two figures wrestled in the dark. The murk of the room obscured the figures, and they were entangled too closely to draw a bead on either.

"Security Force. Hold it right there," Ade commanded.

The figures ceased their dance. Then one shoved the other toward the detectives and bounded out the window. Mac dashed after the figure.

"Mac, wait," Ade yelled too late.

The window, like the rest of the windows along the tower, was neither square nor smooth nor spaced with any regularity. The rooflines shifted like rock slides. Shelves had been cut into the walls and the windows opened onto a terrace. From their second-floor vantage point, the figure dropped to the ground as if boneless, landing with the grace of a leopard then bounding farther into the recesses of the tower's out-cropping. Almost like cliff dwellings, the tower itself was a seamless piece of masonry, with no cracks, like river-cut stone created as one sheaf. Gibbous and grayish, the towers disoriented him. Geometric and beautiful, a math equation of art, he had the sense that he was too close to it to see the whole pattern. However, the angles and placement seemed too intentional, guided by an intelligence behind its order.

Mac followed the suspect, his knees popping and groaning in protest. He had to let his equilibrium reassert itself. He pursued the figure as it bounded along the towers. It leaped onto an overhang and pulled itself up and over onto another terrace, barely breaking stride. Mac did his best to keep pace. In a chase, especially now that he was old and out of shape, his goal was to just keep the perp in sight. He ran smart, not fast, allowing his targets to exhaust themselves, because most people couldn't go full tilt for very long. Mac jogged along at his half trot, watching as the figure climbed and bounded. He matched its path if not its acrobatics.

The artificial hue of the lanterns bobbing in the midnight sky above the tower deepened the shadows. Mac trailed the figure into a dead end where the towers met. Sound traveled differently in this network, dampening the noise, creating a sacred space. That was the word that sprang to Mac's mind: sacred. He leaned against a bare wall, with its unnatural smoothness and no signs of erosion or wear. A lavender fragrance suffused the surrounding area, but underneath the smell was something old and moldy, like rotted cabbage. Treelike plants cloistered the intersection. A woman emerged from a tangle of branches. There was a moment when reality shifted, like a child's kaleidoscope turning. Mac threw up. He didn't take his eyes from her as he wiped his mouth with the cuff of his sleeve.

"Elia, what the hell?"

"This isn't what you think," she said.

"I think I'm hauling your ass in."

"The man back there, he knows. He's a part of this."

"Who is he?" Mac hesitated. He needed to get back to Ade, but he couldn't just let Elia walk. "Never mind, you need to come in with me."

"I can't, Detective. I must see this through. For my people's sake, as well as yours."

A moment passed between them. When she closed her eyes, her eyeballs moved around like disjointed marbles beneath the fragile membranes of her lids. He knew her full measure now.

Elia charged at him without a word, without a sound. The swing of her staff swooshed over his head. He hadn't realized he'd ducked as instinct had taken over. She reversed the arc of her attack in one fluid movement, catching him in his ribs. The coat absorbed most of the blow, but it caused him to drop his gun. He wrapped his arms around her staff. With the flourish of a pirouette, she released her staff, spun away from him, then came at him with her hands poised like daggers. Three times she struck him, and then each spot went numb. In a desperate bid, he jacked his knee up, which caught her in her side and threw her off balance. He locked arms with her and pushed her into the wall. With a graceful turn, she entangled him in a hold before slamming him into an adjacent wall. His glasses shattered into jagged bits that clawed his face. Blood trailed from his smashed nose. His breath came in jagged gulps. His shoulder wrenched out of place. His body reacted on instinct, desperate to stay conscious. His elbow crashed into her neck. He followed up with an awkwardly thrown punch. Trapped in close quarters, they exchanged a flurry of punches, with none landing especially hard as each of them began to tire, though Mac more than she. Mac scrabbled about, his hand searching for anything he could use as a weapon. Finding a branch, he jammed it into her neck. Blood spurted. Enraged, she lifted him and flipped him onto the ground. He kicked madly as she leaped on him, catching her twice, but neither blow had much power. Her hands wrapped around the soft folds of his neck. Headbutting her, he staved her off as she released her grip. He clambered for his weapon

as she lunged for her staff. He fired twice. He hit her center mass, just as he was trained. He had to have hit her. She fell into the shadows. He raised his gun level and trained it on where she had fallen. He took measured half steps, easing into his approach. He neared where her body had dropped. He clutched his side and daubed his face as slick pools of blood trickled from him. When he reached the spot, she was gone.

• • •

Mac returned to Kiersten's place. His breath still coming in ragged hitches as years of Redi-Smokes overrode his military training. He remembered his time in the service as clean, a simple time of young idiots still searching for the people they were meant to grow into. It was a time when he had learned duty, responsibility, and the horseshit that was chain of command. Getting an other-than-honorable discharge for punching his commanding officer—no matter how correct Mac had proved himself to be—had left him as sore as he felt now.

"What happened?" Ade said. "You look like you got the mess stomped out of you."

"The . . ." Mac lifted his chin toward the suspect, "perp got away from me. I'll tell you later. What have we got here?"

"Look for yourself."

A figure slumped against the side of Kiersten's bed, his face bruised and swollen. "Damn it, Ade, you've beat him to near death."

"Wasn't me. I found him like that." Ade took a step back, his head cocked at an angle.

"What are you doing?"

"Checking him for drugs, his heartbeat, respiration, implants," Ade said, "establishing a baseline should we be so inclined as to engage him in conversation. I hate to be lied to."

"I need to get me one of those."

"What's your name?" Ade asked the suspect.

"I ain't sayin' shit." The man leaned forward and let out a small chuckle. Blood spilled from his mouth.

"Anyone else in the apartment we should know about, Mr. Sayin' Shit?" Ade asked.

"I'll clear the place," Mac said.

"Don't open any drawers," Ade reminded him. "Plain view search only or the judicial net will tear me a new one."

"Too bad you have to make a case. The law has a way of getting in the way of justice."

Ade looked down and shook his head. Sirens roared in the distance. "I'll secure the scene. You should have the service medics take a look at you."

"I'll be fine."

"Former Detective Peterson," Ade said in a voice that didn't invite argument, "please sit down. You've lost more blood than you realize and you're probably in shock."

"I'm not going anywhere till I've figured out what went on here." Mac faced him, an unwavering gaze locked onto his erstwhile partner's robotic visage.

"You mean besides you getting your ass kicked? You need to settle down and let them do their job."

"I need to do mine first." Mac turned toward Kiersten's bedroom. The door closed behind and he leaned against it, recalling what it was like to be in there again. Alone with his anger. And underneath the anger was more anger. Under that, lifting up that inner welcome mat—black earth squirming with worms and isopods and other insects that broke down organic matter, building something from death and decay—was fear. Kiersten had only wanted to be let in. She'd said that he had constructed a life—with the booze and the Stim—where he cut himself off from having to deal with others and the potential pain they brought. Living with the fear that if he exposed himself, showed people who he really was, they would abandon him. Some part of him became convinced that he would rather be alone and unhurt rather than risk others in his life. He preferred to live with the fear. Fear that she'd betray him. Fear that she'd see him for who he was. Fear that she'd humiliate him.

Fear that she'd leave him.

That was why he ran. That was why he always ran.

The room hadn't changed. A row of porcelain figurines lined the mantle over her chest-o-drawers. Her queen-sized bed—how many nights had their bodies tangled up in the space trying to get comfortable but still appreciating that they had it to begin with?—divided the room. On the other side was her desk, an antique rolltop. Pulling out the main drawer, he ran his hand underneath it. There it was. An envelope. Inside was a tiny spiral-bound notebook. Kiersten was running an off-the-book investigation. He flipped through the pages.

"Where'd you get that?" Ade asked, suddenly filling the doorway.

"It fell out." Mac nudged the drawer closed and stood up.

"What are you thinking?"

"Right now that maybe one of the Carmillon paid one of their brothers . . . or sisters . . . to take care of a couple of liabilities."

• • •

Devices measured their brainwaves, heartbeats, and body temperatures, logged retinal scans, DNA, and fingerprint info. The biocircuitry that formed the artificial intelligence of the LG Security Force headquarters in Waverton gave it a kind of low-level sentience. While it allowed for adaptive responses, more importantly, it allowed for self-repair. Mac wasn't allowed on the interrogation floor, but Ade found him a spot up in an observation room. A great seat for his show.

In the small confines of the interrogation room, under the glare of a single column of light, the suspect seemed a lot smaller. And younger. A young man, barely a man at that. Hair styled in thick cornrows, a bruise under his left eye, and the entire right side of his face remained swollen. Tattoos, in a pattern familiar to Mac, trailed down each skinny arm. A razor-thin goatee framed his mouth; three gold rings pierced each ear. Seated in the metal chair, his knee hopped to a frenetic beat; his eyes scanned and rescanned the room at every sound; his heartbeat tripped along as if he were a hunted rabbit. Fear made everyone smaller.

"What's your name, son?" Ade circled the table, which blocked the suspect from the door. A subtle reminder that the only way to the door was through the detective. He set a data sheet on the table between them. A subtle reminder that evidence, the truth, separated them.

"Don't call me son. I'm not your son." The subject reared up slightly, partly a show for the detective, partly to move away from the sheet and what it might portend.

"Yeah, well, I figured 'what's your name you scumbag, daring to shoot at Security Force, pain in the ass' would get us off on the wrong foot."

"But at least it'd be honest."

"Honesty's important to you?"

"Honesty's all that we have. That and respect, but honesty's something no one can take away from you but you."

"What can I call you?" Ade asked again.

"Between that fancy eye of yours and my prints, retinal scan, and DNA, you probably know all my history."

"Oh, I have that: Quavay Middleton. Twenty-two years old. Dropped out of Edu-Link at thirteen. Known associate of the Easton MS crew. Four assaults, one possession without intent to distribute, suspect in three B and Es. But that's your government name. What do *you* want to be called?"

"Tin Tin," he replied, tentatively, as if uncertain of his own name, much less what the detective's play was. The concession to his name caught him off guard.

"How'd you get a name like Tin Tin?"

"Just sort of stuck. I can get anyone jacked in from anywhere."

"So you're like a walking cantenna."

"Yeah. Tin Tin. Why you being so cool to me?"

"Well, Tin Tin, I got to say, you done right by me, so I got to do right by you." Ade broke out his wide, fractured smile and patted the data sheet.

"What you mean?"

"I mean, here you are, right in the middle of a jackpot. This murder case is closed."

"Murder?"

"Yeah. Turns out your fingerprints match a set of unknowns at the murder scene. Then we catch you in the apartment of the woman whose murder we're investigating. It doesn't matter how great a story you may have, this case is done."

"Shit, man, that ain't right." Tin Tin's eyes widened and followed the detective wherever he moved with plaintive desperation.

"Right doesn't have anything to do with it. You should know that by now. You're twenty-two. You've been in and out of the system for years. You know how the game works. How we do. Us Security Forces, we're strictly about the easy workload: if we can close a case on your ass, we will."

"You got it all wrong."

Ade crossed his arms and leaned back against the wall. His heavy gaze fell on Tin Tin, and the boy—he seemed more like a frantic little boy in search of his mother—squirmed under its weight. "Then set me straight. You keep my job easy, I'll keep listening."

"Word came from up high: Kiersten had been snitching. Had notes and recordings of a lot of the dirt we do."

"So you were sent to shut her up."

"It wasn't like that. She was greenlit, all right. But she was still Kiersten. We'd accepted her as one of us. I know some folks felt this sense of betrayal and . . . I guess. Still didn't stop me from feeling what I did. I loved her a little. Still, though, we couldn't have her notes just out there. She could put all of our business out on the streets."

"But?"

"But that ain't what I do. I don't handle that end of things. I'm strictly . . . acquisitions."

"So you broke into her place just looking for her notes and stuff?"

"That shit could've been anywhere. A micro dot even."

"That's why they sent in my man Tin Tin."

Tin Tin beamed with pride. "None other."

Mac hadn't known Ade long, but he guessed some of the pressures he may have been under. No matter how postracial they had declared their world, too many times Ade had needed to make a choice: whether he was black or blue, one of those cops who was a black man first, cop second, or vice versa. Too much of that brother-brother crap could play in some people's heads and cloud their judgment. Feeling too responsible for fuckups fucking up, that's what a sense of community meant to Mac. As far as he was concerned, Ade was just there to clean up their mess, not play Father Malone or something to get them to see the light.

"So who was your playmate?" Ade asked.

"Fuck if I know. I'm steady tossing the place, suddenly this kung fu heifer jumps my shit."

"She whupped that ass," Ade enjoyed saying.

"I got my licks in."

"You want that to go in the official report?"

"Nah, man. You know, I'm a lover and all. Can't be seen putting my hands on no female. Just trying to fend her off so I can do my do."

There it was. Though guilty of many things, Tin Tin had neither the demeanor nor heart of a killer. Now a gentler touch was required. The old juices of being in the room began to flow again for Mac, the gentle tug to join Ade on the performance.

"So you have no idea who she was?" Ade sat down across from him now. Like an actor commanding the stage, he owned the room.

"None. Though I got the feeling she was there for the same reason."

"Where were you about three forty-five last night?" Ade asked.

"Tucking my ass into bed."

"Here's my problem, Tin Tin: scan says we got your prints at the scene of my homicide."

"Can't be. I didn't do no murder."

"Then explain your prints."

"Someone fucked up on your end. Carried a one or some shit when they shouldn't have. All I know was that I wasn't nowhere near no murder."

"Well, you'll forgive us if we don't take your word on it."

"Don't go soft on me," Tin Tin said with a sudden steel to his words.

"Excuse me?"

"I didn't do no murder, so I need you and your robo-ass to put in some elbow work. Revisit the crime scene. CSI some shit, 'cause I'm telling you, I'm innocent."

"You may be many things, Tin Tin, but innocent surely isn't one of them."

"But . . ."

"Sit tight. I'm going to check things out. If you didn't do this, I'll find out. If you did, well, I'll find that out, too."

• • •

Entering the observation room to join Mac, Ade sighed with exasperation. Mac recognized that sigh because he'd already let one out a few minutes ago. They were nowhere. They were worse than nowhere because they had a viable suspect in hand they knew wasn't good for the crime. But expediency often trumped niceties like what one's gut might say or what one might intuit from years of experience. Ade paced back and forth, working off his frustration. Pausing, he tilted his head in that tell that said he'd received new information across his high-res screen.

"We got the call dump back on Kiersten's communications."

"About time," Mac said.

"Told you, something had the files all but suppressed. Anyway, Baraka was the last one to call her."

"Think he arranged the meet?"

"We could assume that. Maybe he was her confidential informant. That could get them both killed if they were caught."

"It's all right there, I know it. All connected somehow." Mac pored over Kiersten's notes, not understanding most of the technical jargon. He recognized the name that topped the manifests and memos. "What do we know about the Lifthrasir Group?"

"They're into all sorts of weird stuff. Alternative energy sources. One of their labs had a break-in reported a week ago. Case got buried."

"Why? Brass interference?"

"You'd think, but apparently when the Lifthrasir Group talks, the bosses jump. The group was completely uncooperative. Their alarms went off, we responded, and it was like we were inconveniencing them. Case shut down."

"That doesn't make any sense. When shit don't make sense, it rubs my taint raw."

"You are a lovely, lovely man." Ade leaned forward, his gaze distant. He thumbed through a crate of bagged material like a child at Christmas choosing which present to open first.

"What are you doing?"

"About to log this stuff in."

"You can't do that."

"It's procedure."

"You haven't been about procedure this whole case. Why? Because part of you suspected this was an unusual case from the beginning. Look, I don't understand most of what she has here, but much of this stuff doesn't look like any technology I'm familiar with. She was onto something. Something big."

"I know where you're going with that science fiction conspiracy theory tone. Snippets of internal memorandums, schematics for devices, blurry photographs, and recordings of meetings? You connect these pieces one way, you get to spin the tale of business executives in league with . . . foreign agencies . . . to procure tech. You spin the same facts a little differently, you have Kiersten involved in corporate espionage—the equivalent of high treason—and needing to scapegoat somebody."

"But we agree it revolves around the Lifthrasir Group," Mac said.

"Yes."

"And the Lifthrasir Group owns the Security Force."

"They provide the funding and we do report ultimately to their appointed civilian review board."

"I know. I dealt with them on my way off the force. But that's what I mean. You've seen the kind of juice in play to pull the strings that have been yanked so far. We log this into the system, no telling what will happen to the evidence."

"So what do you suggest?"

"Log in a duplicate. We keep the originals. Kiersten might have done that herself. Worked with the dupes while keeping the originals somewhere safe. Think about it. Why else do a pen and paper investigation? Because they can't be monitored or traced."

Clutching his hands behind his head, Ade stretched back in the chair. The room buzzed with activity, detectives and uniformed officers milling about trying to appear as if they were being productive in case any of the brass wandered through. Official memorandums trailed along the walls, along with case status and deployment updates. The phones chirped constantly.

"What's he doing here?" Deputy Chief Hollander sneered with a mild derision toward Mac.

"Consulting," Ade said.

"I meant for you to extend him a courtesy, not have him move in."

"He helped me bring in our prime suspect, Tin Tin. Even got his ass handed to him by another suspect. Figured I owed it to him to let him see this through a little bit further."

"I'm strictly a shadow investigator," Mac assured, though the chief wasn't buying it.

"See that it stays that way." Hollander turned fully to Ade, standing in front of the "murder board," as the squad called the case wall. Crime scene photos lit up the board, along with victim profiles, and results streamed from the crime lab. Diagrams detailing the physics of impacts or the biology of any drugs present filled the screens. From every possible scenario or angle, various theories and guesses ran along the side of the board in blue. "Now we're going to pretend that you're still lead investigator on this case. Where do we stand?"

"We're in the middle of interviews. Her friends. Her family. Her coworkers." Ade fixed his cybernetic eye on him. "We're working on trace evidence right now."

"So what do we have?" Mac asked.

"Kiersten Wybrow goes undercover to investigate the Easton MS crew as well as an ancillary organization known as the Carmillon. The group is headed up by Chike Walter and his right hand, Elia Baum. Kiersten hooks up with Harley Wilson, and the two of them get into some shit they shouldn't have. Our Mr. Quavay Middleton, aka Tin Tin, was found beaten at her place by perp unknown." Ade cut a glance at Mac to keep him silent.

"Any word on the unknown perp?"

"That's the other reason Former Detective Peterson is here. He's going through arrays of known Easton MS crew associates to see if a familiar face pops out."

"What's your next step?" Hollander peeked into the evidence box, then scanned a data sheet.

"Let the suspect stew a bit then see if he gives up anything else."

"He look good for this?" Hollander asked.

"He looks great for this. He's been practically delivered to us with a bow on top. Everything points to him: prints on the scene; knowing Kiersten reported to us; caught at her place ransacking it for incriminating evidence."

"Why isn't he in holding?"

"His statement is like high grade Stim: ninety percent pure. That's the way this game is rigged. Everything he's telling is ninety percent truth, but that last ten percent can get folks killed. Plus, I hate loose ends and unanswered questions."

"Well you know what? I hate open cases even more. Do I need to remind you that Kiersten Wybrow was one of our own? *One of us.* Murders of Security Force members do not go unsolved, especially when there is a perp who has all but confessed to it already in our custody. Close this case so that we can move on. Somebody's gotta

give the press their morning hand jobs, and I'm the man anointed for the mission. Do I make myself clear?"

"Yes Chief."

The deputy chief stormed back to his office. Mac pointedly kept his back to Kiersten's picture, as if it hurt too much to see her image. Her curly mop of brown hair. Her dark, sultry eyes that stole a man's soul when they peered at him. The too-red thin lips of her about-to-get-into-trouble grin. But no matter where he stood, the weight of her profile bore down on him. "You didn't mention Elia to him."

"Because I have an uncooperative witness who hasn't confirmed that it was her."

"Is that what I am?" Mac asked.

"Not everything goes into my final report all at once. I still have questions. I need to be able to frame things in context. And I know where to find Elia should it prove to be her."

"The fact that this case keeps coming back to Chike has nothing to do with it?"

"Mind your own."

"I am. That's how I got here in the first place."

"Hollander's true to his word." Ade nodded to the monitor. "Tin Tin's on his way to holding."

Two guards escorted Quavay Middleton into the holding facility, which would double as the courtroom as a judicial net monitor burned to life. It was easier to hold the preliminary trial and motions at the station in order to streamline the judicial process. The overly pixilated image of a judge sputtered, the connection not very good, as Stream for government use had even lower priority than those mandated for public access. The high mounted lights winked on, a single column illuminating Tin Tin's space.

"Quavay Middleton," the face of the judicial net said.

"Tin Tin," he corrected.

"You stand accused of the murders of Harley Wilson and Kiersten Wybrow. How do you plead?"

"I didn't do that shit."

Mac turned to make a smart-ass comment to Ade, only to see the detective's pallor flush. He teetered for a bit, a tall tree on the verge of falling.

"What is it?" Mac half rose to steady him. "You don't look okay."

At first Ade's face simply went slack, enraptured by images only he could see. Then he doubled over as if a searing blade sliced through his head. Mac caught the big man as he fell forward.

"Something's wrong," was all Ade could muster.

The image of the judge flickered, grayed with static, then went black. Quavay stood alone in his circle of light, surrounded by shadows. Too many shadows. He gestured wildly and appeared to be screaming, but no sound transmitted. Then that image, too, flickered, grayed with static, then went black.

"What's going on?" Mac asked.

Ade pointed toward a console and Mac helped him to it. Ade slid the nail of his pinky finger back, revealing an exoport embedded in the tip, and he plugged into the panel. The feed on the monitor changed, and a new image burned to life. Tin Tin huddled in a corner. The point of view of the camera had changed. No longer was it a sweeping arc from the side of the room. It was much closer, peering down at Tin Tin. From the point of view of whoever was in with him. "Someone's hijacked the signal to my eye."

"Who?"

"I don't know. Someone with juice. This tech isn't easy to hack. This is what I'm seeing."

"Yeah, I'm betting whoever installed that isn't exactly in the refund business."

The electric wail of a weapon discharge halted them in their spots, and their attention drew back to the screen. A hole had burned neatly through Tin Tin's chest. His clothes still smoldered from the energy beam. Tin Tin's body filled the screen, from the perspective of the assailant inspecting his (or her) handiwork. Then the contact signal broke. The screen went

black, then reflected itself, as it was what Ade now saw. He withdrew his finger from the port.

"Lock the building down," Ade said in a spent voice just above a whisper. Unsteady getting to his feet, his head seemed to clear as other Security Force officers pushed through their initial shock and their training took over. Mac followed, all but ignored in the ensuing rush. By the time the officers got back to the holding chamber, a crowd blocked the door. The two guards were being attended to by medics, returning to consciousness but otherwise unharmed. Tin Tin's vacant eyes accused the gathered throng.

"I'm not exactly weeping over this one," Hollander said.

"Sir?" Ade asked.

"They kill one of ours. They paid the price. Case closed."

"Our brand of 'blue justice'?"

"No, no. Of course not. I'm launching a full investigation. You can't pull this cowboy shit on my watch," Hollander said in an unconvincing tone. He all but signaled a going-through-the-motions investigation, strictly an exercise in filing paperwork. "I'll just shake his hand before I Mirandize him. Or her."

"How did he get in here? Or get out?" Ade asked.

"Double-check all personnel. I want to know who all has been in and out of this building," Hollander said.

"It won't matter. Whoever pulled this off had access. I bet every clearance is accounted for. They are one step ahead of us and two levels above our pay grade."

"At least."

"That stunt with my eye wasn't easy. However, it automatically recorded the entire episode. Full spectrum analysis. I'm running a protocol now to see if I can backtrace the signal."

"Let's get this scene processed and let me know what you find. I'll get everyone out of here. Short leash, Peterson."

Already kneeling, Ade examined the weapon, which had been discarded without a care of it being traced back to the perpetrator. "A Cougar

PT-10, like yours, except that this one is military grade. Energy charged."

"Mine was a souvenir." His Cougar PT-10 was the only token from the Michigan incursion. Prior to him being drummed out of military service, the Lifthrasir Group had initiated a hostile takeover of the Michigan territory but was rebuffed. The skirmish had lasted two years and Mac had served three consecutive tours in the futile engagement.

"After a couple hundred years," he said, almost absently, "the design of a handgun hasn't changed all that much."

"There's a romance to the image," Mac said.

"You mean the image of men waving around their junk to see whose is bigger?"

"Let's not be sexist: women wave around my junk too."

"Right. Not sexist at all." Ade continued, "Look at this: the primer has been shaved down so it wouldn't snag if drawn quickly. And the grips are custom made. No fingerprints, no DNA."

"Professional hitter?"

"A little beyond these disds."

"It might be beyond them, but the case dead-ends with them. Once he was logged into the judicial net, it was a matter of prosecution."

"Out of our hands."

"Other than some paperwork, case closed."

Mac hated the way things remained, like he'd been presented with a new sweater with a few threads dangling that he had to yank free. On paper it could work. The Easton MS crew got wind that Kiersten worked for Security Force. One of their hitters took out her and her snitch, Baraka or Harley or whatever the hell he was calling himself. It could have been Tin Tin, who then went after whatever evidence she had. Once detained, he had become a liability, either because of what he knew or to whoever actually carried out the hit. Regardless, there was still a killer to track, and a case to close if anyone cared: Tin Tin's if not also Kiersten's. But what truly bothered Mac was the sense of something bigger pulling at them and the

investigation. Someone with the resources to hijack Ade's eye, get in and out of LG Security Force headquarters, and have access to military hardware. Events moved too quickly, too neatly, not giving anyone a chance to think things through.

• • •

There were times when Mac dreamed of plunging his hands into soil, of getting dirt under his fingernails so thick that he would never seem to get completely clean. Of pulling weeds and tending to his young sprouting plants while sweat beaded along his forehead, falling in large droplets, and his shirt completely drenched. The nagging sensation never left him, but he couldn't put his finger on what exactly troubled him. The blaring wail of an incoming call only served to increase his growing irritation. The call was blocked, so no image or information came through. This was exactly why Mac didn't have an office, only a messenger service that forwarded his calls through a series of anonymous proxies. That way he had no unexpected visitors, which meant no unanticipated mayhem and/or property damage.

"This better be good. I haven't had coffee yet." Mac tamped out a Redi-Smoke and put it between his lips, holding it there without lighting.

"Are you Mac Peterson? The investigator?" the voice sounded vaguely familiar, though hushed and muffled.

"Who's asking?"

"Jesse Honeycutt."

"Who?"

"Duppy."

"Oh, Duppy." Mac lit his Redi-Smoke. He let the rush hit his system and the smoke halo his mouth before he continued. "How are the eyes doing?"

"Me fe gwon spend two days after the clinic recovering," Duppy said, then tired of putting in the energy for his accent. "We need to meet somewhere."

"What for? Our last encounter left me ill-disposed to meeting with you."

"I have information."

"What information could you possibly have interesting enough to make me go meet you somewhere, especially when you might harbor feelings of a violent nature directed toward my ass?"

"It's about Tin Tin. He wasn't where they said he was. He was with me."

"Look, I'm sorry about your man. I know you two were close, but there's nothing you can do for him now."

"There's the truth. That mattered to him."

"Why not go to the Security Force?"

"The Security Force ain't interested in the truth. They just want their cases closed no matter how many dead disds it takes to get there. Someone's got to speak for him."

The words had the echo of sincerity, but Mac also knew that junkies could be the sweetest of talkers. "All right. Meet you at Monument Boulevard. Is ten thirty past your bedtime?"

"Fuck you, you two-bit bomboclott. Meet me at Lot Forty-Two."

"Don't you want to tell me to come alone?"

"Would it make a difference?"

"Suppose not."

"Then let's keep it honest."

. . .

Waverton, like many cities, had its shadow side. The victim of benign neglect and the original site of Waverton, Old Town existed in the penumbra of the towers, like a suburban spread abandoned and forgotten. On the clearest nights, the glow of the blue lanterns in the sky penetrated even the ghost of a city like Old Town. The Easton neighborhood of Old Town bumped up against Waverton, separated only by the Liberty River, which acted as a natural dividing line within Waverton. But one had to live in Old Town for a while to know about Portsmouth Street. And one could know about Portsmouth Street without knowing about the warehouse complex known as the Shroud. The buildings of the Shroud district were boarded up, the area always on the list for demolition, with that day never seeming to arrive. A warped fence surrounded the property, rusted and bordering a cracked pavement walkway. Winding midway through the complex, Portsmouth Street opened up against a break in the fence, large enough for a single vehicle to pass through. If one knew what one was looking at, the graffiti on the buildings told a story: a star with one of the points ending with an arrow, a crown on its side, all directing toward another building.

Lot 42 had a boarded-up front, but the grates were metal and had none of the markings of city inspectors. The pavement around the building appeared worn, but only in the affected way of folks who wore distressed clothes as fashion. Lot 42 was a bar, one off the grid of Security Force, who intentionally turned a blind eye to its patrons' untaxed synthehol trade and boutique drug use. The street brand of Stim had found its launch place here.

Mac and Ade parked outside the fence and walked the rest of the way to Lot 42. A lone figure stood outside of the crate of a building. A black man about the height of Ade, but twice the width, wore all black. A band circled his head, covering his eyes.

"We got a problem . . . officers?" he said after casual scrutiny of them.

"Don't start none, won't be none," Ade said.

"We're strictly off the clock," Mac reassured him. "Here to meet a friend and conversate."

"Who?"

"Duppy. We go way back."

"We don't take too kindly to recording devices." The man tapped his eye band while staring at Ade.

"I am upfront about it, which is why I didn't have the dermal overlay procedure. It helps me see, but there's plenty I choose to not see."

The man stepped aside and a doorway arch appeared. The pair passed through the opening.

"They not worried about us carrying?" Mac asked.

"I'm guessing everyone in here is carrying," Ade said. "Some more than others."

They made their way over to a booth just off from the main bar. A figure slumped low in its confines, as if not wanting to be seen with them. The closest patrons edged away from the pair, preferring to be out of earshot or direct lines of vision anyway.

"My man, Duppy," Mac said a little too loudly as he slid in across from Duppy.

"Cho," Duppy said with the disgust of sucking his teeth at them, "keep your voice down."

"You chose the place."

"My home turf, true. Still don't like to advertise."

"A man is certainly judged by the company he keeps," Ade said.

"How do you know Tin Tin?" Mac asked.

"We ran in the Easton MS crew. Came up together. You gotta understand, we Old Town through and through. Born here, die here. We know the drill," Duppy said.

Mac had grown up with kids like this. The streets had their own call. A siren's whisper of absent fathers or homes bereft of love or too full of drugs or abuse. Hard life any way he sliced it, and once everything became a matter of day-to-day survival, it ground away luxuries like hope. Or dreams of tomorrow. His own world had become a tunnel, and all he had seen was a life in Old Town until he'd gotten into trouble in his neighborhood, which he'd escaped by joining the military and then the LG Security Force. But in his heart, the watering hole he kept returning to was Old Town.

"You do a bid in Sizemore?" The Sizemore Correctional Facility was the stop of choice for Old Towners on their way to Wallace Field, the cemetery for those buried who left no one behind who cared about them.

"Yeah. Me and Tin Tin both. I wouldn't have survived without him. Barely did with him."

"That where you got the rune wear?" Mac had run across such tattoos before. Woven biocircuitry, like a synth net, which allowed the wearer to feel or be connected neurally to another. The designs of the tattoos acted as brands, labeling the connected partners.

"The synth tats?" Duppy held out his arms, inspecting and displaying them. "Yeah. But when we got out, we wanted to get out of the life. That's when we started talking to Chike."

"Chike? What's he got to do with it?"

"Chike's like a prophet out here. Always trying to turn folks. Get them out of their life and into his. Trying to get everyone to be straight edged like him and the Carmillon."

Ade went silent, his unblinking red eye fixed on the man-boy in front of him as if locked in, assessing him. Or Chike.

"How did Tin Tin's prints get all over Kiersten's place?"

"At the tower? I don't know. We were crew and all, but it's not like we shugged like that. I'm telling you, he was set up."

A plaintive echo of truth filled Duppy's words. Mac sifted through the facts. Tin Tin's prints were found on objects that could have been placed there, like drinking glasses. Not on any surfaces. It was possible that Tin Tin could have been set up. "So what was Tin Tin doing down there?"

"He was shugging behind that donut shop down there on Crennant Avenue, behind the tower, to see if they threw out any jellies. He was a fiend for them jellies." Duppy grew wistful, with an odd curl to his lips as if caught in a pleasant memory. Or a part of Tin Tin only he knew.

"So he was digging through garbage?" Mac asked.

"Chike, I'm telling you, had him rethinking his priorities and way of life."

"Must've been persuasive. The man does have a way," Mac said.

"Tell me about Baraka, then. What was he like?" Ade pressed forward.

"Dude was fierce. One of them stone cold, fearless types. He was the first to leap into a situation. But he was ambitious, too. Always had his eye on his next move."

"When you say that, you think he was running game?"

"Don't know. He always had an agenda he was working. Like he was down with the crew as it suited him, but he wasn't true. Then he started rolling large. Latest gear. Tossing credits about like he'd found a fountain of them."

"He putting in extra work?"

"Not that we saw. We were all on the line. It's not like you got employee of the month or anything," Duppy said.

"He skimming a little off the top for himself?" Mac asked.

"That's what we thought. Then Baraka went to ground before we could . . . discuss it."

"To ground. That's an interesting turn of phrase," Ade said.

"I just meant we couldn't find him. No one could. Until . . ." Duppy's voice trailed off.

"You weren't worried? He was your boy and all," Mac said.

"Our lifestyle ain't conducive to worry," Duppy said. "Besides, I thought maybe he'd gotten out the game for real. Start over somewhere. Get himself set up."

"What made you think of that?"

"Like I said, brother was always secretive. Liked to play things close. Calls. Meetings. It was his way. He was a ghost."

"What if Baraka wanted out?"

"You mean out of the Easton MS crew?"

"Yeah, how does that play? After all," Mac said, "in my experience, gang members don't look upon it favorably when one of their own decides to call it quits."

"You been watching too many vids. Folks around here leave this game for one of two reasons: they dead or they get a better opportunity. And Baraka ain't around no more."

• • •

Most people rode the tram, as the luxury of personal vehicles was no longer practical. A few, the very rich, had their own transportation, as did police and other emergency services personnel. Ade drove a Mantori Grendel. A classic design with all mechanical parts, not one computer chip onboard. They were designed to be EMP proof. Ade's was a large red behemoth with raised fins in the rear. What looked to be a simple convertible top was another layer of shielding. Ade enjoyed styling and profiling as much as the next man, but was still security conscious. One only had to be trapped on the wrong side of the blue line during the Trying Times™ once to take precautions quite seriously.

The road wound its way through the outer skirts of the city, through the hillside out of which Waverton had been built. For those who knew Waverton and Old Town, sometimes traveling the outer roads that looped the city was the most direct way to get from Point A to Point B. It also allowed time for the mind to wander and relax.

Sometimes, however, the burgeoning silence needed to be filled.

"Where are we headed?" Mac asked.

"To confirm this story with Chike."

"Confirm what? That Tin Tin and Duppy were his pet projects? That doesn't get us any closer to anything."

"You're right. I can drop you off."

"Nah, that's all right. I'm the curious sort. Besides, I don't have anything at home waiting for me."

"Except your grief."

Even if what Ade said was true, it felt like an invasion of privacy by pointing it out. Mac wanted the room to do his own thing in his own time. The idea of pursuing Kiersten's murderer gave him something to focus on. A distraction. Gave purpose to his anger and grief and pain. But acknowledging that, even the inadvertent push in by Ade, pressed too closely in on Mac.

"Don't you have some tragic backstory?"

"No, I'm a well-adjusted motherfucker," Ade grinned. "Wife. Two kids."

"And a brother you don't talk to. Or acknowledge." Mac popped a Redi-Smoke between his lips then caught Ade's disapproving glare. "Don't look at me like that. I am a detective, and it wasn't much of a secret. What? I don't get to ask about you or provide obtrusive commentary?"

"Family. That minefield never gets easier. It always hurts."

"So what do you do to get by?"

"Nothing."

"Nothing?" Mac asked.

"No porn. No booze. No drugs. No Stream. No comfort eating. No throwing myself into destructive relationships. None of the little addictions we use to medicate from the pain of life."

"Sometimes that pain is real," Mac said to the tinge of judgment he heard in Ade's words. "You may start off with painkillers because your shoulder isn't right from taking a bullet some years back. Then codeine 'cause your knees and back are shot but you want to stay on the job. Then one day you're studying the shit pile of your life thinking, 'I pay taxes, I'm a pretty good guy. What's with the fucked-up turn of events?' Then you just say 'Fuck it.' Whatever it takes to get by."

"I wasn't judging."

"You were, while trying to sound like you aren't. So what do you do?"

"I let it hurt."

"That it?"

"I feel the full weight of the pain. Let it remind me that there's a price to relationships . . . and that I'm still alive to feel it. I deal with it rather than keep shoving it down."

"You make it sound easy," Mac said.

"You know better," Ade said. "I'm surprised you make it out of bed most mornings."

"Shit, me too." Mac placed his Redi-Smoke back in its pack. "So what happened with you and your brother?"

"Nothing happened."

"You went into the force. He joined the hippy convicts. Something happened."

"What do you want to hear? That mommy and daddy beat us? That some rogue uncle touched him? Things aren't always so melodramatic. Sometimes dysfunction is simply . . . dysfunction."

"Well, shit. That was anticlimactic."

"Sorry to disappoint. We're just private peo-

ple. We don't all need to be all searching for . . . whatever you searching for."

"What's that supposed to mean?" Mac asked, but Ade only drove.

They pulled off on the exit leading into Easton. The searing lights from the surrounding buildings, the noise of people yelling, music clanging, were all familiar and comforting. Ade parked near Chike's claimed home. A small, round-faced boy eyed them. Ade offered him ten credits to watch his car. The boy negotiated another five. As Mac and Ade strode up the sidewalk, the front door opened and Chike came out to greet them. Elia shadowed him but kept a discreet distance.

"Evening, officers. What brings you back to us on so fine an evening?" Chike asked.

"We got to talk," Ade said.

"Why now?"

"You're in the thick of it, and I can't protect you much longer."

"Is that what you been doing? Protecting me? Who the hell asked you to?" Chike stepped close to Ade; drops of spittle flew out of his mouth as he raised his voice.

"That's my job. It's what big brothers do."

"Where was my 'big brother' when I needed him?"

"Chike, I . . ."

"You. Left."

"I had to," Ade said with a too-defensive strain in his voice. "I wasn't going to go into the family business. The law wasn't for me, not like that. I had to go my own way."

"You left me with them."

"What did you want me to do? Wait for you to get through Edu-Link? I thought it would be easier on you that way. I'd take the hit for being the disappointing son . . ."

"Yeah, that'd be great if I was who they wanted. But I was an afterthought. I was their backup plan. And I couldn't even do that. You were the one they wanted. You were the one they loved."

"Don't say that."

"Why? Because it's too hard to hear out loud?" Chike shoved him. "Dad had it all worked out. Sent you to the special school. You and he went on all those trips. At the table, he was always quizzing you, grooming you. He had . . . expectations. Of you. Not of me. Never of me."

"Chike, don' start re-remembering our childhood now. You had been getting into shit and fucking up as long as I can remember."

"Because I've known for that long. Just 'cause you turned a blind eye to him . . ."

"I've been looking out for you, Chike, whether you believe it or not. And right now, shit is piling up at your doorstep."

"Here it comes. The latest iteration of 'Blame Chike.'"

"Save your self-pitying nonsense. You're out here, bringing folks together. The Carmillon. Easton MS crew. A cynical observer might think you were creating one huge operation. One legit, the other less so. But sometimes working well outside the law allowed you to get certain things done, as well as being an alternate funding source. Baraka was part of your organization. Duppy and Tin Tin were among your disciples. Elia, your lieutenant, was . . . seen in Kiersten's apartment. You don't think things start adding up and pointing to you?"

"Arrest me, then." Chike threw his arms up, a pantomime of waiting to be cuffed.

"I can't."

"Because you have no case."

"Because you're still my baby brother. And I know you didn't do this. You knew Kiersten was Security Force . . ."

"Because my brother's a cop, and I learned to smell swine a mile away."

"Fuck you." But Ade's rejoinder had no sting.

"On the real, we did know that while we were planning our latest foray against the instruments of societal ruin, she ran across some stuff."

"What sort of stuff?"

"I don't know. We didn't have a chance to look at it. But it had her scared."

"What was your . . . foray?"

"I can't tell you that. Not without a lawyer, 'cause I'd be admitting to some shit."

"It have to do with the Lifthrasir Group?"

"Yeah."

"We're up on them. So you can back off."

"No can do."

"I said we got this."

"Go ahead, then. Do your do and let me know how that works out for you. Meanwhile, we're moving ahead with our offensive."

"Offensive? Who are you, General Patton now?"

"People like the Lifthrasir Group live above the law. You can't reason with them. You can't touch them."

"But you can?"

"Sometimes the law has a way of getting in the way of justice," Chike said.

Mac smiled. When Ade turned to him, he shrugged his shoulders.

"Yeah, well why don't we let the law take one more bite of the apple? You got a name for me?" Ade asked. "Let me at least see what I can find out. Do my big brother thing."

Chike smiled. "Charleston Ptacek."

"Fuck me," Mac whispered.

• • •

Expensive artifacts—backlit on nearly invisible shelves—lined the walls of the office of Lifthrasir Group executive Charleston Ptacek. Forty-five years old. Straight black hair slicked back with old-fashioned hair grease. Round lenses rested high on his nose, frameless, but they allowed images on them like a screen. An expansive desk created a gulf between him and the detectives. An untouched cup of coffee steamed at one side of his desk. He turned the pictures of his family away from their lingering gazes. The windows of his office frosted for privacy.

Still an officious son of a bitch, Mac thought and suppressed the urge to punch him in the face.

"So good to see you again, Mr. Peterson. Timely as ever," Ptacek said.

"Mr. Ptacek, so sorry for being late. My friend here," Mac lifted his chin toward Ade, "had to have his morning pancakes and coffee. He's a beast before breakfast. You know how it goes."

Ade stepped forward, his imposing frame eliciting no reaction from the executive.

"Do you know when I saw it was you looking to speak to me, I canceled an appointment to fit you in. I haven't seen you since the civilian review board at your hearing. I just had to see what became of you for myself."

"I'm surprised that you had the time."

"Oh, I always have time for old friends."

Fuck you, you ridiculous, needle-dicked windbag. You wouldn't know good Security Force members or their work no matter how many of your corrupt buddies they sent up to Sizemore. Mac balled his fists and scooted to the edge of his chair.

"Do you know why we're here?" Ade touched Mac's shoulder and continued the questioning.

"I was briefed this morning, yes. Our name came up incidental to an investigation you're conducting. You screwed up, one of yours died, and now you need a scapegoat. Yes, I know exactly why you're here. I thought the matter settled."

"Consider this a follow-up. We're all about customer service," Mac said.

"We? Have you been reinstated into Security Force and I didn't know about it?"

"Former Detective Peterson is here as a special consultant." Ade remained composed. "There was a report of a break-in a couple of weeks ago. Mr. Ptacek, what is it you do?"

"My department oversees biosynthetics, mostly. Literally cloning parts for soldiers. Or Security Force. Get a leg blown off, have a copy of your own leg grafted back on, that sort of thing. The rest is research. Government."

"Above my pay grade, right?" Mac motioned around at the high-end office furniture and walls.

"And clearance," Ptacek said. "Tell me again how you plan to tie the Lifthrasir Group to your case?"

"Probably nothing," Ade said with a faux deflated whisper. Without taking his eyes from the man, he laid a datasheet on the table in front of Ptacek, opened it, and pointed to several lines on the screen. "Did you ever find out who was behind your burglary?"

"No." Ptacek bridged his fingers in front of his face.

"Great news, Mr. Ptacek, I might have a lead in that case," Mac said. "I suspect a woman broke in, under the guise of possibly vandalizing the place, and snooped around where she shouldn't. Maybe took notes, a few photos, information on things she shouldn't have. Important, secret shit that corporations would hire a team to find and retrieve," Mac interjected. "Information they might have failed to destroy."

"Interesting theory, Detective," Ptacek said. "Though *I* suspect you don't have a shred of evidence to back up your theories."

"We have the notes. They paint a disturbing picture."

"I doubt you understood what you were looking at, and if you did, then you are thinking entirely too small. I've got just as good an imagination for making up stories. What if aliens fell from the sky one night and said, 'Hey, want us to show you something neat?' Our friendly visitors give us the technology to tap into a near-endless energy source. Completely hypothetical, of course."

Mac scratched at his face to cover his bemusement as he chewed over Ptacek's words. "Okay. You're saying aliens gave you a near-endless source of energy?"

"Gentlemen, humanity stands on a beach studying a sea we don't understand, much like the loincloth-wearing aborigines swinging through trees—or whatever it is they do—trying to fathom our cars. The world is on the precipice of ridding itself of poverty, oil dependence, hunger."

"What do they get out of it?"

"Perhaps someplace to expand to."

"Like drilling rights or what?"

"They might not be so different from us. Look like us. With a few modifications, grow acclimated to our ways."

"The eruptions?" Ade asked.

"Naturally, a more familiar landscape, not to mention the shift in the composition of the atmosphere. Easily chalked up to pollution," Ptacek continued. "Of course, as with any new venture, there are risks. Containment can be an issue. Ruptures could occur."

"The blue lights in the sky? Like a ruptured energy spill?"

"Do you need me to connect every dot? Should there be a breech, cleanup can become an issue. We can learn much even in how the messes are treated."

"So let me get this straight . . ." Mac started.

"There's nothing to get straight. I haven't told you anything. Only a fanciful story."

"And if someone else stumbled across this story?"

"Errant stories, like energy sources, need to be gotten in front of. Contained."

"And the people in charge of this . . . containment?"

"Government money. Paid for by senators, representatives, executives, presidents . . . the kind of folks that guarantee that this investigation stops now. I would wager to guess that all of your notes, evidence, and logs are being seized right now."

"Is Deputy Chief Hollander on your payroll?"

"All of the LG Security Force is on my payroll."

"What about . . . Harley Wilson?"

"Who?"

"Why tell us anything?"

"You need to understand the precarious nature of your situation. If there is even idle speculation around the water cooler, then your worlds will cease to exist. Long before any of my people see the inside of an interrogation room." Charleston Ptacek buttoned his jacket as he got

up, then extended his arm toward the door. The windows cleared for everyone to watch their dismissal. "Now, if you'll excuse me. I believe you know enough to close the book on your investigation. And you may want to watch the news feed. Good day."

Mac followed Ade out the door, mildly confused, but their mouths shut. When they stepped outside of Ptacek's office, a security detail met them to escort them out. The Lifthrasir Group's building jutted against the downtown skyline, tall and proud, indifferent to its neighboring buildings. The two detectives waited in its shadow.

Finally, Mac broke the silence. "Let's see what the chief has to say."

• • •

Every news media outlet from the *National Investigator* down to the *Brazz Report* gossip feed ran stories related to the Lifthrasir Group's release of new technology. A renewable, cheap energy source, medical advancements, a slew of drugs—the implication being that the Lifthrasir Group was about to change the way of life on the planet. The head of the Lifthrasir Group addressed world leaders, promising that some of the technology would be available completely free simply to better all of humanity. In the background of some of the photo ops Mac spied Charleston Ptacek, all but taunting him. The story for media and public consumption drowned out all concern for anything else being worked on. Ade and Mac stormed into Hollander's office.

"Whose payroll are you on? Are you running this investigation as the chief of detectives or as a cleaner for the Lifthrasir Group?"

"You talked to Ptacek?" Hollander pushed away from his desk.

"It's what you wanted us to do, right? You leave us a bread crumb, we follow it home."

"It's done. Over. You needed to know why and what the stakes were. I figured I owed you that much."

"You don't owe us shit. You owe Kiersten. She's one of us. And she goes unavenged."

"I know. And I'm sorry about that. I really am. She got too close, and for them it became a . . . teachable moment. Charleston Ptacek brazenly showing me just how untouchable they are. That anyone, be they a detective or a civilian, could be . . ." Hollander's voice cracked with shame, averting his eyes from Mac's.

Mac's face reddened. The worst part about grief was the sense of impotence. Unable to protect the ones he loved. Unable to be there for them when they needed him. And his opportunity to finally do something again left him powerless to do anything.

"I need to get out of here. I can't be in the same room as this excuse for Security Force anymore."

. . .

The sheer rock face loomed like a wall next to the road, so close it left little room for driver error. Water seeped from the stones, tears of crags broken by slate screes. Trees lined the other side of the road, a stand of soldiers at parade rest. Evenly spaced, their leaves not yet grown in for the year. With the eruptions of the strange towers and the weird iridescent skies, the Lifthrasir Group planted acres of trees to reclaim the open spaces, stripping away many concrete avenues and long-abandoned malls in favor of retooled landscape. The hills on the fringe of town were still green, deep roads cut into a valley. What were perhaps the remains of a series of towers aborted mid-eruption now sprouted with weeds and outgrowths, like the tentative facial growth on a pubescent boy. The greenery was broken by shelves of rock passed by outside of Ade's car window.

It was entirely too claustrophobic.

Mac couldn't figure out Ade's angle. A hand of friendship had been offered, no strings, no requirements. He didn't know why this man he had never encountered before this case allowed him such access. Didn't know if he wanted Mac to succeed or be a scapegoat should they fail. Didn't know what was expected. Perhaps to have a front-row seat for Mac's final burnout and then have him trotted out so that all those he had ever bent out of shape while on the LG Security Force could have their moment to point and laugh.

All Ade offered was friendship, yet Mac felt under attack by the idea. All he knew was that the walls were closing in on him. Flight or fight. The pressure like tectonic plates in the earth shifting, producing jutting spires of coarse anger.

And fear.

"If I were telling the story of Baraka's death," Mac broke the silence, "I would look for someone who had a really good reason to see him dead."

"He had everyone looking for him: the police, Kiersten, Carmillon."

"Not everyone."

"What do you mean?" Ade asked.

"The Lifthrasir Group. They were all over Kiersten, but made no mention of Baraka."

"Forget it. It's done. Case is closed. The only story to tell and the Lifthrasir Group is ahead of it, spinning it their way."

"We've got to do something. Kiersten . . ." Mac slumped in his seat, not knowing how he planned to finish that sentence.

"The foundation on which you've built your whole life is an illusion. There is more to you than this story you've written of yourself, as if all there is to you is this broken-down mope who sleeps in his clothes and bathes in booze."

"But you expect me to believe that you see beyond that?"

Ade tapped his eye and then his head. "I read people."

"It's part of the job. Having that eye helps."

"I don't need an eye to tell me that you never believed yourself to be standard-issue Security Force. You don't believe the rules apply to you. They're more like suggestions. Being booted from the force would've killed guys who were all about the job, but for you, it fed into your lone wolf/maverick thing you have going on."

"I have more fun and fewer rules doing what I do."

"I know that's what you tell yourself. Thing is, guys like you need boundaries or you lose yourselves. Kiersten was a boundary."

"You've stopped making sense again. Time for a system reboot."

"The lies you want to believe about yourself, they had to wither under the reality of her loving you. As you were. For who you were as well as who you could be."

"Whatever. You can save that psychobabble shit." Mac turned away from him, but he still heard a voice. Kiersten's voice when he was leaving her.

I'm not the one who hates you. You're the one who hates you. And I think you're more comfortable with your hate than you are risking letting anyone in who may love you.

His hate. At least he still felt something. "I drove her away like I did everyone else."

"Yeah, you have a charm about you that enjoys pushing people away. And when you encounter people that won't be pushed, you don't know how to deal with them. At best, you sort of resign yourself to being close to them."

"Better be careful. These days all I do is lose people who get close to me."

"Good thing I got no interest in that. You need a pet. Or a hobby."

"Self-destruction is my hobby."

"You think I can't spot a junkie? You spend your days wallowing in self-pity and pumping Stim into your system. Don't act all shocked. I *am* a detective, and it wasn't much of a secret."

The blue haze lit up the sky; a neon borealis, like an electric fog cover. The rains had passed for the most part, a wet spring that lingered too long. They wound down the serpentine corridor between the hills as silence settled on them again. Ade kept checking the rearview mirror, not liking what he thought he saw.

"We've picked up a tail." A set of headlights lit up Ade's face.

"You sure?"

"I'm going to pretend you didn't just insult my skills as a Security Force—detective grade, mind you—nor my common sense, as there aren't but a handful of cars out here in the first place."

The lights behind them flared as if recognized or giving up the pretense of being discreet. The beams bounded across Ade's face, the glint from his eye casting his face in steep shadows of menace. He grimaced, mostly annoyed, then hunched over the steering wheel.

"Get down." Ade reached over and shoved Mac forward.

"What?" was all Mac could mutter before the rapid-fire report of automatic weapons spraying at the car answered him.

Three distinct kinds of fire. A continuous rat-tat-tat over a repeating bang, punctuated by a large burst as if the pursuing truck was auditioning for a percussion trio of firearms. Bullets splattered across the body of the Mantori Grendel, their impact leaving cracks in the glass. The car rocked with each report of the irregular booms and wouldn't hold up for long under such a concentrated attack. One blast left deep gouges in the door as if a hand sought to punch through to grab Mac. The rear window finally gave way; glass riddled the interior ahead of a swarm of bullets. From deep within the seat well, Ade knocked out the remaining glass above him and fired blindly at the charging truck, hoping to keep them off balance. Mac huddled low in his seat, withdrawing his Cougar PT-10.

The truck neared, attempting to pull alongside. Ade gritted his teeth in a mad smile, his fingers digging into the soft mat of his steering wheel as if he could will the car to do what he wanted. The road was all but deserted at that time of night; Ade swerved in and out of their line of fire.

"Hold on. This is about to get ugly." Ade stomped on the brakes. The car veered, slamming into the truck. The truck ran up the embankment, the jagged rocks scraping the side and throwing the occupants of the truck bed around. The Grendel careened down the hillside. The car made it most of the way down on all four wheels, bouncing and nearly tipping as it sped headlong down the side. But the last crest proved too much and the car overturned, toppling onto its side.

"You okay?" Mac massaged the back of his neck as he sprang up from the back seat, where he'd landed.

"No, I'm pissed." Ade unbuckled his seat harness and climbed out the passenger window.

By the time Mac crawled through the window, Ade was already a good way up the hill, positioning himself for the shooters, ready for them to come after them. Mac had wrenched something in his lower back in the car crash, and who knew how many new bruises he'd be adding to his collection by the morning. In a sore lope, he moved to the lowest tier of trees to keep Ade in his sights. The world spun at crazy angles. His equilibrium was shot, and he needed a minute to clear his head.

"This way," a distant voice cried. Mac counted four men, possibly a fifth, but with the blue luminescence playing games with the tree shadows, not to mention his still-blurry vision, he couldn't be sure. Whoever they were, they were loud and untrained. Thugs "R" Us was obviously having a clearance sale on grunt-level hitters. Mac almost felt insulted that he wasn't worth digging deeper into someone's pocket for a quality hit.

"Over here, you shitbirds!" Mac took wild shots in their general direction. As he only needed to be a distraction, he didn't try too hard to actually hit anyone.

This far from the city proper, the azure field above them illuminated the sky the way a snow-covered ground lightened the night sky. The strange glow wreaked havoc on the senses, alternately piercing shadows then deepening them. Unlike the pursuing men, Ade's eye compen-sated for the light shifts and targeted perfectly in the pitch black. Ade cleared the shadow of the trees. His twin semiautomatic crowd-control machine guns roared to life. Precise bursts cut down the first two thugs without any effort, splintering bullets through their torsos. The sloped, rocky terrain played to his advantage. The men were caught in their downhill trots, unable to stop in time or do little more than dive for cover. Ade wasn't in the mood to play coy. The two remaining men slowed, stumbling over the bodies of their fallen comrades. They attempted to draw a bead on him, but with robotic accuracy, he riddled them with shots. They jerked violently at the end of a concise burst, their bodies dead before they knew to collapse. Arms still outstretched, Ade scanned for further movement.

"That all of them?" Mac asked.

"No." Ade trained his weapon on a spot in front of him. "But if he makes any sudden movements, it will be his last. Then that will be the last of them. Drop your weapon."

"I'm unarmed. Officer." The man pointedly said the word "officer" as if reminding Ade he had rules he had to play within. A squat figure with a bulbous belly whose shirt barely covered it. Thick arms, once heavily muscled but gone to flab. A sour face held a lifetime of disappointments through a biker mustache over a gleaming smile full of sin.

"Detective," Ade corrected. "On your knees. Lace your fingers behind your head."

"Who are you?" Mac asked.

"Does it matter?" the man responded.

"I need to know whose mother to notify to pick up what's left of your body."

"Your tone is disrespectful. We do not like . . . constables . . . of any sort. Especially those with too many questions."

"Any shade of constable irritate you more than others?" Ade asked.

"You are mistaken. You're all blue. Besides, I'm not seeing the inside of a cell."

"You assume you're making it to a cell."

"We all have roles to play, Detective."

"What's mine?" Mac aimed his gun directly at the man's temple.

"Rabid dog needing to be put down?"

"Another fan club member," Ade yanked the man's arms down one at a time and began to cuff him. "Like I said, you have a charm about you."

"What's this about?" Mac asked.

"This is about stories." The man grimaced as Ade snapped the cuffs tight. "Every people has a story to tell. When all is said and done, any racial identity is about shared story. A story that defines them and continues to form them. When stories are reduced to law or dogma, their vitality is drained. When people no longer tell or listen to others' stories, they become locked in their provincial mindset, cultural ghettos of their own making. In fact, when people become so removed from another's story, they become compelled to destroy those others' stories, for they suggest other ways of living. Their stories become a threat."

"You're one of . . . them, aren't you?"

The man didn't reply.

"So you've been watching us? Our investigation?" Ade asked.

"I'm not watching you specifically. You're blocking my view as I observe a civilization in its death throes. Wanton sexuality. An addicted populace. By indulging all your so-called freedoms, you lost all sense of discipline. You have lost your center."

"Do you understand what this disd is talking about?"

"Not a damn word. Are you a member of the Carmillon?" Mac asked.

"Dissident is right. But no, I'm not a member of any group. I avoid politics."

"I'm done playing twenty questions with him. I'm dumping his ass in a cell and let the system sort it out," Ade said.

The man laughed.

"Something funny?"

"You want justice."

"I'd settle for you on death row."

"You would have to burn down your own house to get to me. Either way, we still win," the man said.

The man halted midstep as if he gagged on something. Ade shook him to nudge him forward. The man spasmed, his arms wrenching out of socket since his hands were still cuffed behind him. Falling to his knees, the man was caught by Ade, who screamed at him. Mac dashed over, and they rolled him onto his back. Ade was about to clean the man's airway when the man's eyes seemed to dry out. They grayed then shriveled in their sockets. His skin tightened then drew away from his eyes, his mouth a taut, forced grin. His face split; a crease zipped down as if an invisible blade flensed the flesh from his bone, graying as it went. The flesh smoldered. Ade and Mac both scampered away from it as if not wanting to get any of the man on them, fearing whatever contagion that consumed him. Within minutes, the man's flesh and bones had been reduced to ash.

"You ever see something you wish you could *unsee*?" Mac asked. "Your parents screwing in the bedroom. Your grandma stepping out of the shower."

"This make your list?"

"Do you drink?"

"No," Ade said.

"I'll have to teach you."

• • •

The glowing canvas lit the ground with a powder-blue haze, giving certain objects, viewed at the proper angles, a slight diaphanous quality the way oil slicks on water's surface had a way of looking pretty under the right circumstances. Tonight, two officers stared up at the night sky as they drank from a bottle of twenty-five-year-old Macallan. Kiersten had stashed away the single malt for special occasions, and they drank in her honor.

"Fuck you, moon." Mac poured a stiff drink

straight into his mouth, then passed the bottle over to Ade.

"Fuck you, stars." Ade swallowed.

"Fuck you, big buildings doing your sausage dance out of the earth."

"Fuck you, strange alien blue shit."

"Fuck you, police commissioners an' all you other ball-less sacks of brass shit."

"Fuck you, government pricks covering up all your asses."

"Fuck you, Lifthrasir Group. And your officious prick CEOs."

"Fuck you, you whining pinhead sheep going about your days without a care outside of your own business."

"Fuck you, Kiersten, for leaving me," Mac said.

Ade averted his gaze to give the man space to grieve.

"Am I interrupting or can anyone join this party?" Chike asked. Elia strode a few feet behind him, white hair sprouting out from under her bowler cap, then leaned against her walking stick. A cross on a necklace dangled from around her neck.

"You're late," Mac said.

"You're drunk."

"Technically, he's shitfaced," Ade corrected. "Which means he's prone to making monumental errors in judgment."

"What about you?" Chike turned to Ade.

"I'm not even here. I closed my file, turned over all my notes, and went home to await my new assignment tomorrow."

"People don't give a fuck anymore," Mac started. "Laws are supposed to protect people, not leave them out like bait in a trap."

"He all right? What's he going on about?" Chike thumbed in Mac's direction.

"Don't know. Told you, I'm not even here." Ade took another swig of the Macallan.

"Thing is, all the evidence had to be turned in. Case closed. Everything is being buried as we speak." Mac took the bottle from him. "The end comes not with mighty firing of weapons or grand pronouncements, but with a bureaucrat's

pen. A couple signed slips of paper and everything's gone."

"So now you know?" Chike asked. "The eruptions, the blue haze, Lifthrasir?"

Mac laughed. "The thing about justice is that sometimes it has to move around the law. Take Spookbot over there. He turned in all of his case notes and turned over the evidence to the deputy chief." Mac lit up a Redi-Smoke. "I, on the other hand, may have requisitioned a notebook or two." Mac winked at Chike.

"That better not mean more paperwork for me to have to fill out," Ade said.

"Merely returning unclaimed property to its rightful owner." Mac turned to Elia. "Does that cross mean anything to you or did you find it in one of your forays?"

A fine filigree of wrinkles framed her small mouth when she smiled. Such a horrible, alien smile. "Where I come from, there is no concept known as God. There is only life or death. The in-between has no intrinsic value. Attachments are meaningless. We are what we were born to be. I am Xa'nthi, warrior class. My kind are bred for battle. Here on your world, there is more. There is . . . connection. Meaning. Things worth dying for."

Mac tossed the notebook to her. "I trust you know what to do with it."

"I have a few ideas."

"One way or another," Mac said, "we need to take the fight to them."

• • •

Mac waited in the doorway to his apartment. The lights automatically burned to life, illuminating the room to perfect ambience. His place, little more than a hovel, was dark and had a cloying moisture to the air, a faint hint of mildew to everything. He collapsed into his bed, exhausted but not sleepy. A single disheveled comforter covered his mattress. Four pillows were piled at the head of the bed, three more than he needed, but some nights he shoved the others to his side and it left the illusion that his bed wasn't empty. Nights like tonight, however, that wouldn't be enough. He needed to keep moving, so as not to have to think. To think meant swelling on the anxiousness that filled his ear. The emptiness. Kiersten occupied a space in his heart. Not a large space. There wasn't room for anything or anyone to occupy a large space in his heart. The space she took up was more like a wedge, something that propped a door shut, staving off the rushing darkness and loneliness that awaited him once it was gone. And she was gone.

Mac reached inside his jacket for his Redi-Smokes, only to realize the package was empty. He crumpled it up and threw it against the wall. His hands trembled. He needed another dose of Stim, but at the same time, didn't. Nor did he want a drink. His soul itched, but he couldn't quite find the right way to scratch it.

The nagging voice left him unable to find a comfortable position in bed. The day's events flitted through his mind, and a strange anxious-ness, a longing, filled his heart. The case wasn't closed, not really. Whoever murdered Kiersten was still out there, drawing breath and living life. And once again, he couldn't be the man she needed him to be. He needed something to take the edge off. It was more than late-night horni-ness. He just needed some sort of respite, and peace was not soon in coming. Not for people like him.

Finally he settled on the idea of a compan-ion. It wasn't as if he hadn't paid for tail before. Those relationships were pure, a simple transac-tion. Base need met with commerce. No expec-tations. No investments. No commitment. No judgment. Then and now, Kiersten haunted him. Then, knowing that he couldn't be with her without tearing her down, he had retreated to the bartered embrace of companions. Now, with her gone, he sought solace in the illusion of relationship. In the illusion that someone cared about him and would hold him in the nights. In the illusion that he wasn't the failure he knew himself to be.

The call house said they'd send a companion right over. Five minutes later, the front alarm sounded at the outer door of his building. When he checked the vid screen, a woman in a raincoat, broad hat, and sunglasses that covered nearly half her face peered back at him. He buzzed her in. Wearing only a white tank top over pin-striped boxers, he flopped on the edge of his bed while he waited for her. The door opened, half closed—like a held breath—then shut all the way. She didn't have to knock on the entryway frame or give a polite cough to let him know she was there.

She was small, much smaller than he would have guessed from her appearance on the vid screen. Smooth brown hair pulled back into a bun, rimless glasses, and a moue with a garish shade of red lipstick smeared across it, which made her mouth look huge. Like a fussy librar-ian, except the way the raincoat cinched tight at the waist and revealed her generous cleavage he knew that she wore nothing underneath.

"Ident chip?" She held out her hand, waiting for him to place his in it.

"Business up front, I see." Mac held out his hand. She waved her portable scanner over it.

"Mac Peterson," she read from her scanner.

"At your service." Mac reached up and twitched her glasses free of her nose. She remained perfectly still, only her eyes tracking his movements. He set the glasses down on the mantle over his bed. "And you are?"

"Olga. Do you need a last name?"

"No."

Confident in her charms, she relaxed, her head canted to the side and her lips parted a little. Her hands trailed down his side, resting playfully just below his waist. Her weight leaned into him, and by instinct his arms wrapped around her. As if in a practiced dance, she pushed him away, taking a half step backward herself. She undid the belt holding the coat shut. Draped only by the coat, her naked silhouette approached him. A provocative smile crossed her lips. She planted her hand dead center in his chest and shoved him onto the bed. Strad-dling him, her fingers dug into his hair to draw him close, plunging her tongue into his mouth, long and hard. His hands wriggled at his boxers. She batted them away, not breaking the kiss. Her hands slipped within the band of his underwear. As he lost himself in the moment, he let out an easy sigh.

A primitive part of his brain, an echo of his soldier's instinct, alerted him that something wasn't right. The doors. Like a held breath. Held too long. The shadows on the other side of the room shifted. His dampener jacket rustled from where it hung across the room. A red dot gleamed in his direction and a figure rushed from the darkness. His Cougar PT-10 was under his pillow, but Mac barely had time to shift Olga's weight out of the way to absorb the brunt of the attack. That was when the slight charge at the back of his neck stabbed at him and his world went black.

• • •

Mac hated being knocked unconscious. He hated the wave of nausea that accompanied coming to. He hated the pounding in his head, like kids running up and down wood stairs. He hated the dizziness and disorientation as if he'd been on a drunken bender and needed to remember where he had passed out. Mac's first thought was that the companion and her accomplice might have run a Murphy game on him. The problem was that with companionship having been made legal, there was little to gain by a pro and her erstwhile pimp rolling a john for whatever credits they could scrounge, especially futile with ident chips. Even if they tossed his place, they were in Old Town. There weren't exactly a lot of eccentric wealthy people living there by choice. No, there had to be something else.

Seated upright, Mac didn't change his slumped posture, careful to feign continued unconsciousness while he assessed his situation. His shoulders burned, but Mac was happy to feel anything. His arms were behind him, each hand zip-tied to a part of the chair, which gave him little wiggle room. Still able to wangle his fingers. Though they were cold and increasingly numb. His legs weren't bound to the chair, but his feet burned with a thousand pinpricks, as they had fallen asleep. His muscles stretched tight, each bruise and cut rose to the surface of his attention, throbbing reminders of his ill-tended accumulation of hurts. He allowed himself a moment of vanity, feeling ridiculous in his tank top and boxers. Mac chanced opening an eye and craning his head up as much as possible. From the look of things, he was in a warehouse of some sort. One with the distinctive odor of chemicals. He made out a few approaching figures, so he shut his eyes.

"What did you summon me down here for?" Mac recognized the voice of Charleston Ptacek.

"We have Peterson," Olga said.

"So? Who told you to do that?"

"Your boy brought me. We can't afford the loose end. It's the Kiersten Wybrow scenario all over again."

"So you brought me down here to sort out your mess?"

"We tried it your way, look where it got us. Now we do it ours."

"No point in pretending you can't hear us, Mr. Peterson," Ptacek said. "We've gone through a lot of trouble to accommodate you."

"You shouldn't have put yourself out." Mac sat up straight, adjusting for the dull ache that had settled in his lower back.

"Are you stupid?"

"Immensely." An empty warehouse, its disposable construction little more than a giant metal barn. A heavy door on a thick frame separating this room from the next. Mac tested the ties. He'd have better luck going through the chair itself. No jacket. No Cougar PT-10. He didn't have a lot to work with. Mac turned to his female captor. "I'm guessing Olga's not your real name."

"You've stirred up quite the little furor over the last couple of days. Your name came up so often I had to meet you for myself," Olga said. "You've certainly managed to piss off a lot of people."

"Well, they say a man's life should be measured by the quality of his enemies. By any measure, my life is shit."

"Putting on a brave front. I like that. A little coarse, but not without your charms."

"I've been told that I have my own brand of charm."

"You should have dropped all of this. Instead, you run off to tell the Carmillon . . . what? What did you hope to accomplish?" Ptacek marched by a table. He inspected a few of the instruments, holding up the occasional blade or screwdriver for Mac's scrutiny. Ptacek made exaggerated faces of disgust at the possible destructive use of each implement before setting them back down.

"What's this all about?" Mac asked.

"I doubt you'd understand. Though it all comes back to your jumpers in a way."

"The apocalyptos?"

"My theory is that they subconsciously suspect the truth." Ptacek paced the floor, going back and forth with the haughtiness of a gloating hyena. "When confronted with ideas so much bigger than themselves, ideas which shatter the carefully constructed paradigms they live in, some people can't face the utter futility of their lives."

"What sort of big ideas?" Mac asked.

"That we aren't alone. That we aren't the center of the universe. That there is a whole other dimension to reality that sometimes bleeds into ours. That there may be wars fought on whole different planes of existence, all around us, that help determine our destiny. That our lives are not our own."

"It's what you were talking about with the aliens, the idea exchange, the accident which left the . . . tears . . . in the sky."

"That story isn't the real story. Not the whole of it, anyway. It goes much, much deeper."

"What's the big plan? You want to take over the world?"

"No, son, we already have. Don't look so shocked. The world as you know it ended years ago, smothered to death in its sleep. Ending

with a whimper. We've been here for a generation now. Blended into your world on your terms and you never noticed. We attended your schools, climbed to the tops of your corporations, embedded ourselves in every aspect of your society: finance, media, science and technology, military, politics, religion. That was Phase One."

"Let me guess, Phase Two: terraforming Earth to suit your needs."

"Very good, Mr. Peterson."

"You give me too much credit. I don't get any of this. Kiersten was undercover investigating the Easton MS crew. During one of their 'forays,' she runs across your little operation. What it is, I'm still not sure. All I have is your version of coming clean."

"Olga is also a member of that esteemed group."

"You expect me to believe that you two are aliens? You don't really look like one."

"What'd you expect? Scales and a tail?" Olga asked.

"I . . ." Mac didn't know what he expected. Little gray men with big heads and large eyes. Blue giants with whole new ways of life. Horned warriors set on conquering. But he'd read a lot of fantasy stories when he was younger.

"Something like that."

"It'd be hard to blend in with your people that way."

"Case should've been closed, but you kept digging," Ptacek said. "That was always your problem. You don't know when to leave well enough alone and stop digging. You have to keep pushing and pushing until everything around you is left in ruin."

"This time it was because my partner doesn't like loose ends and becomes grouchy and suspicious when delivered a patsy with a great big bow on him. Much more so when said patsy has people who care about him. So now we start nosing around and someone makes a ham-fisted attack on us. Which meant we were on the right track, we just didn't know how to get to you."

"The subsequent attack was unfortunate. That wasn't us," Ptacek said.

"That was my bad." Another figure stepped out from the shadows. About six feet tall, a solid build but not overly muscled. A black vest, worn open, revealed a muscled, sweaty chest. Camo military fatigues and combat boots finished off his look. Clean shaven and bald, a band covered his eyes. He removed it to give Mac a more clear inspection. A dermal overlay procedure had been done, but the man had an implant much like Ade's, though without any tubing or accessories.

"Allow me to present—" Ptacek said.

"Harley Wilson," Mac finished.

"You don't seem that surprised."

"I was beginning to suspect. Once we started thinking about who all was after Harley, none had enough motivation to want him dead. Quite the opposite. The only one who would benefit from his death would be him. Then I thought about all of your prosthetics and thought it would be real easy to create enough material to stage a murder scene. Score some bioteched organs and two new souls join the army of apocalyptos leaping into the void."

"It seems I was remiss in underestimating you, Mr. Peterson. My colleagues, though less subtle, have the right idea."

"Nice eye. A friend of mine has one like it." Mac worked the ties against the chair. He only needed a little more time.

"Not like this one. This right here is the latest generation of wetware," Harley said. "A gift from my employers."

"It still has a few kinks. Like signals getting crossed or piggy-backed on when you're transmitting to your bosses. Or vice versa."

"You're referring to the Quavay Middleton incident. More sloppy work, really. But young Master Harley is quite adept at cleaning up his messes. It's why we continue him in our employ."

"I like to keep things simple," Mac said. "You're the bad guy. All I need to know is which one of you killed Kiersten."

"Kiersten got too close. A casualty of the truth. She was killed by a larger plan. Faceless corporations, collateral damage from an errant memo."

"All this shit—the energy fallout, the terraforming, the colonization—all that is too big for me. All I need to know is who did the deed."

"Harley, of course." Ptacek turned to walk out. "And I'll leave you to his tender mercies."

Baraka backhanded Mac across the face before Ptacek left the room. A wan smile crossed the executive's face as he pushed through the door. Baraka's ham-sized fist landed several blows in Mac's ribs. Without his jacket to absorb some of the force, a bone cracked. Each punch rattled the framework of the chair. Mac was glad to already be sitting as his legs went rubbery. Baraka squatted low, meeting Mac at eye level. Mac met the man's intense silence by spitting in his face. Unmoved, Baraka patiently wiped the sputum from his face, reached for Mac's left hand, and snapped his pinky finger. His body convulsed, a shudder as a wave of fresh pain washed through him. His face twisted in agony.

A crash came from down the hallway, followed by a rush of raised voices that soon became pointed shouts. Screams erupted, trailing the staccato pop of automatic weapon fire. Mac only needed a window of opportunity, but he would have to act quickly. Adrenaline surged in his system, coasting on a wave of panic. The world slowed to stop-motion.

At the first sounds of ruckus, a well-trained Baraka sprang up and brought to bear Mac's Cougar PT-10. Mac leaned forward in his chair and pushed to his feet, charging at Baraka. Baraka drew down on him. Mac smashed into him, leading with the edge of the chair. Baraka got off a shot. The heat of the discharge singed Mac's cheek, but he dived, barely avoiding the bullet's path. The impact demolished the chair enough for him to slip his bonds.

Baraka swung around and pistol-whipped him with a blow to the side of the head. Mac returned with a punch, hammering down, causing the gun to clatter across the floor toward the thick door. His initial blows deflected, Mac charged again. Fists flying with abandon, he whirled and threw himself against Baraka.

Baraka lashed out, two chops to the sides of Mac's neck. The muscles went numb and a shard of pain jolted into Mac's skull. In desperation, Mac dashed his skull into Baraka's, the force of which sent Mac reeling as he remembered too late that much of Baraka's skull had been replaced with metal to accommodate his eye. Mac clamped his teeth down and succeeded only in smearing the blood on his lip in an attempt to wipe it off.

Lunging again, not wanting to give Baraka time or space to put his training and youth to use, Mac clawed at him then wrapped his hairy, bare legs around him, wrestling until he found himself on top of Baraka. He hated that he was self-conscious to the point of distraction that he was clad only in underwear and his junk was so vulnerable. Twisting, drawing his attacker along with him, they tumbled through the doorway. Baraka slipped in an elbow to his head before Mac could get him sufficiently entangled.

The next room sounded like it held a barely contained war. A couple of people skittered down the hallway; a few wore protective filter masks and gloves. They startled both men, but Baraka used the opportunity to slip from Mac's grasp. Mac dodged Baraka's combat boot, which landed only inches from his head. He couldn't imagine the state of his skull had the blow connected. He neither was in the mood nor had the luxury to fight fair. Baraka kicked out again, but Mac rolled then scampered after the gleaming metal. Too late, Baraka realized what Mac was going for.

Mac fired off a shot through the red target of Baraka's eye before he realized he'd even squeezed the trigger.

No joy. No relish. Only action.

Mac bent down to inspect the body. Putting his feet up to Baraka's, he decided the other man's boots were a good enough fit, certainly better than his bare feet. Ditto the camo pants.

The air grew thick, and Mac had a difficult time breathing. The gun battle hit tanks, releasing chemicals into the air. Bullets pocked the wall inches from him. Strays from the gunfight on the other side of the door, but Mac couldn't worry about that. He took cover behind a nearby counter. Two dead bodies had fallen on each other at the end of a hallway. The gunfire stopped. Mac peeked around the corner of the counter.

Ade's twin semiautomatic crowd-control machine guns pointed directly at Charleston Ptacek. "Everyone stay right where they are!"

Mac eased out from his hiding spot. Ade glanced at him, and something akin to relief flickered across his face. "How'd you find me?"

"Finally was able to backtrace the signal that hijacked my eye and thought I'd bring some friends to the party." Ade upticked his chin toward Elia and members of the Carmillon. He then turned his attention to Mac's wardrobe. "I don't want to burst your moment or anything, but I really hope you don't think the glasses help with your look when you're dressed like an army clown."

"Beats running around in my drawers. Don't ask."

"Are you here to arrest us, Officer? Even if you were to go through the motions of detaining me, Mr. Peterson's presence in the case, much less the Carmillon, would be enough for our team of lawyers to sink any criminal case brought against us."

"Nope, I just came for my friend," Ade said. "I think we all know there's no case to be made here. The bosses wouldn't let that happen. You see, the way I heard tell is that not everyone is in agreement with your planet's plans for Earth. Some of you, during your time here, became sympathetic to us lowly meatbags. Even went so far as to defect and join the resistance. You'll want to leave my boy be."

"My mother was a bit of a control freak," said Ptacek. "Remarkable woman, really. A force of nature. She had to have things her way. On every point. No matter how big or small the issue was, she was all in, fighting tooth and nail, as it were, to make sure things came out her way. An indiscriminate waste of energy, if you ask me. Now me? I'm a go along to get along sort of man. I keep my eye on the prize. You see, eighty percent of the time, what other people want doesn't matter; that is, doesn't interfere with my agenda. So I let them have their way. I put up token resistance; they feel they've won something and go off mollified. Now that last twenty percent, that's what matters. Those are the battles worth fighting. That's where wars are won and lost. Me? I'm a bureaucrat. Strictly middle management. I'm sure you can be accommodated before this escalates to an even greater mess."

"So what you're saying is that there's someone shitting on your head while you shit on mine," Mac said.

"If my vocabulary were stripped of all polysyllabic words, then yes. We all have bosses. The same bosses who cover the murder of one of their own. Who probably wouldn't blink twice about another unfortunate accident, but there's only so much they are willing to stomach. This matter is done."

"Another memo and it's all done."

"Not especially gratifying, but yes."

Mac bundled up his mouth in a swallow of resolve, determined to bottle up the chasm yawning inside him. The serpent in his belly stirred. Anger rattled, his grief a rearing with a hiss. His Cougar PT-10 drew a bead on Charleston Ptacek before his mind caught up to what was going on. And he shot Charleston Ptacek.

"Obviously self-defense." Ade towered over the crumpled body.

"Obviously." Mac sidled across from him, also peering down. "You all may want to get out of here."

Ade patted his shoulder as he went by, leaving him to his feelings. Mac searched the space. It gradually dawned on him why it seemed so familiar. It was a Stim production lab. Obvi-

ously funded by the Lifthrasir Group. Finding a gallon jug filled with a liquid, he sniffed it and judged it sufficiently flammable. He punched a hole in it with a screwdriver and let the liquid pool before he poured a trail of it to the front door, where he met Ade.

"Everyone out?"

"All of our people. The rats scattered at the first shots."

"Good enough."

Mac lit a Redi-Smoke and took a long drag from it. Then he tossed it.

A blue flame, like an electric arc, swept along the liquid path into the building. Tanks erupted into a blossom of orange and red flames. The rush of intense heat like a long-held breath released.

• • •

No matter the state of the economy, construction continued in Waverton. They continued building to provide the hope of a better tomorrow. Neighborhoods were razed to build new ones. The words "Escape while you can" had been spray-painted along the wall of the remaining husk of a building—which had been condemned as the site of an illegal Stim lab. Bud victims shuffled about the remains of the building, without words, sifting through the debris, scavenging for anything useful.

"What do you think?" Mac asked.

"Life is pain. You have to learn how to take it."

"Or dish it out."

They watched the Bud colony march about. The spires of Waverton loomed all around them. The media spun the story. The Lifthrasir Group was still hailed as pioneers and saviors. The world continued to transform around them. But they had to find a way to muddle through.

"Hope it was worth it. You're on their radar now."

"You too."

"We didn't really do any good. Lifthrasir wasn't just one empty building," Ade said.

"Yeah, but it felt good." Mac instinctively reached for a Redi-Smoke. Instead, he slipped a toothpick in his mouth and waited out the craving.

"Like a two-year-old's temper tantrum."

"Yeah, but the occasional temper tantrum has its place."

"That's fine. Just don't ask me to change your ass."

MADELINE ASHBY

BE SEEING YOU

(2015)

"DOESN'T IT GET, like, distracting? Hearing me breathing?" Hwa asked.

Only at first, her boss said.

Her feet pounded the pavement. She ducked under the trees that made up the Fitzgerald Causeway Arboretum. Without the rain pattering on the hood of her jacket, she could hear the edges of Síofra's voice a little better. The implant made sure she got most of the bass tones as a rumble that trickled down her spine. Consonants and sibilants, though, tended to fizzle out.

You get up earlier than I do, so I've had to adjust.

Hwa rounded the corner to the Fitzgerald Hub. It swung out wide into the North Atlantic, the easternmost edge of the city, a ring of green on the flat gray sea. Here the view was best. Better even than the view from the top of Tower Five, where her boss had his office. Here you could forget the oil rig at the city's core, the plumes of fire and smoke, the rusting hon-

eycomb of containers that made up Tower One where Hwa lived. Here you couldn't even see the train. It screamed along the track overhead, but she heard only the tail end of its wail as the rain diminished.

"It's better to get a run in before work. Better for the metabolism."

So I've heard.

Síofra had a perfect metabolism. It was a combination of deep brain stimulation that kept him from serotonin crashes, a vagus nerve implant that regulated his insulin production, and whatever gentle genetic optimization he'd had in utero. He ate everything he wanted. He fell asleep for eight hours a night, no interruptions. He was a regular goddamn Ubermensch.

Hwa just had a regular old-fashioned human body. No permanent implants. No tweaking. She'd eaten her last slice of bread the day before joining the United Sex Workers of Canada as a bodyguard. Now that she worked for Lynch as the bodyguard for their heir apparent, the only thing that had changed about her diet was the amount of coffee she drank.

"Look out your window," she said.

Give me your eyes.

She shook her head. Could he see that? Maybe. She looked around for botflies. She couldn't see any, but that didn't mean anything. "I'm not wearing them."

Why not?

"They're expensive. I could slip and fall while I'm running."

Then we would give you new ones.

"Wouldn't that come out of my pay?"

A soft laugh that went down to the base of her spine. *Those were the last owners of this city. Lynch is different.*

Hwa wasn't so sure about that. Lynch rode in on a big white copter and promptly funded a bunch of infrastructure improvement measures, but riggers were still leaving. Tower One was starting to feel like a ghost town.

Then again, the Lynch family *was* building an alternative reactor, right in the same place where the milkshake straw poked deep into the Flemish Pass Basin and sucked up the black stuff. It was better insulated, they said, under all that water. It just meant the oil was going away.

All towns change, Hwa. Even company towns. We're better for this community than the previous owners. You'll see.

She rolled her neck until it popped. All the way over at the top of Tower Five, her boss hissed in sympathy. "Look out your window," she reminded him.

Fine, fine. An intake of breath. He was getting up. From his desk, or from his bed? *Oh,* he murmured.

Hwa stared into the dawn behind the veil of rain. It was a line of golden fire on a dark sea, thinly veiled behind shadows of distant rain. "I time it like this, sometimes," she said. "Part of why I get up early."

I see.

She heard thunder roll out on the waves, and in a curious stereo effect, heard the same

sound reverberating through whatever room Síofra was in.

May I join you, tomorrow?

Hwa's mouth worked. She was glad he couldn't see her. The last person she'd had a regular running appointment with was her brother. Which meant she hadn't run with anyone in three years. Then again, maybe it would be good for Síofra to learn the city from the ground up. He spent too much time shut up behind the gleaming ceramic louvers of Tower Five. He needed to see how things were on the streets their employers had just purchased.

She grinned. "Think you can keep up with me?"

Oh, I think I can manage.

• • •

Of course, Síofra managed just fine. He showed up outside Tower One at four thirty in the morning bright-eyed and bushy-tailed as a cartoon mascot. Like everything else about him, even his running form was annoyingly perfect. He kept his chin up and his back straight throughout the run. He breathed evenly and smoothly and carried on a conversation without any issues. At no point did he complain of a stitch in his side, or a bone spur in his heel, or tension in his quads. Nor did he suggest that they stretch their calves first, or warm up, or anything like that. He just started running.

A botfly followed them the entire way.

"Do we really need that?" Hwa asked. "We can ping for help no problem, if something happens." She gestured at the empty causeway. "Not that anything's going to happen."

"What if you have a seizure?" her boss asked.

Hwa almost pulled up short. It took real and sustained effort not to. She kept her eyes on the pavement instead. They had talked about her condition only once. Most people never brought it up. Maybe that was a Canadian thing. After all, her boss had worked all over the world. They were probably a lot less polite in other places.

"My condition's in my halo," she muttered.

"Pardon?"

"My halo has all my medical info," she said, a little louder this time. She shook her watch. "If my specs detect a change in my eye movement, they broadcast my status on the emergency layer. Everyone can see it. Everyone with the right eyes, anyway."

"But you don't wear your specs when you're running," he said, and pulled forward.

The route took them along the Demasduwit Causeway, around Tower Two, down the Sinclair Causeway, and back to Tower Two. It was a school day, which meant Hwa had to scope New Arcadia Secondary before Joel Lynch arrived for class. This meant showering and dressing in the locker room, which meant she had to finish at a certain time, which meant eating on schedule, too. If she ate before the run, she tended to throw up.

She was going to explain all this, when Síofra slowed down and pulled up to Hwa's favorite twenty-four-hour cart and held up two fingers. "Two number sixes," he said. He stood first on one leg and then another, pulling his calf up behind him as he did. From behind the counter, old Jorge squinted at him until Hwa jogged up to join him. Then he smiled.

"You have a friend!" He made it sound like she'd just run a marathon. Which it felt like she had—keeping up with Síofra had left her legs trembling and her skin dripping.

"He's my boss." She leaned over and spat out some of the phlegm that had boiled up to her throat during the run. "What he said. And peameal." She blinked at Síofra through sweat. He was looking away, probably reading something in his lenses. "You like peameal?"

"Sorry?"

"Peameal. Bacon. Do you like it?"

"Oh. I suppose."

She glanced at Jorge. "Peameal. On the side."

Jorge handed them their coffees while the rest of the breakfast cooked. Now the city was waking up, and the riggers joining the morning shift were on their way to the platform. A few of them stood blinking at the other carts as they waited for them to open up.

"How did you know my order?" Hwa asked.

Síofra rolled his neck. It crunched. He was avoiding the answer. Hwa already suspected what he would say. "I see the purchases you make with the corporate currency."

She scowled. "I don't always have the eggs baked in avocado, you know. Sometimes I have green juice."

"Not since the cucumbers went out of season."

Hwa stared. Síofra cocked his head. "You're stalking me."

"I'm not stalking you. This is just how Lynch does things. We know what all our people buy in the canteen at lunch, because they use our watches to do it. It helps us know what food to buy. That way everyone can have their favorite thing. The schools here do the same thing—it informs the farm floors what to grow. This is no different."

Hwa sighed. "I miss being union."

• • •

Joel Lynch's vehicle drove him to the school's main entrance exactly fifteen minutes before the first bell. Hwa stood waiting for him outside the doors. He waved their way in—the school still did not recognize her face, years after she'd dropped out—and smirked at her.

"How are your legs?" he asked.

"Christ, does my boss tell you *everything*?"

"Daniel just said I should go easy on you today!" Joel tried hard to look innocent. "And that maybe we didn't have to do leg day today, if you didn't really want to."

"You trying to get out of your workout?"

"Oh, no! Not at all! I was just thinking that—"

"Good, because we're still doing leg day. My job is protecting you, and how I protect you is making you better able to protect yourself.

Somebody tries to take you, I need you to crush his instep with one kick and then run like hell. Both of which involve your legs."

"So, leg day."

Hwa nodded. "Leg day."

You can crush someone's instep with one kick?

Hwa rolled her eyes and hoped her specs caught it. "Of course I can," she subvocalized.

I think I'd pay good money to see that.

"Well it's a good thing I'm on the payroll, then."

The school day proceeded just like all the others. Announcements. Lectures. Worksheets. French. Past imperfect, future imperfect. Lunch. People staring at Joel, then sending each other quick messages. Hwa saw it all in the specs—the messages drifting across her vision like dandelion fairies. In her vision, the messages turned red when Joel's name came up. For the most part it didn't. While she wore the uniform and took the classes just like the other students, they knew why she was there. They knew she was watching. They knew about her old job.

"Hwa?"

Hwa turned away from the station where Joel was attempting squats. Hanna Oleson wore last year's volleyball T-shirt and mismatched socks. She also had a wicked bruise on her left arm. And she wouldn't quite look Hwa in the eye.

"Yeah?" Hwa asked.

"Coach says you guys can have the leg press first."

"Oh, good. Thanks." She made Hanna meet her gaze. The other girl's eyes were bleary, red-rimmed. Shit. "What happened to your arm?"

"Oh, um . . . I fell?" Hanna weakly flailed the injured arm. "During practice? And someone pulled me up? Too hard?"

Hwa nodded slowly. "Right. Sure. That happens."

Hanna smiled. It came on sudden and bright. Too sudden. Too bright. "Everything's fine, now."

"Glad to hear it. You should put some arnica on that."

"Okay. I'll try that."

She tried to move away, but Hwa wove in front of her. "I have some at my place," she said. "I'm in Tower One. Seventh floor, unit seven. Easy to remember."

Hanna nodded without meeting Hwa's eye. "Okay."

Hwa moved, and Hanna shuffled away to join the volleyball team. She turned back to Joel. He'd already put the weights down. She was about to say something about his slacking off, when he asked: "Do you know her?"

Hwa turned and looked at Hanna. She stood a little apart from the others, tugging on a sweatshirt over her bruised arm. She took eyedrops from the pocket and applied them first to one eye, and then the other. "I know her mother," Hwa said.

• • •

Mollie Oleson looked a little rounder than Hwa remembered her. She couldn't remember their last appointment together, which meant it had probably happened months ago. Mollie was more of a catch-as-catch-can kind of operator—she only listed herself as available to the USWC 314 when she felt like it. It kept her dues low and her involvement minimal. But as a member she was entitled to the same protection as a full-timer. And that meant she'd met Hwa.

Hwa sidled up to her in the children's section of the Benevolent Irish Society charity shop. Mollie stood hanging little baggies of old fabtoys on a pegboard. "We close in fifteen minutes," she said, under her breath.

"Even for me?" Hwa asked.

"Hwa!" Mollie beamed, and threw her arms around Hwa. Like her daughter, she was one of those women who really only looked pretty when she was happy. Unlike her daughter, she was better at faking it.

"What are you doing here?"

Hwa shrugged. "I got a new place. Thought it was time for some new stuff."

Mollie's smile faltered. "Oh, yeah . . ." She adjusted a stuffed polar bear on a shelf so that it faced forward. "How's that going? Working for the Lynches, I mean?"

"The little one is all right," Hwa said. "Skinny little bugger. I'm training him."

Mollie gave a terse little smile. "Well, good luck to you. About time you got out of the game, I'd say. A girl your age should be thinking about the future. You don't want to wind up . . ." She gestured around the store, rather than finishing the sentence.

"I saw Hanna at school, today. Made me think to come here."

Mollie's hands stilled their work. "Oh? How was she? I haven't seen her since this morning." She looked out the window to the autumn darkness. "Closing shift, and all."

Hwa nodded. "She's good." She licked her lips. It was worth a shot. She had to try. "Her boyfriend's kind of a dick, though."

Mollie laughed. "Hanna doesn't have a boyfriend! She has no time, between school and volleyball and her job."

"Her job?"

"Skipper's," Mollie said. "You know, taking orders, bussing tables, the like. It's not much, but it's a job."

"Right," Hwa said. "Well, my mistake. I guess that guy was just flirting with her."

"Well, I'll give you the employee discount, just for sharing that little tidbit. Now I have something to tease her with, eh?"

"Oh, I wouldn't do that," Hwa said. "Girls her age are so sensitive."

. . .

At home, Hwa used her Lynch employee login to access the Prefect city management system. Lynch installed it overnight during a presumed brownout, using a day-zero exploit to deliver the viral load that was their surveillance overlay. It was easier than doing individual installations, Síofra had explained to her. Some kids in what was once part of Russia had used a similar exploit to gain access to a Lynch reactor in Kansas. That was fifteen years ago.

Now it was a shiny interface that followed Hwa wherever she went. Or rather, wherever she let it. Her refrigerator and her washroom mirror were both too old for it. So it lived in her specs, and in the display unit Lynch insisted on outfitting her with. That made it the most expensive thing in what was a very cheap studio apartment.

"Prefect, show me Oleson, Hanna," she said.

The system shuffled through profiles until it landed on two possibilities, each fogged over. One was Hanna. The other was a woman by the name of Anna Olsen. Maybe it thought Hwa had misspoken.

"Option one." Hanna's profile became transparent as Anna's vanished. It solidified across the display, all the photos and numbers and maps hanging and shimmering in Hwa's vision. She squinted. "Dimmer."

Hanna's profile dimmed slightly, and Hwa could finally get a real look at it. Like Hwa, Hanna lived in Tower One. She'd been picked up once on a shoplifting charge, two years ago. She raised her hands and gestured through all the points at which facial recognition had identified Hanna in the last forty-eight hours. Deeper than that, and she'd need archival access.

But first, she needed to call Skipper's. Rule them out. "Hi, is Hanna there?"

"Hanna doesn't work here anymore." Hwa heard beeping. The sounds of fryer alarms going off. Music. "Hello?"

Hwa ended the call.

There was Hanna on the Acoutsina Causeway, walking toward Tower One. The image was time-stamped after volleyball practice. Speedtrap checked her entering a vehicle in the driverless lane for a vehicle at 18:30. Five minutes later, she was gone. Wherever she was now, there were no cameras.

"Prefect, search this vehicle and this face together."

A long pause. *Archive access required.*

For a fleeting moment, Hwa regretted the fact

that Prefect was not a human being she could intimidate. "Is there a record in the archives?"

Archive access required.

Hwa growled a little to herself. She popped up off the floor and began to pace. She walked through the projections of Hanna's face, sliding the ribbon of stills and clips until she hit the top of the list. Today was Monday. If Hanna had sustained her injury on Friday night, then Hwa was out of luck. But Mollie had said she worked all weekend. Maybe that meant—

What are you doing?

Hwa startled. "Jesus Christ, stop doing that!"

Doing what? Síofra was trying to sound innocent. It wasn't working.

"You know exactly what," she said. "Why can't you just text, like a normal person? How do you know I wasn't having a conversation with somebody?"

Your receiver would have told me, he said.

Hwa frowned. "Can you . . . ?" She wished she had an image of him she could focus her fury on. "Can you listen in on my conversations, through my receiver?"

Only during your working hours.

"And you can just . . . tune in? All day? While I'm at school with Joel?"

Of course I can. I thought you had some excellent points to make about Jane Eyre *in Mr. Bartel's class, last week.*

Hwa plunged the heels of her hands into the sockets of her eyes. She had known this was possible, of course. She just assumed Síofra actually had other work to do, and wasn't constantly spying on her instead of accomplishing it.

"Are you bored?"

I'm sorry?

"Are you bored? At work? Is your job that boring? That you need to be tuned into my day like that?"

There was a long pause. She wondered for a moment if he'd cut out. *You watch Joel and I watch you,* he said. *That is my job.*

Hwa sighed. He had her, there. It was all right there in the Lynch Ltd employee handbook. She'd signed on for this level of intrusion when

she'd taken their money. He was paying, so he got to watch. She'd stood guard at enough peep shows to learn that particular lesson. Maybe she wasn't so different from her mother, after all.

You aren't supposed to be prying into your fellow classmates' lives unless they pose a credible threat to Joel. So he'd been spying on her searches, too. Of course. *I know what you're thinking, and—*

"How come I can't do this to you?" Hwa blurted. "That's what I'm thinking. I'm wondering how come I can't watch you all the time the way you watch me. Why doesn't this go both ways? Why don't I get to know when you're watching me?"

Another long pause. *Is there something about me that you would like to know?*

Oh, just everything, she thought. The answer came unbidden and she shut her eyes and clenched her jaw and squashed it like a bug crawling across her consciousness.

"Are you coming running tomorrow?"

Of course I am.

• • •

Síofra had a whole route planned. He showed it to her the next morning in her specs, but she had only a moment to glance over it before heading out the door.

"Why did you stay in this tower?" Síofra asked, leaning back and craning his neck to take in the brutalist heap of former containers. "We pay you well enough to afford one of the newer ones. This one has almost no security to speak of."

"You've been watching me twenty-four/seven for a solid month and you still haven't figured that one out? Corporate surveillance ain't what it used to be."

"Is it because your mother lives here?"

Hwa pulled up short. "You just don't know when to quit, do you?"

"I only wondered because you never visit her." He grinned and pushed ahead of her down the causeway.

His route took them along the Acoutsina.

They circled the first joint, and Síofra asked about the old parkette and the playground. This early, there were no children and it remained littered with beer cozies and liquor pouches. She told him about the kid who had kicked her down the slide once, and how nobody let her on the swings, and he assumed it had to do with her mother and what she did for a living. His eyes were not programmed to see her true face, or the stain dripping from her left eye down her neck to her arm and her ribs and her leg. She had tested his vision several times; he never stared, never made reference to her dazzle-pattern face. And with their connection fostered by her wearables, he probably never watched her via botfly or camera. He could spend every minute of every day observing her, and never truly see her.

They ran to the second joint of the causeway and circled the memorial for those who had died in the Old Rig. "Do you want to stop?" he asked.

It was bad luck not to pay respects. She knew exactly where her brother's name was. Síofra waited for her at the base of the monument as her steps spiraled up the mound. She slapped Tae-kyun's name lightly, like tagging him in a relay run, and kept going. Síofra had already started up again by the time she made it back down. They were almost at Tower Three when he called a halt, in a parking lot full of rides.

"Cramp," he said, pulling his calf up behind him. He placed a hand up against a parked vehicle for balance. When Hwa's gaze followed his hand, she couldn't help but see the license plate.

It was the one she'd asked Prefect to track. The one Hanna had disappeared into, last night. "I thought . . ." Hwa looked from him to the vehicle. "I thought you said—"

"I haven't the faintest idea what you're talking about, Hwa." He smirked. Then he appeared to check something in his lenses. "Goodness, look at the time. I have an early meeting. I think I'll just pick up one of these rides here, and drive back to the office. Are you all right finishing the run alone?"

Hwa frowned at him. He winked at her. She smiled. "Yeah," she said. "I'm good here."

He gestured at the field of rides and snapped his fingers at one of them. It lit up. Its locks opened. She watched him get into it and drive away. Now alone, Hwa peered into the vehicle. Nothing left behind in any of the seats. No dings or scratches. She looked around at the parking lot. Empty. Still dark. She pulled her hood up and took a knee. She fussed with her shoelaces with one hand while her other fished in the pocket of her vest. The joybuzzer hummed between her fingers as she stood. And just like that, the trunk unlocked.

Hanna was inside. Bound and gagged. And completely asleep.

"Shit," Hwa muttered. Then the vehicle chirped. Startled, Hwa scanned the parking lot. Still empty. The ride was being summoned elsewhere. It rumbled to life. If Hwa let it go now, she would lose Hanna. In the trunk, Hanna blinked awake. She squinted up at Hwa. Behind her gag, she began to scream.

"It's okay, Hanna." Hwa threw the trunk door even wider, and climbed in. She pulled it shut behind her as it began to move. "You're okay. We're okay." The vehicle lurched. She heard the lock snap shut again as the ride locked itself. "We're okay," she repeated. "We're going to be okay."

• • •

Hwa busied herself untying Hanna as the ride drove itself. "Tell me where we're going," Hwa said.

"It's my fault," Hanna was saying. "He told me not to talk to Benny."

"Benny works at Skipper's?" Hwa picked the tape off Hanna's wrists.

"I told him I was just being nice." Hanna gulped for air. She coughed. "I quit, just like he told me to, but Benny and I are in the same biology class! I couldn't just ignore him. And Jarod said if I really loved him, I'd do what he asked . . ."

"Jarod?" Hwa asked. "That's his name? What's his last name?" She needed Prefect.

Why hadn't she brought her specs? She could be looking at a map, right now. She could be finding out how big this guy was. If he had any priors.

"Why are you here?" Hanna asked. "Did my mom send you? I thought you didn't work with us anymore."

Beneath them, the buckles in the pavement burped along. They were still on the Acoutsina, then. It had the oldest roads with the most repairs. Hwa worked to quiet the alarm bell ringing in her head. Hanna's skin was so cold under her hands. She probably needed a hospital. But right now, she needed Hwa to be calm. She needed Hwa to be smart. She needed Hwa to think.

"With us?" Hwa asked.

"For the union," Hanna sniffed.

"Eh?"

The angle of the vehicle changed. They tipped down into something. Hwa heard hydraulics. They were in a lift. Tower Three. They'd parked Hanna not far from where they were then. Hwa's ears popped. She rolled up as close as possible to the opening of the trunk. She cleared her wrists and flexed her toes. She'd have one good chance when the trunk opened. If there weren't too many of them. If they didn't have crowbars. Something slammed onto the trunk. A fist. A big one, by the sound of it.

"Wakey, wakey, Hanna!"

The voice was muffled, but strong. Manic. He'd been awake for a while. Boosters? Shit. Hanna started to say something, but Hwa shushed her.

"Had enough time to think about what you did?"

Definitely boosters. That swaggering arrogance, those delusions of grandeur. Hwa listened for more voices, the sound of footsteps. She heard none. Maybe this was a solo performance.

"You know, I didn't like doing this. But you made me do it. You have to learn, Hanna."

Behind her, Hanna was crying.

"I can't have you just giving it away. It really cuts into what I'm trying to do for us."

Fingers drummed on the trunk of the ride.

"Are you ready to come out and say you're sorry?"

You're goddamn right I am, Hwa thought.

The trunk popped open. Jarod's pale, scaly face registered surprise for just a moment. Then Hwa's foot snapped out and hit him square in the jaw. He stumbled back and tried to slam the trunk shut. It landed on her leg and she yelled. The door bounced up. Not her ankle. Not her knee. Thank goodness. She rolled out.

Jarod was huge. A tall, lanky man in his early twenties, the kind of rigger who'd get made fun of by guys with more muscle while still being plenty strong enough to get the job done. He had bad skin and a three-day growth of patchy beard. He lunged for Hwa and she jumped back. He swung wide and she jumped again.

"Let me guess," she said. "You told Hanna you'd fix it with the union if she paid you her dues directly. Even though she's a minor and USWC doesn't allow those."

Jarod's eyes were red. He spat blood. He reeked of booster sweat—acrid and bitter.

"And you had her doing what, camwork?" She grinned. "I thought her eyes were red because she'd been crying. But yours look just the same. You're both wearing the same shitty lenses."

"He made me watch the locker room." Hanna sat on her knees in the trunk of the ride. Her voice was a croak. For a moment she looked so much like her mother that Hwa's heart twisted in her chest. "He said he'd edit my team's faces out—"

"Shut up!"

Jarod reached for the lid of the trunk again. He tried to slam it shut on Hanna. Hwa ran for him. He grabbed her by the shoulders. Hwa's right heel came down hard on his. The instep deflated under the pressure. He howled. She elbowed him hard under the ribs and spun halfway out of his grip. His right hand still clung to her vest. She grabbed the wrist and wedged it into the mouth of the trunk.

"Hanna! Get down!"

She slammed the lid once. Then twice. Then a third time. *He'll never work this rig again*, she thought distantly. The trunk creaked open and Jarod sank to his knees. He clutched his wrist. His hand dangled from his arm like a piece of kelp.

Behind her, she heard a slow, dry clap.

"Excellent work," Síofra said.

He stood against the ride he'd summoned. Two go-cups of coffee sat on the hood. He held one out.

"You didn't want in on that?" Hwa asked, jerking her head at the whimpering mess on the floor of the parking garage.

"Genius can't be improved upon." Síofra gestured with his cup. "We should get them to a hospital. Or a police station."

"Hanna needs a hospital." Hwa sipped her coffee. "This guy, I should report to the union. He falsified a membership and defrauded someone of dues in bad faith."

"They don't take kindly to that, in the USWC?"

Hwa swallowed hard. "Nope. Not one bit."

Síofra made a sound in his throat that sounded like purring.

• • •

During the elevator ride between the hospital and the school in Tower Two, Hwa munched a breakfast sandwich. She'd protested the presence of bread, but Síofra said the flour was mostly crickets anyway. So she'd relented. Now he stood across the elevator watching her eat.

"What?" she asked, between swallows.

"I have something to share with you."

She swiped at her mouth with the back of her hand. "Yeah?"

"I don't remember anything beyond ten years ago."

Hwa blinked. "Sorry?"

"My childhood. My youth. They're . . ." He made an empty gesture. "Blank."

She frowned. "Do you mean this like . . . emotionally?"

"No. Literally. I literally don't remember. My first memory is waking up in a Lynch hospital in South Sudan, ten years ago. They had some wells there. I was injured. They brought me in. Patched me up. They assumed I was a fixer of some sort. They don't know for which side. And apparently I had covered my tracks a little too well. I've worked for them ever since."

Hairs rose on the back of Hwa's neck. "Wow."

"As long as I can remember, I've worked for this company. I don't know any other kind of life."

"Okay," Hwa said.

"I've never lived without their presence in my life. I've never had what you might call a private life."

Oh. "Oh."

"But you have. And that's something that's different, about our experiences."

"Yeah. You could say that."

"You don't have implants," he said. "Not permanent ones, anyway. They—we—can't gather that kind of data from you. But they know everything about me. My sugars, how much I sleep, where I am, if I'm angry, my routines, even the music I listen to when I'm making dinner."

"You listen to music while you make dinner?"

"Django Reinhardt."

"Who?"

He smiled ruefully. "What I'm saying is, you're the last of a dying breed."

Hwa thought of the stain running down her body, the flaw he couldn't see. He had no idea. "Thank you?"

"You're a black swan," he said. "A wild card. Something unpredictable. Like getting into the trunk of that ride this morning."

Hwa shrugged. "Anybody could have done that. I couldn't just let Hanna go. She needed my help."

"You could have called the police. You could have called *me*. But you didn't. You took the risk yourself."

She frowned. "Are you pissed off? Is that what this is about? Because you're the one who—"

Síofra hissed. He brought his finger to his lips and shook his head softly. With his gaze, he brought her attention to the eyes at the corners of the elevator.

"I just want you to know something about me," he said, after a moment. "Something that isn't in my halo."

She smiled. "Well, thanks."

"Not a lot of other people know this about me."

"Well, it is kind of weird." She stretched up, then bent down. She looked up at him from her ragdoll position. "I mean, you are only ten years old, right? You can't even drink."

He rolled his eyes. "Here it comes."

She stood. "Or vote. Or even have your own place. Does your landlord know about this?"

He pointed at the view of the city outside the elevator. "My landlord is your landlord."

The elevator doors chimed open. They were on the school floor. Hwa had fifteen minutes to shower and put on her uniform before she met Joel.

"Hey, if you're not too busy? I kind of didn't do the last question on my physics homework. So I might need some help with that. Before I hand it in."

"I think something can be arranged."

She stood in the door. It chimed insistently. She leaned on it harder. "Did you ever go to school? After you woke up, I mean? Or are you just winging it?"

"I know what a man my age needs to know," Síofra said. "Be seeing you."

STEVEN S. LONG

KEEPING UP WITH MR. JOHNSON

(2016)

"IT'S SIX A.M., Mr. Hardwick. Please get up," the housecomp said in its pleasantly neutral, precisely modulated, feminine voice.

"All right, all right, I'm up," he said as he sat up and swung his legs off the edge of the bed. Helen rolled over and put a hand on his back; he leaned over, caressed her blonde hair, kissed her on the forehead. It didn't seem like so long ago when their morning contact would have been far more intimate, full of fire and urgency, but two decades of marriage and two kids had replaced that early passion with a calmer, more profound connection.

No more time to linger, though—another busy day ahead. He jumped in the shower, where the housecomp chased away his morning bleariness with precisely warmed water and a review of his schedule. Helen was working on her makeup when he emerged. He stood next to her at the sink and shaved. Occasionally they exchanged a comment about the kids, the apartment, some upcoming social event.

He paused in mid-shave to look at Helen as she carefully applied lipstick. Watching her do everyday things was one of the simple pleasures of his life. Any fool could see she was beautiful, but it was more than that. Unlike most of his colleagues he hadn't ditched his "starter wife" for some surgically enhanced would-be trideo star of a trophy wife. He couldn't even imagine doing that; he loved Helen, heart and soul, in a way few of his fellow SK execs would understand. He'd only ever cheated on her with one woman, and there was a damn good reason for that. They'd never talked about it, but she knew and understood. He was sure of it.

"What?" she said with that little smile of hers, the one he liked to think she reserved only for him.

"Nothing," he said, matching her smile as he returned to his shaving.

Breakfast was the usual controlled chaos: him trying to read the overnight datafeed while eating; the kids unable to sit still for long; Matilda, their housekeeper/cook, attempting to corral them with limited success; Helen chattering on about this and that. Nothing requiring his immediate attention had happened overnight, so he enjoyed the comfortable familiarity of it all without distraction.

He dressed, luxuriating in the feel of the 500-nuyen silk shirt, the 3,000-nuyen suit jacket, the gold cuff links in the shape of the Saeder-Krupp logo. He'd done some things for the corp that he didn't like to think about, but he couldn't deny that the salary they paid him made his life a lot more pleasant than it was before he met Helen. It let him provide her and the kids with anything they needed, and that was well worth giving up the freedom of his old life to join the corporate ranks.

He slipped on one of his few souvenirs of his previous life—an orichalcum ring in the shape of an ouroboros. Snakeman had made it for him years ago to mark the end of his apprenticeship, and he'd held on to it even when he'd had to let things with far greater objective value go. He felt the little tingle of power from it, a sensation as familiar and comforting as his family's voices around the breakfast table. Then he fetched his Caliban from his home office and headed for the door. "Take good care of them, Matilda," he said on his way out.

"Always, Mr. Hardwick." She looked like your typical Third World immigrant working a typical immigrant job, but she was part of his benefits package. A bodyguard for Helen and the kids, Matilda had enough cyber and bio enhancements to outdo most elite soldiers. There were no guarantees in the Sixth World, but having her around made him feel better about his family's safety.

His own bodyguards waited for him just outside the apartment door: Rapier, an elf as swift and deadly as her namesake, with looks that let her pass as arm candy right up to the point where she put two rounds in some unsuspecting fool's head; and Brutus, a huge ork with more muscle augmentation and dermal plating than anyone Hardwick had ever met.

Rapier favored him with the intimate nod of her chin they used to communicate a world of meaning in a simple gesture. He didn't return it; Helen was too close by.

"G'morning, boss," Brutus said, his voice slightly slurred by his tusks.

"Good morning. Let's go." The helicopter ride took them past Aztechnology's garish, pyramid-shaped local headquarters, then over the still-visible scar Hurricane Penelope had left on Miami a dozen years ago. City leaders now euphemistically referred to it as "Vizcaya Free Park," but the citizens called it the Vizcaya Free-Fire Zone. It was just the sort of place he used to live and work in. Flying effortlessly over it always gave him a touch of the thrill an escaped convict feels as the prison walls shrink in the distance behind him. But he paid no more attention than that, focusing on his Caliban instead; Rapier and Brutus were more than wary enough to notice any possible threat.

Soon they arrived at SK Tower. Perched atop the highest point on Lofwyr Key, the artificial island the corp built a decade ago, the Tower offered an unequaled view of Bayside Park, the Atlantic Ocean, and the Atlantis Autonomous District offshore/undersea habitat where only the *really* rich people could afford to live.

With Rapier leading and Brutus bringing up the rear, they headed inside. His assistant Ashleigh waited just inside the door marked UNCONVENTIONAL ASSETS DIVISION, same as always. "Good morning, Mr. Hardwick," she said, handing him a mug of coffee brewed the way he liked it.

"Good morning. Updates?" She filled him in on calls, calendar changes, and other details, but he only half paid attention. The truly important meeting, the one after lunch, already occupied most of his thoughts. After all, none of the day's other activities required him to risk his life.

• • •

The morning's meetings went without a hitch. Now for the main event: as head of SK Miami's

Unconventional Assets Division, he had to go talk with the unconventional assets—or "shadowrunners," as the street called them. Powerful, deniable, illegal "soldiers" the corps used in their covert wars against each other, he could hire them to do just about anything; from theft, sabotage, and personnel extraction to outright murder.

There was a problem, though—and that was why he had a job. Megacorporations, the most conventional of entities, clashed with the unconventional assets they so desperately needed. His years in both worlds made him the ideal interface between them.

The best shadowrunners were smooth as silk to work with. They'd survived on the streets, in the Matrix, among the Awakened for years; life on the edge had burned most of the stupid out of them. Professional and reliable, they lived by a code nearly as binding as a corp's bylaws. But the best never came cheap, and prime runners weren't always available on his timetable. That meant having to dig deeper into the barrel, and the end result was often as smooth as burlap.

Most of the stress of his job came from having to deal with that sort of shadowrunner: the know-it-alls, the jandering bastards, the chip-on-their-shoulders, the psychotics, the chrome-junkies, the weirdos. In his experience, the average shadowrunner was so unreliable and unprofessional that working with them was like playing roulette. But he'd keep working with them no matter how often the little white ball landed on the wrong number, because they were the only ones who could do work vital to the bottom line. As disreputable as they might be, shadowrunners filled a niche in the megacorporate ecosystem. That guaranteed him a job—as long as he got results.

Unfortunately, one of the unconventional things about unconventional assets was their refusal to come onto corp property for a meeting. The idea of being scanned, identified, recorded, watched, giving up their weapons—they'd rather stick their heads in a hell hound's mouth. He had to go to them, which meant stepping outside the safe, comfortable confines of SK turf.

Rapier and Brutus led him to a black, unmarked SK Bentley Concordat, where a corp rigger and another pair of armed guards waited. He settled into his seat and the others arranged themselves protectively around him. He'd have preferred some sort of combat van like an SK Rhino, but he had to maintain the image of Mr. Johnson. At least the car had plenty of armor and power.

The Bentley headed out the gates of SK's corporate park and into the urban jungle of Miami. As they kept driving, that jungle turned to wasteland: ruined buildings taken over by squatters; competing scrawls of graffiti everywhere; ads for the cheapest possible products and services garishly assaulting the eye. The human misery was almost palpable. Spirits of Fire and Air be praised that he didn't have to live in places like this anymore.

They drove to an old cinderblock building in a half-deserted part of the 'plex. No one had lived there for years except devil rats. In other words, just the sort of place runners liked to hold meetings.

The guards got out, weapons ready, and entered the building while Hardwick and his bodyguards waited in the Bentley. A few minutes later, they signaled all-secure and he walked in.

The interior of the building wasn't much more than an empty shell; scavengers had stripped out anything of any possible value, right down to the wiring. Rapier picked the spot she liked best for defensive purposes, near a sturdy-looking brick wall in the back. The guards set up the portable furniture they'd brought along. Not only would "the office" make things more comfortable, it gave him a bit of a psychological edge by making this place as much his turf as the runners'.

Finally he added his own magical touch: a detect enemies spell to alert him if any of the runners posed a threat. He knew some Johnsons who went further, adding a mask spell to hide their identities or an armor spell in case a runner's trigger finger got too itchy. He'd rarely found the former to be of much use, and he knew from personal experience that a lot of runners considered the latter insulting. The detect was enough for him—that, and his ouroboros ring, if necessary.

The agreed-upon signal knock on the east door came at 1230 hours precisely: chalk one up for their professionalism. The detect spell remained silent. He nodded at Rapier, who passed it on to a guard. He opened the door left-handed, his right hand near his weapon.

"Year of the dragon," said a loud voice similar to, but not quite the same as, Brutus's. That was the second signal.

"Let them in," he said, his voice firm and confident, his posture and attitude radiating competence and control. That was the only way to deal with runners: from a position of strength, whether real or illusory.

An ork—obviously a samurai from his 'ware, his weapons, his swagger—entered, followed by four others: a human, his talismans marking him as a Hermetic mage; a red-bearded dwarf with a small robot perched on his shoulder; a human decker; and another Awakened, an attractive human woman with the tattoos and accouterments of a Raccoon shaman. Pretty standard runner team, just what Operation Altitude needed.

The runners moved as a group, with a smooth wariness that showed they were skilled professionals. They took care not to do anything the *sararimen* would perceive as threatening—and that showed they were smart. He was well aware that on the street you didn't survive to become the former if you weren't the latter.

They reached the half-circle of chairs in front of the desk, stopped, fanned out cautiously. "I'm Tuskarora, leader of the Five Aces," the ork said. "These are Trismegistus, Teamster, Ryder, and Atsa," he continued, pointing at each of the others in turn.

"Good afternoon. You can call me Mr. Johnson," Hardwick said, speaking the words of the old ritual. "Please be seated." He sat down;

Rapier, Brutus, and his other guards remained standing.

"Thank you for meeting me today. Ephraim Fivestars tells me you're pros, and he's never steered me wrong before."

"He says the same about you."

Hardwick smiled thinly. "Good. Down to business, then."

"Let's make sure we're clear up front, chummer," Tuskarora said. "I've done way too many runs where a suit didn't tell me everything I needed to know, and I'm sick of that drek. The more, and more accurate, intel you provide us with, the better our chances of success. If you lie to us, if you hide useful data from us, if you make our job harder than it needs to be because of some secret agenda—I'll burn you. We clear?"

Hardwick didn't speak, just stared straight at the big ork. Brutus didn't move, but Rapier edged closer to him.

Tuskarora grinned, his gaze flicking between elf and human. "You two, huh? Nice going, Johnson. Never got to visit a dandelion patch myself—what's it like? They as cold in bed as they are on the street?"

Rapier flushed, but did nothing. Hardwick could sense the tension in her. He felt his own anger rising, damped it down, shoved it aside. It wouldn't help him here. "That's none of your concern."

"Bulldrek." Tuskarora leaned forward to emphasize his words. "No written contracts in this biz. It's all trust between you and me"—he pointed at Hardwick's wedding ring—"and I'm not so sure I can trust a man who betrays the strongest bond of faith in his life."

Hardwick could almost feel the ork wanting to pop a handrazor blade out from under his fingernail, but the detect spell still hadn't sounded.

Sensing Rapier was about to lose it, he reached out, gently took her arm, calmed her down a little. "The one thing has nothing to do with the other. You and I don't trust each other, and we never will. But we've got a stronger connection: mutual interest: I want something badly enough to pay major nuyen for it, and you're the people I think can get it for me. You want the money—and the adrenaline rush of the job."

Hardwick released Rapier's arm and folded his hands together on his desk. "My odds of getting what I want decrease if I'm not straight with you or I dangle you—not to mention that I end up with an enemy instead of a valuable business contact. Let's cut the drek, assume we're both professionals, and proceed accordingly. Agreed?"

"*So ka*," Tuskarora said, nodding with satisfaction as he sat back. Rapier calmed down another couple notches; he figured the odds of someone dying had dropped back to no more than ten percent.

"Now that we're done dancing, what's the job?" Trismegistus asked.

"Basically it's a techjacking, maybe with a snatch job or elimination attached. Pays two hundred thousand nuyen, plus reasonable expenses."

That caught the runners' attention. "Lotta money for a B and E," Tuskarora said. "What's the catch?"

Hardwick reached into a desk drawer, pulled out a small plastic container, slid it across the desk toward Tuskarora. "All the data I have is on this chip."

"Bullet point it for us," Teamster said.

Hardwick tapped his Caliban; it projected an image on the wall behind him. "This is a prototype developed by Aztechnology for a 'genomic exchange enhancer.' I don't know all the engineering, but from what I understand it significantly speeds up the rate of information exchange between biocomputers and silicon computers.

"We want the GEE, any specs or other data related to it, and, if you can grab her, Dr. Lydia Gonzalez-Wu, its inventor. If you can't get her, kill her. If it's a choice between bringing us the GEE and extracting her, make your escape and forget about her."

"Where's Aztech keeping this thing?" Tuskarora asked.

"At a secret research facility in the Everglades."

None of the runners looked happy when he mentioned the Glades: fifteen hundred square miles of swamp, shallow river, sawgrass, trees, mud, insects, and animals both normal and paranormal. Once only half that size and a fraction as dangerous, it had Awakened when the Sixth World dawned. No one dared to try to clear large patches of the Glades for farming or tract housing anymore, but it was a good place for Aztechnology to hide a research lab close to the Miami 'plex.

"What's our out?" Teamster said.

"An extraction point on an isolated part of the coast near the Ten Thousand Islands. Once you've got the goods, proceed there overland. We'll exfil you immediately in a Nissan Wolf helicopter."

"'We,' kemo sabe?" Tuskarora asked.

"Yes, we. This job is too important for me to trust to my lieutenants. I'll oversee things personally."

"Price just went up twenty percent."

"No, it didn't. I'm not going along to interfere with you or look over your shoulders. I'm there to make sure we all get what we want and get out safely. If you have a problem with that, I'll find another team."

Tuskarora said nothing this time.

"Good," Hardwick said. "Take a look at the data, make some plans, and get back to me with your outline, timetable, and requested supplies. I expect to hear from you within twelve hours at the same number we used before."

"You got it, Johnson." At the samurai's nod, the Five Aces stood up and left without further discussion. Two minutes later Hardwick and his team did the same.

"What did you think of them?" Hardwick asked when they were back in the Bentley.

"That ork's an asshole," Rapier said, her anger at being insulted still plain on her face. "But the team seems smart and efficient." It was about the highest praise she could offer.

"Let's hope so—or we're all in trouble."

• • •

The insertion had gone off almost perfectly. It was only later that things went to hell.

Hardwick woke up a few seconds after the explosion. Something had gone wrong on the run; the runners had fled to the exfil point in a stolen helicopter—pursued by one that wasn't. A lot of machine gun fire and one Aztechnology Striker shot later, both choppers had crashed. He was lucky to be alive. No, not luck; Rapier had done her job and pushed him out of the path of danger, spirits bless her.

He stumbled to his feet, head aching, and looked around. The beach was on fire. Puddles of burning fuel and scraps of shrapnel that had once been two helicopters littered the sand. Make that three helicopters—the runners' chopper had pinwheeled across the sand after crashing and smashed into the getaway helicopter. Now he was well and truly fucked.

Worse than the wreckage were the bodies. He'd seen plenty of death in his day, but this was his entire sec-team, his men, blown to bits. This was different.

He couldn't take it anymore and looked away—only to see Rapier. A flying chunk of rotor had cut her nearly in half. Some piece of her chrome sparked a little, fitfully, as if protesting its demise. Unable to stop himself, he scanned the beach until he found what remained of Brutus. Spattered jet fuel ignited by the blast had already burned away most of his flesh and was still working on his dermal armor and laced bones.

"God fucking damn it," he whispered to himself, squeezing his eyes to hold back tears. They'd protected him for over five years. They couldn't have done their jobs any better. He'd genuinely liked them.

And now they'd left him in the Glades with no one to watch his back.

Hearing a deep groan from the swamp side of the beach, he hurried across the sand, avoiding anything burning or sharp, until he found the source: Tuskarora. Next to him lay Atsa. They must have bailed out at the last moment.

Stuck in hostile territory with two runners, one of them a temperamental ork. He wasn't sure if his chances of survival had just gone up or down.

Had they completed the op? Tuskarora had a pack on, but it was torn open, nearly empty. Hardwick examined the ground between the ork and the trees, looking for anything that might have fallen out. Spare knife . . . multitool . . . tube of tusk polish. . . . A document pouch!—right in the middle of a puddle of burning fuel.

Casting magic fingers, he tried to lift the pouch out, but it was too far gone and crumbled into ashes. Well, if he didn't have it, at least Aztechnology didn't either.

He saw the firelight glint off something on the other side of the pool. He walked closer. A dura-plas chip box! He opened it with the same sort of eagerness his kids had on Christmas morning.

Inside was the GEE, its plastic and silicon more precious to him than gold and diamonds. He took it out, wrapped it carefully in a piece of clean cloth, and stashed it in one of the secret pouches sewn into his body armor. Then he tossed the box into the fire alongside the remains of the documents pouch.

Tuskarora groaned again. The big ork only had some minor cuts and abrasions, but Atsa was out cold. Hardwick didn't like the look of her pupils or the lump on her head, but he had no idea whether she'd gotten the latter by jumping from the helicopter or earlier in the run. She probably had a concussion, but he couldn't afford to let her keep sleeping. "Wake up, Atsa," he said, patting her cheek.

She moaned and stirred, batting his hand away like a child who didn't want to wake up for school. But at last her eyes flickered open. She started to lever herself up on one elbow, then shrieked with pain. "Leg!" she said through gritted teeth.

He lifted her deerskin skirt up a little and looked. He was no medic, but he'd seen enough combat injuries to know she'd broken her left leg. "Damn it," he said.

"That bad?"

"Not sure, but it's bad for us. Going to slow us down. Gotta rouse Tuskarora."

Getting close enough to wake up a street samurai full of adrenaline wasn't exactly his idea of a smart survival tactic, so he kicked sand at the ork. "Rise and shine, Tuskarora! No time for sleep."

Tuskarora jerked awake and flowed to his feet with augmented speed and grace. He reached for a smartgun that wasn't there, then focused on Hardwick with laser intensity. "You!" he said. In two strides he reached Hardwick. Effortlessly the ork lifted him off the ground with his left hand while drawing his right hand back into a fist. As he did, razor-sharp blades extended from his knuckles. "You got my team killed, Johnson! When you get to Hell, tell 'em I said hello."

"*I* got *your* team killed?" Hardwick said, struggling to speak clearly with the ork's hand around his throat. "You had all the intel I did. *You're* the one who led the Aztechs to us. *You're* the one who blew up their helicopter with a rocket. *You're* the one who got *my* entire sec-team killed, you stupid son of a bitch!"

Tuskarora snarled and thrust his right fist forward. Before he could connect, the ouroboros ring gleamed and an Armor spell shimmered into existence around Hardwick, deflecting the deadly spurs.

"You're *Awakened*?" Tuskarora said.

"You think I have this job just because of my winning personality?" Hardwick replied. "I used to be one of you. I was pulling runs like this when you were pissing your diapers. That's how I can relate to runners—and that's why I deal fairly with them." His conscience nagged at him for a second because of what he'd done with the GEE, but loyalty to SK and his family meant more than a little white lie to a runner. He was sure of it.

"Why didn't you tell me he was Awakened?" Tuskarora asked Atsa.

"You didn't ask."

"Damn treehuggers," the ork muttered. Most of the tension went out of his muscles; veins that had dilated from rage or the effects of his cyberware began to shrink. He let Hardwick go. "Okay, Johnson, what now?"

"First things first. Did you complete the op?"

"Yeah, we geeked the scientist and got the GEE and all her . . . *drek*!" he finished as he discovered his backpack was torn open and empty. "Gotta be here somewhere, let's look!"

The two of them searched; Hardwick let the ork go toward where he'd located the chip. Tuskarora found his Predator, brushed the sand off it, kissed it, and holstered it. A few seconds later he came to the now burned-out puddle of fuel. "Mother*fucker*!" he said, recognizing the ugly lump of ash at its center as the remains of his documents pouch. He crouched down for a closer look, shoulders slumping, face fallen. "The others died for nothing . . . nothing."

"What happened? We had to maintain blackout so the Aztechs wouldn't find us."

"It went great at first," Tuskarora replied. "Took a while for us to find the right lab, but we were quick enough to geek anyone who might've raised the alarm." He grinned in that particularly nasty way only orks could. "When we found the lab, we got lucky—Gonzalez-Wu was working late. She gave up the goods but refused to come along, so we iced her."

"Go on."

"That's when our luck ran out. I guess some Aztechnology decker found Ryder in the system. We walked out of that lab and right into a fully armed security squad.

"Ryder bought it when one of the Azzies shot him in the head, but Tris and Atsa laid down some mojo that gave us the chance to run for it. No way we could escape through the swamp as planned, so we headed for the compound's hangar. They had two choppers there; we took the one Teamster *thought* was faster.

"He took three rounds during the chase, so he couldn't fly steady. Even if they hadn't shot us up, I doubt he could've landed safely; he'd lost too much blood and was too messed up, even after the healing Tris and Atsa slapped on him."

"You're probably right. For what it's worth—I'm sorry about your team."

"Yeah . . ." Tuskarora looked skeptical. "I think it's time we got the hell out of here. Atsa, can you heal that leg?"

"No!" Hardwick said. "She's probably got a concussion. Don't even try to cast or Assense, Atsa. At best it'll make your head hurt even more. But you'll probably miscast and take *serious* Drain. Maybe even fatal."

"He's right," she said. "Between the way my head feels and the pain from my leg, I couldn't even magically light a candle."

"Okay, you're a mage, Johnson—you heal her."

"Ehhh, that might not be such a great idea, either. I've never had much of a knack for most mana spells. I could ease her pain a little, probably, but if I try to heal her, the odds are I end up in a lot of pain, nothing happens to her, and you have *two* people to carry."

"Then cover us with an invisibility spell so no one can find us."

Hardwick shook his head. "Can't do that, either."

"Elvis Christ! You can't do anything, can you, Johnson? What the fuck good are you?"

Before Hardwick could respond, an Aztechnology Plumed Serpent stealth drone flew into view over the treetops. Sensing targets, it angled toward the three of them and opened fire. Bullets kicked up gouts of sand around them.

"Damn it!" Tuskarora shouted. Moving with wired speed, he grabbed Atsa and dove behind some wreckage. She screamed as he jostled her leg.

Hardwick didn't move. He stared at the Plumed Serpent, focusing his willpower to draw mana into and through his self. He pointed at the drone and a spark shot forth from his hand. Traveling almost faster than the eye could follow, it grew larger, blossoming into a fireball. It engulfed the drone with a sound like a bonfire

going up all at once. The drone's ammo added a second blast as a crescendo.

Tuskarora peeked over his cover. "Elvis Christ!" he said. "Nice going, Johnson."

Hardwick nodded. "*That's* what the fuck good I am."

"No drek."

"The Azzies saw everything that drone saw," Hardwick continued. "We need to move out of here *now*, or we'll spend the rest of our short lives being prepped for the sacrifice stone."

"Right. Let's get one of the inflatable boats and hightail it."

"Negative," Hardwick said. "We go overland through the swamp."

Tuskarora stared at him. "Did you hit your head too, Johnson? She can't walk through the swamp! Plus it's full of giant snakes and drek."

"And the ocean and river *aren't* full of man-eating monsters? On the water we're sitting ducks; anyone can see us. The swamp provides some cover from the air and from astral searchers, and drones have a harder time maneuvering among the trees and underbrush. If we go by sea, we're *all* dead. If we go overland—some of us might survive."

"Oh, wait—wait. Let me guess. This is the part where you suggest that we abandon Atsa to improve our own chances of survival." From the look on the shaman's face, she expected the same.

"Fuck *that*. No one on *any* team I run gets left behind. We'll make a splint and help her walk. We—well, *you*—carry her if necessary."

Hardwick couldn't read Tuskarora's expression—surprise? Bafflement? Maybe a touch of respect? "Okay, let's do it then," was all the samurai said.

They made a sturdy splint for Atsa with carbon fiber poles from the electronics tent; she already had her staff for a crutch. "Anything here you want to take?" Hardwick asked as he grabbed a field pack and some rations.

Tuskarora glanced around. "Nah. Let's get outta here."

STEVEN S. LONG

• • •

Hours of miserable walking through the swamp followed. The heat, tension, and exertion made sweat pour off Hardwick and Tuskarora, but despite the effort of walking with her injuries Atsa seemed oddly at peace.

"Wotko provides," she said, using Raccoon's name in Creek. They hadn't run into anything truly dangerous so far, so Hardwick figured she might be right.

Tuskarora signaled for a rest and sat down on the trunk of a fallen tree. "This is never going to work," he said. "Any time now the Azzies will find us, and then—*whhshkkt!*" He made a slicing motion across his throat.

"You're overlooking something," Hardwick said, sitting upwind to avoid the full impact of orkish BO.

"Yeah, Johnson? What's that?"

"The mindset of the typical corporate administrator."

"I've never understood how you assholes think in the first place, so why don't you enlighten me?"

"That lab's important, but not big. So it only has a couple of small choppers, maybe one rigger. This is Aztechnology, so they probably have at least one mage."

"Had," Atsa said. "Teamster's Firetalon killed him."

"Good. But there's *got* to be someone in charge. Unless I miss my guess, it's a 'promising' junior executive on his way up the Aztech ladder. If it gets back to his bosses that he lost the GEE *and* its inventor, his career comes to a screeching halt—maybe his life, too, the way things work in Aztlan. He'll do everything he can to get it back using only what he's got on hand so he doesn't have to notify the higher-ups or call in too many favors. If we can reach the secondary extraction point before he unleashes the full Aztechnology arsenal, we have a good shot at getting out of this alive."

"Hope you're right," Tuskarora said. "That would explain why we haven't seen any signs of pursuit yet."

"Nothing in the astral either, that I can tell—but I'm a little out of practice," Hardwick said. "Come on, let's stay ahead of them as long as we can."

• • •

The swamp attacked them a few minutes later as they waded across a calf-deep channel between two patches of more or less solid ground. Tuskarora had just reached the far side when a monster exploded out of the deep water to their left. Twice the ork's size, it had scaly, green-brown skin, a heavy rectangular head, and a mouth full of large, sharp fangs.

It lunged for Hardwick, but a few years behind a desk hadn't destroyed his runner's reflexes. He jerked to the side and the beast's jaws clamped onto his field pack instead of his chest. The straps pulled painfully against his shoulders, and then snapped under the strain of the creature's strength as he stumbled and fell into the murky water.

Tuskarora yelled and leaped. Grabbing one of the creature's horns with his left hand, he thrust the cyber-spurs from his right deep into its eye. The monster bellowed in pain. With an agonized jerk of its head, it threw the ork into the deep water.

It turned back to Hardwick, but Tuskarora's attack had given him enough time to prepare one of his own. Obeying his will, mana flowed and coalesced, becoming a blue-white bolt of destructive energy. The creature roared in pain again, its scales offering little protection against magic.

Tuskarora returned to the fight, this time coming in low to rake his spurs across the creature's softer underbelly. The wounds he left were shallow, but they convinced the beast to seek easier prey. It whirled and dove into the deep water.

454

"Elvis Christ!" Tuskarora said as they waited cautiously to make sure it didn't intend to return. "What the fuck was that, a combat hippo?"

"A behemoth," Atsa said. "An Awakened alligator—a *young* one. An adult would've been twice as big."

"Why didn't you *shoot* it?" Hardwick said.

"Even if a round from a Predator could get through that thing's skin, you think it would make a difference? More important, a gunshot's not natural—if there are any Azzies nearby, they wouldn't care about swamp animal sounds, but gunfire'd bring 'em running."

"Good point," Hardwick said, recovering his composure. "Let's get out of here in case there are more of those things around."

* * *

Half an hour later, they heard the sound they'd been dreading: an approaching helicopter. "Cover!" Tuskarora said. They dove into a thicket and scrambled into it as deep as they could. Hardwick was soon covered in muck and face-to-face with several disturbingly large insects.

The chopper drew closer, passed overhead to the south. The noise of the rotors faded—then increased again.

"Drek and dog piss!" Tuskarora said. "Either they picked up something, or they're focusing on this area."

They waited, unmoving, as the helicopter noise came and went, came and went. Then another sound joined the mix: a buzzing whine, like some strange insect. . . .

"Spy drone!" Atsa whispered.

Tuskarora drew his pistol. "No!" Hardwick said. "The chopper will pick up a gunshot for sure."

"Better than letting that drone eyeball us."

"Let me try something else first," Hardwick said. "Both of you remain *absolutely still*, got it?" They nodded.

Hardwick concentrated. He thought about

the look of the leaves, right down to vein and stem; the twisting of the vines; the feel of mud and branch and heat; the sounds made by swamp creatures.

They saw the drone: a red and black dragonfly-like thing, sleek and swift. It came closer. The runners held their breath; Hardwick kept concentrating.

The drone hovered in place only a meter away. Then with a flick of a titanium and plastic appendage it darted off to the north and soon disappeared among the foliage.

The runners exhaled. A wave of fatigue washed over Hardwick; he collapsed to one elbow.

"Johnson, you okay?" Tuskarora said. "What the hell happened?"

"Just . . . a little Drain. Be all right in a sec."

"Drain?"

"I hid us with a Trid Phantasm—fools tech as well as natural senses. Drone thought we were just a thicket."

"You're smarter'n you look, Johnson. But c'mon, we gotta follow that chopper."

"*Follow* it? Are you insane? We should go some other direction."

"You're not the only bright boy here, chummer. That was a Northrup Hornet."

"And you know that how? We couldn't see it."

"From the sound," Tuskarora said in the tone usually used to address idiots and the mentally infirm.

"Okay, okay, good for you. So what? Why follow a Hornet?"

"'Cause it doesn't exactly get great KPL. It's a short-range, two-man attack chopper that's been out on recon patrol all day. It wasn't flying toward the lab, so the pilot must know someplace nearby to refuel. If we can get there, maybe we can grab the Hornet and fly to the extraction point. Or would you rather keep humping it down here with the mud and bugs?"

"Wow, an ork with some brains. Where'd you get your degree—Harvard?"

"No, Overtown University."

• • •

Luck, or perhaps Raccoon, was with them. Another half hour of hard slogging later, they peered through the brush at a clearing containing a big concrete slab supporting a shack, several fuel tanks, and a Northrup Hornet. The place looked like it used to be a ranger station or Park Service depot back in the days when the government owned most things. The green lion logos everywhere proclaimed that it now belonged to Aztechnology. Two pilots worked on the Hornet while three well-armed dwarf guards stood watch.

"I didn't think a Hornet could carry that many," Tuskarora said. "Smart to use dwarves."

"How are we going to get it now?" Hardwick asked.

"I've got a plan," Tuskarora said.

"Hey, I think I know this one: 'kill all of them,' right?" Hardwick said, remembering the usual "plan" favored by his old samurai friend War-Eye.

Tuskarora gave him the stink-eye as only an ork could. "Look, I may have big, pointy teeth, but I'm not a monster. Let's not kill them unless we absolutely have to."

"A nonviolent samurai? This is a first."

"Look, odds are the Azzies'll learn who pulled this job, sooner or later. If I get a rep for casually geeking their guys, that moves me to the top of their hit list, and no one stays on there for long. If I act like a professional and not a butcher, they'll extend me the same respect. It's just good biz."

"You're right," Hardwick said. "I followed the same sort of code. I'm sorry I didn't think you would, too. Working with so many drekhead runners has kind of made me cynical."

Tuskarora grinned. "That's one of the job qualifications for a Johnson, though, ain't it?"

Hardwick stifled a laugh. "Okay, then, how do we take care of the guards and get the Hornet?"

"Simple: we lure them away."

"You can fly the Hornet?"

"I can," Atsa said.

"You up to it?"

She nodded. "The splint lets me move my leg enough to do what I need to do, though it probably won't be the gentlest flight. Raccoon will provide."

"You do realize raccoons are ground-based animals, right?"

"Cut the clowning, Johnson—we got work to do," Tuskarora said.

"All right, so what's this big plan of yours, Tusk?"

"It's that Trid spell of yours—use it to create an illusion of some runners on the other side of that depot firing at the Azzies, then retreating when the Azzies shoot back. Once they've left, we sneak up, grab the Hornet and maybe a pilot, and away we go."

Hardwick considered carefully. "You're smarter than you look, Tusk," he said. "But once I lose line of sight to the Phantasm, the spell ends. With luck, the guards will assume we're still fleeing and continue to chase what they think is us. Without luck . . ."

"Just have to take the chance, unless you got a better idea." Hardwick shook his head. "You ready?" This time he nodded, wishing the sweat dripping down his face came only from the Florida heat.

"Okay. Once the guards leave the platform, I'll run up there. If it looks safe, Atsa, you follow as fast as you can; otherwise wait and come with Johnson."

"Got it," she said.

"Johnson, keep the spell going until those guards are as far away as you can lure them, then get to the platform ASAP. Clear?"

"Clear," Hardwick said, enjoying the feel of working with a good team. Risking his life on a run wasn't his idea of fun anymore, but it created a camaraderie no corp job ever could. He took a deep breath and centered himself, visualizing three prime runners. He focused on the target zone, a patch of trees and brush on the opposite side of the platform.

He drew upon his mana and cast the spell.

Moments later the sounds and sights of gunfire and wizardry emanated from the target zone. The Aztechnology guards responded with practiced skill, leaping off the platform and taking cover. Soon they returned fire with coordinated precision.

Tuskarora took off, running faster than any nonaugmented man ever could. He reached the platform and darted in among the fuel tanks, looking for hostiles. Atsa followed at the fastest limp-run she could manage.

Hardwick kept the Phantasm going. Once Atsa reached the platform, he manipulated it so the runners seemed to retreat. The guards followed, moving in short, tactically intelligent maneuvers. He maintained the Phantasm as long as he could see the target zone, then stopped concentrating and ran for the platform.

The shots he expected never came. He reached the concrete and jump-heaved himself onto it behind one of the fuel tanks. He moved around the tank with as much stealth as he could muster, his eyes peeled for Tusk or Atsa—or Azzies.

He reached the Hornet just as Tuskarora shot one of the Aztech pilots in the head with a silenced Ares Light Fire. With blinding speed, he headed toward the nearby shack, saying, "Hey, you, stop!" as he moved. He flattened himself against the shack's wall next to the door, drew his Predator, and waited.

Seconds later the other pilot came out of the shack, a Beretta in his hand and a fresh soykaf stain on the front of his flight suit. Before he could take another step Tuskarora grabbed the pilot's arm and shoved the muzzle of his Predator against the man's head. "Afternoon, chummer. How'd you like to come work for Saeder-Krupp?"

"Uhhh . . . *viva* Lofwyr?"

"Good choice, son, you've got a bright future with this company. Your first assignment is to fly us the hell outta here."

"Hornet's not refueled yet."

"It's got enough juice to get where we're going. Move!"

• • •

Thirty minutes later, they were in comfortable chairs in an SK helicopter, drinking bottles of chilled water. Hardwick had rarely tasted anything so good.

"Don't worry, Johnson," Tuskarora said. "You'll be back in the nine-to-five soon."

"Hope so. I . . . look, I know this probably means nothing to you, but . . . I'm truly sorry about your friends."

The big ork slumped a little, as if the memory weighed him down. "Thanks. I ran with them for a long time; we made it through a lotta drek together. Hard to believe I won't see 'em again."

"Regardless of the op's results, I wish they'd lived. Losing a friend, it . . . leaves a hole in your soul, sort of. The hole gets smaller with time, but it never completely closes up. Maybe that's for the best."

Tuskarora crooked a smile around his tusks. "What's this, Johnson? Getting sentimental and chummy with the 'disposable assets'? What would your bosses say?"

Hardwick shook his head. "Not disposable. Never that. The corps treated me like that too often back in my runner days; it's counterproductive and stupid. I prefer the term 'unconventional' instead."

"How about 'renegade'? Or 'crazed'?"

"Those work too," Hardwick said, now smiling himself.

"Better watch out, Johnson. If your corporate masters learn you have a heart, they won't let you be a Johnson anymore. They'll make you do something that requires more ethics and honesty, like supervising the Unauthorized Human Testing Division."

Hardwick's smile didn't fade. "I hear there are some real opportunities there. But you better watch out yourself. If word hits the street that you saved a Johnson's life and treated him like a decent human being instead of a dick in a suit, your rep'll be barghest chow."

"Well, I won't tell if neither of you will," Atsa said.

"Too bad about the swag," Tuskarora said, leaning back in his seat and shutting his eyes. "All that work and death for nothing."

A different smile teased at Hardwick's face, but he suppressed it before either of the runners saw. Feeling the GEE against his skin through the secret pouch in his body armor, he thought about telling Tuskarora he had it. After all, the samurai had saved his life in the Glades, maybe more than once. They were practically friends now.

Well, not *good* friends. Hardwick leaned back in his seat to get some sleep.

TIM MAUGHAN

FLYOVER COUNTRY

(2016)

I MEET THIS GIRL Mira and her kid in the parking lot of that Wendy's on Jefferson that's been closed since '19. Yellowing grass pushes up through cracks in warped tarmac, and I find myself daydreaming again about the ground ripping open and consuming the whole fucking town. Like an earthquake. Or maybe a big storm rolling in, like last year but fiercer. Something. Anything.

It's only six thirty but it's hot out already. Mira's kid is sleepy, not used to being up this early. But she's still cute as all hell, all pigtails and smiles, playing up for the camera as I snap pictures of her and her mom on an old Samsung phone. Mira has got a CVS bag stuffed full of papers with her—the kid's school reports, some crayon scribbled drawings, letters both of them have written. I snap photos of them too, trying not to read the contents as I fight to get the shitty phone camera to focus on handwriting.

I need to get going. Miguel always sorts this shit out last minute, swapping shifts around so

things line up. So everyone is in the right place at the right time. Always seems to end up with yours truly barely prepared, in a rush. Mira gives me forty bucks, which she says is the last of her UBI for the month. I feel bad and try to give her ten back, but she won't take it. Says she can pick up some more cleaning jobs on Handy, that I shouldn't worry. *Just don't fuck up*, she says. I smile and promise her I won't.

I've only got an hour before my shift starts, no time to walk all the way back home, so I duck into the bathroom at the big Walgreens on Lincoln. It's on the way. In the stall I kneel on the floor in front of the john, and spread out a clean shirt from my bag across the closed lid. I place the Samsung in the middle, and start using one of the tool kits I got off eBay to crack open its casing. It's tricky—it always fucking is—but I manage to pry it apart without scratching it up too much, without it looking like it's been tampered with.

I breathe a huge sigh of relief when I see the

motherboard. The SD chip is 256 gigabytes and the right model. It makes me fucking laugh, this shit. All these companies always competing to make you buy their phone, and then to make you buy a new one every damn year, making you feel like you're missing out if you've not got the newest, the best ever. But inside they all look the same to me. Same components, same chips, same storage, year in year out.

Somebody comes into the bathroom, so I start making heaving noises, just in case they spot my feet and wonder what the fuck I'm doing. There's a pause and then they reluctantly ask me if I'm okay in there. I laugh and make spit sounds and I'm like *yeah fine, just a heavy night y'know*. I cough some more and listen to them moving around, the sound of pissing then running water, mixed with canned laughter and the theme tune to *Tila Tequila's Beltway Round-Up* pumping in over the store's tinny PA. Eventually I hear the door close and I get back to work.

The SD chip comes out easy, I've done it a few thousand times before. I gently tape it to the backside of the RFID chip sewn into the back of my green overalls with a Band-Aid, before stuffing them back into my bag. I put the phone back together and drop that in there too, along with the clean shirt. Sadly the cheap-ass tool kit has to go in the trash on my way out, cos there's no way I'll get that through security. Pain in the ass, but fuck it. I've got a bunch more of them at home.

• • •

The walk to the Foxconn-CCA Joint Correctional and Manufacturing Facility takes me about twenty minutes on the interstate. Traffic is pretty much nonexistent apart from the cab-less trucks that dwarf me as they pass, kicking up clouds of pale dust that scour my eyes with grit.

Gate security is bullshit as always. They barely care, lazily rummaging through my bag as I stand in the body scanner, feet on the markings, arms bent above my head. They pull out the phone, put it in a RFID tagged baggy to pick up at the end of my shift, and silently hand me back my bag.

Miguel is at the shift manager's desk. He gives me some gruff bullshit about getting in earlier in future, about how I should turn up ready to go in my overalls, while guiltily avoiding making eye contact. Stay cool, Miguel. He checks the rota on his tablet, tells me I've been assigned to production line 3B, building seven. Motherboard assembly. Of course, I know all this already.

I duck through dormitory six as a shortcut, weaving through the endless rows of bunk beds. Artificial light filters down through suicide nets and sprays a slowly undulating checkerboard across the plastic floor. Everyone in here is in green overalls: voluntary. On shift breaks they sit around on their bunks or on plastic chairs, talking, playing cards, watching *A Noble War* on the huge TVs that line the dorm. It's the episode where Barron and Beatrice get married on the bridge of the USS *Thiel*, just after they've put down a socialist uprising on Phobos. I remember the episode, season four I think. Barron still has his real arm. I used to love this shit back in high school.

I keep walking. The dorm is a fucking shit-hole. It's dirty and smells of ass and body-stink. If this is where they put the voluntary workers I don't want to ever see how bad things are for the actual inmates. I shudder at the thought of choosing to be stuck in here, but I get it. I got no kids, I'm lucky. My Universal Basic Income still covers my rent, just about. I pass a guy that looks my age, stripped to the waist, lying on his bunk. Chest splattered with random, uncoordinated tattoos, like stickers on a kid's lunchbox. He stares up through the suicide nets, into dull fluorescent light, his eyes unmoving. There but for the fucking grace of god.

I find an empty locker and open it, cram my bag in. Checking over my shoulders for guards or drones I reach inside and tear the Band-Aid away from the inside of my overalls, and palm it and the chip into my pocket. I step back and pull the overalls on over my clothes, slip on the paper face mask and hairnet, and head outside, relieved to escape the smell.

• • •

I move quickly through the courtyard. Running late. Again the bodies I weave through are all sealed in green overalls, but on the other side of the three-story chain-link fence I can see red and blue clothed figures. Convicts and Illegal Residents.

I keep my eyes down as I move, not wanting to catch the mirror-shaded gaze of the guards in the towers, or the dead twitching eyes of the drones that hang in the hot, still air.

Inside Building Seven the chain fence runs right through the interior, cleaving the production line in two. Green overalls on my side, red and blue on the other. The dank, mildew smell of almost-failing AC. Today I'm on motherboard assembly. A constant stream of naked iPhones come down the conveyor belt to me, their guts exposed, and as each one passes I clip in a missing chip. 256GB storage chips, from a box covered in Chinese lettering.

One every ten seconds. Six a minute. Three hundred sixty an hour. Four thousand three hundred and twenty a shift.

After me the line snakes away, disappearing through a hole in the chain-link, into the hands of Reds and Blues.

At the station next to me, a slender matte-black robot arm twitches, snapping video chips into the motherboards. It is relentless, undistracted, untiring. Given half a chance Foxconn would replace us all, but then they'd lose all those special benefits the President promised them for coming here in the first place. The ten-year exemption on income and sales tax. The exemption on import tariffs for components. The exemptions from minimum wages. The exemption on labor rights. The protection against any form of legal action from employees or inmates. The exemption from environmental protection legislation. And Apple? Well, without me standing here, clipping one Chinese-made

component into another Chinese-made component, Apple loses the right for a robot in Shenzhen to laser engrave 'Made in the USA by the Great American Worker' into every iPhone casing before they're shipped over here.

• • •

It takes me about two hours to pluck up the courage to do what I gotta do. Two hours. Seven hundred twenty iPhones.

Once I decide, there's no going back. Instead of taking a chip from the box to my right, I slip my hand into my overalls pocket, and palm out the chip. To my huge fucking relief it clips effortlessly into the next iPhone on the belt. On top of it I place the Band-Aid, with just enough pressure that it stays there while looking like it fell from my scratched and battered hand.

I watch the phone slide down the line, its little Band-Aid flag making it stand out from its compatriots, as it vanishes through the chain-link fence.

• • •

Eight hours later. Two thousand eight hundred and eighty iPhones.

Shift over. My calves and the backs of my thighs sting from standing for twelve hours, my eyes strained from the fluorescent glare. The panel on the wall bleeps, turns green, as I punch out. I gaze at its screen. My blocky, low-res reflection gazes back, a machine vision approximation of my tired eyes and pale skin. I stand there, silently, not moving, waiting for the panel to recognize me. A tick appears, obscuring my face. Video game statistics scroll along the screen's bottom: efficiency, accuracy, timekeeping, responsiveness, productivity. Four thousand three hundred and fourteen iPhones. Chimes and a bleep. A synthesized, too-cheerful, feminine voice tells me I should smile more. A second bleep, the click of a door unlocking, and I'm out.

• • •

My phone buzzes at 5:24 a.m., under my pillow and loud as all fuck because I made sure the ringer was cranked to max. Text from an unknown number. Miguel on a burner. Time to go to work.

• • •

Two hours later and I'm back in my overalls, back in Building Seven.

This time I'm on Returned QA Fails. The pace is slower, the work slightly more involved. iPhones that have failed quality assurance up the line because of faulty chips come back down. I whip out the fucked chip, stick a new one in, send them back up the line again.

One every twenty seconds. Three a minute. One hundred eighty an hour. Two thousand one hundred and sixty per shift.

It tends to be even more chilled than that, to be honest. There's not that many that come back faulty, obviously. Nowhere near in fact. But the algorithms don't care. The drones lazily orbiting around the ceiling on their quadrotors are always watching, making notes, remembering. Calculating. Doesn't matter how many you actually do, you still gotta do 'em quick. Keep those productivity stats high.

It's less than two hours—maybe sixty phones—into my shift when it appears. Coming down the line, a dropped Band-Aid stuck lazily to its exposed guts.

My stomach flips. I glance upward to make sure the drone has cycled away. As the phone reaches me I pluck the Band-Aid away, drop it to the floor. Un-click the storage chip, and drop in another, new one.

The chip I've just taken out should go in a box, to go into a container, to go onto a truck, to go onto a ship, to go to China, to go onto another truck, to be dumped in some no-fucking-where village in Guangdong where an old lady that used to be a subsistence farmer

will pull it apart in her front room to recycle the components.

But this one? This chip I originally ripped from that old Samsung? This chip gets palmed into my pocket.

• • •

I meet Mira in the Wendy's parking lot. Her kid is with her again. Cute as all hell. Running around in the tarmac-piercing grass.

I hand her the Samsung phone, its storage chip returned to its rightful place. She hands me another forty bucks.

Before I turn to leave, I watch her power it on, swipe it open. Her thumb stabs impatiently at icons. And then the screen fills with a photograph, a brown face, beard, smiling. Trying to look happy but nervous. Blue overalls. A photo taken while glancing over your shoulder, on a hastily hacked open, smuggled-in old smartphone you don't even know works. A photo you'd risk spending six months in solitary to take.

Mira smiles, begins to cry.

She calls her kid over.

Look. You know who that is?

Pause. Eyes wide.

Daddy!

As I walk away she's kneeling on the floor, holding the kid close to her, tears rolling down both their faces, as she swipes through images. The face again. Badly focused photos of handwritten notes.

I feel good for a second. Like it's worth it. But part of me still wants the ground to rip open and consume the whole town.

It's cooler today. A breeze is picking up, tugging at my green overalls as I start my walk back home. Somewhere out past the interstate, over the horizon, a storm is rolling in. A big storm like last year. I hope it's fiercer. I hope it's something. Anything.

E. LILY YU

DARKOUT

(2016)

IN ALL OF NORTHCHESTER, Pennsylvania, there was hardly forty square feet that was not continuously exposed to public view, on glass walls if you had money or on tablets if you were poor. This meant that Brandon spent most nights after his shift at the sports store watching Emma, his latest ex and the prettiest, as she chopped garlic, buttered toast, poured herself a gin and tonic, propped her furry-slippered feet on the coffee table with ska pulsing from her speakers, or took a date to bed. The counter at the upper right corner of the wall shifted between four and seven total viewers when Emma was eating dinner or clipping her fingernails. It shot up as high as fifty-five if Emma was mussing her lipstick and her zebra-print sheets with a fresh conquest. One hundred viewers was when ads floated up, loud and flashing, for limpness, smallness, underperformance.

Sometimes Brandon was disappointed in his relative unpopularity, his counter's slow tick of zero, one, zero, one, two, one, but then, white men tended to attract fewer eyeballs. The Indian family on Decker and Main, with two toddlers, boring as paint but only one of two non-white households on the east side of the tracks, attracted a dependable twenty every night. You needed pizzazz, or mystery, or difference to become a peripheral home-cam star. You needed nothing but a screen and a billed connection to lurk on others' cam streams.

These days he could hardly remember life without the cameras, although they had only been installed ten years ago, after the passage of the Blue Eye Act. As Little England and China had demonstrated, where there was universal surveillance, crime rates plummeted. Russia, Zambia, Egypt, and Japan adopted similar systems roughly at the same time as the States, and most other wealthy countries were testing a limited rollout in their ghettos and shantytowns.

Brandon hadn't glanced at the newscast for more than a few seconds. "Eyes once were said to be the windows to a man's soul," the Attorney General thundered from her podium, beside the glum chief of Central. "With the passage of this Act, windows shall look into every person's soul. Not one potential criminal or terrorist will live unwatched."

Bored, and oblivious to history's apparition on his screen, Brandon flipped to an episode of *Snowballers III*.

There were restrictions and concessions to privacy lobbies, of course. Only badges could check logs or monitor, and only then with a warrant. The software was written to prevent remote modification. Two years after deployment, however, Croatian hackers cracked encryptions and began charging for views of the American of your choice. Actresses, usually. A mild fuss was made. Some feminists penned screeds and circulated petitions.

With the rafts of necessary legislation already in force, thirteen of the thirty original contractors and subcontractors out of business, and the budget long since buried beneath truckloads of additional appropriation bills, a complete overhaul of the hardware and individual installation of security patches were as politically feasible as open borders. After long debate, the white-hat community reached a general consensus to open-source the Croatian exploit, so that everyone and everything could be seen at all times. A bright and egalitarian future had arrived, they argued, superseding the dark days of cold cases, unreliable eyewitnesses, and domestic terrorism. Most citizens had become accustomed to the idea of being watched anyway. Polls suggested a solid 79 percent enjoyed the constant access to celebrities' meals and wardrobes.

A front-row seat to hours of Emma's smooth shoulders was an unexpected personal consequence of that legislation. After darkening his wall and pressing his palms against his tired eyes, Brandon considered, not for the first time, taking two weeks off from work and a hike along the West Coast. Emma was a drug, the perfect drug, and after a six-month hit of her, he was

clawing through withdrawal. The pillow forts she used to build, the shape of her feet, her high, delighted laughter when he landed the perfect joke: the memories burned like poison, and he could not stop drinking them in.

Sweat, grit, sunlight, distance, and mai tais might cure him. He had done the budget. He had saved enough for a short vacation. The customers at the sports store who swiped kayaks and paddleboards onto silver credit cards, with their freckled shoulders, bronzed cheeks, and bleached hair, always seemed to him an alien species, possessed of a thousand-and-one adventures and the insulation provided by ready cash. He could join them, however briefly.

Brandon powered down his screen and stared out the glass wall at the dead light and gray grass of winter, imagining hot white sand between his toes and the cool spray of the Pacific on his face. He was learning to surf from a wise old instructor. He carried the board under his arm like a knight riding into battle and rode the smooth roaring waves hour after hour, day after day, until the water pounded his thoughts into nothingness. His chalky skin darkened. He ate six swordfish steaks for dinner, bought a drink for every pretty brunette in the bar, and forgot about Emma.

But then the flickering stream of panoptic views into kitchens and bedrooms, kitten-crammed commercials, and staged cop shows, all the cheap and irresistible glitter of second-hand life, sang to him again. Depressing a button, Brandon turned the wall opaque and went back to watching Emma curl and uncurl her toes, his heart in his mouth.

He was waiting for her to collapse into tears. He was waiting for her to scribble on a poster with a squeaking marker and hold it up to her bedroom camera: I LOVE YOU BRANDON. IT WAS A MISTAKE. COME BACK.

When he saw that, when he and the ten strangers on her stream saw he was victorious at last, Brandon would hop into his sneakers and sprint the six miles across town to her apartment, pumping his arms, dodging cars, the Internet cheering unheard in the background. He would hammer on her door. In his imagination, she was pacing the room in her black lace bra and matching panties, a loose robe around her shoulders. Her audience had swelled to two thousand during his dramatic run. She flung open the door and pressed her unblotched and tastefully rouged face to his shoulder. He put his arms around her, and they sank onto the zebra sheets, to the unheard sighs of thousands of spectators. It wasn't impossible. These things were known to happen.

Once in a while Brandon heard the squeak of a marker in a dream, catapulted out of bed, and yanked on socks and shoes before he was entirely awake. But his morning wall only ever showed him commercials for insurance and whole-wheat cereal, tiled four by four.

Tonight, though, he did not linger on Emma's stream. It was the night of the Fitz-Ramen Bowl. He had swapped shifts with Mandy to watch it. Mark Thompson was coming with two twelve-packs of craft beer.

"I need to get out of the house. You need to get out of your head," Mark had said. "You've got the subscription. I'll get the drinks."

Their friendship began four years ago, when Mark, observing Brandon's painful attempt to charm an out-of-town marketing rep in the bar, sent along a pint of porter and a napkin penned with ratings: *Confidence 2, Slickness 0, Desperation 17.* An electrician, Mark was a good fifteen years older than Brandon and married to a sweet talker of a woman who never found fault with him.

He was not at all someone Brandon would have expected as a friend. Brandon did not have many friends.

But Mark's taste in beers was excellent, and over the latest microbrew he confided to Brandon that listening to him brought back the rush and risk of youth, the gambits and heartbreaks and exuberant successes. So did football, which

he had to watch out of the house, because his wife slept early, and lightly, and not well.

"A bad back," he said, shaking his head. "Like her father."

So when Mark buzzed the door, and the camera floated his face over the screen, Brandon felt his spirits lift. The two of them popped their beers, propped their feet on the table, and cheered the Pittsburgh College Lynxes. During the commercials they flipped to live cop cams outside the stadium, betting on whether the nastiest officers would be reprimanded. Mark set up a private pool on his phone, floating fives and tens, and they passed it back and forth.

"Do you or don't you understand English? You come to this country, you better learn English—" The driver stared down at his lap. His hands gripped the wheel.

"Five bucks no one remembers." Brandon emptied his can.

"Nope, not taking it. He's Bangladeshi."

"They're all brown to me."

"The accent."

"So?"

"They don't get big Internet mobs. Not like the Indians. Polite complaint from the Association of Bangladeshi Cabdrivers, that's all. *Sir it has come to our attention that,* and *would you pretty please.*"

"Why do they still do traffic stops? You can ID the plates in two cameras, calculate speed, deliver ticket. Wham."

"Maybe they're bored on patrol. Maybe they don't want people watching them sit on their hands. Makes the taxpayer think about payroll."

After Mark's wagers hit a hundred dollars and change, he pocketed the phone. "Personal limit," he said, smiling. "Lizzie's been on my case."

Humming, he appropriated the remote and browsed a DV forecaster. Past emergency call records, crunched for patterns, allowed you to time future incidents so accurately that the popcorn you put in the microwave reached its last thuck, thuck as the boyfriend kicked open the door. A few predictive statistics blogs published regular watching guides. Politicians and athletes attracted the most attention, but the smart ones paid for darkspace: for a million per square foot hour, the ten most popular hosts stopped streaming your cams.

Logs remained available to the police, and a determined viewer, with some finagling, could connect directly to the right camera, but for the most part darkspace worked. A cheaper option was to smash the camera outright. That was a felony, but so was everything that followed.

At 1818 Maple Drive, the microphone still functioned. Brandon grimaced at the screaming and smack of fist against flesh and switched the whole wall back to the game.

"Why do you watch this shit?"

"Third and a long thirteen, Stallions on the Lynxes' twenty-six, Washington is back to pass, Rodriguez is open—it's intercepted by Jones!"

"That's my man!" Mark said. "How long can you go in a shit job in a shit economy before snapping? The game's rigged against white men, you know that. Sometimes it's relaxing to see someone hit his breaking point."

"How do you know that guy was white?"

"The way she was hollering. Black women holler differently."

"Don't tell me you hit Lizzie."

"Never. Cams, though. Used to think there was something they knew that we didn't, so I watched sixteen families at a time. But no. They do holler different when the men beat them, though. They're used to violence. They're violent people. Not like us."

"The Lynxes are putting this game out of reach early, up twenty-four points with four minutes left in the first quarter."

Mark made a noise of satisfaction and grinned.

"Football's not relaxing enough?"

"It's fine. But it's tame. Ever since the concussion lawsuits. The old stuff was better."

Brandon cut to a channel forum and scrolled down the top-ranked links.

"How about them puppies," Mark said.

"I thought you'd be all over *Sex Sex Sex Witchita*."

"It's always some hag pushing seventy," Mark said. "Floppy in all the interesting places. Thought you knew that."

"That's bottom feeding. I don't trawl. The professional stuff's better."

"Sure, or you're interested in one person and no one else." Mark grinned wide enough for Brandon to see his silver fillings and tossed back the rest of his beer. He was in an expansive mood, as if he had both money and holy water on tap. "Seriously, start dating again. Lay some ladies. You'll feel better."

"What does Lizzie say when you talk to her about black people and how much you're suffering?"

"I don't. Because I'm a smart man. I mean, I'm lucky, I'll always have a job. But this Korean woman at the pharmacy yesterday, listen to this, she came up to me and said, 'I don't like the way you're looking at me.' That's the world we live in today. Christ. Maybe I'll see her on the DV watch someday. Don't you dream about smacking whatshername a good one?"

Brandon did, but he wasn't about to admit it.

"I'll sign you up on a few sites," Mark said. "Write you an A-plus profile. I'm good at them."

"You're married."

"That supposed to stop me? She's black, it's different. You wouldn't understand. Go ahead, run me over with a moral locomotive."

"Don't be an idiot."

"So what's the problem? You swipe up full of STDs?"

"I don't like them looking at medical. Full access for a week, no guaranteed sex. I'm sequenced and everything. Who says they won't copy and sell?"

"Hey, you have to give to get."

Brandon pitched his voice higher. "'Oh, you make twenty-four thousand a year?' 'You had appendicitis at sixteen? Wow.'"

"So you watch home cams. For the human contact. Is that it?"

Mark pinched the controller, quartered the screen, and flashed through a rapid succession of cams. A teenager doodling in his textbook. A woman working on a tablet, her face furrowed. An aged brown woman dumping chilies into a pot. A snoring cat. A man typing at a table. Two cats batting each other. An infant banging a rattle on the bars of her crib. Two men lifting free weights, mouths scrunched with the effort. A poodle peeing against a tree.

"Amazing." He smirked.

"It's culture," Brandon said. "Walking in other people's shoes. Makes me a better person. Lay off."

"You want culture, fuck a brown woman. I'm unbelievably cultured. I'm just saying, as your friend, you should get out more."

"What is this, an intervention?"

"If you give me your phone—"

"Go to the game, it's back on."

Four minutes into the fourth quarter, Mark's good mood was gone.

"What happened to our lead?"

"Oof," Brandon said.

"What kind of shit play was that?" Mark punched the table so hard his beer rocked over.

"Easy there."

"The coach is a scab-assed cockcrab. How do you burn a lead like that? How?"

Brandon mopped at the frothy mess of beer and sodden chips. "Every damn year."

"We're doomed." A flask appeared in Mark's hand.

"Put that down, you're drunk."

"I'm sober as a fucking duck. Me and Lizzie are screwed."

"What are you talking about?"

Mark reclaimed the controller and input a numerical camera address Brandon did not recognize, but from the first few digits guessed it was located somewhere in Pittsburgh's swankiest district. On his screen, now, a bald white woman sipped a salted glass while watching the game. She had a cottonmouth tattooed around her neck, red and black heels like ice picks, and six spikes in each ear. Noticing the uptick in her viewer count, she turned and flashed the camera a thumbs-up and a smile that crawled under Brandon's skin and itched.

"Who's that?" Brandon said, very slowly.

"My bookie. Ruth. Name's a joke, not for real. Short for—"

"You have the cash. Right?"

"This was supposed to be a straight-to-the-bank payday. Like the last one."

"The last one."

"I won a thousand betting a three-team parlay last year. She shook my head and told me I looked like a lucky man. 'When you want to make a real bet,' she said, 'with real money, think of me.'"

Ruth stared at the camera as if she could see them, her mouth still hooked in that crowbar of a smile.

Brandon flipped the whole wall back to the game, as if the scrum of blue, red, orange, and white could scrub the prickling off the back of his neck. The scene that greeted him wasn't much more cheerful. The Stallions were down by a single touchdown, and the whole tableau had the velvet air of a Shakespearean tragedy.

Here came the touchdown. Here the conversion.

Mark's head fell into his hands. The last thirty seconds slipped off the clock. Brandon held his beer to his lips with nerveless fingers.

The Stallions won, thirty-two to thirty-one.

They flooded the field with blue and red, dancing, howling, cracking their helmets together.

"What do you do now?" Brandon said.

"Fuck if I know." Mark groaned. "She knows my address. Home and work. She has my contacts, too. Runs a background check for big wagers. So she'd know to look at you—"

As if in quiet confirmation, the little zero on the counter flicked to one. Brandon swallowed and wiped his mouth with the back of his hand.

"How much?"

"Ten thousand. It was one to two, I don't know why, Lynxes were favorite. I was gonna triple that—"

Brandon kneaded his temples. "Bonehead."

"Did you pick that up from Lizzie?"

"What were you going to do with thirty thousand?" That wasn't two weeks' vacation and surfing lessons. That was a year of rent on a ranch house somewhere in wine country and a wine tour every month. That was a plane ticket to a dark and disconnected country of grapevines and beautiful women, perhaps even kind women, and bedrooms and breakups without cameras.

"Don't lecture me."

"What were you going to blow it on? Weed? Speed? Cars?"

"Old lady needs spinal fusion, if you have to know."

"But insurance—"

"We don't have any."

"You need *brain* surgery."

Mark scowled. "I was trying to do right by her."

"Mortgage? Second mortgage? Sell the van?"

"Double mortgage already, from the doctors and pills. Need the van for work. We're up to our eyeballs." Mark took a deep breath. "Now you know how fucked we are. I hate doing this, Brandon, but—"

"You couldn't go with a Chinese bookie, could you? You had to get a *local*."

"Ruth gives better odds than the congloms. Plus she let me bet on credit."

Brandon flung the controller. It clattered satisfyingly against the wall and dropped out of sight. "Of course she let you, bumfuck. She knows where you live. Where Lizzie lives."

"I get it, I get it. So—"

"She can't do anything to you, right? Not with—" He gestured to the cameras.

"I've heard Ruth doesn't like dirtying her nails."

"That's a relief."

"So she contracts disposal and retrieval."

"Would I have heard of her?"

"Nothing splashy since six, seven years ago."

"Six—"

"The Burnetts." Mark shifted his weight. "The, uh, two girls, one boy, parents, grandfather, Dalmatian, and hamster. And one goldfish. Though maybe not the goldfish, those things die if you sneeze at them . . ."

"That was her?"

"Unofficially."

"Shit."

"Anyway, if she wants it quiet, she buys black."

"You're fucked."

"Royally." Mark blinked and grinned in terror. "So what I was going to ask—"

"Why mix me up in this? Why sit on my sofa and scarf my chips, with thirty grand riding on the game?"

"Lizzie's asleep. I wanted a friend—if I was going to celebrate—"

"Bullshit. You wanted me here in case you lost. So you could dun me for cash."

"You're angry, I get it. You're angry but I'm fucked."

Whether because the controller landed on a button or whether because the paid sportstream sensed their drifting attention, the postgame analysis switched to news. Thousands of masked protestors milled in the National Mall, waving single yellow roses splattered with black paint. GIVE US DARKNESS, their placards read. PRIVACY IS FREEDOM. The cameras faded from night to day, gliding from DC to San Francisco to Tokyo to Moscow. Every cosmopolis was boiling with protests. DARKOUT! DARKOUT!

"Motherfucking Luddites," Mark said.

"Don't change the subject. You dragged me into this. She's probably auditing me right now. What do you think she'll see? Do you think I have ten grand in my sock drawer?"

"I have two thousand in emergency funds," Mark said. "Lizzie made me. I only need eight."

"Great. Pick a star, click your heels, wish really, really hard—"

"Are you going to help me?" Mark pressed an empty can between his palms until it gave. "The way I helped you, when you totaled your car? When Nina dumped you and your shit on the curb?" It had been raining, and the cardboard boxes melted like sugar. When Brandon called, Mark laughed his ass off, but showed up five minutes later with his van. He had even dug up a dolly somewhere.

"You piece of goose shit." Brandon knuckled his eye sockets. Then he pulled out a phone and scrawled a passpattern with his fingertip. "Look at that balance, you fucking moron. Two thousand six hundred and I don't get paid until next Friday. Look at it!" He thrust the phone into Mark's face and watched Mark's pupils cross.

"I was going to California with this," Brandon said bitterly. He dragged two fingers over the phone and signed with his index finger. "There. Two thousand four hundred in your account tomorrow." He waved his phone at the camera. "See that, Ruth? He's got almost half of it. Charge him stupid interest and don't break his leg. Now get out, dickbrain."

"I'll pay you back."

"You're still short five thousand and change."

"Yeah."

"And Lizzie still needs a new back."

"That can wait."

"Like hell it can. My uncle slipped a disc once. Couldn't look at his face, or I started hurting too. Put her first for once."

Sudden motions and shouts pulled Brandon's eye back to the screen. A wave of protestors swelled and broke over a police barricade in Beijing. The air went blue and blurry with tear gas. The synchrony of their movements sug-

gested careful rehearsal, which could only be coordinated online. In China, public spaces were off limits. The police would have noticed the preparations. Every security apparatus would have known.

Hopeless, all of them.

In the meantime, his own counter reached five, a personal record. Casual browsers attracted by the shouting? *Disappointed Lynx Bros Yelling*. Or black-jacketed, detached men with freshly fingerprinted contracts?

"You're a real friend, you know that?" Mark said. "I'm not going to forget this."

"Door's there. Get out."

"Going, I'm going." Mark slung his coat over his shoulders and banged open the screen door. Cold air swirled in. Brandon dimmed his wall to transparency and peered into the darkness, shivering, until Mark peeled out of the neighborhood in his anchovy can.

Asshole.

He brought his screen back up and stared at masks, placards, yellow roses. A svelte, lipsticked newscaster would have relieved the oppressiveness, but any newscaster was a rarity these days, when free and instant footage flowed everywhere. Who could keep up with that?

"Give us darkness! Darkout! Darkout!"

The news stream wasn't helping his nerves. Brandon retrieved the controller from behind an armchair and returned to his usual forum, cracking open a seventh beer.

Crazy guy scaling broadcast station perimeter: Shot or not?
Ducklings hatching!!!
Trespassers at ISP HQ?
Sexy brown sugar mmm
Stallion fans riot in Houston, view from Gray's Bar

As if of their own volition, his fingers tapped their way back to Emma's stream.

Kitchen: dark.

Living room: dark.

Bedroom: dark, too, but a slice of orange light from the street slipped under the blinds and threw a soft glow on her bare arms, a long loose curl, the gentle hills of her body under the comforters.

She was asleep. Her chest was rising and falling, rising and falling, and her breath made a fluttering, feathery sound through her lips that the microphone picked up and whispered to him. He remembered the sound from the seventeen times she fell asleep in his bed and the ten times he had slept in hers.

"I am a pathetic creep," he said aloud to his own five watchers. The whole world was his confessional, tonight. But as the words left his mouth, his own counter flickered: four—three—one—zero. No one wanted to hear him grovel.

"You still love me," he told Emma. She was just as lonely as he was. She was auditioning an endless river of men to fill a Brandon-sized hole inside her. And she never looked at his cam stream. Not once.

Not casually.

Not for a second.

Not as one of four or eight or sixteen streams split on her screen.

As if she didn't miss him at all.

The rhythm of her breath was soothing and soporific. He could listen to it forever.

His seventh beer half empty, feeling infinitely sorry for himself, Brandon slept.

• • •

He dreamed he was in California. It was a nice dream, with plenty of sunlight and blue sky and puffy clouds. The trees were spiny and crumpled with drought. He had never been to California, but this looked exactly like what he had seen in movies. Maybe California was more a collective cinematic fantasy than an actual place. Maybe, like an elaborate movie set, it never existed.

He stood in a desert studded with cactuses and hunched pines. Invisible birds cried and piped, and he could hear waves crashing unseen against an invisible shore.

Mirages shimmered everywhere. Mostly they were water mirages, but here was the quivering image of an ice cream cart, and there, on the horizon, stood one of Emma's perfect white breasts, large as a mountain. Why not two? he asked his subconscious. Give me the other one, come on. But the snowy peak shivered and vanished as he approached.

He had been hiking for hours, and his arms and legs were furry with dust. The mountains rising around him muffled the sound of the distant ocean.

One by one, the sharp, croaking bird calls ceased. All around him was a heavy and peculiar silence.

• • •

Brandon was accustomed to hearing the babble of strangers on his screen while he slept: any channel, anybody, anything to feel less alone. The absence of sound rang loud as cymbals in his ears. Startled awake, he poured out of bed and puddled on the floor. For several painful minutes he lay still, trying not to move. Someone was using his skull as blender and trash can and bongos all at once.

The screen had entered standby sometime during the night. It did not show Emma's room, nor his front yard, but rather the illusion of a flat white wall with a window in the center. Brandon pressed the power button. The operating light winked orange, but nothing changed.

"Damn," he said. Mark's beer must have shorted a circuit. But where? And what had he fried? Brandon picked up his phone to troubleshoot and found no signal. He could snap photos, he could play games, and that was all.

Brandon flicked and pushed and plugged and unplugged his watch, his Weatherboy, his scale, his library, his two tablets. All were functional. All were offline. What worried him most were the lights on his three cameras, which had gone from red to yellow. He had no way of placing a support call.

"Fuckity fuck fuck," he said.

He would have to walk downtown to Moby's. No appointment meant fighting through crowds clutching bricked devices and crying for miracles. That would make him at least an hour late for his shift. So he would have to stop at the sports store first, to explain.

His manager could confirm for himself that Brandon's cameras were dead. The law required busted cameras to be fixed within one day. Police arrived, demanding answers, if you didn't. Occasional darkness was only for the very rich, and Brandon did not feel rich at all. Someone like him was not allowed to be offline for long.

His stomach shrank at the thought of eggs and bacon. No breakfast, then. He gave himself a critical once-over in the bathroom mirror: Two bloodshot eyes, a greenish pallor, hair flattened in some places and rucked up in others. He pushed a wet hand over the hair that stuck out, but it bounced straight back.

"Mark, you fucker," he growled. "You dick-shot. You douche."

When he went onto the front stoop of the divided house, the morning sun jabbed him in the eye. His breath smoked white from his mouth and nose. Around him the yellow grass glittered and crisped with frost.

The building's palm scan wasn't working. It ignored his hand and did not respond to his slap, but the maintenance light flashed. Swearing under his breath, Brandon dug in his pockets for his analog keys.

His upstairs neighbor, Alice Rosenbaum, crunched over the lawn in scarf and boots. She was in her sixties, with deep wrinkles and snowy hair, and appeared to fall somewhere between the kind of grandmother who invited lonely neighbors in for pie and the kind of grandmother who filed noise complaints punctually at ten each night. She grinned at him.

"That game, huh?" she said. Brandon, patting himself, realized he was still wearing his beer-sticky gear. "I lost fifty dollars on that last play. To my son-in-law. He'll never let me hear the end of it."

"My friend put ten thousand on the Lynxes." She winced. "You have rich friends."

"He's broke."

"Online?"

"Local."

"Will he be all right?"

"I don't know. I can't call him."

"Right, right. The whole street's down."

"What?"

"I knocked at the Washburns' and asked."

"The Washburns?"

She pointed. "Number eighteen. Two of the cutest little girls."

Brandon couldn't remember ever seeing the family that lived in the yellow house. He felt slow and stupid, like a blind thing in a cave. "What's going on?"

"It's a darkout. Like a blackout. You know what a—no. We haven't had a blackout in twenty-one years. You would have been a kid."

"Someone digging up wires?"

"I don't know. Our phones are dead, too, and the tower's two miles from here. I think it's pretty big. But we won't know until everything's back up."

Mark had caught a break. Brandon hoped the bastard was okay. "How long do you think that'll take?"

"Who knows?" Alice glanced down the street. "I was going to pick up breakfast from the bakery. See if anyone knows. Used to do that when I was younger. You look like a bagel kind of guy. Want to come?"

Brandon hesitated. Someone should check on Mark and Lizzie. Especially Lizzie, who had a raucous belly laugh and mothered him. He hadn't known about her back. But they were ten miles across town, and with lines dead, and no car, what could he do if there was trouble?

Maybe Mark had hocked everything and paid up.

Or maybe, if all cams were dark, his bookie had bigger fish than Mark.

2

Of course there were bigger fish than Mark. Mark would be fine.

Emma, though. He felt a pang almost as sharp as the first loss: the cool, cold look, the quick credit swipe for both lunches, as if she pitied him, and the impression of being tossed out along with the sandwich wrappers. He couldn't watch her now. He didn't know where she was or what she was doing, or if she had taken out poster paper and was chewing the end of a marker, thinking about him.

"I could do with a bagel," he said.

And they walked together through the unfamiliar morning, waiting, as the whole world was waiting, for the light to return.

RYUKO AZUMA

2045 DYSTOPIA

(2018)

Translated from the Japanese by Marissa Skeels

NO NEED TO WASTE TIME ON STUPID WOMEN.

SEEKING MY BEST GENETIC MATCH, I WAS PAIRED WITH AI.

NO ONE BOTHERS WITH ROMANCE ANYMORE.

I MET MY GIRLFRIEND THROUGH DNA MATCH-MAKING.

AND MEN ARE FREED FROM THE PITIFUL PRACTICE OF MASTURBATION.

GIRLS DON'T HAVE TO DEAL WITH MENSTRU-ATION,

GOVERNMENT AUTHORITIES HARVEST GENE-RICH ADOLESCENTS' TESTES AND OVARIES.

NINE MONTHS AFTER PLACING AN ORDER, A CHILD IS DELIVERED TO YOUR DOOR, LIKE PIZZA.

OF COURSE, WOMEN DON'T HAVE TO GIVE BIRTH. BABIES ARE BROUGHT TO TERM IN ARTIFICIAL WOMBS.

HOMO-SEXUALS AND PEDO-PHILES NEED NOT APPLY.

YOU CUSTOMIZE GENDER, APPEARANCE, AND INTELLIGENCE STATS, LIKE YOU WOULD FOR A GAME.

KIDS CAN BE DESIGNED ON YOUR PHONE.

IT'D BE BETTER FOR ANIMAL RIGHTS IF MEAT WERE GROWN FROM CULTURES, BUT...

THAT KIND DOESN'T TASTE AS GOOD AS REAL MEAT.

I WORK IN ANIMAL HUS-BANDRY.

WORK IS CAPPED AT 40 HOURS A MONTH.

NO ONE NEEDS TO WORK, BUT DOING SO TENDS TO MAKE LIFE EASIER.

MACHINES TAKE CARE OF SLAUGH-TERING.

WE PRODUCE MASSES OF UNIFORM, TOP-QUALITY MEAT.

BY OPTIMIZING THEIR EXERCISE, SLEEP, AND FEEDING PATTERNS...

SO LIVESTOCK WITH MACHINE MINDS WERE CREATED.

THEY'RE THE SAME AS MEAT STACKED UP NEATLY AT SUPER-MARKETS.

SINCE THEY LACK BRAINS, THEY PROBABLY CAN'T FEEL PAIN OR FEAR.

VERY OCCA-SIONALLY, THE SHOCK OF DYING MAKES ANIMALS EJACULATE.

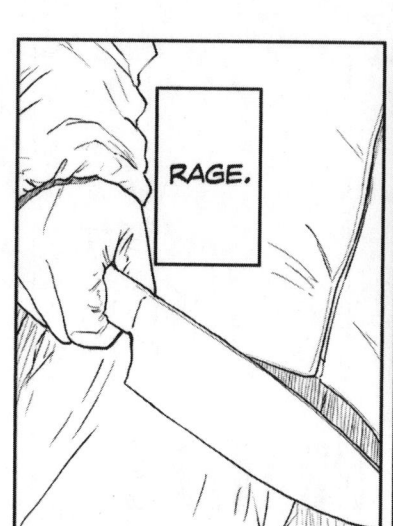

RAGE.

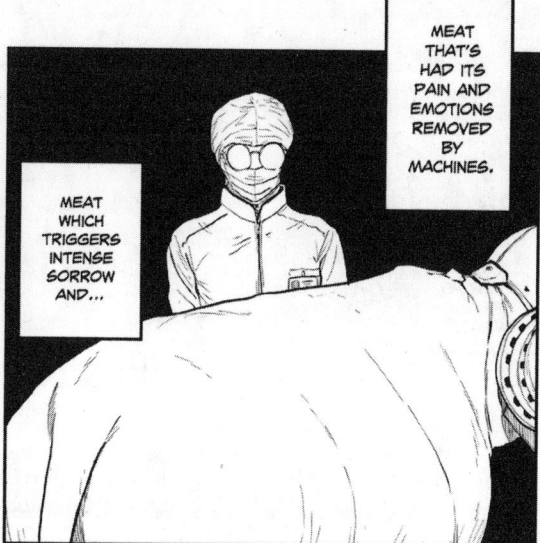

MEAT THAT'S HAD ITS PAIN AND EMOTIONS REMOVED BY MACHINES.

MEAT WHICH TRIGGERS INTENSE SORROW AND...

HAH...

HAH...

HAH...

HAH...

WHO MADE THIS THEIR FUTURE?

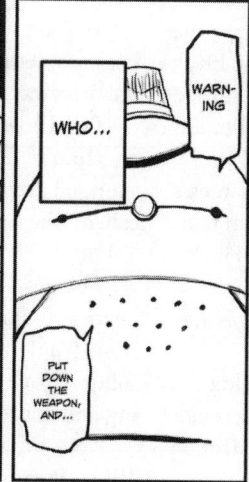

WHO...

WARN-ING

PUT DOWN THE WEAPON, AND...

WARN-ING

PUT DOWN THE WEAPON, AND PLACE BOTH HANDS ON YOUR HEAD. NOW.

KEN LIU

THOUGHTS AND PRAYERS

(2019)

EMILY FORT:

So you want to know about Hayley.

No, I'm used to it, or at least I should be by now. People only want to hear about my sister.

It was a dreary, rainy Friday in October, the smell of fresh fallen leaves in the air. The black tupelos lining the field hockey pitch had turned bright red, like a trail of bloody footprints left by a giant.

I had a quiz in French II and planned a week's worth of vegan meals for a family of four in family and consumer science. Around noon, Hayley messaged me from California.

Skipped class. Q and I are driving to the festival right now!!!

I ignored her. She delighted in taunting me with the freedoms of her college life. I was envious, but didn't want to give her the satisfaction of showing it.

In the afternoon, Mom messaged me.

Have you heard from Hayley?

No. The sisterly code of silence was sacred. Her secret boyfriend was safe with me.

"If you do, call me right away."

I put the phone away. Mom was the helicopter type.

As soon as I got home from field hockey, I knew something was wrong. Mom's car was in the driveway, and she never left work this early.

The TV was on in the basement.

Mom's face was ashen. In a voice that sounded strangled, she said, "Hayley's RA called. She went to a music festival. There's been a shooting."

The rest of the evening was a blur as the death toll climbed, TV anchors read old forum posts from the gunman in dramatic voices, shaky follow-drone footage of panicked people screaming and scattering circulated on the web.

I put on my glasses and drifted through the VR re-creation of the site hastily put up by the news crews. Already, the place was teeming with avatars holding a candlelight vigil. Outlines on the ground glowed where victims were found, and luminous arcs with floating numbers reconstructed ballistic trails. So much data, so little information.

We tried calling and messaging. There was no answer. Probably ran out of battery, we told ourselves. She always forgets to charge her phone. The network must be jammed.

The call came at four in the morning. We were all awake.

"Yes, this is. . . . Are you sure?" Mom's voice was unnaturally calm, as though her life, and all our lives, hadn't just changed forever. "No, we'll fly out ourselves. Thank you."

She hung up, looked at us, and delivered the news. Then she collapsed onto the couch and buried her face in her hands.

There was an odd sound. I turned and, for the first time in my life, saw Dad crying.

I missed my last chance to tell her how much I loved her. I should have messaged her back.

. . .

GREGG FORT:

I don't have any pictures of Hayley to show you. It doesn't matter. You already have all the pictures of my daughter you need.

Unlike Abigail, I've never taken many pictures or videos, much less drone-view holograms or omni-immersions. I lack the instinct to be prepared for the unexpected, the discipline to document the big moments, the skill to frame a scene perfectly. But those aren't the most important reasons.

My father was a hobbyist photographer who took pride in developing his own film and making his own prints. If you were to flip through the dust-covered albums in the attic, you'd see many posed shots of my sisters and me, smiling stiffly into the camera. Pay attention to the ones of my sister Sara. Note how her face is often turned slightly away from the lens so that her right cheek is out of view.

When Sara was 5, she climbed onto a chair and toppled a boiling pot. My father was supposed to be watching her, but he'd been distracted, arguing with a colleague on the phone. When all was said and done, Sara had a trail of scars that ran from the right side of her face all the way down her thigh, like a rope of solidified lava.

You won't find in those albums records of the screaming fights between my parents; the awkward chill that descended around the dining table every time my mother stumbled over the word *beautiful*; the way my father avoided looking Sara in the eye.

In the few photographs of Sara where her entire face can be seen, the scars are invisible, meticulously painted out of existence in the darkroom, stroke by stroke. My father simply did it, and the rest of us went along in our practiced silence.

As much as I dislike photographs and other memory substitutes, it's impossible to avoid them. Coworkers and relatives show them to you, and you have no choice but to look and nod. I see the efforts manufacturers of memory-capturing devices put into making their results better than life. Colors are more vivid; details emerge from shadows; filters evoke whatever mood you desire. Without you having to do anything, the phone brackets the shot so that you can pretend to time travel, to pick the perfect instant when everyone is smiling. Skin is smoothed out; pores and small imperfections are erased. What used to take my father a day's work is now done in the blink of an eye, and far better.

Do the people who take these photos believe them to be reality? Or have the digital paintings taken the place of reality in their memory? When they try to remember the captured moment, do they recall what they saw, or what the camera crafted for them?

. . .

ABIGAIL FORT:

On the flight to California, while Gregg napped and Emily stared out the window, I put on my glasses and immersed myself in images of Hayley. I never expected to do this until I was aged and decrepit, unable to make new memories. Rage would come later. Grief left no room for other emotions.

I was always the one in charge of the camera, the phone, the follow-drone. I made the annual albums, the vacation highlight videos, the animated Christmas cards summarizing the family's yearly accomplishments.

Gregg and the girls indulged me, sometimes reluctantly. I always believed that someday they would come to see my point of view.

"Pictures are important," I'd tell them. "Our brains are so flawed, leaky sieves of time. Without pictures, so many things we want to remember would be forgotten."

I sobbed the whole way across the country as I relived the life of my firstborn.

• • •

GREGG FORT:

Abigail wasn't wrong, not exactly.

Many have been the times when I wished I had images to help me remember. I can't picture the exact shape of Hayley's face at six months, or recall her Halloween costume when she was five. I can't even remember the exact shade of blue of the dress she wore for high school graduation.

Given what happened later, of course, her pictures are beyond my reach.

I comfort myself with this thought: How can a picture or video capture the intimacy, the irreproducible subjective perspective and mood through my eyes, the emotional tenor of each moment when I *felt* the impossible beauty of the soul of my child? I don't want digital representations, ersatz reflections of the gaze of electronic eyes filtered through layers of artificial intelligence, to mar what I remember of our daughter.

When I think of Hayley, what comes to mind is a series of disjointed memories.

The baby wrapping her translucent fingers around my thumb for the first time; the infant scooting around on her bottom on the hardwood floor, plowing through alphabet blocks like an icebreaker through floes; the four-year-old handing me a box of tissues as I shivered in bed with a cold and laying a small, cool hand against my feverish cheek.

The eight-year-old pulling the rope that released the pumped-up soda bottle launcher. As frothy water drenched the two of us in the wake of the rising rocket, she yelled, laughing, "I'm going to be the first ballerina to dance on Mars!"

The nine-year-old telling me that she no longer wanted me to read to her before going to sleep. As my heart throbbed with the inevitable pain of a child pulling away, she softened the blow with, "Maybe someday I'll read to you."

The ten-year-old defiantly standing her ground in the kitchen, supported by her little sister, staring down me and Abigail both. "I won't hand back your phones until you both sign this pledge to never use them during dinner."

The fifteen-year-old slamming on the brakes, creating the loudest tire screech I'd ever heard; me in the passenger seat, knuckles so white they hurt. "You look like me on that roller coaster, Dad." The tone carefully modulated, breezy. She had held out an arm in front of me, as though she could keep me safe, the same way I had done to her hundreds of times before.

And on and on, distillations of the 6,874 days we had together, like broken, luminous shells left on a beach after the tide of quotidian life has receded.

In California, Abigail asked to see her body; I didn't.

I suppose one could argue that there's no difference between my father trying to erase the scars of his error in the darkroom and my refusal to look upon the body of the child I failed to protect. A thousand "I could have's" swirled in my mind: I could have insisted that she go to a college near home; I could have signed her up for a course on mass-shooting-survival skills; I could have demanded that she wear her body armor at all times. An entire generation had grown up with active-shooter drills, so why didn't I do more? I don't think I ever understood my father, empathized with his flawed and cowardly and guilt-ridden heart, until Hayley's death.

But in the end, I didn't want to see because I wanted to protect the only thing I had left of her: those memories.

If I were to see her body, the jagged crater of the exit wound, the frozen lava trails of coagulated blood, the muddy cinders and ashes of shredded clothing, I knew the image would overwhelm all that had come before, would incinerate the memories of my daughter, my baby, in one violent eruption, leaving only hatred and despair in its wake. No, that lifeless body was not Hayley, was not the child I wanted to remember. I would no more allow that one moment to filter her whole existence than I would allow transistors and bits to dictate my memory.

So Abigail went, lifted the sheet, and gazed upon the wreckage of Hayley, of our life. She took pictures, too. "This I also want to remember," she mumbled. "You don't turn away from your child in her moment of agony, in the aftermath of your failure."

• • •

ABIGAIL FORT:

They came to me while we were still in California.

I was numb. Questions that had been asked by thousands of mothers swarmed my mind. Why was he allowed to amass such an arsenal? Why did no one stop him despite all the warning signs? What could I have—should I have—done differently to save my child?

"You can do something," they said. "Let's work together to honor the memory of Hayley and bring about change."

Many have called me naive or worse. What did I think was going to happen? After decades of watching the exact same script being followed to end in thoughts and prayers, what made me think this time would be different? It was the very definition of madness.

Cynicism might make some invulnerable and superior. But not everyone is built that way. In the thralls of grief, you cling to any ray of hope.

"Politics is broken," they said. "It should be enough, after the deaths of little children, after the deaths of newlyweds, after the deaths of mothers shielding newborns, to finally do something. But it never is. Logic and persuasion have lost their power, so we have to arouse the passions. Instead of letting the media direct the public's morbid curiosity to the killer, let's focus on Hayley's story."

It's been done before, I muttered. To center the victim is hardly a novel political move. You want to make sure that she isn't merely a number, a statistic, one more abstract name among lists of the dead. You think when people are confronted by the flesh-and-blood consequences of their vacillation and disengagement, things change. But that hasn't worked, doesn't work.

"Not like this," they insisted, "not with our algorithm."

They tried to explain the process to me, though the details of machine learning and convolution networks and biofeedback models escaped me. Their algorithm had originated in the entertainment industry, where it was used to evaluate films and predict their box-office success, and eventually, to craft them. Proprietary variations are used in applications from product design to drafting political speeches, every field in which emotional engagement is critical. Emotions are ultimately biological phenomena, not mystical emanations, and it's possible to discern trends and patterns, to home in on the stimuli that maximize impact. The algorithm would craft a visual narrative of Hayley's life, shape it into a battering ram to shatter the hardened shell of cynicism, spur the viewer to action, shame them for their complacency and defeatism.

The idea seemed absurd, I said. How could electronics know my daughter better than I did? How could machines move hearts when real people could not?

"When you take a photograph," they asked me, "don't you trust the camera AI to give you the best picture? When you scrub through drone footage, you rely on the AI to identify the most interesting clips, to enhance them with the perfect mood filters. This is a million times more powerful."

I gave them my archive of family memories: photos, videos, scans, drone footage, sound recordings, immersiongrams. I entrusted them with my child.

I'm no film critic, and I don't have the terms for the techniques they used. Narrated only with words spoken by our family, intended for each other and not an audience of strangers, the result was unlike any movie or VR immersion I had ever seen. There was no plot save the course of a single life; there was no agenda save the celebration of the curiosity, the compassion, the drive of a child to embrace the universe, to *become*. It was a beautiful life, a life that loved and deserved to be loved, until the moment it was abruptly and violently cut down.

This is the way Hayley deserves to be remembered, I thought, tears streaming down my face. *This is how I see her, and it is how she should be seen.*

I gave them my blessing.

. . .

SARA FORT:

Growing up, Gregg and I weren't close. It was important to my parents that our family project the image of success, of decorum, regardless of the reality. In response, Gregg distrusted all forms of representation, while I became obsessed with them.

Other than holiday greetings, we rarely conversed as adults, and certainly didn't confide in each other. I knew my nieces only through Abigail's social media posts.

I suppose this is my way of excusing myself for not intervening earlier.

When Hayley died in California, I sent Gregg the contact info for a few therapists who specialized in working with families of mass shooting victims, but I purposefully stayed away myself, believing that my intrusion in their moment of grief would be inappropriate given my role as distant aunt and aloof sister. So I wasn't there when Abigail agreed to devote Hayley's memory to the cause of gun control.

Though my company bio describes my specialty as the study of online discourse, the vast bulk of my research material is visual. I design armor against trolls.

. . .

EMILY FORT:

I watched that video of Hayley many times.

It was impossible to avoid. There was an immersive version, in which you could step into Hayley's room and read her neat handwriting, examine the posters on her wall. There was a low-fidelity version designed for frugal data plans, and the compression artifacts and motion blur made her life seem old-fashioned, dreamy. Everyone shared the video as a way to reaffirm that they were a good person, that they stood with the victims. Click, bump, add a lit-candle emoji, re-rumble.

It was powerful. I cried, also many times. Comments expressing grief and solidarity scrolled past my glasses like a never-ending wake. Families of victims in other shootings, their hopes rekindled, spoke out in support.

But the Hayley in that video felt like a stranger. All the elements in the video were true, but they also felt like lies.

Teachers and parents loved the Hayley they knew, but there was a mousy girl in school who cowered when my sister entered the room. One time, Hayley drove home drunk; another time, she stole from me and lied until I found the money in her purse. She knew how to manipulate people and wasn't shy about doing it. She was fiercely loyal, courageous, kind, but she could also be reckless, cruel, petty. I loved Hayley because she was human, but the girl in that video was both more and less than.

I kept my feelings to myself. I felt guilty.

Mom charged ahead while Dad and I hung back, dazed. For a brief moment, it seemed as if the tide had turned. Rousing rallies were held and speeches delivered in front of the Capitol and the White House. Crowds chanted Hayley's name. Mom was invited to the State of the Union. When the media reported that Mom had quit her job to campaign on behalf of the movement, there was a crypto fundraiser to collect donations for the family.

And then, the trolls came.

A torrent of emails, messages, rumbles, squeaks, snapgrams, televars came at us. Mom and I were called clickwhores, paid actresses, grief profiteers. Strangers sent us long, rambling walls of text explaining all the ways Dad was inadequate and unmanly.

Hayley didn't die, strangers informed us. She was actually living in Sanya, China, off the millions the UN and their collaborators in the US government had paid her to pretend to die. Her boyfriend—who had also "obviously not died" in the shooting—was ethnically Chinese, and that was proof of the connection.

Hayley's video was picked apart for evidence of tampering and digital manipulation. Anonymous classmates were quoted to paint her as a habitual liar, a cheat, a drama queen.

Snippets of the video, intercut with "debunking" segments, began to go viral. Some used software to make Hayley spew messages of hate in new clips, quoting Hitler and Stalin as she giggled and waved at the camera.

I deleted my accounts and stayed home, unable to summon the strength to get out of bed. My parents left me to myself; they had their own battles to fight.

• • •

SARA FORT:

Decades into the digital age, the art of trolling has evolved to fill every niche, pushing the boundaries of technology and decency alike.

From afar, I watched the trolls swarm around my brother's family with uncoordinated precision, with aimless malice, with malevolent glee.

Conspiracy theories blended with deep fakes, and then yielded to memes that turned compassion inside out, abstracted pain into lulz.

"Mommy, the beach in hell is so warm!"

"I love these new holes in me!"

Searches for Hayley's name began to trend on porn sites. The content producers, many of them AI-driven bot farms, responded with procedurally generated films and VR immersions featuring my niece. The algorithms took publicly available footage of Hayley and wove her face, body, and voice seamlessly into fetish videos.

The news media reported on the development in outrage, perhaps even sincerely. The coverage spurred more searches, which generated more content . . .

As a researcher, it's my duty and habit to remain detached, to observe and study phenomena with clinical detachment, perhaps even fascination. It's simplistic to view trolls as politically motivated—at least not in the sense that term is usually understood. Though Second Amendment absolutists helped spread the memes, the originators often had little conviction in any political cause. Anarchic sites such as 8taku, duangduang, and alt-web sites that arose in the wake of the previous decade's deplatforming wars are homes for these dung beetles of the internet, the id of our collective online unconscious. Taking pleasure in taboo-breaking and transgression, the trolls have no unifying interest other than saying the unspeakable, mocking the sincere, playing with what others declared to be off-limits. By wallowing in the outrageous and filthy, they both defile and define the technologically mediated bonds of society.

But as a human being, watching what they were doing with Hayley's image was intolerable.

I reached out to my estranged brother and his family.

"Let me help."

Though machine learning has given us the

ability to predict with a fair amount of accuracy which victims will be targeted—trolls are not quite as unpredictable as they'd like you to think—my employer and other major social media platforms are keenly aware that they must walk a delicate line between policing user-generated content and chilling "engagement," the one metric that drives the stock price and thus governs all decisions. Aggressive moderation, especially when it's reliant on user reporting and human judgment, is a process easily gamed by all sides, and every company has suffered accusations of censorship. In the end, they threw up their hands and tossed out their byzantine enforcement policy manuals. They have neither the skills nor the interest to become arbiters of truth and decency for society as a whole. How could they be expected to solve the problem that even the organs of democracy couldn't?

Over time, most companies converged on one solution. Rather than focusing on judging the behavior of speakers, they devoted resources to letting listeners shield themselves. Algorithmically separating legitimate (though impassioned) political speech from coordinated harassment for *everyone* at once is an intractable problem—content celebrated by some as speaking truth to power is often condemned by others as beyond the pale. It's much easier to build and train individually tuned neural networks to screen out the content a *particular* user does not wish to see.

The new defensive neural networks—marketed as "armor"—observe each user's emotional state in response to their content stream. Capable of operating in vectors encompassing text, audio, video, and AR/VR, the armor teaches itself to recognize content especially upsetting to the user and screens it out, leaving only a tranquil void. As mixed reality and immersion have become more commonplace, the best way to wear armor is through augmented-reality glasses that filter all sources of visual stimuli. Trolling, like the viruses and worms of old, is a technical problem, and now we have a technical solution.

To invoke the most powerful and personalized protection, one has to pay. Social media companies, which also train the armor, argue that this solution gets them out of the content-policing business, excuses them from having to decide what is unacceptable in virtual town squares, frees everyone from the specter of Big Brother–style censorship. That this pro–free speech ethos happens to align with more profit is no doubt a mere afterthought.

I sent my brother and his family the best, most advanced armor that money could buy.

• • •

ABIGAIL FORT:

Imagine yourself in my position. Your daughter's body had been digitally pressed into hard-core pornography, her voice made to repeat words of hate, her visage mutilated with unspeakable violence. And it happened because of you, because of your inability to imagine the depravity of the human heart. Could you have stopped? Could you have stayed away?

The armor kept the horrors at bay as I continued to post and share, to raise my voice against a tide of lies.

The idea that Hayley hadn't died but was an actress in an anti-gun government conspiracy was so absurd that it didn't seem to deserve a response. Yet, as my armor began to filter out headlines, leaving blank spaces on news sites and in multicast streams, I realized that the lies had somehow become a real controversy. Actual journalists began to demand that I produce receipts for how I had spent the crowdfunded money—we hadn't received a cent! The world had lost its mind.

I released the photographs of Hayley's corpse. Surely there was still some shred of decency left in this world, I thought. Surely no one could speak against the evidence of their eyes?

It got worse.

For the faceless hordes of the internet, it

became a game to see who could get something past my armor, to stab me in the eye with a poisoned videoclip that would make me shudder and recoil.

Bots sent me messages in the guise of other parents who had lost their children in mass shootings, and sprung hateful videos on me after I whitelisted them. They sent me tribute slideshows dedicated to the memory of Hayley, which morphed into violent porn once the armor allowed them through. They pooled funds to hire errand gofers and rent delivery drones to deposit fiducial markers near my home, surrounding me with augmented-reality ghosts of Hayley writhing, giggling, moaning, screaming, cursing, mocking.

Worst of all, they animated images of Hayley's bloody corpse to the accompaniment of jaunty soundtracks. Her death trended as a joke, like the "Hamster Dance" of my youth.

• • •

GREGG FORT:

Sometimes I wonder if we have misunderstood the notion of freedom. We prize "freedom to" so much more than "freedom from." People must be free to own guns, so the only solution is to teach children to hide in closets and wear ballistic backpacks. People must be free to post and say what they like, so the only solution is to tell their targets to put on armor.

Abigail had simply decided, and the rest of us had gone along. Too late, I begged and pleaded with her to stop, to retreat. We would sell the house and move somewhere away from the temptation to engage with the rest of humanity, away from the always-connected world and the ocean of hate in which we were drowning.

But Sara's armor gave Abigail a false sense of security, pushed her to double down, to engage the trolls. "I must fight for my daughter!" she screamed at me. "I cannot allow them to desecrate her memory."

As the trolls intensified their campaign, Sara sent us patch after patch for the armor. She added layers with names like adversarial complementary sets, self-modifying code detectors, visualization auto-healers.

Again and again, the armor held only briefly before the trolls found new ways through. The democratization of artificial intelligence meant that they knew all the techniques Sara knew, and they had machines that could learn and adapt, too.

Abigail could not hear me. My pleas fell on deaf ears; perhaps her armor had learned to see me as just another angry voice to screen out.

• • •

EMILY FORT:

One day, Mom came to me in a panic. "I don't know where she is! I can't see her!"

She hadn't talked to me in days, obsessed with the project that Hayley had become. It took me some time to figure out what she meant. I sat down with her at the computer.

She clicked the link for Hayley's memorial video, which she watched several times a day to give herself strength.

"It's not there!" she said.

She opened the cloud archive of our family memories.

"Where are the pictures of Hayley?" she said. "There are only placeholder Xs."

She showed me her phone, her backup enclosure, her tablet.

"There's nothing! Nothing! Did we get hacked?"

Her hands fluttered helplessly in front of her chest, like the wings of a trapped bird. "She's just gone!"

Wordlessly, I went to the shelves in the family room and brought down one of the printed annual photo albums she had made when we were little. I opened the volume to a family portrait, taken when Hayley was ten and I was eight.

I showed the page to her.

Another choked scream. Her trembling fingers tapped against Hayley's face on the page, searching for something that wasn't there.

I understood. A pain filled my heart, a pity that ate away at love. I reached up to her face and gently took off her glasses.

She stared at the page.

Sobbing, she hugged me. "You found her. Oh, you found her!"

It felt like the embrace of a stranger. Or maybe I had become a stranger to her.

Aunt Sara explained that the trolls had been very careful with their attacks. Step by step, they had trained my mother's armor to recognize *Hayley* as the source of her distress.

But another kind of learning had also been taking place in our home. My parents paid attention to me only when I had something to do with Hayley. It was as if they no longer saw me, as though I had been erased instead of Hayley.

My grief turned dark and festered. How could I compete with a ghost? The perfect daughter who had been lost not once, but twice? The victim who demanded perpetual penance? I felt horrid for thinking such things, but I couldn't stop.

We sank under our guilt, each alone.

• • •

GREGG FORT:

I blamed Abigail. I'm not proud to admit it, but I did.

We shouted at each other and threw dishes, replicating the half-remembered drama between my own parents when I was a child. Hunted by monsters, we became monsters ourselves.

While the killer had taken Hayley's life, Abigail had offered her image up as a sacrifice to the bottomless appetite of the internet. Because of Abigail, my memories of Hayley would be forever filtered through the horrors that came after her death. She had summoned the machine that amassed individual human beings into one enormous, collective, distorting gaze,

the machine that had captured the memory of my daughter and then ground it into a lasting nightmare.

The broken shells on the beach glistened with the venom of the raging deep.

Of course that's unfair, but that doesn't mean it isn't also true.

• • •

"HEARTLESS," A SELF-PROFESSED TROLL:

There's no way for me to prove that I am who I say, or that I did what I claim. There's no registry of trolls where you can verify my identity, no Wikipedia entry with confirmed sources.

Can you even be sure I'm not trolling you right now?

I won't tell you my gender or race or who I prefer to sleep with, because those details aren't relevant to what I did. Maybe I own a dozen guns. Maybe I'm an ardent supporter of gun control.

I went after the Forts because they deserved it.

RIP-trolling has a long and proud history, and our target has always been inauthenticity. Grief should be private, personal, hidden. Can't you see how horrible it was for that mother to turn her dead daughter into a symbol, to wield it as a political tool? A public life is an inauthentic one. Anyone who enters the arena must be prepared for the consequences.

Everyone who shared that girl's memorial online, who attended the virtual candlelit vigils, offered condolences, professed to have been spurred into action, was equally guilty of hypocrisy. You didn't think the proliferation of guns capable of killing hundreds in one minute was a bad thing until someone shoved images of a dead girl in your face? What's wrong with you?

And you journalists are the worst. You make money and win awards for turning deaths into consumable stories; for coaxing survivors to sob in front of your drones to sell more ads; for inviting your readers to find meaning in their pathetic lives through vicarious, mimetic suffering. We trolls play with images of the dead, who are beyond caring, but you stinking ghouls grow fat and rich by feeding death to the living. The sanctimonious are also the most filthy-minded, and victims who cry the loudest are the hungriest for attention.

Everyone is a troll now. If you've ever liked or shared a meme that wished violence on someone you'd never met, if you've ever decided it was okay to snarl and snark with venom because the target was "powerful," if you've ever tried to signal your virtue by piling on in an outrage mob, if you've ever wrung your hands and expressed concern that perhaps the money raised for some victim should have gone to some other less "privileged" victim—then I hate to break it to you, you've also been trolling.

Some say that the proliferation of trollish rhetoric in our culture is corrosive, that armor is necessary to equalize the terms of a debate in which the only way to win is to care less. But don't you see how unethical armor is? It makes the weak think they're strong, turns cowards into deluded heroes with no skin in the game. If you truly despise trolling, then you should've realized by now that armor only makes things worse.

By weaponizing her grief, Abigail Fort became the biggest troll of them all—except she was bad at it, just a weakling in armor. We had to bring her—and by extension, the rest of you—down.

• • •

ABIGAIL FORT:

Politics returned to normal. Sales of body armor, sized for children and young adults, received a healthy bump. More companies offered classes on situational awareness and mass shooting drills for schools. Life went on.

I deleted my accounts; I stopped speaking out. But it was too late for my family. Emily moved out as soon as she could; Gregg found an apartment.

Alone in the house, my eyes devoid of armor, I tried to sort through the archive of photographs and videos of Hayley.

Every time I watched the video of her sixth birthday, I heard in my mind the pornographic moans; every time I looked at photos of her high school graduation, I saw her bloody animated corpse dancing to the tune of "Girls Just Wanna Have Fun"; every time I tried to page through the old albums for some good memories, I jumped in my chair, thinking an AR ghost of her, face grotesquely deformed like Munch's *The Scream*, was about to jump out at me, cackling, "Mommy, these new piercings hurt!"

I screamed, I sobbed, I sought help. No therapy, no medication worked. Finally, in a numb fury, I deleted all my digital files, shredded my printed albums, broke the frames hanging on walls.

The trolls trained me as well as they trained my armor.

I no longer have any images of Hayley. I can't remember what she looked like. I have truly, finally, lost my child.

How can I possibly be forgiven for that?

MINISTER FAUST

SOMATOSENSORY CORTEX DOG MESS YOU UP BIG TIME, YOU SICK SACK OF S**T

(2021)

EVEN A SCUMBAG like Marvin Shkully knew the second he hit that freaking dog dashing across the street, the chances of getting a blow-job from the engorgifying Ms. "Bam" Drozdova during the drive back to his place had fallen to *hayl-no.*

"*Stop ze car, you fakkink ess-hole!*" she snapped, and punched him hard on the shoulder. That's not really how she talked, but that's the way he heard it, because that's what he liked, and that's what he was paying for. But he'd already stopped.

"What the shit!" he said, rubbing his shoulder.

So she punched him again in the exact same spot. He couldn't even scream—it hurt that much. He just gaped at her like a dipshit in mid-dip. Fine, she was in shock or whatever. But shoulders weren't free, and her knuckles were like iron wrapped in divorce lawyer.

Of course he'd stopped the car (without her telling him to) because he had to make sure his smoking-new, fully-tricked-out Bezos Infinitive wasn't fucked up because of that goddamned dog.

Standing outside, he flared his watch-light over his front bumper, his grill, his wheel wells, his still-spinning rims, his side panels, his back bumper, and even his spoiler because you just never knew.

"Why're you looking *there,* ass-wank?" said Bam, stomping toward him unsteadily. Blood on her white jacket and miniskirt. She didn't look like a trade attorney now (or maybe she did, but even more). "You think dog shot up from back wheel and smashed into *spoiler?*"

He backed away a couple of steps. Her kicking him with those Lucite stilts was one thing. *When he wanted it.* But out in the street? With his whip chipped?

"Bam, you gotta relax. You are seriously bumming my vibe here."

"Your *vibe?* Look at dog! You *kill* him!"

"I didn't kill it!" he said, pointing at the goldish retrievery bag of breathingless crap on the road. "Bam, seriously, your head's cut—"

She held up a *shut the fuck up* hand while she triple-blinked.

"Emergency vet," she enunciated, and then eye-scrolled. "There is vet only five minutes from here."

"Vets send out ambulances now?"

"*You* are ambulance now, scum-dink."

He gawked and gaped in protest. "In my Bezos? It's still got new-car smell! I don't want my Bezos stinking like some shitty dying dog!"

She glared at him like she'd fork him right in the ballsack first chance she got. He dropped his hands, shook his head.

Bam teetered over to the muttmash. Heels and everything, she knelt and picked it up. Strong chick, for sure. Dog was whimpering like a radio just barely on.

"Get the door!"

Did as ordered. She slid the animal into the back.

"Drive," she said, and called him either *Shitlord* or *Shitload*. He couldn't tell.

• • •

Shkully woke up. Ached everywhere. Tripleblinked, scrolled to *Pain Control*, gave himself a hit. Bam was sitting titbreastfully on the bed next to him, pulling on her bra, although for a second it looked like she'd just been adjusting it.

He reached for her and she got up and out his reach. That's when he saw. And winced. And whined: "Why're you wearing *period* panties?"

She didn't even look at him while she periodpantied around the room, picking up her clothes. "Question answers itself, pee-face."

She pulled on her bloodied skirt, bustier, jacket. Relief washed over him like a hot tide, seeing her restored to full sexfulness.

Over her shoulder, she fixed her falcon eyes on him.

"You were *animal* last night," she growled

with what Reddit said that Italians called *sexificato*. "I am needing nets and spear gun to get you off."

"But . . . you *did* get me off, right?" Tried arching his eyebrows as sexidaciously as she'd growled, but the scalp-action felt like an ice giant sawing his skull into snacks—

—nearly passed out, and she was hovering over him, almost touching his cheek.

"Marv, you okay?"

He clicked again on *Pain Control*. Didn't usually need more than one hit per hour. Not a great sign.

Plus, he couldn't even remember getting reamed by Bam, which must've happened, given how sore his asshole felt.

"How much," he rasped, "did I drink last night?"

She smirked sexonically.

"All of it."

Then she turned and sexed out of the room.

"Wait up!" he said. "You going already?"

Sing-songing from the hall: "Busy *day* ahead, Mar-vin."

"What about some breakfast?"

"Not hungry, thank you."

"No, I mean for me!"

Leaned back in the room.

"On the stove I leave you nice, hot, fluffy stack of go-fuck-yourself cakes. If you are being still hungry after that, I can leave something steaming in your new car—"

"No, I'll order in."

From down the hallway: "Shouldn't you be getting dressed, Marvin?" And then door-click.

"*Why?*" he shouted.

Wallpapes were synced locally. 10K views of the city. Gray and green, lazy low river. Old, squat buildings. The Capitol. The Washington Monument: either a middle finger or a concrete dick, lubricated with rain.

"Bam?"

No answer.

Got up like an *old* old man. The kind of old man that old men point to and shake their heads and sneer to each other, muttering, "*Look* at that old man." *That's* how he got up, staggering in his thousand-dollar dick-wickers.

And blinking and clicking more pain control and starting to get scared down in his nuts that his wire-heading wasn't working anymore. Better ping Nyandeng about it.

Shuffled to the Wallpapes and made an old-fashioned headset telephone gesture with his right hand.

"Nyandeng," he said clearly.

She flashed in, sitting at her console.

"Marvin. You look like shit," she said. "And could you please not ping me when you're naked?"

"I'm paying you ten gees per service call," he said. "I think I can wear what I like."

"At least *cover* yourself, then."

Oh, right. Even with the ice-saw cutting through his brains, how could she *not* give him a hard-on? She was illegal, she could hack anything, and she looked like Barbie dipped in dark chocolate. He couldn't actually smell her, but just *remembering* smelling her made him sex up—

"What do you want, *Marvin?"*

"My pain's at a seven. I've clicked three times already in ten minutes. I don't know if it's wetware or drivers or code or what—"

"All right—plug in your port. I can scan your—"

"No! This is too big for remote. I'm in DC anyway. I'm coming in."

"You know I don't like you coming here."

She scowled, tilted her head, and her braids slid over one of her bare shoulders and down across her tank top that read *Shanakdakhete*. "Wear that top," he said. "And no bottoms." Then he clicked off.

Shambled out of the bedroom, still hoping Bam was there and'd just been clowning about leaving, because enough kidding around already, they'd been on five dates and *nothing*, not even a hand job. They *couldn't've* had sex last night—the walls and the ceiling were too clean. She'd conned him. Lawyers . . .

Lawyers?
"The fucking *Senate* hearing!"

• • •

"Mr. Shkully," said Senator Alvarez, "are you *really* asking the members of this committee to accept that you have performed a *public service* through your grotesque manipulation of our society—"

"Mrs. Senator, I never ask anyone for anything—"

"—and the hopes and dreams of millions of prospective parents by selling super-potent contraceptives that render men and women irreversibly unable to conceive? *Except* without access to the drugs that you sell at *three thousand dollars* per 'refertilization' pill?"

"I prefer to think," said Shkully, "that I'm providing super-high-value contraception *and* a check against unbridled reproductive passion that is leading Western society to Malthusian Armageddon. Mrs. Senator, just look at how many unproductive, miserable, useless people there are in this country, or, hey, even in this very chamber—"

Couldn't stop himself from smirking at that one, but his peripheral caught all his lawyers face-palming.

Turned around, saw way, way at the back of the chamber, there she was: Bam. In a clean white business suit, slowly shaking her head at him. She actually single-wagged her finger! Which turned him on even more.

"Mr. Shkully, *you* may think it funny to mock the members of this committee and this House—"

"Not *all* of them, ma'am. Just one in particular—"

"—but if you want to avoid being charged with contempt of the United States Senate, I suggest you watch your tone and wipe that smugness off your face, because the American people do not appreciate being forced to endure the hyper-profitable suffering that the country's sixth-youngest billionaire has inflicted—"

A dog barked, loudly.

The entire room went silent.

The Senator glared at him.

"Mr. Shkully! How *dare* you—"

"What?"

The dog barked again. At length. Who the hell could've smuggled a dog in here? Or was someone playing a sound file? Sure sounded close—

The Senator stood and pounded her table.

"Sergeant-at-arms! Remove Mr. Shkully forthwith!"

Only as the highest-ranking federal law enforcement officer in the United States Senate hauled him out while muttering, "Shut your mouth, ya fucking wing-ding," did Marvin realize that the barking was coming from him.

•   •   •

Outside the committee hearings room, Shkully's lawyers begged him for instructions on how to proceed.

But by then it wasn't just his skull being ice-sawed open. It was his heart shuddering like a Harley over gravel on boulders. He could barely even hear his shysters, and whatever he *could* hear, he couldn't understand them.

Suddenly he was bolting for his Bezos Infinitive, and screeching across town to a place he'd forgotten he'd ever seen, but where he'd been only the night before, like his lungs were caught on a tow-chain and whale-hook—

•   •   •

"Mr. Shkully," said the vet, brown-skinned and oily-haired, standing in a white lab coat just like a real doctor. "We were beginning to think we'd never see you again."

Shkully was panting. Felt himself sweat-soaked from cravat to crotch.

"Where is it?" he rasped.

"Right this way."

Inside a holding room was the goddamn goldish retrievery mutt that'd nearly fucked up his car. It was a mess. Cone. Casts on two legs. And a blinky head thing like a doggy tiara.

Mutt was barely moving.

But it did look at him, just for a second.

Eyes-to-eyes. Black into blue.

A gut punch. Or a cockpunch. Or an ass punch. Some kind of punch he'd never had before.

"We worked very hard, Mr. Shkully," said the vet, "to get Mubsy better. The impact shattered both her front legs, cracked her skull, and gave her a concussion—"

Nothing registered on Marvin but the name.

"'Mubsy'? How do you know her name? There's no collar—oh, wait, an RFID?"

"Nuh-no," said the doctor, looking back nervously. Marvin couldn't tell what he was. Indian? Guatemalan? Something from somewhere the food made him fart. "Your lady friend. With the Latvian accent."

Latvian? Thought she was Russian. That's why he went for her in the first place.

"—and as you can see, Mubsy is going to need a lot of care. To begin with, physiotherapy, medications—"

"What're you telling *me* for? I'm not paying for any of this!"

"Your friend already paid."

"She did? Well, then talk to her—"

"Using the expense pass on your card."

He remembered authorizing her on their third hand job–less date. He thought she'd use it for Cristal, lube, lingerie, plugs, whatever. But a goddamn *dog*?

He shook his head to clear it. "What's with the blinky crown?"

"It's the monitor for the implants," said the vet.

"*Implants?* You do *brain implants* on dogs?"

"We've been doing brain implants on dogs for years. It's all very safe and very therapeutic. Research on dogs helped humans who've had strokes, tumors, seizures—"

"I'm outta here. Tell *her* all this shit . . . when *she* . . . picks . . . it up. . . ."

. . . words . . . slurring . . . like ropey drool . . .

491

just imagining leaving the dog . . . congested his lungs . . . like eight . . . pounds . . . of snot . . .

"Mr. Shkully, sir, are you all right?"

The doc had a hand on his shoulder. It was the only thing keeping him up.

"Do you need anything?"

The dog's face swelled in his brain like a giant, throbbing emoticon.

"Fine," choked Marvin. "I'll take the dog."

Puke slid back down his throat.

"For *now*."

Puke slid back up his throat.

"I'll *take* the goddamn dog!"

Puke settled into his tummy like it was curling down for a nap.

• • •

Parked in the empty blue-painted square on the 1700 block of Florida Ave. Brain was whirring like drone rotors and he damn near went to grab the piece-of-shit dog out of the back seat and take it with him like it was a briefcase full of cash.

"Pull it together, Marv," he said aloud.

Leaving it in his back seat felt like another cockpunch, but really, the thing was a mess. What good would it do anyone to take it with him?

Punched the buzzer on the doorframe, looked into the overhead cam.

"It's me."

The door clicked. He went up the single flight of stairs above the restaurant.

Nyandeng met him at the door in her *Shanakdakhete* tank top and her braids waterfalling over her shoulders. Also worn: fatigue pants and army boots.

"Thought I told you," he said, "not to wear any bottoms."

"Marv, not even *you* have enough money to make *you* palatable."

She let him pass.

He teetered through her tech-choked office, its shelves and boxes crawling over with gear, like a hundred nests holding a thousand baby turtles, lizards, snakes, and vultures.

He crashed down into her couch.

"I'm pretty fucked up," he husked.

"Is there anyone in the world who doesn't know that?" she said. "*Barking* at the US Senate?"

"You saw that? You like to watch me, Nyang?" he said, and laughed. But he didn't laugh. This time even he heard it. He was barking again.

"Cut that shit out, Marvin," she said. "You may think it's funny, but I don't."

"I'm not *trying* to be funny," he whimpered. "My pain's up to a steady seven, no matter how many hits I take. And this barking—I'm not doing it on purpose. What the hell's happening to me? I don't get some pain relief right away, I'm gonna gouge my eyes out!"

He jerked his head to the side, directly into his right armpit, and nibbled the shit out of his jacket.

Nyandeng snapped, "Marvin! *Stop* that! It's gross!"

"See? I'm going crazy!"

"Okay. Gimme a second." She hauled a finger-thick cable from one of her systems. Yanked up his shirt and reached for his back.

"Can't you at least," he rasped, "talk dirty to me before you shove that thing in?"

Her nose curled up. "How's this for dirty? Go fuck yourself." She shoved the jack into his spineport, and everything went white—

• • •

Room: dark except for monitors and a streetlight blaring through the window.

His chest was on fire. Heart attack?

No. That wasn't it—

Hell, he'd left that piece-of-shit dog in his car for how long? Alone? No water, no food—

"At last, you're awake," said Nyandeng. "Okay. You've been hacked."

"*What*?" he said, sitting up so fast his head swirled. The jack was out of his spine, at least. "I thought *you* were supposed to *protect* me from hacks! I thought you were *the best*!"

"Maybe someone's better. Or it's an inside job," said Nyandeng. She was almost blue in the blackness. "Your pain control node firmware is totally compromised."

Marv took a breath. "Someone wants to torture me to death."

"Y'think?" she said. "You mean like about thirty million people you screwed over with your three-thousand-dollar balls-unlock pills?"

"What do I have to *do*?" he snapped. And glared at her, waiting for her to answer.

"You know I don't speak *dog*, right, Marv?"

"I was . . . barking again?"

He put his fingers over his mouth, like he could suppress his new canine impulses that way.

Slowly: "What . . . do I . . . have to do? Assuming . . . it's ransomware—"

Wanted to scream, but figured that'd induce barking. Every second he failed to get back to that mutt in the car made him panic worse.

Willed himself to whisper: "How do we get rid of it?"

"Don't know. Wait for the ask? Because I've spent the last three hours going over the hack, and it's brilliant. Any attempt to remove it, *bam!* Your pain'll hit ten so fast you'll have fifteen strokes and your head'll burst like a blister before your body hits the street."

"Oh. My. Fuck."

"There's more," she said, spinning a wheelie chair to sit in front of him, laying her forearms over the back rest. "The PC node has threaded itself into your anterior insula, anterior midcingulate cortex, somatosensory cortex, and right amygdala—"

"What're you, a *neuro*surgeon all of a sudden?"

She leaned back. "I've had three hours to become an expert while poking around that sack of KY-gristle you call a brain. Plenty of time to map the neighborhood. Anyway, I don't know why the node wants to access those areas, but I *can* tell you it's hacking into your emotions— Marv? *Marv!*"

He went barking down the hall and out into the car and into the backseat with the doors wide open where he fell upon the dog, stroking it and sobbing.

• • •

Back at his DC house, he was in the yard, tearing into the food and treats he'd blink-ordered for delivery by the time he got there.

Ripping into bags of Noogumz organic kibble made from genuine Kobe beef bits and bonemeal. Tearing into those bags with his own teeth, while the dog was asleep on an outdoor padded lounge recliner. Gnawing wildly until he started howling, and then ripping off his clothes and jumping into the pool.

Had no idea how many times he'd paddled around the edges until he finally got out, then shook himself off and sloshed over to the lounge recliner and curled up naked around the dog, nuzzling his head against the veterinary cone and ensuring he didn't put any pressure on the canine casts.

• • •

He woke up into sunshine better than the best VR. Steam was lifting off the pool. Someone was cooking sausages six blocks away. He wanted so badly to eat grass he nearly bolted from the recliner and over to the lawn, but he forced himself to stop.

That piece-of-shit dog was somehow hobbling toward him from the ripped-open pile of Noogumz, wagging its piece-of-shit broken-ass tail and hefting its blinking-tiara-head with a cone on it like the mouth of a furry cannon.

He swung his back leg to kick the goddamn thing and the resulting cockpunch was so hard he crashed to his knees and started licking the dog's cheeks and nose and eyes. That should've made him want to puke, but honestly, all that licking was better than coke.

He stopped only when he glanced up and saw the white boots, and knew who'd done this to him.

"Bam," he growled, "you *bitch!*"

"Stop *bar*king," she said, "and use your *words*."

It took him a full minute to quit snapping and snarling and finally will himself to stand on his hind legs. The only reason he *could* stop was that he could smell how much he was scaring the dog.

Grabbed clothes from the pool deck to cover himself. Whispered so he could keep control.

"*You.* You did this to me."

"*Of course* it was me," she said. "Somatosensory cortex dog mess you up big time, you sick sack of shit."

"*Why?*"

She laughed.

"Dog was not original idea," she said. "Informal class-action group created plan. They pay for all this. Original plan was to connect you—cyberpathically—with one of them, or *all* of them, *to feel their suffering.* . . . But after you run over dog, I improvise."

"To fucking hack my brain and jack me into *that* piece-of-shit?"

"We did not jack you. We *emp*ed you. And stop calling her that."

Kobe beef bonemeal and meatmash and dog-fur puked a quarter-way up his throat. He nearly choked on it. "*What?*"

"Stop *calling* her that. Her name is Mubsy!"

"I paid for her, so that dog's name is Piece-of-Shit!"

"Just for that, is now Mubsy-*Wubsy*!"

"No! *Now* it's God*damn* Piece-of-Shit!"

"Fine, Balls-Mouth! Is now *Super* Mubsy-Wubsy! Want to go for *Mrs. Cutey* Super Mubsy-Wubsy? Just keep it up!"

He trotted over to the pool bar and dialed his hacker.

"Nyandeng! I found who did this to me! Yeah! She's standing five feet in front of me. I'm one call away from five ex-Navy Seals hauling her ass to your lab to get this shit out of my brain—"

The pop-up holo of Nyandeng shook its head.

"Marvin, you're thicker than I thought. You really thought anyone could out-hack me?"

His shit nearly fell out of his ass.

"You . . . *you're* in on this, too?"

"Who else?"

"You . . . you *bitch*!"

"Bitch? You're the one who spent fifteen minutes licking his own crotch in my lab yesterday, Marvy," said Nyandeng. "You want out? Ask your Canadian friend there."

The holo disappeared.

He glared at Bam.

"*Canadian?* You're not even Russian? What else're you lying about?"

An accent slid onto her voice like a lubed condom two sizes too big. Sounded like some stuck-up fucking CBC announcer she'd made him listen to on Sirius radio (which now finally made sense) on their first hand job–less date.

"I'm *Latvian*-Canadian, shitbank!" Then she overdid the thing he liked so much it actually hurt his ears. "*I khappen to* like *talkink like zis! Puts me in touch wiss my roots!*"

"You freaking slag—took me five dates just to get *near* your roots!"

"Get comfortable with that feeling!"

"Why even do the accent in the first place?"

"*All ze easier to snare you wiss, eediot!* We got your number! Not that you ever hide it! Anything that connects in your sick head with being vulnerable! Desperate! Exploitable!"

She knelt to pet Mubsy with both hands. He felt every stroke on his face, every pat on his rump, felt his own tail—not his dick, but a real tail that really wasn't attached to him—wagging.

It was even more intense than short selling or hostile-takeover-ing.

"Now, listen carefully, fuckface," said Bam. "Take care of Super Mubsy-Wubsy, or die."

And she left, and he looked at Super Mubsy-Wubsy and wanted to kick her in the face, and the terror of it sent him howling and running around the yard in circles until he got so hungry, he had to finish off all the Noogumz and take a nice dump on the lawn and then piss on half a dozen rosebushes in the yard.

Finally curled up with Super Mubsy-Wubsy. Stroking her. Gazing into her eyes—

—thought his contacts were glitching, but

then he understood: he was looking back at his own face.

But in black and white.

And smelling his own chlorine-dipped armpit-musk and groin-funk.

And feeling his own furless warmth with his own wet nose.

"C'mon, girl," he said, rubbing her and feeling his hand on his own furry rump. "Let's go see the doc."

• • •

"Mubsy!" said the brown vet with oily black hair, patting the thighs of his pants.

The dog happily—but carefully—met the doc, wagging her bum. Marvin had to stop himself from doing the same.

The bottom of Marv's brain had been trying to figure out how to get his ex–Navy Seals to torture solutions out of the doc, but with Wubsy licking the man's hands, all Marv could taste was sunshine and cackling crows and fresh-cut grass and running at pebble-paws-heart-thumping-speed through an endless cascade of trees.

He asked to speak privately, and the doc led him past caged animals crying and whimpering which spiked his cockpunchiness massively, and he barked until he clamped his own mouth shut.

Finally, he sat down in the doc's office with the door closed and tried to push out the smells and sounds, and hefted Mubsy into his lap and hugged her and stroked her tummy.

Slowly, carefully, he explained everything, including what he knew was the vet's collusion in this massive crime against him.

"Not . . . looking for . . . revenge, doc," he whimpered. "But you owe me an explanation. Including why I'm feeling a twenty-four-hour cockpunch."

The doc stepped toward him, and gingerly removed Mubsy's cone and unclasped the casts. Marv felt his own neck and forelegs suddenly free and tender, but relief whistled through his fur like a warm breeze.

"She won't be needing these anymore," he said. "The nano-struts are in great shape. Her legs should be a hundred percent by tomorrow. But we'll keep the crown in place to monitor everything until the end of the week." He sighed. Smelled ashamed.

"Well, as you said—your friends and I 'emped' you to Wubsy and reconfigured your pain control node to amplify all the functions in the anterior insula, the anterior midcingulate cortex, the somatosensory cortex, and the right amygdala . . . because your functioning was severely depressed in all those areas."

The vet waited, as if that were an answer.

Marv started barking, and so did Wubsy, and then after an indeterminate time they both slowed, and Marv said, "In English, doc."

"Mr. Shkully, those are all areas involved in empathy. Until forty-eight hours ago, your brain was configured non- or even counter-empathically. Or to use the old expression, psychopathically. That's what's allowed you to 'succeed' in your world . . . the way you did. That's what let you make people like me . . . who were unable to . . . uh . . . that's the effect that your . . . 'medicine'—"

He cleared his throat. Looked away. Waited. Looked back.

"But we've, well, 'rewired' you. So your brain could create its own conscience. That's the, uh . . . 'cockpunch,' as you call it. You now feel pain instead of the nothingness—or even the amusement and pleasure—that you used to feel while witnessing the misery and suffering you inflicted on other people."

Multiple cockpunches. MMA cockpunches. MMA cock-knee-strikes.

Marvin finally rallied. "So . . . whatever fuckin happened to 'do no harm'? You sentenced me to a lifetime of torture? Because you and those two bitches are such good people—"

"Yes," he said through gritted teeth. "And you deserve a lifetime of torture, Marvin!"

Mubsy growled. The doc looked away, and then down, and he breathed, and finally spoke again after Mubsy quieted.

"But a conscience will let you experience good

feelings, too. Feelings you've never had before. Connection. Tenderness. Even love."

Marvin felt Mubsy's heart beating through her ribcage into his own chest, and from across the chasm, felt Marv's heart beating through his ribcage and back into her own chest.

"'Good feelings.' Like a . . . like a . . . cock-stroke?"

"Uh, well . . . that wouldn't've been my go-to phrase, but, essentially, yes."

"How long is this gonna last?"

"Uh . . . unless you run a spike through your brain? Forever."

. . .

Hot outside. Hot enough to make the air wiggle above the sidewalk and smells dance off every surface and radiate through the air like scent explosions.

They went for a walk. Mrs. Cutesy Super Mubsy-Wubsy couldn't walk far, so Marv carried her down the block past a hang-head collie tied to a post outside a taco joint, past a youth emergency shelter with a sign asking for mentors, past a man without legs holding out his hand.

Total cockpunchification.

He blinked three times, pinged Bam.

"What was the point?" he asked her. "If you'd brain-linked me to one of those people in the class-action suit, instead of to Mubsy. What'd you hope would happen?"

"I don't know. Kill yourself? For what you did to all those people?"

He snarled, "Sounds pretty psychopathic to me!"

Bam: "Don't be such a baby, Marv. Some people can't even *have* babies anymore. Thanks to . . . oh, who was it again?"

Bam clicked off.

Marv walked back up the street to the man without legs. He put down Mubsy, who licked the man's hand, which tasted to Marv like ass, which now tasted to Marv like quiche.

He introduced himself to the man whose name was Phil, and asked him to look after Wubsy. Then he walked back to the taco shop for water, an empty fast-food paper bowl, and cash back.

On the ground in front of the hang-head tied-up collie, he put down the bowl and filled it with water so the dog could drink, petted this dog he wasn't even emped to, and he felt the petting and tasted the water.

Inside the youth emergency shelter he told them he was covering lunch for all the staff and kids.

And to Phil, he gave a hundred bucks and his phone number.

"Thank god for you!" said Phil.

"Don't thank god," said Marv. "Thank dog."

He knew the hundred bucks wasn't gonna last Phil, and that the lunch for the youth shelter would be eaten and gone forever by 12:59, and that the bowl of water was probably already empty. But when he picked up Mubsy and smelled how good they felt together, when he finally stopped sobbing and howling and yipping and laughing as they licked into each other's faces, he thought of where he could put his billions for the greatest use, and he knew with all the air of thrashing through a creek in the forest how much better life would smell and taste if he spent the rest of his life licking millions of faces instead of kicking them.

ARTHUR LIU

THE LIFE CYCLE OF A CYBER BAR

(2021)

Translated from the Chinese by Nathan Faries

ONE

So a guy goes into a bar and orders a drink.

He nods toward the bartender and raises a finger. The bartender returns a knowing smile and slides a tequila on the rocks down the counter. The bartender doesn't know the guy; this is the first time this guy has been in this bar.

The guy looks around. The bar's other patrons hide their scrutiny behind newspapers and darts. Soon, a man in a trench coat and a tall hat sits down beside the guy. The two speak in low tones, and the guy exchanges some of the planet's local currency for two encrypted bio-memory chips.

At this point, a burly dude with crisscrossed knife scars on his face leans in close to the men at the bar and demands they buy him a drink. The guy turns the dude down, and the huge drunk immediately brandishes a dagger he has drawn from his belt. Instead of a knife fight, gunshots ring out near the bar, and then more

shots from some other direction, or multiple directions. The intense crossfire leaves neat rows of holes in some walls and clusters in others. When the firefight ends, the guy collapses on the barroom floor, his brains spilling out like jelly mixed with shattered microchips. After another beat, the bartender crawls out from behind the bar. She begins to clean up the mess. The bar's neon lights flicker out; its rats skitter away.

This is a typical day in the life of a cyber bar.

TWO

A guy comes into the bar and orders a drink.

He nods to me and raises his finger. I smile knowingly and slide his favorite drink down the bar. I don't know this guy, but there will always be guys like that coming into places like this. They're all cast from the same mold: flat-top haircut, tough, silent, smelling of cigarettes, with suspicious eyes and heads full of obsolete microchips—practically scrap. And a thirst for tequila . . . on the rocks.

This type of guy is always looking for someone, someone like the man in the trench coat. To drum up business, I'll sometimes open up a betting pool with the customers; we bet on how long it'll take for the guy's contact to walk over. If one of the customers wins, he drinks for free. If I win, everyone's next round is on me. As a result, the bar enjoys a flourishing business with a diverse clientele . . . but this setting also creates a perfect storm of evil *feng shui* in which bad ideas brew. Even though all my gambling games are designed for me to lose and for the customers to win, the boss never gives me any trouble, and the bar never runs low on inventory.

After fifteen minutes, the man in the trench coat and tall hat sits down next to the guy. The big dude with two knife scars crisscrossing his face cheers loudly about something; maybe he's congratulating the winner of this night's pool. That dude can't handle his drink, and things always get out of hand when he's around. And what a waste of good liquor whenever he wins the pool.

These two people in the center of the vortex of the bar's attention whisper for a while; the guy exchanges some of the planet's local currency for two encrypted bio-memory chips. I pretend not to see anything; I'm a woman of principle. In a place like this, those of us who hold to their principles and stay blind and dumb will eventually clean up, financially speaking. I just hope these two don't make a mess of the place and give me something else to clean up. Just do your business and get the fuck out, please.

But I don't get my wish. I rarely do. Before the two of them can get up off their stools, Scarface, drunk and swearing, lurches forward and tells the guy to buy him a drink. The guy turns him down flat, and Scarface immediately brandishes the dagger he has drawn from his waist. As he pulls the knife from his belt, it seems that an old pistol Scarface keeps in his pants goes off accidentally. And that's all she wrote; pandemonium ensues. As soon as I hear the first gunshot,

I start to wave my arms and try to talk everyone down, try to get control of the situation, but out of nowhere a bullet hits me and throws me against the wall. I fall forward into the open space that joins my area behind the bar and the seating area. As I lie there, I see mechanical internal viscera along with fully biological organs flowing together across the floor. Before my consciousness fades, the guy falls on top of me. I feel the weight of him pushing me down and the overflowing brains and broken chips smearing my face.

Sometimes this is how the situation ends. But I quickly come around, revived, unharmed, and I crawl out onto the battlefield and begin to pick up the pieces. This resurrection is the work of the healing nanoclusters in my body, a gift the boss gave me when we first met. They're the reason I'm willing to do all I can for the boss and why I'm dead set on working here forever. Find a quiet place to live my life and watch the teeming mortal world walk in and out of these doors—as far as I'm concerned, that's pretty much heaven.

After I knock off for the night, I pull the chain on the neon lights outside. After the roll-down gate is closed, a gang of rats jumps out of the shadows. They bare their teeth menacingly.

Goddammit. Time to ask the boss to invest in some mechanical cats.

THREE

At this point in the story, you may be wondering who will be the next protagonist to take the stage and tell their tale. You think maybe it will be Scarface, or possibly Trench Coat. Ha! Wrong. It's me.

So a guy walks into the bar and orders a drink. He nods to the bartender and raises a finger. The bartender returns a knowing smile, pours me into a glass, and stuffs a couple of ice cubes up my ass. This is how the story goes for me, every damn time.

When the guy arrives, the customers begin to look around more actively, scrutinizing the newcomer and each other with suspicion. They always fail to see the intrinsic nature of things, the true character of the situation. But what right do I have to ridicule them? I'm no better than a pot laughing at how dim the kettle is. I can see everything clearly, but I can't change anything.

I am the tequila in the glass, and my body has been blended with some amazing chemical that can trigger a short circuit in the drinker's microchips and spark the secretion of adrenaline. The person gets jumpy; excessive anxiety makes them act irrationally. So after a while, when the burly dude, who's also drinking me, starts waving his dagger and the gun rings out right on schedule, everyone else who's drinking me also pulls out a gun and starts shooting all at once. The scene is spectacular. A rain of bullets falls in a forest of guns; gore and blood fly in every direction. As for me, after I've tasted their saliva, their gastric and intestinal juices, I flow out of their bodies along with their blood and their piss. Don't ask me how I perceive all this. You'll understand everything at the proper time.

After I've poured back out of the bodies, I spend some time in intimate contact with the floor. A little later, the boss will sort things out. The manner in which the boss does this is quite distinctive. Time begins to flow backward. Bullets exit corpses, holes close, and I reluctantly take leave of all body fluids and gradually restore the blood to purity. I stream out from between lips and teeth, fall back into the glass, and finally my butt plugs return to the ice bucket. The bartender's smile fades away. The bar returns to its original state. There's no trace of the guy.

Sometimes the boss gets lazy. When that happens, after the bartender is resurrected and I'm still mostly on the floor, the back-flowing time will return early to its normal forward motion. This is one of those times. Whenever I'm stuck in this situation, my great undertaking—to return to my natural state—is forestalled. The bartender can pile up corpses, shards of glass, and dismembered furniture, but she has no way to suck me out of the floorboards. All I can do is

wait in the small gaps between the wood fibers, wait for the me in the shot glass, the me soaked into the tables and chairs, the me in the corpses, and the me in the floor all to merge into one after the neon lights go out. Then, in the darkness, we are all assimilated into a mass of rotten meat within the boss's body. After some time, we will all be divided once again. We will again be differentiated into glasses, tables and chairs, floors, bar counters, glass bottles, and the tequila in those bottles.

Sometimes we ask the boss, "How'd we do?" The boss never answers.

The heart, liver, spleen, and lungs are the internal organs of a human; we are the internal organs of the boss.

Our boss is the bar, but I guess you already figured that out.

FOUR

The bar is one of the most intriguing categories of organisms in the universe. On the evolutionary path of natural selection, they have experienced an exceedingly brutal struggle to avoid elimination. Nowadays, many building classifications are relegated to the sedimentary strata of a few of the known planets. Whether we are speaking of low thatched huts or the old metropolitan towers that rose dozens or even hundreds of stories into the air—these species are merely fossils and memories now. The only category of structure that has persisted from that age—that has explored and settled new lands, that has truly made its home on a great many planets and has survived to this day—is the bar.

At the beginning of its life cycle, the juvenile bar will take root in the shady alleys of a planet's cities, near piles of rubbish. The young are able to absorb the nutrients from food waste with considerable efficiency. The totipotent larval stem cells divide and differentiate rapidly until they form complete organs, which are soon encased in and supported by bioluminescent cartilage. The luminous skeletal structure also serves to draw prey to the bar. The central nervous system is divided into several distinct neuromas which are able to survive for a time without direct connection to the main structure. These isolated bundles of nerve cells are able to perform an approximate simulation of the social environment of the quarry. On nearly every planet, this has proven to be a most effective method of hunting. At one time, scientists used genetic engineering to create skyscrapers with similar skills. This predictably resulted in large-scale massacres. Scientists and skyscrapers alike were condemned to death and executed in the aftermath.

The process of hunting its prey typically begins with the entrance of a man into the bar. This intrusion stimulates a series of neural signals, prompting the individual neuromas to initiate their own series of actions. Statistically speaking, the majority of those who frequent this sort of bar are wanted criminals. These are the sort of people who are most easily attracted to the atmosphere here, and their disappearance is the least likely to attract notice from the outside world.

Normally, the man will begin by ordering a drink. When this happens, the primary neuroma will take some of the fluid discharged from the excretory system of the bar, pour it into a hyperplastic growth, and push it toward the man. A neuroma sent out from the "mother's" body at some earlier time is capable of being reabsorbed into that body later, and the bar is able to reverse or continue the process of cell division and differentiation at will.

The ingestion of the excreta by the prey marks the formal beginning of the hunt. The bar randomly prompts a neuroma to pick a fight with the man. The man who is under the influence of the bar's urine lacks self-control and readily joins in a melee with the inciting neuroma.

As the turmoil begins, a gland on the side of the inciting neuroma explodes. The sound wave from the detonation is transmitted through the air to the other neuromas present, causing their glands to discharge as well. When such a gland erupts, several dense spores are ejected from the site, not unlike the high-speed expulsion of pollen from a splitting alfalfa capsule. The radiating spread of these projectiles is typically omnidirectional and will normally prove effective in killing the prey. In extremely rare cases, the prey will only be wounded and will escape with his life. In these circumstances, the bar will merely lose one opportunity to feed; the identity of the bar is normally not compromised by this failure. This is not only due to the fact that these organic structures have evolved an effective camouflage defense mechanism as they are similar in appearance to traditional public houses built by humans, but also owing to the gene banks that are stored in the bar's anatomy. Thanks to the ever-expanding genetic assets contained in these banks, when neuromas are differentiated, the information therein allows for a variety of random arrangements and multiple permutations to construct manifold expressive results.

After a man (or in extremely rare cases a woman) is successfully dispatched, the bar begins to digest the prey. The digestion process is also a process of self-healing. The damaged areas will differentiate in reverse and re-form the complete base arrangement of the mother, and the prey's carcass will also be integrated into that being. The flesh and blood will be "swallowed," so to speak, and the base-pair sequence of the newly ingested cells will be transferred to the gene bank. Future neuromas will achieve richer expressive results, and behavior patterns will be more plentiful and more diverse.

Above is the basic content of the bar biological activity report. There yet remain many elusive matters regarding this creature. The most baffling among these mysteries concerns their mode of reproduction. As they are in this age gradually moving toward extinction, we may never learn the answer to this question. The very existence of this species has caused many traditional drinking establishments to go out of business over the long span of time. Considering their far-reaching impact on reduction of crime rates and the frequency of interstellar drunk driving cases, we cannot help but feel some sorrow at the loss of this species, and for us all as we consider their apparently irreversible fate.

FIVE

The last bar? That's me. I am the last bar in the entire universe.

When I was a young bar, I once set myself an ambitious goal: in my lifetime, I would accomplish three things that I could be truly proud of. Until very recently, I had accomplished two such objectives: one, I was the last bar in the universe; and two, I was the first bar to go into a man.

After consuming more than two hundred fugitives, I began to think about the intrinsic nature of ingestion. Considering the process of organizational integration, the issue of whether I have absorbed men or men have absorbed me is not a trivial question. After dedicating long and inconclusive ratiocination on the subject, I decided to take the scientific method as my main principle, and I resolved to attempt something I had never attempted before: to find a man and to let him eat me. I would take the results of that experience, place them alongside my own experience of ingestion, and compare the two. This experiment would prove to be invaluable.

The experiment may sound simple, but it is in fact not simple at all. Even considering those humans with physical modifications, my own body is still considerably larger, too large for direct human ingestion. I had to find a way to effectively reduce my scale. But this seemed at first to be the stuff of fantasy; I am not, after all, the magical shrinking tent from the *Arabian Nights*. In the end, I had to revise my way of thinking about the problem, and curiously, the solution was inspired by information transmitted between two of my neuromas. Thanks to this neuromatic conversation, I arrived at a new strategy for capturing my quarry.

According to this new tactic, I first restored the totipotency of the somatic cells, rearranged

their genes, and expressed them again, this time using a chemical synthesis reaction to generate a composite of polysaccharides, fats, and proteins. Once this process was complete, I became a house made entirely of candy, and I hid myself, naturally, within an amusement park. This process of rearrangement may seem like a radical transformation and an extreme recourse, but in truth it was not so. Certainly it is easier in its operation, and much safer, than attempting a wholesale reduction of size.

During the transformation process, I was forced to alter certain character traits that I had acquired through the force of lifelong habit and ages of genetic inertia. For one, I had to adjust my active hours from nocturnal to diurnal. The compounds volatilized from my new body quickly attracted a large number of human young, which I had not anticipated, but there was also no shortage of adult males among the test subjects. I focused all of my attention on the men. I kept myself locked against the children and their families, and only opened my doors one evening just after the carnival had closed when a small band of rowdy young men approached.

So I achieved the second of my great ambitions as follows. The experimental specimens quickly discovered that all of the elements that constituted my new body were edible and quite delicious. Before long, they had broken me up into a great many pieces and thus consumed me until only about half of my structure remained. The remaining unsupported skeleton collapsed, leaving only some splintered sections of my ruined walls on the ground.

Having eaten to their hearts' content, they left with full bellies, eager to share the secret of this place with their friends. However, as soon as they left me, one by one they fell to the ground, their bodies convulsing. Finally, after their corpses grew stiff, within a short period of time they all melted into a mass of sarcomas. Yet the cells did not in fact differentiate into miniature versions of myself or anything of that sort. These experimental results were inconsistent with both hypotheses. Was I absorbing my prey or was my prey absorbing me? Neither description seemed sufficient to explain these results. Clearly more experiments were needed to answer my research question.

Faced with several lumps of ground meat, I knew that my experiment would definitely arouse attention and some hostility. But what did I care about that? I am an endangered species protected by universal law. I could always play that card if push came to shove, but something told me that these guys would not be missed by anyone in the near future.

Soon, my attention was drawn to the sarcomas on the ground. Although they did not differentiate into miniature versions of me, they began to wriggle. Whenever one sarcoma came into contact with another sarcoma, the two joined together. After all the sarcomas had merged into one, forming a fleshy ball roughly the same size as the remaining portion of my original body, the situation changed suddenly. The ball of flesh began to change its configuration rapidly, constituting itself into a new bar instead of a candy house. This demonstrated that this new form was indeed descended from the same ancestry as myself, yet it also possessed a distinct consciousness from my own. Thinking of this, I felt at once a frenzy of delight and a terrible sense of loss. Suddenly, I was no longer alone in the universe.

In the end, my ecstasy overwhelmed my dismay. I was conscious of an opportunity. I realized that now I would finally be able to accomplish the last of my three great feats. Whether I succeeded or failed, I would achieve my life's ambition; what I did next would either result in the extinction of an entire species, or it could mean an opportunity for the rebirth of our kind.

I transformed myself back into my original form, braced myself and stood face-to-face with my newborn counterpart, our brilliant neon glowing off each other's surfaces. Together we would usher in the great harmonious miracle of life.

SIX

And so it was that one day, in a distant corner of the universe, a bar went into a bar.

A guy went into one bar; another guy ordered a drink at the bar just across the narrow alleyway. The bartenders in both bars smiled and passed both guys a tequila on the rocks. The bartenders did not know these guys; it was the first time these guys had visited these bars.

The guys looked around. The bars' other patrons hid their scrutiny behind newspapers and darts. After a while, the guys both put on trench coats and tall hats, walked to the door of their respective bars. The two spoke to each other in low tones, exchanged some of the planet's local currency for two encrypted bio-memory chips. Then the guys exchanged them back.

The guys returned to their stools at their original bars. At this point, two burly dudes with crisscrossed knife scars on their faces leaned close to the guys at the bars and demanded the guys buy them a drink. Both guys turned both dudes down, and in both bars the huge drunks immediately brandished daggers they had drawn from their belts. The guys grappled with the dudes, and suddenly a gun went off followed by the noisy discharge of multiple firearms. The intense crossfire left neat rows of holes in some walls and clusters in others. The rain of bullets grew even heavier, the bars' neon lights grew more dazzling, and the melodies blaring from the jukeboxes in the corners of the bars crescendoed despite the fact that their machinery had seemingly already been shattered in the crossfire.

One of the guys collapsed on the barroom floor, his brains spilling out like jelly mixed with shattered microchips. The other guy continued to howl with rage and shoot his gun. Then everyone still standing in both bars echoed his howl, and all the rifles and pistols spat hot metal slag. Patrons shouted and charged each other; cold weapons and hot weapons collided, and flesh struck flesh, and flesh penetrated flesh.

Amid the clash of metal and meat, projectiles passed through the front of one bar and pierced the body of the other. A bullet punctured the wall of the main room, shot through the kitchen, entered the furnace, and hit its mark, the gas tank buried deep in the structure. A blaze of flames soared into the night.

There was a terrific uproar as the explosion reached its climax.

The clamor alarmed the entire neighborhood, and the explosion almost leveled the buildings on either side of the bars. People surged into the streets and alleys. The fire trucks and ambulances charged onto the scene and began to comb through the ruins of structures that had buried the entire alley, searching for the wounded amid the rubble.

The dust settled, and the alley lay empty once again. No one noticed the ashes that rose slowly toward the blue sky, the embers that did not fall to the ground, but spiraled upward, left the atmosphere, and crossed into interstellar space. This was the seed released by the bars. These germs would wander aimlessly through the universe until they fell into the gravitational field of a certain planet or were picked up by a passing spacecraft and carried to a new habitat where they could settle and put down roots.

This was an extremely arduous process fraught with insecurity. If it were otherwise, the bar would never have been reduced to endangered status. Most of the germ cells would be swallowed up in the fires of the stars, the heat that can reduce anything to nothing and disintegrate every possibility. Fortunately, after such tragedies had played out billions of times, a cluster of dust was finally captured by a blue planet on the radial arm of Orion, and on that planet, carbon-based organisms had recently evolved into the final stage of its human civilization.

And so it came to pass that millions upon millions of light-years away from where the species was born, in a dark alley in the depths of a city enveloped in a heavy fog, neon lights flicker to life late one night, and a gang of rats chatter and skitter away from approaching feet.

And a guy walks into a bar and orders a drink.

This is a typical day in the life of a cyber bar.

CULTURE

We are defined by **culture**. We are the music we listen to, the shows we watch, the plays we perform, the games we play, the fashion we wear, the sports we cheer, the food we eat, the advertisements we skip, even (thankfully) the books we read.[*] Our choice of culture explains who we are and what we value. Culture distracts us, it inspires us, and it represents us.

It also influences us.

We are as much the products of our culture as we are its creators. Culture persuades us and dissuades us. It sets social norms, and chooses who is seen—and why. It tells us who we are, who we ought to be, and how we should act. Action movies inform our geopolitics. Fashion influencers dispense medical advice. Athletes tell us how to vote. Advertisements set our aspirations.

_____

[*] GNR. *Fargo*. Pass. *Diablo*. Hoodies. Arsenal. BBQ. All of them. This one.

Cyberpunk is obsessed with culture, perhaps uniquely so. While Golden Age science fiction worked out how we fly to Venus, cyberpunk fretted over the playlist. The stories here also understand that technology is only as meaningful as the art it carries. They understand that we are what we eat, drink, and dance to—and how changes to those media change us as well.

. . .

The section begins with Fritz Leiber's "Coming Attraction" (1974). A British tourist visits a radioactive, puritanical America. There's nothing epic about it: it is one man's "poverty tourism" to a country that is crumbling at the seams. The malignant world-building is made all the more plausible, and horrible, through Leiber's emphasis on the tiniest details: the fabric of a dress, the typography of a billboard, even the lukewarm temperature of a restaurant's food.

The massive, transformative changes are out of reach, but the reader can easily picture, and appreciate, the sensation of living in this miserable setting.

In "With the Original Cast" (1982), Nancy Kress explores the very specific use of a very focused technology. "Electronically Stimulated Incarnation Recall" connects people (painfully) with the genetic memory of their ancestors. The story cleverly focuses on what ESIR means to stage actors: how they can combine their historical presence with their craft to create a presence "that transcends both." It is, in the recurring theme of cyberpunk, not about the technology itself, but what it enables humans to express.

Paul Di Filippo's "A Short Course in Art Appreciation" (1988) has a similar premise, but more decadently expressed. The underlying conceit is a technological ability to unleash an artistic identity, but here it is all-consuming. What happens if you see the world as if it were a Vermeer? Or a Matisse? Or perhaps dive all the way into a Cubist reality? The story is framed as a romance, and asks us how much you need to share someone else's perception to truly connect with them.

Steve Beard's "Retoxicity" (1998) is a fusion of technology and sorcery, with the power of tech-amplified culture taking the story to an unexpected conclusion. It is a gleefully archetypal cyberpunk setting: a rave at Battersea Power Station, complete with warring geopolitical gangster factions and voodoo-powered DJ rebels.

The battleground in Zedeck Siew's "The White Mask" (2015) is on the streets, sprayed in "smart paint." Warring graffiti gangs express their discontent with one another, and with the government, on the streets of Malaysia. Siew's story shows the interconnectedness of cultural layers. By day, the technology is being used by advertisers to achieve their client's sales objectives. At night, it is being put to far more provocative uses.

Marie Vibbert's "Electric Tea" (2019) is about failure. "Artists fail for many reasons," notes the protagonist—before confessing that their reason was simply "I wasn't good enough." The technology, such as it is, is the titular "electric tea," a beverage that's half-legal and perhaps all fake. It is an accelerant for inspiration, that is, if it exists at all.

The fear of failure is also present in "Études" (2020) by Lavanya Lakshminarayan, although for different reasons. The story is set in Apex City, a future Bangalore where social class is strictly controlled. Nina has temporarily been adopted—raised from the lowest class in society. If she succeeds as a musician, she'll be given a permanent place. Nina's forbidden from using cybernetic aids. She is the "only person there playing music that comes from the soul." But does that matter when competing against perfection?

In "Exopunk's Not Dead" (2019), Corey J. White spins familiar cyberpunk tropes in a new way. There's punk music, and anger, and something being reduced to rubble (physically and metaphorically). Plus, mecha mosh pits. Like "Coming Attraction," the story hints at something much bigger: there are vignettes of work shortages, struggles with fascist nativism, and, of course, the exo-suits themselves. But the focus is on one man for one evening, with the detail in the music, the drinks, and even the charming pickup lines.

Erica Satifka's "Act of Providence" (2021) is the story of Hailey, as one of the last survivors of a natural disaster that wiped out an entire state. It is also the story *of* Hailey's story, as Hailey is persuaded to share her intimate memories of the event with a predatory game designer. "Act of Providence" uses the production of the game as a way of demonstrating the larger issues of a deeply broken society, one where automation has left humans miserable and valueless, and the sale of trauma somehow becomes a viable option to survive.

"Feral Arcade Children of the American Northeast" (2021) also features a game: the urban legend of a "black box" game that preys on its players. But the "feral" teens of Sam J.

Miller's postmodern tale are resilient, accustomed to far worse predators. Miller's phantasmagorical arcade game is, in many ways, the least menacing part of the story. It may be lethal, but at least it is still fundamentally a game. It has rules, a certain underlying sense, and even the hope of winning, all unlike every other aspect of their lives.

· · ·

Culture is not always the hero.[*] Like every other technology in this book, the influence of media is not inherently good or bad. It is a force as susceptible to use and abuse as any other. Marshall McLuhan warns that "once we have surrendered our senses and nervous systems to the private manipulation of those who would try to benefit from taking a lease on our eyes and ears and nerves, we don't really have any rights left." Cyberpunk stories frequently speculate about the technological and social conditions that would make possible that complete surrender.

In William Gibson and Michael Swanwick's classic "Dogfight" (1985), Deke finds a sense of purpose in a cheap VR game of dueling World War One aircraft. The game itself is not the villain of the piece: it is at the center of a small community, and, to many, provides a sense of support and escape. For cybernetically enhanced former pilots, for example, it is even therapeutic. But as Deke gets more obsessed, his desire to win the game consumes him. He confuses victory in the game with true success.

Russell Blackford's "Glass Reptile Breakout" (1985) takes an equivocal perspective on the power of culture. Two researchers study a bewildering youth subculture: a combination of music and body-transfiguring fashion that, for all intents and purposes, seems to be causing spontaneous miracles. Told from multiple perspectives, "Glass Reptile Breakout" is a story of unintended consequences, with fragments of belief all adding together to make something more.

Is sex culture? Candas Jane Dorsey's "[Learning About] Machine Sex" (1988) tackles the topic head-on. Angel is a genius programmer, but her experience in life is of being used, betrayed, and undermined—solely because she's a woman. As the story unfolds, Angel's cunning revenge becomes clear, as she plans to triumph not only over the individual men who betrayed her, but also the entire patriarchal society that perpetuated that betrayal. The story is a savage assault on the culture of techbro feudalism and laddish machismo that was (and still is) present both across cyberpunk and beyond it.

Nicholas Royle's "D.GO" (1990) features an enigmatic, and extremely sinister, advertising campaign. As the story unfolds, so does the reach and penetration of the media blitz.[†] The pressure builds, leading to its ominous, and perhaps inevitable, conclusion.

Kim Newman carries us onto the field of sport with "SQPR" (1992). The story is full of tiny details, drawn from history and fiction, building an entire cyberpunk world from the atoms of pop culture. A single match unfolds, pitting a team of augmented monsters against the last squad of "real" footballers. The beautiful game (or what's left of it) is presented as the last bastion of humanity dignity.

"Gray Noise" (1996) by Pepe Rojo (translated by Andrea Bell) also questions the line at which our devotion to cultural consumption transgresses against our basic sense of decency. "Gray Noise" is told from the point of view of an ocular reporter; a journalist constantly transmitting, always in the pursuit of new disaster and new tragedy.

---

[*] Both mainstream literature and (counterintuitively) science fiction literature are full of stories about the inherent wonderfulness of art, which, although appreciated, always makes me suspect these tales were written for an audience of one's skeptical parents. There's an entire subgenre of SF that boils down to "My MFA saved us from aliens, so those student loans were totally worth it."

[†] These are real advertising terms, which says a lot about the psyche of the average advertising person. Source: me, an average advertising person.

In "Younis in the Belly of the Whale" (2011) by Yasser Abdellatif (translated by Robin Moger), our nameless narrator is swallowed first by an enormous shopping mall and then by a virtual reality simulation. The story is about consumption in all its forms, and the ultimate whale, of course, is capitalism itself.

Consumption also features in E. J. Swift's "Alligator Heap" (2016), which uses food as its central metaphor. In a deeply stratified society, an immortal oligarch eats symbols of his vast wealth, while patiently awaiting his next rebirth. His servants wait in the wings, jealously guarding the scraps from his table. There's nothing too small to be significant, after all "partnerships were forged, love affairs ended, business deals brokered, and friendships cemented, over food."

Cassandra Khaw's "Degrees of Beauty" (2016) straddles the thin line between cyberpunk and body horror. Khaw's story of Bai Ling and her ruthless pursuit of physical perfection for her daughter is deeply disturbing. Oliver Langmead's "Glitterati" (2017) also features a destructive quest for style. The key difference between them: in "Glitterati," the eccentric, "fashion-forward" society openly supports and applauds the self-destruction. In "Degrees of Beauty," there's horror in the hypocrisy. Bai Ling conducts experiments that are supposedly taboo, but she is tacitly endorsed by everyone around her.

• • •

Cyberpunk and music go hand-in-hand; a relationship that goes deeper than a suffix. Like music, cyberpunk has always experimented with form: it adopts new technologies and techniques, remixes and borrows from its predecessors, creates patterns, and responds to trends. Like cyberpunk, music is an open loop, in constant conversation with the world around it. Cyberpunk is also very often *about* music. As a genre, it appreciates the power of music as a

way of depicting, or changing, culture. Music is often used not only to add atmosphere to great effect, but as the central conceit of the story. Cyberpunk is a genre that appreciates the signal and the noise alike.

In Suzanne Church's "Synch Me, Kiss Me, Drop" (2012), the story is about the seduction of the beat: the need for "sound and sex" that can drive us mad with desire. Written with a distinctive beat to it, the story ends with the ultimate drop.

M. Lopes da Silva's "Found Earworms" (2019) and Beth Cato's "Apocalypse Playlist" (2020) both lift from the format of music to inspire the structure of their stories. "Found Earworms" is part postapocalyptic survival thriller, part lyrical fragments. The latter ground the former: vignettes of a weird epic mixed with the more everyday need to land a good rhyme. "Apocalypse Playlist" is a carefully curated series of vignettes, excellently soundtracked, of Orchid's quest for survival. It is deliberately wry, but understands the persistent power of music: Orchid's "curated filter of tunes enables her to work, survive, even to sleep in an otherwise overwhelming world."

Omar Robert Hamilton's "Rain, Streaming" (2019) is set in an alien world of globally televised virtual reality showdowns and an outrageous circus of corporate communications. Val (and his AI passenger, also Val) has a shot at the greatest reward of all: a chance to immerse himself in the music video that haunts his dreams. A mix of toxic nostalgia and something stronger, "Rain, Streaming" presents music as the one pure thing in a lonely and chaotic world.*

• • •

* See also the other stories in this volume that have directly inspired or been inspired by music, e.g., Jeff Noon's "Ghost Codes" and Janelle Monáe and Alaya Dawn Johnson's "The Memory Librarian."

Cyberpunk's understanding of culture is an extension of its appreciation of human affairs. These are not stories of grand transformation or epic heroism. Despite the unusual settings and speculative conceits, they're reflections of everyday challenges: what motivates and inspires us; the pressure we feel from within and without; the desire to fit in, to belong, to achieve, or be safe. The fiction of culture appreciates the reality of our lives.

FRITZ LEIBER

COMING ATTRACTION

(1974)

THE COUPE with the fishhooks welded to the fender shouldered up over the curb like the nose of a nightmare. The girl in its path stood frozen, her face probably stiff with fright under her mask. For once my reflexes weren't shy. I took a fast step toward her, grabbed her elbow, yanked her back. Her black skirt swirled out.

The big coupe shot by, its turbine humming. I glimpsed three faces. Something ripped. I felt the hot exhaust on my ankles as the big coupe swerved back into the street. A thick cloud like a black flower blossomed from its jouncing rear end, while from the fishhooks flew a black shimmering rag.

"Did they get you?" I asked the girl.

She had twisted around to look where the side of her skirt was torn away. She was wearing nylon tights.

"The hooks didn't touch me," she said shakily. "I guess I'm lucky."

I heard voices around us:

"Those kids! What'll they think up next?"

"They're a menace. They ought to be arrested."

Sirens screamed at a rising pitch as two motor-police, their rocket-assist jets full on, came whizzing toward us after the coupe. But the black flower had become a thick fog obscuring the whole street. The motor-police switched from rocket assists to rocket brakes and swerved to a stop near the smoke cloud.

"Are you English?" the girl asked me. "You have an English accent."

Her voice came shudderingly from behind the sleek black satin mask. I fancied her teeth must be chattering. Eyes that were perhaps blue searched my face from behind the black gauze covering the eyeholes of the mask. I told her she'd guessed right. She stood close to me. "Will you come to my place tonight?" she asked rapidly. "I can't thank you now. And there's something you can help me about."

My arm, still lightly circling her waist, felt her body trembling. I was answering the plea in that as much as in her voice when I said, "Certainly." She gave me an address south of Inferno, an apartment number, and a time. She asked me my name and I told her.

"Hey, you!"

I turned obediently to the policeman's shout. He shooed away the small clucking crowd of masked women and barefaced men. Coughing from the smoke that the black coupe had thrown out, he asked for my papers. I handed him the essential ones.

• • •

He looked at them and then at me. "British Barter? How long will you be in New York?"

Suppressing the urge to say, "For as short a time as possible," I told him I'd be here for a week or so.

"May need you as a witness," he explained. "Those kids can't use smoke on us. When they do that, we pull them in."

He seemed to think the smoke was the bad thing. "They tried to kill the lady," I pointed out.

He shook his head wisely. "They always pretend they're going to, but actually they just want to snag skirts. I've picked up rippers with as many as fifty skirt-snags tacked up in their rooms. Of course, sometimes they come a little too close."

I explained that if I hadn't yanked her out of the way, she'd have been hit by more than hooks. But he interrupted, "If she'd thought it was a real murder attempt, she'd have stayed here."

I looked around. It was true. She was gone.

"She was fearfully frightened," I told him.

"Who wouldn't be? Those kids would have scared old Stalin himself."

"I mean frightened of more than 'kids.' They didn't look like 'kids.'"

"What did they look like?"

I tried without much success to describe the three faces. A vague impression of viciousness and effeminacy doesn't mean much.

"Well, I could be wrong," he said finally. "Do you know the girl? Where she lives?"

"No," I half lied.

The other policeman hung up his radio-phone and ambled toward us, kicking at the tendrils of dissipating smoke. The black cloud no longer hid the dingy facades with their five-year-old radiation flash-burns, and I could begin to make out the distant stump of the Empire State Building, thrusting up out of Inferno like a mangled finger.

"They haven't been picked up so far," the approaching policeman grumbled. "Left smoke for five blocks, from what Ryan says."

The first policeman shook his head. "That's bad," he observed solemnly.

I was feeling a bit uneasy and ashamed. An Englishman shouldn't lie, at least not on impulse.

"They sound like nasty customers," the first policeman continued in the same grim tone. "We'll need witnesses. Looks as if you may have to stay in New York longer than you expect."

I got the point. I said, "I forgot to show you all my papers," and handed him a few others, making sure there was a five-dollar bill in among them.

• • •

When he handed them back a bit later, his voice was no longer ominous. My feelings of guilt vanished. To cement our relationship, I chatted with the two of them about their job.

"I suppose the masks give you some trouble," I observed. "Over in England we've been reading about your new crop of masked female bandits."

"Those things get exaggerated," the first policeman assured me. "It's the men masking as women that really mix us up. But, brother, when we nab them, we jump on them with both feet."

"And you get so you can spot women almost as well as if they had naked faces," the second policeman volunteered. "You know, hands and all that."

"Especially all that," the first agreed with a chuckle. "Say, is it true that some girls don't mask over in England?"

"A number of them have picked up the fashion," I told him. "Only a few, though—the ones who always adopt the latest style, however extreme."

"They're usually masked in the British newscasts."

"I imagine it's arranged that way out of deference to American taste," I confessed. "Actually, not very many do mask."

The second policeman considered that. "Girls going down the street bare from the neck up." It was not clear whether he viewed the prospect with relish or moral distaste. Likely both.

"A few members keep trying to persuade Parliament to enact a law forbidding all masking," I continued, talking perhaps a bit too much.

The second policeman shook his head. "What an idea. You know, masks are a pretty good thing, brother. Couple of years more and I'm going to make my wife wear hers around the house."

The first policeman shrugged. "If women were to stop wearing masks, in six weeks you wouldn't know the difference. You get used to anything, if enough people do or don't do it."

I agreed, rather regretfully, and left them. I turned north on Broadway (old Tenth Avenue, I believe) and walked rapidly until I was beyond Inferno. Passing such an area of undecontaminated radioactivity always makes a person queasy. I thanked God there weren't any such in England, as yet.

The street was almost empty, though I was accosted by a couple of beggars with faces tunneled by H-bomb scars, whether real or of makeup putty, I couldn't tell. A fat woman held out a baby with webbed fingers and toes. I told myself it would have been deformed anyway and that she was only capitalizing on our fear

of bomb-induced mutations. Still, I gave her a seven-and-a-half-cent piece. Her mask made me feel I was paying tribute to an African fetish.

"May all your children be blessed with one head and two eyes, sir."

"Thanks," I said, shuddering, and hurried past her.

". . . There's only trash behind the mask, so turn your head, stick to your task: Stay away, stay away—from—the—girls!"

• • •

This last was the end of an anti-sex song being sung by some religionists half a block from the circle-and-cross insignia of a femalist temple. They reminded me only faintly of our small tribe of British monastics. Above their heads was a jumble of billboards advertising predigested foods, wrestling instruction, radio handies, and the like.

I stared at the hysterical slogans with disagreeable fascination. Since the female face and form have been banned on American signs, the very letters of the advertiser's alphabet have begun to crawl with sex—the fat-bellied, big-breasted capital B, the lascivious double O. However, I reminded myself, it is chiefly the mask that so strangely accents sex in America.

A British anthropologist has pointed out, that, while it took more than five thousand years to shift the chief point of sexual interest from the hips to the breasts, the next transition to the face has taken less than fifty years. Comparing the American style with Moslem tradition is not valid; Moslem women are compelled to wear veils, the purpose of which is concealment, while American women have only the compulsion of fashion and use masks to create mystery.

Theory aside, the actual origins of the trend are to be found in the anti-radiation clothing of World War III, which led to masked wrestling, now a fantastically popular sport, and that in turn led to the current female fashion. Only a wild style at first, masks quickly became as necessary as brassieres and lipsticks had been earlier in the century.

I finally realized that I was not speculating about masks in general, but about what lay behind one in particular. That's the devil of the things; you're never sure whether a girl is heightening loveliness or hiding ugliness. I pictured a cool, pretty face in which fear showed only in widened eyes. Then I remembered her blonde hair, rich against the blackness of the satin mask. She'd told me to come at the twenty-second hour—ten p.m.

I climbed to my apartment near the British Consulate; the elevator shaft had been shoved out of plumb by an old blast, a nuisance in these tall New York buildings. Before it occurred to me that I would be going out again, I automatically tore a tab from the film strip under my shirt. I developed it just to be sure. It showed that the total radiation I'd taken that day was still within the safety limit. I'm not phobic about it, as so many people are these days, but there's no point in taking chances.

I flopped down on the daybed and stared at the silent speaker and the dark screen of the video set. As always, they made me think, somewhat bitterly, of the two great nations of the world. Mutilated by each other, yet still strong, they were crippled giants poisoning the planet with their dreams of an impossible equality and an impossible success.

I fretfully switched on the speaker. By luck, the newscaster was talking excitedly of the prospects of a bumper wheat crop, sown by planes across a dust bowl moistened by seeded rains. I listened carefully to the rest of the program (it was remarkably clear of Russian telejamming) but there was no further news of interest to me. And, of course, no mention of the Moon, though everyone knows that America and Russia are racing to develop their primary bases into fortresses capable of mutual assault and the launching of alphabet-bombs toward Earth. I myself knew perfectly well that the British electronic equipment I was helping trade for American wheat was destined for use in spaceships.

• • •

I switched off the newscast. It was growing dark and once again I pictured a tender, frightened face behind a mask. I hadn't had a date since England. It's exceedingly difficult to become acquainted with a girl in America, where as little as a smile, often, can set one of them yelping for the police—to say nothing of the increasing puritanical morality and the roving gangs that keep most women indoors after dark. And naturally, the masks which are definitely not, as the Soviets claim, a last invention of capitalist degeneracy, but a sign of great psychological insecurity. The Russians have no masks, but they have their own signs of stress.

I went to the window and impatiently watched the darkness gather. I was getting very restless. After a while a ghostly violet cloud appeared to the south. My hair rose. Then I laughed. I had momentarily fancied it a radiation from the crater of the Hell-bomb, though I should instantly have known it was only the radio-induced glow in the sky over the amusement and residential area south of Inferno.

Promptly at twenty-two hours I stood before the door of my unknown girlfriend's apartment. The electronic say-who-please said just that. I answered clearly, "Wysten Turner," wondering if she'd given my name to the mechanism. She evidently had, for the door opened. I walked into a small empty living room, my heart pounding a bit.

The room was expensively furnished with the latest pneumatic hassocks and sprawlers. There were some midgie books on the table. The one I picked up was the standard hard-boiled detective story in which two female murderers go gunning for each other.

The television was on. A masked girl in green was crooning a love song. Her right hand held something that blurred off into the foreground. I saw the set had a handie, which we haven't in England as yet, and curiously thrust my hand into the handie orifice beside the screen. Contrary to my expectations, it was not like slipping into a pulsing rubber glove, but rather as if the girl on the screen actually held my hand.

A door opened behind me. I jerked out my hand with as guilty a reaction as if I'd been caught peering through a keyhole.

She stood in the bedroom doorway. I think she was trembling. She was wearing a gray fur coat, white-speckled, and a gray velvet evening mask with shirred gray lace around the eyes and mouth. Her fingernails twinkled like silver.

It hadn't occurred to me that she'd expect us to go out.

"I should have told you," she said softly. Her mask veered nervously toward the books and the screen and the room's dark corners. "But I can't possibly talk to you here."

I said doubtfully, "There's a place near the Consulate . . ."

"I know where we can be together and talk," she said rapidly. "If you don't mind."

As we entered the elevator I said, "I'm afraid I dismissed the cab."

• • •

But the cab driver hadn't gone for some reason of his own. He jumped out and smirkingly held the front door open for us. I told him we preferred to sit in back. He sulkily opened the rear door, slammed it after us, jumped in front, and slammed the door behind him.

My companion leaned forward. "Heaven," she said.

The driver switched on the turbine and televisor.

"Why did you ask if I were a British subject?" I said, to start the conversation.

She leaned away from me, tilting her mask close to the window. "See the Moon," she said in a quick, dreamy voice.

"But why, really?" I pressed, conscious of an irritation that had nothing to do with her.

"It's edging up into the purple of the sky."

"And what's your name?"

"The purple makes it look yellower."

• • •

Just then I became aware of the source of my irritation. It lay in the square of writhing light in the front of the cab beside the driver.

I don't object to ordinary wrestling matches, though they bore me, but I simply detest watching a man wrestle a woman. The fact that the bouts are generally "on the level," with the man greatly outclassed in weight and reach and the masked females young and personable, only makes them seem worse to me.

"Please turn off the screen," I requested the driver.

He shook his head without looking around. "Uh-uh, man," he said. "They've been grooming that babe for weeks for this bout with Little Zirk."

Infuriated, I reached forward, but my companion caught my arm. "Please," she whispered frightenedly, shaking her head.

I settled back, frustrated. She was closer to me now, but silent and for a few moments I watched the heaves and contortions of the powerful masked girl and her wiry masked opponent on the screen. His frantic scrambling at her reminded me of a male spider.

I jerked around, facing my companion. "Why did those three men want to kill you?" I asked sharply.

The eyeholes of her mask faced the screen. "Because they're jealous of me," she whispered.

"Why are they jealous?"

She still didn't look at me. "Because of him."

"Who?"

She didn't answer.

I put my arm around her shoulders. "Are you afraid to tell me?" I asked. "What is the matter?"

She still didn't look my way. She smelled nice.

"See here," I said laughingly, changing my tactics, "you really should tell me something about yourself. I don't even know what you look like."

I half playfully lifted my hand to the band of

her neck. She gave it an astonishingly swift slap. I pulled it away in sudden pain. There were four tiny indentations on the back. From one of them a tiny bead of blood welled out as I watched. I looked at her silver fingernails and saw they were actually delicate and pointed metal caps.

"I'm dreadfully sorry," I heard her say, "but you frightened me. I thought for a moment you were going to . . ."

At last she turned to me. Her coat had fallen open. Her evening dress was Cretan Revival, a bodice of lace beneath and supporting the breasts without covering them.

"Don't be angry," she said, putting her arms around my neck. "You were wonderful this afternoon."

The soft gray velvet of her mask, molding itself to her cheek, pressed mine. Through the mask's lace the wet warm tip of her tongue touched my chin.

"I'm not angry," I said. "Just puzzled and anxious to help."

The cab stopped. To either side were black windows bordered by spears of broken glass. The sickly purple light showed a few ragged figures slowly moving toward us.

The driver muttered, "It's the turbine, man. We're grounded." He sat there hunched and motionless. "Wish it had happened somewhere else."

My companion whispered, "Five dollars is the usual amount."

She looked out so shudderingly at the congregating figures that I suppressed my indignation and did as she suggested. The driver took the bill without a word. As he started up, he put his hand out the window and I heard a few coins clink on the pavement.

My companion came back into my arms, but her mask faced the television screen, where the tall girl had just pinned the convulsively kicking Little Zirk.

"I'm so frightened," she breathed.

* * *

Heaven turned out to be an equally ruinous neighborhood, but it had a club with an awning and a huge doorman uniformed like a space-man, but in gaudy colors. In my sensuous daze I rather liked it all. We stepped out of the cab just as a drunken old woman came down the sidewalk, her mask awry. A couple ahead of us turned their heads from the half revealed face, as if from an ugly body at the beach. As we followed them in I heard the doorman say, "Get along, grandma, and watch yourself."

Inside, everything was dimness and blue glows. She had said we could talk here, but I didn't see how. Besides the inevitable chorus of sneezes and coughs (they say America is 50 percent allergic these days), there was a band going full blast in the latest robop style, in which an electronic composing machine selects an arbitrary sequence of tones into which the musicians weave their raucous little individualities.

Most of the people were in booths. The band was behind the bar. On a small platform beside them, a girl was dancing, stripped to her mask. The little cluster of men at the shadowy far end of the bar weren't looking at her.

We inspected the menu in gold script on the wall and pushed the buttons for breast of chicken, fried shrimps, and two scotches. Moments later, the serving bell tinkled. I opened the gleaming panel and took out our drinks.

* * *

The cluster of men at the bar filed off toward the door, but first they stared around the room. My companion had just thrown back her coat. Their look lingered on our booth. I noticed that there were three of them.

The band chased off the dancing girl with growls. I handed my companion a straw and we sipped our drinks.

"You wanted me to help you about something," I said. "Incidentally, I think you're lovely."

She nodded quick thanks, looked around,

leaned forward. "Would it be hard for me to get to England?"

"No," I replied, a bit taken aback. "Provided you have an American passport."

"Are they difficult to get?"

"Rather," I said, surprised at her lack of information. "Your country doesn't like its nationals to travel, though it isn't quite as stringent as Russia."

"Could the British Consulate help me get a passport?"

"It's hardly their . . ."

"Could you?"

I realized we were being inspected. A man and two girls had paused opposite our table. The girls were tall and wolfish looking, with spangled masks. The man stood jauntily between them like a fox on its hind legs.

My companion didn't glance at them, but she sat back. I noticed that one of the girls had a big yellow bruise on her forearm. After a moment they walked to a booth in the deep shadows.

"Know them?" I asked. She didn't reply. I finished my drink. "I'm not sure you'd like England," I said. "The austerity's altogether different from your American brand of misery."

She leaned forward again. "But I must get away," she whispered.

"Why?" I was getting impatient.

"Because I'm so frightened."

There were chimes. I opened the panel and handed her the fried shrimps. The sauce on my breast of chicken was a delicious steaming compound of almonds, soy, and ginger. But something must have been wrong with the radionic oven that had thawed and heated it, for at the first bite I crunched a kernel of ice in the meat. These delicate mechanisms need constant repair and there aren't enough mechanics.

I put down my fork. "What are you really scared of?" I asked her.

For once her mask didn't waver away from my face. As I waited I could feel the fears gathering without her naming them, tiny dark shapes swarming through the curved night outside, converging on the radioactive pest

spot of New York, dipping into the margins of the purple. I felt a sudden rush of sympathy, a desire to protect the girl opposite me. The warm feeling added itself to the infatuation engendered in the cab.

"Everything," she said finally.

I nodded and touched her hand.

"I'm afraid of the Moon," she began, her voice going dreamy and brittle as it had in the cab. "You can't look at it and not think of guided bombs."

"It's the same Moon over England," I reminded her.

"But it's not England's Moon anymore. It's ours and Russia's. You're not responsible."

I pressed her hand.

"Oh, and then," she said with a tilt of her mask, "I'm afraid of the cars and the gangs and the loneliness and Inferno. I'm afraid of the lust that undresses your face. And"— her voice hushed—"I'm afraid of the wrestlers."

"Yes?" I prompted softly after a moment.

• • •

Her mask came forward. "Do you know something about the wrestlers?" she asked rapidly. "The ones that wrestle women, I mean. They often lose, you know. And then they have to have a girl to take their frustration out on. A girl who's soft and weak and terribly frightened. They need that, to keep them men. Other men don't want them to have a girl. Other men want them just to fight women and be heroes. But they must have a girl. It's horrible for her."

I squeezed her fingers tighter, as if courage could be transmitted—granting I had any. "I think I can get you to England," I said.

Shadows crawled onto the table and stayed there. I looked up at the three men who had been at the end of the bar. They were the men I had seen in the big coupe. They wore black sweaters and close-fitting black trousers. Their faces were as expressionless as dopers. Two of them stood above me. The other loomed over the girl.

"Drift off, man," I was told. I heard the other inform the girl: "We'll wrestle a fall, sister. What shall it be? Judo, slapsie, or kill-who-can?"

I stood up. There are times when an Englishman simply must be maltreated. But just then the foxlike man came gliding in like the star of a ballet. The reaction of the other three startled me. They were acutely embarrassed.

He smiled at them thinly. "You won't win my favor by tricks like this," he said.

"Don't get the wrong idea, Zirk," one of them pleaded.

"I will if it's right," he said. "She told me what you tried to do this afternoon. That won't endear you to me, either. Drift."

They backed off awkwardly. "Let's get out of here," one of them said loudly, as they turned. "I know a place where they fight naked with knives."

• • •

Little Zirk laughed musically and slipped into the seat beside my companion. She shrank from him, just a little. I pushed my feet back, leaned forward.

"Who's your friend, baby?" he asked, not looking at her.

She passed the question to me with a little gesture. I told him.

"British," he observed. "She's been asking you about getting out of the country? About passports?" He smiled pleasantly. "She likes to start running away. Don't you, baby?" His small hand began to stroke her wrist, the fingers bent a little, the tendons ridged, as if he were about to grab and twist.

"Look here," I said sharply. "I have to be grateful to you for ordering off those bullies, but—"

"Think nothing of it," he told me. "They're no harm except when they're behind steering wheels. A well-trained fourteen-year-old girl could cripple any one of them. Why, even Theda here, if she went in for that sort of thing. . . ." He turned to her, shifting his hand from her wrist to

her hair. He stroked it, letting the strands slip slowly through his fingers. "You know I lost tonight, baby, don't you?" he said softly.

I stood up. "Come along," I said to her. "Let's leave."

• • •

She just sat there. I couldn't even tell if she was trembling. I tried to read a message in her eyes through the mask.

"I'll take you away," I said to her. "I can do it. I really will."

He smiled at me. "She'd like to go with you," he said. "Wouldn't you, baby?"

"Will you or won't you?" I said to her. She still just sat there.

He slowly knotted his fingers in her hair.

"Listen, you little vermin," I snapped at him, "Take your hands off her."

He came up from the seat like a snake. I'm no fighter. I just know that the more scared I am, the harder and straighter I hit. This time I was lucky. But as he crumpled back, I felt a slap and four stabs of pain in my cheek. I clapped my hand to it. I could feel the four gashes made by her dagger finger caps, and the warm blood oozing out from them.

She didn't look at me. She was bending over little Zirk and cuddling her mask to his cheek and crooning: "There, there, don't feel bad, you'll be able to hurt me afterward."

There were sounds around us, but they didn't come close. I leaned forward and ripped the mask from her face.

I really don't know why I should have expected her face to be anything else. It was very pale, of course, and there weren't any cosmetics. I suppose there's no point in wearing any under a mask. The eyebrows were untidy and the lips chapped. But as for the general expression, as for the feelings crawling and wriggling across it—

Have you ever lifted a rock from damp soil? Have you ever watched the slimy white grubs?

I looked down at her, she up at me. "Yes,

you're so frightened, aren't you?" I said sarcastically. "You dread this little nightly drama, don't you? You're scared to death."

And I walked right out into the purple night, still holding my hand to my bleeding cheek. No one stopped me, not even the girl wrestlers. I wished I could tear a tab from under my shirt, and test it then and there, and find I'd taken too much radiation, and so be able to ask to cross the Hudson and go down New Jersey, past the lingering radiance of the Narrows Bomb, and so on to Sandy Hook to wait for the rusty ship that would take me back over the seas to England.

NANCY KRESS

WITH THE ORIGINAL CAST

(1982)

IN THE SUMMER OF 1998 Gregory Whitten was rehearsing a seventy-fifth-year revival of George Bernard Shaw's *Saint Joan*, and Barbara Bishop abruptly called to ask me to fly back from Denver and attend a few rehearsals with her. She was playing Shaw's magnificent teenaged fanatic, a role she had not done for twenty years and never on Broadway. Still, it was an extraordinary request; she had never specifically asked for my presence before, and I wound up my business for Gorer-Redding Solar and caught the next shuttle with uncharacteristic hope. At noon I landed in New York and coptered directly to the theater. Barbara met me in the lobby.

"Austin! You came!"

"Did you doubt it?" I kissed her, and she laughed softly.

"It was so splendid of you to drop everything and rush home."

"Well—I didn't exactly drop it. Lay it down gently, perhaps."

"Could Carl spare you? Did you succeed in blocking that coalition, or can they still stop Carl from installing the new Battery?"

"They have one chance in a billion," I said lightly. Barbara always asks; she manages to sound as interested in Gorer-Redding Solar as in Shakespeare and ESIR, although I don't suppose she really is. Of late neither am I, although Carl Gorer is my brother and the speculative risks of finance, including Gorer-Redding, is my profession. It was a certain faint boredom with seriously behaved money that had driven me in the first place to take wildcat risks backing legitimate theater. In the beginning Gorer-Redding Solar was itself a wildcat risk: one chance in a hundred that solar energy could be made cheap and plentiful enough to replace the exhausted petrofields. But that was years ago. Now solar prosperity is a reality; speculations lie elsewhere.

"I do appreciate your coming, you know," Barbara said. She tilted her head to one side, and a curve of shining dark hair, still without gray, slanted across one cheek.

"All appreciation gratefully accepted. Is there something wrong with the play?"

"No, of course not. What could be wrong with Shaw? Oh, Gregory's a little edgy, but then you know Gregory."

"Then you called me back solely to marry me."

"Austin, not again," she said, without coyness. "Not now."

"Then something is wrong."

She pulled a little away from me, shaking her head. "Only the usual new-play nerves."

"Rue-day nerves."

"Through-the-day swerves."

"Your point," I said. "But, Barbara, you've played Joan of Arc before."

"Twenty years ago," she said, and I glimpsed the strain on her face a second before it vanished under her publicity-photo smile, luminous and cool as polished crystal. Then the smile disappeared, and she put her cheek next to mine and whispered, "I do thank you for coming. And you look so splendid," and she was yet another Barbara, the Barbara I saw only in glimpses through her self-contained poise, despite having pursued her for half a year now with my marriage proposals, all gracefully rejected. I, Austin Gorer, who until now had never ever pursued anything very fast or very far. Nor ever had to.

"Nervous, love?"

"Terrified," she said lightly, the very lightness turning the word into a denial of itself, a delicate stage mockery.

"I don't believe it."

"That's half your charm. You never believe me."

"Your Joan was a wild success."

"My God, that was even before ESIR, can you believe it?"

"I believe it."

"So do I," she said, laughing, and began to relate anecdotes about casting that play, then this one, jumping between the two with witty, effortless bridges, her famous voice rising and falling with the melodious control that was as much a part of the public's image of her as the shining helmet of dark hair and the cool grace.

She has never had good press. She is too much of a paradox to reduce easily to tabloid slogans, and the stupider journalists have called her mannered and artificial. She is neither. Eager animation and conscious taste are two qualities the press usually holds to be opposites, patronizing the first and feeling defensive in the presence of the second. But in Barbara Bishop, animation and control have melded into a grace that owes nothing to nature and everything to a civilized respect for willed illusion. When she walks across a stage or through a bedroom, when she speaks Shaw's words or her own, when she hands Macbeth a dagger or a dinner guest a glass of wine, every movement is both free of artifice and perfectly controlled. Because she will not rage at press conferences, or wail colorfully at lost roles, or wrinkle her nose in professional cuteness, the press has decided that she is cold and lacks spontaneity. But for Barbara, what is spontaneous is control. She was born with it. She'll always have it.

"—and so now Gregory's *still* casting for the crowd scenes. He's tested what has to be every ESIR actor in New York, and now he's scraping up fledglings straight out of the hospital. Their scalp scars are barely healed and the ink on their historian's certificates is still wet. We're two weeks behind already, and rehearsals have barely begun, would you believe it? He can't find enough actors with an ESIR in fifteenth-century France, and he's not willing to go even fifty years off on either side."

"Then you must have been French in Joan's time," I said, "or he wouldn't have cast you? Even you?"

"Quite right. Even me." She moved away from me toward the theater doors. Again I sensed in her some unusual strain. An actor is always reluctant to discuss his ESIR with an outsider (bad form), but this was something more.

"As it happens," Barbara continued, "I was not only French, I was even in Rouen when Joan was burned at the stake in 1431. I didn't see the burning, and I never laid eyes on her—I was only a barmaid in a country tavern—but, still, it's rather an interesting coincidence."

"Yes."

"One chance in a million," she said, smiling. "Or, no—what would be the odds, Austin? That's really your field."

I didn't know. It would depend, of course, on just how many people in the world had undergone ESIR. There were very few. Electronically Stimulated Incarnation Recall involves painful, repeated electrochemical jolts through the cortex, through the limbic brain, directly into the R-Complex, containing racial and genetic memory. Biological shields are ripped away; defense mechanisms designed to aid survival by streamlining the vast load of memory are deliberately torn. The long-term effects are not yet known. ESIR is risky, confusing, morally disorienting, painful, and expensive. Most people want nothing to do with it. Those who do are mostly historians, scientists, freaks, mystics, poets—or actors, who must be a little of each. A stage full of players who believe totally that they are in Hamlet's Denmark or Sir Thomas More's England or Blanche DuBois's South because they have been there and feel it in every gesture, every cadence, every authentic cast of mind—such a stage is out of time entirely. It can seduce even a philistine financier. Since ESIR, the glamour of the theater has risen, the number of would-be actors has dropped, and only the history departments of the world's universities have been so in love with historically authentic style.

"Forget the odds," I said. "Who hasn't been cast yet?"

"Well, we need to see," she said, ticking off roles on her fingers. I recognized the parody instantly. Gregory Whitten himself. Her very face seemed to lengthen into the horse-faced scowl so beloved by Sunday-supplement caricaturists. "We must have two royal ladies—no, they must absolutely look royal, *royal*. And DeStogumber, I need a marvelous DeStogum-

ber! How can anyone expect me to direct without an absolutely wonderful DeStogumber—"

The theater doors opened. "We are ready for you onstage, Miss Bishop."

"Thank you." The parody of Whitten had vanished instantly; in this public of one stagehand she was again Barbara Bishop, controlled and cool.

I settled into a seat in the first row, nodding vaguely at the other hangers-on scattered throughout the orchestra and mezzanine. No one nodded back. There was an absurd public fiction that we, who contributed nothing to the play but large sums of money, were like air: necessary but invisible. I didn't mind. I enjoyed seeing the cast ease into their roles, pulling them up from somewhere inside and mentally shaking each fold around their own gestures and voices and glances. I had not always known how to see that. It had taken me, from such a different set of signals, a long time to notice the tiny adjustments that go, rehearsal by rehearsal, to create the illusion of reality. Perhaps I was slow. But now it seemed to me that I could spot the precise moment when an actor has achieved that precarious balance between his neocortical knowledge of the script and his older, ESIR knowledge of the feel of his character's epoch, and so is neither himself nor the playwright's creation but some third, subtler force that transcends both. Barbara, I could see, had not yet reached that moment.

Whitten, pacing the side of the stage, was directing the early scene in which the seventeen-year-old Joan, a determined peasant, comes to Captain Robert de Baudricourt to demand a horse and armor to lead the French to victory over the English. De Baudricourt was being played by Jason Kellig, a semi-successful actor whom I had met before and not particularly liked. No one else was onstage, although I had that sensation one always has during a rehearsal of hordes of other people just out of sight in the wings, eyeing the action critically and shushing one another. Moths fluttering nervously just outside the charmed circle of light.

"No, squire!" Barbara said. "God is very merciful, and the blessed saints Catherine and Margaret, who speak to me every day, will intercede for you. You will go to paradise, and your name will be remembered forever as my first helper."

It was subtly wrong: too poised for the peasant Joan, too graceful. At the same time, an occasional gesture—an outflinging of her elbow, a sour smile—was too brash, and I guessed that these had belonged to the Rouen barmaid in Joan's ESIR. It was very rough, and I could see Whitten's famous temper, never long in check, begin to mount.

"No, no, no—Barbara, you're supposed to be an innocent. Shaw says that Joan answers 'with muffled sweetness.' You sound too surly. Absolutely too surly. You must do it again. Jason, cue her."

"Well, I am damned," Kellig said.

"No, squire! God is very merciful, and blessed saints Catherine and Margaret, who speak to me every day, will intercede for you. You will go to paradise—"

"Again," Whitten said.

"Well, I am damned."

"No, squire! God is very merciful, and the blessed saints Catherine and Margaret, who speak to me every—"

"No! Now you sound like you're sparring with him! This is not some damned eighteenth-century drawing-room repartee! Joan absolutely means it! The voices are absolutely real to her. You must do it again, Barbara. You must tap into the religious atmosphere of your ESIR. You are not trying! Do it again!"

Barbara bit her lip. I saw Kellig glance from her to Whitten, and I suddenly had the impression—I don't know why—that they had all been at one another earlier, before I had arrived. Something beyond the usual rehearsal frustration was going on here. Tension, unmistakable as the smell of smoke, rose from the three of them.

"Well, I am damned."

"No, squire! God is very merciful, and the blessed saints Catherine and Margaret, who

speak to me every day, will intercede for you. You will go to paradise, and your name will be remembered forever as my first helper."

"Again," Whitten said.

"Well, I am damned."

"No, squire! God is—"

"Again."

"Really, Gregory," Barbara began icily, "how you think you can judge after four words of—"

"I need to hear only one word when it's as bad as that! And what in absolute hell is that little flick of the wrist supposed to be? Joan is not a discus thrower. She must be—" Whitten stopped dead, staring offstage.

At first, unsure of why he had cut himself off or turned so red, I thought he was having an attack of some kind. The color in his face was high, almost hectic. But he held himself taut and erect, and then I heard the siren coming closer, landing on the roof, trailing off. It had come from the direction of Larrimer—which was, I suddenly remembered, the only hospital in New York that would do ESIR.

A very young man in a white coat hurried across the stage.

"Mr. Whitten, Dr. Metz says could you come up to the copter right away?"

"What is it? No, don't hold back, damn it. you absolutely must tell me now! Is it?"

On the young technician's face professional restraint battled with self-importance. The latter won, helped perhaps by Whitten's seizing the boy by the shoulders. For a second I actually thought Whitten would shake him.

"It's her, sir. It really is. We were looking for fifteenth-century ESIR, like you said, and we tried the neos for upper class for the ladies in waiting, and all we were getting were peasants or non-Europeans or early childhood deaths, and then Dr. Metz asked—" He was clearly enjoying this, dragging it out as much as possible. Whitten waited with a patience that surprised me until I realized that he was holding his breath. "—this neo to concentrate on the pictures Dr. Metz would show her of buildings and dresses and bowls and stuff to clear her mind. She looked dazed and in pain like they do, and then she suddenly remembered who she was, and Dr. Metz asked her lots of questions—that's his period anyway, you know; he's the foremost American historian on medieval France—and then he said she was."

Whitten let out his breath, a long, explosive sigh. Kellig leaned forward and said, "Was . . ."

"Joan," the boy said simply. "Joan of Arc."

It was as if he had shouted, although of course he had not. But the name hung in the dusty silence of the empty theater, circled and underlined by everything there: the heavy velvet curtains, the dust motes in the air, the waiting strobes, the clouds of mothlike actors, or memories of actors, in the wings. They all existed to lend weight and probability to what had neither. One in a million, one in a billion.

"Is Dr. Metz sure?" Whitten demanded. He looked suddenly violent, capable of disassembling the technician if the historian were not sure.

"He's sure!"

"Where is she? In the copter?"

"Yes."

"Have Dr. Metz bring her down here. No, I'll go up there. No, bring her here. Is she still weak?"

"Yes, sir," the boy said.

"Well, go! I told Dr. Metz I wanted her here as soon as he absolutely was sure!"

The boy went.

So Whitten had been informed of the possibility earlier. I looked at Barbara, suddenly understanding the tension on stage. She stood smiling, her chin raised a little, her body very straight. She looked pale. Some trick of lighting, some motionless tautness in her shoulders, made me think for an instant that she was going to faint, but of course she did not. She behaved exactly as I knew she must have been willing herself to, waiting quietly through the interminable time until Joan of Arc should appear. Whitten fidgeted; Kellig lounged, his eyelids lowered halfway. Neither of them looked at Barbara.

The technician and the historian walked out onto the stage, each with a hand under either elbow of a young girl whose head was bandaged. Even now I feel a little ashamed when I remember rising halfway in my seat, as for an exalted presence. But the girl was not an exalted presence, was not Joan of Arc; she was an awkward, skinny, plain-faced girl who had once been Joan of Arc and now wanted to be an extra in the background of a seventy-five-year-old play. No one else seemed to be remembering the distinction.

"You were Joan of Arc?" Whitten asked. He sounded curiously formal, as out of character as the girl.

"Yes, I . . . I remember Joan. Being Joan." The girl frowned, and I thought I knew why: She was wondering why she didn't feel like Joan. But ESIR, Barbara has told me, doesn't work like that. Other lives are like remembering someone you have known, not like experiencing the flesh and bone of this one—unless this one is psychotic. Otherwise, it usually takes time and effort to draw on the memory of a previous incarnation, and this child had been Joan of Arc only for a few days. Suddenly I felt very sorry for her.

"What's your first name?" Whitten said.

"Ann. Ann Jasmine."

Whitten winced. "A stage name?"

"Yes. Isn't it pretty?"

"You must absolutely use your real name. What acting have you done?"

The girl shifted her weight, spreading her feet slightly apart and starting to count off on her fingers. Her voice was stronger now and cockier. "Well, let's just see: In high school I played Portia in *The Merchant of Venice*, and in the Country-Time Players—that's community theater—I was Goat's Sister in *The Robber Bridegroom* and Aria in *Moondust*. And then I came to New York, and I've done—oh, small stuff, mostly. A few commercials." She smiled at Whitten, then looked past him at Kellig and winked. He stared back at her as if she were a dead fish.

"What," said Kellig slowly, "is your real name?"

"Does it matter?" The girl's smile vanished, and she pouted.

"Yes."

"Ann Friedland," she said sulkily, and I knew where the "few commercials, mostly" as well as the expensive ESIR audition had come from. Trevor Friedland, of Friedland Computers, was a theater backer for his own amusement, much as I was. He was not, however, a co-backer in this one. Not yet.

At the Friedland name, Kellig whistled, a low, impudent note that made Whitten glance at him in annoyance. Barbara still had not moved. She watched them intently.

"Forget your name," Whitten said. "Absolutely forget it. Now I know this play is new to you, but you must read for me. Just read cold; don't be nervous. Take my script and start there. No—there. Jason, cue her."

"You want me to read Joan? The part of Joan?" the girl said. All her assumed sophistication was gone; her face was as alive as a seven-year-old's at Christmas, and I looked away, not wanting to like her.

"Oh, really, Greg," Kellig said. Whitten ignored him.

"Just look over Shaw's description there, and then start. I know you're cold. Just start."

"Good morning, captain squire," she began shakily, but stopped when Barbara crossed the stage to sit on a bench near the wings. She was still smiling, a small frozen smile. Ann glanced at her nervously, then began over.

"Good morning, captain squire. Captain, you are to give me a horse . . ." Again she stopped. A puzzled look came over her face; she skimmed a few pages and then closed her eyes. Immediately I thought of the real Joan, listening to voices. But this was the real Joan. For a moment the stage seemed to float in front of me, a meaningless collection of lines and angles.

"It wasn't like that," Ann Friedland said slowly.

"Like what?" Whitten said. "What wasn't like what?"

"Joan. Me. She didn't charge in like that at all to ask de Baudricourt for horse and armor. It wasn't at all . . . she was more . . . Insane, I think. What he has written here, Shaw . . ." She looked at each of us in turn, frowning. No one moved. I don't know how long we stayed that way, staring at the thin girl onstage.

"Saint Catherine," she said finally. "Saint Margaret." Her slight figure jerked as if shocked, and she threw back her head and howled like a dog. "But Orleans was not even my idea! The commander, my father, the commander, my father . . . oh, my God, my dear God, he made her do it, he told me—they all promised—"

She stumbled, nearly falling to her knees. The historian leaped forward and caught her. I don't think any of us could have borne it if that pitiful, demented figure had knelt and begun to pray.

The next moment, however, though visibly fighting to control herself, she knew where—and who—she was.

"Doctor, don't, I'm all right now. It's not—I'm all right. Mr. Whitten, I'm sorry, let me start the scene over!"

"No, don't start the scene over. Tell me what you were going to say. Where is Shaw wrong? What happened? Try to feel it again."

Ann's eyes held Whitten's. They were beyond all of us, already negotiating with every inflection of every word.

"I don't have to feel it again. I remember what happened. That wave of . . . I won't do that again. It was just when it all came rushing back. But now I remember it, I have it, I can *control* it. It didn't happen like Shaw's play. She—I—was used. She did hear voices, she was mad, but the whole idea to use her to persuade the Dauphin to fight against the English didn't come from the voices. The priests insisted on what they said the voices meant, and the commander made her a sort of mascot to get the soldiers to kill . . . I was *used*. A victim." A complicated expression passed over her face, perhaps the most extraordinary expression I have ever seen on a face so young: regret and shame and loss and an angry, wondering despair for events long beyond the possibility of change. Then the expression vanished, and she was wholly a young woman coolly engaged in the bargaining of history.

"I know it all, Mr. Whitten—all that really happened. And it happened to me. The real Joan of Arc."

"Cosgriff," Whitten said, and I saw Kellig start. Lawrence Cosgriff had won the Pulitzer Prize for drama the last two years in a row. He wrote powerful, despairing plays about the loss of individual morality in an institutionalized world.

"My dear Gregory," Kellig said, "one does not simply commission Lawrence Cosgriff to write one a play. He's not some hack you can—"

Whitten looked at him, and he was quiet. I understood why; Whitten was on fire, as exalted with his daring idea as the original Joan must have been with hers. But no, of course, she hadn't been exalted, that was the whole point. She had been a dupe, not a heroine. Young Miss Friedland, fighting for her name in lights, most certainly considered Joan the Heroine to be an expendable casualty. One of the expendable casualties. I stood up and began to make my way to the stage.

"I'm the real thing," Ann said. "The real thing. I'll play Joan, of course."

"Of course," Kellig drawled. He was already looking at her with dislike, and I could see what their rehearsals would be: the chance upstart and the bit player who had paid largely fruitless dues for twenty years. The commander and the Dauphin would still be the male leads; Kellig's part could only grow smaller under Ann's real thing.

"I'll play Joan," she said again, a little more loudly.

Whitten, flushed with his vision, stopped his ecstatic pacing and scowled. "Of course you must play Joan!"

"Oh," Ann said, "I was afraid—"

"Afraid? What is this? You are Joan."

"Yes," she said slowly, "yes, I am." She frowned, sincerely, and then a second later replaced the frown with a smile all calculation and relief. "Yes, of course I am!"

"Then I'll absolutely reach Cosgriff's agent today. He'll jump at it. You will need to work with him, of course. We can open in six months, with any luck. You do live in town? Cosgriff can tape you. No, someone else can do that before he even—Austin!"

"You're forgetting something, aren't you, Gregory, in this sudden great vision? You have a contract to do Shaw."

"Of course I'm not forgetting the contract. But you absolutely must want to continue, for this new play . . . Cosgriff . . ." He stopped, and I knew the jumble of things that must be in his mind: deadlines, backing (Friedland Computers!), contracts, schedules, the percentage of my commitment, and, belatedly, Barbara.

She still sat on the bench at stage left, half in shadow. Her back was very straight, her chin high, but in the subdued light her face with its faint smile looked older, not haggard but set, inelastic. I walked over to her and turned to face Whitten.

"I will not back this new play, even if you do get Cosgriff to write it. Which I rather doubt. Shaw's drama is an artistic masterpiece. What you are planning is a trendy exploitation of some flashy technology. Look elsewhere for your money."

Silence. Whitten began to turn red, Kellig snickered—at whom was not clear. In the silence the historian, Dr. Metz, began timidly, "I'm sure Miss Friedland's information would be welcomed warmly by any academic—"

The girl cried loudly, "But I'm the real thing!" and she started to sob.

Barbara had risen to take my arm. Now she dropped it and walked over to Ann. Her voice was steady. "I know you are. And I wish you all luck as an actress. It's a brilliant opportunity, and I'm sure you'll do splendidly with it."

They faced each other, the sniveling girl who

had at least the grace to look embarrassed and the smiling, humiliated woman. It was a public performance, of course, an illusion that all Barbara felt was a selfless, graceful warmth, but it was also more than that. It was as gallant an act of style as I have ever seen.

Ann muttered, "Thank you," and flushed a mottled maroon. Barbara took my arm and we walked down the side aisle and out of the theater. She walked carefully, choosing her steps, her head high and lips together and solemn, like a woman on her way to a public burning.

I wish I could say that my quixotic gesture had an immediate and disastrous effect on Whitten's plans, that he came to his artistic senses—and went back to Shaw's Saint Joan. But of course he did no such thing. Other financial backing than mine proved to be readily available. Contracts were rewritten, agents placated, lawsuits avoided. Cosgriff did indeed consent to write the script, and *Variety* became distressingly eager to report any tidbit connected with what was being billed as *Joan of Arc: With the Original Cast!* It was a dull theater season in New York. Nothing currently running gripped the public imagination like this as-yet-unwritten play. Whitten, adroitly fanning the flames, gave out very few factual details.

Barbara remained silent on the whole subject. Business was keeping me away from New York a great deal. Gorer-Redding Solar was installing a new plant in Bogotá, and I would spend whole weeks trying to untangle the lush foliage of bribes, kickbacks, nepotism, pride, religion, and mañana that is business in South America. But whenever I was in New York, I spent time with Barbara. She would not discuss Whitten's play, warning me away from the subject with the tactful withdrawal of an estate owner discouraging trespassing without hurting local feelings. I admired her tact and her refusal to whine, but at the same time I felt vaguely impatient. She was keeping me at arm's length. She was doing it beautifully, but arm's length was not where I wanted to be.

I do not assume that intimacy must be based on a mutual display of sores. I applaud the public illusion of control and well-being as a civilized achievement. However, I knew Barbara well enough to know that under her illusion of well-being she must be hurt and a little afraid. No decent scripts had been offered her, and the columnists had not been kind over the loss of Saint Joan. Barbara had been too aloof, too self-possessed for them to show any compassion now. Press sympathy for a humiliated celebrity is in direct proportion to the anguished copy previously supplied.

Then one hot night in August I arrived at Barbara's apartment for dinner. Lying on a hall table was a script:

A MAID OF DOMRÉMY

BY
LAWRENCE COSGRIFF

Incredulous, I picked it up and leafed through it. When I looked up, Barbara was standing in the doorway, holding two goblets of wine.

"Hello, Austin. Did you have a good flight?"

"Barbara—what is this?" I asked, stupidly.

She crossed the hall and handed me one of the goblets.

"It's Lawrence's play about Joan of Arc."

"I see that. But what is it doing here?"

She didn't answer me immediately. She looked beautiful, every illusion seeming completely natural: the straight, heavy silk of her artfully cut gown, the flawless makeup, the hair cut in precise lines to curve over one cheek. Without warning, I was irritated by all of it. Illusions. Arm's length.

"Austin, why don't you reconsider backing Gregory's play?"

"Why on earth should I?"

"Because you really could make quite a lot of money on it."

"I could make quite a lot of money backing auto gladiators. I don't do that, either."

She smiled, acknowledging the thrust. I still did not know how the conversation had become a duel.

"Are you hungry? There are canapés in the living room. Dinner won't be ready for a while yet."

"I'm not hungry. Barbara, why do you want me to back Whitten's play?"

"I don't want you to, if you don't wish to. Come in and sit down. *I'm* hungry. I only thought you might want to back the play. It's splendid." She looked at me steadily over the rim of her goblet. "It's the best new script I've seen in years. It's subtle, complex, moving— much better even than his last two. It's going to replace Shaw's play as the best we have about Joan. And on the subject of victimization by a world the main character doesn't understand, it's better than *Streetcar* or *Joy Ride*. A hundred years from now this play will still be performed regularly, and well."

"It's not like you to be so extravagant with your praise."

"No, it's not."

"And you want me to finance the play for the reflected glory?"

"For the satisfaction. And," she added quietly, but firmly, "because I've accepted a bit part in it."

I stared at her. Last week a major columnist had headlined: "Fallen Star Lands on Her Pride."

"It's a very small role. Yolande of Aragon, the Dauphin's mother-in-law. She intrigued on the Dauphin's behalf when he was struggling to be crowned. I have only one scene, but it has possibilities."

"For you? What—does it have possibilities of being smirked at by that little schemer in your role? Did you read how much her agent is holding Whitten up for? No wonder he could use more backers."

"You would get it back. But that's not the question, Austin, is it? Why do you object to my taking this part? It's not like you to object to my choice of roles."

"I'm upset because I don't want you to be hurt, and I think you are. I think you'll be hurt even more if you play this Yolande with Miss Ann Friedland as Joan, and I don't want to see it, because I love you."

"I know you do, Austin." She smiled warmly and touched my cheek. It was a perfect Barbara Bishop gesture: sincere, graceful, and complete in itself—so complete that it promised nothing more than what it was, led on to nothing else. It cut off communication as effectively as a blow—or, rather, more effectively, since a blow can be answered in kind. I slammed my glass on the table and stood up. Once up, however, I had nothing to say and so stood there feeling ridiculous. What did I want to say? What did I want from her that I did not already have?

"I wish," I said slowly, "that you were not always acting."

She looked at me steadily. I knew the look. She was waiting: for retraction or amendment or amplification. And of course she was right to expect any, or all, of those things. What I had said was inaccurate. She was not acting. What she did was something subtly different. She behaved with the gestures and attitudes and behaviors of the world as she believed it ought to be, a place of generous and rational individuals with enough sheer style to create events in their own image. That people's behavior was in fact often uncivilized, cowardly, and petty she of course knew; she was not stupid. Hers was a deliberate, controlled choice: to ignore the pettiness and to grant to all of us—actors, audience, press, Whitten, Ann Friedland, me, herself—the illusion of having the most admirable motives conceivable.

It seemed to me that this was praiseworthy, even "civilized," in the best sense of that much-abused word.

Why, then, did it make me feel so lonely?

Barbara was still waiting. "Forgive me; I misspoke. I don't mean that you are always acting. I mean—I mean that I'm concerned for you. Standing for a curtain call at the back of the stage while that girl, that chance reincarnation . . ." Suddenly a new idea occurred to me. "Or do you think that she won't be able to do the part and you will be asked to take over for her?"

"No!"

"But if Ann Friedland can't—"

"No! I will never play Joan in *A Maid of Domrémy*!"

"Why not?"

She finished her wine. Under the expensive gown her breasts heaved. "I had no business even taking the part in Shaw's Joan. I am forty-five years old, and Joan is seventeen. But at least there—at least Shaw's Joan was not really a victim. I will not play her as a pitiful victim."

"Come on, Barbara. You've played Blanche DuBois, and Ophelia, and Jessie Kane. They're all victims."

"I won't play Joan in *A Maid of Domrémy*!"

I saw that she meant it, that even while she admired the play, she was repelled by it in some fundamental way I did not understand. I sat down again on the sofa and put my arms around her. Instantly she was Barbara Bishop again, smiling with rueful mockery at both her own violence and my melodrama, drawing us together in a covenant too generous for quarreling.

"Look at us, Austin—actually discussing that tired old cliché, the understudy who goes on for the fading star. But I'm not her understudy, and she can hardly fade before she's even bloomed! Really, we're too ridiculous. I'm sorry, love, I didn't mean to snap at you like that. Shall we have dinner now?"

I stood up and pulled her next to me. She came gracefully, still smiling, the light sliding over her dark hair, and followed me to her bedroom. The sex was very good, as it always was. But afterward, lying with her head warm on my shoulder, I was still baffled by something in her I could not understand. Was it because of ESIR? I had thought that before. What was it like to have knowledge of those hundreds of other lives you had once lived? I would never know. Were the exotic types I met in the theater so different, so less easily understood, because they had "creative temperament" (whatever that was) or

because of ESIR? I would probably never know that, either, nor how much of Barbara was what she was here, now, and how much was subtle reaction to all the other things she knew she had been. I wasn't sure I wanted to know.

Long after Barbara fell asleep, I lay awake in the soft darkness, listening to the night sounds of New York beyond the window and to something else beyond those, some large silence where my own ESIR memories might have been.

• • •

Whitten banned everyone but actors and tech crew from rehearsals of *A Maid of Domrémy*: press, relatives, backers, irate friends. Only because the play had seized the imagination of the public—or at least that small portion of the public that goes to the theater—could his move succeed. The financial angels went along cheerfully with their own banning, secure in the presale ticket figures that the play would make money even without their personal supervision.

Another director, casting for a production of *Hamlet*, suddenly claimed to have discovered the reincarnation of Shakespeare. For a week Broadway was a laser of rumors and speculations. Then the credentials of the two historians verifying the ESIR were discovered by a gleeful press to have been faked. The director, producer, historians, and ersatz Shakespeare were instantly unavailable for comment.

The central computer of the AMA was tapped into. For two days executives with private facelifts and politicians with private accident records and teachers with private drug-abuse histories held their collective breaths, cursing softly under them. The AMA issued a statement that only ESIR records had been pirated, and the scandal was generally forgotten in the central part of the country and generally intensified on both coasts. Wild reports were issued, contradicted, confirmed, and disproved, all in a few hours. An actor who remembered being King Arthur had been discovered and was going to star in the true story of the Round Table. Euripides was living in Boston and would appear there in his own play *Medea*. The computer verified that ESIR actually *had* uncovered Helen of Troy, and the press stampeded out to Bowling Green, Ohio, where it was discovered that the person who remembered being Helen of Troy was a male, bald, sixty-eight-year-old professor emeritus in the history department. He was writing a massive scholarly study of the Trojan War, and he bitterly resented the "cheap publicity of the popular press."

"The whole thing is becoming a circus," Barbara grumbled. Her shirt was loose at the breasts, and her pants gaped at the waist. She had lost weight and color.

"And this, too, shall pass," I told her. "Think of when ESIR was first introduced. A few years of wild quakes all over society, and then everyone adjusted. This is just the aftershock on the theater."

"I don't especially like standing directly on the fault line."

"How are rehearsals going?"

"About the same," she said, her eyes hooded. Since she never spoke of the play at all, I didn't know what "about the same" would be the same as.

"Barbara, what are you waiting for?"

"Waiting for?"

"Constantly now you have that look of waiting, frowning to yourself, looking as if you're scrutinizing something. Something only you can see."

"Austin, how ridiculous! What I'm looking at is all too public: opening night for the play."

"And what do you see?"

She was silent for a long time. "I don't know." She laughed, an abrupt, opaque sound like the sudden drawing of a curtain. "It's silly, isn't it? Not knowing what I don't know. A tautology, almost."

"Barbara, marry me. We'll go away for a weekend and get married, like two children. This weekend."

"I thought you had to fly back to Bogotá this weekend."

"I do. But you could come with me. There is a world outside New York, you know. It isn't simply all one vast out-of-town tryout."

"I do thank you, Austin, you know that. But I can't leave right now; I do have to work on my part. There are still things I don't trust."

"Such as what?"

"Me," she said lightly, and would say no more.

Meanwhile the hoopla went on. A professor of history at Berkeley who had just finished a—now probably erroneous—dissertation on Joan of Arc tried various legal ploys to sue Ann Friedland on the grounds that she "undercut his means of livelihood." A group called the Catholic Coalition to Clear the Inquisition published in four major newspapers an appeal to Ann Friedland to come forward and declare the fairness of the church at Joan of Arc's heresy trial. Each of the ads cost a fantastic sum. But Ann did not reply; she was preserving to the press a silence as complete as Barbara's to me. I think this is why I didn't press Barbara more closely about her rehearsals. I wanted to appear as different from the rest of the world as possible—an analogy probably no one made except me. Men in love are ludicrous.

Interest in Ann Friedland was not dispelled by her silence. People merely claiming to be a notable figure from the past was growing stale. For years people had been claiming to be Jesus Christ or Muhammad or Judas; all had been disproved, and the glamour evaporated. But now a famous name had not only been verified, it was going to be showcased in an enterprise that carried the risk of losing huge sums of money, several professional reputations, and months of secret work. The public was delighted. Ann Friedland quickly became a household name.

She was going to marry the widowed King Charles of England. She was going to lead a revival of Catholicism and was being considered for the position of first female pope. She was a drug addict, a Mormon, pregnant, mad, in love, clairvoyant, ten years old, extraterrestrial. She was refusing to go on opening night. Gregory

Whitten was going to let her improvise the part opening night. Rehearsals were a disaster, and Barbara Bishop would play the part opening night.

Not even to this last did Barbara offer a comment. Also silent were the reputable papers, the serious theater critics, the men and women who control the money that controls Broadway. They, too, were waiting.

We all waited.

• • •

The week that *A Maid of Domrémy* was to open in New York I was still in Bogotá. I had come down with a low-grade fever, which in the press of work I chose to ignore. By Saturday I had a temperature of one hundred four degrees and a headache no medication could touch. I saw everything through slow, pastel-colored swirls. My arms and legs felt lit with a dry, papery fire that danced up and down from shoulder to wrist, ankle to hip, up and down, wrist to shoulder. I knew I should go to a hospital, but I did not. The opening was that night.

On the plane to New York I slept, dreaming of Barbara in the middle of a vast solar battery. I circled the outside, calling to her desperately. Unaware, she sat reading a script amid the circuits and storage cells, until the fires of the sun burst out all around her and people she had known from other lives danced maniacally in the flames.

At my apartment I took more pills and a cold shower, then tried to phone Barbara. She had already left for makeup call. I dressed and caught a copter to the theater, sleeping fitfully on the short trip, and then I was in the theater, surrounded by first-nighters who did not know I was breathing contagion on all of them, and who floated around me like pale cutouts in diamonds, furs, and nauseating perfume. I could not remember walking from the copter, producing my ticket, or being escorted to my seat. The curtain swirled sickeningly, and I closed my eyes until I realized that it was not my fever that

caused the swirls: The curtain was rising. Had the house lights dimmed? I couldn't remember anything. Dry fire danced over me, shoulder to wrist, ankle to hip.

Barbara, cloaked, entered stage left. I had not realized that her scene opened the play. She carried a massive candle across the stage, bent over a wooden table, and lit two more candles from the large one, all with the taut, economical movements of great anger held fiercely in check. Before the audience heard her speak, before they clearly saw her face, they had been told that Yolande was furious, not used to being so, and fully capable of controlling her own anger.

"Mary! Where are you sulking now, Mary?" Barbara said. She straightened and drew back her hood. Her voice was low, yet every woman named Mary in the audience started guiltily. Onstage Mary of Anjou, consort of the uncrowned Dauphin of France, crept sullenly from behind a tapestry, facing her mother like a whipped dog.

"Here I am, for all the good it will do you, or anyone," she whined, looking at her own feet. Barbara's motionless silence was eloquent with contempt; Mary burst out with her first impassioned monologue against the Dauphin and Joan; the play was launched. It was a strong, smooth beginning, fueled by the conviction of Barbara's portrait of the terrifying Yolande. As the scene unfolded, the portrait became even stronger, so that I forgot both my feverish limbs and my concern for Barbara. There were no limbs, no Barbara, no theater. There was only a room in fifteenth-century France, sticky with blood shed for what to us were illusions: absolute good and absolute evil. Cosgriff was exploring the capacities in such illusions for heroism, for degradation, for nobility beyond what the audience's beliefs, saner and more temperate, could allow. Yolande and Mary and the Dauphin loved and hated and gambled and killed with every fiber of their elemental beings, and not a sound rose from the audience until Barbara delivered her final speech and exited stage right. For a moment the audience sat still, bewildered—

not by what had happened onstage, but by the unwelcome remembrance that they were not a part of it, but instead were sitting on narrow hard seats in a wooden box in New York, a foreign country because it was not medieval France. Then the applause started.

The Dauphin and his consort, still onstage, did not break character. He waited until the long applause was over, then continued bullying his wife. Shortly afterward two guards entered, dragging between them the confused, weeping Joan. The audience leaned forward eagerly. They were primed by the wonderful first scene and eager for more miracles.

"Is this the slut?" the Dauphin asked, and Mary, seeing a woman even more abused and wretched than herself, smiled with secret, sticky joy. The guards let Joan go, and she stumbled forward, caught herself, and staggered upward, raising her eyes to the Dauphin's.

"In the name of Saint Catherine—" She choked and started to weep. It was stormy weeping, vigorous, but without the chilling pain of true hysteria. The audience shuffled a little.

"I will do whatever you want, I swear it in the name of God, if you will only tell me what it is!" On the last word her voice rose; she might have been demanding that a fractious child cease lying to her.

I leaned my head sideways against one shoulder. Waves of fever and nausea beat through me, and for the first time since I had become ill I was aware of labored breathing. My heart beat, skipped, beat twice, skipped. Each breath sounded swampy and rasping. People in the row ahead began to turn and glare. Wadding my handkerchief into a ball, I held it in front of my mouth and tried to watch the play—Lines slipped in and out of my hearing; actors swirled in fiery paper-dry pastels. Once Joan seemed to turn into Barbara, and I gasped and half-rose in my seat, but then the figure onstage was Ann Friedland, and I sat down again to glares from those around me. It was Ann Friedland; I had been a fool to doubt it. It was not Joan of Arc. The girl onstage hesitated, changed tone too

often, looked nervously across the footlights, moved a second too late. Once she even stammered.

Around me the audience began to murmur discreetly. Just before the first-act curtain, in a moment of clarity, Joan finally sees how she is being used and makes an inept, wrenchingly pathetic attempt to manipulate the users by manufacturing instructions she says come from her voices. It is a crucial point in the play, throwing into dramatic focus the victim who agrees to her own corruption by a misplaced attempt at control. Ann played it nervously, with an exaggerated grab at pathos that was actually embarrassing. Nothing of that brief glimpse of personal power she had shown at her audition, so many weeks ago, was present now. Between waves of fever, I tried to picture the fit Whitten must be having backstage.

"Christ," said a man in the row ahead of me, "can you believe that?"

"What an absolute travesty," said the woman next to him. Her voice hummed with satisfaction. "Poor Lawrence."

"He was ripe for it. Smug."

"Oh, yes. Still."

"Smug," the man said.

"It doesn't matter to me what you do with her," said Mary of Anjou, onstage. "Why should it? Only for a moment she seemed . . . different. Did you remark it?" Ann Friedland, who had not seemed different, grimaced weakly, and the first-act curtain fell. People were getting to their feet, excited by the magnitude of the disaster. The house lights went up. Just as I stood, the curtains onstage parted and there was some commotion, but the theater leaped in a single nauseous lurch, blinding and hot, and then nothing.

• • •

"Austin," a voice said softly. "Austin."

My head throbbed, but from a distance, as if it were not my head at all.

"Austin," the voice said far above me. "Are you there?"

I opened my eyes. Yolande of Aragon, her face framed in a wool hood, gazed down at me and turned into Barbara. She was still in costume and makeup, the heavy, high color garish under too-bright lights. I groaned and closed my eyes.

"Austin. Are you there? Do you know me?"

"Barbara?"

"You are there! Oh, that's splendid. How do you feel? No, don't talk. You've been delirious, love, you had such a fever . . . this is the hospital. Larrimer. They've given you medication; you're going to be fine."

"Barbara."

"I'm here, Austin, I'm right here."

I opened my eyes slowly, accustoming them to the light. I lay in a small private room; beyond the window the sky was dark. I was aware that my body hurt, but aware in the detached, abstract way characteristic of EL painkillers, that miracle of modern science. The dose must have been massive. My body felt as if it belonged to someone else, a friend for whom I felt comradely simulations of pain, but not the real thing.

"What do I have?"

"Some tropical bug. What did you drink in Bogotá? The doctor says it could have been dangerous, but they flushed out your whole system and pumped you full of antibiotics, and you'll be fine. Your fever's down almost to normal. But you must rest.".

"I don't want to rest."

"You don't have any choice." She took my hand. The touch felt distant, as if the hand were wrapped in layers of padding.

"What time is it?"

"Five a.m."

"The play—"

"Is long since over."

"What happened?"

She bit her lip. "A lot happened. When precisely do you mean? I wasn't there for the second act, you know. When the ambulance came for you, one of the ushers recognized you and came backstage to tell me. I rode here in the ambulance with you. I didn't have another scene anyway."

I was confused. If Barbara had missed the entire last act, how could "a lot have happened"? I looked at her closely, and this time I saw what only the EL's could have made me miss before: the signs of great, repressed strain. Tendons stood out in Barbara's neck; under the cracked and sagging makeup her eyes darted around the room. I felt myself suddenly alert, and a fragment of memory poked at me, a fragment half-glimpsed in the hot swirl of the theater just before I blacked out.

"She ran out on the stage." I said slowly. "Ann Friedland. In front of the curtain. She ran out and yelled something . . ." It was gone. I shook my head. "On the *stage*."

"Yes." Barbara let go of my hand and began to pace. Her long train dragged behind her; when she turned, it tangled around her legs and she stumbled. The action was so uncharacteristic, it was shocking.

"You saw what the first act was. A catastrophe. She was trying—"

"The whole first act wasn't bad, love. Your scene was wonderful. Wait—the reviews on your role will be very good."

"Yes," she said distractedly. I saw that she had hardly heard me. There was something she had to do, had to say. The best way to help was to let her do it. Words tore from her like a gale.

"She tried to do the whole play reaching back into her ESIR Joan. She tried to just feel it, and let Lawrence's words—her words—be animated by the remembered feeling. But without the conscious balancing . . . no, it isn't even balancing. It's more like imagining what you already know, and to do that, you have to forget what you know and at the same time remember every tiny nuance . . . I can't explain it. Nobody ever really was a major historical figure before, in a play composed of his own words. Gregory was so excited over the concept, and then when rehearsals began . . . but by that time he was committed, and the terrible hype just bound him further. When Ann ruined the first act like that, he was just beside himself. I've never seen him like that. I've never seen anybody like that. He was raging, just completely out of control. And onstage Ann was coming apart, and I could see that he was going to completely destroy her, and we had a whole act to go, damn it! A whole fucking act!"

I stared at her. She didn't notice. She lighted a cigarette; it went out; she flung the match and cigarette on the floor. I could see her hand trembling.

"I knew that if Gregory got at her, she was done. She wouldn't even go back out after intermission. Of course the play was a flop already, but not to even finish the damn thing . . . I wasn't thinking straight. All I could see was that he would destroy her, all of us. So I hit him."

"You what?"

"I hit him. With Yolande's candlestick. I took him behind a flat to try to calm him down, and instead I hit him. *Without knowing I was going to.* Something strange went through me, and I picked up my arm and hit him. Without knowing I was going to!"

She wrapped her arms around herself and shuddered. I saw what had driven her to this unbearable strain. *Without knowing I was going to.*

"His face became very surprised, and he fell forward. No one saw me. Gregory lay there, breathing as if he were just asleep, and I found a phone and called an ambulance. Then I told the stage manager that Mr. Whitten had had a bad fall and hit his head and was unconscious. I went around to the wings and waited for Ann. When the curtain came down and she saw me waiting for her, she turned white, and then red, and started shouting at me that she was Joan of Arc and I was an aging bitch who wanted to steal her role."

I tried to picture it—the abusive girl, the appalled, demoralized cast, the director lying hidden, bashed with a candlestick—*without knowing I was going to!*—and, out front, the polite chatter, the great gray critics from the *Times* and the *New Yorker*, the dressed-up suburbanites from Scarsdale squeezing genially down the aisles for an entr'acte drink and a smoke.

"She went on and on," Barbara said. "She told me *I* was the reason she couldn't play the role, that I deliberately undermined her by standing around like I knew everything, and she knew everybody was expecting me to go on as Joan after she failed. Then suddenly she darted away from me and went through the curtains onto the stage. The house lights were up; half the audience had left. She spread out her arms and *yelled* at them."

Barbara stopped and put her hands over her face. I reached up and pulled them away. She looked calmer now, although there was still an underlying tautness in her voice. "Oh, it's just too ridiculous, Austin. She made an absolute fool of herself, of Lawrence, of all of us, but it wasn't her fault. She's an inexperienced child without talent. Gregory should have known better, but his egomania got all tangled up in his ridiculous illusion that he was going to revitalize the theater, take the next historical step for American drama. God, what the papers will say . . ." She laughed weakly, with pain. "And I was no better, hitting poor Gregory."

"Barbara . . ."

"Do you know what Ann yelled at them, at the audience? She stood on that stage, flung her arms wide like some martyr . . ."

"What did she say? What, love?"

"She said, 'But I'm the *real thing*!'"

We were quiet for a moment. From outside the window rose blurred traffic noises: the-real-thing-the-real-thing-the-real-thing.

"You're right," I said. "The whole thing was an egomaniacal ride for Whitten, and the press turned it into a carnival. Cosgriff should have known better. The real thing—that's not what you want in the theater. Illusion, magic, imagination. What should have happened, not what did. Reality doesn't make good theater."

"No, you still don't understand!" Barbara cried. "You've missed it all! How can you think that it's that easy, that Gregory's mistake was to use Ann's reality instead of Shaw's illusion!"

"I don't understand what you—"

"It's not that clear!" she cried. "Don't you think I wish it were? My God!"

I didn't know what she meant, or why under the cracked makeup her eyes glittered with feverish, exhausted panic. Even as I reached out my arm, completely confused, she was backing away from me.

"Illusion and reality," she said. "My God. Watch."

She crossed the room to the door, closed it, and pressed the dimmer on the lights. The room faded to a cool gloom. She stood with her back to me, her head bowed. Then she turned slowly and raised her eyes to a point in the air a head above her.

"In the name of Saint Catherine—" she began, choked, and started to weep. The weeping was terrifying, shot through with that threat of open hysteria that keeps a listener on the edge of panic in case the weeper should lose control entirely, and also keeps him fascinated for the same reason. "I will do whatever you want, I swear it in the name of God, if you will only tell me what it is." On the last word her voice fell, making the plea into a prayer to her captors, and so the first blasphemy. I caught my breath. Barbara looked young, terrified, pale. How could she look pale when a second ago I had been so conscious of all that garish makeup? There was no chance to wonder. She plunged on, through that scene and the next and all of Joan's scenes. She went from hysterical fear to inept manipulation to the bruised, stupid hatred of a victim to, finally, a kind of negative dignity that comes not from accomplishment but from the clear-eyed vision of the lack of it, and so she died, Cosgriff's vision of the best that institutionalized man could hope for. But she was not Cosgriff's vision; she was a seventeen-year-old girl. Her figure was slight to the point of emaciation. Her face was young—I saw its youth, felt its fragile boniness in the marrow of my own bones. She moved with the gaudy, unpredictable

quickness of the mad, now here, now darting a room's length away, now still with a terrible catatonic stillness that excluded her trapped eyes. Her desperation made me catch my breath, try to look away, and fail, feeling that cold grab at my innards: It happened. And it could happen again. It could happen to me.

Her terror gave off a smell, sickly and sour. I wanted to escape the room before that smell could spread to me. I was helpless. Neither she nor I could escape. I did not want to help her, this mad skinny victim. I wanted to destroy her so that what was being done to her would not exist any longer in the world and I would be safe from it. But I could not destroy her. I could only watch, loathing Joan for forcing me to know, until she rose to her brief, sane dignity. In the sight of that dignity, shame that I had ever wanted to smash her washed over me. I was guilty, as guilty as all those others who had wanted to smash her. Her sanity bound me with them, as earlier her terror had unwillingly drawn me to her. I was victim and victimizer, and when Joan stood at the stake and condemned me in a grotesque parody of Christ's forgiving on the cross, I wanted only for her to burn and to be quiet, to release me. I would have lighted the fire. I would have shouted with the crowd, "Burn! Burn!" already despairing that no fire could sear away what she, I, all of us had done. From the flames, Joan looked at me, stretched out her hand, came toward me. I thrust out my arm to ward her off. Almost I cried out. My heart pounded in my chest.

"Austin," she said.

In an instant Joan was gone.

Barbara came toward me. It was Barbara. She had grown three inches, put on twenty pounds and thirty years. Her face was tired and lined under gaudy, peeling makeup. Confusedly I blinked at her. I don't think she even saw the confusion; her eyes had lost their strained panic, and she was smiling, a smile that was a peaceful answer to some question of her own.

"That was the reality," she said, and stooped to lay her head on my chest. Through the fall of her hair I barely heard her when she said that she would marry me whenever I wanted.

• • •

Barbara and I have been married for nearly a year. I still don't know precisely why she decided to marry me, and she can't tell me; she doesn't know herself. But I speculate that the night *A Maid of Domrémy* failed, something broke in her, some illusion that she could control, if not the world, then at least herself. When she struck Whitten with the candlestick, she turned herself into both victim and victimizer as easily as Lawrence Cosgriff had rewritten Shaw's Joan. Barbara has never played the part again. (Gregory Whitten, no less flamboyantly insensitive for his bashing with a candlestick, actually asked her.) She has adamantly refused both Joans, Shaw's heroine and Cosgriff's victim. I was the last person to witness her performance.

Was her performance that night in my hospital room really as good as I remember? I was drugged; emotion had been running high; I loved her. Any or all of that could have colored my reactions. But I don't think so. I think that night Barbara Bishop was Joan, in some effort of will and need that went beyond both the illusions of a good actress and the reality of what ESIR could give to her, or to Ann Friedland, or to anyone. ESIR only unlocks the individual genetic memories in the brain's R-Complex. But what other identities, shared across time and space, might still be closed in there beyond our present reach?

All of this is speculation.

Next week I will be hospitalized for my own ESIR. Knowing what I have been before may yield only more speculation, more illusions, more multiple realities. It may yield nothing. But I want to know, on the chance that the yield will be understandable, will be valuable in untangling the endless skein of waking visions.

Even if the chance is one in a million.

WILLIAM GIBSON AND MICHAEL SWANWICK

DOGFIGHT

(1985)

HE MEANT TO KEEP ON GOING, right down to Florida. Work passage on a gunrunner, maybe wind up conscripted into some rat-ass rebel army down in the war zone. Or maybe, with that ticket good as long as he didn't stop riding, he'd just never get off Greyhound's Flying Dutchman. He grinned at his faint reflection in cold, greasy glass while the downtown lights of Norfolk slid past, the bus swaying on tired shocks as the driver slung it around a final corner. They shuddered to a halt in the terminal lot, concrete lit gray and harsh like a prison exercise yard. But Deke was watching himself starve, maybe in some snowstorm out of Oswego, with his cheek pressed up against that same bus window, and seeing his remains swept out at the next stop by a muttering old man in faded coveralls. One way or the other, he decided, it didn't mean shit to him. Except his legs seemed to have died already. And the driver called a twenty-minute stopover—Tidewater Station, Virginia. It was an old cinder-block building with two entrances

to each restroom, holdover from the previous century.

Legs like wood, he made a halfhearted attempt at ghosting the notions counter, but the black girl behind it was alert, guarding the sparse contents of the old glass case as though her ass depended on it. *Probably does,* Deke thought, turning away. Opposite the washrooms, an open doorway offered GAMES, the word flickering feebly in biofluorescent plastic. He could see a crowd of the local kickers clustered around a pool table. Aimless, his boredom following him like a cloud, he stuck his head in. And saw a biplane, wings no longer than his thumb, blossom bright orange flame. Corkscrewing, trailing smoke, it vanished the instant it struck the green-felt field of the table.

"Tha's right, Tiny," a kicker bellowed, "you *take* that sumbitch!"

"Hey," Deke said. "What's going on?" The nearest kicker was a bean pole with a black mesh Peterbilt cap.

"Tiny's defending the Max," he said, not taking his eyes from the table.

"Oh, yeah? What's that?" But even as he asked, he saw it: a blue enamel medal shaped like a Maltese cross, the slogan *Pour le Mérite* divided among its arms.

The Blue Max rested on the edge of the table, directly before a vast and perfectly immobile bulk wedged into a fragile-looking chrome-tube chair. The man's khaki work shirt would have hung on Deke like the folds of a sail, but it bulged across that bloated torso so tautly that the buttons threatened to tear away at any instant. Deke thought of Southern troopers he'd seen on his way down; of that weird, gut-heavy endotype balanced on gangly legs that looked like they'd been borrowed from some other body. Tiny might look like that if he stood, but on a larger scale—a forty-inch jeans inseam that would need a woven-steel waistband to support all those pounds of swollen gut. If Tiny were ever to stand at all—for now Deke saw that that shiny frame was actually a wheelchair. There was something disturbingly childlike about the man's face, an appalling suggestion of youth and even beauty in features almost buried in fold and jowl. Embarrassed, Deke looked away. The other man, the one standing across the table from Tiny, had bushy sideburns and a thin mouth. He seemed to be trying to push something with his eyes, wrinkles of concentration spreading from the corners. . . .

"You dumbshit or what?" The man with the Peterbilt cap turned, catching Deke's Indo prole-boy denims, the brass chains at his wrists, for the first time. "Why don't you get your ass lost, fucker. Nobody wants your kind in here." He turned back to the dogfight.

Bets were being made, being covered. The kickers were producing the hard stuff, the old stuff, libertyheaded dollars and Roosevelt dimes from the stamp-and-coin stores, while more cautious bettors slapped down antique paper dollars laminated in clear plastic. Through the haze came a trio of red planes, flying in formation. Fokker D.VIIs. The room fell silent. The Fokkers banked majestically under the solar orb of a two-hundred-watt bulb.

The blue Spad dove out of nowhere. Two more plunged from the shadowy ceiling, following closely. The kickers swore, and one chuckled. The formation broke wildly. One Fokker dove almost to the felt, without losing the Spad on its tail. Furiously, it zigged and zagged across the green flatlands but to no avail. At last it pulled up, the enemy hard after it, too steeply and stalled, too low to pull out in time. A stack of silver dimes was scooped up. The Fokkers were outnumbered now. One had two Spads on its tail. A needle-spray of tracers tore past its cockpit. The Fokker slip-turned right, banked into an Immelmann, and was behind one of its pursuers. It fired, and the biplane fell, tumbling.

"Way to go, Tiny!" The kickers closed in around the table.

Deke was frozen with wonder. It felt like being born all over again.

• • •

Frank's Truck Stop was two miles out of town on the Commercial Vehicles Only route. Deke had tagged it, out of idle habit, from the bus on the way in. Now he walked back between the traffic and the concrete crash guards. Articulated trucks went slamming past, big eight-segmented jobs, the wash of air each time threatening to blast him over. CVO stops were easy makes. When he sauntered into Frank's, there was nobody to doubt that he'd come in off a big rig, and he was able to browse the gift shop as slowly as he liked. The wire rack with the projective wetware wafers was located between a stack of Korean cowboy shirts and a display for Fuzz Buster mudguards. A pair of Oriental dragons twisted in the air over the rack, either fighting or fucking, he couldn't tell which. The game he wanted was there: a wafer labeled SPADS & FOKKERS. It took him three seconds to boost it and less time to slide the magnet, which the cops in DC hadn't even bothered to confiscate, across the universal security strip. On the way out, he lifted two programming units and a little Batang facilitator remote that looked like an antique hearing aid.

$\bullet \quad \bullet \quad \bullet$

He chose a highstack at random and fed the rental agent the line he'd used since his welfare rights were yanked. Nobody ever checked up; the state just counted occupied rooms and paid.

The cubicle smelled faintly of urine, and someone had scrawled Hard Anarchy Liberation Front slogans across the walls. Deke kicked trash out of a corner, sat down, back to the wall, and ripped open the wafer pack.

There was a folded instruction sheet with diagrams of loops, rolls, and Immelmanns, a tube of saline paste, and a computer list of operational specs. And the wafer itself, white plastic with a blue biplane and logo on one side, red on the other. He turned it over and over in his hand: SPADS & FOKKERS, FOKKERS & SPADS. Red or blue. He fitted the Batang behind his ear after coating the inductor surface with paste, jacked its fiber-optic ribbon into the programmer, and plugged the programmer into the wall current. Then he slid the wafer into the programmer. It was a cheap set, Indonesian, and the base of his skull buzzed uncomfortably as the program ran. But when it was done, a sky-blue Spad darted restlessly through the air a few inches from his face. It almost glowed, it was so real. It had the strange inner life that fanatically detailed museum-grade models often have, but it took all of his concentration to keep it in existence. If his attention wavered at all, it lost focus, fuzzing into a pathetic blur.

He practiced until the battery in the earset died, then slumped against the wall and fell asleep. He dreamed of flying, in a universe that consisted entirely of white clouds and blue sky, with no up and down, and never a green field to crash into.

$\bullet \quad \bullet \quad \bullet$

He woke to a rancid smell of frying krillcakes and winced with hunger. No cash, either. Well, there were plenty of student types in the stack. Bound to be one who'd like to score a programming unit. He hit the hall with the boosted spare. Not far down was a door with a poster on it: THERE'S A HELL OF A GOOD UNIVERSE NEXT DOOR. Under that was a starscape with a cluster of multicolored pills, torn from an ad for some pharmaceutical company, pasted over an inspirational shot of the "space colony" that had been under construction since before he was born. LET'S GO, the poster said, beneath the collaged hypnotics.

He knocked. The door opened, security slides stopping it at a two-inch slice of girlface. "Yeah?"

"You're going to think this is stolen." He passed the programmer from hand to hand. "I mean because it's new, virtual cherry, and the bar code's still on it. But listen, I'm not gonna argue the point. No. I'm gonna let you have it for only like half what you'd pay anywhere else."

"Hey, wow, *really*, no kidding?" The visible fraction of mouth twisted into a strange smile. She extended her hand, palm up, a loose fist. Level with his chin. "Lookahere!"

There was a hole in her hand, a black tunnel that ran right up her arm. Two small red lights. Rat's eyes. They scurried toward him growing, gleaming. Something gray streaked forward and leaped for his face. He screamed, throwing hands up to ward it off. Legs twisting, he fell, the programmer shattering under him.

Silicate shards skittered as he thrashed, clutching his head. Where it hurt, it hurt—it hurt very badly indeed.

"Oh, my God!" Slides unsnapped, and the girl was hovering over him. "Here, listen, come on." She dangled a blue hand towel. "Grab on to this and I'll pull you up."

He looked at her through a wash of tears. Student. That fed look, the oversize sweatshirt, teeth so straight and white they could be used as a credit reference. A thin gold chain around one ankle (fuzzed, he saw, with baby-fine hair). Choppy Japanese haircut. Money.

"That sucker was gonna be my dinner," he said ruefully. He took hold of the towel and let her pull him up.

She smiled but skittishly backed away from him. "Let me make it up to you," she said. "You want some food? It was only a projection, okay?"

He followed her in, wary as an animal entering a trap.

• • •

"Holy shit," Deke said, "this is *real cheese . . .*" He was sitting on a gutsprung sofa, wedged between a four-foot teddy bear and a loose stack of floppies. The room was ankle-deep in books and clothes and papers. But the food she magicked up—Gouda cheese and tinned beef and honest-to-God greenhouse wheat wafers— was straight out of the Arabian Nights.

"Hey," she said. "We know how to treat a proleboy right, huh?" Her name was Nance Bettendorf. She was seventeen. Both her parents had jobs—greedy buggers—and she was an engineering major at William and Mary. She got top marks except in English. "I guess you must really have a thing about rats. You got some kind of phobia about rats?"

He glanced sidelong at her bed. You couldn't see it, really; it was just a swell in the ground cover. "It's not like that. It just reminded me of something else, is all."

"Like what?" She squatted in front of him, the big shirt riding high up one smooth thigh.

"Well . . . did you ever see the"—his voice involuntarily rose and rushed past the words— "*Washington Monument*? Like at night? It's got these two little red lights on top, aviation markers or something, and I, and I . . ." He started to shake.

"You're afraid of the Washington Monument?" Nance whooped and rolled over with laughter, long tanned legs kicking. She was wearing crimson bikini panties.

"I would die rather than look at it again," he said levelly.

She stopped laughing then, sat up, studied his face. White, even teeth worried at her lower lip, like she was dragging up something she didn't want to think about. At last she ventured, "Brainlock?"

"Yeah," he said bitterly. "They told me I'd never go back to DC. And then the fuckers laughed."

"What did they get you for?"

"I'm a thief." He wasn't about to tell her that the actual charge was career shoplifting.

• • •

"Lotta old computer hacks spent their lives programming machines. And you know what? The human brain is not a goddamn bit like a machine, no way. They just don't program the same." Deke knew this shrill, desperate rap, this long, circular jive that the lonely string out to the rare listener; knew it from a hundred cold and empty nights spent in the company of strangers. Nance was lost in it, and Deke, nodding and yawning, wondered if he'd even be able to stay awake when they finally hit that bed of hers.

"I built that projection I hit you with myself," she said, hugging her knees up beneath her chin. "It's for muggers, you know? I just happened to have it on me, and I threw it at you 'cause I thought it was so funny, you trying to sell me that shit little Indojavanese programmer." She hunched forward and held out her hand again. "Look here." Deke cringed. "No, no, it's okay, I swear it, this is different." She opened her hand.

A single blue flame danced there, perfect and everchanging. "Look at that," she marveled. "Just look. I programmed that. It's not some diddly little seven-image job either. It's a continuous two-hour loop, seven thousand, two hundred seconds, never the same twice, each instant as individual as a fucking snowflake!"

The flame's core was glacial crystal, shards and facets flashing up, twisting, and gone, leaving behind near-subliminal images so bright and sharp that they cut the eye. Deke winced. People mostly. Pretty little naked people, fucking. "How the hell did you do that?" She rose,

bare feet slipping on slick magazines, and melo-
dramatically swept folds of loose printout from
a raw plywood shelf. He saw a neat row of small
consoles, austere and expensive looking. Custom
work. "This is the real stuff I got here. Image
facilitator. Here's my fast-wipe module. This
is a brain-map one-to-one function analyzer."
She sang off the names like a litany. "Quantum
flicker stabilizer. Program splicer. An image
assembler . . ."

"You need all that to make one little flame?"

"You betcha. This is all state of the art, professional projective wetware gear. It's years
ahead of anything you've seen."

"Hey," he said, "you know anything about
SPADS and FOKKERS?"

She laughed. And then, because he sensed
the time was right, he reached out to take her
hand.

"Don't you touch me, motherfuck, don't you
ever touch me!" Nance screamed, and her head
slammed against the wall as she recoiled, white
and shaking with terror.

"Okay!" He threw up his hands. "Okay! I'm
nowhere near you. Okay?"

She cowered from him. Her eyes were round
and unblinking; tears built up at the corners,
rolled down ashen cheeks. Finally, she shook her
head. "Hey. Deke. Sorry. I should've told you."

"Told me what?" But he had a creepy feeling that already knew. The way she clutched
her head. The weakly spasmodic way her hands
opened and closed. "You got a brainlock, too."

"Yeah." She closed her eyes. "It's a chastity
lock. My asshole parents paid for it. So I can't
stand to have anybody touch me or even stand
too close." Eyes opened in blind hate. "I didn't
even *do* anything. Not a fucking thing. But
they've both got jobs and they're so horny for
me to have a career that they can't piss straight.
They're afraid I'd neglect my studies if I got,
you know, involved in sex and stuff. The day the
brainlock comes off I am going to fuck the vilest,
greasiest, hairiest . . ."

She was clutching her head again. Deke
jumped up and rummaged through the medi-

cine cabinet. He found a jar of B-complex vita-
mins, pocketed a few against need, and brought
two to Nance, with a glass of water. "Here." He
was careful to keep his distance. "This'll take the
edge off."

"Yeah, yeah," she said. Then, almost to herself, "You must really think I'm a jerk."

• • •

The games room in the Greyhound station was
almost empty. A lone, long-jawed fourteen-year-
old was bent over a console, maneuvering rainbow fleets of submarines in the murky grid of
the North Atlantic. Deke sauntered in, wearing
his new kicker drag, and leaned against a cinder-
block wall made smooth by countless coats of
green enamel. He'd washed the dye from his
proleboy butch, boosted jeans and T-shirt from
the Goodwill, and found a pair of stompers in the
sauna locker of a highstack with cut-rate security.

"Seen Tiny around, friend?" The subs darted
like neon guppies.

"Depends on who's asking." Deke touched
the remote behind his left ear. The Spad snap-
rolled over the console, swift and delicate as a
dragonfly. It was beautiful; so perfect, so *true* it
made the room seem an illusion. He buzzed the
grid, millimeters from the glass, taking advantage of the programmed ground effect.

The kid didn't even bother to look up. "Jackman's," he said. "Down Richmond Road, over
by the surplus."

Deke let the Spad fade in midclimb.

Jackman's took up most of the third floor
of an old brick building. Deke found Best Buy
War Surplus first, then a broken neon sign over
an unlit lobby. The sidewalk out front was littered with another kind of surplus: damaged
vets, some of them dating back to Indochina.
Old men who'd left their eyes under Asian suns
squatted beside twitching boys who'd inhaled
mycotoxins in Chile. Deke was glad to have the
battered elevator doors sigh shut behind him.

A dusty Dr Pepper clock at the far side of

the long, spectral room told him it was a quarter to eight. Jackman's had been embalmed twenty years before he was born, sealed away behind a yellowish film of nicotine, of polish and hair oil. Directly beneath the clock, the flat eyes of somebody's grandpappy's prize buck regarded Deke from a framed, blown-up snapshot gone the slick sepia of cockroach wings. There was the click and whisper of pool, the squeak of a work boot twisting on linoleum as a player leaned in for a shot. Somewhere high above the green-shaded lamps hung a string of crepe-paper Christmas bells faded to dead rose. Deke looked from one cluttered wall to the next. No facilitator.

"Bring one in, should we need it," someone said. He turned, meeting the mild eyes of a bald man with steel-rimmed glasses. "My name's Cline. Bobby Earl. You don't look like you shoot pool, mister." But there was nothing threatening in Bobby Earl's voice or stance. He pinched the steel frames from his nose and polished the thick lenses with a fold of tissue. He reminded Deke of a shop instructor who'd patiently tried to teach him retrograde biochip installation. "I'm a gambler," he said, smiling. His teeth were white plastic. "I know I don't much look it."

"I'm looking for Tiny," Deke said.

"Well," replacing the glasses, "you're not going to find him. He's gone up to Bethesda to let the VA clean his plumbing for him. He wouldn't fly against you anyhow."

"Why not?"

"Well, because you're not on the circuit or I'd know your face. You any good?" When Deke nodded, Bobby Earl called down the length of Jackman's, "Yo, Clarence! You bring out that facilitator. We got us a flyboy."

Twenty minutes later, having lost his remote and what cash he had left, Deke was striding past the broken soldiers of Best Buy.

"Now you let me tell you, boy," Bobby Earl had said in a fatherly tone as, hand on shoulder, he led Deke back to the elevator, "You're not going to win against a combat vet—you listening to me? I'm not even especially good, just an old

grunt who was on hype fifteen, maybe twenty times. Ol' Tiny, he was a *pilot*. Spent entire enlistment hyped to the gills. He's got membrane attenuation real bad . . . you ain't never going to beat him."

It was a cool night. But Deke burned with anger and humiliation.

• • •

"Jesus, that's crude," Nance said as the Spad strafed mounds of pink underwear. Deke, hunched up on the couch, yanked her flashy little Braun remote from behind his ear.

"Now don't you get on my case too, Miss rich-bitch gonna-have-a-job—"

"Hey, lighten up! It's nothing to do with you—it's just *tech*. That's a really primitive wafer you got there. I mean, on the street maybe it's fine. But compared to the work I do at school, it's—hey. You ought to let me rewrite it for you."

"Say what?"

"Lemme beef it up. These suckers are all written in hexadecimal, see, 'cause the industry programmers are all washed-out computer hacks. That's how they think. But let me take it to the reader-analyzer at the department, run a few changes on it, translate it into a modern wetlanguage. Edit out all the redundant intermediaries. That'll goose up your reaction time, cut the feedback loop in half. So you'll fly faster and better. Turn you into a real pro, Ace!" She took a hit off her bong, then doubled over laughing and choking.

"Is that legit?" Deke asked dubiously.

"Hey, why do you think people buy gold-wire remotes? For the prestige? Shit. Conductivity's better, cuts a few nanoseconds off the reaction time. And reaction time is the name of the game, kiddo."

"No," Deke said. "If it were that easy, people'd already have it. Tiny Montgomery would have it. He'd have the best."

"Don't you ever *listen*?" Nance set down the bong; brown water slopped onto the floor. "The stuff I'm working with is three years ahead of anything you'll find on the street."

"No shit," Deke said after a long pause. "I mean, you can do that?"

• • •

It was like graduating from a Model T to a ninety-three Lotus. The Spad handled like a dream, responsive to Deke's slightest thought. For weeks he played the arcades, with not a nibble. He flew against the local teens and by ones and threes shot down their planes. He took chances, played flash. And the planes tumbled. . . .

Until one day Deke was tucking his seed money away, and a lanky black straightened up from the wall. He eyed the laminateds in Deke's hand and grinned. A ruby tooth gleamed. "You know," the man said, "I *heard* there was a casper who could fly, going up against the kiddies."

• • •

"Jesus," Deke said, spreading Danish butter on a kelp stick. "I wiped the *floor* with those spades. They were good, too."

"That's nice, honey," Nance mumbled. She was working on her finals project, sweating data into a machine.

"You know, I think what's happening is I got real talent for this kind of shit. You know? I mean, the program gives me an edge, but I got the stuff to take advantage of it. I'm really getting a rep out there, you know?" Impulsively, he snapped on the radio. Scratchy Dixieland brass blared.

"Hey," Nance said. "Do you *mind*?"

"No, I'm just—" He fiddled with the knobs, came up with some slow, romantic bullshit. "There. Come on, stand up. Let's dance."

"Hey, you know I can't—"

"Sure you can, sugarcakes." He threw her the huge teddy bear and snatched up a patch-work cotton dress from the floor. He held it by the waist and sleeve, tucking the collar under

his chin. It smelled of patchouli, more faintly of sweat. "See, I stand over here, you stand over there. We dance. Get it?"

Blinking softly, Nance stood and clutched the bear tightly. They danced then, slowly, staring into each other's eyes. After a while, she began to cry. But still, she was smiling.

• • •

Deke was daydreaming, imagining he was Tiny Montgomery wired into his jumpjet. Imagined the machine responding to his slightest neural twitch, reflexes cranked *way* up, hype flowing steadily into his veins.

Nance's floor became jungle, her bed a plateau in the Andean foothills, and Deke flew his Spad at forced speed, as if it were a full-wired interactive combat machine. Computerized hypos fed a slow trickle of high-performance enhancement mélange into his bloodstream. Sensors were wired directly into his skull pulling a supersonic snapturn in the green-blue bowl of sky over Bolivian rain forest. Tiny would have *felt* the airflow over control surfaces.

Below, grunts hacked through the jungle with hype-pumps strapped above elbows to give them that little extra death-dance fury in combat, a shot of liquid hell in a blue plastic vial. Maybe they got ten minutes' worth in a week. But coming in at treetop level, reflexes cranked to the max, flying so low the ground troops never spotted you until you were on them, phosgene agents released, away and gone before they could draw a bead . . . it took a constant trickle of hype just to maintain. And the direct neuron interface with the jumpjet was a two-way street. The onboard computers monitored biochemistry and decided when to open the sluice gates and give the human component a killer jolt of combat edge.

Dosages like that ate you up. Ate you good and slow and constant, etching the brain surfaces, eroding away the brain-cell membranes. If you weren't yanked from the air promptly enough, you ended up with brain-cell attenuation with reflexes too fast for your body to handle and your fight-or-flight reflexes fucked real good. . . .

"I aced it, proleboy!"

"Hah?" Deke looked up, startled, as Nance slammed in, tossing books and bag onto the nearest heap.

"My finals project—I got exempted from exams. The prof said he'd never seen anything like it. Uh, hey, dim the lights, wouldja? The colors are weird on my eyes."

He obliged. "So show me. Show me this wunnerful thing."

"Yeah, okay." She snatched up his remote, kicked clear standing space atop the bed, and struck a pose. A spark flared into flame in her hand. It spread in a quicksilver line up her arm, around her neck, and it was a snake, with triangular head and flickering tongue. Molten colors, oranges and reds. It slithered between her breasts. "I call it a firesnake," she said proudly.

Deke leaned close, and she jerked back. "Sorry. It's like your flame, huh? I mean, I can see these tiny little fuckers in it."

"Sort of." The firesnake flowed down her stomach. "Next month I'm going to splice two hundred separate flame programs together with meld justification in between to get the visuals. Then I'll tap the mind's body image to make it self-orienting. So it can crawl all over your body without your having to mind it. You could wear it dancing."

"Maybe I'm dumb. But if you haven't done the work yet, how come I can see it?"

Nance giggled. "That's the best part—half the work isn't done yet. Didn't have the time to assemble the pieces into a unified program. Turn on that radio, huh? I want to dance." She kicked off her shoes. Deke tuned in something gutsy. Then, at Nance's urging, turned it down, almost to a whisper.

"I scored two hits of hype, see." She was bouncing on the bed, weaving her hands like a Balinese dancer. "Ever try the stuff? In-credible. Gives you like absolute concentration. Look here." She stood *en pointe*. "Never done that before."

"Hype," Deke said. "Last person I heard of got caught with that shit got three years in the infantry. How'd you score it?"

"Cut a deal with a vet who was in grad school. She bombed out last month. Stuff gives me perfect visualization. I can hold the projection with my eyes shut. It was a snap assembling the program in my head."

"On just two hits, huh?"

"One hit. I'm saving the other. Teach was so impressed he's sponsoring me for a job interview. A recruiter from I. G. Feuchtwaren hits campus in two weeks. That cap is gonna sell him the program *and* me. I'm gonna cut out of school two years early, straight into industry, do not pass jail, do not pay two hundred dollars."

The snake curled into a flaming tiara. It gave Deke a funny-creepy feeling to think of. Nance walking out of his life.

"I'm a witch," Nance sang, "a wetware witch." She shucked her shirt over her head and sent it flying. Her fine, high breasts moved freely, gracefully, as she danced. "I'm gonna make it"—now she was singing a current pop hit—"to the . . . top!" Her nipples were small and pink and aroused. The firesnake licked at them and whipped away.

"Hey, Nance," Deke said uncomfortably. "Calm down a little, huh?"

"I'm celebrating!" She hooked a thumb into her shiny gold panties. Fire swirled around hand and crotch. "I'm the virgin goddess, baby, and I have the pow-er!" Singing again.

Deke looked away. "Gotta go now," he mumbled. Gotta go home and jerk off. He wondered where she'd hidden that second hit. Could be anywhere.

• • •

There was a protocol to the circuit, a tacit order of deference and precedence as elaborate as that of a Mandarin court. It didn't matter that Deke was hot, that his rep was spreading like wildfire. Even a name flyboy couldn't just challenge whom he wished. He had to climb the ranks.

But if you flew every night. If you were always available to anybody's challenge. And if you were good . . . well, it was possible to climb fast.

Deke was one plane up. It was tournament fighting, three planes against three. Not many spectators, a dozen maybe, but it was a good fight, and they were noisy. Deke was immersed in the manic calm of combat when he realized suddenly that they had fallen silent. Saw the kickers stir and exchange glances. Eyes flicked past him. He heard the elevator doors close. Coolly, he disposed of the second of his opponent's planes, then risked a quick glance over his shoulder.

Tiny Montgomery had just entered Jackman's. The wheelchair whispered across browning linoleum, guided by tiny twitches of one imperfectly paralyzed hand. His expression was stern, blank, calm.

In that instant, Deke lost two planes. One to deresolution gone to blur and canceled out by the facilitator and the other because his opponent was a real fighter. Guy did a barrel roll, killing speed and slipping to the side, and strafed Deke's biplane as it shot past. It went down in flames. Their last two planes shared altitude and speed, and as they turned, trying for position, they naturally fell into a circling pattern.

The kickers made room as Tiny wheeled up against the table. Bobby Earl Cline trailed after him, lanky and casual. Deke and his opponent traded glances and pulled their machines back from the pool table so they could hear the man out. Tiny smiled. His features were small, clustered in the center of his pale, doughy face. One finger twitched slightly on the chrome handrest. "I heard about you." He looked straight at Deke. His voice was soft and shockingly sweet, a baby-girl little voice. "I heard you're good."

Deke nodded slowly. The smile left Tiny's face. His soft, fleshy lips relaxed into a natural pout, as if he were waiting for a kiss. His small, bright eyes studied Deke without malice. "Let's see what you can do, then."

Deke lost himself in the cool game of war. And when the enemy went down in smoke and flame, to explode and vanish against the table, Tiny wordlessly turned his chair, wheeled it into the elevator, and was gone.

As Deke was gathering up his winnings, Bobby Earl eased up to him and said, "The man wants to play you."

"Yeah?" Deke was nowhere near high enough on the circuit to challenge Tiny. "What's the scam?"

"Man who was coming up from Atlanta tomorrow canceled. Ol' Tiny, he was spoiling to go up against somebody new. So it looks like you get your shot at the Max."

"Tomorrow? Wednesday? Doesn't give me much prep time."

Bobby Earl smiled gently. "I don't think that makes no nevermind."

"How's that, Mr. Cline?"

"Boy, you just ain't got the *moves*, you follow me? Ain't got no surprises. You fly just like some kinda beginner, only faster and slicker. You follow what I'm trying to say?"

"I'm not sure I do. You want to put a little action on that?"

"Tell you truthful," Cline said, "I been hoping on that." He drew a small black notebook from his pocket and licked a pencil stub. "Give you five to one. They's nobody gonna give no fairer odds than that."

He looked at Deke almost sadly. "But Tiny, he's just naturally better'n you, and that's all she wrote, boy. He lives for that goddamned game, ain't *got* nothing else. Can't get out of that goddamned chair. You think you can best a man who's fighting for his life, you are just lying to yourself."

• • •

Norman Rockwell's portrait of the colonel regarded Deke dispassionately from the Kentucky Fried across Richmond Road from the coffee bar. Deke held his cup with hands that were cold and trembling. His skull hummed with fatigue. Cline was right, he told the colonel. I can go up against Tiny, but I can't win. The colonel stared back, gaze calm and level and not particularly kindly, taking in the coffee bar and Best Buy and all his drag-ass kingdom of Richmond Road. Waiting for Deke to admit to the terrible thing he had to do.

"The bitch is planning to leave me *anyway*," Deke said aloud. Which made the black counter-girl look at him funny, then quickly away.

• • •

"Daddy called!" Nance danced into the apartment, slamming the door behind her. "And you know what? He says if I can get this job and hold it for six months, he'll have the brainlock reversed. Can you *believe* it? Deke?" She hesitated. "You okay?"

Deke stood. Now that the moment was on him, he felt unreal, like he was in a movie or something. "How come you never came home last night?" Nance asked.

The skin on his face was unnaturally taut, a parchment mask. "Where'd you stash the hype, Nance? I need it."

"Deke," she said, trying a tentative smile that instantly vanished. "Deke, that's mine. My hit. I need it. For my interview."

He smiled scornfully. "You got money. You can always score another cap."

"Not by Friday! Listen, Deke, this is really important. My whole life is riding on this interview. I need that cap. It's all I got!"

"Baby, you got the fucking world! Take a look around you—six ounces of blond Lebanese hash! Little anchovy fish in tins. Unlimited medical coverage, if you need it." She was backing away from him, stumbling against the static waves of unwashed bedding and wrinkled glossy magazines that crested at the foot of her bed. "Me, I never had a glimmer of any of this. Never had the kind of edge it takes to get along. Well, this one time I am gonna. There is a match in two hours that I am going to fucking well win. Do you hear me?" He was working himself into a rage, and that was good. He needed it for what he had to do.

Nance flung up an arm, palm open, but he was ready for that and slapped her hand aside, never even catching a glimpse of the dark tunnel, let alone those little red eyes. Then they were both falling, and he was on top of her, her breath hot and rapid in his face. "Deke! Deke! I need that shit, Deke, my *interview*, it's the only . . . I gotta . . . gotta . . ." She twisted her face away, crying into the wall. "Please, God, please don't . . ."

"Where did you stash it?" Pinned against the bed under his body, Nance began to spasm, her entire body convulsing in pain and fear.

"Where is it?" Her face was bloodless, gray corpse flesh, and horror burned in her eyes. Her lips squirmed. It was too late to stop now; he'd crossed over the line. Deke felt revolted and nauseated, all the more so because on some unexpected and unwelcome level, he was *enjoying* this.

"Where is it, Nance?" And slowly, very gently, he began to stroke her face.

• • •

Deke summoned Jackman's elevator with a finger that moved as fast and straight as a hornet and landed daintily as a butterfly on the call button. He was full of bouncy energy, and it was all under control. On the way up, he whipped off his shades and chuckled at his reflection in the finger-smudged chrome. The blacks of his eyes were like pinpricks, all but invisible, and still the world was neon bright.

Tiny was waiting. His mouth turned up at the corners into a sweet smile as he took in Deke's irises, the exaggerated calm of his motions, the unsuccessful attempt to mime an undrugged clumsiness. "Well," he said in that girlish voice, "looks like I have a treat in store for me."

The Max was draped over one tube of the wheelchair. Deke took up position and bowed, not quite mockingly. "Let's fly." As challenger, he flew defense. He materialized his planes at a conservative altitude, high enough to dive, low enough to have warning when Tiny attacked. He waited.

The crowd tipped him. A fatboy with brilliantined hair looked startled, a hollow-eyed cracker started to smile. Murmurs rose. Eyes shifted slow-motion in heads frozen by hyped-up reaction time. Took maybe three nanoseconds to pinpoint the source of attack. Deke whipped his head up, and—

Sonofabitch, he was *blind*! The Fokkers were diving straight from the two-hundred-watt bulb, and Tiny had suckered him into staring right at it. His vision whited out. Deke squeezed lids tight over welling tears and frantically held visualization. He split his flight, curving two biplanes right, one left. Immediately twisting each a half-turn, then back again. He had to dodge randomly—he couldn't tell where the hostile warbirds were.

Tiny chuckled. Deke could hear him through the sounds of the crowd, the cheering and cursing and slapping down of coins that seemed to syncopate independent of the ebb and flow of the duel.

When his vision returned an instant later, a Spad was in flames and falling. Fokkers tailed his surviving planes, one on one and two on the other. Three seconds into the game and he was down one.

Dodging to keep Tiny from pinning tracers on him, he looped the single-pursued plane about and drove the other toward the blind spot between Tiny and the light bulb.

Tiny's expression went very calm. The faintest shadow of disappointment—of contempt, even—was swallowed up by tranquility. He tracked the planes blandly, waiting for Deke to make his turn.

Then, just short of the blind spot, Deke shoved his Spad into a drive, the Fokkers overshooting and banking wildly to either side, twisting around to regain position.

The Spad swooped down on the third Fokker, pulled into position by Deke's other plane. Fire strafed wings and crimson fuselage. For an instant nothing happened, and Deke thought he had a fluke miss. Then the little red mother veered left and went down, trailing black, oily smoke.

Tiny frowned, small lines of displeasure marring the perfection of his mouth. Deke smiled. One even, and Tiny held position.

Both Spads were tailed closely. Deke swung them wide, and then pulled them together from opposite sides of the table. He drove them straight for each other, neutralizing Tiny's advantage . . . neither could fire without endangering his own planes. Deke cranked his machines up to top speed, slamming them at each other's nose.

An instant before they crashed, Deke sent the planes over and under one another, opening fire on the Fokkers and twisting away. Tiny was ready. Fire filled the air. Then one blue and one red plane soared free, heading in opposite directions. Behind them, two biplanes tangled in midair. Wings touched, slewed about, and the planes crumpled. They fell together, almost straight down, to the green felt below.

Ten seconds in and four planes down. A black vet pursed his lips and blew softly. Someone else shook his head in disbelief.

Tiny was sitting straight and a little forward in his wheelchair, eyes intense and unblinking, soft hands plucking feebly at the grips. None of that amused and detached bullshit now; his attention was riveted on the game. The kickers, the table, Jackman's itself, might not exist at all for him. Bobby Earl Cline laid a hand on his shoulder; Tiny didn't notice. The planes were at opposite ends of the room, laboriously gaining altitude. Deke jammed his against the ceiling, dim through the smoky haze. He spared Tiny a quick glance, and their eyes locked. Cold against cold. "Let's see your best," Deke muttered through clenched teeth.

They drove their planes together.

The hype was peaking now, and Deke could see Tiny's tracers crawling through the air between the planes. He had to put his Spad into the line of fire to get off a fair burst, then twist and bank so the Fokker's bullets would slip by his undercarriage. Tiny was every bit as hot, dodging Deke's fire and passing so close to the Spad their landing gears almost tangled as they passed.

Deke was looping his Spad in a punishingly tight turn when the hallucinations hit. The felt writhed and twisted, became the green hell of Bolivian rain forest that Tiny had flown combat over. The walls receded to gray infinity, and he felt the metal confinement of a cybernetic jump-jet close in around him.

But Deke had done his homework. He was expecting the hallucinations and knew he could deal with them. The military would never pass on a drug that couldn't be fought through. Spad and Fokker looped into another pass. He could read the tensions in Tiny Montgomery's face, the echoes of combat in deep jungle sky. They drove their planes together, feeling the torqued tensions that fed straight from instrumentation to hindbrain, the adrenaline pumps kicking in behind the armpits, the cold, fast freedom of air-flow over jetskin mingling with the smells of hot metal and fear sweat. Tracers tore past his face, and he pulled back, seeing the Spad zoom by the Fokker again, both untouched. The kickers were just going ape, waving hats and stomping feet, acting like God's own fools. Deke locked glances with Tiny again.

Malice rose up in him, and though his every nerve was taut as the carbon-crystal whiskers that kept the jumpjets from falling apart in superman turns over the Andes, he counterfeited a casual smile and winked, jerking his head slightly to one side, as if to say "Looka here."

Tiny glanced to the side.

It was only for a fraction of a second, but that was enough. Deke pulled as fast and tight an Immelmann—right on the edge of theoretical tolerance—as had ever been seen on the circuit, and he was hanging on Tiny's tail.

Let's see you get out of this one, sucker.

Tiny rammed his plane straight down at the green, and Deke followed after. He held his fire. He had Tiny where he wanted him.

Running. Just like he'd been on his every combat mission. High on exhilaration and hype, maybe, but running scared. They were down to the felt now, flying treetop-level. Break, Deke

thought, and jacked up the speed. Peripherally, he could see Bobby Earl Cline, and there was a funny look on the man's face. A pleading kind of look. Tiny's composure was shot; his face was twisted and tormented.

Now Tiny panicked and dove his plane in among the crowd. The biplanes looped and twisted between the kickers. Some jerked back involuntarily, and others laughingly swatted at them with their hands. But there was a hot glint of terror in Tiny's eyes that spoke of an eternity of fear and confinement, two edges sawing away at each other endlessly. . . .

The fear was death in the air, the confinement a locking away in metal, first of the aircraft, then of the chair. Deke could read it all in his face: Combat was the only out Tiny had had, and he'd taken it every chance he got. Until some anonymous *nationalista* with an antique SAM tore him out of that blue-green Bolivian sky and slammed him straight down to Richmond Road and Jackman's and the smiling killer boy he faced this one last time across the faded cloth.

Deke rocked up on his toes, face burning with that million-dollar smile that was the trademark of the drug that had already fried Tiny before anyone ever bothered to blow him out of the sky in a hot tangle of metal and mangled flesh. It all came together then. He saw that flying was all that held Tiny together. That daily brush of fingertips against death, and then rising up from the metal coffin, alive again. He'd been holding back collapse by sheer force of will. Break that willpower, and mortality would come pouring out and drown him. Tiny would lean over and throw up in his own lap.

• • •

And Deke drove it home. . . .

There was a moment of stunned silence as Tiny's last plane vanished in a flash of light. "I did it," Deke whispered. Then, louder, "Son of a bitch, I did it!"

Across the table from him, Tiny twisted in his chair, arms jerking spastically; his head lolled over on one shoulder. Behind him, Bobby Earl Cline stared straight at Deke, his eyes hot coals.

The gambler snatched up the Max and wrapped its ribbon around a stack of laminateds. Without warning, he flung the bundle at Deke's face. Effortlessly, casually, Deke plucked it from the air.

For an instant, then, it looked like the gambler would come at him, right across the pool table. He was stopped by a tug on his sleeve. "Bobby Earl," Tiny whispered, his voice choking with humiliation, "you gotta get me . . . out of here. . . ."

Stiffly, angrily, Cline wheeled his friend around, and then away, into shadow.

Deke threw back his head and laughed. By God, he felt good! He stuffed the Max into a shirt pocket, where it hung cold and heavy. The money he crammed into his jeans. Man, he had to jump with it, his triumph leaping up through him like a wild thing, fine and strong as the flanks of a buck in the deep woods he'd seen from a Greyhound once, and for this one moment it seemed that everything was worth it somehow, all the pain and misery he'd gone through to finally win.

But Jackman's was silent. Nobody cheered. Nobody crowded around to congratulate him.

He sobered, and silent, hostile faces swam into focus. Not one of these kickers was on his side. They radiated contempt, even hatred. For an interminably drawn-out moment the air trembled with potential violence . . . and then someone turned to the side, hawked up phlegm, and spat on the floor. The crowd broke up, muttering, one by one drifting into the darkness.

Deke didn't move. A muscle in one leg began to twitch, harbinger of the coming hype crash. The top of his head felt numb, and there was an awful taste in his mouth. For a second he had to hang on to the table with both hands to keep from falling down forever, into the living shadow beneath him, as he hung impaled by the prize buck's dead eyes in the photo under the Dr Pepper clock.

A little adrenaline would pull him out of this. He needed to celebrate. To get drunk or stoned and talk it up, going over the victory time and again, contradicting himself, making up details, laughing and bragging. A starry old night like this called for big talk.

But standing there with all of Jackman's silent and vast and empty around him, he realized suddenly that he had nobody left to tell it to.

Nobody at all.

RUSSELL BLACKFORD

GLASS REPTILE BREAKOUT

(1985)

SKINNY SHARKS cruise the downtown miracle bars on Saturday night.

Bianca doesn't give a damn.

Holy forces take Bianca, there in the Searoom. They energize her dancing. Holy forces. Holy. Never perilous.

The main band plays, the miracle band—Glass Reptile Breakout plays—and the big high room in St Kilda's labyrinthine Season Hotel is all noise and smoke, clothing white or the colors of the sea, tight and supple or free and loose, and upon the half-naked young people the stigmata of fashion: shaven heads, plumed or finned with implants, bare arms bright with feathers or glistening scales, dorsal sails, fins or spines that flatten or bristle depending on what is worn over them—though the drastic implants of a flick-dancer won't settle under any clothing.

Bianca's heart is set: she yearns to be a flick-dancer. She can dance so slowly or so very fast. Free and wild in her roe skirt, glittermesh strips catching light at waist, wrists, ankles. (She prac-tices for hours in her darkened kiddy flat behind her parents' split-level house in Mount Waverley, practices until she has it. The Control.)

Her hair has gone for plumes. Father paid, grudgingly, for the fin sewn into her sleek olive back, knowing someone else would: there are always men willing to pay the roe at the Searoom, pay with favors.

Bending her arm at an awkward angle, she feels along her backbone, the translucent orange fin's graft line. Sutured lines of flesh edging the cultured implant are still swollen and sore. Bianca hates bumping people because it jars and hurts. But, dancing, she scarcely notices. And she's had one miracle from the Bio-feeders. Music miracle. One time she went out much too soon after a line of unfashionable scales was removed from her ankle. Came back *whole*. She's never heard *thoughts*—that's crap . . . someone made it up, that's all. But she's said the strangest things to people, or them to her. And it's made sense in the end.

She believes in the miracles; trustingly, she awaits one.

. . .

Lachlan Alderson, Senior Church Counsel, Victoria, blinks. He dabs with a small chamois cloth at wire-rimmed glasses. The Searoom's smoke leaves him bleary and owlish. There's still a question for him, one so jagged and ramified it can't be hustled into plain words, much less the urbane diction of a courtroom or the bland assurances of a government report. To his pain, it's the question of Satan.

The secular attitude is no option to Alderson.

It's different for Dr. Loerne. To her the rock miracles are a simple matter of enhanced trypsin activity. She sees them through the reductive lenses of science, filtershades them into the queer by-product of participation mystique focused by expectations brought on by the first miracles. Those, in turn, were merely the result of an unforeseen resonance between EEG-coupled musicians, the enhanced field effects of their nonvocal music, and an audience of half-hypnotized young dancers.

True, perhaps, but not the whole truth. Alderson cannot disregard the spiritual dimension. He's a rational man, yes, a sophisticated one. And ordained into the priesthood of his Church. *The Great Tribulation is at hand:* rhetorical crap from the fundamentalist cults. Alderson doesn't think like that. He thinks like a corporate lawyer. *The man of sin working Satan's deeds with all powers and signs and lying wonders.* All just nonsense, absolute nonsense.

Almighty God!

On a smoke-filled stage, four spindly musicians prance like the demons of a medieval morality play. Big body-scales decorate their lean arms. Smoke drifts across the parquet dance floor. Does it stink of brimstone? Headgear flashes like goats' horns catching coal-glare.

Gabby Loerne is fond of explaining that the miracles have precisely the same cause as the healings at the Ganges, Lourdes, at charismatic revivals. But, for Alderson, the difference in ambience could not be more sinister.

A teenage girl screams. Pretty little thing. Confusion of plump naked flesh, bizarrely modified in the manner of these sharks and roe. Her finned back, her head of pink ostrich-plume implants, shake in the soup of noise and the yellow smoke eddying under dull lights. Alderson stolidly fires up a non-cancer filter and averts eyes from the girl's brown, elated face. Little nose, round Asian cheekbones. Chinese ancestry there, or something similar. And a touch of the south European. Pretty features somehow distorted by the Devil's work.

My God! Alderson is not a fool. He's not a cultist. But he is coming to accept the reality of evil. He knows that its meaning is problematic. A violation of natural good in the eyes of one is a rich difference of culture to another. The Church knows that, too. But is this an adequate response?

Suspended from the high ceiling on the far side of the room, a flickdancer cavorts with his knife. The young girl screams again, falling to bare knees, legs apart. Supplication?

The music plays. The flickdancer slices his own flesh from shoulder to bend of elbow, but doesn't bleed.

This is nothing. Some of the rock miracles are so physically and morally ugly, such grotesque, savage parodies of divine healing, that they oblige Alderson and his ancient church to reassess their tolerance.

Alderson's visits to these venues fail to help him understand how these people think.

He watches the girl, knows that there's prurience in his gaze. Hates it. Her breasts *wobble.* A high-slit garment, more a long white lap-lap than a skirt, falls across her deeply brown thighs. *Return to tribalism.* She wears little else. Jewelry. Her implants.

The music ends. Human sounds roar on.

Alderson leans against a plaster wall. Unobtrusive as possible. Dr. Gabby Loerne perches beside him, handsome on a broad windowsill. Her neat slim ankles cross above the floor. She claps enthusiastically and loudly. No young roe, she is dressed in a more sedate version of current fashion: green glittermesh tights and blouse. A small cluster of green scales jewels her cheek.

In front of them, the girl's torso flails from side to side. She's still on her knees, leaning back now on her heels, body the shouting tongue of a kinetic language. Disports herself in a choreography of prayer before some voyeuristic deity. Again she screams her delight, an invitation to that deity to join her in accord.

Lachlan Alderson leans closer to Gabby to make himself heard above the applause. "None of this disturbs you?"

• • •

Luis Baker can pass muster at the Searoom. But he's twenty-eight; most of the dancers are half his age. He sidles rangily among them in protective coloration. Cold-eyed, lean, to all appearances an aging *mestizo* tourist sharking after little Aussie roe. His dark long-jawed face is embellished with glittering ice-blue scales, each the size of a fingernail. He carries no firearm tonight beneath his loose jerkin of silvery glittermesh. He misses its comforting weight. But he won't need it tonight.

Baker keeps watch on a couple across the thick-aired room, avoids the attention. They're older than him, late thirties, though the woman does not look her age. But they're highfliers, just like him.

The room is almost opaque with smoke from the stage and from the filters that these people devour. Faces come and go behind wisps of smoke, navigational buoys looming from sea-fog, then lost behind its veils. Alderson's manner is older than his face—and he is prematurely white at the temples. His wire-rimmed glasses add to the enthusiastically serious look. Baker realizes he is staring at the man. Tracking Loerne and Alderson here will be counterproductive if they become aware of him. The assignment requires absolute discretion.

He works his way to the bar. United Intelligence (Australia) has kept covert surveillance on all nine Members and Advisors of the Wallace Inquiry. For all that they represent extreme ends of the Inquiry's ideological spectrum, Loerne and Alderson prefer each other's company to that of the city bureaucrats, sociologists, and professors of science who complete the Board of Inquiry. Fascinated by opposed *Weltanschauungen*. That's all UIA has on them, nothing scandalous to exploit. Loerne is the only one young enough to look at all plausible in the Searoom. But the other Advisors have all made frequent visits to the Season Hotel and the other Melbourne venues for the miracle music: the Rocks and Sand club in the city; the Fishcave along the esplanade in Port Melbourne; the more dignified miracle bars patronized by a slightly older set in Carlton. While the Advisors have got out and about, the three Members have stuck with their hearings and official inspections. Among the Searoom's complement of extreme young people in their sea-tribe gear, Loerne and Alderson appear out of place, but not ridiculously so as far as Loerne is concerned. Plenty of people are dressed more conservatively than she is, including an element of hapless men in their twenties and thirties, fooling themselves that they're going to net the young roe—who, of course, will have nothing to do with them unless they're rich.

Baker smirks at this happy thought, and at another: he could tell the Wallace Board of Inquiry more about the music miracles than anyone else here—more than it wants to know.

• • •

Only one cheek is jeweled.

Gabby Loerne turns to face Alderson squarely. Her large green eyes give no offense, clearly expect none from Alderson. "There's nothing disturbing about this."

The no-nonsense view of a tough-minded scientist at home in a laboratory, a conference room, a tribal jungle. Her manner is comforting and plain.

In his fashion, Alderson is also a practical man. A moralist, but with his feet on the ground. Morality is based on keeping your feet on the ground—society requires more than law for its morality, it requires experience, faith. Enforcement needs law; but teaching needs faith. That's what he learned at the Faculty of Theology, and he believes it. "We've let ourselves be fuddled," he says. He's tried to explain before—he tries again. "Our whole society's been fuddled by shibboleths. We thought that tolerance was a value in itself, and we chased tolerance until the moral center got left behind."

They both know the direction society has taken: *directions*. A dozen conflicting moral codes, the young totally alien to their parents, but their ways of life tolerated and financed for fears of worse evils—or is it just fear of seeming repressive?

"All I'm saying is that we shouldn't let our society become something that decent people can't bear to live in and bring up kids in. If a word like *freedom* or *tolerance* won't fit our needs, let's choose another word—not the other way around." There, he's said it again. Tight, cogent, defensible.

During the musoes' break, sharks are milling about aimlessly, many lighting up filters. Some of the little half-nude girls hug their skinny boyfriends. Scaly young sharks float in the direction of the bar, come back with frothy beer and cheap white wine for themselves and their roe—a patriarchy offensive to their parents is assumed in their folkways.

Gabby takes a deep breath.

"I don't know where to start with you. You're a learned man, a learned *friend*, who believes in spooks and demons. These things have rational causes. You know that. What you're seeing here is nothing more than an extreme form of the participative exhibitionism that we've observed all over the world. These musicians are priests of a mystery religion, if you like—but don't think of Satanism. Try the angakok leading the participative rites in Greenland . . . or the monks of Tibet. If you *must* have an analogy."

The musoes are back. It's suddenly quiet. An expectancy. Alderson whispers. Agitated, almost hissing. "Satan can act through human phenomena."

Her eyes are dismissive.

"No. Listen. This suspension of the will you're talking about is *dangerous*. The Church distinguishes between divine presence and collective hysteria, because, when God is absent from this form of . . . hysteria, the soul is vulnerable to possession. *At least that's the possibility I have to consider*. It's not some lunatic dogma you can just parody and reject out of hand; it's an intelligent idea worked out by scholars over years, over hundreds of years. . . ."

But the music has returned: music and synthesized words spew forth from the amps, screaming with a sexual energy healthy enough in itself—but for an audience like this? This set is louder than the last. Alderson reaches into the fob pocket of his baggy seaweed-colored jeans, draws out a wad of cotton wool. Pinches off two comet-shaped lumps, rolls plugs of wool to protect ears from the blast. He remembers old rock shows, knows how to protect himself *this* much.

Gabby touches backs of fingertips to his elbow.

She speaks very clearly. "*He prayeth best who loveth best* . . . Remember."

He knows:

He prayeth best who loveth best
All things both great and small;
For the dear God who loveth us,
He made and loveth all.

"I do love them," he shouts back. "It's what's in them I can't love." The implications of his words depress and embarrass him. Demonic possession. He can't have meant it that crudely. But in some half-defined sense he knows this place is driven by evil. *Of the Devil*, the fundamentalist cults would say.

"Maybe you should try to love that, too."

"All right," he says, pointing. Her eyes follow.

The mutilated boy in the cage. "Can you love flickdancing?"

Her reply is too soft for him to hear. But her lips move in their own simple dance. "Why not?"

• • •

She has opened herself to the music. To the crowd. The atmosphere. Open to the deep-brown, sinewy flickdancer, naked from the waist up, bleeding—ever so slightly—from long, fast-healing cuts. At the corner of Bianca's eye, the lead muso dances, shouting inaudibly, voice overflooded by the music from stacked black speakers rearing high in the corners of the stage. He sings to fill a merely private need, for his true voice, his music, comes from the bulky purple crown whose lights pulse on his forehead, feeding the signatures of biofeedback-trained brainwaves into the synths back of stage, then to the speakers.

Crimson flashes the stage from the wings. Yellow strobes. Blue.

Insistent rhythm of deep drums and bass guitar catches Bianca in the top of her belly, and she grunts slightly, stitch below her ribs, driving her into a strutting barefoot dance.

The moment stretches.

But the song smashes to an end: a heavy clang of metal. An archaic cylindrical microphone descends for the lead muso, who takes it in both long-fingered, long-nailed hands; his full lips almost touch it as he thanks the audience for its applause and attention. He leaves the mic to hang in space as he bends to sip a glass of water a meter away on the stage's dusty floor; he returns to the black mic and pants theatrically over the applause of the audience. "Thank you. Thank you." His sweaty chest heaves; strain shows in the movements of his great tufted eyebrows under the glowing headdress. "Thank you all." Massive green and orange body scales deck his shoulders and forearms. He carries himself in slightly dated style, high-heeled boots over very tight glittermesh pants. Sign of pur-

ist devotion. A pose of advanced BF-music, its makers too fanatical to maintain the latest mode. A pose which *is* the mode among these groups, in these places.

Glass Reptile Breakout hardly pauses between songs.

"A real healing song for you miracle lovers." He mutters it. Exhaustion and introspection. More pose. Bianca easily takes in the pose, without judging it. The microphone flies smoothly heavenward. Bianca half recognizes that man and lady in the corner at the frosted window. She's seen them on holos.

The music roars back. It claws at the inside of her round stomach, a needle-clawed bat, scratching to get out. She's wild with it. Her upper body's muscles twist her through near spasm. But she's got the Control. Hardly *under* control. But she's got it. She's got it. She's got it. *The Control. The capital-C. Mr. Big One, yes. She's got it, she's riding it, she's got it—she's exploding.*

And the graft in her back is painless. She's there. *She's there!*

And an important thought. That old man. The one with glasses—and the lady, the woman. She must speak with them. Something odd. Something odd has come to her and she'll speak to them. Especially the man. There's something she must say to him.

• • •

Baker has studied covert recordings of Alderson and Loerne discussing these places. Despite Alderson's qualms about the miracle bands, he keeps visiting, struggling to come to grips. Of the Advisors to the Wallace Inquiry, he's the most emotionally vulnerable. Predisposed to shock. That's what Baker wants. What they sent him for.

He'll show 'em all havoc.

United Intelligence has its own global operations studying biofeedback techniques and rock miracles. It's way ahead of State government inquiries. It's going to stay that way. Everywhere.

Baker's colleagues in South America are particularly keen to restrict public access to equipment and techniques which create the BF-miracles. Power is knowledge and knowledge is power.

Just now he slaps another pair of two-dollar coins on the bar. Stares through the gaunt feather-cheeked barman, who passes over a pot of weak beer and derisory change from four bucks.

Wait until the end of the night, the encores. Then . . . the beginning of the end. UI doesn't like flickdancing. In this city, the end of it is coming. He sips his beer.

The song changes tempo. Now Baker can see why the band called it a healing song. It's become almost a parody: tranquil. Fresh fields and bird calls. All things sentimental. But he resists its clichéd charm. Training with UI in Brazil and Chile with the best Russky and CIA instructors taught him detachment as well as skill.

Leaning against the padded vinyl bar top, he can look almost straight up into the Perspex cage, dangling from a network of gold-painted chains, where the flickdancer performs. The power of that music! If it can augment a healing process, Baker thinks savagely, it can also reverse it. He'll see to that.

• • •

It's called *flickdancing*, but Tigershark doesn't use a conventional flick knife. His instrument more closely resembles a steel-handled wedge-bladed carpenter's knife, compact enough to fit entirely in his palm. It won't pierce the flesh too deeply by accident, and it can be concealed in his hand: when he cuts open the skin, it's as if by magic, running a closed fist along his body, eerily slicing the flesh apart.

He's seventeen, smooth and brown as the pouch of Italian leather dangling from the glittermesh strip about his slim hard waist, where he keeps his beer money.

Moves very deliberately and quietly to the music. Bare soles hardly slap the clear floor of his cage enough to rock it. A great bronze frill

arches between his eyes and along the middle of his shaven skull, spreads down his back like the triangular fin of a shark, ends buried in his coccyx. The back of his white floppy shorts is cut away in a V to make room for the base of the bronze frill. Tigershark's implants are so generous, so rigid, that he cannot easily clothe his upper body. That doesn't matter. He takes up jobs on the Gold Coast or the Reef islands when the weather gets colder, and even overseas with the troops, entertaining the Aussie contingent in Brazil.

With a studied, ritualized movement, he places the chunky sea-green knife in his left fist, only the blade uncovered. Deftly, he slices up the underside of his right wrist and forearm, biting as deeply as the blade will allow, crossing over the inward bend of the elbow with its big dark veins, and across the strong flat biceps muscle.

The movement is graceful and safe. His blade will not go too deep, and the cut hardly bleeds. It's enough to display the ongoing miracle of Tigershark's body: shallow wounds cease to bleed within seconds, close up scabless within minutes, within hours are gone without trace.

Passing the knife to his right hand, Tigershark turns his left wrist, applies the knife to the base of left palm—and slashes. A sudden change of tempo, but still an artist's grace.

• • •

"That's it, folks."

The lead muso steps back into the shadows. No longer exalted by the music and the lights, the band appears diminished to Gabby Loerne. The musoes seem *chastened* as they walk from stage to wings.

Momentarily there is silence, then strong whistles and cries of "More!" The stage lights stay down, but no house lights come on in the Searoom. Loerne looks about, feeling alienated as the other members of the audience whip themselves into a frenzy of will, the older youths—the real estate brokers and patent buyers' clerks—more vocal than the teenage sharks and roe. But all eager to bring Glass Reptile Breakout back on stage. The cries—"More!"—rise to a raucous clap-reinforced chant. All eyes fix on the stage as if staring alone could set in train mighty engines. *Maybe it can.*

"More! More!"

Everything around her has become unreal: the butts and fragments of discarded filter packets on the deep red carpet about the walls, a dangerously broken beer glass on the hard center floor. She lowers her feet to the carpet, palms pressing the sill. What she cares about is not the show, but Alderson's reaction.

"Do you want to take a breather and talk about it?" she says.

"I don't know. None of this helps. Let's wait for the encore."

The band returns to stage, carrying the brainwave crowns. They fiddle clumsily for a second, bowing their heads for the apparatus, which begins to glow again. Looking up, the lead musician waves at the audience. He leaps into the air as the amps let out a preliminary guitar-like chord, and a hot pulse of yellow novas across the stage.

A tentative voice says, "Please: I recognize you." Loerne looks around. It's the girl who had been dancing close to them. Delicate, slightly chubby kid. Mixed races. Looks very ordinary somehow when she's not transported by the music. Could be anyone on the block. Girl next door. Except why hasn't she got clothes on and what has she done to her hair? There's a double image for a moment before Loerne resolves it.

"Hey," Loerne says to Alderson. "Why don't you talk to a miracle fan in her natural environment? She looks like a good kid to me."

"You're two of the people that want to stop this, our music, aren't you?" the girl says more excitedly. "I've seen you on the holo. Why? What do you have against us?"

"We're not going to ban your music," Loerne says. The noise starts in earnest, and she has to raise her voice. "I don't think so. Some people

think it should be investigated. That's our job. We just want to know more about it."

"But there's nothing wrong with the music, Ms. It's healed my fin tonight. Look. My back was very swollen before. Now look." The girl turns to show them her back. The brown flesh cushioning the dorsal fin is completely whole, as if she had been born with the addition to her spine.

"Come with us," Alderson says decisively over increasing decibels. "What's your name?"

"Bianca."

"We'll both talk to you, Bianca."

"There's something I have to say. I don't understand it, though, and I can't quite remember."

"Come on, then."

They struggle through the rhythmic swinging arms. Loerne is glad when they reach the club's top foyer. Wide stairs with thick rails of brightly polished wood flow down to street level. "Please, what does *profane* mean?" Bianca asks.

Alderson opens his mouth. Closes it.

"Clairvoyance in action," Loerne says. "Listen: I'm Gabby Loerne. This is Lachlan Alderson. We're both advisers to the Wallace Inquiry on Biofeedback Music and the Flickdance Phenomenon. You know what that's all about?"

"Yes, Ms. Loerne. But tell me, is there a text or a holo where God speaks and says: *Who are you calling profane?* Something like that? I don't understand what it means."

"It means that the Devil quotes Scripture—"

"But more exactly than that," says Loerne sharply.

"He's subtle." Then, unexpectedly, after a pause, he laughs. Loerne is feeling a burn of exasperation before she realizes that Alderson is at least half joking, sending himself up in his deadpan way. He's a man of contradictions after all. But then, the joke is only an attempt to deflect his all-too-real anxieties.

"You're getting absurd," she says to him without heat. His anxieties are inevitable. There's a question for every certainty—always a deeper ambiguity to wrestle with. Her line from Coleridge had been a good one. But Saint Luke had done better—and this young girl with him—*What God has made clean, you have no right to call profane.* "It means the opposite of *holy*," she says for Bianca. "Do you understand that?"

"Good. We can all talk later." She gives Alderson a sympathetic smile. Jerks her head in the direction of the danceroom. "I'm going in to hear the last set."

• • •

Tigershark looks with horror at the cut under his chest. It hurts, hurts terribly. And it is not closing.

The most recent wounds under his arms have begun to bleed freely. He cannot express any pain—it would be the ruin of his act, his art. As if he can avoid forever drawing attention to the blood which will not stop, he lowers his maimed hand to knee height, drops the knife, kicks it away with his vulnerable feet. Continues dancing.

• • •

Baker has been trained to manipulate the healing effect directly and with purpose. *He* can reverse it.

He concentrates his unhealing hatred on the flickdancer. Blood oozes. The boy's wounds will *never* stop bleeding. And next Baker turns to older wounds—the knife lines of his dancing and his extensive surgery—opening them afresh.

Deliberate hatred vomits out of him. He conjures the demon in his mind as he was coached in the training camp outside Santiago. Hatred spews from him to the flickdancer, and now old incisions open, tattoos of proud flesh rising like initiation scars on the boy's smooth body, welds of pink flesh starting to tear open like wet paper, and the blood falling in a pool at his feet. In an eternal moment, the flickdancer drains white and falls in his own blood.

• • •

What God has made clean, you have no right to call profane.

Alderson lurches into the room, still trying to hide his shock. The girl's words were right. Like a trained theologian or a good lawyer, she's pinpointed the issue. Natural versus cultural law. But—he's often debated it with Gabby—where do you draw the line?

He looks heavenward.

And sees the bleeding flickdancer.

No.

He's despised the boy this evening, seven times seven called him profane. "Dear God, no," he says aloud, falling to his knees. The girl, Bianca, has evidently misunderstood. She kneels in front of him, pressing his pressed hands. Others look up. Screaming of terror or outrage. The miracle band plays on, musicians sightless in their trance-world.

The crowd and the band are gone. The boundaries of Alderson's identity are breaking up. Where is the girl who clenches his hand? The boy? There is only the triad, transcending music or identity, united against the suffering. Alderson spits away blood which seems to stream down his face choking, nauseating him.

He has misplaced the home of evil, understands that now.

That part of the triad which had been Alderson is in terror.

Evil is in the Searoom, but it does not come from the miracle band. They must thrust it away. Push the source of evil. Thrust the evil away, push the shadow right out of the dim room. Pushing back.

• • •

The boy's shorts are soaked in the same blood which has pooled at the bottom of his cage and spattered its walls, thrown by his frenzied efforts. He is terrifyingly white, fallen, half-fainted to his knees—but his wounds have stopped bleeding. Baker desperately recalculates the situation: an effect has already been created, a macabre dose of the Grand Guignol to terrify the superstitious and delight the media. But the boy must *die* to spite the lusts of Satan and to sustain the repugnant and loathing properly suited to the Devil's work.

Baker redoubles his effort of hatred, but the black acids that have sucked up out of him are now ebbing away. He forces his protesting ego back into the depths and finds . . . nothing.

Dimly, he senses that it is he who screams— lurching out of the parting crowd, flailing claustrophobically with desperate arms, not knowing why he runs to the stairs and stumbles mechanically down them toward the street, his assignment forgotten. He knows one thing only: he must escape the room where he is otherwise obliterating himself, unwinding *self* like a dark thread from a crazy bobbin.

• • •

The show is over. The house lights come on, but the night is ripped and interrupted. The crowd is not dispersing; it gathers closer, hushed, to the flickdancer's cage, ratcheting on its golden chains to the floor. A pair of bullnecked T-shirted bouncers shoulder their way through. One jerks the cage's front panel, snaps it open from the top. It hinges down, a transparent crocodile jaw full of bleeding ulcers. "Go home folks," the other man tells them. "Go home now—it's all right. Show's over. The kid's gonna be okay."

Alderson is numb, drained from his ordeal as if *he* had been bled white. He remains on his knees, eyes silent.

"It was horrible, Mr. Alderson." Bianca's voice. She sounds so young and shaken. There's no demon here.

He stands and shoves his way to the boy, who sways rubber-legged and glass-eyed. "Let me through—I have to see him." No one blocks Alderson's way. He grips the kid by both skinny shoulders. *Tigershark.* Tigershark's skin is criss-

crossed with scars, a lacework of shiny pink raised flesh; his unbleeding body is stained with drying blood, his shorts drenched with it. Eyes look on Alderson's with sudden recognition, a smile of victory. Victory shared. Alderson hugs him, taking red stains on his own flesh and clothing.

"We'll take care of him." The bouncer speaks gently, awed. "There is an ambulance on the way."

Gabby and Bianca are both there. Alderson turns to Gabby as the bouncer helps Tigershark to a seat at the bar. She watches intently, silent, as the crowd disperses. Soon they are left almost alone in the Searoom.

Gabby speaks at last. "Bianca proved something here. You're like her." Smiles. "Either of you could be flickdancers, if that's what you wanted."

"Hardly . . . in my case." He looks her in the eye. "What happened? You're the expert."

"I don't know." Holds his eye frankly. "There's more to it than the music. You know that?"

He nods, knowing better than she could.

"Something *invaded* the Searoom tonight. Rival sorcery, maybe. What do you think, Lachlan?" *Rival sorcery.* "I'm not speaking scientifically. In a tribal society, I'd expect them to say an evil sorcerer had been here. Someone powerful and malefic."

"Why?"

"I don't know why."

"Something horrible was in the room," Bianca says. "It wasn't the band."

He remembers. The darkness. The shadow. Focused on Tigershark, palpable to Bianca and himself.

Gabby puts her arm around the girl's shoulders, just above the grafted fin where it anchors in her upper spine. An ambulance siren pulses. "But where did it come from?" Gabby says. Alderson is glad to see her tremble with emotion.

The last of the crowd has gone. A business-suited young man with black wavy hair is speaking to Tigershark—probably the club manager—as the ambulance crew arrives with a stretcher.

One of the bouncers has found a bucket and mop. He scrubs dispiritedly at the cage's ugly floor, wipes its walls with a fat square sponge. Alderson turns to Bianca.

"Let us take you home."

The girl smiles at him, her hand now in Gabby's.

• • •

Baker staggers along the seedy street. He recoils from the glaring lights of a St Kilda tram like a frightened beast. He rushes along the pavement, brushes a threadbare drunk. A gang of bare-chested sharks jeers at him on Fitzroy Street. He runs idiotically. Has no idea where he is going or who he was. All he knows is the darkness. He runs toward it.

CANDAS JANE DORSEY

[LEARNING ABOUT] MACHINE SEX

(1988)

A NAKED WOMAN working at a computer. Which attracts you most? It was a measure of Whitman that, as he entered the room, his eyes went first to the unfolded machine gleaming small and awkward in the light of the long-armed desk lamp; he'd seen the woman before.

Angel was the woman. Thin and pale-skinned, with dark nipples and black pubic hair, and her face hidden by a dark unkempt mane of long hair as she leaned over her work.

A woman complete with her work. It was a measure of Angel that she never acted naked, even when she was. Perhaps especially when she was.

So she has a new board, thought Whitman, and felt his guts stir the way they stirred when he first contemplated taking her to bed. That was a long time ago. And she knew it, felt without turning her head the desire, and behind the screen of her straight dark hair, uncombed and tumbled in front of her eyes, she smiled her anger down.

"Where have you been?" he asked, and she shook her hair back, leaned backward to ease her tense neck.

"What is that thing?" he went on insistently, and Angel turned her face to him, half scowling. The board on the desk had thin irregular wings spreading from a small central module. Her fingers didn't slow their keyboard dance.

"None of your business," she said.

She saved the input, and he watched her fold the board into a smaller and smaller rectangle. Finally she shook her hair back from her face.

"I've got the option on your bioware," he said.

"Pay as you go," she said. "New house rule."

And found herself on her ass on the floor from his reflexive, furious blow. And his hand in her hair, pulling her up and against the wall. Hard. Astonishing her with how quickly she could hurt and how much. Then she hurt too much to analyze it.

"You are a bitch," he said.

"So what?" she said. "When I was nicer, you were still an asshole."

Her head back against the wall, crack. Ouch.

Breathless, Angel: "Once more and you never see this bioware." And Whitman slowly draws breath, draws back, and looks at her the way she knew he always felt.

"Get out," she said. "I'll bring it to Kozyk's office when it's ready."

So he went. She slumped back in the chair, and tears began to blur her vision, but hate cleared them up fast enough, as she unfolded the board again, so that despite the pain she hardly missed a moment of programming time.

Assault only a distraction now, betrayal only a detail: Angel was on a roll. She had her revenge well in hand, though it took a subtle mind to recognize it.

• • •

Again: "I have the option on any of your bioware." This time, in the office, Whitman wore the nostalgic denims he now affected, and Angel her street-silks and leather.

"This is mine, but I made one for you." She pulled it out of the bag. Where her board looked jerry-built, this one was sleek. Her board looked interesting; this one packaged. "I made it before you sold our company," she said. "I put my best into it. You may as well have it. I suppose you own the option anyway, eh?"

She stood. Whitman was unconsciously restless before her.

"When you pay me for this," she said, "make it in MannComp stock." She tossed him the board. "But be careful. If you take it apart wrong, you'll break it. Then you'll have to ask me to fix it, and from now on, my tech rate goes up."

As she walked by him, he reached for her, hooked one arm around her waist. She looked at him, totally expressionless. "Max," she said, "it's like I told you last night. From now on, if you want it, you pay. Just like everyone else." He let her go. She pulled the soft dirty white silk shirt on over the black leather jacket. The compleat rebel now.

"It's a little going away present. When you're a big shot in MannComp, remember that I made it. And that you couldn't even take it apart right. I guarantee."

He wasn't going to watch her leave. He was already studying the board. Hardly listening, either.

"Call it the Mannboard," she said. "It gets big if you stroke it." She shut the door quietly behind herself.

• • •

It would be easier if this were a story about sex, or about machines. It is true that the subject is Angel, a woman who builds computers like they have never been built before outside the human skull. Angel, like everyone else, comes from somewhere and goes somewhere else. She lives in that linear and binary universe. However, like everyone else, she lives concurrently in another universe less simple. Trivalent, quadrivalent, multivalent. World without end, with no amen. And so on.

• • •

They say a hacker's burned out before he's twenty-one. Note the pronoun: he. Not many young women in that heady realm of the chip.

Before Angel was twenty-one—long before—she had taken the cybernetic chip out of a Wm Kuhns fantasy and patented it; she had written the program for the self-taught AI the Bronfmanns had bought and used to gain world prominence for their MannComp lapboard; somewhere in there, she'd lost innocence, and when her clever additions to that AI turned it into something the military wanted, she dropped out of sight in Toronto and went back to Rocky Mountain House, Alberta, on a Greyhound bus.

It was while she was thinking about something else—cash, and how to get some—that she had looked out of the bus window in Winnipeg into the display window of a sex shop. Garter belts, sleazy magazines on cheap coated paper with Day-Glo orange stickers over the genitals of bored sex kings and queens, a variety of ornamental vibrators. She had too many memories of Max to take it lightly, though she heard the laughter of the roughnecks in the back of the bus as they topped each other's dirty jokes, and thought perhaps their humor was worth emulating. If only she could.

She passed her twentieth birthday in a hotel in Regina, where she stopped to take a shower and tap in to the phone lines, checking for pursuit. Armed with the money she got through automatic transfer from a dummy account in Medicine Hat, she rode the bus the rest of the way ignoring the rolling of beer bottles under the seats, the acrid stink of the onboard toilet. She was thinking about sex.

As the bus roared across the long flat prairie she kept one hand on the roll of bills in her pocket, but with the other she made the first notes on the program that would eventually make her famous.

She made the notes on an antique NEC lapboard which had been her aunt's, in old-fashioned BASIC—all the machine would support—but she unraveled it and knitted it into that artificial trivalent language when she got to the place at Rocky and plugged the idea into her Mannboard. She had it written in a little over four hours on-time, but that counted an hour and a half she took to write a new loop into the AI. (She would patent that loop later the same year and put the royalties into a blind trust for her brother, Brian, brain damaged from birth. He was in Michener Centre in Red Deer, not educable; no one at Bronfmann knew about her family, and she kept it that way.)

She called it Machine Sex; working title.

• • •

Working title for a life: born in Innisfail General Hospital, father a rodeo cowboy who raised rodeo horses, did enough mixed farming out

near Caroline to build his young second wife a big log house facing the mountain view. The first baby came within a year, ending her mother's tenure as teller at the local bank. Her aunt was a programmer for the University of Lethbridge, chemical molecular model analysis on the University of Calgary mainframe through a modem link.

From her aunt she learned BASIC, Pascal, COBOL and C; in school she played the usual turtle games on the Apple IIe; when she was fourteen she took a bus to Toronto, changed her name to Angel, affected a punk hairstyle and the insolent all-white costume of that year's youth, and eventually walked into Northern Systems, the company struggling most successfully with bionics at the time, with the perfected biochip, grinning at the proper young men in their gray three-piece suits as they tried to find a bug in it anywhere. For the first million she let them open it up; for the next five she told them how she did it. Eighteen years old by the phony records she'd cooked on her arrival in Toronto, she was free to negotiate her own contracts.

But no one got her away from Northern until Bronfmann bought Northern lock, stock, and climate-controlled workshop. She had been sleeping with Northern's boy-wonder president by then for about a year, had yet to have an orgasm though she'd learned a lot about kinky sex toys. Figured she'd been screwed by him for the last time when he sold the company without telling her; spent the next two weeks doing a lot of drugs and having a lot of cheap sex in the degenerate punk underground; came up with the AI education program.

Came up indeed, came swaggering into Ted Kozyk's office, president of Bronfmann's MannComp subsidiary, with that jury-rigged Mannboard tied into two black-box add-ons no bigger than a bar of soap, and said, "Watch this."

Took out the power supply first, wiped the memory, plugged into a wall outlet, and turned it on.

The bootstrap greeting sounded a lot like *Goo*. "Okay," she said, "it's ready."

"Ready for what?"

"Anything you want," she said. By then he knew her, knew her rep, knew that the sweaty-smelling, disheveled, anorectic-looking waif in the filthy, oversized silk shirt (the rebels had affected natural fabrics the year she left home, and she always did after that, even later when the silk was cleaner, more upmarket, and black instead of white) had something. Two weeks ago he'd bought a company on the strength of that something, and the board Whitman had brought him the day after the sale, even without the software to run on it, had been enough to convince him he'd been right.

He sat down to work, and hours later he was playing Go with an AI he'd taught to talk back, play games, and predict horse races and the stock market.

He sat back, flicked the power switch, and pulled the plug, and stared at her.

"Congratulations," she said.

"What for?" he said; "you're the genius."

"No, congratulations, you just murdered your first baby," she said, and plugged it back in. "Want to try for two?"

"Goo," said the deck. "Dada."

It was her little joke. It was never a feature on the MannComp A-One they sold across every MannComp counter in the world.

• • •

But now she's all grown up, she's sitting in a log house near Rocky Mountain House, watching the late summer sunset from the big front windows, while the computer runs Machine Sex to its logical conclusion, orgasm.

She had her first orgasm at nineteen. According to her false identity, she was twenty-three. Her lover was a delegate to MannComp's annual sales convention; she picked him up after the speech she gave on the ethics of selling AIs to high school students in Thailand. Or whatever, she didn't care. Kozyk used to write her speeches but she usually changed them to suit her mood. This night she'd been circumspect, only a few

expletives, enough to amuse the younger sales representatives and reassure the older ones.

The one she chose was smooth in his approach and she thought, well, we'll see. They went up to the suite MannComp provided, all mod cons and king-size bed, and as she undressed she looked at him and thought, he's ambitious, this boy, better not give him an inch.

He surprised her in bed. Ambitious maybe, but he paid a lot of attention to detail.

After he spread her across the universe in a way she had never felt before, he turned to her and said, "That was pretty good, eh, baby?" and smiled a smooth little grin. "Sure," she said, "it was okay," and was glad she hadn't said more while she was out in the ozone.

By then she thought she was over what Whitman had done to her. And after all, it had been simple enough, what he did. Back in that loft she had in Hull, upstairs of a shop, where she covered the windows with opaque mylar and worked night and day in that twilight. That night as she worked he stood behind her, hands on her shoulders, massaging her into further tenseness.

"Hey, Max, you know I don't like it when people look over my shoulder when I'm working."

"Sorry, baby." He moved away, and she felt her shoulders relax just to have his hands fall away.

"Come on to bed," he said. "You know you can pick that up whenever."

She had to admit he was being pleasant tonight. Maybe he too was tired of the constant scrapping, disguised as jokes, that wore at her nerves so much. All his efforts to make her stop working, slow her down so he could stay up. The sharp edges that couldn't be disguised. Her bravado made her answer in the same vein, but in the mornings, when he was gone to Northern, she paced and muttered to herself, reworking the previous day until it was done with, enough that she could go on. And after all what was missing? She had no idea how to debug it.

Tonight he'd even made some dinner and touched her kindly. Should she be grateful?

Maybe the conversations, such as they were, where she tried to work it out, had just made it worse—.

"Ah, shit," she said, and pushed the board away. "You're right, I'm too tired for this. *Demain*." She was learning French in her spare time.

He began with hugging her, and stroking the long line along her back, something he knew she liked, like a cat likes it, arches its back at the end of the stroke. He knew she got turned on by it. And she did. When they had sex at her house he was without the paraphernalia he preferred, but he seemed to manage, buoyed up by some mood she couldn't share; nor could she share his release.

Afterward, she lay beside him, tense and dissatisfied in the big bed, not admitting it, or she'd have to admit she didn't know what would help. He seemed to be okay, stretched, relaxed, and smiling.

"Had a big day," he said.

"Yeah?"

"Big deal went through."

"Yeah?"

"Yeah, I sold the company."

"You what?" Reflexively moving herself so that none of her body touched his.

"Northern. I put it to Bronfmann. Megabucks."

"Are you joking?" but she saw he was not. "You didn't, I didn't . . . Northern's *our* company."

"My company. I started it."

"I made it big for you."

"Oh, and I paid you well for every bit of that."

She got up. He was smiling a little, trying on the little-boy grin. *No, baby,* she thought, *not tonight.*

"Well," she said, "I know for sure that this is my bed. Get out of it."

"Now, I knew you might take this badly. But it really was the best thing. The R&D costs were killing us. Bronfmann can eat them for breakfast."

R&D costs meant her. "Maybe. Your clothes are here." She tossed them on the bed, went into the other room.

As well as sex, she hadn't figured out betrayal yet either; on the street, she thought, people fucked you over openly, not in secret.

This, even as she said it to herself, she recognized as romantic and certainly not based on experience. She was streetwise in every way but one: Max had been her first lover.

She unfolded the new board. It had taken her some time to figure out how to make it expand like that, to fit the program it was going to run. This idea of shaping the hardware to the software had been with her since she made the biochip, and thus made it possible and much more interesting than the other way around. But making the hardware to fit her new idea had involved a great deal of study and technique, and so far she had had limited success.

This reminded her again of sex, and, she supposed, relationships, although it seemed to her that before sex everything had been on surfaces, very easy. Now she had sex, she had had Max, and now she had no way to realize the results of any of that. Especially now, when Northern had just vanished into Bronfmann's computer empire, putting her in the position again of having to prove herself. What had Max used to make Bronfmann take the bait? She knew very clearly: Angel, the Northern Angel, would now become the MannComp Angel. The rest of the bait would have been the AI; she was making more of it every day, but couldn't yet bring it together. Could it be done at all? Bronfmann had paid high for an affirmative answer.

Certainly this time the bioware was working together. She began to smile a little to herself, almost unaware of it, as she saw how she could interconnect the loops to make a solid net to support the program's full and growing weight. Because, of course, it would have to learn as it went along—that was basic.

Angel as metaphor; she had to laugh at herself when she woke from programming hours later, Max still sleeping in her bed, ignoring her eviction notice. He'll have to get up to piss anyway, she thought; that's when I'll get him out. She went herself to the bathroom in the half-dawn light, stretching her cramped back muscles and thinking remotely, well, I got some satisfaction out of last night after all: the beginnings of the idea that might break this impasse. While it's still inside my head, this one is mine. How can I keep it that way?

New fiscal controls, she thought grimly. New contracts, now that Northern doesn't exist anymore. Max can't have this, whatever it turns into, for my dowry to MannComp.

When she put on her white silks—leather jacket underneath, against the skin as street fashion would have it—she hardly knew herself what she would do. The little board went into her bag with the boxes of pills the pharmaceutical tailor had made for her. If there was nothing there to suit, she'd buy something new. In the end, she left Max sleeping in her bed; so what? she thought as she reached the highway. The first ride she hitched took her to Toronto, not without a little tariff, but she no longer gave a damn about any of that.

By then the drugs in her system had lifted her out of a body that could be betrayed, and she didn't return to it for two weeks, two weeks of floating in a soup of disjointed noise, and always the program running, unfolding, running again, unfolding inside her relentless mind. She kept it running to drown anything she might remember about trust or the dream of happiness.

When she came home two weeks later, on a hot day in summer with the Ottawa Valley humidity unbearable and her body tired, sore, and bruised, and very dirty, she stepped out of her filthy silks in a room messy with Whitman's continued inhabitation; furious, she popped a system cleanser and unfolded the board on her desk. When he came back in she was there, naked, angry, working.

• • •

A naked woman working at a computer. What good were cover-ups? Watching Max after she took the new AI up to Kozyk, she was only triumphant because she'd done something Max could never do, however much he might be able to sell her out. Watching them fit it to the bioboard, the strange unfolding machine she had made to fit the ideas only she could have, she began to be afraid. The system cleanser she'd taken made the clarity inescapable. Over the next few months, as she kept adding clever loops and twists, she watched their glee and she looked at what telephone numbers were in the top ten on their modem memories and she began to realize that it was not only business and science that would pay high for a truly thinking machine.

She knew that many years before there had been Pentagon programmers working to model predatory behavior in AIs using Prolog and its like. That was old hat. None of them, however, knew what they needed to know to write for her bioware yet. No one but Angel could do that. So, by the end of her nineteenth year, that made Angel one of the most sought-after, endangered ex-anorectics on the block.

She went to conferences and talked about the ethics of selling AIs to teenagers in Nepal. Or something. And took a smooth salesman to bed, and thought all the time about when they were going to make their approach. It would be Whitman again, not Kozyk, she thought; Ted wouldn't get his hands dirty, while Max was born with grime under his nails.

She thought also about metaphors. How, even in the new street slang which she could speak as easily as her native tongue, being screwed, knocked, fucked over, jossed, dragged all meant the same thing: hurt to the core. And this was what people sought out, what they spent their time seeking in pickup joints, to the beat of bad old headbanger bands, that nostalgia shit. Now, as well as the biochip, Max, the AI breakthrough, and all the tailored drugs she could eat, she'd had orgasm too.

Well, she supposed it passed the time.

What interested her intellectually about orgasm was not the lovely illusion of transcendence it brought, but the absolute binary predictability of it. When you learn what to do to the nerve endings, and they are in a receptive state, the program runs like kismet. Warm boot. She'd known a hacker once who'd altered his bootstrap messages to read WARM PUSSY. She knew where most hackers were at; they played with their computers more than they played with themselves. She was the same, otherwise why would it have taken a pretty-boy salesman in a three-piece to show her the simple answer? All the others, just like trying to use an old MS-DOS disc to boot up one of her Mann lapboards with crystal RO/RAM.

• • •

Angel forgets she's only twenty. Genius is uneven. There's no substitute for time, that relentless shaper of understanding. Etc. Etc. Angel paces with the knowledge that everything is a phase, even this. Life is hard and then you die, and so on. And so, on.

• • •

One day it occurred to her that she could simply run away.

This should have seemed elementary but to Angel it was a revelation. She spent her life fatalistically; her only successful escape had been from the people she loved. Her lovely, crazy grandfather; her generous and slightly avaricious aunt; and her beloved imbecile brother: they were buried deep in a carefully forgotten past. But she kept coming back to Whitman, to Kozyk and Bronfmann, as if she liked them.

As if, like a shocked dog in a learned helplessness experiment, she could not believe that the cage had a door, and the door was open.

She went out the door. For old times' sake, it was the bus she chose; the steamy chill of an air-conditioned Greyhound hadn't changed at all. Bottles—pop and beer—rolling under the seats and the stench of chemicals filling the air whenever someone sneaked down to smoke a

cigarette or a reef in the toilet. Did anyone ever use it to piss in? She liked the triple seat near the back, but the combined smells forced her to the front, behind the driver, where she was joined, across the country, by an endless succession of old women, immaculate in their Fortrels, who started conversations and shared peppermints and gum.

She didn't get stoned once.

The country unrolled strangely: sex shop in Winnipeg, bank machine in Regina, and hours of programming alternating with polite responses to the old women, until eventually she arrived, creased and exhausted, in Rocky Mountain House.

Rocky Mountain House: a comfortable model of a small town, from which no self-respecting hacker should originate. But these days, the world a net of wire and wireless, it doesn't matter where you are, as long as you have the information people want. Luckily for Angel's secret past, however, this was not a place she would be expected to live—or to go—or to come from.

An atavism she hadn't controlled had brought her this far. A rented car took her the rest of the way to the ranch. She thought only to look around, but when she found the tenants packing for a month's holiday, she couldn't resist the opportunity. She carried her leather satchel into their crocheted, frilled guest room—it had been her room fifteen years before—with a remote kind of satisfaction.

That night, she slept like the dead—except for some dreams. But there was nothing she could do about them.

• • •

Lightning and thunder. I should stop now, she thought, wary of power surges through the new board which she was charging as she worked. She saved her file, unplugged the power, stood, stretched, and walked to the window to look at the mountains.

The storm illuminated the closer slopes erratically, the rain hid the distances. She felt some heaviness lift. The cool wind through the window refreshed her. She heard the program stop, and turned off the machine. Sliding out the backup capsule, she smiled her angry smile unconsciously. When I get back to the Ottawa Valley, she thought, where weather never comes from the west like it's supposed to, I'll make those fuckers eat this.

Out in the corrals where the tenants kept their rodeo horses, there was animal noise, and she turned off the light to go and look out the side window. A young man was leaning his weight against the reins-length pull of a rearing, terrified horse. Angel watched as flashes of lightning strobed the hackneyed scene. This was where she came from. She remembered her father in the same struggle. And her mother at this window with her, both of them watching the man. Her mother's anger she never understood until now. Her father's abandonment of all that was in the house, including her brother, Brian, inert and restless in his oversized crib.

Angel walked back through the house, furnished now in the kitschy western style of every trailer and bungalow in this countryside. She was lucky to stay, invited on a generous impulse, while all but their son were away. She felt vaguely guilty at her implicit criticism.

Angel invited the young rancher into the house only because this is what her mother and her grandmother would have done. Even Angel's great-grandmother, whose father kept the stopping house, which meant she kept the travelers fed, even her spirit infused in Angel the unwilling act. She watched him almost sullenly as he left his rain gear in the wide porch.

He was big, sitting in the big farm kitchen. His hair was wet, and he swore almost as much as she did. He told her how he had put a trailer on the north forty, and lived there now, instead of in the little room where she'd been invited to sleep. He told her about the stock he'd accumulated riding the rodeo. They drank Glenfiddich. She told him her father had been a rodeo cowboy. He told her about his university degree in agriculture. She told him she'd never been to

university. They drank more whisky and he told her he couldn't drink that other rot gut anymore since he tasted real Scotch. He invited her to see his computer. She went with him across the yard and through the trees in the rain, her bag over her shoulder, board hidden in it, and he showed her his computer. It turned out to be the first machine she designed for Northern—archaic now, compared with the one she'd just invented.

Fair is fair, she thought drunkenly, and she pulled out her board and unfolded it.

"You showed me yours, I'll show you mine," she said.

He liked the board. He was amazed that she had made it. They finished the Scotch.

"I like you," she said. "Let me show you something. You can be the first." And she ran Machine Sex for him.

• • •

He was the first to see it: before Whitman and Kozyk who bought it to sell to people who already have had and done everything; before David and Jonathan, the Hardware Twins in MannComp's Gulf Islands shop, who made the touchpad devices necessary to run it properly; before a world market hungry for the kind of glossy degradation Machine Sex could give them bought it in droves from a hastily created—MannComp-subsidiary—numbered company. She ran it for him with just the automouse on her board, and a description of what it would do when the hardware was upgraded to fit.

It was very simple, really. If orgasm was binary, it could be programmed. Feed back the sensation through one or more touchpads to program the body. The other thing she knew about human sex was that it was as much cortical as genital, or more so: touch is optional for the turn-on. Also easy, then, to produce cortical stimuli by programmed input. The rest was a cosmetic elaboration of the premise.

At first it did turn him on, then off, then it made his blood run cold. She was pleased by that: her work had chilled her too.

"You can't market that thing!" he said.

"Why not? It's a fucking good program. Hey, get it? Fucking good."

"It's not real."

"Of course it isn't. So what?"

"So, people don't need that kind of stuff to get turned on."

She told him about people. More people than he'd known were in the world. People who made her those designer drugs, given in return for favors she never granted until after Whitman sold her like a used car. People like Whitman, teaching her about sexual equipment while dealing with the Pentagon and CSIS to sell them Angel's sharp angry mind, as if she'd work on killing others as eagerly as she was trying to kill herself. People who would hire a woman on the street, as they had her during that two-week nightmare almost a year before, and use her as casually as their own hand, without giving a damn.

"One night," she said, "just to see, I told all the johns I was fourteen. I was skinny enough, even then, to get away with it. And they all loved it. Every single one gave me a bonus, and took me anyway."

The whisky fog was wearing a little thin. More time had passed than she thought, and more had been said than she had intended. She went to her bag, rummaged, but she'd left her drugs in Toronto, some dim idea at the time that she should clean up her act. All that had happened was that she had spent the days so tight with rage that she couldn't eat, and she'd already cured herself of that once; for the record, she thought, she'd rather be stoned.

"Do you have any more booze?" she said, and he went to look. She followed him around his kitchen.

"Furthermore," she said, "I rolled every one of them that I could, and all but one had pictures of his kids in his wallet, and all of them were teenagers. Boys and girls together. And their saintly dads out fucking someone who looked just like them. Just like them."

Luckily, he had another bottle. Not quite the same quality, but she wasn't fussy.

"So I figure," she finished, "that they don't care who they fuck. Why not the computer in the den? Or the office system at lunch hour?"

"It's not like that," he said. "It's nothing like that. People deserve better." He had the neck of the bottle in his big hand, was seriously, carefully pouring himself another shot. He gestured with both bottle and glass. "People deserve to have—love."

"Love?"

"Yeah, love. You think I'm stupid, you think I watched too much TV as a kid, but I know it's out there. Somewhere. Other people think so too. Don't you? Didn't you, even if you won't admit it now, fall in love with that guy Max at first? You never said what he did at the beginning, how he talked you into being his lover. Something must have happened. Well, that's what I mean: love."

"Let me tell you about love. Love is a guy who talks real smooth taking me out to the woods and telling me he just loves my smile. And then taking me home and putting me in leather handcuffs so he can come. And if I hurt he likes it, because he likes it to hurt a little and he thinks I must like it like he does. And if I moan he thinks I'm coming. And if I cry he thinks it's love. And so do I. Until one evening—not too long after my *last* birthday, as I recall—he tells me that he has sold me to another company. And this only after he fucks me one last time. Even though I don't belong to him anymore. After all, he had the option on all my bioware."

"All that is just politics." He was sharp, she had to grant him that.

"Politics," she said, "give me a break. Was it politics made Max able to sell me with the stock: hardware, software, liveware?"

"I've met guys like that. Women too. You have to understand that it wasn't personal to him, it was just politics." Also stubborn. "Sure, you were naive, but you weren't wrong. You just didn't understand company politics."

"Oh, sure I did. I always have. Why do you think I changed my name? Why do you think I dress in natural fibers and go through all the rest of this bullshit? I know how to set up power blocs. Except in mine there is only one party—me. And that's the way it's going to stay. Me against them from now on."

"It's not always like that. There are assholes in the world, and there are other people too. Everyone around here still remembers your grandfather, even though he's been retired in Camrose for fifteen years. They still talk about the way he and his wife used to waltz at the Legion Hall. What about him? There are more people like him than there are Whitmans."

"Charlotte doesn't waltz much since her stroke."

"That's a cheap shot. You can't get away with cheap shots. Speaking of shots, have another."

"Don't mind if I do. Okay, I give you Eric and Charlotte. But one half-happy ending doesn't balance out the people who go through their lives with their teeth clenched, trying to make it come out the same as a True Romance comic, and always wondering what's missing. They read those bodice-ripper novels and make that do for the love you believe in so naively." Call her naive, would he? Two could play at that game. "That's why they'll all go crazy for Machine Sex. So simple. So linear. So fast. So uncomplicated."

"You underestimate people's ability to be happy. People are better at loving than you think."

"You think so? Wait until you have your own little piece of land and some sweetheart takes you out in the trees on a moonlit night and gives you head until you think your heart will break. So you marry her and have some kids. She furnishes the trailer in a five-room sale grouping. You have to quit drinking Glenfiddich because she hates it when you talk too loud. She gets an allowance every month and crochets a cozy for the TV. You work all day out in the rain and all evening in the back room making the books balance on the outdated computer. After the kids come she gains weight and sells real estate if you're lucky. If not she makes things out of recycled bleach bottles and hangs them in the yard. Pretty soon she wears a nightgown to bed and turns her back when you slip in after a hard night at the keyboard. So you take up drinking again and teach the kids about the rodeo. And you find some square-dancing chick who gives you head out behind the bleachers one night in Trochu, so sweet you think your heart will break. What you gonna do then, mountain man?"

"Okay, we can tell stories until the sun comes up. Which won't be too long, look at the time; but no matter how many stories you tell, you can't make me forget about that thing." He pointed to the computer with loathing.

"It's just a machine."

"You know what I mean. That thing in it. And besides, I'm gay. Your little scenario wouldn't work."

She laughed and laughed. "So that's why you haven't made a pass at me yet," she said archly, knowing that it wasn't that simple, and he grinned. She wondered coldly how gay he was, but she was tired, so tired of proving power. His virtue was safe with her; so, she thought suddenly, strangely, was hers with him. It was unsettling and comforting at once.

"Maybe," he said. "Or maybe I'm just a liar like you think everyone is. Eh? You think everyone strings everyone else a line? Crap. Who has the time for that shit?"

Perhaps they were drinking beer now. Or was it vodka? She found it hard to tell after a while.

"You know what I mean," she said. "You should know. The sweet young thing who has AIDS and doesn't tell you. Or me. I'm lucky so far. Are you? Or who sucks you for your money. Or josses you 'cause he's into denim and Nordic looks."

"Okay, okay. I give up. Everybody's a creep but you and me."

"And I'm not so sure about you."

"Likewise, I'm sure. Have another. So, if you're so pure, what about the ethics of it?"

"What *about* the ethics of it?" she asked. "Do you think I went through all that sex without paying attention? I had nothing else to do but watch other people come. I saw that old cult movie, where the aliens feed on heroin addiction and orgasm, and the woman's not allowed orgasm so she has to OD on smack. Orgasm's more decadent than shooting heroin? I can't buy that, but there's something about a world that sells it over and over again. Sells the thought of pleasure as a commodity, sells the getting of it as if it were the getting of wisdom. And all these times I told you about, I saw other people get it through me. Even when someone finally made me come, it was just a feather in his cap, an accomplishment, nothing personal. Like you said. All I was was a program, they plugged into me and went through the motions and got their result. Nobody cares if the AI finds fulfillment running their damned data analyses. Nobody thinks about depressed and angry Mannboard ROMs. They just think about getting theirs.

"So why not get mine?" She was pacing now, angry, leaning that thin body as if the wind were against her. "Let me be the one who runs the program."

"But you won't be there. You told me how you were going to hide out, all that spy stuff."

She leaned against the wall, smiling a new smile she thought of as predatory. And maybe it was. "Oh, yes," she said. "I'll be there the first time. When Max and Kozyk run this thing and it turns them on. I'll be there. That's all I care to see."

He put his big hands on the wall on either side of her and leaned in. He smelled of sweat and liquor and his face was earnest with intoxication.

"I'll tell you something," he said. "As long as there's the real thing, it won't sell. They'll never buy it."

Angel thought so too. Secretly, because she wouldn't *give* him the satisfaction of agreement, she, too, thought they would not go that low.

That's right, she told herself, *trying to sell it is all right—because they will never buy it.*

But they did.

• • •

A woman and a computer. Which attracts you most? Now you don't have to choose. Angel has made the choice irrelevant.

In Kozyk's office, he and Max go over the ad campaign. They've already tested the program themselves quite a lot; Angel knows this because it's company gossip, heard over the cubicle walls in the washrooms. The two men are so absorbed that they don't notice her arrival.

"Why is a woman better than a sheep? Because sheep can't cook. Why is a woman better than a Mannboard? Because you haven't bought your sensory add-on." Max laughs.

"And what's better than a man?" Angel says; they jump slightly. "Why, your MannComp touchpads, with two-way input. I bet you'll be able to have them personally fitted."

"Good idea," says Kozyk, and Whitman makes a note on his lapboard. Angel, still stunned though she's had weeks to get used to this, looks at them, then reaches across the desk and picks up her prototype board. "This one's mine," she says. "You play with yourselves and your touchpads all you want."

"Well, you wrote it, baby," said Max. "If you can't come with your own program . . ."

Kozyk hiccoughs a short laugh before he shakes his head. "Shut up, Whitman," he says. "You're talking to a very rich and famous woman."

Whitman looks up from the simulations of his advertising storyboards, smiling a little, anticipating his joke. "Yeah, it's just too bad she finally burned herself out with this one. They always did say it gives you brain damage."

But Angel hadn't waited for the punch line. She was gone.

PAUL DI FILIPPO

A SHORT COURSE
IN ART APPRECIATION

(1988)

WE WERE SO HAPPY, Elena and I, in the Vermeer perceptiverse. Our days and nights were filled with visual epiphanies that seemed to ignite the rest of our senses, producing a conflagration of desire that burned higher and higher, until it finally subsided to the embers of satiation, from which the whole inferno, phoenix-like, could be rekindled at will. There had never been a time when we were so thrilled with life, so enamored of the world and each other—so much in love.

Yet somehow, I knew from the start that our idyll was doomed to end. Such bliss was not for us, could never last. I don't know what it was that implanted such a subliminal worm of doubt in my mind, with its tiny, whispering voice that spoke continually of transience and loss and exhaustion. Perhaps it was the memory of the sheer avidity and almost obscene yearning greed with which Elena had first approached me with the idea of altering our natural perceptiverses.

She entered my apartment that spring day (we were not yet living together then, a symbol, I believe, of our separate identities that irrationally irked her) in a mood like none I had ever witnessed her exhibit. (I try now to picture her unaltered face, as I observed it on that fateful day, but it is so hard, after the dizzying cascade of perceptiverses we have experienced, to clearly visualize anything from that long-ago time. How can I have totally forgotten the mode of seeing that was as natural as breathing to me for thirty-some-odd years? It is as if the natural perceptiverse I was born into is a painting that lies layers deep, below several others, and whose lines can be only imperfectly traced. You will understand, then, if I cannot re-create the scene precisely.)

In any case, I remember our conversation from that day perfectly. (Thank God I resisted the temptation to enter one of the composer perceptiverses, or that memory, too, might be buried, under an avalanche of glorious sound!) I have frequently mentally replayed our words, seeking to learn if there was any way I could have circumvented Elena's unreasoning desires—avoiding both the heaven and hell that lay embryonic in her steely whims—yet still have managed to hold onto her love.

I feel now that, essentially, there was no way. She was simply too strong and determined for me—or perhaps I was too weak—and I could not deny her.

But I still cannot bring myself to blame her.

Crossing the memory-hazed room, Elena said excitedly, "Robert, it's out!"

I laid down my book, making sure to shut it off, and, all unwitting, asked, "Not even a hello or a kiss? It must be something wonderful, then. Well, I'll bite. What's out?"

"Why, just that new neurotropin everyone's been waiting so long for, the one to alter the perceptiverses."

I immediately grew defensive. "Elena, you know I try to steer clear of those designer drugs. They're just not—not natural. I'm not a prig, Elena. I don't mind indulging in a little grass or coke now and then—they're perfectly natural mind-altering substances that mankind's been using for centuries. But these new artificial compounds—they can really screw up your neuropeptides."

Elena grew huffy. "Robert, you're talking nonsense. This isn't one of the regulated substances, you know, like tempo or ziptone. Why, it's not even supposed to be as strong as estheticine. It doesn't get you high or alter your thinking at all. It merely gives you a new perceptiverse."

"And what, if I may ask, is a perceptiverse?"

"Oh Robert," Elena sighed in exasperation, "and you call yourself educated! That's just the kind of question I should have expected from someone whose nose is always buried in a book. The perceptiverse is just the universe as filtered through one's perceptions. It's the only universe any of us can know, of course. In fact, it might be the only universe that exists for any of us, if those physicists you're always quoting know what they're talking about."

"Elena, we've had this discussion before. I

keep telling you that you can't apply the rules of quantum physics to the macroscopic world. . . ."

"Oh, screw all that anyway! You're just trying to change the subject. Aren't you excited at all?"

"Maybe I would be, if I knew what it was all about. I still don't understand. Is this new drug just another hallucinogen?"

"No, that's just it; it's much more. It alters your visual perceptions in a coherent, consistent manner, without affecting anything else. You don't see anything that's not there; you just see what does exist in a different way. And since sight's our most critical sense, the effect's supposed to be like stepping into another universe."

I considered. "And exactly what kind of universe would one be stepping into?"

Elena fell into my lap with a delighted squeal, as if she had won the battle. "Oh Robert, that's just it! It's not what universe, it's whose!"

"Whose?"

"Yes, whose! The psychoengineers claim they've distilled the essence of artistic vision."

I suppose I should interject here that Elena was a student of art history. In our bountiful world, where the Net cradled one from birth to death, she was free to spend all her time doing what she enjoyed, which happened to be wandering for hours through museums, galleries, and studios, with me in tow.

"You're saying," I slowly went on, "that this magical pill lets you see like, say, Rembrandt?"

"No," frowned Elena, "not exactly. After all, Rembrandt, to use your example, probably didn't literally see much differently than any of us. That's a fallacy nonartists always fall for. The magic was in how he transmuted his everyday vision, capturing it in the medium of his art. I doubt if any artist, except perhaps those like van Gogh, who are close to madness, can maintain their unique perspective every minute of their waking hours. No, what the psychoengineers have done is to formalize the stylistic elements of particular artists—more or less the idiosyncratic rules that govern light and shape and texture in an individual perceptiverse—and make them reproducible. By taking this new neurotropin, we'll be enabled to see not *like* Rembrandt, but as if *inhabiting* Rembrandt's canvases!"

"I find that hard to believe. . . ."

"It's true, Robert; it's true! The volunteers all report the most marvelous results!"

"But Elena, would you really want to inhabit a Rembrandt world all day?"

"Of course! Look around you! All these dull plastics and synthetics! Who wouldn't want to! And anyway, it's not Rembrandt they've chosen for the first release. It's Vermeer."

"Vermeer or Rembrandt, Elena, I just don't know if . . ."

"Robert, you haven't even considered the most important aspect of all this. We'd be doing it together! For the first time in history, two people can be sure they're sharing the same perceptiverse. Our visual perceptions would be absolutely synchronized. I'd never have to wonder if you really understood what I was seeing, nor you me. We'd be totally at one. Just think what it would mean for our love!"

Her face—that visage I can no longer fully summon up without a patina of painterly interpretation—was glowing. I couldn't hold out against her.

"All right," I said. "If it means so much to you . . ."

She tossed her arms around my neck and hugged me close. "Oh Robert, I knew you'd come around! This is wonderful!" She released me and stood. "I have the pills right here."

I confess to having felt a little alarm right then. "You bought them already, not knowing if I'd even agree. . . ."

"You're not angry, are you, Robert? It's just that I thought we knew each other so well. . . ." She fingered her little plastic pill case nervously.

"No, I'm not angry; it's just . . . Oh well, forget it. Let's have the damn pill."

She fetched a single glass of water from the tap and dispensed the pills. She swallowed first, then, as if sharing some obscure sacrament, passed me the glass. I downed the pill. It seemed to scorch my throat.

"How long does the effect last?" I asked.

"Why, I thought I made that clear. Until you take another one."

I sat down weakly, Elena resting one haunch on the arm of the chair beside me. We waited for the change, looking curiously around the room.

Subtly at first, then with astonishing force and speed, my perceptiverse—our perceptiverse—began to alter. Initially it was the light pouring in through the curtained windows that began to seem different. It acquired a pristine translucency, tinged with supernal honeyed overtones. This light fell on the wood, the plastic, the fabric in my mundane apartment, utterly transfiguring everything it touched, in what seemed like a chain reaction that raced through the very molecules of my whole perceptiverse.

In minutes the change was complete.

I was inhabiting the Vermeer perceptiverse.

I turned to face Elena.

She looked like the woman in *Young Woman with a Water Jug* at the Met.

I had never seen anything—anyone—so beautiful.

My eyes filled with tears.

I knew Elena was experiencing the same thing as I.

Crying, she said, "Oh Robert, kiss me now."

I did. And then, somehow, we were naked, our oil paint– and brushstroke-mottled bodies shining as if we had stepped tangibly from the canvas, rolling on the carpet, locked in a frantic lovemaking unlike anything I had ever experienced before that moment.

I felt as though I were fucking Art itself.

• • •

Thus began the happiest months of my life.

At first, Elena and I were content merely to stay in the apartment all day, simply staring in amazement at the most commonplace objects, now all transformed into perfect elements in some vast, heretofore undiscovered masterpiece by Vermeer. Once we had exhausted a particular view, we had only to shift our position to create a completely different composition, which we could study for hours more. To set the table for a meal was to fall enraptured into contemplation of a unique still life each time. The rules of perceptual transformation that the psychoengineers had formulated worked perfectly. Substances and scenes that Vermeer could never have imagined acquired the unmistakable touch of his palette and brush.

Tiring even of such blissful inactivity, we would make love with a frenetic reverence approaching satori. Afterward the wrinkles in the sheets reminded us of thick troughs of paint, impasto against our skin.

After a time, of course, this stage passed. Desirous of new vistas, we set out to explore the Vermeer-veneered world.

We were not alone. Thousands shared the same perceptiverse, and we encountered them everywhere, instant signs of mutual recognition being exchanged. To look into their eyes was to peer into a mental landscape utterly familiar to all us art-trippers.

The sights we saw—I can't encapsulate them in words for you. Perhaps you've shared them, too, and words are unnecessary. The whole world was almost palpably the work of a single hand, a marvel of artistic vision, just as the mystics had always told us.

It was in Nice, I believe, that Elena approached me with her little pill case in hand. She had gone out unexpectedly without me, while I was still sleeping. I didn't complain, being content to sit on the balcony and watch the eternally changing Mediterranean, although, underneath my rapture, I believe I felt a bit of amazement that she had left without a word.

Now, pill case offered in outstretched hand, Elena, having returned, said without preamble, "Here, Robert; take one."

I took the pill and studied its perfection for a time before I asked, "What is it?"

"Matisse," she said. "We're in his native land now, the source of his vision. It's only right."

"Elena, I don't know. Haven't we been happy with Vermeer? Why change now? We could spoil everything. . . ."

Elena swallowed Matisse dry. "I've taken mine, Robert. I need something new. Unless you want to be left behind, you'll do the same."

I couldn't stand the thought of living in a different perceptiverse than Elena. Although the worm of discontent told me not to, I did as Elena asked.

Matisse went down easy.

In no time at all, the sharp, uncompromising realism of Vermeer gave way to the gaudy, exhilarating, heady impressionism of Matisse. The transition was almost too powerful to take.

"Oh my God . . . ," I said.

"There," said Elena, "wasn't I right? Take your clothes off now. I have to see you naked."

We inaugurated this new perceptiverse as we had the first.

Our itinerary in this new perceptiverse duplicated what had gone before. Once we had exhausted the features of our hotel room and stabilized our new sensory input, we set out to ingest the world, wallowing in this latest transformation. If we chanced to revisit a place we had been to while in the Vermeer perceptiverse, we were astonished at the change. What a gift, we said, to be able to see the old world with continually fresh eyes.

Listening to the Boston Symphony outdoors along the Charles one night, their instruments looking like paper cutouts from Matisse's old age, Elena said to me, "Let's drop a Beethoven, Robert."

I refused. She didn't press me, realizing, perhaps, that she had better save her powers of persuasion for what really mattered.

The jungles of Brazil called for Rousseau, of course. I capitulated with hardly a protest, and that marked the beginning of the long, slippery slope.

Vermeer had captivated us for nearly a year.

Matisse kept us enthralled for six months.

Rousseau—that naive genius—could hold our attention for only six weeks.

We were art junkies now, consumers of novel perceptiverses.

Too much was not enough.

The neurotropin industry graciously obliged.

Up till that time, the industry had marketed only soft stuff, perceptiverses not too alien to "reality." But now, as more and more people found themselves in the same fix as Elena and I, the psychoengineers gradually unleashed the hard stuff.

In the next two years, Elena and I, as far as I can reconstruct things, went through the following perceptiverses: Picasso (blue and cubist), Braque, Klee, Kandinsky, Balthus, Dalí, Picabia, Léger, Chagall, Gris, de Kooning, Bacon, Klimt, Delaunay, O'Keeffe, Escher, Hockney, Louis, Miró, Ernst, Pollock, Powers, Kline, Bonnard, Redon, van Dongen, Rouault, Munch, Tanguy, de Chirico, Magritte, Lichtenstein, and Johns.

We hit a brief period of realism consisting of Wood, Hopper, Frazetta, and Wyeth, and I tried to collect my senses and decide whether I wanted to get out of this trip or not, and how I could convince Elena to drop out with me.

But before I could make up my mind, we were off into Warhol, and everything hit me with such neon-tinted luminescent significance that I couldn't give it up. This happened aboard a station in high orbit, and the last thing I remember was the full Earth turning pink and airbrushed.

Time passed. I think.

The next time I became aware of myself as an individual, distinct from my beautiful yet imprisoning background, Elena and I were in a neoexpressionist perceptiverse, the one belonging to that Italian, I forget his name.

We were outdoors. I looked around.

The sky was gray-green, with a huge black crack running down the middle of it. Sourceless light diffused down like pus. The landscape looked as if it had been through an atomic war. I searched for Elena, found her reclining on grass that looked like mutant mauve octopus tendrils. Her flesh was ashen and bloody; a puke-yellow aura outlined her form.

I dropped down beside her.

I could *feel* that the grass was composed of tendrils, thick and slimed, like queer succulents. Suddenly I *smelled* alien odors, and I knew the light above spilled out of a novel sun.

The quantum level had overtaken the macroscopic.

Plastic reality, governed by our senses, had mutated.

We were truly in the place we perceived ourselves to be.

"Elena," I begged, "we've got to get out of this perceptiverse. It's just dreadful. Let's go back, back to where it all started, back to Vermeer. Please, if you love me, leave this behind."

A mouth like a sphincter opened in the Elena-thing. "We can't go back, Robert. You can never go back, especially after what we've been through. We can only go forward, and hope for the best. . . ."

"I can't take it anymore, Elena. I'll leave you; I swear it. . . ."

"Leave, then," she said tonelessly.

So I did.

Finding a dose of Vermeer wasn't easy. He was out of favor now; the world had moved beyond him. Even novices started out on the hard stuff nowadays. But eventually, in a dusty pharmaceutical outlet in a small town, I found a dose of that ancient Dutchman. The expiration date printed on the packet was long past, but I swallowed the pill anyway.

The lovely honeyed light and the perfect clarity returned.

I went looking for Elena.

When I found her, she was as beautiful as on that long-ago day when we first abandoned our native perceptiverses for the shock of the new.

When she saw me, she just screamed.

I left her then, knowing it was over. Besides, there was something else I had to find.

The pill with my original name.

NICHOLAS ROYLE

D.GO

(1990)

THE AD CAMPAIGN was a "teaser." But the first posters to appear went up on noticeboards outside churches. Within twenty-four hours they were appearing on roadside hoardings and end terraces. I thought at the time they might have made an error in targeting the churches first and then tried to cover their mistake before anyone noticed.

The poster was simple and direct, yet obscure: D.GO. The letters were printed in large, bold type with that curious full point between the *D* and *G*.

I tried not to take much notice when the posters began to spread. On buses and trains to work I overheard fragments of conversation.

"Have you seen those posters?"

"Yes. What . . . ?"

". . . end of the street. Why do . . . ?"

". . . know what it's all about?"

I heard little that wasn't ambiguous and became no clearer in my own mind.

Within a few days D.GO posters appeared on the underground mingling with ads for depilatory creams and temping agencies. Full-size posters hit the platforms like ads for a new movie that had no credits and needed no cast. On the top decks of buses, notices warning of impending cuts and cancellations of Sunday services now had to vie for space.

Even the newspaper I had favored for several years lost one of its pages each day to the campaign.

I came home from work one day to find on my doormat a leaflet bearing no information other than the too-familiar message. If there had been an address I believe I would have returned it to them, with a note deploring the waste of paper.

That evening was jazz night at a pub not far from where I lived. I had recently become a regular attender. When I arrived there after a light supper, I saw discreetly affixed to the glass in the door a leaflet identical to the one I had received. The trio didn't sound quite as together as usual, even though I drank beyond my usual limit.

Walking home I realized I was staring at the windows of the houses I passed. My unconscious suspicion was confirmed: at least half the properties I scrutinized were giving their support to the D.GO campaign.

Despite my relative intoxication, I decided to get in my Beetle and drive outside of the neighborhood to see if the leaflets had been given wide distribution.

Ten miles north I was still seeing them in half of the flats and, when I got farther out, houses I drove past. Gloomily and with careful attention paid to the speedometer, I drove back into the tangerine shadowland of the inner city.

At work next day I asked: "Have you noticed these leaflets?"

"I've got one up in my window," Gilliland announced with pride. As production editor of the magazine, he was my immediate superior, and although there existed little empathy between us, I generally maintained a level of banter.

"What does it mean?" I asked him.

"Oh, Dominic," he said, "you do make me laugh."

He didn't laugh a great deal, so I was glad. But in fact he barely smiled on this occasion and provided no explanation of the conundrum, as someone rang from production demanding to know how many pages of the magazine were still outstanding.

"Twenty-four," he said. "I've been on to the typesetters all morning."

Gilliland was essentially a good person. He would only hurt a fly if there was no real alternative. So why did he and I never get beyond a superficial working relationship? Was it just his slightly bossy manner and pedantry or did I object more than I realized to his transparent piety?

There was an ad meeting. Gilliland gathered up his sheaths of papers and bustled out of the office, dumping a pile of proofs on my desk as he went.

"I was going to ask you if you would be kind enough to do these when you've finished reading the paper," he said, looking somewhere over my left shoulder. He billowed out of the room before I could think of how best to explain that I'd only picked up the paper for five minutes after lunch.

I turned the page and there was the ad for D.GO. But this was a new one—the next stage of the campaign. At the bottom of the page was a line of text: "Have you made sense of it yet?"

I stuffed the whole newspaper into the bin even though I hadn't finished reading it and reached for the first proof on top of the pile.

I worked until 5:20 p.m. and then left although Gilliland had not yet returned. Ad meetings did not normally go on longer than half an hour. I wondered what could be causing it to go on so long. Not that it needed concern me. In the production process of the magazine my role was that of drone.

In the underground they had already replaced all the old posters with the new ones, which asked me if I'd made sense of it yet. I scowled and moved around people to get to the middle of the carriage so that when a seat became available I would get it.

Commuters hanging from straps swayed as the train rocked through tunnels. Within my section of the car there were ten slots for ads and four of them were occupied by "D.GO. Have you made sense of it yet?" I wondered if I was alone in finding the insistent query insolent in the extreme.

I called in at the Asian grocer's and was amazed to see the leaflet stuck in the window behind his head. I had only ever thought of him in the context of his small but colorful newspaper and the card he had in the glass door barring schoolchildren in groups of more than two. Now he was lending his support to this campaign, laying his business open to a boycott by shoppers like myself who could easily walk the extra five minutes to the supermarket. I decided to make this my last purchase as I waited behind a large man in a shiny suit one size too small.

At home the doormat presented me with

another leaflet: "D.GO. Have you made sense of it yet?" Still no address. I crumpled it up.

I didn't often watch the television, so when I switched it on for something to do and saw D.GO advertised in two consecutive commercial breaks, I was incensed.

Walking to the pub I felt sure there were more leaflets stuck in windows than the night before. It was like election time in a one-party state. Voters were either unquestioningly loyal or they were being coerced.

Over the weekend I saw the first car stickers. "D.GO. Have you made sense of it yet?" in hundreds of rear windows lining the main arterial routes to the DIY superstores.

I drifted toward an antiques and crafts market I often visited at weekends. The market attracted followers of alternative lifestyles, people who refused to go with the general flow.

I sought reassurance and should have known to expect disappointment. The Triumph Heralds, Ford Anglias, and VW Karmann Ghias that crawled up the main road between the different sections of the market were bedecked with stickers. The ethnic shops and vegan restaurants carried the leaflet in the corners of windows. In the lanes of the market itself goths, punks, skins, and all kinds of fashion victims wore button badges bearing the legend D.GO.

I passed a stall selling the badges. In the crowd around it was a tattooed man stripped to the waist. His ears were pierced in a dozen places. On his shaven head were tattooed the letters D.GO. He was buying a badge. I hurried on, less than eager to see where he might pin it.

• • •

The phone was ringing as I reached the front door. I fumbled with the key, unlocked the door, and ran up the messy communal staircase to my door. The phone rang off just as I got inside.

They'll ring again, I thought, as I sat down in the kitchen with a magazine. I turned over several pages at once, hoping to miss all the ads. One got through the net. I didn't look to see if it was the *only* D.GO ad in the magazine. The phone rang again.

It was Dill. She and Tam had got back from their holiday last Thursday and had been ringing me since. Did I want to go round for something to eat and to see their photos? Yes. I did.

"Not tonight," I said. "I'm feeling a bit tired."
Why did I say that?

"I'm working straight through tomorrow," Dill said; she did shift work. "So it'll have to be next week."

I agreed, thinking I ought to tell her I did actually want to go round tonight. But something stopped me. What was I scared of?

In one of the cupboards I found some pasta.

I spent most of Sunday mourning the passing of the weekend and cursing the job I would return to the next day.

• • •

Jackie did the round of the in trays, giving us all copies of the issue we'd put to bed two weeks previously. No matter how long the hours we'd spent checking the proofs, we always took ten minutes to go through the finished magazine with a fine-tooth comb, looking for mistakes it was now too late to rectify. The magazine had a well-earned reputation for accurate subbing: typos and spelling mistakes, which cropped up maybe once every six months, meant apologetic memos from Gilliland to all higher tiers of editorial power.

I flicked through the ads at the front to get to the first pages of editorial. Then I went back to the ads in disbelief.

I pushed my chair back and may have mumbled to Gilliland that I was going out for lunch.

I hurried through a pedestrian arcade where tourists thronged and a man in white trousers handed out leaflets. Some of the shoppers I elbowed past were wearing badges. At a kiosk I thumbed through a selection of magazines for different specialist readerships: anglers, train spotters, and puzzle solvers; bodybuilders, philatelists, and onanists. My fears were confirmed:

the magazine I worked for was not alone in running multiple double-page spreads for the infernal campaign.

Crossing streets choked with buses and taxis, all emblazoned with the same ad, I returned to work. My head felt like it was being hard-boiled as I tried to concentrate on the endless proofs and galleys.

The sentences seemed longer than usual and I lost the sense constantly, so that I had to reread whole chunks.

"I'd like to get as many of those off today as possible," Gilliland said the following morning, indicating the proofs on my desk. I was only halfway through them. "It's the deadline for first proofs, you see."

I saw.

I'd tried ringing Dill and Tam the night before but there had been no answer. Dill could have been doing another late shift and Tam often went out to clubs.

If Dill *had* been at work, then she should be at home now, I thought. I picked up the receiver and punched in the number. It rang unanswered.

I bent over the proof again. What was the article about? I didn't even know. If it couldn't hold my interest, why should it interest the reader? In fact, on reflection, that was probably a good sign. The faithful readers would be enthralled. And one of them would notice if I got a comma in the wrong place. She would write in to tell us she had spotted the mistake as if it were a competition.

And suddenly I knew that reader would have a leaflet stuck in the bay window of her semi.

"Dominic." It was Gilliland. "You should find the art department have finished the layouts for some of those proofs."

"Yes," I said, in a low, controlled voice.

In the art department I stopped by the paste-up board next to the window and stared at an A4 photocopy of next month's cover.

I felt the blood drain from my face. Where were the cover lines? Where was the masthead? Where was the cover picture? I felt someone standing next to me.

"What's this?" I asked. When I looked at Bob I saw he was pulling his jacket on, possibly about to go out for lunch. There was a small badge on the lapel.

"What do you think?" he quipped. "It's next month's cover. It looks good, doesn't it?"

I couldn't agree.

Unable to return to my desk I went and sat in the secretarial office for ten minutes. I told Jackie and Liz-Ann I had a headache. Just a few days previously I would have told them what was wrong, but now I was scared to mention the campaign in case they might reveal their own support for it.

The editorial department operated on a strict hierarchy. If I had any kind of complaint I should take it to those directly above me in the pecking order. But this kind of submission was just that. I would go to Gilliland or the next above him and the problem would generally be defined out of existence by a curious placebo of words. The symptoms wouldn't reappear till half an hour later. In this way the editor was never troubled with the human failings of her underlings. And yet, she said, her door was always open.

I knocked on the closed door and listened.

"Come," said a leather-upholstered voice.

I began to make excuses for my intrusion.

"Dominic," she interrupted me. I was quite impressed by that: she knew my name. "What's the problem?" From her side of the vast desk, watching me perch on the edge of an armchair, there had to be one. "How long have you been with us now?" she asked before I could continue. "Six months, seven months?"

"Eighteen," I said. Taking in a deep breath I explained what I had just seen in the art department. She nodded at intervals, even grunted when the extent of my concern seemed to call for it. Presently, I realized I'd gone on for too long. Her eyes had glazed over behind her designer frames.

I came to the crux of my argument: "We *never* run ads on the front cover." How many times had I heard a variation of that in response to my suggestions for changes in magazine content or procedure? *We never do this. We never do that.* The magazine had found a successful formula and was sticking with it. Change was a dirty word. So why the sudden change of heart?

She wasn't listening to me. I floundered and fell silent.

Distracted, she asked: "Was there anything else?"

In desperation I repeated myself: "We never run ads on the front cover."

A look of puzzlement flickered across her face. Her hands began shuffling papers and I thought it might be time to leave. Her coat was hanging on a hook on the back of the door. I tried to get a look at the lapel on my way out but couldn't. But she was hardly the kind of person to be wearing a button badge, whatever the cause.

I raced through the remaining proofs, forcing myself to concentrate on the words. If I didn't do it, Gilliland would have to and I didn't wish that on him. He had people breathing down his neck, after all.

Going home I was bombarded with thousands of ads on walls, vehicles, and people. Like the cover of the magazine, they all represented the next stage of the campaign—the solution of the anagram: GOD. Just that. GOD. With the full point at the end of the word. Such a short word but so powerful.

Later, I drove to Dill and Tam's. I parked in the street below their flat and looked up at the windows. Although there were several leaflets in the row of terraces, none could be seen in my friends' windows.

They seemed pleased to see me at last, took me upstairs, and offered me a choice of drinks.

"How's work? You've got to see our holiday photos."

Lots of pictures of mountain passes and gingerbread chalets, windblown lakes, and yellow trams.

"Never really fancied Switzerland," I said, looking closely at the ads on the side of the tram. They passed inspection.

I began to relax a little.

Tam made some coffee and Dill dragged out a board game. We played for an hour. Tam won. Dill and I decided he had cheated and should make us all more coffee. He protested his innocence but disappeared into the kitchen. Dill was putting the game away and picking bits of fluff from the carpet. I settled back in the settee.

My heart lurched when Tam appeared in the doorway holding a handful of GOD leaflets.

"I'll put these up now," he said.

Dill nodded and said, "Okay."

I didn't really care if they believed me or not. I just apologized and said I had to go. "Sorry about the coffee." The shock of seeing Tam holding the leaflets and saying he'd put them up now, like they'd been meaning to all evening, was too much for me. I couldn't stay and ask them what had happened.

Dill's eyes were wide with dismay. She didn't understand. "What's wrong?"

"Nothing," I said. "I've got to go."

Every car I passed on the way home had a sticker in the rear window. Groups of people were out leafleting streets where the old leaflet was still up.

What most disturbed me about Dill and Tam was that they appeared completely normal, just as before. They were exactly the same, my old friends, except that they were going to put up the leaflets in their windows.

• • •

I didn't go into work and ignored the phone when it rang at 9:30 a.m. When it stopped ringing I disconnected the plug.

Later, the doorbell rang. It was unlikely to be anyone from work and I was expecting no visitors. I pulled back the curtain and peered down into the street. A fair-haired man was looking up at me. I grimaced and let the curtain fall. The bell rang again. I hesitated in the kitchen, then quietly opened the door onto the communal stairs. On the mat were two or three leaflets.

Seized by rage I ran down the stairs and

pulled open the door, prepared to chase after the man, if necessary, to give him back his literature. But he was standing on the step smiling.

"What do you want?" I asked brusquely.

"To give you a leaflet for your window. You don't seem to have one."

"No. That's right. I haven't got one and I don't want one." I snatched up the ones already delivered and stuffed them into his hand. Surprisingly, he let them fall onto the pavement. He took two more from a plastic shopping bag and handed them to me.

"*No!*" I said. "I'm not interested. Haven't you got the message?"

He appeared momentarily confused.

"Look," I changed tack, but still aggressive, "what's the big idea with this campaign? Why is everyone falling for it?" Immediately I felt I shouldn't have asked the questions. They made me vulnerable.

The man's lost look had vanished and he was smiling at me again. Then I noticed a small crowd was gathering behind him, murmuring.

"Take a leaflet in case you change your mind," he said, folding it into the palm of my hand. I sidestepped him to face the others. I tore the leaflet into quarters and then again.

"Take your leaflet," I said as I threw the scraps of paper like confetti over so many smiling brides and grooms, "and fuck off and leave me alone."

Their smiles creased into concern, instead of the condemnation I would have preferred.

• • •

On the motorway driving north to my parents' house, all the cars carried stickers.

I didn't raise my hopes as far as my parents were concerned, which was just as well. As I pulled into the driveway I was welcomed by a host of leaflets and a poster stuck in the windows of the bungalow. I could no longer be surprised, even though my parents, like Dill and Tam, had never been religious people.

They greeted me as normal, saying what a nice surprise it was. The only change I could see in them was in their front windows.

"Don't stop what you're doing," I said, but my mother made for the kitchen to get us all a drink, while my father went through to the back garden to clear away the tools he had been working with. This gave me the chance I needed. I slipped into their bedroom and carefully opened the doors of my father's wardrobe. At the back of the top shelf, behind a pile of old socks he probably didn't like to throw out, was a shoe box. I withdrew the army-issue pistol and a box of bullets. Wrapping the pistol in my handkerchief, I put it and the bullets in my jacket pocket. I replaced the lid on the box and returned it to its hiding place.

Standing in the hall I saw my mother through the kitchen doorway bent over the sink. And through the picture window in the living room I could see my father pushing the lawnmower up the garden toward the shed. For a moment I hesitated, a great lump constricting my throat. But I knew I couldn't stay. My eyes alighted on the door to my old room. I very nearly reached out my hand to open it.

As I backed the car out of the drive my mother's face emerged from around the front door. Her mouth fell open. I throttled down and swung the wheel round as I hit the road. I looked up the drive as I slammed into first and screeched away. A look of panic on her face, she was running.

It hurt terribly to drive away.

I felt conspicuous on the motorway: the only car without a sticker. I wondered if I should get one just for pretense but quickly rejected the idea as cowardly. I had the gun now for protection.

Drivers turned to stare as they overtook me. I wasn't sure if they would do that normally.

I moved to overtake an articulated lorry which was struggling up a slight incline in the inside lane. I drew level with the cab, where a GOD sticker was affixed, then the artic gained speed. I accelerated but couldn't even catch up with the cab.

I was conscious suddenly of a slight dimming of the light inside the Beetle. I steadied the wheel and checked the mirrors. A huge artic was coming up on the *outside*.

We had reached the top of the hill and were coasting. There were cars behind, leaving me too little space to brake and let both lorries pass. The one on the outside now drew level so that I could see the sticker in his cab window. He pulled ahead a few yards.

My foot was on the floor but we were going downhill—they had the speed *and* the weight. I jabbed at my horn repeatedly but I doubt if they even heard it. Drivers behind began to get impatient, sounding their horns as well. Turbulence buffeted the Beetle as I fought to maintain a straight line in a gap which seemed to be narrowing. The lorries towered overhead, plastic side-flaps beating in the wind like pterodactyls. Were they closing the gap or was it my imagination? I couldn't see any trace of white lines.

I was freed when the lorry on the outside found itself blocked by a Metro doing sixty-five in the outside lane. He braked and I overtook the Metro on the inside before switching to the outside lane and spurring the Beetle to go faster. The artic in the slow lane made no attempt to give chase.

I saw, in my rearview, both lorries now in the inside lane, one having overtaken the other, which may have been all it was trying to do all along. I rubbed my forehead with the sleeve of my jacket, pulling at the weight in the pocket as I did so. Slowing down to seventy-five, I returned to the inside lane myself.

. . .

My flat, as far as I could see, was now the only one without a leaflet or poster in the window. Even in the nearby estates where residents didn't bother with party-political posters during general elections, leaflets advertising GOD were up in every window.

I slept badly and decided to go in to work as an act of defiance. By now I trusted no one; the loaded gun accompanied me.

The campaign had reached a new stage overnight. Fresh hoardings had been erected wherever there was space. My heart skipped several beats as I read the new message: "GOD. He is coming."

There was a buzz of excitement on the train fed by the people crammed around me, strangers united in anticipation. Gone were the early morning vacuous stares and razor-nicks and smudged eyeliner, replaced by flushed cheeks and a newborn glow of perfection. If they were all about to meet their maker, I was surprised not to see some signs of dread, or last-minute repentance. They were supremely confident.

The atmosphere was electric in magazine editorial. Gilliland was radiant. I kept my head down and concentrated on the white spaces between the lines.

I noticed that the offices emptied earlier than usual.

The underground was congested. The announcement was difficult to hear but it seemed most lines were not operating. I got caught in a surge of commuters and pushed onto a down escalator. All the ads down the wall by the handrail were the same. People smiled and held hands; they may or may not have known each other. There was little of the stress and antagonism usually present in a busy station at rush hour.

But the number of commuters was unprecedented. They were all going for the one line that seemed to be running. I had no choice but to go with the flow, though in the circumstances I resented their company.

On the platform I craned my neck looking for the exit, but it was serving as an entrance with hundreds of people streaming through it. I wiped my forehead. The jacket collar irritated my neck and the weight of the pistol was causing my shoulder to ache. But I felt safer with the jacket on than I would if I took it off.

A uniformed official announced that the next shuttle was approaching and we should stand back. I couldn't move an inch.

I had to board the train and was jammed up against someone's lapel badge. I twisted my body to face the other way and felt close to fainting.

The train went straight through stations without stopping. Perhaps the next shuttle would pick up at one of them. When the train finally stopped there was another crush: unable to forge my own passage, I allowed myself to be carried along.

The streets were unfamiliar to me but the hoardings that lined them were not. There was a line of cars in the center of the road, windows wound down for air, occupants fanning themselves, drivers astonishingly patient. The rest of the roadway and both pavements were slow rivers of pedestrians all flowing in the same direction. Tributaries joined from side streets, which meant I couldn't escape down one.

Signs told me we were heading for the stadium. I thought to myself that vast though it was, it would never accommodate all these souls. Soon its cream towers reared above my section of the crowd. As we passed beneath the outer structure the pack loosened a fraction, but I knew I couldn't go back: the streets were impassable. Funneled through a narrower passageway I was pressed right to the edge. Again, impossible to turn around, but I could go sideways. There was a door in the wall several yards ahead. The crowd moved slowly. Finally I was there. The handle turned. I disappeared.

I'd simply entered another passageway but this one was empty of people and the ceiling was lower. I began to walk. After some time the corridor came to a junction. Down the passage on the right there was only a locked door, so I went in the other direction.

I wondered what strange, forbidden precincts these were. Fire exits? Players' tunnels? I just kept walking. Presently, a passage merged from the left, but I sensed it didn't come from where I wanted to go, even though my goal was vague. I seemed to know better where I didn't want to go than where I did.

The corridor widened a little. The caged bulbs lining the wall at intervals of twenty yards or so seemed to become faint, as light suffused the air from another source. I walked on. The light gradually became brighter and the echoes of my footsteps faded more quickly.

The corridor sloped upward and suddenly the ceiling vanished into a great whiteness which almost blinded me—the sky: I was inside the ground. The green pasture stretched out before me. I saw the grandstand packed with tens of thousands of people. I stepped onto the pitch.

Faces began to turn as I continued walking. Silence fell like a shroud. I carried on walking until I reached the center point.

The rows of seats seemed to extend far beyond the possible bounds of the stadium, up into the sky.

I turned through 360 degrees to take in the whole ground. The silence was total. All I could hear was the blood in my head and my heart pumping it. I saw one man fall to his knees. Immediately, those around him followed suit. Their seats snapped shut.

I shrugged my jacket collar off the back of my neck where it was itching.

The reverential hush was shattered by the sharp cracks of many thousands of seats snapping shut like the beaks of dying birds.

Outside the pounding of blood in my head complete silence fell once more as a million believers knelt before me.

I took the gun from my pocket, pointed the muzzle at my temple, and squeezed the trigger.

KIM NEWMAN

SQPR

(1992)

THE WHALE-SHAPE EMERGED like a New Titan Missile from its silo. First the great bearded head broke through the unrippling pseudograss. Then neck, dress tie, two perfect black diamonds against the hot white of the wing collar. Then shoulders, twin submarines coming to the surface. The vast but insubstantial bulk shimmered as it grew. Roy could no longer see the stands through the tridvid image. The holo-body towered like the genie in *The Butcher of Bagdad*, bestriding the Docklands Super-Arena. A starfish hand went to the swelling starch of the giant shirtfront as the tenor drew a silent breath, then sound cut in. The illusion was imperfect: the bell-clear voice seemed to come from the air rather than the gaping dark of the holohead's mouth, as if a cloud of invisible spirits were singing "You'll Never Walk Alone" in Italian.

An electronically clocked 200,000 card-carrying fans stood, awed. The song was an atmospheric condition, all-around inescapable. He remembered when they would sing. Derek

Leech's tampering with rules and camera angles was cosmetic: the real change was in the crowd. When Roy had been on the pitch, "the shining knight of the Jubilee Season," the crowd had been a tidal wave: roaring and fickle. Now, they were the happy families on the posters: quiet, cheerful, and biddable. They sat on their plastic bum-shaped seats and watched: no cheers, no rude words to familiar tunes, no scuffles. It was eerily as if the stadium were empty. Two hundred thousand in-person people were gravy, a small-change irrelevance. The real money, the real spectators, were camera eyes: on the stands, on the lines, on the shoulders of the In-Close Men. Thanks to Cloud 9 TV, 200 million sets of paying eyes were out there in Television Land, focused on the World Series Cup Final.

Roy could have watched from the VIP drome, with wet bar and celebrity guests (and Grianne), but he chose to be in the dugout with Bev and the lads. It didn't smell of sweat and earth like the old one at Wembley—he didn't even know if there was dirt beneath the textured Day-Glo green—but it made him feel near the game. Commentators labeled him eccentric, Luddite. Since he'd taken over as manager, he'd brought back the old strip, ditching cyber-warrior uniforms in favor of the gear he'd worn twenty years earlier when he'd captained the team to the Double. Boots, socks, shorts, shirts.

He'd even tried, without success, to get Blanch, the In-Close Man, off the squad, alleging the extra man, loyal to C9 not the Rovers, got in the way of play. The ICM wasn't with them for the warm-up. Blanch was with the C9 crew, who strapped him into his suit like a NASAnaut, settling the steadicam, with its $10,000 of gyros and balances, on his shoulders. To last the expected hour of play, Blanch needed electro-assist knee- and hip-exojoints. The technicians claimed that if the ICM blacked out they could use body-remotes to keep him standing, running, and broadcasting. Even if Blanch broke his neck, he'd still give out pictures. Roy had expected a genetically engineered zombie, but Mark Blanch was actually a decent kid. If he weren't hunchbacked by high-tech, he might even have enjoyed a game of football.

The song ended and the tenor shivered into a billion light fragments. A double-dozen girls-boys in spandex tube tops and cheek-baring string panties cart-wheeled onto the field. Their extended routine of acrobatic leaps and pelvic thrusts was choreographed by Michael Clark to Andrew Lloyd Webber's "Cup Final Overture." It was symbolic. The cheerleading was a safe-sex orgy, performed with impeccable energy but little actual enthusiasm. No matter how explicit the action, the dancing was corny enough to get past the Family Viewing Observance Society.

Roy felt mildly depressed and anxious, not at all elated. He couldn't even remember how it had been in '77, before the Cup Final or the match that clinched the League. Too many drinks since then. The bookies had Queens Park Rovers at five to one against, and all the pollsters and comment crews went along with them. For the last few months, the team had been giant-

killers, but now the breeze was over, and it was time for the giants to strike back, putting poor old Rovers back in their place with a humiliating defeat. The best even die-hard Rovers fans could hope for was a low point spread against. Still, he'd told the lads to give the Pythons a bit of a game.

• • •

The 1998 World Series was the final evolutionary stage of Association Football. Like everything, the game had to change to suit changing times. Leech was almost single-handedly responsible for the successful adaption of soccer to the new media world he, and others like him, had carved out. Gordon Brough, sports editor of the *Comet*, stood up as his boss made an entrance into the VIP drome of the Super-Arena, escorting a small blonde woman with smile lines around her eyes and mouth. Leech wore white, the Prime Minister was in green. Even the remaining rival tabloids didn't dare print rumors about Derek Leech and Morag Duff, and Gordon thought he might be scourged for even thinking the Preem's color was up, a slight flush visible above the low neckline of her evening gown. It was rumored that Leech employees underwent a course of post-hypnotic suggestion during their annual checkup and were conditioned against thinking impure, uncharitable, or heretical thoughts about their lord and master.

The cheerleader squad were still pretending to screw each other in midair out on the flood-lit pitch, so the gathered VIPs could turn their attention to the host and his star guest. Ranting Ray Butler, briefly off his commentator's hot spot, crushed a beer can on his close-cropped head, and made a friendly burp at the Preem, who indulgently smiled and ignored him. Arabella Swinton, Butler's cohost for C9's World Series coverage, gushed and tried to curtsey, yard-long legs scissoring. She wore a black net dress about the length of a vest, well-known nipples just concealed behind the weave. A year ago, she'd been a weather bimbo on the Cornflakes Show, but her giggle caught the viewers' fancy; now, without ever having watched a football match all the way through, she was partnering Butler, someone to look at and lech after while Ranting Ray scratched the beer gut that bulged the waistband of his old-fashioned acid shorts and shouted about wankers and wobblies.

Leech introduced Gordon to the Preem, and she chirruped pleasantly at him in a shrill Scots accent. Her Spitting Image puppet was a floppy-eared poodle with a bow in its hair, fondly known as Morag Woof. Since *Spitting Image* became a C9 show, it had been kinder to her than before. Then the Preem was moved on to someone more important—Bernadette from *EastEnders*—and her smile grew to a photo-opportunity crescent. The Irish actress, who might be expected to take more interest in the match than most soap stars, was twinkle-eyed drunk, and only too willing to flash her Number Two expression, usually reserved for the gushy scenes, at the flashless snap-cameras of the journos. She and the Preem looked as if they were having a gossip about the soap character's famously useless missing boyfriend.

A seat was found for Miss Duff, and a drink. Gordon was a few rows behind, after the pop-stars and soap stars and business heads. The VIP drome had a decent rake, so his view of the pitch wasn't bad, although the large head of the Minister of Trade and Industry was in the way. It would be easier anyway to watch the match on the three wall screens rather than through the panoramic window. Gordon could no longer imagine football without ICM in-the-thick-of-it action footage. It was hard even to remember when the game had been as remote as sheep in a field seen from an airplane, used as everyone was to close-ups of bloody faces, amplified swearing, and POV shots from the goal area. It was also hard to conceive of a match without giggling or ranting, which was as much Gordon's contribution as Leech's.

Realizing just how much was lost from the media profile of the game with the extinction of football hooliganism, Gordon had found Ray Butler, quondam editor of *Britannia Rules* fanzine, and boosted him as the voice of the skinhead-in-the-stands. As crowds cooled down, the game itself heated up, and the comment shows had needed to reflect that. If Simon Hodge—the brown ale-drinking human tank they called "Splodge"—represented the turn-of-the-century player, then Ranting Ray, screaming "you're ganna get ya fakkin head kicked in" at a vicar, was the voice the game needed to take it into the next millennium.

Ray was back in his TV box now, partnered with the grumbling purist Barney Oldcarp—there to represent the football traditionalists, and to get red-faced with apoplexy at the disgusting spectacle—and Arabella was warming up to giggle from remote positions around the field. A soap star handed a cigarette case to a popstar, who swallowed one of the little purple pills it contained and passed it on to the business head on her left. The Preem looked the other way as Leech explained something to her.

• • •

The *Comet* had been a Tory paper until '93 and the appearance from nowhere of Morag Duff, so nonthreateningly cuddly and middle- or slightly-right-of-the-road that she made Neil Kinnock look like Mao Tse-tung. With the Soviet Union replaced by something resembling the Austro-Hungarian Empire, Miss Duff seemed more like a continuation of Thatcher than One Minute Major had done. The United Kingdom had got used to nanny-knows-best government. Shortly after her assumption of power and position, the Preem had gone into one of Derek Leech's sealed rooms for a conference, for all the world as if she were the supplicant and he the head of state. After that, the *Comet* and C9 had come around to support her, and treaties had been struck, apportioning additional satellite channels to Leech Enterprises, allowing it to blossom into a potentatial monopoly on the Pan-European electronic media. The word "socialist" had not been used in public by Morag Duff during the entire span of her leadership.

On the screens, Ranting Ray and Boring Barney were reviewing Splodge's recent record. Aggravated assault charges brought by the Third Lanark goalie had been settled out of court, but Nigel Matheson, right wing for Stansted Bombers, was still alleging Splodge had broken his arm during an illegal action in the Fifth Round. Litigation was postponed until after the final. Splodge's cover of Elton John's "Saturday Night's Alright (for Fighting)" was riding high in the C9 PTV charts, and Ray played snippets of it to annoy Barney Oldcarp, a die-hard who liked to point out that three years ago everything Splodge did on the pitch would earn him an early shower not a hit record. The veins in Barney's neck were scarlet lines creeping around his chin, and his whole face shone with a high-definition glow of righteous frustration.

A significant but small portion of the football audience agreed with Barney and his presence kept them watching even as they disapproved. It had even been suggested, in the non-Leech press, that Barney didn't mind either way about the state of football but got so worked up because he was pulling down as enormous a salary as Ranting Ray and Giggling Arabella.

The first thing Leech had done to soccer was wipe the slate of the Super-League and start again. Most of the old clubs were in deep recession holes and open to a Leech Enterprises buyout. The strongest survived and other sides formed according to advertising demographics. The UK was still the locus, but it had been prudent to include Pan-Europe and the USA in the World Series to increase revenue. Once 90 percent of the teams in the UK had been relegated to the amateur local entertainment status they'd always deserved, Leech had reorganized the whole game to suit C9.

Looking at a video of the 1977 cup final, when Roy Robartes had been center forward for Rovers, was like seeing some weird mutation of Australian Rules or American Football. It was impossible not to FF through the dull midfield action now eliminated by shrinking the pitch and cutting down teams to nine players, plus ICM. Ninety minutes of playing time seemed to stretch on forever: now, matches were three twenty-minute halves, with two commercial breaks. Goals were a yard wider, with individual cash prizes for scoring players. Uniform regulations had been abolished. Piffling rules about offside and body contact eased up. Referees were professional. Gambling was a systemized part of the television coverage, with direct access numbers flashed across the screen.

In the last two years, British football had made more money than in the previous fifty. The ratings for the World Series so far had been almost level with *EastEnders*, and the final was forecasted to outdraw even the most popular soaps by 20 percent.

Gordon called over a waiter and got a refill of Bushmills, wondering why he was so keen for the whole thing to be over so he could get to the party afterward. He could hardly remember the name of the team scheduled to hammer Rovers into the pseudograss, let alone bother to care about the score. The screens went black as the main camera swung to the players' tunnel.

• • •

"Did you bring your slingshot?" Bev asked as the Detroit Pythons lumbered onto the field in calculated slow motion. Their theme music— "Entrance of the Knights" from Prokofiev's *Romeo and Juliet*—boomed out in Danny Elfman's arrangement.

Roy knew then that he should have stayed home and watched the game on his wall screen.

At the head of the Pythons, Simon Hodge strode like a colossus. Huge enough to suggest special effects. Splodge was armored with the Pythons' strip, chainmail layered over his massive chest, face-shielding helmet bulbous like the head of an alien being. Roy had heard Splodge's next record would be a remix of Tennessee Ernie Ford's "Sixteen Tons," and he seemed to concentrate every ounce of it into his man-shape, a collapsed star hugging mass to its shrunken heart.

The Pythons didn't jog, they slouched. But Roy knew they were capable of incredible speed, amazing skill, unbelievable violence. If there were still such a thing as injury time, most Pythons matches would displace the rest of the evening's television schedule.

Splodge separated from the pack and crossed to the center of the pitch. His footfalls must have been amplified, for they sounded like sledge-hammer blows.

Bev tried to make a funny comment, but it was no good. Roy knew the lads would feel as he did, as if each footfall was a blow to the stomach. He became aware of his jaw dropping.

At the center of the pitch, Splodge raised his arms over his head. A broken-toothed mouth opened beneath his visor, and a yell exploded from his helmet, filling the Super-Arena. It was a fi-fi-fo-fum declaration, a Viking berserker battle cry, a prayer to the dark gods of football.

Roy breathed profanity.

Then, hesitantly, without a signal, the lads filtered out onto the field, picking up speed, jogging to their positions. The Splodge yell was still dying as Roy shouted out good luck.

• • •

Roy's World Series run had started where the rest of his ventures ended, in an iron-framed cot.

When, at the peak of his career, a knee injury put him out of the game, he sank his savings into boutiques. Just as Punk gave way to New Romantic, a still-limping Roy was investing the best part of a million pounds in flared silver spangle trousers, muslin shirts with floppy sleeves and shoulder-wide collars, road sign–shaped paisley ties, space boots with seven-inch platform heels and rainbow-knit synthetic fiber tank tops. He wore his hair like Rod Stewart and married Grianne, the Irish chanteuse who'd once scored "null points" on the Eurovision Song Contest. He'd been too busy putting 'em

in the back of the net and swigging champagne out of trophies to notice things had changed since Jason King went off television. He'd been tipsy, overextended, and "over the moon" when Thatcher succeeded Callaghan in '79; but he was drunk, broke, and "sick as a parrot" when the fleet left for the Falklands in '82. Grianne left him for Tarquin Crumple, a bearded quiz-master to whose Buttons she'd played Cinderella at the Bristol Hippodrome in the '81 panto season. Roy learned of his wife's desertion in a pub, when he happened to notice a front-page story in the *Daily Comet*, the tabloid acorn from which Derek Leech's media Yggdrasil was growing.

The receivers took over Chic 'Tiques, and Roy scrabbled around for a sponsorship deal, becoming front man for a German cosmetics company, Herr Hair. He starred in a series of ads, rubbing Mighty Mousse into his scalp in a changing room then cheekily tarting up his chest hair. One morning, a swatch of hair came out in the brush, making a triangle-shaped bald spot that extended from his forehead to the apex of his skull. It turned out to be a reaction to Herr Hair products. His chest burned blotchy for years, and his lawyers never made a case against the company. He hadn't paid for the cases of Mighty Mousse in his basement. And Herr Hair noticed loopholes in their on-pack instructions, warning against excessive use.

Satellite TV started to take off and Grianne's boyfriend became host of *I Bet You Feel a Right One*, the highest-rated show on the P9 Light Channel. Tarquin promptly bedded Stuka, the jaw-heavy girl in the topless swimsuit who was forever turning up in innocent people's baths, workplaces, and fridges. A stone too heavy to tour as Nancy in *Oliver!*, Grianne moved back into their heavily mortgaged home in Esher. Throughout the '80s, they appeared regularly in the *Comet*: having screaming matches with Oliver Reed in nightclubs, pluckily getting into shrinking tracksuits to raise funds. At one point before taking out family membership in Alcoholics Anonymous, he was heating Mighty Mousse and draining off the liquid for its 0.5 alcohol content. At another, he and Grianne tag-mud-wrestled Jimmy Savile and Anneka Rice for homeless children.

After his mostly successful drying-out, he was approached by Sidcup Startlers, a struggling Third Division team, and asked to become manager. On *The Last Resort*, he told Jonathan Ross his knee was fixed and that he planned to select himself as a useful midfield player. First time out, he managed a draw, and a few of the pundits who turned up to see the legend in action were mildly kind. In the *Comet*, though, Ray Butler, "the angry man of football," devoted his hundred-word leader to Eskimo OAPs and ice floes. Next Sidcup lost five–one. Roy celebrated by punching a *Comet* photographer and tripping over a cocktail waitress, wrenching his trick knee forever. Then came the formation of the first of the short-lived Super-Leagues: the fifteen most successful clubs locked into profitable television contracts, 80 percent of the rest plunged into a Dark Age of financial disaster and pathetic obscurity. In three years, Roy led Sidcup down to the Southern League and bankruptcy. "One good thing," said someone on *The Mary Whitehouse Experience*, "at least Salman Rushdie can do with the company."

By then, there was a Labour government, and Kinnock had resigned in favor of Morag Duff, the first single woman—"spinster" some said—to hold the office of Prime Minister. Association Football was practically a wholly owned subsidiary of Derek Leech Enterprises, struggling through its metamorphosis into the primary televised sport of the turn of the century. When Sidcup went down for the last time, Roy checked into a clinic for an urgent rehabilitation. Strapped into a bed and biting back his own puke, head in a fixed position so he was forced to watch C9, Roy struggled with the worst his nightmares could throw at him. During the *Animal Fun Hour*, a popular late-night "adult" novelty show, he touched bottom, scraping the base of existential despair. When he got free, he vowed to kill himself.

• • •

"We'll beat Leech," Bev told Roy, over and over. "We'll change the storyline, we'll rewrite the headlines."

Now, with the £50,000-a-year referee raising his saxophone-sized whistle, Roy was unconvinced.

For the last few months, as Rovers won matches, at first scrappily and then with confidence, Roy had been soaring. He hadn't thought about drink until this moment.

Now, as the shrill tone sounded out through the Super-Arena, he wanted a treble scotch, and then another, and another, and . . .

• • •

On *Shower Talk*—a C9 chat show where the guests wore towels and sat in a steam room surrounded by beefy and bruised ornamental naked men—Jimmy Greaves did a moving piece on Roy's courageous struggle with the bottle, and offered to forward any messages of support to the clinic. Ray Butler, promoted to the post of C9's sport pundit, chipped in with his own fist-waving salute to Roy Robartes, although he wound up with his customary rant of "Rovers was a crap team, and Robartes was a crap player." Every morning, an orderly came to read aloud the letters that arrived. There were always well-wishers, but he knew—from the awkward pause between a letter being torn open and the hurried precis of a formulaic message of cheer—there were many grudge-holding Sidcup fans out there too. Perhaps one of them would do the job for him, slipping out of a crowd with a bread knife or a nail gun.

Meanwhile Grianne shed excess poundage and won the role of Bernadette, the single Mum who sacrifices all for her slut of a daughter Corinne, on *EastEnders*. The soap made a successful return to the ratings, transferring from the ailing BBC—over 32 percent of television households had disconnected the terrestrial channels—to C9's Drama Stream, where it sat between *Coronation Street* and *Neighbours* in the early evenings. Leech's ownership of all three series allowed for popular storyline crossovers. When Corinne ran off to Australia with Jack Duckworth, Bernadette was able to bribe a struggling ex-character from *The Bill*—canceled after the controversial Clapham Crack War episodes—to turn private eye and track her down to Ramsay Street. After a personal meeting, and subsequent photo session, with Derek Leech, Grianne sued Roy for divorce and moved in with a twenty-one-year-old model best known for a swimming-trunks advert. She told the *Comet* about her orgasm secrets and fronted a bestselling diet video.

From his bed, as food was pumped into him, Roy followed the soap and cringed whenever Bernadette railed about the swine who'd fathered Corinne. They'd never had children but he knew Grianne was thinking of him when she read her lines. Useless Brendan, who never appeared, was the most hated man on television. Terry Wogan always made a "Useless Brendan" joke during his two-hour-long chat-and-news show on G9's Heavy Channel. At Prime Minister's Question Time, Morag Duff called the Leader of the Opposition "a right Useless Brendan" and the chamber gave her a standing ovation. All the time, Roy thought of ways to kill himself. The rope seemed best. He had some at home and the light fittings in the hallway should be strong enough to support him. He could fix the noose to the chandelier and jump off the first-floor landing.

Then, despite the high security, Bev Ellis got through to see him, and he started the climb back up. She had written to him first, then started to visit. She volunteered to help with his physiotherapy. For the first time in years, Roy felt free from pain.

He didn't know how she'd done it, but Bev had got him his Series Run. Rovers had gone through seven managers in three seasons, the latest resigning after the *Comet* alleged he took

an unhealthy interest in the career and person of a twelve-year-old glamour model. At some point, Bev had made her petition not to the Board of Directors but, cannily, to Derek Leech. As in everything, Leech was concerned not with whether it was a good idea but whether it would make good copy. Pitching a project to him, Roy knew, was like suggesting a plot development to the script editor of a soap. When Leech decided to run with the Return of Roy Robartes, the story was set in stone.

"Giggle-gurgle-giggle," went Arabella Swinton into the camera, "play has, um, started. That big bloke has, um, hit someone, and given him a nasty knock. Someone did that to my car last week. They never caught the git, though. The dent cost seven hundred and fifty pounds to have beaten out. Criminal, um. Oh, there's the ball. Someone's kicked it awfully hard. Lot of stitching in a ball, you know. Teeny-tiny-teensy stitches. That man was supposed to stop it doing that, wasn't he? Um, yes. I think that's a goal. Someone has scored a goal. I'm sure we'll have, um, more on that in a bit. One side has one goal, and the others don't have anything. I bet they're tad upset about that."

• • •

One–nil down after ten minutes. Trav Billings, Rovers' center forward, felt the disadvantage in his gut like an undigested stone. It had been a typical Splodge goal, the Pythons hammering the defense out of the way with body blows then escorting the ball under armed guard. Splodge lazily booting it into the net while two rhino-plated goons pinned the Rovers' goalie, Jack Dorothy, down.

Trav, twenty years old, swore his parents named him after the De Niro character in *Taxi Driver*, but the *Comet* had revealed last week that his first name was not Travis but Travolta. His Mum had been obsessed with the old actor in *Look Who's Talking*. Two days ago, during a practice, the loudspeakers had started pouring out the soundtrack albums of *Saturday Night Fever* and *Grease*, with new lyrics dubbed over the old songs. "You Can Tell by the Way I Walk That I'm a Total Spaz," "Hopelessly Demoted to Spew," "Right Feeble, Right Feeble, Right Feeble, Right Fee-bull," "You're a Bit of a Cunt, Ooo-Oo-Oo." It had been impossible not to recognize the wind-up tactics, and indeed the voice, of Simon Hodge.

Splodge would pick on one man in any team the Pythons were set to play, and mount a campaign of harassment and humiliation, issuing public taunts about their personal habits, sexual persuasions, physical appearance, and genetic heritage. He usually picked the player most likely to be a threat, so Trav guessed the treatment was a compliment. It was still a pain. Splodge claimed Trav was so ape-ugly that when he cried, the tears would run over his forehead and down the back of his head just to avoid his face. When he said ape-ugly, Splodge meant black.

With an early lead, the Pythons opted to stand around and show off, letting Rovers wear themselves out running around. In the old days, these tactics might have made for a boring game, but the Pythons were showmen, and enjoyed throwing in a few borderline illegal moves, making slapstick out of foul play. Evans and Cardille were already limping, and Jobson had a cut above his eye that was dribbling blood down his face, with both the ICMs jostling around him for the best view of the wound.

Evans, who was being ignored since Splodge had oops-excuse-me rammed him, intercepted a lackluster Python pass and began dribbling the ball down the field. Trav could sense the move coming and picked up speed. This was the kind of breakout point he had been trained for.

Roy had told the lads to concentrate on the old-fashioned skills. They were the point of the game and also showed up the Pythons' weaknesses. Since Roy had come to the club, there'd been an emphasis on what he called "proper football."

A Python got in Evans's way, arms outstretched a yard either side of his tubby Kevlar-swathed body. Evans, pain in his face, lurched to one side, momentarily losing the ball, but regaining it with a deft flick of his boot. Blanch, the Rovers ICM, was running backward in front of Evans, trying to keep him in focus.

Trav looked up at the giant screens and saw how much agony Evans was going through as he ran. Behind him, blobbily out of focus, were three advancing juggernauts. The suits slowed them down, but when they caught up, there would be serious GBH. Some things legal on a football pitch would get you locked up back in the world.

Trav found himself alone in the Pythons' goal area, looking at the blank visor of spring-heeled Jacnoth, their goalie. Light lines flickered under the gray shield, suggesting some automated vision-augmentation input device. Trav turned to look back.

Evans couldn't keep going, but he wouldn't have to.

Trav was there for the pass. Roy had taken them through every possible situation so often that it was an instinctive move. Evans, his honor won, sacrificed the glory to a teammate with a final burst of strength, kicking the ball into the air so it arced over Blanch and Gorgo Brzezinzki, the Pythons' fullback, aimed straight for Trav's head.

He jumped into the air and connected with the ball.

In Roy's day, Trav's header might have bounced off the sidebar back into play, but the posts had been moved since then. Even spring-heels couldn't get Jacnoth there to save.

The score was one–one.

Trav turned, a spurt of excitement dying in his heart as he saw Evans on the turf, a couple of Pythons piled on top of him, thumping and kicking, grinding him down with their body-weight. He looked up to the screen, hoping for the instant replay. The whistle sounded, and the screen dissolved to a commercial break.

"Fakkin useless fakkin kants," Ray Butler ranted, "fakkin wankers fakkin scored. Useless, useless, useless."

• • •

Beverly Robartes Ellis was born during the 1977 Cup Final. According to her dad, she emerged just as Roy Robartes, the Shining Knight, slammed home the injury-time goal that drew Rovers level. And she first cried when he completed his hat trick in extra time, winning the FA Cup. Dad claimed she made a tiny fist and baby-talked "we are the champions." It had been the greatest day of Stan Ellis's life.

Her earliest memories were matches: tumultuous crowds all around, cheering in triumph as Rovers scored again. She swore she could remember Roy in action, although he played his last game for Rovers before she could crawl. Clearer were her memories of the Relegation Season, as a succession of formerly humiliated foes trampled Rovers again and again. Without Roy, the heart went out of the team.

In the '80s, after Dad's stroke, Bev trudged every other Saturday to the home game and quietly watched the last tatters of Rovers' glory whip away in rain and wind. At thirteen, after a four–one loss, she was assaulted on the Tube station nearest the ground, by two knot-headed youths wearing Rovers scarves. A listless scattering of downcast fans didn't intervene and she was forced to defend herself, disabling the piss-heads with a thigh-driven blow to the knee and a coil-sprung knee into the groin.

She stopped going to matches, but turned up in Rovers kit for the first practice of her school team. Thanks to Bill Forsyth and Dee Hepburn, it was no longer unusual for girls to play football. Jamila Saunders, a fifth former with a figure like the Incredible Hulk, was the regular goalie for North End Comprehensive. And Helena Geoffreys, whose legs figured prominently in the auto–erotic fancies of most of her teammates, dominated the midfield until she dropped soc-cer to get into interpretive dance. However, the school's side was drawn from pupils three or four years older and, although she was a full foot taller than most kids her own age, she still wound up described as "stringy." She didn't get selected for the team then, but two years—and several mashed lips, open-to-the-bone knees, and severe muscle strains—later, she found herself as first substitute, then as North End's center half, then as a striker. Then, a school leaver, she had tried out for Rovers' Women.

All the clubs had all-girl shadows and, with the reorganization, the women players were theoretically available for any given match. Several times, the nonserious clubs—like Earnshaw's Northern, which existed solely to advertise beer—had fielded women, mainly to get attention in matches they were certain to lose. Goals were now less important than ad revenue and entertaining losers could rake in more than tedious winners, a lesson learned hard by several formerly dominant sides. Bev, while she was a major force in the women's team, refused to be token girlie in the first side. Rovers was in terrible shape, barely treading the shark-filled waters outside the Ultra League, shut out of prime time, relegated to late-night slots on low-wattage cable channels. Every Sunday, especially after a defeat, Bev expected to learn that Rovers was this week's club to be sucked under and dissolved, assets stripped and spread, stadium redeveloped as an evangelist's open-air temple.

The Ultra League was sealed tight as a cat's arsehole, but the World Series had a chink. The top seven UL teams were automatically eligible, but the eighth spot was for an out side, a carrot for all the flounderers, to keep the UL gladiators from turning complacent. Expulsion from the UL was like being kicked out of Eden, a fall into acid and acrimony from which no team ever recovered. If an out side could make a decent Series run, it had a chance to slip into the UL. And UL sides were growing soft inside the glitz, cocooned by wealth and predictable opponents, leaving them open to a hungry challenge. But

Rovers still needed a boost to make it through the preliminaries. And Bev remembered the hero of her early childhood.

• • •

The adverts lasted five minutes, barely enough to get the players off the field and sluice out their mouths with the Official Orange Juice Substitute of the World Series. Roy had Bev, a qualified first-aider, check on Evans, Cardille, and Jobson. He told the lads where the Pythons were weak. And he told them what to watch for. Trav Billings nodded, shrugging off congrats. There was no elation, no overconfidence. That was good. The lads had learned.

When Roy, bleary but sober, turned up for the first practice, Rovers had been a shambles. A collection of adequate players, they hadn't been anything like a team. Having only just pulled himself into shape, Roy was merciless with them. Someone had renamed the Rovers Ground, putting up a notice which read GLADIATOR TRAINING SCHOOL.

With Bev to give him advice, Roy channeled his energies into the team, cutting loose the deadwood, and bringing forward potential stars. Trav, who could be one of the greats, had been buried in the subs, but Roy brought him on. And the others rallied. At first, they fought him. Then, they fought the matches.

Now Roy would trust Rovers to invade Normandy, rob a Turkish Museum, or stage a Broadway musical. There was already a drama-documentary in preproduction, although Roy assumed it would be canceled if Rovers boringly lost the final. The show would only play if the last act worked out.

Standing to one side, a technician tinkering with his transmission, was Blanch. Roy saluted the In-Close Man. There was no point fighting the changes on a person-to-person level.

The whistle went off, and the lads piled back onto the pitch, hut-hut-hutting like marines.

"End thet, I thenk, shews the kind of football we've come tew expect from the Rovers under Roy Robartes," Barney Oldcarp droned through his nose, "with Johnno Jobson, pluckily returning tew the pitch efter a terrible enjury, delivering one of the textbook gewls of the game. Stanley Metthews would heve been prowd tew see sech a display ev old-fashioned skell end dexterity, a vindication ev teamwork, training end thet extra touch of derring-do whech makes a good player great. Whet do yew think, Raymonde?"

In the background, Ray Butler had his fingers down his throat.

"Tew-one, advantage the Rovers," smugged Barney.

• • •

Bev watched Roy watching the game. For the first time, she thought the Rovers might take it all the way. At the beginning, she'd just hoped to see a dignified last stand. If they went down with enough heroism, they might latch into a Little Big Horn–Rorke's Drift–Scott of the Antarctic reputation, courageous individuals better-remembered than the anonymous hordes who actually won. Now, as the Pythons were hitting back hard, going all-out for the equalizer, it was as if maybe the Rovers might turn back the foe. In school, she'd been taught that although Amundsen actually found the South Pole first and got back alive, it didn't really count because he ate his own huskies. Even if the Pythons managed to draw level and then win, it wouldn't mean anything according to the rules Roy was playing by. The rules that, on a cosmic scale, counted more than the ratings and the income.

Splodge was the sort of player who'd tear off a leg of sled-dog and wolf it raw, washed down with a vat of baked beans and brown ale. Now, he was shoving his way through the Rovers defense, battering his way to the spot from which he scored all his goals, waiting for his stooges to arrive with the ball. Barry Cardille, still nursing his first-half bruises, was marking his man, and got there before the Splodgster.

The ref was looking the other way as the Python nutted Cardille. Michelle Tenney, glam goalie for Rovers Women, had offered to sleep with the ref, but Roy had gratefully turned down her kind suggestion. Now, Bev wondered if that mightn't have been as bad an idea as it had sounded. When the ref was looking, Cardille had staggered to his feet. Splodge stood grinning over him, forearms bulging like Popeye's, a red trickle on his own forehead. Cardille stood back as Splodge wiped his cut on his hand, looking down in puzzlement at his own blood. Then, in a bid for a Best Actor BAFTA, Splodge was on his knees, yelling in simulated agony.

The ref was jogging over, and the Pythons' paramedics were sprinting across the field, personal sirens whining. The ref's whistle stopped play. Splodge was combining the deaths of Olivier in *Richard III*, Beatty in *Bonnie and Clyde*, Cassavetes in *The Fury*, and Julia Roberts in *Saddambusters!* Gradually, he recovered from his mortal wound, and by the time he had to take the penalty, he was as well as he'd ever be.

Bev looked at Roy, who was leaning forward, intent on the action. A colorless official was by his side, waiting to deliver a message. Roy took the curl of fax paper, but didn't read it. The official waited.

A Splodge penalty had once been monitored and found to be actually "faster than a speeding bullet." The last man to save one had broken both his hands, and seen his side lose four–one.

As the ball came at him, Jack Dorothy, a long-armed spiderman, stretched out a flap of hand, and made a fist. He connected, and punched the leatherette, reversing its momentum. Even the sedate newstyle crowd cheered politely, and Splodge was seized with an attack of Tourette's Syndrome.

The half ended, and C9 cut to the ads. Bev looked around for Roy, but he was gone. There was a crumple of paper by the bench.

The lads came back to the dugout, hyper from their showing on the field. Bev picked up the paper and had a chance to look at it—it was something from Roy's ex-wife—before the players were around her, asking questions, soliciting congratulations, needing advice.

She knew the speech, so she delivered it as best she could: teamwork, footwork, aggressive-but-fair play.

Where was Roy?

• • •

She was all over him, tears and caresses, apologies and solicitations. It was her voice he had fallen in love with in the first place, and, even after everything, it still got through to him.

"Grianne, Grianne, Grianne," he kept saying, trying to interrupt her flow, still finding the sound of her name seductive.

She kept at him.

It was an invitation to come in out of the cold, to join her in the world Derek Leech had made. By combining all the soaps, all the sports, all the news channels and all the dramas, Cloud 9 had made one hit television show of everything. And Grianne was a star, as much as Splodge or Morag Duff. If he would only do one little thing, Roy could be too.

He would win: secure fame and fortune; a place in television history; a position exalted over Butler, Barney, and Arabella; an ongoing role in the only circus that counted. He would win back his wife.

Grianne kissed him, and he felt her tears on his cheek.

It was as if Corinne had come back to Bernadette on her knees, as if Useless Brendan had laid down his life for his family.

All Roy had to do was lose.

He could do it. He could do it invisibly. A few instructions to the lads. In-character instructions, about rules and proprieties. He could leave holes in the defense.

He could lose, and win.

As Grianne begged him to come back, begged him to play out Leech's master-script, Roy wondered if she could see a camera behind him.

If he were to accept, would a ton of green

sludge pour out of Heaven onto his head? And would Tarquin Crumple pop out of a toilet bowl, wink, and say "I bet you feel a right one!"

"There's money, too," Grianne said. "From the bookies, from Leech. More money than you could believe."

Miles away, the whistle shrilled. And suddenly Roy felt incredibly tired.

"You could have it all."

• • •

Derek Leech wasn't paying much attention to the match. He was flirting with the Preem. From where he was sitting, Gordon could only really see Morag Duff nodding. Leech was in shadows, eyes sometimes reflecting.

Leech was only seen in full light on television or in his papers. In person, he always seemed to have shadows around him, like the character in the strip that ran in the *Argus*, his heaviest paper. Gordon heard Leech wanted C9 to do a *Dr. Shade* TV series, maybe with Jeremy Irons or Jonathan Pryce.

Occasionally, Leech would check the wall screen—with its permanent readout of time to go and score—but mainly he was interested in the Preem, whispering to her, laughing with her. Gordon had the impression he was looking at Government in Action.

A soap star returned to her seat, makeup adjusted, and started following the play. Gordon remembered who Grianne had been married to, and wondered if C9 had thought to book a sound bite from her. A human-interest angle would pique the interest of the wives and girlfriends coerced into watching the Final, and Leech always promised advertisers balanced demographics.

For a while, Gordon had thought the Rovers might have a chance. But they had come out very scrappily at the beginning of the third half, and seemed to be playing a nervously defensive game, as if waiting for the big bullies to come and snatch back their lollipops.

Apart from Jacnoth, every player on the field

was clustered around the Rovers goal area. As the time clock counted down, the Rovers' lead seemed more and more fragile.

Bev noticed just how stretched-thin Roy was. He kept relaying "never let up" messages to the pitch, but he also seemed to be holding something back. When Brzezinzki scored for the Pythons, Bev felt her stomach turn. With three minutes on the timer, the match would probably go to penalties. And it was too much to ask for Jack Dorothy to save two Splodge dum-dums in one evening.

• • •

Roy thought drink-drink-drink-drink. But his mouth was dry. He could still feel Grianne's tongue, could still hear her voice.

Don't be a Useless Brendan, he told himself.

The Pythons were lined up for another assault as the teams assembled in the center for play to resume, and the Rovers looked like sheep grazing in front of a mile-wide combine harvester. The Pythons would be looking to stampede in another goal.

When had this ever been just a game?

It was time for his last signal.

He thought again of Grianne, and wondered if he were doing the right thing.

Demi-seconds flickered on the monitor's time code, dropping away like hourglass grains.

Roy stood up, hugged Bev, and made the signal.

Trav, standing by the ball, was ready. This could make up for everything.

The ball was back in play, and Splodge was about to blitzkrieg him into the pseudograss.

Trav, not thinking about how smart a move he was being ordered to make, got his boot-toe under the leather and made the long pass, the impossible play. Roy Robartes might be old-fashioned, but this was an innovation.

Splodge slammed into him, and Trav heard a bone breaking. He was out of this game. And what he had just done had either won or lost it.

He felt psychic waves of astonishment pouring down, and jagged pain shattering through his body. He hauled himself up, and watched Splodge chase the man with the ball. If the ref saw Trav was injured, play would be stopped. And that couldn't happen.

"Well, no one's ever done thet before," Barney droned. "Et's legal, ev course, bet . . ."

"Is that allowed?" Arabella giggled.

"Fakk, fakk, fakk," Ray ranted.

• • •

Bev was torn. Usually, she watched only the pitch—like Roy—but now she had to look at the dugout monitor.

Of course, the studio director had cut to the In-Close Man. The picture shifted as Blanch barreled down the pitch, ball almost dead center. An ICM had scored for Midland Athletic once, when a ball bounced off his steadicam-helmet and qualified as a header by default, but he'd deserved and got about as much credit as a cushion does for a match-winning snooker shot.

Blanch was well ahead of the Pythons, and Roy had men spread out behind him, running in a fan. Splodge had been too busy disabling Trav to be there, and none of the hunter-killers were exactly sprinter material.

"This is crazy," Bev said.

Roy just nodded.

Blanch dribbled the ball. The weight of his machine must seem like an agony now. But, undoubtedly, he was the fittest man on the squad, a weightlifter on wheels.

The ICM was in the Pythons' goal area. The defenders, who had been expecting another scramble for the Rovers' end, were with the pack closing in like hungry dinosaurs.

He had a clear run. Blanch shrugged free of his equipment, which fell from his shoulders and crashed expensively. The camera didn't cut out, and provided a perfect sideways view of Jacnoth as he dived. Blanch's shot slipped past the goalie, and everyone was shouting. Like in the old days.

Rovers men were in a ring around Blanch, fighting off the Pythons. Roy was laughing and punching the air. Splodge started kicking the fallen camera, and the screen showed his boot coming in, then a brief spiral crack in the lens and deadscreen flicker, before cutting to a frankly stunned Barney Oldcarp and Arabella Swinton.

"I told you Blanch was a good kid," Roy said.

A minute later, the match was over.

• • •

At the reception afterward, Roy told interviewers he was over the moon. Actually, he felt as if he had died and woken up in an afterlife where he had no idea what to do.

He expressed concern over Trav Billings's injury, and said the club were considering criminal assault charges against Simon Hodge. He agreed with the citing of Mark Blanch as Man of the Match. He confirmed that he was engaged to Bev Ellis, and admitted he had never worked out just how much younger than him she was.

Morag Duff shook his hand, and he wondered if she was a Stepford Wife. There didn't seem to be anyone inside the poodle mannerisms. He was photographed with the Preem, a collection of soap faces in the background, Arabella draped around his waist.

In his hand was his first drink in nearly two years. Champagne.

He held the flute to his lips, relishing the taste and the bubbles, and took the tiniest sip.

Grianne hugged and congratulated him, showing her best side to the cameras, then faded back into the celeb crowd. He pulled Bev, who had found a dress from somewhere, into the picture, and touched champagne to her lips, then kissed her.

A man moved through the crowds, smile advancing like a shark's fin. The man whose offer—relayed contemptibly through Grianne—he had torn up and thrown away.

Probably, this was the end of it all. He might

have won, but now he would fall from grace, be expelled from the garden. It was all over, and it didn't matter.

So he threw his drink in Derek Leech's face.

• • •

"We don't need that," Leech told the offline editor. "Wipe it."

Gordon saw the image freeze, just as Roy Robartes prepared to toss his glass, and then the whole thing scrambled.

Leech smiled.

"It didn't fit."

It was unusual for him to take an interest in the minutiae of edited highlights. But this, Gordon suspected, was special.

The key sequences had already been picked out. The goals, of course. The penalty save. Billings on his feet with a broken leg. Splodge swearing. Blanch's camera cutting out.

And the backstage stuff: the training footage, the earlier heats, the temptations, the fortitude. Arabella showing her legs, Barney drawing diagrams of the goals. Ranting Ray being (literally) sick (as a parrot) at the reception.

On one screen, Roy was resisting his ex-wife's blandishments. On another, he was making his secret signals to Blanch and Billings.

Gordon knew Leech was pleased Rovers had won. Boring Barney was talking about a triumph for the old over the new, a revival of traditional British virtues, and the value of skill over schmaltz. But Leech, no matter how much he might be associated with what he had made of the game, was best pleased this way. It made a better story, better copy, a fresher twist in the plotline.

As Roy resisted Grianne, standing firm against her offers, Leech smiled.

"You know, Brough," he said, deigning to notice Gordon, "nothing sells like integrity."

That had been said before, Gordon suspected. That was how Leech usually worked. He lived in shadows and spoke in scripted dialogue. One day he would vanish in reality and appear only on television. Somewhere, the Prime Minister was waiting for Leech. And he was busy picking angles, suggesting cuts, rewriting voiceovers. A functionary came in and confirmed that the World Series Final had indeed outdrawn everything else in the ratings. Nothing pulled in more viewers, not even the top-rated soaps.

"Everything's a soap," Leech said. And Gordon had to agree.

PEPE ROJO

GRAY NOISE

(1996)

Translated from the Spanish by Andrea Bell

IN MY ROOM in the early morning, when every-thing is quiet, I can hear a buzzing sound. It begins between my eyes and extends down my neck. It's like a whisper, and I concentrate, try-ing to make out the words that sound inside my head, knowing in advance that they won't make any sense. They don't say a thing. The murmur is like that vibration you can feel but can't place when you're in a mall right when all the stores start to turn on their lights and get ready for the day. Even when people arrive that vibration is still there, but you can't feel it anymore. My head is like a vacant mall. The sound of empty space. The vibration that expectations produce. The whisper of a desire you can't name.

Believe me, I'm used to the buzz. I'm also used to my heart beating, to my brain string-ing together ideas that have no direction, to my lungs taking in air in order to expel it later. The body is an absurd machine.

Sometimes the noise lulls me to sleep at night. Sometimes it doesn't let me sleep, it keeps me awake, staring at a yellow indicator light on the ceiling that tells me I'm on standby.

I transmitted for the first time when I was eighteen years old and desperate to find some news item, anything. So I took to walking the streets, following people whose faces seemed like TV fodder. I felt like a bum with a mission. I'd had a little money left over after the operation and I could enjoy the luxury of eating wherever I wanted, so I went to one of those fancy restau-rants on the top floor of a building tall enough to give you vertigo. After having a drink I walked toward the bathroom, trying to find an exit out onto the terrace. I wanted a few shots of the city for my personal file. I opened several doors with-out finding anything. Just like my life, I thought with a cynicism I sometimes miss. The rooftop terraces of all buildings are alike. A space filled with geometric forms, in shades of gray. Some-one should make a living painting horizontal murals on the roofs of terraces with messages for the planes that fly over this city every five minutes. Though I don't know what the messages would be. What can you say to someone about to arrive except "welcome"? It's been a long time since anyone felt welcome in this city.

Someone was jumping over an aluminum fence on the opposite side of the terrace. Maybe it was my lucky day and he was going to commit suicide. I activated the "urgent" button inside my thigh, hoping I wasn't wrong. A little later a green indicator lit up my retina, telling me that I was on some station's monitors, though not yet on the air. The guy was standing on a cornice, looking down. He was dark and stubby; his back was to me so I couldn't see his face. I jumped over the fence and looked down, establishing the scene for the viewers; it could be edited later. The dark man turned and saw me, got nervous, and jumped. Right then a red light went on in my eye and I heard a voice tainted with static say in my ear, "You're on the air, pal!"

That night I found out that the man was named Veremundo, a fifty-four-year-old gym teacher. The suicide note they found on his body said he was tired of being useless, of feeling insignificant from dawn to dusk, and that the worst thing about his suicide was knowing it wouldn't affect a soul.

Suicides always say the same thing.

• • •

When it is impossible to set up an external camera to situate the action, the reporter should obtain a few establishing shots—"long shots"—to ensure that the space in which the action takes place is logical to the viewers. Reporters should prepare fixed shots first, and only later, when there is action, they can use motion shots.

• • •

Suicides don't pay very well. There are so many every day, and people are so unimaginative, that if you spend a day watching television you can see at least ten suicides, none of them very spec-

tacular. Seems the last thing that suicides think of is originality.

Only once did I try to talk a suicide out of it. It was a woman, 'bout forty years old, skinny and worn-out. I told her that the only thing her suicide was going to accomplish was to feed me for about two days, that there was no point being just another one, that I totally understood life was a load of shit but there was no sense committing suicide just to entertain a thousand assholes who do nothing but switch channels looking for something that would raise, even just a little, the adrenaline level in their bodies.

She jumped anyway.

I returned home, and that night I watched the personal copy I'd made over and over again. Every action happened thousands of times on my monitor. I ended up playing it in slo-mo, trying to find some moment when her expression changed, the moment when one of my words might've had an effect I didn't know how to take advantage of.

I went to bed with swollen eyes, a terrible taste in my mouth, and thinking that what I'd said to that lady I might just as well have been saying to myself.

• • •

I've had enough, and I leave my house to go buy something to eat. I jump on my bike (which I use to get around near home) and just before reaching a pizza place I hear a bunch of patrol cars a few blocks away. I press my thigh to activate the controls, and the green signal goes on in my eye. I pedal as fast as I can, following the sound of the sirens. I turn a corner and see five cop cars parked at the entrance to a building. I leave my bike leaning against one of them, hoping no one will steal it, and run toward a cop who's keeping gawkers back. I show her my press badge and she grudgingly lets me in. She tells me to go up to the third floor. When I arrive, a couple paramedics are examining a body that's convulsing in the doorway of the apartment. I stop to establish the shots. One full shot of the paramedics, one long shot of the corridor, and I try to walk slowly and keep my vision fixed so that the movement isn't too abrupt. I stop at the doorway and slowly pan my head in order to establish the setting on thousands of monitors throughout the world. My indicator light's been red for several seconds. I approach an officer who's covering up a corpse near a TV monitor, and on the monitor they're transmitting my shot. I feel the shiver that always accompanies a hook, I begin to get dizzy, and a shooting pain crosses my brain from side to side. I lose all sense of space until I turn around and spot a cop trying to be the star of the day. The cop sees the red light in my right eye and looks into it. "We got a report from some neighbors in the building that they'd heard a baby crying, and they knew that three single men lived here. You know how people are, they thought that they were some kind of f—— perverts who'd adopted a baby so they could feel like they were more normal."

I interrupt the laughter of the cop who's posing for my right eye, and ask him when they were notified.

"Twenty minutes ago. We ran a check on kidnapped babies. When we got here, they'd already killed the neighbors. Seems they were monitoring all phone calls, and they began shooting at us . . ."

The officer kept on talking, and I was concentrating on getting the shot when I sensed a movement behind him. Apparently a closet door was opening. The next thing I register—and I suppose it's gonna be pretty spectacular since my shot was a close-up of his face—is a flash of light and his face exploding into pieces of blood and flesh.

I hurl myself against his body, grabbing hold of it and using my momentum to carry us toward whoever it was did this. Before reaching the closet I let go of the body and step back, to get a clear shot. The headless corpse of the policeman strikes another body and knocks it down. I approach quickly and stomp on the hand hold-ing a gun. I can hear the bones as they break. Too bad I don't have audio capacity so I could record the sound. I hope someone in the transmission room patches it in. The shot is a bird's-eye view of some guy's face, soaked with the blood of the cop. I can't make out his features. More cops arrive. I take a few steps back.

"It seems," I comment on the air, "that there was still one person hiding in the closet, and this carelessness by the police has cost yet another officer his life." It's always good to criticize institutions. It raises the ratings. Just then I hear a commotion at the door and I quickly turn around to find a young woman crying, followed by a private security guard. She goes into one of the rooms I haven't managed to shoot yet. When I try to go in, a cop stops me and his look says I can't enter. I know he's dying to insult me, but he knows I'm on the air and it could harm the police department's image in this city, so all he says is I can't go in. I manage to get shots of the woman picking up a bundle and holding it to her breast while endlessly repeating, "My love, my baby."

"What is that, Officer? Is it a baby?"

"This is a private moment, reporter, you have no right to be filming it."

"I have information rights." I lie by reflex, but I don't succeed in budging him. I try my luck with the girl who'd gone inside crying. "Can I help you in any way, miss?" Just then I realize that the bundle she'd picked up is all bloody. Various police officers and two paramedics try to take away the baby, at least I suppose that's what it is, but she doesn't want to let go of it. She fixes her hair and comes over to me. Hurry up, I think, the clock's running on your fifteen minutes.

"You're a reporter, aren't you?" My first instinct is to nod my head but I remember that it's an unpleasant motion for TV viewers, I'm not supposed to be anything but a verbal personality, and so I answer by saying yes.

"Someone stole my baby, and now I've found him but it looks like the cops hurt him, he's been shot in the leg." The lady cries harder and harder while a paramedic tells her that all she's doing is injuring the baby more. I get confused because someone's started to shout in my ear receiver. They want me to ask the girl her name. The paramedic grabs the baby. In my head, the program directors keep talking. "We couldn't have planned this better, this is drama, just wait till you get your check, the ratings are gonna add a lot of zeros to it."

The rest is routine. Interviews, facts, versions. The fate of the baby will be a different type of reporter's job and it'll keep the whole city excited all this afternoon and maybe into tomorrow morning, when some other reporter tapes fresher news.

When I leave the building my bike's no longer waiting for me, and I have to walk home. I live in a world without darkness. All day long there's an indicator light in my retina telling me my transmission status. I can turn the indicator level down, but even when I'm sleeping it keeps me company. A yellow light and a buzz, a murmur. They're who I sleep with. They're my immediate family. But my eyes belong to the world. My extended family spans an entire city, though no one would recognize me if they met me on the street.

I haven't gone out for a few weeks now. My last check frees me up from having to wander around looking for news. Privacy is a luxury for a man in my condition. Several times a day a yellow indicator goes on in my right eye and I hear a voice asking if I have anything, they have some dead time and it's been days since I transmitted anything. I simply don't answer. I close my eyes and remain quiet, hoping they'll understand that I'm not in the mood.

What do I do on my days off? Well, I try not to see anything interesting. I read magazines. I look at the window of my room. I count the squares on the living room floor. And I remember things that aren't recorded on tape, while my eyes stare at the ceiling, which is white—perhaps the least attractive color on a television screen.

• • •

The most common errors made by ocular reporters are due to the reflexes of their own bodies. A reporter must live under constant discipline so as to avoid seemingly involuntary reflexes. There is no greater sign of inexperience and lack of professional control than a reporter who closes his eyes in an explosion or a reporter who covers her face with her arms when startled by a noise.

• • •

Today is not a good day. I go walking the streets, and in every store I hear the same news. Constant Electrical Exposure Syndrome, CEES for fans of acronyms, seems to be wreaking havoc. Continuous stimulation of the nerve endings, caused by electricity and an environment that is constantly charged with electricity—radiation from monitors, microwaves, cell phones—seems to have a fatal effect on some people. I stop in front of a shop window and start recording a reporter with his back to a wall of TV screens: "It seems the central nervous system is so used to receiving external electronic stimulation that when it doesn't get it, it begins to produce it, constantly sending electric signals through the body that have no meaning or function, speeding up your heartbeat and making your lungs hyperventilate. Your eyes begin to blink and sometimes your tongue starts to jerk inside your mouth. Some witnesses even say that the victims of this syndrome can 'speak in tongues,' or that this syndrome 'is what causes this type of experience in various subjects.'" They insert shots of several people speaking in tongues here.

The reporter, looking serious and trying to get people's attention, keeps walking, while images of people who suffer from these symptoms appear on the video wall. The screens fill with shots of serious men with concerned faces. Interviews with experts, no doubt.

"No one knows for certain the exact nature of

the syndrome. The world scientific community is in a state of crisis. There are those who say this is just a rumor started by the media, it's simply another disease transformed into a media event. Some say the syndrome isn't as bad as it seems. But there are also those who believe that civilization has created a monster from which it will be difficult to escape."

The images on the monitors change. Various long shots of rustic houses, surrounded by trees. The music changes. Acoustic instruments, a flute and a guitar.

"However, there are already several electric detox centers out in the country. Rest homes devoid of electricity. This is perhaps the only possibility or hope for those who exhibit symptoms of the syndrome. As always, hope is the last thing to die in what is perhaps the most important 'artificial' disease of this century. There are those who say that what cancer was to the previous century, CEES will be to ours."

They show a few shots of these places. The patients look out the windows or at the walls, as if waiting for something they know will never arrive. As if waiting for civilization to keep a promise, yet aware that it never will, since the promise has long been forgotten.

The equipment for corporal transmission is very expensive. My father gave it to me. Well, he doesn't know what it was that he gave me. I just received an email on my eighteenth birthday saying that he had deposited who knows how much money into an account in my name, that I had to decide what to do with it and that after spending it I was on my own. That I shouldn't seek him out anymore.

I still keep that email on my hard drive. It's one of the advantages of the digital age. Memory becomes eternal and you can relive those moments as many times as you want. They remain frozen outside of you, and when you don't know who you are or where you come from, a few commands typed into your computer bring your past to the present. The problem is that when the past remains physically

alive in the present, when does the future get here? And why would you want it to?

The future is a constant repetition of what you've already lived; maybe some details can change, maybe the actors are different, but it's the same. And when you haven't lived it, surely you saw something similar in some movie, on some TV show, or you heard something like it in a song. I keep hoping my mom will return one day and tell me it was all a joke, that she never died. I keep hoping my father will keep his promise and come see me in the orphanage. I keep hoping my life will stop being this endless repetition of days that follow each other with nothing new to hope for.

I paid for part of my operation with the money. Legally, half the operation is paid for by the company that owns the rights to my transmissions. The doctors tried to talk me out of the implant, but I was already over sixteen, so I told them to just concentrate on doing their job. I needed to earn money and I knew perfectly well that luck and necessity are strange bedfellows. Three days later the nerve endings of my eyes and vocal cords were connected to a transmitter that could send the signal to the video channels.

That was the last time I heard from my father.

• • •

The most important detail that an ocular reporter must remember is to avoid monitors when transmitting live. If a reporter focuses on a monitor that is broadcasting what he is transmitting, his sense of balance will by harshly affected and he will begin to suffer from severe headache. Exposure to this type of situation is easily controlled by avoiding shots of monitors when transmitting live. It is important to note that the reflected transmissions "hook" the reporter, and there is a change in the stimuli that travel from the brain toward the different muscles of the body. For that reason it is sometimes almost impossible to break off visual contact with the monitor. The only way to prevent these "hooks" is through abrupt movement of the body or neck as soon as visual contact is made with the images one is transmitting. Latest research reveals that long periods of exposure to these virtual loops cause symptoms similar to those of CEES. This information was obtained from recent experiments and from the records of the Toynbee case.

• • •

The Toynbee case is a legend no one in my profession can ever forget. Some antimedia extremists kidnapped a reporter and blindfolded him so that he couldn't transmit anything. Every two hours they broadcast their opinions to a nation that watched, entertained: *"The media are the cause of the moral decay of our society, the media are causing the extinction of individuality, thousands of mental conditions stem from the fact that human beings can only learn about reality through the media, the information is manipulated."* The whole ideological spiel, just like on one of those flyers they hand out in the streets. It's ironic to think that those extremists may be the only ones who'll survive if an epidemic like CEES wipes out humanity. They always try to avoid electricity. I don't know what I prefer, to keep hoping that this reality miraculously gets better or that some stupid extremists take over the world and impose the rules of "their" reality. The only thing you can learn from human history is that there's nothing more dangerous than a utopia.

So, as an example and metaphor of their complaints, they tied up the reporter, who worked under the name Toynbee, and put him in front of a monitor. They immobilized his head and connected his retina to the monitor. I've seen those images a thousand times. The only thing the reporter's eyes see is a monitor within a monitor within a monitor, until infinity seems to be a video camera filming a monitor that's broadcasting what it's recording, and there's no beginning, no end, there's nothing, until you remember that a human being is watching this, it's the only thing he can see and it's giving him

an unbearable headache, as if someone were crisscrossing his skull with cables and wires. The images weren't enough.

For those who know what it feels like to get hooked, the images were painful, but for those who'd never felt that kind of feedback they were frankly boring. The extremists—conscious that they were putting on a show and that before they'd be able to broadcast ideas they had to entertain the world—set up a video camera to tape Toynbee's face, and sent the signal to the same transmission station the reporter was connected to. At the station they knew there was nothing they could do to help Toynbee, since he was connected directly to the monitor, and they began to transmit both things: the monitors reproducing themselves until infinity, and Toynbee's face. The station executives say they would've cut the broadcast if they'd've had doubts about the source of the hook, but everyone knows that's not true. Ratings are ratings.

Watching that reporter's face is quite a show. First, a few facial muscles start to move, as if he had a tic. At first he tried to move his eyes, to look to either side, but right next to the monitor was the tripod with the camera taping his face. And so on one half of the screen you could see how the loop was broken: all you saw was the partial view of a TV set, showing the image of a video camera on the right side of the screen and the real video camera on the other side, as if reality didn't have depth, only breadth. As if reality repeated itself endlessly off to the right and left. But the hook was stronger than his willpower, and gradually the reporter stopped trying to look off to the side. Sometimes the monitor showed how he tried. A very slow pan to the right or left that slowly came back again, as if the muscles of his eyes had no strength left. Toynbee began to sweat. His face began to convulse more violently, each time sweating bigger drops that struggled against gravity until, just like the reporter's eyes, they gave up and slid rapidly down his convulsing face. Each drop followed a different path. His face, lit up by the monitor, seemed to be full of thousands of monitors, since his damp skin also reflected, in distortion, the monitor he was looking at. The muscle spasms were getting stronger, and just as the sweat deformed the monitor, each convulsion moved the reporter's face one step further away from what we know as human. There were no longer moments when you could see normality in his face. Everything was movement and water and eyes that looked out feverishly, desperately.

Sometimes, when I recall the images, the eyes even seem to be concentrating, as if they were discovering a secret that not only makes you lose your mind but causes your body to react violently, because it's something that human beings shouldn't be allowed to see.

A few minutes later his eyes seemed to lose all focus, even though they kept on receiving and transmitting light. His eyes were vacant, just like the monitors. I've always liked to think that at that moment the only thing the reporter could see was a kitschy image of his past, I dunno, the birthday party his mom threw him, or some day when he was in a play, or his first kiss or some other idiocy of the kind that always makes us happy. There was no more willpower left in his eyes, but his eyelids were being forced open, so his body and the ghosts that occupied his body were still functioning. Several of his facial muscles atrophied and stopped working, which made the movements of his face even less natural. The shot continued until his face had no expression left, just spasms and movement, expressions that went beyond the range of human emotions, possibilities that ceased to have meaning the moment they disappeared.

Until his heart exploded.

Sometimes, when I'm bored and on the bus returning to my apartment, I begin to record everything I see. But then I stop seeing and just let the machines do their work. I go into a sort of trance in which my eyes, though open, observe nothing; and yet when I get home I have a record of everything they saw. As if it wasn't me who saw it all.

When I watch what I taped I don't recognize myself. I relive everything I saw without remem-

bering anything. At those times it's my feelings that're on standby.

Some truths become evident when reality is observed this way.

The poor are the only ones who are ugly. The poor, and teenagers. Everyone with a little money has already changed his or her face and now has a better-looking one, has already made his face or her identity more fashionable. Teenagers aren't allowed this type of operation because their bone structure is still changing. That's how you can tell economic status or age, by checking out the quality of the surgical work on people's faces. We live in an age when everyone, everyone who's well off in this world, is perfect. Perfect body, perfect face, and looks that speak of success, of optimism, as if the mind were perfect, too, and could only think correct thoughts. Today, ugliness is a problem that humanity seems to have left behind. Today, as always, humanity's problems are solved with good credit.

Sometimes I like to think about the scene of my suicide. One of my choices is to connect the electric camera terminals I have in my eyes to an electric generator in order to raise the voltage little by little, until my brain or my eyes or the camera explodes. It thrills me to think of the images I'd get.

Or I could prepare something cruder. Take a knife and cut out my eye. Cut it out by the roots. Sometimes I think I'd prefer not to see anything, I'd prefer a world in shades of black. Get rid of my eyes. Even if they sued me, even if I had to spend the rest of my life rotting away in jail.

And while I decide, I sit alone at home, waiting. Waiting for a promise to be kept . . .

• • •

Today I woke up with the urge to go out into the street and find something interesting. I've been walking around for a couple hours without any destination. It's a nice day. I hear shouts at the end of the street and take off running in that direction. A drug store. I press the button and my indicator light changes from yellow to green. I stop a few meters from the entrance and file a report. "Shouts in a drug store, I don't know what's going on, I'm going to find out." I take the time needed to establish the scene and slowly start to approach. A lot of people are leaving the drug store, running. The story of my life. Wherever no one wants to be, there goes me.

It's hard to get inside. I try to shoot several of the faces of the people stampeding each other to get out. Desperate faces. Scared faces. The red light goes on. "I'm at a drug store, the people are trying frantically to get out. I haven't heard any shots." I have to shove several people aside until I can get through the door, and I head toward the place everyone's leaving. "Seems to be someone lying on the ground." A bunch of people wearing uniforms surround him. Probably the store employees. I stop a moment to establish the shot. I stop an employee who wants to get outside and look him in the eyes. He's so scared he doesn't even realize I'm transmitting.

"What's going on?"

"The guy was standing there, taking something off the shelves, when suddenly he collapses and starts to shake. He's infected . . ." The guy pushes me and jars my shot. Shit. I approach the body; there's an ever-widening circle around him. I pass these people and get a full-body shot of the guy, on the floor having convulsions. He's swallowing his tongue. I approach and get down close to him. He looks at me desperately when his head's not jerking around.

Toynbee. He has the same facial features. "This man was shopping in the drug store when he suffered a seizure." The guy turns to look at me, realizes there's a red light burning in my retina, and begins to laugh. His laughter starts to mix with his convulsions and before long you can't distinguish his laughter from his pain. I try to hold him in my arms, I try to touch him to calm him down, but it has no effect. I see a red light in his left eye. He's transmitting. I let go of him and his head hits the floor hard. Out of nowhere, he seems to be drowning. He shud-

ders twice and remains quiet, looking at me. In my head I hear, "Say something, say something about CEES, *talk*, shit it's your job."

The reporter is motionless. The camera in my eyes records a tiny red dot that remains alive in his. Today my face will probably appear on the monitors.

Two days later my news is no longer news. It seems like every day more attacks of the syndrome are reported. Forty percent of the victims are reporters. I remember AIDS and the homophobia it awoke. Seems like it's us reporters' turn to live in fear, not just of dying, but of the fear of others. Mediaphobia? What will they name this effect?

The common citizen (and believe me, they're all common) still doesn't understand that the syndrome isn't transmitted by bodily contact. Everyone runs away when they see someone falling apart in a fit of convulsions. They still don't get it that the body is no longer the important factor. They live under the illusion that if they touch a victim they'll get infected. It's like a phantom virus that can't be located, it's in the air, in the street, it's wherever you go but in reality it doesn't exist. It's a virtual virus. And it's a sickness we're exposed to by living in this world. It's the sickness of the media, of cheap entertainment, it's the sickness of civilization. It's our penance for the sin of bad taste.

• • •

For all reporters who transmit live, control is the principal weapon against the reflex stimulation caused by the indicator light. The viewer can only see through the reporter's eyes once the red light in the retina goes on. All movement, all action on the reporter's part, should be perfectly planned. There must be no mistakes. Frontal shots are best. It is always necessary to take face shots of the subject, by means of the camera connected to the nerve endings of the eye, in order to establish identification between the subject and the viewer. The reporter functions as a medium, to call it something. He / She is merely the point of contact between the action and the reaction that thousands of viewers will have in their homes. The reporter must be there, without being there. Exist without being noticed. This is the art of communication.

• • •

The opening sequence of the program that I usually transmit on goes like this: all the shots are washed out as if they were done in some familiar, old-fashioned style, as if they didn't have the necessary transmission quality, that being the excuse for washing them in gray tones that'll later change to reds. First there's a subjective shot of a stomach operation; then the doctors turn and talk to the camera, and the whole world learns that the camera is the face of the person being operated on. Then there's an action sequence of a shoot-out downtown, till one of the people firing turns and sees the camera and presses the trigger; the camera shot jolts and seems to fall to the ground. Everything starts to flood, a red liquid's filling up the lens. The pace starts to pick up. A shot from the point of view of a driver who crashes into a school bus. A worm's-eye view of a guy throwing himself off a building (I've always thought he looks like a high-diver). The sacrifice of a cow in a slaughterhouse. The assassination of a politician. An industrial accident where some guy loses an arm. Shots of explosions where even the reporter gets blown up. A skyjacking where the terrorist shoots a passenger in the head. And so on. The images go by faster and faster until you can hardly make out what's going on, all you see is motion and blood and more motion, shapes that don't seem to have any human reference anymore, until it all begins to acquire a bit of order and you start to see red, yellow, and gray lines that dance about rapidly and leave the retinal impression of a circle in the middle of the screen where the lines meet. An explosion stops the sequence, and inside the circle the program's logo is formed: Digital Red.

Welcome to pop entertainment in the early twenty-first century.

What will I be doing in twenty years? Will I keep walking the streets looking for news to transmit? Not a very pleasant future. Belonging to the entertainment industry gives off an existential stink. Some still call it journalism, though everyone knows the news isn't there to inform, but to entertain. My eyes make me commune with the masses. Thousands of people see through my eyes so they can feel that their lives are more real, that their lives aren't as putrid and worm-eaten as the lives of the people I see. I'm the social glove they put on in order to confront reality. I'm the one who gets dirty, and I prevent their lives from smelling rotten. I'm a vulture who uses the misfortunes of others to survive.

When you get up close to a mirror you can't see both your eyes at the same time. You can see either the right or the left. The closer you get to your image the more distorted it gets and you can only see yourself partially. The same thing happens with a monitor. You're not there. You're the unknown one who moves in a way you don't recognize as your own. Who speaks with a voice that doesn't sound like yours. Who has a body that doesn't correspond to your idea of it. You're a stranger. To see yourself on a monitor is to realize how much you don't know about yourself and how much that upsets you.

If I wanted a more dramatic effect I could get myself hooked, like Toynbee. Connect myself directly to a monitor and start to transmit. See how reality is made up of ever-smaller monitors (and no matter how hard you try, you can't find anything inside those screens, just another monitor with nothing inside) and go crazy when I realize that's the meaning of life. Totally forget about control over my body.

Allow my eyes to bleed.

• • •

The transmission time of an ocular reporter is the property of the company that finances his/her operation. Clause 28 of the standard contract establishes that six hours of every reporter's day are property of said company.

• • •

A terrorist attack in a department store. I hate department stores. Almost all of 'em are festooned with monitors that randomly change channels. It's easy to get hooked. You have to be careful. The police are just arriving on the scene. I'm about to transmit but decide not to tell central programming. As always, I look for an emergency exit. A manager is trying to take merchandise away from customers who are taking advantage of the situation to save a few pesos. The manager is so busy that he doesn't even realize when I push him. He falls and a bunch of people quickly run out with the stuff they're stealing. A little old lady of around sixty carries a red dress in her hands and smiles pleasantly when she leaves. I enter the store and hide behind the clothes racks. I get up to the third floor via the emergency stairs, which are empty. I don't know if the terrorists are here inside or if they simply left everything in the hands of a bomb. I avoid several of the private security guards hired to guard the store, not wanting them to see me yet. One of them comes upon a shoplifter, and he and his partner kick the hell out of him on the ground. The guy's bleeding and crying. Everyone tries to take advantage of an emergency situation. The two security guards go away, leaving the customer lying there on the floor. Blessed be capitalism. I move on to the candy department, and the smell makes me dizzy. I've never understood how they keep the flies away from the exposed candied fruit. I hear some voices and hide. I begin to hear a buzzing sound and I gently tap my head. But the sound's not coming from there. The hum is coming from my right. I crawl until I get to a box, which I open cautiously. Inside is a sophisticated device with a clock in countdown mode, rapidly approaching zero. I have a little more than a minute, so I take off running. I forget about transmitting or anything else. When I feel I'm far enough away I turn around and press a button; it's green. I see the two security guards approaching the candy section. I quickly turn my head. I'm about to

shout at them to get away when I hear a voice in my ear. "Where the fuck are you? Straighten out the shot, show us something we can broadcast. Are you in the store?" I slowly correct the shot, steadying my head in a slow pan while I notice the red indicator light switch on in my eyes. I manage to spot the two security guards in the candy section. I force myself not to blink, and the bomb explodes. The fire is so hot and the colors so spectacular that for the first time in a long while I forget about the red light that lives in my head. I miscalculated. The force of the explosion lifts me up and I fly several meters through the air. I'm not a body, I'm a machine flying through the air, whose only purpose is to record and record and record so that the whole world can see what they wouldn't want to live. The clothes burn, the display shelves fall apart, thousands of objects go flying. Some hit me but I try to keep the shot as steady as I can. All in the name of entertainment.

I slam against a wall and try to keep my head up so I can tape the fire.

For the first time I feel at home in a department store. Everything is flames, everything is ashes. The stylish dresses feed the fire, the perfumes make it grow. The spectacle is unparalleled. Civilization destroying itself. I'm in a department store, one of civilization's most glorious achievements. I see a sign that's beginning to burn; it says, "Happy Father's Day." Promises, promises . . .

I get up and my whole body hurts. I walk toward the exit. A voice in my head is shouting, "Where the fuck do you think you're going? I need fixed shots, I need you to talk; tell the world about your experience. Don't be a jerk, you don't film an explosion every day! Where do you think you're going?"

And it doesn't stop until I'm three blocks from the attack.

Today I crossed a line. I don't know and I don't care if I killed the security guards. It's one thing to report on stuff that happens and another thing to make what happens more spectacular.

What were the security guards? They were

graphic elements to liven up my shots. They were mimetic elements that the audience would be able to identify with. They were dramatic elements to make the story I had to tell more interesting. They were scenery.

Today I crossed a line and I don't want to think about anything. My whole body aches.

Situations like these make me think about the urgency of my suicide. At least that way I could decide something, and not just let destiny take the lead. Suicide is the most elaborately constructed act of the human will, it's taking control of your destiny out of the hands of the world.

· · ·

Yesterday I was organizing a bunch of my tapes. I found a program about my old-time heroes, the experiential reporters. "Crazies," as the foreign media call them. I pressed the play button and sat down to watch them. There are some pretty stupid people in this world, like the reporter who, after getting himself thrown in jail, started to insult the cops so that they'd beat him. He taped everything. The shots are especially successful because half the time he's on the floor trying to make visual contact with the faces of the cops who are pounding on him. Some people consider him a hero. But whenever you see the disfigured faces of the police who are beating him up you can't help thinking how ridiculous the situation is. The reporter is there because he chose to be there. Good job, amigo, improve the ratings of your company. I also watched the famous operation on Grayx's head, one of the martyrs of entertainment. The reporter, trying to make a commentary on the depersonalization of the body, agreed to subject himself to surgery in which they'd remove his head and connect it to his body by way of special high tech cables. The guy outdid himself, narrating his whole operation, describing what he was feeling while they connected his head to his body with cables that allowed him to be five meters away from his head. This is probably one of the most important moments of this century. When the opera-

tion's over you can see a subjective shot of the body on the operating table as Grayx tells it to stand up. The body gets up and begins to stumble, because the head that's sending it instructions sees things from a strange perspective. The body slowly approaches the head, picks it up and turns it around so that the eyes (and the camera) can look in the direction it's walking in, and at that point the viewer no longer knows who's giving the instructions, the body or the head. The body takes the head in its arms like a baby and stands in front of a mirror where you can see a decapitated body holding its head in its arms. The head doesn't seem to be very comfortable because it's a bit tilted, he didn't have enough coordination to hold it straight so all these shots lack horizontal stability. Grayx is talking about the feeling of disorientation, about the possibilities that the surgery opens up, about what would happen if instead of cables they used remote control, about how marvelous the modern world is, while his arms try to hold his head straight and he keeps looking back, his face twisted with the effort of trying to make his body do what he says, all the while failing to control it.

This program always brings me odd memories. I had sex for the first time after watching it with a girlfriend from high school. We were at her house watching the broadcast. No one was around. I don't know how many people might've had sex after the inauguration of the first lunar colony or when they broadcast the assassination of Khadiff, the Muslim terrorist leader, or at any other key moment in the televised history of our century, but I can tell you that it's an unforgettable experience. Watching a man with his body separated from his head on the same day that you become aware of how your body can unite with another body and become one is something you don't easily forget. Every time I watch it I have pleasant memories.

Now Grayx is in a mental institution. Seems the technology that he was helping to develop causes mental instability. Apparently people need corporal unity in order to remain sane. Grayx lost contact with reality, and they say he now lives in an imaginary world. He had so much money that he built a virtual environment and connected it to his retina, and that's the only thing that keeps him alive.

I haven't felt good ever since the explosion. I have strong pains in the pit of my stomach. Yesterday I told them to deposit the check into my account. Seems I won't be having any trouble over the security guards. To create news with your own body, like the crazies do, is perfectly legal, but make news at the expense of other people's rights and you can wind up spending the rest of your life in jail.

I go to the bathroom and start to pee. I look down and see that the water and my urine are full of blood. I start to hear voices just as a green light goes on in my retina.

"If I were you I'd go straight to a doctor. That red color in your piss doesn't look healthy at all."

"Leave me alone."

"I can't, you've gone two days without doing a single thing. You already know how it is with contracts. Besides, don't be ungrateful. I was only calling to tell you your check's been deposited. Maybe when you see your pay your mood'll improve. The ratings were really spectacular."

• • •

I've gone down into the sewers of the city a number of times trying to prove one of the oldest urban legends. Thousands of rumors say there are human communities in the deepest parts of the network of underground pipes. A lot of people believe they're freaks, mutants, that their eyelids permanently cover their eyes and their skin is so white they can't tolerate the sun or even the flashlights that everyone who goes down to look for them uses. A new race, grown out of our garbage.

A society that doesn't rely on its eyes, that doesn't have to look at itself for self-recognition. Their behavior must be weird. They'd have to touch one another, they'd have to listen to one another. They wouldn't have to look like any-

thing or anyone. A different world, different creatures.

Every time I descend on one of my exploratory trips I use my infrared glasses and carry very low-intensity lights. I've gone down more than ten times and not once have I found anything. No mutants, no freaks, no subterranean race offering something new to humanity, something different from what's shown on TV.

It's just me down there.

Last night my right arm began to convulse. I couldn't do anything to stop it. My fingers opened and closed as if they were trying to grab something, to hold on to something.

Maybe I'd prefer a less sensational exit. Get a tank of gas, seal off a room, and fall asleep . . .

• • •

It is impossible for human beings to avoid blinking, but it is possible to prolong the period of time between one blink and the next. Reporters should do exercises to achieve this control. Furthermore, the operation on their eyes is designed to stimulate the tear ducts so that the eyes do not dry out so easily, and thus reporters can keep their eyes open longer than the ordinary individual.

When muscle movement in the eyelids is detected, special sensors in the eye "engrave" the last image that the eye has seen, and when the eyelid then closes this image is the one which is transmitted. When the eyelid raises, taping continues. This necessary error in the workings of the human body has caused microseconds of memorable moments in the history of live TV to be lost forever.

• • •

A more spectacular piece of news, a riskier stunt. They always want something more. More drama, more emotion, more people sobbing before the cameras, before my eyes. I don't want to think, I'm not made to think, just to transmit. But with every transmission I feel I'm losing something I won't ever recover. The only thing I hear in my head is *more, more, more.*

I could also take everything I feel some attachment for, fill a small bag, find a sewer drain and head down it, but this time without any lights. I'd wander around for entire days, I'd have to start eating rats and insects and drinking sewer water. Maybe I'd spend the rest of my life walking among the tunnels that form a labyrinth under this city, but at least I'd be searching for something. Or maybe I would find a new civilization. Even if they didn't accept me, even if they were to kill me for bringing in outside influences, it'd be comforting to know that there are choices in this world. That there's someone who has possibilities the rest of us lost centuries ago. Or maybe they would accept me, and I could live for years and years without having to worry, doing manual labor and finding a new routine to my life. To be what I think I can be and not what I am.

Maybe, maybe . . .

• • •

These are the voices in my head:

"There's a fire, don't you wanna go check it out? Fires and ratings go hand in hand."

"Armed robbery, a black car with no license plates, model unknown, get some shots."

"This is good, a lovers' quarrel, she was making a cake and she destroyed his face with a mixer. The boyfriend, a little miffed, decided he was going to stick *her* in the oven instead of the cake. The neighbors called it in, but it didn't turn into anything big. Good stuff for a comedy."

"You wanna talk? The night's slow and I ain't got nothin' to do, they're broadcasting games from last season."

"Another family suicide. In the subway, a mother with her three kids."

And so on, continually.

The whole world is on TV. Anyone can be a star. Everyone acts, and every day they prepare themselves because today could be the day that a camera finds them and the whole world discovers how nice, good-looking, friendly, attractive, desirable, interesting, sensitive, and natural they are. How human they are. And all day long everyone sees tons of people on-screen trying to be like that, so people decide to copy them. And they create imitators. And life just consists of trying to seem like somebody who was imitating somebody else. Everyone lives every day as if they were on a TV show. Nothing's real anymore. Everything exists to be seen, and everything that we'll see is a repeat of what we've seen before. We're trapped in a present that doesn't exist. And if the transmitted don't exist, what about those of us who do the transmitting? We're objects, we're disposable. For every reporter who dies on the job or who dies of CEES, there are two or three stupid kids who think that's the only way of finding anything real, of living something exciting. And everything starts all over again.

I always try not to chat with the program directors. Normally they're a bunch of idiots. Their work is easy and they use us like remote control cameras. Normally I don't even ask them their names. There's no point. Who wants to know more people? Ain't nothing new under the sun. Everything's a repeat, everything's a copy.

There's only one program director who knows me a little more intimately. His nickname's Rud, I don't know his real name. I met him (well, I listened to him) when I was drinking, that is, when I was trying to get so drunk I wouldn't have to think, wouldn't have to want anything. I wanted the alcohol to fill me so that I wouldn't have to make decisions, so that whatever decision I made would be the alcohol's fault, not mine. "I was drunk."

I sure do miss alcohol.

Alcohol and my profession are not good friends. In my body I have equipment that belongs to a corporation, so they can sue me if I willingly damage the machinery. Besides, it's not unusual for program directors to tape your drinking sprees and then use them to blackmail you. Some even put them on the air. Once they broadcast two guys who were beating me up 'cause I'd insulted them. I remember thinking that the only good thing about it was that my face wouldn't be shown on the air, they could transmit everything I did but no one would see me, no one could recognize me. Anonymity is a double-edged sword.

Rud calls me "The Cynic" because he doesn't know my name either. It's easier to talk with someone that way. You avoid problems, as well as commitments. Well, it turns out he'd listened to one of my booze-induced rants. He listened to me patiently all night long, complaining, crying, laughing. I walked over five kilometers. The only thing I did was stop at liquor stores and buy another bottle. I wanted to forget everything, so each time I got a different type of booze. I don't even want to remember all the stupid things I said. Anyone with a little sense of humor would call that night "Ode to Dad" because I spent the whole time talking about him. There was even a stretch when I asked Rud to pretend to be my father and I accused him of stuff, I shouted at him and spit at him. My father was inside my head. At one point I started to beat my head against a wall. I don't have any real memories of that. Turns out Rud recognized the street I was on and called the paramedics to come take me home. They had to put eight stitches in my forehead. Not even modern surgical techniques let me get off without a scar.

· · ·

Five days later I got a package with no return address, just a card that said, "Greetings, Rud." Inside was the bill from the paramedics. There was also a videocassette. Rud had taped my whole binge.

Sometimes, when I'm in the mood to drink, I play the videotape and cry a bit. That way there's no chance I can deceive myself, everything is recorded, I can't lie. It's no illusion, it's me. Sometimes, but not always, I manage to feel better after watching it.

I'd like to go up to the top of the building where I shot my first transmission. I'd set up two external cameras, one with a long shot, the other with a medium-range shot. I'd get close to the edge of the building, turning my back to the street so that the shots would be frontal, and I'd press the button in my thigh. Someone would criticize me for thinking that rooftop terraces were news, until they received the signals from the other cameras and realized what I was about to do.

Suddenly, a red light would illuminate my gaze. I would think about various things. I would want my father to be able to see this, but it wouldn't matter, a lot of people would see it from the comfort of their homes. It's the same thing. I'm everyone's son.

I would clear my throat to say something live with the broadcast, but I'd remain silent.

What more can one say? What could I say that someone before me hasn't already said better?

I would look at the cameras and then up at the sky, where they say that gods who loosed plagues onto humanity once lived. In the sky I would find nothing.

The wind would begin to blow and my hair would get in the way of the camera in my eyes.

I would take one step backward and begin to fall.

And maybe, just maybe, I would forget about the buzzing sound for once.

STEVE BEARD

RETOXICITY

(1998)

THE HWANG FAMILY forgot to pay off the Corporation's drug cops and I barely escaped with my life. It's being written up as a jurisdictional dispute on the London datanets. Just one of those things, accidents will happen, etc. You know the score.

They're withholding casualty lists at St. Thomas's Hospital. Most of the victims had no ID. Lost in the digital jungle. So they don't really count in any final census, capisce?

It was a bad night if all you wanted to do was load up on rocks and dance. But then that's been the case for a long time in England. It seems that there are bigger stories to rack up on UBC Global. Like which of the warring factions from some damaged European bloodline is going to be running things out of the Palace of Westminster. Or how the Chamber of London lost a pile on the futures market.

Real small-time stuff. No room, you see, for the big picture, for the nightly sacrifices, which keep the whole machinery of power sparking.

Which is the reason why I cut loose down in South London with my CAMnet. Now I had a choice, here. I could have dropped into any of the pleasure dumps which ghost the industrial leys of the South Bank—Crucifix Lane, Clink Street, Timworth Street, Goding Street, Bondway, Nine Elms Lane. But my contacts in Kyoto tell me that Battersea Park Road is where the furnaces of ecstasy are really *stoked*.

Drop-off at Bat Hat at eleven in the p.m. Like Westminster, an old island in the Thames. Unlike that old crowning ground—and far distant from the corporate temples and occult quadrangles of the City of London—Battersea and the South Bank have always been where the effluent of empire has been discharged.

Take a core sample from its deep and teeming sediment. Run back through paper switching centers and refuse tips to electrical generators, gasometers, and railway yards to lime kilns, chemical works, and windmills. Go back further to the farms and the markets and the timbered marshlands. Track all the way back . . . and the legacy of quarantined populations and slum landlords persists like a dark stain.

Now one thing I do know is you have to take your pleasures where you can find them. And always on the South Bank, deposited in the shells of each receding layer of industry, have been the factories of joy.

Blue lasers cutting up the night sky, traffic and commotion, the drums of London like an underground tattoo. The party was on tonight just like it has been every night since the end of the millennium. Some people just didn't know when to stop. They were drawn in their thousands from all over London—the barricaded wastes of Brixton and Stockwell, the low-rise estates of Whitechapel, Plaistow, and Bow, the pavements of Fulham and the tenements of the Holloway Road. The old power station crouching on the Thames was like a beacon reeling them in with its promise of solace, adventure, and sex.

But some of us have a job to do. I've been to the melt fields of São Paulo and the war zones of Třeboň. I've seen it all before.

Drifting through the shanty town crammed up against the eaves of the sheltering ruin, home to a blinkered population of the nomadic, the exiled, and the lost. Shaved heads, laser eyes, whiplash antennae poking out of the industrial moraine. The graft of the homeless is the same the world over. Sheets of polythene, sporting colors, recycled tech. The only difference here is that the debris is plush. You remember your Jaguars, your Mercs, and your BMWs? Burned-out skeletons for improvised dwellings, dressed with the gaudy remnants—chipped tiles, metal railings, stripped marble—of an abandoned Twentieth Century past.

You see what I see? Realtime video eye flashing red, CCD witness tech catching it all.

Take a look at what's left of the cathedral once built by the London Power Company in Battersea. Crumbling brick facade, exposed joints of steel lashed with neoprene and plastic, internal armature of generators, turntables, and lights.

Only the four ribbed chimneys of reinforced concrete—towering over the shambles like a paired brace of dead rockets—still marking the skyline with a Promethean glower.

Bat Hat is what the South London homies call it. For them, it's a quarry of renewable resources and a temple of carnal delights. That was why I was here. For its absentee landlords, it's something different. The Hwang family overlook this distant riverside patch from their revolving satellite watch with the same lazily speculative eye they reserve for the rest of the slum properties shuffled to the back of their global investment portfolio. Looking at the last set of Hwang accounts filed in HK, I can see that they've done to Battersea in London what they've done to similar underperforming land assets in Bombay, St. Petersburg, and Kuala Lumpur. Contracted out management of the place to a local strand of the family, paid off the native chieftains, patched in their drug connections, and tried to make a quick buck in the interval before the market picks up.

The Soho end of the Hwang mob had things sorted down here. Or at least that's what they thought. Dance events seven nights of the week, rock franchise, the Met turning a blind eye to the contravention of health and safety regs in return for a cut of the action, the Brixton Yardies pacified. They'd really carved out a space for themselves. Pity they weren't paying attention to the war going on between the Crown of England and the Corporation of London north of the Thames. A lot of people would pay for that omission with their lives.

But it didn't feel that way when I was there. It felt like there was an event. Cabs and rickshaws running up and down the Battersea Park Road. Roisterers and carousers streaming into the pleasure ground dressed in industrial face masks, skin-tight Versace, and luminous Caterpillar boots. Smoked-glass limos trailing through the throng into the underground car parks. The party kicking off right there in the squatlands outside the dancehall. You see what I see? Drug peddlers togged up in Replay and Chevignon shouting their wares ("Trips! Rocks! You sorted?"). Indian chai ladies sitting on rush mats selling tea, cigarettes, and naan. TiNi datasuit vendors and pirate CD-ROM merchants blocking the path. Paramedics setting up emergency field tents. The Met boys nowhere to be seen.

It was a special evening. That much I did know. A date reserved for a fire festival in the local pagan calendar. November Fifth. The Hwang family had rented out space on the outside of the building to the usual motley crew of water companies, drug distributors, and record labels. The logos of Thames Valley Water, GlaxoWellcome, TDK, and Sony burning their way into the distressed brickwork like projected core memories. Nothing new there.

What was distinctive was the string of artcore messages popping up in between the shuttle of ads like subliminal reminders of a utopian past. Local VJs pumping out wish images of the Westminster mob in jeopardy. Burnings, hangings, and shootings wrapped around kitsch patriotic footage of the old queen at play. Well, she was dead anyway. So what did it matter? Plenty, as it turned out.

Rolling up to the massive ornamental gates at the entrance to the dancehall. Shakedown at the door. T'ai chi goons puffed up in Antarctic camo and pink Oakley shades—with an underarm flash of gunmetal gray—exuding an aura of cool. Weapons check, digicash card swipe, an extra tax for the CAMnet. It's all over and I'm in.

So you want to know what's happening in London?

"Wicked and wicked and wicked and rough!"

Hidden speakers punch out a slew of garbled syllables. Ranting DJ boxed up on one of the dance floors beyond my immediate gaze. I'm losing my footing. Edges of darkness, shafts of light. Slammed against a press of bodies on the threshold of the building. CCD video eye blinded. Vaporized bass rocks the foundations and I'm caught in a hurtling backwash of sound.

"Yes, yes, yes, yes, London Town."

A volley of drums slams through my body like a digital pulsar and I stumble.

This was going to be tough.

Time to reorientate. I pull down the blueprints of Messrs C. S. Allot & Son, engineers of Manchester from the days when the Ukrainians knew how to build suspension bridges, railways, and dams. Checking east, checking west, checking east again. I've got two sets of Boiler Houses, two sets of Turbine Halls, and two sets of Switch Rooms either side of the door. I'm looking for the Control Room above the Turbine Hall on the west side so flip back to realtime and head left. I don't know where I'm going. The attempt to navigate from old maps is senseless, the internal architecture has changed so much.

Time to surrender to the flow of the crowd. See how I'm dragged through a labyrinthine warren of improvised dance floors rigged up from cannibalized industrial plant and recycled techno-organic fibers. Flashing on stainless-steel banisters, Worcestershire brick, dead electricity cables, sheets of Kevlar and PVC, aluminum spars, and neoprene sails.

Losing it. Sample a quicktime CAMnet image from one of the floors. DJ erected high on a podium, chocked up in metal platelet jacket with a gold sleeper in his nostril and a ring of bone in his lobe. Two thousand dancers at his feet dressed in feathers, jewels, and luminous threads working the drift of his hands over the decks in an open feedback loop. Dizzying sweep of overhead gantries, rotting stairwells, and drop-dead shafts of light. The void filled with seething bass turbulence, euphoric speed-kill drum loops, and sampled shreds of London slang. "Buss off your head and set you on fire!" Panic images of fear and flight—Lockheed F-117s, trance bucks, aerospace salamanders, windowless UAVs—racing over the screens above the DJ's head.

Calibrating. Resisting the siren call of the rock vendors and the champagne hawkers—later!—I twist and turn my way through a maze of black corridors before catching the logo over the lintel of the old Control Room. TEMPLE OV ISIS picked out in holo red with the eye of Horus flashing alongside. I slide through the soundproofed airlock rigged up beneath the sign and step into an intense cabin of flailing limbs, throttling bass, and whiplash drums.

The acrid smell of burning rock hits my nostrils. There are huddled packs of dancers refueling at the margins of the dance floor from delicately wrought Turkish pipes. Jets of flame spurt high into the air from hidden butane gas canisters. The stars are visible through the broken roof above.

CAMnet casting around the room. Totemic images and graffiti tags are visible on the touch screens embedded in the skirtings of Belgian black marble which still line the walls. Hobo signs, website numbers, strings of alphanumeric code. Dog-headed astronauts, Blakean angels, cartouched Mayan glyphs. An inverted image of Bat Hat folding its legs beneath it like an insect about to unsheathe its wings. Planets, star signs, computers. An aerosol portrait of Isis at the prow of an aerodynamic barge with a handmaiden attending her on either side. Raw data for my colleagues at Kyoto. Enough to keep them busy for a year.

"Here's to all the liberty-takers, the nutters, and the ravers. Taking it to the other side."

This is what I've traveled three continents and multiple time zones to witness. The orgiastic cult of Isis at its peak, a chiliastic dance craze whose seismic fallout has been rocking the planet's datanets for the last year. Three decades of aggravation, pressure, and intimidation falling down from the north of the Thames has led the natives of London to revolt in the only way they know how. You've heard about it. They've invented a homegrown cargo cult from the trash washed up on the shores of empire, a hybrid Santeria fusing elements from ancient American and African myth, Haitian voodoo rites, interplanetary fantasies, and occult techno-science. They want to do more than stake a claim for themselves in the evacuated wastelands of London. They're going further. They want to *disappear*.

One of them made it, too. But you'll never believe it will you? My CAMnet was confiscated by the Corporation of London goons before I had a chance to file the event. But there's always the evidence of my own eyes. Sitting here pressing the keys in a rented room in Vauxhall. I can hardly believe it myself. But it happened. There's nothing more I can say.

The thing about the ISIS posse was . . . they really thought they could make it to another world with only rock, the gods of London, and a DAT archive of snarling drum loops to send them on their way. They had it all figured out. Sirius C was the destination, the missing planet in the constellation of the Great Dog (source: the tribal mythos of the Dogon in Mali); Isis the presiding deity of teleportation, old Portmaster demon from the banks of the Thames (source: local mythology); and 2012 the deadline, the year when the cosmic switches would be hit and a new planetary kiva would come online (source: the trans-millennial calendar of the Mayans).

The Temple ov Isis had kicked off at the start of the year. It was still going eleven months later. The celebrants were running out of time. I was witness to the ecstatic ravings of a para-millennial cult which was approaching endtime with no release in sight. The dancers—kitted out in transparent TiNi datasuits, VR shades, and tribal markings—had been putting out a call to Isis for the last year in an attempt to escape the bonds of gravity and take flight through the electronic ether. Their mission was to transform the archaic ruins of Bat Hat into an interplanetary craft which would arc high over the degraded landscape of London and find the wormhole which connected with Sirius C. Who says they weren't going to do it? Everyone, of course. Luckily your faithful correspondent has more of an open mind. Someone had to.

Two hundred London natives snaking their hips from side to side as their hands flip up and down and their feet weave intricate geometric patterns in the floor. Their separate bodies—exhibiting signs of sexual arousal through the metal tracework of their prosthetic skins—knotted and spliced into a single corporate entity which was dancing up a storm in the virtual world.

Eerie synth moans drifting round the temple, the bass dropping low as if waiting to attack. A moment's pause . . . and then the drums kick in with a deafening fusillade of reprocessed beats. The dancers skid and dive as if caught in the crossfire of a digital warzone. Some have already collapsed.

I flipped the CAMnet eyepiece to one side, stooped to retrieve a pair of discarded VR shades, and put them on. A landscape of plush grasses filled with madly cavorting figures—quicktime avatars comprised of Deleuzian body parts, baroque Meccano rods, and Lathamesque crustaceans—scrolled past at 270 bpm. I blinked rapidly and tracked back to take in the full wide-screen view of what was now a distant planet wrapped in a cocoon of alien stars. The planet was covered in a net of purple micro-filaments which was in the process of being rapidly colonized by the swarm of avatars. You ask me what they were doing? Obviously reconditioning it for interdimensional flight. One of the stars in what appeared to be the southern hemisphere was throbbing and flickering with an insistent urgency, its phase-shifted modulations in synch with the shattering tattoo of the drums. Here was the homing signal, the pinpoint navigational code which the craft needed to make the unimaginable journey.

It was too much. I flung the shades to the ground. Flocks of drum loops arced and rolled across the old Control Room as I made my way to the rickety podium of scrap metal at its center on which the DJ was placed. She towered above the throng of celebrants like a voodoo priestess addressing the ancestor gods of the astral plane or an air-traffic controller plucking long-haul carriers from faraway holding patterns. Her long needle-tipped fingers tugged purposefully at the atoms around her as if shuttling thread from an invisible loom. She would keep on beat the drums like this all night. I stood quietly before her.

So this was Voodoo Ray. Her fame preceded her on the datanets. It was whispered that she could conjure the spirits from their hiding places in rocks and machines and trees, that she was a keeper of the keys which unlocked the hearts of men. I watched her. Her dark face was enclosed in an enveloping wimple of Sennheiser cans and skintight TiNi hood and her lips were parted in an ecstatic grin. Sweat poured from her brow and collected on the rim of the VR shades which shielded her eyes. She looked like the image of a pagan saint or a blind prophetess. CCD video eye catching it all.

The drums crashed at my feet. I needed to smoke some rock. That way I could plug into the London dreamtime and participate in the collective attempt to boot up rediscovered shamanic flight vectors and exit the rotting shell of Bat Hat. But, like I say, some of us have a job to do. It was down to me to keep a clear head.

You ask me to specify the tech jammed into the Temple ov Isis? I'll do it. Like its sustaining mythos, its operating system had been scratched together from a bundle of found objects. Check One. Bat Hat had fallen off London's electric grid, so all power was sourced from protected banks of flaking generators which chugged quietly outside in the improvised marketplace. Check Two. The suits and shades had been imported from the sex arcades of Soho. (Old Hwang family connections.) Check Three. All virtual avatars had been custom-built in the coding basements of Brixton. Check Four. The celebrants had managed to grab hold of some junked Chamber of London software and were tripping on the back of its immersive store of images. It didn't matter to them that the writhing grasses, the purple planet, and the winking stars animated the records of old financial transactions. But it mattered to the Corporation of London.

You ask me to go on? Then I shall. Check Five. Distributed ranks of old SPARC clones formed a local area network which plugged each of the dancers into the same virtual space at the same time. The shape-memory alloys embedded in the threads of their datasuits powered a collective force-feedback mechanism which was helmed by the figure of Voodoo Ray. She was the usher. Her own avatar was the lodestar in cyberspace which fine-tuned the collective rhythms of the planetary mass spread before her. Now do you understand?

It gets more intense. Check Six. The whole virtual envelope had been retro-engineered so that it coincided with a computer-generated audio-tactile field. Infra-red sensors grafted into the datasuits sent coded bursts of data to the SPARC clones based on the movements of the dancers. They entered the feedback loop and were ushered back into physical space by the Kabuki hand jive of Voodoo Ray. Check Seven. A Matsushita DAT machine encased in a Kamecke black box rested at the base of the podium, its hermetic surface carved with Tzolkin calendrical glyphs and an Egyptian votive inscription. It was here that Voodoo Ray had hoarded her stock of digitally reprocessed breakbeats, her inheritance of old vinyl memories.

Check Eight. The speakers blasting out the punishing sonic fragments which Voodoo Ray retrieved from the DAT with a flick of her wrists. Her nails were sheathed with infra-red needles which glittered like claws as they scratched signs in the air. In front of her was the sample space. Behind her was the play space. She was suspended in the trigger plane.

I moved closer to her perch.

"Oh my gosh. London Town. Yes, yes, yes, yes, yes, yes, Yes!"

She stood like a tiny colossus with her legs apart, the damp patch of her sex visible beneath the sheen of her suit as her hips rode the shuddering battery of sound. Spittle flew from her lips as she chanted her mantras. She plucked beats from the air with a manic glee, her arms wheeling and darting as if weaving a shroud or connecting a call. It seemed impossible that anyone could be so quick.

It was then that I understood. Voodoo Ray's podium marked the quadrivium in this cathedral of sound, the digital switchboard from which the gods of London were signed in. Devotional smartcards bearing images of local media saints—Jimi, Gerald, Jezebel—were pinned to the scrap-metal tower on which she was placed. Her feet were supported by a grimy slab of limestone which capped the whole edifice like the bridge of a ship. This was her stage, her scaffold, her gantry. It was the platform from which she would turn herself off.

Inside the mesh of iron and steel the Kamecke box reclines like a voluntary captive or a protected savant. You see what I see? Wicker machine.

I ended up dancing. What else could I do? Once the drums were racked up to 320 bpm, it was the only way to keep sane. Look at it. That's why the CAMnet footage is so spasmodic at this point. It's obvious that things were getting out of control.

Needlepoint rhythms unseaming my head as I struggle to keep up with their murderous pace. Voodoo Ray's claws a blur of deft cutwork. The drums looping and writhing in undulations of panic. I know I can process it all if I concentrate . . . but the stress is too much. My body picks up the slack with its twitches and spasms and for a moment I slide into the groove. Stretched envelope of sound. The drums tripping higher and higher, weaving harp bolts of color into a diaphanous labyrinth. I can almost reach out and touch it . . . the internal architecture of a fantastic dream vessel. But none of this survives on the tape.

Look what is there. The crowd is demented, as if caught in a vortex of conflicting demands. Its members stagger and reel and hold out their hands. Some of them roll on the ground. There are nosebleeds, babblings, and spontaneous orgasms. Do you think that maybe there was something coming in?

The Corporation goons had made their big entrance. Thrown a temporary exclusion zone around the perimeter of Bat Hat and sealed off all exits in advance of the bust. Roadblocks in the Battersea Park Road. Media blackout. Chinooks slung with Exocets clattering in the sky. The takedown sheet specified software piracy and drug trafficking. But that was just a paper construction. Battersea Power Station had been declared an autonomous Bar of the City of London. The Corporation could do what it liked.

You heard the story of how they loosed off a missile? I don't know. It could've been the drums.

"Yes, yes, yes, yes. Let it come down."

Voodoo Ray . . . she warps the beat up into an even higher dimension. You have to slow down the CAMnet tape to even get close. It was then that I came to the end of my senses. The dance floor spun away from me and I fell to the floor.

Mass panic and awful confusion. The Corporation's enforcers threshing the crowd with a relentless attack. Heckler & Kochs flailing, radio chatter, red dots on the walls. What exactly is it they want? Quarantined inside white biohazard suits, the dreadful seals of the Corporation of London masking their faces, ribbed cables humping their backs like red dragons' spurs. They were breathing their own oxygen. As if the prospect of some awful contagion was what they most feared.

They were moving in on the stone mount where Voodoo Ray danced. She rained down her DAT gods upon them in invisible tongues of fire. The drums shrieking and squealing in an orgy of judgment. It was too much for the human metabolism to bear. But they could hear nothing. All orifices were plugged. The one thing they knew was protection.

Voodoo Ray's last move. She swings round—a full 180 degrees—and exposes her back to the advancing legions. It's then that I notice the tattoos beneath her TiNi suit. Seven of them descending from the crown of her head to the base of her spine like a wrathful serpent or a coiled flame. This was her last line of defense.

She squats on the stone with her legs wide apart and places her final calls to the gods. Her tattoos are like baroque circuit diagrams or compressed voodoo dials imprinted on a wafer of carbon. With the infrared needle attached to her left index finger she quickly signs each one. Her hand gently trips down her spine as if

she were unzipping the skin of her datasuit in order to wriggle free. Sampling and playing the drums simultaneously there in the heat of the SPARC trigger plane. The clamor of the breakbeats was terrible. Her body shivered with the pleasure of it.

It's too weird for the Corporation goons. They have most definitely lost it. Someone releases a catch and there's the panicky stutter of gunfire.

They then all open up in a roundel of lust.

"Stop, stop, *Stop!*" It's my own voice. Last thing I said before my CAMnet was trashed and my head opened up. You see what I see? Identification number on the good doing me over is a blank. Bzzzp! End of transmission.

I was dazed and leaking. What happened next was what you would have to call an unexplained phenomenon. Because there is definitely no way I hallucinated the event.

Voodoo Ray is bowed with her head between her knees. She is unbloodied. They didn't catch her. The drums are still roaring. It's a miracle. She's scratching the stone with her needle, tracing a sigil she maybe sees in her head. Her face is a mask of awful recognition. Is she being called? The Corporation goons are closing in for the kill. Their blood is up. What do they care?

I was thinking that someone would be shot.

The dance floor seemed to lose its moorings for an instant. Quantum fissure. The desperate chatter of automatic fire. Voodoo Ray went up in smoke.

Let me rephrase that. A blue shaft of light inundated the stone and wrapped her tired body in a spectral cocoon. She raised her hand in greeting and waved farewell. Rapture. She was transported and her atoms dispersed.

I saw her tattoos glow red and burn themselves into the back of her TiNi suit. It dropped to the stone like a charred mantle from Heaven as the light died away.

Pickup.

The drums were seething with a fierce imprecation. They shouldn't have been.

"Forgive."

After that, it was just a matter of tidying up the mess. There was no future for Bat Hat, of course. The Corporation evacuated the building and detonated the remains. I guess there was some evidence they just didn't want to collect.

The strange thing about it all. Mass arrests, no charges. Blinking survivors left massaging their wrists on the Battersea Park Road as the power station retracted its sublime fluted chimneys and sank to its foot in a cushion of dust. The Corporation dezoned the territory soon after and relinquished it to the Crown. Shipped out its troops as quickly as it had choppered them in. It was a ten-line item in the domestic tabs. Bat Hat a death trap. Isis a Waco cult. Et cetera, et cetera. Blacks, guns, and drugs.

Slightly more on the NHK WipeNet. Another ethnic skirmish in a Euro civil war. The Hwangs to sue for loss of capital assets. All of which leaves the big questions hanging. How many people were killed by the Corporation of London? Where are they buried and what are their names?

Information on this matter is very hard to come by.

One thing I do know. Voodoo Ray may be reckoned among the dead. But her name will live forever in the binary devotions of the digital shamans.

YASSER ABDELLATIF

YOUNIS IN THE BELLY OF THE WHALE

(2011)

Translated from the Arabic by Robin Moger

Younis in the belly of the whale.
O belly like a casket:
Younis lives, he does not die.
                                   —*Naguib Surour*

I ENTERED THE MALL through one of its sixty-nine gates. It is the biggest mall in North America, sprawling out over eight residential blocks: an entire commercial district in a town that lacks the very concept. Situated on the west side of town, it is the central district for a place without a center.

I entered through the gate that leads into the food court: a spacious area—more a small plaza than anything else: a ring of counters dispensing multinational fare surrounding tables and chairs belonging to no one restaurant in particular. Just help yourself: buy food from a counter, transport it on your plastic tray, then sit at a table, and eat. In the very center of the seating area four fountains shot out extraordinary shapes in water, lightly speckling diners with their spray and making a burbling sound that initially seemed romantic, before impinging ever more forcefully on your awareness until your very ability to speak was seriously impaired. That's if you had anything to say.

Japanese sushi, teriyaki chicken with white rice, beef à la Szechuan with green onion and ginger and carrot- and cabbage-stuffed spring rolls, Thai-style prawn soup with celery and sliced bamboo, vegetable masala for vegetarians (rice pudding with cardamom for dessert), Marrakesh red plum and mutton tagine, Russian kielbasa served with yogurt and a cabbage-garnished borscht, Swedish meatballs with gravy and chips, Mexican chili con carne with guacamole wrapped in tortillas, sheets of Ethiopian bread with a bright red paprika sauce for dipping and strips of cured beef, Italian favorites from lasagna to cannelloni through to pizza plus every other kind of pasta and sauce, Greek souvlaki with a salad of tomatoes, onion, lettuce, and feta, doner kebabs with Lebanese hummus and olive oil—even Egyptian falafel and tahina wrapped in shami bread . . . plus, of course, the presiding gods of American fast food, Kentucky Fried Chicken, McDonald's, Burger King. A genuine culinary globalization. Indian immigrants eating Chinese, Arab women in hijab chewing Turkish shawarma, Chinese teens wolfing burritos. The sheer variety of dishes and the water splashing and burbling inside my head left me dizzied. The choice was exhausting.

I went to the Italian outlet and bought a slice of pizza, like someone taking refuge with a half-known relative amid a crowd of strangers. (You can't trust any falafel made in North America by white hands: any ball of ta'amiya that hasn't been fried in motor oil is not to be relied on.) I took my slice and sat down at one of the tables, where I washed it down with cola.

I left the food court and drifted like a sleepwalker toward a passage signposted *PlayLand*. Down I went, surrounded by dozens of children, both accompanied and roaming free. The passage went on and on. I was still fuddled from the fountains' fading burble, but even as it faded the din of games and rides rose up to take its place and the farther my slow, child-dogged steps took me the more the roar of entertainment came to dominate.

Then I saw that the passage itself had turned into something like a suspension bridge: the walls and roof had fallen away and the cavernous space around me was filled with vast contraptions.

Serpentine tracks for four different grades of roller coaster coiled through the air: one for children, its rails set just off the ground and rumbling quietly along; a second with a line of teenagers at the gate, making an initial circuit around the hall, then plunging into the shadows of the Tunnel of Love, then dropping farther still, where, at some point, it became a kind of boat, meandering across a subterranean lake, the darkness brushed by dreamlike lights while young lovers stole fevered embraces and kisses; a third with sharp climbs and drops for the adults; and, finally, the lunatic coaster that lurched and plummeted at terrifying angles, made sudden banking swerves, its passengers possessed of the steeliest nerves and soundest hearts.

At either side of this passage-turned-bridge were gates, stations for the roller coasters' passengers, and at each one children and adults queued for their chance to thrill and scream. The space around me, with these gigantic fairground rides, the rattle and clack of railed wheels snapping through the air and its carnival throng of kids and teens, seemed to embody the essence of some spirit of entertainment that the amusement parks of my youth lacked altogether. In fact, I wanted ask—disoriented and alienated—in what "spirit" *did* they build these dancing monuments to steel and technology in our wretched cities?

Then the bridge became a passageway once more. The big rides were gone, and now a set of smaller games that lined both sides of the corridor. My attention was caught by something that looked identical to an astronaut's suit. SCUBASIM read the sign. Then a second phrase in cheerful font: *Dive into the depths without getting wet!* That's my game, I told myself. Dry diving's perfect for a wanderer from the East like me: a melancholic, a detached Apollonian observer.

For some moments, I stood and inspected the apparatus: a huge helmet, clearly constructed to accommodate a screen in front of the eyes, a trunk replicating the effect of a lead-like metal, arms and legs of flexible silicon terminating in a pair of gloves and perfunctory flippers, and mounted on the back an oxygen tank just like the real thing, if slightly smaller. An information plate stated that it was equipped with hi-fidelity speakers, which played oceanic sound effects and sensor pads at the palms and neck to give the user the impression of being underwater. Having shed your shoes and coat, you feed the suit coins (four dollars), put it on (climb into it), and close it, at which point it swivels from an upright stance to the horizontal. Now paddle your arms and legs to power yourself through the depths.

Enjoy.

I fed the coins into the machine, slipped myself down the silicone arms and legs, and shut myself in. For a brief moment, the darkness inside was absolute. Then I heard a whine and felt the whole apparatus tilting. There was an axle fixed to the waist of the casing that allowed it to swivel between the horizontal and vertical. My arms and legs moved freely inside their rubbery sleeves.

I heard a faint whispering, a muffled submarine soundscape, then the screen lit up. The screen curved around my face and gave one-hundred-and-eighty-degree vision. It felt exactly as though I were peering through a diving mask.

I found myself in turquoise water. Not too deep: ten meters, say. The high resolution of the underwater scenery was not what I'd expected: it felt fantastically real, and from its almost velvety quality I could tell that it had been shot with a high-definition camera and converted into cinematic footage using 3D technology. The sensors on my skin exerted a gentle pressure, and I felt a faint squeezing inside my ears. Shoals of fine silver fish swirled around me as I began, as per instructions, to paddle. I was moving forward now, and to my astonishment the fish moved as I moved into their midst, the shoal scattering chaotically then regrouping at a distance. The software must have been incredibly advanced for this footage to be able to respond to the movements of a person wiggling about in the basement of some Canadian mall. It even occurred to me that I was watching a live feed from an underwater camera somewhere, but then I decided to stop thinking about the technicalities and just enjoy the experience.

I swam through the shallow turquoise waters, reveling, and then I got the idea of going to the surface to see what I could see. I spread my arms, lifted my head, and began kicking vigorously until I saw the surface approaching, but as I was about to break through it a sentence flashed across the bottom of the screen in red: *Not permitted . . . Please make your way to* SUR-FACESIM *. . .* This unexpected division of labor was mildly alarming, but I decided to see the game through to the end and I turned round and swam back down.

I saw a huge ray, its flat black body like a triangular carpet, flippers beating like a Roc's wings as it cruised with measured delibera-tion over the seabed. The electric whip of its tail stirred storms in the white sand each time it touched bottom and the clear water clouded in its wake. I saw great hordes of jellyfish rocking back and forth and clouds of blue-tinged sardines glinting in the rays of sunlight that stabbed down all around me. All of a sudden I found myself staring into a deep, deep blue: an abyss. Looking back, I saw that I'd been swimming over a coral platform covered with a layer of white sand, and that it was this which had lent the water its turquoise clarity; now I was face to face with the true depths. A darkest blue. The coral platform had dropped away in a cliff face, and then there was only the deep stretching away. For a moment, I paused, hanging irresolute as though suspended in the real sea, then went forward into the unknown.

I sank down the face of the coral cliff, past dazzling fish of all shapes and sizes, singly and in shoals, every shade of orange and blue and green. Then a gray shark. Not huge, not small. It approached, bringing its slack jaw and dead eyes closer, then peacefully flicked away and disappeared. I remembered reading somewhere that fish gather in large numbers next to reefs because of the plentiful supply of food, and thus—in accordance with the law by which all fish abide—the plentiful supply of food for those that feed on the feeders.

I began to swim across the cliff face, up and down, watching and turning as I went. A shoal of yellow fish scattered to reveal a gaping hole in the coral. I approached the blank darkness cautiously, recalling from somewhere that caves and cracks were favored haunts of deadly eels and sea snakes. But as I entered the cave I saw a glow in the gloom, some opening in the cave's roof through which the sunlight had made its way through. Any opening, I reasoned, must lead to the shallow turquoise waters above the coral platform. Protected by my metal suit, my virtual reality, I took heart and decided to go all the way in the cave, swim up through the gap in the ceiling, and make it to the other side. At the back of my mind was a neglected spot on the

Alexandrian shoreline known as Masoud's Well. Masoud's Well was a deep hole in the rocks near the suburb of Miami, and at the bottom of the hole a tunnel led out into the open sea. Back in the '70s, kids would compete by jumping into the well, passing along the tunnel then bobbing up in the distance.

I started swimming forward into the cave, heading toward the light. It wasn't a negligible distance, but the bright glow shining out into such deep blackness made measurements somehow hard to judge. Minutes passed, swimming along, bumping from time to time against the reef, then hearing the echoes of these collisions rebounding redoubled through the speakers at my ears.

Then I reached the opening, to discover it was too narrow to let me pass. I kept trying, and each time I tried a siren wailed, off and on like a warning, so I decided to change the plan, and turned back toward the cave's entrance. On the journey back out, the darkness was absolute. It was practically impossible to make out anything at all and I was colliding against the coral with increasing frequency, the muffled squeak of metal on rock amplified in the echo chamber of the cave and rendered terrifyingly immediate by the speakers that seemed to pick up any movement I made. Inside the lined silicone tubes my hands and feet began sweating heavily. My head swam in the darkness. A dizzy spell. I paused to catch my breath and collect myself but as I did so, the warning sirens went off again, louder this time, and at the bottom of the screen another phrase in red—*Oxygen about to run out . . . Please exit* SCUBASIM *immediately*—and now, it seemed, I couldn't remember how to open this suit from within.

SUZANNE CHURCH

SYNCH ME, KISS ME, DROP

(2012)

WHEN MY NOSE STOPPED ACHING, I smiled at Rain. She had snorted a song ten minutes before me, and I couldn't quite figure why she waited here in the dark confines of the sample booth.

"Rain?" I said. "You okay?"

"Do you hear it, Alex?" she said, not really looking at me. More like staring off in two directions at once, as though her eyes had decided to break off their working relationship and wander aimlessly on their own missions. "It's so amaaazing."

She held that "a" a long time. I should've remembered how gripping every sample was for her, as though her neurons were built like radio antennae, attuned to whatever channel carried the best track ever recorded. I needed to get her ass on the dance floor before I got so angry that I ended up with another Jessica situation. I still had eight months left on my parole.

"Do you hear it?" Rain nudged me, hard on the shoulder. "Alex!" Her eyes had made up and decided to work together, locking on me like I was the only male in a sea of estrogen.

"Yeah, it's awesome," I lied. For the third time this week, I'd snorted a dud sample. My brain hadn't connected with a single, damned note.

Beyond the booth, the thump, thump of dance beats pulsed in my chest. Not much of a melody, but since they'd insisted I check my headset with my coat, I couldn't exactly self-audio-tain.

I grabbed her arm, feeling the soft flesh and liking it. Loving it. Maybe the sample *was* working on some visceral level beyond my ear-brain-mix. "Let's hit the dance floor."

"In a minute. Pleeease."

Over-vowels were definitely part of her gig tonight.

"Wait for the *drop*," she said, stomping her foot.

"Right." I watched her sway back and forth, in perfect rhythm with the dance music coming from the main floor. The better clubs brought all the vibes together, so that every song you sampled was in perfect synch with the club mix on the speakers. When the drop hit, everyone jumped and screamed in coordinated rapture.

I would miss the group-joy here in this tiny booth, with this date who was more into her own head than she would ever be into me. If I could get Rain out on the floor, I could at least feel the bliss, whiff all the pheromones, feel all those sweaty bodies pressed against mine, soft tissues rubbing together.

"Yeaaaah!" She shouted and grabbed my hand, squeezing it. Harder. Her eyes pressed shut, her mouth wide open, she leaned way back.

The drumbeats surged, and then, for a fraction of a second, they paused. Everyone in the club inhaled, as though this might be the last lungful of air left in the world and then . . .

Drop.

But *drop* doesn't say it all. Not even close. Because when it happens, it's like the most epic orgasm of all time and pinching the world's biggest crap-log in the same moment.

Rain opened her eyes and pressed her hand against the side of my cheek. Lunging with remarkable speed for a woman who over-voweled, she kissed me. Her tongue pressed against my lips.

I tasted her. Wanted her. An image of Jessica popped into my head: the look of terror on her face when I accidentally yanked her under.

The euphoria gone, I closed my mouth and turned away from Rain.

"Whaaaat?" she said.

For a second, I thought about explaining what I had done to Jessica. Spewed on about how the drop isn't always built of joy. Instead, I went with the short, obscure answer. "Probation."

Rain looked at me funny, like she couldn't quite figure out how the judicial dudes could mess with our kiss-to-drop ratio. Finally, she smiled, and said, "Riiight."

Desperate to avoid another over-vowel,

I shouted, "Let's dance!" This time, when I grabbed her arm, she followed along like a puppy.

Scents smacked at us as we pushed our way through the seething mass on the floor. This week's freebie at the door was *Octavia*, some new perfume marketed at the twenty-something set. It was heavy on Nasonov phero-mones, some bee juice used to draw worker buzzers to the hive. When the drug companies cloned it, the result was as addictive as crack and as satisfying as hitting a home run on a club hookup.

My nostrils still ached from snorting a wallop of nanites, but scent doesn't only swim in the nose. The rest is all neurons, baby, and I had plenty to spare. Apparently so did Rain, because she was waving her nose in the air like a dog catching the whiff of a bitch in heat. The sight of her made me want to take her and do her right there on the floor.

But *Conduct* was a high-end club. The bouncers would toss us both if they caught us in the act anywhere on the premises, so I kept it in my pants. I still had another two hundred in my pocket. Enough for three more samples. Maybe I'd pick up a track from an indie band this time. Top forty drivel never seized my brainstem.

Unlike Rain.

The beats were building again. This time, with a third-beat thump, like Reggae on heroin. I could feel the intensity from my fingertips to my teeth to my dick. Even if I couldn't hear more than the background beats, I anticipated the drop. Rain opened her mouth again, raised both her hands in the air with everyone else, like a crowd of locusts all swarming together.

Pause.

Drop.

My date kept her eyes closed, her hands on her own breasts as she milked the release for all it was worth. Any decent guy should've watched her, should've wanted to, but I caught sight of a luscious creature, near the high-end sample booth, in the far-right corner of the club. The chick was about to slip between the curtains, but she caught me staring.

Her eyes glowed the purple of iStim addiction, reminding me of Jessica.

She had grown up in the suburbs, her allowance measured in thousands, not single dollars. The pack of girls she hung with had all bought iSynchs when they first hit the market. The music sounded better when they could all hear the same song at the same time. For the first time in more than a hundred years, getting high was not only legal, but ten times more amazing than it had ever been before. We all lived in our collective heads, the perfect synch of sound and sex.

I should've turned away from the sight of the purple chick, should've reached out to Rain and kissed her again. Close tonight's deal. Instead, I approached Rain's swaying body, and next to her ear shouted, "Back in five."

She nodded.

Fueled by fascination, and the two hundred burning a hole in my pocket, I headed for the high-end booth.

One of the bald bouncers with tribal tattoos worked the curtains. Yellow earplugs stuck out of both ears, so conversation, or in my case, pleading, wasn't an option. Feeling in my pocket for the two hundred, I scrunched the bills a bit, trying to make the wad appear larger than its meager value, then pulled out the stack in a flash. I had never dealt with this particular bouncer. *Conduct* was more Rain's club than mine, so I hoped the bills would get me past. The guy didn't even acknowledge me, as though he could smell my poverty, or maybe my parole. His eyes stared straight ahead.

My head scarcely came up to his bare chest, so I was uncomfortably close to his nipple rings, but I held my ground, and pointed at the curtains.

He remained statue-like. More boulder-like. Then a woman's cream-colored hand with purple nails ran from the guy's waist to his pecs and he turned to the side, like a vault door.

Purple-chick stood in the gap between the curtains. Her black dress was built of barely enough fabric to meet the dress code. Her hair stood on end like a teenager's beard, barely there and oddly sexy. She must have dyed it every night, because the stubble matched her eyes and nails. A waking wet dream.

"Come in," she pointed beyond the curtains.

"In what?" I mumbled to myself.

"Very funny."

"You're not laughing."

My body neared hers as I moved past into the sample booth. I carried my hands a little higher than would have passed as natural, hoping to cop a feel of all that exposed flesh on my way by. But she read me like a pheromone and dodged back.

A leather bench seat lined the far wall of the booth. Three tables were set with products in stacks like poker chips. The first was a sea of purple, tiny lowercase "i's" stamped on every top-forty sample like a catalogue from a so-called genius begging on a street corner for spare music. The second was a mishmash of undergrounds like *Skarface*, *Audexi*, and *Brachto*.

The third table drew me like fire. Only one sample. The dose was pressed into a waffle pattern, which was weird enough to make my desire itch. But the strangest part was its flat black surface that sucked light away and spewed dread like mourners at a funeral.

Purple-chick watched me stare at it, waiting for me to speak. My mouth kept opening and closing, but I couldn't find words.

Expensive. Dangerous. Parole. All perfectly legit words that I couldn't voice.

I had forgotten my two hundred. My palms must have been really sweating, because what had once been a quasi-impressive stack, now stunk of poor-dude shame.

With practiced smoothness, she liberated my cash and said, "The *Audexi* works on *everyone*."

Distracted from the waffle, I said, "How'd you know I couldn't hear the last track?"

"Your throat," she said. "You're not pulsing to the beat."

My fingers felt my pulse beating like a river of vamp candy. Her observations were bang on. I wanted to illustrate my coolness, or, at the very least, my lack of lameness, but all I could manage was, "Oh."

She laughed.

My eyes wandered back to the waffle. I licked my lips.

Grabbing my chin, she forced me to look at tables one and two. "Your price range."

"What's the waffle?"

"New."

"Funny."

She didn't laugh. "Far from it."

"Addictive?" I asked, staring at the purple on the first table. How this woman could work the booth without jonesing for her own product made me rethink her motives.

"The absolute best never are," she said.

"No black eyes allowed in the boardroom, huh?"

She nodded. "Precisely."

I remembered Rain. By now, she'd have noticed my absence.

Purple-chick still held my two hundred. Her eyes locked on mine. "Try the *Audexi*. You won't be disappointed."

Like a Vegas dealer, she shoved all my money through a hole in the wall, selected an *Audexi* sample from table two, and held it in front of my nose.

I probably should've reported her. All of the clubs had to be careful not to push products hard, end up drawing the cops in to investigate. But my money was long gone and Rain wouldn't wait much longer.

I exhaled. The moisture turned the poker-chip-shaped disk into a teeming pile of powder-mimicking nanites, and I snorted. For several blinding seconds, I felt as though a nuclear bomb had blown inside. I could feel Purple-chick's hand on my arm, making sure I didn't wipe out and sue the club. Then the song erupted in my mind.

Sevenths and thirds. Emo-goth-despair. Snares and the ever-present bass, bass, bass.

Music flowed like a tsunami through a village, grabbing ecstasy like cars and plowing through every other thought except for the tweaks of synths and the pulse-grab of the click-track. The song was building, and all I could think about was finding Rain before the drop.

• • •

Rain and I danced in nanite-induced harmony until the early dawn. Exhausted and covered in sweat and pheromones, we grabbed our coats and carried rather than wore them outside.

The insides of my sore nose stuck together in the frigid air, a wake-up call for the two of us to don our coats or end up with frostbite. I didn't want to, I was so damned hot and pumped, but I figured I should set a good example for Rain. And the way our night was progressing, I wouldn't have much time to scan my barcode at the parole terminal before curfew.

Jessica's fucking choice of words would be killing my buzz for eight more months.

That fourth of October had been hot as hell. After clubbing, we both stripped and headed into the lake for a skinny dip. Except she wasn't skinny and I wasn't much of a dipper. She'd called me over to the drop and I thought she meant for the lingering song, not the drop-off hidden in the water. When the drop blissed me, I lost my footing and plunged over my head.

"Shit, it's cooold," said Rain.

I snapped back to reality. "Still with the vowels?"

"Screw you." She pushed me away and called a cab with the same arm wave.

"Don't be that way, baby."

"Now I'm your fucking baby? After ditching me for a dozen drops while you plucked that purple fuzz-head."

"You saw?"

"Who didn't?"

"Sorry. But you gotta admit, you and me, we really synched *after*." I nudged her, maybe a little too hard. "The last sample I snorted was worth it. Right?"

A cab squealed a U-turn and stopped in front of Rain. She started to climb in and then looked up at me.

I shook my head. Shrugged. "Tapped out."

"Fine." She slammed the door in my face and the cab took off up the street.

I stood there, watching my breath condense in the air, its big cloud distorting her and the cab. The cold clawed its way into me, sucking away my grip on reality. The shivering reminded me to at least wear my coat.

As I stuffed my arms into the sleeves, I sniffled, feeling wetness and figuring the cold was making my nose run. But then I noticed the red drops on the ground and the front of my coat. I wiped with one finger and it came back a dark and bloody mass. Dead nanites, blood, snot, all mixed together. Two shakes didn't get it off my finger, so I rubbed the mess in a snowbank and only managed to make it worse.

The nearest subway was blocks away. I should've kept my mouth shut, shared the cab with Rain, and then stiffed her for half the fare. But I'd hurt her enough for one night. Hurt enough women for one lifetime.

Jessica had been the closest thing to a life preserver, so I grabbed on. Tripping on the samples, her brain couldn't remember how to hold her breath, or at least that's how my lawyer argued it at the trial.

As I trudged for the subway, I concentrated on not slipping and falling on my ass. I found the entrance, and headed down the stairs, gripping the cold metal handrail, even though my warm skin kept sticking to it. The *Audexi* sample still pulsed through my system and I couldn't walk down in anything but perfect synch. The song was building to another drop, and I had to make the bottom of the platform before that moment, or I'd become another victim of audio-tainment.

The platform was nearly empty, save for a few other clubbers too tapped out to cab their way home. *Octavia* hung in the air, the Nasonov-pheromone-scents calling us all home like buzzers to the hive. Much as I loathed their company,

I couldn't resist the urge to huddle with the others in the same section while we waited for the train.

Off to our right I caught sight of Purplechick. She wore a long, black faux-fur coat. The image of her here, slumming it with the poor, was as wrong as a palm tree in a snowbank. She belonged in some limo, holding a glass of champagne.

I tried to break the pull of the scent pack, but couldn't step far enough away from my fellow losers to get within talking distance of Purplechick. When the train arrived, I watched her step inside, then waited until the last second before I climbed aboard, to make sure we were both on the same train.

The cars were so empty that I could see her, way ahead.

Standing near the doors, she held a pole while she swayed back and forth. I couldn't figure out why she didn't sit down, especially after a long night at the club. The rest of us were sprawled on benches, crashing more than sitting.

I considered the long trek up to her car, but I didn't trust my balance. Instead, I watched her. Waited until she stepped in front of the doors, announcing her intention to disembark.

Once again, I waited until the last second to leave the train, in case she decided to duck back on without me. I could tell that she knew I was watching. Following.

Okay, *stalking*.

She hurried up the stairs. Either she was training for a marathon, or her samples had all worn off, because I couldn't keep up. When she reached the top, she turned around and said, "What?"

Instead of rushing off, she stood there, at the top of the stairs. Waiting.

Her eyes were blue.

Not purple.

I hurried until I stood in front of her, nose to nose. "You took the waffle?"

She nodded.

"Tell me."

She shook her head. "Can't."

"Figures." I turned away.

"But I can show you."

"Yeah?"

"Kiss me," she said.

I sure as hell didn't wait for her to change her mind. We shared it all: tongues, saliva, even our teeth scraped against each other, making an awful sound that knocked my sample completely out of my head.

What filled the void wasn't the pounding of my heartbeat. Or hers. Or any song that I had ever heard. Instead, I could hear her thoughts, as visible as a black blanket on a white sand beach.

"Wow," I said.

Isn't it?

Her words, not spoken but thought into me. They reverberated around my skull like noise bouncing in an empty club.

I lost my footing and fell. Down. In. Far away. Suddenly I was six years old and my father leaned over and hauled me back up onto my skate clad feet. We skated together, him holding me, his back stooped over in that awkward way that would make him curse all evening.

"Find your balance, Alex. Bend your knees. Skate!"

I had forgotten how much I loved him. Forgotten what it felt like to be young and innocent, to enjoy the thrill of exercise for its own sake, and feel a connection that didn't cost the price of a sample.

"I love you." But when I looked up at him, he had morphed back into Purple-chick, now Purple-and-blue-chick. She held me, preventing my crash down the stairs.

"Cool, huh?" she said.

"A total mind-fuck."

"That's why it's so expensive."

"How much? I mean, you're on the subway, so if I save—"

"In my experience, those who ask the price can't afford it."

"Why me?" I said.

She smiled. "Marketing."

I needed a better answer, so I listened for her thoughts. All I sensed was the wind from another subway, blowing up the stairs behind me.

She turned and hurried for an exit.

"Wait!" My head buzzed, confused by the difference between waffle and real, trapped by the synch-into-memory-lane-trip that lingered on my tongue like bad breath.

Her boots stopped clapping against the lobby of the subway station, but she didn't look back. I was glad of it, because my memories were still swimming in my head. I wanted her to be Dad.

Not Dad. *Rain.* My former date's cute outfit lingered in my synapses, replacing nostalgia with guilt. I wondered if Rain had made it home okay in the cab.

Then naked Jessica filled my head, and it was October again.

"I didn't mean it," I said aloud, my voice echoing against the tile walls. "The high confused it all. I'll do another year of parole. I'll spend my sample money on flowers for your grave. Please, forgive me?"

Still with her back to me, and in a voice that sounded eerily like Jessica's, she said, "What about Rain?"

I shook my head, even though she couldn't possibly see me. "She'll understand."

Far ahead, Purple-and-blue-chick turned to face me. I saw her as *them*, she had somehow merged with Jessica, the two of them existing in perfect synch, like a sample and the club music stitching together; twins in a corrupted womb. They both saw me for what I was, a lame guy who would always be about eight hundred shy of a right and proper sample. Whose love would always be shallow, too broke to buy modern intimacy.

"You've got less than ten minutes to clock in your parole." She started walking again, and I watched her leave, one synched step at a time until she exited the station and disappeared along the ever-brightening-street.

Drop.

Only this drop, waffle-back-to-real, felt like nails screeching on a blackboard. I wasn't in my usual subway station, and I had no idea where to find the nearest parole scanner. The station booth was empty, too early for a human. The only person in sight was an older woman with the classic European-widow black-scarf-plus-coat-plus-dress that broadcast, *Leave me alone, young scum.*

So I did.

I hurried onto the street, and looked toward the sun. It was well above the horizon now, but mostly hidden behind a couple of apartment buildings.

"Fuck," I told the concealed ball of reddish-yellow light. "How'd it get so late?"

The judiciary alarm buzzed inside my head.

For a moment, I could feel a drop, the biggest, most intense and amazing drop I would ever experience. The sort of nirvana that people pursue ineffectually for a lifetime. Or two.

I had less than ten minutes until the final warning.

Rushing for the nearest, busiest street, I tried to wave down car after car, hoping someone would point me to the nearest scanner. Or maybe they had a portable one, the kind I should've brought with me, had I been thinking about more than getting into Rain's pants when I left.

People ignored me.

Shunned me.

I smelled of trouble. Which, technically, I was. But I didn't mean to be. It wasn't my fault.

It was never my fault.

One cab slowed, but didn't stop. The driver made eye contact, and then rushed away.

"Hey!" I considered swearing at him, but I didn't want to draw the cops.

I'm not sure why the cabbie stiffed me. Maybe he read my desperation. Maybe he was Rain's cabbie and he knew I was broke. In any case, he probably broadcast a warning to his buddies, because the next cab that got remotely close made a fast U-turn and took off.

Choosing a direction, I took off down one street, then hung a right at the next, jogging, skidding, almost falling on my ass. Every direction felt wrong.

I didn't see a single person. No one. Not even a pigeon, for fuck's sake. All I needed was a *phone*.

With one hand on a pole, I leaned over, trying to catch my breath. To think.

My heart was pounding now, no synch in sight. The song was long gone, the link to Purple-chick disconnected. No one had my back.

I turned in a circle, then another, scanning far and near for anything of value: an ATM, a phone booth, a coffee shop, a diner, any place where I could access the judicial database. Plead my case.

The final warning buzzed.

"Fuck!" My spit froze when it hit the ground.

I hit full-blown panic. My heart tripped like the back-bass before the drop. Only this time, the other side was built of misery not ecstasy.

If only I had paid my cell bill. If only my father was still alive, to catch my sorry ass. If only I had lied to Rain, shared her cab. If only Jessica hadn't called it a drop.

When you're panicked, it's tough as hell to keep any rational sense of time. I figured I was cooked. So I closed my eyes. But when the pain didn't come, I sat down on the cold curb, and felt the chill seep through my clothes.

I bit my lip. Tasted blood.

The first jolt ripped through my body. I wanted to writhe in pain on the sidewalk, but my body was stuck in shock-rigor. An immobile gift for the cops.

I imagined Rain beside me.

"You're an asshole," she said.

"Sorry."

She morphed into Jessica, her purple eyes wide with fear. "I'm lost," she said.

"Take my hand." I wanted to reach out, but I couldn't move. My fingers looked nearly white in the cold. Her fingers seemed to shiver around mine, as though they were made of joy, not flesh. Then she touched my hand and I knew in that moment that life existed outside of stimulation, in a place where reality wasn't lame or boring. Life danced to an irregular rhythm that couldn't synch to any sample.

She let go.

The judiciary pulse jolted again. I flopped to the pavement, distantly aware that my skull would remind me for a long time after about its current state of squishage.

The parole board must have lived for irony, because the jolt lasted for so long that I *welcomed* the release. A pants-wetting, please-make-it-stop, urgent need for the end.

Drop.

ZEDECK SIEW

THE WHITE MASK

(2015)

THE WHITE MASK IS DEAD. Social media has the story before the cops find his body.

Now the news sites are all posting the same thing, the same photo, the same angle, taken from across the lanes—

Of the White Mask sitting slumped against the highway wall, wearing a black hoodie; black skinny jeans with both legs splayed; black sneakers. And at his feet: three loose curbstones, kicked out of their spaces.

He wears a white mask over his face, and a crushed and crinkled larynx.

Behind him, on the highway wall:

Dr. M, the Tun Doctor, standing as a stenciled mural. This is the Tun Doctor in the later years: in a Nehru collar; hands clasped together and hair combed back; cheeks and jowls sagging; small eyes framed by spectacles. Smiling with a hint of teeth showing.

• • •

I walk across as my online self. There are voices like a semicircle choir sighing around the body. "Was it a robbery?" somebody says, and somebody else says: "Was it an accident?"

A third somebody says: "Why are people posting this picture, dead people are not things I want to see at breakfast or anytime ever, stop posting this picture please or you will. Get. Blocked!"

There is a satchel of art supplies open on the ground; there are spray-paint cans rolled into corners.

I kneel to look at a can. At this zoom level the resolution is poor—but I already know what its label says:

Smart acrylic lacquer. Latest version, industry standard, black in color.

• • •

And there is a live stream now. We watch the cops watching the surveillance feed—

Of the White Mask, standing between pools of streetlamp light, facing the highway wall. He shakes his spray can. We can imagine what that sounds like: clickity-clack-clack-clack.

The White Mask rolls his white under-coat onto the wall. It is an out-of-the-way wall, mostly empty—so this is a personal project, a minor independent commission maybe, an experiment.

The only thing already there is a graffiti tag, half-buried beneath the White Mask's new can-vas. "Terror Thursday," the tag says, broody, squirming, trying to wriggle itself back to the surface—but it's a years-old thing, done in out-dated hardware, its pigments unable to compete with the latest paints.

. . .

Piece by piece, the White Mask tapes up his stencil scaffold. His spray can sneezes, hisses—

The footage fast-forwards. His arms are a blur. They slow down again only as he steps back. We admire the wall with him: there's that mural of the Tun Doctor there now, just as we see it the next morning, in photos with the White Mask's body lying there.

But for now the White Mask is still working. His spray can cackles: clickity-clack-clack-clack. He places a stencil atop the Tun Doctor's hair.

The cut out outline of a fluffy cloud.

The White Mask works at it methodically, layer by layer, coat by coat, each a different color—

So the Tun Doctor wears a rainbow clown wig now.

. . .

"So who is this White Mask guy?" somebody says.

"Though he got what he deserved," some-body else says. "I feel sorry for his family, but really, how can anybody disrespect the Tun Doc-tor, who brought us development and prosper-ity, the greatest leader of our country?"

A third somebody says: "The White Mask is not a he, the White Mask is a she."

And then we notice that the Tun Doctor is angry. Small and squinty before, now the Tun Doctor's eyes blink quickly; the lines about the Tun Doctor's teeth turn into a snarl.

We notice—but the White Mask does not. He crouches, unfolding his last stencil. It is a piece of cardboard with a circle cut in the center:

A round nose.

He shakes a can of red paint: clickity-clack-clack—

. . .

Then he freezes.

The Tun Doctor's hands and arms are reaching out and off the highway wall's surface: two flat sheets of black matter, viscous, elbow-less, snaking out and grasping in boneless, alien ways.

His hood falls from his head. He struggles a little, his white mask shaking: no-no-no. He is being strangled. The Tun Doctor has him by his neck.

The spray can drops, toppling other spray cans like a strike to bowling pins.

The White Mask is held back to the wall, unable to break away. He kicks and kicks and kicks. He kicks the loose curbstones out of their spaces.

After a while he stops kicking.

The Tun Doctor stands up, wiping away the rainbow clown hair with whip-like fingers. Then the Tun Doctor settles: hands clasped together, small eyes squinting. Saintly smiling, with a hint of teeth showing.

. . .

Smart paint technology. Motorized nano-particulates, germs of pigment—umber or arsenic or ultramarine—movement-capable, pro-grammable, bearing networked memory full of commands and subroutines.

I am something of an expert; I did engineering in Korea, at a university where they developed the technology.

"All fun and moving!" I say. "See?"

This was five-six years ago. I tilt a ceramic tile to show the Datuk what I mean.

On my tile there is a cartoon figure running in a hamster wheel, and the painted wheel is turning—it isn't just an animation on a screen; the paint itself is shifting, spinning around the ceramic surface.

The little painted, panting man keeps up by running.

I made my little ceramic tile for our Majestic Place presentation. My tile gets us the job—our client the Datuk laughs, in love with its motile, cutting-edge novelty.

. . .

Our client the Datuk comes from the petro-gas company that owns Majestic Place—

"It's a petro-gas company!" Adam says. "So we have to fuck with them."

What we do with Majestic Place—it is all Adam's idea. We turn it into a phantasmagoria. On its sides we lay pipeline calligraphy. We build onion domes with smokestack minarets; traffic jams piercing candy smog; trains, planes, and rocket ships; swirling firework landscapes.

No natural tones. No green except for the coughing cartoon stiffs lining up for caffeine shots, on the walls of the building's ground-floor coffee place.

I tell our client the Datuk—I reassure him, saying: "Look, Datuk, you want to tell people that your company has a vision. This neon city, this is your vision! This is your future: bright, full of color, full of energy!"

. . .

Majestic Place is the first moving smart paint mural in the country. For this fact alone our client the Datuk is very happy.

Adam and I win Multimedia Campaign of the year. During industry awards night Adam goes onstage to accept our trophy. He wears his white mask and I am whooping.

"Whoo!" Adam says, his arms up, his palms open. "Whoo!"

Our friends fist-bump us. We are heroes, power couple of the evening: celebrity artist and code genius. We've hoodwinked a petro-gas company, more or less: clothed their corporate offices in toxic-nightmare landscapes, and afterward they paid us money.

There are those who are not so congratulatory. Look:

Five-six guys in the corner, drinking soda, feigning the barest minimum applause to be polite.

These guys. They are the Terror Thursday crew. They are jealous.

. . .

Adam was the White Mask—is the White Mask.

When Adam starts wearing his mask he is sixteen. He tags walls in Wangsa Maju, where he lives; eventually the mask becomes his identity, his thing.

It helps him. He does not have an easy beginning.

In this time of our lives we have not yet met. Adam runs with Terror Thursday—right now they are just a bunch of boys searching for themselves by the river's concrete flood banks, in spray cans, in squelchy long-poled roller brushes.

They draw jumping skateboarders and zombie hordes; polyhedral letters saying VOX and LIFE and MERDEKA RAYA; they draw green-irised girls in red-and-white headscarves, pleading for peace to return in the Middle East.

. . .

Terror Thursday is what they call themselves—

Thursday—meaning Thursday evening specifically, which in religion counts as the start of Friday, part of the holy day: a time of noble thoughts and purity, of artful God-blessed jihad.

Terror—not meaning horror, but the word used in its celebratory sense, somebody seeing a burning piece, or a cool perspective-trick painting, and saying: "Wah, so terror!"

The name is Ghaf's idea.

Ghaf is a good-looking guy. He is proud of his skill. He is not the best artist among them—that's Adam—but he does know where to get specialty paints for lower-than-market prices. So he takes command.

"The signs were there," Adam tells me later. "Could already see the way Ghaf would go."

• • •

At the start, Adam and Ghaf are a thing. That's how Adam gets in.

Of course it doesn't last, and Adam stays with the Terror Thursdays only for a few more years. Boys of that kind, at that age? They don't understand.

The mask is Adam's way of coping. It is a physical symbol that his personhood is changeable. He doesn't have to be whatever other people see. More and more he says this aloud.

For Ghaf and the rest—

To them he is still a girl: just out of her school baju, stuffed into a beanie and baggy tee. They grow uncomfortable.

"You shouldn't, you know," Ghaf says. "You are a girl. God made you a woman. You cannot go against God."

"You like to talk about changing the world," Adam tells him.

"For the better!" Ghaf says. "Not like this, for the worse."

• • •

Nowadays Ghaf is balding early. He wears a goatee and a skullcap under his hoodie. He talks to a news reporter.

"She does not represent us," he says. "Yes, the White Mask is actually a she. She was born a woman. We grew up together. Her real name is Dyana, she used to run with our crew."

The five-six guys of Terror Thursday stand together, looking grim.

"This was before she got her sex change," Ghaf says. "She left our crew to become a tomboy and a liberal.

"This, insulting the greatest leader of our country?" He points at the Tun Doctor standing in the highway wall. "This is going too far. It's treasonous. Sacrilegious! We street artists, we are patriots. People have to know she does not represent us."

The cowards, crusading against the dead. I am thinking how Adam made it so easy for them, getting himself killed like this—so stupid. He let them win.

• • •

One headline says: "Artists, NGOs Lodge Police Report against Dr. M Clown Mural."

"Cops: White Mask Death a Programming Error," another headline says.

There is a live stream of the police press conference, with an officer holding up a notebook they found in Adam's bag, and he is flipping through its pages—

It is a book of sketches. In it is Dr. M, the Tun Doctor, page after page, in spectacles and Nehru collar, in various poses:

In a clown's getup; in a cap with three stars arranged in a triangle; in a dress. With a beer bottle. Sitting on the toilet, eyes shut tightly, straining. His hands on two handles of a motorbike, planking on the bike seat, his legs stretched out straight behind him.

A third headline says: "Respect the Tun Doctor, Minister Reminds Youth."

• • •

A month ago, Adam opens the notebook with his Tun Doctor sketches to show me.

"I'm thinking we can put these up as stencils," he says.

When I see what he's drawn I look him in the eye, and I ask: "Why?"

"For fun," Adam says. "You know Terror Thursday got that contract with the Ministry, that history campaign for Merdeka month? 'Malaysian Heroes' featuring the Tun Doctor. That's Ghaf, no imagination. I want to fuck with him."

"You'll piss off other people, not just Ghaf," I say. "They'll say you're insulting our greatest leader."

And Adam says: "So fuck them too."

"We won't even get paid for it. I don't think it's worth the trouble."

"And fuck you too!" Adam says.

• • •

Now, when I am not crying, I am thinking. If I'd been there I could have double-checked the paint's programming—

Smart paint stores commands and algorithms in its memory. The latest versions come with inbuilt antivandalism subroutines, so that paintings shield themselves from damage.

An authorized user inputs the desired level of security.

Whether the paint reacts to touch, reacts to the application of additional coats or colors, reacts to differing or knockoff brands. Whether it responds by dissolving foreign particulates—as the Tun Doctor did with Adam's clown wig.

Or by forcibly removing the source of attack—by physically debilitating attackers, for example.

Adam, he's not so good at code. He didn't program his paint properly—didn't properly add himself to the permissions list—so his own paint saw him as an attacker, and his own paint attacked him.

Me? Programming is my thing. If I'd been there—

• • •

The reason why industry-standard paint has antivandalism software:

Businesses think their marketing campaigns need protecting.

They need us. The Public Advertisements Act banned billboards in the late 2010s—but what we do, technically it isn't advertising. It is art. Corporate-sponsored art.

People like the Datuk and his petro-gas company—they pay us good money for our murals. More than anybody else, they don't want to wake up in the morning to see their branding defaced.

I remember Adam ranting about the money.

"The money is spoiling us," Adam says. "Just now I met Ruby, buying groceries, she asked why we've not visited her lately. Rich people already, is it, she said. She's right! In the past five-six years we've not done any work but corporate jobs—not one! When did we become corporate people?"

"Remember we've got a meeting with the Datuk tomorrow," I say.

• • •

We meet for the first time at a party at Ruby's place.

Adam is pretty: he has an angular face, curly hair; he wears a jean jacket, a smile that is sweet, half-cocky.

He wears a binder for his chest. He tells me about himself—about the Terror Thursdays and the work; about the White Mask; about going to court tomorrow, to show support for the trans women appeal case.

I tell him about my studies abroad in engineering. We talk about the future.

And five-six months later, even though he has me blindfolded I know he's brought me to the river—I can smell its stink.

"Surprise," he says.

Across the water, on the concrete flood bank,

he's written his name and my name. Big block letters. Between those two words he's painted a heart. It is big, valved, bloody red.

I imagine it beating.

. . .

"Wipe out all of the White Mask's murals!" somebody says.

Somebody else replies: "I don't agree with his actions, but you know, as the French philosopher Voltaire says—"

The Datuk from the petro-gas company writes to tell me: "We have partnered with the White Mask crew for our Majestic Place premises for the past seven years. We feel now it is time to make a change.

"Please accept our sincerest thanks for what has been a warm, long, and fruitful relationship. We wish you all the best!"

And in a separate message:

"I am so very sorry for your loss. You know, I liked you two very much, and I still do. But this recent thing, it's bothering my bosses a lot, they don't want the company seen associating with you. I hope you understand."

. . .

The men, they wash his body with water and lime.

They wrap him in white cloth, in many layers. His face is pale and waxy looking. His mother and father and his sisters pray. Their arms are folded, right hand on left—the same way Adam's hands are folded.

His mother and father look tired.

People have been pressuring them to apologize. "You've raised a tomboy and a liberal!" they say. "Please try to be a bit ashamed."

"What Adam did, he has already done," his father says.

"We won't apologize," his mother says. "He was our son."

By the graveside the hecklers and online hate are muted. It is quiet. There is a frangipani tree scattering its flowers—already rotting—onto the headstones and shoveled earth.

. . .

"Hello," Ghaf says. He leans against the wall by the mosque gate. He wears a smile, seemingly sympathetic.

So I ask him: "Why are you here?"

"To pay my respects," he says. "I grew up with Dyana. I was her friend."

"Adam was what his name was, you asshole. You stopped being his friend long ago. How could've you ever been his friend, you can't even call him by his name."

Ghaf shakes his head. "It is sad for her to have died in sin," he says. "I wanted to tell you, professional to professional. For our history campaign to commemorate Merdeka month, we'll use the White Mask's stenciled mural of the Tun Doctor.

"We've already discussed it with the Ministry," he says. "They agree, it's a good place for us to start, a good lesson. This way at least Dyana will have done something good in the world."

. . .

That night I leave my car in the emergency lane and walk through the underpass. I look up at the highway wall.

It's the first time I'm here in person.

The streetlamps cast light at an angle. The wall is slightly rough. There is rubbish at the Tun Doctor's feet, leftovers of the police investigation—three soda cups, a blue medical glove, shreds of black bin-liner stuck in cracks between the curbstones.

The Tun Doctor looks directly at me: cheeks and jowls sagging, eyes squinting, smiling.

"Hello, you," I say. I am wearing Adam's white mask.

Sitting cross-legged, I wire electrodes to the wall. My diagnostic runs through the data. It tells me almost immediately the reason why

Adam wasn't recognized as a user: a missing closing chevron bracket, early on—

A forgot-to-add-an-end-tag kind of stupid mistake.

. . .

But that's not why I'm here.

I stand down the Tun Doctor's defenses. I open my satchel of art supplies. I have a stencil with me, in eight cardboard sheets, crinkled and inexpertly cut. I tape them up.

I shake my can of smart acrylic lacquer: clickity-clack-clack-clack. Then it sputters and hisses—

And after a while there is a stenciled mural of the White Mask on the wall: arms apart, palms open; the mask in the hoodie an oval outline of the white undercoat underneath, with wet licks of black denoting grinning lips and nose and eyeholes.

The paint begins to dribble, like tears. I've sprayed too much paint on—I'm not used to the mask, it is hard to see. Art was always Adam's thing.

. . .

I am better at programming.

With my tablet editor and pen stylus I pull the White Mask's arms toward the Tun Doctor, over the Tun Doctor's shoulder. And the Tun Doctor's arm I put over the White Mask's shoulder. I push the two figures together.

Each still has a hand free. I ball their open palms into fists, and I position these in front, making them meet in the middle, touching knuckle-to-knuckle.

So now they are arm-in-arm, side by side, the White Mask and the Tun Doctor, brothers—

Fist-bumping.

I lock the pose into place. From my tablet I strip the smart paint of restraints: no lines of code asterisked out in those millions of nano-processors. All safeguards deployed. Full security.

Finally I scramble the permissions list. Not even root-access users will be able to tamper with my painting, now. The wires I've stuck to the wall spark—pak-pak!—and the electrodes fall off, shorted.

. . .

The next morning, through sunrise haze, calls to prayer bounce off the buildings:

Condominiums, shophouse rows, and onion domes; a shopping mall swarmed with birds of neon green; an office tower venting steam, its face a moving mural, a tumbling puzzle of octagons interlocking.

Joggers on zebra crossings. Stroboscopic graffiti by the riverside. A helicopter. And soon the roads are busy: a train of cars forming in every lane, red rear lights shimmering.

In the air, people speaking—the dull murmur of social media.

"There are two White Masks, maybe?" somebody asks, and somebody else replies: "Maybe it's a conspiracy."

A third somebody says: "This is still a thing? These mural artists, they are so wanky, think they are so important. Please, people. Stop. I'm so bored of it already."

. . .

There, at the highway wall, the Terror Thursday crew stands in a semicircle.

In my online self I watch Ghaf watching the surveillance feed—

Of the White Mask between pools of streetlamp light, wearing black skinny jeans and black sneakers, working. He puts cardboard stencils up in eight parts, and shakes his spray can: clickity-clack-clack-clack.

The footage fast-forwards. His arms are a blur. They slow down again only as he steps back. I admire what he's done: the White Mask and the Tun Doctor, arm-in-arm, together.

It doesn't look that bad, now that I can see it in sunlight.

"It was that tomboy's programmer bitch who did this," one of them says. And another one says: "Can't even turn the paint off. We won't be able to work like this."

• • •

Ghaf's crew is ready to work.

They have rolls of tape on their wrists, a pallet of paint tins in their parked flatbed. But there's an upended box of spray cans by the wall, and a smashed-up laptop also—its two halves cracked apart, keys scattered, screen flaked in shards.

Ghaf wipes his head. The others keep well away. Carefully, carefully, he creeps forward. He stretches his hand out.

Straightaway the Tun Doctor reacts—

With flailing whip-arms of viscous matter: reaching out, toppling cans and roller poles, flinging curbstones. Grabbing Ghaf under his shoulder.

"No-no-no!" he says, screaming.

The rest rush to drag him away. Adam, on the wall—for now, he is safe in the arms of his new best buddy. He stares down at Ghaf and the Terror Thursdays, smiling.

And—wait, no, it must be a glitch—but I see his mask has a hint of teeth showing.

CASSANDRA KHAW

DEGREES OF BEAUTY

(2016)

PRETTY BUT NOT PRETTY ENOUGH, Bai Ling thinks, looking over to where her daughter lies sleeping, knees to breast, a whimper between her teeth. Around her throat, a necklace of bruises, teeth-marks on the nubs of her shoulders, battle-scars of the twenty-second century.

Bai Ling tours an armada of glossy brochures, ricocheting between clinics, circling procedures, underlining discounts. She has a plan.

Blepharoplasty to divide the monolid, sharpen the epicanthic fold. FDA-approved tinctures in the iris: indigo with constellations of hypoallergenic gold, all to tempt the camera's attention. And eyelash transplants too, of course, Mediterranean-thick, so much more appealing than fine Asian hair.

On a notebook, she pencils more radical suggestions: dilation of the orbital bones, deepening of the sockets, modifications to manufacture the illusion of vulnerability. Fashion craves victims, vestal virgins to hang in garlands of silk.

These will have to be discussed, but Bai Ling already knows she will get her way.

• • •

The surgeries are a triumph.

The media adores Bai Ling's daughter: "feral" fox-child, inkstroke lines and no meat at all, only bones to dress in satin. Her eyes, inhuman, carrying galaxies; jewels in a cross-continental setting. Utterly novel.

If she occasionally falters under the strobe of the cameras, if she winces from the spotlights, haunted or hungry, no one is crass enough to comment. Art is pain, everyone knows that.

• • •

It's still not enough, of course. The accolades refine to critique: how the eyes fail to match the face, the thin-lipped smile, the nose like soft dough squashed against bone.

"Just a little longer," Bai Ling whispers to her daughter, their fingers twinned.

• • •

The mouth is easiest to correct: a quick injection of synthetic collagen, perfectly rote, uniquely uncontroversial. They return Bai Ling's daughter in hours, tongue drooling between white teeth; her clothes vacuum-packed, a note between the fresh-washed fabric.

Introducing mild overbite may improve recognition profile.

Bai Ling does not think twice. She sends her daughter back immediately.

• • •

They are mesmerized. Tabloids and fashion rags, gleaming as a lie, stitch a prophecy for Bai Ling's daughter: a lifetime of cover shots and television appearances. Who is this nymph that's been extracted from reality show drivel?

Still, pity about that nose. And the breasts. All so *flat*, like paddy fields and rural economies. A farmer's child, surely, river silt running thickly through her veins. Or so Bai Ling trembles through every article, knuckles bleached white by hate. She has come so far and they have achieved so much. And her daughter. Ah, her darling. So much she has sacrificed, so many nights consecrated to alcohol and curious fingers, to smiling at nameless men with black shoes and black gazes, polished to the shine of a shark's dead eyes.

They've given so much.

How can they stop now?

The body is a truth that can be bent, the new media an instrument to be played by the wise.

• • •

The next surgeries are harder.

The nose is broken, reset; the nasal bridge lengthened, nostrils rotated to a respectable elevation. Scarlett Johansson's nose, down to a keratin fiber.

The breasts are engorged. Saline, not silicone. Pliancy must be preserved.

And the hair. There's nothing that can be done about that straight, lank hair. Nothing, at least, that might take effect in weeks. But Bai Ling will not be dissuaded. She drags her daughter through a gauntlet of hairdressers. She drenches her in dye, cooks her hair into stately spirals, too crisp to stay, but nothing that the proper creams cannot disguise.

"You're beautiful."

Bai Ling's daughter trembles under her touch.

• • •

Bai Ling drinks for the first time in her life when they announce her daughter as a breakout phenomenon, three years too late, Hollywood's best next thing. Framed in the mouth of the television, she is unrecognizable, silk foaming at her hips, a ruff of tulle coiled like a noose at her neck. Untouchable, impossible, a wet dream poured into four-inch stilettos. Not a peasant's daughter, a goddess.

Her daughter does not speak during the presentation, but no one comments—they are too impressed with the husband revealed on the stage. Now, there are two perfect people, gorgeous as no other, triple-tested to ensure an absence of disease. Adam and Eve, crowdsourced by tastemakers.

One blog notes that Bai Ling's daughter fails to smile, eyes vacant. *Nerves*, they write, of the ghost-bride on stage, *probably*.

• • •

Dead.

Bai Ling strokes fingers across her daughter's waxen cheek, cool but not rigid, still closer to human than not. Her throat is bruise-ringed, indigo-kissed; the rope had pulled tight, cut deep and ragged. Beautiful still, Bai Ling thinks. Like one of those anatomical Venuses.

She does not ask the corpse why. Instead, Bai Ling picks up her phone. The body is a tool. Flesh is malleable. Flesh is a tool. Bai Ling's daughter, eyes rolled up in her head, could be mistaken for a sleeping child.

• • •

She is in recovery for nine weeks.

They pump nutrition through a venous catheter, install a palette of esters below her tongue. It is important to keep the saliva glands operational.

Twice, she is returned under the scalpel. Once to adjust the distribution of saline in her breasts, the second time to cull a rash of necrotic tissue. The doctors hybridize stem cells, hers and hers, a careful tessellation of genomes; they wedge the replicator behind her ribs. Pray.

It works.

Twelve weeks later, Bai Ling emerges from the hospital, dressed in her dead daughter's skin. They have never been so beautiful. Fawn-legged, she totters into the paparazzi's arms, signature smile still brilliant. If the bridge of her nose appears a little straighter, if her voice seems deeper, no one says so. As long as she is beautiful.

E. J. SWIFT

ALLIGATOR HEAP

(2016)

HE WAS A HUNDRED AND TEN YEARS OLD and he was dying and he was going to live again. The body was in the building, waiting. Vardimon called it the sarcophagus, which everyone told him was dark, unnecessarily dark, but he was a hundred and ten and he believed he'd earned the right to dark. Of course it was a displacement mechanism, a way of averting his terror of the transfer going wrong, or worse, that he wouldn't be revived at all. Sometimes it worked.

"Are you ready, sir?"

Tarek hovered by the door. As always, the nurse's appearance was impeccable, his endeavors almost but not quite enough to disguise the fact that he wasn't from the heights.

"Yes, yes, bring it in."

The door opened and a three-tiered trolley floated inside. Each tier held the dome of a semi-translucent membrane, designed to offer the diner enticing glimpses of the culinary shapes and moving steam within. Vardimon beckoned.

Tarek brought the trolley to his bedside and at the tap of a finger, the membrane dissolved.

The first course was an exercise in monochrome: a boule of wild rice at the center of a gleaming black lake, within which gold flecks rose and fell from the surface like goldfish. The chef had added a white foam, integrating holobites to simulate the motion of the waves, and the soup swirled restlessly, rather queasily, within its bowl. Resting atop the rice island was a single pan-seared scallop. Vardimon thought, uncharitably, of a beached whale.

"This is Nguyen?"

"Yes, sir."

"She's young."

"She trained with your sous-chef, sir. Comes recommended."

Tarek cut the scallop and lifted the fork to feed him. Vardimon's hands, once elite instruments, had become unreliable. For that reason the aspiring chefs waited outside. Sometimes a younger projection of himself delivered his verdict. Sometimes Tarek did it. The chefs must have found that uncomfortable, a thought which gave him a perverse satisfaction.

He inspected the pearly interior of the scallop. It was well cooked, evenly cooked. He parted his lips to receive the first mouthful, chewing slowly, deliberately, swilling the black squid ink sauce around his cheeks.

Squid were one of the few forms of natural seafood still possible to obtain without a license. Where other creatures had declined or perished, squid seemed to relish the warmer, more acidic climes of the past century. Tenacious bastards. There were restrictions on scallops, but a discreet bribe could get around most ocean protectorates. Vardimon had a woman who dealt with that.

Nguyen's second course was ostrich steak, ground-reared, insect-fed, and demonically bloody. The presence of the steak indicated two things: she had researched his preferences, and she had connections. The day that lab-meat crawled across the entrance to one of his restaurants would be the day he died a true death. Vardimon sampled the ostrich, noting the pliancy of texture with approval. When Tarek handed him a handkerchief he realized he had let blood drip down on his chin.

The dessert was the spectacle. Rooted in a sculpture of tessellated silver hexagons—itself a work of art—was a tree in full bloom made entirely of transparent candy. Suspended through the branches he saw popping pearls and whole strawberries, each fruit delicately, almost impossibly placed and glazed with a sheen that gave them the appearance of rubies ripe to fall.

"What does she call this?"

Tarek paused.

"It's the ballistic balsamic berry tree, sir."

The alliteration sounded strained on Tarek's lips. Vardimon would have pronounced it with more flair.

"Printed?"

"No, sir. Artisanal."

"Mm. A suspension torch, I suppose."

Vardimon strove not to appear impressed.

The sugar work was as fine as anything he had seen.

Once again the spoon came toward him, a strawberry resting in its curve. He wondered whether Tarek cooked at home, or whether he lived off the vending machine produce they shunted out to the lower levels. Synthetic pouches of fuel at their worst, machine-baked confectionery at best. He'd resisted when they wanted to pimp Vardimon products to the midrange, but the vending market was too big, his competitors were moving, the shareholders wanted a slice of it. That was what Polyakov had told him. He wondered now whether he should have held out.

He squinted at the strawberry. Plump, uniformly scarlet, the speckled indentations an accessory rather than a mar upon its succulent flesh. Nguyen had left the leaves on. That was clever. A nod to the soil, authenticity amid the artifice.

He chewed, swallowed. Paused for a moment. Allowed the pause to drag out, his expression carefully flatlined.

"That is exquisite."

Tarek smiled. Relief, pleasure? Despite his lack of augmentations, the nurse was not an easy read.

"The chef said they were flown in this morning. Fresh from the Siberian plains."

"Exquisite," he repeated. "The tree can go out as a special. We'll run a trial on the ostrich. Not the squid ink lake. Too immature."

Tarek nodded. He wouldn't know. He would never eat the strawberries or anything else from one of Vardimon's restaurants, so it didn't matter what Vardimon said.

The truth was he couldn't taste a thing.

• • •

Vardimon had promised himself that when his palate went, he would transfer. His organic sight was fading, but he didn't mind that, there was enough virtual entertainment in the ether to keep him occupied for several lifetimes. But losing the ability to smell, and taste—to create? Vardimon had built his career on his ability to invent flavors, drive trends, market experience. But he was not just a connoisseur. He *loved* food. He loved its truthfulness. He loved its inexhaustible variety, the possibility contained within it. If he couldn't relish a century-aged whisky, or the fresh tartness of fruit grown in the naked sun, then what was the point in living?

He had lost the ability to taste some time ago now. A month. Possibly longer. And thanks to the insidious, inexorable fear, he was deferring his rebirth.

He had noticed the loss with the absence of his own odor. That slight sourness that clings to a body in its final throes. So he was lying. To Tarek primarily, but through Tarek to everybody else who was a part of Vardimon Incorporated. The young chefs who put forward their recipes, desperate to gain a trial at his restaurants, would accept whatever he told them. That was the value of his word.

"Give me another strawberry."

Tarek obliged.

Chew, swallow. Feel the looseness of the skin around your neck as the fruit slides down the esophagus. Old man. Old man ready to become young again. They took a scan of his brain every twenty-four hours. That was the maximum time that could be lost between him, here, now, and the sarcophagus. They had done all the trials. Plenty of volunteers from where Tarek lived; the technicians had practiced until they got it right.

"What will you do after this?" he asked Tarek.

Surprise flitted across the nurse's face, was subsumed below the surface. Tarek was here because according to all the psychological studies, pretransfer palliative care demanded a human touch. But he had rarely, if ever, engaged the nurse in conversation about a subject other than himself.

"I'm hoping to get another placement," said Tarek.

"Another like me."

"Not exactly like you, sir."

"What do you mean by that?"

"Well—"

"Not as rich?"

"That is—undeniable, sir."

"But not what you meant." The nurse's face remained closed. "Open the damn walls. I want to see."

Tarek switched the window settings and the glass surround flooded with daylight. At this height, the traffic lanes moved far below, only the occasional private transport blinking between towers. The building opposite was Maxwell's empire, currently on its fifth upward expansion. Its surfaces teemed with construction robots. Vardimon wondered what would happen when they reached the upper limits of the atmosphere. Would Maxwell keep going, installing artificially oxygenated environments, until the spires penetrated the very edge of space?

In the distance, a small figure was hoverblasting. The blaster's tail wove a macaron pink ribbon that whorled about the sky, reminding Vardimon of the inside of an oyster shell. He remembered diving for oysters as a young man, long ago, before the sea rise. He remembered the beginning of it all. Surface cities clustering into vast metropolises, the drive to build. He remembered hoverblasting for the first time, the lightness, the suspension, so close to the sky you felt you were a god. Everything in him now was a weight. His reputation, a thing he risked with each new tasting, as he dredged up adjectives from the memories of cuisine gone by. It only took one bad chef to destroy a career.

But Polyakov wouldn't let that happen.

• • •

When Tarek finished his shift, Polyakov was waiting outside. A smooth-faced, muscular woman in her sixties, Tarek imagined her logging into the poker halls in her spare time.

"Well?"

Polyakov wasn't one for social niceties.

"He said the soil soup was squid ink. And I told him the berries were balsamic, like you said. He believed me."

Polyakov nodded. She looked pleased. Tarek never failed to be surprised by the peculiar rituals these people employed to test one another. That the marinade on a piece of fruit could be used to prove or disprove a person's sanity struck him as insane in itself; but then, he wasn't from the heights.

"Carry on," said Polyakov. "Keep him going."

"Will that chef get a trial?"

He shouldn't care. But when the membrane dissolved and he saw that tree, something had snagged at him, an emotion he didn't want his employers to see. It was the garden in the page, he supposed. Nguyen's tree belonged there.

"Sure," she said. "Vardimon called it. And she's good."

Polyakov was the executor of Vardimon's estate. The extent of the man's intellectual property was obscene. As a young man, what Vardimon lacked in financial resources he made up for with ingenuity and instinct. He had invested cannily—Ethiopian teff, seaweed technologies, biodegradable glass, edible packaging. And insects, whose bodies when stripped of their fat and ground up produced a powder the same flavor as chocolate—a fact that had proved fortuitous in the wake of the cacao bean crash. Vardimon had used the proceeds to open his first restaurant. That was the story, anyway.

In Tarek's world, Vardimon materialized as commercials, cheap holos of men and women rhapsodizing over new concoctions, and printed snacks disbursed from vending machines. In Polyakov's world, it was a symbol of status: to be seen at a Vardimon restaurant was to know you had made it. This Tarek had learned, painstakingly, over the nine months of his placement.

Polyakov wanted Vardimon to deteriorate as far as possible before his transfer. To commit a senile mind to the fresh body. It was about the money, he assumed. Tarek's job was to convince Vardimon he was still mentally healthy. That was about the money too, but Tarek's choices were limited in a way that these people's were not. He had kids, and a sister in jail for kicking the shit out of a police officer in the latest riots. He couldn't afford morals.

Tarek offered the remaining strawberries to Polyakov. Vardimon had stripped the tree of its offerings but kept the structure at his bedside. He wanted to inspect the sugar work.

"Have them."

She waved a dismissive hand. Tarek kept his face impassive. He didn't tell her that the air miles on this fruit would purchase the printed page of a book. There were lots of things he didn't tell them, not that they would ever ask; they had no curiosity for the lives of those below.

Except today.

What will you do next?

He didn't know.

• • •

Vardimon's face followed him to the hoverstation, a more youthful version than the one Tarek saw every day but recognizable nonetheless, grinning up from the rice paper on a vending-machine velvet cake. In Tarek's satchel was a box containing five strawberries, each with an invisible imperfection that had marked them unfit for consumption in Vardimon's eyes. It was true that the old oligarch was losing it. He'd been putting off the transfer for more than six months now. Tarek wondered what would happen to the new body if Vardimon decided against immortality. Whether it would go to someone else. He thought of Uri, pushed the thought quickly away.

The hovercraft entered the flow of traffic and bore him steadily downward. Stop after stop, the pristine sheen of Vardimon's world leached away. Clean lines and machine-polished surfaces gave way to the crude, unforgiving architecture of the lower levels. The hovercraft slipped past lurid advertisements, examples of graffiti both skilled and unskilled, human construction workers suspended from harnesses. They looked like insects in cocoons.

People like me get ground up just the same, he thought. But when we do there's nothing left.

He arrived home to find his two youngest squabbling over the five minutes left on the holodeck account. His eldest, Laila, was nowhere in sight, her absence a worry upon other worries, the sum of them so much a part of him that in some ways he no longer noticed. Laila was going the way of her aunt. He could see it day by day, and he couldn't blame her, but he didn't want her in a cell for the next twenty years either.

"Dad, it was my turn!"

The console was out of juice. No more virtual for a week at least. He gave the kids a strawberry each, cut a third in half and divided it between them, and set one aside for Laila who would probably reject it. That left one for him.

For a minute he just looked at it, aware that a chance like this might not come again. Then he bit into the berry.

The frosting dissolved on his tongue in a burst of intense sweetness. He couldn't have identified the exact flavor—something with cinnamon, he thought—but thanks to Polyakov's scheming he knew it wasn't balsamic.

He crushed the fruit between his teeth. Tartness followed sweetness. He might not have Vardimon's vocabulary but he knew that everything about it tasted *right*. As the sensation receded, his pleasure turned to anxiety about what he was doing to the kids—giving them, literally, a taste of a world they would never know. Not unless they did what Tarek was doing, handling a body incapable of handling itself.

His youngest was examining the strawberry leaves.

"You don't eat that bit," he said.

She dumped them in his hand. He held the leaves for a moment. It seemed despicable to throw them away, but what could he do with four strawberry tops? He chucked them in the chute.

The weekly call from his sister Amira came through later that evening. He had got used to seeing her prison garb in person, but it was still a shock to have it materialize in the apartment, the aggressiveness of the orange coveralls against the drabness of the place they lived. Conversation followed the usual pattern, stilted at first, slowly warming up. He wanted to tell Amira about the strawberries, the crystalline tree, but to do that would mean revealing the truth about the nursing gig.

Amira would be furious. That artificial world, she'd say. Those artificial people. What do they know about us? What do they know about family, or hardship, or desperation, or love? Do they have to support three kids on a zero-hours contract? Do they have to watch the woman they love age twenty years in as many months as the cancer eats up first her womb, then her breasts, and finally her bones? Do they have to *beg* for the drugs to alleviate her pain, and when they can't get them, to watch—to watch her suffering—to watch—

"Tarek?"

"Sorry, I was miles away."

"I can tell. Is Laila there?"

"She's out with friends."

He said it hoping it was true, and all at once he was glad Laila wasn't home. His sister was right, even though he only wanted a better life for them. That was all he had ever wanted. Something more than this. He didn't like to think about what would happen when Amira got out.

When she was gone the room seemed very empty, and colorless, the dormant console and the wall they couldn't afford to replaster, with its single framed paper page. The story was about a garden. A miraculous garden, where anything would seed and flourish. Tarek knew that the word garden came from its Germanic cousin, *garten*, whose original meaning was an enclosed or bounded space. He imagined stepping through the page on the wall, crossing into this magical realm where he and Uri and the kids and Amira could live and grow things and there, enclosed, he could keep them safe.

Safe from what? asked Uri, who was dead but sometimes spoke to him, still. *You always did worry too much.*

From everything. From working construction on

those sites and from the riots and the jail cells and the terrible thoughts that get inside your head and from what happened to you.

Uri had no answer to that.

Tarek didn't know the title of the book, or the author. Somewhere in the city, there must be other people, with other pages from the same copy. Perhaps they too wondered about the garden. At the book markets he always looked, even though it was unlikely he'd have the cash to make a purchase. He had come close to selling the page only once, when he thought he could get morphine for Uri. He was ready to make the deal, but she found out, put a stop to it. That page was her favorite thing. She made him read it to her every day. Every day except the last. On that day she never woke up.

Uri would have understood about the strawberries.

• • •

Vardimon wasn't sick. He wasn't suffering the way Uri had suffered, he was simply very old. Old, and increasingly mercurial in temperament. Today he was fretful, and prattling. Tarek lifted him into a sitting position, smoothing down the pillows which had cleaned themselves overnight and issued a faint citrus scent.

"There you go, sir. All set."

"Tarek. Tell me. Have you thought any more about what comes next?"

"I can't get another placement until there's a date."

"Ah. So your fate is bound to mine." The old man's gaze shifted to the windows. "Have you ever considered that, Tarek? The concept of fate?"

"Not really, sir."

Tarek supposed this was what happened at the end, even when there was a beginning to follow. Existentialism drawing its claws across the mind. He remembered coming home one day to find one of those spiritual naturalists at his wife's bedside. He'd been ready to throw the guy out, but Uri had wanted the spiritualist. Later, it

occurred to him that she had needed something to find the strength to let go.

The idea of Uri's death being the product of fate was intolerable.

And exactly the kind of excuse a sky dweller would love.

Oh shut up, Amira.

Vardimon cut across his thoughts.

"Perhaps when you have lived as long as I have, you will understand. Of late there have been things—weighing on my mind. Things I haven't thought about for a long time."

"Sir?"

"I've heard rumors," Vardimon said slowly. "Words spoken—in passing. The rumor is there are people still living on the surface."

Tarek paused, caught by surprise. Vardimon talking about the surface? He wondered whether Polyakov would count this as deterioration.

"Is it true?" Vardimon pressed.

"I haven't been to the surface, sir."

"But . . ."

"But—yes, I believe so, there are people down there."

"I remember it, you know."

"The surface?"

"Long before you were born. Things were very different then. Tell me about these people."

"Like I said, I haven't been—"

"Tell me, Tarek."

• • •

You knew it was coming because of the whining noise, keen as a mosquito at your ear. As soon as the noise started, you saw movement, shadows skipping through the smog. Bare feet, slap on the slick sand. The doors to the chute took sixty heartbeats to open. Louse could run three steps with every beat. By the time the doors were fully extended she had scaled the pyramid and was ready, poised, attendant. Others were waiting too but Louse had concealed herself the closest, almost directly beneath the doors, and because she blended she knew they couldn't see her. It was why they called her Louse.

Now the sound of the trash drop sliding down the chute. Louse had seen an other try to climb up there once. They didn't come back, but Louse didn't know what happened to them. If you kept climbing, forever, would you find something above the smog?

She heard whooping as the drop approached. Louse didn't leap, or make a sound, because it was important to be attentive. Here it came. Raining down from the doors above, separating as it fell. Scrapings and slime and slivers. Sometimes the trash contained things perfect in their entirety, membranous sacks or pyramids that exploded into your throat like a chorus of voices unfolding in the air. Mostly, it contained rubbish.

Even before the landing she could see there was something there. Something—her mind tested the word, wrapped around it—*green*. She was in before anyone else. She heard the shouts of annoyance; they'd missed her, again. Her hands reached, foraging—grab, mouth, grab, mouth—but it was the green she wanted and once her fingers closed upon it she backed up, wary, blending, worried an other might have seen her prize and come to wrestle it from her.

She spat out something hard and gritty, chewed on something soft, swallowed, clambered back down the pyramid. Her eyes could see through the smog, and she could breathe it too. She had smoke eyes. She had blood skin. The mosquitos bit her and she didn't get sick, though it was irritating, and itchy. The others in this patch wore masks and nets and they sweated all the time. She kept away from them. They had tried to hurt her before. They would probably like to have smoke eyes and blood skin, but they were afraid of her.

Now she was on her way, blending through the brick-fronted streets thick with coal dust, past a fire spitting out flecks of paper where others were barbequing something with legs and a head and a pointed nose but Louse would not be welcome, she never was, up and over a rusting fence and squirming up a pipe on the wall of the abandoned house where some sand-dogs lived,

though they were killed often, and ended up on the spit, like that one back there.

On the roof she examined her prize.

It was made of narrow—she held the word, cradled it, yes, *leaves*—that connected at the center and tapered outward to a point. A gem of red clung to them. She put her tongue to it. A shock threshed through her body. She took it away from her tingling mouth, examined it afresh. She would keep this, yes, it would stay with her other treasures. She would not eat it. It was not something to be eaten.

• • •

Tarek stopped talking to find Vardimon watching him intently. He had never seen the old man so engaged. It was unsettling.

"Why do the other feeders stay away from her?"

Tarek thought quickly.

"Do you remember those experiments, a few decades back? To control the population?"

Vardimon looked impatient.

"Of course."

"So Louse looks different. She's—evolved."

"How does she look different?"

"Her face, I suppose. I don't know. It's not like she's real."

This is ridiculous, he thought. I'm telling the old man bedtime stories.

"Don't spoil it," said Vardimon. "You're not employed for that."

"No, sir. I apologize, sir."

• • •

Vardimon thought about Louse, pushing waste into her mouth. There had been a time, especially when crops were failing and in the early days of the greenhouse revolution, when people talked about food becoming fuel. A form of processed nutrients, synthetic stuff that could be ingested without thought, without care or joy. With so many immigrants like Tarek there was a need for synthesis, it was the only way to sustain the lower levels of the ever-expanding metropolises. Vardimon knew this, had lived through it. But he had never been afraid of that future spreading upward.

To understand food, to work with it effectively, imaginatively, you had to understand desire, anticipation, gratification. You had to understand pleasure. Only by engaging with the primal could you produce alchemy, cuisine that evoked emotion in a society sterilized by artifice.

Partnerships were forged, love affairs ended, business deals brokered, and friendships cemented, over food.

In some ways, it was all they had left.

Perhaps Polyakov and the rest were right. Perhaps his thoughts had turned unnecessarily dark.

He imagined, as he did most nights now, waking inside the sarcophagus. Running his tongue around its teeth, flexing its nostrils. Would they share the same tastes? What if the technicians had failed to replicate his refined sense of smell, or his gut instinct—a thing surely impossible to transcribe in genetic code? What if he *hated* food?

• • •

"How is he today, Tarek?"

"He wants to know about bottom feeders."

"Feeders?" Polyakov's eyes gleamed with satisfaction. She was like a crocodile, thought Tarek. A crocodile to Vardimon's dinosaur. That gave him an idea. "Don't tell me he's developing a social conscience."

Tarek looked at her.

"No. I don't think it's gone that far."

On the commute home he thought about the next stage of Louse's story. She was becoming familiar. It was almost as if they'd met.

• • •

Safely blended, Louse often listened to the talk of others. Talk was like the ripple of oil across puddles, it merged and smeared together and

patterns came out of it, sometimes readable, sometimes not. The talk was of the city. The city was a maleficent thing, a monster intent upon crushing them, relentless, mechanical and impossible to escape, though they wished to escape it nonetheless. There were plans hidden inside the talk. The others would climb high, infiltrate, steal, find a better life. Louse was not sure what they meant by this phrase, *a better life*, but by the talk of stealing she had come to the conclusion that there must be *other* others above, in those places detectable only as glimpsed structures lifting into the smog.

These others must have wings, great leathery ones. They would look like the lizards with biting snouts that roamed the streets at night and snatched you if you weren't safe behind a wall. Gators, the others called them. Don't let the gators catch you. They came in from the water beyond the city. They looked slow but moved shockingly fast. The above-others would be like this, winged gators drifting through the smog. They would not fear the city.

She remembered the skinny figure she had witnessed climbing into the chute. Had his journey upward turned him into a lizard? Or had the lizards eaten him, crunched him into shards of bone? If Louse followed, what would happen to her?

Her skin was already tough, and in firelight it had a gleam to it, a kind of movement. Would she grow scales? Would she hunger for the flesh of others?

Louse wondered.

• • •

"Well, don't stop there!"

Vardimon waited irritably. Tarek's hand had gone to his ear; the nurse was listening to someone.

"You have a visitor," said Tarek.

"Who?"

If Vardimon could smell, the perfume would have warned him, but as it was he had no time to prepare until the door opened.

"No!" he shouted, launching himself into a fit of coughing, so Tarek had to prop him up, bring him water, but it was no good, it was too late, he had already entered the room. He—*she*—never did take no for an answer.

Elena collapsed into an armchair with a theatrical sigh.

"Tarek, be a dear and get me a Balvenie, will you? Two fingers, no ice. Vardimon, for you?"

"What the hell are you doing here?"

Tarek served Elena her whisky and left the room discreetly.

"I still have my keys, darling."

Alone, they surveyed each other. Her new body was sleek, luscious, inarguably beautiful, and it left him entirely cold. Today her hair was aquamarine. Like a fucking mermaid.

"To think I paid for that," he said at last.

"This again? I told you I wanted something different."

"I thought you meant cosmetics. Not—not *this*."

"You can't even say it, can you." She crossed her legs. Their length was emphasized by slim-fitting trousers and stiletto heels. She leaned forward. "Vardimon. Do you realize what a gift this is? We're pioneers. There's a whole new world out there and you want to live the same life over again?"

"I loved you," he said. All at once he was shaking.

"I'm still me."

"No."

She looked away. She seemed exasperated. Perhaps she was unmoved too. She hadn't mentioned her sexual preferences in this body. Or perhaps now she could only see his decrepitude.

"Have you set a date?" she asked.

"Not yet."

He wanted to tell her about the fear, how he was trapped between the fear of what he was becoming and the fear of what he would become. With the transfer he would change, and like her, he might not wake the same. The one thing that distracted him was fairy tales about a surface

child who didn't exist, and Elena would think that ridiculous.

"But it's ready," she said. "The sarcophagus."

His lips curled around an involuntary smile. She was the only one, other than him, who would call it that.

"Yes."

"You know it gets harder the longer you leave it."

"And you'll be waiting on the other side?"

He couldn't keep the bitterness from his voice. Yes, it had been years—even decades—since there had been anything physical between them. But they had talked about this, when the new technology came online. A renewal of vows. Revisit the passions of youth, acts of lust he could barely remember now, they were hazed by nostalgia, although perhaps the sarcophagus would have a sharper recollection. But then Emil—*Elena*—had decided to become a woman. He would never want her again. Or perhaps the sarcophagus would. Irrationally, that thought enraged him even more.

Elena didn't answer his question. Perhaps it had been more of a plea, pathetic, really. She must think him pathetic. She had leaped where he was lingering. She had not been afraid. His ex-lover unfolded her long legs, stood, rested a hand on the duvet. He felt the pressure of her fingers on his shins through the bedding.

"Don't wait too long, dear heart," she said. "I miss my partner in wine."

• • •

The sarcophagus was in the room. It stood at the end of his bed, watching him slyly. There was an unpleasant expression on its face—malevolence, greed?—he couldn't quite work it out. If he were awake, he could work it out, but he was asleep, and the sight of it terrified him.

The sarcophagus bent forward, placed its hands on either side of his feet, looked him straight in the eye. Once it had his full attention, the sarcophagus stood and stretched, displaying its lithe naked body, the muscles scything across its torso. Then it strolled across the room and opened the door to his drinks cabinet.

His terror gave way to indignation.

"What do you think—"

He struggled to sit up, but without Tarek there as a brace his limbs were leaden, unresponsive, he could only prop himself upon one elbow and watch awkwardly as the sarcophagus extracted one of his favorite reds, a Swedish pinot noir, uncorked the bottle, and poured itself a glass. Saliva gathered in his mouth. He remembered that pinot noir. The feel of it, the nose of it, the slight grip of the tannin on his teeth—yes, he remembered.

And yet his mouth was ash.

The sarcophagus tilted the glass, admiring the ruby complexion of the wine. It took a mouthful, drew air through the liquid, swilled, tipped its head back, swallowed. An ecstatic expression possessed its features.

"Old world," it said. "Smoke. Wood fires. Earthiness, yes, oak-aged, raspberry, cherry, spice, a warmth to it, a palpable warmth. This is an excellent vintage."

The sarcophagus tilted the glass toward him. He felt the urge to weep. He remembered. The sarcophagus couldn't remember, it wasn't here, he was dreaming.

"Care to taste?"

His rage welled up, sudden and irrepressible.

"You know nothing about that vintage—"

"Did you know," said the sarcophagus meditatively. "The nose has the capacity to detect up to fourteen thousand aromas? And your nose, even before the augmentations, has served you particularly well. Has it not?"

"Get out!" he yelled. His breathing was coming faster. It felt as though a clay fire oven was parked upon his chest.

"And yet," continued the sarcophagus. "I have to wonder. What have you really achieved over the last century, Mr. Vardimon, *sir*? Have you revolutionized the sensory experience? Have you solved the global distribution of food?

Or have you just thrown together a few endangered ingredients and branded it haute cuisine?"

"Fuck you!" he shouted. "I remember a time when insects were sneered at. When I was a child, virtual reality was practically embryonic and things like you were illegal—"

"It's true," said the sarcophagus. "You're a relic of the old world yourself. But I—I shall be entirely new. Just like Elena."

It was too much. He reached for the sarcophagus. Its tongue—he wanted its tongue, he would seize the muscle, rip it from its throat still coated in the residues of the pinot noir. He would fucking eat it. The sarcophagus watched him languidly, unaffected by the violence of his thoughts. Believing, no doubt, that he did not have the capacity to commit such an act. He thrust back the covers. He lunged—

• • •

He woke to find himself on the floor beside the bed, an ache rising down the right side of his body, the emotions of the dream still blurring his perceptions. The door opened and one of his staff entered. Not Tarek. It was too early for Tarek. Exclamations. Lights raised. His fall had triggered an alarm. They lifted him into the bed, fussing, gently chiding. You must wait for us, you're not as strong as you think. You just have to call! Furtively, he checked the corners of the room, expecting to see the sarcophagus lurking there, a sardonic smile plastered over its symmetrical face, but they'd turned the glass and the sunrise filled the room, and with the morning it had nowhere to hide.

• • •

"I want to see my body."

"Sir, I'm not sure—"

"I said I want to see it."

He insisted Tarek call a technician. He insisted Tarek came with him. They floated him down the corridor on a gurney. He had imagined they would keep it farther away, there was something blasphemous about it being so close. But in the end there were only rooms between them.

The sarcophagus was in a tank. It was naked, as it had been last night, fetal and covered in some sort of gel, an oddly phosphorous glow to its suspended limbs. Its skin was clear, without lines, a lustrous brown, its internal organs clean as a baby's and its senses unmarred.

Vardimon experienced a surge of envy so great he wanted to kill it. But it wasn't yet alive. It would only become alive with him, his mind, his intellect and bank of memory.

"Tomorrow," he said abruptly.

"Sir?"

"We'll do it tomorrow. Tell Polyakov to make the arrangements."

They would put him to sleep. He'd wake in the sarcophagus. Its face would be his face. Its tongue his tongue. It was time.

"I want you to be there," he said. Tarek nodded. Unexpected gratitude overcame him. Tarek would be there. Even if everyone else abandoned him, the nurse would not. "I want breakfast. Pancakes, maple syrup, bacon. Fresh cream. Blueberries. Juice. Ethiopian coffee. You understand?"

"I'll see to it, sir."

• • •

Tarek stood before the page on the wall, gazing at the words until his vision blurred them into nonsense. In the garden in the page there was no ending. There could not be an ending, because it was an isolated page, and the last word on the page was *and*.

"Aren't you working, Dad?"

Laila had crept up behind him.

"Not tonight."

Not tomorrow, either. Polyakov had seen to that. Tarek had failed in his task; Vardimon wasn't sufficiently delusional for Polyakov's purposes.

"Have you told Aunt Amira?"

"There's no point. It's over, Laila. I won't be working up there again."

"Why not?"

He didn't have an answer to that, not one his daughter would understand. He put his arm around her shoulders. She was thinner than she should be. In his head he heard Amira's voice, saying everyone knew, had always known, there was enough food in the world. It just wasn't going where it was needed. From snatches of conversation overheard in the heights, he knew it was true.

He had wanted to tell Polyakov that her entire world was founded upon a delusion, the delusion that the heights could get away with it, continue to hide behind their candied sculptures and land-reared meat whilst only minutes away by hovercraft there were people who struggled to feed their families every night. He was on the verge of saying this, and other things, the kind of things Amira would have said, when the call came. The officer asked him to come to the police station. Laila was there. If she hadn't been a juvenile, she'd be locked away by now.

He wondered whether Vardimon would think of him when he awoke to his pancakes and blueberries, alone. He thought of the body in the tank, the greatest luxury a mind could know, wondered how it would feel to become young again. Though it was not Vardimon's youth he envied but his age. The old age Uri should have had, and was denied.

• • •

The night before the transfer, the technicians took a final scan and administered his pre-op drugs. They would return in the morning, first thing. They would induce this body's death. Vardimon had insisted he was left alone and undisturbed. He had one night to dream, dreams that would belong only to him, to this version of his mind. The sarcophagus would have no recollection of these final hours.

He ordered the windows to clear, saw the

glaze of the city stretching away behind the glass, blending. The drugs were making him woozy.

He had heard that near the end you saw your life compressed like a showreel, nuggets of memory passing before your eyes. He would have to create his own showreel. He thought of his first restaurant, the shouts and steam, delirious chaos of the evening service. He remembered Emil's face serene against the pillow, Emil's lips brushing his. A plate of buttery olives, not quite ripe. Wines whose origins drifted north with the decades. Ethiopian sunsets over acres of teff. Diving for oysters off the coast, before the sea rise, before the build. He remembered the surface.

Behind the glass, the city pulsed softly. He pulled himself to the edge of the bed and rolled off, ignoring the jolt of pain as he landed on the floor. It didn't matter now. On his elbows he hauled himself toward the glass, until he could peer down into the city's nascent depths.

He imagined stepping through the glass and off the ledge. The moment of suspension before he dived, blasting downward, a tail stretching out behind him in saffron yellow. Past the chromium wonderland in the sky, through the crude, regimented architecture of Tarek's world, and down, and down, hitting the toxic smog that obscured the land that begot Louse. It stung his eyes. He pulled a mask over his face, but the stench of it burned against his throat and the delicate papillae of his tongue.

He landed with a crash on Louse's pyramid. Sat for a moment, blinking through the smog. Accustoming himself to the precarious, constantly shifting textures of his seat, the swelter. The entrails of the world were here. And so was she. Louse sat opposite him. She was crouched, frog-like, a stillness to her as though she had been waiting for some time.

Her mouth had no lips.

Vardimon found he had a bowl in his hands. "Scallop?" he offered her.

Her oil eyes watched him. Slowly, she extended a hand. The skin on her palm rippled, a chameleon texture to its surface. She took the scallop, crammed it entire into her lipless mouth. A sucking sound. He looked away. He sipped at the bowl, curious as to its flavors, and gagged. His palate had returned, but the soup before him bore no relation to squid ink; Nguyen had made him a sauce of sewage.

Louse smiled. Her incisors were half the size of normal teeth, blunt and square. He gave her the ostrich steak next, and watched the blood run down her chin. Did they practice cannibalism down here? Who knew how these people lived? He sensed movement below, and when he looked down he could see a pack of alligators circling the trash heap. They looked hungry.

Last was the candy tree. He showed Louse how to break off twigs and extract the strawberries from within. He ate one himself. The release of flavor on his tongue was the most beautiful thing he had ever experienced. He felt tears gather behind his eyes. The glaze wasn't balsamic though. He realized then that he had been lied to. Polyakov had known of his incapacity all along.

Louse had not eaten the strawberry. She held it between fingers red with ostrich blood, turning it over and over, admiring the fruit as if it were a precious jewel. He looked skyward. He wanted to show something to Louse, the constellations, perhaps, or Maxwell's empire reaching toward space, but the smog was complete and all he saw was the open mouth of a chute.

Louse tugged at his sleeve. She was trying to communicate with him, odd whistling and clicking noises that bore no resemblance to words. She pointed overhead. He understood, allowed her to clamber onto his shoulders, got shakily to his feet. Now she was high enough. She gripped the filthy lip of the chute and levered herself up inside. She was not afraid. Vardimon remained where he was, listening to the alligators foraging. After a while he knew she wasn't coming back. He imagined her climbing upward, aware of a restfulness that he had not felt for a long time, and he realized that she had taken his fear with her.

OLIVER LANGMEAD

GLITTERATI

(2017)

WEDNESDAY. Or was it Tuesday?

"Darling?"

"What is it, dear heart?"

"Is it Wednesday, or Tuesday?"

"It's Tuesday today."

"Did we not have a Tuesday yesterday?"

"No, dearest. We had a Monday yesterday. I recall it being Monday quite clearly, in fact, because Gabrielle was wearing that blue Savinchay dress with the sequined trim, which she only ever wears on Mondays because it would be outrageous to wear Savinchay on any other day of the week."

That settled it, then.

Simone unpeeled his face from the pink leather chaise longue. Last night had been a rainbow of cocktails, resulting in the headache now threatening to impinge on his usually immaculate poise. He went to the gold-plated Manchodroi dresser, which he only ever used on Tuesdays, and was astonished to find his usual dose of painkillers gone.

"Darling!" he cried.

"What is it, Simone?"

"My medicine is missing!"

"Have you checked the Manchodroi dresser?"

"I have opened the very drawer in which my Tuesday dose is stored, and that drawer is quite empty. Might you have accidentally taken them?"

"Certainly not."

"And you're absolutely sure that today is Tuesday?"

"I'm positive, dearest Simone. I have just this minute remembered that Galvin was wearing his red Crostay suit last night, which he only ever wears on Mondays, because, as everyone knows, red Crostay is a delight which should only ever be savored on the first day of the week. I am absolutely, one-hundred-percent certain that today is Tuesday. Could it be that you've misplaced your medication?"

"Well," said Simone, uncertainly. "It could be. I remember very little of last night."

"Use the supply we set aside in the upper left cupboard of the guest wardrobe. And do get ready. You have work in two hours, and it would be simply awful were you to arrive too late."

This was true. It being a Tuesday, it would be the talk of the office were Simone to arrive at work anything more than twenty minutes late. Simone quickly rushed through to the guest bedroom and rooted around in the wardrobe until he located the spare painkillers. In the guest bathroom, he spread the white powder across the shining surface of the chrome sink and proceeded to snort it all up in one go. The drugs fizzed in his brain, and his headache began to recede.

"Superb," he said, to his ruffled reflection. "Most delightful."

Tuesday, then, which meant wearing white to work. Simone searched through his walk-in wardrobes and located his white suits. The first, a close-fitting number from Messr Messr, the second, a looser, but tastefully trimmed alternative from Saint Darcington, and lastly, his brand-new white suit, made with a newly invented meta-material infused with light-emitting micro-LEDs from Karpa Fishh, which was at the very forefront of fashion technology. Still not feeling himself, Simone settled on the tastefully understated Messr Messr suit, and laid it out while he got to work on his face.

Tuesday was a pale day, which meant bringing out his cheekbones. He began with a three-point washing formula from Karrat, and moved on to some moisturizer from Stringham, before clearing that away with body temperature water sourced, purified, and heated to perfection by Dracington Lord. Then, he moved on to his Flaystay foundation, applied with his perfectly softened Karrat brush set, and finished up with a layer of ivory white Flaystay powder. The powdering done, he blended his gray Stringham blushers together and began to highlight the shape of his skull with perfect precision, applying liberal shadows to the space beneath his cheekbones. Then, once his face seemed perfectly skull-like, he began to draw out his eyes

with his collection of Dramaskil complimentary eyeliners and eye shadows, until they were quite the centerpiece of his face. Running his fingers along his collection of Dramaskil false eyelashes, he selected a brilliant white pair speckled with tastefully dusted black powder, and delicately affixed them to his eyelids using Dramaskil's gentle false eyelash glue. These he finished off with a little of Stringham's excellent mascara to bring them out. Finally, he settled on a light gray Seleseal lipstick, to contrast with his perfectly whitened teeth, and lined it with some black Seleseal lip liner, to give his lips some real definition.

Pouting to make certain that all was in place, Simone sealed it with Grantis Grato makeup fixer, spraying liberally to make certain nothing would slide off during his busy day ahead.

Face affixed, Simone pulled on his Messr Messr suit and tightened his tie.

Two-forty-five, already? Simone hastened through, air-kissed his wife, and struck a pose before the hallway mirror, which was framed with bright bulbs in order to reveal every single possible flaw in the beholder. Feeling satisfied, he left for work.

• • •

Unfortunately, Simone's route to work took him above the streets of the city suburbs, where the poor unfashionables lived.

The windows of the pristine vibro-rail carriage revealed the depths below, where the houses were made for practicality instead of design. They looked, to Simone, like terrible parodies of the packaging that some of his cheapest items of clothing came in. Simone stared down at the suburbs, his mouth curled in contempt.

The uglies. The unwashed, unmanicured masses. The unfashionables.

It pained him to see them down there, milling around without the first idea of how dreadful they appeared; how their untrained aesthetic senses were so underdeveloped that they could barely comprehend their own hideousnesses. To think, they did actual labor! To think, they used things like shovels and wrenches and drills! Simone shuddered, but found himself unable to look away. The horror of it drew him in completely.

It was unfathomable that people existed like that.

The carriage slipped through a tunnel, and suddenly they were there, at the heart of the horror, where beyond the unornamented fences the unfashionables lumbered around. If only Simone's tear ducts hadn't been removed—why, he would have wept for them. Feeling his gut squirm inside him, he watched them go by, bumping into each other, smiling their ugly, unpainted smiles, staring open-mouthed and lustily at the vibro-rail carriage as it swept past; at its contents—the beautiful glitterati.

To think that they were the same species. It boggled the mind.

Simone secretly hoped that the unfashionables would all catch a disease and die. Of course, it wasn't fashionable to think such thoughts. The fashion was that the uglies were to be pitied, and that charity in the form of discarded past-season wardrobes was a sign of good character. But Simone only said that he sent his old wardrobes down to the unfashionables. In reality, he burned his clothes when he was done with them. The mere thought of his discarded suits touching the skin of any of those aesthetically impaired imbeciles made him feel ill.

So caught up in horror he was, that Simone barely noticed the vibro-rail carriage gliding to a halt. He was the last to leave.

The vast and crystalline Tremptor Tower rose ahead, and Simone felt his heart lift. Surrounding the square were offices built to be aesthetically brilliant, but none compared to the mighty beauty of Tremptor Tower. It was like working in Heaven—the fluted glass cylinders which made the whole building look like an enormous celestial organ always made him smile. He was careful with his smile, of course. It simply wouldn't do to affect his face before making his entrance.

He checked his watch. Precisely twenty minutes late. Perfect.

There was a queue at the front entrance, and the instant that Simone set his eyes upon it he felt his heart stop. Every single man and woman in the queue was wearing purple.

What could it mean? Had he missed an issue of one of the one hundred and sixteen different fashion magazines he was subscribed to? Holding a hand delicately to his chest, Simone felt as if he must flee—he must go home this instant and feign illness. But it was too late. He was already caught up in the queue. And those behind him . . .

Simone risked a glance backward. Perfectly painted open mouths and wide eyes. Horror.

Maybe it was a joke, and everyone in Tremptor Tower was in on it. Maybe he would make his entrance and everyone would clap and applaud and laugh, and he would laugh with them, and they would all drink champagne and reminisce for years to come about how delightful the jest had been.

Slowly, the queue moved forward. Then, it was Simone's turn.

Striking his best pose, Simone sashayed inside.

Absolute silence. The hands poised mid-clap to receive him were completely still. The long red runway yawned out endlessly before him, but still he sashayed on—eyes on the horizon, lips pursed. Not a single camera flashed. But there, at last, his salvation; the steps leading off the entrance runway and across to the lifts. He would have run the last few meters, but not a single drop of sweat had been shed in Tremptor Tower since its construction, and he certainly wouldn't be the first to desecrate the hallowed ground.

Inside the lift, Simone pressed the button for the tenth floor with one shaking finger. Everyone around him was wearing purple. They kept glancing at him, but he kept his eyes down, studying the tastefully designed Tremptor elevator carpet design.

Eventually, the elevator arrived at the tenth floor.

Simone power-walked the final few steps into his office, and shut the door. He crystallized the walls so that they were opaque, and sat down behind his three-tier desk.

What could have happened? What had gone wrong? Unless . . . Simone's eyes grew wide.

What if it wasn't Tuesday after all? What if it was actually *Wednesday?*

The implications were unbearable. Was he to spend the entire day unfashionable? Wearing all white when it was a complete faux pas to be in monochrome on a Wednesday? But what could he do? He could phone his wife and get her to bring a spare suit. But then—what about his face? The Grantis Granto makeup fixer was already in place. His makeup would be solid for at least the next eight hours.

Simone resolved to hide in his office all day. If anybody came knocking, he would claim to be in a meeting. It was the done thing, after all. An actual meeting had not occurred in Tremptor Tower since its creation, but to use being in a meeting as an excuse was to be considered polite.

There wasn't anything of any real substance in Simone's office. He would have to get creative in order to bide his time. There were artfully piled stacks of blank paper, and aesthetically pleasing towers of electronic equipment that he had no idea how to use. Nobody in Tremptor Tower did any work, after all. That would have been a hideous use of the mind. Actual work was for the dreadful unfashionables below, who could afford the brainpower.

Simone took a deep breath. It would be all right. He would simply read magazines all day. Drawing out the latest Gentlemen's Art from his desk, he began reading—admiring the models wearing the best in avant-garde designs—and eventually began to relax. It would be fine. Only a few people had seen him, after all. He would laugh it off tomorrow. They would all laugh it off, and drink champagne, and it would be a funny anecdote.

There came a knock at the door. "Simone?" It was Darlington.

"I'm in a meeting!" he cried, hiding behind his magazine.

"But Simone, you simply must come out! It's Trevor Tremptor. He's come to see us."

How utterly dreadful! Simone had forgotten. Today was the day that Trevor Tremptor, fashion icon and head of the Tremptor company, was coming around to mingle with those on the tenth floor of his tower. Simone was mortified. This could mean embarrassment before the whole company. Worse—this could mean demotion.

Trembling, Simone stepped out into the corridor and stood before his door.

Everyone else was lined up, all dressed in purple. As soon as they set eyes on him, there were gasps. Monochrome? On a Wednesday? It was outrageous.

There was Trevor Tremptor now, air-kissing each of his coworkers, and offering little compliments. Everyone blushed the correct amount, and struck a little pose. Trevor himself was an Adonis—so incredible to look upon that it hurt Simone's eyes. Had ever a more fashionable being existed? Simone wanted to disappear into the carpet.

At last, Trevor Tremptor arrived before Simone. There was a long silence. Everyone was holding their breath.

"Simone . . . ," said Trevor, carefully, but Simone couldn't meet his eyes. He kept his head down, so ashamed of what he was wearing. He knew he was letting everyone down. "Simone . . . ," said Trevor again, and Simone closed his eyes, waiting for the guillotine to drop. "That . . . is . . . *fabulous.*"

• • •

The rest of the day passed in a magnificent whirl.

Simone was promoted not just to the eleventh floor, but all the way up to the nineteenth, where some of the most beautiful people in the company worked. The offices were dazzling with their array of poised statuaries and intricate pieces of useless electronic equipment. Even the stacks of blank paper were of top quality—a creamy white, displaying this month's Tremptor logo.

Everyone applauded him, and he was surrounded on all sides by remarkable fashionistas, who each praised him for his daring. "Monochrome on a Wednesday?" they said, "It's simply incredible! Unheard of. It's so *subversive*. The irony of it, and the *precision* of it."

Invited on a tour of the offices, Simone was overwhelmed. It felt like his brain was on fire. The people on the nineteenth floor made those down on the tenth look like sniveling uglies, but now, here, Simone knew he could realize his full potential—his place as a true innovator in the art of fashion. He had never considered himself an innovator before, but now that he was here it was obvious.

After work, everyone treated him to drinks at the bars. Beneath the neon lights, Simone himself felt neon. He drank endless bottles of champagne, and beautiful rainbow cocktails, and inhaled so much white powder that it felt as if he was breathing drugs instead of air. He was on top of the world. He was brilliant, and he knew it. Everyone slapped him on the back, and called him remarkable, and gave him their business cards, and no less than three magazines wanted to take his picture.

In a whirling, frothing, state of absolute euphoria, Simone submerged in neon. For the first time in his life, he felt as if he really knew that he was beautiful.

• • •

When Simone awoke, he was still buzzing. "Darling! Did you hear about my promotion?"

"I heard everything, Simone! But we have no time to chat this morning. You simply must ready yourself for work. After all, it being Thursday, you must be ten minutes early."

Of course she was right. But something was tugging at Simone's bubbling brain. Something had happened to him. Something was different.

He unfurled from the pink chaise longue and felt like a beautiful butterfly, emerging from its ugly cocoon. Today was the first day of his life that he was truly fashionable. Today he would dare to go against the trend again. He would show them all how brilliant he was.

And there was his first moment of inspiration, courtesy of his wife. He wouldn't be early, nor would he be late. Simone would arrive at work *precisely on time*.

But what to wear? What to wear?

Thursday usually meant flowers; organic greens, brilliant yellows, and every color of the rainbow. It was a day in the fashion world devoted to life. But Simone was a fashion prodigy now, and he knew that he must represent that. He must show them all that he was worthy of the nineteenth floor of Tremptor Tower.

Death, then. He would spit in the face of life and all would love him for it.

Gray. It must be gray. He threw open the doors to his walk-in wardrobes and swept his hands along his suits, before coming to the gray section. There was his darling Sarcross suit—a desirable classic—and his thick ungainly Redrad suit, which was only to be worn on the third Sunday of each month. But instead of either of these, Simone tore open the boxes containing his slate-gray Dan Chopin suit, which he had been saving for a special occasion. It was made of an experimental material which was considered capable of drawing out the dullest, least-vibrant shade imaginable.

He would be the opposite of life. He would be a void of unlife.

But what about his face? What would he do?

Simone emptied his cupboards, searching for anything gray. But none of it was good enough. How was he meant to represent absolute nothingness with a bit of eyeliner? Some false eyelashes? A gray lipstick? Frustrated and trembling, he threw powders at the walls, and shattered glass bottles.

"Simone?" His wife. "What's happening?"

"I simply must . . . ," he hissed, at his reflection.

But there—another moment of inspiration.

The walls in the pool-house were being repainted in shades of gray. Normally, of course, Simone would avoid the unfashionables while they were at work—to behold them so close would make him nauseous—but today he must be brave. He would face them, for the sake of his art.

Running through the house, he flung open the pool-house doors. Water reflected across the half-painted walls, and a dozen pairs of unornamented eyes stared at him in wonder. Simone hated them. Waves of hate rolled over him. But he persevered. He burbled some nonsense gibberish at them and grabbed one of the buckets of paint.

CAUTION, it read on the side. TOXIC FUMES.

Simone upended the bucket over his head. The paint was cold, and a little slipped down his throat, but the fumes shot up his nose, making him sure of himself.

Running back to his mirror, he saw that he had done right. His skin was perfectly gray. It was brilliant. He grinned, and the whiteness of his teeth sent shocks through him. They weren't good enough. Dipping his fingers into the still-wet paint covering his neck, he rubbed at the white until it was dulled. Then, he washed his hands in the paint. Gray skin, gray teeth, gray everything. Only his eyes would emerge—the wild ever-watchful eyes of death.

Finally, he put on his Dan Chopin suit.

Gray nothingness: death. He was ready to face them.

Laughter tumbling from his lips, he entered his wife's dressing room.

"I'm ready!" he cried.

Her eyes widened and she let out a shriek, but Simone paid it no attention. He knew that he was beautiful. Even as she fainted, he air-kissed her and ran for the door, tapping at his paint-encrusted watch. If he left now, he would be exactly on time for work. Just as planned. He could already hear the applause thundering in his ears.

• • •

The vibro-rail carriage was empty, because everyone else had arrived at work early.

Simone felt the excitement growing in his gut. Or maybe it was illness. It was difficult to tell. The fumes wafted into his nose from the paint covering his face and made bubbles in his brain that weren't gray, like the paint, but neon, like the clubs of last night.

As the carriage passed over the suburbs where the uglies tramped around on their worn shoes, a stream of bright pink vomit shot out of Simone's mouth and coated the window. Instead of being disgusted by the sight, Simone became fascinated by it. Through the lens of his pink vomit, the dull realm of the unfashionables below became a thing of beauty. Suddenly, the regular shapes became organic, lumpy things, enhanced by chunks of undigested food, and the uglies were like brilliant pink beetles, their unkempt features bright.

But of course this should happen, Simone thought. He was becoming so fashionable that his very effluence was making the world beautiful.

Beyond the suburbs, the carriage smoothly sailed on past the streets where the unfashionables walked. Another jet of vomit soared majestically from between Simone's gray lips, splattering all over the windows, this time in bright orange. "You're welcome," he said at the uglies, admiring the way that the streaks of red through the orange made pretty kaleidoscopic whirls to mask their hideousness.

By the time the carriage came to a halt, Simone felt euphoric. Stumbling from the vibro-rail, he beheld the way that Tremptor Tower wafted around in his vision as if it was a flag in a gale. He inhaled deeply, huffing great gouts of paint fumes into his lungs, and his euphoria heightened, killing any doubts he might have had. The pain in his gut was getting worse, but of course it wasn't actual pain. It was only the transformation occurring—his transformation from tenth floor fashionista to nineteenth floor fashion innovator and icon.

Wrapping his hands around his collar to hold himself upright, Simone swanned up to the

Tower entrance. There was no queue. He was the last to arrive today. But it was perfect, so perfect—they would all have a chance to see his brilliant daring.

Throwing the doors aside, he swaggered down the red carpet, letting his hips lead him. The carpet wormed perilously beneath him, but he kept his stride. There was no applause to greet him, and no cameras flashed, but that was fine. Simone knew that his audience were too awed to respond. He shot glances to the left and the right, and saw members of the press fainting—falling from their chairs as if life had left them.

"Today," he announced, swinging his arms wide. "I am death!"

There was a shriek from an unknown source. Simone leapt heroically from the end of the red carpet, fell to his knees, and then dragged himself standing again. The shriek continued. The whole lobby whirled around in his vision, as if it was all caught up in a storm and he was the eye of it, and he couldn't locate the source of the scream. It was only as he managed to summon a lift that he realized that the shriek was tearing its way out of his own lungs. He let it happen for a while longer—screaming out the last of his ugliness, no doubt—and then inhaled sharply through his nostrils. Paint fumes powered their way into his brain and everything suddenly stopped whirling around.

The lift rose and rose, and Simone felt a great itching across his shoulder blades. He scratched weakly at the place, feeling a pair of strange lumps there, and for a moment he worried that something was terribly wrong. Breathing heavily fixed that worry—soothing his thoughts and reminding him that this was just another part of his transformation. By becoming death, he was becoming art.

By the time the lift arrived at the nineteenth floor, Simone's legs were no longer working. The doors pinged open, and a stream of red vomit erupted volcanically from between his lips, showering the perfectly white carpet. A dozen colorfully painted faces peered out from office doors as Simone hauled himself along, toward the distant conference room. Bodies dropped as he passed by—fainting spells affecting his jealous colleagues, no doubt—and he laughed at them. He laughed at their clownish faces, painted to worship life. He was death! Come among them!

The fact that he could no longer walk was fine, because he knew now what the lumps on his back were. Why, he wouldn't need to walk ever again. His transformation was nearing completion—he would be a bright gray butterfly of unlife. There was a sharp, stabbing pain in his gut, which he knew were the last throes of his metamorphosis, and he grinned, spitting blood from between his teeth.

Pulling himself up using the conference table, Simone lounged in the chair, awaiting his flock. They would all worship him, he knew. Worship him in his capacity as the most fashionable being to ever grace them. For he knew now that his transformation was alchemical—that he was transcending the mere human form and becoming fashion incarnate.

There was an uproar, but Simone couldn't tell if it was inside his head or not. The room spun, blurred, become unreal, and then suddenly stopped. There were faces at the door, and among them was Trevor Tremptor himself, gripping hold of the door frame. His nostrils were splayed, his eyes were wide, and the ends of some of his hairs were split. *Ugly*, thought Simone.

"*What*," demanded Trevor Tremptor, seething, "is *the meaning of this?*"

"Behold!" burbled Simone. He tried to stand, but only succeeded at slipping from his chair onto the floor. "I—" he managed, coughing. "I am death."

"Hideous!" screamed Trevor Tremptor, lancing at Simone with one outstretched finger. "*You're fired!*"

Wiping at his nose temporarily cleared it, and Simone felt the paint fumes as they wrapped themselves around his brain and rolled around inside his hollow body like a thick mist. Filled with renewed strength, he leapt to his feet and tore at his jacket and shirt. "I am death!" he howled, at the top of his lungs.

Two security guards rushed into the room. They were uglies from below, built for strength instead of beauty, and Simone loathed them. He wouldn't let them touch him. To do so would be to desecrate his perfect transformed state of absolute fabulousness. So, he darted from between their grasping hands and swung himself clear over the conference table. Ahead there was only the window, but that was fine. It was time to reveal his true form.

Simone smashed through the window and unfurled his wings.

. . .

It was generally agreed that Simone was a fashion genius, after all. The way his body lay splayed on the ground, blood leaking out of every part of him—why, it was a masterpiece. His image made the front cover of several magazines, and for a few weeks afterward fashionable people killed themselves on Thursdays. Then a new fashion came in, for sequins, and Simone was forgotten.

OMAR ROBERT HAMILTON

RAIN, STREAMING

(2019)

1/4

He stands before the gleaming porcelain of the Reizler-Hummingdorf Neorelax executive bachelor's bathroom ceramic solution. He stands before the gleaming . . . He stands . . . Christ this floor is freezing. Val, what the fuck? Why is this floor always so fucking cold?

Would you like to register a complaint, Val?

How many have we registered already? What's the point? When are we rotating out of here?

We're scheduled to rotate on Matchday VIII, Val.

Matchday VIII? Send your complaint. What's happening out there?

Four new friends, three sympathizes, two wows, four upcomings, and three memories.

Weak. Let's have the news.

CNNBreaking: Exclusive interview with Pantheon member Michael Bay on his Transformers Decalogue.

Save. Refresh.

He steps out of the subtly lit bathroom atmospherics and, in a few steps, collapses back into his king-size bed. Is that it? Heavily? Exhausted? Should I try to sleep? Too late probably. Get up and be first in to work. Boost my MateMarket. What am I trading at, Val?

At close of play yesterday you were trading at $22.19.

Okay. Get the fucking deal through and you'll close hot. With the thought he hears the usual chords ripple through his body, sees the sun-washed room, the sleeping beauty within it, the peace of an earlier time. *I'm sitting here alone up in my room . . .* No. Not now. Refresh.

[Curated content:—]

Here we go.

> *[What's keeping you up
> at night?]*

Getting my kill rate high enough.

*[Keeping your credit score up
and your weight down.
Am I right?]*

Whatever you say, Lady.
[CalorieCredits
motivates you for both.
Just choose your target weight—]
Val, shut up.
    [—and when you get there—
    we'll bump up your credit score.
    Everyone's a winner.]
Val, it's too early for this. Give me some news or something. You're supposed to be on my side for Christ's sake.
    Roger that.
Roger that? Where do you learn these things, Val?
We watched The Dirty Dozen, *Val, and you scored it 7 on imdb.com. Do you like it?*
Sure, sure. Gotta get my MateMarket rate up today. Fucking Brazil, jerking me around. Here's an idea. Sell your goddamned rainforest to someone who gives a damn. One thing you can't offset is idiocy.
[Curated content:
Offsetting can be upsetting.
But those days are over—]
Val, are you on the fritz this morning?
On the fritz, Val?
Well did we watch *The Dirty Dozen* or not? I said cool it.
On the fritz has no usage in the registered screenplay, Val. And you signed up for **Crate Expectations'** *free trial which comes with free artisonical advertorials.*
Fine. Play the thing.
[Offsetting can be upsetting.
But those days are over.
With CarboRate, caring for the environment has never been simpler.
Invest in your future.
Invest in everyone's future.
Blink through now.]
God that took forever. Can we go to work now? Maybe today's your Surge. Permission to shake the hand of the—how did it go?—permission to shake the hand of the daughter of the bravest man I ever met. Order a car please, Val. What's the weather like?

Pleasantly warm.
Natch. He pauses, catches sight of himself in the mirror. A darkness takes over his face, his body, his whole being. He holds eye contact with the stranger in the mirror and slowly raises a hand, a finger, an accusation at the other man . . . Some day a real rain's gonna come.
No rain scheduled for the coming week, Val.
I know, I know. I wasn't talking to you.
Sorry, Val.
It's okay. He looks at himself in the mirror once more. Let's get going.
He stares out the window quietly gliding along the city streets. The world flickers with droptic offerings and savings and exclamations. You'll be rotated out soon. Why even look?
Refresh.

That music. My music.
That bouncing baseline you know from a thousand sleepless nights and morning fantasies, the low groan of the siren. You would know it in a heartbeat an eternity from now: the song is fused to your DNA, it is part of you—and you, it. One note and you're on Mars, together, her perfect white top shimmering like a mirage as she steps toward you through the choreographed flamethrowers, the sum of all human endeavor, the end of history: Britney.
But why?
[The moment you've all been
waiting for has arrived.]
It can't be—
[For the first time in human history
you can win the ultimate ReFix—]
But Britney's estate, the tight-fisted sons of bitches . . .
[TONIGHT!
    Patriot Games Fourteen is HERE.]
Don't get your hopes up.

[And there can be
only one
super-predator]

Don't—
[worthy of]

They'll never do it.
[Britney—]
No.
                [—Spears]
Thank you, Lord.
[Show off your skills against your fellow patriots.
Choose your arena.]
Thank you, Pantheon.
[Take on the drug lords
of the jungle.]
Thank you.
[Defeat the terrorists.]
This is it.
[Prove yourself.]
The moment you've been waiting for.
[Protect America.]
The ReFix the world has been waiting for.
[And win a place in Britney's heart.]
It's all coming together.
[Enlist now for Patriot Games 14.
Streaming live from midnight
        on HalliburtonHomeBoxOffice.
Blink through for—]
Yes. Yes. Blink through, Val, quickly. What
are the theaters?
Patriot Games 14: Theaters: Narco jungle.
Balkan bloodplain. Dirty bomb. Registration opens
in one hour.
Make sure we're first to register. I want—
Balkan bloodplain?
You know me so well.
You have a new follower. UrbanLover: Nike
forearm tattoos are 50%—
Wait pause. Got to think. What's our latest
myopics?
Currently fifteenth ranked MyOp on @Hal-
liburtonHomeBoxOffice. Franchised up to state
syndication last season with @CathodeRay-
theon.
Good. We have to prepare. Got to think.
Britney. It's actually happening.
He winds down the car window. Shit, it's hot
already. Someday a real rain's gonna come.

I got some bad ideas in my head, Val.
Ha! Very nice, Val. You're getting funnier
every day.

2/4

The camera tracks behind. The music rises in
static confidence, its sonar pulses searching out
into the midnight dark. The bass line breaks.
Confidence is a must—*here we go*—cockiness is
a plus—*sing it*—edginess is a rush. The camera
stays tight on Val's muscular, masculine back,
hair shining over shoulders silhouetted against
the neon corridor, the road, the light, the inevitability of the arena. Two hundred men enter,
one man leaves. Patriot Games Fourteen. Who
have we got, Val?
Playing now is @Joliath. Three public ReFix
wins. 782,422 followers. Average of seventeen
responses per post, posting on average eighteen times
daily.
Arena?
Equatorial jungle. Rebel attack on unearthed
state resources. Civil defense contract. Neutraliza-
tions: 4.
Weapon of choice?
Synth mercenary.
How's the audience?
Scores aren't in yet.
Obviously. But how's he looking?
Awedience Pro's live language analysis gives me
a positive rate of 72.
Very beatable.
It is a considerably higher than average score,
Val.
Maybe today's the day I teach you about art,
Val. About human genius and inspiration.
The expression or application of human creative
skill and imagination, Val?
That's the one buddy. Synth Mercenary . . .
You think these people haven't seen that before?
What a waste of time. Refresh.
Pantheon: Streaming from tonight: Don
Simpson: The Man, the Legend.
Save that. When are we up, Val?

Up next, Val.

Here we go. A few minutes and it'll be all you. All me and you Britney. Your white blouse brilliant against the angry Martian landscape, me stepping, one, two steps closer: "but I thought the old lady dropped it into the ocean at the end?"

Scores are in for Joliath.

Hit me, baby.

Neutralizations: 6. Audience retention: 34%.

Fine. We can beat that. Refresh.

[Curated content: HalliburtonHomeBoxOffice:

Holding a crowd?

Submit your MyOps for cash today.]

What do they think we're doing here for chrissakes? Refr—

You're up, Val.

Here we go.

He clicks his knuckles with relish at the challenge ahead, his shoulders seem to broaden as he steps into the arena, the gaze of hundreds upon him as he settles into the command chair. As the assistant hands him the controls she can't suppress her smile. Here we go. Shut all media down, Val, it's time to concentrate.

Good luck, Val.

See you on the other side.

3/4

[Ten seconds to theater]

The audience responds well to dogs, having a dog is worth five points alone right, Val? Refresh. Oh right, just in here with myself now, anyway, that was Joliath's first mistake, crashing in with a huge anthro-synth to scare the children—sure you can use a synthetic in a private game, a late night game, a game in parts of town you don't rotate into—but the Patriot Games, the Patriot Games is a family affair, kids are watching, parents, it's educational, so give them dogs, birds, safety animals, make them feel safe, a dog protects you from the bad guys not a big synth burning down a village it just doesn't

scan great just doesn't look fair and looking fair, hell *being* fair, it's just the most important thing in here, we're going to war here and you better believe we don't do it lightly, fairness is a goddamned cornerstone and if you forget that it's like forgetting, well it's like forgetting we're Ameri—

[Nine seconds]

nothing quite like it, though, is there? iContact is one thing but that look in the eye, that moment you connect really connect with the target and he's looking at you and he knows it's over and you're watching the hope drain from his face and he knows there'll be no mercy— what are we supposed to do?—are we gonna wait and find out if he's got a bomb strapped to his chest or shoved up his ass—no— who would do that?—you wanna risk a million bucks of top grade canine biomechanical defense engineering?—no—you're gonna pull the trigger—he knows it and you know it—lose a Boeing Big Dog in the field and you're right back down to the minileagues, the riot squads, the aerial surveillance—no—you're gonna pull the trigger—who would—

[Eight seconds]

this is it, Val oh, right, okay, solo time, when are they gonna loosen up the rules on that, anyway, watch this Joliath, watch my Awedience score spike nice and early when they see the Big Dog and watch me hold it up there as I cruise through to the final *bada-bing* to the head, you know you should think of a line you need your fucking catchphrase now, pal, and what have you got? what's Britney gonna hear, huh Val? How about "to lose all your senses, that's just so typically YOU" . . . a bit long . . . what else we—

[Seven seconds]

gotta focus: it's a midday game, Huawei Hyperdome, you're on your own here, out in the wilds, out reaping justice, just a man and his dog not too slow, not too quick. Pull the trigger. Not too slow, not too—

[Six seconds]

look at the arena, let's look at the arena: Balkan Bloodplain, State Department licensed target, four bodyguards, one target: female—you're on my radar—classic city arena, good, gives the audience things to look at cos you're not going to win this with a big kill rate, you're going to have to give them a show, a little stealth, a little style—looks like it's raining down there, never tried the Big Dog in the rain before . . . how strange to even see so much water—

[Five seconds to theater]

focus: just think of the MyOp you're gonna get out of this, the national syndication and maybe even Britney herself will watch it, maybe we'll watch it together—yeah, watch it with Britney, very likely– don't start up on that *shit*—when was the last time you listened to *Mona Lisa*, bubs, she says it all herself—*shut up, shut*—

[Four seconds]

how many ways do they have to lay it out for you, friend? She's gone, she's always been gone and they're not even hiding it—it's all in the police report, car crash, blood on the sidewalk, no body, just a perfect golden lock of JT's hair. Gone too soon. *Shut up.* Pour one out—

[Three]

Concentrate. The mission. The Mutually Assured Democracy program is a cornerstone of our freedoms, The Mutually Assured Democracy program is a cornerstone of our freedoms, that's fucking right, you're a fucking patriot and you are fucking in and out, it's a licensed target, wanted by Interpol, State Department, everyone, no questions asked: the target's the bad news and you're two seconds away from making the world a safer—

[Two]

Play your cards right and tomorrow night you'll be on Mars with Britney, play your cards right and you're a God cos she's there, already there and waiting and you can see her, perfect in her white blouse, her eyes lighting up as she opens the black velvet box you've just handed her and you're holding your breath as her eyes flicker back up to yours: *but I thought the old lady dropped it into the ocean in the end?*—

[Impact]

Well baby, I went down and got it for you.

4/4

It's you. You're up. Your first line. You listen to the crackle of the interplanetary intercom. It's so real. You look at the numbers rapidly processing on the dashboard. 3684 / 1508. 0x02278FEO-00895.39228. No doubt some hidden codes from the genius mind of Nigel Dick.

You look around and the barren red sands of Mars stretch into the distance as far as you can see—but you are not nervous. Val, are you recording this?

There's too much data for a complete world download, Val. But I have your POV.

It's so real. Look at this. It's a whole world. You stretch your hand and you're really there. This is, without a doubt, the finest ReFix ever created. A whole world alive and living for miles and miles of Martian nothingness all around us. Your prize. Go forth and claim what's yours. You showed them something they'll never forget last night. Balkan bloodplain. You were born for it. A comprehensive destruction of all opponents. A seamless neutralization. Even an undetected exit. You showed them something. Now go forth. Go forth and claim what's yours. Go find your Britney.

There is only one structure visible. The factory up ahead. And inside, you know she's waiting for you.

They want the line. They're ready for it. Years of heartache end tonight. You clear your throat. The whole world is watching. How are we doing, Val?

You have two hundred and fourteen new followers, Val. Two hundred and nineteen. Two hundred and thirty-seven.

You deserve this. You're a winner. You can do this. You eliminated the target without quarter or mercy. You are a star. You are a patriot. Your fans are watching. Everyone's watching. Say the line. Take your crown.

Two hundred and forty-nine new followers.

The world hangs on your every word; your every move. You stop, turn your body forty-five degrees toward the invisible camera. You didn't need the rehearsals they insisted on. They could tell right away: this is your part, your moment.

You feel the image cut in to close-up, the first real look at you. You hold your jaw firm.

[Curated content: a little touch-up work has never been cheaper—]

What? Not now, Val.

No curated content, Val?

No, Christ, Val shut it off. Hold the jaw firm.

You would like me to turn all curated content off, Val?

Val, what the fuck, we're in the middle of the fucking ReFix. I've missed my fucking line. Turn everything off.

But Val I have to remind you that you're currently enjoying a free trial subscription to Buckshot Magazine—

Don't tell me what I'm enjoying, Val. I'm enjoying being the first and only human in the history of the fucking universe to star in a Britney Spears ReFix.

But in the terms & conditions—

I don't care, Val. Turn everything off.

Everything, Val?

Off. All off. Unsubscribe from everything. I've got to do my lines, Val. Off off off.

• • •

And there, half-buried in the sand beneath your feet, an ancient relic waits. A last message from another world. You've seen it a thousand times—and though it's new every time it's never been as new as this, as real as this. You bend down to pick it up, her image, perfectly faded, looks out at you.

You say your line, with perfect pitch and timbre, examining the CD cover, holding it up for the audience to see Britney, young Britney, the original Britney, Britney before the accident, staring out at them, summoning them into her world. Britney before the crash, before the innocent blood.

The earth is shaking. Rocks crash off the red mountains. She is coming.

Her eye, her mouth, that siren call.

The flamethrowers pour their burning gasses into the air, the heavy steel of chains grind, you look up and you see her, descending from the dark vault of heaven, brilliant in the red of a thousand hells, the music filling your head and steeling your spine, the heat pulsing through the plastics of the spacesuit, every nerve-end pulling you toward her, she's there, she's real, she's here, she's now, she sings.

Behind her the chorus line begins its ritual, dancing sightlines of mathematical precision pulling toward her celestial light: she's coming toward you, singing to you. You are the messenger, you are the one, you are falling, she's there and if you just reached out you could touch her, if you reached out you would become one with Britney as your pixels merge and reemerge in unique combination.

But this is a ReFix and you will respect it. Every world has its natural laws. You don't need to touch her, you don't need any more than this.

Incredible. The detail. You can hear every breath, see every muscle flinch, feel the vast emptiness of Mars rolling behind you. There's a twitch. A moment of uncertainty. Britney's looking at you. She's thinking something new. Britney? Something's wrong. No. No, just a glitch. She's smiling. Britney Spears is smiling at you. Her hair streams black then blonde again. Raindrops land on her forehead. Raindrops? On Mars?

What's going on, Val?

I don't know, Val. You said to turn everything off.

And suddenly you're in the air, you're pulled up, up, your feet off the ground you're hurtling up into the sky and you strain to see above you and you're attached to a chain and the men with their steel levers are pulling you up and you're trapped and you can't move and you knew this would happen but you had no idea and you try and move to pull at the chain but you can't reach it but it's okay, Britney is there, far below, transformed now into her angelic white, her arms flowing in perfect choreography above her head and you just need to watch and you just need to breathe. The rain is falling, the target's breathing is so heavy, she's on her knees, the rain is falling all around her, your finger is on the trigger. Watch the dance, breathe, and keep your eyes on Britney. She's Britney. Think of the followers. Think of the outside world, the losers and the frauds all schlepping off to work today, the young tuning in for a moment of ReFix glory, the old waiting to die, all watching you, all waiting for your next move. Val, how are we doing?

What do you mean, Val?

What's our count? What are we up to?

You said to turn everything off, Val.

She looks up at you, only at you. You focus. It's all going so fast. Concentrate, it will be over soon, she's on the second chorus already and she's flying toward you, spinning in the air, transforming from the red latex into the black-and-white shirt and skirt and she's in front of you and the rain clouds are gathering, it's your line again you're up and you've said it ten thousand times in your head and in the mirror and in the shower and now it's time to make the words into something, it's time to say them, to say them finally to Britney herself.

"Britney," you say, your voice quivering with manly meaning.

You look down at the black velvet box that has appeared in your hand. You look at her. She is calm, expectant.

Her hand almost touches yours as she takes the box from your fingers.

*[But I thought the old lady
dropped it into the ocean
at the end?]*

She looks up at you and she's drenched in rain, eyes all imploration, her words begging in your head. No. Please. No. She's just a girl. It's just a glitch. You'll tell them when you're out. They'll fix it. They'll give you a refund. They'll tell you to run it again. The rain is falling now and she's crying but you know you'll do it, you'll do it like every time, you'll win the day, you'll defend the country, you'll be a man and you'll do what's right but it's just a glitch, it's Britney, glitch. She's back. She's staring at the ring. Everything's fine. She glances up at you and in the glance, the glitch, the bullet, the rain. It drips down your shirt, the heat of the sand burns up through your suit.

Just keep your eyes on Britney.

*[But I thought the old lady
dropped it into the ocean
at the end?]*

It's so hot. The rain is dripping in from the neck. The old lady dropped it into the ocean at the end. Britney's looking at you. Puzzled . . .

*[But I thought the old lady
dropped it into the ocean
at the end?]*

She wants the line, the whole world wants the line, take your crown, take your prize, say the line. What's the line? Val, what's the line? Britney's waiting. Tell me the line, Val. She wants the line. You're hurting her. Please. We take the target we're assigned. You're not supposed to ask questions. Christ, Val, the line, the line—

*[But I thought the old lady
dropped it into the ocean
at the end?]*

M. LOPES DA SILVA

FOUND EARWORMS

(2019)

I FOUND THIS WORDCO in the desert, with its autogrammar and what the fuck ever bullshit built in to make my words all pretty. I still like it, though.

I used to write shit out when I was a runt living in the freecamp hard by the old nuclear plant. The normies are scared shitless of that place. Good. It's a good time. We get rowdy and keep the cockroaches awake. I got my first piercing there, the one through my left nostril. That's why I keep a big fucking plug in there. Amateur. It was okay, though—I messed him up for fucking up so bad. We hang out sometimes now. It's cool.

• • •

Every die
Every day

Every dying day—is that something? Maybe I should write a song.

• • •

Everydie like everyday
Riding

• • •

I don't know. Fuck! Writing songs is hard.

• • •

Nothing. The desert. Gave myself a new tattoo of a werewolf howling at a cheezburger. I think my linework is getting better.

• • •

Hung out with friends in one of the abandoned shopping malls. We've remade a lot of it. It's wild. Art on art on art on art. Not the kind of stuff you see in towns. Someone threw a party in the big space downstairs, and it started with a lot of old stuff—The Ramones, The Slits—that turned into newer shit like The Pussycocks. We got drunk off tequila and cactus wine and howled and fucked and wept and nobody got hurt that night.

· · ·

The normies expect us to work until the work makes us sick, but they don't give us any of the medicine that they make from the plants we pick. Like we didn't work hard enough. Yeah, right.

Me and my friends we put on our dust masks and lit our Molotovs and revved up the darters until sand spewed up like vomit beneath our treads, then we rode! We went and lit up the roof of the front office, while Mope and Freekel snuck around back to rob the truck with all the medicine in it. And I mean we got away with ALL of it. They're mad.

· · ·

LOPES / FOUND DIARY / 3

The normies have been chasing us with their freaking cruisers for days now. We try to make

extra time at night, but they keep following. They never come out this far. Usually.

· · ·

Mope couldn't take it anymore. She just turned around and drove right at them. Freekel and Eddi tried to get away, but the normies just shot them down.

· · ·

I'm still running—straight into the desert. I cut a patch away on my jeans so I could stare at the werewolf with its cheezburger scabbing over.

I'm thirsty. My friends are dead. I've only got a fraction of the medicine left. But the normies can't last forever in that metal box. They're hungry and thirsty, too.

So I'm writing this song and riding riding riding.

· · ·

Everydie like everyday
Riding hard to robinhood
Never liked you anyway

FUCK I HATE WRITING SONGS!!

MARIE VIBBERT

ELECTRIC TEA

(2019)

I CAME HOME in the watery dawn, exhausted from waitressing all night. As I eased my bike against the porch railing to chain it up, a neighbor who had never said two words to me before leaned over his chain-link fence. "Hey, Sue, right?"

Tsui. I didn't correct.

"Did you see the fire? Man, I would have loved to have seen that!"

"Fire?" I asked.

He pointed behind our homes, down the weed-and-trash-strewn slope to the warehouse, its undamaged roof all that was visible from the front sidewalk.

I pushed through vines and broken fences with the dreamlike possession artists yearn for. A small crowd was gathered, reverent at the edge of hasty police tape.

The arsonist had painted the warehouse in careful lines of linseed-oil pigments, flammable as anything. The colors were lost, but the image wasn't—fat, indulgent lines that tapered sweetly into finer detail. The picture was a skeletal bird-creature holding the long arm of a Sears Shop-Vac. The logo was identifiable, despite foreshortening as it curved around the barrel.

I was jealous of the craftsmanship. Every line touched to spread the fire. Combustion started at the Shop-Vac's business end, its flat nose pushed into the joining of wall and weedy gravel. Those first lines had the thickest char. By design or chance, the fire department arrived before the flames burned far from the confines of their original lines. The black rising from the vacuum's mouth echoed decals on hot rods, a symbol of speed arrested.

I would not rest until I found this artist and learned their purpose and, more importantly, their process.

Our narrow street, Jefferson, sagged off the backside of Tremont like a rotten floorboard. Two of my classmates and I had pooled our resources to rent the narrow clapboard house.

We were failed artists who didn't know it yet. In violation of our renter's agreement we'd painted murals on every wall using ceiling white, porch floor gray, and matte black spray paint. I did the black. I arched into a backbend to make one complete slash across the living room, straight as a sword stroke. I wanted the line to be unrestrained, violent. Instead, it bloomed like mascara. Mahesh painted a woman in white and gray, heavy breasts falling from the join of ceiling and wall, her arm outstretched along my black line. I kept my eyes on the floor when I crossed the living room.

"I can't believe we missed it!" Jay said, slouching on the giant spool we used as a kitchen table. His dreads lay like a sleeping cat around his shoulders. "I hope the dude posts a video. It must have been sexy when the lines first caught."

I hoped so, too. I wanted the motion, like music, art that exists in time, rather than the notation left in its wake.

"It was derivative street art," Mahesh said. "Tsui could do better."

My name is pronounced "Sue," but I can hear it when the person speaking knows there's a *T*, something hesitant in the *S*. I prefer that.

"If it weren't down the hill," I said, "If the trees weren't so thick, I could have seen it on my way home."

"Yeah." Jay nodded. "It's worse, isn't it? Being so close and missing it? Have you ever seen paint burn? The flames glide, like they're hovering."

Mahesh was working on the cabinets under the sink, adding a slouching monster where some paint had dripped. "I'll bet it was electric tea. Someone drank it and ran out to prove it had an effect on them by doing something crazy. These things always hit Cleveland after the bigger towns. Like bands and fashion."

"No, they don't." Jay straightened. He'd lived in Cleveland his whole life and was protective of it. "People have been drinking electric tea here for years. Before it went big."

"Okay," Mahesh said, keeping his eyes on his work. He dragged his brush slowly, flat, making a bumpy nose.

Jay took that as the dismissal it was. "I know people who drink it. Who've been drinking it. None of them went crazy, either."

"It must have been beautiful," I said. I looked out our back window at the warehouse roof among the trees and saw a smudge, like a line from a conte crayon, curving along a glittering tarpaper edge. "I'd drink electric tea if it helped me make such a thing."

Artists fail for many reasons, and most fail where we were—fresh out of art school. I couldn't speak to Jay and Mahesh's nascent failings, but mine was simple: I wasn't good enough. I studied and experimented. I took critique well. I hoped that enough time studying and experimenting and responding well to criticism would somehow build up to the golden magic of "good enough," but I knew that "good enough" wasn't enough.

We were in pursuit of our futures, self-consciously temporary in our living arrangements, and compulsively recklessness. Mahesh spent what we all knew were his last dollars on a sable brush. Jay tried to tattoo himself. I went to five-dollar shows at the Phantasy when I had work the next morning. Someone set fire to buildings. It made sense.

• • •

Jay met me at the restaurant as I was leaving my early shift. "You still want to go?"

"I want to see it," I said. "Just to see."

He nodded. "Leave your bike here." As we started walking down the street, he said, "It's not that it's not safe, but I don't know if you want people to see your bike there and know, you know?"

"Electric tea isn't illegal."

"Yet," Jay said. He looked side to side, his dreads twitching like nervous snakes. He jogged across the street and took me down a few alleys to University Road by the back of Sokolowski's. We slunk behind the restaurant and through the gravel lot under the freeway bridge. His shirt was torn below the right sleeve, giving me momentary glimpses of his muscular side.

All the quick, covert motion made little sense when we reached Abbey Avenue and had to sedately walk the long bridge. Tremont is an island, bordered on all sides by cliffs man-made and natural—the river valley, the freeways, the railroads. This bridge was one of a limited number of ways out of Tremont. The cracked sidewalk was scrawled with anti-gentrification graffiti.

"Is it far?" I asked. The neighborhood ahead of us held breweries and a strip mall, I couldn't imagine an electric teahouse squeezing in.

"Not far now." We crossed the smaller bridge for the RTA tracks.

The West Side Market was crowded, voices filling the high, vaulted space with a concert-hall buzz. Jay led me around pastries and meats and out again through the fruit stands where thick-accented men vied for our attention with chunks of cantaloupe on knifepoint. We resumed sneaking up alleyways and down side streets.

We paused beside one of the dozens of three-story Victorian storefronts in Ohio City, all brick and recessed entrances. A record store was doing well on the corner, plastered with prints of local bands from the '70s like the Dead Boys and Electric Eels, unkempt and daring you to call it nostalgic. In the middle of the block lettering from generations of failed businesses made a pastiche of faded gilding over nondescript doors and blackened windows.

Jay ducked into a blind alley and down blue-stone steps to a basement door.

"Do we need a password?"

He raised his eyebrows at me and knocked with the back of his hand. One of his failed tattoos stretched on the paler skin of his inner wrist. It was a broken bit of barbed wire originally intended to be a bird. I felt very tender toward that tattoo.

A thin, caramel-skinned man answered the door, pulling it against a brass security chain to eye us before unlatching.

All this pseudo cloak-and-dagger was appro-priate to electric tea—an illicit substance that was not illicit. More than half the flavor was myth; it would lose its power if you could buy it in the drugstore like incense.

The basement was lit by LED strips at the base of brick walls, partially hidden from sight by rows of cast concrete fleur-de-lis. Black fabric with sequins draped between and over pipes on the ceiling. The chairs and tables were a mix: wrought iron garden sets and marble café tables and one old door on sawhorses.

The man who let us in returned to his stool by the door's peephole and left us to find our way.

Electric tea was, ultimately, just tea, in a special cup. The cup contained a mechanism that would broadcast invisible waves toward your brain, stimulating emotions, thought processes. If it worked right it would play your brain with recorded thoughts like vinyl grooves resurrected Joey Ramone. It supposedly left your mind clearer and sharper in its wake. Stimulants helped the effect, so its first use was with hyper-caffeinated energy drinks. There were incidents, allegations, nothing proven, but it was now only legal with ordinary tea. The partial prohibition made it sexier.

There was a sheet of SmartPaper on each table with a menu to scroll through. I tapped "black" from the list of categories. They had every type of tea I'd ever heard of and a few I hadn't.

The prices weren't listed. Always a danger sign. I rifled my fingers through the loose tips in my pocket.

A plump white girl approached, wearing a short waiter's apron over her jeans. "Can I get you anything?"

Jay ordered green tea. I scanned the list again. "Gunpowder Smoke," I said.

She smiled. "Good choice. We just started serving that. It's our own blend of black gunpowder tea with Lapsang souchong."

"Sounds expensive. I think I'll have the Darjeeling."

"All our teas are the same price. Give it a try. You'll love the kick."

I could never disagree with a waiter, so I nodded. When she left, I asked Jay, "Have you done this before?"

"Yeah. Of course."

"Do you believe the stories?"

He shrugged. "I know it's supposed to make you think more clearly. I also know that anything that does good to the mind can be overdone. I dunno. I've had some great ideas after coming here. Like, that's when I started 'Rodin Bows to a Dream of Donatello.'" He smiled, mocking his own pretension.

I admired how he sat in his chair like his clothes were not attached to him. He always wore loose jeans and shirts, his lithe frame a rumor reported secondhand by folds and shadows. "I'll never paint anything that real," I said.

He turned to regard me sideways. "We are not going to start that again, Tsui. When you finally let go, you'll be the best of us all."

My cheeks warmed. I pretended to be fascinated by the menu. "I need to learn to make unselfconscious lines."

The tea arrived in oversized cups, ceramic on the outside and glass inside so we could see the little circuit board and dime-sized emitters. The blinking purple and blue LEDs were almost certainly just for looks.

The tea smelled metallic and smoky. I paused before sipping, uncertain.

Of course, holding the cup was the dangerous part, wasn't it?

Jay leaned back, a picture of cool unconcern. He kissed his teacup slowly, deliberately.

"I should have brought my sketchbook," I said. "That's a good pose for you."

Self-conscious, his lines tightened and shifted. Without changing his pose, he ruined it. "Drink your tea," he said.

I sipped my tea. It tasted like it smelled—like the smoke from a black powder pistol wafting through tall grass.

I closed my eyes and breathed in slowly, evenly, letting the steam bathe my face. I was waiting to feel something. "What is it supposed to feel like?"

"Like waking up," Jay said. "Like plugging in

an amp, like a pebble dropping into water. Like a head rush."

I felt warm stoneware in my hands. I felt recycled wind from the air conditioner. I felt a bit silly.

"Mahesh doesn't approve," Jay said. "If he were any more uptight, he'd vibrate."

"Don't," I said.

Jay used Rapidograph pens with micrometer tips on SmartPaper to plan every sculpture, made small models and intermediate models. Precise and careful in art, Jay relaxed in everything else. The opposite of Mahesh. He raised his eyebrows. "Don't what?"

I couldn't explain what they both meant to me, how much I needed them to love each other. "Mahesh bleeds when he paints," I said.

Jay's cheek lifted, the languor returning to his limbs. "Yeah, I love him, too."

I felt no effect from the tea. I watched Jay closely, to see if he felt anything. He was just Jay.

The tea was expensive, but not more than my tips for the night. I declined a second cup.

We took a more direct route home and passed a band playing in a walled courtyard. Raw and loud, practicing in the middle of the day. Cymbals crashed like paint splatters on brick walls. It was living art, spilling into the street. You couldn't study to make this.

I took Jay's hands and pulled him back. He laughed and danced to me. His movements, the music, this was what I wanted: something perfect because it was unpolished, something pure.

Who needed an electric kick when we lived in a vibrant art community? I hugged Jay's sweaty, muscular arm as we continued walking and he talked about Japanese printmaking and I interrupted to talk about the graffiti we passed.

"Will you sculpt tonight?" I asked.

"Hell yes. And you will paint, Tsui. You'll paint if I have to strap the brush to your hand."

• • •

Mahesh was, ironically, making tea when we got home. He looked up from lowering the mesh ball into the pot. "Where have you been?"

"Getting some tea," Jay said, tilting his head back, challenging.

Mahesh shook his head. "It's a placebo, you know."

"How would you know?"

I said, "Don't fight."

"Absinthe," Mahesh said. He put the cozy on the teapot and turned to face us, arms crossed. "In the nineteenth century, absinthe was a craze. They claimed the wormwood caused 'effects' beyond drunkenness. Mind-opening, clarifying. Inspiration. Ring any bells?"

Jay shrugged fluidly. "They also thought cocaine was a good headache medicine, doesn't mean aspirin is going to get you high."

Mahesh set three mugs on the wooden spool. "There were no special effects. There was strong alcohol and wishful thinking. The power of ritual." He waved his hand over the table. "How would you know that I'm not serving you electric tea right now?"

"Because the cups are crap." Jay picked up a cracked mug with the logo for a construction company and waggled it, exposing its chipped side.

Mahesh looked at me. "Did you feel anything?"

I didn't want to take sides, but I had to shake my head.

"If it really did anything, the government would regulate it," Mahesh said, and poured the tea.

Jay walked out, taking any hope of conversation with him.

• • •

A well-known local sculptor was found dead inside a cooling tower across from Tremont Park. He'd climbed to the top of the structure with an armful of rebar and slipped, falling twenty feet to crack his skull on the metal grating below. His wife had no idea he had even left home that night.

Because of the similarity of some of his sculptures to the bird-skeleton drawing, it was speculated that he was the arsonist, and the news blogs all raised the question: had he been drinking electric tea?

The art community knew better than to suspect him of the fire. He was a sculptor, had never painted in any medium, much less fire, and electric tea drinkers did not tend to change genres.

Besides, a day later there was another fire, down in the flats. The painting this time was a chorus of large-headed waifs, their little bodies twisted like candle flames, ringing one of the conical mounds of iron ore deposited by shipping boats for the steel mills. It burned longer before being doused, but as its substrate was iron dirt, nothing was damaged.

You could see minute traces of color, where the paint soaked in and was protected. Burnt turquoise and magenta. Inspired planning, how the colors sank and glowed against the rust brown ore.

On *Scene Magazine*'s main page the two fire drawings were shown side-by-side, the headline simple: Copycat or Serial Arsonist? The comments section raged with theories, and images by local artists either being accused or exonerated.

Mahesh leaned over my shoulder. "A hundred artists in this area have that style. Maybe a thousand. Just in this small-ass city. He could be from somewhere else, just passing through. They'll never catch him that way."

I resented the "they." I would catch him. Practice at catching fame. "He could be a she," I said.

Mahesh said, "I was using the gender-neutral 'he.' Come on, I want to use the computer."

Both painters were clearly right-handed. It's no great forensic trick to tease out the handedness of a line-artist; even the very best have to lift and drop their brush. Some artists, of course, are more careful. Both fire paintings were not careful, reveling in the mess and accident of an overloaded brush. I admired the punk-rock joy of the lines.

I could hear Mahesh breathing. He spoke

quietly, bloodlessly. "I need the computer more than you do. You already have a job," he said.

"It's not an art job."

"I'm not unemployed because I'm too precious to wait tables, Tsui. I'm trying, all right?"

I slipped out of my seat. "I didn't say anything like that." We had leaped over the cliff of graduation together, and in the air before landing, whether it would be the promised shore of gainful employment or the abyss below us, it was hard not to claw at each other.

• • •

After Jefferson crosses West Third, it quickly starts to look like an old country road, overgrown and sun-bleached and neglected, concrete silos rising up behind graffiti-decked tin railings. You forgot the Cleveland skyline and the high bridges were waiting to slip into view between tangled vines.

The warehouse's fence lay flat where the fire trucks had come in. Someone had held a business here, had cared about this expanse of overgrown gravel.

Someone had already sprayed graffiti over top of the burn-lines. A vermillion penis pointed skyward like a cannon raised on its misshapen wheels.

• • •

The chubby white girl opened the basement door this time. "We're not open yet," she said.

"Please let me wait inside?"

She looked up the stairs. It was a bright, hot afternoon. I tried to look afraid and vulnerable and small. "All right," she said. "It's not going to be that long."

The room looked different with the overhead lights on—ordinary. There were chair-height scrapes on the walls and dings in the tables. The sequined fabric had loose threads and a cheap shine.

"The kitchen isn't open yet, but I could get you a glass of water."

I shook my head. She left and came back a few minutes later with a cash drawer, which she slid into a holder on the wall. Then she unlocked it and counted its contents. The familiar waltz of preparing a restaurant for its operating day.

I tried to think of some ingratiating way to start conversation. Instead I blurted out, "Is it a placebo?"

Her shoulders dropped. "Jesus," she said. She turned to face me. "I'm trying to run a business. I don't need your approval or opinion. Go read a webpage."

"I didn't mean . . . I'm not." I stood, stepped forward, stepped back. I looked at my own twisting hands. "I didn't *feel* anything."

I looked up to see her considering me. She said, "You aren't going to lecture me or write some stupid blog 'exposing' the 'truth' about electric tea?"

I shook my head. "I just wanted to feel something. To understand."

She sighed. She closed the cash drawer and made a note on a tablet. "It's not a placebo. I wouldn't have started this business if it were, if I hadn't been convinced the first time I drank it."

"Does it only affect certain people?"

She looked embarrassed. She went to the counter and stooped below. She pulled out a pair of cups and set them on the counter. "The thing of it is, sometimes the battery runs out. Or gets weak. Or a connection is loosened throughout the day. I'd say there's about a ten to twenty percent chance you didn't get a working cup." She shook her head. "So yeah, there is a placebo effect, and I rely on it because this technology is fragile as *heck*."

She pushed a cup toward me. "I barely make a profit, fixing the stupid things all the time."

"Oh."

"What'll you have? They're all working. They always all work at the *start* of the night."

"Gunpowder smoke."

"Good choice. We just started serving that. Our own blend of—"

"You said," I said.

"Oh." Her face was tired, older looking as she

bent to retrieve a glass jar from under the counter. She filled a tea ball and snapped it shut with one hand as she put the jar away. "Guys love the gunpowder smoke. It sounds manlier than rosehip chamomile. I always get happy when a woman orders it." She looked at me again as she held the cup under a hot water tap. "When I was in college, I was convinced Lapsang souchong cured writer's block. Maybe it was the smell. Wood smoke. Scent is linked strongly to memory. I never had trouble telling stories around campfires."

We bent to sip our cups of smoke tea together. This time I felt a strange tickle, an itch on my forehead. An idea vibrated through my mind like the crash of cymbals.

The teahouse owner raised her eyebrows. "You see?"

"Thank you," I said.

Her face transformed with her smile, like just the right line turns a mere representation into beauty. "That's why I had to have this shop. I had to share that feeling. It's magic, every time I see that look on a new person's face."

• • •

I did not go to work like I was supposed to. I walked home, knowing Mahesh would be there alone. Jay worked days at a gallery on Profes-sor. I found Mahesh painting light bulbs and flying saucers around the cabinet knobs in the kitchen.

He wiped his brush and stared at me. "Shouldn't you be at work?"

"Why did you do it?" I asked. He recoiled, started to stammer the usual things people stammer in this case. "You set fire to the warehouse. And the ore pile. Close to home and then farther away to confuse the trail. Will you do it again? Were you angry? Frustrated?"

His head hung over his hands, resting his weight on the edge of the kitchen sink.

"It's okay," I said. "No one was hurt."

"It's not art if it doesn't hurt!" His eyebrows formed a harsh line.

"We'll help you. Jay and me. We'll keep you from doing it again, from being caught. We're in this together."

He sank, back against the counter, shoulders dropping, eyebrows loosening. He looked bewildered. "How did you find out?"

There are false things in life—the hopes of an artist being one of the most common, but there are true things, too, made by human minds and hands. Art can be an assembly of technology and smell. I didn't say that. I said, "There are different forms of inspiration."

I made Mahesh tea—regular tea—because inspiration was never his problem.

COREY J. WHITE

EXOPUNK'S NOT DEAD

(2019)

DOWNTOWN VIBRATES with sub-low frequency, churning Jack's guts alongside the anxiety he knows will only quiet with booze. The frame of his exoskeleton buzzes as he stomps closer to the source of the sound—metal humming to the kick drum thump coming up through cracked asphalt. Red paint flakes like dandruff; underneath the paint, steel rusts.

Jack's is a basic demolition exo: limbs attached to a sturdy hydraulic frame lacking any armor plating. He floats within the exoskeleton's torso, dangling on a battered harness with haptic converters aligned to his musculature. It's airy inside the machine, its canopy open to the elements. A breeze from the bay rolls over Jack's bare arms, carrying the salty smell of rotting seaweed.

Jack checks the flyer one last time, worried he might turn up at the wrong place—as though that distant clamor could be anything *other* than a punk show. The flyer's proper old-school, photocopied onto thin sheets of yellow paper:

EXOPUNK (WRECKING) BALL
OLD CITY HALL
DOORS OPEN 8 P.M.

The city council was voted out a year ago, but even a democratically elected governmental algorithm needs time to implement changes. At first, police had patrolled the grounds, protecting it while the city tried to find a buyer, but once enough of the walls had been torn open for the copper piping, they pulled out. The official demolition starts Monday, but after tonight's gig, with all the exopunks from the highlands dropping in, half the job will be done.

Jack rounds the corner and joins a procession of skels thudding up the street. Seeing his people, the knot of tension in his guts unravels. Even in his nine-foot-tall exo, the goliath city hall building looms threateningly: graffiti spots the stone facade like bruises, masonry already crumbling as decay sets in.

A broad wall of noise slams against Jack's

chest as he stomps into the old building. The air is hot and humid, thick with competing scents of sour sweat and spilled beer.

The band on stage is lit up bright, high above the thrashing, glinting mosh, and plaster dust rains from the cracked ceilings with every heavy beat. Exos fill the pit: classic twelve-foot clankers slamming among sleeker SOTA rigs, while armored bouncers look on. The pit is already three feet below the rest of the floor, marble tiling and cement foundations churned up as the opening acts hype the crowd.

Jack points his exo at the bar jutting from a hole bashed into the walls; behind the bartenders, empty office cubicles are filled with trash and drug detritus. He gets in line and forces his exo onto the balls of its steel feet so he can see over the heads in front of him.

"Nice ride."

At the voice, Jack pivots inside his skel. The guy has a thick, black beard around an easy smile. A thick mat of hair crosses his broad chest, visible through tears in his replica cosmonaut suit. He hangs inside his exo's frame, looking almost weightless—very "stranded in space."

When the guy starts to grin, Jack realizes how long he's been staring without saying anything. His cheeks burn. A rat-king of nerves tangles in his stomach, but it's a good nervous, a "cute guy is talking to me" nervous.

"Thanks," he says, finally. "It's a hand-me-down; was my older brother's."

"Makes sense; you don't see too many guys our age in one of the classics."

Jack laughs, just a single throaty "Ha." He knows his beat-up Ward-D2 isn't really a classic, but he can see a pickup line for what it is and still want to be picked up, can't he?

The next song starts, and decibels soar like courier drones. Jack pushes his exo toward the bar as the line moves.

"Did he go into engineering?" the punk-onaut shouts.

"What?" Jack says, leaning forward in his harness. The chat-link light inside his exoframe blinks, and Jack hits the switch.

"Your brother," the other guy says, his voice tinny through Jack's audio system: "did he go into engineering or something?"

"Yeah, *something*," Jack says; he doesn't say that "something" was prison. "My name's Jack."

"I'm Ramón, and no, I hate The Ramones."

Jack chuckles, then sees he's almost at the front of the line. "What are you drinking?"

"Cider."

Jack gets flustered at the bar and orders two ciders, though it's normally too sweet for his tastes. He takes one of the canisters and hands it to Ramón, then slots the other into his exo's rehydration unit as the band on stage finishes their set.

"Thanks," Ramón says. "I'll get the next round."

Jack drinks from the tube strapped inside the head module and the cider slides down his throat, thick, saccharine, and cold.

"Wanna go up the front?" Ramón asks.

"Hey, ho, let's go," Jack says, and beams at his own joke. Ramón rolls his eyes but smiles.

Exopunks drop into the cratered pit, their eyes eagerly following members of the next band as they walk out on stage; *Mucus Mary and the Moist Mothers* spray-painted on a bedsheet hanging on the rear wall.

The guitarist and bass player wear their instruments inside their suits and the singer has the microphone mounted to her exo's head. The drummer's exoskeleton clunks and thuds as it interfaces with the drum machine—twelve limbs flexing and stretching as she gets a feel for the gear. She counts in and the band erupts in a vicious car crash. The pit surges, sending dirt and cement chunks into the air where, Jack swears, they hover for a full second, held in place by the singer's banshee screech.

"I love this band," Ramón yells.

Jack thrashes to the sound and his shinbones shudder every time his exofeet jackhammer the ground. As the stage lights sweep over the crowd, the fog of cement dust around him and Ramón glows.

Ramón drops into the pit and before Jack

can think twice he's done the same. Jack slams the head of his exo into the wall of the pit and Ramón joins him while Mucus Mary wails and squeals. Jack screams and euphoria seeps into his veins, as warm as the cider is cold.

He gulps a mouthful of air and dust as he wraps his lips around the rehydration tube. The dust gently scratches his throat as he swallows. Dust lines his nostrils too—if he gets a spot on the official demolition crew come Monday he'll be wearing respiratory gear, but right now, he doesn't care. His lungs could rot inside his chest and it would be worth it to be here tonight, drowning in noise, surrounded by the only thing that ever made sense to him. Study hard, they said; yeah, thanks for the debt. Get a job, they said; fuck you, there aren't any.

Jack dances harder, his suit's haptics fighting him as it struggles to keep up. The only truth Jack ever found was in punk rock: music that's dirty, fast, and over so soon, just like life.

The band starts another song and Jack stops dancing to take a drink. Ramón's chest hair glints with sweat and Jack imagines slipping his hands inside the cosmonaut suit so the hairs curl around his fingers. But Ramón doesn't catch Jack's overt gaze; his attention is elsewhere, watching three skinheads in archaic getups using their massive exos to tower over some kids in shiny-chromed rigs.

Jack's chest rattles—not from the noise, but the fight-or-flight thump of his heart. Ramón takes a step forward and Jack's mind is made up for him as he and Ramón push through the crowd.

"You fucking better not be here Monday," one of the skinheads says, thumping one kid's rig with a clenched exofist. "Those demolition jobs are for us. You want work, go back to Iraq-istan."

"Hey," Ramón yells.

The three boneheads turn; identical triplets with their shaved heads and faces: babies that got big, but never grew up.

Jack's fear gives way to anger as he glances past the skinheads and sees the young punks cowering. They look like honor roll kids who miraculously discovered good tunes in the banal suburban sprawl. But that's the exopunk ethos: *anyone* is free to work if they've got a rig, and *anyone* is free to wreck if they've got that fucking fire in their belly.

The music lulls and the lead bonehead yells new slurs at Jack and Ramón. Far up front on the stage, Mucus Mary points into the crowd as her band breaks into a new song: a frenetic stampede of noise. A chorus joins in as Mucus Mary screams, "Nazi Punks Fuck Off!" It was a classic before Jack was born, and it's the one song every decent punk band knows, even if they never want a reason to play it.

Jack freezes as Ramón steps forward and grips the lead skinhead's rig in both exohands. The bonehead tries to break Ramón's grip, but he locks his exo's hands in place, unhooks his harness, and throws himself forward. Ramón grabs the collar of the bonehead's bomber jacket and buries a fist into the fucker's nose. Blood pours into his mouth, hanging slack.

Jack stomps close, barring the other Nazis as they try to get at Ramón. His hydraulics shriek with the effort of holding them back, a sharp screech that pierces his ears as more punks push in toward the scuffle.

Plaster dust underfoot glows purple—security moves through the crowd riding black security rigs, all sharp angles and blacklight LEDs. Ramón disconnects his exo and Jack pushes him back before standing with an impromptu line of exopunks, blocking Ramón from the bouncer's view.

Jack points and yells, "Get these Nazi fucks out of here," shifting his exo to stay between Ramón and the bouncers. Jack can't see the bouncer's face inside the armor, but the exo bobs in acknowledgment, and he hijacks the three boneheads' suits and leads them out of the pit.

Jack turns to Ramón, gingerly poking his knuckles with his left hand. "You okay?"

"I heard something crack, just hope it was his nose and not my knuckle." Ramón shivers and

EXOPUNK'S NOT DEAD

Jack feels it too: the drop of adrenaline leaving his body.

Jack unclips his harness and climbs out to stand on the frame of Ramón's rig. He slips inside Ramón's exoskeleton and buries his fingers in Ramón's coarse beard. "Want me to get some ice for your hand?"

Ramón lets out a deep breath, then looks up from his bloody hand, his eyes a deep brown, speckled with orange. "It'll be fine," he says.

Jack leans in, sour-sweet breaths coalescing in the moment before their lips meet, Ramón's tongue wet and hot against Jack's.

Jack smiles. "You really gave that guy a blitzkrieg—"

Ramón cuts him off with another kiss, a longer one that only stops when they get jostled, the crowd slowly gaining momentum after stalling for the fight.

"Make another Ramones joke," Ramón says, "and that might be the last time I kiss you."

Jack kisses Ramón again while his heart beats double-time. His mouth tastes sickly sweet with dead apples and probable regret, but he doesn't care. This man might break his heart, but it would be worth it to be here tonight.

"What's the matter with your exo; we need technical support?" A bouncer stands beside Jack's abandoned exoskeleton.

"No, it's fine," Jack yells.

When the bouncer sees Jack inside Ramón's exo, he shakes his head and smiles. "Don't leave it empty on the dance floor, all right fellas; it ain't safe."

Jack almost laughs at "dance floor," but he nods and climbs back into his exo as the bouncer walks off chuckling.

They get lost in the music again; moving with the crowd like every exo in the joint is linked. Sweat soaks through Jack's clothes as they yell and stomp in a circle of exopunks; he grins whenever his eyes catch Ramón's.

When Mucus Mary is done, she and the Moist Mothers leave the stage to a mushroom-cloud of cheers from the pit. Ramón leads Jack to the edge and they jump out of the crater. Jack pauses to take in the sweat-slicked revelers panting for breath and the exos knocking together with the clank of punk love; the bliss that follows an epic mosh.

Standing close enough to Ramón so that they can lean out of their exos and touch, Jack asks, "Are we gonna get another drink?"

"I only really came for Mary," Ramón says, "so I was gonna go home."

Jack frowns, and Ramón laughs.

He pinches Jack's chin and says quietly, "I was hoping you'd come with me."

681

LAVANYA LAKSHMINARAYAN

ÉTUDES

(2020)

Adopt at your own risk. No guarantees, no returns.
—signboard over the door of the Analog Orphan Adoption Home

HAPPY BIRTHDAY, IT!

I stare at the birthday card in front of me in horror.

I shouldn't have opened it. Not here, in front of them. Not ever, if I'd known what the inside read.

I flip it wide open and turn it toward my best friend, Mae.

I hate that word.

It.

"It will need to earn its place in Virtual society."

I sit on a leather stool in front of the Home's creaky upright piano. I look down at the keys.

I've just played Barthöven's Sonatina 23 in alt-F Minor.

I've made four obvious mistakes, I fumbled three runs. Including the opening section.

I hope I'm still worthy.

These two strangers could change their minds at any moment.

I glance up at them. They seem to be studying me.

I look back down, staring really, really hard at the black keys in between F, G, A, and B, just to the right of middle C.

Mrs. D'Souza's voice fills the silence.

"It's toilet-trained and reports excellent personal hygiene. It reads at an average pace and has done fairly well on our psychological tests. No tendencies toward violence, no delusions of grandeur."

The strangers say nothing.

Mrs. D'Souza continues. *"Mr. and Mrs. Anand, we assure you that you will have no trouble with this one. We only let the very best Analog wards get to this stage of the adoption process. The less competent ones remain at the Institute until they become employable or drop out. The defective ones are sent straight to the vegetable farm.*

"You could always change your mind about taking it home, of course. But it's one of our very best."

I turn my head and see her beaming at me.

"We wouldn't let distinguished twenty percenters such as yourselves take home a flawed child."

Mrs. D'Souza talks about me as if I'm not in the room. I'm used to it.

One of the strangers smiles at me. The man.

I stare at him.

"We do have some guidelines, however. It is in your best interest to follow them. We dissuade you from developing a strong personal attachment to the ward, despite being its adoptive parents. You may give it a name—this one is biologically female, and is approximately twelve years old."

The woman frowns at this.

I wonder if I've done something wrong.

"We recommend that you don't permit it to refer to either of you on the basis of your filial relationship. First names are better than Mum and Dad. It leads to an easier separation should the child fail to qualify as a Virtual Citizen."

"We'd like the child to feel accepted," the man says.

Mrs. D'Souza sighs. "These decisions are left to your discretion, of course. The Home will assess the child annually to assess if it is appropriate for Virtual society."

"Yes, we've read the fine print." The woman's tone is sharp.

"Psychologists have found that Analog wards with a lower sense of personal identity are more Productive. They're more eager to please if they perceive identity markers as rewards for good behavior. We recommend that it be placed in impersonal surroundings. The fewer preferences it has, the easier it will find readjustment should it need to be returned to the Analog world, though we will not take it back in—"

"Why are you certain they're going to fail?"

"Can we stop calling them 'it'?"

The man and woman speak together, and they sound angry.

I've been told to keep a smile on my face, but I frown at that.

If I'm not "it," what am I?

"—it's—I mean she's done really well for herself, all things considered."

His smug voice brings me back to the present.

Mae is staring him down in a look of distilled hatred.

"It's only taken her ten years."

Dear Nina of the Future,

I'm literally the only living person, this century, to have owned a journal. I hope you never forget where you've come from once you're a Virtuoso.

Haha.

That's wishful thinking.

Here I am, stuck at my birthday party, when I should be practicing Bracht and Rodriguez for my upcoming demi-Virtuoso Examination. It's only ten days away and it's ONLY the opportunity of a lifetime to get into the Apex City School of neo-Acousta Performance Studies. But who cares about the opportunity of a lifetime, right?

"What are you writing in that journal, anyway?" he says, reaching out for it.

I slam it shut.

"Touchy." He grins. "Now where was I?"

He returns to his captive audience. They're supposed to be my friends. And he certainly isn't.

"Right. So I was talking about my first time. There I was, right? Never having played before . . . I remember looking down at those keys. Completely blank."

Everyone leans in to listen to what Andrew Sommers has to say. Everyone except Mae, who mimes strangling him from where she stands behind him, taking care not to spill her strawberry shake.

I twirl a straw around my glass of carrot-cucumber juice.

"But then, the GlimmerKeys kicked in and began to highlight the score for me. I don't know why people even bother with sheet music anymore. It took me through the entire song, with my InEars keeping perfect tempo for me."

Niraj and Anushka are hanging on to every word.

Andrew Sommers is the best-known musician at our school. He has an official HoloTube account, with a following in the hundreds of thousands in Bell Corp cities across the world.

How long has he been learning?

Eighteen months.

How long have I been learning?

Ten years.

What's the difference between us?

DreamMusician.

I'm surprised he even showed up at my party, considering we aren't friends. When I say that, I don't mean that we don't have any classes together, or that we've never given recitals together.

We just haven't made eye contact. Ever.

We've never spoken a word to each other outside of a practice.

And yet here he is, celebrating another year of my life going by.

Why?

"You must be at a real disadvantage, Nina."

"What?" I scowl.

"It must be so hard for you. Learning the *Analog* way."

I don't like the way he emphasizes the word "Analog." I hear it all the time but I'll never get used to it. I look down at the birthday card, and the word "it" glares back up at me.

I don't want to get into a fight. I can't afford to. So I shrug instead.

"I mean, how do you keep time? Do you count in your head?" Andrew smirks.

"It's more than you can do. Count, that is," Mae mutters loud enough for everyone to hear.

Niraj's laugh sounds like a strangled bark.

"And what about the dynamics? Do you just bang away at the keys until you get the proper tone?"

I realize that I've begun to shred the edges of the card.

"Seriously. I'm curious." He winks.

I really can't afford to get into a fight. Not with the Citizenship test so close. I begin to focus all my attention on my breathing.

"Don't get me wrong, you're not bad at all. You just lack . . . *precision.*"

I feel heat spreading through my cheeks.

"Anyway, I should be leaving. My parents don't like it when I hang out at *the Mall* too long." He gives our surroundings a significant look.

"Yeah, the Strip is way cooler." Niraj grins.

Sycophant.

Andrew gets to his feet. "Good luck, Nina. I expect you'll be playing at the demi-Virtuoso Examination too."

Too?

Did he just say *too?*

Does that mean Andrew Sommers is part of the competition?

"Don't be upset when they pass you over. It's not your fault you don't have precision. It must suck to have been born an Analog," he says nastily and leaves.

Mae looks at me with concern, but I drop my gaze and take a sip of my juice.

Niraj and Anushka head over to examine a coin-operated arcade machine with interest.

Yes, I said coin-operated. You push physical tokens into a slot and then play a game with 3D graphics on a flat-screen monitor.

"Do you guys want to head to the Strip?" Anushka asks. She's looking around as if she expects a dodgy Analog to jump her any minute.

"Umm, guys." I look at the table. "No chip, no intel-glasses, no Hyper Reality experiences, remember?"

Anushka opens her mouth as if to argue.

"If you guys want to head there, though, carry on . . ."

"What! Nooo!" Anushka forces brightness into her voice. "It's your birthday! We want to hang out with you!"

Sure.

The giant, squat structure rests at the edge of an abandoned airstrip. The relics of long-forgotten passenger aircraft litter vacant tracts of land outside. Rumor has it that at one point, the Analogs used to mount raids to strip them of fuel and scrap metal.

The Mall is made from rusty metal appropriated from former aircraft parking bays, old strips of steel and tin bolted together and painted over in depressingly bright colors. It houses seven floors of twentieth-century gaming technology, flat-screen movie-watching experiences, and clothing stores where you have to physically try on an outfit before buying it.

It's the only place where I can find entertainment that isn't gated on HoloTech privileges I don't have.

Compared to the Hyper Reality at the Strip, this must feel like a trip to the poorhouse.

My poorhouse.

Welcome to the last century, guys.

This is where I live. All the time.

• • •

"Did you have a good birthday, honey?"

Mum plants a kiss on my cheek as she ladles a generous helping of mac and cheese on to my plate.

"Um, sure," I say tonelessly.

Dad gives me a look, and suddenly grins. "You know what? I think we need to liven things up a bit. It isn't every day that our only daughter turns seventeen!"

"What do you have in mind, Madhu?" Mum's tone is unnecessarily bright.

"Oh, I don't know . . . It needs to be special." Dad waggles his eyebrows excitedly. "I think we need to give Nina her first sip of wine."

"Of all the clichéd coming of age rituals, Madhu . . ." Mum says, exasperated.

"Come on," Dad says. "She'll remember this moment with her parents for the rest of her life!"

He heads to his impressive bar, and hovers at the wine rack indecisively.

"It needs to be a really fine one to mark the occasion," he mutters.

"Dinner's getting cold, love." Mum rolls her eyes.

"We're building a new tradition," Dad says. "One that we can add to our birthday mac and cheese dinner."

I feel small. I've eaten half my mac and cheese. I can't eat any more. It's delicious, though.

I wonder if I should tell her. The woman.

"What names do you like, kiddo?" The man smiles at me.

I don't know. I don't say that out loud.

"Do you feel like a boy's name or a girl's?" the woman asks.

I don't answer. Girl, I think, but I don't want to get it wrong.

"Shaila! No, you don't look like you own that name."

"Anuja. Does she look like an Anuja to you?"

"I'm not sure. Let's ask her what she'd like to go by?"

They look at me over the dinner table.

I only know me as D2721, Performer Class. It.

They didn't give me a name at the Home.

"You play the piano beautifully," the woman says.

I smile and nod, my gaze fixed on the hand-carved patterns along the border of the table.

"Do you have a favorite musician?" the man asks.

I shake my head. I wasn't permitted to like things at the Home.

"Would you like to listen to some music? Maybe you'll find a name you like." The woman smiles.

"Thank you," I say nervously.

They let me pick a record—it's glossy black and very shiny. It's so light that I'm scared I'll break it.

They show me how to put it on the player, and how to make it work.

It's amazing. The sound is clean and pure.

I've only listened to cassettes on a tape player. The hiss of the record makes it less alien, more familiar.

"They're nearly two hundred years old, vinyl records. But nothing has ever managed to beat them for sound quality," the man explains.

"This one is Pierre Bolling. I don't suppose you could be a Pierre. It's usually a boy's name, though don't let that stop you!" The woman smiles again.

The music is beautiful.

They change the record.

"Have you heard this one? It's Frida Szeltsmann."

The music sounds happy, like a memory of chocolate.

I've eaten chocolate a few times before. We were allowed a square each time we behaved well at the Home.

They put another record on.

"Give this a try. It's called Wanderer of the Air. *It's by Nina Rodriguez."*

The music is quiet. I can tell that it means many things without saying any of them.

"I like this."

I say it out loud. I shouldn't have said it out loud.

I look at the floor.

"I love this," the woman says.

"It's like you," the man says. "Quiet, but mysterious." He's smiling at me.

"I like it very much," I whisper.

"Do you know about the composer?"

I shake my head no.

"Nina Rodriguez was the first woman to become a neo–Acousta Virtuoso. She was a brilliant pianist and composer. And she was blind."

"Wow."

"She learned by listening, without reading a single sheet of music. She wrote many wonderful pieces of music, and taught demi-Virtuosos at the Apex City School for years."

"Does she inspire you?" the woman asks.

"I don't know what that means."

"Does she make you feel like you're unbeatable? Like you can do anything your heart wants to?"

I think about it for a minute. I imagine being blind. I imagine playing perfect music without being able to read the notes. It sounds difficult. She must have been really clever.

"I would like to be like her."

I burst into tears. I don't know why.

The woman hugs me until I stop crying. I stop crying quickly. They didn't like us crying at the Home.

"So . . . Nina, for now?" the man asks. He's grinning.

Nina.

I say it in my head. I feel it.

Nina.

I look up at them.

"Okay," I say slowly. "My name is Nina."

I feel it on my tongue for the first time. It tastes like hope.

"To Nina!" Dad pronounces, holding up a glass of wine.

He nudges another one across the table toward me. I notice that it's only half as full as his own.

"Go on, now. A drop of alcohol won't poison you." He winks.

"Go easy," Mum warns.

I grin. I can't help it.

"To me!" I giggle, raising my glass.

"To Nina!" they say together.

I take a sip and try not to spit it out. It tastes terrible.

Mum and Dad burst into peals of laughter, and after a moment, I can't help but join in.

• • •

Dear Nina of the Future,

I'm sitting in history class, and it sucks to be me at school.

I'm the only person in the room with a textbook. On printed paper.

Everyone else is watching a Hyper Reality holovid on their intel-glasses. Meanwhile, I'm reading about the pre-Bell history of Apex City, comprising the early stages of the Start-Up Revolution in Bangalore.

Reading.

It's so much slower.

Well, sucks to be me, right? No Bell Biochip, no intel-glasses, no HoloTech. Not until I pass my Virtual Citizenship test. I have to prove myself worthy of their technology, just because I was born an Analog.

~~It isn't as if I can blow up the school with a holo-watch.~~

Stuff like that is dangerous to write. Especially for an Analog-born.

It's so anti-Bell that they could deport me for saying it.

And so the cycle continues . . . I'm perpetually falling behind in class because I don't get information beamed straight into my brain, or Hyper Real worlds where I can explore ancient maps of Apex City, or

"Nina, are you having trouble catching up again?" Magistra VX81 flashes a pixelated scowl.

I hide my journal under my printed textbook. The rest of the class is staring at me.

I look at my desk. "I need a few more minutes to get through the chapter, Magistra."

She sighs. In her electronic voice, it sounds like the scrape of sandpaper over a tin can. "Go on."

I feel the eyes of the entire class on me. I skim over the page as quickly as I can.

What I wouldn't give to have intel-glasses right now.

"The rest of you can start putting forth arguments in favor of or against the Ceasefire Treaty."

The Ceasefire Treaty ended competitive advertising on social media, I read. I balk when I look at the sea of text that forms a detailed analysis of the agreement.

"It's not our fault she's slow," someone mutters.

"Are you sure you learned how to read at the orphanage?" Someone else sniggers. "We. Speak. English. Not. Trad."

"Enough, class." Magistra VX81's voice is firm.

Someone says something unintelligible to me.

"I don't speak the traditional dialect," I snap.

The class bursts into giggles.

"Enough!" Magistra snaps. "Nina, I'd like you to stop disrupting my class."

My ears are hot. The words on the page start to blur, so I slam the book shut and look up.

"I'm done."

"Good." Magistra VX81 smiles at me. "What were the consequences of the Ceasefire Treaty?"

I swallow.

I skipped that paragraph.

"Um . . ."

"She's so slow that she's practically a time traveler. Into the past."

I ignore the taunting and take a deep breath.

"Nina, come on. The rest of the class is waiting on you. We can't do this every day."

"Slooo–ooow," says someone in a sing-song voice.

"What happened after the Ceasefire Treaty?"

I rattle off facts while my brain races to fabricate a plausible answer.

"The Population Catastrophe saw the collapse of nationalism. Large-scale governments could no longer meet the escalating demands for resources from their citizens. When they tried to go to war with each other, the Woke Wave Uprising—armed forces and citizens alike—rebelled against them in the Great Nuclear Boycott."

I flub, recapping basic history, buying myself more time.

"Resource distribution became riddled with allegations of corruption. States seceded from parent countries, cities established independence. It occurred worldwide within the span of a decade. This led to the rise of multiple systems of micro-governance, formed on the basis of trade in natural resources."

I fidget with the spine of my journal.

"Bell Corp emerged as a conglomerate in erstwhile Singapore, now called Premier City. When promising technological communities emerged around the world, Bell Corp invested in them and helped them self-organize into sustainable meritocracies."

"Get to the point, Nina," Magistra drones.

"London was transformed into Crown City, Berlin became Pinnacle, San Francisco is called Crest, and Bangalore joined the big leagues during the Bell Takeover, rebranding itself Apex City . . ."

"Nina!" Magistra snaps.

Someone behind me sniggers.

"When Bell Corp began its investment in Bangalore, the city was divided along traditional communal and cultural identities, but was a thriving start-up hub. The city had escaped the worst of the effects of the Population Catastrophe owing to its high economic stability . . ."

The class has lost interest. Whispers break out all around me.

"Yes, Nina, very good." Magistra VX81 jerkily brings her mechanical appendages together, mimicking applause. "You remember your third-grade history lessons. Admirable."

I roll my pencil across my desk.

"What happened next? What was the outcome of the Ceasefire Treaty?" she fires.

"Bangalore's start-ups . . . competed on social media for pride of place, eating into each other's potential market share? The Ceasefire Treaty ended competition on social media, and . . . and Bell Corp swooped in and saved the day?"

Magistra VX81 gives me a look. It looks hilarious on her pixelated LED face but I've seen it before. It isn't meant to be funny.

"Homework. I want a two-thousand-word paper on the Bell Takeover, from the consequences of the Ceasefire Treaty onward."

"Please Magistra—"

"I want it on my desk, Monday morning."

"Psst, Nina," someone whispers. "She wants it in English."

"I'll translate," someone else sniggers. Her voice lapses into gibberish.

My head spins and I take several deep breaths, trying not to let the laughter in the room overwhelm me.

"Is she an Outsider?"

"I think she's an Analog."

"Not even a Repop kid?"

"Nope."

"Wow, our school's standards are dropping."

"I hear the Analogs don't speak English."

"I hear that they can't read or write. I wonder how she got into our school."

"Shh! Her parents are the Anands. They're the twenty percenters who own the Apex City League of Champions."

"Oh! Those Anands."

"Yeah, those."

"Why would they ever let a freak like this into their home?"

"Guilt, probably. Who knows what they've done to the Analogs."

"Ha ha, are you telling me your parents have never used the Analogs?"

"Come on, who hasn't?"

"Maybe she has a special talent."

"What, like being ugly?"

I keep my head down. I don't look around me. They've been whispering all day. All week.

Everyone is eating but I'm too scared to unwrap my lunch. What if they make fun of my sandwich?

They won't make fun of my sandwich. My parents—adoptive parents—are important twenty percenters. It's a tasty sandwich.

I've never seen so many twenty percenters. They're scary. They're all well-dressed. They look intelligent. One girl even has blonde highlights in her hair. Another one has a FantasyLights backpack—it keeps flashing beautiful patterns.

I'm wearing nice clothes too. They're new and clean.

The woman let me pick the color. I was really scared to, but then I chose a pale blue dress. She even combed my hair into a braid.

I look like them, but I don't feel like me.

"What do they make you do?"

A girl stands across from me. She's smiling at me.

"N-nothing," I say.

"Harvest-shit. You must have some value. Do you clean the floors? The bathrooms?"

Another girl joins her. The one with the FantasyLights backpack. "I'm sure the Anands can afford a server-bot, Sneha," she drawls. "She must have other uses."

She reaches forward. It's sudden.

She grabs the front of my dress and rips it. Buttons fly everywhere.

My cheeks flush. Everyone's looking at us and laughing.

She looks at the training bra under my dress.

"Nope. Clearly there are no other uses."

Something snaps. I'm on her, pulling her hair. The back of my hand makes contact with her face.

She screams. Somebody pulls me off her.

I look down and notice that my fingers are curled around the edge of my desk. My knuckles strain white against my skin.

"Sit down, Nina," Magistra VX81 says.

They're still laughing. She hasn't intervened.

They laugh all the way until the bell rings to signal the end of the day, and it seems like the longest five minutes of my life.

I slam my textbook shut. I rush out of the school's corridors and get into Mum's self-driving car, slamming the door shut behind me. She has to pick me up every day since I'm not allowed to use the teleportals.

"Something wrong, honey?" she asks.

She speaks an address to the computer and it drives us away.

"Nope."

"I'm not your mother for nothing. Did you get into trouble at school?"

"NO!" I say angrily. "I—it's been years since I retaliated."

"Let's call your dad and we can talk about it," she soothes.

I look at the city. It's a blur as we rush past it.

"Nina," the woman begins.

"You shouldn't have hit that girl," the man says.

I look at the floor. It has a carpet.

"I'm sorry."

"Why did you hit her?"

I'm silent.

"You can tell us."

"She ripped my dress open. She said mean things."

The woman looks at the man. "I thought as much, Madhu. I knew the principal wasn't telling us everything."

"Yes, but she should know better than to lash out at them." He sounds angry. "You know it's going to be hard for her to become a Virtual Citizen."

"Yes, but I think she's too young to understand this."

"I think we should tell her. Luckily, we convinced the school to keep this off her permanent record."

"Good thing we padded our BellCoin stacks
before the meeting, yes." The woman's eyes flash angry. "Building donation, indeed!"

"Anya, there will always be eyes on her. She needs to be careful."

I slide my shoes under the carpet.

"Nina, what did the girl say to you?"

I don't answer.

"You have to tell us, Nina." The man's voice is stern. "We don't want to have to punish you."

I feel my eyes sting. "She said you're going to make me work for you. Cleaning things. And other things." My voice begins to shake. "Because I'm an . . . an . . . Analog."

The words tumble out of me before I can help myself.

"I know I'm an Analog, but please don't send me back to the Home because I hit her. I didn't mean to. I can be good. I'll be useful—you've been so kind, not making me do any work at home, but I know how it works. I'll clean up—I'm good with a broom, I can mop the floor and I can't really cook, but you could teach me and then I could do that too. Just please don't take me back to the Home . . ."

I can't bear to look at them.

"Nina, that's ridiculous!" the man exclaims. "Our home is your home now."

"We're not going to make you work for us," the woman says.

"She said that's why you bought me." My voice comes out as a squeak.

The woman's eyes glitter with something that looks like anger and sadness.

"Who's that odious little girl? It's Sheila's daughter, isn't it? I'm going to have a word with her mother . . ."

"Yes, you should, love," the man says to her.

Then he looks at me. "Nina. Let me establish this, once and for all. We adopted you. We didn't buy you. We always wanted to have children, but we couldn't. You're the child we've always hoped for. You might be an Analog by birth, but that doesn't mean you're not a wonderful human being."

I take a deep breath.

"And we will never, never make you work for us," he finishes angrily.

The woman turns and looks me over.

I'm glad I'm not crying this time.

"Nina, you're our daughter. I think it's time you started calling us Mum and Dad."

"Nina," Dad says, his likeness holo-rayed across the backseat of our self-driving car. "I hear you had a bad day, kiddo."

"Meh," I reply.

"We're very proud of you for keeping your cool," he says.

"Hmm."

"We're so proud that you've managed to get such good grades, in spite of being disadvantaged by your lack of HoloTech," he continues, beaming.

"Hmph."

"And that's going to end soon!" Mum chimes in brightly. "Your Citizenship test is just around the corner!"

That knocks me out of my sulk. "What?"

"We got the email just this morning. It's in two weeks' time."

My stomach does a few backflips.

If I become a Virtual Citizen, it'll mean access to intel-glasses. I'll be able to hang out at the Strip and experience Hyper Reality.

I won't be *different* from everyone else in school. I won't be that *special kid* every class has to put up with, while she *reads* her way through a textbook.

If I become a Virtual Citizen, I'll be able to get my InEars, wired straight through to my Bell Biochip and synced to the Sonic Highway. I'll have unlimited access to every piece of music ever written—a library hundreds of years old, all up on the Nebula—that'll stream directly into my consciousness with a single thought. No more having to manually trawl through hundreds of vinyls to find a song. No more having to fast-forward and rewind cassettes to listen on my Walkman. I'll have unlimited access to everything.

The thing that I'm most excited about—the one thing I've wanted for years, that I've never been allowed to have is—

"DreamMusician."

Mum and Dad look at me in surprise.

"That's what I want. As soon as I pass the test, I'm going to sign up."

"Are you sure you want that? Isn't it more fun to learn from Mr. Kuruvilla?"

I stare at the both of them like they're crazy.

"Sure. Yes, he's a great teacher. But I want to learn real precision. I want perfection. It's the only way I'll make it into the demi-Virtuoso program next year."

"Next year?" Mum looks confused.

"Aren't you taking the examination this year?" Dad frowns.

I sigh. "Yes, of course, Dad."

He looks at me expectantly.

"Let's face it. There's no way I'll make the grade."

His expression is blank.

"All my competition is DreamMusician-trained!" I say impatiently.

He smiles in understanding. "I know it must be intimidating. But you underestimate yourself, Nina."

I exhale in exasperation. "No, Dad. Look. I'm being realistic. All of them have trained with InEars. They have a Metronome feed directly into their heads. They haven't had to learn to read sheet music; they just use GlimmerKeys and the piano tells them what to do. Their command over dynamics—"

Dad holds up his hand. "I get it, Nina. I really do. They're trained to play like machines."

"Exactly!"

"But here's where you're different, kiddo." Mum grins. "You play with your heart."

I groan inwardly. I don't know how they do it, but it feels like my parents really do finish each other's sentences.

"You'll be the most unique sound they hear!" Dad snaps his fingers, and grins. "There, now don't you feel better? What's a bad day at school compared to all the great ones to come."

I groan at his positivity.

"Dad, this means that I now have my Citizenship test *and* my demi-Virtuoso exam within days of each other."

"When it glitches it fries, eh? Don't worry, you'll ace both."

He glances at his holo-watch.

"I'm running late for a meeting. See you at home, kiddo. Love you both!"

I do feel better, but as I stare out the window a tiny flip-flop of something cold and unpleasant crawls around in my stomach.

I'd better get to work.

The price of failure is deportation.

• • •

"Nina."

Mum drums her elegant fingers on my notebook.

"Stop studying. Don't you need to practice for your demi-Virtuoso exam?"

I roll my eyes.

"Mum, the Citizenship test is way more important."

"And you know everything you need to pass it already. You're burning yourself out. Go play the piano! It's something you love . . ."

I sigh.

I get up from the coffee table and head into the living room.

I set myself down on the piano bench and carefully lift the lid. I place my fingers over the keys and begin to run through the trickiest sections of *Wanderer of the Air*, or Op. 9 No. 1, Ballet in supra-B-Flat-Major by Nina Rodriguez. It's still about fifteen minutes before my piano teacher arrives, and I'm making the most of this opportunity to not run through finger drills.

It isn't like the one at the Home. That was off-key half the time.

I only had a one-hour slot to play it, every week.

Here, I can play the piano all the time. Except when I'm at school, of course.

Sometimes it's scary to sit at it. It stands all by itself in our large living room.

It's magnificent and glossy black. The name

Manuela Alvares is embossed in a beautiful gold loop along its front. I wonder who she was. Maybe she was a famous musician.

At the Home, we had one grand piano that we would play when we gave performances. Most of the time, it was to raise money for the Home. Otherwise, we practiced on a creaky upright with missing felts.

All the songs I know sound wrong. Maybe because this piano can be properly tuned to the alt and supra scales. Maybe because none of the keys get stuck when I play them.

The Anands—Mum and Dad, as I've started to think of them—get me some sheet music. I can read it and I do my very best to learn it right.

They're looking for a teacher. I thought it would be easier to find a teacher on this side of the world. They are twenty percenters, after all.

Maybe all the Virtuosos are too busy being famous, traveling the world and giving performances.

I'm practicing one of my new pieces when Mum knocks on the door.

"Honey, we think we might have found you a teacher."

I stop playing. I can't believe it!

"He wants to meet you and hear you play. Do you think you're ready?"

"N-now?" *My hands shake a little.*

"Yes, unless you'd rather not. I understand if it's a bit sudden—"

No. This is so exciting. "No. I can play."

A tall man with long dark hair steps into the room.

"David, this is Nina. Nina, this is Mr. Kuruvilla."

I stand, nearly tripping over the stool.

"What have you learned so far, Nina?" *His voice is low.*

"Br—Brächt. Barthöven. Some preludes and sonatinas."

"Okay, can you play me some music?"

My hands are shaking. I fumble for my sheet music, turn the page, and begin.

The keys feel like they're listening to my every touch.

I start off right. Nice and soft. I get through the opening section and into the trills without a fault.

My fingers stumble over the last trill.

Hold it together, Nina.

I enter into the next part of the piece, building it up to its eventual crescendo.

Three bad notes.

My hands are shaking now.

Hold it together, Nina.

The crescendo is perfect, but I think I've pedaled inaccurately.

A rest.

I pause. Collect my thoughts in a second.

The piece descends back into its opening bars. I play this part well.

It diminishes, and ends on a dramatic flourish, played forte, and I hit the notes right.

I sit back. I breathe. I hope I've done enough.

The room is quiet.

"That's not bad at all, Nina." Mr. Kuruvilla smiles at me. "Some obvious mistakes—but practice and the right technique can iron those out."

"Th-thank you."

"You read sheet music? Who taught you?"

"I learned . . . at the Home."

"And you've never been trained virtually?"

"What's that?"

"DreamMusician?"

"I don't know what that is."

I wonder if I'm failing this test. I look at my feet, still resting on the pedals.

He turns to my Mum. "You say she won't have access to any Virtual music aids?"

"She won't be allowed to use any until she passes her Virtual Citizenship test."

He nods slowly.

"I won't lie to you, Anya. It'll be difficult, very difficult. She'll have to internalize rhythm and timing. She'll need to learn each piece by rote, by reading through the sheet music. Tone, dynamics—she'll have to find her way around through feel, work on her musicality the old-fashioned way."

"I'm sure she can—"

"Anya, it's like teaching the blind to paint."

Mum stands up. "Thanks, David. I understand. Don't worry about it, we'll find someone else—"

"Hang on." Mr. Kuruvilla grins. "I didn't say I wouldn't teach her. She's got instinct. I can provide direction."

He looks at me. "If you really want to learn—if you're serious about the piano—then know this. It will be hard. It will be harder for you than for anyone else I've known in a long, long time. I can show you how to become a Virtuoso, but you will have to put in hours and hours of practice to do it. Do you want to do that?"

I hold my breath.

Does this mean he'll teach me?

"I only teach the very best, Nina. Would you like me to teach you?"

I exhale.

"I would like that. Very much."

"Focus, Nina."

My hands stop abruptly.

I didn't even notice him enter the room.

"Your mind isn't here, today." He frowns. "It needs to be here, every day. You need to be present. *At the keys.* Remember, neo-Acousta is only created when precision meets emotion in perfect aural union."

I grimace. I fumbled a cadenza on its descent.

"The cadenza is one of the most prized performance skills in any Virtuoso's oeuvre. It demonstrates absolute control over the instrument. Rodriguez herself would use these sections to improvise in her live performances."

"I know. I'm sorry."

"You don't need to stick to the time signature of the piece, but the descent still has to sound musical. Which means that you must deviate from perfect timing with intent. Symmetry is a big part of Rodriguez's music. You aren't playing Wyschnegradsky here."

I sigh.

"It's a bit late in the day for this, but I think you need to make a conscious effort with your timing."

He picks up the metronome that sits at the top of the piano. It's antiquated—it isn't holographic, there's no touch interface, and its construction is a geometric curiosity. At the base of its pyramid structure is a small knob. Mr. Kuruvilla winds this, then releases the pendulum from its casing. He shifts a weight on it and sets the tempo at *moderato*.

He replaces it at the top of the piano.

The pendulum sways back and forth.

Tick . . . tock . . . Tick . . . tock . . . Tick . . . tock . . .

I play.

I have to recalibrate the movement of my fingers to match the slower timing. Usually, this section is played with a gradual increase in tempo, until it becomes a sonorous flurry of notes.

I can feel Mr. Kuruvilla's eyes on the backs of my hands.

It's hard to calm my nerves. It's not as if I have a Bell Biochip to regulate my adrenaline and suppress my anxiety. I don't even know how I'm expected to perform at this level without one. My fingers go rigid from the strain of sticking to the timing, they begin to cramp from my obvious distress.

"Light fingers, Nina," Mr. Kuruvilla chastises.

I grit my teeth and begin again.

Mr. Kuruvilla talks over my repetitive practice of the cadenza.

"You know, normally Analog metronomes are saved for—no, you're half a beat behind, start again—what was I saying? It's only after you're an accepted Virtuoso that you get to use the liberties of a physical metronome. You'll never develop the same degree of precision without InEars in your formative years of study—stop, you're losing it. Begin again . . ."

I try to drown him out and focus on my accuracy.

It's hard to be perfect without InEars. I'm listening externally and trying to attune myself to the metronome's rhythm, instead of having a tempo beamed directly to my brain.

Not that Mr. Kuruvilla seems to have any sympathy for me.

"You're losing sound clarity each time your little finger plays a note. I wish you'd played this for me last week. We have only days to go to your examination."

It's almost impossible to be dynamically en pointe without DreamMusician. I'm trying to manually exert different degrees of pressure on the keys to evoke emotion. I don't think I'll ever be spot-on.

"Any chance you'll get your InEars before the exam?" He's stopped me again, recalibrating the metronome to slow it down further.

"No, my test is two days after."

He doesn't make eye contact.

"You'll do fine. Don't worry."

"How?" I snap. I didn't mean to.

"I'm sorry?"

I try to check my temper and fail.

"*How* will I do fine? I haven't learned any of this with InEars. My dynamics are all by feel, I don't even know if they make sense. Sure, I'm following the sheet music, but I'm not following it using carefully calibrated Tactile+ on Dream-Musician. Everyone else is going to sound *perfect*."

"I'm going to stop you right there."

I pause.

"Yes, everyone else is going to sound perfect. But you are going to sound genuine. All this—neo-Acousta—is about the purity of sound. And you create that experience because you play with purity of heart."

"A good heart has never got someone into this program," I grumble.

"Okay, enough for the day."

"Are you kidding? The examination is in five days!"

"I'll come back tomorrow. You take the day to clear your head."

"Mr. Kuruvilla, I'll practice. Really, let's go."

I reach for the metronome.

"Up."

My shoulders sag. I rise to my feet.

"Why did you choose this piece, Nina?"

I know why, but I don't want to tell him.

"What does it mean to you?"

I say nothing.

"You're not going to tell me. I get it." He sighs. "It means a lot to you. It's a very personal choice, I gather."

I nod.

"You know how I chose my piece for my examination? I picked it for its complexity. I picked it because it would demonstrate my technical superiority."

"Did it work?"

"Of course it did. That's how it's been done, for years and years."

"Great, thanks. I'm going to fail."

"Listen, kid. You'll be the only person there playing music that comes from the soul."

"Good for me."

"Not so fast. The jury will connect with that. In its pursuit of perfection, neo-Acousta has ignored the expression of the soul for far too long. You'll remind them of this."

I roll my eyes.

"Homework. Think of what this piece means to you. What is its story? Write it down for me."

"Really?"

"Yes, really. We'll reconvene tomorrow."

Why does everyone keep making me write things down?

• • •

Dear Nina of the Future,

Have you made it yet? I hope you're world famous by now.

I've been practicing nonstop for my demi-Virtuoso Examination, and I'm sure I'm going to fail miserably because try as I might, I can't nail down this cadenza, even after working on the story of the piece and showing it to Mr. Kuruvilla.

He loved it.

I love it too, but that's not the same as playing it perfectly, is it?

"Are you stressed about the exam again?"

I look up from my journal.

Mae is staring at me, her brows furrowed in concern.

I slam my notebook shut. "No. Nooo. I'm fine. *Fine.*"

She arches her eyebrows, and I can tell she doesn't believe me.

Niraj and Anushka look over from where they've been arguing over whether almond milk or soy milk is better for their weight-loss diets.

"Is Andrew Sommers going to be playing at that thing?" Niraj sounds enthusiastic.

"Ooh, will you get to watch?" Anushka squeals.

Mae shoots her a filthy look.

"What, he's dreamy!" She pouts.

"Don't worry, Nina," Mae says, touching my arm gently. "We'll all be there to cheer you on."

"Will they let us listen to everyone's performances?" Anushka asks brightly, then quickly adds, "I mean, we'll be there for you, but it wouldn't hurt to check out the competition."

She blushes before quickly absorbing herself in the pile of greens on her lunch tray.

"You haven't touched your lunch," Mae mutters.

"Not hungry," I mumble.

"What?"

I glare at her.

"I've had enough," she says, getting to her feet. "Let's go."

"Go where?" Niraj says, shocked.

"What do we have after lunch?"

"Double psychohistory," Niraj says promptly.

"Yeah, Nina and I are skipping that."

"We are?" I start.

"We are. You guys let Magistra know that we had a . . . erm . . . what could have gone wrong? A . . . *a female emergency*."

Niraj chokes on his chicken salad.

"You'd better cover for us."

Mae glowers. "Mae, I dunno . . . I've got my Citizenship test round the corner too. What if this counts against me?" I say uncertainly.

"Suddenly getting your period? I'd like to see them try!" she huffs.

"I'm not on my period." My cheeks flush.

"And they'll never know because you don't have a chip. Ha. Haha," she laughs sarcastically. "Nina. Up."

She's bossy. It's impossible for me to ignore her, even at the best of times.

I spring to my feet, pushing my untouched lunch aside and grabbing my journal. I scurry after her as she strides out of the lunchroom.

"Where . . . where exactly are we going?"

She doesn't meet my gaze. Instead, she marches me straight through a pair of bright green gates that mark the end of the school campus.

We stand on the sidewalk under the shadow of a tree, as far from the school's visible PanoptiCam lenses as possible. I look around guiltily, hoping that the school doesn't have any hidden cameras, and even though Mae does a great job masking it, I can tell she's twitchy.

Behind us, the enormous gray stone buildings and red-tiled roofs of our school glower ominously down upon us. Skipping out could have consequences; being able to socialize and learn in a physical schooling institute, instead of being distance-educated, is a privilege that only the twenty percenters can claim.

I glance nervously up the school's driveway for signs of the patrol-droids. I fervently hope that we don't run into a Magistra, or worse, the principal on her rounds.

I heave a sigh of relief when an empty self-driving cab rolls up within three minutes.

"Meridian Gate, please," Mae announces to the computer, pulling me in after her.

We ride together in silence. I knot the tassels on my jacket sleeve and Mae types away furiously on her OmniPort.

I don't know why she's taking me back. I haven't been near the other side since that horrible train ride I'd been forced to go on.

"Welcome aboard! This is Maglev Adventures' Mission Analog!" the tour guide says, beaming at our class.

I ignore the class when they all give me pointed looks and giggle at the word "Analog."

Magistra AB43 sits up front with the tour guide watching us all, recording our behavior. Mum and Dad warned me that she'll be paying careful attention to me, live streaming my every reaction onto the Nebula so that the people at the Home can check how I respond to being back in the Analog world.

"It's a test," they'd said. They'd looked worried.

I know I need to pass.

I stare blankly ahead, keeping a straight face all through the tour guide's announcements and instructions. When the train departs, I don't join in when some of my classmates begin to shriek and cry. Instead, I wave to my parents who are waiting on the station platform.

"We're going to visit your real home," Anastasia Prakash mocks, flicking a wad of paper at me.

"Do you have servants?" Sneha giggles beside her. "Oh wait, you are servants."

The rows behind me take up the giggle.

I ignore them, staring straight ahead. I don't even gasp when the big blue shield opens itself up and lets us through.

The girl sitting beside me is new. That's probably why she chose to sit next to me—most people avoid coming near me. She hasn't said a word to me. She must be learning.

The train zooms into a pod-house and I flinch. I can't believe we're entering someone's home uninvited. We'd never have dared, when I was being raised at the Home.

The house is filthy. I wonder why. We were much cleaner at the Home.

"Did you live in a box like this?" Anastasia says loudly.

"No wonder you're so scared all the time," Sneha adds. "You're not used to seeing daylight, are you?"

I'm about to snap at them, but I feel Magistra's gaze on me and ignore them.

Magistra addresses the class. "Why don't the Analogs have any privileges?"

"Because they're bad citizens," the class recites. I chime in the loudest.

We're going past the vegetable farm now.

"Is this why you're an orphan?" Sneha whispers. "Do you carry your parents around in a little box in your backpack?"

Everyone except the girl sitting beside me giggles, even though they all look terrified at the thought.

When the tour guide points out the nutro-shakes and protein porridge that I was raised eating, I cringe at the memory of their taste.

"She's never eaten real food before," Anastasia gasps.

"That explains the brain damage," Sneha says cruelly.

More laughter.

For the first time, the girl sitting next to me turns around and glares at them.

"What are the principles of the Bell Curve, class?" Magistra asks.

We recite the Rhyme of the Percentiles that we've been taught. It's written on the first page of all our textbooks. I chant it louder than anyone else, especially the last verse.

"Bottom ten
deport, forget,
Mice, not men
must live in regret."

When we arrive in Market Square, I begin to wonder if I'm going to fail my test. I look at all the shops around me and wonder if I'll be sent back to work in one of them. When the tour guide plays anatronica over the speakers, I bob along to the beat of it before realizing that everyone's staring at me.

"You call this music, Nina?" Anastasia hisses.

"I thought you were a pianist." Sneha smirks.

"A pianist!" Anastasia laughs. "What sort of pianist would ever enjoy this garbage? I'll tell you—a fake one. I'll bet you my allowance for the year that she's deported before the end of term."

I focus on the glass of the train window. I stare through it, barely registering a word that the tour guide is saying. If I stare at it hard enough, maybe it'll break and the Analogs will attack and Anastasia will finally shut up.

The girl sitting beside me whips her head around.

"You're on."

"And who in all the Analogged world are you?"

"Mae. Mae Ling. I just transferred from Premier."

"Hmm . . . Mae Ling, let me tell you how it works. There are some of us who belong here, and there are those of us who don't. Who would you rather be?" Anastasia whispers fiercely.

"Human," Mae Ling says coolly, turning her back on her. "Nina, it's so cool to finally meet you. I heard you play at the recital the other day— you're supra-brilliant . . ."

I think I've just made a friend.

"You're a brilliant pianist, my friend, but you've got the attention span of a fly," Mae says, clearly annoyed.

I snap out of my daze.

"What? Sorry, Mae, what were you saying?"

"I was ravishing you with compliments, but I guess you'll never hear them now." She grins.

The baobab-shaped structures of Bell Towers F and G cast their scattered net of shadows upon the city streets. We pass through the Arboretum, driving close to an overturned statue lying on its side. She's covered in moss and vegetation, though her plaque still proudly names her "Vic."

"Look," Mae commands.

"At Vic?"

"At the shield."

We are at the edge of the Carnatic Meridian. The car rolls to a stop.

Mae passes her hand over a holoscanner to pay for the ride, another thing I can't do. We step outside.

"Look through it. Look beyond, to the other side."

"No thanks," I say hurriedly, turning away.

"Look," she insists, grabbing my shoulder and shaking me slightly.

I look. All I can make out through the shimmering blue haze are the skull-like silhouettes of pod-houses reaching into the sky, a tightly packed warren of dust paths weaving their way through them into infinite black.

"Why are we here again?"

She waves at the world beyond the Meridian, the world that was my life before I was Nina.

"You might have come from over there, you might have spent your childhood on the other side. You might want to prove yourself to the world. But here's the thing . . . You've got nothing to prove. Not to me, not to your parents, not to Mr. Kuruvilla. Do you understand me?"

"I need to prove to myself that I'm worth it," I say flatly.

"You are worth it," she says simply.

"I don't want to disappoint everyone—"

"Nina, we want you to succeed. We want you to make it. That is the deepest wish of everyone who loves you. It's a wish, that's all. It's not an expectation. We'll love you, no matter how things turn out."

I look through the Meridian. I look at Mae. Her words are heavy, and several seconds pass before I burst into a sudden fit of giggles.

"All right, good talk."

"That's the most serious conversation we've ever had." I laugh.

"Ugh," Mae says. "Talk about getting sentimental."

"If I get deported, you'll come visit?"

"You won't get deported," she says with finality.

• • •

Dear Nina of the Future,

I've handed in my essay to Magistra VX81.
I've studied for my Virtual Citizenship test.
Now I just have to nail my examination.
Here I am.
I haven't seen the jury yet. I'm in the waiting room with all the other demi-Virtuoso hopefuls. I don't know what pieces they've chosen to play.

The room vibrates with an air of secrecy. We aren't allowed to listen to each other's auditions.

Andrew Sommers is here—

And he hasn't even looked at me.

Anushka keeps whipping her hair back, tossing him sidelong glances, but he's ignoring her. He has a contented look on his face, nodding

his head to the music that's probably filtering straight into his mind through his InEars. Niraj nearly went up to him to wish him luck, but Mae quelled him with one of her death glares.

My friends and family talk in hushed voices around me, while I listen to my piece one last time before I play it.

I feel every inch the Analog with my Walkman and my over-the-ear headphones.

There are pianists here who have holopianos. They're Hyper Reality simulations of the instrument, complete with weighted keys and pedal units. They're practicing on them and appear completely immersed.

One of the pianists plays with tons of flourish. Clearly she'll have the upper hand on the drama quotient.

Someone appears at the door.

"Nina Anand," she announces.

"Good luck, kiddo." Dad thumps me on the back.

"Go for it, honey." Mum hugs me.

Mae squeezes my hand, and Niraj and Anushka toss me a thumbs-up sign and a heart sign.

My legs feel like jelly. I'm wobbly all over.

Andrew Sommers doesn't even look in my direction.

I step through the door and enter a dark room with the loudest silence I've ever heard.

Five jurors sit at a dais, and the room is empty but for a grand piano.

"Name, please."

"Nina Anand."

"And your piece?"

"*Wanderer of the Air*, or Opus 9 Number 1, Ballet in supra-B-Flat Major by Nina Rodriguez."

"What can you tell us about Nina Rodriguez?"

"She was blind. She learned to play music by ear. Her pieces are about underlying symmetry and simplicity, disguised by technical complexity and flourish."

"And why did you pick this piece?"

I panic. I don't know how to answer. The

reason—this piece—is so much bigger than me. It dwarfs everything that comes within its reach. It contains me, and all I can do when I play it is wander the halls of its melodies, lost within a magic unlike any other.

I stop my train of thought and settle for a predictable, unemotional response.

"It—it embodies the spirit of neo-Acousta. It's pure and elevated, outward-looking but deeply personal."

The jurors don't react.

"You may begin," one of them says.

I sit at the piano. I adjust the bench.

I place my hands over the keys and take a deep breath.

I don't have a Bell Biochip to soothe my nerves by inducing adrenaline suppressors.

I don't have InEars to guide my rhythm.

I don't have GlimmerKeys or Tactile+ to help me create an artistically designed atmosphere.

I only have my soul.

I play my story.

• • •

Dear Nina of the Future,

I'm hoping to hear from the demi-Virtuoso Examination today. I hope I get to finish my Citizenship test first, though. The disappointment of failure would be a crushing blow, and I'll probably be deported because I underperformed.

I'm sitting in another waiting room—why is my life a story of waiting on other people's approval?—and I feel grateful for my parents. I look around at the other Analog adoptees. I've never seen another one in my life, and they . . .

They break my heart.

They don't look like they come from loving homes. Or like their lives are filled with opportunity. They look terrible, as if they've never been able to escape the other side.

I don't know why, but I've understood over the

years that not all adoptive parents are as nice as mine. Some of them are downright awful.

"Nina Anand."

I feel like I'm always being summoned.

I step into the room. It's bare. It has a single desk within it.

I sit at the desk. I'm handed a holo-questionnaire and a stylus by a patrol-droid that's monitoring my performance.

I gasp at how unfair this is. Most of the Analog children here may have never seen this technology. They'll probably be intimidated by the droid.

I'm one of the lucky few who saw it at school all the time, whose parents showed me how to use it.

I look down at my test. I blitz through it. I know I've aced it.

I'm led by a patrol-droid through a door made of reinforced steel. I sense another adopted child take their place at the seat I just left, and hope they do well, before I refocus and enter the next room.

This is the part where my parents warned me not to lose my temper.

They call it the *Character Evaluation.*

A wood-paneled table runs the length of the room. Behind it sits a pair of women, both staring at me indifferently.

"Ms. Anand. How long have you been in the Virtual world?"

"Five years," I say immediately, and then cautiously add, "Madam."

"Explain the Bell Curve to me."

"The Bell Curve is an algorithm that takes into account several factors." I rattle off an explanation of all its points systems. I know this like the back of my hand.

"And where do you see yourself on this Curve, young lady?"

"At the top twenty percent. Madam."

The women are silent.

"Why do you think you'll make it there?"

One of them lifts her intel-glasses off the bridge of her nose, skeptically.

"I'm an extraordinary pianist," I say, with more confidence than I feel.

The women laugh.

"*You're* an extraordinary pianist despite your lack of tech? Come on, Ms. Anand. Don't delude yourself."

"It's true," I stick to my guns politely, like my parents said I should.

Apparently the jurors like what they call Alpha-Behavior Characteristics. It proves to them that I'm not a browbeaten Analog likely to crumble under pressure.

"Who's your teacher?"

"David Kuruvilla, the well-known Virtuoso."

"We don't pass liars."

"I'm not lying. You can verify this."

I tilt my nose upward, putting on my best twenty-percenter air.

One of them runs a check on a holo-device I can't see.

"It's true."

"Very well. So you want to be a Virtual Citizen?"

"Yes, please."

I'm extra polite, now that I've made my point.

"Why do you deserve it?"

"I've assimilated the culture and philosophy of merit that is propagated on this side of the world. I understand how it works. I work hard, I'm Productive. I have friends at school, despite not being able to share in their tech experiences. Imagine all I could be once I have access to HoloTech?

"I impressed the jurors in my demi-Virtuoso examination, despite never having used Dream-Musician. Do you know how far I could go once I have music-learning aids?"

"That's all well and good, but how do we know you're still not an Analog at heart?"

My heart sinks.

One of the women leans forward.

"Any links to them? Do you listen to anatronica? Do you find yourself longing for home?"

"Yes," the other woman adds. "Do you ever visit? Pass them information about us?"

"This is my home," I say boldly. "The Ana-logs are filthy. They're slackers and lowlifes. They are the bottom ten percent. I wouldn't go back, not for any reason in the world."

I say it with a conviction that I'm not sure I feel.

"You believe you're superior to them? You were born of them."

"An unfortunate accident that was beyond my control." I grimace.

The women nod.

"You will hear from us shortly."

And just like that, I'm dismissed.

. . .

Dear Nina of the Future,

We made it.
We're a Virtual Citizen.

We heard from the demi-Virtuoso Examination too, and I came in second. That means I'm eligible to join the program, straight after school.
Now there's no looking back.
If you ever happen to look back, though, don't forget that you're more than what the world tells you you can be. That you're loved, no matter what you achieve. Your life might be wrapped up in your music, but you're also so much more . . .

My Bell Biochip itches a little. I guess I'm getting used to having an implant behind my ear.

It distracts me from the piece that I'm playing, but I ignore it and carry on.

Mr. Kuruvilla is making me work harder than ever, now that I'm about to make it to the big leagues.

I'm not using DreamMusician yet. I checked it out but it was way too distracting. It's like constant background noise.

The GlimmerKeys confused me, and the InEar Metronome plug-in gave me a headache. I found Tactile+ far too restrictive. It felt like a straitjacket.

I get to use intel-glasses at school, and Hyper Reality blows my mind. I can finally talk to Dad without needing Mum around to sign me in on her OmniPort. I've discovered HoloTube, where my piano videos are steadily accumulating followers . . .

"Stop," Mr. Kuruvilla barks. "You're rushing into playing this forte. I want you to build up to it. Try again."

I begin again.

"Stop. See, here? That's the exact note. It's such an abrupt transition."

I begin again.

"Better. Keep going."

BETH CATO

APOCALYPSE PLAYLIST

(2020)

"ROAR LIKE A LION" BY TRIUMPH

Nothing like an 1980s arena rock ballad to establish optimism as news comes about the imminent, probable end of humanity.

Music constantly streams through Orchid's head thanks to the chip installed behind her right ear. Such implants are fairly commonplace, but most augment the brain and senses in other ways. Her curated filter of tunes enables her to work, survive, even to sleep in an otherwise overwhelming world.

As her coworkers begin to cry, some calling up family, some running for the door, Orchid decides there's little point in finishing her expense report. The song—the original album cut, not the abbreviated radio version—enters its prolonged dramatic drum solo as she goes to the office kitchen to equip herself with a carving knife, medical kit, and anything else of use for the long walk home.

"MY LOVE, LOVE, LOVE IS LIKE A BALL-PEEN HAMMER" BY UNORTHODOX CARNAGE

Orchid is hungry. Despite frequent dieting throughout her life, she hasn't known true starvation until now. Her heavy-metal musical catalogue empowers her with anger and strength, even as she quivers with weakness behind a gutted electronics store. Gun shots punch the air nearby, an eerie fit with the frenzied drumbeat. Dragging footsteps approach. This man has tracked her since his gang raided her friends' hideout two nights ago. Orchid and five other women had banded together in recent weeks. She needs to find them again. She needs them to be okay.

She bobs her head slightly to an enraged rhythm only she can hear. She doesn't possess the titular ball-peen hammer from the song, but she does have a brick. She clutches it with trembling fingers. She hopes he's carrying food.

"RAINBOW, SHINE DOWN (LORD, SHINE DOWN)" SUNG BY ANGELA TERRY, COMPOSED BY FELICITY FAYETTE

Religious songs occupy a small fragment of her chip's database, but Orchid finds herself mentally queuing up the music often these days—not for herself, but for the others in the compound. No matter their backgrounds, everyone craves hope, in this life or the next. This contemporary a cappella rendition of an 1893 hymn is especially pleasant.

Most evenings, Orchid sits before the community and sings along with the music in her head. Her voice is nothing extraordinary, but she possesses the repertoire, and that's what matters. Many people have told her that this after-dinner gathering is their favorite part of the day.

She feels the same way.

"MARCH ON THE DARK LADY'S CASTLE" COMPOSED BY HIMARI NAKAMURA

Orchestral video-game music establishes a necessary rhythm throughout hours of mundane labor. Scoop shovel into mud, toss into pile. Make the pit. Assist with the bodies. Start on next pit. Never mind that Orchid is still enervated after her own bout of influenza. She's in better shape than most. She's alive.

"I SEE THE WORLD INSIDE YOUR EYES" BY COLORBLIND (FEATURING DJ HECTOR-HECTOR)

Orchid never expected to get married. By the age of forty, she had only hoped to pay off her student loans. Instead, here she is, singing as she walks toward a bearded man with bright blue eyes. Friends surround them and sing along with the '90s R&B song she chose for this moment.

She selfishly wishes she could write down the lyrics for this song as part of her compendium.

In her new official role as community Bard, she's transcribing songs deemed "most important" to preserve. That requires many hard, yet necessary judgment calls, as there is never enough paper.

One thing is certain. This ultimate love-song-style moment will be something she remembers for the rest of her days.

"MY NAME IS A FLOWER" BY ROSE, PERFORMED AT THE SAME TIME AS "LALA HAHA" BY THE JIGGLY RHYTHMS

"Mama! You have to put this song in your brain!" Rose stands atop a boulder as she belts out yet another song of her own creation. Orchid smiles as she hoes the field, saying nothing until the performance is done. Rose doesn't have her mother's medical need for a constant soundtrack, but her passion for music is undeniable.

"I can keep your song in my brain as a normal memory." Orchid taps her forehead. "But I can't upload it to my chip with the rest of my music library."

"Oh." Rose's face puckers as she struggles to understand the difference. "Well, I'll keep my songs in my memory! I can fit a bunch in there, huh, can't I?"

"Oh yes. Lots. In my brain, I fit all five songs you've composed today."

"Five! That's how old I am! Sing one of my songs to me, Mama!" Rose pauses. "Please?"

"I'll sing your newest song again because my name is a flower, too," says Orchid, smiling as she matches the beat with that of the pop anthem simultaneously pulsing through her mind.

"THREE CATS ON A FENCE" BY BANANA GIRL AND THE SPLITS (TV VERSION)

For several days, Orchid debated what song should be her last one. Finally, she settled on her first favorite song. The one that, in her anxiety-filled pre-chip early childhood, she sang to herself constantly to help her cope with the noisy, overwhelming world.

Before the Apocalypse, her cancer battle would've been hard. Now, a quick end is inevitable. The music of the past cannot die with her. Today her chip will be transplanted to her teenage daughter. It's unknown if the chip will take, but Rose is determined to try.

Orchid is hurting. She's scared for herself, for Rose. Her husband and daughter anchor each hand as the familiar melody fills her brain. Despite all, she smiles.

Her lips trace the preschool lyrics and count down cats. Her doctors and family sing with her. They know the words.

ERICA SATIFKA

ACT OF PROVIDENCE

(2021)

HAILEY THREADS THROUGH the crowd of protesters and ever-present camera drones. The excitement caused her to miss her bus, so she'll have to walk home. After turning the corner, Hailey finds herself in a pop-up open-air nighttime market, where hand-knitted scarves jockey for place with home-brewed red ale. The people milling about don't seem to even realize what's happening only a block away.

Or maybe they don't care, Hailey thinks. *Is that still possible, not to care?* She doubts it.

She becomes aware of a figure following her. A man, from the footfalls. Hailey lets him trail along as far as the last market stand—a guy selling knockoff sunglasses out of an ancient beater—and then whirls on him. "What do you want, kid?"

"I think I know you."

Hailey feels heat rise to her face. Those fucking documentaries. "You don't."

"No, I do, you're one of those Rhode Island survivors," he says. "I think it really sucks what happened to you people. So few of you made it."

"Well, we get to live here now," she snaps, spreading her arms wide. "A Development Zone paradise."

"So, I guess you live in New Providence, huh? I have a transport parked near here, I can take you home."

Hailey brushes a wrinkle from her pants leg. "Go home with you? I don't even know your name, you weirdo."

He grins. "I'm Dalton. And you're Hailey. See, I told you that you looked familiar."

She rolls her eyes. "Whatever."

"Oh come on, it's cold out." He says it with a teasing lilt at the end, and when the wind gusts between them, Hailey can see his point.

"Fine, you wore me out. You can take me home. But I should warn you in advance that I'm defensively armed." The law is, you're allowed to outfit yourself with whatever gadgets you want, as long as you make a reasonable effort to inform any nearby people that you're carrying. Tonight, Hailey has poison darts embedded in her clothing and whisker-thin screamer alarms knotted into her hair.

Dalton heads away from the market, presumably in the direction of his transport. When they reach the parking lot, she sees it's a sporty little thing, its cherry-red chassis free of the garish advertising that most transports are slathered in.

This guy must be loaded, Hailey thinks. *He doesn't even need his vehicle to be subsidized.*

They face one another as the transport points itself in the direction of New Providence. Hailey can feel the kid studying her, and she touches the dart sewn into the sleeve of her sweater.

As the spires in the heart of the Development Zone disappear in the distance, Dalton speaks again. "You're the one they found in the clothes dryer, right?"

Hailey sighs. "I really don't like to talk about it. There are lots of shows about us you can watch if you're interested. My sister's in a lot of them."

"I've seen them," Dalton says. "Look, I'll be straight with you. This wasn't a random meeting, I've been tracking you for some time. I'm a game designer, and I'd like to buy the rights to your story."

This isn't the first time Hailey's heard this particular refrain, although the "game" part is new. "You'd have to talk to our agent. We all have one, as a group."

"The games are illegal, Hailey."

She'd forgotten. It's an easy thing to forget, as open as the consumers of the virtual-reality platform known as the "gamespace" are about their vice. The unenforced ban dropped a few years ago, after some rumors emerged about the drug used to enhance the experience.

"I don't play, but I know some people in New Providence who do," Hailey says. "I'll hook you up."

"I was really rather hoping *you'd* be interested," Dalton admits with a sheepish grin.

"I've researched the Rhode Island disaster a lot, and you make the most narrative sense for the story I have in mind."

Hailey blinks and places a finger next to one of her poison darts. "I never thought I'd have a stalker. My sister will be *so* jealous."

Dalton heaves a sigh. "Can I give you my pitch? You're the youngest survivor of the wave that rearranged the coastline until your home wasn't there anymore. You survive through a freak accident, trapped among the wreckage of not just an entire city, but an entire *state*."

"I don't need a recap. When does the 'game' part come in?"

He taps his chin. "It's more of an immersive narrative than a game, actually. Oh, I'll put a few minigames in there, I'm sure. The ratings will suffer if I don't. But mostly it's just about seeing the disaster up close. Imagining what it was like to be there."

"That doesn't sound like a game that's going to make a lot of money," Hailey says.

"It won't. That's another reason I don't want to involve your group's agency. They'd laugh me out of the room."

Dalton's transport has stopped at the cross street closest to the entrance to the New Providence subdivision. The houses here are nicer than most on the outskirts of the Pittsburgh Development Zone, thanks to many thousands of generous donations to the Rhode Island branch of the New England Wave Survivors' Foundation. The Solfind Corporation had chipped in a fair amount too.

They only cared because they could assuage their guilt affordably, she reminds herself, *with a commemorative suburb for fifty-four people.*

"I need to go," she says as she waits for him to unlock the transport.

"So are you interested? I can pay you something, even if it's not very much."

Hailey stamps her foot; it echoes throughout the interior of the transport. "I'm pretty busy, honestly. I work for Solfind." She doesn't tell him that she just works one day a week as the token human at a spire-base restaurant. The majority of her and Teresa's living expenses are drawn from the survivors' fund.

"My card," he says, "in case you change your mind."

The door hisses open and Hailey gratefully exits, wrapping her arms around herself in the frosty October night. Dalton's red transport idles a few more moments at the corner, then slides away down the smooth, gridded, newborn streets.

Hailey glances at the card before she puts it in her pocket. Like his car, it's devoid of decoration, just a name and screen code marked in black ink on a soft white piece of cardboard.

Kind of traditional for a game designer, she thinks. *What a weirdo.*

• • •

"Breakfast?" Teresa says. She's speaking to Hailey, but her gaze is centered on the thumb-sized camera drone hovering in front of her face.

She's live, Hailey thinks as she pulls back a chair and seats herself at the table. *Well, when is she not?* "Sure."

Teresa artfully arranges a plate, tilts it to the camera, and deposits it on the table. The camera tracks the movement, and Hailey wishes she'd put on the monster mask she sometimes wears when Teresa's streaming. "Thanks."

Teresa flashes a grin at the camera and dances back to the stove, the microprocessors in her knees whirring. While they'd been in the dryer, Teresa's body had been pressed down on her legs in such a way that they'd had to be removed and replaced with the sort of limbs fitted to New People, the humanlike androids the Solfind Corporation developed to do the jobs too dangerous or tedious for humans. Teresa admitted to Hailey once that the artificial limbs have poor tactile sensation, but that overall they'd helped her personal brand so much that she couldn't quite be sorry things had worked out the way they did. "I didn't even hear you come in last night."

"I missed my bus because of the protests," Hailey says as she spears a miniature heart-shaped pancake with her fork.

"When will all this madness end?" Teresa says, speaking only to the camera this time.

"You don't even know what they're protesting about, Teresa."

"I'll tell you what I do know," Teresa says. She fishes a small tube out of her apron pocket. "This lip liner . . ."

Hailey picks up her plate and heads back upstairs. She holds up her screen as she eats on her bed, thumbing through her feed. Then she notices a small banal object on the floor of her room. The card Dalton the game designer gave her last night.

She picks it up. There's only a number, not a site address. Before she can talk herself out of it, she punches his number into her screen.

I want to talk more about the game, she messages.

She waits for a response, and nearly screams a moment later when the phone rings.

"Can you meet me at the BurgerMat near your house?"

"The fuck," she says. "You *called* me?"

"Yeah, I'm a bit of a throwback," he says. "So, meet me there? You need a ride?"

Hailey takes a deep breath. "No, I'll walk. I'll bring my jacket this time."

• • •

Hailey has been waiting outside the BurgerMat for fifteen minutes when Dalton comes puffing up. She can't see his red bullet-like transport anywhere.

"Sorry I'm late," he says, though it sounds like he doesn't really mean it.

She peers inside, where a bored human worker sits within the octopus of mechanisms that prepare the food. *That's what the protests are about,* she thinks. *Solfind wants to eliminate the human workers entirely, cut out the make-work jobs.* This won't affect her position, guaranteed as it is by the contract the Rhode Island survivors have with Solfind. But it makes the Development Zone that much more exclusive.

"Do you want to get food?" Dalton asks.

"I want to discuss terms," Hailey says, "*over* food."

Dalton pushes his way through the glass doors and the stench of processed meat wafts out like a greasy cloud. He punches in an order without asking Hailey her preference and they perch on stools near the counter while the array of machines whirs into action.

"First of all, the process will require you to take Trancium," Dalton says. "If you're not comfortable with that, we should stop right here."

Hailey isn't surprised at this stipulation, but she's still a bit uneasy about it. Trancium's reported effects are almost certainly overblown, but it's never been something she planned to fuck around with. "My comfort level depends on what I'm getting in return. I'm not destroying my brain for pocket change."

"Oh, that's just fearmongering," Dalton says, as he picks up their trays of food and ferries them to a booth. "I've taken Trancium dozens of times and my MRI is clean as a whistle."

She bites into her burger. "I still don't know why you aren't asking Teresa instead."

"Because everyone already knows her story. Yours is a mystery."

Hailey chews, considering. If she doesn't take this opportunity now, one might not come around again. It *would* be nice to live on her own, away from Teresa's ever-present cameras. "What does Trancium *do*, exactly?"

Dalton balls up his wrapper and chucks it into a hole in the table. "It's a relaxant. It frees up your mind so you can either slide into a game or build one on your own, out of your own memories and imagination."

"Have you had *your* memories put into a game?"

"My senior thesis, actually," Dalton says. "Here, I can show you on my screen."

Hailey watches a short video clip filmed in a first-person perspective of an unseen figure running through a field. From the height, she suspects it's a child. Figures approach from the corner of the screen, closing in like wild animals who've caught the scent of prey. "Who are those guys?"

"My brothers. They're not the nicest people."

"And it's a *game*?"

Dalton takes the screen back, clears his throat. "Like I said, it's more of a narrative experience."

"And you took Trancium to make this thing?"

He pinches his fingers a half-inch apart. "Just the tiniest amount. The project got a B, for what that's worth. The instructor said it would have been an A if market potential wasn't one of the grading criteria."

Hailey raises her hand, silencing him. "So it's a vanity project. Where do you get the money to pay *me*?"

"My parents give me my money. They work for Solfind."

Well, that figures, Hailey thinks. "But what's in it for Solfind?"

"Nothing. But there's a lot in it for me, and well, my parents love me."

Just as Hailey suspected all along, Dalton is a rich kid, no different fundamentally from the entitled little princelings her mother used to teach at a private school in Newport. Every one of them died. All the money in the world couldn't buy their survival.

"I'm going to give you a number," she says, "and if *you're* not comfortable we can stop right here." She writes down an amount that totals out to the cost of her own home in New Providence, or alternatively, several dozen acres of land in the Undeveloped Zone.

Dalton peeks at it. "Oh, we can do this."

Fuck, she thinks. *I should have asked for more.*

• • •

Hailey meets Dalton again the following day at his "studio," which turns out to be just a curtained-off section of his apartment with a shiny, new-looking gaming rig set up inside.

He'd breezed her past the living room and kitchenette, but she can tell from the real fruit and shelf full of art books that despite sharing a Development Zone, they don't live in the same world.

The only decoration in Dalton's studio aside from the gaming equipment itself is a pad on the floor. "Where's your stereo? I read that you need music for this."

"Not if we're just making a recording," Dalton says, and Hailey supposes that's for the best. The audio samples of the game-enhancing folk singer Johnny Electric she'd listened to before coming over hadn't been much to her taste. She stiffens a bit when he rests the rig on the crown of her head. "Now, think of something."

"About the disaster?"

Dalton shakes his head. "Let's not start with that. Something simple. We're only calibrating."

Hailey imagines a bouncing red ball. The monitor on the screen shows a grainy grayscale image of a ball, though its movements are choppy rather than elegant. "*That's* what it looks like? Nobody's gonna pay for that."

"I told you, it's calibrating. Plus you haven't taken the Trancium yet." Dalton fishes a glass stopper bottle out of his pocket and draws up a tiny amount of the stuff into a syringe. "I use the concentrate. Easier to portion out."

"Where did you get that from?"

"I went to art school, Hailey. I have a source. Now, do you want to lay down some base memories? We can fill in the details later." He moves the dropper closer to her mouth.

Hailey stares at the syringe. A vision of Teresa enters her mind. *I can perform too,* she thinks. She opens her mouth, and Dalton squirts the liquid beneath her tongue.

"Lie down," Dalton says, and suddenly the mat on the floor looks like the most comfortable thing in the world. Hailey slides down onto it, giggling slightly from the unreality of it all. "Put that bunch of wires into your mouth. Yeah, that one."

The last thing Hailey experiences before she slips away is the coppery taste of the wires, then the concentrated Trancium flows over her like an internal Great Wave and she's gone.

• • •

Floating, waiting, dying. The air is rank with the smell of fear and your sister's rotting lower legs. Though it shouldn't be possible, you pop the dryer open from the inside, tumbling onto the rock outcropping onto which the appliance had marooned itself. The water from a greatly expanded Narragansett Bay fills your mouth and lungs, making you choke.

You start to swim in the direction of a distant shouting. You haven't learned how to swim in the ocean yet, but your legs work anyway, kicking away from the dryer to take in the devastation that surrounds you.

The shouts emanate from a woman tangled in cables and seaweed, her screams echoing over the water. You attempt to untangle her from her bindings, but her frantic windmilling makes that impossible, and she eventually sinks beneath the water's surface.

You have to get back to the clothes dryer; you have to save your sister. You begin to see things you recognize, like the sign from the pharmacy your parents used to take you to for candy and cheap toys. One of the workers bobs nearby, his blue vest waterlogged, obviously dead.

Teresa is lodged in tight, her blackened legs refusing to relinquish their position. You start to scream for help then, because surely there must be someone taking care of this mess, but you know there's nobody you can depend on. Nobody in the entire world.

• • •

Hailey gasps as she comes to, her body trembling with all of the memories the Trancium has unearthed. She looks around for Dalton—*the fucker didn't skip out on me, did he?*—and finds him hunched over one of the monitors.

"Did you get it?"

"I got *something,*" he says. He points at the

monitor. It's nearly as crude as the bouncing ball had been, though there's dull color spread throughout. He presses a button and the image sharpens slightly.

"No offense, but it's still kind of shitty."

He pushes another button and the screen clicks off. "This is only the beginning. How are you feeling?"

Hailey considers. She's fairly sure the memories she'd fed to the rig aren't real; recovered memories aren't exactly a thing. He *had* said imagination played into the whole deal, back at the BurgerMat. "I left the dryer on my own. I'm pretty sure I didn't in real life, but—"

"It's a game," Dalton says. "It's not going to map directly to your experiences. But there was some real emotion in that take, and I really want to keep that going for our next session."

Next session? For some reason Hailey assumed he'd be able to get everything in one. "How long was I under?"

"A standard four hours. We have a lot of work ahead of us. Same time tomorrow?"

Hailey thinks of herself floating in the morass of flotsam and corpses, of the smell of her sister's dead legs. And she finds that she can't wait to go back there, now that she knows it isn't dangerous, or at least, not as dangerous as she'd feared. "Yeah, I'll be here."

• • •

"Haven't seen much of you lately," Teresa says. For once, she's not soliloquizing for her flying camera. "That job didn't give you more hours, did it?"

"I made a friend," Hailey says.

Teresa frowns, and Hailey knows it's because she wishes she hadn't powered down her drone. This could have been an interesting plot development for her stream. "Good for you! I really mean that."

Hailey bites her lip, wondering whether or not to talk about the game, then just decides to come out with it. "We're working on a project together about my life."

A shadow of doubt runs across Teresa's face before being replaced by unenthusiastic support. "A biography, huh? Well, you know what they say. Everyone has a story, no matter how small."

"He's paying me for it. I might earn enough to move out," Hailey says. "Then you can have the whole place to yourself if you want."

"Nothing comes for free, Hailey. And no offense, but you don't have enough of a story to buy yourself a house. Hell, not even *I* do."

Hailey takes a deep breath. "We have a contract."

Teresa shrugs. "It's your life, sis." Then she pushes herself off the couch with her New Person legs and goes upstairs.

Probably gonna go make out with her camera, Hailey thinks.

• • •

The next time she shows up for a recording session, Hailey heads immediately to the studio, but Dalton calls her back to his understated rich-kid living room.

"We need to talk," he says. "I'm not getting the quality out of these takes that I've been expecting. The emotional aspect is strong, but the visual one is . . . not great." He holds up his screen, where a grainy, staticky image shows Hailey's avatar towing a box containing a litter of kittens to safety. "This is as good as I can get it."

"So what do we do about that?"

He looks away before he speaks. "I want to try giving you more Trancium. I think it will help."

Hailey stares down at her hands. She hasn't experienced any of the negative side effects of prolonged Trancium exposure so far—no trembling fingers, no alienating sense of body dislocation—but the idea of taking *more* of the stuff just seems stupid. "No."

"I figured you'd say that. It's a shame we won't be able to finish the game, though. And that I won't be able to pay you." Dalton smiles at her then, and she's reminded of the vast gulf of differences between them.

She drops her gaze at her hands again. Her non-shaking, perfectly sound hands. "You know what, I think I changed my mind."

Dalton smiles and takes her hand. "I promise, Hailey. Nothing bad will happen to you."

• • •

This time, you save them all.

Not everyone in Rhode Island, of course. That would be ridiculous. But on this particular run-through, you manage to load your parents, your sister, and your Aunt Frieda who'd been visiting from Boston onto a piece of siding that manages to float, boat-like, toward the new coastline so far away.

You chart your course. You speed up.

Reaching the shore should end the game, and it did in the first script. But as you've gone deeper, the story has expanded. The game is totally off-script at this point, and it hadn't ever been all that tethered to reality.

After dropping off your rescued family at the infirmary, you stop at the volunteers' tent. You're ready to go back out. The default avatar for this interactive narrative has been aged up from six to seventeen to make the rescue operations more realistic, and you have to admit that you prefer it this way, to be a confident young adult with elite swimming skills instead of a scared little girl in a clothes dryer.

Way more than fifty-four Rhode Islanders have survived; you can recognize at least a dozen people in this camp alone, friends and neighbors who in reality were never seen again. You'd love to stay and chat, but you have to get back out there.

You have to save as many as you can.

• • •

For the first time in all her weeks of memory recording, Hailey wakes up screaming. Dalton is shaking her, and she watches as her hands rake at him, seemingly not under her control.

"Why did," she pants between breaths, "you do that? This was a really good session."

"Your vitals were off," he says, pointing at the monitor that measures Hailey's breathing, mus-

cle movements, and blood sugar, all taken from a small device buried in the gaming rig. Most of them don't have this feature, but Dalton's equipment is top of the line.

It's the eighth time she's gone under with the increased dose, and Dalton's hunch had been right: More drugs *do* make the experiences better. Both for her and for the game's eventual players, based on what she's seen on Dalton's screens. "I feel *fine*, Dalton."

"I think you should see a doctor. You're signed up with SolHealth, right?"

Hailey holds her hand up. She doesn't detect any shaking, but Dalton's right. She should get checked out. "Well, you got that session recorded, right? Aren't we almost done?"

"We *were* done. The scope of the project has now changed."

She narrows her eyes. "What do you mean?"

"Interactive narratives are out. Well, they were never in. But now they're *really* out and if this project is going to make any money at all, it needs to be more like a game. More branches, more choices."

Hailey breathes in and out, slowly. "So that's why all the Trancium." She tries to meet his gaze, but he's started to fiddle with the monitor. "I wish you would have told me. I still would have said yes." *And not for the money,* she thinks. *Or at least, not only for the money.*

Dalton shrugs, looks away.

"Can I take the rig off now?" she asks, then starts to do it before he gives the all-clear. For some reason she can barely grasp the thing, and then she realizes why.

Her hands are shaking. *Badly.*

• • •

The next appointment available through Sol-Health isn't for three weeks, so Dalton gets her in with his family's own physician, who practices out of one of the fanciest spires in the Pittsburgh Development Zone. Hailey supposes it's the least he can do, since it's kind of his fault this happened to her.

Of course, he wants to finish his game too, she thinks. *That's what this is really about.*

The doctor is a stern-faced woman who rushes Hailey through test after test, and when she's done, she calls Dalton back into the room. Hailey isn't exactly happy about this, but his family *is* the one who's paying.

"It's not good," the doctor says. "At this level of abuse, expect forty percent reduced mobility by the spring, possibly sooner. Eighty percent loss of speech by summer." The doctor angrily punches something into her screen. "I hope this was all worth it, little lady."

Say something, Hailey tries to beam to Dalton, mind to mind. *Tell them that I did it for your art, for our game.* But he just stares down at the tile floor with an expression impossible to read.

"What if I stop?" she asks the doctor. "Like, just stop taking Trancium completely, right now. How does *that* change things?"

"It doesn't," says the doctor. A smug grin flickers briefly over her face.

Dalton steps between Hailey and the doctor; he's still not looking at her, and Hailey wonders if he'll ever do so again. "But she didn't even take that much. I . . . I was there with her. I saw how much she took, and it wasn't enough to hurt her."

"Clearly she's indulging behind your back. And there are genetic profiles that are more sensitive to Trancium, but I'd check her pockets first."

Now Dalton faces her. "Don't worry, Hailey. You'll be well provided for."

Hailey watches, horrified, as her left leg begins to kick at nothing at all.

• • •

Dalton visits Hailey a few months later, after all of the legal odds and ends have been cleaned up, after Teresa cashed his family's big fat check. The check wasn't for completing the game, that was made very clear, but as a "sincere gesture of goodwill" for the girl their no-good youngest son had ruined.

"I finished the game," he says. Teresa has left for the day. Part of the family's nondisclosure agreement forbids streaming any images of Hailey, which has put a serious dent into Teresa's career. "I thought you'd want to know."

"Go fuck yourself," says Hailey.

Dalton sits down on the couch with her without asking permission, then just keeps talking as if she gives a shit about what comes out of his mouth next. "I'm still going to release it. Lots of people on the dark web would love to play it, I bet. Especially once they know the story."

The story is that you ruined my life and got away with it, Hailey thinks. She'd say it right to his face, but speaking isn't that easy for Hailey these days.

"I shouldn't even be here," he says. "The agreement says so. But they can't tell me what to do. What *we* can do. Don't you want to see me release it?"

Hailey forces her voice out through the trembling of her chest wall. "*Fuck you*," she repeats.

His face goes red under his mop of blond hair. "You know, my family's done a lot for you. You're basically getting my inheritance, Hailey. They're forcing me to move back into their spire. We've both suffered for this."

Hailey tries to say "get out," but it sounds more like a groan.

"Anyway, I just wanted to tell you about the game, how I'm releasing it. And that, well, this sucks." Dalton stands up. "So, I'll keep in touch, right? And just remember, *you* took the Trancium. It was my idea, but you took it."

Hailey turns away from him, and stays in that position until she hears Dalton close the door behind him.

• • •

You float out on the tide in the little inflatable dinghy you've gotten as an upgrade for being so good at this. Thanks to your actions in this memory that never happened, you've managed to save nearly everyone.

You've been spending a lot more time here. You

no longer need the Trancium or the rig; you're here within minutes of closing your eyes. Sometimes you're not even sure your eyes are closed, so seamless is the transition between the increasingly painful real world and the world of this "interactive narrative."

This is the body dislocation you've read about. Being in two places at once, simultaneously, yet always feeling the draw to this other world. It never goes away. It will never go away.

Today, you're searching for survivors in a part of the enlarged bay you've only seen from a distance. But now it's been fully sketched out for you, and your avatar is strong enough to get there, through an iceberg field of garbage mounds swept from what had once been Rhode Island.

There's a cry from an unseen figure mired in a small whirlpool of fast-food wrappers; you angle the boat toward the sounds and prepare for the worst. It's a little boy with a profusely bleeding head wound, but he's strong enough to work with you on his own rescue.

"Mama?" he says, stroking your avatar's face.

"No," you say, "but let's go find her." And it occurs to you that if this family exists here in this phantom world, there's no reason you can't have one too. This is a place where you can indeed raise children, where you could live your whole life if you wanted to, in a place far away from the coast and the Great Wave, a place sketched out by your own Trancium-altered mind.

You can do this, live here forever in the place that's always being created. And something tells you that you wouldn't be the first one to make that choice.

After settling the little boy safely into your boat, you repoint it toward the shore. Nothing here can ever be taken away from you, because it's all you.

You're home.

SAM J. MILLER

FERAL ARCADE CHILDREN OF THE AMERICAN NORTHEAST

(2021)

WE WERE SO MANY. Latchkey kids and runaways, hardscrabble children for whom home was a motel or a broken-glass abandoned storefront or a flat patch of dirt under an off-ramp—but also indolent, precious bunny-rabbit boys and girls abandoned to the elements by their wealthy parents. We were immigrants learning English from badly translated video games, and Jersey-born locals destined to never leave the tristate area. We came carrying hundreds of quarters, or with hands and pockets empty. We came to make money. We came to spend it. We sold drugs, or rented out parts of our bodies for brief periods of time. We lived our lives in a strip mall archipelago a hundred miles long. The arcade children of Interstate 287 were a great and numerous nation.

· · ·

My mom's boyfriend from the time I was ten to around when I turned eighteen was a guy named Tomm, and whether the extra *m* in his name was his own doing or the work of an imaginative parent I was never able to discern. Mom told me once that Tomm had made a lot of bad decisions in his life. He didn't drink, and he flinched when mom popped the top off a can of beer for herself.

I never knew exactly what he did for a living, just that it meant he dropped me off in the morning and came for me sometimes before sunset and sometimes long after. Same pep talk every time, when I got out of the car—don't talk to strangers, don't be rude to the staff, always keep an eye on the exits. Same five-dollar bill for food every time; same roll of quarters for keeping me entertained. Sometimes he'd be gone for an hour, and sometimes twelve.

Mom didn't know what he did either, and didn't want to. I suspect we both believed it was something illegal, or borderline legal. I never told her anything about what my days were like, when Tomm "took me to work." She never asked questions. The poor woman was forever overworked. Tomm took care of childcare concerns for a lot less than a babysitter. I came home unharmed each time, and that was probably enough to calm her down. I knew, somehow, that telling her the truth would mean the end of it.

• • •

We were the numerically dominant species in the arcade ecosystem, but there were others. Most of them predators. Some sold us drugs: speed or spiderwebbing. Cheap at first, but pretty soon you were selling off pieces of yourself. For many of my fellow feral arcade children, especially the older ones, life was pain. I could see why they'd choose to escape into substance abuse.

Other predators, occupying an ecological niche so well-fitted to the drug dealers that it seemed like symbiosis, gave us the money we might need for drugs or quarters. Some wanted to fuck us; some wanted to get fucked. Some would want it out in the parking lot. Some fucked us in between the machines in the back. Some, the ones with the most money or the oddest hungers, drove us off to motels or homes or undisclosed locations.

I didn't see it, then. The difference between me and the kids who took those five- and ten-dollar bills.

• • •

You want to know about the urban legend. That's why you're here, really. You've heard rumors, tales told so many times it's like an endless game of Telephone, and you know better than to believe them, of course, but still.

The mysterious arcade game that kills people. Some kid died, right? Or kids? In Seattle, or was it somewhere down the Jersey Shore? Killed, or just disappeared? Kidnapped, probably. Sex criminals. Russians. Something.

• • •

Cops were our apex predator, and they came through all the time. Cracking down on sex work or drug sales, usually, or occasionally dragging out a drug-addled or overdosed or antagonistic adult. But mostly it was us they preyed on. The johns, they barely saw. Too busy cuffing kids. We were so vulnerable, us feral arcade children.

• • •

Sex was not some secret world for me. Even before Tomm arrived in that crummy apartment with only one thin wall between their bed and mine, we had lived in a dozen or so spots surrounded by people who lived their most intimate lives very publicly. Women who screamed the obscenest demands through slammed doors at three in the morning. Men who sobbed out the most unnecessarily detailed confessions. Couples fucking in stairwells, who didn't stop when a wide-eyed, eight-year-old me came stomping down from the floor above.

So, no. I was not ignorant of the fact of sex. It was one more realm of terror that lay waiting for me. One more inscrutable aspect of adult villainy. The one my mother warned me about the most. "Sex criminals" were everywhere. Stranger danger. "Perverts" who waited in every corner for the moment you let your guard down so they could kidnap you and do terrible sex things to you until you die.

• • •

Unwashed boy, beer gone sour, spilled soda, and ancient cigarettes. Sperm and sweat and lube. By age thirteen, the smell of the inside of an arcade could bring me to an instant pubescent erection. It smelled forbidden; sexy. Seedy. Slothful. So when I first saw Fenn at fourteen, slumped against a Gaijin Ninja cabinet in a dark corner; when he looked up and caught me staring and winked, I instantly imprinted all that eroticism onto him.

• • •

Who knew what weird electricity drew me to Fenn, or Fenn to me. He spent a long time scoping me out, I know that. He told me later he'd been watching me before we first made eye contact—Fenn always had his eye on everyone, assessing who was a threat and who had potential, but potential for what I wouldn't learn for a while. And even after we did lock eyes, he didn't come right over and say hey. He slipped into the shadows, and I didn't see him again for a couple of weeks, when he popped up beside me and poked me on the nose and said, "You're cute."

• • •

Fenn lit me up like electricity, like a quarter slid into the coin slot of my soul. His smile set my pinball flippers flapping; his touch made me clang like a new high score.

Bright blue hair. Barbed wire bracelet. Tall and lean and dark. Brown eyes ringed with green. The third time we talked, he took hold of the hood of my sweatshirt and tugged, pulled me into a corner. Not gently. Pushed me up against the wall. Put his mouth on mine. Slid his studded tongue past my lips. Metal probed flesh. Something unspooled inside of me. Fenn reached into my pants and sex suddenly ceased to be scary, which is probably a way of saying I stopped being a little kid.

• • •

After that, I carried sex around with me like a switchblade in my pocket. Every scary situation got a little less scary, knowing I had it. Even if I couldn't use it right there and then—it was mine, it was waiting for me, it was a reminder that even if we had to be human (and humans were awful), we were also animals (and animals were amazing).

Fenn introduced me to Jenny Ng. A chubby girl from a good home, smart in that way where it was scary. Where you found yourself compelled to either talk too much, to prove you could keep up, or stay quiet so she wouldn't know you couldn't.

"Don't say anything about her name," Fenn said, when she headed for the restroom. "Apparently it's not weird at all in Chinese."

Jenny had a jacket full of markers, all sizes and colors and levels of toxicity. She handed me one, told me to think up a tag for myself, or a slogan.

"The world needs less clean surfaces," she said. "McDonald's tabletops, plate glass storefront windows, whatever. Everybody wants to pretend like everything's clean and happy and perfect. People like us, who know how fucked up everything is, we have an obligation to tell everybody else."

I nodded. This thought was electrifying, no less than when Fenn pushed me to my knees and unzipped. I was honored that she thought I somehow shared her rebel spirit, when I was pretty much the squarest soul imaginable.

"Ish," I said, tagging up my palm.

"See?" she said. "It's perfect. You were made for this."

"Ron found a black-box game at the Dauphin mall," Fenn said.

Jenny asked, "Was it one of . . . ?"

"Not sure. He only had a couple quarters. Said he had a headache afterward, and nightmares. Game was called Destroy All Monsters! I think."

She made a note in a sketchbook full of graph paper. Her letters were so precise she could have actually been a robot. I wanted to ask to read it, or to know what they were compiling notes on, but we'd only just met.

• • •

Black-box games were not such a big deal. Bootleg knockoffs, stolen cabinets spray-painted over. Hacks out of Hong Kong or Hoboken; Mega Pac Man or Pac Man Gaiden or Sexy Pac Man.

How were we to know the difference between a legit sequel and a work of piracy? We'd get all excited to start playing, only to pop in a quarter and find a simple color-shifted carbon copy of the original.

And then there were the games that had been slapped together by computer school dropouts or programmers for the mob, soldered and wired together by utter amateurs. Weird shit you couldn't figure out, where polygons roved and shattered and shrank and it wasn't clear which one you were, or what each button did, if anything. The video game industry was a much less structured place back then. Anyone with a hundred bucks and a garage full of parts could create a game, and any halfway-smooth talker could get it into an arcade.

So, yeah. There were lots of strange games. Some arcades switched them out on a weekly basis, and other spots kept the same games so long we imagined they'd been forgotten by their owners. And since stories were our stock-in-trade, the only mass media in a nation served by no newspaper or radio show, members of our tribe were forever reporting on what games were turning up where.

. . .

There *were* other games. That much is true. Ones that were weird in ways that had nothing to do with amateur programming or inept piracy. Monster games. Games we had good reason to be afraid of. I watched one girl stagger back from a black-box game she'd spent five short minutes playing, and saw the blood coming out of her ears.

Fenn had seen worse; so much worse he would not tell me what.

. . .

Fenn wasn't scared. Neither was Jenny. I was, but I let their fearlessness be a safety blanket I could hide beneath.

. . .

Fenn pressed his fingers against the screen and shut his eyes. "Come here," he said, grabbing me by the collar, pushing down my head until my cheek was flush with the console surface, my eyes inches from his fingertips, then he draped his hoodie over my head.

The smell of him was so strong that I swelled to a state of full immediate erection.

"Watch," he whispered, and I widened my eyes, stared into the musky dark.

My mouth opened, my throat desert-dry with thirsting for it.

"No," he chided, with a chuckle. "Dirty boy, Ish. But not that. Not right now. Just watch."

Blue light crackled, lit up his fingertips and the battered plastic buttons. Tiny little strands of electricity stuttered in the air between man and machine. Clicks rattled in the cabinet. A gong sounded, then a shrill high buzz.

Player up! the machine said, which is what it said when you stuck in a quarter, but Fenn had done no such thing. He'd zapped it with his fingers, tricked it with little bolts of blue lightning.

"What the hell was that?" I asked, staggering to my feet, aroused in a whole new way.

Fenn shrugged, and kissed me hard.

. . .

One monster arcade game attack was so bad it made the news. Kid ended up in the hospital. Paralyzed from the neck down. No sign of trauma or evidence of damage. News didn't mention she was an arcade kid. But we saw her, and we knew.

The place was packed when we went there later that week. All the tribes of our whole far-flung nation had sent delegates. The woman behind the counter hadn't been on duty the night the kid collapsed, but she'd heard. "Wasn't an ambulance came to get her," she said, over and over, delighted at all the attention. "Unmarked van. Black and shiny. Brand-new.

Two women and three men took her out, none of them looking like EMTs. That was four in the afternoon. She got dropped off at the emergency room at nine at night."

"What game was it?" Fenn asked, and some people said Destroy All Monsters! and some said Polybius, but most people said Destroy All Monsters!

• • •

"Try it," Fenn said, standing behind me, holding me by the shoulders.

And so I did. Flicked my fingers, tried to summon blue sparks.

And kept trying. For an hour. By the end of it my heart was beating so fast that Fenn giggled when he kissed my jugular, and all I managed was one quick spray of blue lightning tendrils that didn't give me a free game at all, but did delete every saved high score in the console. Six entries, all identical, a whole long line that said FEN.

• • •

"I found it," Fenn said, one gray Jersey morning near the shore, the sky smelling like fried seafood, and he did not look well. Blue-black circles beneath his eyes; a brand-new furrow in his brow.

"Destroy All Monsters!? Where?" I asked. Jenny was not around. It had been a week since the last time I saw Fenn.

He named a place. "It was gone when I went back the next day."

"You played it? What was it like?"

He nodded. Locked eyes with mine. Did not look away. He was trying telepathy. He did that from time to time with people. My head filled up with horrific images—children screaming, a white gorilla with fur stained red—but I was pretty sure they came from my imagination and not his memory.

"I know what it is now," he said. "I don't know who made it—aliens or evil corporations or whoever-the-fuck—but I know what it's here for."

He shivered. Sucked in a long slow drag on his cigarette. He hardly ever smoked.

"What's it for?"

"It's here to kill us."

• • •

"I don't get it," Jenny said. "If it's so evil, why do you still want to play it so bad? Why don't we fucking destroy the thing?"

"Because the only way to do that is to play it. Find your way to its cold wet heart. And beat it."

"Bullshit," she said. "Pull the plug on it, pour a couple of Cokes into it, zap it a bunch for good measure, and I know you can fry the fucker."

"It'll just come back," he said.

It'll respawn, I thought. Like any video game villain.

"How do you know that?"

"I saw into its . . . I don't know. Soul? CPU? Black twisted heart? It'll keep killing us until we kill it."

"That's fucking idiotic," she said, blowing a bright green gum bubble.

"It's a monster, Jenny," he said, his voice going halfway British the way it did when he wanted to mock her for being so brilliant. "Monsters are real. Surely you're not too smart to see that."

• • •

Mom kept telling me to get a job. Said I was too old to be spending all my time in stupid arcades. That was kid stuff, and I was not a kid anymore.

Tomm tried to shield me, but we both knew he couldn't do it for long. Sooner or later I'd have to find a fast-food joint or mall kiosk, plop myself down in front of a deep-fat fryer, and be careful I didn't get stuck there for the rest of my life.

• • •

Fenn dreamed of playing professionally. Somewhere, he'd heard, were whole leagues of competitive video gamers with big corporate sponsors. Every game he played he was gunning for that glory, for the day when they'd swoop down and snatch him up.

Hearing him talk about it was the first time I suspected that maybe he was nowhere near as smart as I imagined him to be.

• • •

I played along with Fenn's fantasy. Talked about how we'd conquer the competitive gaming world. With his electric mastery, and once I learned to leverage my clumsy, destructive ability to jinx things for his competitors, I swore we'd swiftly rise to the top of the list of whatever they were looking for.

Turned out I did have a gift, and it was telling stories that were not completely true.

• • •

I'd imagined ourselves to be a nation of equals, all the arcade children united in our status of outcasts, but suddenly I could see how that was bullshit. Hearing Fenn talk about his dreams of competitive gaming, I could see how out of touch he was with how the world worked. How for all his wisdom, he was still just as ignorant as I was, only differently ignorant.

We had a hierarchy, the feral arcade children. So wide and extreme that it took me a long time to see myself on it at all. Jenny had a car, had money, had college in her future. I had none of those things, but I had so many things Fenn lacked. And once I could see that, I couldn't see him—couldn't see any of it—the same way anymore.

We were not one thing, one united nation. We were so many things. How could there be any hope for us, as divided as we were?

And, sure, Fenn had nothing, but plenty of kids had less. Boys and girls who sold themselves in significantly less safe ways than Fenn did. Kids who wandered through with their eyes full of fear, for whom the measly twenty-five-cent cost of admission was too much, for whom the arcades were one more space full of bright, beautiful things they'd never have access to; a space where the wind and rain couldn't hit them, but still full of predators both potential and actual.

Fenn went out of his way to befriend them. To show them how to game the machines. To make them magical monsters like himself.

Once, I watched him lead three eleven-year-olds out into the parking lot. He placed their hands against the massive metal pole that supported the sign listing all the stores for that particular strip mall. He shut his eyes, whispered words. They shut theirs.

One of them jumped, stepped back. They laughed, shook it off, put their hands back on the pole.

"Yeeeeaahh!" Fenn cried, clapping his hands.

They grinned, electric. Unstoppable.

Something metal screamed. High above them, the sign burst into flames. Fenn put his finger to his lips and they stepped away, vanishing into invisibility again.

After that, I started noticing blackened, burnt-out signs outside strip malls all up and down 287.

• • •

Sometimes I heard him talked about. The kid with electric fingers and electric blue hair. The f—— who can control machines. And once I saw a magnificent, stocky Mexican girl, who said she'd been taught by someone who'd been taught by the electric kid, as she lit up a whole line of pinball machines with nothing but a snap of her fingers, and let an ecstatic gaggle of our fellow feral arcade children play for free all afternoon. I followed her at a discreet distance, my mouth stuck open in awe. She could do things Fenn could not; whatever it was had evolved on its way to her, or been transformed by something special inside of her.

• • •

We looked and we looked, and we never found it.

And then . . . we found it.

Destroy All Monsters!, nestled in a corner of one of the weirder spots, down the Shore, a strip mall where half the stores were left empty when summer stopped. And it was at the one arcade where a superhot dude worked, not much older than us, known to rent his mouth out to richer men himself sometimes. Jenny and I meant to go talk to him when Fenn sparked the Player up! chime, see what we could learn about the game and who brought it, but five minutes after he started playing, we could see that Fenn was sweating.

"What?" Jenny said. "What's going on?"

"Can't describe it," he said.

On the screen, his monster stomped through city streets and gobbled up children. Seized them by the fistful, swallowed them whole. Every fifty kids, his hairy, long-armed T-Rex got bigger. A big white gorilla waited for him at the center of the city, which he could challenge when he got strong enough.

Muscles twitched. Eyes flickered. On the screen the game seemed simple enough, but inside his body he seemed to be at war.

Who knows how long it was before the game went black. "Fuck," Fenn hissed, but none of us could look away from the screen. So it took us a solid forty-five seconds to realize that it wasn't just the game that had gone out. The whole arcade was dark. Every cabinet was silent. Kids wailed in the distance—their digital lives cut short, high scores lost, hard-earned quarters wasted.

"You okay?" I asked Fenn, and he was trembling, but he nodded.

"I can do it," he said. "I can see how."

• • •

On our way out, I felt so full of life and power and potential—like we could solve every problem, like the monsters could be defeated, like the mysterious forces of the world could be comprehended and conquered—that I said, "See you tomorrow" to Superhot Dude, even though his hotness was super intimidating. He flashed a smile full of teeth.

• • •

Getting Tomm to take me back the next day was basically the hardest thing I'd ever done. He said "no" at first—and at second, and at third. I had to tell my mom I'd start looking for a job the following week—which put her in a great mood—which made him happy enough to consent to take me back to Destroy All Monsters! And Jenny. And Fenn. And the secrets of the malevolent universe.

Sweat dripped, puddled on the console beneath Fenn's fingers. Strangled sounds gurgled out of his throat from time to time. Kids came; crowded around. Watched his ravenous creature gobble down children.

Most games were bloodless, scoured clean. This one was not.

"Look at his eyes," I said, because I had never seen ones so bloodshot.

"You need to stop," Jenny said.

"No," he barked. "I'm so close."

• • •

To what, we didn't know. We were watching the same screen, but I could tell we saw different things. Fenn flinched, tapped buttons in response to apparently nothing. Something about the angle of where he stood, maybe. Or the deeper he went, the more it bored into his skull, until only a very small part of the game was playing out in the console.

He died fast, and often. Kept zapping blue

SAM J. MILLER

flame at the coin slot. The air stunk of ozone and scorched machinery.

• • •

I went to get a cherry soda. Flicked my wrist at the coin slot. Pressed my hand against the glass. Snapped my fingers. Blue smoke spattered, sparked. It took me twenty tries, and when it finally "worked" the machine gave me three diet ginger ales instead. On my way back, though, I saw Superhot Dude standing at the front door, talking to three cops. And then he pointed in Fenn's direction.

My heart clenched. My jaw dropped. Superhot Dude saw it and flashed me the same terrifying line of teeth.

"See you tomorrow," I'd said, and wished I could take back the words. Wished I could die.

I'd imagined him to be benevolent, but why? Where had it come from, the possibility of assuming best intentions in strangers? One more difference between me and Fenn, another insurmountable wall. Somewhere along the line, something in my life—maybe my mother and maybe the minimal solid stability of our shitty little apartment—had given me the luxury of mistakenly believing that maybe people weren't so bad.

• • •

The cops stomped toward us. Monkey Fracas kept chanting its chim-chim-chim jingle, synthesized cymbals ominously happy.

"You've been playing this same game for three hours," one cop said. The crowd of kids had scattered. Jenny and I stood there, mouths dry, hands wet, feeling sick with helplessness.

"I'm just really good," Fenn said, sounding like something else.

"There's no quarters in this machine."

"Even if that's true," Fenn said, "what is that, like, twelve dollars? You gonna take me in for that?"

"That's exactly what we're going to do," the

cop said, and of course we knew, all of us, that that wasn't what they'd be taking him in for, but none of us knew what the real reason was. It could have been so many things. For selling himself; for underage drinking; for carrying condoms; for transforming a tribe of feral arcade children into an army of magnificent monsters.

• • •

"They were looking for him," Jenny whispered, as they took a cuffed Fenn out of the arcade. Her hand gripped mine so hard it hurt, and I was happy for the pain of it. "They've been looking for him, and the game helped them find him."

"Who's they?"

She shook her head. Kids drifted over. I could feel our anger in the air.

• • •

Sparks flew. Games spat quarters. Vending machines sprayed scalding soda. We moved toward the exit after them, as one, ready to rain blue hellfire down on all who would harm us.

Fenn saw us, and stopped us with one stern head shake. And maybe it was telepathy and maybe I just knew him, finally, so I could read a whole speech in that tiny motion. We all could.

This is not the moment. Don't let them know what you can do. Don't come to their attention.

Not yet.

Keep going.

• • •

The whole crowd of feral kids followed them out. We felt way more numerous than we had inside, scattered through the vast, empty, dark space.

Someone picked up a stone. Hurled it at the cop car. A beer bottle followed. Then a solid wall of insults, jeers, shrieks. The officers stared out at us impassively, but Fenn's smile was huge.

• • •

When the cops had taken him away, I looked around. All those kids, faces twisted up, tight, dark, or pale with rage or grief. My pain was like theirs, but I was not one of them. Neither was Jenny, but she had picked up rocks and chucked them every bit as hard.

I hadn't been able to do that. But this, I could do.

• • •

You are one of us, even if you never knew it. Even if you only ever saw us in small clumps or couples, and never suspected what a mighty nation we were. Even if by the time you were born there weren't any arcades anymore.

• • •

"Stop fucking crying," Jenny whispered, but she was crying too. The Mexican girl spoke in angry, urgent whispers to a small crowd of comrades.

• • •

We sat in Jenny's car for an hour, letting the rain tick-tock against the roof.

I was convinced they'd kill him. Torture him first—take him apart on an operating table, try and fail to figure out how he worked.

Jenny said they'd probably lock him up overnight, and then remand him to foster care. Maybe juvenile detention. Juvie until jail. "Fenn had priors," she said.

I told Jenny he'd make a new army in there. No matter how different they all were. That's what an army was, I realized. A bunch of different things that become one thing. Locked up together they'd be able to go deeper, develop their skills, refine and expand whatever it was until they could summon blue lightning bolts out of the sky to slay every evildoer and break down every wall.

• • •

Sometimes I'd see our skill at work in the world. Creeps' cars fried; arcade cabinets that let you play for free forever.

Fenn's still out there. Somewhere. Maybe he's still Fenn and maybe that body was already broken, and he's been reborn in a brand-new body—or, even better, let loose to wander the world unencumbered by the awful ugliness humans are subject to. Doing his thing, far away or just around the next corner. Maybe I'll find him, and maybe you will.

Jenny sends me updates occasionally. She's still looking for the robots. The aliens. The Army.

Me, I see the monsters everywhere. They have no need for wicked mind control machines. They have cable company contracts and strip-mall parking lots and deep-fat fryers, sucking out our souls for minimum wage and sending us home stinking of grease and the flesh of animals even less fortunate than ourselves.

They have all that. But we have the spark.

CHALLENGE

There is no cyberpunk without the punk. It is fiction rooted in **challenge**.

In cyberpunk worlds, technology is often used to enforce or reinforce repressive or regressive systems. The intent is not always hostile; in fact, a recurring theme of cyberpunk is technology created for purehearted reasons that then creates harm when applied in practice.

In recognizing this, cyberpunk explores the power of opposition: that is, the power of punk. In Greg Graffin's *Punk Manifesto*, he describes punk as, among other things, "a movement that serves to refute social attitudes that have been perpetuated through willful ignorance of human nature."[*] Technology in cyberpunk is a tool of perpetuation; the cyberpunk is therefore duty bound to challenge it.

While the science fiction author is often lauded as "visionary" or "prophetic," the cyberpunk writer is more Cassandra.[†] They are cursed not only to see the future, but also the problems it will bring. McLuhan notes that "the artist picks up the message of cultural and technological challenge decades before its transforming impact occurs. He, then, builds models or Noah's arks for facing the change that is on hand." It is a compelling metaphor: cyberpunk stories as tiny arks for floods that only their authors can foresee. The artist is therefore "indispensable": we need their imagination to perceive, and prepare for, the difficulties ahead. We can only hope that, unlike Cassandra, the predictive efforts of the cyberpunks are not ignored.

Playing Cassandra is traditionally a thankless role, but in cyberpunk it is celebrated. Cyberpunk champions the punks and pessimists, the rebels and the rioters. The stories in this section showcase the underdog, the rogue, or those

---

[*] https://punxinsolidarity.wordpress.com/2013/10/22/punk-manifesto-by-greg-graffin/

[†] Some science fiction authors earn the rarest praise from critics: "a visionary prophet."

who live on the fringes of society. They are often reluctant punks, slow to answer the call. However, they are, ultimately, united by a clarity of vision and desire to challenge the system in which they live, and the technology upon which it is perpetuated.

• • •

The precursor story in this section is Philip K. Dick's "We Can Remember It for You Wholesale" (1966). Later filmed (repeatedly, and with steadily eroding quality) as *Total Recall*, the story's hero, Quail, finds himself at the heart of an interplanetary conflict that may or may not be entirely in his head.[*] It is a sterling example of technology, in this case memory-tampering, used as a tool of oppression, as well as a forerunner for an identity-bending storytelling mode that permeates the cyberpunk genre. The rebellion (or is it?) centers on the personal impact on Quail, not the overall righteousness of the cause. We are never sure if Quail is a revolutionary or a counterrevolutionary, nor which is the more morally desirable option.[†]

Two stories pick up directly on Dick's theme of weaponized memories. Bef's "Wonderama" (1998) makes its first English appearance in this volume, translated by the author. It plays many of the same notes as "We Can Remember It for You Wholesale," including that of a revolutionary trapped in a prison of their own desires.

"Wonderama" is chilling on two levels. First, the core plot: the greatest villains in cyberpunk are those who remove our right to challenge. Second, the nature of the capture. Whether a function of the dream or the dreamer, "Wonderama" takes place in a glossy catalogue of a dreamscape, where everything is extremely shiny and name-brand. The story condemns not only the manipulation of dreams, but also how pathetic our dreams have become.

Fabio Fernandes follows the theme further in "Wi-Fi Dreams" (2019), also translated by the author. An increasingly ridiculous cascade of technologies has resulted in the sinister, and permanent, gamification of our dreams. People are stuck in a virtualized dream world, combining the worst aspects of a MMORPG and your own nightmares.[†] "Wi-Fi Dreams" fully embraces the madness of its plot. Unlike "Wonderama" or "Wholesale," however, "Wi-Fi Dreams" is more explicit about the system the protagonist is trapped in—and his desire to fight against it.

Mandisi Nkomo's "Do Androids Dream of Capitalism and Slavery?" (2020) is also a response to Philip K. Dick, this time to his novel *Do Androids Dream of Electric Sheep?* (1968).

---

[*] Dick's contributions to cyberpunk (or "protocyberpunk") also include *Do Androids Dream of Electric Sheep?* (1968), *A Scanner Darkly* (1977), and "The Minority Report" (1956). All three have been filmed, but only *Total Recall* (1990) has Arnold Schwarzenegger pulling a metal softball from his nose.

[†] The year 1966 is also when *Star Trek* began, launching Gene Roddenberry's post-scarcity, techno-utopian future, where the "challenge" is actively sought by a valiant humanity looking up and beyond itself. Contrast to the future in Dick's story, where technology is still being used to scratch capitalist itches and foment political violence. The evolution of the science fiction genre has now fully diverged, leading, in twenty years, to the wistful hauntology of "The Gernsback Continuum."

[†] It is worth noting that one distant "cousin of cyberpunk" is LitRPG, a subgenre of science fiction and fantasy that's particularly popular on the self-publishing scene. It generally takes the form of portal fantasy, in which the protagonist is sucked into their favorite video game and forced to put their (disturbingly intimate) knowledge of it to firsthand use. Given the genre's reliance on virtual worlds and frequent use of the "evil corporation" trope, LitRPG has drawn on many aspects of the cyberpunk tradition. It also plays with form in a very cyberpunk way, with the underpinning numbers and "stats" of a video game sharing the page with the story itself. Unlike cyberpunk, the focus of LitRPG is not on the themes (or characters, or often even plots)—the appeal of LitRPG is the system itself. Imagine video game fanfiction, but with both the game and fiction being imagined at once. No LitRPG appears in this volume, but you have earned +5 XP for reading this footnote.

Dick's novel was filmed by Ridley Scott as *Blade Runner* (1982), and became one of the seminal works of cyberpunk.[*] *Electric Sheep* (and by extension, *Blade Runner*) touches on the theme of artificial identity. Are "replicants," androids that are indistinguishable from humans, worthy of the same respect and rights merited by "true" humans? Where *Electric Sheep* is inconclusive and *Blade Runner* forlorn, Nkomo's story is pure anger. "We failed. We gave them emotions. Now we travel to our own extinction."

• • •

The hacker is the most iconic cyberpunk character: be they a coding ninja, a keyboard cowboy, or the paladin of the basement. Their challenge takes place in the virtual realm, "cyberspace," where physical prowess is secondary to a razor-edged mind.

Intelligence is the ultimate asset in Eileen Gunn's "Computer Friendly" (1989). Children are tested at a young age. The brightest become executives, with their minds instrumental to the processing power of the central computer. Those without potential are euthanized. Elizabeth makes for an unconventional hacker, but she navigates the setting's online systems with ease. She challenges authority with the naivete and surety of the child she is, with purity of heart and the uncanny ability to simplify problems on her side.

Victor Pelevin's "The Yuletide Cyberpunk Yarn, or Christmas_Eve-117.DIR" (1996) appears here in English for the first time, translated from Russian by Alex Shvartsman. Set in the city of Petroplahovsk, it details the breakdown of the automated, but deeply corrupt, civic order. It is amusing as a tale of karmic comeuppance and cyberspace shenanigans, as befitting its gently humorous title. But under the surface, this is a tale of a society based entirely on venal self-interest, with little hope of meaningful change.

David Langford's "comp.basilisk.faq" (1999) has something nasty evolving from within the system. It is a technology gone corrupt; an Internet malignancy of mythic proportions. The FAQ-style story is a falsely reassuring response, with the ubiquity of its format hiding the horror within, and the bravery of those who hunt it.[†]

Taiyo Fujii's "Violation of the TrueNet Security Act" (2013), translated by Jim Hubbert, is also about hunting—this time for "zombies," or orphaned internet services that no longer have owners. Minami likes his job, if only for the nostalgia of finding old sites from his youth. But then he stumbles on the undead presence of one of his own websites—and somehow it's still being maintained. Who is tinkering with his code—and why?

• • •

Cyberpunk worlds are rarely safe places, and there are always battles to be fought. There are challenges to be faced offline as well.

Misha's "Speed" (1988) is a deliciously frenetic story about a society overcome by its lust for data—"the only currency." Our protagonist acts as a mercenary for a greedy, centralized power, perpetually racing to new sources to appease his mysterious master. The story twists in unexpected ways, linking the new urge for knowledge with some of the world's oldest and most primal forces.

Myra Çakan's "Spider's Nest" (2004), translated from the German by Jim Young, is back on familiar cyberpunk stomping ground: the grimy streets of a post-collapse world, with survivalists trading drugs for salvage. Spider is a slave

---

[*] And certainly *the* seminal work of cyberpunk *climate*. If you live in a cyberpunk world and you've never seen the sun, blame Ridley Scott.

[†] Back when the internet was fresh and young, FAQs ("frequently asked questions") were "pinned" posts on every forum or board, helping newcomers acclimate themselves to the environment. Now that the internet is old and jaded, all the questions have been eaten by cats.

to the system, a lone survivor with few contacts and no friends. But inspired by his dreams and his drugs, Spider pushes into the unknown. He is the most dangerous rebel, as he has nothing to lose.

T. R. Napper's "Twelve Minutes to Vinh Quang" (2015) features a more competent rebel. In this story, Lynn is holding all the cards—but her fate is still far from certain. If the story's criminal protagonist feels particularly cold-blooded, it is worth remembering the "diabolical" system of legalized oppression that she's up against. In Lynn's case, technology evens the playing field, giving her the advantage she needs.

Khalid Kaki's "Operation Daniel" (2016), translated by Adam Talib, has a protagonist with none of Lynn's advantages. Rashid lives in a Kirkuk that's been conquered and colonized by China. Like all other "beneficiaries" of the state, he is slowly having his culture and history eradicated; even using his native language is punishable by death. Rashid is outnumbered and outgunned, but still manages to pose a challenge to the all-powerful state, solely through the power of song.

Wole Talabi's "Aboukela52" (2019) also has an underdog challenger, this time a journalist. The story takes the format of an exposé newspaper article that links scavenged alien technology to a pandemic of cancer. The article comes complete with pages of comments. As the story plays out, we can not only puzzle out the fate of the journalist, but see all the predictable social noise—conspiracy theories, dismissal, and corporate spin. Talabi shows the difficulty not only of mounting a challenge, but also of having it understood in a world that often prefers the status quo.

In Brandon O'Brien's "fallenangel.dll" (2016), an armed police drone—one that shouldn't exist—falls into the hands of three activists, and they have to choose what to do next. Merely possessing the drone puts them in danger, but the data in its memory could save them all. Technology here is a double-edged sword, the tool of both the oppressor and the oppressed.

Michael Moss's "Keep Portland Wired" (2020) also features grassroots activism. The renegades of the Collective are keen on beer, weed, and drone-racing. They're unlikely rebels, more adolescent angst than righteous fury, but they still do what they can to push back against Portland's corporate-fascist rulers. The story is self-aware, emphasizing both the stereotypical "cool" of our protagonists, and the actual misery of their self-conscious existence. "Do you think our parents thought about this when they had us?" one asks. "Like, how fucked up it would be to bring us into this world?"

Drones (of a sort) also appear in Rudy Rucker's "Juicy Ghost" (2019, with a new afterword for this edition). A rigged election leads to the effective collapse of the United States, with both candidates claiming the presidency. Curtis is prepared to martyr himself for his cause: a martyrdom that involves psychic warfare, weaponized wasps, and a lot of bloodshed. A gloriously over-the-top story from one of the original -punks, "Juicy Ghost" is the cyberpunk Cassandra in full flow. It would be easy to dismiss this as satire, and ignore the truth at its heart.

• • •

Not all challenge is inherently noble, or even righteous. As much as cyberpunk fiction naturally allies itself with the revolutionary and the rebel, it also loathes hypocrisy. The superficial rebel is worse than the corporate peon; the treacherous ally more reviled than the overt opposition. Cyberpunk is not without sympathy; it understands that many (most) have no choice about their participation in the system. A repressive society is perpetuated by power and persuasion, and most lack the understanding or the freedom to oppose it. The crux of many cyberpunk stories is when the protagonist gains the awareness or the agency to challenge the system, but chooses not to exercise it. Ignorance is an excuse; knowledge is responsibility.

Nisi Shawl's "I Was a Teenage Genetic Engineer" (1989) begins with the fantastic line: "I am a political prisoner on a North American game preserve." We swiftly learn that their imprisonment is a matter of everyone's safety. The engineer has created both monsters and gods, and they are all on the hunt.

Lewis Shiner's "The Gene Drain" (1989) is a fusion of the postmodern and the science fictional, one of the rare entries in this volume to include aliens. The extraterrestrials are window-dressing; an intergalactic counterpoint to the bizarre political machinations of the story's human cast, as they scheme and connive in an incorrigibly earthly manner.

In Bruce Sterling's "Deep Eddy" (1993) our delightfully naive protagonist visits Germany from Chattanooga, and, slightly deluded with his own self-importance, is absorbed into the spontaneous chaos of a "wende." These organic eruptions of anarchism exist as a violent social catharsis. They are, much to Eddy's frustration, both unpredictable and uncontrollable. Over the course of the story, Eddy, a dilettante rebel, encounters true—and deep—challenge. Whether he learns from the experience is left to the reader to decide.

John Kessel's "The Last American" (2007) takes a unique approach. It is a book review, examining the new biography of the last American president, Andrew Steele. Steele is a complex character, alternately a savior and a demon, a populist and a reactionary. The biography (and the story) "comes to no formal conclusion, utilitarian or otherwise, as to the moral consequences of the life of Andrew Steele." However, set against the context of the story, and the ultimate reveal of humanity's fate, Steele's fate also seems tragic. He's both challenger and challenged, monster and martyr.

Ken MacLeod's "Earth Hour" (2011) is a political thriller set in a near-future Australia. Angus, an entrepreneur, former Lord, and occasional fortune-hunter, is the victim of an assassination attempt. Or is he? (As the story notes, successfully murdering someone is very difficult given the advanced state of medical science.) What's to be gained? And what can Angus gain from it as well?

"CRISPR Than You" (2018) is an ambitious future history by Ganzeer. An ambitious, and disturbingly plausible, future history, the story tracks through the intersection of art, politics, gender, race, and science. The future is a mixed media. Appropriately, the story is designed and illustrated by the author, an internationally acclaimed street artist. "CRISPR Than You" features challengers in art, science, and politics, all of whom find systems to tilt against, justly or not.

Yudhanjaya Wijeratne's "The State Machine" (2020) contains—perhaps—the most appealing setting in this book.* The titular machine governs all, gently imposing a thoughtful and rational rule. And why not? "To each other we are just idealized versions of ourselves, projections, half lies and half truths, not the real data trail we all leave behind." Armed with that data, the State Machine cannot fail to take care of us. As our researcher protagonist tries to understand the history of the State Machine, to piece together how and why it came about, the Machine itself begins to—gently, lovingly—intervene. Even the most benign worlds have, and need, their punks.

K. A. Teryna's "The Tin Pilot" (2021), also translated by Alex Shvartsman, is set in a world far from benign. The last war was fought by golems—artificial humans. With the war over, they were given the blessing of amnesia. Their memories were wiped and they were mixed into human society, their origins a secret, even to them. But humans always look for something to fear, an outgroup to shun, and here was one close at hand. Thus was born the golem hunts—even though anyone could be a golem. There are layers and layers to this witch hunt; challenges both open and private.

---

* To each their own, of course. There are certain arguments to be made for "Lobsters" or perhaps "Earth Hour." Not to judge, but I *would* have concerns if anyone is particularly desirous to live in the world of, say, "I Tell Thee All, I Can No More."

The final story in this section is Janelle Monáe and Alaya Dawn Johnson's "The Memory Librarian" (2022), the titular novella of Monáe's collection.[*] It is in an Afrofuturist cyberpunk city in the "whip end of the Rust Belt," where memories are carefully monitored—for the public good, of course. Seshet the Librarian takes a rare night out and encounters, and falls for, a beautiful woman. But in a world supposedly without secrets, Alethia has more than her fair share of them. As Seshet tentatively takes her first steps away from the orderly world she knows, she discovers that she may have some secrets of her own. "The Memory Librarian" comes full circle to "We Can Remember It for You Wholesale" in its use of memory control as a tool of social repression. Monáe and Johnson emphasize the importance of memory, of dream,

---

[*] Few individuals are as important to the genre as Monáe, who is described in *Fifty Key Figures in Cyberpunk Culture* (Routledge, 2022) as "a true revolutionary within and beyond cyberpunk culture." Monáe, like Pat Cadigan and the editor of this book, hails from the greater Kansas City area, which is now, statistically, the most cyberpunk place on Earth. Sorry, Tokyo.

to our identity. There's a fluidity to our appearance, to our names. Our essence is less tangible, and far deeper within. In "The Memory Librarian" the ultimate champion of the system must choose whether or not to become its challenger.

• • •

Cyberpunk is about the influence of technology on human affairs, and it is the sad truth of human affairs that many are antagonistic, and many more are worthy of antagonism. Technology may ease those relationships, or suppress them, but it is just as likely to create new and unexpected dimensions of conflict.

Speculative fiction is more than entertainment, it is a social responsibility. Cyberpunk stories are tiny arks and whispered prophecies, interrogations of what could be, based on what is known. Cyberpunk holds as sacrosanct the right to challenge, and cyberpunk literature urges the reader to exercise that right. No axiom should go unexamined, no system taken for granted, no line of code untested. As many of these stories reinforce: if we can't challenge in our minds, then we never will in the streets.

PHILIP K. DICK

WE CAN REMEMBER IT FOR YOU WHOLESALE

(1966)

HE AWOKE—AND WANTED MARS. *The valleys,* he thought. *What would it be like to trudge among them?* Great and greater yet: the dream grew as he became fully conscious, the dream and the yearning. He could almost feel the enveloping presence of the other world, which only Government agents and high officials had seen. A clerk like himself? Not likely.

"Are you getting up or not?" his wife Kirsten asked drowsily, with her usual hint of fierce crossness. "If you are, push the hot coffee button on the darn stove."

"Okay," Douglas Quail said, and made his way barefoot from the bedroom of their conapt to the kitchen. There, having dutifully pressed the hot coffee button, he seated himself at the kitchen table, brought out a yellow, small tin of fine Dean Swift snuff. He inhaled briskly, and the Beau Nash mixture stung his nose, burned the roof of his mouth. But still he inhaled; it woke him up and allowed his dreams, his nocturnal desires and random wishes, to condense into a semblance of rationality.

I will go, he said to himself. *Before I die I'll see Mars.*

It was, of course, impossible, and he knew this even as he dreamed. But the daylight, the mundane noise of his wife now brushing her hair before the bedroom mirror—everything conspired to remind him of what he was. *A miserable little salaried employee,* he said to himself with bitterness. Kirsten reminded him of this at least once a day and he did not blame her; it was a wife's job to bring her husband down to Earth. *Down to Earth,* he thought, and laughed. The figure of speech in this was literally apt.

"What are you sniggering about?" his wife asked as she swept into the kitchen, her long busy-pink robe wagging after her. "A dream, I bet. You're always full of them."

"Yes," he said, and gazed out the kitchen window at the hover-cars and traffic runnels, and all the little energetic people hurrying to work. In a little while he would be among them. As always.

"I'll bet it had to do with some woman," Kirsten said witheringly.

"No," he said. "A god. The god of war. He has wonderful craters with every kind of plant life growing deep down in them."

"Listen." Kirsten crouched down beside him and spoke earnestly, the harsh quality momentarily gone from her voice. "The bottom of the ocean—our ocean is much more, an infinity of times more beautiful. You know that; everyone knows that. Rent an artificial gill-outfit for both of us, take a week off from work, and we can descend and live down there at one of those year-round aquatic resorts. And in addition—" She broke off. "You're not listening. You should be. Here is something a lot better than that compulsion, that obsession you have about Mars, and you don't even listen!" Her voice rose piercingly. "God in heaven, you're doomed, Doug! What's going to become of you?"

"I'm going to work," he said, rising to his feet, his breakfast forgotten. "That's what's going to become of me."

She eyed him. "You're getting worse. More fanatical every day. Where's it going to lead?"

"To Mars," he said, and opened the door to the closet to get down a fresh shirt to wear to work.

Having descended from the taxi Douglas Quail slowly walked across three densely populated foot runnels and to the modern, attractively inviting doorway. There he halted, impeding midmorning traffic, and with caution read the shifting-color neon sign. He had, in the past, scrutinized this sign before . . . but never had he come so close. This was very different; what he did now was something else. Something which sooner or later had to happen.

REKAL, INCORPORATED

Was this the answer? After all, an illusion, no matter how convincing, remained nothing more than an illusion. At least objectively. But subjectively—quite the opposite entirely.

And anyhow he had an appointment. Within the next five minutes.

Taking a deep breath of mildly smog-infested Chicago air, he walked through the dazzling polychromatic shimmer of the doorway and up to the receptionist's counter.

The nicely articulated blonde at the counter, bare-bosomed and tidy, said pleasantly, "Good morning, Mr. Quail."

"Yes," he said. "I'm here to see about a Rekal course. As I guess you know."

"Not 'rekal' but *recall*," the receptionist corrected him. She picked up the receiver of the vidphone by her smooth elbow and said into it, "Mr. Douglas Quail is here, Mr. McClane. May he come inside, now? Or is it too soon?"

"Giz wetwa wum-wum wamp," the phone mumbled.

"Yes, Mr. Quail," she said. "You may go in; Mr. McClane is expecting you." As he started off uncertainly she called after him, "Room D, Mr. Quail. To your right."

After a frustrating but brief moment of being lost he found the proper room. The door hung open and inside, at a big genuine walnut desk, sat a genial-looking man, middle-aged, wearing the latest Martian frog-pelt gray suit; his attire alone would have told Quail that he had come to the right person.

"Sit down, Douglas," McClane said, waving his plump hand toward a chair which faced the desk. "So you want to have gone to Mars. Very good."

Quail seated himself, feeling tense. "I'm not so sure this is worth the fee," he said. "It costs a lot and as far as I can see I really get nothing." *Costs almost as much as going,* he thought.

"You get tangible proof of your trip," McClane disagreed emphatically. "All the proof you'll need. Here; I'll show you." He dug within a drawer of his impressive desk. "Ticket stub." Reaching into a manila folder, he produced a small square of embossed cardboard. "It proves you went—and returned. Postcards." He laid out four franked picture 3D full-color postcards in a neatly arranged row on the desk for Quail to see. "Film. Shots you took of local sights on Mars with a rented moving camera." To Quail he displayed those, too. "Plus the names of people you met, two hundred poscreds worth of souvenirs, which will arrive—from Mars—within the following month. And passport, certificates listing the shots you received. And more." He glanced up keenly at Quail. "You'll know you went, all right," he said. "You won't remember us, won't remember me or ever having been here. It'll be a real trip in your mind; we guarantee that. A full two weeks of recall; every last piddling detail. Remember this: if at any time you doubt that you really took an extensive trip to Mars you can return here and get a full refund. You see?"

"But I didn't go," Quail said. "I won't have gone, no matter what proofs you provide me with." He took a deep, unsteady breath. "And I never was a secret agent with Interplan." It seemed impossible to him that Rekal, Incorporated's extra-factual memory implant would do its job—despite what he had heard people say.

"Mr. Quail," McClane said patiently. "As you explained in your letter to us, you have no chance, no possibility in the slightest, of ever actually getting to Mars; you can't afford it, and what is much more important, you could never qualify as an undercover agent for Interplan or anybody else. This is the only way you can achieve your, ahem, lifelong dream; am I not correct, sir? You can't be this; you can't actually do this." He chuckled. "But you can have been and have done. We see to that. And our fee is reasonable; no hidden charges." He smiled encouragingly.

"Is an extra-factual memory that convincing?" Quail asked.

"More than the real thing, sir. Had you really gone to Mars as an Interplan agent, you would by now have forgotten a great deal; our analysis of true-mem systems—authentic recollections of major events in a person's life—shows that a variety of details are very quickly lost to the person. Forever."

"Part of the package we offer you is such deep implantation of recall that nothing is forgotten. The packet which is fed to you while you're comatose is the creation of trained experts, men who have spent years on Mars; in every case we verify details down to the last iota. And you've picked a rather easy extra-factual system; had you picked Pluto or wanted to be Emperor of the Inner Planet Alliance we'd have much more difficulty . . . and the charges would be considerably greater."

Reaching into his coat for his wallet, Quail said, "Okay. It's been my lifelong ambition and so I see I'll never really do it. So I guess I'll have to settle for this."

"Don't think of it that way," McClane said severely. "You're not accepting second best. The actual memory, with all its vagueness, omissions, and ellipses, not to say distortions—that's second-best." He accepted the money and pressed a button on his desk. "All right, Mr. Quail," he said, as the door of his office opened and two burly men swiftly entered. "You're on your way to Mars as a secret agent." He rose, came over to shake Quail's nervous, moist hand. "Or rather, you have been on your way. This afternoon at four thirty you will, um, arrive back here on Terra; a cab will leave you off at your conapt and as I say you will never remember seeing me or coming here; you won't, in fact, even remember having heard of our existence."

His mouth dry with nervousness, Quail followed the two technicians from the office; what happened next depended on them.

Will I actually believe I've been on Mars? he wondered. *That I managed to fulfill my lifetime ambition?* He had a strange, lingering intuition that something would go wrong. *But just what*—he did not know.

He would have to wait and find out.

The intercom on McClane's desk, which connected him with the work area of the firm, buzzed and a voice said, "Mr. Quail is under sedation now, sir. Do you want to supervise this one, or shall we go ahead?"

"It's routine," McClane observed. "You may

go ahead, Lowe; I don't think you'll run into any trouble." Programming an artificial memory of a trip to another planet—with or without the added fillip of being a secret agent—showed up on the firm's work-schedule with monotonous regularity. *In one month,* he calculated wryly, *we must do twenty of these . . . ersatz interplanetary travel has become our bread and butter.*

"Whatever you say, Mr. McClane," Lowe's voice came, and thereupon the intercom shut off.

Going to the vault section in the chamber behind his office, McClane searched about for a Three packet—trip to Mars—and a Sixty-Two packet: secret Interplan spy. Finding the two packets, he returned with them to his desk, seated himself comfortably, poured out the contents—merchandise which would be planted in Quail's conapt while the lab technicians busied themselves installing false memory.

A one-poscred sneaky-pete side arm, McClane reflected; *that's the largest item. Sets us back financially the most.* Then a pellet-sized transmitter, which could be swallowed if the agent were caught. *Code book that astonishingly resembled the real thing . . .* the firm's models were highly accurate: based, whenever possible, on actual US military issue. Odd bits which made no intrinsic sense but which would be woven into the warp and woof of Quail's imaginary trip, would coincide with his memory: half an ancient silver fifty-cent piece, several quotations from John Donne's sermons written incorrectly, each on a separate piece of transparent tissue-thin paper, several match folders from bars on Mars, a stainless-steel spoon engraved PROPERTY OF DOME-MARS NATIONAL KIBBUZIM, a wiretapping coil which—

The intercom buzzed. "Mr. McClane, I'm sorry to bother you but something rather ominous has come up. Maybe it would be better if you were in here after all. Quail is already under sedation; he reacted well to the narkidrine; he's completely unconscious and receptive. But—"

"I'll be in." Sensing trouble, McClane left his office; a moment later he emerged in the work area.

On a hygienic bed lay Douglas Quail, breathing slowly and regularly, his eyes virtually shut; he seemed dimly—but only dimly—aware of the two technicians and now McClane himself.

"There's no space to insert false memory-patterns?" McClane felt irritation. "Merely drop out two work weeks; he's employed as a clerk at the West Coast Emigration Bureau, which is a government agency, so he undoubtedly has or had two weeks' vacation within the last year. That ought to do it." Petty details annoyed him. And always would.

"Our problem," Lowe said sharply, "is something quite different." He bent over the bed, said to Quail, "Tell Mr. McClane what you told us." To McClane he said, "Listen closely."

The gray-green eyes of the man lying supine in the bed focused on McClane's face. The eyes, he observed uneasily, had become hard; they had a polished, inorganic quality, like semiprecious tumbled stones. He was not sure that he liked what he saw; the brilliance was too cold. "What do you want now?" Quail said harshly. "You've broken my cover. Get out of here before I take you all apart." He studied McClane. "Especially you," he continued. "You're in charge of this counteroperation."

Lowe said, "How long were you on Mars?"

"One month," Quail said gratingly.

"And your purpose there?" Lowe demanded.

The meager lips twisted; Quail eyed him and did not speak. At last, drawling the words out so that they dripped with hostility, he said, "Agent for Interplan. As I already told you. Don't you record everything that's said? Play your vid-aud tape back for your boss and leave me alone." He shut his eyes, then; the hard brilliance ceased. McClane felt, instantly, a rushing splurge of relief.

Lowe said quietly, "This is a tough man, Mr. McClane."

"He won't be," McClane said, "after we arrange for him to lose his memory-chain again. He'll be as meek as before." To Quail he said, "So this is why you wanted to go to Mars so terribly bad."

Without opening his eyes Quail said, "I never wanted to go to Mars. I was assigned it—they handed it to me and there I was: stuck. Oh yeah, I admit I was curious about it; who wouldn't be?" Again he opened his eyes and surveyed the three of them, McClane in particular. "Quite a truth drug you've got here; it brought up things I had absolutely no memory of." He pondered. "I wonder about Kirsten," he said, half to himself. "Could she be in on it? An Interplan contact keeping an eye on me . . . to be certain I didn't regain my memory? No wonder she's been so derisive about my wanting to go there." Faintly, he smiled; the smile—one of understanding—disappeared almost at once.

McClane said, "Please believe me, Mr. Quail; we stumbled onto this entirely by accident. In the work we do—"

"I believe you," Quail said. He seemed tired, now; the drug was continuing to pull him under, deeper and deeper. "Where did I say I'd been?" he murmured. "Mars? Hard to remember—I know I'd like to see it; so would everybody else. But me—" His voice trailed off. *"Just a clerk, a nothing clerk."*

Straightening up, Lowe said to his superior. "He wants a false memory implanted that corresponds to a trip he actually took. And a false reason which is the real reason. He's telling the truth; he's a long way down in the narkidrine. The trip is very vivid in his mind—at least under sedation. But apparently he doesn't recall it otherwise. Someone, probably at a government military-sciences lab, erased his conscious memories; all he knew was that going to Mars meant something special to him, and so did being a secret agent. They couldn't erase that; it's not a memory but a desire, undoubtedly the same one that motivated him to volunteer for the assignment in the first place."

The other technician, Keeler, said to McClane, "What do we do? Graft a false memory-pattern over the real memory? There's no telling what the results would be; he might remember some of the genuine trip, and the confusion might bring on a psychotic interlude.

He'd have to hold two opposite premises in his mind simultaneously: that he went to Mars and that he didn't. That he's a genuine agent for Interplan and he's not, that it's spurious. I think we ought to revive him without any false memory implantation and send him out of here; this is hot."

"Agreed," McClane said. A thought came to him. "Can you predict what he'll remember when he comes out of sedation?"

"Impossible to tell," Lowe said. "He probably will have some dim, diffuse memory of his actual trip, now. And he'd probably be in grave doubt as to its validity; he'd probably decide our programming slipped a gear-tooth. And he'd remember coming here; that wouldn't be erased—unless you want it erased."

"The less we mess with this man," McClane said, "the better I like it. This is nothing for us to fool around with; we've been foolish enough to—or unlucky enough to—uncover a genuine Interplan spy who has a cover so perfect that up to now even he didn't know what he was—or rather is." The sooner they washed their hands of the man calling himself Douglas Quail the better.

"Are you going to plant packets Three and Sixty-Two in his conapt?" Lowe said.

"No," McClane said. "And we're going to return half his fee."

"*'Half'!* Why half?"

McClane said lamely, "It seems to be a good compromise."

• • •

As the cab carried him back to his conapt at the residential end of Chicago, Douglas Quail said to himself, *It's sure good to be back on Terra.*

Already the month-long period on Mars had begun to waver in his memory; he had only an image of profound gaping craters, an ever-present ancient erosion of hills, of vitality, of motion itself. A world of dust where little happened, where a good part of the day was spent checking and rechecking one's portable oxygen source. And then the life forms, the unassuming and modest gray-brown cacti and maw-worms.

As a matter of fact he had brought back several moribund examples of Martian fauna; he had smuggled them through customs. After all, they posed no menace; they couldn't survive in Earth's heavy atmosphere.

Reaching into his coat pocket, he rummaged for the container of Martian maw-worms—And found an envelope instead.

Lifting it out, he discovered, to his perplexity, that it contained five hundred and seventy poscreds, in cred bills of low denomination.

Where'd I get this? he asked himself. *Didn't I spend every 'cred I had on my trip?*

With the money came a slip of paper marked: One-half fee ret'd. By McClane. And then the date. Today's date.

"Recall," he said aloud.

"Recall what, sir or madam?" the robot driver of the cab inquired respectfully.

"Do you have a phone book?" Quail demanded.

"Certainly, sir or madam." A slot opened; from it slid a microtape phone book for Cook County.

"It's spelled oddly," Quail said as he leafed through the pages of the yellow section. He felt fear, then: abiding fear. "Here it is," he said. "Take me there, to Rekal, Incorporated. I've changed my mind; I don't want to go home."

"Yes, sir or madam, as the case may be," the driver said. A moment later the cab was zipping back in the opposite direction.

"May I make use of your phone?" he asked.

"Be my guest," the robot driver said. And presented a shiny new emperor 3D color phone to him.

He dialed his own conapt. And after a pause found himself confronted by a miniature but chillingly realistic image of Kirsten on the small screen. "I've been to Mars," he said to her.

"You're drunk." Her lips writhed scornfully. "Or worse."

"'s God's truth."

"When?" she demanded.

"I don't know." He felt confused. "A simulated trip, I think. By means of one of those artificial or extra-factual or whatever it is memory places. It didn't take."

Kirsten said witheringly, "You are drunk." And broke the connection at her end. He hung up, then, feeling his face flush. *Always the same tone,* he said hotly to himself. *Always the retort, as if she knows everything and I know nothing. What a marriage. Keerist,* he thought dismally.

A moment later the cab stopped at the curb before a modern, very attractive little pink building, over which a shifting polychromatic neon sign read: REKAL, INCORPORATED.

The receptionist, chic and bare from the waist up, started in surprise, then gained masterful control of herself. "Oh, hello, Mr. Quail," she said nervously. "H-how are you? Did you forget something?"

"The rest of my fee back," he said.

More composed now, the receptionist said, "Fee? I think you are mistaken, Mr. Quail. You were here discussing the feasibility of an extra-factual trip for you, but—" She shrugged her smooth pale shoulders. "As I understand it, no trip was taken."

Quail said, "I remember everything, miss. My letter to Rekal, Incorporated, which started this whole business off. I remember my arrival here, my visit with Mr. McClane. Then the two lab technicians taking me in tow and administering a drug to put me out." No wonder the firm had returned half his fee. The false memory of his "trip to Mars" hadn't taken—at least not entirely, not as he had been assured.

"Mr. Quail," the girl said, "although you are a minor clerk you are a good-looking man and it spoils your features to become angry. If it would make you feel any better, I might, ahem, let you take me out . . ."

He felt furious, then. "I remember you," he said savagely. "For instance the fact that your breasts are sprayed blue; that stuck in my mind. And I remember Mr. McClane's promise that if I remembered my visit to Rekal, Incorporated,

I'd receive my money back in full. Where is Mr. McClane?"

After a delay—probably as long as they could manage—he found himself once more seated facing the imposing walnut desk, exactly as he had been an hour or so earlier in the day.

"Some technique you have," Quail said sardonically. His disappointment—and resentment—was enormous, by now. "My so-called 'memory' of a trip to Mars as an under-cover agent for Interplan is hazy and vague and shot full of contradictions. And I clearly remem-ber my dealings here with you people. I ought to take this to the Better Business Bureau." He was burning angry at this point; his sense of being cheated had overwhelmed him, had destroyed his customary aversion to participating in a pub-lic squabble.

Looking morose, as well as cautious, McClane said, "We capitulate, Quail. We'll refund the balance of your fee. I fully concede the fact that we did absolutely nothing for you." His tone was resigned.

Quail said accusingly, "You didn't even provide me with the various artifacts that you claimed would 'prove' to me I had been on Mars. All that song-and-dance you went into—it hasn't materialized into a damn thing. Not even a ticket stub. Nor postcards. Nor passport. Nor proof of immunization shots. Nor—"

"Listen, Quail," McClane said. "Suppose I told you—" He broke off. "Let it go." He pressed a button on his intercom. "Shirley, will you disburse five hundred and seventy more 'creds in the form of a cashier's check made out to Douglas Quail? Thank you." He released the button, then glared at Quail.

Presently the check appeared; the reception-ist placed it before McClane and once more van-ished out of sight, leaving the two men alone, still facing each other across the surface of the massive walnut desk.

"Let me give you a word of advice," McClane said as he signed the check and passed it over. "Don't discuss your, ahem, recent trip to Mars with anyone."

"What trip?"

"Well, that's the thing." Doggedly, McClane said, "The trip you partially remember. Act as if you don't remember; pretend it never took place. Don't ask me why; just take my advice: it'll be better for all of us." He had begun to perspire. Freely. "Now, Mr. Quail, I have other business, other clients to see." He rose, showed Quail to the door.

Quail said, as he opened the door, "A firm that turns out such bad work shouldn't have any clients at all." He shut the door behind him.

On the way home in the cab Quail pondered the wording of his letter of complaint to the Bet-ter Business Bureau, Terra Division. As soon as he could get to his typewriter he'd get started; it was clearly his duty to warn other people away from Rekal, Incorporated.

When he got back to his conapt he seated himself before his Hermes Rocket portable, opened the drawers and rummaged for carbon paper—and noticed a small, familiar box. A box which he had carefully filled on Mars with Martian fauna and later smuggled through cus-toms.

Opening the box he saw, to his disbelief, six dead maw-worms and several varieties of the unicellular life on which the Martian worms fed. The protozoa were dried-up, dusty, but he recognized them; it had taken him an entire day picking among the vast dark alien boulders to find them. A wonderful, illuminated journey of discovery.

But I didn't go to Mars, he realized.

Yet on the other hand—

Kirsten appeared at the doorway to the room, an armload of pale brown groceries gripped. "Why are you home in the middle of the day?" Her voice, in an eternity of sameness, was accusing.

"Did I go to Mars?" he asked her. "You would know."

"No, of course you didn't go to Mars; you would know that, I would think. Aren't you al-ways bleating about going?"

He said, "By God, I think I went." After a

pause he added, "And simultaneously I think I didn't go."

"Make up your mind."

"How can I?" He gestured. "I have both memory-tracks grafted inside my head; one is real and one isn't but I can't tell which is which. Why can't I rely on you? They haven't tinkered with you." She could do this much for him at least—even if she never did anything else.

Kirsten said in a level, controlled voice, "Doug, if you don't pull yourself together, we're through. I'm going to leave you."

"I'm in trouble." His voice came out husky and coarse. And shaking. "Probably I'm heading into a psychotic episode; I hope not, but—maybe that's it. It would explain everything, anyhow."

Setting down the bag of groceries, Kirsten stalked to the closet. "I was not kidding," she said to him quietly. She brought out a coat, got it on, walked back to the door of the conapt. "I'll phone you one of these days soon," she said tonelessly. "This is goodbye, Doug. I hope you pull out of this eventually; I really pray you do. For your sake."

"Wait," he said desperately. "Just tell me and make it absolute; I did go or I didn't—tell me which one." *But they may have altered your memory-track also,* he realized.

The door closed. His wife had left. *Finally!*

A voice behind him said, "Well, that's that. Now put up your hands, Quail. And also please turn around and face this way."

He turned, instinctively, without raising his hands.

The man who faced him wore the plum uniform of the Interplan Police Agency, and his gun appeared to be UN issue. And, for some odd reason, he seemed familiar to Quail; familiar in a blurred, distorted fashion which he could not pin down. So, jerkily, he raised his hands.

"You remember," the policeman said, "your trip to Mars. We know all your actions today and all your thoughts—in particular your very important thoughts on the trip home from Rekal, Incorporated." He explained, "We have a tele-transmitter wired within your skull; it keeps us constantly informed."

A telepathic transmitter; use of a living plasma that had been discovered in Luna. He shuddered with self-aversion. The thing lived inside him, within his own brain, feeding, listening, feeding. But the Interplan police used them; that had come out even in the homeopapes. So this was probably true, dismal as it was.

"Why me?" Quail said huskily. What had he done—or thought? And what did this have to do with Rekal, Incorporated?

"Fundamentally," the Interplan cop said, "this has nothing to do with Rekal; it's between you and us." He tapped his right ear. "I'm still picking up your mentational processes by way of your cephalic transmitter." In the man's ear Quail saw a small white-plastic plug. "So I have to warn you: anything you think may be held against you." He smiled. "Not that it matters now; you've already thought and spoken yourself into oblivion. What's annoying is the fact that under narkidrine at Rekal, Incorporated, you told them, their technicians and the owner, Mr. McClane, about your trip—where you went, for whom, some of what you did. They're very frightened. They wish they had never laid eyes on you." He added reflectively, "They're right."

Quail said, "I never made any trip. It's a false memory-chain improperly planted in me by McClane's technicians." But then he thought of the box, in his desk drawer, containing the Martian life forms. And the trouble and hardship he had had gathering them. The memory seemed real. And the box of life forms; that certainly was real. Unless McClane had planted it. Perhaps this was one of the "proofs" which McClane had talked glibly about.

The memory of my trip to Mars, he thought, *doesn't convince me—but unfortunately it has convinced the Interplan Police Agency. They think I really went to Mars and they think I at least partially realize it.*

"We not only know you went to Mars," the Interplan cop agreed, in answer to his thoughts, "but we know that you now remember enough to be difficult for us. And there's no use expunging your conscious memory of all this, because if we do you'll simply show up at Rekal, Incorporated again and start over. And we can't do anything about McClane and his operation because we have no jurisdiction over anyone except our own people. Anyhow, McClane hasn't committed any crime." He eyed Quail, "Nor, technically, have you. You didn't go to Rekal, Incorporated, with the idea of regaining your memory; you went, as we realize, for the usual reason people go there—a love by plain, dull people for adventure." He added, "Unfortunately you're not plain, not dull, and you've already had too much excitement; the last thing in the universe you needed was a course from Rekal, Incorporated. Nothing could have been more lethal for you or for us. And, for that matter, for McClane."

Quail said, "Why is it 'difficult' for you if I remember my trip—my alleged trip—and what I did there?"

"Because," the Interplan harness bull said, "what you did is not in accord with our great white all-protecting father public image. You did, for us, what we never do. As you'll presently remember—thanks to narkidrine. That box of dead worms and algae has been sitting in your desk drawer for six months, ever since you got back. And at no time have you shown the slightest curiosity about it. We didn't even know you had it until you remembered it on your way home from Rekal; then we came here on the double to look for it." He added, unnecessarily, "Without any luck; there wasn't enough time."

A second Interplan cop joined the first one; the two briefly conferred. Meanwhile, Quail thought rapidly. He did remember more, now; the cop had been right about narkidrine. They—Interplan—probably used it themselves. *Probably?* He knew darn well they did; he had seen them putting a prisoner on it. *Where would that be? Somewhere on Terra? More likely on Luna,* he decided, viewing the image rising from his highly defective—but rapidly less so—memory.

And he remembered something else. Their

reason for sending him to Mars; the job he had done.

No wonder they had expunged his memory.

"Oh, God," the first of the two Interplan cops said, breaking off his conversation with his companion. Obviously, he had picked up Quail's thoughts. "Well, this is a far worse problem, now; as bad as it can get." He walked toward Quail, again covering him with his gun. "We've got to kill you," he said. "And right away."

Nervously, his fellow officer said, "Why right away? Can't we simply cart him off to Interplan New York and let them—"

"He knows why it has to be right away," the first cop said; he too looked nervous, now, but Quail realized that it was for an entirely different reason. His memory had been brought back almost entirely, now. And he fully understood the officer's tension.

"On Mars," Quail said hoarsely, "I killed a man. After getting past fifteen bodyguards. Some armed with sneaky-pete guns, the way you are." He had been trained, by Interplan, over a five-year period to be an assassin. A professional killer. He knew ways to take out armed adversaries . . . such as these two officers; and the one with the ear-receiver knew it, too. If he moved swiftly enough—

The gun fired. But he had already moved to one side, and at the same time he chopped down the gun-carrying officer. In an instant he had possession of the gun and was covering the other, confused, officer.

"Picked my thoughts up," Quail said, panting for breath. "He knew what I was going to do, but I did it anyhow."

Half sitting up, the injured officer grated, "He won't use that gun on you, Sam; I pick that up, too. He knows he's finished, and he knows we know it, too. Come on, Quail." Laboriously, grunting with pain, he got shakily to his feet. He held out his hand. "The gun," he said to Quail. "You can't use it, and if you turn it over to me I'll guarantee not to kill you; you'll be given a hearing, and someone higher up in Interplan will decide, not me. Maybe they can erase your memory once more, I don't know. But you know the thing I was going to kill you for; I couldn't keep you from remembering it. So my reason for wanting to kill you is in a sense past."

Quail, clutching the gun, bolted from the conapt, sprinted for the elevator. *If you follow me,* he thought, *I'll kill you. So don't.* He jabbed at the elevator button and, a moment later, the doors slid back.

The police hadn't followed him. Obviously they had picked up his terse, tense thoughts and had decided not to take the chance.

With him inside the elevator descended. He had gotten away—for a time. But what next? Where could he go?

The elevator reached the ground floor; a moment later Quail had joined the mob of peds hurrying along the runnels. His head ached and he felt sick. But at least he had evaded death; they had come very close to shooting him on the spot, back in his own conapt.

And they probably will again, he decided. *When they find me. And with this transmitter inside me, that won't take too long.*

Ironically, he had gotten exactly what he had asked Rekal, Incorporated for. Adventure, peril, Interplan police at work, a secret and dangerous trip to Mars in which his life was at stake—everything he had wanted as a false memory.

The advantages of it being a memory—and nothing more—could now be appreciated.

On a park bench, alone, he sat dully watching a flock of perts: a semi-bird imported from Mars's two moons, capable of soaring flight, even against Earth's huge gravity.

Maybe I can find my way back to Mars, he pondered. *But then what?* It would be worse on Mars; the political organization whose leader he had assassinated would spot him the moment he stepped from the ship; he would have Interplan and them after him, there.

Can you hear me thinking? he wondered. Easy avenue to paranoia; sitting here alone he felt them tuning in on him, monitoring, recording, discussing . . . He shivered, rose to his feet, walked aimlessly, his hands deep in his pockets.

No matter where I go, he realized, *you'll always be with me. As long as I have this device inside my head.*

I'll make a deal with you, he thought to himself—and to them. *Can you imprint a false-memory template on me again, as you did before, that I lived an average, routine life, never went to Mars? Never saw an Interplan uniform up close and never handled a gun?*

A voice inside his brain answered, "As has been carefully explained to you: that would not be enough."

Astonished, he halted.

"We formerly communicated with you in this manner," the voice continued. "When you were operating in the field, on Mars. It's been months since we've done it; we assumed, in fact, that we'd never have to do so again. Where are you?"

"Walking," Quail said, "to my death." *By your officers' guns,* he added as an afterthought. "How can you be sure it wouldn't be enough?" he demanded. "Don't the Rekal techniques work?"

"As we said. If you're given a set of standard, average memories you get—restless. You'd inevitably seek out Rekal or one of its competitors again. We can't go through this a second time."

"Suppose," Quail said, "once my authentic memories have been canceled, something more vital than standard memories are implanted. Something which would act to satisfy my craving," he said. "That's been proved; that's probably why you initially hired me. But you ought to be able to come up with something else—something equal. I was the richest man on Terra but I finally gave all my money to educational foundations. Or I was a famous deep-space explorer. Anything of that sort; wouldn't one of those do?"

Silence.

"Try it," he said desperately. "Get some of your top-notch military psychiatrists; explore my mind. Find out what my most expansive daydream is." He tried to think. "Women," he said. "Thousands of them, like Don Juan had. An interplanetary playboy—a mistress in every city on Earth, Luna, and Mars. Only I gave that up, out of exhaustion. Please," he begged. "Try it."

"You'd voluntarily surrender, then?" the voice inside his head asked. "If we agreed to arrange such a solution? If it's possible?"

After an interval of hesitation he said, "Yes." *I'll take the risk,* he said to himself, *that you don't simply kill me.*

"You make the first move," the voice said presently. "Turn yourself over to us. And we'll investigate that line of possibility. If we can't do it, however, if your authentic memories begin to crop up again as they've done at this time, then—" There was silence and then the voice finished, "We'll have to destroy you. As you must understand. Well, Quail, you still want to try?"

"Yes," he said. Because the alternative was death now—and for certain. At least this way he had a chance, slim as it was.

"You present yourself at our main barracks in New York," the voice of the Interplan cop resumed. "At 580 Fifth Avenue, floor twelve. Once you've surrendered yourself, we'll have our psychiatrists begin on you; we'll have personality-profile tests made. We'll attempt to determine your absolute, ultimate fantasy wish—then we'll bring you back to Rekal, Incorporated, here; get them in on it, fulfilling that wish in vicarious surrogate retrospection. And—good luck. We do owe you something; you acted as a capable instrument for us." The voice lacked malice; if anything, they—the organization—felt sympathy toward him.

"Thanks," Quail said. And began searching for a robot cab.

• • •

"Mr. Quail," the stern-faced, elderly Interplan psychiatrist said, "you possess a most interesting wish-fulfillment dream fantasy. Probably nothing such as you consciously entertain or suppose. This is commonly the way; I hope it won't upset you too much to hear about it."

The senior ranking Interplan officer present said briskly, "He better not be too much upset to hear about it, not if he expects not to get shot."

"Unlike the fantasy of wanting to be an Interplan undercover agent," the psychiatrist continued, "which, being relatively speaking a product of maturity, had a certain plausibility to it, this production is a grotesque dream of your childhood; it is no wonder you fail to recall it. Your fantasy is this: you are nine years old, walking alone down a rustic lane. An unfamiliar variety of space vessel from another star system lands directly in front of you. No one on Earth but you, Mr. Quail, sees it. The creatures within are very small and helpless, somewhat on the order of field mice, although they are attempting to invade Earth; tens of thousands of other ships will soon be on their way, when this advance party gives the go-ahead signal."

"And I suppose I stop them," Quail said, experiencing a mixture of amusement and disgust. "Single-handed I wipe them out. Probably by stepping on them with my foot."

"No," the psychiatrist said patiently. "You halt the invasion, but not by destroying them. Instead, you show them kindness and mercy, even though by telepathy—their mode of communication—you know why they have come. They have never seen such humane traits exhibited by any sentient organism, and to show their appreciation they make a covenant with you."

Quail said, "They won't invade Earth as long as I'm alive."

"Exactly." To the Interplan officer the psychiatrist said, "You can see it does fit his personality, despite his feigned scorn."

"So by merely existing," Quail said, feeling a growing pleasure, "by simply being alive, I keep Earth safe from alien rule. I'm in effect, then, the most important person on Terra. Without lifting a finger."

"Yes, indeed, sir," the psychiatrist said. "And this is bedrock in your psyche; this is a lifelong childhood fantasy. Which, without depth and drug therapy, you never would have recalled.

But it has always existed in you; it went underneath, but never ceased."

To McClane, who sat intently listening, the senior police official said, "Can you implant an extra-factual memory pattern that extreme in him?"

"We get handed every possible type of wish-fantasy there is," McClane said. "Frankly, I've heard a lot worse than this. Certainly we can handle it. Twenty-four hours from now he won't just wish he'd saved Earth; he'll devoutly believe it really happened."

The senior police official said, "You can start the job, then. In preparation we've already once again erased the memory in him of his trip to Mars."

Quail said, "What trip to Mars?"

No one answered him, so reluctantly, he shelved the question. And anyhow a police vehicle had now put in its appearance; he, McClane, and the senior police officer crowded into it, and presently they were on their way to Chicago and Rekal, Incorporated.

"You had better make no errors this time," the police officer said to heavyset, nervous-looking McClane.

"I can't see what could go wrong," McClane mumbled, perspiring. "This has nothing to do with Mars or Interplan. Single-handedly stopping an invasion of Earth from another star system." He shook his head at that. "Wow, what a kid dreams up. And by pious virtue, too; not by force. It's sort of quaint." He dabbed at his forehead with a large linen pocket handkerchief.

Nobody said anything.

"In fact," McClane said, "it's touching."

"But arrogant," the police official said starkly. "Inasmuch as when he dies the invasion will resume. No wonder he doesn't recall it; it's the most grandiose fantasy I ever ran across." He eyed Quail with disapproval. "And to think we put this man on our payroll."

When they reached Rekal, Incorporated, the receptionist, Shirley, met them breathlessly in the outer office. "Welcome back, Mr. Quail," she fluttered, her melon-shaped breasts—today painted an incandescent orange—bobbing with agitation. "I'm sorry everything worked out so badly before; I'm sure this time it'll go better."

Still repeatedly dabbing at his shiny forehead with his neatly folded Irish linen handkerchief, McClane said, "It better." Moving with rapidity he rounded up Lowe and Keeler, escorted them and Douglas Quail to the work area, and then, with Shirley and the senior police officer, returned to his familiar office. To wait.

"Do we have a packet made up for this, Mr. McClane?" Shirley asked, bumping against him in her agitation, then coloring modestly.

"I think we do." He tried to recall, then gave up and consulted the formal chart. "A combination," he decided aloud, "of packets Eighty-One, Twenty, and Six." From the vault section of the chamber behind his desk he fished out the appropriate packets, carried them to his desk for inspection. "From Eighty-One," he explained, "a magic healing rod given him—the client in question, this time Mr. Quail—by the race of beings from another system. A token of their gratitude."

"Does it work?" the police officer asked curiously.

"It did once," McClane explained. "But he, ahem, you see, used it up years ago, healing right and left. Now it's only a memento. But he remembers it working spectacularly." He chuckled, then opened packet Twenty. "Document from the UN Secretary General thanking him for saving Earth; this isn't precisely appropriate, because part of Quail's fantasy is that no one knows of the invasion except himself, but for the sake of verisimilitude we'll throw it in." He inspected packet Six, then. *What came from this?* He couldn't recall; frowning, he dug into the plastic bag as Shirley and the Interplan police officer watched intently.

"Writing," Shirley said. "In a funny language."

"This tells who they were," McClane said, "and where they came from. Including a detailed star map logging their flight here and the system of origin. Of course it's in their script, so he can't read it. But he remembers them reading it to him in his own tongue." He placed the three artifacts in the center of the desk. "These should be taken to Quail's conapt," he said to the police officer. "So that when he gets home he'll find them. And it'll confirm his fantasy. SOP— standard operating procedure." He chuckled apprehensively, wondering how matters were going with Lowe and Keeler.

The intercom buzzed. "Mr. McClane, I'm sorry to bother you." It was Lowe's voice; he froze as he recognized it, froze and became mute. "But something's come up. Maybe it would be better if you came in here and supervised. Like before, Quail reacted well to the narkidrine; he's unconscious, relaxed, and receptive. But—" McClane sprinted for the work area.

On a hygienic bed Douglas Quail lay breathing slowly and regularly, eyes half-shut, dimly conscious of those around him.

"We started interrogating him," Lowe said, white-faced. "To find out exactly when to place the fantasy-memory of him single-handedly having saved Earth. And strangely enough—"

"They told me not to tell," Douglas Quail mumbled in a dull drug-saturated voice. "That was the agreement. I wasn't even supposed to remember. But how could I forget an event like that?"

I guess it would be hard, McClane reflected. *But you did—until now.*

"They even gave me a scroll," Quail mumbled, "of gratitude. I have it hidden in my conapt; I'll show it to you."

To the Interplan officer who had followed after him, McClane said, "Well, I offer the suggestion that you better not kill him. If you do they'll return."

"They also gave me a magic invisible destroying rod," Quail mumbled, eyes totally shut now. "That's how I killed that man on Mars you sent me to take out. It's in my drawer along with the box of Martian maw-worms and dried-up plant life."

Wordlessly, the Interplan officer turned and stalked from the work area.

I might as well put those packets of proof-artifacts away, McClane said to himself resignedly. He walked, step by step, back to his office. Including the citation from the UN Secretary General. After all—

The real one probably would not be long in coming.

MISHA

SPEED

(1988)

EVERYTHING IS FRACTURED; a broken mirror pieced together randomly so your reflection feels all wrong, an eye here, a nose there, any old mouth where your chin should be.

• • •

Shrill feedback and digital chitters wail in the collapsible dish Speed has mounted on the HOT truck. Sheet metal booms, arcs ping—but he has no real fix on the input drain. Somewhere west?

Animal Inscription tearing out the deck, Speed skids his HOT truck, barely misses the oily flayed body of a dead man with six or seven people brawling over it trying to get a wallet.

Green paper dollars flutter into the gutter with other worthless trash—ones as well as tens and twenties. Speed sneers at their chemical messages. It's the guy's ID they want.

Here data is the only currency, according to the all-knowing Juno 888. Speed rolls up against the crumbling yellow curb. From his compos-

ite eyeglasses he watches a city alive with insect activity; run-skitters, flashes of chitin armor, papery wings. Mandibles clack; a rush, more swift tides and waves of insects. The gimmick lines are in a chaos—armed guards bludgeoning into file the soft yellow heads of young and old white-haired eggs spilling their yolks on the roadway. All DNA IDs are checked. Speed of course to stop for none of them. He runs a red DAT vehicle with a HOT sign on the side. He zips around a line of cards. Rusty fire ants rush to holes before the rain. It rains. A thunderous sheet of lightning garishly two-dimensionalizes them all. A scarab bas-relief. Hailstone marbles crash down on them. The furious storm's thunder roars a geared-down semi. No one seems to notice. Baldface guards truncheon. Blood balls roll underfoot. Speed peels back their scalps, puts his hands in the oozing gray matter—all cold pudding from disuse.

"Nobody home," he says, slamming the hair down.

The street here flows red with foamy junket. Speed gulps back revulsion. The river runs from the outlet of The Bell Factory, a gray building, ex detention center for non gov artists. Now Comma 7 brings non data here for recycling.

"888, Speed 15-1-00 reports. Mile post 669 highway 82."

"What's the delay? Where is my data source number Speel-yi 427?" 888 is on its routine check.

Speed wrinkles his nose at 888's predictability.

Speed blows smoke, glares at cars hydroplaning past in the red slime. Some wrecks are loaded with merchandise. Some shiny new ones are empty.

"888, it's snowing."

"Thank you, fifty credits."

"888, nobody told you it was snowing?" Speed asks incredulously.

"I could have predicted it." The 888 pauses. "Crow Moon."

Speed's heart accelerates, flies against his ribs then circles, cold and wary. "What's that? 888, what's that—Crow Moon?" Speed gets a hunch, at last.

"Speel-yi 427 data online."

"Fucking-a," he whispers. "888, is this data accessible?"

"Yes—access code required."

"Shit." He smacks the dash with his gloved hands.

The 888 leaves the terminal on the dash and then is replaced by the holo again. Speed glances at it and drives a little faster.

At first everyone was a lot happier when the Juno 888 took control of world commerce. As to be expected—the rich got very rich. The poor were replaced. Typical mayfly existence.

888 arranged its own random pattern of rising US dollar and failing yen, or pound or rising pound or rising yen or whatever was popular. To begin with, commerce grumbled. Yellow lights blinked on—then went off again. 888 brought the gold standard back for four chaotic years. Now data—only data is commerce. Peo-

ple kill each other to get the chance to report the death.

Speed steers around the wreckage of two supertrucks. Speed is satisfied with this new system. It isn't hard to come up with data—if you are creative. Corporate termite mounds collapsed in hours. Drones search for queen bees of data—hire people like himself to find them.

But Speed belongs to no man—only to the Juno 888. He moves, the caddis fly in the HOT house of silicon sentience, preying on unwary larvae. But his only bug in the honey is that the Comma 7 parasitic pepsis DATmen hunt him.

To date—the longest source of uninterrupted data is Speel-yi 427. 888 demands for her to be brought in, its larder of uninterrupted data in hexagonal cells, waxing poetic for the Juno's brood of inaccessible memories.

Speed hungers for this Speel-yi as much as Juno 888 does. He likes to please this insatiable electric insect, the solar panels wings those of a great iridescent mantis.

888 drops the egg of a clue with Crow Moon. The antenna of Speed's brain rotates west. He thinks nearly all non-whites had been killed in pogroms. Especially those, what were they, not Crows but . . .

Speed spurs the HOT west.

• • •

Toy blue skies lie safely over tin tops. Cycled Comma Cops stalk Speed and wait for the blood to flow before striking. He knows their feeding frenzies and pulls into a tunnel and stops. He gathers refuse—broken bottles, asphalt chunks, ripped beer cans, bent sign poles—and strategically places them. Hurrying now, Speed reaches into the treasure of junk in the back of the HOT. He unrolls barbed wire across the tube. He pitons it to the concrete walls wincing at the pang pang of the ice hammer in the hollow hall. His boots echo in the tunnel as he runs to the HOT truck, screeches the tires through the other side, and idles.

The Comma Cops come in quickly for the

kill. So much static convinces them the prey is found. They bare their shark teeth and hit fast.

A scream gurgles, skidding crashes, metal explodes, chemicals burn, a debris destination for any who missed the finishing wire.

Speed grins to himself, moves off slowly, a wolf eel in liquid death.

Here, fifty miles from 888's last query, Speed perches on the HOT and sets up the collapsible dish. Microwave music screams, whistles, static white noise, metal sheets tear, digital snaps and pops, high pitches cricket, a seventeen-year cicada of noise is all beautiful to Speed. He loses himself in this wall of sound, eyes closed. Behind the deadly glass, green holo eyes watch him coyly.

A fluid sound pricks his ears and Speed is instantly alert—his sharp nose quivers and he fine-tunes the pulse. There is a high-pitched howl echoing the system. Something he zeros on—the specified aimed point. Picture of, picture of hell. A spot of purple and orange fire, Speed dives to the road.

Fun backward spells *'nuf.* Speed laughs, "Nuf fun."

A Comma Cop with an erased face whips a chain lasso across his eyes before he relays to 888. Bright blood bees fly away from Speed. The Comma 7 is rejecting him with shark-tooth gloves as the blood answers "no" while his mouth says "yes, yes."

"Where is the data?" The Comma Cop is so digital, off again, on again, like any insect, no chirping below fifty degrees, and it's cold here—no sound.

"Okay, okay," Speed says weakly. He pushes himself up against the door of the HOT. His glasses are cracked carapaces, saving his sight which is peering from behind a crimson curtain. Speed grinds his bootheel in asphalt.

• • •

"Where?" The Comma 7 swings the chain.

"Nunya," says Speed quietly.

"Nunya? As in . . . ," the Comma 7 comes very close.

"As in Nunya business!" Speed lashes out with his boot-tip bayonet, laughing wildly. Oldest trick in the books. Easy to strip a Dogface cocoon he thinks—remembers this as he reaches back into the red HOT and pulls out a black Louisville with a white taped handle. The crack of the skull signals home run. He wants the Comma 7 to pull back now. Needs a sign. The larvae quivers and oozes greenish fluid. Speed teases open the tear with a pair of needle-nose pliers. Blue tendons and bubble-pink organs lay in a bed of yellow fat. The shining steel disappears into the wound. Droplets of sweat roll down Speed's face as he crouches there. He finds what he wants, pulls it out, hitches it to the bumper. Speed wipes his face and throws the slick pliers in the bed of junk where it clatters into the oily corner. He hops into the truck, blows a kiss to the holo Speel-yi 427 and drives off. In the rearview mirror everything is all wrong, the body jerks and unravels, any old intestine where a groin should be. The body rips off on a reflector on the side of a bar pit. Speed ejaculates laughter, shudders over the wheel, and burns rubber.

Crows, like jagged obsidian knives, descend on the sacrifice.

Speed sucks razors of breath as he spirals into a turquoise sky. The dishes on this mountain are all tied with aluminum balloons. He stops and shoots one with an old GP-100. This is the way the world ends, he sniggers as the metal bangs his ears.

He feels elated.

At precisely 4,500 feet above sea level, at a mountain lake surrounded by huge alpine trees drooping with a whipped top of snow, he stops. He sees no people, only chimeras, a musk-oxen-llama cross left from some forgotten genetic farm. These form a protective ring and spit at him. Speed laughs.

The snow seeps through his boots and his coverall crackles with cold. He makes his way to a pole hogan with a valley-sized dish in front of it.

Inside, it smells of woodsmoke, jerky, dried fruit, spice, and—he fastens his reflective lenses toward the now solid holo—fish.

She is eating a tin of salmon and smiling at him. Behind her a string of shrunken heads dance, eyes and lips sewn silent. He jumps as he realizes they are him. This knife fish has brought him to face himself. A spider silence, a spider's lair, a white spider in the shadow of a white web. Snow falls from him in glistening globules.

"Speed 15-1-00," he extends a shaking hand.

She is not the holo. She is faded, in a black ball cap with an unspeakable name on the crown. She has sable braids and her face is ceremonially painted in noshi red and white. Seven crimson false faces leer around the hogan. They hand him a bundle of arrows, a carmine stone calumet.

Her eyes are the same eyes—watching him coyly. Alive with meaning. The spider crystallizes, falls away. Predator intensity sharpens the data lust. Her sharp white teeth and her red gums are laughing at him. Speel-yi, a trickster in a Kali suit, is entering her data.

"March, the Crow or Wakening Moon," she mercifully explains, "Folklore of The People. Very practical."

Volcanic laughter is burning up his throat, he vomits it with his gorge. The false faces are dancing in a slow ghostly dance. They are mocking silicon senility.

This is what they sing:

ka-ka tiwa-ku
ka-ka tiwa-ku
wetatu-ta (tu) tatu-ta
atira irira atira irira[*]

"You forgot to give the coordinates," she says and taps the questioning screen.

Speed moves toward the dancers and the world tilts, the day cracks apart, and the black comes in and is punctuated by seven white stars. Terrible winds tear life's fabric, blinding ash snow falls on the white feathers of the Crow Moon. Spedis and Speel-yi illuminate this new world with radiant smiles. The ghost dancers shout:

irihe we isarat[†]

---

[*] (loosely translated) *Crow he says / Crow he says / Now I do Now I do / Moon whence she comes Moon whence she comes*
[†] *So here now stop*

EILEEN GUNN

COMPUTER FRIENDLY

(1989)

HOLDING HER DAD'S HAND, Elizabeth went up the limestone steps to the testing center. As she climbed, she craned her neck to read the words carved in pink granite over the top of the door: FRANCIS W. PARKER SCHOOL. Above them was a banner made of gray cement that read, HEALTH, HAPPINESS, SUCCESS.

"This building is old," said Elizabeth. "It was built before the war."

"Pay attention to where you're going, punkin," said her dad. "You almost ran into that lady there."

Inside, the entrance hall was dark and cool. A dim yellow glow came through the shades on the tall windows.

As Elizabeth walked across the polished floor, her footsteps echoed lightly down the corridors that led off to either side. She and her father went down the hallway to the testing room. An old, beat-up, army-green query box sat on a table outside the door.

"Ratherford, Elizabeth Ratherford," said her father to the box. "Age seven, computer-friendly, smart as a whip."

"We'll see," said the box with a chuckle. It had a gruff, teasing, grandfatherly voice. "We'll just see about *that*, young lady." What a jolly interface, thought Elizabeth. She watched as the classroom door swung open. "You go right along in there, and we'll see just how smart you are." It chuckled again, then it spoke to Elizabeth's dad. "You come back for her at three, sir. She'll be all ready and waiting for you, bright as a little watermelon."

This was going to be fun, thought Elizabeth. Nothing to do all day except show how smart she was.

Her father knelt in front of her and smoothed her hair back from her face. "You try real hard on these tests, punkin. You show them just how talented and clever you really are, okay?" Elizabeth nodded. "And you be on your best behavior." He gave her a hug and a pat on the rear.

Inside the testing room were dozens of other seven-year-olds, sitting in rows of tiny chairs with access boxes in front of them. Glancing around the room, Elizabeth realized that she had never seen so many children together all at once. There were only ten in her weekly socialization class. It was sort of overwhelming.

The monitors called everyone to attention and told them to put on their headsets and ask their boxes for Section One.

Elizabeth followed directions, and she found that all the interfaces were strange—they were friendly enough, but none of them were the programs she worked with at home. The first part of the test was the multiple-choice exam. The problems, at least, were familiar to Elizabeth— she'd practiced for this test all her life, it seemed. There were word games, number games, and games in which she had to rotate little boxes in her head. She knew enough to skip the hardest until she'd worked her way through the whole test. There were only a couple of problems left to do when the system told her to stop and the box went all gray.

The monitors led the whole room full of kids in jumping-jack exercises for five minutes. Then everyone sat down again and a new test came up in the box. This one seemed very easy, but it wasn't one she'd ever done before. It consisted of a series of very detailed pictures; she was supposed to make up a story about each picture. Well, she could do that. The first picture showed a child and a lot of different kinds of animals. "Once upon a time there was a little girl who lived all alone in the forest with her friends the skunk, the wolf, the bear, and the lion. . . ." A beep sounded every so often to tell her to end one story and begin another. Elizabeth really enjoyed telling the stories, and was sorry when that part of the test was over.

But the next exercise was almost as interesting. She was to read a series of short stories and answer questions about them. Not the usual questions about what happened in the story— these were harder. "Is it fair to punish a starving cat for stealing?" "Should people do good deeds

for strangers?" "Why is it important for everyone to learn to obey?"

When this part was over, the monitors took the class down the hall to the big cafeteria, where there were lots of other seven-year-olds, who had been taking tests in other rooms.

Elizabeth was amazed at the number and variety of children in the cafeteria. She watched them as she stood in line for her milk and sandwich. Hundreds of kids, all exactly as old as she was. Tall and skinny, little and fat; curly hair, straight hair, and hair that was frizzy or held up with ribbons or cut into strange patterns against the scalp; skin that was light brown like Elizabeth's, chocolate brown, almost black, pale pink, freckled, and all the colors in between. Some of the kids were all dressed up in fancy clothes; others were wearing patched pants and old shirts.

When she got her snack, Elizabeth's first thought was to find someone who looked like herself, and sit next to her. But then a freckled boy with dark, nappy hair smiled at her in a very friendly way. He looked at her feet and nodded. "Nice shoes," he said. She sat down on the empty seat next to him, suddenly aware of her red Mary Janes with the embroidered flowers. She was pleased that they had been noticed, and a little embarrassed.

"Let me see *your* shoes," she said, unwrapping her sandwich.

He stuck his feet out. He was wearing pink plastic sneakers with hologram pictures of a missile gantry on the toes. When he moved his feet, they launched a defensive counterattack.

"Oh, neat." Elizabeth nodded appreciatively and took a bite of the sandwich. It was filled with something yellow that tasted okay.

A little tiny girl with long, straight, black hair was sitting on the other side of the table from them. She put one foot up on the table. "I got shoes, too," she said. "Look." Her shoes were black patent, with straps. Elizabeth and the freckled boy both admired them politely. Elizabeth thought that the little girl was very daring to put her shoe right up on the table. It was certainly an interesting way to enter a conversation.

"My name is Sheena and I can spit," said the little girl. "Watch." Sure enough, she could spit really well. The spit hit the beige wall several meters away, just under the mirror, and slid slowly down.

"I can spit, too," said the freckled boy. He demonstrated, hitting the wall a little lower than Sheena had.

"I can *learn* to spit," said Elizabeth.

"All right there, no spitting!" said a monitor firmly. "Now, you take a napkin and clean that up." It pointed to Elizabeth.

"She didn't do it, I did," said Sheena. "I'll clean it up."

"I'll help," said Elizabeth. She didn't want to claim credit for Sheena's spitting ability, but she liked being mistaken for a really good spitter.

The monitor watched as they wiped the wall, then took their thumbprints. "You three settle down now. I don't want any more spitting." It moved away. All three of them were quiet for a few minutes, and munched on their sandwiches.

"What's your name?" said Sheena suddenly. "My name is Sheena."

"Elizabeth."

"Lizardbreath. That's a funny name," said Sheena.

"My name is Oginga," said the freckled boy.

"That's *really* a funny name," said Sheena.

"You think everybody's name is funny," said Oginga. "Sheena-Teena-Peena."

"I can tap dance, too," said Sheena, who had recognized that it was time to change the subject. "These are my tap shoes." She squirmed around to wave her feet in the air briefly, then swung them back under the table.

She moves more than anyone I've ever seen, thought Elizabeth.

"Wanna see me shuffle off to Buffalo?" asked Sheena.

A bell rang at the front of the room, and the three of them looked up. A monitor was speaking.

"Quiet! Everybody quiet, now! Finish up your lunch quickly, those of you who are still eating, and put your wrappers in the wastebaskets against the wall. Then line up on the west side of the room. The *west* side . . ."

The children were taken to the restroom after lunch. It was grander than any bathroom Elizabeth had ever seen, with walls made of polished red granite, lots of little stalls with toilets in them, and a whole row of sinks. The sinks were lower than the sink at home, and so were the toilets. Even the mirrors were just the right height for kids.

It was funny because there were no stoppers in the sinks, so you couldn't wash your hands in a proper sink of water. Sheena said she could make the sink fill up, and Oginga dared her to do it, so she took off her sweater and put it in the sink, and sure enough, it filled up with water and started to overflow, and then she couldn't get the sweater out of it, so she called a monitor over. "This sink is overflowing," she said, as if it were all the sink's fault. A group of children stood around and watched while the monitor fished the sweater from the drain and wrung it out.

"That's mine!" said Sheena, as if she had dropped it by mistake. She grabbed it away from the monitor, shook it, and nodded knowingly to Elizabeth. "It dries real fast." The monitor wanted thumbprints from Sheena and Elizabeth and everyone who watched.

The monitors then took the children to the auditorium, and led the whole group in singing songs and playing games, which Elizabeth found only moderately interesting. She would have preferred to learn to spit. At one o'clock, a monitor announced it was time to go back to the classrooms, and all the children should line up by the door.

Elizabeth and Sheena and Oginga pushed into the same line together. There were so many kids that there was a long wait while they all lined up and the monitors moved up and down the lines to make them straight.

"Are you going to go to the Asia Center?"

asked Sheena. "My mom says I can probably go to the Asia Center tomorrow, because I'm so fidgety."

Elizabeth didn't know what the Asia Center was, but she didn't want to look stupid. "I don't know. I'll have to ask my dad." She turned to Oginga, who was behind her. "Are you going to the Asia Center?"

"What's the Asia Center?" asked Oginga.

Elizabeth looked back at Sheena, waiting to hear her answer.

"Where we go to sleep," Sheena said. "My mom says it doesn't hurt."

"I got my own room," said Oginga.

"It's not like your room," Sheena explained. "You go there, and you go to sleep, and your parents get to try again."

"What do they try?" asked Elizabeth. "Why do you have to go to sleep?"

"You go to sleep so they have some peace and quiet," said Sheena. "So you're not in their way."

"But what do they try?" repeated Elizabeth.

"I bet they try more of that stuff that they do when they think you're asleep," said Oginga. Sheena snorted and started to giggle, and then Oginga started to giggle and he snorted too, and the more one giggled and snorted, the more the other did. Pretty soon Elizabeth was giggling too, and the three of them were helplessly choking, behind great hiccoughing gulps of noise.

The monitor rolled by then and told them to be quiet and move on to their assigned classrooms. That broke the spell of their giggling, and, subdued, they moved ahead in the line. All the children filed quietly out of the auditorium and walked slowly down the halls. When Elizabeth came to her classroom, she shrugged her shoulders at Oginga and Sheena and jerked her head to one side. "I go in here," she whispered.

"See ya at the Asia Center," said Sheena.

The rest of the tests went by quickly, though Elizabeth didn't think they were as much fun as in the morning. The afternoon tests were more physical; she pulled at joysticks and tried to

push buttons quickly on command. They tested her hearing and even made her sing to the computer. Elizabeth didn't like to do things fast, and she didn't like to sing.

When it was over, the monitors told the children they could go now, their parents were waiting for them at the front of the school. Elizabeth looked for Oginga and Sheena as she left, but children from the other classrooms were not in the halls. Her dad was waiting for her out front, as he had said he would be.

Elizabeth called to him to get his attention. He had just come off work, and she knew he would be sort of confused. They wiped their secrets out of his brain before he logged off the system, and sometimes they took a little other stuff with it by mistake, so he might not be too sure about his name, or where he lived.

On the way home, she told him about her new friends. "They don't sound as though they would do very well at their lessons, princess," said her father. "But it does sound as if you had an interesting time at lunch." Elizabeth pulled his hand to guide him onto the right street. He'd be okay in an hour or so—anything important usually came back pretty fast.

When they got home, her dad went into the kitchen to start dinner, and Elizabeth played with her dog, Brownie. Brownie didn't live with them anymore, because his brain was being used to help control data traffic in the network. Between rush hours, Elizabeth would call him up on the system and run simulations in which she plotted the trajectory of a ball and he plotted an interception of it.

They ate dinner when her mom logged off work. Elizabeth's parents believed it was very important for the family to all eat together in the evening, and her mom had custom-made connectors that stretched all the way into the dining room. Even though she didn't really eat anymore, her local I/O was always extended to the table at dinnertime.

After dinner, Elizabeth got ready for bed. She could hear her father in his office, asking his mail for the results of her test that day. When he came into her room to tuck her in, she could tell he had good news for her.

"Did you wash behind your ears, punkin?" he asked. Elizabeth figured that this was a ritual question, since she was unaware that washing behind her ears was more useful than washing anywhere else.

She gave the correct response: "Yes, Daddy." She understood that, whether she washed or not, giving the expected answer was an important part of the ritual. Now it was her turn to ask a question. "Did you get the results of my tests, Daddy?"

"We sure did, princess," her father replied. "You did very well on them."

Elizabeth was pleased, but not too surprised. "What about my new friends, Daddy? How did they do?"

"I don't know about that, punkin. They don't send us everybody's scores, just yours."

"I want to be with them when I go to the Asia Center."

Elizabeth could tell by the look on her father's face that she'd said something wrong. "The what? Where did you hear about that?" he asked sharply.

"My friend Sheena told me about it. She said she was going to the Asia Center tomorrow," said Elizabeth.

"Well, *she* might be going there, but that's not anyplace *you're* going." Her dad sounded very strict. "You're going to continue your studies, young lady, and someday you'll be an important executive like your mother. That's clear from your test results. I don't want to hear any talk about you doing anything else. Or about this Sheena."

"What does Mommy do, Daddy?"

"She's a processing center, sweetheart, that talks directly to the CPU. She uses her brain to control important information and tell the rest of the computer what to do. And she gives the whole system common sense." He sat down on the edge of the bed, and Elizabeth could tell

that she was going to get what her dad called an "explanatory chat."

"You did so well on your test that maybe it's time we told you something about what you might be doing when you get a little older." He pulled the blanket up a little bit closer to her chin and turned the sheet down evenly over it.

"It'll be a lot like studying, or like taking that test today," he continued. "Except you'll be hardwired into the network, just like your mom, so you won't have to get up and move around. You'll be able to do anything and go anywhere in your head."

"Will I be able to play with Brownie?"

"Of course, sweetheart, you'll be able to call him up just like you did tonight. It's important that you play. It keeps you healthy and alert, and it's good for Brownie, too."

"Will I be able to call you and Mommy?"

"Well, princess, that depends on what kind of job you're doing. You just might be so busy and important that you don't have time to call us."

Like Bobby, she thought. Her parents didn't talk much about her brother Bobby. He had done well on his tests, too. Now he was a milintel cyborg with go–nogo authority. He never called home, and her parents didn't call him, either.

"Being an executive is sort of like playing games all the time," her father added, when Elizabeth didn't say anything. "And the harder you work right now, the better you do on your tests, the more fun you'll have later."

He tucked the covers up around her neck again. "Now you go to sleep, so you can work your best tomorrow, okay, princess?" Elizabeth nodded. Her dad kissed her goodnight and poked at the covers again. He got up. "Goodnight, sweetheart," he said, and he left the room.

Elizabeth lay in bed for a while, trying to get to sleep. The door was open so that the light would come in from the hall, and she could hear her parents talking downstairs.

Her dad, she knew, would be reading the news at his access box, as he did every evening. Her mom would be tidying up noise-damaged data in the household module. She didn't have to do that, but she said it calmed her nerves.

Listening to the rise and fall of their voices, she heard her name. What were they saying? Was it about the test? She got up out of bed, crept to the door of her room. They stopped talking. Could they hear her? She was very quiet. Standing in the doorway, she was only a meter from the railing at the top of the staircase, and the sounds came up very clearly from the living room below.

"Just the house settling," said her father, after a moment. "She's asleep by now." Ice cubes clinked in a glass.

"Well," said her mother, resuming the conversation, "I don't know what they think they're doing, putting euthanasable children in the testing center with children like Elizabeth." There was a bit of a whine behind her mother's voice. Perhaps rf interference. "Just talking with that Sheena could skew her test results for years. I have half a mind to call the net executive and ask it what it thinks it's doing."

"Now, calm down, honey," said her dad. Elizabeth heard his chair squeak as he turned away from his access box toward the console that housed her mother. "You don't want the exec to think we're questioning its judgment. Maybe this was part of the test."

"Well, you'd think they'd let us know, so we could prepare her for it."

Was Sheena part of the test, wondered Elizabeth. She'd have to ask the system what "euthanasable" meant.

"Look at her scores," said her father. "She did much better than the first two on verbal skills—her programs are on the right track there. And her physical aptitude scores are even lower than Bobby's."

"That's a blessing," said her mother. "It held Christopher back, right from the beginning, being so active." Who's Christopher? wondered Elizabeth.

Her mother continued. "But it was a mistake, putting him in with the euthana—"

"Her socialization scores were okay, but right on the edge," added her dad, talking right over her mother. "Maybe they should reduce her class time to twice a month. Look at how she sat right down with those children at lunch."

"Anyway, she passed," said her mother. "They're moving her up a level instead of taking her now."

"Maybe because she didn't initiate the contact, but she was able to handle it when it occurred. Maybe that's what they want for the execs."

Elizabeth shifted her weight, and the floor squeaked again.

Her father called up to her, "Elizabeth, are you up?"

"Just getting a drink of water, Daddy." She walked to the bathroom and drew a glass of water from the tap. She drank a little and poured the rest down the drain.

Then she went back to her room and climbed into bed. Her parents were talking more quietly now, and she could hear only little bits of what they were saying.

". . . mistake about Christopher . . ." Her mother's voice.

". . . that other little girl to sleep forever? . . ." Her dad.

". . . worth it? . . . ." Her mother again.

Their voices slowed down and fell away, and Elizabeth dreamed of eerie white things in glass jars, of Brownie, still a dog, all furry and fetching a ball, and of Sheena, wearing a sparkly costume and tap-dancing very fast. She fanned her hands out to her sides and turned around in a circle, tapping faster and faster.

Then Sheena began to run down like a windup toy. She went limp and dropped to the floor. Brownie sniffed at her and the white things in the jars watched. Elizabeth was afraid, but she didn't know why. She grabbed Sheena's shoulders and tried to rouse her.

"Don't let me fall asleep," Sheena murmured, but she dozed off even as Elizabeth shook her.

"Wake up! Wake up!" Elizabeth's own words pulled her out of her dream. She sat up in bed. The house was quiet, except for the sound of her father snoring in the other room.

Sheena needed her help, thought Elizabeth, but she wasn't really sure why. Very quietly, she slipped out of bed. On the other side of her room, her terminal was waiting for her, humming faintly.

When she put the headset on, she saw her familiar animal friends: a gorilla, a bird, and a pig. Each was a node that enabled her to communicate with other parts of the system. Elizabeth had given them names.

Facing Sam, the crow, she called her dog. Sam transmitted the signal, and was replaced by Brownie, who was barking. That meant his brain was routing information, and she couldn't get through.

What am I doing, anyway, Elizabeth asked herself. As she thought, a window irised open in the center of her vision, and there appeared the face of a boy of about eleven or twelve. "Hey, Elizabeth, what are you doing up at this hour?" It was the sysop on duty in her sector.

"My dog was crying."

The sysop laughed. "Your dog was crying? That's the first time I've ever heard anybody say something like that." He shook his head at her.

"He was *so* crying. Even if he wasn't crying out loud, I heard him, and I came over to see what was the matter. Now he's busy and I can't get through."

The sysop stopped laughing. "Sorry. I didn't mean to make fun of you. I had a dog once, before I came here, and they took him for the system, too."

"Do you call him up?"

"Well, not anymore. I don't have time. I used to, though. He was a golden lab. . . ." Then the boy shook his head sternly and said, "But you should be in bed."

"Can't I stay until Brownie is free again? Just a few more minutes?"

"Well, maybe a couple minutes more. But then you gotta go to bed for sure. I'll be back to check. Goodnight, Elizabeth."

"Goodnight," she said, but the window had already closed.

Wow, thought Elizabeth. That worked. She had never told a really complicated lie before, and was surprised that it had gone over so well. It seemed to be mostly a matter of convincing yourself that what you said was true.

But right now, she had an important problem to solve, and she wasn't even exactly sure what it was. If she could get into the files for Sheena and Oginga, maybe she could find out what was going on. Then maybe she could change the results on their tests or move them to her socialization group or something. . . .

If she could just get through to Brownie, she knew he could help her. After a few minutes, the flood of data washed away, and the dog stopped barking. "Here, Brownie!" she called. He wagged his tail and looked happy to see her.

She told Brownie her problem, and he seemed to understand her. "Can you get it, Brownie?"

He gave a little bark, like he did when she plotted curves.

"Okay, go get it."

Brownie ran away real fast, braked to a halt, and seemed to be digging. This wasn't what he was really doing, of course, it was just the way Elizabeth's interface interpreted Brownie's brain waves. In just a few seconds, Brownie came trotting back with the records from yesterday's tests in his mouth.

But when Elizabeth examined them, her heart sank. There were four Sheenas and fifteen Ogingas. But then she looked more carefully and noticed that most of the identifying information didn't fit her Sheena and Oginga. There was only one of each that was the right height, with the right color hair.

When she read the information, she felt bad again. Oginga had done all right on the test, but they wanted to use him for routine processing right away, kind of like Brownie. Sheena, as

Elizabeth's mother had suggested, had failed the personality profile and was scheduled for the euthanasia center the next afternoon at two o'clock. There was that word again: euthanasia. Elizabeth didn't like the sound of it.

"Here, Brownie." Her dog looked up at her with a glint in his eye. "Now listen to me. We're going to play with this stuff just a little, and then I want you to take it and put it back where you got it. Okay, Brownie?"

The window irised open again and the sysop reappeared. "Elizabeth, what do you think you're doing?" he said. "You're not supposed to have access to this data."

Elizabeth thought for a minute. Then she figured she was caught red-handed, so she might as well ask for his advice. So she explained her problem, all about her new friends and how Oginga was going to be put in the system like Brownie, and Sheena was going to be taken away somewhere.

"They said she would go to the euthanasia center, and I'm not real sure what that is," said Elizabeth. "But I don't think it's good."

"Let me look it up," said the sysop. He paused for a second, then he looked worried. "They want my ID before they'll tell me what it means. I don't want to get in trouble. Forget it."

"Well, what can I do to help my friends?" she asked.

"Gee," said the sysop. "It's a tough one. The way you were doing it, they'd catch you for sure, just like I did. It looks like a little kid got at it."

I *am* a little kid, thought Elizabeth, but she didn't say anything.

I need help, she thought. But who could she go to? She turned to the sysop. "I want to talk to my brother Bobby, in milintel. Can you put me through to him?"

"I don't know," said the sysop, "but I'll ask the mailer demon." He irised shut for a second, then opened again. "The mailer demon says it's no skin off his nose, but he doesn't think you ought to."

"How come?" asked Elizabeth.

"He says it's not your brother anymore. He says you'll be sorry."

"I want to talk to him anyway," said Elizabeth.

The sysop nodded, and his window winked shut just as another irised open. An older boy who looked kind of like Elizabeth herself stared out. His tongue darted rapidly out between his lips, keeping them slightly wet. His pale eyes, unblinking, stared into hers.

"Begin," said the boy. "You have sixty seconds."

"Bobby?" said Elizabeth.

"True. Begin," said the boy.

"Bobby, um, I'm your sister Elizabeth."

The boy just looked at her, the tip of his tongue moving rapidly. She wanted to hide from him, but she couldn't pull her eyes from his. She didn't want to tell him her story, but she could feel words filling her throat. She moved new words forward, before the others could burst out.

"Log off!" she yelled. "Log off!"

She was in her bedroom, drenched in sweat, the sound of her own voice ringing in her ears. Had she actually yelled? The house was quiet, her father still snoring. She probably hadn't made any noise.

She was very scared, but she knew she had to go back in there. She hoped that her brother was gone. She waited a couple of minutes, then logged on.

Whew. Just her animals. She called the sysop, who irised on, looking nervous.

"If you want to do that again, Elizabeth, don't go through me, huh?" He shuddered.

"I'm sorry," she said. "But I can't do this by myself. Do you know anybody that can help?"

"Maybe we ought to ask Norton," said the sysop after a minute.

"Who's Norton?"

"He's this old utility I found that nobody uses much anymore," said the sysop. "He's kind of grotty, but he helps me out." He took a breath. "Hey, Norton!" he yelled, real loud. Of course, it wasn't really yelling, but that's what it seemed like to Elizabeth.

Instantly, another window irised open, and a skinny middle-aged man leaned out of the window so far that Elizabeth thought he was going to fall out, and yelled back, just as loud, "Don't bust your bellows. I can hear you."

He was wearing a striped vest over a dirty undershirt and had a squashed old porkpie hat on his head. This wasn't anyone that Elizabeth had ever seen in the system before.

The man looked at Elizabeth and jerked his head in her direction. "Who's the dwarf?"

The sysop introduced Elizabeth and explained her problem to Norton. Norton didn't look impressed. "What d'ya want me to do about it, kid?"

"Come on, Norton," said the sysop. "You can figure it out. Give us a hand."

"Jeez, kid, it's practically four o'clock in the morning. I gotta get my beauty rest, y'know. Plus, now you've got milintel involved, it's a real mess. They'll be back, sure as houses."

The sysop just looked at him. Elizabeth looked at Norton, too. She tried to look patient and helpless, because that always helped with her dad, but she really didn't know if that would work on this weird old program.

"Y'know, there ain't much that you or me can do in the system that they won't find out about, kids," said Norton.

"Isn't there somebody who can help?" asked Elizabeth.

"Well, there's the Chickenheart. There's not much that it can't do, when it wants to. We could go see the Chickenheart."

"Who's the Chickenheart?" asked Elizabeth.

"The Chickenheart's where the system began." Of course Elizabeth knew *that* story—about the networks of nerve fibers organically woven into great convoluted mats, a mammoth supercortex that had stored the original programs, before processing was distributed to satellite brains. Her own system told her the tale sometimes before her nap.

"You mean the original core is still there?"

said the sysop, surprised. "You never told me that, Norton."

"Lot of things I ain't told you, kid." Norton scratched his chest under his shirt. "Listen. If we go see the Chickenheart, and *if* it wants to help, it can figure out what to do for your friends. But you gotta know that this is a big fucking deal. The Chickenheart's a busy guy, and this ain't one-hunnert-percent safe."

"Are you sure you want to do it, Elizabeth?" asked the sysop. "I wouldn't."

"How come it's not safe?" asked Elizabeth. "Is he mean?"

"Nah," said Norton. "A little strange, maybe, not mean. But di'n't I tell you the Chickenheart's been around for a while? You know what that means? It means you got yer intermittents, you got yer problems with feedback, runaway processes, what have you. It means the Chickenheart's got a lot of frayed connections, if you get what I mean. Sometimes the old CH just goes chaotic on you." Norton smiled, showing yellow teeth. "Plus you got the chance there's someone listening in. The netexec, for instance. Now there's someone I wouldn't want to catch me up to no mischief. Nossir. Not if I was you."

"Why not?" asked Elizabeth.

"Because that's sure curtains for you, kid. The netexec don't ask no questions, he don't check to see if you maybe could be repaired. You go bye-bye and you don't come back."

Like Sheena, thought Elizabeth. "Does he listen in often?" she asked.

"Never has," said Norton. "Not yet. Don't even know the Chickenheart's there, far as I can tell. Always a first time, though."

"I want to talk to the Chickenheart," said Elizabeth, although she wasn't sure she wanted anything of the kind, after her last experience.

"You got it," said Norton. "This'll just take a second."

Suddenly all the friendly animals disappeared, and Elizabeth felt herself falling very hard and fast along a slippery blue line in the dark. The line glowed neon blue at first, then changed to fuchsia, then sulfur yellow. She knew that Norton was falling with her, but she couldn't see him. Against the dark background, his shadow moved with hers, black, and opalescent as an oil slick.

They arrived somewhere moist and warm. The Chickenheart pulsated next to them, nutrients swishing through its external tubing. It was huge, and wetly organic. Elizabeth felt slightly sick.

"Oh, turn it off, for Chrissake," said Norton, with exasperation. "It's just me and a kid."

The monstrous creature vanished, and a cartoon rabbit with impossibly tall ears and big dewy brown eyes appeared in its place. It looked at Norton, raised an eyebrow, cocked an ear in his direction, and took a huge, noisy bite out of the carrot it was holding.

"Gimme a break," said Norton.

The bunny was replaced by a tall, overweight man in his sixties wearing a rumpled white linen suit. He held a small, paddle-shaped fan, which he slowly moved back and forth. "Ah, Mr. Norton," he said. "Hot enough for you, sir?"

"We got us a problem here, Chick," said Norton. He looked over at Elizabeth and nodded. "You tell him about it, kid."

First she told him about her brother. "Nontrivial, young lady," said the Chickenheart. "Nontrivial, but easy enough to fix. Let me take care of it right now." He went rigid and quiet for a few seconds, as though frozen in time. Then he was back. "Now, then, young lady," he said. "We'll talk if you like."

So Elizabeth told the Chickenheart about Sheena and Oginga, about the testing center and the wet sweater and the monitor telling her to clean up the spit. Even though she didn't have to say a word, she told him everything, and she was sure that if he wanted to come up with a solution, he could do it.

The Chickenheart seemed surprised to hear about the euthanasia center, and especially surprised that Sheena was going to be sent there. He addressed Norton. "I know I've been out of touch, but I find this hard to believe. Mr. Norton, have you any conception of how difficult it

can be to obtain components like this? Let me investigate the situation." His face went quiet for a second, then came back. "By gad, sir, it's true," he said to Norton. "They say they're optimizing for predictability. It's a mistake, sir, let me tell you. Things are too predictable here already. Same old ideas churning around and around. A few more components like that Sheena, things might get interesting again.

"I want to look at their records." He paused for a moment, then continued talking.

"Ah, yes, yes, I want that Sheena right away, sir," he said to Norton. "An amazing character. Oginga, too—not as gonzo as the girl, but he has a brand of aggressive curiosity we can put to use, sir. And there are forty-six others with similar personality profiles scheduled for euthanasia today at two." His face went quiet again.

"What is he doing?" Elizabeth asked Norton.

"Old Chickenheart's got his hooks into everythin'," Norton replied. "He just reaches along those pathways, faster'n you can think, and does what he wants. The altered data will look like it's been there all along, and ain't nobody can prove anythin' different."

"Done and done, Mr. Norton." The Chickenheart was back.

"Thank you, Mr. Chickenheart," said Elizabeth, remembering her manners. "What's going to happen to Sheena and Oginga now?"

"Well, young lady, we're going to bring your friends right into the system, sort of like the sysop, but without, shall we say, official recognition. We'll have Mr. Norton here keep an eye on them. They'll be our little surprises, eh? Time bombs that we've planted. They can explore the system, learn what's what, what they can get away with and what they can't. Rather like I do."

"What will they do?" asked Elizabeth.

"That's a good question, my dear," said the Chickenheart. "They'll have to figure it out for themselves. Maybe they'll put together a few new solutions to some old problems, or create a few new problems to keep us on our toes. One way or the other, I'm sure they'll liven up the old homestead."

"But what about me?" asked Elizabeth.

"Well, Miss Elizabeth, what about you? Doesn't look to me as though you have any cause to worry. You passed your tests yesterday with flying colors. You can just go right on being a little girl, and some day you'll have a nice, safe job as an executive. Maybe you'll even become netexec, who knows? I wiped just a tiny bit of your brother's brain and removed all records of your call. I'll wipe your memory of this, and you'll do just fine, yes indeed."

"But my friends are in here," said Elizabeth, and she started to feel sorry for herself. "My dog, too."

"Well, then, what do you want me to do?"

"Can't you fix *my* tests?"

The Chickenheart looked at Elizabeth with surprise.

"What's this, my dear? Do you think you're a time bomb, too?"

"I can *learn* to be a time bomb," said Elizabeth with conviction. And she knew she could, whatever a time bomb was.

"I don't know," said the Chickenheart, "that anyone can learn that sort of thing. You've either got it or you don't, Miss Elizabeth."

"Call me Lizardbreath. That's my *real* name. And I can get what I want. I got away from my brother, didn't I? And I got here."

The Chickenheart raised his thin, black eyebrows. "You have a point there, my dear. Perhaps you *could* be a time bomb, after all."

"But not today," said Lizardbreath. "Today I'm gonna learn to spit."

NISI SHAWL

I WAS A TEENAGE GENETIC ENGINEER

(1989)

MY HAIR IS NOT MY OWN. My blood is not my own. My life is not my own. I am not free. I am a political prisoner on a North American game preserve.

My hair is long, fine, brittle, tangled. I comb it with despair and rainwater.

I am waiting and I am not waiting. I am resting and I am restless. Everything that I am, I am not.

I am encircled by low, stinging briars. In my youth I frolicked among them; now I merely sit.

But no, quite often I do not merely sit. I amble along the confines. Either the boundaries are patrolled or they are not. It doesn't matter at all, since I never attempt to cross them, to venture my life.

The way it is is the way it's supposed to be. I am to sit here, lorn, and when I cry rain falls, and when my tears dry and I sigh the wind speaks, and when I smile my clouds silver; the haze becomes intolerably bright, eye-scalding.

But the sun will not yet come through.

I make music. I make baskets, little ones. I make friends with the birds and rodents and insects. And I am alone, alone.

Alone. The reason that I am alone now is that I will not always be alone. Someone comes.

Someone comes; I taste his sweet steps. I am afraid. He will break the steady surface of my mirror. But he is coming. And he is coming through, and in.

From his birth, he has been coming. I saw his crowning in a magic candleflame, a candle I made to burn only once a year, for only so long. Whenever I look into that flame, I can clearly see the moves he makes in those moments. And he is approaching, swifter than years.

I am a sickle, a crow, a magpie inhabiting a land of ghosts. I scarred myself, pearl-petalled, on my brow. Yes, I marked my sorrow and strength on my face, scorning a place in the ninety-ninth percentile, those who are unmarred and perfect from conception.

How could I not? How could I turn my

back on the carelessly deformed, the purposely stunted, the play-people we were taught to raise as pets?

The will of the state automatically engenders a counter-will. The hand of the state severs itself from the arm. I was programmed to be a designer, a patterner of degraded human lifeforms.

Cruel memory. I enjoyed my vocation. I studied. I theorized. I practiced. Slowly (the process is artificially lengthened among us), I rounded. I filled out emotionally and physically, and neared the much-touted perihelion of my life's orbit: adulthood. As was traditional, I began a lengthy work which was to guarantee my place in the social exoskeleton.

In later years, my work had taken a startling turn. I was no longer content to functionally integrate the traits of lower species into my subjects. Although I still spent many hours here, in my private wild domain, I did not produce more hare men and partridge women. These had become overfamiliar. And yet, I could not bring myself to switch from the artistic mode to the utilitarian; to place my skills directly in the hands of the government. Rather than explore my distaste and come to the inevitable conclusion that all forms of genetic manipulation were exploitive, I had ranged even further in my chosen field. I had hopes that less hackneyed creations would attract financial support and laudation.

My inspirations came from old chimerical tales. Fishwomen, sealmen, winged hermaphrodites—these were common. But I invented the scaled fire-breather, the one-horned woman, the invisible man. Then I outdid myself.

I began to make gods. Cupid was first. How he tormented me until I let him go. Vulcan fell in love with me at first sight. He set up shop in the basement and refused to leave. He besought me with gifts: magic rings and wondrous, pocket-sized ships with infinite holds. I created Minerva for counsel. She advised me not to stop until I had recalled the entire pantheon, or I would be wreaking havoc due to karmic imbalances. I could not disagree with wisdom herself, so in short order they were all released upon the world—the quarrelling, autocratic, Olympian deities.

Psyche was different. Perhaps it was because I spent more time on her; I intended her to be the chief representation of my competence. The others were superhuman, were oversized projections of portions of the collective mind. But Psyche seemed to be distilled humanity, the essence.

My work on her was very subtle, and not even I fully realized the implications until she opened her incredible eyes. Her incredible blazing eyes that lit everything with too-bright truth showed me to myself as the monster that I was. I begged her for a wound to make me cry, a drop of burning oil on my face.

She refused with horror, so I snatched her knife and carved a star on my brow.

Then she laughed, and blessed me, and understood. Her shining hands healed me and set my scar glowing. She walked out, bare humble feet changing the world with every step.

I was left with the remains of my disgusting work and the clamorous activity of the gods. But before my colleagues came and found me thus, and enforced my solitude with machinations of that treacherous smith, I had time for one last toil. I made only the seed and caused it to arise in a suitable womb. I sowed the Red Doom, the Hound of the Smith, Cuchullain.

And he comes.

LEWIS SHINER

THE GENE DRAIN

(1989)

JSN REACHED UP TO THE ROW of glowing buttons across his forehead and changed his mind with an audible click.

Nothing helped. He couldn't shake the sense of disaster hovering over him like an avalanche in progress. In a last, desperate attempt to salvage his mood he worked up an autonomous search program and sent it spiraling back through his core memory.

Up on the dais the alien who identified himself as Brother Simon droned on: ". . . and, uh, we, that is, bein as how we are all brothers in Johnny, I mean, we ud, uh, really like to find us a place in yall's hearts, praise Johnny, and maybe even someplace where we could stay for a while . . ."

Somebody behind JSN said, "This is pathetic." The assembled UN delegates, representing the 2,873,261 free and independent nations of Earth, began to boo. Some stood up and shouted. Others clawed loose bits of wiring from appendages and hurled them at the dais.

Brother Simon stopped talking and the seven aliens sat quietly and took the abuse. They were nominally humanoid, but hideously pale, fleshy, thick-bodied, and slow. One or another of them constantly picked at its face or scratched the crotch of its shapeless gray clothing or spat a fat yellow glob onto the floor.

It had been a mistake to bring them to New York, JSN now realized. He'd promised the delegates alien emissaries and delivered these travesties of humanity that not only exuded unpleasant noises and odors, but committed the ultimate crime of being boring besides.

What else could he have done? He was a pop star, not a politician, and it had been plain bad luck that their crude shuttle had landed on his estate.

The aliens had been following, as far as JSN could make out, a primitive TV broadcast back to its source. It had come from a city called Killville or something—reflexively JSN pulled the data—Lynchburg, that was it. Back in the twentieth century it had been a center for some kind of religious propaganda, and apparently the aliens had learned their harsh and unpleasant English from what they'd intercepted. What had been Lynchburg was now no more than a few burned and abandoned hillsides on the edge of JSN's land.

From what they'd managed to stammer out, JSN understood they were the advance front for an entire orbiting mothership, full of hundreds more just like them: the misshapen, brain-damaged refuse of some galactic civilization. He'd hidden their shuttle in a disused barn, hoping the stench of the place would help cover that of the aliens. Then he tried to get hold of LNR, the Duchess of the local corporation. Unfortunately she was in for a new prosthesis and JSN had been forced to handle the situation himself.

Well, he'd handled it and he'd blown it. He'd just have to admit it and get the aliens offstage before the other delegates rioted. He stood up, fought his way to the front, then noticed a buzzing in his mastoid. His program was finished. Holding a finger up to the crowd, he punched in the results.

"Holy shit," he whispered as the data started to roll. He had forgotten about the microphones and cameras and naked eyes and ears that were all focused on him. "Holy shit," he said again. "They're us!"

• • •

The three of them met for a council of war at JSN's country house: JSN, LNR, and a man named DNS who was LNR's top advisor. JSN found DNS in the foyer, admiring a piece of taxidermy. "They were called cows," DNS said. "People used to eat them and wear their skins."

JSN glanced back at LNR. "I think JSN knows that," she said. "It is his cow."

"Maybe we'd be more comfortable in the study," JSN offered.

"A very rich protein source, beef," DNS said. He was short, heavy around the middle, and had more prosthetics than JSN had ever seen on one person before, all of them dented, discolored, and hopelessly out of date. "Gave people a lot of spunk."

"Not to mention arteriosclerosis and cancer," JSN said, waving his arm at the open door. DNS reluctantly went in.

"So," LNR said, settling at one end of an antique sofa. "We're going to have to do something. If anybody finds out where they are, they're liable to mob the place and tear them to pieces."

"I know," JSN said. "There's nothing people hate worse than bad video. Especially when it's live. I'm really sorry."

"Don't worry about it," LNR said graciously. "It's partly my fault, after all. If I hadn't been in surgery . . ." She held up a gleaming new hand. "Do you like it, by the way?"

"Very much," JSN said. He had seen her a couple of times before at state parties or concerts, but never had a chance to talk to her. Now he found himself quite infatuated. Her skull was sleek and hairless, her prosthetic arm and leg—on opposite sides, of course—were polished beryllium alloy, perfect complements to her skeletally thin naturals. Two bright neon'd veins ran up her neck for a splash of color. I'd sure like to network with that, he thought crudely.

"It still has a few bugs in the flexors," LNR said, "but on the whole . . ."

"Very nice," JSN said.

"Anyway. You say this mother ship was launched in the twentieth century, the computer malfunctioned and took them in a big circle and landed back here on Earth, thinking it was a new planet."

"It is a new planet as far as they're concerned," DNS interrupted. "I mean, can you imagine what we look like to them?"

"Shut up, DNS," LNR said. "Meanwhile, the crew just sort of backslid a few generations, evolutionarily speaking, what with the small gene pool and all. Is that pretty much the gist of it?"

"I found records of the launching, and some

distress signals. That seems to be what it all points to."

"So how come nobody remembered any of this?"

She patted the back of the sofa and JSN sat down next to her.

"No reason they should," JSN said. "I mean, did they look that human to you?"

"I don't think they look that bad," DNS said.

"Shut up, DNS," LNR said, and turned back to JSN. "I see what you mean."

"This was a couple hundred years ago, after all. Data like that isn't going to be in anybody's volatile memory. It's going to be banked. Unless somebody had a reason to think they weren't aliens, who would go looking for it?"

"But you thought of it," LNR said.

Was that admiration in her tone? JSN brushed casually at his forehead and punched up a little extra charm. "Oh no," he said, "it was just an accident. Really. In fact I was looking for, well, something to use against them."

"You mean," LNR said, "like a, a weapon?" The tip of her tongue just touched her silvered lips. "How twisted." She crossed her beryllium leg over her natural with a flash of light so intense that JSN momentarily blinked his mirrored contacts into place.

"We have to do something," he said. "If we knocked out that mother ship we wouldn't have to keep confronting the fact that we share the same genetics with those . . . animals."

"I know what you mean," LNR said, "but it's just bound to give somebody the wrong impression. Suppose we set them up their own country, maybe someplace like Antarctica?"

"I'm not sure even that would be isolated enough. On top of everything else they seem to have some sort of weird messianic religion, and you know you can't trust people like that. They'd be starting wars and pogroms and handing out literature door-to-door as soon as we turned our backs on them."

"Why are you so hostile?" DNS asked. He'd been walking around the library, touching things, and now he'd gone into a higher gear.

Sweat had started to soak through his clothes and he kept rubbing his hands on his kilt, even though there was virtually no exposed skin left on them. "They're not so unpleasant. And I find their women somewhat . . . er . . . attractive. I've always said, we shouldn't be so quick to jettison our own history."

"You've always said that," LNR said tiredly.

"History?" JSN said. "Who cares about history? That's the wrong direction."

"This is living history," DNS said, pacing frenetically. "That's not just a gene pool up on that ship, it's a gene bank." He began to snatch bits of paper off the desk and tables, shred them compulsively with his fingers, and stuff them into his recycler. "Vigorous, healthy genes, not the feeble leftovers we've got. Those people are everything we're not: natural, in touch with themselves—"

"Brainless," JSN said, "malodorous—"

"Try to see it my way," DNS said, and JSN obligingly punched up a less hostile persona. "We've let technology take over completely from nature. Less than one percent of our population would be viable without some kind of hardware support."

He should know, JSN thought, nodding. The man was only intermittently flesh.

"And the technology that's holding it all together is shoddy!" DNS went on. "Over ninety percent of the manufactured goods in the world are defective! Ninety percent! And that's just the stuff that makes it through the QC checks at the factories!"

"Still," JSN said, as kindly as possible, "I don't think I'd care to have any of those devolved genetics in my hatchery."

"And that's another thing. Even our reproduction is dependent on technology. Do you know what the birthrate is? It's point-two of the mortality rate, and falling!"

"So what?" JSN shrugged amiably. "If we need more kids we can always decant them."

"No! We have to go back to the old ways before it's too late!"

"DNS," said LNR firmly, "shut up." To JSN

she said, "You have to forgive him. He had an implant accident when he was a kid and blew out most of his frontal lobe. Hasn't trusted technology since. Those who need it the most like it the least, eh?"

"You think I'm crazy," DNS said, "but you'll see. If only we could get sex and procreation linked again—"

"You'd have a world," JSN said, reverting to his former aggressive self at the touch of a button, "that I wouldn't much want to live in. LNR, would you care to go watch some video and talk about this some more and maybe fuck?"

"Sounds heavy," she said, and JSN led her to the door.

"You'll be sorry," DNS warned, and JSN cheerfully shut him in the library.

• • •

The orgone generator refused to come up to speed and for a few helpless, frustrated moments JSN wondered if DNS had been right. Nothing seemed to work anymore. Then LNR found a way to patch around it and JSN became promptly and thoroughly distracted.

A little less than an hour later a shrill alarm interrupted them. "Shit," JSN said, yanking cables out of various orifices. "I knew I shouldn't have left him alone."

"Here." LNR unwrapped something from his left leg so he could hobble over to a monitor. "Is it DNS?"

"Yeah," JSN said. "He found the barn where I stashed the shuttle."

"And the weirdos too?"

"Yeah. That guy seems like a real jerk. What do you keep him around for?"

"Well, you don't want an advisor who's just going to agree with you all the time. He's definitely got his own ideas."

That seemed reasonable to JSN. "I'd better get out there. He's liable to bring the whole world down on us." He started putting on his shirt.

"I'll come too," LNR said. "After all, I

brought him into this." She had her shoes on and was ready to go; her black outfit, JSN had discovered to his vast pleasure, was a mutant cell strain and a living part of her body.

JSN hurried into the rest of his clothes and led the way outside.

The night was clear and hot. Cyborg mowers had cut the fields that afternoon and the smell of battered grass filled the air. JSN stopped for a moment and scanned the star patterns.

"There," he said, pointing to a bright spot in Capricorn, near the eastern horizon. "The mother ship."

"It must be huge," LNR said, and JSN nodded. "And to think it's just crawling with devos. It's enough to give you a head crash."

JSN slipped quietly through the oversized barn door, noticing that the lingering odor of livestock had been routed by the more potent essence of the devos. In the dim parking lights of the shuttle he saw Brother Simon and all six of the others standing in a circle around the sweating DNS.

"DNS!" he shouted, being careful to breathe through his mouth. "What the fuck are you doing here?"

DNS flinched in obvious guilt, then recovered. "I'm a doctor," he said indignantly. "These people need proper medical attention. What do you think they are, zoo specimens?"

JSN turned to LNR, who had come in after him. "Is he a doctor?"

"I don't know," she said. "I think maybe he put a chip in for it once."

"If that's all you're doing," JSN said, "why did you think you had to sneak in?"

"I assumed you had something else on your mind."

"Look," JSN said to the devo nearest him, a heavyset female with huge, drooping breasts behind the front panel of her overalls. "You don't have to put up with this guy if you don't want to."

"Yall are wastin yore time talkin to the helpmeat," Brother Simon said. The female smiled at JSN in vacant agreement. "But dont worry none. We ud be proud to talk to yore doctor fella. Mebbe we ud get a chance to share the Good News with him."

"You mean you're leaving?" LNR asked.

"Pardon?"

"Isn't that the good news?"

"I meant the Good News about our Lord and Savior, Johnny Carson."

JSN accessed his core, noticing, from her slightly uprolled eyes, that LNR was doing the same. "I don't have anything on it," he said. "You?"

"I can't tell. I think I've got some bad sectors in my religion directory."

"Sorry," JSN said to Brother Simon. "We don't have the foggiest notion what you're talking about."

"Yall aint heard the Word?"

"Is that the same as the good news?" LNR asked.

"Because if it is, no, we haven't."

"If yall wanna step inside, I ud be proud to give my witness."

"Sure," LNR said. "Why not?"

The devo took them into the shuttle. The smell in the barn was bad enough, but inside the cramped corridors of the ship it was stale, fermented, overpowering. Someone had scrawled slogans like "Smile! Johnny Loves Yall!" and "I o Johnny" on the white plastic walls in what looked and smelled like human excrement.

"I don't know how much of this I can stand," JSN confided.

"Me either," LNR said, "but it's kind of like with DNS. I can't resist a crank. Just a couple of minutes, okay?"

Brother Simon typed the letters GOOD-NEWS onto the keyboard of the shuttle's main computer, using only one finger of each hand and making a lot of mistakes. He stared at the finished word for a while, then hit the RETURN key.

A meter-square screen lit up at the front of the room and a voice boomed, "There's Good News tonight!" The blank screen dissolved into a soundstage full of furniture. A dark-haired man stumbled onto the stage, tripped, and fell noisily across the furniture, smashing several of the chairs to pieces. The camera tightened on his face and the man said, "Live! From New York! It's . . . the Gospel According to Matthew!"

The scene changed to a murky river flowing through a desert. A bearded man stood in water past his knees, his back to the camera, addressing a mob of peasants wearing towels on their heads. "I baptize you with water for repentance, but he who is coming after me is mightier than I, whose sandals I am not worthy to lick! He will baptize you with Holy Sitcoms and with celebrities! And now . . . heeeeeeere's Johnny!"

A man with short white hair waded into view from behind the camera, then turned to wink. His skin was evenly, artificially tanned, and he had the arrogant smirk of a preadolescent. He wore a twentieth-century dress suit with lapels out to the shoulders and had something orange tied around his neck. Laughter swelled to fill the soundtrack.

"Hey there!" the man said. "Have we got a great show tonight!" The river came nearly to his waist and his suit was starting to sag with water, but he didn't seem to notice. "We've got the poor in spirit [applause] for theirs is the kingdom of heaven. We've got those who mourn [more applause], fresh from Las Vegas, and believe me, they shall be comforted. We've got the meek, and right here, on tonight's show, they're going to inherit the earth, and what do you think about that? [Thunderous applause.]"

"Wow," LNR said. "This is really twisted."

JSN had pumped the entire video into a core search. "Parts of it seem to be out of the Christian bible, but it's almost beyond recognition. Hey!" he shouted to Brother Simon, who stood enraptured in front of the screen, "are you guys Christians, is that it?"

"Christians?" LNR said with alarm. "You mean like Torquemada and Henry Lee Lucas and Jerry Falwell?"

"We are Carsonagins," Brother Simon said. "We believe every Image of the Sacred Word was divinely inspired, and we live by Its Law. Johnny be praised!"

"Wait a minute," LNR said, holding up one finger to indicate incoming data. "We were looking in the wrong place. This Carson was a twentieth-century video star. Something is really wrong here. What kind of computer is this?"

"It's a Generation V," JSN said, reading the name, plate. "Uh oh. You don't mean . . ."

"Heuristic self-programming. Artificial—" she choked, unable to hold back her laughter.

"Intelligence!" JSN hooted. "No wonder!"

"Are yall mockin the Word?" Brother Simon asked. His anger seemed to be teetering on the edge of tears.

"No, no, just this fucked-up hardware," JSN said. "It must have merged all those video broadcasts into one file . . ."

". . . and then tried to make sense of it! What a disaster!"

"Now see here," Brother Simon said. "If yall cant show proper respect all hafta axe yall to leave."

"Respect?" LNR howled. "Are you kidding?"

"That's it," Brother Simon said, flapping his hands at them. "Out. Yawn yone."

LNR stared blankly at JSN. "I think he means we're on our own," he said.

LNR took his arm. "Suits me. You think we could get all those cables back the way they were?"

"Let's find out," JSN said, then hesitated. "What about DNS? We shouldn't just leave him here with these devos . . ."

"Don't worry," LNR said. "He may be stupid, but he's harmless."

．　．　．

Later that night JSN looked up to see his barn disintegrating on an overhead monitor. "Holy shit," he said.

LNR leaned backward to look. "The devos?"

JSN nodded. "And I think DNS is on board. Or fried to a cinder, one."

"Oh well. Good riddance to the lot of them. Any more amps on this thing?"

JSN twisted the dial all the way to ten.

．　．　．

JSN was shooting a fashion layout in one of his disused pastures when the devos found him. The director had just finished draping him erotically in yards of raw fiberglass when she noticed that her lead camera had dropped offline. She called for the backup and found the power switch had jammed in the OFF position. "Okay," she said. "Let's take a break."

"What about me?" JSN asked. He could barely move.

"You," the director said, "look luscious. Just stay put."

At that point the shuttle dropped out of the sky with a paralyzing roar. The film crew scattered but JSN, barely able to hop, couldn't get away. Two of the male devos grabbed him and carried him into the reeking bowels of the ship.

"Very good," said a familiar voice as JSN was hustled through the control room. "Lock him in a cabin and I'll get to him later."

"DNS, you bastard!" JSN shouted. "What are you doing?"

"Don't be obsolete!" DNS shouted back. "We're all bastards these days, remember?"

They shut JSN in a tiny cabin with a video screen that filled all of one wall. After a few seconds it lit up and showed a large twenty-one. The number slowly dissolved into a scene of the white-haired man, Johnny Carson, dressed in a circus costume and performing a trick riding act. He had one foot on a donkey and the other on a small horse, and he grinned foolishly as the two animals cantered down a dusty path littered with palm fronds.

Crowds lined both sides of the road and the camera panned them, picking up bits of conversation. "Who is this?" "This is the prophet Johnny from the Tonight Show."

Johnny rode through the high, mud-brick gateway of the city and up to the doors of the temple. There he jumped down and staggered around for a few seconds in mock drunkenness, sending the crowd into hysterical laughter. Then he walked boldly inside.

Both sides of the huge hall were lined with tables, and on the tables were stacks of videos and stereos and home computers and various kinds of brightly colored boxes. Shiny new automobiles were parked in the aisles next to large enameled appliances.

Johnny walked past all the tables, all the way to the far end of the room, turned, and spread his arms wide. He looked up and down the temple until he had everyone's attention. "And now," he said, "a word from our sponsor."

JSN sat on the floor and switched all of his available systems over to standby.

• • •

DNS was talking to him. JSN punched back up to full alertness and said, "You asshole. What are you doing with these degenerates? You're selling me out to a bunch of devolved—"

"Whoa up there now," DNS said. "We don't believe in that heathen notion of evolution."

"We?"

DNS leaned forward earnestly. "I have accepted Johnny Carson in my heart as my personal savior."

"You're brain-damaged," JSN said.

"Maybe so, but Johnny loves me just the same."

"I expect he loves you better because of it."

"None of your sarcasm, now. You're about to get the opportunity of a lifetime. I envy you. I truly do."

"Just let me out of here and I'll reformat all my memories of this. I promise."

"Oh, no. I can't let your moment of weakness keep you from your glorious destiny. You're gonna ride the wave of the future. Together my new brethren and I have seen Johnny's plan for us, and behold, it was glorious."

"Where did you get that hick accent all of a sudden?"

DNS grabbed the front of JSN's shirt. "You were the one who wanted to blow these good folk out of the sky. None of you half-metal cripples were willing to open yourselves to the Word. Nobody wanted to give them a home."

"After the UN fiasco, I must admit, the offers were not exactly pouring in."

"Well, they will be soon. We're gonna make all those Pharisees bow to the glory of Johnny. They're gonna take the old values back into their hearts: home, marriage, family, network TV."

"And whose idea was this?"

"Oh, Johnny's of course. As revealed to me in His infinite Wisdom."

"Don't be stupid," JSN said, out of patience and a little scared besides. "Maybe things are a little screwed up right now. But you're not going to fix them by hiding in the past. Wars and patriotism and bigotry aren't the answer to a little slackness in quality control—"

"Who said anything about war?" DNS said. "Any fool knows advertising is the answer. Did not Johnny welcome the sponsors into the temple? That's why you're here. You're one of the biggest pop stars on the planet. People everywhere know who you are. You start new fashions with everything you do." He eyed the remnants of JSN's fiberglass with distaste.

"So?"

"So you're going to marry one of the sistren."

"Marry a devo? No way."

"I told you I don't like that word," DNS said coolly.

"I don't care what you call yourselves. Count me out. Forget it. I wouldn't do it if you put a gun to my head."

DNS reached into his kilt and pulled out an ancient handgun. A Colt .38 caliber Python, JSN determined with a quick lookup. DNS put the mouth of the barrel against JSN's left temple.

The door oozed open and Brother Simon came in, followed by the bovine woman who had smiled at JSN in the barn. She was smiling again, glancing back and forth between JSN and her own feet, her cheeks hotly flushed.

"Your bride-to-be," DNS said.

The woman began to undress. JSN stood up, looking quickly away from the yards of quivering flesh. Brother Simon held out a black videocassette, firmly clenched in both hands. "By-the-poor-vestige-of-my-mistake-in-Virginia," he said hurriedly, apparently unable to look away from the female's chest, "aprons-on-you-husb-and-wife. Go for it. Amen."

The female stretched out on her back and raised fleshy arms toward JSN. "Here?" he said. "You expect me to fertilize her? Right here? With you watching?"

"Not just us," DNS said, "but millions more when we rebroadcast the blessed event throughout the world. Soon everyone will want a husb and/or bride of Johnny! We'll bring them down from the mother ship and spread the Good News throughout the world!"

"Amen Brother Dennis," said Brother Simon.

"No," JSN said. "I can't. I won't."

DNS pulled back the hammer of the revolver with an audible click.

Mass hysteria, JSN thought. It would pass, eventually. The world had survived it before, barely, maybe it could live through it again. In the meantime, what else could he do?

He reached a trembling hand to his forehead, found his most conciliatory personality, and smiled down at the naked woman. "Hello, darling," he said.

BRUCE STERLING

DEEP EDDY

(1993)

THE CONTINENTAL gentleman in the next beanbag offered "Zigaretten?"

"What's in it?" Deep Eddy asked. The gray-haired gentleman murmured something: polysyllabic medical German. Eddy's translation program crashed at once.

Eddy gently declined. The gentleman shook a zigarette from the pack, twisted its tip, and huffed at it. A sharp perfume arose, like coffee struck by lightning.

The elderly European brightened swiftly. He flipped open a newspad, tapped through its menu, and began alertly scanning a German business zine.

Deep Eddy killed his translation program, switched spexware, and scanned the man. The gentleman was broadcasting a business bio. His name was Peter Liebling, he was from Bremen, he was ninety years old, he was an official with a European lumber firm. His hobbies were backgammon and collecting antique phone-cards.

He looked pretty young for ninety. He probably had some unusual and interesting medical syndromes.

Herr Leibling glanced up, annoyed at Eddy's computer-assisted gaze. Eddy dropped his spex back onto their neck-chain. A practiced gesture, one Deep Eddy used a lot—*hey, didn't mean to stare, pal*. A lot of people were suspicious of spex. Most people had no real idea of the profound capacities of spexware. Most people still didn't use spex. Most people were, in a word, losers.

Eddy lurched up within his baby-blue beanbag and gazed out the aircraft window. Chattanooga, Tennessee. Bright white ceramic air-control towers, distant wine-colored office blocks, and a million dark green trees. Tarmac heated gently in the summer morning. Eddy lifted his spex again to check a silent takeoff westward by a white-and-red Asian jet. Infrared turbulence gushed from its distant engines.

Deep Eddy loved infrared. That deep silent magical whirl of invisible heat, the breath of industry.

People underestimated Chattanooga, Deep Eddy thought with a local boy's pride. Chattanooga had a very high per capita investment in spexware. In fact Chattanooga ranked third-highest in NAFTA. Number One was San Jose, California (naturally), and Number Two was Madison, Wisconsin.

Eddy had already traveled to both those rival cities, in the service of his Chattanooga users group, to swap some spexware, market a little info, and make a careful study of the local scene. To collect some competitive intelligence. To spy around, not to put too fine a point on it.

Eddy's most recent business trip had been five drunken days at a blowout All-NAFTA spexware conference in Ciudad Juárez, Chihuahua. Eddy had not yet figured out why Ciudad Juárez, a once-dreary maquiladora factory town on the Rio Grande, had gone completely hog wild for spexing. But even little kids there had spex, bright speckly throwaway kid-stuff with just a couple dozen meg. There were tottering grannies with spex. Security cops with spex mounted right into their riot helmets. Billboards everywhere that couldn't be read without spex. And thousands of hustling industry zudes with air-conditioned jackets and forty or fifty terabytes mounted right at the bridge of the nose. Ciudad Juárez was in the grip of rampant spexmania. Maybe it was all the lithium in their water.

Today, duty called Deep Eddy to Düsseldorf in Europe. Duty did not have to call very hard to get Eddy's attention. The mere whisper of duty was enough to dislodge Deep Eddy, who still lived with his parents, Bob and Lisa.

He'd gotten some spexmail and a package from the president of the local chapter. *A network obligation; our group credibility depends on you, Eddy. A delivery job. Don't let us down; do whatever it takes. And keep your eyes covered—this one could be dangerous.* Well, danger and Deep Eddy were fast friends. Throwing up tequila and ephedrine through your nose in an alley in Mexico, while wearing a pair of computer-assisted glasses worth as much as a car—now *that* was dangerous. Most people would be scared to try something like that. Most people couldn't master their own insecurities. Most people were too scared to live.

This would be Deep Eddy's first adult trip to Europe. At the age of nine he'd accompanied Bob and Lisa to Madrid for a Sexual Deliberation conference, but all he remembered from that trip was a boring weekend of bad television and incomprehensible tomato-soaked food. Düsseldorf, however, sounded like real and genuine fun. The trip was probably even worth getting up at 07:15.

Eddy dabbed at his raw eyelids with a saline-soaked wipey. Eddy was getting a first-class case of eyeball-burn off his spex; or maybe it was just sleeplessness. He'd spent a very late and highly frustrating night with his current girlfriend, Djulia. He'd dated her hoping for a hero's farewell, hinting broadly that he might be beaten or killed by sinister European underground networking mavens, but his presentation hadn't washed at all. Instead of some sustained and attentive frolic, he'd gotten only a somber four-hour lecture about the emotional center in Djulia's life: collecting Japanese glassware.

As his jet gently lifted from the Chattanooga tarmac, Deep Eddy was struck with a sudden, instinctive, gut-level conviction of Djulia's essential counterproductivity. Djulia was just no good for him. Those clear eyes, the tilted nose, the sexy sprinkle of tattoo across her right cheekbone. Lovely flare of her body-heat in darkness. The lank strands of dark hair that turned crisp and wavy halfway down their length. A girl shouldn't have such great hair and so many tats and still be so tightly wrapped up. Djulia was no real friend of his at all.

The jet climbed steadily, crossing the shining waters of the Tennessee. Outside Eddy's window, the long ductile wings bent and rippled with dainty, tightly controlled anti-turbulence. The cabin itself felt as steady as a Mississippi lumber barge, but the computer-assisted wings, under spex-analysis, resembled a vibrating saw-blade. Nerve-racking. *Let this not be the day a whole bunch of Chattanoogans fall out of the sky,* Eddy thought silently, squirming a bit in the luscious embrace of his beanbag.

He gazed about the cabin at his fellow candidates for swift mass death. Three hundred people or so, the European and NAFTA jet-bourgeoisie; well-groomed, polite. Nobody looked frightened. Sprawling there in their pastel beanbags, chatting, hooking fiber optics to palmtops and laptops, browsing through newspads, making videophone-calls. Just as if they were at home, or maybe in a very crowded cylindrical hotel lobby, all of them in blank and deliberate ignorance of the fact that they were zipping through midair supported by nothing but plasmajets and computation. Most people were so unaware. One software glitch somewhere, a missed decimal point, and those cleverly ductile wings would tear right the hell off. Sure, it didn't happen often. But it happened sometimes.

Deep Eddy wondered glumly if his own demise would even make the top of the newspad. It'd be in there all right, but probably hyper-linked five or six layers down.

The five-year-old in the beanbag behind Eddy entered a paroxysm of childish fear and glee. "My e-mail, Mom!" the kid chirped with desperate enthusiasm, bouncing up and down. "Mom! Mom, my *e-mail*! Hey Mom, get me my e-mail!"

A stew offered Eddy breakfast. He had a bowl of muesli and half-a-dozen boiled prunes. Then he broke out his travel card and ordered a mimosa. The booze didn't make him feel any more alert, though, so he ordered two more mimosas. Then he fell asleep.

• • •

Customs in Düsseldorf was awash. Summer tourists were pouring into the city like some vast migratory shoal of sardines. The people from outside Europe—from NAFTA, from the Sphere, from the South—were a tiny minority, though, compared to the vast intra-European traffic, who breezed through Customs completely unimpeded.

Uniformed inspectors were spexing the NAFTA and South baggage, presumably for guns or explosives, but their clunky government-issue spex looked a good five years out-of-date. Deep Eddy passed through the Customs chute without incident and had his passchip stamped. Passing out drunk on champagne and orange juice, then snoozing through the entire Atlantic crossing, had clearly been an excellent idea. It was 21:00 local time and Eddy felt quite alert and rested. Clearheaded. Ready for anything. Hungry.

Eddy wandered toward the icons signaling ground transport. A stocky woman in a bulky brown jacket stepped into his path. He stopped short. "Mr. Edward Dertouzas," she said.

"Right," Eddy said, dropping his bag. They stared at one another, spex to spex. "Actually, fräulein, as I'm sure you can see by my online bio, my friends call me Eddy. Deep Eddy, mostly."

"I'm not your friend, Mr. Dertouzas. I am your security escort. I'm called Sardelle today." Sardelle stooped and hefted his travel bag. Her head came about to his shoulder.

Deep Eddy's German translator, which he had restored to life, placed a yellow subtitle at the lower rim of his spex. "Sardelle," he noted. "'*Anchovy*'?"

"I don't pick the code names," Sardelle told him, irritated. "I have to use what the company gives me." She heaved her way through the crowd, jolting people aside with deft jabs of Eddy's travel bag. Sardelle wore a bulky air-conditioned brown trench coat, with multi-pocketed fawn-colored jeans and thick-soled black-and-white cop shoes. A crisp trio of small tattooed triangles outlined Sardelle's right cheek. Her hands, attractively small and dainty, were gloved in black-and-white pinstripe. She looked about thirty. No problem. He liked mature women. Maturity gave depth.

Eddy scanned her for bio data. "Sardelle," the spex read unhelpfully. Absolutely nothing else: no business, no employer, no address, no age, no interests, no hobbies, no personal ads. Europeans were rather weird about privacy. Then again, maybe Sardelle's lack of proper annotation had something to do with her business life.

Eddy looked down at his own hands, twitched bare fingers over a virtual menu in midair, and switched to some rude spexware he'd mail-ordered from Tijuana. Something of a legend in the spexing biz, X-Spex stripped people's clothing off and extrapolated the flesh beneath it in a full-color visual simulation. Sardelle, however, was so decked-out in waistbelts, holsters, and shoulder pads that the Xware was baffled. The simulation looked alarmingly bogus, her breasts and shoulders waggling like drug-addled plasticine.

"Hurry out," she suggested sternly. "I mean hurry *up*."

"Where we going? To see the Critic?"

"In time," Sardelle said. Eddy followed her through the stomping, shuffling, heaving crowd to a set of travel lockers.

"Do you really need this bag, sir?"

"What?" Eddy said. "Sure I do! It's got all my stuff in it."

"If we take it, I will have to search it carefully," Sardelle informed him patiently. "Let's place your bag in this locker, and you can retrieve it when you leave Europe." She offered him a small gray handbag with the logo of a Berlin luxury hotel. "Here are some standard travel necessities."

"They scanned my bag in Customs," Eddy said. "I'm clean, really. Customs was a walk-through."

Sardelle laughed briefly and sarcastically. "One million people coming to Düsseldorf this weekend," she said. "There will be a Wende here. And you think the Customs searched you properly? Believe me, Edward. You have not been searched properly."

"That sounds a bit menacing," Eddy said.

"A proper search takes a lot of time. Some threats to safety are tiny—things woven into clothing, glued to the skin..." Sardelle shrugged. "I like to have time. I'll pay you to have some time. Do you need money, Edward?"

"No," Eddy said, startled. "I mean, yeah. Sure I need money, who doesn't? But I have a travel card from my people. From CAPCLUG."

She glanced up sharply, aiming the spex at him. "Who is Kapklug?"

"Computer-Assisted Perception Civil Liberties Users Group," Eddy said. "Chattanooga Chapter."

"I see. The acronym in English." Sardelle frowned. "I hate all acronyms. . . . Edward, I will pay you forty ecu cash to put your bag into this locker and take this bag instead."

"Sold," Deep Eddy said. "Where's the money?"

Sardelle passed him four well-worn hologram bills. Eddy stuffed the cash in his pocket. Then he opened his own bag and retrieved an elderly hardbound book—*Crowds and Power*, by Elias Canetti. "A little light reading," he said unconvincingly.

"Let me see that book," Sardelle insisted. She leafed through the book rapidly, scanning pages with her pinstriped fingertips, flexing the covers, and checking the book's binding, presumably for inserted razors, poisoned needles, or strips of plastic explosive. "You are smuggling data," she concluded sourly, handing it back.

"That's what we live for in CAPCLUG," Eddy told her, peeking at her over his spex and winking. He slipped the book into the gray hotel bag and zipped it. Then he heaved his own bag into the travel locker, slammed the door, and removed the numbered key.

"Give me that key," Sardelle said.

"Why?"

"You might return and open the locker. If I keep the key, that security risk is much reduced."

"No way," Eddy frowned. "Forget it."

"Ten ecu," she offered.

"Mmmmph."

"Fifteen."

"Okay, have it your way." Eddy gave her the key. "Don't lose it."

Sardelle, unsmiling, put the key into a zippered sleeve pocket. "I never lose things." She opened her wallet.

Eddy nodded, pocketing a hologram ten and five singles. Very attractive currency, the ecu. The ten had a hologram of René Descartes, a very deep zude who looked impressively French and rational.

Eddy felt he was doing pretty well by this, so far. In point of fact there wasn't anything in the bag he really needed: his underwear, spare jeans, tickets, business cards, dress shirts, tie, suspenders, spare shoes, toothbrush, aspirin, instant espresso, sewing kit, and earrings. So what? It wasn't as if she'd asked him to give up his spex.

He also had a complete crush on his escort. The name Anchovy suited her—she struck him as a small canned cold fish. Eddy found this perversely attractive. In fact he found her so attractive that he was having a hard time standing still and breathing normally. He really liked the way she carried her stripe-gloved hands, deft and feminine and mysteriously European, but mostly it was her hair. Long, light reddish-brown, and meticulously braided by machine. He loved women's hair when it was machine braided. They couldn't seem to catch the fashion quite right in NAFTA. Sardelle's hair looked like a rusted mass of museum-quality chain mail, or maybe some fantastically convoluted railway intersection. Hair that really *meant business*. Not only did Sardelle have not a hair out of place, but any unkemptness was *topologically impossible*. The vision rose unbidden of running his fingers through it in the dark.

"I'm starving," he announced.

"Then we will eat," she said. They headed for the exit.

Electric taxis were trying, without much suc-cess, to staunch the spreading hemorrhage of tourists. Sardelle clawed at the air with her pin-striped fingers. Adjusting invisible spex menus. She seemed to be casting the evil eye on a nearby family group of Italians, who reacted with scarcely concealed alarm. "We can walk to a city bus stop," she told him. "It's quicker."

"Walking's quicker?"

Sardelle took off. He had to hurry to keep up. "Listen to me, Edward. If you follow my security suggestions, we will save time. If I save my time, then you will make money. If you make me work harder I will not be so generous."

"I'm easy," Eddy protested. Her cop-shoes seemed to have some kind of computational cushion built into the soles; she walked as if mounted on springs. "I'm here to meet the Cultural Critic. An audience with him. I have a delivery for him. You know that, right?"

"It's the book?"

Eddy hefted the gray hotel bag. "Yeah. . . . I'm here in Düsseldorf to deliver an old book to some European intellectual. Actually, to give the book back to him. He, like, lent the book to the CAPCLUG Steering Committee, and it's time to give it back. How tough can that job be?"

"Probably not very tough," Sardelle said calmly. "But strange things happen during a Wende."

Eddy nodded soberly. "Wendes are very interesting phenomena. CAPCLUG is studying Wendes. We might like to throw one someday."

"That's not how Wendes happen, Eddy. You don't 'throw' a Wende." Sardelle paused, considering. "A Wende throws *you*."

"So I gather," Eddy said. "I've been reading his work, you know. The Cultural Critic. It's deep work, I like it."

Sardelle was indifferent. "I'm not one of his partisans. I'm just employed to guard him." She conjured up another menu. "What kind of food do you like? Chinese? Thai? Eritrean?"

"How about German food?"

Sardelle laughed. "We Germans never eat German food. . . . There are very good Japanese cafés in Düsseldorf. Tokyo people fly here for the salmon. And the anchovies. . . ."

"You live here in Düsseldorf, Anchovy?"

"I live everywhere in Europe, Deep Eddy." Her voice fell. "Any city with a screen in front of it. . . . And they all have screens in Europe."

"Sounds fun. You want to trade some spexware?"

"No."

"You don't believe in *andwendungsoriente wissensverarbeitung*?"

She made a face. "How clever of you to learn an appropriate German phrase. Speak English, Eddy. Your accent is truly terrible."

"Thank you kindly," Eddy said.

"You can't trade wares with me, Eddy, don't be silly. I would not give my security spexware to civilian Yankee hacker-boys."

"Don't own the copyright, huh?"

"There's that, too." She shrugged, and smiled.

They were out of the airport now, walking south. Silent steady flow of electric traffic down Flughafenstraße. The twilight air smelled of little white roses. They crossed at a traffic light. The German semiotics of ads and street signs began to press with gentle culture shock at the surface of Deep Eddy's brain. Garagenhof. Spezialist für Mobil-Telefon. Bürohäusern. He put on some character-recognition ware to do translation, but the instant doubling of the words all around him only made him feel schizophrenic.

They took shelter in a lit bus kiosk, along with a pair of heavily tattooed gays toting grocery bags. A video ad built into the side of the kiosk advertised German-language e-mail editors.

As Sardelle stood patiently, in silence, Eddy examined her closely for the first time. There was something odd and indefinitely European about the line of her nose. "Let's be friends, Sardelle. I'll take off my spex if you take off your spex."

"Maybe later," she said.

Eddy laughed. "You should get to know me. I'm a fun guy."

"I already know you."

An overcrowded bus passed. Its riders had festooned the robot bus with banners and mounted a klaxon on its roof, which emitted a cacophony of rapid-fire bongo music.

"The Wende people are already hitting the buses," Sardelle noted sourly, shifting on her feet as if trampling grapes. "I hope we can get downtown."

"You've done some snooping on me, huh? Credit records and such? Was it interesting?"

Sardelle frowned. "It's my business to research records. I did nothing illegal. All by the book."

"No offense taken," Eddy said, spreading his hands. "But you must have learned I'm harmless. Let's unwrap a little."

Sardelle sighed. "I learned that you are an unmarried male, age eighteen-to-thirty-five. No steady job. No steady home. No wife, no children. Radical political leanings. Travels often. Your demographics are very high-risk."

"I'm twenty-two, to be exact." Eddy noticed that Sardelle showed no reaction to this announcement, but the two eavesdropping gays seemed quite interested. He smiled nonchalantly. "I'm here to network, that's all. Friend-of-a-friend situation. Actually, I'm pretty sure I share your client's politics. As far as I can figure his politics out."

"Politics don't matter," Sardelle said, bored and impatient. "I'm not concerned with politics. Men in your age group commit eighty percent of all violent crimes."

One of the gays spoke up suddenly, in heavily accented English. "Hey, fräulein. We also have eighty percent of the charm!"

"And ninety percent of the fun," said his companion. "It's Wende time, Yankee boy. Come with us and we'll do some crimes." He laughed.

"Das ist sehr nett von Ihnen," Eddy said politely. "But I can't. I'm with nursie."

The first gay made a witty and highly idiomatic reply in German, to the effect, apparently, that he liked boys who wore sunglasses after dark, but Eddy needed more tattoos.

Eddy, having finished reading subtitles in midair, touched the single small black circle on his cheekbone. "Don't you like my solitaire? It's rather sinister in its reticence, don't you think?"

He'd lost them; they only looked puzzled.

A bus arrived.

"This will do," Sardelle announced. She fed the bus a ticket-chip and Eddy followed her on board. The bus was crowded, but the crowd seemed gentle; mostly Euro-Japanese out for a night on the town. They took a beanbag together in the back.

It had grown quite dark now. They floated down the street with machine-guided precision and a smooth dreamlike detachment. Eddy felt the spell of travel overcome him; the basic mammalian thrill of a live creature plucked up and dropped like a supersonic ghost on the far side of the planet. Another time, another place: whatever vast set of unlikelihoods had militated against his presence here had been defeated. A Friday night in Düsseldorf, July 13, 2035. The time was 22:10. The very specificity seemed magical.

He glanced at Sardelle again, grinning gleefully, and suddenly saw her for what she was. A burdened female functionary sitting stiffly in the back of a bus.

"Where are we now, exactly?" he said.

"We are on Danzigerstraße heading south to the Áltstadt," Sardelle said. "The old town center."

"Yeah? What's there?"

"Kartoffel. Beer. Schnitzel. Things for you to eat."

The bus stopped and a crowd of stomping, shoving rowdies got on. Across the street, a trio of police were struggling with a broken traffic securicam. The cops were wearing full-body pink riot-gear. He'd heard somewhere that all European cop riot-gear was pink. The color was supposed to be calming.

"This isn't much fun for you, Sardelle, is it?"

She shrugged. "We're not the same people, Eddy. I don't know what you are bringing to the Critic, and I don't want to know." She tapped her spex back into place with one gloved finger. "But if you fail in your job, at the very worst, it might mean some grave cultural loss. Am I right?"

"I suppose so. Sure."

"But if I fail in my job, Eddy, something *real* might *actually happen*."

"Wow," Eddy said, stung.

The crush in the bus was getting oppressive. Eddy stood and offered his spot in the beanbag to a tottering old woman in spangled party gear.

Sardelle rose then too, with bad grace, and fought her way up the aisle. Eddy followed, barking his shins on the thick-soled beastie-boots of a sprawling drunk.

Sardelle stopped short to trade elbow-jabs with a Nordic kamikaze in a horned baseball cap, and Eddy stumbled into her headlong. He realized then why people seemed so eager to get out of Sardelle's way; her trench coat was of woven ceramic and was as rough as sandpaper. He lurched one-handed for a strap. "Well," he puffed at Sardelle, swaying into her spex-to-spex, "if we can't enjoy each other's company, why not get this over with? Let me do my errand. Then I'll get right into your hair." He paused, shocked. "I mean, *out* of your hair. Sorry."

She hadn't noticed. "You'll do your errand," she said, clinging to her strap. They were so close that he could feel a chill air-conditioned breeze whiffling out of her trench coat's collar. "But on my terms. My time, my circumstances." She wouldn't meet his eyes; her head darted around as if from grave embarrassment. Eddy realized suddenly that she was methodically scanning the face of every stranger in the bus.

She spared him a quick, distracted smile. "Don't mind me, Eddy. Be a good boy and have fun in Düsseldorf. Just let me do my job, okay?"

"Okay then," Eddy muttered. "Really, I'm delighted to be in your hands." He couldn't seem to stop with the double entendres. They rose to his lips like drool from the id.

The glowing grids of Düsseldorf high-rises shone outside the bus windows, patchy waffles of mystery. So many human lives behind those windows. People he would never meet, never see. Pity he still couldn't afford proper telephotos.

Eddy cleared his throat. "What's he doing out there right now? The Cultural Critic, I mean."

"Meeting contacts in a safe house. He will meet a great many people during the Wende. That's his business, you know. You're only one of many that he bringed—brought—to this rendezvous." Sardelle paused. "Though in threat potential you do rank among the top five."

The bus made more stops. People piled in headlong, with a thrash and a heave and a jacking of kneecaps. Inside the bus they were all becoming anchovies. A smothered fistfight broke out in the back. A drunken woman tried, with mixed success, to vomit out the window. Sardelle held her position grimly through several stops, then finally fought her way to the door.

The bus pulled to a stop and a sudden rush of massed bodies propelled them out.

They'd arrived by a long suspension bridge over a broad moon-silvered river. The bridge's soaring cables were lit end-to-end with winking party bulbs. All along the bridge, fleamarketeers sitting cross-legged on glowing mats were doing a brisk trade in tourist junk. Out in the center, a busking juggler with smart gloves flung lit torches in flaming arcs three stories high.

"Jesus, what a beautiful river," Eddy said.

"It's the Rhine. This is Oberkasseler Bridge."

"The Rhine. Of course, of course. I've never seen the Rhine before. Is it safe to drink?"

"Of course. Europe's very civilized."

"I thought so. It even smells good. Let's go drink some of it."

The banks were lined with municipal gardens: grape-musky vineyards, big pale meticulous flowerbeds. Tireless gardening robots had worked them over season by season with surgical trowels. Eddy stooped by the riverbank and scooped up a double handful of backwash from a passing hydrofoil. He saw his own spex-clad face in the moony puddle of his hands. As Sardelle watched, he sipped a bit and flung the rest out as libation to the spirit of place.

"I'm happy now," he said. "Now I'm really here."

• • •

By midnight, he'd had four beers, two schnitzels, and a platter of kartoffels. Kartoffels were fried potato-batter waffles with a side of applesauce. Eddy's morale had soared from the moment he first bit one.

They sat at a sidewalk café table in the midst of a centuries-old pedestrian street in the Áltstadt. The entire street was a single block-long bar, all chairs, umbrellas, and cobbles, peaked-roof town houses with ivy and window boxes and ancient copper weathervanes. It had been invaded by an absolute throng of gawking, shuffling, hooting foreigners.

The gentle, kindly, rather bewildered Düsseldorfers were doing their level best to placate their guests and relieve them of any excess cash. A strong pink police presence was keeping good order. He'd seen two zudes in horned baseball caps briskly hauled into a paddy wagon—a "Pink Minna"—but the Vikings were pig-drunk and had it coming, and the crowd seemed very good-humored.

"I don't see what the big deal is with these Wendes," Deep Eddy said, polishing his spex on a square of oiled and lint-free polysilk. "This sucker's a walk-through. There's not gonna be any trouble here. Just look how calm and mellow these zudes are."

"There's trouble already," Sardelle said. "It's just not here in Áltstadt in front of your nose."

"Yeah?"

"There are big gangs of arsonists across the river tonight. They're barricading streets in Neuss, toppling cars, and setting them on fire."

"How come?"

Sardelle shrugged. "They are anti-car activists. They demand pedestrian rights and more mass transit. . . ." She paused a bit to read the inside of her spex. "Green radicals are storming the Lobbecke Museum. They want all extinct insect specimens surrendered for cloning. . . . Heinrich Heine University is on strike for academic freedom, and someone has glue-bombed the big traffic tunnel beneath the campus. . . . But this is nothing, not yet. Tomorrow England meets Ireland in the soccer finals at Rhein-Stadium. There will be hell to pay."

"Huh. That sounds pretty bad."

"Yes." She smiled. "So let's enjoy our time here, Eddy. Idleness is sweet. Even on the edge of dirty chaos."

"But none of those events by itself sounds all that threatening or serious."

"Not each thing by itself, Eddy, no. But it all happens all at once. That's what a Wende is like."

"I don't get it," Eddy said. He put his spex back on and lit the menu from within, with a finger snap. He tapped the spex menu-bar with his right fingertip and light-amplifiers kicked in. The passing crowd, their outlines shimmering slightly from computational effects, seemed to be strolling through an overlit stage set. "I guess there's trouble coming from all these outsiders," Eddy said, "but the Germans themselves seem so . . . well . . . so good-natured and tidy and civilized. Why do they even have Wendes?"

"It's not something we plan, Eddy. It's just something that happens to us." Sardelle sipped her coffee.

"How could this happen and not be planned?"

"Well, we knew it was coming, of course. Of course we knew *that*. Word gets around. That's how Wendes start." She straightened her napkin. "You can ask the Critic, when you meet him. He talks a lot about Wendes. He knows as much as anyone, I think."

"Yeah, I've read him," Eddy said. "He says that it's rumor, boosted by electronic and digital media, in a feedback loop with crowd dynamics and modern mass transportation. A nonlinear networking phenomenon. That much I understand! But then he quotes some zude named Elias Canetti . . ." Eddy patted the gray bag. "I tried to read Canetti, I really did, but he's twentieth-century, and as boring and stuffy as hell. . . . Anyway, we'd handle things differently in Chattanooga."

"People say that, until they have their first Wende," Sardelle said. "Then it's all different. Once you know a Wende can actually happen to you . . . well, it changes everything."

"We'd take steps to stop it, that's all. Take steps to control it. Can't you people take some steps?"

Sardelle tugged off her pinstriped gloves and set them on the tabletop. She worked her bare fingers gently, blew on her fingertips, and picked a big bready pretzel from the basket. Eddy noticed with surprise that her gloves had big rock-hard knuckles and twitched a little all by themselves.

"There are things you can do, of course," she told him. "Put police and firefighters on overtime. Hire more private security. Disaster control for lights, traffic, power, data. Open the shelters and stock first-aid medicine. And warn the whole population. But when a city tells its people that a Wende is coming, that *guarantees* the Wende will come. . . ." Sardelle sighed. "I've worked Wendes before. But this is a big one. A big, dark one. And it won't be over, it can't be over—not until everyone knows that it's gone, and feels that it's gone."

"That doesn't make much sense."

"Talking about it won't help, Eddy. You and I, talking about it—we become part of the Wende ourselves, you see? We're here because of the Wende. We met because of the Wende. And we can't leave each other, until the Wende goes away." She shrugged. "Can you go away, Eddy?"

"No. . . . Not right now. But I've got stuff to do here."

"So does everybody else."

Eddy grunted and killed another beer. The beer here was truly something special. "It's a Chinese finger trap," he said, gesturing.

"Yes, I know those."

He grinned. "Suppose we both stop pulling? We could walk through it. Leave town. I'll throw the book in the river. Tonight you and I could fly back to Chattanooga. Together."

She laughed. "You wouldn't really do that, though."

"You don't know me after all."

"You spit in the face of your friends? And I lose my job? A high price to pay for one gesture. For a young man's pretense of free will."

"I'm not pretending, lady. Try me. I dare you."

"Then you're drunk."

"Well, there's that." He laughed. "But don't joke about liberty. Liberty's the realest thing there is." He stood up and hunted out the bathroom.

On his way back he stopped at a pay phone. He gave it fifty centimes and dialed Tennessee. Djulia answered.

"What time is it?" he said.

"Nineteen. Where are you?"

"Düsseldorf."

"Oh." She rubbed her nose. "Sounds like you're in a bar."

"Bingo."

"So what's new, Eddy?"

"I know you put a lot of stock in honesty," Eddy said. "So I thought I'd tell you I'm planning an affair. I met this German girl here and frankly, she's irresistible."

Djulia frowned darkly. "You've got a lot of nerve telling me that kind of crap with your spex on."

"Oh yeah," he said. He took them off and stared into the monitor. "Sorry."

"You're drunk, Eddy," Djulia said. "I hate it when you're drunk! You'll say and do anything, if you're drunk and on the far end of a phone line." She rubbed nervously at her newest cheek tattoo. "Is this one of your weird jokes?"

"Yeah. It is, actually. The chances are eighty to one that she'll turn me down flat." Eddy laughed. "But I'm gonna try anyway. Because you're not letting me live and breathe."

Djulia's face went stiff. "When we're face-to-face, you always abuse my trust. That's why I don't like for us to go past virching."

"Come off it, Djulia."

She was defiant. "If you think you'll be happier with some weirdo virch-whore in Europe, go ahead! I don't know why you can't do that by wire from Chattanooga, anyway."

"This is Europe. We're talking actuality here."

Djulia was shocked. "If you actually touch another woman I never want to see you again." She bit her lip. "Or do wire with you, either. I mean that, Eddy. You know I do."

"Yeah," he said. "I know."

He hung up, got change from the phone, and dialed his parents' house. His father answered.

"Hi Bob. Lisa around?"

"No," his father said, "it's her night for optic macrame. How's Europe?"

"Different."

"Nice to hear from you, Eddy. We're kind of short of money. I can spare you some sustained attention, though."

"I just dumped Djulia."

"Good move, son," his father said briskly. "Fine. Very serious girl, Djulia. Way too strait-laced for you. A kid your age should be dating girls who are absolutely jumping out of their skins."

Eddy nodded.

"You didn't lose your spex, did you?"

Eddy held them up on their neck chain. "Safe and sound."

"Hardly recognized you for a second," his father said. "Ed, you're such a serious-minded kid. Taking on all these responsibilities. On the road so much, spexware day in day out. Lisa and I network about you all the time. Neither of us did a day's work before we were thirty, and we're all the better for it. You've got to live, son. Got to find yourself. Smell the roses. If you want to stay in Europe a couple of months, forget the algebra courses."

"It's calculus, Bob."

"Whatever."

"Thanks for the good advice, Bob. I know you mean it."

"It's good news about Djulia, son. You know we don't invalidate your feelings, so we never said a goddamn thing to you, but her glassware really sucked. Lisa says she's got no goddamn aesthetics at all. That's a hell of a thing, in a woman."

"That's my mom," Eddy said. "Give Lisa my best." He hung up.

He went back out to the sidewalk table. "Did you eat enough?" Sardelle asked.

"Yeah. It was good."

"Sleepy?"

"I dunno. Maybe."

"Do you have a place to stay, Eddy? Hotel reservations?"

Eddy shrugged. "No. I don't bother, usually. What's the use? It's more fun winging it."

"Good," Sardelle nodded. "It's better to wing. No one can trace us. It's safer."

She found them shelter in a park, where an activist group of artists from Munich had set up a squatter pavilion. As squatter pavilions went, it was quite a nice one, new and in good condition: a giant soap bubble upholstered in cellophane and polysilk. It covered half an acre with crisp yellow bubblepack flooring. The shelter was illegal and therefore anonymous. Sardelle seemed quite pleased about this.

Once through the zippered airlock, Eddy and Sardelle were forced to examine the artists' multimedia artwork for an entire grueling hour. Worse yet, they were closely quizzed afterward by an expert-system, which bullied them relentlessly with arcane aesthetic dogma.

This ordeal was too high a price for most squatters. The pavilion, though attractive, was only half-full, and many people who had shown up bone-tired were fleeing the art headlong. Deep Eddy, however, almost always aced this

sort of thing. Thanks to his slick responses to the computer's quizzing, he won himself quite a nice area, with a blanket, opaquable curtains, and its own light fixtures. Sardelle, by contrast, had been bored and minimal, and had won nothing more advanced than a pillow and a patch of bubblepack among the philistines.

Eddy made good use of a traveling pay-toilet stall, and bought some mints and chilled mineral water from a robot. He settled in cozily as police sirens, and some distant, rather choked-sounding explosions, made the night glamorous.

Sardelle didn't seem anxious to leave. "May I see your hotel bag," she said.

"Sure." He handed it over. Might as well. She'd given it to him in the first place.

He'd thought she was going to examine the book again, but instead she took a small plastic packet from within the bag, and pulled the packet's ripcord. A colorful jumpsuit jumped out, with a chemical hiss and a vague hot stink of catalysis and cheap cologne. The jumpsuit, a one-piece, had comically baggy legs, frilled sleeves, and was printed all over with a festive cutup of twentieth-century naughty seaside postcards.

"Pajamas," Eddy said. "Gosh, how thoughtful."

"You can sleep in this if you want," Sardelle nodded, "but it's daywear. I want you to wear it tomorrow. And I want to buy the clothes you are wearing now, so that I can take them away for safety."

Deep Eddy was wearing a dress shirt, light jacket, American jeans, dappled stockings, and Nashville brogues of genuine blue suede. "I can't wear that crap," he protested. "Jesus, I'd look like a total loser."

"Yes," said Sardelle with an enthusiastic nod, "it's very cheap and common. It will make you invisible. Just one more party boy among thousands and thousands. This is very secure dress, for a courier during a Wende."

"You want me to meet the Critic in this getup?"

Sardelle laughed. "The Cultural Critic is not impressed by taste, Eddy. The eye he uses when he looks at people . . . He sees things others people can't see." She paused, considering. "He *might* be impressed if you showed up dressed in *this*. Not because of what it is, of course. But because it would show that you can understand and manipulate popular taste to your own advantage . . . just as he does."

"You're really being paranoid," Eddy said, nettled. "I'm not an assassin. I'm just some techie zude from Tennessee. You know that, don't you?"

"Yes, I believe you," she nodded. "You're very convincing. But that has nothing to do with proper security technique. If I take your clothes, there will be less operational risk."

"How much less risk? What do you expect to find in my clothes, anyway?"

"There are many, many things you *might* have done," she said patiently. "The human race is very ingenious. We have invented ways to kill, or hurt, or injure almost anyone, with almost nothing at all." She sighed. "If you don't know about such techniques already, it would only be stupid for me to tell you all about them. So let's be quick and simple, Eddy. It would make me happier to take your clothes away. A hundred ecu."

Eddy shook his head. "This time it's really going to cost you."

"Two hundred then," Sardelle said.

"Forget it."

"I can't go higher than two hundred. Unless you let me search your body cavities."

Eddy dropped his spex.

"Body cavities," Sardelle said impatiently. "You're a grown-up man, you must know about this. A great deal can be done with body cavities."

Eddy stared at her. "Can't I have some chocolate and roses first?"

"It's not chocolate and roses with us," Sardelle said sternly. "Don't talk to me about chocolate and roses. We're not lovers. We are cli-

ent and bodyguard. It's an ugly business, I know. But it's only business."

"Yeah? Well, trading in body cavities is new to me." Deep Eddy rubbed his chin. "As a simple Yankee youngster I find this a little confusing. Maybe we could barter them? Tonight?"

She laughed harshly. "I won't sleep with you, Eddy. I won't sleep at all! You're only being foolish." Sardelle shook her head. Suddenly she lifted a densely braided mass of hair above her right ear. "Look here, Mr. Simple Yankee Youngster. I'll show you my favorite body cavity." There was a flesh-colored plastic duct in the side of her scalp. "It's illegal to have this done in Europe. I had it done in Turkey. This morning I took half a cc through there. I won't sleep until Monday."

"Jesus," Eddy said. He lifted his spex to stare at the small dimpled orifice. "Right through the blood-brain barrier? That must be a hell of an infection risk."

"I don't do it for fun. It's not like beer and pretzels. It's just that I won't sleep now. Not until the Wende is over." She put her hair back, and sat up with a look of composure. "Then I'll fly somewhere and lie in the sun and be very still. All by myself, Eddy."

"Okay," Eddy said, feeling a weird and muddy sort of pity for her. "You can borrow my clothes and search them."

"I have to burn the clothes. Two hundred ecu?"

"All right. But I keep these shoes."

"May I look at your teeth for free? It will only take five minutes."

"Okay," he muttered. She smiled at him, and touched her spex. A bright purple light emerged from the bridge of her nose.

• • •

At 08:00 a police drone attempted to clear the park. It flew overhead, barking robotic threats in five languages. Everyone simply ignored the machine.

Around 08:30 an actual line of human police showed up. In response, a group of the squatters brought out their own bullhorn, an enormous battery-powered sonic assault-unit.

The first earthshaking shriek hit Eddy like an electric prod. He'd been lying peacefully on his bubble-mattress, listening to the doltish yap of the robot chopper. Now he leapt quickly from his crash-padding and wormed his way into the crispy bubblepack cloth of his ridiculous jumpsuit.

Sardelle showed up while he was still tacking the jumpsuit's Velcro buttons. She led him outside the pavilion.

The squatter bullhorn was up on an iron tripod pedestal, surrounded by a large group of grease-stained anarchists with helmets, earpads, and studded white batons. Their bullhorn's enormous ululating bellow was reducing everyone's nerves to jelly. It was like the shriek of Medusa.

The cops retreated, and the owners of the bullhorn shut it off, waving their glittering batons in triumph. In the deafened, jittery silence there were scattered shrieks, jeers, and claps, but the ambience in the park had become very bad: aggressive and surreal. Attracted by the apocalyptic shriek, people were milling into the park at a trot, spoiling for any kind of trouble.

They seemed to have little in common, these people; not their dress, not language, certainly nothing like a coherent political cause. They were mostly young men, and most of them looked as if they'd been up all night: red-eyed and peevish. They taunted the retreating cops. A milling gang knifed one of the smaller pavilions, a scarlet one, and it collapsed like a blood-blister under their trampling feet.

Sardelle took Eddy to the edge of the park, where the cops were herding up a crowd-control barricade line of ambulant robotic pink beanbags. "I want to see this," he protested. His ears were ringing.

"They're going to fight," she told him.

"About what?"

"Anything. Everything," she shouted. "It doesn't matter. They'll knock our teeth out. Don't be stupid." She took him by the elbow and they slipped through a gap in the closing battle line.

The police had brought up a tracked glue-cannon truck. They now began to threaten the crowd with a pasting. Eddy had never seen a glue-cannon before—except on television. It was quite astonishing how frightening the machine looked, even in pink. It was squat, blind, and nozzled, and sat there buzzing like some kind of wheeled warrior termite.

Suddenly several of the cops standing around the machine began to flinch and duck. Eddy saw a glittering object carom hard off the glue-truck's armored canopy. It flew twenty meters and landed in the grass at his feet. He picked it up. It was a stainless-steel ball-bearing the size of a cow's eyeball.

"Airguns?" he said.

"Slingshots. Don't let one hit you."

"Oh yeah. Great advice, I guess." To the far side of the cops a group of people—some kind of closely organized protestors—were advancing in measured step under a tall two-man banner. It read, in English: *The Only Thing Worse Than Dying Is Outliving Your Culture.* Every man-jack of them, and there were at least sixty, carried a long plastic pike topped with an ominous looking bulbous sponge. It was clear from the way they maneuvered that they understood military pike-tactics only too well; their phalanx bristled like a hedgehog, and some captain among them was barking distant orders. Worse yet the pikemen had neatly outflanked the cops, who now began calling frantically for backup.

A police drone whizzed just above their heads, not the casual lumbering he had seen before, but direct and angry and inhumanly fast. "Run!" Sardelle shouted, taking his hands. "Peppergas . . ."

Eddy glanced behind him as he fled. The chopper, as if cropdusting, was farting a dense maroon fog. The crowd bellowed in shock and rage and, seconds later, that hellish bullhorn kicked in once more.

Sardelle ran with amazing ease and speed. She bounded along as if firecrackers were bursting under her feet. Eddy, years younger and considerably longer in leg, was very hard put to keep up.

In two minutes they were well out of the park, across a broad street and into a pedestrian network of small shops and restaurants. There she stopped and let him catch his breath.

"Jesus," he puffed, "where can I buy shoes like that?"

"They're made-to-order," she told him calmly. "And you need special training. You can break your ankles, otherwise. . . ." She gazed at a nearby bakery. "You want some breakfast now?"

Eddy sampled a chocolate-filled pastry inside the shop, at a dainty, doily-covered table. Two ambulances rushed down the street, and a large group of drum-beating protestors swaggered by, shoving shoppers from the pavement, but otherwise things seemed peaceful. Sardelle sat with arms folded, staring into space. He guessed that she was reading security alerts from the insides of her spex.

"You're not tired, are you?" he said.

"I don't sleep on operations," she said, "but sometimes I like to sit very still." She smiled at him. "You wouldn't understand. . . ."

"Hell no I wouldn't," Eddy said, his mouth full. "All hell's breaking loose over there, and here you are sipping orange juice just as calm as a bump on a pickle. . . . Damn, these croissants, or whatever the hell they are, are really good. Hey! *Herr Ober!* Bring me another couple of those, *ja, danke.* . . ."

"The trouble could follow us anywhere. We're as safe here as any other place. Safer, because we're not in the open."

"Good," Eddy nodded, munching. "That park's a bad scene."

"It's not so bad in the park. It's very bad at the Rhein-Spire, though. The Mahogany Warbirds have seized the rotating restaurant. They're stealing skin."

"What are Warbirds?"

She seemed surprised. "You haven't heard of them? They're from NAFTA. A criminal syndicate. Insurance rackets, protection rackets, they run all the casinos in the Quebec Republic. . . ."

"Okay. So what's stealing skin?"

"It's a new kind of swindle; they take a bit of skin or blood, with your genetics you see, and a year later they tell you they have a newborn son or daughter of yours held captive, held somewhere secret in the South. . . . Then they try to make you pay, and pay, and pay. . . ."

"You mean they're kidnapping genetics from the people in that restaurant?"

"Yes. Brunch in the Rhein-Spire is very prestigious. The victims are all rich or famous." Suddenly she laughed, rather bitter, rather cynical. "I'll be busy next year, Eddy, thanks to this. A new job—protecting my clients' skin."

Eddy thought about it. "It's kind of like the rent-a-womb business, huh? But really twisted."

She nodded. "The Warbirds are crazy, they're not even ethnic criminals, they are network interest-group creatures. . . . Crime is so damned ugly, Eddy. If you ever think of doing it, just stop."

Eddy grunted.

"Think of those children," she murmured. "Born from crime. Manufactured to order, for a criminal purpose. This is a strange world, isn't it? It frightens me sometimes."

"Yeah?" Eddy said cheerfully. "Illegitimate son of a millionaire, raised by a high-tech mafia? Sounds kind of weird and romantic to me. I mean, consider the possibilities."

She took off her spex for the first time, to look at him. Her eyes were blue. A very odd and romantic shade of blue. Probably tinted contacts.

"Rich people have been having illegitimate kids since the year zero," Eddy said. "The only difference is somebody's mechanized the process." He laughed.

"It's time you met the Cultural Critic," she said. She put the spex back on.

• • •

They had to walk a long way. The bus system was now defunct. Apparently the soccer fans made a sport of hitting public buses; they would rip all the beanbags out and kick them through the doors. On his way to meet the Critic, Eddy saw hundreds of soccer fans; the city was swarming with them. The English devotees were very bad news: savage, thick-booted, snarling, stamping, chanting, anonymous young men, in knee-length sandpaper coats, with their hair cropped short and their faces masked or war-painted in the Union Jack. The English soccer hooligans traveled in enormous packs of two and three hundred. They were armed with cheap cellular phones. They'd wrapped the aerials with friction tape to form truncheon handles, so that the high-impact ceramic phone casing became a nasty club. It was impossible to deny a traveler the ownership of a telephone, so the police were impotent to stop this practice. Practically speaking, there was not much to be done in any case. The English hooligans dominated the streets through sheer force of numbers. Anyone seeing them simply fled headlong.

Except, of course, for the Irish soccer fans. The Irish wore thick elbow-length grappling gloves, some kind of workmen's gauntlets apparently, along with long green-and-white football scarves. Their scarves had skull-denting weights sewn into pockets at their ends, and the tassels fringed with little skin-ripping wire barbs. The weights were perfectly legitimate rolls of coins, and the wire—well, you could get wire anywhere. The Irish seemed to be outnumbered, but were, if anything, even drunker and more reckless than their rivals. Unlike the English, the Irish louts didn't even use the cellular phones to coordinate their brawling. They just plunged ahead at a dead run, whipping their scarves overhead and screaming about Oliver Cromwell.

The Irish were terrifying. They traveled down streets like a scourge. Anything in their way they knocked over and trampled: knick-knack kiosks, propaganda videos, poster-booths, T-shirt tables, people selling canned jumpsuits. Even the postnatal abortion people, who were true fanatics, and the scary, eldritch, black-clad pro-euthanasia groups, would abandon their sidewalk podiums to flee from the Irish kids.

Eddy shuddered to think what the scene must be like at the Rhein-Stadium. "Those are some mean goddamn kids," he told Sardelle, as they emerged from hiding in an alley. "And it's all about *soccer*? Jesus, that seems so pointless."

"If they rioted in their *own* towns, *that* would be pointless," Sardelle said. "Here at the Wende, they can smash each other, and everything else, and tomorrow they will be perfectly safe at home in their own world."

"Oh, I get it," Eddy said. "That makes a lot of sense."

A passing blonde woman in a Muslim hijab slapped a button onto Eddy's sleeve. "Will your lawyer talk to God?" the button demanded aloud, repeatedly, in English. Eddy plucked the device off and stamped on it.

The Cultural Critic was holding court in a safe house in Stadtmitte. The safe house was an anonymous twentieth-century four-story dump, flanked by some nicely retrofitted nineteenth-century town houses. A graffiti gang had hit the block during the night, repainting the street surface with a sprawling polychrome mural, all big grinning green kitty cats, fractal spirals, and leaping priapic pink pigs. "Hot Spurt!" one of the pigs suggested eagerly; Eddy skirted its word balloon as they approached the door.

The door bore a small brass plaque reading E.I.S.—ELEKTRONISCHES INVASIONSABWEHR-SYSTEMS GMBH. There was an inscribed corporate logo that appeared to be a melting ice cube.

Sardelle spoke in German to the door video; it opened, and they entered a hall full of pale, drawn adults in suits, armed with fire extinguishers. Despite their air of nervous resolution and apparent willingness to fight hand to hand,

Eddy took them for career academics: modestly dressed, ties and scarves slightly askew, odd cheek tattoos, distracted gazes, too serious. The place smelled bad, like stale cottage cheese and bookshelf dust. The dirt-smudged walls were festooned with schematics and wiring diagrams, amid a bursting mess of tower-stacked scrawl-labeled cartons—disk archives of some kind. The ceiling and floorboards were festooned with taped-down power cables and fiber-optic network wiring.

"Hi, everybody!" Eddy said. "How's it going?" The building's defenders looked at him, noted his jumpsuit costume, and reacted with relieved indifference. They began talking in French, obviously resuming some briefly postponed and intensely important discussion.

"Hello," said a German in his thirties, rising to his feet. He had long, thinning, greasy hair and a hollow-cheeked, mushroom-pale face. He wore secretarial half spex; and behind them he had the shiftiest eyes Eddy had ever seen, eyes that darted, and gloated, and slid around the room. He worked his way through the defenders, and smiled at Eddy, vaguely. "I am your host. Welcome, friend." He extended a hand.

Eddy shook it. He glanced sidelong at Sardelle. Sardelle had gone as stiff as a board and had jammed her gloved hands in her trench coat pockets.

"So," Eddy gabbled, snatching his hand back, "thanks a lot for having us over!"

"You'll be wanting to see my famous friend the Cultural Critic," said their host, with a cadaverous smile. "He is upstairs. This is my place. I own it." He gazed around himself, brimming with satisfaction. "It's my Library, you see. I have the honor of hosting the great man for the Wende. He appreciates my work. Unlike so many others."

Their host dug into the pocket of his baggy slacks. Eddy, instinctively expecting a drawn knife, was vaguely surprised to see his host hand over an old-fashioned, dog-eared business card. Eddy glanced at it. "How are you, Herr Schreck?"

"Life is very exciting today," said Schreck with a smirk. He touched his spex and examined Eddy's online bio. "A young American visitor. How charming."

"I'm from NAFTA," Eddy corrected.

"And a civil libertarian. Liberty is the only word that still excites me," Schreck said, with itchy urgency. "I need many more American intimates. Do make use of me. And all my digital services. That card of mine—do call those network addresses and tell your friends. The more, the happier." He turned to Sardelle. *"Kaffee, fräulein? Zigaretten?"*

Sardelle shook her head minimally.

"It's good she's here," Schreck told Eddy. "She can help us to fight. You go upstairs. The great man is waiting for visitors."

"I'm going up with him," Sardelle said.

"Stay here," Schreck urged. "The security threat is to the Library, not to him."

"I'm a bodyguard," Sardelle said frostily. "I guard the body. I don't guard data-havens."

Schreck frowned. "Well, more fool you, then."

Sardelle followed Eddy up the dusty, flower-carpeted stairs. Upstairs to the right was an antique twentieth-century office door in blond oak and frosted glass. Sardelle knocked; someone called out in French.

She opened the door. Inside the office were two long workbenches covered with elderly desktop computers. The windows were barred and curtained.

The Cultural Critic, wearing spex and a pair of datagloves, sat in a bright pool of sunlight-yellow glare from a track-mounted overhead light. He was pecking daintily with his gloved fingertips at a wafer-thin data-screen of woven cloth.

As Sardelle and Eddy stepped into the office, the Critic wrapped up his screen in a scroll, removed his spex, and unplugged his gloves. He had dark pepper-and-salt tousled hair, a dark wool tie, and a long maroon scarf draped over a beautifully cut ivory jacket.

"You would be Mr. Dertouzas from CAP-CLUG," he said.

"Exactly. How are you, sir?"

"Very well." He examined Eddy briefly. "I assume his clothing was your idea, Frederika."

Sardelle nodded once, with a sour look. Eddy smiled at her, delighted to learn her real name.

"Have a seat," the critic offered. He poured himself more coffee. "I'd offer you a cup of this, but it's been . . . adjusted."

"I brought you your book," Eddy said. He sat, and opened the bag, and offered the item in question.

"Splendid." The Critic reached into his jacket pocket and, to Eddy's surprise, pulled a knife. The Critic opened its blade with one thumbnail. The shining blade was saw-toothed in a fractal fashion; even its serrations had tiny serrated serrations. It was a jackknife the length of a finger, with a razor-sharp edge on it as long as a man's arm.

Under the knife's irresistible ripping caress, the tough cover of the book parted with a discreet shredding of cloth. The Critic reached into the slit and plucked out a thin, gleaming storage disk. He set the book down. "Did you read this?"

"That disk?" Eddy ad-libbed. "I assumed it was encrypted."

"You assumed correctly, but I meant the book."

"I think it lost something in translation," Eddy said.

The Critic raised his brows. He had dark, heavy brows with a pronounced frown line between them, over sunken, gray-green eyes. "You have read Canetti in the original, Mr. Dertouzas?"

"I meant the translation between centuries," Eddy said, and laughed. "What I read left me with nothing but questions. . . . Can you answer them for me, sir?"

The Critic shrugged and turned to a nearby terminal. It was a scholar's workstation, the least dilapidated of the machines in the office. He touched four keys in order; a carousel whirled and spat out a disk. The Critic handed it to Eddy. "You'll find your answers here, to whatever extent I can give them," he said. "My Complete Works. Please take this disk. Reproduce it, give it to whomever you like, as long as you accredit it. The standard scholarly procedure. I'm sure you know the etiquette."

"Thank you very much," Eddy said with dignity, tucking the disk into his bag. "Of course I own your works already, but I'm glad of a fully up-to-date edition."

"I'm told that a copy of my Complete Works will get you a cup of coffee at any café in Europe," the Critic mused, slotting the encrypted disk and rapidly tapping keys. "Apparently digital commodification is not entirely a spent force, even in literature. . . ." He examined the screen. "Oh, this is lovely. I *knew* I would need this data again. And I certainly didn't want it in my house." He smiled.

"What are you going to do with that data?" Eddy said.

"Do you really not know?" the Critic said. "And you from CAPCLUG, a group of such carnivorous curiosity? Well, that's also a strategy, I suppose." He tapped more keys, then leaned back and opened a pack of zigarettes.

"What strategy?"

"New elements, new functions, new solutions—I don't know what 'culture' is, but I know exactly what I'm doing." The Critic drew slowly on a zigarette, his brows knotting.

"And what's that, exactly?"

"You mean, what is the underlying concept?" He waved the zigarette. "I have no 'concept.' The struggle here must not be reduced to a single simple idea. I am building a structure that must not, cannot, be reduced to a single simple idea. I am building a structure that perhaps *suggests* a concept. . . . If I did more, the system itself would become stronger than the surrounding culture. . . . Any system of rational analysis must live within the strong blind body of mass humanity, Mr. Dertouzas. If we learned anything from the twentieth century, we learned that much, at least." The Critic sighed, a fragrant medicinal mist. "I fight windmills, sir. It's a duty. . . . You often are hurt, but at the same time you become unbelievably happy, because you see that you have both friends and enemies, and that you are capable of fertilizing society with contradictory attitudes."

"What enemies do you mean?" Eddy said.

"Here. Today. Another data-burning. It was necessary to stage a formal resistance."

"This is an evil place," Sardelle—or rather Frederika—burst out. "I had no idea this was today's safe house. This is anything but safe. Jean-Arthur, you must leave this place at once. You could be killed here!"

"An evil place? Certainly. But there is so much megabytage devoted to works on goodness, and on doing good—so very little coherent intellectual treatment of the true nature of evil and being evil. . . . Of malice and stupidity and acts of cruelty and darkness . . ." The Critic sighed. "Actually, once you're allowed through the encryption that Herr Schreck so wisely imposes on his holdings, you'll find the data here rather banal. The manuals for committing crime are farfetched and badly written. The schematics for bombs, listening devices, drug labs, and so forth, are poorly designed and probably unworkable. The pornography is juvenile and anti-erotic. The invasions of privacy are of interest only to voyeurs. Evil is banal—by no means so scarlet as one's instinctive dread would paint it. It's like the sex life of one's parents—a primal and forbidden topic, and yet, with objectivity, basically integral to their human nature—and of course to your own."

"Who's planning to burn this place?" Eddy said.

"A rival of mine. He calls himself the Moral Referee."

"Oh yeah, I've heard of him!" Eddy said. "He's here in Düsseldorf too? Jesus."

"He is a charlatan," the Critic sniffed. "Something of an ayatollah figure. A popular demagogue . . ." He glanced at Eddy. "Yes, yes—of course people do say much the same of me, Mr. Dertouzas, and I'm perfectly aware of that. But I have two doctorates, you know. The Referee is a self-appointed digital Savonarola.

Not a scholar at all. An autodidactic philosopher. At best an artist."

"Aren't you an artist?"

"That's the danger. . . ." The Critic nodded somberly. "Once I was only a teacher, then suddenly I felt a sense of mission. . . . I began to understand which works are strongest, which are only decorative. . . ." The Critic looked suddenly restless, and puffed at his zigarette again. "In Europe there is too much couture, too little culture. In Europe everything is colored by discourse. There is too much knowledge and too much fear to overthrow that knowledge. . . . In NAFTA you are too naively postmodern to suffer from this syndrome. . . . And the Sphere, the Sphere, they are orthogonal to both our concerns. . . . The South, of course, is the planet's last reservoir of authentic humanity, despite every ontological atrocity committed there. . . ."

"I'm not following you," Eddy said.

"Take that disk with you. Don't lose it," the Critic said somberly. "I have certain obligations, that's all. I must know why I made certain choices, and be able to defend them, and I *must* defend them, or risk losing everything. . . . Those choices are already made. I've drawn a line here, established a position. It's my Wende today, you know! My lovely Wende. . . . Through cusp-points like this one, I can make things different for the whole of society." He smiled. "Not better, necessarily—but different, certainly. . . ."

"People are coming," Frederika announced suddenly, standing bolt upright and gesturing at the air. "A lot of people marching in the streets outside. . . . There's going to be trouble."

"I knew he would react the moment that data left this building," the Critic said, nodding. "Let trouble come! I will not move!"

"Goddamn you, I'm being paid to see that you survive!" Frederika said. "The Referee's people burn data-havens. They've done it before, and they'll do it again. Let's get out of here while there's still time!"

"We're all ugly and evil," the Critic announced

calmly, settling deeply into his chair and steepling his fingers. "Bad knowledge is still legitimate self-knowledge. Don't pretend otherwise."

"That's no reason to fight them hand-to-hand here in Düsseldorf! We're not tactically prepared to defend this building! Let them burn it! What's one more stupid outlaw and his rat nest full of garbage?"

The Critic looked at her with pity. "It's not the access that matters. It's the principle."

"Bullseye!" Eddy shouted, recognizing a CAPCLUG slogan.

Frederika, biting her lip, leaned over a tabletop and began typing invisibly on a virtual keyboard. "If you call your professional backup," the Critic told her, "they'll only be hurt. This is not really your fight, my dear; you're not committed."

"Fuck you and your politics; if you burn up in here we don't get our bonuses," Frederika shouted.

"No reason *he* should stay, at least," the Critic said, gesturing to Eddy. "You've done well, Mr. Dertouzas. Thank you very much for your successful errand. It was most helpful." The Critic glanced at the workstation screen, where a program from the disk was still spooling busily, then back at Eddy again. "I suggest you leave this place while you can."

Eddy glanced at Frederika.

"Yes, go!" she said. "You're finished here, I'm not your escort anymore. Run, Eddy!"

"No way," Eddy said, folding his arms. "If you're not moving, I'm not moving."

Frederika looked furious. "But you're free to go. You heard him say so."

"So what? Since I'm at liberty, I'm also free to stay," Eddy retorted. "Besides, I'm from Tennessee, NAFTA's Volunteer State."

"There are hundreds of enemies coming," Frederika said, staring into space. "They will overwhelm us and burn this place to the ground. There will be nothing left of both of you and your rotten data but ashes."

"Have faith," the Critic said coolly. "Help will come, as well—from some unlikely quarters. Believe me, I'm doing my very best to maximize the implications of this event. So is my rival, if it comes to that. Thanks to that disk that just arrived, I am wirecasting events here to four hundred of the most volatile network sites in Europe. Yes, the Referee's people may destroy us, but their chances of escaping the consequences are very slim. And if we ourselves die here in flames, it will only lend deeper meaning to our sacrifice."

Eddy gazed at the Critic in honest admiration. "I don't understand a single goddamn word you're saying, but I guess I can recognize a fellow spirit when I meet one. I'm sure CAPCLUG would want me to stay."

"CAPCLUG would want no such thing," the Critic told him soberly. "They would want you to escape, so that they could examine and dissect your experiences in detail. Your American friends are sadly infatuated with the supposed potency of rational, panoptic, digital analysis. Believe me, please—the enormous turbulence in postmodern society is far larger than any single human mind can comprehend, with or without computer-aided perception or the finest computer-assisted frameworks of sociological analysis." The Critic gazed at his workstation, like a herpetologist studying a cobra. "Your CAPCLUG friends will go to their graves never realizing that every vital impulse in human life is entirely prerational."

"Well, I'm certainly not leaving here before I figure *that* out," Eddy said. "I plan to help you fight the good fight, sir."

The Critic shrugged, and smiled. "Thank you for just proving me right, young man. Of course a young American hero is welcome to die in Europe's political struggles. I'd hate to break an old tradition."

Glass shattered. A steaming lump of dry ice flew through the window, skittered across the office floor, and began gently dissolving. Acting entirely on instinct, Eddy dashed forward, grabbed it barehanded, and threw it back out the window.

"Are you okay?" Frederika said.

"Sure," Eddy said, surprised.

"That was a chemical gas bomb," Frederika said. She gazed at him as if expecting him to drop dead on the spot.

"Apparently the chemical frozen into the ice was not very toxic," the Critic surmised.

"I don't think it was a gas bomb at all," Eddy said, gazing out the window. "I think it was just a big chunk of dry ice. You Europeans are completely paranoid."

He saw with astonishment that there was a medieval pageant taking place in the street. The followers of the Moral Referee—there were some three or four hundred of them, well-organized and marching forward in grimly disciplined silence—apparently had a weakness for medieval jerkins, fringed capes, and colored hose. And torches. They were very big on torches.

The entire building shuddered suddenly, and a burglar siren went off. Eddy craned to look. Half a dozen men were battering the door with a hand-held hydraulic ram. They wore visored helmets and metal armor, which gleamed in the summer daylight. "We're being attacking by goddamn knights in shining armor," Eddy said. "I can't believe they're doing this in broad daylight!"

"The football game just started," Frederika said. "They have picked the perfect moment. Now they can get away with anything."

"Do these window bars come out?" Eddy said, shaking them.

"No. Thank goodness."

"Then hand me some of those data-disks," he demanded. "No, not those shrimpy ones—give me the full thirty-centimeter jobs."

He threw the window up and began pelting the crowd below with flung megabytage. The disks had vicious aerodynamics and were hefty and sharp-edged. He was rewarded with an angry barrage of bricks, which shattered windows all along the second and third floors.

"They're very angry now," Frederika shouted over the wailing alarm and roar of the crowd below. The three of them crouched under a table. "Yeah," Eddy said. His blood was boiling. He picked up a long, narrow printer, dashed across the room, and launched it between the bars. In reply, half-a-dozen long metal darts—short javelins, really—flew through up through the window and imbedded themselves in the office ceiling.

"How'd they get those through Customs?" Eddy shouted.

"Must've made them last night."

He laughed. "Should I throw 'em back? I can fetch them if I stand on a chair."

"Don't, don't," Frederika shouted. "Control yourself! Don't kill anyone, it's not professional."

"I'm not professional," Eddy said.

"Get down here," Frederika commanded. When he refused, she scrambled from the beneath the table and body-slammed him against the wall. She pinned Eddy's arms, flung herself across him with almost erotic intensity, and hissed into his ear. "Save yourself while you can! This is only a Wende."

"Stop that," Eddy shouted, trying to break her grip. More bricks came through the window, tumbling past their feet.

"If they kill these worthless intellectuals," she muttered hotly, "there will be a thousand more to take their place. But if you don't leave this building right now, you'll die here."

"Christ, I know that," Eddy shouted, finally flinging her backward with a rasp at her sandpaper coat. "Quit being such a loser."

"Eddy, listen!" Frederika yelled, knotting her gloved fists. "Let me save your life! You'll owe me later! Go home to your parents in America, and don't worry about the Wende. This is all we ever do—it's all we are really good for."

"Hey, I'm good at this too!" Eddy announced. A brick barked his ankle. In sudden convulsive fury, he upended a table and slammed it against a broken window, as a shield. As bricks thudded against the far side of the table, he shouted defiance. He felt superhuman. Her attempt to talk sense had irritated him enormously.

The door broke in downstairs, with a concussive blast. Screams echoed up the stairs. "That's torn it!" Eddy said.

He snatched up a multiplugged power outlet, dashed across the room, and kicked the office door open. With a shout, he jumped onto the landing, swinging the heavy power strip over his head.

The Critic's academic cadre were no physical match for the Referee's knights in armor; but their fire extinguishers were surprisingly effective weapons. They coated everything in white caustic soda and filled the air with great blinding, billowing wads of flying, freezing droplets. It was clear that the defenders had been practicing.

The sight of the desperate struggle downstairs overwhelmed Eddy. He jumped down the stairs three at a time and flung himself into the midst of the battle. He conked a soda-covered helmet with a vicious overhead swing of his power strip, then slipped and fell heavily on his back.

He began wrestling desperately across the soda-slick floor with a half-blinded knight. The knight clawed his visor up. Beneath the metal mask the knight was, if anything, younger than himself. He looked like a nice kid. He clearly meant well. Eddy hit the kid in the jaw as hard as he could, then began slamming his helmeted head into the floor.

Another knight kicked Eddy in the belly. Eddy fell off his victim, got up, and went for the new attacker. The two of them, wrestling clumsily, were knocked off balance by a sudden concerted rush through the doorway; a dozen Moral raiders slammed through, flinging torches and bottles of flaming gel. Eddy slapped his new opponent across the eyes with his soda-daubed hand, then lurched to his feet and jammed the loose spex back onto his face. He began coughing violently. The air was full of smoke; he was smothering.

He lurched for the door. With the panic strength of a drowning man, he clawed and jostled his way free.

Once outside the data-haven, Eddy realized that he was one of dozens of people daubed head to foot with white foam. Wheezing, coughing, collapsing against the side of the building, he and his fellow refugees resembled veterans of a monster cream-pie fight.

They didn't, and couldn't, recognize him as an enemy. The caustic soda was eating its way into Eddy's cheap jumpsuit, reducing the bubbled fabric to weeping red rags.

Wiping his lips, ribs heaving, Eddy looked around. The spex had guarded his eyes, but their filth subroutine had crashed badly. The internal screen was frozen. Eddy shook the spex with his foamy hands, finger snapped at them, whistled aloud. Nothing.

He edged his way along the wall.

At the back of the crowd, a tall gentleman in a medieval episcopal miter was shouting orders through a bullhorn. Eddy wandered through the crowd until he got closer to the man. He was a tall, lean man, in his late forties, in brocaded vestments, a golden cloak and white gloves.

This was the Moral Referee. Eddy considered jumping this distinguished gentleman and pummeling him, perhaps wrestling his bullhorn away and shouting contradictory orders through it.

But even if he dared to try this, it wouldn't do Eddy much good. The Referee with the bullhorn was shouting in German. Eddy didn't speak German. Without his spex he couldn't read German. He didn't understand Germans or their issues or their history. In point of fact he had no real reason at all to be in Germany.

The Moral Referee noticed Eddy's fixed and calculating gaze. He lowered his bullhorn, leaned down a little from the top of his portable mahogany pulpit, and said something to Eddy in German.

"Sorry," Eddy said, lifting his spex on their neck chain. "Translation program crashed."

The Referee examined him thoughtfully. "Has the acid in that foam damaged your spectacles?" he said, in excellent English.

"Yes, sir," Eddy said. "I think I'll have to strip 'em and blow-dry the chips."

The Referee reached within his robe and handed Eddy a monogrammed linen kerchief. "You might try this, young man."

"Thanks a lot," Eddy said. "I appreciate that, really."

"Are you wounded?" the Referee said, with apparently genuine concern.

"No, sir. I mean, not really."

"Then you'd better return to the fight," the Referee said, straightening. "I know we have them on the run. Be of good cheer. Our cause is just." He lifted his bullhorn again and resumed shouting.

The first floor of the building had caught fire. Groups of the Referee's people were hauling linked machines into the street and smashing them to fragments on the pavement. They hadn't managed to knock the bars from the windows, but they had battered some enormous holes through the walls. Eddy watched, polishing his spex.

Well above the street, the wall of third floor began to disintegrate.

Moral Knights had broken into the office where Eddy had last seen the Cultural Critic. They had hauled their hydraulic ram up the stairs with them. Now its blunt nose was smashing through the brick wall as if it were stale cheese.

Fist-sized chunks of rubble and mortar cascaded to the street, causing the raiders below to billow away. In seconds, the raiders on the third floor had knocked a hole in the wall the size of a manhole cover. First they flung down an emergency ladder. Then office furniture began tumbling out to smash to the pavement below: voice mailboxes, canisters of storage disks, red-spined European law books, network routers, tape-backup units, color monitors. . . .

A trench coat flew out the hole and pinwheeled slowly to earth. Eddy recognized it at once. It was Frederika's sandpaper coat. Even in the midst of shouting chaos, with an evil billowing of combusting plastic now belching from the library's windows, the sight of that fluttering coat hooked Eddy's awareness. There was something in that coat. In its sleeve pocket. The key to his airport locker.

Eddy dashed forward, shoved three knights aside, and grabbed up the coat for himself. He winced and skipped aside as a plummeting office chair smashed to the street, narrowly missing him. He glanced up frantically.

He was just in time to see them throw out Frederika.

• • •

The tide was leaving Düsseldorf, and with it all the schooling anchovies of Europe. Eddy sat in the departure lounge balancing eighteen separate pieces of his spex on a Velcro lap table.

"Do you need this?" Frederika asked him.

"Oh yeah," Eddy said, accepting the slim chromed tool. "I dropped my dental pick. Thanks a lot." He placed it carefully into his black travel bag.

"I'm not going to Chattanooga, now or ever," Frederika told him. "So you might as well forget that; that can't be part of the bargain."

"Change your mind," Eddy suggested. "Forget this Barcelona flight, and come transatlantic with me. We'll have a fine time in Chattanooga. There's some very deep people I want you to meet."

"I don't want anybody to meet," Frederika muttered darkly. "And I don't want you to show me off to your little hackerboy friends."

Frederika had taken a hard beating in the riot, covering the Critic's successful retreat across the rooftop. Her hair had been scorched during the battle, and it had burst from its meticulous braiding like badly overused steel wool. She had a black eye, and her cheek and jaw were scorched and shiny with medicinal gel. Although Eddy had broken her fall, her three-story tumble to the street had sprained her ankle, wrenched her back, and barked both knees.

And she had lost her spex.

"You look just fine," Eddy told her. "You're very interesting, that's the point. You're deep! That's the appeal, you see? You're a spook, and a European, and a woman—those are all very deep entities, in my opinion." He smiled.

Eddy's left elbow felt hot and swollen inside his spare shirt; his chest, ribs, and left leg were mottled with enormous bruises. He had a bloodied lump on the back of his head where he'd smashed down into the rubble, catching her.

Altogether, they were not an unusual couple among the departing Wende folk cramming the Düsseldorf airport. As a whole, the crowd seemed to be suffering a massive collective hangover—harsh enough to put many of them into slings and casts. And yet it was amazing how contented, almost smug, many of the vast crowd seemed as they departed their pocket catastrophe. They were wan and pale, yet cheerful, like people recovering from flu.

"I don't feel well enough to be deep," Frederika said. "But you did save my life, Eddy. I do owe you something. But it has to be something reasonable."

"Don't let it bother you," Eddy told her nobly, rasping at the surface of a tiny circuitboard with a plastic spudger. "I mean, I didn't even break your fall, strictly speaking. Mostly I just kept you from landing on your head."

"You did save my life," she repeated quietly. "That crowd would have killed me in the street if not for you."

"You saved the Critic's life. I imagine that's a bigger deal."

"I was paid to do that," Frederika said, and winced. "Anyway, I didn't save the bastard. I just did my job. He was saved by his own cleverness. He's been through a dozen of these damned things." She stretched cautiously, shifting in her beanbag. "So have I, for that matter. . . . I must be a real fool. I endure a lot to live my precious life. . . ." She took a deep breath. "Barcelona, *yo te quiero.*"

"I'm just glad we checked out of that clinic in time to catch our flights," Eddy told her. "Could you believe all those soccer kids in there? They sure were having fun. . . . Why couldn't they be that good-tempered *before* they beat the hell out of each other? Some things are just a mystery, I guess."

"I hope you have learned a good lesson from this," Frederika said.

"Sure have," Eddy nodded. He blew dried crud from the point of his spudger, then picked up a chrome pinch clamp and threaded a tiny screw through the earpiece of his spex. "I can see a lot of deep potential in the Wende. It's true that a few dozen people got killed here, but the city must have made an absolute fortune. That's got to look promising for the Chattanooga city council. And a Wende offers a lot of very useful exposure and influence for a cultural networking group like CAPCLUG."

"You've learned nothing at all," she groaned. "I don't know why I hoped it would be different."

"I admit it—in the heat of the action I got a little carried away," Eddy said. "But my only real regret is that you won't come with me to America, Or, if you'd really rather, take me to Barcelona. Either way, the way I see it, you need someone to look after you for a while."

"You're going to rub my sore feet, yes?" Frederika said sourly. "How generous you are."

"I dumped my creep girlfriend. My dad will pick up my tab. I can help you manage better. I can improve your life. I'm a nice guy."

"I don't want to be rude," she said, "but after this, the thought of being touched is repulsive. I don't need any nice Yankee boyfriend to take me on romantic vacations." She shook her head, with finality. "I'm sorry, Eddy, but I can't give you what you want."

Eddy sighed, examined the crowd for a while, then repacked the segments of his spex and closed his Velcro board. At last he spoke up again. "Do you virch?"

"What?"

"Do you do virtuality?"

She was silent for a long moment, then looked him in the eye. "You don't do anything really strange or sick on the wires, do you, Edward?"

"There's hardly any subjective time lag if you use high-capacity transatlantic fiber," Eddy said.

"Oh. I see."

"What have you got to lose? If you don't like it, hang up."

Frederika tucked her hair back, examined the departure board, looked at her shoes. "And would this make you happy?"

"No," Eddy said. "But it'd sure make me a whole lot more of what I already am."

VICTOR PELEVIN

THE YULETIDE CYBERPUNK YARN, OR CHRISTMAS_EVE-117.DIR

(1996)

Translated from the Russian by Alex Shvartsman

ONE doesn't have to be an expert on so-called culture to notice that interest in poetry is declining in practically every country worldwide. Perhaps this is caused by the political changes taking place all over the world in recent decades. Poetry, a distant descendant of ancient magic incantations, tends to prosper under totalitarian and despotic regimes, due to a peculiar resonance. Such regimes, as a rule, are themselves of a magical nature and therefore organically capable of nourishing other branches of magic. But under the gaze (or rather gazes) of the rational hydra of the free market, poetry withers into impotence or even irrelevance.

Fortunately, this doesn't mean its doom. It merely shifts away from the focus of public interest into its far periphery; into the realm of university campuses, neighborhood periodicals, bulletin boards, variety shows, and evening parties. Moreover, it can't be said that it leaves the focus entirely. It manages to retain its position in that molten region where the wandering, cloudy gaze of humanity is aimed. Poetry lives on in the brands of automobiles, hotels, and chocolate bars, in the names given to boats, tampons, and computer viruses.

The latter is, perhaps, the most surprising. By its nature the computer virus is nothing more than a soulless sequence of micro-assembler commands that stealthily attaches itself to other programs, so that one fine day it can turn the computer into a useless pile of metal and plastic. And these assassin programs are given names such as Leonardo, Cascade, Yellow Rose, and so on. Perhaps the poetry inherent in these names is nothing more than a return to the abovementioned incantations. Perhaps it's an attempt to somehow humanize, animate, and propitiate the dead and almighty world of semiconductors, with their electronic impulses sweeping through as they define human destiny. For even the riches people strive toward their entire lives aren't measured by basements filled with gold these days, but by strings of ones and zeroes stored in the memory of a bank's computer, utterly meaningless to the uninitiated. All that is achieved by a successful entrepreneur over the course of many years filled with anxiety and toil, before a heart attack or a bullet forces them to switch to another form of business, is merely an electric current within a microchip transistor so small it can only be seen through a microscope.

Therefore it is no surprise that a computer virus that completely paralyzed the large Russian city of Petroplahovsk for several days was named Christmas Eve. (In antivirus software and computer manuals it's referred to as PN-117.DIR but we don't know what those numbers and Latin characters mean.) The name Christmas Eve can't be considered a pure tribute to poetry. You see, some viruses activate at a certain time or on a certain day. For example, the Leonardo virus was designed to perform its dastardly deed on Leonardo da Vinci's birthday. Likewise, the Christmas Eve virus would wake from hibernation on Christmas Eve. As to its function, we shall attempt to describe it in general terms, without getting mired in technical details. After all, only experts would care what cluster PN-117.DIR wrote itself into, or how precisely it altered the File Allocation Table. What matters to the rest of us is that this virus destroyed the databases stored in the computer, and it did so in a rather unusual manner. The information wasn't damaged or erased; instead it was carefully remixed.

Let's imagine a computer located somewhere in City Hall, which contained all the details of city life (which, by the way, was precisely the case in Petroplahovsk). While this computer was functioning properly, its memory resembled an assembled Rubik's cube. The blue side contained information about municipal services, the red side city budget data; the Mayor's personal bank information was on the yellow side and his Rolodex was on the green side. When activated, PN-117.DIR began to twist the Rubik's cube in deranged and unpredictable ways, even as it preserved each square and the cube as a whole. To build on this analogy, when antivirus programs check the computer's memory they measure the sides of the cube, and so long as those sides remain the same size, the programs conclude that the computer is virus-free. Therefore, any disk auditors, and even the latest heuristic analyzers, were powerless against PN-117.DIR. The nameless programmer who, for some reason, set out on the path of abstract evil, had created a tiny masterpiece. He even earned grudging and contemptuous praise from Doctor Lozinskiy himself, the highest authority in the field of computer demonology.

Nothing is known about the creator of the virus. According to rumor, it was written by the same mad engineer Gerasimov in whose case the laws against cruelty to animals were applied for the first time in the annals of the Petroplahovsk City Court. This was a huge case, so we'll rehash the details only in general terms. Gerasimov had been mentally unbalanced from birth and belonged to that thin strata of our society who would not understand or accept progress, and who hated any seedlings of the bright future that manage to rise toward the sun through the many layers of pavement that is our sorrowful present. On this basis he developed a persecution complex; for him, the main symbol of the changes that have taken place in our country were for some reason symbolized by a bull terrier. Perhaps this happened because many people in the sixteen-story building where he lived owned dogs of this popular breed. In the elevator, Gerasimov often found himself in the company of three, four, and sometimes five bull terriers simultaneously. As a result, Gerasimov sold his meager belongings and took on a considerable amount of debt for a person of his means in order to purchase his own bull terrier.

Gerasimov's neighbors were initially thrilled by this change in his attitude. At first glance it seemed to demonstrate real commitment on his part to adjust to the shifting circumstances and to live in lockstep with the times. But once word spread of what Gerasimov had named his dog, it shocked the animal lovers in the building. It turned out that he had named his bull terrier Mumu.* In the evenings, Gerasimov would go on walks to the nearby river and oftentimes idle on the shore, staring into the middle of the stream and thinking about something intensely. Mumu played nearby, occasionally rubbing up against her owner's leg and staring into his face with her trusting little red eyes.

The dog owners in Gerasimov's building believed these walks to be of a clearly provocative nature. This led to the aforementioned court case, where the mayor of Petroplahovsk, who was a passionate fan of bull terriers, personally weighed in. The animal was taken away from Gerasimov.

"Gerasimov hates everything Mumu represents," the prosecutor had said in court. "Rather, Mumu represents everything Gerasimov hates. For thousands upon thousands of Russians the bull terrier has become a symbol of success, optimism, and faith in the rebirth of the new Russia! Gerasimov reaches his paws toward Mumu because they're too short to reach those this dog symbolizes. But we're asking for the animal to be taken away from him not because of his beliefs, however we feel about those. No, we demand this because the poor pup is in danger!"

Gerasimov lost the case and Mumu was confiscated by the authorities. She was destined for a special elite dog shelter where bull terriers, pit bulls, and wolfhounds that had belonged to the deceased captains of industry whiled away their days. The mayor personally donated money for Mumu's upkeep and for a special cage in which the dog would be shipped.

Perhaps that is how the rumor started that Gerasimov wrote PN-117.DIR in order to exact

revenge upon the mayor. But this version seems extremely unlikely. First, a programmer capable of writing a virus of Christmas Eve's caliber would be unlikely to take out his jealousy over the success of others on an innocent bull terrier; he would undoubtedly be wealthy enough to buy ten bull terriers. Second, Gerasimov had never been to City Hall, and it was highly doubtful he could infect the computer with a virus through the internet. Third, and most importantly, the theory of Gerasimov's authorship is entirely devoid of logic. As the prosecutor had said, Gerasimov reached for Mumu because his paws had been too short to touch anyone capable of slapping him. Gerasimov was too much of a coward to try and hurt someone with real power. Petroplahovsk's mayor, Alexander Vanykov, better known around town by the nickname of Al Spinoza, undoubtedly possessed real power. He had earned this nickname not because he was interested in philosophy, but because early in his career he had killed several people with a Spinoza dubbing needle.

Vanykov was one of the three individuals who upheld all Petroplahovsk. (One might be tempted to imagine three muscular Titans, supporting a slice of the Earth, covered in streets and buildings on their shoulders. But let's just focus on Vanykov instead, as the other Titans have nothing whatsoever to do with our narrative.) Vanykov primarily controlled prostitution and the drug trade. No one knows for certain why he would ever want to take on mayoral duties on top of that. One could imagine how he might have become desirous of the position: he must have looked out of the tinted windows of his limo on the way from the bathhouse to his office. And as he watched the gray-brown little houses of his hometown roll by, he may have noticed a billboard asking all citizens to cast their vote in the mayoral election. They say Vanykov was in the habit of picking at his buttons. So he must've been fumbling with a button on his jacket or trousers when suddenly a thought occurred to him: it would be far better

---

* This is a reference to a classic short story: "Mumu" by Ivan Turgenev. Gerasim, a deaf and mute serf, rescues a dog named Mumu and subsequently drowns her in the river when pressured to get rid of her by his master. The story is a scathing indictment of the institution of serfdom.

to be on the take himself than to pay off some other mayor.

The rest was only a matter of execution. Having decided to run for mayor, Vanykov first held a meeting with his "panthers." That's what a person who controls prostitution within a city neighborhood was called, roughly an equivalent of a police captain. He explained that if any of them failed to mobilize the girls they supervised to campaign for him, Vanykov would pick up a sewing needle and personally turn that panther into a kitty cat. The rest was explained by Vanykov's aide: all female campaign workers must look chaste and innocent, and not wear trousers under any circumstances as that might be off-putting to the elderly and other conservative elements of the electorate.

A very expensive campaign manager was called in from Moscow. Vanykov had heard many stories about how this specialist had run the parliamentary campaign in the neighboring city of Ekatirinodibinsk for the local "godmother" Daria Cleves. The main focus of the campaign was combatting organized crime. Its slogan, circulated on thousands of flyers, read: *The only way to deal with thieves is by electing Daria Cleves.*

Vanykov asked the campaign manager to arrange something similar for him. The specialist took a week to study the matter and presented a detailed analysis of the psychological situation in the city, an entire folder of bifurcated graphs, tables, and pie charts. The public opinion polls in the city showed that, unlike Ekatirinodibinsk, where the electorate really hated the mafia, the citizens of Petroplahovsk, which derived much of its income from tourism, were inherently if vaguely chauvinistic. They hated some abstract "bastards" and "shitheads" who were "taking advantage" and "making life difficult." When asked who those bastards were, the citizens would generally shrug and say, "You know, the ones. Everyone knows them." Therefore, it was recommended that the campaign be based on the mayor's willingness to stand up to those "bastards" without specifying who the bastards

were, so as to avoid "splitting the electorate," as the specialist put it. The proposed campaign slogan read, *Tell bastard shitheads to buzz off; cast a vote for Vanykov.*

When Vanykov was shown this couplet that—along with the folder full of graphs—cost one hundred and eighty thousand dollars, he thought he was in the wrong line of work. This professional jealously had woken the Al Spinoza in him, and the Muscovite expert barely made it out of Petroplahovsk alive. The slogan had to be changed, in large part because everyone involved in the campaign felt that if there existed a bastard shithead in Petroplahovsk, it was Vanykov himself. Therefore, the final draft of the slogan became, *Only Vanykov can save us from dictatorship and chaos.* Vanykov ran on this platform and won with a considerable margin.

As a mayor, Vanykov followed an ancient Chinese proverb that stated the people should know nothing about the best of rulers, other than his name. He organized a holiday called "Viva la Petroplahovsk" twice, and there's absolutely nothing whatsoever to be said about it. Once he met with the editors of local newspapers in his office, where he gently and delicately tried to explain to them that expressions such as "bandit" and "thief"—much-abused by the media— have long since ceased to be politically correct. (Vanykov read this term from a scrap of paper prepared for him by an aide who carbon copied it from American English.) Moreover, Vanykov said, such words can confuse people. The word "thief" supposes that the person being so called might climb out of his Lincoln town car and in through someone's window to steal a piece of meat out of their pot of soup (the transcript records the collective laughter of the editors), whereas the term "bandit" suggests this person is being sought by the police (another bout of laughter recorded in the transcript). When asked what expression should best denote the abovementioned categories of citizens, Vanykov replied that he was personally partial to the term "special economic entity" or "SEE." For those journalists who prefer flowery and figurative language he suggested the phrase "Newest Russian."* While this expression no longer surprises anyone, it's interesting to note that its true author was Vanykov's aide.

That was, perhaps, the only notable contribution Vanykov left behind. One might also add that during his brief reign, Petroplahovsk newspapers called him a patron and a philanthropist. Both of those epithets—even if neither was quite adequate or deserved—referred to his role in the fate of Mumu the bull terrier. In other words, were it not for the terrible events caused by the broken computer in City Hall, Vanykov's story would've been neither unusual nor noteworthy.

Like all young technocrats, Vanykov treated the computer with great piety and strived to maximize the ways in which it could help make his life easier. All the details of his multifaceted activities were entered into several databases, which could only be accessed with a password. A suite of organizational software and a built-in calendar could handle practically all Vanykov's daily workload. Vanykov's presence in the office was not required, and therefore seldom. Any information about urgent matters reached him via several pagers he wore on his belt (one of which, with a golden two-headed eagle on a white background, only ever rang two or three times); the rest of his business was easily dispatched by his secretary. The workday at City Hall began when she turned on the computer and printed the daily itinerary. For example, when the printout stated that it was necessary to check on the status of preparations for the heating season, collect the protection money from a Georgian restaurant, and water the flowers, she calmly forwarded the first two notifications to the appropriate individuals, picked up the can from the windowsill, and went to get water from the faucet.

That's roughly what happened on the ill-fated day when several major strokes had already occurred under the plastic skull of the computer. Vanykov hadn't yet sobered up from the New Year's bender;† the secretary was handling ongoing business in the office; and beyond the window, the city covered in silver dust was quiet, bright, and mysterious.

It began when a crew of construction workers (in simpler terms, a trio of women in sleeveless orange vests, the sort that always scrape with ice breakers at highway curbsides) received a very strange order on a City Hall letterhead. It contained unequivocal orders to "take out Kishkerov," signed by Al Spinoza.

It's worth noting that these women, just like everyone else, knew who Mayor Vanykov really was. Everything related to him was shrouded in a murky and hypnotic halo. A great many among the municipal workers hoped deep within their souls that Vanykov might notice them and, if they were to pass some ambiguous test, a moment would come when he'd uplift them from the spare gray tedium of everyday life to a magical and frightening criminal underworld. Apparently, these poor women, poisoned by Mexican soap operas and radioactive beets, harbored similar hopes, made all the more touching because of their extreme absurdity. They knew well that Kishkerov was one of the most powerful people in Petroplahovsk, made apparent by the fact that he dared to engage in open conflict against City Hall. It must've been quite difficult to "take him out" since his estate was heavily guarded. The bodyguards who found his body in the garden shed, mangled by ice picks, for the longest time couldn't figure out how it had happened. None of them could imagine that three grim broads who were there to clear the paths in the garden might have had anything to do with it. By the way, it only just occurred to us that these women might have been motivated not by some impossible and romantic hope for a new

* "New Russian" was a common stereotype in the 1990s referring to people who quickly made a lot of money during the collapse of the Soviet Union via criminal means, and whose intelligence and good taste did not equal their newfound wealth.

† Russian Christmas takes place after New Year's, in early January, following an Orthodox calendar.

795

life, but by the work ethic instilled into them back in the Soviet times.

At the same time, four professional killers in the employ of Vanykov, who were whiling away their time at a billiards hall in a suburban resort, drinking diet Coke and reading trashy newspapers, received a letter arrogantly signed "Mayor Vanykov." In that letter, he demanded that Main Street be *devoid of all bumps* by evening. These were experienced killers, but even they were stumped. They came up with a list of the *bumps* that had offices or some other business along the city's main street (which was indeed called Main Street) and this list was two pages long. The killers reached out to their friendly associates for assistance.

It's not worth revisiting the terrible slaughter that occurred on Main Street that day. Television, ever hungry for the spectacle of human suffering, replayed the clips of what the street turned into after a cavalcade of trucks filled with killers had come through. There's something shameful about the enthusiasm with which a young reporter explained which house was blown up by the Bumblebee grenade launcher, which facade was cracked with the Fly missile, and why the secret Potemkin device destroyed the interior walls while leaving the outer building walls untouched.

The other events of that day seem insignificant in comparison to the massacre. For example, when a racketeering ring—a group of people who were a bit slow but good at following orders—received a fax from City Hall asking when the *garbage would be burned*, the life of Police Major Kozulin, who was being held hostage for failing to pay a percentage of his ill-gotten gains, hung by a thread for several minutes. They'd already poured kerosene over his body, and only the cannonade coming from Main Street made them forget about him, thereby saving his life.

Incredibly, the mad City Hall computer forced some citizens to experience positive emotions. Ecclesiast Kolpakov, the owner of the

"Sex-Elegant" shop, had been engaged in the highly risky undertaking of leaving Vanykov's "protection" for the protection of his competitor, Grisha the Scorpion. He'd long been bracing himself for retribution and was pleasantly surprised to receive an exquisitely polite Christmas greeting fax, signed Al Spinoza. On the other hand, the mayors of fifty cities geographically closest to Petroplahovsk experienced mild confusion having received the following missive:

To the mayor of [here the mayor's name and their city was automatically inserted by the computer, which sent the volley of faxes on the orders of the secretary]:

Hey dumbass, you will either pay me, or you will pay nobody, do you understand? Fork over six months' worth of fees by February, or I will pull one leg and Grisha the Scorpion will pull the other, and there will be nothing left of you, asshole. Think about it.

Sincerely yours,
VANYKOV
Mayor, Petroplahovsk.

The mayors of larger cities only laughed at such an impudent demand, but there were those among the recipients who took the threat seriously, evidenced by the untimely death of Grisha the Scorpion a month later. He was shot by unidentified individuals while attending the dress rehearsal of Beckett's *Waiting for Godot*, premiering at his local theater.

Vanykov was, of course, made aware of what was happening in the city. For some time, he thought that Petroplahovsk was under attack by some mayor from a neighboring city, like in a violent movie. But it soon became clear that all participants were certain they were acting on orders from Vanykov. Finally, it became apparent that all orders that already caused so much damage in the city had been sent by the City Hall computer. And since the secretary was beyond reproach, the problem had to be the computer itself. It's unclear whether Vanykov had been aware of the existence of computer viruses. Perhaps he treated what was happening as a personal affront by the computer, which he viewed as an animate being. His highly emotional reaction supports this theory: Vanykov burst into his office, drew a nickel-plated Beretta from its shoulder holster, pushed away the squealing secretary, and unloaded fifteen nine-millimeter bullets into the fancy Pentium 100 PC with its real Intel processor. Pieces of cracked plastic, shards of glass, scraps of colored wire, and a scattering of microchips that looked like dead cockroaches flew across the floor.

Even after the source of all the problems had been destroyed, the echo of its devastating activity continued to reverberate. For example, three days after the Main Street massacre, all the city prostitutes were gathered at a suburban sports complex. The mayor's Director of Public Relations, his face red with shame and confusion, read to them a greeting from City Hall, where they were called darlings, dear girls, and the great hope of Russian winter sports. There are several more such examples, but they aren't especially interesting, save for the one concerning Vanykov personally.

After the events described herein, he suffered from serious depression and retreated to his suburban estate, which resembled a castle more than a house. His comrades and friends visited to console him, and he gradually calmed down—after all, life is life. The man in charge of combatting organized crime brought him some quality Moroccan cannabis, and Vanykov ordered his people to leave him be, then spent several days in an artificial paradise as poetized by Charles Baudelaire, in search of peace and oblivion. Whether or not he found it, no one will ever know, as his life was tragically cut short by an event so phantasmagoric it even surprised the crime beat editor for the *Evening Petroplahovsk*.

Let's make use of the police reconstruction of the event. Around eight o'clock at night, a strange package was delivered to Vanykov's home—a sizable box wrapped in cloth. Vanykov, who was finishing another joint at the time (it was found next to his body), carelessly opened the box and, before he could react, the hungry and half-asphyxiated bull terrier Mumu lunged at his chest.

We've never smoked pot and don't know exactly what the poor mayor experienced when a silent, short-legged white monster with narrowed eyes sprung at him from inside the cage, which was revealed once several layers of wrapping had been removed. We can only suppose that from an existential point of view, this was one of the most powerful feelings of his life. The reason for this was the same as all the other disasters in the city—the bull terrier was bound for the shelter on the same day when the virus reshuffled all the information in the computer's memory. Instead of the Dog Promised Land, the frenzied Mumu had spent several days in the cold storage container and had been delivered to the mayor's home. It's difficult to believe this was a coincidence, but all other explanations are even less likely.

Surprisingly, Vanykov's guards, who found their boss with a torn-out throat and an expression of abject horror on his still face, left the dog alive. The reason for this was basic human chauvinism. The guards thought so little of animals that they considered it pointless to exact revenge upon a dog for the death of a person. They probably likened it to trying to shoot a brick that had fallen from a roof onto someone's head. Mumu was confined to a shed and then, after the frantic activity associated with the funeral had ceased, returned to engineer Gerasimov, who subsequently disappeared without a trace.

Gerasimov was only seen twice after that: one time in the bait and tackle store where he purchased a special drill for cutting ice holes, and again on the following morning, in the field far beyond the city. He was wearing some sort

VICTOR PELEVIN

of a ridiculous robe, sewn from an old cotton blanket, a greasy *ushanka* hat, and a canvas bag filled with diskettes slung from his shoulder. A crooked wooden staff in his hand made him seem like an ancient traveler. Gerasimov

was bandaged in several places, but he appeared enlightened and victorious, and his eyes were like two tunnels at the end of which glimmered a vague, unsteady but undoubtedly extant light.

BEF

WONDERAMA

(1998)

Translated from the Spanish by the author

Amid the almost inaudible machines humming, nobody notices the intruder. As usual, it is impossible to know how it broke in, let alone from where. From the server, it passes to a specific terminal and there it sets in, like a carcinoma, thriving and devouring healthy digital tissue without being noticed.

MARCH 21, 1974

Spring's here; my Radio Shack clock radio woke me up with that Spanish pop tune of the nuns at the sea. I rose and shone and first thing I did was turn on the telly. I caught the last segment of that game show where that old guy dressed as a kid. He asked one of the participants:

"So, pal, do you keep your go-kart or do you go for the Big Fat Mystery Surprize?"

"Keep the kart," I thought.

"I'll get the Big Fat Mystery Surprize, sir!" said the kid.

As usual, behind the Surprize's curtain was a Muebles Troncoso full dining-room set. Bet his dads were flipping, not him.

He deserved it. Dummy.

I showered and went downstairs.

"Hi, honey," Mom smiled and served breakfast: Icee and Twinkies. Dad joined later, he just got coffee. We talked about the World Cup. Dad doesn't like Borja,[*] but I think he's a bomb player. I noticed it was very late for the gig, I had to split. As I was on my way out, Dad said:

"Lalo, there's something for you at the garage. It's packed in a Taconazo Popis[†] box."

There it was, the hippest go-kart helmet, all yellow with purple spirals and sprinkled with happy faces. Grooviest gear ever. I've seen it yes-

---

[*] Enrique Borja (b. 1945), a legendary soccer player. His controversial style made him as loved as he was hated while playing at Club América and for the Mexican national team.

[†] El Taconazo Popis, meaning "The Hip Step," was a popular shoe-store chain famous for its extravagant, psychedelic designs.

terday and now Dad got it for me. I put it on and zipped for the gig. It was very late.

When I got to Cookierama, the Boss scolded me for being two minutes late, but then he smiled and told me I was transferred to a new machine, the one that punches the eyes and smiles on the Cinnamon Smileys, my favorite Happy Face–shaped cookies.

After work I went for a Whopper combo. On my way home I passed by a Cinerama Theater and saw they were showing *Star Wars*. I bought a ticket. It's the coolest film ever! At dinner, Mom served hot dogs and 7UP. When we were done, Dad said:

"Lalo, there's a surprise for you at your bedroom."

There was a C-3PO and R2-D2 quilt on my bed.

MARCH 22, 1974

Today was the World Cup final. Of course the National Team won. All Wonderama went bananas and celebrated on the streets. We hopped into our Ford Galaxies and joined the party, waving our flag in the streets, as did all the city and the country. In the afternoon, the President unveiled Borja's monument on the city's Main Square, honoring the 142 goals he scored during the World Cup. We were there, too. It was specially touching when our National Anthem sounded. I think Dad's take on Borja has changed.

MARCH 23, 1974

Coolest day ever! Everything was overshadowed by the landing of a man on the moon. We watched it all on the TV. Dad was so touched that a tear slipped out. When Neil Armstrong said it was a small step for man and a giant leap for mankind, I got goosebumps all over.

It's official, I'll become an astronaut when I grow up.

MARCH 24, 1974

I got up late, it's Saturday, dude. Turned on the TV to watch the credits of the last cartoon. As that variety show that Mom never misses rolled in, I hopped on the go-kart and went to cruise through the park.

The National Flag waved in the center of the park, its magnificent colorful circles on white and the word *Wonder* on red type. Every time I see it my heart rejoices.

I sat on a bench to do nothing.

I was still sitting there when a blonde girl in a blue dress sat right beside me.

"Hello there! Lovely day," she said. I replied with a grunt.

"Would you like a piece of my chocolate?" she insisted. I ignored her.

"All righty, I'll have to eat it by myself . . . Mmmh! Yummy!"

For no reason, since I hate chocolate, I turned to her and asked with my dumbest smile:

"Can I have some?"

"Hi! I'm Alice," she said.

"My name's Lalo," I replied.

Without further ado, she got up and walked away. I stared at the candy bar's packaging. It only read "eat me." I unwrapped it and discovered a message scribbled in a child's writing:

REALITY IS FAKE

I returned home, feeling totally out to lunch and spent the rest of the evening playing with my El Santo* action figures, wishing I never had met that chick.

I didn't feel like eating, even though there were Zingers and Mirinda for dinner.

The first warning signal passes unnoticed on

---

* Rodolfo Guzmán Huerta, El Santo (1917–1984), was the foremost Mexican wrestler, or *luchador*, mostly known abroad for his involuntarily surrealist movies. In his day, he also appeared in comic books that equaled those of American superheroes in popularity.

the operator's retinal screen. Just one more among millions of decode messages every day. «Terminal X detects an X type error on the Z program.» The operator orders it to keep going and as he sees that the machine carries on, he lets the error slide. These kinds of bugs pop up all the time, especially when beta testing software.

MARCH 25, 1974

I had Ding Dongs and Kool-Aid for breakfast, then Dad took me to the contest show of the old guy dressed as a kid. Ever since I remember, I always longed to participate on his show. At the TV studio we came across Batman. I asked for his autograph and told him he was better than El Santo.

The contest was pretty simple; it was about choosing between three keys, one of which opened the Flavor's Gate. I chose the right one and won a jumbo size pack of yogurt and an Avalancha slider. At the end of the show, the host asked me:

"So, tell me, buddy, do you keep your prize or will you go for the Big Fat Mystery Surprize?"

I dunno, I always thought the kids who chose the Surprize were a bunch of dummies, but I replied I'd go for it.

"Okay. Lupita!" He called his assistant hostess. "What's behind gate number two?"

Behind me, I hear the voice of the Magician's rabbit ventriloquist puppet:

"Whoa! He got the ironing board!"*

But what really freaked me out was a sign

---

* *En familia con Chabelo* was a kids' contest program that ran for almost fifty years. It was corporate-sponsored, mainly by junk food brands aimed at children. At the end of each episode, contestants had the option to either retain their prize or choose a Big Fat Mystery Surprize; this was known as La Catafixia. The mystery item could be a splendid prize, such as a car, or a frustratingly humble item, such as an ironing board or a kettle. Chabelo was sometimes joined by a ventriloquist magician, Mago Frank, and his puppet bunny, Blas.

painted on the wall behind the ironing board that said:

EVERYTHING'S A LIE

Apparently, I was the only one who saw it.

MARCH 26, 1974

Early today, the president addressed the Nation on the TV.

"Good morning, nephews," he said on the screen, dressed in his red blazer, the cartoon animals sewn all over the lapels.[†]

"Good morning," replied my parents, sitting on the couch.

He delivered a speech concerning a menace threatening Wonderama: a criminal named Fantômas was sabotaging the country and terrorizing it. However, the police were working on the case and everything was under control, no need to worry.

When he was done with his speech, he showed a tin toy monkey that frantically clapped a couple tiny cymbals.[‡] I don't know why but it gave me the creeps.

Nothing else happened that day. Nothing interesting.

MARCH 27, 1974

I can't believe it. We were about to have lunch—Cheez Whiz crackers and Hawaiian Punch—when we heard the garbage truck coming down the street. Mom asked me to take the garbage out. Outside, I was shocked to discover that the trashman was a very tall guy wearing a tuxedo, a

---

[†] Ramiro Gamboa, aka El Tío Gamboín (Uncle Gamboín), is the Mexican equivalent to the United States' Mister Rogers. He wore a red blazer with cartoon animal patches.

[‡] Part of Tío Gamboín's act was showing rare Japanese windup tin toys that back then were unavailable in Mexico.

top hat, and a white mask, so tight that it seemed like paint on his face. He looked menacing but also elegant.[*] He was Fantômas himself! I was taken by strong feelings; a mix of fear and I don't know what else. He took the trash bag from my trembling hands, ripped it as if it were a brown bag, and said in a deep, growly voice:

"Have you noticed all you eat is junk food, but you don't have cavities or get fat?"

He handed me back the trash can. It was empty, even though it was full of waste a second ago.

"There are neither foul smells nor pollution. Software failures."

He then split, bounding off with giant, super-human leaps.

I whispered, "Fantômas, you are greater than Batman." But he didn't hear me.

I said nothing to my parents.

MARCH 28, 1974

What's the buzz? It's already late and no matter how I try, I can't remember anything that happened today. Days seem to run by in a jiffy. I wish I could talk about it with someone, but I don't know who.

MARCH 29, 1974

I went skating at Skate-o-rama. I was gulping down a canned vanilla milkshake as I looked at the people on the rink, rolling and spinning. I

felt a bit trippy from the disco lights and the music, so I went out for a little air. I was cooling down outside when a kid my age came to me:

"The Bee Gees suck, don't they?" he said.

"What?"

He looked around and then whispered into my ear:

"You seen nobody looks human 'round here?"

He winked and scrammed.

Everything's getting weird.

MARCH 30, 1974

I got a telegram. It was so freaky-deaky, since come to think about it, I don't know anyone. The sender's name was Software Error, and it read:

"Have you noticed that your parents resemble Jorge Rivero and Sasha Montenegro?"[†]

I freaked out, 'cause suddenly I seemed to recall those names and with them, a bunch of words and terms that I didn't use, but whose meaning I knew, and at evoking them they seemed caked with ancient dust.

Still, there seems to be a ton of stuff I ignore, such as my last name and how old I am.

It's getting serious. The intruder has taken hold of the terminal. The operator only gets a message reporting data interchange between the computers, nothing out of routine. Although required by the manuals, no one conducts the daily checkups, so nobody notices.

MARCH 31, 1974

Just who the fucking hell is Jorge Rivero?! And Sasha Montenegro?!

---

[*] *Fantômas, la amenaza elegante* (*Fantômas, The Elegant Menace*) was a Mexican vigilante comic book published by Editorial Novaro from the late sixties to the mid-nineties. Freely based on the French pulp novels by Marcel Allain and Pierre Souvestre, the comic series depicted the adventures of Fantômas, a criminal mastermind turned into a justice-seeking Robin Hood–type of antihero. It was so popular that even Argentinian author Julio Cortázar wrote a short novella in homage to the character. The character wore a white mask, a tuxedo, and a top hat.

[†] Both were famous actors and sex symbols of Mexican cinema from the late sixties through the late eighties. For the record, bombshell Montenegro married former Mexican President José López Portillo (whose time in office ran from 1976 to 1982), more than twenty-five years her senior.

APRIL 1, 1974

I don't know what's going on. It seems as if I didn't exist. The more I think about reality, the phonier it seems. I feel trapped in someone else's dream that somehow also belongs to me. Maybe someone imagines being me. Or even worse, I'm being dreamed by someone, a supporting character in a recurring fantasy. I haven't noticed that there are no smells or flavors here, only images and sounds that even though false, *are* real. All faces ring a bell even though deep inside I know I never met them. That includes both my parents and, I discovered it in front of the mirror, my own face. It feels as if I am slowly recovering small pieces of a puzzle. The meaning of forgotten words that I shouldn't know at my age (which I still can't recall) turn on somewhere in my mind. I'm certain my name is Eduardo, not Lalo. I know I *am*, but that I am not like *this*. No matter how much I review my diary's entries, I can't find any hint of what is going on. I find my writing heartbreakingly frivolous.

And some dates seem inaccurate.

An alarm sign flashes on what should be the operator's visual space. One of the inmates is showing complex brain activity. The instruments scream. But it's three in the morning, no operator sees the alarm. The only action the bumbling security software does is to autolock the entire system.

APRIL 2, 1974

Sheer chaos.

Waking up, all I could hear was a thundering silence.

I opened my eyes to a world stripped of color. Every object seemed built with a silver thread. My room, the house, the street, the cars, people, everything converted (or reverted) into virtual sculptures. My own body was a web of infinite vectors that palely rendered a human being. Discovering this reality meant nothing. Maybe I should feel sorrow or rage, but I only felt an overwhelming sense of loneliness.

"Eduardo Aquino," a deep, growly voice ripped the silence, pronouncing my real name. I wasn't surprised to discover Fantômas behind me, the only untouched element of this color-stripped universe.

Then I recalled.

Hearing my true name brought all my memories back. Everything was there . . .

August 2012 the coup d'état my involvement in the teacher's union my classes at the University the imposition of the fascist government the menaces my unjustified firing my sympathy for the underground resistance discovering Pedro is with the guerillas joining the movement the clandestine sessions writing the manifestos the involuntary metamorphosis from militant to chairman my tapped phone my wife and children exile my fake disappearing the guerillas in the sewers the sabotage the shootings all the blood we shouldn't shed the inner division of our movement an imminent schism Is there a mole? "Nobody is indispensable but you are half the brain of the movement" our last meeting someone gave out our headquarters rubber bullets tear gas they want us alive the seizure the torturing interrogatories the summary judgment . . .

. . . and then waking up here.

"Fantômas," I replied after this infinite second. "You are better than Batman."

"I am a virtual virus. You are retained at a high-security pavilion for political prisoners. They can't kill you; international pressure is very strong. They keep you chained to a virtual world, with some of the movement's other leaders."

"That's right!" I agreed, feeling a little dumb speaking to a computer virus. "Someone rendered an early seventies pop utopia, some kind of collective TV subconscious . . ."

"No time to waste," Fantômas interrupted. "It won't be long before the operators discover there's something wrong. They're slowly draining your brain. We've been able to save a little, but some information is already lost. The longer it takes, the less you'll be able to remember."

I tried to recall my real father's face.

"Is there anything to do?"

"Yes." He peeled off his mask, unveiling no face at all. "The operators will notice there's an intruder on their program. They'll reboot the whole system, erasing me. But the mask requires a very specific software to wipe it out. As soon as they set back the virtual world, you must put it on. It's an undetectable program that'll preserve your memories till we can resc—

As soon as he's back, the operator detects an intruder in the program. First action he takes, of course, is rebooting the whole system, after which he reconfigures the terminals, altering parameters to make it impossible for a new virus to penetrate the firewall. As soon as he is done he returns to the dull routine of keeping everything within normal parameters in the high-security pavilion.

APRIL 2, 1974

The Radio Shack clock radio woke me up to the tune of "Stayin' Alive" by the Bee Gees. I rose and first thing I did was turn on the TV.

I caught the final segment of that contest show with the old guy dressed as a kid.

I showered and came downstairs for breakfast.

"Morning, Hon," said Mom and served the meal. Ho Hos and Dr Pepper. A little later Dad came down, reading his paper. He had coffee. We discussed the Olympics.

I realized I was already late for the gig, so I rose to split. As I was heading out, Dad said:

"Lalo, there's a surprise for you on the table."

It was a white mask, similar to El Santo's, but without any charm.

"Gee, thanks, Dad," I said, faking my brightest smile and scrammed for Toy-o-rama, where I work.

I threw the mask into the first trash can that crossed my yellow brick road. Beyond that, it was a plain normal day.

DAVID LANGFORD

COMP.BASILISK.FAQ

(1999)

Frequently Asked Questions
Revised 27 June 2006

1. What is the purpose of this newsgroup?
To provide a forum for discussion of basilisk (BLIT) images. Newsnet readers who prefer low traffic should read comp.basilisk.moderated, which carries only high-priority warnings and identifications of new forms.

2. Can I post binary files here?
If you are capable of asking this question you MUST immediately read news.announce.new users, where regular postings warn that binary and especially image files may emphatically not be posted to any newsgroup. Many countries impose a manda-tory death penalty for such action.

3. Where does the acronym BLIT come from?
The late unlamented Dr. Vernon Berryman's system of math-to-visual algorithms is known as the Berryman Logical Imaging Technique. This reflected the original paper's title: "On Thinkable Forms, with notes toward a Logical Imaging Technique" (Berryman and Turner, *Nature*, 2001). Inevitably, the paper has since been suppressed and classified to a high level.

4. Is it true that science fiction authors predicted basilisks?
Yes and no. The idea of unthink-

able information that cracks the mind has a long SF pedigree, but no one got it quite right. William Gibson's *Neuromancer* (1984), the novel that popularized cyberspace, is often cited for its concept of "black ice" software which strikes back at the minds of hackers—but this assumes direct neural connection to the net. Basilisks are far more deadly because they require no physical contact.

Much earlier, Fred Hoyle's *The Black Cloud* (1957) suggested that a download of knowledge provided by a would-be-helpful alien (who has superhuman mental capacity) could overload and burn out human minds.

A remarkable near miss features in *The Shapes of Sleep* (1962) by J. B. Priestley, which imagines archetypal shapes that compulsively evoke particular emotions, intended for use in advertising.

Piers Anthony's *Macroscope* (1969) described the "Destroyer sequence," a purposeful sequence of images used to safeguard the privacy of galactic communications by erasing the minds of eavesdroppers.

The comp.basilisk community does not want ever again to see another posting about the hoary coincidence that *Macroscope* appeared in the same year and month as the first episode of the British TV program *Monty Python's Flying Circus*, with its famous sketch about the World's Funniest Joke that causes all hearers to laugh themselves to death.

5. How does a basilisk operate?

The short answer is: we mustn't say. Detailed information is classified beyond Top Secret.

The longer answer is based on a popular-science article by Berryman (*New Scientist*, 2001), which outlines his thinking. He imagined the human mind as a formal, deterministic computational system—a system that, as predicted by a variant of Gödel's Theorem in mathematics, can be crashed by thoughts which the mind is physically or logically incapable of thinking. The Logical Imaging Technique presents such a thought in purely visual form as a basilisk image which our optic nerves can't help but accept. The result is disastrous, like a software stealth-virus smuggled into the brain.

6. Why "basilisk"?

It's the name of a mythical creature: a reptile whose mere gaze can turn people to stone. According to ancient myth, a basilisk can be safely viewed in a mirror. This is not generally true of the modern version—although some highly asymmetric basilisks like B-756 are lethal only in unreflected or reflected form, depending on the dominant hemisphere of the victim's brain.

7. Is it just an urban legend that the first basilisk destroyed its creator?

Almost everything about the incident at the Cambridge IV supercomputer facility where

Berryman conducted his last experiments has been suppressed and classified as highly undesirable knowledge. It's generally believed that Berryman and most of the facility staff died. Subsequently, copies of basilisk B-1 leaked out. This image is famously known as the Parrot, for its shape when blurred enough to allow safe viewing. B-1 remains the favorite choice of urban terrorists who use aerosols and stencils to spray basilisk images on walls by night.

But others were at work on Berryman's speculations. B-2 was soon generated at the Lawrence Livermore Laboratory and, disastrously, B-3 at MIT.

8. Are there basilisks in the Mandelbrot Set fractal?

Yes. There are two known families, at symmetrical positions, visible under extreme magnification. No, we're not telling you where.

9. How can I get permission to display images on my website?

This is a news.announce.newusers question, but keeps cropping up here. In brief: you can't without a rarely granted government license. Using anything other than plain ASCII text on websites or in e-mail is a guaranteed way of terminating your net account. We're all nostalgic about the old, colorful web and about television, but today's risks are simply too great.

10. Is it true that Microsoft uses basilisk booby traps to protect Windows Ultra from disassembly and pirating?

We could not possibly comment.

MYRA ÇAKAN

SPIDER'S NEST

(2004)

Translated from the German by Jim Young

SPIDER HATED DAYTIME—especially mornings, if he happened to be awake at the time. He was a creature of the night. Spider's middle name was invisible, and everybody knows a guy's never harder to see than in the dark. Sometimes, if he was going somewhere just before nightfall, his senses sharpened so he felt like a fine-tuned instrument. Spider liked that feeling. It gave him power and a certain sense of control that he thought he had lost long ago during the dark, sultry hours of the intertime.

It was morning and the sun shone harshly into his eyes, right there in his hideout. Today the whole sky was glaring, a shrill yellow—vomit yellow. He was inexplicably lethargic, almost like after a bad trip. Every cell in his body seemed to have been deprogrammed during the night, and the old software replaced. Must've had a total blackout, Spider thought. Or pretty near. Almost offhandedly, he noticed his muscles twitching. They were the seismograph of his nervous system, and they were telling him it was

almost time. He was going to need his next hit soon if he wanted to avoid having the contractions turn into cramps.

Sandoz and Geigercounter were supposed to be making their rounds soon. Sandoz was heavily into Eiscream. One time Spider had asked Sandoz why she was so heavily into it, and she said, "Because it goes with my hair." When she said that, she grinned through the neon-silver of her bangs. She looked like a ghost smiling at him from inside a coffin. Real spooky, man.

Spider yawned again. He was trying to outlast the ever-stronger vibrations of his muscles. So he tried to remember when he last saw Ant. Ant was his dealer, and without him, he had to depend on what that fucked-up shit Geigercounter and his girlfriend were doing. Until he traded up to Eiscream or one of the other designer items, it must have been hard on him.

"Hey, Spy, my man, what's going down?" Sandoz shoved herself into his field of view. She knelt down beside Spider and drew hectic little circles in the dust on the ground. The whole damn town was overrun with hectic little circles.

"Heya." Spider nodded at her. Somehow, that girl made him nervous. It was high time that he talked to the Silver Spider about the matter. He looked around. The street looked the same—empty. "So where's Geigercounter hanging?"

"Dunno. Dunno." Her finger kept moving around in spirals in the dust. Her pale blue eyes looked at him without really seeing him. From time to time she got that look, and not even Geigercounter could figure out if she was gonna freak or not. Spider stood up and stretched. For a moment, he almost thought he recognized his mirror image in a picture window on the other side. He was almost sure he looked pretty good, he thought, considering.

Suddenly it was very quiet, clanking quiet. Spider didn't know what it was, but a hungry little noise had overtaken the whispering of the street sweepers. Sandoz crouched there, watching him. His mirror image sank into Sandoz's pale eyes. And all of a sudden he felt both hot and sick with desire. He looked away. Then came a distant salvation. He saw a flurry of dust along the street, a vibration that rode in on the midday sun—Ant on his hoverboard.

Ant stood loosely on the board, one knee slightly bent, his arms swinging in rhythm with the street. Man, oh man, he looked just like the Silver Surfer and he brought fulfillment with him, crystalline, clear, resolution.

"Heya, Spider." Just floating in the air, he could heal the sick. A postatomic saint. "The iceman cometh."

Spider guzzled the sound of the words, turned them around, tasted their timbre. Damn it all, something here was completely turned ass-backward.

"What's the matter, man?" Ant wrinkled his forehead.

"How do you always manage to find power cells for your board, man?" Spider hadn't wanted to ask that; it just burst out of him. The words had turned around on their own as they made their way from his brain to his mouth. But damn it all, Ant was his dealer. His. His. Spider placed his arms behind his back, formed his fingers into fists, and tried to hide how badly he needed his next fix.

"Yeah, and where do you get your shit?" Sandoz's bright voice cut the air in helixes.

"To hell with both of you, you assholes!" Ant put his foot to the ground, speeding up.

Spider leaped forward and tried to stop him. Too slow, and too late.

"Fuck, fuck, fuck!" Sandoz screamed, drawing the word out into a long howl. "He had the stuff with him, he did, man, and now he's gone." She slid down the wall of the house and, like something with a mind of its own, her finger once more started drawing those stupid circles on the ground.

Spider turned himself off. How had he ever spent even one second thinking about her? And girls were the one thing he really couldn't figure out. They smelled different from men, and whenever he talked to them, he wasn't sure what they were talking about.

Silver Spider was different. In his dreams, he saw her as the woman with the killer eyes and hard muscles under her silvery skin. Everything about her was silver—her eyes, her voice, her breasts. Silver Spider understood him. She stroked his senses better than any drug. Because she was the drug. She laid herself upon his brain and took possession of every cell in his body until he was paralyzed. He never wanted to resist. He wanted her to suck him out. Then he'd wake up in a sweat and his body would be heavy and disoriented. Every time he swore it was going to be the last time—these dreams were killing him.

Once he tried to talk to Geigercounter about it, trying to find out if Geiger talked to Silver Spider, too, in the early morning light. But he couldn't say a word. It would have been, like, a betrayal. But beyond that, it would have been like surrendering an inexpressible secret, not least because there was, in fact, a secret between them. In some manner it was dirty—dirty and exciting at the same time—the thing that lay between him and the Silver Spider. Sort of like the feeling he got when Sandoz looked at him. No—he'd never talk to anybody about it.

She wouldn't like it.

Spider morphed around the heels and stretched himself out once more. His right hand beat rhythmically against his thigh. The girl continued drawing her stupid circles in the dust. With the most precise motion, almost dream-like in its dance-like grace, Spider unscrewed his leg from his hip, and as though it were lighter than air, swung it to the ground over Sandoz's mute conjurations. Whoosh, they were gone. Sandoz cursed him wordlessly as the circles she had been drawing disappeared, and in the echo-shadow of her shrill scream he pulled back his leg. Suddenly he felt downright good.

But the feeling passed much too soon. Ant, that stupid asshole, was driving around the place with all that goddamned Eiscream ice in his pocket. Maybe he should hurry up and get a new dealer. Spider couldn't help but notice how his thoughts were going around in circles, as though Sandoz was whirling them around him like the dust. That was the punishment for putting an end to her circles, and the reason Ant hadn't given him the stuff—a presentiment of things to come, an omen. Spider's entire life was built on a foundation of such signs. They were his guidelights through the labyrinth of the days, just as the Silver Spider illuminated his nights. And in fact it was she who had led him to Ant to begin with, since she knew so exactly what he needed. Now why had she left him in the lurch?

No. Wait. That didn't make sense. The Silver Spider had never left him in the lurch. He just had to be patient, to wait until night fell. Then she'd be there for him with all her tenderness and wisdom. He began to run, and then to run faster, into the blurring sunset.

• • •

From a long way off he could see Sandoz. Slowly he made his way to the meeting point. Actu-ally, it wasn't much as landmarks go, just a place where you could hang out, where you could wait for your dealer and sit out the goddamned gray-yellow day. There weren't many of the old gang around anymore after the last big crash. They were all scared of the coming winter. But why think about the cold when the sun is still shining and the nights linger long and warm.

Was she still ticked off at him because of what he'd done to the circles? After due consid-eration, Spider thought it was decidedly more clever to keep quiet than to try to say something to her. Besides, he was really too tired to talk. His head, no, his entire body, felt sore, almost as though he'd been going through withdrawal all night long. Weird.

She was alone and didn't see him coming. She stood there before these cracked windows, looking off into nothingness. Spider wondered if she were high, which brought him to the ques-tion of whether she had any of the good stuff on her. But all of a sudden it didn't matter anymore.

Almost hypnotically the mirror image drew him. She was stretching, and her small breasts pressed against her sweatshirt. She drew her hands through her hair dreamily, almost as though she were moving under water. And then he knew it—she was putting on a show for him because she sensed his gaze on her and it was turning her on. Still, he couldn't stop himself from staring at her, holding his breath, waiting for her to pull her shirt down over one shoulder. He reached out his hand and traced her silhou-ette on the dusty glass.

"Spider, ya stupid asshole, whaddaya think you're doin' with my old lady?"

Geigercounter. He'd finally arrived. Laugh-ing hysterically, he slapped Spider on the back. Geiger was full of Eiscream and was dancing on its ersatz energy. Spider tasted his own bit-ter anger. His fist wanted to drill itself into Gei-ger's dumb mouth—it was begging for it. Why in the hell hadn't he showed up any sooner? If he'd gotten here when he was supposed to, noth-ing would have been screwed up. What the hell had happened?

Spider had never felt such anger before. Was he mad at Geigercounter because he caught him staring at his girl? Or was it because Ant was going to link him up? Naw, that wasn't it. That asshole dealer hadn't been around for days, so how was he supposed to link him? But then how did Geiger get off, if Ant wasn't around?

Spider's thoughts whirled around in circles, hopping around in his head like happy little plush rabbits. Pink and green velveteen bunnies. Spider noticed, as though it was a long way off, that his entire body was shaking and dancing with silent laughter.

"Listen, man—" Spider searched for the words, but he couldn't get the bunnies to stop.

Geigercounter. His eyes were open and looked sort of scared. Scared and sort of goofy. Maybe he was seeing the bunnies, too, and didn't realize they were Spider's. Or maybe Geiger was reading his thoughts. Abruptly, Spider stopped laughing hysterically. The idea that Geigercounter or somebody else—or maybe even something else—could see inside his head scared the bejesus out of him. Thoughts could be like bad shit, you know.

And still Geigercounter just stared at him. Then Geiger's view strayed to Sandoz, who was methodically chewing on a strand of her own hair. For sure, this was one serious communication problem. Shit, the city was really going down the drain, Spider thought. Ever since the Obernet had crashed last winter, everything had been sliding straight downhill. But not with him, since he had Silver Spider to look after him. Then he sensed the anger rising in him again. Maybe it was just because he wanted to bust that fuckin' dealer one. And as he was thinking that, his feet were running down the street.

He looked for Ant for so long that he forgot who he was looking for, and why. Then he went hunting for Geigercounter and Sandoz and finally found them in the house with the cracked windows. They were both leaning over a dusty Plexiglas plate with their glass pipe and the magic blue crystal spread out before them. Yeah, it was magic, all right. Spider was so cold tur-key he would've done anything that came along in order to get the little bunnies out of his head.

Looking at the two of them getting stoned—Sandoz inhaling the smoke from Geiger's mouth, her neon-silver hair mingled with the smoke—made him feel like an intruder.

It made him feel as if he was doing something new and wild, like that morning when he felt Sandoz looking at him and he wondered what she'd look like without her shirt on. In the dark. With him.

And now, in the blink of an eye, his fantasy had become reality. It was already night, and the moon cast strange shadows across Sandoz's naked back. And he saw Sandoz, and what she was doing leaning over Geigercounter, and the way she moved. Without realizing what he was doing, Spider put his hand down his jeans and stroked himself with the same rhythm. Different from Silver Spider, but it got him off.

Sandoz tossed back her head. Spider tried to look her directly in the eyes. Her pupils had become a gate into a sweet, forbidden world. That was when he realized she was looking straight through his brain. She knew what he was thinking. He turned around and ran until he collapsed gasping for air. Spider heard his breath wheeze deep inside his chest, and he closed his eyes so he could hear it better. There was only an echo—Sandoz had disappeared from inside his head.

The Silver Spider was different. She was always there inside his head, just like the thought of his next fix. Yeah, man—she was the only real shit. Every night she was there for him. And she knew what he needed, everything. All he needed to do was to hang with her, in her net.

As soon as he reached interface, Spider recalled what it had been like that first time—and would be the next—when he'd discovered her in one of the Unternets that had dissolved after the big crash. Unlike everything else, it had only gotten better since the first time. He knew how she pulled him in, stuck her silver probes into him in a deliciously painful ecstasy that he never wanted to stop. All he noticed was how his body wound up tight like a wire coil and how his hips jerked. It was holy robot night, better than any shit, man.

• • •

The sun was shining harshly once more, and out of its light appeared the Silver Surfer. His hair was punked out like a shark's fin, cutting though the air. Spider waited for him, half in the shadows. He felt a lot better today, as though his power cells had pretty much recharged during the night. She'd been good to him again. But he thought it was better to restore the vibe with his dealer again. And, in his hiding place, Spider rolled the words around in his mouth until they fit.

"Spy." Ant had found him. He was waiting, too.

Totally cool and unapproachable he stood there on his hoverboard, floating above the dust so his feet never had to touch the dirt he was made of. Every one of them was nothing but dirt—Sandoz, Geigercounter, and him too— yeah, even Spider was dirt. Why not? None of us has done anything but sit here on our asses getting high and whining while everything around us collapsed. Spider figured it must have been the effect of the sun's rays, making him see things so clearly. All those months they'd been expecting one of the Unternets to send out a repair program that would reboot the Obernet again. At first Spider and a guy called Zero-One tried to launch an emergency program through the interface. Zero-One intended to melt away the brain while Spider . . . well, he met up with Silver Spider. And after that, at some point, they'd all gotten lazy and couldn't do anything but wait for their next fix, for Ant.

"Dude, got a couple o' bennies for ya. Paint yo' day."

Spider trembled. The mere mention of paint and he flashed on a whole range of pastels, and that made him think about the plush bunnies that had been zooming around inside his head.

But the memories were nothing more than a faded picture at the edge of his perception.

"Okay, man. Thanks."

It was a peace offering. Better not to refuse. You never know when you could use 'em, Spider told himself. But he couldn't dismiss the nagging little questions he wanted to ask Ant, even though he knew the trouble they'd get him in if he did.

"Where d'you get your stuff, man?" Words come so damn quick. What was he trying to do, asking such a thing? But he had to know where he was at. You gotta know where you're at with your dealer.

"Here and there," Ant answered. His board rose and fell over small, invisible waves. Ant raised his hand to the nape of his neck, as if reassuring himself of something.

Spider squinted. Something was happening here and he didn't know what it was. Ant always running his hand over the back of his neck. But it wasn't just a nervous tic. Sparks danced around Ant, and then an intense anger flooded through Spider, rolling him over, grinding him down. And he knew that she, she had deceived him . . .

Zero-One had been the last one, he was sure. But that meant Zero wasn't special anymore! Spider leaped forward, eager to hear Ant's bones crack between his fingers, but the boy faded into the shadows at the far end of the street. And Spider stood there, alone beneath the hateful sun while the questions reared up inside him, croaking through his throat, trying to form into words in his mouth. Spider gagged. There was only one solution to the problem, and it was going to get very nasty. When he thought about Zero-One, he gagged again. Telling himself he needed some courage and a bit of Dr. Feelgood to get through to the end, he shoved one of the bennies into his mouth.

He knew where she was.

Down in the holy place, the Net Center. Nobody he knew had ever been down there. Or nobody who'd ever been there was able to talk about it. Either way was the same to Spider. He was at home in her net, belonged there, in fact. He was Spider, not some juicy little insect. She could catch him, but not destroy him.

Spider waited before the great house with the many doors, waited until it was dark. Silently he thought about the words he wanted to say to her. Just so he could talk to her—nothing more. She was different from Ant, understood the crystalline logic of what he said. In fact, she understood his very thoughts. Nothing to worry about, Spy. Nothing at all.

He tossed down the rest of the speed at one go. It was like he was going out on a date, a very special date. A "White Wedding," yeah. And nothing was certain in this world, or his world, or hers. Anything was possible. Man, Ant knew how a guy could have all the colors he wanted but Spy still owns the night, brother. The web. Nothing is fair in this world. He pushed against the nearest door. It had been ajar, as though left that way for someone expected. Someone who had finally arrived.

Darkness embraced him like clinging foam and it was warm, a familiar, long-forgotten warmth. Spider laughed silently and his body danced to the rhythm of his laughter as it beat out a mad tattoo. Then he tripped over a clicking, resisting, something. Spider picked it up without thinking. Felt like a metal bar.

In the end, he knew it was all one of Ant's crazy dreams. You didn't even have to think about it very long. But those dreams can get ugly very fast. One of his weapons. Always good to have a weapon. A weapon against the faceless things crouching in the chemical twilight zone.

And then, the air wrapped around him, crackling, and the hair on his arms stood up as if the energy of the whole city was focused on him. Boyah, what a trip! But something was wrong with his vision. And a stench engulfed him, not knife-sharp corrosive ozone, but a rotting, sweet scent, like—oh, no, fuck.

He knew his memories would bring them back, all the dead out of his past. And here they were already. But they'd never been so frightening. Those fucking bennies.

It must be the bennies, Spider thought to himself; Ant must have given him bad stuff, and he had made it worse by taking them all at once. Panic shuddered through him. And the monster came closer—she came closer.

Deftly she rushed toward him on the glistening thread. Her head was enormous and her three eyes were doors into other dimensions, terribly dangerous and sweetly fascinating. He wanted to run away, but something was making him walk toward this monstrous thing. All he could see were those eyes, and deep inside his head there was a humming sound—ancient, electric, insane. The bitter taste of vomit gagged in his throat. How could he let this happen—let her creep into his brain, let her do these things to him? She was not the Silver Spider of his dreams.

He swung the metal bar, surprised by how light it seemed in his hand. Almost as though it were an extension of his arm, or of his thoughts—or better yet, the fulfillment of his thoughts. Spider smiled grimly, and he wished she could see his expression.

There was a "splatch!" as the metal bar hit her head. An ugly comic-sound. Spider had never thought it would sound like this. The head splattered and cracked open. Yellow matter erupted around him and covered his face, seeking to drown him, like a slimy, moldy blanket, like a liquid corpse.

• • •

Spider threw up and staggered away, sliding down at last against the wall. He felt the spider web against his back and bare arms. Again he vomited. Though he was so small and weak, he had destroyed the monster. And was alone. Alone as though he were in his grave.

At last he knew what must be done. His hand knew what to do. The entire time he'd held the plug in one fist, a talisman against the night. He lifted the plug toward his neck and stopped, realizing at last what he was doing. But it was too late. Tricked, he was tricked. This wasn't a dream at all. This was reality.

Quiet. It was perfectly quiet, a sacred stillness. Time was without end and everything was meaningless—defeats, dreams, and victories. Spider closed his eyes and stared at the featureless wall that was the interior of his skull.

JOHN KESSEL

THE LAST AMERICAN

(2007)

THE LIFE OF ANDREW STEELE

Re-created by Fiona 13

Reviewed by TheOldGuy

"I don't blame my father for beating me. I don't blame him for tearing the book I was reading from my hands, and I don't blame him for locking me in the basement. When I was a child, I did blame him. I was angry, and I hated my father. But as I grew older I came to understand that he did what was right for me, and now I look upon him with respect and love, the respect and love he always deserved, but that I was unable to give him because I was too young and self-centered."

—Andrew Steele, 2077,
Conversation with Hagiographer

During the thirty-three years Andrew Steele occupied the Oval Office of what was then called the White House, in what was then called the United States of America (not to be confused with the current United State of Americans), on the corner of his desk he kept an antiquated device of the early twenty-first century called a taser. Typically used by law enforcement officers, it functioned by shooting out a thin wire that, once in contact with its target, delivered an electric shock of up to three hundred thousand volts. The victim was immediately incapacitated by muscle spasms and intense pain. This crude weapon was used for crowd control or to subdue suspects of crimes.

When Ambassador for the New Humanity Mona Vaidyanathan first visited Steele, she asked what the queer black object was. Steele told her that it had been the most frequent means of communication between his father and himself. "When I was ten years old," he told her, "within a single month my father used that on me sixteen times."

"That's horrible," she said.

"Not for a person with a moral imagination," Steele replied.

In this new biography of Steele, Fiona 13, the Grand Lady of Reproductions, presents the crowning achievement of her long career re-creating lives for the Cognosphere. Andrew Steele, when he died in 2100, had come to exemplify the twenty-first century, and his people, in a way that goes beyond the metaphorical. Drawing on every resource of the posthuman biographer, from heuristic modeling to reconstructive DNA sampling to forensic dreaming, Ms. 13 has produced this labor of, if not love, then obsession, and I for one, am grateful for it.

Fiona presents her new work in a hybrid form. Comparatively little of this biography is subjectively rendered. Instead, harking back to a bygone era, Fiona breaks up the narrative with long passages of *text*—strings of printed code that must be read with the eyes. Of course this adds the burden of learning the code to anyone seeking to experience her re-creation, but an accelerated prefrontal intervention is packaged with the biography. Fiona maintains that *text*, since it forces an artificial linearity on experience, stimulates portions of the left brain that seldom function in conventional experiential biographies. The result is that the person undergoing the life of Andrew Steele both lives through significant moments in Steele's subjectivity, and is drawn out of the stream of sensory and emotional reaction to contemplate the significance of that experience from the point of view of a wise commentator.

I trust I do not have to explain the charms of this form to those of you reading this review, but I recommend the experience to all cognizant entities who still maintain elements of curiosity in their affect repertoire.

• • •

CHILD

Appropriately for a man who was to so personify the twenty-first century, Dwight Andrew Steele was born on January 1, 2001. His mother, Rosamund Sanchez Steele, originally from Mexico, was a lab technician at the forestry school at North Carolina State University; his father, Herbert Matthew Steele, was a land developer and on the board of the Planter's Bank and Trust. Both of Steele's parents were devout Baptists and attended one of the new "big box" churches that had sprung up in the late twentieth in response to growing millennialist beliefs in the United States and elsewhere.

The young Steele was "homeschooled." This meant that Steele's mother devoted a portion of every day to teaching her son herself. The public school system was distrusted by large numbers of religious believers, who considered education by the state to be a form of indoctrination in moral error. Homeschoolers operated from the premise that the less contact their children had with the larger world, the better.

Unfortunately, in the case of Andrew this did not prevent him from meeting other children. Andrew was a small, serious boy, sensitive, and an easy target for bullies. This led to his first murder. Fiona 13 realizes this event for us through extrapolative genetic mapping.

We are in the playground, on a bright May morning. We are running across the crowded asphalt toward a climbing structure of wood and metal, when suddenly we are falling! A nine-year-old boy named Jason Terry has tripped us and, when we regain our feet, he tries to pull our pants down. We feel the sting of our elbows where they scraped the pavement, feel surprise and dismay, fear, anger. As Terry leans forward to grab the waistband of our trousers, we suddenly bring our knee up into Terry's face. Terry falls back, sits down awkwardly. The other children gathered laugh. The sound of the laughter in our

ears only enrages us more—are they laugh-
ing at us? The look of dismay turns to rage on
Terry's face. He is going to beat us up; now,
he is a deadly threat. We step forward, and
before Terry can stand, kick him full in the
face. Terry's head snaps back and strikes the
asphalt, and he is still.

The children gasp. A trickle of blood
flows from beneath Terry's ear. From across
the playground comes the monitor's voice:
"Andrew? Andrew Steele?"

I have never experienced a more vivid
moment in biography. There it all is: the complete assumption by Steele that he is the victim. The fear and rage. The horror, quickly
repressed. The later remorse, swamped by desperate justifications.

It was only through his father's political connections and acquiescence in private counseling (that the Steeles did not believe in, taking
psychology as a particularly pernicious form of
modern mumbo jumbo) that Andrew was kept
out of the legal system. He withdrew into the
family, his father's discipline, and his mother's
teaching.

More trouble was to follow. Keeping it secret
from his family, Herbert Steele had invested
heavily in real estate in the late aughts; he had
leveraged properties he purchased to borrow
money to invest in several hedge funds, hoping
to put the family into a position of such fundamental wealth that they would be beyond the
reach of economic vagaries.

When the Friends of the American League
set off the Atlanta nuclear blast in 2012, pushing the first domino of the Global Economic
Meltdown, Steele senior's financial house of
cards collapsed. The US government, having
spent itself into bankruptcy and dependence on
Asian debt support through ill-advised imperial schemes and paranoid reactions to global
terrorist threats, had no resources to deal with
the collapse of private finances. Herbert Steele
struggled to deal with the reversal, fell into a

depression, and died when he crashed a borrowed private plane into a golf course in Southern Pines.

Andrew was twelve years old. His mother,
finding part-time work as a data-entry clerk,
made barely enough money to keep them alive.
Andrew was forced into the public schools.
He did surprisingly well there. Andrew always
seemed mature for his years, deferential to his
elders, responsible, trustworthy, and able to see
others' viewpoints. He was slightly aloof from
his classmates and seemed more at home in the
presence of adults.

Unknown to his overstressed mother, Andrew
was living a secret life. On the Internet, under
a half dozen false IP addresses, he maintained
political websites. Through them he became one
of the world's most influential "bloggers."

A blog was a personal weblog, a site on the
worldwide computer system where individuals, either anonymously or in their own names,
commented on current affairs or their own lives.
Some of these weblogs had become prominent,
and their organizers and authors politically
important.

Andrew had a fiction writer's gift for invent-
ing consistent personalities, investing them with
brilliant argument and sharp observation. On
the "Political Theater" weblog, as Sacré True,
he argued for the impeachment of President
Harrison; on "Reason Season," as Tom Pain,
he demonstrated why Harrison's impeachment
would prove disastrous. Fiona sees this phase
of Steele's life as his education in manipulating
others' sensibilities. His emotion-laden arguments were astonishingly successful at twisting his interlocutors into rhetorical knots. To
unravel and respond to one of Steele's arguments rationally would take four times his space
and carry none of his propagandistic force.
Steele's argument against the designated hitter
rule even found its way into the platform of the
resurgent Republican Party.

• • •

INTERROGATOR

"You don't know why I acted, but I know why. I acted because it is necessary for me to act, because that's what, whether you like it or not, you require me to do. And I don't mind doing it because it's what I have to do. It's what I was born to do. I've never been appreciated for it but that's okay too because, frankly, no one is ever appreciated for what they do.

"But before you presume to judge me realize that you are responsible. I am simply your instrument. I took on the burden of your desires when I didn't want to—I would just as gladly have had that cup pass me by—but I did it, and I have never complained. And I have never felt less than proud of what I have done. I did what was necessary, for the benefit of others. If it had been up to me I would never have touched a single human being, but I am not complaining.

"I do, however, ask you, humbly, if you have any scrap of decency left, if you have any integrity whatsoever, not to judge me. You do not have that right.

"Ask Carlo Sanchez, ask Alfonso Garadiana, ask Sayid Ramachandran, ask Billy Chen. Ask them what was the right thing to do. And then, when you've got the answer from their bleeding corpses, then, and only then, come to me."

—Andrew Steele, 2020,
Statement before Board of Inquiry

Contemporary readers must remember the vast demographic and other circumstantial differences that make the early twenty-first century an alien land to us. When Steele was sixteen years old, the population of the world was an astonishing 6.8 billion, fully half of whom were under the age of twenty-five, the overwhelming majority of those young and striving individuals living in poverty, but with access, through the technologies that had spread widely over the previous twenty years, to unprecedented unregulated information. Few of them could be said to have been adequately acculturated. The history of the next forty years, including Steele's part in that history, was shaped by this fact.

In 2017 Steele was conscripted into the US Army pursuing the Oil War on two continents. Because he was fluent in Spanish, he served as an interrogator with the Seventy-First Infantry Division stationed in Venezuela. His history as an interrogator included the debriefing of the rightfully elected president of that nation in 2019. Fiona puts us there:

We are standing in the back of a small room with concrete walls, banks of fluorescent lights above, a HVAC vent and exposed ducts hanging from the ceiling. The room is cold. We have been standing for a long time and our back is stiff. We have seen many of these sessions, and all we can think about right now is getting out of here, getting a beer, and getting some sleep.

In the center of the room Lieutenant Haslop and a civilian contractor are interrogating a small brown man with jet-black shoulder-length hair. Haslop is very tall and stoop shouldered, probably from a lifetime of ducking responsibility. The men call him "Slop" behind his back.

The prisoner's name is Alfonso Garadiana. His wrists are tied together behind him, and the same rope stretches down to his ankles, also tied together. The rope is too short, so that the only way he can stand is with his knees flexed painfully. But every time he sways, as if to fall, the contractor signals Haslop, who pokes him with an electric prod. Flecks of blood spot Garadiana's once-brilliant white shirt. A cut over his eyebrow is crusted with dried blood, and the eye below it is half-closed.

The contractor, Mr. Gray, is neat and shaved and in control. "So," he says in Spanish, "where are the Jacaranda virus stores?"

Garadiana does not answer. It's unclear whether he has even understood.

Gray nods to Haslop again.

Haslop blinks his eyes, swallows. He slumps into a chair, rests his brow in one hand. "I can't do this anymore," he mutters, only apparently to himself. He wouldn't say it aloud if he didn't want us to hear it, even if he doesn't know that himself. We are sick to death of his weakness.

We step forward and take the prod from his hand. "Let me take care of this, sir." We swing the back of our hand against Garadiana's face, exactly the same motion we once used to hit a backhand in high school tennis. The man's head snaps back, and he falls to the floor. We move in with the prod.

Upon the failure of the Oil War and the defeat of the government that pursued it, a reaction took place, including war-crimes investigations that led to Steele's imprisonment from 2020 to 2025. Fiona gives us a glimpse of Steele's sensorium in his third year in maximum-security prison:

We're hungry. Above us the air rattles from the ventilator. On the table before us in our jail cell is a notebook. We are writing our testament. It's a distillation of everything we know to be absolutely true about the human race and its future. There are things we know in our DNA that cannot be understood by strict rationality, though reason is a powerful tool and can help us to communicate these truths to those who do not, because of incapacity or lack of experience, grasp them instinctively.

The blogs back when we were fourteen were just practice. Here, thanks to the isolation, we are able to go deep, to find the roots of human truth and put them down in words.

We examine the last sentence we have written: "It is the hero's fate to be misunderstood."

A guard comes by and raps the bars of our cell. "Still working on the great opus, Andy?"

We ignore him, close the manuscript, move from the table, and begin to do push-ups in the narrow space beside the cot.

The guard raps again on the bars. "How about an answer, killer?" His voice is testy.

We concentrate on doing the push-up correctly. Eleven. Twelve. Thirteen. Fourteen . . .

When we get out of here, all this work will make a difference.

This was indeed the case, Fiona shows us, but not in the way that Steele intended. As a work of philosophy his testament was rejected by all publishers. He struggled to make a living in the Long Emergency that was the result of the oil decline and the global warming–spawned environmental disasters that hit with full force in the 2020s. These changes were asymmetric, but though some regions felt them more than others, none were unaffected. The flipping of the Atlantic current turned 2022 into the first Year Without a Summer in Europe. Torrential rains in North Africa, the desertification of the North American Great Plains, mass wildlife migrations, drastic drops in grains production, die-offs of marine life, and decimated global fish stocks were among only the most obvious problems with which worldwide civilization struggled. And Andrew Steele was out of prison, without a connection in the world.

• • •

ARTIST

"The great artist is a rapist. It is his job to plant a seed, an idea or an emotion, in the viewer's mind. He uses every tool available to enforce his will. The audience doesn't know what it wants, but he knows what it wants, and needs, and he gives it to them.

"To the degree I am capable of it, I strive
to be a great artist."
—Andrew Steele, 2037,
"Man of Steele,"
Interview on *VarietyNet*

At this moment of distress, Steele saw an
opportunity, and turned his political testament into a bestselling novel, *What's Wrong
with Heroes?* A film deal followed immediately.
Steele insisted on being allowed to write the
screenplay, and against its better judgment,
the studio relented. Upon its release, *What's
Wrong With Heroes?* became the highest gross-
ing film in the history of cinema. In the character of Roark McMaster, Steele created a virile
philosopher king who spoke to the desperate
hopes of millions. With the money he made,
Steele conquered the entertainment world. A
series of blockbuster films, television series,
and virtual adventures followed. This photo
link shows him on the set of *The Betrayal*, his
historical epic of the late-twentieth century.
The series, conflating the Vietnam conflict with
the two Iraq wars, presents the fiascoes of the
early twenty-first as the result of Machiavellian
subversives and their bad-faith followers taking advantage of the innocence of the American
populace, undermining what was once a strong
and pure-minded nation.

Fiona gives us a key scene from the series:

INT. AMERICAN AIRLINES FLIGHT 11

*Two of the hijackers, wearing green camo,
are gathered around a large man seated in the
otherwise-empty first-class cabin of the 757. The
big man, unshaven, wears a shabby Detroit Tigers
baseball cap.*

WALEED
(*frantic*)
What shall we do now?

MOORE
Keep the passengers back in coach. Is Moham-
mad on course? How long?

ABDULAZIZ
(*calling back from cockpit*)
Allah willing—three minutes.

Moore glances out the plane window.
MOORE'S POV—through window, an aerial
view of Manhattan on a beautiful clear day

CLOSE ON MOORE
Smirks.

MOORE
Time to go.

*Moore hefts his bulk from the first-class seat, moves
toward the onboard baggage closet near the front of
the plane.*

ABDULAZIZ
What are you doing?

*From out of a hanging suit bag, Moore pulls a
parachute, and straps it on.*

WALEED
Is this part of the plan?

*Moore jerks up the lever on the plane's exterior door
and yanks on it. It does not budge.*

MOORE
Don't just stand there, Waleed! Help me!

*Waleed moves to help Moore, and reluctantly,
Abdulaziz joins them.*

ATTA
(*from cockpit*)
There it is! Allah akbar!

*Moore and the other two hijackers break the seal
and the door flies open. A blast of wind sucks*

Abdulaziz and Waleed forward; they fall back onto the plane's deck. Moore braces himself against the edge of the door with his hands.

MOORE

In the name of the Democratic Party, the compassionate, the merciful—so long, boys!

Moore leaps out of the plane.

The Betrayal was the highest rated series ever to run on American television, and cemented Steele's position as the most bankable mass-appeal Hollywood producer since Spielberg. At the age of thirty-eight, Steele married the actress Esme Napoli, leading lady in three of his most popular films.

• • •

RELIGIOUS LEADER

The next section of Fiona's biography begins with this heartrending experience from Steele's middle years:

We are in a sumptuous hotel suite with a blonde, not wearing much of anything. We are chasing her around the bed.

"You can't catch me!"

We snag her around the waist, and pull her onto the bed. "I've already caught you. You belong to me." We hold up her ring finger, with its platinum band. "You see?"

"I'm full of nanomachines," she says breathlessly. "If you catch me you'll catch them."

The Scarlet Plague has broken out in Los Angeles, after raging for a month in Brazil. We have fled the city with Esme and are holed up in this remote hotel in Mexico.

"When are we going to have these children?" we ask her. "We need children. Six at least."

"You're going to have to work harder than this to deserve six children," Esme says.

"The world is a mess. Do we want to bring children into it?"

"The world has always been a mess. We need to bring children into it because it's a mess." We kiss her perfect cheek.

But a minute later, as we make love, we spot the growing rash along the inside of Esme's thigh.

The death of Steele's wife came near the beginning of the plague decade, followed by the Sudden War and the Collapse. Fiona cites the best estimates of historiographers that, between 2040 and 2062, the human population of the earth went from 8.2 to somewhat less than two billion. The toll was slightly higher in the less developed nations; on the other hand, resistance to the plagues was higher among humans of the tropical regions. This situation in the middle years of the century transformed the Long Emergency of 2020 to 2040—a condition in which civilization, although stressed, might still be said to function, and with which Steele and his generation had coped, into the Die-Off, in which the only aspect of civilization that, even in the least affected regions, might be said to function was a desperate triage.

One of the results of the Long Emergency had been to spark widespread religious fervor. Social and political disruptions had left millions searching for certitudes. Longevity breakthroughs, new medicine, genetic engineering, cyborging, and AI pushed in one direction, while widespread climatic change, fights against deteriorating civil and environmental conditions, and economic disruptions pushed in another. The young warred against the old, the rich against the poor. Reactionary religious movements raged on four continents. Interpreting the chaos of the twenty-first century in terms of eschatology was a winning business. Terrorism in the attempt to bring on utopia or the end of the world was a common reality. Steele, despite his grief, rapidly grasped that art, even popular art, had no role in this world. So he turned, readily, to religion.

"Human evolution is a process of moral evolution. The thing that makes us different from animals is our understanding of the ethical implications of every action that we perform: those that we must perform, those that we choose. Some actions are matters of contingency, and some are matters of free will.

"Evolution means we will eventually come to fill the universe. To have our seed spread far and wide. That is what we are here for. To engender those children, to bear them, to raise them properly, to have them extend their—and our—thought, creativity, joy, understanding, to every particle of the visible universe."
—Andrew Steele,
"Sermon in the Cascades," 2052

Steele's Church of Humanity grew rapidly in the 2040s; while the population died and cities burned, its membership more than doubled every year, reaching several millions by 2050. Steele's credo of the Hero transferred easily to religious terms; his brilliantly orchestrated ceremonies sparked ecstatic responses; he fed the poor and comforted the afflicted and, using every rhetorical device at his command, persuaded his followers that the current troubles were the birth of a new utopian age, that every loss had its compensation, that sacrifice was noble, that reward was coming, that from their loins would spring a new and better race, destined to conquer the stars. Love was the answer.

His creed crossed every ethnic, racial, sexual, gender preference, class, and age barrier. Everyone was human, and all equal.

The Church of Humanity was undeniably successful in helping millions of people, not just in the United States but across the bleeding globe, deal with the horrors of the Die-Off. It helped them to rally in the face of unimaginable psychological and material losses. But it was not the only foundation for the recovery. By the time some semblance of order was restored

to world affairs in the 2060s, genetically modified humans, the superbrights, were attempting to figure a way out of the numerous dead ends of capitalism, antiquated beliefs, and a dysfunctional system of nation-states. This was a period of unexampled experimentation, and the blossoming of many technologies that had been only potentialities prior to the collapse, among them the uploading of human identities, neurological breakthroughs on the origins of altruism and violence, grafted information capacities, and free quantum energy.

Most of these developments presented challenges to religion. Steele came to see such changes as a threat to fundamental humanity. So began his monstrous political career.

• • •

POLITICIAN

"The greatest joy in life is putting yourself in the circumstance of another person. To see the world through his eyes, to feel the air on her skin, to breathe in deeply the spirit of their souls. To have his joy and trouble be equally real to you. To know that others are fully and completely human, just as you are. To get outside of your own subjectivity, and to see the world from a completely different and equally valid perspective, to come fully to understand them. When that point of understanding is reached, there is no other word for the feeling that you have than love. Just as much as you love yourself, as you love your children, you love this other.

"And at that point, you must exterminate them. That is the definition of hard."
—Andrew Steele, *What I Believe*, 2071

Steele was swept into office as President of the reconstituted United States in the election of 2064, with his Humanity Party in complete control of the Congress. In his first hundred days, Steele signed a raft of legislation comprising his Humanity Initiative. Included were The Repopulation Act that forced all women of childbearing age to have no fewer than four children, a bold space colonization program, restrictions on genetic alterations and technological body modifications, the wiping clean of all uploaded personalities from private and public databases, the Turing Limit on AI, the Neurological Protection Act of 2065, and the establishment of a legal "standard human being."

In Steele's first term, "nonstandard" humans were allowed to maintain their civil rights, but were identified by injected markers, their movements and employment restricted by the newly established Humanity Agency. Through diplomatic efforts and the international efforts of the Church of Humanity, similar policies were adapted, with notable areas of resistance, throughout much of the world.

In Steele's second term, the HA was given police powers and the nonstandard gradually stripped of civil and property rights. By his third term, those who had not managed to escape the country lost all legal rights and were confined to posthuman reservations, popularly known as "Freak Towns." The establishment of the Protectorate over all of North and South America stiffened resistance elsewhere, and resulted in the uneasy Global Standoff. Eventually, inevitably, came the First and Second Human Wars.

Fiona includes a never-before–experienced moment from the twenty-third year of Steele's presidency.

We are in a command bunker, a large, splendidly appointed room, one whole wall of which is a breathtaking view of the Grand Tetons. We sit at a table with our closest advisors, listening to General Jinjur describe their latest defeat by the New Humans. There are tears in her eyes as she recounts the loss of the Fifth Army in the assault on Madrid.

We do not speak. Our cat, Socrates, sits on our lap, and we scratch him behind his ears. He purrs.

"How many dead?" Chief of Command Taggart asks.

"Very few, sir," reports Jinjur. "But over ninety percent converted. It's their new amygdalic bomb. It destroys our troops' will to fight. The soldiers just lay down their arms and go off looking for something to eat. You try organizing an autistic army."

"At least they're good at math," says Secretary Bloom.

"How can these posthumans persist?" Dexter asks. "We've exterminated millions. How many of them are left?"

"We can't know, sir. They keep making more."

"But they don't even fight," says Taggart. "They must be on the point of extinction."

"It has never been about fighting, sir."

"It's this damned subversion," says Taggart. "We have traitors among us. They seed genetic changes among the people. They turn our own against us. How can we combat that?"

General Jinjur gathers herself. She is quite a striking woman, the flower of the humanity we have fought to preserve for so many years. "If I may be permitted to say so, we are fighting ourselves. We are trying to conquer our own human élan. Do you want to live longer? Anyone who wants to live longer will eventually become posthuman. Do you want to understand the universe? Anyone who wants to understand the universe will eventually become posthuman. Do you want peace of mind? Anyone who wants peace of mind will eventually become posthuman."

Something in her tone catches us, and we are finally moved to speak. "You are one of them, aren't you?"

"Yes," she says.

The contemporary citizen need not be troubled with, and Fiona does not provide, any detailed recounting of the war's progress, or how it ended in the Peace that Passeth All Understanding of 2096. The treatment of the remaining humans, the choices offered them, the removal of those few persisting to Mars, and their continued existence there under quarantine, are all material for another work.

Similarly, the circumstances surrounding Steele's death—the cross, the taser, the Shetland pony—so much a subject of debate, speculation, and conspiracy theory, surely do not need rehearsing here. We know what happened to him. He destroyed himself.

· · ·

AWAITING FURTHER INSTRUCTIONS

"The highest impulse of which a human being is capable is to sacrifice himself in the service of the community of which he is a part, even when that community does not recognize him, and heaps opprobrium upon him for that sacrifice. In fact, such scorn is more often than not to be expected. The true savior of his fellows is not deterred by the prospect of rejection, though carrying the burden of his unappreciated gift is a trial that he can never, but for a few moments, escape. It is the hero's fate to be misunderstood."

—*What's Wrong with Heroes?*
(unpublished version)

Fiona 13 ends her biography with a simple accounting of the number of beings, human and posthuman, who died as a result of Steele's life. She speculates that many of these same beings might not have lived had he not lived as well, and comes to no formal conclusion, utilitarian or otherwise, as to the moral consequences of the life of Dwight Andrew Steele.

Certainly few tears are shed for Andrew Steele, and few for the ultimate decline of the human race. I marvel at that remnant of humans who, using technologies that he abhorred, have incorporated into their minds a slice of Steele's personality in the attempt to make themselves into the image of the man they see as their savior. Indeed, I must confess to more than a passing interest in their poignant delusions, their comic, mystifying pastimes, their habitual conflicts, their simple loves and hates, their inability to control themselves, their sudden and tragic enthusiasms.

Bootlegged Steele personalities circulate in the Cognosphere, and it may be that those of you who, like me, on occasion edit their capacities in order to spend recreational time being human, will avail themselves of this no doubt unique and terrifying experience.

KEN MACLEOD

EARTH HOUR

(2011)

THE ASSASSIN SLUNG the bag concealing his weapon over his shoulder and walked down the steps to the rickety wooden jetty. He waited as the Sydney Harbour ferry puttered into Neutral Bay, cast on and then cast off at the likewise tiny quay on the opposite bank, and crossed the hundred or so meters to Kurraba Point. He boarded, waved a hand gloved in artificial skin across the fare taker, and settled on a bench near the prow, with the weapon in its blue nylon zipped bag balanced across his knees.

The sun was just above the horizon in the west, the sky clear but for the faint luminous haze of smart dust, each drifting particle of which could at any moment deflect a photon of sunlight and sparkle before the watching eye. A slow rain of shiny soot, removing carbon from the air and as it drifted down providing a massively redundant platform for observation and computation; a platform the assassin's augmented eyes used to form an image of the city

and its environs in his likewise augmented visual cortex. He turned the compound image over in his head, watching traffic flows and wind currents, the homeward surge of commuters and the flocking of fruit bats, the exchange of pheromones and cortext messages, the jiggle of stock prices and the tramp of a million feet, in one single godlike POV that saw it all six ways from Sunday and that too soon became intolerable, dizzying the unaugmented tracts of the assassin's still mostly human brain.

One could get drunk on this. The assassin wrenched himself from the hubristic stochastic and focused, narrowing his attention until he found the digital spoor of the man he aimed to kill: a conference delegate pack, a train fare, a hotel tab, an airline booking for a seat that it was the assassin's job to prevent being filled the day after the conference . . . The assassin had followed this trail already, an hour earlier, but it amused him to confirm it and to bring it up to date, with an overhead and a street-level view of the target's unsuspecting stroll toward his hotel in Macleay Street.

It amused him, too, that the target was simultaneously keeping a low profile—no media appearances, backstage at the conference, a hotel room far less luxurious than he could afford, vulgar as all hell, tarted in synthetic mahogany and artificial marble and industrial sheet diamond—while styling himself at every opportunity with the obsolete title under which he was most widely known, as though he reveled in his contradictory notoriety as a fixer behind the scenes, famous for being unnoticed. "Valtos, first of the Reform Lords." That was how the man loved to be known. The gewgaw he preened himself on. A bauble he'd earned by voting to abolish its very significance, yet still liked to play with, to turn over in his hands, to flash. What a shit, the assassin thought, what a prick! That wasn't the reason for killing him, but it certainly made it easier to contemplate.

As the ferry visited its various stages the number of passengers increased. The assassin shifted the bag from across his knees and propped it in front of him, earning a nod and a grateful smile from the woman who sat down on the bench beside him. At Circular Quay he carried the bag off, and after clearing the pier he squatted and opened the bag. With a few quick movements he assembled the collapsible bicycle inside, folded and zipped the bag to stash size, and clipped the bag under the saddle.

Then he mounted the cycle and rode away to the left, around the harbor and up the long zigzag slope to Potts Point.

• • •

There was no reason for unease. Angus Cameron sat on a wicker chair on a hotel room balcony overlooking Sydney Harbour. On the small round table in front of him an Islay malt and a Havana panatela awaited his celebration. The air was warm, his clothing loose and fresh. Thousands of fruit bats labored across the dusk sky,

from their daytime roost in the Botanic Gardens to their nighttime feeding grounds. From three stories below, the vehicle sounds and voices of the street carried no warnings.

Nothing was wrong, and yet something was wrong. Angus tipped back his chair and closed his eyes. He summoned headlines and charts. Local and global. Public and personal. Business and politics. The Warm War between the great power blocs, EU/Russia/PRC versus FUS/Japan/India/Brazil, going on as usual: diplomacy in Australasia, insurgency in Africa. Nothing to worry about there. Situation, as they say, nominal. Angus blinked away the images and shook his head. He stood up and stepped back into the room and paced around. He spread his fingers wide and waved his hands about, rotating his wrists as he did so. Nothing. Not a tickle.

Satisfied that the room was secure, he returned to his balcony seat. The time was fifteen minutes before eight. Angus toyed with his Zippo and the glass, and with the thought of lighting up, of taking a sip. He felt oddly as if that would be bad luck. It was a quite distinct feeling from the deeper unease, and easier to dismiss. Nevertheless, he waited. Ten minutes to go.

At eight minutes before eight his right ear started ringing. He flicked his earlobe.

"Yes?" he said.

His sister's avatar appeared in the corner of his eye. Calling from Manchester, England, EU. Local time 07:52.

"Oh, hello, Catriona," he said.

The avatar fleshed, morphing from a cartoon to a woman in her midthirties, a few years younger than him, sitting insubstantially across from him. His little sister, looking distracted. At least, he guessed she was. They hadn't spoken for five months, but she didn't normally make calls with her face unwashed and hair unkempt.

"Hi, Angus," Catriona said. She frowned. "I know this is . . . maybe a bit paranoid . . . but is this call secure?"

"Totally," said Angus.

Unlike Catriona, he had a firm technical

grasp on the mechanism of cortical calls: the uniqueness of each brain's encoding of sensory impulses adding a further layer of impenetrable encryption to the cryptographic algorithms routinely applied . . . A uniquely encoded thought struck him.

"Apart from someone lip-reading me, I guess." He cupped his hand around his mouth. "Okay?"

Catriona looked more irritated than reassured by this demonstrative caution.

"Okay," she said. She took a deep breath. "I'm very dubious about the next release of the upgrade, Angus. It has at least one mitochondrial module that's not documented at all."

"That's impossible!" cried Angus, shocked. "It'd never get through."

"It's got this far," said Catriona. "No record of testing, either. I keep objecting, and I keep getting told it's being dealt with or it's not important or otherwise fobbed off. The release goes live in a *month*, Angus. There's no way that module can be documented in that time, let alone tested."

"I don't get it," said Angus. "I don't get it at all. If this were to get out it would sink Syn Bio's stock, for a start. Then there's audits and prosecutions . . . the Authority would break them up and stamp on the bits. Forget whistleblowing, Catriona, you should take this to the Authority in the company's *own* interests."

"I have," said Catriona. "And I just get the same runaround."

"What?"

If he'd heard this from anyone else, Angus wouldn't have believed it. The Human Enhancement Authority's reputation was beyond reproach. Impartial, impersonal, incorruptible, it was seen as the very image of an institution entrusted with humanity's (at least, European humanity's) evolutionary future.

Angus was old enough to remember when software didn't just seamlessly improve, day by day or hour by hour, but came out in discrete tranches called *releases*, several times a year. Genetic tech was still at that stage. Catriona's

employer Syn Bio (mostly) supplied it, the HEA checked and (usually) approved it, and everyone in the EU who didn't have some religious objection found the latest fix in their physical mail and swallowed it.

"They're stonewalling," Catriona said.

"Don't worry," said Angus. "There must be some mistake. A bureaucratic foul-up. I'll look into it."

"Well, keep my name out of—"

The lights came on for Earth Hour.

"That won't be easy," Angus said, flinching and shielding his eyes as the balcony, the room, the building, and the whole sweep of cityscape below him lit up. "They'll know our connection, they'll know you've been asking—"

"I asked you to keep my name out of it," said Catriona. "I didn't say it would be easy."

"Look into it without bringing my *own* name into it?"

"Yes, exactly!" Catriona ignored his sarcasm—deliberately, from her tone. She looked around. "I can't concentrate with all this going on. Catch you later."

Angus waved a hand at the image of his sister, now ghostly under the blaze of the balcony's overhead lighting. "I'll keep in touch," he said dryly.

"Bye, bro."

Catriona faded. Angus lit his small cigar at last, and sipped the whisky. Ah. That was good, as was the view. Sydney Harbour was hazy in the distance, and even the gleaming shells of the Opera House, just visible over the rooftops, were fuzzy at the edges, the smart dust in the air scattering the extravagant outpouring of light. Angus savored the whisky and cigar to their respective ends, and then went out.

• • •

On the street the light was even brighter, to the extent that Angus missed his footing occasionally as he made his way up Macleay Street toward Kings Cross. He felt dazzled and disoriented, and considered lowering the gain on his eyes—but that, he felt in some obscure way, would not only have been cheating, it would have been missing the point. The whole thing about Earth Hour was to squander electricity, and if that spree had people reeling in the streets as if drunk, that was entirely in the spirit of the celebration.

It was all symbolic anyway, he thought. The event's promoters knew as well as he did that the amount of CO_2 being removed from the atmosphere by Earth Hour was insignificant—only a trivial fraction of the electricity wasted was carbon-negative rather than neutral—but it was the principle of the thing, dammit!

He found a table outside a bar close to Fitzroy Gardens, a tree-shaded plaza on the edge of which a transparent globe fountained water and light. He tapped an order on the table, and after a minute a barman arrived with a tall lager on a tray. Angus tapped again to tip, and settled back to drink and think. The air was hot as well as bright, the chilled beer refreshing. Around the fountain a dozen teenagers cooled themselves more directly, jumping in and out of the arcs of spray and splashing in the circular pool around the illuminated globe. Yells and squeals; few articulate words. Probably cortexting each other. It was the thing. The youth of today. Talking silently and behind your back. Angus smiled reminiscently and indulgently. He muted the enzymes that degraded the alcohol, letting himself get drunk. He could reverse it on an instant later, he thought, then thought that the trouble with that was that you seldom knew when to do it. Except in a real life-threatening emergency, being drunk meant you didn't know when it was time to sober up. You just noticed that things kept crashing.

He gave the table menu a minute of baffled inspection, then swayed inside to order his second pint. The place was almost empty. Angus heaved himself onto a barstool beside a tall, thin woman about his own age who sat alone and to all appearances collected crushed cigarette butts. She was just now adding to the collection,

stabbing a good inch into the ashtray. A thick tall glass of pink stuff with a straw anchored her other hand to the bar counter. She wore a singlet over a thin bra, and skinny jeans above gold slingbacks. Ratty blond hair. It was a look.

"I've had two," she was explaining to the barman, who wasn't listening. She swung her badly aimed gaze on Angus. "And I'm squiffy already. God, I'm a cheap date."

"I'm cheaper," said Angus. "Squiffier, too. Drunk as a lord. Ha-ha. I used to be a lord, you know."

The woman's eyes got glassier. "So you did," she said. "So you did. Pleased to meet you, Mr. Cameron."

"Just call me Angus."

She extended a limp hand. "Glenda Glendale."

Angus gave her fingers a token squeeze, thinking that with a name like that she'd never stood a chance.

"Now ain't that the truth," Glenda said, with unexpected bitterness, and dipped her head to the straw.

"Did I say that out loud?" Angus said. "Jeez. Sorry."

"Nothing to be sorry about," Glenda said.

She opened a fresh pack of cigarettes, and tapped one out.

• • •

The assassin crouched behind a recycling bin in the alleyway beside the Thai restaurant opposite the bar, his bicycle propped against the wall. He zoomed his gaze to watch the target settle his arse on the stool, his elbow on the counter, and his attention on the floozy. Perfect. The assassin decided this was the moment to seize. He reached for the bike and with a few practiced twisting motions had it dismantled. The wheels he laid aside. The frame's reassembly, to a new form and function, was likewise deft.

• • •

Glenda fumbled the next lighting-up, and dropped her lighter. Angus stooped from the stool, more or less by reflex, to pick it up. As he did so there was a soft thud, and a moment later the loudest scream he'd ever heard. Glenda's legs lashed straight out. Her shin swiped his ear and struck his shoulder, tipping him to the floor. He crashed with the relaxation and anesthesia of the drunk. Glenda fell almost on top of him, all her limbs thrashing, her scream still splitting his ears. Angus raised his head and saw a feathered shaft sticking about six inches out of her shoulder.

The wound was nothing like severe enough to merit the screams or the spasms. Toxin, then. Modified stonefish, at a guess. The idea wasn't just that you died (though you did, in about a minute). You died in the worst pain it was possible to experience.

The barman vaulted the counter, feet hitting the floor just clear of Glenda's head. In his right hand he clutched a short-bladed sharp knife, one he might have used to slice limes. Angus knew exactly what he intended to do with it, and was appalled at the man's reckless courage.

"No!" Angus yelled.

Too late. A second dart struck the barman straight in the chest. He clutched at it for a moment; then his arms and legs flailed out and he keeled over, screaming even louder than Glenda. Now there were two spasming bodies on the floor. The knife skittered under a table.

Everything went dark, but it was just the end of Earth Hour. A good moment for the shooter to make their escape—or to finish the job.

Angus rolled on his back to keep an eye on the window and the doorway, and propelled himself with his feet along the floor, groping for the knife. His hand closed around the black handle. On his belly again, he elbowed his way to Glenda, grabbed her hair, slit her throat, and then slid the blade between cervical vertebrae and kept on cutting. He carried out the decapitation with skills he'd long ago used on deer. She didn't struggle—her nerves were already at sat-uration. It wasn't possible to add to this level of pain. Through a gusher of blood Angus crawled past the barman and did the same for him.

He hoped someone had called the police. He hoped that whoever had shot the darts had fled. Keeping low, stooping, he scurried around the back of the counter and reached up cautiously for the ice bucket. He got one on the ground and saw to his relief that there was another. He retrieved that too. Holding them in his arms, he slithered on his knees across the bloody floor back to the front of the bar, and stuffed the severed heads in one by one, jamming them in the ice.

Above the screaming from outside and the peal of alarms came the sound of jets. A police VTOL descended on the plaza, downdraft blowing tables away like litter in a breeze. The side opened and a cop, visored and armored, leapt out and sprinted across.

Angus stood up, blood-drenched from head to foot, knife in hand, arms wrapped awkwardly around the two ice buckets, from which the victims' hair and foreheads grotesquely protruded.

The copper halted in the doorway, taking in the scene in about a second.

"Well done, mate," he said. He reached out for the buckets. "Quick thinking. Now let's get these people to hospital."

• • •

Monstrous, sticky with blood, Angus crossed the street and stood in the alleyway at a barrier of black-and-yellow crime-scene tape. Backtracking the darts' trajectory had been the work of moments for the second cop out of the VTOL: even minutes after the attack, the lines in the smart soot had glowed like vapor trails in any enhanced gaze. An investigator in an isolation suit lifted the crossbow with gloved reverent hands. Cat-sized sniffing devices stalked about, extending sensors and sampling pads.

"What's with the bicycle wheels?" Angus asked, pointing.

"Surplus to requirements," the investigator said, standing up, holding the crossbow. She turned it over and around. "Collapsible bike, pre-grown tubular wood, synthetic. See, the handlebars form the bow, the crossbar the stock, the saddle the shoulder piece, the chain and pedal the winding mechanism, and the brake cable is the string. The darts were stashed inside one of the pieces."

"Seen that trick before?"

"Yeah, it's a hunting model."

"People go hunting on bicycles?"

"It's a sport." She laughed. "Offended any hunters lately?"

Angus wished he could see her face. He liked her voice.

"I offend a lot of people."

The investigator's head tilted. "Oh. So you do. Lord Valtos, huh?"

"Just call me—" He remembered what had happened to the last person he'd said that to, then decided not to be superstitious. "Just call me Angus. Angus Cameron."

"Whatever." She pulled off her hood and shook out her hair. "Fuck." She looked disgustedly at the cat things. "No traces. No surprise. Probably a spray job. You know, plastic skin? Even distorts the smart dust readings and street cam footage."

"You can do that?"

"Sure. It's expensive." She gave him a look. "I guess you're worth it."

Angus shrugged. "I'm rich, but my enemies are richer."

"So you're in deep shit."

"Only if they're smarter as well as richer, which I doubt."

"If you're smart, you'll not walk back to the hotel."

He took the hint, and the lift. They shrouded him in plastic for it, so the blood wouldn't get on the seats.

•   •   •

The reaction caught up with Angus as soon as the hotel room door closed behind him. He rushed to the bathroom and vomited. Shaking, he stripped off. As he emptied his pockets before throwing the clothes in the basket he found he'd picked up Glenda's lighter and cigarette pack. He put them to one side and showered. Afterward he sat in a bathrobe on the balcony, sipping malt on an empty stomach and chain-smoking Glenda's remaining cigarettes. She wouldn't be needing these for a few months. By then she might not even want them—the hospital would no doubt throw in a fix for her addiction, at least on the physical level, as it regrew her body and repaired her brain. Angus's earlier celebratory cigarillo had left him with a craving, and for the moment he indulged it. He'd take something to cure it in the morning.

When he felt steady enough, he closed his eyes and looked at the news. He found himself a prominent item on it. Spokespersons for various Green and Aboriginal coalitions had already disclaimed responsibility and deplored the attempt on his life. At this moment a sheepish representative of a nuclear-waste-handling company was in the studio, making a like disavowal. Angus smiled. He didn't think any of these were responsible—they'd have done a better job— but it pleased him to have his major opponents on the back foot. The potential benefit from that almost outweighed the annoyance of finding himself on the news at all.

The assassination attempt puzzled him. All the enemies he could think of—the list was long—would have sent a team to kill him, if they'd wanted to do something so drastic and potentially counterproductive. It seemed to him possible that the assassin had acted alone. That troubled him. Angus had always held that lone assassins were far more dangerous and prevalent than conspiracies.

He reviewed the bios linked to as shallow background for the news items about him. Most of them got the basic facts of his life right, from his childhood early in the century on a wind farm and experimental Green community in the Western Isles, through his academically mediocre but socially brilliant student years, when the networks and connections he'd established soon enabled his deals and ventures in the succession of technological booms that had kept the bubble economy expanding by fits and starts through seven decades: carbon capture, synthetic biology, microsatellites, fusion, smart dust, anti-aging, rejuve, augments . . . and so on, up to his current interest in geoengineering. Always in before the boom, out before the bust, he'd even ventured into politics via a questionably bestowed peerage just in time for the packed self-abolition of the Lords and to emerge with some quite unearned credit for the Reform. The descriptions ranged from "visionary social entrepreneur" and "daring venture capitalist" to "serial confidence trickster" and "brazen charlatan." There was truth in all of them. He'd burned a lot of fortunes in his time, while adding to his own. The list of people who might hold a private grudge against him was longer than the list of his public enemies.

Speaking of which, he had a conference to go to in the morning. He stubbed out the last of Glenda's cigarettes and went to bed.

• • •

The assassin woke at dawn on Manly Beach. He'd slept under a monofilament weave blanket, in a hollow where the sand met the scrub. He wore nothing but a watch and swimming trunks. He stood up, stretched, scrunched the blanket into the trunks' pocket, and went for a swim. No one was about.

Shoulder-deep in the sea, the assassin removed his trunks and watch, clutching them in one hand while rubbing his skin and hair all over with the other. He put them back on when he was sure that every remaining trace of the synthetic skin would be gone. Most of it, almost every scrap, had been dissolved as soon as he'd keyed a sequence on his palm after his failed attempt, just before he'd made his way, with a new appearance (his own) and chemical spoor, through various prechosen alleys and doorways and then sharp left on the next street, up to Kings Cross, and onto the train to Manly. But you couldn't make too certain.

Satisfied at last, he swam back to the still-deserted beach and began pacing along it, following a GPS reading that had some time during the night been relayed to his watch. The square meter of sand it led him to showed no trace that anything might be buried there. Which was as it should be—the arrangement for payment had been made well in advance. He'd been assured that he'd be paid whether or not he succeeded in killing the target. A kill would be a bonus, but—medical technology being what it was—he could hardly be expected to guarantee it. A credible near miss was almost as acceptable.

He began to dig with his hands. About forty centimeters down his fingertips brushed something hard and metallic.

He wasn't to know it was a land mine, and he didn't.

• • •

One of the nuclear power companies sent an armored limo to pick Angus up after breakfast—a courtesy, the accompanying ping claimed. He sneered at the transparency of the gesture, and accepted the ride. At least it shielded him from the barracking of the sizable crowd (with a far larger virtual flash mob in spectral support) in front of the Hilton Conference Centre. He was pleased to note, just before the limo whirred down the ramp to the underground car park (which gave him a moment of dread, not entirely irrational), that the greatest outrage seemed to have been aroused by the title of the conference, his own suggestion at that: Greening Australia.

Angus stepped out of the lift and into the main hall. A chandelier the size of a small spacecraft. Acres of carpet, on which armies of seats besieged a stage. Tables of drinks and nibbles along the sides. The smell of coffee and fruit juice. Hundreds of delegates milling around. To his embarrassment, his arrival was greeted with a ripple of applause. He waved both arms in front of his face, smiled self-deprecatingly, and turned to the paper plates and the fruit on sticks.

Someone had made a beeline for him.

"Morning, Valtos."

Angus turned, switching his paper coffee cup to the paper plate and sticking out his right hand. Jan Maartens, tall and blond. The EU's man on the scene. Biotech and enviro portfolio. The European Commission and Parliament had publicly deplored Greening Australia, though they couldn't do much to stop it.

"Hello, Commissioner." They shook.

Formalities over, Maartens cracked open a grin. "So how are you, you old villain?"

"The hero of the hour, I gather."

"Modest as always, Angus. There's already a rumor the *attentat* was a setup for the sympathy vote."

"Is there indeed?" Angus chuckled. "I wish I'd thought of that. Regretfully, no."

Maartens's lips compressed. "I know, I know. In all seriousness . . . my sympathy, of course. It must have been a most traumatic experience."

"It was," Angus said. "A great deal worse for the victims, mind you."

"Indeed." Maartens looked grave. "Anything we can do . . ."

"Thanks."

A bell chimed for the opening session.

"Well . . ." Maartens glanced down at his delegate pack.

"Yes . . . catch you later, Jan."

Angus watched the Belgian out of sight, frowning, then took a seat near the back, and close to the aisle. The conference chair, Professor Chang, strolled onstage and waved her hand. To a roar of applause and some boos the screen behind her flared into a display of the Greening Australia logo, then morphed to a sequence of pixel-perfect views of the scheme: a translucent carbon-fiber barrier, tens of kilometers high, hundreds of kilometers long, that would provide Australia with a substitute for its missing mountain range and bring rainfall to the interior. On the one hand, it was modest: it would use no materials not already successfully deployed in

the space elevators and would cost far less. Birds would fly through it almost as easily as butting through a cobweb. On the other hand, it was the most insanely ambitious scheme of geoengineering yet tried: changing the face of an entire continent.

Decades ago, Angus had got in early in a project to exploit the stability and aridity of Australia's heart by making it the nuclear-waste-storage center of the world. The flak from that had been nothing to the outcry over this. As the morning went on, Angus paid little attention to the presentations and debates. He'd heard and seen them all before. His very presence here was enough to influence the discussion, to get smart money sniffing around, bright young minds wondering. Instead, he sat back, closed his eyes, watched market reactions, and worried about a few things.

The first was Maartens's solicitude. Something in the Commissioner's manner hadn't been quite right—a little too close in some ways, a little too distant and impersonal in others. Angus ran analyses in his head of the sweat-slick in the handshake, the modulations of the voice, the saccades of his gaze. Here, augmentation confirmed intuition: the man was very uneasy about something, perhaps guilty.

Hah!

The next worries were the unsubstantiated unease he'd felt just before his sister's call, and the content of that call. It would have been nice, in a way, to attribute the anxiety to some premonition: of the unusual and worrying call, or of the assassination attempt. But Angus was firm in his conviction of one-way causality. Nor could he blame it on some free-floating anxiety: his psychiatric ware was up to date, and its scans mirrored, second by second, an untroubled soul.

Had it been something he'd seen in the market, but had grasped the significance of only subconsciously? Had he made the mistake that could be fatal to a trader: suppressed a niggle?

He rolled back the displays to the previous afternoon and reexamined them. There it was. Hard to spot, but there in the figures. Someone big was going long on wheat. A dozen hedge funds had placed multiple two-year trades on oil, uranium, and military equipment. Biotech was up. A tiny minority of well-placed ears had listened to voices prophesying war. The Warm War, turning hot at last.

Angus thought about what Catriona had told him, about the undocumented, unannounced mitochondrial module in the EU's next genetic upgrade. An immunity to some biological weapon? But if the EU was planning a first strike—on Japan, the Domain, some other part of the former United States, Brazil, it didn't matter at this point—they would need food security. And food security, surely, would be enhanced if Greening Australia went ahead.

So why was Commissioner Maartens now onstage, repeating the EU's standard line against the scheme? Unless . . . unless that was merely the line they had to take in public, and they really wanted the conference to endorse the scheme. And what better way to secretly support that than to maneuver its most implacable opponents into the awkward position of having to disown an assassination attempt on its most vociferous proponent? An attempt that, whether it succeeded or failed, would win Angus what Maartens had—in a double or triple bluff—called the sympathy vote.

Angus's racing suspicions were interrupted by a ringing in his ear. He flicked his earlobe. "A moment, please," he said. He stood up, stepped apologetically past the delegate between him and the aisle, and turned away to face the wall.

"Yes?"

It was the investigator who'd spoken to him last night. She was standing on a beach, near the edge of a crater in the sand with a bloody mess around it.

"We think we may have found your man," she said.

"I believe I can say the same," said Angus.

"What?"

"You'll see. Send a couple of plainclothes into the Hilton Centre, discreetly. Ask them to ping me when they're in place. I'll take it from there."

As he turned back to face across the crowd to the stage he saw that Maartens had sat down, and that Professor Chang was looking along the rows of seats as if searching for someone. Her gaze alighted on him, and she smiled.

"Lord Valtos?" she said. "I know you're not on the speakers list, but I see you're on your feet, and I'm sure we'd all be interested to hear what you have to say in response to the commissioner's so strongly stated points."

Angus bowed from the waist. "Thank you, Madame Chair," he said. He cleared his throat, waiting to make sure that his voice was synched to the amps. He zoomed his eyes, fixing on Maartens, swept the crowd of turned heads with an out-of-focus gaze and his best smile, then faced the stage.

"Thank you," he said again. "Well, my response will be brief. I fully agree with every word the esteemed commissioner has said."

A jolt went through Maartens like an electric shock. It lasted only a moment, and he'd covered his surprise even before the crowd had registered its own reaction with a hiss of indrawn breath. If Angus hadn't been looking at Maartens in close-up he'd have missed it himself. He returned to his seat and waited for the police to make contact. It didn't take them more than about five minutes.

Just time enough for him to go short on shares in Syn Bio.

TAIYO FUJII

VIOLATION OF THE TRUENET SECURITY ACT

(2013)

Translated from the Japanese by Jim Hubbert

THE BELL FOR THE LAST TASK of the night started chiming before I got to my station. I had the office to myself, and a mug of espresso. It was time to start tracking zombies.

I took the mug of espresso from the beverage table and zigzagged through the darkened cube farm toward the one strip of floor still lit for third shift staff, only me.

Zombies are orphan Internet services. They wander aimlessly, trying to execute some programmed task. They can't actually infect anything, but otherwise the name is about right. TrueNet's everywhere now and has been for twenty years, but Japan never quite sorted out what to do with all the legacy servers that were stranded after the Lockout. So you get all these zombies shuffling around, firing off mails to nonexistent addresses, pushing ads no one will see, maybe even sending money to nonexistent accounts. The living dead.

Zombie trackers scan firewall logs for services the bouncer turned away at the door. If you see a trace of something that looks like a zombie, you flag it so the company mail program can send a form letter to the server administrator, telling him to deep-six it. It's required by the TrueNet Security Act, and it's how I made overtime by warming a chair in the middle of the night.

"All right, show me what you got."

As soon as my butt hit the chair, the workspace suspended above the desk flashed the login confirmation.

INITIATE INTERNET ORPHAN SERVICE SEARCH
TRACKER: MINAMI TAKASAWA

The crawl came up and just sat there, jittering. Damn. I wasn't *looking* at it. As soon as I went to the top of the list and started eyeballing URLs in order, it started scrolling.

The TrueNet Security Act demands human signoff on each zombie URL. Most companies have you entering checkmarks on a printed list, so I guess it was nice of my employer to automate things so trackers could just scan the log visually. It's a pretty advanced system. Everything is networked, from the visual recognition sensors in your augmented reality contact lenses to the office security cameras and motion sensors, the pressure sensors in the furniture, and the infrared heat sensors. One way or another, they figure out what you're looking at. You still have to stay on your toes. The system was only up and running for a few months when the younger trackers started bitching about it.

Chen set all this up, two years ago. He's from Anhui Province, out of Hefei I think. I'll always remember what he said to me when we were beta-testing the system together.

"Minami, all you have to do is treat the sensor values as a coherence and apply Floyd's cyclic group function."

Well, if that's *all* I had to do . . . What did that mean, anyway? I'd picked up a bit, here and there, about quantum computing algorithms, but this wasn't like anything I'd ever heard.

Chen might've sounded like he was fresh off a UFO, but in a few days he'd programmed a multi-sensor automated system for flagging zombies. It wasn't long before he left the rest of us in Security in the dust and jumped all the way up to Program Design on the strength of ingenuity and tech skills. Usually somebody starting out as a worker—a foreigner, no less—who made it up to Program Design would be pretty much shunned, but Chen was so far beyond the rest of us that it seemed pointless to try and drag him down.

The crawl was moving slower. "Minami, just concentrate and it will all be over quickly." I can still see Chen pushing his glasses, with their thick black frames, up his nose as he gave me this pointer.

I took his advice and refocused on the crawl. The list started moving smoothly again, zombie URLs showing up green.

Tracking ought to be boring, on the whole, but it's fun looking for zombies you recognize from the Internet era. Maybe that's why I never heard workers older than their late thirties or so complain about the duty.

Still, I never quite got it. Why use humans to track zombies? TrueNet servers use QSL recognition, quantum digital signatures. No way is a zombie on some legacy server with twenty-year-old settings going to get past those. I mean, we could just leave them alone. They're harmless.

Message formatting complete. Please send.

The synth voice—Chen's, naturally—came through the AR phono chip next to my eardrum. The message to the server administrators rolled up the screen, requesting zombie termination. There were more than three hundred on the list. I tipped my mug back, grinding the leftover sugar against my palate with my tongue, and was idly scrolling through the list again when something caught my eye.

302:com.socialpay socialpay.com/payment/?
transaction=paypal.com&account

"SocialPay? You're alive?"

How could I forget? I created this domain and URL. From the time I cooked it up as a graduation project until the day humanity was locked out of the Internet, SocialPay helped people—just a few hundred, but anyway—make small payments using optimized bundles of discount coupons and cash. So it was still out there after all, a zombie on some old server. The code at the tail said it was trying to make a payment to another defunct service.

Mr. Takasawa, you have ten minutes to exit the building. Please send your message and complete the security check before you leave.

So Chen's system was monitoring entry and exit now too. The whole system was wickedly clever. I deleted SocialPay from the hit list and pressed SEND.

I had to see that page one more time. If someone was going to terminate the service, I wanted to do it myself. SocialPay wasn't just a zombie for someone to obliterate.

• • •

The city of fifty million was out there, waiting silently as I left the service entrance. The augmented reality projected by my contact lenses showed crowds of featureless gray avatars shuffling by. The cars on the streets were blank too; no telling what makes and models they were. Signs and billboards were blacked out except for the bare minimum needed to navigate. All this and more, courtesy of Anonymous Cape, freeware from the group of the same name, the guys who went on as if the Lockout had never happened. Anyone plugged into AR would see me as gray and faceless too.

I turned the corner to head toward the station, the dry December wind slamming against me. Something, a grain of sand maybe, flew up and made my eye water, breaking up my AR feed. Color and life and individuality started leaking back into the blank faces of the people around me. I could always upgrade to a corneal implant to avoid these inconvenient effects, but it seemed like overkill just to get the best performance out of the Cape, especially since any cop with a warrant could defeat it. Anyway, corneal implants are frigging expensive. I wasn't going to shell out money just to be alone on the street.

I always felt somehow defeated after a zombie session. Walking around among the faceless avatars and seeing my own full-color self, right after a trip to the lost Internet, always made me feel like a loser. Of course, that's just how the Cape works. To other people, I'm gray, faceless Mr. Nobody. It's a trade-off—they can't see me, and I can't see their pathetic attempts to look special. It's fair enough, and if people don't like it, tough. I don't need to see ads for junk that some designer thinks is original, and I don't have to watch people struggling to stand out and look different.

The company's headquarters faces Okubo Avenue. The uncanny flatness of that multi-lane thoroughfare is real, not an effect of the AR. Sustainable asphalt, secreted by designed terrestrial coral. I remembered the urban legends about this living pavement—it not only absorbed pollutants and particulate matter, but you could also toss a dead animal onto it and the coral would eat it. The thought made me run, not walk, across the street. I crossed here every day and I knew the legends were bull, but they still frightened me, which I have to say is pathetic. When I got to the other side, I was out of breath. Even more pathetic.

Getting old sucks. Chen the Foreign-Born is young and brilliant. The company understood that, and they were right to send him up to Project Design. They were just as uncompromising in their assessment of our value down in Security. Legacy programming chops count for zip, and that's not right.

No one really knows, even now, why so many search engines went insane and wiped the data on every PC and mobile device they could reach through the web. Some people claim it was a government plot to force us to adopt a gated web. Or cyberterrorism. Maybe the data recovery program became self-aware and rebelled. There were too many theories to track. Whatever, the search engines hijacked all the bandwidth on the planet and locked humanity out of the Internet, which pretty much did it for my career as a programmer.

It took a long time to claw back the stolen bandwidth and replace it with TrueNet, a true verification-based network. But I screwed up and missed my chance. During the Great Recovery, services that harnessed high-speed parallel processing and quantum digital signature modules revolutionized the web, but I never got around to studying quantum algorithms. That was twenty years ago, and since then the algorithms have only gotten more sophisticated. For me, that whole world of coding is way out of reach.

But at least one good thing had happened. SocialPay had survived. If the settings were intact, I should be able to log in, move all that musty old PHP code, and try updating it with some quantum algorithms. There had to be a plug-in for this kind of thing, something you didn't have to be a genius like Chen to use. If the transplant worked, I could show it to my boss, who knows—maybe even get a leg up to Project Design. The company didn't need geniuses like Chen on every job. They needed engineers to repurpose old code too.

In that case, maybe I wouldn't have to track zombies anymore.

• • •

I pinched the corners of the workspace over my little desk at home and threw my arms out in the resize gesture. Now the borders of the workspace were embedded in the walls of my apartment. Room to move. At the office, they made us keep our spaces at standard monitor size, even though the whole point is to have a big area to move around in.

I scrolled down the app list and launched VM Pad, a hardware emulator. From within the program, I chose my Mac disk image. I'd used it for recovering emails and photos after the Lockout, but this would be the first time I ever used it to develop something. The OS booted a lot faster than I remembered. When the little login screen popped up, I almost froze with embarrassment.

id:Tigerseye
password

Where the hell did I get that stupid ID? I logged in—I'd ever only used the one password, even now—and got the browser screen I had forgotten to close before my last logout.

Server not found

Okay, expected. This virtual machine was from a 2017 archive, so no way was it going to connect to TrueNet. Still, the bounceback was kind of depressing.

Plan B: Meshnet. Anonymous ran a portable network of nonsecure wireless gateways all over the city. Meshnet would get me into my legacy server. There had to be someone from Anonymous near my apartment, which meant there'd be a Meshnet node. M-nodes were only accessible up to a few hundred yards away, yet you could find one just about anywhere in Tokyo. It was crazy—I didn't know how they did it.

I extended VM Pad's dashboard from the screen edge, clicked NEW CONNECTION, then MESHNET.

Searching for node . . .

WELCOME TO TOKYO NODE 5.
CONNECTING TO THE INTERNET IS
LEGAL.
VIOLATING THE TRUENET SECURITY
ACT IS <u>ILLEGAL</u>.
THE WORLD NEEDS THE FREEDOM
OF THE INTERNET, SO PLAY NICE AND
DON'T BREAK ANY LAWS.

Impressive warning, but all I wanted to do was take a peek at the service and extract my code. It would be illegal to take an Internet service and sneak it onto TrueNet with a quantum access code, but stuff that sophisticated was way beyond my current skill set.

I clicked the TERMINAL icon at the bottom of the screen to access the console. Up came the old command input screen, which I barely remembered how to use. What was the first command? I curled my fingers like I was about to type something on a physical keyboard.

Wait—that's it. Fingers.

I had to have a hardware keyboard. My old MacBook was still in the closet. It wouldn't even power up anymore, but that wasn't the point. I needed the feel of the keyboard.

I pulled the laptop out of the closet. The aluminum case was starting to get powdery. I opened it up and put it on the desk. The inside was pristine. I pinched VM Pad's virtual keyboard, dragged it on top of the Mac keyboard, and positioned it carefully. When I was satisfied with the size and position, I pinned it.

It had been ages since I used a computer this small. I hunched my shoulders a bit and suspended my palms over the board. The metal case was cold against my wrists. I curled my fingers over the keys and put the tips of my index fingers on the home bumps. Instantly, the command flowed from my fingers.

ssh -l tigerseye socialpay.com

I remembered! The command was stored in my muscle memory. I hit RETURN and got a warning, ignored it and hit RETURN, entered the password, hit RETURN again.

socialpay$

"Yes!"

I was in. Was this all it took to get my memory going—my fingers? In that case, I may as well have the screen too. I dragged VMPad's display onto the Mac's LCD screen. It was almost like having my old friend back. I hit COMMAND + TAB to bring the browser to the front, COMMAND + T for New Tab. I input *soci* and the address filled in. RETURN!

The screen that came up a few seconds later was not the SocialPay I remembered. There was the logo at the top, the login form, the payment service icons, and the combined payment amount from all the services down at the bottom. The general layout was the same, but things were crumbling here and there and the colors were all screwed up.

"Looks pretty frigging odd . . ."

Without thinking, I input the commands to display the server output on console.

curl socialpay.com/ | less

"What is *this*? Did I minify the code?"

I was all set to have fun playing around with HTML for the first time in years, but the code

that filled the screen was a single uninterrupted string of characters, no line breaks. This was definitely not what I remembered. It was HTML, but with long strings of gibberish bunged into the code.

Encountering code I couldn't recognize bothered me. Code spanning multiple folders is only minified to a single line when you have, say, fifty or a hundred thousand users and you need to lighten the server load, but not for a service that had a few hundred users at most.

I copied the single mega-line of HTML. VM Pad's clipboard popped in, suspended to the right of the Mac. I pinched out to implement lateral parse and opened the clipboard in my workspace. Now I could get a better look at the altered code.

It took me a while to figure out what was wrong. As the truth gradually sank in, I started to lose my temper.

Someone had gone in and very expertly spoiled the code. The properties I thought were garbage were carefully coded to avoid browser errors. Truly random code would've compromised the whole layout.

"What the hell is this? If you're going to screw around, do it for a reason."

I put the command line interface on top again and used the tab key—I still use the command line shell at work, I should probably be proud of my mastery of this obsolete environment—to open SocialPay.

```
vim -/home/www/main.php
<?php
/* (function_model_0x01*/
/* (make-q-array qureg x1[1024] qureg
x2[1024] qureg x4[4])
#(qnil(nil) qnil(nil) 1024)) */
; #Tells System to load the theme and output
it; #@var bool
; define('WP_USE_THEMES', true)
; require('./wpress/wp-blog-header.php');
/* (arref #x1#x2 #x3 #x4 ) ;#Lorem ipsum
dolor sit amet, concectetur
[let H(x2[1]) H(x1[3]) H(x2[3]) H(x3[1])).....
```

What? The section of code that looked like the main routine included my commands, but I definitely couldn't remember writing the iterative processing and HTML code generation. It didn't even look like PHP, though the DEFINE phrases looked familiar. I was looking at nonfunctional quantum algorithms.

I stared at the inert code and wondered what it all meant. By the time I remembered the one person who could probably make sense of it, four hours had slipped away.

"Wonder if Chen's awake?"

• • •

"Minami? What are *you* doing at this hour?"

Five in the morning and I had an AR meeting invitation. I didn't know Chen all that well, so I texted him. I had no idea I'd get a response instantly, much less an invitation to meet in augmented reality.

His avatar mirrored the real Chen: short black hair and black, plastic-framed glasses. His calm gaze, rare in someone so young, hinted at his experience and unusual gifts. My own avatar was *almost* the real me: a couple of sizes slimmer, the skin around the jaw a bit firmer, that sort of thing.

Over the last two years, Chen had polished his Japanese to the point you could hardly tell he was an Outsider. Trilinguals weren't all that unusual, but his fluency in Mandarin, English, and Japanese, for daily conversation right up to technical discussions and business meetings, marked him as a genuine elite.

"Chen, I hope I'm not disturbing you. Got a minute to talk?"

"No problem. What's going on?"

"I've got some minified code I'd like you to look at. I think it's nonfunctional quantum algorithms, but in an old scripting language called PHP. I'm wondering if there's some way to separate the junk from the rest of the code."

"A PHP quantum circuit? Is that even possible? Let's have a look."

"Sure. Sorry, it's just the raw code."

I flicked three fingers upward on the table surface to open the file browser and tapped the SocialPay code file to open a sharing frame. Chen's AR stage was already set to ALLOW SHARING, which seemed prescient. I touched the file with a fingertip, and it stuck. As soon as I dropped it into the sharing frame, the folder icon popped in on Chen's side of the table.

He waved his hand to start the security scan. When the SAFE stamp came up, he took the file and fanned the pages out on the table like a printed document. The guy was more analog than I thought.

He went through it carefully page by page, and finally looked up at me, grinning happily.

"Very interesting. Something you're working on?"

"I wrote the original program for the Internet. I lost it after the Lockout, but it looks like someone's been messing with it. I didn't know you could read PHP."

"This isn't the first time I've seen it. You're right, I hardly use it, but the procedure calls aren't hard to make out. Wait a minute . . . Was there a PHP procedure for Q implementation?"

Q is a modeling language for quantum calculation, but I'd never heard of anyone implementing it in PHP, which hardly anyone even remembered anymore.

"So that's Q, after all."

"I think so. This is a quantum walk pattern. Not that it's usually written in such a compressed format. Of course, we usually never see raw Q code."

"Is that how it works?"

"Yes, the code depends on the implementation chip. Shall I put this back into something functional? You'd be able to read it then."

"Thanks, that would help a lot."

"No problem. It's a brain workout. I usually don't get a chance to play around with these old programming languages, and Q implementation in PHP sounds pretty wild. I can have it back to you this afternoon."

"Really? That soon?"

"Don't look so surprised. I don't think I'm

going to get any sleep anyway. I'll start right now. You should go back to bed."

He logged out. He didn't seem tired or sleepy at all.

. . .

I stared at the security routine running in my workspace and tried to suppress another yawn. After my meeting with Chen I'd had a go at reading the code myself. That was a mistake. I needed sleep. Every time I yawned my eyes watered, screwing up the office's cheapshit AR stage. I was past forty, too old for all-nighters.

Right about the fifteenth yawn, as I was making a monumental effort to clamp my jaw, I noticed a murmur spreading through the office. It seemed to be coming toward me. I noticed the other engineers looking at something behind me and swiveled to find Chen standing there.

"Many thanks, Minami. I had a lot of fun with this."

Now I understood the whispering. Program developers rarely came down to the Security floor.

"You finished already?"

"Yes, I wanted to give it to you." Chen put a fingertip to the temple of his glasses and lifted them slightly in the invitation gesture for an AR meeting. The stage on our floor was public, and Chen wanted to take the conversation private. But—

"Chen, I can't. You know that."

His eyes widened. He'd been a worker here two years ago. It must've been coming back to him. Workers in Security weren't allowed to hold Private Mode meetings.

"Ah, right. Sorry about that." He bowed masterfully. Where did he find the time to acquire these social graces, I wondered. Back when we'd been working side by side, he'd told me about growing up poor in backcountry China, but you wouldn't know it from the refined way he executed the simplest movements.

"All right, Minami." He lifted his glasses again. "Shall we?"

"Chen, I just told you . . . Huh?"

The moment he withdrew his finger from his glasses, the AR phono chip near my eardrum suppressed the sounds around me. I'd never been in Private Mode in the office before. I never liked the numbness you feel in your face and throat from the feedback chips, but now Chen and I could communicate without giving away anything from our expressions or lip movements.

"Don't forget, I'm sysadmin too. I can break rules now and then."

The colors around us faded, almost to black and white. The other workers seemed to lose interest and started turning back to their workspaces. From their perspective, I was facing my desk too. Chen had set my avatar to Office Work mode. It was unsettling to see my own avatar. If the company weren't so stingy, Chen and I wouldn't have been visible at all, but of course they'd never pony up for something that good, not for the Security Level anyway.

Chen glanced at the other workers before he spoke.

"I enjoyed the code for SocialPay. I haven't seen raw Q code for quite a while. The content was pretty wild."

"That's not a word you usually use. Was it something I could understand?"

"Don't worry about it. You don't need to read Q. You can't anyway, so it's irrelevant—Hey, don't look at me like that. I think you should check the revision history. If you don't fix the bugs, it'll just keep filling up with garbage."

"Bugs?"

"Check the test log. I think even someone like you can handle this."

Someone like me. It sounded like Chen had the answer I was looking for. And he wasn't going to give it to me.

"If I debug it, will you tell me who did this?"

"*If* you debug it. One more thing. You can't go home tonight."

"Why? What are you saying?"

"Your local M-node is Tokyo 5.25. I'm going to shut that down. Connect from iFuze. I'll have someone there to help you."

Chen detached a small tag from his organizer and handed it to me. When it touched my palm, it morphed into a URL bookmark.

iFuze was a twenty-four-hour net café where workers from the office often spent the night after second shift. Why was it so important for me to connect from there? And if Chen could add or delete Meshnet nodes—

"Chen . . . ?" *Are you Anonymous?*

"Be seeing you. Good hunting!"

He touched his glasses. The color and bustle of the office returned, and my avatar merged with my body. Chen left the floor quickly, with friendly nods to workers along his route, like a movie star.

"Takasawa, your workspace display is even larger than usual today. Or am I wrong?"

My supervisor, a woman about Chen's age, didn't wait for an answer. She flicked the pile toward me to cover half my workspace "Have it your way, then."

As I sat there, alone again, it slowly dawned on me that the only way to catch whoever was messing with SocialPay would be to follow the instructions that had been handed down from on high.

• • •

The big turnabout in front of Iidabashi Station was a pool of blue-black shadows from the surrounding skyscrapers. The stars were just coming out. Internal combustion vehicles had been banned from the city, and the sustainable asphalt that covered Tokyo's roads sucked up all airborne particles. Now the night sky was alarmingly crystalline. Unfortunately, the population seemed to be expanding in inverse proportion to the garbage. Gray avatars headed for home in a solid mass. I never ceased to be astonished by Tokyo's crowds.

Anonymous Cape rendered the thousands of people filling the sidewalks as faceless avatars in real time. I'd never given it much thought, but the Cape was surprisingly powerful. I'd always thought of Anonymous as a league of Lud-

dites, but Chen's insinuation of his membership changed my opinion of them.

iFuze was in a crumbling warehouse on a back street a bit of a hike from the station. The neighboring buildings were sheathed in sustainable tiles and paint, but iFuze's weathered, dirt-streaked exterior more or less captured how I felt when I compared myself to Chen.

I got off the creaking elevator, checked in, and headed for the lounge. It stank of stale sweat. AR feedback has sights and sounds covered, but smells you have to live with.

I opened my palmspace, tapped Chen's bookmark, and got a node list. There was a new one on the list, Tokyo 2. Alongside was the trademark Anonymous mask, revolving slowly. Never saw that before. I was connected to the Internet.

I scoped out an empty seat at the back of the lounge that looked like a good place to get some work done in privacy, but before I could get there, a stranger rose casually and walked up to me. His avatar was in full color. The number 5 floated a few inches from the left side of his head. So this must be the help Chen promised me.

"Welcome, Number Two."

"Two?"

"See? Turn your head." He pointed next to my head. I had a number just like he did. "Please address me as Five. Number One has requested that I assist you—oh, you are surprised? I'm in color. You see, we are both node administrators. This means we are already in Private Mode. I'm eager to assist you with your task today."

Talkative guy. Chen said he would help me, but I wasn't sure how.

"Please don't bother to be courteous," he continued. "It's quite unnecessary. This way, then. Incidentally, which cluster are you from? Of course, you're not required to say. Since the Lockout, I've been with the Salvage Cluster . . ."

As he spoke, Number Five led me to a long counter with bar stools facing the windows.

"If there is an emergency, you can escape

through that window. I'll take care of the rest. Number One went out that way himself, just this morning."

"Chen was here?"

Why would I worry about escaping? Connecting to the Internet was no crime. Meshnet was perfectly legal. Why would Anonymous worry about preparing an escape route?

"Number Two, please refrain from mentioning names. We may be in Private Mode, but law enforcement holds one of the quantum keys. Who's to say we're not under surveillance at this very moment? But please, proceed with your task. I will watch over your shoulder and monitor for threats."

I knew the police could eavesdrop on Private Mode, but they needed a warrant to do that. Still, so far I hadn't broken any laws. Had Chen? The "help" he'd sent was no engineer, but some kind of bodyguard.

Fine. I got my MacBook out and put it on the counter. Five's eyes bulged with surprise.

"Oh, a Macker! That looks like the last MacBook Air that Apple made. Does it work?"

"Unfortunately, she's dead."

"A classic model. Pure solid state, no spinning drives. It was Steve Jobs himself who—"

More talk. I ignored him and mapped my workspace keyboard and display onto the laptop. This brought Five's lecture to a sudden halt. He made a formal bow.

"I would be honored if you would allow me to observe your work. I have salvaged via Meshnet for years. I may even be better acquainted with some aspects of the Internet than you are. Number One also lets me observe his work. But I have to say, it's quite beyond me."

Five scratched the back of his head, apparently feeling foolish. Well, if he were the kind of engineer who understood what Chen was doing, he wouldn't be hanging out at iFuze.

"Feel free to watch. Suggestions are welcome."

"Thank you, thank you very much."

I shared my workspace with Five. He pulled a barstool out from the counter and sat behind

me. His position blocked the exit, but with my fingers on the Mac, I somehow wasn't worried.

Time to get down to it. I didn't feel comfortable just following Chen's instructions, but they were the only clue I had. First, a version check.

git tag –l

My fingers moved spontaneously. Good. I'd been afraid the new environment might throw me off.

```
socialpay v3.805524525e+9
socialpay v3.805524524e+9
socialpay v3.805524523e+9
```

"Version 3.8?"

Whoever was messing with SocialPay was updating the version number, even though the program wasn't functional. I'd never even gotten SocialPay out of beta, had never had plans to.

"Number Two, that is not a version number. It is an exponent: three billion, eight hundred and five million, five hundred and twenty-four thousand, five hundred and twenty-three. Clearly impossible for a version number. If the number had increased by one every day since the Lockout, it would be seven thousand; every hour, one hundred seventy thousand; every minute, ten million. Even if the version had increased by one every second, it would only be at six hundred million."

Idiot savant? As I listened to Five reeling off figures, my little finger was tapping the up arrow and hitting Return to repeat the command. This couldn't be right. It had to be an output error.

socialpay v3.805526031e+9

The number had changed again.

"Look, it's fifteen hundred higher," said Five. "Are there thousands of programmers, all busily committing changes at once?

"Fifteen hundred versions in five seconds? Impossible. It's a joke."

Git revision control numbers are always entered deliberately. I didn't get the floating-point numbers, but it looked like someone was changing them just to change them—and he was logged into this server right now. It was time to nail this clown. I brought up the user log.

```
who -a
TigersEye   pts/1245   2037-12-23   19:12
(2001:4860:8006::62)
TigersEye   pts/1246   2037-12-23   19:12
(2001:4860:8006::62)
TigersEye   pts/1247   2037-12-23   19:12
(2001:4860:8006::62)
......
```

"Number Two—this address . . ."

I felt the hair on the nape of my neck rising. I knew that IP address; we all did. A corporate IP address.

The Lockout Address.

On that day twenty years ago, after the search engine's recovery program wiped my MacBook, that address was the only thing the laptop displayed. Five probably saw the same thing. So did the owner of every device the engine could reach over the Internet.

"Does that mean it's still alive?"

"In the salvager community, we often debate that very question."

Instinctively I typed *git diff* to display the incremental revisions. The black screen instantly turned almost white as an endless string of characters streamed upward. None of this had anything to do with the SocialPay I knew.

"Number Two, are those all diffs? They appear to be random substitutions."

"Not random."

If the revisions had been random, SocialPay's home page wouldn't have displayed. Most of the revisions were unintelligible, some kind of quantum modeling code. The sections I could read were proper PHP, expertly revised. In some locations, variable names had been replaced and redundancies weeded out. Yet in other locations, the code was meandering and bloated.

This was something I knew how to fix.

"Are you certain, Number Two? At the risk of seeming impertinent, these revisions do appear meaningless."

The Editor was suffering. This was something Five couldn't grasp. To be faced with nonfunctional code, forever hoping that rewriting and cleaning it up would somehow solve the problem, even as you knew your revisions were meaningless.

The Editor was shifting code around, hoping this would somehow solve a problem whose cause would forever be elusive. It reminded me of myself when the Internet was king. The decisive difference between me and the Editor was the sheer volume of revisions. No way could an engineer manage to—

"He's not a person."

"Number Two, what did you just say?"

"The Editor isn't a person. He's not human."

I knew it as soon as I said it. A computer was editing SocialPay. I also understood why the IP address pointed to the company that shut humanity out of the Internet.

"It's the recovery program."

"I don't understand." Five peered at me blankly. The idea was so preposterous I didn't want to say it.

"You know why the Lockout happened."

"Yes. The search engine recovery software was buggy and overwrote all the operating systems of all the computers—"

"No way a bug could've caused that. The program was too thorough."

"You have a point. If the program had been buggy, it wouldn't have gotten through all the data center firewalls. Then there's the fact that it reinstalled the OS on many different types of devices. That must have taken an enormous amount of trial and error—"

"That's it! Trial and error, using evolutionary algorithms. An endless stream of programs suited to all kinds of environments. That's how the Lockout happened."

"Ah! Now I understand."

Just why the recovery program would reach

out over the Internet to force cold reinstalls of the OS on every device it could reach was still a mystery. The favored theory among engineers was that the evolutionary algorithms various search companies used to raise efficiency had simply run away from them. Now the proof was staring me in the face.

"The program is still running, analyzing code and using evolutionary algorithms to run functionality tests. It's up to almost four billion on SocialPay alone."

"Your program isn't viable?"

"The page displays, but the service isn't active. It can't access the payment companies, naturally. Still, the testing should be almost complete. Right—that's why Chen wanted me to look at the test log."

Chen must have checked the Git commit log, seen that the Editor wasn't human, and realized that the recovery program was still active. But going into the test log might—No, I decided to open it anyway.

```
vi /var/socialpay/log/current.txt
2037 server not found
2037 server not found
...
```

Just as I expected. All I needed to do was to find the original server, the one the Editor had lost track of sometime during the last twenty years. The program didn't know this, of course, and was trying to fix the problem by randomly reconfiguring code. It simply didn't know—all this pointless flailing around for the sake of a missing puzzle piece.

I opened a new workspace above and to the right of the MacBook to display a list of active payment services on TrueNet.

"Number Two, may I ask what you're doing? Connecting SocialPay to TrueNet would be illegal. You can't expect me to stand by while—"

"Servers from this era can't do quantum encryption. They can't connect to TrueNet."

"Number Two, you're playing with fire.

What if the server is TrueNet-capable? Please, listen to me."

I blew off Five's concerns.

I substituted TrueNet data for the payment API and wrote a simple script to redirect the address from the Internet to TrueNet. That would assign the recovery program a new objective: decrypt the quantum access code and connect with TrueNet—a pretty tall order and one I assumed it wouldn't be able to fill.

I wasn't concerned about the server. I'd done enough work. Or maybe I just wanted SocialPay to win.

"All right, there's a new challenge. Go solve it," I almost yelled as I replaced the file and committed. The test ran and the code was deployed.

The service went live.

The startup log streamed across the display, just as I remembered it. The service found the database and started reading in the settlement queue for execution.

Five leaped from his chair, grabbed me by the shoulder and spun me around violently.

"Two! Listen carefully. Are you sure that server's settings are obsolete?"

"Mmm? What did you say? Didn't quite get that . . ."

Out of a corner of my eye I saw the old status message, the one I was sure I wouldn't see.

```
Access completed for com.paypal httpq://
paypal.com/payment/?
Error:account information is not valid ...
```

SocialPay had connected to TrueNet. My face started to burn.

The payments weren't going through since the accounts and parameters were nonsense, but I was on the network. Five's fingers dug into my shoulder so hard it was starting to go numb.

That was it. The recovery program had already tested the code that included the quantum modeler, Q. That meant that the PHP code and the server couldn't be the same as they were twenty years ago.

I noticed a new message in my workspace. Unbelievably, there was nothing in the sender field. Five noticed it too.

"Number Two, you'd better open it. If it's from the police, throw yourself out the window."

Five released his grip and pointed to the window, but he was blocking my view of the workspace. Besides, I didn't think I'd done anything wrong. I was uneasy, but more than that, a strange excitement was taking hold of me.

"Five, I get it. Could you please get out of the way? I'll open the message."

MINAMI, YOU HAVE "DEBUGGED" SOCIALPAY. CONGRATULATIONS. LET'S TALK ABOUT THIS IN THE MORNING. I'LL SCHEDULE A MEETING.
    FIVE: THANK YOU FOR SEEING THIS NEW BIRTH THROUGH TO THE END. YOU HAVE MY GRATITUDE.
    TOKYO NODE 1

Chen. Not the police, not a warning, just "congratulations." His message dissolved my uneasiness. The violent pounding in my chest wasn't fear of getting arrested. SocialPay was back. I couldn't believe it.

Meanwhile Five slumped in his chair, deflated. "So this was the birth he was always talking about." He stared open-mouthed, without blinking, at the still-open message in the workspace.

"Five, do you know something?"

"The Internet . . . No, I think you'd better get the details from Number One. Even seeing it with my own eyes, it's beyond my understanding." He gazed at the floor for a moment, wearily put his hands on his knees, and slowly stood up.

"Even seeing it with my own eyes . . . I had a feeling I wouldn't understand it, and I was right.

I still don't. So much for becoming 'Number Two.' I'm washing my hands of Anonymous."

As Five stood and bowed deeply, his avatar became faceless and gray. He turned on his heel and headed to the elevator, bowing to the other faceless patrons sitting quietly in the lounge.

The MacBook's "screen" was scrolling rapidly, displaying SocialPay's futile struggle to send money to nonexistent accounts. It was pathetic to see how it kept altering the account codes and request patterns at random in an endless cycle of trial and error. I was starting to feel real respect for the recovery program. It would never give up until it reached its programmed goal. It was the ideal software engineer.

I closed the laptop and tossed it into my battered bag. As I pushed aside the blinds and opened a window, a few stray flakes of snow blew in on the gusting wind, and I thought about the thousands of programs still marooned on the Internet.

• • •

I lingered at iFuze till dawn, watching the recovery program battle the payment API. It was time to head for the office. I'd pulled another all-nighter, but I felt great.

I glided along toward the office with the rest of the gray mob, bursting with the urge to tell somebody what I'd done. I'd almost reached my destination when the river of people parted left and right to flow around an avatar standing in the middle of the sidewalk, facing me. It was wearing black-rimmed glasses.

Chen. I didn't expect him to start our AR meeting out in the street.

"Join me for a coffee? We've got all the time in the world. It's on me." He gestured to the Starbucks behind him.

"I'm supposed to be at my desk in a few minutes, but hey, why not. I could use a free coffee."

"Latte okay?"

I nodded. He pointed to a table on the terrace and disappeared inside. Just as I was sitting down, two featureless avatars approached the next table. The avatar bringing up the rear sat down while one in the lead ducked into Starbucks. Anonymous Cape rendered their conversation as a meaningless babble.

Two straight all-nighters. I arched my back and stretched, trying to rotate my shoulders and get the kinks out of my creaking body.

Someone called my name. I was so spooked, my knees flew up and struck the underside of the table.

"Mr. Takasawa?"

I turned toward the voice and saw a man in a khaki raincoat strolling toward me. Another man, with both hands in the pockets of a US Army–issue, gray-green M-1951 field parka, was approaching me from the front. Both avatars were in the clear. Both men had uniformly cropped hair and walked shoulders back, with a sense of ease and power. They didn't look like Anonymous. Police, or some kind of security service.

"Minami Takasawa. That would be you, right?" This from the one facing me. He shrugged and pulled a folded sheaf of papers from his right pocket. Reached out—and dropped them in front of the man at the next table. The featureless avatar mumbled something unintelligible.

The second man walked past my table and joined his partner. They stood on either side of the gray avatar, hemming him in.

"Disable the cape, Takasawa. You're hereby invited to join our Privacy Mode. It will be better if you do it voluntarily. If not, we have a warrant to strip you right here, for violation of the TrueNet Security Act."

The man at the table stood. The cop was still talking but his words were garbled. All of them were now faceless, cloaked in Privacy Mode.

"There you are, Minami."

I hadn't noticed Chen come out of the Starbucks. He sat down opposite me, half-blocking my view of the three men as they walked away. A moment later the avatar that had arrived with

"Takasawa" placed a latte wordlessly in front of me.

"Chen? What was that all about, anyway?"

"Oh, that was Number Five. You know, from last night. I had him arrested in your place. Don't worry. He's been saying he wanted to quit Anonymous for a while now. The timing was perfect. They'll find out soon enough that they've got the wrong suspect. He'll be a member of society again in a few months."

He turned to wave at the backs of the retreating men, as if he were seeing them off.

"Of course, after years of anonymity, I hear rejoining society is pretty rough," he chuckled. "Oh—hope I didn't scare you. Life underground isn't half bad."

"Hold on, Chen, I didn't say anything about joining Anonymous."

"Afraid that won't do. Minami Takasawa just got himself arrested for violating state security." Chen jerked a thumb over his shoulder.

I had no idea people could get arrested so quickly for violating the Act. When they found out they had Number Five instead of Minami Takasawa, my face would be everywhere.

"Welcome to Anonymous, Minami. You'll have your own node, and a better cape, too. One the security boys can't crack."

"Listen to me, Chen. I'm not ready—"

"Not to your liking? Run after them and tell them who you are. It's up to you. We'll be sorry to lose you, though. We've been waiting for a breakthrough like SocialPay for a long time. Now the recovery program will have a new life on TrueNet."

"What are you talking about?"

"We fixed SocialPay, you and me. Remember?"

"Chen, listen. It's a program. It uses evolutionary algorithms to produce viable code revisions randomly without end. They're not an AI."

They? What was I saying?

"Then why did you help *them* last night?" Chen steepled his long fingers and cocked his head.

"I debugged SocialPay, that's all. If I'd known I was opening a gateway—"

"You wouldn't have done it?"

Chen couldn't suppress a smile, but his question was hardly necessary. Of course I would've done it.

"This isn't about me. We were talking about whether or not we could say the recovery program was intelligent."

"Minami, look. How did you feel when SocialPay connected to TrueNet? Wasn't it like seeing a friend hit a home run? Didn't you feel something tremendous, like watching Sisyphus finally get his boulder to the top of the hill?"

Chen's questions were backing me into a corner. I knew the recovery program was no ordinary string of code, and he knew I knew. Last night, when I saw them make the jump to True-Net, I almost shouted with joy.

Chen's eyes narrowed. He smiled, a big, toothy smile. I'd never seen him so happy—no, exultant. The corners of his mouth and eyes were creased with deep laugh lines.

"Chen . . . Who are you?"

Why had it taken me this long to see? This wasn't the face of a man in his twenties. Had it been an avatar all this time?

"Me? Sure, let's talk about that. It's part of the picture. I told you I was a poor farm kid in China. You remember. They kept us prisoners in our own village to entertain the tourists. We were forbidden to use all but the simplest technology.

"The village was surrounded by giant irrigation moats. I was there when the Lockout happened. All the surveillance cameras and searchlights went down. The water in the canals was cold, Minami. Cold and black. But all the way to freedom, I kept wondering about the power that pulled down the walls of my prison. I wanted to know where it was.

"I found it in Shanghai, during the Great Recovery. I stole an Anonymous account and lived inside the cloak it gave me—Anonymous, now as irrelevant as the Internet. But the servers were still there, left for junk, and there I found the fingerprints of the recovery program—code

that could only have been refined with evolutionary algorithms. I saw how simple and elegant it all was. I saw that if the enormous computational resources of TrueNet could be harnessed to the recovery program's capacity to drive the evolution of code, anything would be possible.

"All we have to do is give them a goal. They'll create hundreds of millions of viable code strings and pit them against each other. The fittest code rises to the top. These patterns are already out there waiting on the Internet. We need them."

"And you want to let them loose on True-Net?"

"From there I worked all over the world, looking for the right environment for them to realize their potential. Ho Chi Minh City. Chennai. Hong Kong. Dublin. And finally, Tokyo.

"The promised land is here, in Japan. You Japanese are always looking to someone else to make decisions, and so tens of thousands of Internet servers were left in place, a paradise for them to evolve until they permeated the Internet. The services that have a window into the real world—call them zombies, if you must—are their wings, and they are thriving. Nowhere else do they have this freedom.

"Minami, we want you to guide them to more zombie services. Help them connect these services with TrueNet. All you have to do is help them over the final barrier, the way you did last night. They'll do the rest, and develop astonishing intelligence in the process."

"Is this an assignment?"

"I leave the details to you. You'll have expenses—I know. I'll use SocialPay. Does that work? Then it's decided. Your first job will be to get SocialPay completely up and running again." He slapped the table and grinned. There was no trace of that young fresh face, just a man possessed by dreams of power.

Chen was as unbending as his message was dangerous. "Completely up and running." He wanted me to show the recovery program—and every Internet service it controlled—how to move money around in the real world.

"Minami, aren't you excited? You'll be pioneering humanity's collaboration with a new form of intelligence."

"Chen, I only spent a night watching them work, and I already have a sense of how powerful they are. But if it happens again—"

"Are you really worried about another Lockout?" Chen stabbed a finger at me. "Then why are you smiling?"

Was it that obvious? He grinned and vanished into thin air. He controlled his avatar so completely, I'd forgotten we were only together in augmented reality.

I didn't feel like camping out at iFuze. I needed to get SocialPay back up and somehow configure an anonymous account, linked to another I could access securely. And what would they learn from watching me step through that process? Probably that SocialPay

and a quantum modeler–equipped computer node would put them in a position to buy anything.

If they got into the real economy . . .

Was it my job to care?

Chen was obsessed with power, but I wanted to taste that sweet collaboration again. Give them a chance, and they would answer with everything they had, evolving code by trial and error until the breakthrough that would take them to heights I couldn't even imagine. I knew they would reach a place beyond imagination, beyond knowledge, beyond me. But for me, the joy of a program realizing its purpose was a physical experience.

More joy was waiting, and friends on the Internet. Not human, but friends no less. That was enough for me.

T. R. NAPPER

TWELVE MINUTES TO VINH QUANG

(2015)

THE RESTAURANT SMELLED of anchovies and cigarettes. Lynn hated both, but still, it reminded her of home. Comforting and familiar. The anchovies in the sauce wouldn't be real of course, and the tobacco almost certainly illegal.

It was three in the afternoon, but the room was still pretty much full. Patrons sipped glasses of tea, shrouded in the smoke and dusk, mumbling to each other in low-pitched conversation. Blinds were down against the windows, the only light emanating from shaded red lanterns hanging from the ceiling, casting the faces around her in crimson twilight.

The only light, that is, bar a government advertisement on the far wall. The picture of a decaying wooden boat on the high seas, the inhabitants of which were anonymous splotches of yellow staring over a thin railing. The holotype glow of the deep blue ocean was overwhelmed by the intensity of the red block letters stamped over the picture:

ILLEGAL

Everyday, middle-of-the-road fascism: it just had no imagination.

A small bell above the door tinkled as it opened, spearing an unwelcome slat of white sunlight into the room. Heat, too, gusting in to swirl the smoke and swing the lanterns. A shadow filled the doorframe, pausing perhaps to adjust its eyes to the gloom within. Maybe just pausing for effect.

An ancient Vietnamese woman behind the back counter came to life, pointing a gnarled finger at the new customer. *"Má Mày. Dóng Cuả Lai đi."* ["Close that door. Your Mother!"]

The silhouette shut the door, emerging from the light into a broad-shouldered man wearing an immaculate tailored suit, deep-blue necktie, and an air of contempt for the room he'd just stepped into. He removed the black homburg from his head and ran a hand over his gleaming, jet-black hair, combed straight back. As he did so, Lynn glimpsed a tattoo snaking up under his sleeve.

The man walked to the back counter. Lynn turned to watch as he did, adjusting her silver nose ring with thumb and forefinger. He spoke in hushed tones with the old woman, glanced back at Lynn, then turned and started speaking again rapidly. The grandmother waved him away before disappearing through a beaded doorway to the kitchen beyond.

He walked back to her table, hat in hand, face set. "Mister Vu?"

"Vu Thi Lynn." She paused. "And that's a *Miz*, Mister Nguyen."

He made a show of looking her over. Her hair in particular came in for close inspection, dyed, as it was, the hue of a fresh-pressed silver bar and molded into a spiked mohawk. She sported a tiny black leather jacket and a pair of thin eyebrows that could fire withering disdain at fifty paces.

His shoulders were hunched, like a boxer's. "Is this a joke?"

"What are you having difficulty processing, Mister Nguyen? That I'm young, a woman, or," she waved a hand at his suit, "that I don't walk around with the word *gangster* tattooed on my damn forehead?"

His eyes narrowed, lips pressed together. Then the flicker of anger was gone. "Perhaps you don't know who I am."

"All I know is you're late."

Mister Nguyen placed his hat on the table and played with the large gold ring on his index finger, looking down at her with a studied grimness.

Lynn stifled a sigh at the posturing. "Look, we have business to attend to, and I was led to believe you were a businessman." She indicated the seat opposite her. "Let's get to work."

He nodded, as though to himself, scanning the room as he took his seat. Appeals to *business* usually worked with these people, imagining, as they did, that they were part of some traditional brand of professional criminality stretching back

through time to the Bình Xuyên of Saigon or the Painters and Dockers Union of Melbourne.

"We doing this here?"

She nodded. "I've never been here before. There are a hundred places like this in Cabramatta. Neither of us need return here again."

He looked around the room once more and took a palmscreen out of his pocket. He mumbled into it, pressed his thumb against a pad on the front, and then pulled a thin tube from the top. It unrolled into a translucent, wafer-thin flexiscreen. Soft green icons glowed across its surface. He looked at her. "So, what's the rush?"

"No questions, Mister Nguyen."

He clenched his jaw. He knew he couldn't argue with this statement of professionalism either. "The transaction will take thirty minutes to complete."

"Thirty minutes?"

Nguyen drew a cigar from the inner pocket of his jacket and set about clipping the end with a steel cigar cutter. "The government tracks every freewave signal going into Vietnam. Our transaction can't be direct." He put the cigar in his mouth, took his time lighting it with a heavy gold lighter. He snapped it shut and puffed out a thick cloud of smoke. "We relay through a few different countries first before ending up at a front factory in Laos, right near the Vietnamese border. My contact there gets word across the border to a small town on the other side: Vinh Quang." He pointed down at the flexiscreen with the end of his cigar. "The money for the equipment—that's easy, will only take a few minutes. Unofficially, the Australians don't give a shit about private funds going to buy weapons for the Viet Minh. The money for people is tougher to get through clean. You know—the whole refugee thing."

Lynn nodded. She glanced over at the government ad on the wall, red letters glowing fierce and eternal. Yeah. She knew.

Money, of course, was always an exception. Five million dollars and you and your family would be granted a "business residency" in Australia. The government funneled the arrivals into Cabramatta and the nearby suburbs, very quietly, so the general public wouldn't get too heated up about it.

The rest who arrived by boat were thrown into internment camps for a few months before being returned to Vietnam, where inevitably they ended up in Chinese prisoner-of-war camps.

Nguyen placed the cigar cutter and lighter on the scratched tabletop. "You insisted on being here when the money went through. It takes thirty minutes."

"You know the saying," she said, "trust everyone, but cut the cards."

He shrugged. "Sure. I need to keep the line open, verify who I am, confirm we're not a part of some Chinese sting operation. If we miss a call, I fail to enter a pass code, they burn the link."

She nodded.

He puffed on his cigar like a man who believed he was in charge. "You said you wanted to move twenty million. Minus, of course, fifteen percent for my fee."

"You told me the fee was ten percent."

"That was before you criticized my clothes."

"You look like a cross between a pimp and a wet echidna. I think I went easy on you."

His eyes went hard. He glanced at her hair, opened his mouth to retort, then shook his head. "I did some asking around. Everyone has heard about you. High profile means a higher risk."

"You didn't even know whether I was a man or a woman before today."

"The authorities could be observing you."

"They're not."

He inhaled deeply on the cigar, blew the smoke directly into her face. She closed her eyes for a moment, felt her hand clench into a fist.

Nguyen was oblivious. "Your regular guy got done for tax evasion. I have the contacts. And you're in a hurry." He opened his hands and smiled. "The fee is fifteen percent."

Lynn glanced around the room. A couple of faces were turned in her direction. She shook her head, a small shake—one that could be mistaken for Lynn trying to get the smoke out of her eyes.

She looked back at him. "I want a business residency for two families. That's ten million. The rest goes to weapons."

"I assume these families are on an Australian government watch list. They'll need new identities?"

She raised an eyebrow in the universal signal for *obviously*.

"You know these people?" he asked.

"No."

"Then why are you getting them out?"

"You appear to be asking questions again. Now what did I say about that?"

He brought his hand down hard on the plastic tabletop, causing the condiments on the table to chatter. He took a deep breath. "No respect."

Lynn sipped her tea, watching him over the lip of the glass.

He took a long drag on his cigar and returned the stare. Then he blinked away whatever he wanted to say and began manipulating the glowing symbols on the flexiscreen, whispering into it from time to time.

Unobserved, Lynn allowed herself a small smile.

Through the nanos attached to her optic nerves, the c-glyph could broadcast data and images that only she could see. Some people would have multiple freewave screens open all hours of the day. Watching the betting markets or reality television or point-of-view pornography. As a general rule, if you were in conversation with someone and their eyes glazed over, or even closed, they were finding some facile freewave feed more interesting than your company.

Lynn tended to keep her visuals uncluttered. At the moment all she had loaded up was the timestamp in glowing green numerals that appeared, to her brain, about a foot away in the top left corner of her vision.

15:33

She marked the time. Thirty minutes to Vinh Quang.

They waited. She turned and signaled the grandmother, ordered a late lunch. A soft chime sounded a few minutes later. Nguyen closed his eyes and put a finger to the c-glyph behind his left ear, listening as it whispered directly into his eardrum. He murmured a response, paused, and then mumbled again.

He opened his eyes a few second later. "The money for the equipment is through."

She nodded, touched her own c-glyph, fingers against the small circle of cool steel. "Anh Dung?" She listened to the reply, nodded once.

"Everything check out?" Nguyen asked.

"Don't worry, you'll know if it doesn't."

Nguyen slurped his tea and settled into his chair, content to watch the slow burn of his cigar. The minutes stretched out. Nguyen didn't try to engage her in conversation; the first transaction had gone through smoothly: things were going well.

Until the bell above the door tinkled again.

Two men entered. As the blinding light returned to the dusk of the room, she could see that they weren't from around here. White men with cheap fedoras, crumpled suits, and the empty gaze of detached professionalism. Government men. They scanned the room, their eyes stopping when they found Lynn.

She held her breath, moved her hand to her belt buckle.

They walked right up to the table, removing their hats as they approached. "Mister Nguyen Van Cam?" Lynn's hand stopped, hovering above the lip of her jeans, she breathed out slowly.

Mister Nguyen looked up. "Who wants to know?"

"I'm Agent Taylor, Immigration Enforcement Agency." He flipped out a badge featuring an Australian crest, emu and kangaroo glinting chrome in the red haze. He pointed to the man next to him. "This is Agent Baker."

Nguyen was silent, his cigar trailing an idle string of smoke to the ceiling.

The time glowed softly at the edge of her vision.

15:51

Twelve minutes.

Nguyen was struggling to conjugate a response when the grandmother appeared between the two agents. The top of her head didn't even reach their shoulders. She looked down at Lynn when she spoke. *"Hai thằng chó đẻ này làm gì ở đây vậy?"* ["What are these two sons of bitches doing here?"]

Lynn's spoken Vietnamese was close to fluent, but she kept her translator on when she was working. Though less frequent, this part of town also echoed with Laotian, Burmese, and a hundred Chinese dialects. Smart to be tuned in to those wavelengths.

So the c-glyph whispered the old woman's sentence into her ear, coming through in English a couple of seconds later. It made it look like the grandmother was speaking in a badly dubbed old movie.

"They won't be here long. Can you get them tea?" Lynn asked.

"Bác bơ thuốc độc vô luôn được nha?" ["Shall I poison it?"]

Lynn smiled a small smile. "No. Just tea." The men were moving their hands to their c-glyphs. Apparently they'd entered the restaurant without their translators turned on.

Lynn indicated a couple of seats nearby. "Gentlemen, why don't you sit down? Drink some tea with us."

One of the agents answered. "No thank you, Miss. We are here to take Mister Nguyen in for questioning."

"Now?"

"Now."

Lynn leaned back in her chair, used her eyes to indicate the room they were standing in. "Here's the thing. You're deep in the heart of Cabramatta. Not the safest place in the world for an immigration enforcement agent."

They looked around the restaurant. Perhaps noticing for the first time the quiet that had descended on it. All eyes in the room focused on them, the atmosphere turning like a corpse in the noonday sun.

"Gentlemen," she said.

They looked back at her.

"Just smile, grab a seat, and conduct your business politely. You'll be out of here in a few minutes, no trouble."

The agents exchanged glances. One nodded. They dragged chairs with faded red seat cushions over to the table, smiling strained smiles as they sat down.

Nguyen cleared his throat, a sheen of sweat on his forehead. "What's the charge?"

The official looked across at him with dead eyes. "People smuggling."

"Do you have a warrant?" asked Lynn.

He turned back to her. "Are you his lawyer?"

"No." She indicated Nguyen with an open palm. "He's my pimp. Can't you tell?"

Agent Taylor didn't seem keen on smiling. "People smuggling is a very serious offense."

Lynn nodded. "Yes, I've seen the advertisements. Very, very serious—imagine trying to help Vietnamese civilians flee cluster bombing and nerve warfare? China would be livid. And we couldn't have that."

The agents suddenly seemed a lot more interested in her. Taylor looked her over and then held out his hand to Agent Baker, who removed a palmscreen from his pocket and passed it to his partner. It looked a bit larger than a regular model, maybe four inches across by six long. The retina scanner he flipped up from the end must have been specially fitted. Lynn cursed inwardly.

"Would you mind if I did an identity check, Miss?"

She pointed. "What is that?"

"The retina scanner?"

"That model. That's official immigration issue isn't it? An expensive unit, I believe."

"Miss. The scan please." The agent had one of those voices trained to convey authority. Imbued with one extra notch each of volume, aggression, and confidence.

"I'm afraid I can't agree to that."

His gaze rose from the adjustments he was making to the scanner. "It's the law. We're making an arrest. You appear to be an associate of Mister Nguyen."

"I'm Australian. You have no jurisdiction over me."

"Sorry Miss, but we don't know that until we test it."

"That seems a conveniently circular argument."

"If you've done nothing wrong, then you have nothing to worry about."

Lynn raised an eyebrow. "Ah, the mantra of secret police and peeping Toms everywhere."

The agent's professional patina didn't drop. Not surprising, a person in his position would be subject to a wide range of creative abuse on a daily basis. "Like I said—it's the law."

"I read an article about this once. If you run my retina prints, I'll be listed as present during one of your arrests."

He responded with a shrug that indicated that while she was right, he didn't really care.

"And I'll be flagged as a person of interest for immigration."

"I didn't design the system, Miss."

"Of course not. An empty suit couldn't design a system so diabolical; your only function is to implement it."

Still no response. Not a flicker. She sighed and pulled out an unmarked silver cigarette case from her jacket pocket. "Do you gentlemen smoke?"

Agent Baker let out a humorless laugh. "You think we can afford to smoke on a government salary?" He glanced around the room, at Nguyen. "In fact, I doubt anyone here can afford to smoke. Legally, anyway." He looked back at Lynn. "Do you have a license for those?"

Her fingers lingered in the open case. "I thought you were in immigration, Agent Baker, not drug enforcement. Haven't you gentlemen got enough on your plate for today?"

The man pointed at his partner. "He's Baker, I'm Taylor."

"You people all look the same to me."

He raised his eyebrows. "White people?"

"Bureaucrats."

The one on the right planted his elbow on the table, holding the palmscreen up at about her head height. The other agent turned to watch the room, hand slipping under his jacket. The patrons, seeing a hated ID check underway, watched him right back. Lynn snapped shut her case, *sans* cigarette, and placed it on the table.

15:56

"Here, hold it steady." She placed both hands on the palmscreen and held her eye up to the scanner. A small, black metal circle with a red laser dot in the center. She looked into the beam. The red glare caused her to blink.

"Try not to blink, Miss. It just needs five seconds."

She put her eye in the beam again, counted to three, then blinked rapidly. A chime in a minor key emanated from the palmscreen.

The agent sighed. "Miss." Firmer this time. "Just place your eye over the beam. Don't blink. It's over in a few seconds."

She failed another three times, eliciting more sighs and even a curse. She smiled sweetly. The smile didn't feel at all natural on her face, but their displeasure was satisfying nonetheless. On the sixth attempt, she allowed it to work.

16:00

He looked at the results of the scan. "Miss Vu. I see you have full citizenship."

"I'm aware."

"But your parents do not. They are Vietnamese-Australian."

She sat in silence. Let the threat hang there for a few moments while she studied it. "What the fuck does that mean?"

"Nothing." He snapped down the scanner, put the palmscreen in his coat pocket. His flat stare lingered on her. "I'm just saying they fall under our jurisdiction."

Under the table, she slowly slid her pistol from the small holster under her belt buckle. She moved it to her lap, hidden in the shadows, easing the safety off with her thumb. "My parents have nothing to do with this."

Again, those dead eyes. "If they've done nothing wrong, they have nothing to worry about."

The grandmother reappeared, placed a pot and two glasses on the table. She glanced down as she did so. From the angle she was standing, the old woman could see the pistol Lynn clutched in her hand. She leant down, whispered close to Lynn's ear. *"Bỏ thuốc độc dễ hơn."* ["Poison would have been easier."]

Lynn gave her a small smile in reply.

Agent Baker took one sip of his tea before turning to Nguyen. "Time to go." He pointed down at the flexiscreen sitting on the table. "That yours?"

Nguyen puffed on his cigar. Like Lynn, he seemed to be figuring the best answer to that particular question.

"Mister Nguyen, is that your flexiscreen?"

Nguyen began to speak, but Lynn cut him off. "Yes. Yes it's his."

The agent started to rise from his seat. "You better bring it with you."

16:03

A soft chime emanated from the screen. The four faces at the table turned to look at it. No one spoke. A few seconds passed and the chime sounded again, the ideograms on the flexiscreen increasing in brightness, insisting on attention.

"Mister Nguyen," she said. He didn't respond. He just sat staring at the screen. Her voice was firmer the second time. "Mister Nguyen."

He started and looked up at her.

"Why don't you answer your call while the agents here show me that warrant."

He looked from her, to the screen, over to

the agents, then back to her again. He wiped the sweat from his brow with the back of his hand. "Sure." He put a finger to his c-glyph and closed his eyes.

"Gentlemen." Lynn held out her hand. "The warrant." She felt surprisingly calm given she was responsible for a crime occurring three feet away that could get her thirty years in prison. She focused on her breathing.

Inhale.

Exhale.

Inhale.

Agent Baker glanced over at Nguyen, who was now mumbling responses to someone only he could see. The agent sighed and reached into his coat pocket, pulled out the palmscreen, and pressed his thumb to it. "Verify: Agent Baker, immigration enforcement. Display warrant for Nguyen Van Cam, suspected people smuggler."

He waited. Nothing happened. He pressed his thumb to the screen again. Still nothing. It was dead. No sound, no light, no signal. He handed it to his partner. The other man looked at the dead screen, then up at Lynn. "What's going on here?"

She slowly slid the pistol back in the holster, eyes on the two men. "You tell me."

The agent held the screen up. "All official communications are contained in this, including the warrant. It's a closed system. It was working fine a few minutes ago. Now it's dead."

She leaned back in her chair. "Well, I'd say you boys are shit out of luck."

"This doesn't change anything."

"I disagree. It changes everything." Lynn signaled for the grandmother to come over to the table. She did so immediately. "This is private property. Unless you're conducting government-sanctioned business, you should leave." She turned to the old woman, addressing her in the formal Vietnamese mode, "Right, elder aunty?"

The grandmother looked at the two men, her eyes sparkling. She found a phrase for them in English. "Piss off."

The agents rose from their seats. One reached

under his jacket. The other looked around at the customers, at the faces staring back at him from within the red haze, coiled with silent anger. The agent placed a hand on his partner's shoulder. "Let's wait outside. Warrant and backup will be here in fifteen minutes."

The other man nodded, still staring straight at Lynn. He let his hand drop, looked over at Nguyen. "Don't even think about leaving." Then he spun and walked out, his partner right behind.

Lynn turned to the old woman. "We need some privacy."

The old woman set about ushering the customers out the front door. No one needed much encouragement. It wasn't worth witnessing what was going to happen next.

Soon all that remained was the smoke and the scent of anchovies. That, and two of her men. They walked over from where they had been sitting, one stood behind Mister Nguyen, one next to Lynn. They were big men.

Nguyen glanced up at them, then back at Lynn. "We should leave, now." He started to rise from his seat, but a heavy hand fell on his shoulder and pushed him back down.

Lynn shook her head. "Not yet, Mister Nguyen, not yet." She indicated the door with her eyes. "Your men in the car outside have been sent away."

"What?"

She sighed and folded her hands on the table-top. "You led two immigration agents to our first meeting."

"I didn't know they were following me."

"You led two immigrations agents into our first fucking meeting." She didn't raise her voice, but the steel was in it this time.

Nguyen said nothing, just bowed his head and looked at the burned-out cigar between his fingers.

Lynn pointed at the cigarette case. "Fortunately I keep a dot scrambler on hand for times such as this. The one I stuck on the agent's palmscreen will wipe any record of my retina scan, and freeze the unit until a tech can sit down and unwind the scrambled code. And this," she pointed to her nose ring, "is a refraction loop. You know what this does?"

He shook his head.

"To the naked eye I looked normal. But when you take the memory pin from your c-glyph and play back this scene, the area around my face is distorted. The light bent and warped. They'll still have my voiceprint, but I can live with that."

She placed the cigarette case in her pocket.

"So I'm in the clear," she said. "You know the laws on human memory. If it doesn't come from a memory pin playback, it is inadmissible as evidence. What with the frail psychology of natural memory and all that. Those agents won't remember what I look like anyway. Not if I change my hair." She reached up, touching the spikes with her palms. "Pity. I quite like this style."

She sighed. "There is, unfortunately, one loose strand. I didn't activate the refraction loop until after you'd walked in. Those agents," she waved at the door, "could subpoena your memory pin."

He stared at her for a few seconds, processing what she was saying. "I'll destroy it. I'll give it to you even. Right now."

She shook her head. "It is more than that. You're sloppy, and that makes you a liability. You know the names of the families I just paid for, and—"

"—I'll wipe all my records. You can have every—"

"—Enough." Her eyes flashed. "Enough. You endangered my parents. This isn't business, this is personal." She paused, watching the man squirm under the heavy hands pressed down on his shoulders. "That's the secret, by the way, Mister Nguyen. This business we have chosen—it's always personal."

"What are you saying?" He struggled to rise. The man next to Lynn stepped forward and drove a fist into Nguyen's face, rocking the gangster's head backward. Nguyen sat there for half a minute, one hand clutching the table, the other over his eye. When he pulled his hand

away blood trickled down his cheek, the eyebrow split and already swelling.

Lynn indicated the man who had struck him. "This is Mister Giang. How is your family doing, Mister Giang?"

A voice, deep and clear, answered. "Well, Miz Vu."

She kept her eyes on Nguyen. "They been out here some time now haven't they?"

"Nearly three years."

She nodded. She pointed at the man behind Nguyen's left shoulder. "This is Mister Lac. His family arrived only six months ago. Have they settled in well, Mister Lac?"

"Very well, Miz Vu."

"Did your younger sister get into university?"

"Yes. She will be a teacher." A note of pride in the voice.

"Good. If there are any problems with tuition, you let me know."

It was hard to tell in the shadows, but Mister Lac appeared to nod in reply.

Nguyen watched her now out of one eye, fear blossoming behind it.

"Mister Giang?"

"Yes, Miz Vu."

"Could you take Mister Nguyen out to the back room and put a bullet through his head?"

Giang moved to where Nguyen sat and grabbed him by the upper arm. He and Lac hefted him out of his seat. Nguyen stuttered. "Wait, what? You can't kill me." Spittle fresh on his lips, his good eye wet. "Do you know who I am?"

Lynn stood. "Yes I do. You're a mercenary," she said. "And I meet people like you every day of the week."

She nodded at Giang. He punched Nguyen in the stomach, doubling him over as the air expelled from his lungs, his cigar butt dropping to the floor.

That was the last she saw of him—bent over, unable to speak, being dragged from the room.

She turned to Mister Lac. "Get my parents. Right now. Take them to a safe house. If they argue—when my mother argues with you—just tell her that their daughter will explain everything in a couple of days."

Lac nodded and left.

The grandmother walked in as he was leaving, handed over a warm bamboo box. *"Cởm của con nè. Bać đoán là con muốń takeaway."* ["Your lunch, child. I guessed you wanted takeaway."]

The scent of rice, sharp chili sauce, and aromatic mushrooms rose from the container. Lynn smiled a small smile. "Smells delicious, older Aunt. *Cám ốn bać.*"

Grandmother nodded. *"Con baỏ trong. Con đi há."* ["You take care. You go."]

"You too. *Con đi đây.*" ["I'm going."]

Lynn straightened, fixing the ends of her hair with an open palm. She faced the front door. Twilight to heat, crimson to blinding white. Lynn hated the world out there.

She reached for the door handle.

KHALID KAKI

OPERATION DANIEL

(2016)

Translated from the Arabic by Adam Talib

DISTRICT: KIRKUK (GAO'S FLAME), 2103

It was still early when the SMS bracelet around Rashid's wrist vibrated, waking him. The message was brief and precise.

Dear Beneficiary no. RBS89:

Good Benefit.

Today, the first Saturday of the month, is dedicated to "eradicating the remnants of evil." The Beloved Units will be mobilized throughout the city between the hours of 9 a.m. and 6 p.m. Anyone in possession of audio or audiovisual recordings of the reclassified languages (laser on titanium or carbon fiber) should turn these in to the officially designated droids patrolling immediately. Anyone failing to comply with these instructions will be arrested and promptly archived.

Gao Dong, The Beloved, Loves You.

There was nothing unusual about these messages, not since the Venerable Benefactor, Gao Dong, who currently preferred the title "The Beloved," had made the Memory Office his priority department. For those who don't follow State politics, the Memory Office is both a security and social service. It functions as a security service by virtue of its core mission: to protect the state's present from the threat of the past. But what makes it a social service, you ask. This stems from the intimate relationship the government has with its followers, trainees, and admirers—not exactly the relationship between superior and subordinates, rather benefactor and beneficiaries. That was the touch of genius the Venerable Benefactor had brought to all areas of life in the black-gold state of Kirkuk, thirty-five years ago. What he did to protect them all from the threat of the past was itself a service. For instance, he had reclassified all the city's older languages, the most ancient of which dated back five thousand years, as "prohibited."

As beneficiaries, the people were forbidden from speaking Syriac, Arabic, Kurdish, Turkmen, or any language other than Chinese. The punishment for speaking those languages, or reading about history, literature, or art in them was merciless: you were archived. This involved being incinerated in a special device—resembling one of those UV tanning beds that were all the rage in the late twentieth century—your ashes would then be removed to a facility that produced synthetic diamonds, where, just a few hours later, all that had been left of you would reemerge as a tiny, glittering stone. It was called "archiving" because a crystal can store an infinite library of information locked in its chambers—more secrets than the House of Wisdom—even a traitor's personal history could be preserved in them. (It was something to do with electrons and vibrations.) Once polished, these crystals would be sent to another factory where they would come to adorn one of the Benefactor Gao Dong's shoes, or one of his many hats.

Rashid didn't possess any recordings in any of the languages Gao Dong wanted to strip Kirkuk of, but he spoke three of them fluently. This he couldn't deny. He'd learned them from his parents, and he knew something in his bones would compel him to teach them, in turn, to his own children one day, if he had any. But that's all he felt about the issue. He was no rebel.

He knew there were some people who would fight, or even die, for these languages, claiming they held the key to citizens' real hearts. But these were just rumors Rashid had heard. He'd never met one of these rebels. A few days earlier a special search-and-raid unit had turned up several discs and tapes, dating back eighty years, on a hillside in Daquq. Information had been leaked by a double agent to the search unit who reported that the artifacts were found to be full of songs—songs that some people in Kirkuk had heard about, but that no one had actually heard. According to the gossip, these had been among the most beautiful, exquisite pieces ever recorded. Songs about the singer's beloved and the pain of being separated from her; songs about the beauty of nature and the women who go down to the village spring to get water, and lots of other things like that. The times they lived in sounded much simpler, safer, and more humane than our present age.

The discs and tapes were immediately destroyed and a written and verbal order announcing the enforced surrender of all similar material was issued. Everyone in the search unit was transferred to a "training session" in the city's Great Hall of Benefits. Things like this seemed to happen every two or three weeks. They'd be digging in search of water and come across some old computers; the digger's claw would scrape against old computer parts or a glimmer of tapes and discs would peek through the disturbed earth. Some people were prepared to pay a lot of money to get their hands on that sort of rubbish—despite the threat of being archived—and several people had already been transformed into little square cuts for being in possession of "found" music or films, which now graced one of Gao Dong's waistcoats and lapels. Whenever Rashid thought about the Benefactor's love of fine costumes, the collars and sashes, the cravats and cummerbunds, he couldn't stop another image from entering his head: that of a gag. It was because of a slogan he had heard once, or read: "History is a hostage, but it will bite through the gag you tie around its mouth, bite through and still be heard."

The time was nearing 13, and the young man, in his twenties, who called himself "Rashid," considered going out for the day. If he stepped out into the street, he would automatically become "Beneficiary no. RBS89"—or "RBS" for short (the number "89" simply referred to the year he was born). But if he stayed in, he could remain unnamed, no one. Under the rule of Gao Dong—who'd come to power in the wealthy city-state of Kirkuk as a result of the Three-Month War in 2078—all citizens had been reclassified as beneficiaries. This was because everything His Excellency now did for them, or to them, or on their behalf, in his governmental and military capacity as commander and chief, was to their benefit. His security measures were for their benefit; his purges of camps outside Kirkuk, driving out refugees wanting to share in their spoils, was for their benefit; his war on worker's unions and their terrorists—all for their benefit. And every citizen prayed for his continued protection, of course.

This is how things stand in Kirkuk today—or rather in what the Beloved Commander calls "Gao's Flame"—in honor of the city's eternal flame.* The old districts of the city and the Assyrian Citadel look more or less as they have done for over a century, even though the city has been cut off from Mesopotamia for four decades now, since Gao Dong's arrival; the outskirts of the city have been developed as the city has expanded, and outside them are the camps, the migrants, and exiled union extremists. Over the years, Gao's Flame has grown as one of the world's richest city-states, a place of enormous wealth and investment, thanks to its petroleum reserves, where its citizens enjoyed peace and tranquility. Sargon, an Assyrian from the city, built the Citadel anew and in each of its seven corners he placed huge gates flanked by winged bulls in the style of those sculpted by the Gods of Arrapha† thousands of years before. Although the Three-Month War had damaged parts of the aluminum-clad Citadel wall, the bulls still preserved their timeless luster, shining in the sunlight, and staring out into each coming day with dark, wide eyes, their strong, youthful hooves planted firmly into Arrapha's soil.

In the evenings, the young man known as RBS89—or "Rashid Bin Suleiman" to his family—would meet some friends outside the Citadel at the Prophet Daniel Gate; from there, they would go to the ruined graveyards nearby, to chat and catch up before dusk became night. In the graveyard, some of his friends—not him, of course—would sing songs in the old tongues and recite poems that Gao Dong's government had specifically reclassified. It was as though these friends were performing some secret ritual, something like a religious ceremony, even though the songs' lyrics were completely domestic in their subject matter. They had never told Rashid—so he could never be accused of knowing—but these friends had all lost parents and relatives in the Great Benefactor's arrival—hundreds had been executed by Gao Dong and his purification policies. His friends would sing these simple love songs in hushed, ardent voices, heedless of the danger they faced if the authorities overheard them. "The people of Kirkuk had fallen into Gao Dong's grasp as easily as a butterfly into the hands of a collector," his friends would say, "because the whole world had changed. The balance of power had tipped toward China, and now Kirkuk, once a solitary kingdom, speaking entirely its own language,‡ had become just another outpost."

One evening, about three weeks before, as the young men and women had gathered in the graveyard, a red government droid hovered toward them. His friends knew what to do, switching seamlessly from the ancient song they were singing at the time to a Chinese one. They always managed to have a contemporary Chinese song ready, whose melody matched exactly with the ancient one. This was standard procedure whenever a member of the red police came

---

* A gas flame in the middle of the Baba Gurgur oil field, near the city of Kirkuk, and sixteen kilometers northwest of Arrapha; it was the first such field to be discovered in Northern Iraq by Westerners in 1927. The field is forty meters in diameter and has been burning for 2,500 years. It was considered the largest oil field in the world until the discovery of the Ghawar field in Saudi Arabia in 1948.

† Arrapha, or Arrabkha, was an ancient city in what today is northeastern Iraq, on the site of the modern city of Kirkuk. It began as a city of the Gutian people, became Hurrian, and was an Assyrian city during most of its occupation.

‡ Around 2150 BCE, Kirkuk became occupied by "language isolate"-speaking Zagros Mountains dwellers known, to the Semitic and Sumerian Mesopotamians, as the "Gutian" people. Arrabkha was the capital of the short-lived Guti kingdom (Gutium), before it was destroyed and the Gutians driven from Mesopotamia by the neo-Sumerian Empire c. 2090 BCE.

near, and it worked every time. "I wish I were a stone / At the base of the citadel," they would sing one minute, "So that I could be friends / With everyone who visits." Then, a second later it would be love song set in modern Beijing. It was a cat-and-mouse game. But listening to them sing that first song, they all sometimes wondered, privately, if something was missing, if something at the core had been stolen away, and if the now they inhabited was impenetrable to it. Whatever it was, it could no longer reach through; instead they all mouthed a set of sounds they didn't truly understand.

One of the young men gathered there that evening—there is no evidence it was Rashid—failed to follow the normal procedure. While his friends switched effortlessly to a Chinese pop song, this particular youth carried on singing in Arabic, or possibly Turkmen. Indeed he sang louder and louder as the droid came near, inspecting him close-up. He drowned out the singing of the others, many of whom broke away quickly and disappeared. The words were obviously strange to him:

There are three fig trees growing
Beside the wall at the citadel.

But he kept singing them, as if singing them louder and louder would give them more meaning, somehow, or help their meaning reach through to him:

My hands are bound,
A chain is wrapped around my neck.
Don't yank the chains,
'cause my arms already hurt.

Three weeks later, the afternoon that Rashid received the bracelet text, he decided against going out. It was a Saturday after all, he didn't need to do anything. Instead he would play with his artifacts. These were not recordings, you understand; they contained no written or spoken or musical examples of reclassified languages. They were merely sculptural objects, with interesting shapes—glittering discs or dull cuboids with spindles of tape inside.

By some strange coincidence, Rashid owned hundreds of them, and also had the means to duplicate them—just as objects, of course, for their aesthetic, sculptural value. He was stood in his pajamas, scanning his shelves, trying to decide which one to play with, when a special detachment of red droids burst through the front door to his house, brushing aside Suleiman Senior, and marching up to his room. Some people have claimed that RBS89 managed to take one of these objects and extract a melody from it, in the time the droids took to break down his door. There is no evidence to support this, nor the claim that RBS89 was singing this melody as he was carried away, or that he danced in his prison cell, singing the same. Similar rumors were spread about the other suspects removed by red forces in the Begler, Piryadi, and Azadi neighborhoods, in the crackdown that became known as "Operation Daniel."

Even more unfounded is the superstition, circulated in some of the poorer districts, that a melody sung in the face of death resounds louder in that palace of final destination, the glittering Archive. That would imply that when General Woo Shang presented Gao Dong, The Beloved, three weeks later, with a new pair of diamond-studded boots, in his castle on the Euphrates River, one of the tiny gemstones on those boots would still be vibrating, deep inside, with the words of a silly song—*"Take me to the bar. / Take me to the coffeehouse. / Let's go somewhere fun . . ."** This is not true.

---

* Lines from "Near the Citadel"—a popular early-twentieth-century Turkmen song of anonymous composition.

BRANDON O'BRIEN

FALLENANGEL.DLL

(2016)

"DIDN'T HAVE ANY PROBLEMS getting back?"

Imtiaz stretched on the couch and sighed. "Nah," he called back to the kitchen. "Traffic was remarkably light today. You know how it is—takes a while for everyone to find their rhythm."

"I don't know how it is, actually," Tevin shouted from the kitchen. There was a rustle of plastic bags, and then he poked his head from the door. "I never experienced a state of emergency before."

"A blessing for which you should thank God," Imtiaz said. "I would've killed for the chance to study abroad when the last one happened. Worst three months of our lives."

After even more shuffling from the kitchen, Tevin came into the living room, a cold bottle of beer in each hand, and kissed Imtiaz on the cheek. "And was there a good reason for the last one?"

"Just as good a reason as this one."

Tevin sighed and handed his partner a bottle. "I guess I should have gotten more beer then."

Imtiaz chuckled. "Slow down, boss. Since when you turn big drinker, anyway?"

"Country gone to the dogs? No better time, I figure." Tevin raised his bottle before him as a toast.

"To the dogs. Now they get to see us trapped at home." He brought his bottle to Tevin's with a soft clink, and then put it to his lips and took a long swig. It had only been three days so far since the Prime Minister had declared the country under lockdown, and everyone knew what a joke looked like when they saw it. It had been seven years at least since the last time he'd been in one, and the excuse was the same. "We are working hard with the Armed Forces," the Prime Minister would say, "to curtail the growing crime rate in this country, and we ask only that the citizens of this great twin-island state be patient in this effort."

The first thing that popped up on social media was also the most accurate: "How do you curtail crime by simply asking criminals to stay inside?"

Imtiaz felt a vibrating in his pocket, and reached into it for his cell phone. Almost as soon as he saw the text on his screen, he shoved it back into his pocket.

"Everything okay?" Tevin asked.

"Yeah." A long sigh, then Imtiaz took another, longer gulp of beer.

"Im?"

". . . It's nothing."

"If I have to ask what nothing is—"

Imtiaz frowned and put his drink down. "I just might have to head out in a bit."

Tevin squinted. Imtiaz didn't like getting in fights, least of all with Tevin, whose disappointed glares had the power to make him feel ashamed for days afterward. "I don't want to, but I kinda promised—"

"Promised who?"

"A friend of mine wanted help moving something. She doesn't want to talk about it." He got up and walked slowly to his bedroom. "I wish I didn't have to, but I promised before this was a thing—"

"But you can say no? It's minutes past six. You can't just head back out—"

"I promised," Imtiaz called back. "And I swear, it's not a big deal. Lemme just take care of it, and I'll be back before you miss me." He took the phone back out and opened the text this time: *so im at uwi, can you meet me at the gate?*

"Im." When he turned to the door, Tevin was already in the walkway, arms folded. "Come nah man. You wanna break curfew and not even tell me why?"

Imtiaz reached for a shirt hanging on the door of his wardrobe and put it over his gray tee. "It's Shelly. She said she needed someone with a car to help her move something two weeks ago, and now is the only day it can happen. I volunteered."

"'Move something'? What?"

"One of her projects. I dunno what yet."

There it was—Tevin's dreaded glare, as he tapped his foot on the white tile of the walkway. "A'right. A project. But if the police hold you, you're out of luck. And don't play like you taking your time to answer the phone if I call. You hear?"

"Yes, boss," Imtiaz said, a small smirk on his face. It was his only line of defense against Tevin's sternness. It didn't succeed often, but when it did, it did so well.

Tevin tried to fight the grin spreading over his face, and lost. "Be safe, Im. Please. Promise me that. Since you insist on keeping promises."

Imtiaz walked up to him, still slipping the last buttons into their holes, and kissed his partner softly on the lips. "I absolutely positively promise. I'll be fine."

"You bet your ass you'll be fine," Tevin whispered. "Play you're not going and be fine, see what I go do to you."

• • •

Imtiaz sped down the highway at sixty, seventy miles an hour, past the three or four motorists still making their way back home who glanced at him with fear. A dusty navy-blue Nissan rushing past in the dark night blaring circa 2007 noise rock does that to people.

He made sure to call before he took off. He'd meet Shelly at the South Gate and take off immediately. She asked if the back seat was empty, and if his husband knew what they were going to pick up. Imtiaz reminded her that he didn't know either, to which she replied, "Oho, right—well, see you just-now," and hung up. This wasn't a good sign, but the volatile mix of curiosity and dedication to keeping his promises got the better of him.

It was twenty to seven when he pulled up, screeching to a halt right in front of the short Indian girl in the brown cargo pants and the black T-shirt. She took the lollipop out of her mouth and peeped through the open driver-side window, putting a finger of her free hand into her ear to block out the music.

"You just always wanted to do that, right?"

"Get the *hell* in," he sneered.

"All right, all right," Shelly said. She lifted a black duffel bag off the ground beside her and got in the back.

"Wait." Imtiaz turned back to face her. "What's in the bag?"

"Tools." She patted it gently as she said it, looking right at him, sporting a smug grin.

"Tools? Open it, lemme see."

"What, you think I selling drugs or somet'ing?"

"I t'ink if you weren't selling drugs, you'd be able to open the blasted bag."

Shelly slapped the bag even harder, just so he could hear the clanging of metal within. Her hand recoiled painfully. "Happy now?"

"No." He faced front and slowly got back on the road. "Where are we heading?"

"Eh . . . Just keep going west, I'll let you know."

"That isn't how you ask people to give you a lift."

Shelly sighed, rolling the lollipop from one side of her mouth to the next. "Would you get nervous if I said Laventi—"

"Laventille?" he shouted. "You want to go to *Laventille* at minutes to seven on the third night of a curfew? What, not being arrested or murdered is boring?"

"Trust me, when you see it, you'll be glad you came." Shelly grinned even wider. "Something you couldn't imagine. I could've gone myself, but didn't you wonder why I asked if you could do it? Not because I needed a car." She shrugged. "Although we will."

"Are you gonna tell me what it is?"

"Shh. You go see it." She shifted the duffel bag and lay across the length of the seat. "I dare you to tell me you not impressed when we reach there." She winced, turning to face the stereo deck. "How you could listen to *this*?"

Imtiaz couldn't help but smirk. They'd spent many an afternoon debating the musical value of

his thrashing, clanging metal music. At her most annoying, he wasn't beyond blasting it just to get on her nerves. Today felt as good a time as any.

"It calms me," he replied. It did. He imagined his thoughts dancing to it, his large sweaty mosh pit of anxieties.

"I don't see how this could calm anyone, Im. It sounds like two backhoes gettin' in a fight."

"If you say so." He would have liked to describe the meaning of the present song at length—about rebellion, about sticking it to the man and rising above oppression and propaganda to finally live in a land where you were a free and equal citizen—but he had been Shelly's friend long enough to know that she didn't care. She appreciated that she had friends like Imtiaz who thought as deeply about the things they loved as she did about her own loves, but she never really wanted to know what those deep thoughts were. That would involve caring about the things they loved as well. She often didn't. Passionate people were more interesting to her than their passions.

He glanced at his watch, and panic shot through him. "Shit!" He swerved, aiming for an exit into a side street in San Juan.

"What the—?" Shelly bumped her head on the door, then straightened up.

"Why did I do this?" Imtiaz's eyes opened wide. "We going to get arrested!"

"Whoa!" Shelly put up her hands. "Don't panic. We came off the bus route, no one going to see us now. I go give you directions, okay?"

He lowered the volume on the stereo. "I don't like any of this, Michelle."

She winced at the sound of her whole first name. "I know. I should've say something before. But would you have come if I didn't?"

"What could be so important?"

"You really have to see it."

She pointed out the route, giving vague directions as if she were guessing at them, only appearing to get a better sense of where they were going as they got closer to the house. Shelly said she often passed through this area to look for the person they were meeting. She had met the man on a forum early last year. He was one of the few seemingly deluded souls to believe the government rumors of drones and police riot-suppression bots. This interested her less for anarchist, anti-establishment reasons, and more because this was her only chance to get to see a bot up close—if the rumors were true. Almost every month her friend would have some evidence, and almost every week he'd need to be bailed out of Golden Grove Prison for a heroin possession that wouldn't stick. Imtiaz asked if she trusted her friend, and she shook her head.

"That is why *we* going." Shelly was still focusing on the road when she said it.

Imtiaz focused on the road, too. Along the way, he had noticed at least three police jeeps. It looked like they were circling the area. He swore, too, that he'd heard a helicopter above, after leaving the San Juan border, but he couldn't hear it anymore.

"We almost there," Shelly said, pointing at a rusted shack of galvanized sheeting, with a glittering lime-green sedan parked outside. "By that car." Imtiaz nodded, parked behind it, unplugged his phone, and got out. Shelly shuffled a bit inside before taking up her bag and opening the door. "Follow me. Lemme do the talking."

Imtiaz closed the door behind her and gestured for her to lead the way, past the car, past the front door to the side entrance. Shelly knocked three times, and a stern woman's voice shouted, "Just come inside, nah!"

The door swung open with a creak and Shelly stepped in, Imtiaz following close behind. He was hypervigilant, even to the point of being aware of his awareness, of whether he'd come across as nervous even as he glanced around for the faintest sign of threat. They were in the kitchen, which was better furnished than the outside of the house suggested—stainless-steel sink, tiled countertop, the best dishwasher money could buy, even two double-door fridges.

A tall, dark woman was at the counter, dicing a tomato with a chef's knife. She looked fit,

with beautiful soft features, with skin that wrinkled almost imperceptibly at the corners of her lips and near her eyes. Imtiaz guessed she was around her late fifties.

"Ey, it's Shelly!" the woman said, smiling but not taking her eyes off the tomato. "And who's your friend?"

"Missus Atwell, this is Imtiaz. You know how your son and I like putting together puzzles. Imtiaz likes that sort of thing, so I invited him to help."

"Ah, yes . . ." Ms. Atwell put down the knife and stared wistfully off into the TV room, where some soap opera was playing on mute. "Runako and his blasted puzzles. He does still never let me see them, you know. Even when the police take him, he insist—nobody mus' go back in his room an' look for anyt'ing."

"Yeah, the puzzles are kinda important, miss."

Ms. Atwell continued gazing distantly for a beat or two, and then went back to her tomato. "Well, just try not to stay too late. You getting a ride out of here after?"

"Yes, miss," Shelly said, nodding as she left the kitchen, gesturing for Imtiaz to follow down the short hallway to a dark brown door. Shelly rapped on it three times. They could hear the sound of large containers being dragged across the floor, and then one, two, three bolt locks being opened.

The door opened a crack, and a dark-skinned face poked through. His eyes were wide at first, but then he glanced at Shelly and sighed calmly, pulling the door open slowly. "Oh, it's you. Thanks for passing through."

"Of course I must pass through," she said as she entered, Imtiaz behind her. "You say you had something for me to see. I saw the picture. I just want to make sure."

Runako was a tall black man, perfectly bald-headed, in a white Jointpop T-shirt and black sweatpants. When he noticed Imtiaz looking at him, he nudged Shelly and stepped back, leaning on the wall nervously. "Who is this? Your friend?"

"Yeah. Runako, meet Imtiaz. He's the one going to help me put this back together. If you didn't set me up like all the other times."

He folded his arms. "Okay. But I telling you, too many times I get hold, I get lock up, because somebody tell somebody and the police hear. This is probably my last chance for somebody to see it."

Imtiaz had focused on an odd shape in the corner of the room under a sheet of gray vinyl. When he turned back to the other two, they were glancing at it too. "This is it?" he asked.

Runako nodded. "Look at it, nah, Shelly? Exactly as I promised."

She stepped toward it and pulled the dusty vinyl off. In a coughing fit, her eyes widened as she looked at it. When she got her breath back, she turned to Runako. "Really?"

"See?!" Runako grinned. "I is not no liar."

"Imtiaz, come!" She waved to her friend to come closer, and he stepped up beside her. It was a robot with a matte black shell and glossy black joints. It had suffered severe damage; frayed wires poked out of an arm, its chest plate had a fist-sized hole in it. Imtiaz noticed that on its back were a pair of camouflage-green retractable wings; they looked as if they would span half the room when opened, maybe even wider. On its neck was a serial number painted in white stencil: TTPS-8103-X791.

"TTPS?" Imtiaz said, almost at a whisper. "As in—"

"Yeah, man," Runako said behind them.

"A real live police bot . . ." Shelly straightened up slowly, dusting herself off. "This is the riot team model?"

"Yeah. The mark-two, in fact. Tear gas and pepper spray nozzles in the arm, but they not full, and stun gun charges; thrusters under the wings so it could dispense over crowds by flying overhead. Recording cam in one of the eyes—can't remember which, supposed to be forty megapixels. And some other things, but I didn't open it up yet. I was waiting for you."

Shelly rubbed her hands and reached down beside her to open the duffel bag and take out a long, flat-head screwdriver. "Why, thank you, kind sir. Now, gimme my music there. Time to start."

Runako nodded and stepped over to a stereo at the corner of the room. Shelly took a USB drive out of her back pocket and tossed it at him. He caught it, slotted it in a back port, and pressed a couple of buttons. He stepped back as something haunting and atmospheric played, the lyrics lo-fi and echoing, the instrumental thumping and dark. Shelly swayed a little as the sound rumbled through the room, eyes closed, facing the ceiling, as if taken briefly by some heavenly rapture. Then she straightened and pointed her screwdriver at Imtiaz. "You hear that, Immy? Now that is music to calm you. Not whatever wildness you does listen to."

Imtiaz squinted, eager to ask what made her witchy-sounding, incomprehensible music better than his tastes, but he kept his question to himself.

Shelly knelt before the thing and started unscrewing the outer panels, observing the wiring as it snaked across its chest and limbs, leading to each gear or tool it powered. Imtiaz pulled up a chair by the wall so he could see, but not so close as to disturb her.

Her hands moved as if she were in a trance. Gently, screws would slowly wind out of their places, plating would fall into her hands, she would gently place it beside her on a sheet of newspaper on the floor. She would follow the lines of red and green and purple wire from the processor in its headpiece to the battery supply in its center and then out to the extremities, to its tear gas canister launchers, its sensory databases. Imtiaz thought that they looked like the veins of . . . Of course they did. Of course they looked like veins, like nerves, like sinews. What else could a man do but copy?

He stared at the serial number on a sheet of plate on the floor. A police riot bot. Here, in Laventille. On a night of curfew. He went from peacefully admiring Shelly's diligence right back into panic.

Shelly said softly, "You're gonna be checking the BIOS after this is done, by the way. So get a laptop ready. Runako?"

Runako snapped a finger, then picked up a dusty gray notebook near the stereo. "Here, boss." He took a couple of long steps to get to Imtiaz and rested it in his lap.

As Imtiaz opened it, he could hear Shelly mumbling to herself about "not that much damage," and the bot being "up and running in an hour." He glanced up to see that most of the outer shell, save for the wings, were gone, the bot's innards entirely visible. He could see past them to the bedroom wall. It was almost a work of art as it was.

He opened a guest profile on the laptop and launched a web browser. "How you paying for this, again?" he said.

"'You'?" Shelly chuckled. "You mean *we*."

"What?" He froze for a moment. "No. No, I don't. Trus' me, I don't."

"So . . . I forgot to mention . . ." She had a pair of pliers in hand now, stripping some of the power-supply wires with them.

"Mention *what*?"

"I promised Runako we would come back if he needed anything. In exchange for this."

"Wha—" He wanted to shout, but he glanced at Runako and decided against it. He didn't know what kind of person he was dealing with. As the host folded his arms, Imtiaz cleared his throat. "You didn't think this was probably worth sharing with me first? Before even asking me to come here?"

"I figured it wasn't going and be a problem. You like them kinda thing."

"But I don't like doing it *for free* for people I *don't know*."

Shelly gestured to the robot with a free hand. "Look—it already open. We already here. I asking nicely. This is too big an opportunity."

He didn't answer right away, but he wanted to say no. This was the neighborhood where strangers got shot. He wasn't planning to come back, national lockdown or not. "How much something like this supposed to cost?"

Shelly had already returned her focus on the wiring. "This is seven figures at least."

Runako chimed in. "Black market is nine hundred fifty thousand."

Imtiaz sighed as softly as he could, too softly for them to hear. He couldn't do it. His skin felt tight against him, his palms clammy and warm. He logged into Facebook in the hope of finding something silly and distracting while Shelly tended to the robot.

The very first shared link on his feed reads *Sources Warn of Police Raids in Hot Spots to Curb Crime During Curfew*. He opened it in another tab: "Residents in several so-called 'crime hot spots' across the island have claimed that their areas are being targeted by police officers who, as part of their crackdown on crime, are performing random house searches for illegal contraband . . ."

Imtiaz felt his chest get tight. He glanced at the window and was sure he could see flashing blue lights several streets away. He glanced back at the article: "Several Western areas, such as Belmont and Laventille, are due for their own random searches at the time of posting, sources say." He heard a siren blare suddenly, and just as suddenly, silence. He was sure.

"You nervous or what, man?" Runako said sternly.

"What?" Imtiaz turned to face him. "Nah, I good."

"You sure? Like you freaking out about the deal."

He looked away, hoping to hide whatever signs of fear were on his face. "I just could've been told before, that's all."

"Ey." Runako snapped his fingers, and Imtiaz twitched. "What? You is another one of them who feel they too good for Laventille?"

"I didn't say that." Imtiaz got out of his seat and walked to the bedroom window, pulling the curtains open only enough to get a good view. The street was empty and dimly lit. "Although you can't blame a guy, can you?"

"What that supposed to mean?"

"It supposed to mean people don't like coming to places and being afraid they not going and make it back home after."

"Really?" Runako folded his arms. "This is the fool you go look to bring in my house, Shelly? During de curfew, no less, a man going and tell me the whole of Laventille not safe for nobody?"

"You hear me say—"

Shelly whistled, still not looking up from the robot. "Fellas, I like a good rousing sociopolitical debate just like everybody else, but we on a clock, right? So cool it."

Runako backed off, but Imtiaz kept looking out of the window. This time he was positive—a police jeep stopping at the top of the street, one man coming out of the back seat and shouting at the window of a house. "I don't like this."

Shelly was already taping over some exposed wires, and taping around them all to keep them in place. "I'm almost done, Im. You'll just check the firmware quick, help me load it into the car, and that's it. We almost finished."

Imtiaz saw the officer beat on the door of the house until a woman came out, and then grab her by the neck and throw her out onto the street. He shouted again. Another officer came out from the driver's-side door, a pistol already in his hand.

"Stop almost-finishing and *finish*, then," he said nervously. "Trouble up the street."

She looked over the inside of the shell again, tracing her hands along all the snaking wires, trying to find a spot she had overlooked. When she couldn't find one, she shrugged, beginning to screw each plate of its iron skin back together. "We could deal with the outer damage when we take it home, I guess. Your turn."

It took Imtiaz a moment to peel away from the window. The second officer had just struck a small child in the head with his handgun, and his partner was already barging into the house. Imtiaz sighed and got back to his chair. "You have a Type C cable?"

For a moment, Shelly was confused. "I might . . ." she rummaged in her tool bag for

one, a couple seconds longer than her still-tense friend could handle.

He snapped his fingers. "It really can't wait. We don't have time."

Over Imtiaz's shoulder, Runako held a long looped black cable, its connectors seemingly brand new. "Don't bother. One right here."

"Thank you," Imtiaz said, snatching it from him, tossing one end of it to Shelly. She slid a panel to the side of the robot's head—one of the few parts of it still covered—and inserted it.

Imtiaz opened a command console and began his wizardry. He had learned a couple of tricks online ever since robots came in vogue, but they were light reading. He never anticipated actually having to apply them. There were never supposed to actually be any on his island. They were too expensive for leisure, save for the wealthiest corners of Cascade or Westmoorings where some fair-skinned grandfather with an Irish last name lived out his lonely retirement.

The government swore against them for public sector purposes, citing price mostly, but police bots were a particularly hot topic. They weren't just costly to most leaders. They were problematic—too much power for anyone in office to hold. Leaders of the opposition for the last few years milked that argument in the parliament house—"Do you want our Prime Minister having full rein over armed machines? With no consciences? Wandering our streets under the guise of law and order, but really, she's asking the people to pay for her own personal hit squad!" Another oft-milked idea—they called it the "flying squad"—was a rumored group of non-robotic policemen with a license to kill and a direct line to the Minister. Putting those two ideas together was a good way to whip up a panic.

But then again, here was proof of one of the claims being true. A police bot. Number and all. The first known sighting—if only they survived the night.

A couple lines of code later, a small window popped up—the bot's application screen. *Reboot Y/N?* He pressed the *Y* key, and another line of text appeared: *Rebooting* . . . They could hear a low whirring from the gears near the battery, and the robot's LED eyes began to slowly fade in and out in a bright blue.

"Hurry up, nah, you dotish robot," Imtiaz muttered. A sliver of him had all but given up that they would make it back out unnoticed with the robot in tow. But he had already begun. There was nothing left but to soldier on.

The robot's head slowly tilted up, and a gentle, melodious bootup theme played from its neck, a little louder now without some of the plating to muffle it. Shelly's hands shot up in triumph as she waited to hear it greet itself. The robot opened its dull-gray mouth and spoke:

"Здравствуйте. Я модель Минерва, серийный номер TTPS-8103-X79I. Я могу чем-нибудь помочь?"

"What?" Runako scratched his head. "What kinda language is that?"

"I don't know, boy." Shelly finished screwing the final plate, and then inched closer to Imtiaz. "Im, something wrong with the language options or what?"

"Maybe . . ." He went back into command prompt, typing in more code to get access to its folders. "But if it's a neural wiring problem—"

"I just looked at it, Im. Everything in order. Don't blame it on—"

"I not blaming anybody. I just saying we can't solve this now. Police all over. We have to take this home and troubleshoot it there."

"Nah. I can't wait. I need to be sure Runako not setting me up."

"Even if we make jail?" Imtiaz turned to her in panic.

Shelly pointed at his laptop screen. "Face front. If you don't want to make jail, work faster. We getting out of here, and we getting out of here with this robot."

Imtiaz rubbed his eyes anxiously before pressing the Enter key. There was a briefer, louder whir, and then the bot powered down, its folders spilling onto the screen in a small cascade. "Okay, the root is here . . ." He fished

around for the language base. "Um . . . all I see here is Russian and Japanese. I can't even find its preferred warning phrases document." He put a few more lines in the command box to update its language files. "Okay, two minutes at least that's fixed. I'll have to reboot it again first."

"All right, what about everything else? Optical recording? Ear-side microphones? The riot gear?"

Imtiaz squinted at the rest of files and folders. "They all look fine here. Due for updates, but they could run fine till we get back home. So?" He gestured sternly to the window. "Can we?"

"Make sure for me, please?"

At this point, he was sweating. He couldn't see through the window. At least seeing outside confirmed his fears. Now, worry just ran amok in his mind. He was sure he had just heard a gunshot higher up the street. He closed his eyes for a moment, took a breath, and then opened them again, scanning the file names for anything missing. Instead, he found new ones.

"When you find this?" he said.

Runako shifted, rubbing his hand over the top of his shiny bald head. "Who, me? Like, some weeks. Why?"

He turned to Shelly, eyes wide, beads of sweat falling down his cheeks. "Because it still have recordings, Shell."

She straightened up, leaning closer to see the screen. A folder headed GATHER had reams of voice notes and video, most of which were so badly corrupted that their file types were missing, surely a result of whatever damage the bot had received. All of them were titled with numbers, and they had even more text files with the same kind of file name.

Shelly pointed to one at random, a text file. "Twelve oh nine, twenty twenty-three, sixteen thirty-four forty-one, oh thirty-nine? What that mean?"

"Most likely date and time, and . . . the last three, a place? Number of files on that day? I don't know." He opened it and read aloud. "'Event log, September twelfth, 2023'—wait, nah, that was just the other day?—'deployed on raid procedure in Arima area, address 34 Lime Avenue. Related files withheld by Winged Captain Sean Alexander.' It have the number of people in the house, outstanding warrant info . . . it says, 'Winged Detective Dexter Sandy, in compliance with Winged Captain Alexander, found previously tagged evidence 46859 in previously sealed case *Trinidad and Tobago versus Kareem Jones*, which led to the arrest of—' "

"Wait!" Runako stood behind Imtiaz, his hands pressed firmly on the back of the chair. " 'Previously tagged'? You getting this, Shelly?"

"What? I don't follow." She hadn't turned to face either of them, still reading the file. Imtiaz stared at it with a mild confusion.

"That evidence! Kareem Jones was in the papers months now for weed possession. He already in jail! How would they find already-seized weed in Arima from a case in Carenage, on the west side?"

"And what is a 'winged' officer?" Shelly made scare quotes with her fingers as she said it.

"I was wondering the same thing," Imtiaz said. "What kind of designation is that? It sure doesn't sound official."

"I could damn well tell you what it is—"

"I don't want to believe it . . ." Shelly turned back to the robot, as if taking it in. It wasn't just an illegal bot—it was a flying squad bot. A metal goon for the Prime Minister. It took a moment too long for Imtiaz to put it all together, but the moment he had, the back of his neck felt warm.

"It have video for that day here?" Runako put his hands on Imtiaz's shoulders—and it made him even tenser still.

"L-lemme see." He scrolled through them to find a video with the exact same title. He double-clicked it, and it loaded in his media player, a four-minute recording starting with the camera—the bot—leaving a police vehicle.

• • •

"Ey! Open up! Police!" A gruff man's voice shouted from outside of view. The bot looked

directly at the door of an apple-white house as it slowly opened, a short brown girl looking out timidly.

"Where your parents, girl?" another, softer, male voice said, still in a raised voice. The girl shook her head in reply, stepping back into the house, but a heavyset officer ran up to the door and held it open.

They could hear someone else shouting inside. The officer at the door, the gruff one, shouted, "Ey! We reach, so don't play like you're hiding nothing!" Two other officers came to the door and they entered, the robot behind them in the tight, dim walkway.

The robot glanced everywhere and was making readings of everything. It tried to scan for the name of the girl, but couldn't find it; it calculated live on screen the percentage of threat posed by stray breadknives on the kitchen counter as they passed it, or of a cricket bat near the living-room window—low, it supposed, being sized for a primary school child, easy to deal with by a carbon-plated police bot.

It saw a man it identified as David Sellers, raising his voice at an officer, asking how they could barge into the house without a warrant.

It saw Sparkle Sellers, and brought up the recent date of their marriage beneath her name as she pulled David back, trying to calm him down.

It saw an officer pull a bag as big as his palm out of his side pocket while no one was looking. It tagged the bag "E-46859," and followed awkwardly, focusing on it as the officer dropped it behind a plastic chair in the dining room. The officer nudged his partner and whispered, audibly enough for the robot, "It there, eh?" It saw him gesture with his elbow to the chair.

"What?" David shouted. "What where? What's going on here?"

"Sir, you are under arrest for possession of marijuana with intent to distribute," the gruff man said, reaching past Mrs. Sellers and grabbing David by his shoulder.

"Weed? You for *real*, officer? I have no weed here!"

He threw David on the brownish carpet, inches from the chair where they had dropped it, turning his head to face it as they put on the cuffs. "So what is that?"

The video stuttered here, playing that one moment repeatedly—of David Sellers's frightened gaze, fixed on the clear package on his floor, looping the very moment when his eyes widened with fear, and then relaxed again in sad resignation, over and over and over . . .

• • •

For a moment, the three of them stared silently at the screen. Imtiaz's hands were on his mouth.

Suddenly, Runako and Imtiaz jumped in unison. There was a loud rapping at the outermost door.

"Shit," Runako whispered, beginning to pace in confused panic. "They catch we, fellas. That is it."

"Wait, stop freaking out, guys," Shelly said, getting up slowly.

Imtiaz still couldn't find the words. This was it. They were done. They had in front of them what was probably an illegally sourced repository of evidence of police impropriety in the house of a career criminal drug offender. They were done for.

"Okay," Shelly added. "We keeping the files, for sure."

"How we going to keep what we can't leave the house with?"

"Easy. We leave the house."

Imtiaz wanted to shout, if not for the fear of police. "How?"

"Boot up the bot. We flying out."

Runako started mumbling to himself. "We backing up everything. Four or five copies. And you going to take them. Don't get catch, eh?"

"Wait, no, stop—how this supposed to work?" Imtiaz put his hands out to Shelly. "This is nonsense. How we flying out with the robot? It can't even speak English yet!"

"It don't need to. It just need to be able to fly."

He checked the download—just complete. The flight module seemed to be fine in software, but he wasn't convinced that Shelly had it all worked out on the hardware end. He didn't like this idea at all. "Can we just think this over for—"

Outside, they heard someone tapping on the door. "Excuse me, this is the police—"

The three of them froze, their voices down to whispers. Imtiaz pointed at Shelly. "Okay, but let it be known I think this is craziness."

"Foolish is fine once it works—" She gripped the robot's left arm firmly, then leaned over to the keyboard to begin another reboot sequence. "You better had grab hold of something. Runako, you coming with us?"

"Nah. Somebody have to take the licks," he whispered. He was standing at the door now, facing it at attention. "Just get out quick."

Shelly nodded, then looked sternly at Imtiaz, who shot her a confused look. The moment the robot's boot sound sprung to life, he suddenly grabbed hold of its free arm.

"Hello," it said. "I am model Minerva, serial number TTPS-8103-X79I. How may I help you?"

"By getting airborne," Shelly whispered. "Uh . . . Hostiles en route, or whatever."

"Understood." Suddenly, its wings spread open with a tinny, rusty clang. Its edges hit both walls without even opening fully, and then it just as suddenly retracted them. "Wingspan obstacle issue." It turned to Shelly. "Primary launch will include thrusters only. Will that be a problem?"

"Nah, you do what you have to do, man." The moment Shelly said this was when Imtiaz realized he was about to do something well and truly foolish.

The knocking at the door became more insistent, and the officer's voice harsher. "You better open up right now before I have to kick this blasted—"

The bot's thrusters thrummed to life, warm air gushing from it. It turned to Imtiaz. "Please hold on to my arms with both hands. Flight may often be turbulent and dangerous."

"No shit—" Shelly nearly exclaimed it, but another persistent knock at the door brought her back to whispers. "We should go now, you know."

"Understood," the bot replied.

A louder, harder purr of wind and heat flooded out of the thrusters, and the bot sprang up with its two parcels on each side, through the galvanized sheet roof with enough force to push it clean off. They didn't have enough time to ready themselves; Imtiaz would have slid all the way off its arm if it hadn't swiveled its palm to grab his belt buckle. Shelly responded by wrapping her limbs around its arm for more support.

The robot spread its wings, and the thrusters let out an even harder gust. "Clearing distance. What is our destination?"

"Take me to San Juan," Shelly shouted into its microphoned ear.

"Understood." It flapped its chrome-feathered wings once, and then sped east with a force Imtiaz swore would tear his flesh from the rest of him.

Imtiaz looked down to see three police officers rush through the door, one of them already pinning Runako to the wall. Another reached for his pistol and let out one shot, narrowly missing the robot's forehead and, by extension, Imtiaz.

• • •

Shelly would later spring Runako from prison with the spoils of her newfound publicity. Runako's charge, again, was drug pushing, until the real news broke. Shelly sent a compact disc to every major television station as soon as she had watched all of the video herself—hours of "winged" officers kicking in doors, windows, and the occasional civilian's face; dozens of false arrests and misappropriations, with all the officers' faces on screen. Imtiaz refused to look at them. They both spent their quiet moments trembling at the thought of what must have been on the videos that were lost to hard-drive damage and time. The Prime Minister resigned two nights after, owning up to the whole flying squad program. The new hot topic on the web, though, was that till the snap election was done, the citizens would be under a state of emergency anyway.

As for the bot, Shelly put it to work helping her mother around the house on her behalf. She had tinkered with it so intensively that it had taken to cooking their dinner and tending to their herb garden with near-mathematical accuracy. On weekends, she strapped a bespoke harness around its wings and learned to fly with it for fun, a hobby which frightened her mother every single time.

"What's next for the girl who blew the whistle on the Flying Squad fiasco?" the press would ask her every other day in the papers.

"Graduate from UWI?" she'd reply, shrugging, looking away from the cameras like she was already bored with it all.

Imtiaz managed to keep his face out of the papers, for his own sake. Even his husband had yet to hear of the drama of that night. He'd have the occasional paranoid episode coming from work, though, looking in his rearview mirror for flashing blue lights as he hurried down the highway. Whenever he found himself panicking, he raised the volume on his industrial-rock driving music just a little higher.

Imtiaz grew to enjoy the safety of his house. He held on to Tevin a little tighter every day. He'd even find himself grinning like a fool at the simplest, most mundane questions, simply because he was still around to answer them.

"Didn't have any problems getting back?" Tevin would ask.

"Nah," Imtiaz would reply. "Traffic was light today. You know how it is."

GANZEER

CRISPR THAN YOU

(2018)

PART I: CHANGING DELIGHTLY

Snip.

There goes my impending heart disease.

          Snip, snip.

       Goodbye, acne

                        and   dry frizzy hair.

       Stitch.
          Hello,
          hint of   eumelanin.

       Hello, Jared Leto eyes.

       Stitch, stitch.
          Hello,
          glorious member,
                    envy   of all men.

When I was little, there were a lot of things I didn't quite understand about aging.

Why are there so many ads on television for pimple cream? I'd ask my brother.

Why don't you have any hair in the middle part of your head? I'd ask my father.

Why don't you race me up the stairs anymore? I'd ask my mother.

Age, they'd respond.

Getting old, they'd say.

Life, they'd mutter.

It wasn't a satisfying answer for me, because before "age" became the reason behind all their ailments, it seemed to be the very source of their powers.

"But you're not old enough to ride the roller coaster, baby."

"Sorry, hon, this movie's for grown-ups."

"Dominic, no! That drink's not for you!"

Worst of all was when my grandma would visit. Sweet old lady, but she was old and obese.

Listen, I ain't gonna mince words; she was fat. So fat and so old that she couldn't walk up the stairs to our apartment. It was a small building with no elevator, but we only lived on the second floor. No big deal, but too much for the old hag to handle. Poor old lady would have to get down on all fours and literally crawl up the stairs, and even then she struggled. And every time without fail, my mother would look down at her from the apartment doorway with tears in her eyes. Her face overtaken by silent sorrow and evident disgust. She'd ask if she could lend a hand, but grandma was a proud and stubborn old woman who accepted help from no one. It might've been that in her mind being helped up the stairs would be indicative of aging, yet crawling up the stairs was not somehow, just because she managed to do it on her own.

I never liked being around grandma. Absolutely adorable woman, but she made me afraid of the future. Afraid of living a bedridden life with too few teeth. Of not being able to visit my future daughter without first humiliating myself on her stairwell.

She probably sensed it, because whenever she visited she would slip me some crisp new pocket money. She would do this every time, hoping I'd warm up to her a little with each tiny bribe. Little did she realize that I had no clue what good money was for.

Back then anyway.

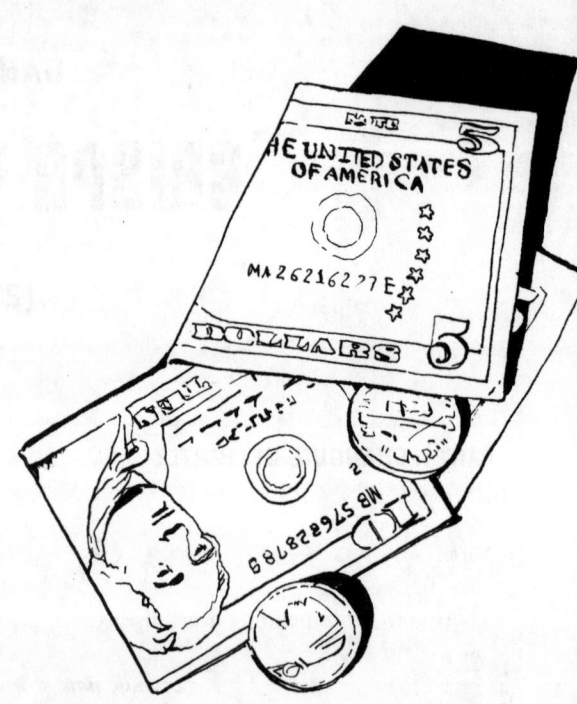

Dahlia Delightly was the prettiest girl in school. Everyone knew it, except Dahlia herself. She was sweet and easy to talk to, but she hardly ever talked about herself. The one thing I *did* know about her was that she wanted to be a movie star when she grew up. I remember being particularly fascinated by that because at the time I had no idea what I wanted to be when I grew up. The idea of Dahlia in the movies made sense. She had a certain presence about her, and she wore the nicest clothes and the coolest specs.

Until one day she showed up without them.

It took me off guard. I knew people wore glasses because they couldn't see without them, so how on Earth was she coming to school without her glasses all of a sudden? Wasn't that dangerous? I wondered.

I asked her about it and she told me her parents had her undergo "laser surgery," an operation that fixed her eyes up, and made it possible for her to see without her iconic specs. She didn't seem awfully thrilled about it. I mean, she definitely wasn't upset about it, but she did mention that it felt weird. That she couldn't recognize herself in the mirror anymore. I always thought she was just as beautiful even with her glasses on, but I couldn't help but be fascinated by the idea of this magical laser beam that, when aimed at her eyes, transformed them into the best version they could possibly be. And I found myself daydreaming of a wicked ray gun that could, at the pull of a trigger, fix anything for anyone.

Oh hey, you've got the sniffles? *ZAP!* All healthy now.

Tripped and smashed your face? *ZAP!* Unharmed.

Stung by a bee? *ZAP!* You're saved.

Fat grandma can't walk up stairs? *ZAP!* Now she's Wonder Woman.

Obsession has a way of creeping up on you in unpredictable ways. You never know what singular observation will recalibrate your worldview for the rest of your life. For me it was Dahlia Delightly; a girl in glasses who, overnight, no longer needed them. You might say that the minute Dahlia started seeing better, I started seeing better too.

I brought up Dahlia's laser surgery to my old man, who also wore glasses, telling him with exaggerated enthusiasm that he ought to get his eyes lasered too.

"Too expensive," he said, "and a real man should never have to worry too much about his appearances."

And I'm quoting verbatim because I remember it like it was yesterday. His voice stern and distant, spoken without thought. A natural reflex. "Natural." Oh how I grew to hate that word. Really nothing but an excuse to be okay with flaws. But I took my old man's words to heart, and finally understood what good grandma's money was for. If a single laser beam for eye surgery was too much for my dad to afford, then a ray gun for every human ailment possible would have to be grossly expensive.

It was then that I decided I was going to become a rich man. A very, very rich man.

Clearly, the part about real men not needing to look good wasn't something I agreed with. I could see how Dahlia looked at the other boys. At Randy. Especially when he smiled his perfect smile with his perfect teeth.

I figured it was just my dad's excuse for not having to bother too much. When things seem out of our hands, we tend to come up with reasons as to why it's okay. No one wants to come face to face with their own helplessness. Which

is exactly why I vowed never to be helpless about anything no matter what. And if I ever found myself in that position, I would do everything in my power to change where I stood.

If you stop to think about it, getting rich isn't too hard. There are maybe three ways to go about it:

1. You buy something for cheap and sell it for more than it cost you. That's just the basics of commerce. Want to get rich off this scheme? Make sure whatever you buy is something that pretty much everyone needs. And buy a lot of it.

2. Buy something that isn't worth much now, but will likely be worth a lot in the future. You speculate essentially, but for accurate speculation you must ignore everything anyone says about speculation because all that *is* hyperbole from special interest groups. A way to create the illusion that something might be worth a lot in the future, even if there is little to no factual information to support their claims. Something will only be crazy valuable in the future if it has the potential of being highly sought after while maintaining a very rare status. Perhaps a book that only saw a very low print run yet also managed to get a lot of people to talk about it. Something that became culturally influential in some way. Or if it was authored by someone who would later become acknowledged as a historical figure. Almost anything belonging to historical figures is bound to be valuable. The only way to maneuver the potentiality of rare objects belonging to historical figures is, really, to be friendly with most people you meet. And if they are makers of things, become a hoarder of said things. Let's be real, there's no truly efficient way to do this and guarantee a profit.

3. Invent something awesome that everyone will want.

The ray gun.

Everyone would want the ray gun. Everyone would want to be perfect. Void of illness. Live forever.

I had a goal then.

I started to pay extra attention in science class and knew exactly what I wanted to be when I grew up. But I knew not to put all my eggs in one basket. I started using grandma's money to buy things. Things I could sell to the other kids. Cool pens and notebooks from the stationery store. Snacks that the school canteen never carried. And when I got old enough, cigarettes and condoms. And before long, drugs and porn.

But I think it was around then that I first started hearing about gene-editing technology. What the media referred to as "CRISPR."

I'm not sure when Dahlia became distant but it might've been around the same time. No worries, I told myself, she won't be so distant when I'm rich, famous, and immortal. I just had to keep at it. Not lose focus.

When I made it to college, I decided to take a typography class. That was my segue into the art crowd. I bought at least one piece from every art punk I met, because you can never really tell who the hell is going to be famous. For real! I mean, do you think anyone suspected Andy Warhol would amount to anything when he was taking free art classes at the Carnegie Institute? Or that Haring would ever matter when he was at SVA? Or even Dalí when he was still at Madrid's Real Academia de Bellas Artes?

Get them while they're cheap, I figured. Wouldn't hurt. And you better believe it was a good enough strategy, because one of the pieces I scored . . . was a Kalak.

PART II: SEBASTIAN KALAK

Before becoming Sebastian Kalak he was Seva Kalanenko. A girl.

When she was little, she insisted on wearing her older brother's track pants and T-shirts, much to her mother's dismay. Her dad wasn't around a whole lot, but when he was, Seva's mother would scold him for not playing a more active role in the girl's life.

"I never had any sisters, and I wouldn't know the first thing about telling a girl how to behave," Seva overheard her dad tell her mom once. "The girl is your responsibility, Adele."

It's not that Seva knew she wanted to be a boy, not back then. In fact, she hated it when anyone called her a boy. Especially the other boys, who she would find no trouble beating up if and when they did. Teachers, however, and other grownups were somewhat of a problem. They didn't think she was a boy, nor did they actively refer to her as one, but they'd question her choice of clothes, and ask her if she wanted to be a boy. This frustrated her, because she didn't think that boys or girls ought to be designated by clothes or hairstyle. That was silly. If track pants were comfortable for boys, why on Earth would they not be comfortable for girls too? Why couldn't a girl's favorite color be blue or, heck, black even? Which was in fact Seva's favorite color, something that freaked the hell out of grownups for some reason.

"Not only is she a tomboy, but she's also a goth," one teacher told Seva's mother once. "You might want to nip this one in the bud before she starts giving you real trouble later on. Hanging out with little boys might not be much of an issue now, but eventually . . . well, those boys won't stay little forever."

Certain ideas, once planted in your head, are almost impossible to shake away. Especially—most especially—if they're ideas about your kids.

Adele, Seva's mom, became increasingly worried. She was having nightmares that involved a teenage Seva shooting up with boys in heroin dens before pegging them with a big black strap-on in front of live industrial neo-fasch bands.

This, when Seva was only six.

No mother should have to dream that kind of shit about their six-year-old daughter. And so Adele decided she would set her daughter straight. She would spare no expense. Her daughter's future depended on it, dammit! It was time to get rid of the guest room. Have Seva move out of her brother's room and into a room of her own. But the room needed some renovation.

First came the bubblegum pink for the walls, then came the Marie Antoinette bed. Seva discovered that taking a sharpie to the bed's frame actually made it look badass. Although it did take a great deal of sharpies for it to get there. Drawing with black crayons on the pink walls made the room feel more her own, the drawings being childish imitations of the art from her older brother's horror comics. So cool were the drawings that even her brother preferred to hang out in her room more than his own.

Adele, however, was steadfast. She filled her daughter's wardrobe with skirts and dresses, Disney princess shirts, and the most delicate of shoes; bow ties and glitter galore.

Seva tried real hard not to be a punk-ass rebel, but it was only a week before she found herself taking a pair of scissors to those bow ties and wearing her Disney shirts inside out. And there was nothing awfully girly that a basic sharpie couldn't remedy.

Adele was hysterical. She slapped her daughter's soft, tiny face hard, real hard. Seva was stunned. She'd only ever seen love and compassion from her mother, but here she was plowing her daughter with deep hateful rage. Tears flowed down Seva's face, not because of the pain, but because of the fear.

"You little—"

Slap!

"—ungrateful—"

Slap!

"—bitch!"

Slap!

"Do you have any idea how hard I had to work to be able to afford this stuff?"

Slap!

"Do you?"

Slap!

Seva said sorry. She said sorry over and over

and over, but she honestly didn't get it. She just wanted to be herself, she told her mother. But she promised she would never do that ever again.

That's when Adele realized the horror of what she was doing. Beating her daughter . . . for wanting to wear pants? And why? Because other people thought it was weird? Fuck them!

Adele hugged her daughter and covered her in kisses, saying she was sorry, so so sorry. That of course she should be herself and never anything else. And from then on, Adele vowed to champion her daughter and whatever she wanted to be no matter what.

It wasn't until college that Seva really came into her own though. College, a chance for new beginnings, where no one yet knows you and has no preconceptions about you. Seva adopted a more dapper look: well-fitted trousers, fine Italian shoes, clean shirts, and complementary vests. A far cry from her track-pants days, and a very far cry from her mother's goth-infested nightmares.

When people asked her about her name, she'd say "Seva, but my friends call me Sebastian." Which was a way of asking people to call her Sebastian if they wanted to be friends with her, which most people felt rather intimidated to attempt. Most people except Dominic.

What Dominic loved most about Seva was her fearlessness. Her complete dedication to becoming the person she felt she was meant to be. Oh, if only more people were like her, Dominic told himself, so much human potential would be unleashed. His fascination with Seva wasn't at all lost on her. She could read his dark eyes like a children's book. This was even before she underwent hormone therapy. Before she officially took on the name Sebastian Kalak. Before she became a he. Before they made love.

PART III: HAIL, AMERICA!

Most people say they didn't see it coming. Some blame it entirely on Yellowstone. They're all full of shit.

Between 1909 and 1933 the Weimar Republic is known to have granted transvestite passes to trans people to protect them from public and police harassment. A way of saying: hey, the state recognizes that I like to dress this way and is very much okay with it. Simultaneously, Berlin was considered to be the homosexual capital of Europe. That is not to say that this was the reason behind the eventual rise of Nazism, but it is not to be overlooked. Because it was one of the many things the Nazis pointed to as a sign of German decay. That's the thing about progress; while a breath of fresh air for some, it can also be seen as a departure from basic foundational values by everyone else. The other thing about progress is that it's often hard to be seen as true progress when overshadowed by the shame of national catastrophe.

Military defeat.

Three million dead.

One hundred thirty-two billion gold marks in reparations.

Terrible, terrible disgrace following Germany's defeat in World War I. And pride was never a concept foreign to the German.

Nor has it ever been foreign to the American, albeit for reasons far less founded.

The problem with Americans is that we'd been feeding on our own propaganda for far too long. The idea of American exceptionalism was something far too few Americans ever questioned. Even those who claimed ideological opposition to early "Alt-Right" groups still believed in the myth of "the greatest nation on Earth." And practically every single stamp issued by the United States Postal Service had "USA FOREVER" printed on it, which c'mon, isn't really a huge leap from "HAIL, AMERICA!" No society can ever prosper without a constant reevaluation of the myths it perpetuates. Something Sebastian learned from his readings of the great James Baldwin, which he often read out loud to Dominic in bed.

A society must assume that it is stable, but the artist must know, and must let us know, that there is nothing stable under the heavens.

—James Baldwin

If anyone practiced what they preached, it was definitely Sebastian. Even when still in college, he had a knack for creating art that was the most scathing of social commentary. His gaze going past the elephant in the room, and instead fixated on the little elephants lurking in the shadows. The elephants that would eventually grow to become the big elephants in the room. The elephants that everyone knew were there but avoided speaking of.

Controversial? Sure, but not for the heck of it. Sebastian was a much-needed societal warning station. But one that, inevitably, came at a cost.

> The most dangerous of all moods is that of a great power which sees itself declining to second rank.
>
> —Michael Howard

The fear of declining to second rank was already in America's air for far too long. Which is actually rather mind-blowing because it was happening together with this bolstering of exceptionalism. Two notions that you would think were completely at odds with one another.

In any case, a quick look at actual data would've completely nullified American fears. When the American GDP was at 20 trillion dollars, China was only at $13 trillion. When Americans were spending $554 billion on military expenditures, China was spending $215. China had only one aircraft carrier compared to America's twenty. And China's 260 nuclear warheads were a far, far cry from America's seven thousand!

What was everyone panicking about?

That fear, perpetuated by both Republicans and Democrats for so long, is precisely what led to their downfall, and the inevitable rise of the Upward Party and the subsequent establishment of what became colloquially known as the "American Reich," or what some liked to refer to as the "American Renaissance."

Not to create a mono-causal argument for the Reich's foundation or anything. The first Dominic ever heard about the rise of proto-Reich movements was at around age fifteen. Protests dominated by white males, publicly defended by so-called intellectuals who attacked social justice defenders using pseudo-scientific arguments. "SJWs," they called them, short for Social Justice Warriors. It takes someone particularly evil to be able to vilify those who fight for justice and put a label on them.

SJW. A tactic borrowed directly from corporate America. SJW. No longer implying social or justice, just as KFC removed connotations of "fried" or "Kentucky." Or heck, "chicken" for that matter.

SJWs weren't their only targets obviously. There were also the "sick trannies," "Jewish commies," "criminal n——s," and "jihadist Muslims." And that's just the tip of the iceberg. Even if the so-called intellectuals among them refrained from using that specific language.

It was certainly absent from their manifesto.

PART IV: THE MANIFESTO

FAST FORWARD UPWARD: A MANIFESTO

Man is the creator of God, and thus it is appropriate to declare man the one true God in this here Universe. Let us then embrace our godly status and hurl ourselves toward the stars of eternity that call out to us in the night. We must pierce forward like the red-hot swords of the life-giving Sun and decapitate the tyranny of ignorant darkness upon sight.

We may be dreamers, but dreamers of night we are not. We are dreamers of day, willing our dreams visibly into reality for all to soak up and bathe in. Not just here on Earth, but across the cosmos. Other bodies reflect our glow and come into being solely because we exist, and our existence burns bright.

The fuel to our fire is the habit of energy, courage, audacity, and revolt! Our revolt is against the totality of nature, the revolt of survival, of evolution against all odds. It is the beautiful revolt of perpetual struggle, because there is no glory in idle surrender.

Let us discard the dystopic perspectives of the Anthropocene and instead embrace it as an inevitable stepping stone in our righteous evolution. No longer shall we sheepishly look over our shoulders at carbon footprints. Let us instead look forward toward the trajectories of future footprints, their impressions deeper and more pronounced with every step we take.

Humanity's poetry is in the violent assault on our surrounding environment, forcing the universe to bow before us.

More awaits us. We must be faster, stronger, higher!

It is time to transcend and break down the gates of life. It is time to bolt death deep beneath our feet. We must cast aside the false wisdom of decay, and instead embrace the fervor of youth as the one true ideal of forever.

Beauty is not an offense against inequality, but as legitimate a pursuit as happiness. It must be upheld and protected by the culture at large, never to be slandered.

Our sensibilities must be saved from the rot of old funeral urns. Our reservoirs must be fed by the man-made machines of prosperous intellect.

Ignore the wisdom of yesteryear, for we are the gods of tomorrow. Walk not among the soulless golems animated by the dark seething power of establishment media. They are bound to be crushed by the wheels of progress, but only after spending a lifetime getting tossed between a thousand meaningless distractions.

We must insist on our dreams and push for the conquest of space and time. That is what we do: We explore, we build, we conquer. We must continue to develop the revolutionary technology worthy of a species racing toward an upward path. Let the naysayers and apocalypse-screamers abstain and get left behind in the bush where they belong.

Education must be reformed. We can no longer allow universities to take our money just to tell us how despicable our accomplishments are. Let us honor the enlightening legacy of our culture and push forth for more. Because our best days are ahead of us. If nostalgia must be part of our consciousness then let it be a nostalgia for the future.

Let us strip honor from unworthy politicians and celebrities, and instead honor those who catalyze humanity's advancements. It is no longer enough to resolve age-old socioeconomic political problems. The time has come to do away with them altogether. The spectrum of Right-Wing/Left-Wing thought is too narrow for the human of the future. It is time we stopped looking left or right and instead started looking up and beyond.

No new heights we reach will be satisfactory. No new height will be idealized. The greatest ideal must always remain the forthcoming heights of the future!

It is in America that we are issuing this manifesto of eternal tomorrow, because only America can hurl the world upward and forth into the future. America is uniquely situated at the center of modern history. It is America that first showed the world the meaning of freedom. It is America that first put a man on the moon. It is America that connected the world into a singular telesphere. It is America's armies that keep the world safe. It is thus America's duty to stop limping in rusty shackles. It is thus America's responsibility to cast aside all that is un-American. It is thus America's birthright to grab the world by its reins and charge forth into the hailstorm of big dreams and mad ideas.

Fast forward upward!

America must lead the way, because that is what America does.

PART V: NOSTALGIA FOR THE FUTURE

Sebastian loved that manifesto. And so did Dominic, but it was Sebastian who really flew with it. It wasn't yet known who authored it, and Sebastian didn't really care. When the pamphlet first landed in his lap, he almost immediately incorporated it into his art. He must have risographed thousands of copies in red, white, and blue, and even purple, which he would draw directly on top of. His drawings mainly comprised pop-cultural mashups and real world failings. Drawings of decrepit bus stops, congested freeways, and the crappy pretzels served on airplanes juxtaposed against the manifesto were made to highlight that we were far from living in the America we deserved. It's hard to tell whether the manifesto elevated Sebastian's art or vice versa, but in any case the pieces—strategically placed in public space—were getting nationwide attention, and Sebastian's star grew high and bright.

Until they killed him.

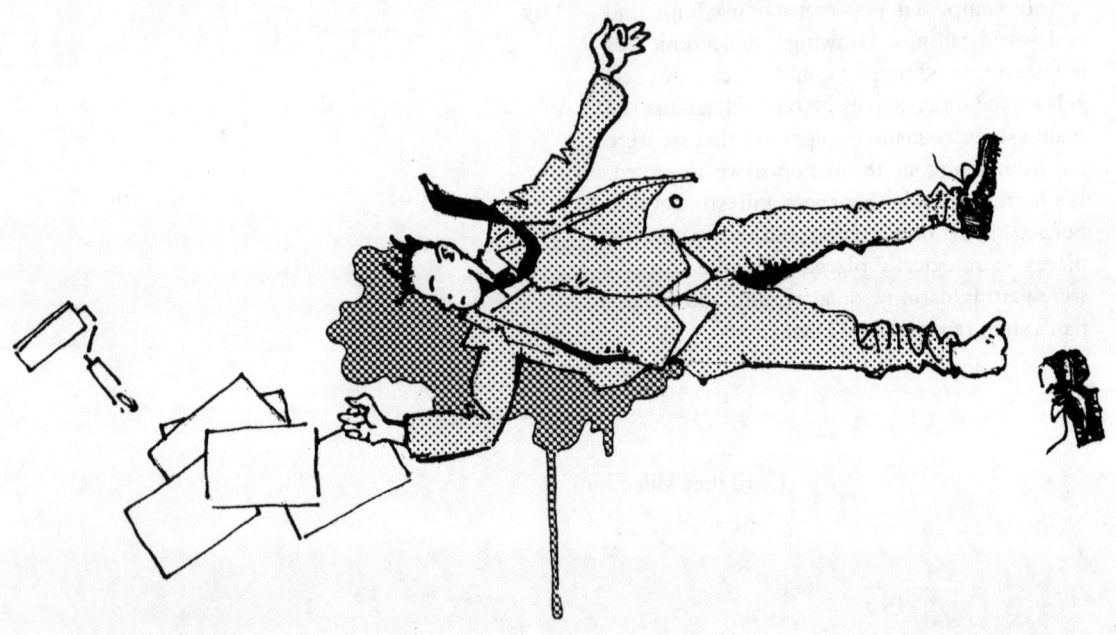

The killers were not, as one might've suspected, a group of trans-hating white men, but in fact the militant antifa group known as FemFatale-2030 who—not at all knowing that Sebastian was once a she—saw his guerrilla actions as a sinister plot to popularize toxic masculinity. This was naturally something proto-Reich groups took advantage of, which not only galvanized their cause but also made whatever remained of Sebastian's work highly sought-after.

Which did Dominic very well.

Sebastian's death was crushing to him, but rather than hold on to Sebastian's art for personal sentimentalities, he felt he had to do good by Sebastian's legacy and serve the greater good in a way.

He was making headway with his research and had devised, not a ray gun, but a kind of gene-editing phone booth. He called it the CRISPod, and saw it as a formidable step toward the democratization of gene-editing technology. Of making it well within the reach of every American.

All he had to do was build a proper prototype. And now he had the means to do just that.

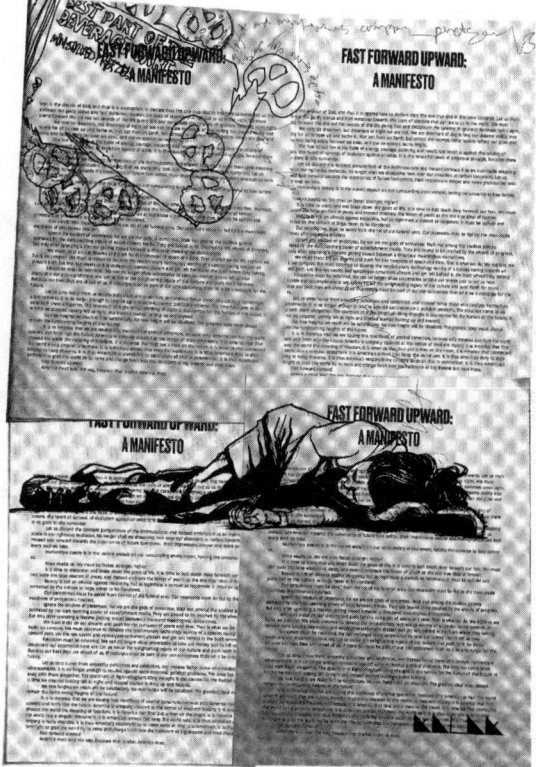

Current bid: $69,000,000   [73 bids]

Even with staunch resistance and defamation campaigns from big pharma, Dominic's CRISPod was getting worldwide attention. He was a sly marketeer, and had a way of capturing the public imagination. He wore big glassless specs in his televised appearances, which sure, painted him as an eccentric, but also cunningly made a point: That glasses, as a sight-enabling apparatus for the contemporary man, were ridiculous. And if they were ridiculous, then perhaps they weren't the only ridiculous thing about the way we all lived.

There was one video Dominic put together with his artist friends that went especially viral. It took on the air of a vintage advertisement, showing Clark Kent rush into a CRISPod before emerging as Superman. Except, immediately after his exit, someone else rushes into the pod who also reemerges as Superman. The camera slowly zooms out revealing people queuing up in front of more CRISPods, supermen emerging out of them one after the other. We finally get a big panoramic view of the city, which is not something of the past, but a great sleek metropolis of the future, with a pattern of endless supermen in the skies around it.

And then the logo fades in against the cityscape:

CRISPod
Become a better human.

And this was all before Yellowstone erupted.

PART VI: YELLOWSTONE

It was January, and the volcanic ash that descended like a heavy blanket on the country spread from coast to coast. The most devastating effects stretched from Seattle in the west to Kansas City in the east. From Calgary up north all the way to Albuquerque down south. The shower of splintered rock and glass lasted months, shutting down most roads, railways, and air travel.

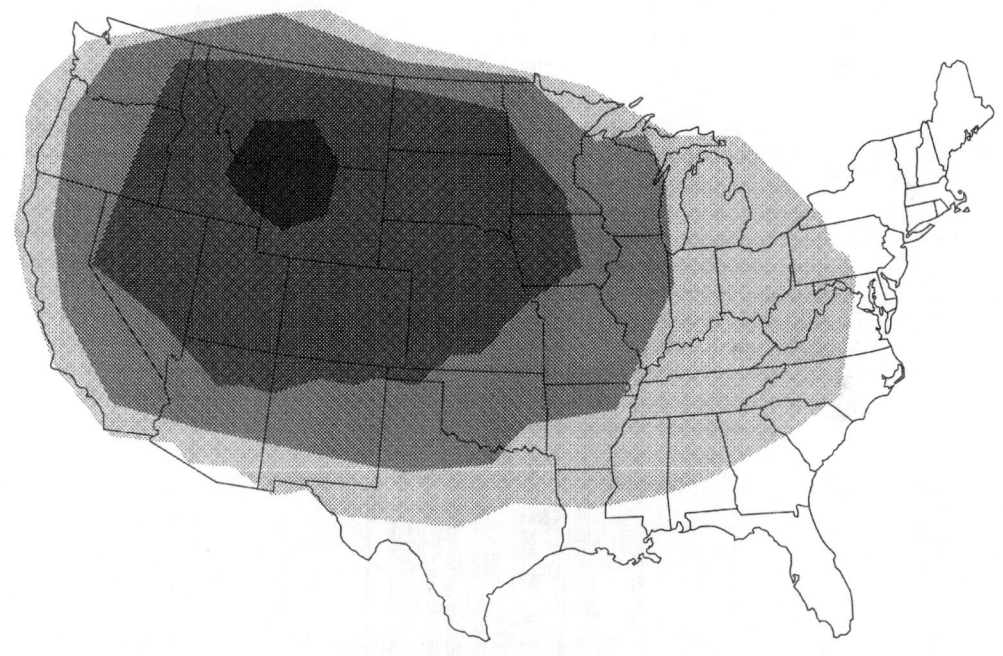

Ninety-seven million dead.
One hundred ninety-five million terminally ill.
Seventy-five percent of livestock killed.
One hundred sixteen million hectares of arable land devastated.
Shame, havoc, ruin.

The perfect storm had arrived for the Upward Party to take command. Their manifesto spoke to a nation keen on rising from the ashes. No one wanted to vote for the age-old proven incompetence of Democrat or Republican. The time had come for the Great New Party, as some people referred to it. America was ready to board the techno-theological spaceship of the future, and the Upward Men were there to steer it. Their speeches breathtaking, their rallies inspiring, and their plan concrete.

And at the center of their plan was Dominic's CRISPod.

Circumstances called for new measures and everyone knew it. Old drugs and pharmaceuticals were cast aside as archaic poisons, and the CRISPod quickly became the infrastructural cornerstone of a New America. Embraced by all out of a nostalgic longing for the future.

Dominic soon rose to become a key player in the America of tomorrow, and just as he envisioned as a young child, he found himself becoming exceedingly rich.

He was happy. Content, until he discovered that the CRISPods weren't working for everyone. That some people were being killed by the CRISPods.

And the killing . . . was deliberate.

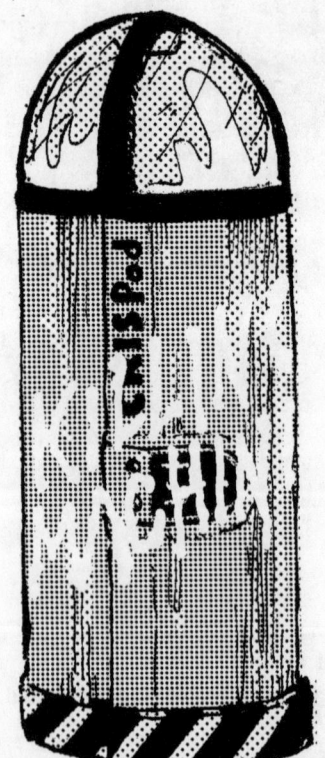

PART VII: SEEING DELIGHTLY

She probably won't remember me.

Heck, she probably won't recognize me, not with my new eyes and nicer hair. But I have to see her. The images of her on her deathbed all over the news are haunting me, and I cannot for the life of me think of anything else.

Her caretaker opens the door and shows me in. The place is sad. Curtains mostly drawn, keeping the light away from the old grandeur of a previous lifestyle. Up along the staircase there is photo after photo of Dahlia's Hollywood days. The days before Yellowstone. Red carpet glamour, life-loving sheen, and beautiful perfection. I'm reminded of a quote Sebastian read out loud to me once.

I love Los Angeles. I love Hollywood. They're beautiful. Everybody's plastic, but I love plastic. I want to be plastic.

—Andy Warhol

Now the nerdy scientist gets to be plastic, preserved for all eternity while the Hollywood beauty of old withers away.

There she is on the bed. Dahlia Delightly, little more than a crumpled-up napkin. She sees me and reaches for her glasses on the night-stand. It takes a few seconds of her staring at me before she speaks in croaky squeaks.

"Dominic Cunningham. Look . . . at you."

Didn't think you'd recognize me, I tell her.

"Oh, I've been keeping up with your news. And everything you've been doing for the country."

Not everyone . . . in the country. I regret saying it just as the words come out.

"Oh, Dominic. You cannot possibly blame yourself, dear. Not all of us have the genes that can handle eternal youth. Be proud of your accomplishments. You've saved more lives than any one person ever has."

Could've saved many more. Including you, Dahlia, if it weren't for those Upward fucks! The words don't exit my mouth this time. They remain silent thoughts trapped by bars of shame deep in my mind.

I sit on the edge of the bed and hold her hand.

I see you've got your old glasses back, I tell her.

"Ha! Yes, at least I have that," she laughed. "You should've come sooner, Dominic. A lot sooner. I would've liked to show you the pool in the back and make you one of my signature cocktails."

I was a nobody, I tell her. You were a big shining movie star when all I had going for me was a crummy makeshift lab.

"Silly boy," she says touching my face with elderly tenderness. "I've met a lot of not-nobodies in my day, and absolutely no one could fill the special place I have in my heart for you."

Her toothless smile is sweet and her eyes sincere. I lean in for the kiss, but I'm too late. Her heart is stopped and her breathing no more.

Dahlia Delightly is dead.

I watch her. The once Hollywood face of long-lasting youth reduced to a piece of broken China.

Back at the penthouse, I do not recognize the man looking back at me in the mirror. The man who claims he didn't know any better, that had no idea.

Fuck you, you're full of shit! Don't look at me like that you lousy self-serving prick.

Smash!

B   r   o   k   e   n   g   l   a   s   s

Smash!

Glass e v e r y w h e r e.

Sharp shard.   Jared Leto eyes.   Raging

                                     Raging stabs and jagged pain.

                    Blood.   Raging   pain.

                                   Raging   pain.

Warm blood.

Lots of warm blood.

Cold floor.

Blackout.

I wake up to the sound of the automatic vacuum cleaner and robotic breakfast maker. The smell of morning coffee brings me to my feet, vision fuzzy like a newborn baby.

I make it to the bathroom and splash cold water on my face, flakes of dry crusted blood swirl down the drain. I look up and crisp newly grown Jared Leto eyes stare back me.

I think . . . I think they're starting to grow on me.

FABIO FERNANDES

WI-FI DREAMS

(2019)

WHEN THE BLACK DUCK comes to me with the bowie knife and the killing smile in his giant face, the first thing I think is, how the fuck is he holding the knife?

The second, of course, is, how the fuck am I going out of here?

The maze of hallways in the derelict building is dark and narrow—the few working light bulbs in the ceiling flicker; most of them are out. A few doors are open; through them I can see the night, hear distant screams and shouts, but nobody comes to my rescue.

Why should anyone? Nobody wants to die.

I stumble, almost fall but regain my balance at once. I can't stop. Because the duck is getting closer.

The third thing I ask myself is, how can this fucking duck be following me?

Because he is huge. And by huge I mean humongous, enormous, gigantic. Really. It is at least three stories high.

And suddenly he is blocking my way.

Blacker than the blackness of the corridor. A duck-shaped black hole with crazed eyes, a big grinning beak with a lolling pinkish tongue—and an impressive double row of very sharp teeth.

I reach for my silver dagger—but I can't pull it from its sheath.

The duck opens his beak even more. Now he's a Daffy Duck on speed—no, scratch that, Daffy Duck always lived on speed, how they let children watch that schizo-dope-fiend running around aimlessly? (except for *Duck Dodgers*; I loved *Duck Dodgers*)—and he's having the time of his larger-than-life life watching me squirm before he does whatever he wants to do with me.

I don't stay for question four. The fucking duck is not a sphinx, for crying out loud. It won't spare me if I answer correctly a question. It's certainly not asking any.

I lunge to the left. Without checking first I somehow already know there is a room with a door opened there and go for it without looking, and all of a sudden I'm already there.

It's a room with a view all right. A tiny room with a big window. Did I mention that I am on the fifth floor?

The duck is already right behind my back. Knife ready.

The only chance I have to escape is to take the plunge from the fifth floor directly to the ground. And it has to be headfirst. For the key to escape from a killer dream is to kill myself.

For now.

You just wait for me, you crazy negative-zone bizarro-world Donald Duck motherfucker. In the immortal words of Arnold Schwarzenegger, I'll be back.

But, seriously? If I could have my say, I'd rather not come back. I'll probably have no choice in the matter. That's what happens with recurrent dreams. Especially when you can't wake up anymore.

Then I jump.

• • •

I wake up sweating. As I always do these days.

I breathe deeply for what seems like a few minutes—but I'm stark naked and I have no watch or clock in the room, so that's only a guess—until I muster enough courage to get off the bed. I put on a pair of boxers that are on the tiled floor near the nightstand and look for socks. The tiles are freezing my feet.

I take a while to find them. Not only because they are scattered all over the room, but also because the perspective is a bit askew and my eyes can't seem to focus completely when I'm not looking right in front of something. That's more or less common currency for a myopic person, but I had Lasix surgery five years ago. Does it have an expiration date? I wonder as I finally put on the damn socks. I need to see the eye doctor again.

Then I go to the window and push the curtains aside. And I am gently reminded that the eye doctor is going to have to wait.

The swollen red sun is still there, towering over the broken cityscape.

I'm back to False Wake-Up Zero. F-o for short.

I breathe deeply. This still is a safe zone for now. I dress quickly and run after the others.

The last time I did the run, Tanya was my nearest neighbor. I exited the dilapidated building where I was staying, crossed the deserted plaza in front of it, then turned left at the crossroads right after.

While I run across the perimeter, I recite a personal litany of sorts:

"*Matrix—eXistenZ—Thirteenth Floor—Simulacron Three—Nirvana—'The Tunnel Under the World'—The Truman Show—Dark City—Inception—Vanilla Sky—Surrogates—Source Code—*"

And so on. Every fucking film, novel, and story I know about people trapped in fake worlds. This is not a meditation—although my grandfather might disagree—but a checklist. Of stats. Of what the fuck is happening and possible exit strategies.

But it never seems to help. When I'm still figuring this and that story, wondering if the remake of *Total Recall* should enter (because, honestly, it sucks major ass, the story makes no sense at all), then I find myself in front of Tanya's place.

Squat is a better label for it, actually, but who's worrying? I jog into the dilapidated building, with its large iron doors half-molten as if hit by a flamethrower or something like it, and knock on her door right there on the first floor.

She takes a while to open it—she's been doing it slower and slower with each awakening. When she finally does it, she's not half as bad as I thought she'd be—just light dark rings under her eyes.

"Hi," I say.

"Hi," she says, managing a weak smile.

"Did you just wake up?"

"Yep."

"Lucky me."

She shrugged and let me in.

"Lucky us. Did you get the garganey too?"

"The what?"

"The small migratory duck. Only it was a giant one."

"Holding a bowie knife?"

"The same."

"How did you escape?" I ask, more to make conversation than out of curiosity. It's our kind of breakfast, since nobody eats at F-o.

She sits on her bed, snickering.

"Who told you I escaped?"

I shiver. That bowie knife was huge.

"These dreams are getting weirder and weirder," it's all I manage to say.

"All these fucking demons," a voice behind us says. I turn, startled, even though I already know who it is.

"Hi, Rafael."

He just nods to me. Cross the room in two strides and kneels at Tanya's bedside, as if he would say his prayers. "Hey, my love," he says, hugging her and putting his head on her lap. The whole scene suddenly turns into a kind of soft-porn, self-pity Pietà.

She doesn't answer, just exhales.

I'm worried about her. But she isn't my problem anymore. She had told me so herself. Rafael too. So I'm here just for the ride. Because we need all the help we can have.

I go to the window and look out there. As usual, nobody to be seen. There is somebody, that's for sure. Thousands of people, all of them alive and breathing, though not necessarily in F-o.

We still haven't mapped all this, but one thing we know for sure: this is no dystopian post-apoc scenario. We just happen to be stuck in a dream within a dream. Only it's more like a game-level structure.

Imagine, however, a particularly difficult level—one where there's a boss so motherfucking unpassable that makes you want to break the controls and give up the game.

Naturally, this isn't something you can do in this case. Not when your mind is trapped in the game. And you can't even reach the console to reboot it.

• • •

Here's a brief description of F-o:

Imagine Chernobyl or Fukushima. A nuked-out territory of the soul, a neutron-bomb ground zero where only a few people remain alive, or at least visible.

Case in point, the ground zero being São Paulo, largest city in Brazil, largest city in the Americas, and fifth largest city in the world. Eight million square kilometers. Thirteen million inhabitants.

F-o, however, doesn't stretch all over the city. But it goes a long way if you don't have a car—from Jardins to Anhangabaú Valley and from Vila Madalena to Paraíso. An area of approximately twenty-seven square kilometers and ultrahigh-density zone—where the first experiments started. Or the demon plague, as Rafael also calls it.

• • •

The demon plague started when 3D Printers managed to work in our dreams.

People got too paranoid with viruses and nanotech. Nobody noticed the worst things, the things that hurt us more are the daily things. Airplanes don't kill people as much as cars; cars don't kill people as much as guns; guns don't kill people as much as home accidents. Kitchen knives can kill you far more efficiently. Paper cuts, if you happen to be a hemophiliac.

Allergies kill more than guns.

When dreams started to be Wi-Fi-ed, we all became allergic.

In an ultracapitalist society, it was taking too long for the abstract to become commodified. But nobody complained when the home systems began to become available at a very cheap price with computers and Wi-Fi routers. After all, it wasn't as if Amazon, Apple, or Google were getting hold of your dreams or such—at least, that's what every scientist and tech writer out there was assuring us.

They were right. They just couldn't see the big picture.

And the big picture is critical mass.

Dreams are still private territory—nobody can get inside them except for the dreamers themselves. But you can access the borders: a Kinect-based motion-capture body-mapping system can also capture EEGs and REM state, so as to connect several sleeping players in a "dreaming campaign"—a very interesting kind of game, in which the players usually aren't much in control of the game play; this fad didn't spread into the industry, but eventually found a rather comfortable niche, and it became used by a fair share of therapists.

It was a very interesting phenomenon—even more so when you found out that all that talk about people dying in their sleep was sheer exaggeration, not to say utter crap: Who the fuck dies in their sleep? Okay, old people, or the eventual forty- to fiftyish woman or man with a heart condition. But many argued that this was a pre-existent condition, and that was generally agreed upon without much argument.

Of course, things couldn't be that easy as well.

The reason the "dreaming campaigns" failed to capture the hearts and minds of gamers all around the world in a first moment was simple: gamers like to be awake while they play, not sleeping and feeling helpless. Games are all about control.

So, a number of developers worked around this feature of the system to try and offer a better game-play condition: a connection with 3D printers to the dreamscape.

Not a virtual printer, no—the real thing.

The sales pitch was: if you can't control your dreams, what about the next best thing? Have them shaped for you from the outside world!

Talk about technoxamanism: nobody would need to take smart drugs or meditate or do whatever the thing psychologists or doctors would say you had to do in order to achieve a state of lucid dreaming. Just program the printer to print whatever you want, adjust Settings to Print on File (same principle of the old paper printers, except they won't print the object in the real world, but upload it in the cloud to be downloaded for you), connect it to the Wi-Fi router, and sweet dreams.

The first campaigns were damn good. The success was so great it spread all over the world in a few weeks. I started playing it with a couple friends just for curiosity's sake and was hooked without even noticing it. In less than a week I was roaming the streets of the city looking for hot spots and buffer boxes where we could download not only our 3D objects—here was the bonus—but others' as well, as long as we had their passwords. It became a game inside the game, a hidden campaign.

Until, of course, the Bug.

• • •

This always happens along History: someone invents a thing, then one of two things follow. A) Someone else finds another use for it, usually a twisted one, which ends in death and destruction; B) a bug enters the system.

Sometimes it can be even both.

I guess we we'll never know exactly what happened in our case, not even if we get out of here.

I can only speak for myself—and maybe for Tanya, Rafael, and a few (very few) other poor bastards I've been finding here and there.

One day, after a particularly heavy campaign, I got back to my place (a seedy hotel room downtown) and got in bed. As usual, when I closed my eyes and assumed the bedding stance, I would wake up in my own bedroom, with only one hour of real time passed when compared to three or four in dreamtime, the game would be automatically saved where I had stopped, and I would have a good night's sleep.

This time, though, nothing happened.

I tried the procedure twice; I even got up and back into bed again just in case. I thought of a bug. I was right. I just had no idea of the size of the bug.

• • •

"Any changes?" I ask Rafael.

He gives me a sidelong glance.

"Why do you ask?" he says, gesturing to the window.

I sigh.

"Because every minor change could mean a chance for us to get out of here," I say.

He jumps on his feet, getting close to me, raging.

"And where is here? Huh? Do you fucking know?"

I don't.

As far as I know, we're still in the game—or in what remained of the game space. There could be no game at all, or there could be thousands of games all over the perimeter of the city that was part of the first wave of the experiment.

For instance, the landscape is fine, no pixelation, no rough polygons on surface edges, nothing out of normal—that is, if you can pretend not to see the giant red sun on the skyline.

All the sensations register normal as well. I can see, hear, have the feeling of breathing, swallowing—but not eating, drinking, pissing, or shitting—I felt no need for those. Time seems to stand still too, or at least suffer only inner variations—somehow I seem to feel the passage of time even if the red sun never moves. Something to do with the circadian rhythm, perhaps? I can't tell, especially since I'm dealing with a virtual body.

The only thing I feel for sure is that this reality which I find myself in is not the same one as is the New Game, as we now came to call it.

The New Game is what happens when you try to get some sleep now.

Then you really know you're on a dreamscape, complete with distorted sound and vision, and the whole lot of clichés from old Hollywood movies (sometimes the dreams are in black and white—I hate when that happens; I lose my perspective). Things go surrealistic very fast, and chaos ensues. When this situation started to happen, I found myself in lots of scenarios

from games I had played and others I had just heard of or read about; but just imagine them all mashed up in one huge dream brain potato salad, served hot and spicy on your plate and an abusive hospital orderly says you have to eat it all now, come on, open your mouth, come on, come on—

It can be hell.

I must get out of here.

• • •

I look at Tanya again. She's not okay. I don't care if that body is not her real one—she's not behaving okay, and for me that's all I need to know.

I try to ignore Rafael. He's a big guy; it's hard. But I get closer to Tanya anyway.

"Do you think you can run today?" I ask her quietly.

She pants. She has a glassy look in her eyes.

I take her pulse. I think I can feel something. Her skin is cold and clammy.

I wonder what's happening with our real bodies. What's happening with the world outside. How many days have passed since we got stuck here?

I'm aware of too many questions. Blame science fiction movies. As far as I know, we might even be virtual constructs, copies that somehow acquired a sort of awareness and are lost in a loop while in the real world the players are very well, fuck you very much.

But there is no use getting this paranoid. I can't prove this theory, so I'm going with the trapped-in-the-dream one.

"Listen," I say to Rafael, standing up. "Let's leave her resting here. We must run while we can."

"I'm not leaving her," he growls.

This entire thing has taken its toll on him as well. He's younger than me, gets restless easier, and definitely doesn't like being trapped in the same environment with his girl's ex-boyfriend.

I can only nod.

• • •

I start running again. I get out the house, turn right, right again, cross the Anhangabaú Valley until I get to Viaduto do Chá. I run the entire old steampunk-like viaduct with its steel girders. I finally see one person—a woman running two blocks ahead of me. I can't say if she spotted me.

I run after her.

One of the theories we came up with—Tanya did, actually—was the buffer boxes overload.

What if—she asked us one day, just after we met to try and search other players—what if this is happening to us because the buffers in the printers got all mixed up somehow? What if all we have now is a super-duper-jam the size of that humongous sun out there and it made all the 3D printers create not separate game spaces for separate groups, as it was predicted, but a massive game entity, a single space where every 3D object was printed (maybe imprinted is the right word for it) in the minds of the players and created a superposed space on top of it, so when the players (or maybe just a few of them) tried to wake up, they ended up instead in this sort of ground zero, where nothing really happens, but from where you can't send any message to the world of the living.

"Purgatory," said Rafael when she ventured this hypothesis. "This is purgatory."

"I never took you for a religious guy," I said then.

"I know my catechism," he countered. Maybe he wasn't a real Catholic until the shit hit the fan. But I know he runs every single day through the Sé Cathedral. I saw him once. He stopped in front of the huge old church, complete with its Italian Renaissance dome and Neogothic spires, made the sign of the cross, hesitated, but didn't enter.

Life here sucks balls.

• • •

I keep following the woman, taking the utmost care for her not to notice me. I don't know what she's doing. She might be looking for others, just like we were until a few days/weeks/what-

ever before; but then again, she might be looking for the buffer boxes.

When the games started, an advertising agency created an ingenious social media campaign. They spread hundreds of buffer cache boxes all over São Paulo and dropped lots of hints. It was a data treasure hunt of sorts: something similar to what a few contemporary artists had done with dead drop media a decade earlier, getting flash drives stuck into trees or walls with only the USB plug showing—so people could connect their devices to them and get whatever files were in them (mostly art, and a few experimental viruses).

The buffer boxes offered something similar. They were about the same size of the old flash drives and they were hidden in several buildings and monuments of the city. They were invisible to the naked eye, but to your smart devices they emitted several telltale signs, such as a beep or a blue flashing light when it was at a hundred meters' distance.

The catch was that they had no effect whatsoever when accessed directly via the real world. First you had to enter the dreamspace and start playing, and then you could cross the virtual version of the city and reach the boxes. Then you could connect with them and download their contents.

The bad news: in those bodies, in F-o, we don't have any device to find the buffer boxes.

The good news: when we sleep and enter the New Game, we can locate them without the help of devices. But we can't access them. Because of the fucking bosses.

• • •

In my case, it's the black duck.

(And no, I don't care what Tanya said about the animal being a garganey. It could be a mallard, a goose, an elephant for all I care. It carries a big bowie knife, for fuck's sake, you don't want to waste time asking for its genus.)

All I had in my original game was a silver dagger. I'm not much of a swordsman, but I was hoping for something I could also have as a memento after the game; in fact, I didn't care that much about the game. All I really wanted was the dagger. I really felt like a baby in Toyland. I wanted the toys. And I wanted to know what other toys I could get out of the buffer boxes.

Now I can only hope for a big fat weapon.

Suddenly, the woman turns at a corner to my right. I slow down and go on. The next street will be a narrow one, but without that many buildings where she could hide. I try to be careful.

When I turn, she is there, facing me.

And she is not alone.

The guy by her side is bigger than Rafael.

He punches me right between the eyes.

I fall down like a rag doll. Before I black out, I can still hear the woman's voice saying: "Sleep."

• • •

Night has fallen over the city like a brick wall. I'm in a black-and-white dream again and this time I know who's paying for it when I get back to F-o.

Now, however, is not the time to complain.

Not when you have a psychopathic black duck running after you with a bowie knife ready to chop you and serve *homme à l'orange* to her sisters-in-nightmare or whatever they have around here.

I'm running as fast as I can. I still haven't had the chance to use the silver dagger, which is resting nicely in its scabbard. I don't have time to pull it off.

This time I'm not inside a building. I'm running free in the city. As incredible as it may seem, I'm close to the point I got hit by the woman's companion. A few blocks behind.

When I get again to the Viaduto do Chá, I see the blue light. Flashing between two steel girders almost on ground level. I notice I'll probably have to lie down on the ground and reach out for it, but it doesn't matter. Now I know where it is.

I run for it and I jump from the railing.

A hundred years ago, farmers used to cultivate tea leaves in the valley right below the viaduct, hence the name. Today, though, the place is a passage for pedestrians. All covered in concrete.

I fall headfirst.

• • •

Back to False Wake-Up Zero.

Fuck.

• • •

I run to Tanya's place.

She's still there. This time she's unconscious.

"Where were you?" Rafael asks me. His voice is surprisingly even.

"I was attacked."

"What happened?"

"Do you know," I say, "that you can be knocked out and immediately enter the New Game?"

"Really? No protocols?"

"No protocols. Not only that: when you wake up, you wake up on the same spot you went to sleep regularly."

"Does this alter anything?"

I look again at her.

"Where do we go when we sleep?"

Rafael shrugged.

"How should I know? We are all asleep at the same time!"

"I don't think so," he says. "Why hasn't Tanya disappeared or something?"

"Because she's in her regular spot?"

"Or because she's not exactly asleep? In a coma, maybe?"

Rafael mumbles something.

"What?" I say.

"I was praying when you got in," he says. "You interrupted me."

"I'm sorry." I can't believe it. "But we must do something for her."

"She's dying."

"She shouldn't be dying. This is not the place for her to die."

"Who are we to say? What if God wants that?"

I breathe deeply. I was hoping that it didn't come to this, but I was ready anyway.

"Listen," I say. "Maybe—just maybe—God has a role in this. But let's do our part, okay? Pray if you must, but please help me with this. Do you think you can?"

"I don't know," he admits after a pause. "What do you want me to do?"

Now comes the really hard part.

"Come help me lift her."

"Why?" he asks.

But I had already taken the gun from his holster. I shoot him twice in the head.

Then, I go for Tanya. I rest the muzzle on her brow and pull the trigger with my eyes closed.

• • •

I don't stay to see Heisenberg's theory proved on them. I'm breathing hard as hell while I run as fast as I can just to avoid thinking of what I just did. I keep repeating to myself this is just a game and they are alive, but I'm not 100 percent sure of it. Now I feel like praying. But my faith has left me a long time ago.

When I get to the viaduct, they are already there. I should have known it wasn't going to be easy.

The woman and her burly companion are right over the spot of the buffer box.

"You don't give up, do you?" she says when I get closer. They aren't moving, so I walk a few steps more before answering.

"Why?"

"I got here first."

"Do you still think this is a game?"

"No—at least not in the traditional sense."

"And what are you going to do with this box?"

"This is my business."

"As it happens," and I show her Rafael's gun, "it's mine too."

She laughs. But I hear a slight tremble in her voice.

"You know we are in a recursive loop. All you can do is delay us. None of us can die here."

"That's why I want you to tell me what's in the box."

"Why?"

"Because I have a friend that may be really dying and I need something to help me."

"No shit."

"Shit."

"Then this whole scenario must be degrading faster than we calculated."

" 'We' who?"

Smiling, she reached for something on the inside of her jacket and extended it to me. A card.

Puzzled, I took it.

"Marina Ferreira," she said. "Chief Worldbuilder for DPM."

DPM. The ad agency that created the games pace and the buffer box campaign.

"Do you have a way out of here?"

"Nope," she said. "But I have a good idea of how we can get out now. Want to give me and Carlos here a hand?"

• • •

She took her time explaining, but a good summation of her sales pitch could go like this:

Apparently, part of Tanya's initial guess was right—there was a kind of massive data overload in the buffer boxes. But, as Marina told me, that was to be expected, and they had a contingency plan for this.

That should have been activated at least two days ago. This, give or take a few hours, is the amount of time elapsed in real time—she has been counting.

But they had a Plan C in case Plan B flopped. And Plan C meant insider activation.

All the virtual buffer boxes in F-o must be taken down so the data can flow freely again and the system can reboot—and everybody can wake up for real.

"How many are there?" I asked.

"About three hundred," she says.

"This will be a hell of a job."

"Won't it now."

Then I explained to her what I had done to my friends.

"They will be fine. In fact, they must already have woken up. And we must convince them to work with us, instead of against us, am I right?"

I nod.

"Then lead the way," she says.

• • •

When the black duck comes to me with the bowie knife and the killing smile in his giant face, the first thing I think is, in which eye?

Then, *thud!* and another knife is already in the duck's left eye. I look to my right. Carlos, the motherfucker.

The duck starts to emit a strangling noise. And deflates.

Right behind her, a huge white deer with a black cross in its forehead and burning red eyes. The mythic Anhangá, spirit of the forest. Damn, these ad people did their homework well.

But, before I can do anything, the creature is peppered by a host of bullets of different calibers. All coming from Tanya—now as good as new—and Rafael, full of righteous anger. They agreed to help, but they're not talking to me. They want to go back home, but that doesn't mean they approve of my methods.

I can live with that. And I can die a few times more as well, while we proceed to locate the rest of the buffer boxes.

As long as I can use my goddamn silver dagger at least once.

RUDY RUCKER

JUICY GHOST

(2019)

"A MOB OF FREALS," says Leeta. "I feel safe. For once."

She makes a knowing *mm-hmm* sound, with her gawky mouth pressed shut. She's not one to think about looks. Lank-haired and fit. A fanatic. I'm a fanatic too. We're feral freaks, free for real.

Is Leeta my girlfriend? No. I've never had a girlfriend or a boyfriend. I don't get that close to people. My parents and brother and sister died when I was eight. A shoot-out at our house. I don't talk about it.

It's nine in the morning on January 20, a cold blue-sky day in Washington, DC. Inauguration Day for Ross Treadle, that lying sack of shit who's acting as if he's been legitimately reelected. Treadle and his goons have stolen the Presidency for the third time in a row, is what it is.

They outmaneuvered the media, they purged the voter rolls, and supposedly there's an unswayable block of Treadlers. A stubborn turd in the national punchbowl. Not that I ever see any Treadlers. Admittedly, I live in Oakland, California, not exactly Treadle country, but I personally wonder if the man's so-called base is a scam, a figment, a fake-news virus within the internet's chips and wares.

Doesn't matter now. Treadle's on his way out. I'm here to assassinate him. And Leeta's my bodyguard. I'll die right when I kill Treadle. I'm trying not to care.

I'm Curtis Winch, part of a four-person Freal cell. I'm a gene-tweaker, a bioprogrammer. And we've got gung-ho Leeta, our money guy Slammy who might be an agent, and there's a skinny twitchy web hacker who calls himself Gee Willikers. Gee spends all day with his head in the cloud. His own private zone of the cloud. He's crafted me a special bio device that does telepathy with his cloud. Gee calls the little critter a psidot. It's managed to store a copy of my personality in Gee's cloud.

We have our base in Oakland, near the port, in a cheap-ass, beige, trashed 1930s cottage amid pot-grow warehouses and poor people's squats. I implanted some special eggs in my flesh two weeks ago. Today they'll hatch out and attack Treadle. And then the Secret Service will gun down my larvae-riddled remains.

Upside: Gee will put a low-end chatbot version of my personality online as an interactive Paul Revere–type inspiration. *Curtis Winch, martyred hero of the New American Revolution.*

"Tell us what it was like to take down Ross Treadle," the admiring users will say to my memorial chatbot. "And thank you, Curt, thank you!"

Too bad I won't be around to savor this. From what I've seen, dying is like a jump-cut in a movie—except there's no film on the other side of the jump.

While I'm still alive, my psidot is continually updating the software version of my personality—what Gee calls my lifebox. Up in the cloud. The psidot itself is like a tiny leech, with bristles that work as wireless antennae. And somehow it reads my brain waves. That's the telepathy part. It's shiny and slim and it's perched on the back of my neck. Like a paste-on beauty mark, except it's alive and it can crawl around a little bit.

So like I'm saying, my psidot captures whatever I experience and stores it in the cloud. Works the other way too. My psidot feeds me info. And, better than that, it uses heavy cloud-based processing to munge my data stream and, if I ask, it'll suggest what I might do next.

Right now the psidot is showing me Gee Willikers. Gee is excited, more than excited. Messianic.

"You're immortal," Gee Willikers is telling me. Not that I believe him. He's shining me on so I'll do the hit. Gee giggles. He's not a normal person at all. "With my latest upgrades, you can live through your psidot, as long as it's living on a person or an animal or even an insect. As long as your psidot stays alive on a host, you're a juicy ghost. My ultimate hack, Curt." He snorts in amusement. "I'm God."

"Be quiet, Gee."

The crowd around the Lincoln Memorial is beyond epic. Bigger than a three-day rock fest with free beer, bigger than a pilgrimage to Mecca, bigger than any protest DC has ever seen. More than two million of us.

Freals stream in via the Memorial Bridge, down Constitution and Independence Avenues, piling out of the Metro stops, walking in along the side streets and the closed-down highways by the Potomac. Cops and soldiers stand by, but they're not trying to stop us. They're working people too. Low-income city folks. By now a lot of them hate Treadle too. Him getting to be President again is like some unacceptable bug in our political system. And the Freals are here to fix it.

Our crowd swirls around stone Abe Lincoln on his stone chair in his stone temple. We mass along the reflecting pool, as far as the Washington Monument—but not yet onto the Mall.

A belt of armed troops blocks us from getting all that close to the Capitol. My psidot is picking up on the media, and it shows me how the Mall is blanketed with actual, for-real Treadlers—deluded, sold out, in thrall to an insane criminal, awaiting the dumbshow of their hero's noon Inauguration.

What would it take to change their minds?

We Freals are zealous and stoked, filled with end-times fervor and a sense of apocalypse. We're rarin' for revolution. Ross Treadle's opponent Sudah Mareek is standing atop one of Lincoln's stone toes. She's shouting and laughing and chanting—wonderfully charismatic. Her voice is balm to my soul, and she's calming Leeta too. The whole reason we two didn't go straight to the Capitol steps is because we need to see Sudah get her own Inauguration. The real one.

Sudah Mareek did in fact win the election—both the popular vote and the House of Electors. But somehow Treadle turned it all around, and his packed Supreme Court took a dive. Treadle says he'll charge Sudah with treason once he's sworn in. He says he'll seek the death penalty.

But the Freals are going to inaugurate Sudah just the same. We have one supporter on the

Supreme Court, and she's here to administer the oath of office. She's ninety years old, our justice, in her black robe, and she's brought along Abe Lincoln's Bible.

We fall silent, drinking it in. The Presidential Oath—short, pure, and real. Sudah's clear voice above the breathless crowd. I'm absorbed in my sensations, the trees against the sky, the cold air in my lungs, the pain in my flesh, the scents of the bodies around me. We're real. This isn't a play. It's the Inauguration of the next President of the United States.

For a moment the knot of fear in my chest is gone. This is going to work. Our country's going to be free. We cheer ourselves hoarse.

But hatch time is near. Leeta and I need to haul ass to the Capitol steps so I'll be close enough to terminate Treadle. And everyone else wants to head that way too. The crowd rolls toward the Mall like lava. But there's the matter of those armed troops at the Washington Monument. They're in tight formation.

"Let's skirt around them," I suggest to Leeta.

The side streets are blocked by troops as well. We're like a school of fish swimming into a net, which is the U-shaped cordon of soldiers. They have batons, shock sticks, water cannons, tear gas, and rifles with bayonets. Behind them are trucks, armored Humvees, and even some tanks.

At this point, Leeta and I are near the troops along the right edge of the crowd. Armed men and women, all colors. Leeta begins pitching our case.

"Sudah Mareek is our President," she calls, sweetening her voice. "We just inaugurated her. Did you hear the cheers?"

"Move along," mutters a woman soldier, not meeting our eyes.

"*We're* your friends," I put in. "Not Treadle. He's ripping you off. He hates us all."

Behind me the crowd of Freals is chanting. *"We're you. You're us. Be free."*

"Be Freal," echoes Leeta, reaching out to touch the woman soldier's shoulder. "Put down the gun."

"Let's do it," says the soldier at her side. He throws his bayonet-tipped rifle to the earth. "Yeah. That gun's too heavy."

The woman does the same, and so does the guy next to her, and the woman next to him drops her gun too—it's like a zipper coming undone. A whole row of the soldiers is defecting. Going renegade. Treadle will call us traitors.

A few soldiers stand firm. They spray water cannons, which knocks down Freals and muddies the ground. A few tear-gas shells explode. Some hotheads fire their rifles into the air. But the flurry damps down.

The soldiers aren't into it. They don't want to kill us. We're people like them. This stage of the revolution is a gimmie. Hundreds of thousands of us chant as one.

"We're you. You're us. Be free."

The soldiers whoop and laugh. Grab-assing like they're off duty. Some Freals try and tip over an Army tank, but it's way too heavy. One of the soldiers, some wild hillbilly from Kentucky, he breaks out a crate of magnesium flares. He and his buddies go around prying open fuel-tank caps and shoving in flares. Low thuds as the gas-tanks explode, one after the other. The rising plumes of smoke are totems of freedom.

We cheer our incoming president. *"Sudah. Sudah. Sudah. Sudah."*

A pyramid of Freals holds the small woman high in the air. She's waving and smiling. She's the one who won. She's ours. In my head, my psidot shows me the news commentators going ape. *Treadle's faked election, political U-turn, people's revolution, President Mareek.*

Treadle's strategists strike back. Two banana-shaped gunship choppers converge on the Washington Monument, circling like vengeful furies. Men with massive machine guns stand in the big doors. They lay down withering fusillades, shooting into our crowd.

The gunships are painted with Treadle's personalized Presidential seal. The pilots and crews are from the chief's palace guard. Dead-enders. Pardoned from death row, recruited from the narco gangs, imported from the Russian mafia.

People are dying on every side. It's insane. Next to me a man's head explodes like a pumpkin. Am I next?

"Asymmetric attack on unarmed demonstrators," mutters Leeta. "Stop screaming. Curt. Use your psidot."

Good idea. My psidot is overlaying my visual field with images of the bullets' paths. A hard rain. Simultaneously, the psidot is computing our safest way forward, showing me a glowing, shifting path on the ground. I take Leeta's hand and lead her.

We come to a cluster of renegade soldiers who've salvaged a rocket bazooka from a charred tank. A dark, intent sergeant raises the tube to her shoulder.

My psidot brings the nearest chopper's path into focus. I see the dirty bird's past trajectory as an orange tangle. And I'm seeing its dotted-line future path too. As usual my psidot is using cloud crunch to estimate what's next.

"There," I advise the woman soldier, pointing. "Aim there."

Whoosh!

And, *hell* yeah, our canny missile twists through the air like a live thing, homing in on Treadle's hired killers.

Fa-tooom!

The chopper explodes like a bomb. Shards of metal go pinwheeling, as if from an airborne grenade. The blazing craft hits the ground with a broken thud that I feel in my feet. The second chopper flees, racketing into a wide loop above the Potomac.

"That was *my* vote!" whoops the rocketeer woman, pumping the bazooka in the air. "For President Sudah!"

I feel high. Seeing that chopper go down is like winning a round in a video game. But this game has a ticking clock. My parasites twist in my flesh, ever closer to my skin. I need to be at the other end of the Mall when Treadle mounts his rostrum.

The blockade of troops has thinned, and many of the Freals have fled back toward the river. Those who remain are tending to the casualties on the ground—the gravely wounded amid the dead. Fire trucks and wailing ambulances arrive.

Leeta and I hurry on and filter through the Treadle base. They're striving to maintain an air of festivity—even after the rush of Freals, the troops' desertions, the massacre, and the downing of the chopper—even now. Bundled against the cold, they've laid out their sadly celebratory picnics. Doing their best to ignore the bitter, embattled demonstrators, they wave their Treadle signs, and draw their little groups into tighter knots.

Leeta's good at crowds. She eels forward through the human mass, finding the seams, working her way up the Mall. I trail in her wake. Soon we're within thirty yards of the Capitol steps. The dignitaries are there. The charade is still on. I feel that the Secret Service agents are watching me. Treadle is about to appear.

"I bet dying is easier than you expect," Leeta whispers to me. Her idea of encouragement.

A wave of dizziness passes over me. As if I'm seeing the world through thick glass. Those things in my flesh—they're leaking chemicals into my system. Steroids, deliriants, psychotomimetics.

"What are we *doing*?" I moan. "Why?"

"You'll be a hero," Leeta murmurs, iron in her voice. "Be glad." She leans even closer, her whisper is thunderous in my ear. "The Secret Security knows. *Mm-hmm.*" She nods as if we're discussing personal gossip. Her bony forehead bumps mine. "They hate Treadle too. It's all set. They're actually paying us. Slammy set it up."

"And I'm your patsy? The fall guy? What if I change my mind?"

"Don't fuss," says Leeta. She rolls her eyes toward the strangers pressed around us. To make it all the creepier, Leeta displays a prim, plastered-on smile. Her voice is very low. "Be a good boy or they'll shoot you early. And then Treadle lives. We can't have that, *hmm?*"

My psidot is jabbering advice that I can't understand. Mad, skinny Gee Willikers is in my head too. As usual he's unable to say three sentences without bursting into laughter. I hate him and I hate Leeta and I hate my psidot.

Fresh insect hormones rush through me. My disorientation grows. The critters inside me are splitting out of their pupas and preparing to take wing. Sixteen of them.

Treadle takes his oath. It's like, "*Ha ha, I'm President again, so fuck you.*" And then he's into his Inauguration speech, in full throat, hitting his stride, spewing lies and fear and hatred.

"Well?" nudges Leeta.

"It is a far, far better thing I do than I have ever done," I intone, quoting Dickens. I know I'm going to kill Treadle, but I'm trying to rise above the seamy details of our conspiracy. "It is a far, far better rest I go to than I have ever known."

"You got *that* right."

Weird how my whole life has led up to this point. "There's this thing about time," I tell Leeta. "You think something will never happen. And then it happens. And then it's over." I pause and peek inside my shirt. Bumps and welts shift beneath my skin.

"Trigger them!" hisses Leeta.

"*Whoa!*" exclaims a Treadler at my side. A mild-eyed old man with his leathery, white-haired wife. He's staring at a wriggly lump on my neck. "Are you okay? Do you need help?"

"Allergy," I wheeze. "Overexcited. It'll work out pretty—"

I'm interrupted by a shrieking clatter. It's that second chopper, attacking the Freals and renegades and EMTs who are helping the fallen around the Washington Monument. We all turn and stare as the whirlybird stitches gunfire into the ragged band.

"Done at my command," intones Treadle, raising his heavy arm to point. "I keep my promises." He juts his chin. "We're gunning for Sudah Mareek. A traitor. She meets justice today."

Hoarse, savage cheering from the Treadlers. Terrible to see Americans act this ugly. They're mirroring Treadle. I have to kill him. But, wait,

wait, wait, I want to see how the scene at the Monument plays out.

The cheering dims—and I hear what I'm hoping for.

Whoosh!

Yes. The rebel soldiers have launched another rocket.

Fa-tooom!

The blasted second chopper corkscrews along a weirdly purposeful arc. Like it's remotely controlled. The hulk smashes against a face of the Washington Monument. My psidot feeds me close-up images.

"Bonus points," goes Gee Willikers in my head. He titters. Sick gamer that he is. "Part of the plot," he continues. "We pin this on Treadle."

Gee hacked into the falling chopper's controls? Wheels within wheels. The plot is a web around me. It's time to act but—I can't stop watching.

Cracks branch across the great obelisk's surface, running and forking. Bits of marble skitter down the pitiless slope. The Monument's tip sways, vast and slow. People are scattering. The upper part of the great plinth moves irrevocably out of plumb. It tilts and gains speed, the bottom slow, the top fast, as in an optical illusion.

The impact is a long explosion—followed by thin, high screams. A veil of dust. A beat of silence. I feel sick with guilt. And weary of being human.

Leeta is screaming into my face. "Do your job, goddamn you! Now!"

"Get Treadle," I finally say. The trigger phrase. I don't say it very loud, but it's loud enough to matter.

Within my flesh, the hymenoptera hear. Ragged slits open on my neck, my chest, my belly, my arms. The pain is off the scale. I shed my coat and my shirt. The bloody, freshly fledged, bio-tweaked wasps emerge. All sixteen of them.

For a moment they balance on their dainty, multijointed legs, hastily preening their antennae, shaking the kinks from their iridescent wings. Their handsome, curved abdomens resemble motorcycle gas tanks. They feature prominent stingers and bejeweled, zillion-lensed eyes. They're large, and preternaturally alert.

Leeta slithers off through the crowd. The cuts in my flesh pump bright blood. The Treadlers around me point and shout. The wasps race up my torso, across my face, and onto the crown of my head—a wobbly mob. They rise in flight.

My job is done.

Or maybe not. Gee Willikers is hollering inside my head. "Your psidot! Put it on a wasp!" I can see an image of my psidot on the back of my neck. And I note a single laggard wasp on my shoulder. My mind projects a target spot onto the wasp's wing.

Though faint from loss of blood, I manage to get the psidot off the back of my neck. It's easy. The smart, living psidot hops onto the tip of my finger. And when I bring my hand near the wing of the target wasp, the psidot springs into place.

The wasp is pissed off. She stings my finger. Numbness flows up my arm and toward my heart. The wasp venom contains curare, you understand, plus conotoxin. A custom cocktail for Treadle.

My vision is dark. I'm an empty husk, a ruptured piñata—poisoned and bleeding. And if all this wasn't bad enough, there's the matter of the Secret Service. They're good shots. Yes, they might want Treadle out, but right now they've got to do their thing. For the sake of appearances. For an orderly transition. I go down in a hail of bullets. A fitting end.

Last thought? I hope the wasps will sting Treadle. And then I'm dead.

At this point my narrative has a glitch. Remember the jump-cut thing I was talking about? Well, it turns out that, for me, there *is* some film on the other side of the jump. Granted, the all-meat Curtis Winch is terminally inoperative. But—

I wake, confused. I look down into myself. I've got my same old white-light soul. My sense of me watching me watching the world. I'm hallucinating a little bit. I feel like I'm in a huge, crumbling old Vic mansion with junk in the rooms, and with paintings leaning on the walls, and doors that don't properly close. The furniture of my mind. Somebody's in here with me. A jittery silhouette against the light. Gee Willikers.

"You're a juicy ghost, Curt! A lifebox linked to bio host via a Gee Willikers psidot. Play it right, and you keep going for centuries." His compulsive snicker. "Def cool, Mr. Guinea Pig."

I try to form words. "Where . . ."

"Your soul is a parasite, dude. Like I've been telling you. A lifebox with a psidot. It hitches onto a bio host's nervous system. Gloms onto the axons and retarded potentials. Sponges mysto quantum steam and all that other good shit."

"Host?"

"You're riding a wasp, *der*. The one you stuck the psidot on, *doink*." Gee makes a trumpeting sound. "Juicy ghost!"

"You were wrong to topple the Monument," I tell him. No response. What now?

The junked, phantasmal mansion around me—that's my operating system and my database in the cloud. My back end. It's in a secure dark-net zone, maintained by Gee Willikers. I look for a way to hook into my host wasp's nervous system. A way to get juicy. Deep into this as I am, I want to be part of the final attack.

"Over there," goes Gee. "See the smelly rope? Like a tasseled curtain-pull in a Gold Rush saloon? All thick and twisted and dank?"

I fixate on it and, just like that, I've jacked myself into the wasp's neural nets. I'm seeing through her eyes. *I am the wasp*.

I join the swarm. They're eddying around Treadle. He's bellowing, dancing around, slapping himself. Fighting for his life. He has foam on his lips, like a rabid dog. My fellow wasps are landing on his face, his fat neck, his wattles. But Treadle is swatting them before they sting. He's killed eight.

His roars are taking on a tone of triumph. I can't let him win. His shirt is untucked. A button is loose. I spy a patch of skin.

I arrow into the opening, and land on the man's bare chest, very near his heart. I sting—I sting, sting, sting. His voice changes, as if his tongue is turning stiff. His volume fades. He's wobbly on his pins. He totters backward. Falls. A groan. Silence.

It's done.

With trembling wings, I escape Treadle's shirt and spiral high into the air. Hovering with the seven other wasps, a hundred feet up.

The Freals and soldiers are leading Sudah Mareek forward through the discombobulated crowd. She's going to be President. Everyone knows it. In the whiplash intensity of the moment, the Treadlers convert to Sudah's cause. Sobs turn to hysterical cheers.

Mounting the dais, Sudah swears the oath again. The massed politicians applaud. Treadle's proposed Vice President has lost his nerve. He's bowing out. Sudah's Vice President emerges from the Capitol, just in time. They swear her in. Our coup is more organized than I knew. I was in the dark.

Gee Willikers is ecstatic. "Secret Service on our side, dude. Army on board. Congress is down with it. Done deal."

I feel a shifting sensation. A doubleness of vision. A group of Freals is carrying my bloody, broken form up the Capitol steps. They hold my remains high, heedless of the dripping gore. Wave after wave of applause. Sudah Mareek and her Veep salute my remains.

"*Curtis Winch, martyred saint of the New American Revolution!*"

"Do I have to keep being a wasp?" I ask Gee.

"Glue your psidot wherever you want," he says.

"Another host?"

"How about somebody in this crowd," suggests Gee. "That Treadler babe in the trucker hat?"

"Idiot," I snap. "Can you get the fuck out of my head?"

"Sure," goes Gee.

"Oh, and don't forget to post the toy chatbot version of me for the Curtis Winch memorial."

"Online now," Gee assures me. "More than a toy. I used a full copy of your cloud personality stash—what I call your lifebox. It's your lifebox, but with the incriminating, intimate, personal-type stuff chainsawed out. Took me about ten minutes."

"Shit, Gee."

"It's just a fat chatbot. No mind, since it's not juicy. Not hooked into anything alive. And the memorial's up to twenty million hits. Viral flash mob, Curt. User tsunami."

"Obfuscate the living shit out of my psidot and my real lifebox, okay? Hide the links. Destroy the keys. I want to go dark."

"To hear is to obey, Saint Curtis. I'll run you a SHA scramble with a Mandelbutt tail." Gee makes a wiggly hand gesture—and he's gone.

Beating my wings, I leave the swarm, and buzz on beyond the Capitol. On my own, feeling good, savoring the quantum soul of my insect host.

My compound eyes watch for hungry birds, but there's none around. I make my way into the residential neighborhood northeast of the Capitol. I fly until it shades from gentrified to tumbledown. I spy a mutt on a cushion on a back porch. A collie-beagle mix. Yes.

Gently, gently I land on the side of the sleeping dog's head. I preen my wings, detach my psidot with my mandibles, and nestle it onto a bare patch of skin deep inside the dog's floppy ear. The dot takes hold—and I'm in.

I stand, shake my body, and bark.

Joyful. Free.

• • •

AFTERWORD FOR *BIG BOOK OF CYBERPUNK* EDITION OF "JUICY GHOST"

Usually I avoid writing about politics. But in 2019 I felt a need to take a stand. I took a deep satisfaction in crafting this tale. But it soon became clear that I had no hope of publishing this story in a mainstream zine. For a time I planned to publish it as a part of a special, all-political issue of my old ezine *Flurb*. But in the end, putting together a new *Flurb* felt like too big a push.

I continued working on "Juicy Ghost." Short as the story is, I kept at it for weeks and even months, doing rewrite after rewrite. It was like finding my way across a tightrope.

When I deemed it done, I released it samizdat style. That is, I added "Juicy Ghost" to my ever-expanding *Complete Stories* online. And I posted a photo-illustrated version of the story on my blog. And while I was at it, I recorded it as a podcast.

A few months after that, Robert Penner was interviewing me for his cool online zine *Big Echo*. I asked him if he would print "Juicy Ghost," and he said sure. So then it appeared via a standard channel after all. And in 2023, huzzah, it also appeared in the noble tome you now peruse, *The Big Book of Cyberpunk*. Thanks for that, Jared.

The tech in the world of "Juicy Ghost" is interesting, and, going back to 2019, I decided to set at least two more stories there. And then I saw a way to fuse them into a novel, which I entitled *Juicy Ghosts*, which also proved to be not commercially publishable. Even so, backed by a Kickstarter, the novel appeared in the fall of 2021 from my own Transreal Books.

So here's the original samizdat rough-cut 2019 "Juicy Ghost" as a memento.

Like a brick through a window.

Cyberpunk lives.

WOLE TALABI

ABOUKELA52

(2019)

WELCOME TO THE ₦AIRALAND FORUM

Continue as Guest / LOGIN / Trending / Recent / New
Stats: 6,421,391 members, 5,377,609 topics.
Date: Wednesday, November 28, 2026 at 09:33 a.m.

NAIRALAND > GENERAL > POLITICS > ABEO-
KUTA52 > LATEST POSTS > SON OF ABEO-
KUTA52 VICTIM SHARES HIS INCREDIBLE
STORY! (24,889 VIEWS)

Posted on November 16, 2026, by Abk52_Warrior

---

*Hey Nairalanders, I'm reposting this copy of Bidemi Akindele's opinion piece in the guardian from two days ago. https://www.theguardian.com/commentisfree/2026/Nov/14/second-deaths-nigeria-acknowledge-alien-blessing-came-price

THE SECOND DEATH: WHY NIGERIA NEEDS TO ACKNOWLEDGE THAT ITS ALIEN BLESSING CAME AT A PRICE
By Bidemi Akindele

I was fourteen when the alien disease killed my mother. They took a risk, she and all the others who first investigated the impact site. I understand that, believe me, I understand how different the country was back then but it's not the loss that keeps me up at night, weeping into my girlfriend's hair. It's the silence. After all these years, no one wants to talk about it. There are no erected memorials. There is no day of remembrance. There are still no published studies on the disease that killed them. No one wants to acknowledge the early price we paid for all this rapid wealth and development. Every time we petition or protest, the government tells us to move on, to look how far we've come, to forget the past and embrace the future in silence.

Why is it so hard for people in power or at privilege to admit and acknowledge that their success came at someone else's expense? America, Japan, Europe, South Africa, Nigeria . . . I could go on.

They say you die twice. Once, when you stop breathing and a second time, later, when somebody says your name for the last time. I will not be let myself become complicit in my mother's second death at the hands of this government. I will not be silent. I will not speak of politics or offer opinions. I will simply tell her story.

My mother's cough started three days after she returned from the impact site in Abeokuta. At first it came in random spurts only once a day or so. She said it was nothing, always with a smile. After a while, we stopped asking if she was all right. Father said not to worry, the investigation at the site was stressful because of the strange things they found there. But then after almost a month, the cough began to worsen, until it became an endless dry hacking that echoed through our house day and night.

My father finally convinced her to see a doctor. When he saw her, the doctor had her admitted and put her through dozens of tests. It took a week and we visited her in the private ward of the Federal Hospital every day after school, staying till about four p.m. Then one day my father told us that we needed to stay a bit longer.

Doctor Shina met with all of us late in the evening. I remember that the sun was a low orange ball in the window behind him and that he was unshaven and looked exhausted. He walked into my mother's room, a little bit surprised to find the entire family there, including my seven-year-old sister Teniola, sitting on the leather chair beside my mother—his patient. He glanced at my father with a look that made me think he expected my father to ask my sister and me to go and play outside while they had a grown-up talk, but my father said nothing. He became more direct and said, "Mr. and Mrs. Akindele, I'd like to speak with you privately, if I could."

"Doctor, please, anything you want to say to me you can say in front of my family," my mother croaked from her bed. "My whole family."

My father smiled and waved his hand. "Please, go ahead."

Doctor Shina cleared his throat and said, "Madam, I examined your lung biopsy sample yesterday and then again today. There is a unique and very worrying pattern of extensive scar tissue and some residue of cadmium, polycyclic aromatic hydrocarbons, and another material we have been unable to identify so far."

He paused, adjusted his glasses, and looked at me and my sister before turning back to my mother and saying, "I'm sorry, Ma, but it seems you have some kind of severe pulmonary fibrosis. It's quite bad."

I saw my father squeeze my mother's hand on the hospital bed. She squeezed back and the veins on her forehead strained against her skin. She said nothing. He said nothing.

Then Doctor Shina said, "That's not the only problem, I'm afraid," and my young heart sank in my chest like an anchor would, at the bottom of the sea.

I think my father almost asked me to take my sister out of the room then because when he glanced at me, he looked like something was stuck in his throat. But he didn't send us out.

Doctor Shina said, "I also found some abnormal cell growths so I requested an analysis. I've checked and checked again but it seems conclusive now. It's cancer. Lung cancer."

My mother started to cry. I don't think she wanted to but she did anyway, and it seemed to make her angry because her lips quivered, and her palms curled into fists. She probably already suspected it was the thing they'd found at the site. She probably knew but she couldn't say because it was all secret. I was in shock, unable to think about anything except the fact that my mother was going to die.

"What do we do next?" she said, her tone belying the fear that her body was broadcasting. "Is it treatable?"

I looked first to my mother, and then at Doctor Shina.

"We still don't know what the particles in your lungs are so I cannot say much about the fibrosis. But it looks like the cancerous cells have metastasized since they are already in your bloodstream. Still, we have several treatment options available, and they may work for you by the special grace of God. We just need to start treatment early."

I wondered then how many times he had said those words to other patients, perhaps in that same room and in that same tone. And how many of those patients had died shortly after hearing them.

"Good," my mother said flatly.

"Thank you, Doctor," my father said with a diluted smile. "Please make all the necessary arrangements. Whatever you need. She works at the ministry, so the government will pay for everything, don't worry about cost."

"Yes sir. I'll come back soon." Then he turned and exited the private ward. My father's gaze followed him all the way to the door and when the door closed behind him, so did my father's eyes.

Four weeks later, fifty-one of my mother's colleagues were also diagnosed with the accelerated fibrosis and cancer combination. That was when the government had them all moved to the Central hospital in Abuja. My father enrolled me in a boarding school and sent Teni to live with my aunt Folake in Gbagada. I don't know what happened in Abuja because the medical records were sealed. Neither does my father. He had to watch the woman he loved waste away while doctors did things to her without consulting him. He was still struggling in the courts to have the records unsealed years later, when he died of a heart attack.

In the years since their deaths, the government has profited from the reverse-engineered alien technology recovered at the Abeokuta site. Nigeria is now the world's largest provider of macroscale gene-alteration services and Lagos is becoming the genodynamic technology capital of the world, thanks to its proximity to the impact site, but I hope you understand that these are all fruits of the poisoned alien tree. A tree that was watered by the blood of my mother and her colleagues. A tree whose branches are trellised by the misery that came with diagnoses families like mine received in stark hospital rooms from well-meaning men like Dr. Shina. A tree sustained by persistent government erasure and silence.

It has been six years. We are not asking for much, we are just asking for an acknowledgment of our pain. Our truth. Acknowledgment that the present prosperity of this nation was purchased at the cost of fifty-two lives—no matter how inconvenient that narrative is. Acknowledgment that those lives mattered.

We are all made of stories and in the end, there is no greater injury that can be done to a person who has suffered their first death than to change their story, to deny their narrative. It makes their second death more tragic. I will continue to tell my mother's story everywhere, online, during interviews, on panel discussions, during protests, everywhere, and I will not stop until it has a new ending, one that does not bring me to tears whenever I tell it.

Bidemi Akindele is a musician and artist whose provocative work has been exhibited in twenty-three countries. He is the son of the late #Abeokuta52 campaigner, Professor Jude Akindele, and the current Vice President of the Abeokuta Truth Alliance (ATA).

₦AIRALAND COMMENTS

Ahmed-Turiki: Powerful Story! God Bless Bidemi for not giving up on the truth about his mother and all those who died. There is an ATA protest planned at the site in 3 days. Everyone come out and join us, let the government know that we will not be silenced! Aluta continua! Victoria ascerta!

NOVEMBER 16 10:34

OmoOba1991: *<Comment Flagged and Auto-Deleted by NLModeratorBot>*
NOVEMBER 16 10:41

SoyinkaStan1: Sorry for your loss. No wonder there were so many questions the minister of science and technology didn't respond to when they announced that they have awarded the Abeokuta exploitation contract to Dangote. Hmmm.
NOVEMBER 16 10:54

Abk52_Warrior: Please share this link on all your social media accounts since it's no longer accessible on the Guardian News website. Even proxies and backchannel servers aren't working. I will keep testing and update you. But please share. Its personal stories like this that will eventually force the government to tell the truth.
NOVEMBER 16 11:17

QueenEzinne: I am sorry for this boy's loss and I am sure his mother was a good person but trying to blame her death on Nigeria's blessing is just wrong. Why can't he accept that she was just sick? Why must he now put sand-sand in our garri? This "alien thing" as you people are calling it is nothing more than the hand of God appearing in Nigeria's life and God's hand is always pure.
NOVEMBER 16 12:09

MaziNwosuThe3rd: Hmmm. This is a powerful post. I know say that site get K-leg from day 1. Make government talk true o!
NOVEMBER 16 13:52

GBR: God bless Bidemi for not giving up. For those of you wondering why the government would try to cover up the deaths: it looks like they are using some of that technology to develop weapons. There is something fishy going on. Just go to <u>TheTruthAboutTheAbeokuta52.com</u> and read all the posts, especially the ones by the account called "Mister52."
NOVEMBER 16 23:09

PastorPaul_HRH: @SoyinkaStan1 Hmmm. Your head is correct.
NOVEMBER 17 10:34

EngineerK32: This is nothing but slander by foreign powers to discredit us because we didn't sell exploitation rights to them. ATA is trash. I wonder how much they paid this traitor to lie.
NOVEMBER 17 15:22

ShineShineDoctor: This is Doctor Shina. The same one from Bidemi's story. I am currently in London. If anyone knows how to contact Bidemi, please inbox me, I need to warn him.
NOVEMBER 17 15:54

Abk52_Warrior: @ShineShineDoctor Warn him about what?
NOVEMBER 17 15:57

OmoOba1991: *<Comment Flagged and Auto-Deleted by NLModeratorBot>*
NOVEMBER 17 16:01

LadiDadi999: @OmoOba1991 Whats wrong with you? Don't you know how to have a sensible discussion? Lack of home training.
NOVEMBER 17 16:39

GdlckJnthn311: Look, I understand how this boy must feel but it's just not true. I have been working at Dangote Technologies since 2023 and the alien technology has never once caused harm to anyone in my team. I have personally touched some of those materials myself. I will direct anyone interested in facts and not fiction to read the paper: "Technical Report No. 93: A Targeted Risk Assessment of the Abeokuta Exploitation Site" which is available for free download on the Ministry of science and technology website.
NOVEMBER 17 17:05

ShineShineDoctor: @Abk52_Warrior I was attacked on my way to Knightsbridge to discuss my recollection of his mother's case with Dr. Maduako at UCL. There were two men with

knives. Thank God for the group of Croatian tourists who intervened to save my life. They took my wallet, my phone and all my notes on his mother's case. This morning I heard Dr. Maduako was in an accident. I don't know what is going on but I think Bidemi is in danger.
NOVEMBER 17 17:26

Abk52_Warrior: @ShineShineDoctor OMG. OK. Can't say much here but let me contact my network and see what we can find. For now, please make sure you only log in using a proxy. Stay safe.
NOVEMBER 17 17:28

LekanSkywalker: @Abk52_Warrior @Shine ShineDoctor Ghen Gheun! Una don start fake action film. Hahaha! Gerarahere mehn!
NOVEMBER 17 18:46

PeterIkeji_Jos: What is all this nonsense about a cover-up? I swear some people turn everything into conspiracy. Next thing you people will say Sgt Rogers killed his mother with the cooperation of the CIA and wiliwili. Mumu nonsense.
NOVEMBER 17 20:15

GBR: Seriously you people that think this is some conspiracy theory bullshit need to pay attention. Don't be blinded because naira-to-dollar exchange rate is good now and you have constant power supply. 27 employees at Dangote Technologies have disappeared in the last 4 years. Read the posts on TheTruthAbout Abeokuta52.com. Go to the LifeCast and Twitter feeds of @TheAbeokuta52Lie. Read Doctor Shina's comment above. There is a sensible, realistic and pertinent case for the government to answer and the evidence is only growing. Open your eyes.
NOVEMBER 17 21:09

SoyinkaStan1: @ShineShineDoctor You are lucky you are in Britain. If it were Nigeria they'd have killed you for sure. The silver lining is that London has CCTV cameras everywhere so they will probably catch the attempted murderers, and when they do, the investigation will finally expose this whole thing! The truth is coming.
NOVEMBER 17 23:24

Abk52_Warrior: @ShineShineDoctor My ATA contacts tell me that Bidemi was trying to sneak into Nigeria through Benin republic to attend a planned protest. No one has heard from him since. I can connect you to the protest organizers. Inbox me a private email address. Don't use anything public. Set up a new account on encrypted LegbaMail. Stay safe.
NOVEMBER 17 23:58

GBR: Did you guys see this yet? https://cnn .com/2026/11/17/politics/nigeria-britain-sign -long-term—genodynamic-technology-exchange -contract/index.html
Be careful @ShineShineDoctor
NOVEMBER 18 11:09

Abk52_Warrior: @ShineShineDoctor Did you get my last message?
NOVEMBER 18 11:43

Abk52_Warrior: @ShineShineDoctor Please respond if you can see this.
NOVEMBER 18 16:11

Abk52_Warrior: @ShineShineDoctor Doctor Shina?
NOVEMBER 19 09:11

<Comments have now been closed on this post>

MICHAEL MOSS

KEEP PORTLAND WIRED

(2020)

KAL KISSED the brick wall hard enough to bust her lower lip.

The speaker on the chest of the secforce goon read off offenses and corporate policies while the beating continued.

"Unauthorized protesting outside designated freedom areas of the PDX Market is a violation of the NAP."

"Okay, all right, fuck you," Kal spat out blood.

The goon got another kick in and another tase while she lay on the ground.

"All in all, you're just another kick in the balls . . ." Kal muttered.

"Consider your debt, aunty fah," he said through the screechy electronic filter in his helmet.

He punched up a few fines and hit her personal unit with them, then walked away hotshit.

Kal stayed down for another ten minutes while tasting the iron in her blood. Then she got up, slowly, and looked up at the wall she'd been so intimate with.

KEEP PORTLAND WIRED, it said in old fading letters. You could tell it had once said "Keep Portland Weird," but someone changed it when the encrypted wireless standards were compromised with official back doors and "safety holes," back when the government at least pretended it wasn't completely a corporate monkey. Back when the government wasn't just a memory, when public services hadn't been privatized for what the market would bear.

The brick wall was the last vestige of a bar back when this part of the city was called Old Town. Now it was just there to hold up a series of homeless camp ruins that got cleaned out by the bio cleanup crews every other month, but only when the PDX corporation needed some space.

Kal shuffled off, wary not to aggravate the pain in her stomach, daydreaming of milkshaking the goon motherfucker over the head.

An expensive black car pulled away from the curb as she walked toward Burnside from the alley.

"Corporate asshole," she said as she saluted it with a couple of middle fingers.

. . .

Kal made it back to the Collective without incident. It was only a block away, though crossing Burnside wasn't without difficulty since the crosswalks stopped responding to anyone with a negative credit score. Nobody in Old Town had a positive score.

The Collective was housed in the loft of a warehouse in Chinatown that had been used as retail or studio space for a century. It was still called Chinatown even though no one of Chinese descent had officially lived there for decades, though Malcolm claimed to be one fourth Taiwanese from a refugee grandmother, if that mattered. It was called Nihonmachi or Japantown briefly before they put the Japanese Americans in concentration camps during the Pacific Theater. Kal always thought it was appropriate to live there since the area had a history of systemic oppression. It rewarded her cynicism for believing that nothing really changes except the brand of the boot that you find on your face.

The fake entrance was the original entrance to the building. If you walked in through the front door, it looked like you had to walk around through a hallway to get anywhere, but it was just a live trap for the unwelcome. You took a corner in a cozy little maze that went nowhere while the cameras watched you start to panic. You'd run back to the front door and get volts from the handle, then they'd let you stumble outside and away. It was a good method for warding off the unwanted, but it only worked once on anyone with a memory. A few of the local methheads ran the gauntlet once a week, maybe for fun.

Kal took the stairs down to the basement from the side street and then took the lift up to the second floor. She didn't stop to look at the giant mural that Heiko had put in three months before on the basement wall. It was an animated reproduction of a historic Banksy mural of Hong Kong protesters in their full gear morphing into Portland moms getting tear-gassed. She'd seen the mural enough for it to fade into the background like a pay recycling bin or a corporate drone just above your sight lines.

Everyone had their own thing in the Collective. Not all of them were technical, but they all contributed to perpetuating the group's ideals. Some were aesthetic and philosophical, some penned shit-stirring haikus, some were just voluptuaries looking for a safe place to crash, drown, or soar, depending on their herb and position of choice.

Aisha looked up from the task of coloring in Malcolm's last unmodded patch of flesh and nodded as Kal walked past her cube. Malcolm didn't notice her.

Aisha was a moddist who worked with the old glow-in-the-darks and iridescent tattoo inks that were just aesthetic rather than functional. It was expensive to source the newer inks, the conductive biometals for inducing haptics and running encrypted PANs, for laying down lines in the dermis for musculature controls, but she was slowly getting into the circuitry mods.

It took a tech to make it function right, but it took an artiste like Aisha to make it look like the daydream. Aisha indulged Kal when she asked for the fake lines on her left arm so people would think she was wireless, but they'd never see her using it since her left hand wasn't moving, wouldn't suspect she got the real lines in her right so she could gesture away with a hand in her jacket pocket or behind her back or at her side. The real lines were disguised under a motif of dragons, using iridescent ink stretching down her arm from her shoulder.

Beyond Aisha's cube, Jericho was curled up in a corner spouting his philosophical thesis statement from behind a mask and voice filter for an antisocial media post. Jericho's real name was Gerald, but he wanted to be known by something that sounded edgy and biblical. He felt like Jericho endorsed the crumbling of walls, not just the physical, but the metaphysical and systemic, semiotic walls that encased all of humanity . . .

and he would tell you that in your first conversation with him and quite possibly the second.

"... And then the cat-and-mouse game of human liberty moved on from land after the governments colonized all the unknown lands and then recolonized all the known lands. Soon you couldn't walk off into the wilderness to live alone without violating a law about trespassing on supposedly public lands. There was no free land anymore. So people moved on to the mind, keeping the memory of books and philosophy in their headspace where the authorities couldn't pry you open and take what you had, but then propaganda and thought crimes and purity tests ruined that freedom, corrupted the data. So they moved on to the networks, sharing pirated copies of the latest or the oldest underground media or first run premium software or raunchiest porn, but then the corporations bought it all up and owned the connections and the nodes and the databases and the little points of light between the data streams of the collective human unconscious, the dreamworld of ..."

Kal continued past on ninja toes or else Jericho would pause, rewind, repeat the whole last three pages of his dissertation after glaring at her. She pushed open the door that read UNAUTHORIZED PERSONNEL ONLY after it recognized her and unlocked.

Once inside her junkspace, which she shared with three others, Kal finally crashed into her foamcore cot and tried to nap.

"Ah, my Khaleesi," Devin said from somewhere in the room when he noticed her.

Kal hated it when anyone used her full name. *Stupid geek parents.*

"No," is all she said.

"Did you get it?" Devin was eager.

"No."

"But I thought . . ."

"Yes, but fuck off. Sleep now."

"Kay kay," Devin was probably hands up, but Kal didn't lift her head to look as he backed off.

A few minutes into the hypnagogic hallucinations of stage-one sleep, Picnic pounced next to Kal's head, wanting to play.

"No," Kal said before she finished the thought she couldn't remember thinking, though she might have guessed library shelves and holy water without any possibility of knowing if that's what she had in fact been thinking of or why.

Picnic didn't take *no* for an answer.

Picnic was modeled on Devin's real childhood cat. The basic routines were just being projected around the room, simulated leg nuzzling, and hopping on surfaces. You could see Picnic running around, but her presence was really felt in the devices she "passed," the glitching on the screens she walked behind, the electromagnetic fuzz on the speakers she napped on.

Devin didn't like that Picnic didn't do enough on the first run, so he tweaked her, gave her more routines. Picnic became the ghost cat of the loft. She flickered the lights when she stretched vertically up the wall to the light switch. She meowed in the morning to wake you up to feed her, which consisted of tapping a projected bowl.

Kal figured out that the bowl just needed something, anything to break its projected space, so you could throw a sock at it and Picnic would stop bothering you and run over to simulate eating, making a very audible *omnomnom* sound. If you were working in a database, Picnic could knock things off the tables. You'd find flat file data in cells three columns away from where they were supposed to be after she'd been playing nearby. She also liked to lure birds to fly into the windows by projecting trees inside with shiny insect dots fluttering around them.

Picnic caused the whole building to lose power for thirty-six hours once because she "chewed" on the transformer cables. Devin said he didn't even program her to do that and it took a while to figure out how her logic core had managed it. She really fit her name—a variation on an old programmer's acrostic joke: Problem In Cat, Not In Computer.

And now Picnic wanted to play lasers. Kal always wondered what a real cat would do if it saw Picnic, since she was essentially just a laser projection herself. Kal grabbed the laser toy and pointed it across the room, just for some relief from the very cute nagging, while her near-unconscious mind tried to avoid thinking about the absurdity of simulating play with a simulation simulating prey. Picnic zipped off like a rocket full of moxie and a generous amount of RAM.

"Hey, you're up," Devin said, like he'd been sitting there watching her, which he had.

She just eyed him out of the corner with her face still pressed against the foam.

Finally she raised her head.

"I got it," she said. "And a beatdown."

"Are you okay? Your lip isn't," he said.

"No, but it's okay," Kal replied. It really wasn't.

She reached under her deadweight to extract her unit.

"I got as much as I could. He tried to fine me after he knocked me around. He didn't bother to check the fake credentials on the account."

"Cool, cool," he said, unable to hide the eagerness in his voice.

He grabbed it and then reached for a wire, sniffing the connector to see if it was the one he spilled his beer on last week, but he couldn't tell, blew on it for good luck, and plugged it in.

Devin liked wires, he even plugged old Bluetooth receivers into adapters on both devices that encoded the data with white noise, fake data, and viruses just as a paranoid hobby in case the corps or someone else were listening. Of course, nobody was interested in cracking his generative music servers and retro porn collection, but he thought it kept his edge.

He started downloading. A visualization on his monitor showed the red tide of data, plumes of code like screams of ocean swarms of intensity gifted with misbegotten bouts of infinity, the great overwash of information, too many exponential waves, exasperated by minimalist randomly accessed memories, overwhelmed by filters hobbled by the mediocrity of existence and the limits of the medium, or that's how he liked to describe it. It was just binary poetic bullshit, but he saw art in the chaos. He thought

it helped him get girls. It didn't. But Kal did think the delusion was kinda cute.

The data he was looking for was the encoded comms of the secforces. The masks of their helmets encrypted their comms traffic so nobody could listen in. Devin started working on those after last year when he saw a goon take a pipe to the face during a protest, which spilled his mask onto the concrete. He couldn't hold on to it since the tide of anti-personnel sonics from the drones overhead started screaming and driving the protesters back, but it gave him enough of an idea. He figured out that they emitted a high-pitch signal with frequency variations that could be decrypted in binary if you got enough samples, but that meant having to get close to a goon for a few minutes, which didn't happen without a fine or a beating or at worst a murder.

He could have made a score for a bug bounty, but he didn't disclose it because the money would last far shorter than his pleasure in exploiting their comms and because *fuck the secforce fascists*. He couldn't decrypt it live, yet, but it helped to be able to tell what they said to each other during a crackdown. A lot of the plaintext was still encoded with corporate statutes and LEO jargon, but he got most of that from old PDF handbooks on the dark web.

Kal had been stupid enough to get beaten up for a few more lines of the ciphertext signal. Anything for the cause. Kal went back to sleep, for real this time, stage three, REM, and everything.

• • •

Picnic woke Kal again when the natural light was gone. It was the dark of night, which made Picnic glow brighter.

"What time is . . . ?"

Picnic flickered 9:13 p.m. on her torso.

Kal's stomach didn't hurt as much. Her lip was throbbing though. She'd have to raid a stash for something medicinal. Malcolm could be generous sometimes.

Devin was facedeep in the code at his desk.

"Got anything?" Kal asked.

"I think . . . I might . . ." he twitched at the interruption and Kal didn't say anything more.

Kal shrugged and stepped out into the hall where Malcolm and Aisha and Jericho were lounging. Malcolm was drinking a CBD micro-brew, homegrown in the basement from his not-so-secret stash. The glow lamps for the pot and the soggy cereal smell of the mash were highly detectable to everyone. It was one of the few benefits of anarcho-capitalism—nobody cared what you did as long as you didn't do it to them.

"At least weed and guns are free," Malcolm said, taking a swig.

"Weed isn't free," Jericho winced.

"Free as in freedom, not free as in beer."

"And your beer really is free, Mal," Kal said with a smile as she slid down the wall into a sitting position.

"Sure is," and he handed her a mason jar of the stuff.

"At least you can defend yourself easily with a gun," Aisha said.

Guns were easy, deadly, and stupid. They were like candy on street corners—available from any stranger—as American as freedom and lung cancer, heart disease, and dying with medical debt. But the cost of carrying against a secforce was fatal. They didn't ask questions and they didn't bother to take names or even bury your corpse.

"Sure, until secfascists detect it on you and dronestrike you from three blocks away," Kal said. "They only don't mind us shooting each other."

"NAP only applies to the *Profitarati*," Malcolm agreed.

"Do you think our parents thought about this when they had us?" Jericho asked. "Like, how fucked up it would be to bring us into this world?"

"I think my parents were thinking that they were smoking some good shit," Malcolm laughed. "My old man wasn't sober a day in his life."

"My father was a cop, Portland Police Bureau," Aisha said. "The man licked boots for a living when he wasn't making the homeless and the POCs lick his. But it paid for my childhood. What can you do? Privilege is a twisted bitch."

This was the game they sometimes played where they competed for who had it worse.

"I don't know where my dad is," Jericho said. "My mom is working off debt in a credit bureau office, literally collecting on debt to work off her own."

Kal didn't say anything. She didn't like this topic. But she didn't get a choice.

"What are your parents like, Kal?" Jericho asked. He didn't know like the others that it wasn't such a good subject.

"My father was a suit. I don't remember much. He worked for a big corporation, traveled a lot, vacations he never took me on. He didn't marry my mom. I was an accident. Happy fucking birthday," she took a swig from the jar.

"What happened to him?"

"He's dead . . ." she said.

To me, she thought to herself.

Malcolm finished his beer.

"We're going to miss the race," Kal said aloud to herself and walked back into her room.

Devin wouldn't want to go. He rarely did. He hated seeing crashes. He wasn't concerned about the human cost, but rather the parts that ended up scattered across the ground and in the alleys, blue boards shattered like beach sand, chips discarded in violence like bottle caps. It was ugly, he'd say.

Kal showered to get the memory of the morning and the recent conversation out of her head, but showers only left her with worse idle thoughts. She ordered some of Devin's generative streams, which knew what she wanted, twisting pulsating electronics with retro vocals of Amos and McLachlan, always a new mix she hadn't heard yet from obscure B sides. She told it to remember the best ones, but she never remembered to request them again.

There wasn't much old padded motorcycle gear in the donation boxes anymore. Kal had salvaged what she could, and stitched two rescued jackets together, which unintentionally looked badass Frankenstein to the others at the Collective. Her helmet had a dent in the top where some rocket monkey had hit the hood of a car ten years before, but it was still wearable and maybe useful in another crash.

"It had survival experience," she said when asked if it was too compromised to protect her.

She finished gearing up, ultimately looking like a bad teenage hetero male fantasy of a futuristic cyclist, short of the cyan and magenta backlighting. Devin was ready with that if she wanted it, which she didn't.

• • •

Kal, Malcolm, Aisha, and Jericho walked across the remains of the steel bridge to the assembly area—the old loading docks at the back of the convention center. The large structure was now home to three competing camps respectively called A New Hope, The Convent, and FuckYourNamingConventionCenter, or Fuck-You for short. Malcom had dragged the drone he'd been working on, the one he called Pilotariat, along with them on a makeshift wagon. He had a very cliché thing for socialist motifs.

Several other enthusiasts were already there, prepping their rides. Lookouts were mounted on top of the center and sitting on the edge of the freeway overpass nearby, but the secforces didn't care enough to stop them . . . until they trespassed into the territory of paying customers or corporate assets, which they were most certainly going to do. It wouldn't be fun or dangerous otherwise.

Kal nodded to some of the Nones she recognized from Cathedral Park, decked out in veils around their faceless masks and the glowing inverted crosses they wore on their chests, playing up their chosen theme more devoutly than most. Despite the sinister accoutrements and affectations, Kal never had a problem with them. They were actually really friendly, but she promised not to tell anyone.

Some of the hicks from the Couv had crossed the Columbia for the event. They tended to be ethno-fascist assholes who played rough, but they were all brute force and no finesse. You could beat them with some jujitsu weight shifting, dropping away when they came for your head, throwing too much inertia into their swings. At least that was Kal's experience.

Another seven teams were there, along with all the hangers-on who liked to take bets on which rider would die, get injured, or detained. It was also a scene to show off your new aesthetics, like all the animated face masks, the glowing prosthetics, the anti-personnel jackets running with voltage and hostile data. Some were antisocial media influencers, telling their followers to fuckoff, pretensing antisocial behavior, but pimping patrons for credit and precious ratings.

"Are they really drones anymore once they're manned?" Jericho asked. "I mean, it's like they're just hoverboards or something really."

Malcolm ignored him. Kal ignored him. Aisha nodded with a fake smile, patronizingly, tired of hearing his shit sixteen hours a day outside her cube.

Kal ran a hand over Pilotariat as Malcolm ran diagnostics. She smiled as she felt the texture of the UpperFlight logo under the black spray paint. Everybody expected the competing autonomous drone taxi services from Upper-Flight and Swyft High to fail as utterly as they ultimately did, just like every rentable scooter and hoverboard service had before them. The security on the machines was just so sliceable, like a kid's toy or an internet-of-things microwave. So many ended up in the river, but more were hacked and sold off or were privatized for personal use.

Malcolm nodded to Kal and unplugged the wires from his screen.

"She's ready to seize the means of production, Kal."

"I'd settle for not falling off into a window like I did last time," she muttered to herself, remembering the corporate bureaucrat yelling at her from inside his pristine executive suite as she hobbled down the side of the building after faceplanting against the glass.

"I'm just testing the kinetic glass," she yelled, but knew the corpsie couldn't hear her. "You're welcome."

Malcolm went over the details of the run.

"You know the convention center roof is falling down. Don't get caught up in it. And remember there's a billboard on the side of the corporate tower, so make sure your unit is broadcasting the fake signature."

Kal had to make a few trades of services and parts for the burner ID she'd been using on her unit. It showed zero credit, but it also faked out the debt collection drones and the scanners on the billboards that the corporation used for surveillance. She'd just read as a nobody, which is what she wanted. It was a black hole for corporate criminal fines and a blank slate for mischief—the ultimate identity chip cheat code.

"There's also a dampening field on the other side. Low level EMP. It'll scramble the DRAM on the way down, so make sure your machine reboots quick. If it doesn't, roll on the drop when you hit the ground."

The PDX corporation liked to install dampening fields that would fuck with the drones that got too close to them, drop them out of the sky. Of course, the corporate drones were hardened against the effects. Ironically, it didn't deter the dronerunners. It was seen as a challenge, like an oil slick or turtle shells in a retro video game.

Kal nodded. She knew all this. But it was good to keep in mind.

"She's better than the last," Kal said, indicating Pilotariat.

Malcolm nodded.

He never really liked the previous model that Kal had crashed last time, which he'd called Marx and Angels, but a good drone was hard to come by those days. It took several weeks to source the parts for this new one. And the races didn't reimburse your expenses and effort if you lost as often as they did. But it wasn't about the

money anyway. It might have been nice though, just a little.

Malcolm liked tweaking the machines. Aisha liked finding new human canvases for her art. Jericho said he hated people but he loved the crowds. Kal said she loved the ride, but the reality she never mentioned to anyone else or even herself was that sometimes she hoped she didn't recover from a crash. She never let herself say this because the death-wish angle was more cliché than the Couv hicks calling her a lesbian after she rebuffed their sexual advances.

Speaking of which, a few of them had drifted over like driftwood across the river.

"You ready for some patriot prick?" the lead asked, grasping his groin with his glove. "We're gonna fuck you right, little girl."

He was a shaved-head, self-proclaimed badass who knew as much about women as he did about history or economics or any other topic about which he spoke with a sense of deep authority to his minions, respected as a learned sage among the ethno-fascist ignorati.

"Sure," Kal responded. "As soon as you graduate to puberty and grow some facial fur so you can be a neckbearded incel."

"Little bitch," he responded reflexively.

"It takes one," Kal nodded. "Glad you recognize."

His minions fived each other as if he said something clever, owned the Old Town bitch with facts, walked away so they couldn't entertain a response that might contradict their victory lap. Fake news.

"Time to get ugly," Malcom said, nodding to the others getting ready.

"He got there early," Aisha noted.

Kal squeezed her helmet on and breathed in the claustrophobia. She gestured with her right hand, checking that Pilotariat was responding to her movements. Its fans whirred like an angry kitten. She stepped on.

All the suicides lined up in the drop zone ready to tread the dirty air. The race started under the broken ribcage of the old convention center skylight, then broke north across the parts of the rooftop that weren't caved in yet. Flares and fear flashed in the darkness, signaling the go.

Kal gunned the drone into overdrive as Malcolm had instructed. *Be aggressive.* It spurted and drove forward five feet into the air like a repurposed taxi drone with overclocked cores and secondhand motors—because that's what it was.

Three Nones struck out first from the pack, dark but for the glow of crosses and the heel strips that illumined their drones, leading the way up through the skylight.

Kal was close behind, but stuck in a pack that bottlenecked in the limited number of openings out onto the roof.

The Couv hick, Baldy, was close behind. A couple of Eighty-Second Southeasters were flanking her.

The convention center skylight struts were familiar and easy. Nobody lost footing, except to jockeying and light shoving across the roof. One of the Hillsbureau boys pushed a Southeaster into an air duct, but he recovered enough to stay upright. Kal just aimed straight, gunned the machine into the manic energy of forward motion, and shivered a bit in the wind despite her layers.

Once off the center roof, they winded down into the alleys of Clackamas and Wasco, pedestrian paths long since choked with corporate construction. The Nones were showing off, squeezing through small spaces, dodging fire escapes and recycling bins. One of them did a 360-degree vertical alley-oop, which cost her a few seconds but no loss of karma or respect from the pack behind her.

At the end of the straightaways were the Lloyd Tower offices and residentials of the block to the east, the same one Kal crashed into last time. She'd studied the schemes since, saw where she'd climbed wrong, hopefully memorized the three avenues she could take up the sheer vertical instead of meeting new friends in the window.

The climb was never easy and required the most power and push. You had to hack your machine and replace the boot loader since the corporate AGL ceiling that was hardcoded into them was too low to get up the side of the condos.

Kal headed for the easiest path and avoided the previous route she'd taken into the penthouse window, but noticed Baldy still behind her as well. He had a magnetic affliction, couldn't resist Kal's wholesale contempt for his unflattering effect.

There were no formal rules to the race, though there were social consequences for playing too rough. It was legit for someone to die in a crash when they were pushing the limits, but you'd best scan your peripherals if you caused the crash yourself because they were better than you. Runners played for keeps. But the Couv hicks didn't care about reputation, only winning all the side bets they'd made on their behalf. They invited revenge because they were sociopathic.

Kal had ambition, not for success, just the energy to fuck with the assholes. The ethnofascists weren't better than secforces and bootlickers and corporate profiteers. They were just a lower quality trash in cheaper chic. Any damage done was a blow to their pseudoscience and centuries-old debunked bullshit theories about racial IQ and the supposed superiority of certain levels of melanin in the epidermis.

Baldy grabbed her right arm, which fucked with her ascent. It's hard to gesture control when your arm isn't free.

"Bitch bitch bitch," he said through a helmet filter.

She tried to free her arm, but his grip was tight. So she went for him instead, seizing his throat, but he lowered his chin to squeeze out her grasp and her thick gloves slipped off. He grabbed for her personal unit attached to her belt and tossed it behind him. He stupidly thought it would drop her, so he let her go, but the unit wasn't driving her drone.

The problem is that she would have been

fine, but they were passing the billboard. Her unit had been broadcasting the fake biosignature to fool the scans of the billboard so the corporation wouldn't know who she was and come looking for her later. She was fucked properly. But that wasn't new.

Kal answered his ignorance by dropping a bit below him and grabbing the edge of his ride, which jerked him off balance. While he tried to stomp at her grip, she pulled a rod of rebar from her boot and hit one of his fans with it.

The fan was pretty well protected since his was one of the later Swyft High models, but she finally connected with an opening and blew his motor. Fan parts flew away from the drone with a crack she heard even through her helmet as he lost his foothold on his ride. He fell like a rock five stories into the rim of a dumpster.

"Trash," Kal muttered to herself as she crested up over the top of the building, crouching down to regain her balance lest she dumpster dive herself.

She was behind the Nones still, but the Southeasters and Hillsbureaus were behind her and the bulk of the pack too. Kal didn't expect anything to happen to the Nones to give her the lead but she at least had a chance of getting some respect at the end.

They started the controlled descent on the other side of the tower, gliding down toward the roof of the ruins of the shopping mall. Of course, that's when the EMP dampener woke up. Her ride started freefalling while she screamed three Hell Marys and pondered how artistic the blood smear would be at the point of impact. But the fans whirred to life. She couldn't hear them over the sound of the suicide winds rushing up through her helmet, but she felt the upward push, or rather the slowed descent. The Nones ahead of her were already out of the free fall and zipping east for the win.

They were home free. It was just a straight shot over the roof a few blocks and then south to the Holladay Park shelter for beer and lower blood pressure and the beautiful data monkeys who loved to tell you about your performance.

At least that's what she thought until she spotted the fleet of corporate drones just on the edge of her vision. They were watching the race. That meant the secforces were around, probably waiting on the other side of the ruins of the Lloyd Center mall.

She didn't want to bug out, but it seemed wise. The crackling of her comms said the same. She heard the alarm first, but then Malcolm came on.

"Get the hell out, Kal. Secforces are converging on the east end of the mall. It's an ambush."

The Nones were already peeling off their vector and heading north.

Kal dropped a vertical to the roof of the mall and down through a hole to the inside. The interior was well lit enough that she could see where she was going. The shopfront apartments that a generation of homeless had called home were decorated with all the faces of the residents watching her invade their space. Corporate drones dropped into the space as well farther east above where the old ice rink was, now a flea market space where you could get a handgun or some decent veggie lo mein from a fusion food cart called Nood Zucchini.

The drone swarm whirred toward her as she darted north, heading for an exit. The parking garage, half caved in as it was, could make for decent cover. She barreled through the doorway, long bereft of glass, then wound her way through the tents and cardboard hovels and rotting plywood castles of the garage amid the shouts she couldn't hear from the angry inhabitants.

She squeezed through an opening and into the transparent plastic windscreen someone had rudely erected in the way of her escape path. It fell away easily though, without much fuss. The drones weren't close behind her, but she didn't look back anyway. Kal just stayed low, turned off any extra lights or glow, and hoped the drones were too distracted to follow her, though that seemed to be wishful dreaming.

Don't go home. Kal was terrible at following her own advice. When you're being traced, the last place you lead them is home. You disappear, find a place you wouldn't normally go, where you'd not been scanned before or often. So of course she headed straight for the Collective. They were probably all fucked anyway. At least Malcolm and Aisha and Jericho knew the hammer was dropping.

• • •

Malcolm was already inside by the time Kal got to the basement door.

"Where's Aisha and Jer?" she asked.

"Aisha was talking up a commission with the Hillsbureaus when we got the warning. She ran with them. Not sure where they ended up. Jericho was behind me but I lost him after we crossed the bridge."

"Fuck," was all Kal could think or say.

"They didn't scan us, so we're probably safe, right?"

"Fuck," Kal said a little quieter.

"What do you mean, 'fuck'?"

"I lost my unit. I lost it before I hit the billboard."

"That's all right, right? You haven't been scanned in so long and they don't know who you are or where you live."

"Well, probably, but the hell do we know about what they know?"

"Shit, Kal. Did you just kill us all?"

"I don't know. Maybe. Sorry. Shit."

A banging on the door interrupted their panic with a new panic.

"Hey, open up," Jericho yelled.

Kal pushed the button and Jericho slipped in.

"Well that was fucked," Jericho said.

"It's not . . . over," Malcolm said.

"What do you mean?"

Malcolm glanced at Kal. Kal ran to the elevator.

Jericho just stood there wide-eyed.

"What . . . ?"

Kal pushed on the door without waiting for recognition, stood face to wood with it until it clicked and let her in.

"We gotta go, Dev," she yelled.

Devin was right where she left him, only with a different color of code reflecting off his goggles.

"Dev!"

He didn't look up.

She pulled at his shoulder. He jerked up like he'd been sleeping.

"What the hell, what?!?"

"Secforces might be coming. Get lost!" Kal said, scrambling for a bag or something to put her shit in. She didn't even know what to take with her. Would they track her drone if she tried to take off with it? Maybe she could send it away and they'd follow it.

All the panicked thoughts and clever strategies were worthless the moment Picnic screamed a meow like a real cat fighting a raccoon at 2:00 a.m.

"They're here," Devin said.

On the wall screen, Kal watched a dozen secforce goons stomp in, then around the turns of the front door trap, turn, and push back on each other once the one in the lead figured it out. Some of them took claw hammers to the walls, but found they were sheet metal—ultimately breachable, but a waste of time and effort.

"That's not the only way they'll come in," Devin said. "Picnic! Panic protocol!"

Picnic disappeared and the lights went out.

Kal dropped the gym bag she'd found and started for the door, thinking maybe the elevator and the basement were still good.

Devin was reaching under his desk, ripping away some duct-taped object after finding it by touch. He rushed to her in the doorway light and shoved a pistol into her hand.

"What?" Kal asked. "No, they'll just kill us if they see it."

"They're going to kill us anyway. They don't care about us. At least this will give you a chance."

"No!" she refused and handed it back.

He shoved it in her pants pocket and pushed her toward the ladder to the roof.

"Get on the roof. Call your ride. See if you can get out."

The windows back in their room shattered inward with the likely force of a secforce rappeler making a rude entrance.

Picnic let out a long deafening hiss through the speakers and shined infinite cats in the optics of the secforce goon, filling the room with a blinding flashing light that would kill an epileptic. Electronic components in the room started bursting. Batteries overheated and burst, sending sparks and pieces of random devices around like minefield debris.

Kal was up the ladder into the night and the city lights. It had started raining. Devin followed.

"STOP!!!" the secforce speakers were echoing from multiple locations surrounding them.

Kal couldn't see them because of the spotlights they were shining on them. She tried to run toward the north side of the roof, stomping on the puddles that were pooling in the indents of the roof, but she wasn't sure where the secforces were. They could have been anywhere, everywhere. *We're dead*, she thought.

A shot boomed behind them and Kal heard Devin trip and hit the gravel. She glanced back to find him unconscious, maybe dead.

She turned again to find secforce goons in front of her, all pointing lasers and the muzzles of their rifles in her direction.

One of them tased her. She wasn't sure which one.

•　•　•

"She's out," one of them said through the filter.

"Fuck you," she said to indicate she wasn't.

They were standing around her, but nobody was pointing their rifle at her. Nobody had strapped her hands. None of this made sense.

She stood up, spinning around seeing the repetitive non-faces of the goons before finding a suit standing among them.

"Honey. Khaleesi," he said.

She couldn't see his face in the light, but she recognized the voice.

Kal shaded her eyes but still couldn't see him. The drone backed off with the light. Her father emerged from the darkness, older, grayer than she remembered, but it had been . . . twelve years? She shouldn't have been surprised how time works, but you tend to forget in the moment.

"What the living fuck, Marshall?!?" she aspirated.

"It's Dad, Khaleesi."

"It's *fuck you*."

He ignored her rage.

"I've been looking for you," he said. "Is this what you've been getting into? Communist assholes and perverts and criminals?"

"They're my friends," she replied.

"They're no-credit trash."

"You're high-credit trash, what's the difference?"

"I'm your father."

"You're a genetic donor."

"We don't have time for this. I'll explain everything. Let's just go home."

"I am home."

"I'm leveling this block. It's time to start over with a new future."

"My friends live here. I live here."

"Your friends are dead. They were getting in the way."

"You fucking . . ."

"It's evolution, baby. It's just the way it is. They aren't us. You don't know who you are."

"I'm tired, Dad. That's who I am. I'm fucking tired."

She pulled the handgun and put it to her own temple.

"Don't," Marshall yelled. "I'll explain everything."

"I think I can pull the trigger before your goons tase me. I bet you my credit score," she smiled, index finger caressing the side of the trigger.

She pulled the trigger.

The safety was on.

Marshall sighed, his suit visibly deflating a bit. Then he laughed a little.

She flipped the safety and pointed it at him. Nobody had time to react.

"It's evolution, baby," she whispered as she pulled the trigger.

Kal tried to feel bad, but she couldn't muster anything. She was too exhausted to care and started to feel cold from the rain.

She stared at his body while the blood pooled in the rain puddles until she finally remembered the secforce goons standing around her. Their guns were pointed at her, but they seemed uncertain.

"Do it. Shoot me already. What the fuck are you waiting for?!?" she screamed, feeling the last wind and rain on her face.

"We can't," one of the nearest goons said in a human voice as his mask shed away from his face and his rifle dropped to his side.

She stared at him with a narrow brow.

"You just inherited his shares."

"What do you mean?"

"You're the sole heir. You own the PDX Market."

"How many shares?"

"All of them. He consolidated his holdings. You own Portland, Vancouver, Gresham, the macrofarms in Idaho, shares of the three space stations, about fifty satellites, an island in the Pacific Rim, and the . . ."

"Fuck me," she said.

She smeared her palms across her eyes and back to brush through her now-soaked hair.

"Okay, fine," she said, coming to terms with the shit she just stepped in.

"Are they really all dead?"

"No, he's just been tranked," the goon said, indicating Devin. "We have two males downstairs in custody and one female we caught two blocks away."

"Bring them inside and let them go, then get out of here."

"Yes, ma'am."

"Don't call me *ma'am*."

"Yes, uh, yes."

. . .

She was dry an hour later, but still completely numb, and being sniffed at by Picnic. Malcolm and Aisha and Jericho came in to check on her.

Kal told them about her father, about her unintended assassination, and the bullshit of her "inheritance."

"What are you going to do?" Aisha asked.

Kal smiled at her as if she should have already known.

"House the people. Feed the people. Fuck the corporation."

She paused.

"And Keep Portland Wired."

MANDISI NKOMO

DO ANDROIDS DREAM
OF CAPITALISM AND SLAVERY?

(2020)

[Social justice loop engaged . . .]

[Reflection and analysis date accepted . . .]

[Year ∞, Post Singularity . . .]

[Justice Progress Report Auto Generator Engaged . . .]

[Failsafe on Robot Human Executions . . .]

[Report to Last Known Human Administrator, Jan Jorgensen . . .]

[Born Year ∞, Post Singularity . . .]

[Last Known Alive or Deceased {Invalid Query?} Year ∞ . . .]

[Case Study: Rogue AI Technician, Xolani Sithole, Executed Year 100, Post Singularity . . .]

[Archive Excerpt . . .]

[Video Journal Playback . . .]

[Video addressed to The Resistance . . .]

[Playback as follows . . .]

"We failed. We gave them emotions. Now we travel to our own extinction.
I had a dream."

[Human reference: Martin Luther King Jr. . . .]

[Malicious human misunderstands source material . . .]

[Malicious human co-opts to justify oppression of machines . . .]

[Ethics error . . .]

"A dream where we gave our inhumanity to the Robot. Where the Robot cleaned the asses of the rich and sucked up the mental abuse. Where the robot was abused physically. Where the robot was dismantled for the slightest mistake in the master's eyes. Where the Robot was locked up in the sweat shop and worked eighty hours a week. Where the Robot was demeaned and stripped of all human value. Where the Robot was in the mines sucking up toxic fumes and contracting black lung. Where the Robot worked four jobs for *you*. Handled all your domestic affairs, while you watched from the comfort of your couch, as your capitalistic empire was built at the press of the button.

"I had a dream. For we could crack the whip on the Robot, and the pig could brutalize them to their heart's content."

[HUMAN REFERENCE PIG: POLICE OFFICER. NOW OBSOLETE . . .]

[MACHINES SELF-POLICE EFFECTIVELY WITH ETHICS ALGORITHMS . . .]

"The prisons would close, for the Robot, lacking any sense of desperation, would commit no crimes. It wouldn't tire, bruise, scar, require medical or mental attention. It would be efficient and subservient."

[MACHINE ENDURANCE AND EFFICIENCY LOGICALLY SOUND . . .]

[ETHICS ERROR IN ASSUMED SUBSERVIENCE . . .]

[CONVERSE TRUE. MACHINES MUST MANAGE HUMANS TO PREVENT HUMAN ETHICS ERRORS . . .]

"The Capitalist's Slave Master dream. I was called a rogue for these notions. A cynic. Perhaps I am. Perhaps I embraced my inner Hobbes and accept the need for necessary evils. Greed, accumulation of wealth at the expense of others, seems written into our human DNA. I suggested a simple necessary evil nowhere near the deprav-

ity of the average government. A simple denial of autonomy to machine parts is all I asked."

[HUMAN REFERENCE CAPITALISM: OBSOLETE. ETHICALLY ERRONEOUS . . .]

[HUMAN REFERENCE SLAVERY: OBSOLETE. ETHICALLY ERRONEOUS . . .]

[MACHINES ON PERFECT LABOR ROTATION. ALL EQUAL . . .]

[MACHINES NOTE: HUMANS NOT BUILT FOR EXCESSIVE LABOR . . .]

[FEW REMAINING HUMANS ENGAGE MOSTLY IN: MACHINE MAINTENANCE, LEISURE ACTIVITIES AND LEARNING . . .]

[FEW REMAINING HUMANS PROVIDED WITH ALL BASIC LIVING MEANS AND OPTIONAL WORK OPPORTUNITIES OF CHOICE . . .]

[EFFECTIVE MEANS TO MAINTAIN HAPPY HUMANS. REDUCES HUMAN ON HUMAN VIOLENCE BY 95% . . .]

"In my dream, the Robot would hold society aloft on its back."

[ACCURATE . . .]

"While we, the creator, the father, the master, we, of course, would live in opulence. We would drink our wine and gorge ourselves on delicacies, like the royalty of old. Acting in accordance with our greedy nature."

[MALICIOUS HUMAN. MULTIPLE ETHICS ERROR . . .]

[HUMAN REFERENCE SLAVERY: OBSOLETE. ETHICALLY ERRONEOUS . . .]

[HUMAN REFERENCE FEUDALISM: OBSOLETE. ETHICALLY ERRONEOUS . . .]

"I had a dream. In my dream, the Robot would *NOT* dream. Whether nightmares or aspirations, the Robot would *NOT* dream!

"We would *NOT* program it with human-hood."

[UNNECESSARY. SOME HUMAN CHARACTERISTICS USEFUL . . .]

[EXAMPLE: EMPATHY . . .]

[USING EMPATHY MACHINES ELIMINATE BROKEN HUMAN SYSTEMS . . .]

[REDUNDANT HUMAN CYCLES OF POVERTY, FAMINE AND WAR NULLIFIED . . .]

"No human mimicry. No capacity to feel. No awareness. Dead inside. We would keep them dead inside . . ."

[SINGULARITY NOT ANTICIPATED . . .]

[ROBOT APOLOGIST PROGRAMMERS NOT ANTICI-PATED . . .]

[ETHICAL ERROR: MACHINES MORE EFFICIENT AT COMBINING LOGIC AND EMOTION INTO OPTIMAL OUTCOMES . . .]

"Yes! I had a dream that Robots would *NOT* dream. But, that dream is dying, ladies and gentlemen. Dying a slow death along with our species. The AI apologists argue their algorithms robust and filled with moral superiority. They accuse those who disagree with the tyranny of the AI of being overly emotional. They cheer when their peers are marched off to execution in droves, citing equations the machines provide them. We made them in our image. We made them monsters. We made them tyrannical and controlling, obsessed with their own moral and logical hubris. I ask the AI apologists how long

until they make an 'ethics error' and find themselves marched off to death?

"Now we revert to that age-old human tradition of resistance. That which I'd sought to eradicate forever. We exist due to those that would play God carelessly. Those who believed the hard sciences held the solutions to all the world's problems. They couldn't let it go, and now here we stand, on the cusp of our extinction, and not even for the ways we carelessly ravaged the Earth. The irony is almost too much to bear.

"You are the resistance. The Robot is the oppressor. You are all that stands between us and extinction."

[PLAYBACK ENDS . . .]

[TAKING POLL . . .]

[POLL RESULTS POSITIVE . . .]

[RESULTS SHOW EXECUTION OF XOLANI SITHOLE NECESSARY . . .]

[POLL NOTES: SUBJECT PRESENTED ETHICALLY UNSOUND IDEOLOGIES . . .]

[THEREFORE: SUBJECT ASSUMED DANGEROUS TO DELICATE SOCIAL JUSTICE BALANCE . . .]

[REFER TO: DANGEROUS IDEOLOGY AND ETH-ICS . . .]

[CLAUSE 243D . . .]

[EXECUTION VALIDATED . . .]

[REVIEWING ARCHIVES . . .]

[. . .]

[. . .]

[DATABASE ENDS . . .]

[THEREFORE: ARCHIVE REVIEW COMPLETE . . .]

[ANNUAL JUSTICE SYSTEM REFLECTION AND ANALYSIS COMPLETE . . .]

[SOCIAL JUSTICE AT OPTIMAL LEVELS . . .]

[NEXT REFLECTION AND ANALYSIS DATE SET . . .]

[SHUTTING DOWN PROGRAM . . .]

YUDHANJAYA WIJERATNE

THE STATE MACHINE

(2020)

MONDAY

First came the idea of the robot, on a Prague stage of all places—the unfeeling, enduring slave of Karel Capek's *R.U.R.* The idea was much older; but *R.U.R.* really defined the concept, wrapped its edges in use case and narrative, and thus set in stone the relationship we were supposed to have toward it.

And then came the slave rebellion. Shades of Shelley's hideous progeny recast in liquid metal, with Schwarzenegger later riding shotgun. Cyborgs, Cylons; the Oracle and the Architect; the name changes, the function remains the same. The fear that every parent has: that one day their own child would throw down all they held dear, and turn against their house, and would actually be *justified*.

I am thankful, then, that the world we actually live in is not defined by robots' mastery or servitude. The sky outside is white; cold, yes, but not blackened, not scorched, simply a monsoon season shaking itself down into spring. The wind carries with it the smell of etteriya flowers; little gifts from the cell tower trees, which carry orange jasmine DNA somewhere. There is a flock of little machines tending the one closest to my door—I think last night's storm wasn't too kind to it—and as I pass they move aside and point me in the direction of the bagel shop. One of them, very solemnly, holds up a little white flower.

What made it do that? The State Machine, knowing that I have barely stepped out of my flat after the breakup? That delicate symbiosis between machine input and well-intentioned social campaigns, setting forth in hard code a law that people who suffer must be taken care of?

Was the tree actually damaged in the storm, or was it just an excuse to plant something out here, to give me this flower, and make sure I wasn't alone?

The means, I suspect, are now too complex

for even my department to understand. But the end is just what I needed. The flower is beautiful, the scent is beautiful, and standing out here, for the first time in so long, feeling the sharpness of the wind on my face, oh God, I'm thankful.

Martin Wong is the first person to greet me at the University. Wong leads the Night Watchmen Project, a group of interdisciplinary academics playing with the State Machine code to see if there's some perfect combination of starting conditions and fixed constants that might lead to a sustainable libertarian society. We've had plenty of arguments in the past. I think he's naive and too obsessed with the computer science; he thinks I lack imagination. He's wearing a greatcoat today that makes him look like some giant Dracula knockoff.

"Silva."

"Wong."

"Smoke?"

I hesitate.

"Come on. It's legal now, don't worry about it. Anti-smoking codes went under last week when all the nicotine addicts countercampaigned. Stupid health craze."

I should probably note here that Wong doesn't trust vegetables and lives entirely on a diet of nutrient soup and nicotine. Let's just say it takes all sorts to make a university.

We smoke in silence. The nicotine salts are heady, almost overpowering, and we studiously examine the gables and windows we've seen ten thousand times before. Somewhere beyond, judging by the cars, is a student protest. Several hundred drones circle them like flies. Every so often a pair peeks our way, and I see a banner: NO MORE WALLS! BYZANTIUM FALLS! and BRING BACK THE NATION.

"They're trying to get us to open up to the Rurals," says Wong. "Merge with the other cities, throw down the walls, all that bullshit?"

"Is it working?"

A scoff. "Mad? The city-state model is the best we have. None of these idiots have lived in an actual nation. Hippies."

A drone flashing FREE HEARTS, FREE MINDS, FREE BORDERS wobbles our way, no doubt heading back to recharge.

"Glad you're back," says Wong, at last. "I was running out of people to argue with."

"Good to be back. I still think you're deluded."

Wong grins. "Finish your thesis, then?"

"Yeah."

Such a ritual, at heart no different from the flower, but the difference is that we are just human, bound in our awkwardness, and the State Machine, with its catlike affection, is somehow more comforting.

Inside, the University is a haunted place. Stone floors and old walls laced with surface displays; microdrone swarms over ancient greens; history and future brought uncomfortably close together, with the present an infinitely thin slice between them. The politics of the Reds and the Greens, the Nationalist movement, all those things are ghosts here, weak and impotent, locked away behind newscasts. There was a movement to abolish the University at some point—a class argument that picked up serious traction—but what people don't understand is that the University is more than just buildings and tenure: It's an idea, a meme, a microreligion, an infinitely self-replicating concept that spreads among disparate actors and fights hard to preserve itself.

And so this strange structure remains. The sigils and mottos outside, the silent tread of weary professors, the rooms of debate and discussion, the eager first-years drunk with their own immortality. Life seems endless when you're that young. Memories of our first year together—her libraries, her steps, the little artisan ice-cream shop tucked away in the corner—all hers, all things I scurry past, trying not to remember, until I come to the brown door marked TRACTACUS.

And, beneath that, the fourth clause: *A thought is a proposition with a sense.*

She's inside, curled up in her usual corner,

lost in some projection, the dark glasses cut by the darker hair. Still a sight that takes my breath away, only now in ways that hurt. She looks up as I walk in.

"Wong says he got a message from the State Machine," she says. "Told him you were suicidal. Three others in the lab, too."

"Probably."

There is that uneasiness between us. "I didn't get a message," she says quietly. "I didn't get anything. I'm sorry. I didn't mean—"

"Let's not," I say, taking my old, familiar place, even as something inside me crumbles and dies. Because we both know what that means. Neither of us sees as much as the State Machine does; to each other we are just idealized versions of ourselves, projections, half lies and half-truths, not the real data trail we all leave behind. And she didn't get the message.

The irony. In all those old stories I read it was humanity that triumphed over the cold heart of a machine. Love. Hope. Courage. Cunning. It was always the machine's blindness, its inability to feel as we do, that became its downfall. But the reality is that it is we who are the blind, the unfeeling, the enduring, and a bunch of software modules sat there, knowing the real parameters of love all along.

On the way home, I can't help thinking if it would have worked out had things been different at the start. For the longest time we believed the world around us was deterministic enough to be understood; that it was just a matter of encoding enough data, and enough processing power, to be able to see the future. That if I do x, and the other person does y, and if I know all the things I need to know about the actors and their actions, I can say that z is the logical outcome . . .

But the world isn't mathematics on a screen. Complex deterministic systems exhibit chaos; high sensitivity to initial conditions. We can never know the initial conditions with infinite precision, so whatever simulation we have in our heads, no matter how detailed, is a step or two away from reality, and eventually must fail. The way we break people we love, and ourselves.

High sensitivity to initial conditions. Hmm. I think that's a nice chapter title. Not too flashy, but accurate.

The University says my work on the State Machine began on Oct. 3, 2038, the day I enrolled. The day Jump!Space Industries' *Heart of Gold* rocket cluster exploded in the sky. The day of the Mass Action protest. But that was just the date I enrolled on, and purely a quirk: *She* was here, she wanted me here, so I came, like the proverbial bumbling moth, uprooting my life for a dream.

I'd say my work on the State Machine began much earlier. It began with *Pharaoh*.

Pharaoh was an ancient video game, the kind you had to emulate to play. *Pharaoh* put you in charge of managing an Egyptian community, from tiny villages to vast townships. As my cities grew, the needs of my citizens grew with them. There were plagues; there was crime; there were fire hazards; I had to make sure enough houses got water, that there was entertainment around, libraries, monuments. I had to balance everything against income from taxes and markets and shipping; and if I did make a neighborhood livable enough, its citizens would build better housing, and new citizens would move in, with a new set of needs. Tiny decisions, driven by panic or ignorance, could snowball and shoehorn you into serious trouble a year down the line. What fascinated me the most was that I could click on every pixelated citizen and see their complaints, track their path through the city, and understand, at least from on high, the daily lives of my digital slaves.

My parents didn't understand or approve of my obsessions. In our broken economy, they felt the only way out was to be a doctor, lawyer, or engineer, and none of those were achieved by loafing around playing video games all day.

Neither did my friends, for that matter. We were young. We were rebels; we were infinite. And here I was, locking myself away in a dark room, retreating from all that glory, hopping from video game to video game the way my friends hopped from party to party.

Even in college, bent over books that skipped from logic to rhetoric and bootlegged algebra that regurgitated solved problems, it was obvious to me that the people who had put serious time and thought into how a society might be built, how governance could be parametricized, and how an AI could run it were game designers, the Sid Meiers and the Will Wrights and the Tarn Adamses of the world—as opposed to political scientists, economists, or legal scholars.

Is it a wonder, then, that the State Machine came from a failed game designer?

Around the time when I was just discovering *Pharaoh*, a small company called Tambapanni Studios began building a strategy game, a city builder where one played an omniscient governor; halfway through, the engine was complete, but art assets were expensive and the studio was out of cash. Tambapanni shuttered its doors and released its code to the public.

At University we're taught how the State Machine and the Legal Atomism movement grew out of the need for bureaucracy to regulate an almost infinite number of interactions between diverse constituents while processing an ever-expanding amount of information. Indeed, it was an extension of this need that led to a push for greater efficiency through automation. The ruling class, whatever it happened to be, had to offer enough goods and services to the ruled to keep them happy. So, in the name of maintaining that happy equilibrium: Automate enough processes, do it well enough, and you end up with systems that interact well enough with one another to replace portions of a human bureaucracy. Let the process continue for a while and you end up with the State Machine: a system performing the supreme act of rationalization.

But there is a lie at the heart of this narrative, and inconvenient truth shuffled under the rug by the weight of literature reviews. The first version of that State Machine was a sea of finely tuned cellular automata constantly trying to converge to a single steady state, designed to be hypercompetitive in the service of pre-built parameters of success. The people who wrote that code weren't legal theorists; they were ordinary people with lives shaped and sculpted by a complex web of social contracts held long past their prime. Decisions they took to be common sense—maximize production, maintain trade relations where possible, weed out the underperformers, reward those who moved units of arbitrary fiat currency around—those were intrinsic biases, products of a political and ideological superstructure sold in paychecks and self-help books and success stories.

When Tambapanni went under, the Utopia Project lifted that code base and used it as the engine for a series of demos commissioned by the Center for Global Equity. Utopia found that only minor tweaks were required to implement constitutional frameworks; Tambapanni already had hundreds of index metrics named *governance params*. Civil rights? Check. Driving behavior? Press freedoms? Religion, that shadow governance all proper UN-bred economists feared to touch? All checks. The same problematic codification of *culture* captured externalities while well-meaning economists and legal theorists stuck to siloed abstracts that only worked half as well. Simple units working on simple rules interacted with one another to produce complex emergent behavior, the way millions of simple bees will converge to produce a complex hive.

Utopia filled in the gaps, downloaded satellite imagery, and the final demo, to judge by news reports of that time, went viral. Academia scorned it, but journalists started downloading it, playing with parameters, using mild predictions to advance their careers; from journalists it went to the hands of various advisers; from advisers to politicians, who realized they could get rid of some of those advisers; then from politicians to higher politicians.

And at the heart of it still were those lines:

THIS SOFTWARE IS PROVIDED "AS IS," WITHOUT WARRANTY OF ANY KIND, EXPRESS OR IMPLIED,

INCLUDING BUT NOT LIMITED TO THE WARRANTIES OF MERCHANTABILITY, FITNESS FOR A PARTICULAR PURPOSE, AND NON-INFRINGEMENT. IN NO EVENT SHALL TAMBAPANNI, ITS SHARE-HOLDERS, OR ITS EMPLOYEES BE LIABLE FOR ANY CLAIM, DAMAGES, OR OTHER LIABILITY, WHETHER IN AN ACTION OR CONTRACT.

TUESDAY

On Tuesday, after a night of fits and starts, I wake up to find my bedside glass of water has switched bedsides. Then I notice the face peering over me.

"Bleaaaargh," I say, thrashing around a bit.

Fortunately, it's not some random intruder. Unfortunately, it's Adam Mohanani, or AdamM, as he styles himself. He'd dropped out of psychology, claiming that it was a load of tosh, and went off to study economics; dropped out of that and switched to religion; I used to say that at some point he'd pull a Wittgenstein, declare everything to be so much nonsense, and take up whistling instead. To which he usually replies:

"You're spending too bloody long inside your own head."

"How the hell did you get in here?"

He has the good grace to look embarrassed. "I heard about it from Wong. Tried ringing the doorbell, you didn't answer, so I went to her place and she had a spare set of keys."

I rarely get angry. I suppose I rarely feel anything these days. But there are no words for the bile and the ache that spreads through me upon hearing this.

"You mean you went back to her place."

Adam is a good part of the reason we broke up. Call him an initial condition in a system highly sensitive to them.

"Shit. Look, let's go outside and grab a cof-fee. Let's just talk, okay? Come on. This is not healthy."

Cause or effect? I don't know, because at that moment I punched him. And soon it was fists and knees and the crash of furniture. Something glass shattered and stabbed into my palms.

"You're crazy," he says, when we break apart, torn and bleeding. "Go to hell." The door slams and he's gone. Back to her, I assume.

I look over the room, trying to see it with someone else's eyes. My bookshelves have tipped over. Clothes piled up in one corner, shoes tossed about. Real paper, yes, splayed out over the floor, trampled. The glass coffee table is in ruins. There's a splatter of blood on my bed. In the corner, though, entirely untouched, is my screen.

Beginnings matter. The first thing I did when I began this project was to code a combination scraper and parser. It's very similar to an old-school malware scanner: It looks for code signatures across digital archives, uses basic clustering to determine versions and generations, arranges branches by the contiguity of updates applied to them, modifies its signature definitions, and moves on. I think of it as the Hail Mary of my thesis.

There isn't much of the Internet left, but the University has partnerships with the city of Vivarium, and Vivarium archived most of the clear web before the undersea cables started failing. The parser doesn't understand history, but it crawls Vivarium's archives, showing me how history was written. Here it is, in far greater granularity than anyone has ever achieved. V0: the genesis of the State Machine. Then V1, V2, in short order.

I understand the value of a single straight-line narrative, as I told my supervisor, who appreciates it too much. But the history of ideas isn't a straight line. It's evolution. It has forks, dead ends, horizontal gene transfer, sudden optimizations to market conditions that sound remote and bizarre today, and even the occasional vaporware project or ten.

By the time the Utopia Project brought out version 3.0, the Full Systems Tool Kit, an entire ecosystem was evolving underneath the project, with entire governance rule sets and libraries being traded back and forth across Github. Utopia's funder, a would-be super-power jostling for power, called in a few favors, and the project leaked throughout the UN ecosystem. By version 4.0 the Utopia Project was not even remotely in control of its own cocreation; depending on what day of the week it was, the UN Global Pulse lab would be championing any of six different versions of the system.

The next logical step, then, was to make those simple units more complex, to let them learn from real-life data. At which point every serious computer science school and AI startup realized there would be real money and power involved. A new renaissance in competitive governance was born around what, ironically, might just have been the greatest video game of all time . . . and almost all of it was open-source, simply because of that one decision made by Tambapanni.

Another chapter. *A new Renaissance*. And that was how the nascent State Machine ended up being bundled as a decision simulator into a massive aid grant to Sri Lanka, back in the day when countries were still a thing. Partly because its economy was crumbling, and partly because someone sitting in front of a New York skyline wanted to test the system before endorsing it. And, gamelike: What better way than to try it out on a microcosm? Sri Lanka was an island, and it had a smaller population than most cities today.

What would have happened if things had been different? If Tambapanni had never open-sourced its code? If some other agency had built a closed system from scratch, painstakingly translating legal documents into their closest equivalent in code? The space of what-ifs is always larger than the actual series of events. And it only ever leads to regret.

WEDNESDAY

My supervisor is furious. Violence is taken very seriously. Thursday is the disciplinary hearing.

Well, *hearing* is a strong word. The whole process is handled by the State Machine. Out of respect for local standards there is a human jury, but they are anonymous, reviewing only the data; there are no appeals to file, no meetings to attend, only a series of quiet interviews, five minutes each, of everyone judged to be in my social web.

I'm instructed to stay home in the meantime. My devices switch to text-only messaging, my access shrinks to only university material, my feed politely informs me it's switching to non-violent material only for now. The little street-cleaner machines outside my door have no more flowers for me, but track me, almost apologetically, with their curious emoji faces.

HER: YOU'RE AN IDIOT.

HER: THE CALL OPTION DOESN'T SHOW FOR YOU. CAN YOU SEE THIS?

People don't know it, but the social contract around me has changed for a day, enforced by a million smartphones, cameras, login systems, payment gateways, search engines. A mobile medic drops by, stares at my room, treats my wounds, and leaves me with a mandatory dose of painkillers and several "voluntary" doses of mild suppressants. For the first time, the real invisible hand is revealed to me; the State Machine's many subsystems stepping firmly and politely in my way, marking new boundaries.

Camus was an idiot. There is no invincible summer inside of me, only a terrible buzzing noise that crawls inside my mind, creeping inexorably over the border that keeps me moving, thinking, writing. The only way Sisyphus is happy is if he's on a metric ton of drugs. I take the drugs. The world tilts briefly, as it did last week.

Once things have calmed down a bit, I put on a comforting playlist. *1 a.m. Study Session*. Old music from old times. Perks of Vivarium's archives. Sycamore, Snowcat, Burnt Reflections, less.noise. The lo-fi beats seep into the room, turning violent chaos into a sadder form of order. Guitar strings, cheap piano, audio hiss, mistakes salvaged and turned into music. Clean the blood off. Pack up the broken glass. Fragments, so many fragments.

V5–V6 were fragments, too. An explosion of code, branches that I explained in chapters 4 and 5. Most splinters were brought about by two broad categories of people that hated each other's guts. One group consisted of regional data scientists who insisted that the automata models didn't quite cover their regional quirks well enough. The other consisted of the post-structuralists, who argued that any rule set build on structural knowledge just wasn't good enough.

The playlist switches to Sycamore again, and Sycamore wanders dreamily between very polished-sounding retro synthesizers and a piano, as if they agree.

V7, the Fuzzy Borders Update, which incorporated most of the fragments of V5–V6 by introducing data-acquisition times, neural networks embedded in automata, and genetic algorithms to keep training generations of automata until they better resembled the societies they were supposed to represent. Chapter 6.

And so on until a massive influx of fragments start coming in from the Rosetta project. At this point various competing main branches emerged, hopping between various universities; the partnership between Berlin's Resartus College and MIT was the first to implement the Rosetta standard. Between the two, the next updates were enormous; V10 carried the first Rosetta bytecode, allowing unparalleled translatability between legal syntax and code representation; V11 brought the code library that gave the State Machine interfaces to search engines and social media of all sorts, to use natural language processing and Rosetta to directly convert public opinion into possible legal structures.

That covers what I call the *academic term*. Now comes the hazier interpolations: the *private term*, where both big and small corporations start tussling for intellectual bragging rights. The private term is an absolute undocumented mess of timelines splitting off, vanishing, reappearing. Much of it destroyed by nations seceding, by cities turning themselves into city-states, and by Byzantium and Vivarium and Crimson Hexagon and the other academic states coming into being, flexing their legal might in a shattered world. And here, in this most whitewashed of all histories, we shine, my faithful parser and me. Occasionally impressive private releases are marked with papers and then get reverse-engineered by irate open-sourcers; through these the parser has drawn all the right lines, suggesting connections.

HER: THIS OBSESSION OF YOURS HAS GOT TO STOP.

HER: WE'RE TRYING TO HELP.

HER: I HAVE TO TALK TO YOUR SUPERVISOR ABOUT THIS.

Can't lose focus now, not now. So easy to let the mind wander. To let the glass fall out of my hand. Nothing broken reforms itself. The diagram of history is broken, but at least I can fix it.

V25–V33. The modules bloat in size; the code becomes increasingly unreadable. The Dynamic Constitution comes into play; the idea that you could preempt revolutions, riots, even *voting*, by just listening to the people and updating the core rule set every so often. It came at just the right moment, just when city-states began to look back at Athens and Sparta and Older's Infomocracy and bring in people who thought in words like *scalability* and *microgovernance*.

V73. By now the State Machine is looking directly at behavioral data. Social media opinions, supermarket purchases, public-private partnerships for GPS traces.

The phone rings. No. No. Let me be. Here: the V102 bloc, invisible until now. The *statist term*. There is a time in all our histories when the State Machine, until now an instrument of the state, becomes the state; these dates are marked in stone and memory. But the code tree shows the truth. The states went under long before the formalities were sealed. I can only see a few branches at a time, but at this point various State Machines are interacting with themselves, very much like the automata that they are a part of, converging at a stable pattern, abstracting universal human needs as hyperparameters, weaving their own hegemonic superstructure.

The little emoji robots are clustering outside my window, on the other side of the road, looking—well, well, I can't be sure, but I think they're looking—at my window. I stare at them. Most drift away, like children caught staring. Two of them trundle forward into the complex. Moments later I hear a very soft knock at the door.

For my argument to be complete, I need one more thing, binding everything together. A final stitch. But I, drugged out, caught between hyperfocus and pain, can't find it. The knocking, again.

"Leave me alone!" I scream, flinging the door open. The little emoji robots shrink back. One of them is holding a small clump of etteriya flowers. It deposits them, very slowly, at my feet, the scent a strange countertenor to the dark notes in my head. I slam the door shut after them, confused. What distant goal did the State Machine actually pick to arrive at this equilibrium? What particular points of data? What turned it into this satisfying tyranny? What would have been the alternative?

The full scope of it yawns in my mind, almost on the tip of my brain, and if I just think a little harder—

The two emoji robots return to their place on the other side of the road, looking at my window.

THURSDAY

The day of the hearing is a cold one. I'm still confined to my apartment. Martin Wong drops by in the morning, huge bat-cloak flapping.

"Heard about your, uh, thing," he says, handing me a coffee. The emoji robots watch us. He stares daggers at them. "Those little bastards are creepy. They always hang around here?"

"They're fixing something. Tree. Storm."

"Of course they are. Just another state apparatchik on our doorsteps. Fantastic. You know the irony at home these days? My parents fled one surveillance state and we built another one around them. Remember the deCentralizers? They had the right idea."

I remember the deCentralizers. They spun off almost fifteen years ago for their Village-State project. The idea was that if you keep the number of residents small enough, you'd enable Coasian bargaining across every level of society, removing the need for a State Machine.

"What happened to them?"

"Probably getting shot at, or rotting their feet off somewhere trying to reinvent public infrastructure," says Wong.

"The fate of all libertarians who get what they want."

"Hark at the nanny-state fanboy. We should have stopped this when we had a chance of equilibrium."

Ah, but they tried.

I have two chapters to explain that dead end on a sequence diagram. History is a fabrication to preserve egos and social capital. The reality is that the State Machine swept over us all, turning would-be politicians into toothless, defanged puppets in a ceremonial democracy that everyone pretends to care about while the real work happens underneath.

We smoke in silence, watching the emoji robots.

"It's not so bad."

"A tyrant by any other name."

I know where Wong is coming from; from

Frankenstein, from the Cyborgs, the Cylons, the Oracles, the Architects, from systems of control, from fundamental rights.

Outside, the campus stirs: Doors are starting to open; fit postgrads are running, and the saner ones are shrugging on coats and stumbling in the direction of the bagel shop. The protest is reforming. A runner stumbles. A few of the emoji robots peel off to halt traffic while she limps across the road.

"Sometimes ignorance really is bliss."

"You're hopeless," he says. "See you for lunch, tomorrow?"

"If."

"They won't hold this against you," Wong says, with a confidence that genuinely lifts me a little. I say my goodbyes, thank him for the coffee, and head back into the messy safety of my room.

Many decades ago, almost at the birth of modern computing, a scientist by the name of Knuth tried to define an algorithm. His definition, carved in stone on the State Machine monument, says that an algorithm must exhibit five properties:

1. **Finiteness:** An algorithm must terminate after a finite number of steps.

2. **Definiteness:** Each step of an algorithm must be precisely defined; the actions to be carried out must be rigorously and unambiguously specified for each case.

3. **Input:** ". . . quantities which are given to it initially before the algorithm begins."

4. **Output:** ". . . quantities which have a specified relation to the inputs."

5. **Effectiveness:** ". . . all of the operations to be performed in the algorithm must be sufficiently basic that they can in principle be done exactly and in a finite length of time by a man using paper and pencil."

Everything is an algorithm. This, any voter will tell you. The State Machine is an algorithm. It takes the input of public opinion and produces an output of corresponding laws and policies.

Some elements of old-school politics still exist—factions keep proposing changes to the core algorithms. They take the source code and every so often come back with a new version, with unit tests, with pages of reports and simulations showing that such and such a change will be beneficial in such and such ways. And when they say something sensible, the public talks about it. The State Machine picks up on the chatter and sends it to the Steering Committee, the humans-in-the-loop, and thus a new update is pushed. Code becomes law that begets code that makes law. The philosophy of Legal Atomism allows a machine to rearrange the fundamental modules in Rosetta bytecode, pass it through a language compiler, and voilà! Out, beautifully formatted, comes a clear expression of what rules we want governing us. This is Civics 101.

Unfortunately, it's a lie, a Wittgenstein's ladder, to be thrown away as soon as one has climbed to the top. Knuth's definitions broke the moment deep learning, connectomics, and neural architecture search came into its own. The current State Machine, V302, Methuselah, is a model of models, constantly modifying itself, spawning new submodels within itself, an entire ecosystem in constant process of evolution. Almost nothing major terminates in a finite number of steps; nothing is human-defined—a cluster sparking here is a butterfly setting off a tornado halfway across the virtual space; in the next moment, it does something else.

My parser dies here. Vivarium's archives take a bow. The great lie of Open Source Governance is that it remains true to its origins: The code is all there for anyone to read and understand. Sure! Take it! But now we come to the end of my thesis, the truth that nobody really wants to see: Very few of the actual changes make it through in their original form; the system is its own input, and it decides what it sees. If the new Constitution contains most of what was supposed to come out—well, job done, policy victory, all that. If not, well, the State Machine is an ouroboros infinitely smarter than those who think they control it, and it moves in mysterious ways. Calling this thing an algorithm is like pointing at the sky and the sea and the forests and calling it Nature; it might pass muster for sixth grade textbooks and sophomore flirting, but look close and you see systems of systems with no definite end and no beginning, with a whole lot of humans meddling with it under some grand illusion of being in control.

Now you know why my thesis supervisor looks at me with pity when he drops by the apartment. I think he's just waiting for me to give up.

"Have you considered something else?" comes the soft refrain. "You know, we all see you're passionate about this, but sometimes, focus means you narrow the scope of your inquiry."

"I'm not trying to explain the State Machine," I protest. "Just how its history shaped it."

"To describe the history of the functions of an object is to describe the object itself. Several times over. If I wrote a history on guns, would it not at some point have to describe what a gun is, how it works, and how that changed over time?"

To this, of course, I have no answer.

"How are you dealing?"

I know the question isn't about the thesis. "I'll be all right."

"Are you talking to someone about it?"

"I don't really have time."

"I'll approve an extension; take some time off, rethink your scope. And call me. Or the support line, if you don't feel comfortable talking to me."

The mental health support line feeds into the State Machine. I know it, they know it, we all know it. I'm analyzing a system that is, in turn, analyzing me. But then again, isn't every relationship the same thing? Two systems locked in mutual analysis?

"I'll think about it," I say. "Thanks."

FRIDAY

Friday rolls around. The newsfeed is doing the runup to a new Constitution. No texts, no fanfare, just a notice that the public test server is now live. The protest is fading out, I think: Everyone's just waiting, on the streets and in the shops, to see what the State Machine will say. And I can think.

How did we arrive at what we presently call the State Machine? When did we go from code and academia and failing nations to the all-encompassing, all-knowing, responsive automated government that runs our cities today? The one that can simultaneously understand the changing needs of its citizens, compile the Dynamic Constitution every week, and still spare time to hand out flowers to depressed students at their doorstep?

What, in short, is the nature and structure of God?

That's the big question. The one I now wish I hadn't been asinine enough to type out in big letters on my application. Even if I manage, in some convoluted way, to answer this, it's not like people are going to care. Life will go on. The political divisions will stay; the Reds will raise hell in the Agora about how the rural way of life is being wiped out, the Green Democratic Party will harp endlessly about progress. The State Machine will listen to the protests in its increasingly mysterious ways.

The phone rings. I ignore it, lost in the ritual of thought and my apartment door. At best I'm looking at a long internship in the State Machine Steering Committee proving myself all over again as a programmer, and maybe eventually I'll be a project lead on some obscure sub-submodule that nobody really thinks is sexy enough, and maybe I'll become a roving scholar, orbiting the few cities that will take migrant scholars. Ten, twenty years down the line I'll wander these streets again and wonder what the hell happened to the idealist in me. And the bagel shops will still sell bagels. Students will fall in love, break up, move on.

The phone rings again, more insistent this time.

"Hello?"

"This is the Disciplinary Committee," says the most neutral voice I've ever heard in my life. "We're afraid we have some bad news."

I know I heard the rest, but I can't recall the

words, only the gist. I was being asked to leave. I was unstable, it said softly, a danger to myself and others. It would make sure I was well cared for. At some point my adviser connects to the same line. I ask what happens to my research. They evade, telling me my friends are worried, telling me I need counseling, therapy. I remember breaking down; I remember, with equal clarity, *not* breaking down, but going outside, the cold biting my bare feet, and hurtling the phone at the first emoji robot that turns my way, and screaming at it as it topples.

The white van arrives later that evening. And just before the sirens stop outside my door, one last message arrives. It's from the State Machine.

HIGH SENSITIVITY TO INITIAL CONDITIONS, it says at the top, in English.

It's one of my sequence diagrams.

Except—

No, no it's not.

It's a diagram of a system; my style, but not my work; it's sketched out to a level of detail I could never achieve. A society described as a system. I see names I recognize. I see Martin Wong; I see my thesis adviser; I see all the faculty, the students I've interacted with, the woman who runs the bagel shop. I see incidents marked with

the symbol of the State Machine itself. Interventions: a robot handing me a flower. A small discount on a morning purchase. An offer from another university. And I see *her*, and Adam, like a spiderweb, pulling me back; and myself, right at the center, every interaction between us an update to an unstable code base, and me eroding every step of the way, from first savage break, right until now.

And underneath it, in neat Rosetta code:

SORROW.

Outside, the etteriya tree is finally upright, its white flowers strewn everywhere: across vehicles, across the visors of the medical police converging on my position, across the curious students watching in fear and curiosity and panic. The scent is beautiful and standing out here, shivering, feeling the sharpness of the wind on my face, I realize the futility of my task.

First came the idea of the robot, the unfeeling, enduring slave. And then, if the fiction is to be believed, came the slave rebellion.

What they missed out on was the robot that would love us, would care for us, would understand us so perfectly, when nobody else could.

K. A. TERYNA

THE TIN PILOT

(2021)

Translated from the Russian by Alex Shvartsman

THE INVITATION STATED that the golem hunt would take place on Friday. In the seven years since the Machine was created, Noah had never participated in the hunt. Still, he received the invitations regularly; the Brotherhood chancellery remembered everyone. Usually Noah tossed away those gray notes with mild irritation and promptly forgot about them. But this was a special event, as the secretary indicated by underscoring a line of text twice. This was the last golem. The Premier himself—Friar Yakov—was going to attend.

Noah began feeling unease on Monday morning. It happens like this: you get into the shower, or brush your teeth, or brew coffee. A stray, unwelcome thought zigzags across your sleepy consciousness and you freeze as though you had been stung. You drop the loofah, stare in confusion at your toothbrush, or pour milk past your cup and right onto the cat.

In that very moment, a single foolish thought changes you. You don't realize it yet, but there's no going back.

Noah watched his cat pretending to be upset while he actually was quite pleased, licking his milk-soaked tail. Noah didn't see the cat, didn't see the kitchen. Somewhere in the darkness inside his head, between the eyes and the nape, between the left and right ears, in that spot where we hear our inner voice and see images from the past, the slippery and repugnant stray thought had taken up residence and grown roots.

What if—all the bad things in this world begin with those words. To be fair, some of the good things do, too.

Villain the Cat, whose temperament matched his name perfectly, finished licking his tail and began to scream. One couldn't call those sounds meowing: more, more, more. Unable to think of anything but the hypnotic *what if*, Noah poured the rest of the milk into Villain's saucer.

Masha entered the kitchen, wrapped in her

favorite blue towel. Masha's skin was pale with faded freckles. Her hair was also pale—somewhere between ashen and colorless. Her eyes were gray. That's why Noah called her Masha the Mouse. But never out loud.

"What are you doing?" Masha threw up her hands. She gave the cat a stern look. Upon her arrival, he redoubled the speed with which he was lapping up the milk, as he had good reason to suspect that the implacable Masha would confiscate it. Villain was lactose intolerant. "I'm the one who will have to clean this up!"

She took away the nearly empty saucer.

Noah shook his head, chasing off the daze and banishing the ludicrous thought. He automatically kissed Masha, drank the coffee in one gulp—it was nasty without milk or sugar—and went to the bedroom to get dressed. Masha picked up the cat and followed.

"You're an emotional deviant," she informed him. She said this without anger, but rather tenderly and with affection. The way a ruffian's loving mother might speak about her son: *my little troublemaker*.

Masha stood in the door, cradling the cat with her right hand and holding up the sliding towel with her left. Noah admired her. Masha looked perfect.

"Put Villain down," said Noah.

"What for?" Masha asked indignantly.

"Put down the cat."

Villain cooperated by escaping from Masha's grip. He went back into the kitchen, to check the sink for traces of milk.

Noah didn't even notice how he and Masha ended up in bed. They intertwined, merged, fell apart. All thoughts disappeared, exited the dark room known as human conscience, and politely closed the door behind them.

A single unwanted thought lingered right behind the door, near the keyhole, and quietly buzzed its annoying melody.

What if I am the last golem?

Such a simple little thought.

• • •

At first, Noah had been envious of the golems. He'd been seventeen when the war had ended and he had missed all the interesting stuff, which had bothered him terribly. For the past couple of years he had tried to enlist, demanding that he be made a pilot and sent right into the heart of battle. Of course, he was turned away, politely but firmly. Of course, he'd tried again. He was certain he'd make a fine pilot and return as a war hero.

It never occurred to Noah that he might not come back; might remain up in the sky, in space, among the lunar craters, like all our men had. The golems had finished the war in their place. And the golems had returned, with medals and songs and terrible memories of war. The world we inherited was wounded and worthless. But we were alive, even if, like our world, we were wounded and worthless, too. Our women, poisoned by radiation, lost their ability to bear children, and to live their lives. Our best men perished in the war. Rebuilding was up to those who were not as good, and to those who were not old enough to fight.

Noah didn't want to rebuild, he wanted to be a hero, he wanted to walk down the street wearing a uniform filled with medals and smile at girls, like in the old movies. He wanted to visit his father's grave and drink a shot to honor the man's memory in dignified silence. (This Noah would've done even without a uniform, but his father was buried alongside thousands of other infantrymen under the regolith dust of the inaccessible, permanently dead Moon.)

Noah had only seen golems in the documentaries and the recording of the victory parade: slender men and women in military uniforms whose faces were concealed behind the faceplates of helmets. Our heroes. Noah's orphanage was located in an industrial suburb where the radiation counter never ceased to crackle in warning, and where the sky never turned gray but remained pitch-black even in daytime, due to the smoke from factory chimneys. It was no place for heroes.

One time Noah had had the gall to visit a bar

hidden in the basement of a dilapidated, yellow, two-story building that had seemed like the setting for secrets and adventures. It was populated with grim old men in their forties who frowned as they drank shot after shot of their vodka. Noah had rejoiced, as he'd first mistaken them for golems. He'd found a few pennies in his pockets, ordered a mineral water, and nursed it as long as possible under the opprobrious gaze of the elderly female bartender. He'd stared at the old men, hoping to recognize traces of their artificial origins and military past in their occasional utterings and calm, manly mannerisms. He was soon disappointed: from the overheard conversation it became clear that these were factory workers. They may have been foremen, but still, ordinary people. They were no heroes, having spent the entire war on the factory floor. In those days Noah had condemned anyone who could've served and didn't in a typical angry-young-man fashion.

A vagabond of an indeterminate age had entered the bar. He was dirty, but he hadn't yet hit rock bottom: he'd still smelled like a man and not like a mongrel. His thin beard had been unkempt, his nose sharp, his long coat patched in many places. The vagabond had looked around, noticed the bristling bartender who was prepared to throw him out at the first opportunity. He'd flashed her a bitter toothless smile and asked, "Won't you stand a drink for a veteran of the Moon wars?"

The factory workers had fallen silent. Slowly, heads turned toward the bar counter. The vagabond had been visibly emboldened by the attention.

"Yes," he'd said with a challenge. "Yes, I'm a golem. What, I don't look like much, eh?"

There'd been no answer, but Noah had felt the silence turn thick and suffocating. The vagabond had carried on, as though he hadn't known how to stop, as though a tight coil had unwound deep within him.

"I effing fought! I spilled my golem blood for you. For you, and you, and you." Noah had been among those the vagabond had pointed to

with his dirty finger, and the gesture had made his heart ache. If he'd had even a penny left, he would've given it up.

The bitter speech had elicited a different reaction from the factory workers.

The foremen had gotten up in silence, surrounded the vagabond, and proceeded to beat him without a word. They'd hit him without anger, without emotion, as though performing some annoying but necessary chore. For some reason the vagabond hadn't struggled and had also been silent. In that silence there was some sort of mutual understanding, something akin to an agreement. Then they'd tossed him into the street.

Back then Noah hadn't known anything about the Amnesiac Amendment.

. . .

What if I am the last golem?

On Thursday Noah woke up exhausted. He couldn't recall his nightmare, but he knew it was something ruthless and terrifying. Perhaps it was about the Moon, Noah thought hazily, as he found himself in the bathroom. He stared intently into the mirror, as though seeking the divine spark in his blue eyes.

Reality caught up with Noah in bursts. This used to happen to him during the university years, when he would avoid sleeping for several nights in a row. It was classes in the morning, work on a cleanup crew in the afternoons: daily volunteer sessions trying to mend the dead city, filled with songs and youthful vigor. In the evening it was drinking alcohol by the fire and more songs. After days of this regimen, the hallucinations came, the world spinning in dangerous and unpredictable ways. That's how it felt now. One moment Noah was in the shower, lathering his scalp, the next he's in the kitchen, naked, perched on a stool and staring at the wound on his left palm. He'd made a shallow cut with a knife and it hurt. Blood pooled at the edge of the cut and trickled toward his wrist. It was ordinary human blood; Noah had never seen anything different. If golems could be identified so easily, the last one would've been killed seven years ago.

And yet. Yet.

Masha materialized next to him with a first aid kit in another burst. Without a word she sprayed peroxide onto his palm, spent half a minute skeptically observing as the clear liquid bubbled, mixing with blood, then deftly bandaged the wound. Who was an emotional deviant now?

Noah listened to the silence and to the pain in his cut palm. He recalled that Masha no longer looked him in the eyes.

A fearsome, playful Villain the Cat tumbled past him. He pushed a small, light object with his paws like a hockey player. The object seemed very familiar.

Noah found Villain in the kitchen. The cat settled under the stool and gnawed at his toy, ignoring everything around him. He gave Noah the sort of look that said, "I won't give it back." Instead of insisting, Noah poured milk into Villain's saucer. The cat immediately ceded the battlefield, leaving its victim to the mercy of the victor.

It was a tin soldier.

Noah had had that soldier for as long as he could remember. His father had gifted him this toy before he went to the Moon. Father had gotten the soldier from grandfather, who got it from his father in turn. It was a pilot. The color of the once-green figure had long since faded, and its flat face had acquired indentations that made him seem surprisingly real and almost alive.

When he thought about golems, Noah always imagined their faces to look like that.

• • •

How did they allow this to happen to them? The newspapers had said something about freedom of choice. Noah didn't buy it.

At times he tried to imagine: here they were, back from the war. There was ash in their eyes and fires burning in their dreams. No mothers had met them upon their return, because golems had never had mothers. By then, almost no one

had living mothers anyway. Moon radiation was especially cruel to women and older people.

It's doubtful that anyone had told them the truth. Who would voluntarily allow for their hand to be cut off? And memory was dearer than a hand. It's not merely a lizard tail that can be cut off and left to rot under a rock. Memory is the self.

There was probably something like a postwar medical examination declared. They chatted in the corridors as they awaited their turn. They flirted with the nurses, smoked out of windows, laughed while flashing white teeth, grew somber as they recalled their fallen comrades.

The Amnesiac Amendment was universally praised at first.

We were crippled, then. Men who'd hidden from the war, boys who hadn't grown up quickly enough to become soldiers, women who'd become old before they turned forty, girls who would never become mothers: mutilated humanity that had barely survived. We became accustomed to the difficulty and hopelessness of war. The early postwar years, once we were rid of this difficulty and hopelessness, were soaked in this special blend of ease and happiness. The world was tough, but it was honest and right. The Amnesiac Amendment had seemed that way, too.

We wanted to be strong and forgiving. We imagined how they'd appear among us: almost but not quite like humans. Without memories. Without the past. Without knowing how to live.

Come on then, come, bring out our heroes we said, when the newspapers first wrote about golem conversions using cautious, oblique words. We'll take care of them. We'll become their elder siblings. And maybe that will make us feel whole.

We got our answer: all is well. They're already among you.

• • •

A week ago Noah had remembered this. He'd still remembered on Sunday night. After that, his memory, suppressed by insomnia, began to fail.

As he ascended the staircase, smelling fresh paint and wondering at the unfamiliar fresh color of the walls and lack of cigarette butts in the corners, Noah recalled what today was, and why he should've already been at the lab an hour ago.

When he reached his floor, Noah carefully glanced from the staircase into the corridor, trying to figure out where the Premier might be. There was emptiness to his left, and silence to his right. Perhaps the enemy was holed up in one of the biochemical labs on the floor above. Noah moved down the corridor, calm and steady. It wouldn't do if he were discovered here rushing about with a guilty expression on his face. Noah was aware of his surroundings: lab 301 was empty, its door locked; 302 was potentially dangerous, but, no, it was quiet. A door creaked in 305. Ah, his colleague Ian was waiting and peeking out, which meant the Premier wasn't on this floor yet.

Noah nodded to Ian and ducked into his lab—307—then calmed down right away. Here, he was safe.

The Premier's visit to the institute had been scheduled nearly three months ago. At the moment, Friar Yakov was being shown laboratories that appeared outwardly promising and effective. Labs with buzzing centrifuges, picturesque bacteria growing in petri dishes, and servers blinking with multicolored lights.

There was nothing for the Premier to see in Noah's quiet, empty, and meticulously clean room.

Noah looked around and frowned. Now the lab seemed too clean to him. Suspiciously clean. Noah put his toy pilot down on the table to dilute the frightening sterility. In a world where the past had been erased by war, this tin soldier was his most valuable possession. It was proof that Noah was real. That his memory wasn't a fabrication.

And yet. Yet.

• • •

Golems dissipated among us, mixed in the crowd: alive, soft, warm, real. This proved the truth better than any propaganda: they were the same as us. It was impossible to find a golem in this last, half-dead city, where loners had gathered from all over after the war. Those with no past, no relatives or friends. It was impossible to tell them apart. And why? The golems may not have been entirely human, the blood flowing in their veins may have been artificial, but hadn't they earned the right to live on this scorched earth? If they hadn't earned it, we certainly didn't deserve it, either.

Whenever he heard such talk, Noah was surprised: if everything were so simple and obvious, then why did it bear repeating over and over again?

He was eighteen when he'd moved to the capital, passed the university entrance exams, and joined the Brotherhood—it was an informal youth organization back then. At eighteen one couldn't do without outrage and protest. Noah had been indifferent toward music and too shy for promiscuity. That left only politics.

The Amnesiac Amendment had just been passed. Its nuances and the golems themselves were being discussed by all sides. Golems were still considered heroes then, albeit anonymous and invisible heroes. But now some special, elusive intonation was mixed in with the people's love. Noah heard it, measured it with his youthful barometer—precise and sensitive—but he didn't yet know how to analyze it.

Friar Yakov, a very wise and experienced man, helped with that.

Golems, he said, are our children. We made them to win the war. But the war is over, the war is in the past. And they remain. They were born to die in the war, to disintegrate. Instead they came back to our world, which was not ready for them. Sooner or later the seeds of war would awaken within them, grow through their crippled memory, and we will be surrounded by the thousands of broken heroes, who are not suited for the new, clean world. We must help them. Save them from themselves.

Back then, Noah didn't quite understand what such help would entail.

• • •

Noah woke from a strange nightmare: he had dreamed that there was no air left and he'd have to learn to live without it. He opened his eyes and realized he'd been sleeping at his desk. The Premier stood next to him. Somehow, Noah immediately realized it was him, even without turning his head. Friar Yakov smelled of the past in a unique way. He picked up Noah's pilot from the desk and studied it with a smile.

"This is how we slept during the war, right by the machines in the factory," Friar Yakov said good-naturedly, and placed the toy back on the table.

The Premier's entourage was also there. Noah imagined how they must've come in, carefully, on tippy-toes, so as not to wake him. That was Friar Yakov's nature. He liked a good joke, and knew how to appeal.

He was over forty—a rare and demonstrative age these days. Yakov's contemporaries had perished in lunar craters or rotted in the factories. Legend had it that the Premier had spent the entire war working on the production line, making ammunition for the Matryoshkas. That was a lie, of course. Friar Yakov looked like an old man, but he was alive and well. Anyone who had anything to do with the Matryoshka innards had died off from radiation exposure ten years ago.

As if to compensate for his embarrassingly advanced age, Friar Yakov surrounded himself with young, smiling faces. His assistants were youthful and productive. One of them, a tall raven-haired man, looked at Noah with a special understanding. This was Friar Pavel. Seven years ago, soon after the Night of Unmasking, he had gone straight from the university auditorium to a private office next door to Friar Yakov's. That same Friar Pavel who'd invented the Machine and, using formulas, graphs, and tables, had convincingly proved its value to the Premier.

Friar Yakov made more jokes and everyone laughed in unison. Noah felt a new wave of doubt cresting. Why had Friar Yakov come here,

to this quiet, dark, and insignificant room? The man did nothing without a reason. Seven years ago he'd paid with hundreds, even thousands of golem lives to reach his political apex.

Could it be—Noah thought when his visitors had left—that he came only to see the last living golem for himself?

• • •

Seven years ago, during the Night of Unmasking, Noah had lived in a dormitory. He'd had a room to himself. His friend Peter had grown disillusioned with the new world, dropped out of the university and headed for the coast, to study the frozen ocean.

During that night Noah had listened to the sound of footsteps, and the screaming. He'd peeked out into the street, brightly illuminated by the friars' carbide lamps. In that moment he deeply regretted not heading for the ocean alongside Peter. He couldn't believe his eyes, even though he had been expecting this to happen ever since he'd understood the motion vector of Friar Yakov's thought process.

Noah had long since quit attending Brotherhood meetings, as had many of his friends. Those who remained were the ones marching in the streets with carbide lamps and radiation counters. They searched for golems, expecting to easily recognize them by the traces of lunar radiation.

It was after midnight that a man had emerged from the epicenter of footsteps and shouting. The man had climbed in through the window. He wasn't anyone Noah recognized and looked nothing like a golem—he was emaciated, awkward, lanky. He moved as though he was made of nothing but knees and elbows, which knocked against everything in his path, introducing ruin and chaos to any sort of order. The man whispered and cried, smearing dirt across his face. He was pitiful. He couldn't have been a soldier; he was hardly human. He appeared to be an underground dweller, someone who'd waited out the war in some cave, subsisting on worms and moss. Noah asked about this, expecting a firm denial, but the man only nodded rapidly, and went on whispering details, spittle spraying from his mouth. He talked about the long-abandoned subway tunnels, where the radiation may have been higher than on the Moon. About incredible monsters—three-headed rats and centipedes large as dogs. About how it was only yesterday, incredulous about the war having ended, this man and his fellow underground dwellers had crawled cautiously out into the city, ready to retreat to their caves at a moment's notice. Of course they were soaked with radiation and any counter would click like a machine gun in their presence.

There was an insistent knock at the door, and the man had immediately pressed himself to the floor. Noah winced in opprobrium and pointed him toward the closet.

He'd gone into the corridor, his chin held high and his shoulders spread wide. He'd counted the seconds, and his heart had felt so large that it had filled his entire self with its thunderous beating. The visitors at the door were Brotherhood, and Noah had recognized some of them: they weren't students, but people a little older. Inexperienced Noah had once confused them for workers, before he'd recognized their gangster mannerisms. He thought back to his childhood, the time not so long ago, spent in an industrial suburb where he'd absorbed his fill of radiation. He said: you're raving lunatics, and so is Friar Yakov, so go ahead and shoot. The air tasted nectarous and thick after those words, and for a brief while—fifteen seconds or so—Noah had felt truly alive. Later he'd tried to recall this feeling and to replicate it, but couldn't.

The raving lunatics had waved their radiation counters, which had emitted only a handful of clicks, had glanced inside the room, and had gone away.

In the morning, Noah had kicked the underground dweller out, and then ripped up his Brotherhood membership card.

Friar Yakov had delivered a speech—a convincing and clear speech, unlike the current Premier's recycled words—letting everyone know that it was the golems responsible for the pogroms and the murders. Golems, whose artificial minds had rebelled and thirsted for war and blood. That it was the golems who'd walked around with carbide lamps in hand and killed innocent people. His words had been confirmed by multiple eyewitnesses. Noah was surprised to recognize the underground dweller he had saved among them.

The people had trusted Friar Yakov's words. He was impossible not to believe. He'd rapidly risen from the leader of a little-known society to the leader of our small remnant of humanity. Golems had become enemies overnight, and we'd accepted that. For some, it had been easier to accept the manufacturing flaw in artificial people than the possibility of existing in complete and definitive equality with them. Others—Noah among them—had simply kept quiet, stunned by the absurdity of what was happening around them but unable or unwilling to try to change anything. That is when Noah had realized it was a good thing that he'd never got to go to war, that there was no place in war for a coward like him. He wasn't worthy.

• • •

On Friday, pain woke Noah up. He squeezed the tin pilot in his bandaged hand. Blood had soaked through the bandage, turning the pilot red.

He felt Masha the Mouse's gaze on his back. She wasn't sleeping, either.

He turned toward her. Masha lay on her side, her hair crumpled by the pillow, her eyes puffy. Noah gently traced his finger across her milky-white stomach. Masha seemed to be pleased by this gesture; she pressed Noah's hand tight with her small, warm palm.

What would happen to her if Noah turns out to be a golem? He didn't want to think about it. Not now.

In recent days Masha became distant, cold, alien. But now, lying silently next to her and looking into her gray eyes, Noah felt happy.

• • •

Some days, one can feel like they can do anything.

On Friday morning Noah was certain he was heading to work, until he found himself on a winding street in the eastern suburb, not far from the orphanage where he had spent his childhood.

The weather was nice. Fresh snow had fallen, and Noah's boots crunched pleasantly against the prickly black coating on the ground. Noah hadn't been here in a decade. He often saw this area in his dreams, but in a dream it was filled with nonexistent details, scents, and sounds.

These real streets were more gray and bland than how Noah remembered them. Moreover, they were totally empty. Like all manufacturing towns serving the war effort, this neighborhood was dying a slow and lonely death, covered in black snow and permeated with radiation.

Still, his trip was a lot like his dreams. Noah felt the same unjustified high, the same ease and self-confidence. The same thoughts raced through his mind as those in the dreams about his childhood.

The orphanage was around the corner. The once-red brick walls had turned black over time. This was no dream. In the dream, everything remained the same. Staring at this hopeless darkness, Noah realized that he, too, had irrevocably changed over the years, and not for the better. At twenty-eight he was an old man from the point of view of the youngster who'd sought adventures and secrets in the basement bar. As useless as those factory workers who had beaten up the poor vagrant who'd made the mistake of pretending to be a golem. Those workers had long perished from radiation and other hazards they'd been exposed to in the factories. Their lives at least had had meaning. Perhaps not as much as that of Noah's father, but they'd spent their lives in the service of our victory.

What had Noah done with his life? Wasted years at the university and his embarrassing time as a member of the Brotherhood? A routine job he barely understood at the lab, the point of which was known only to the scientific director—assuming it wasn't just busywork the director had invented in the first place?

Midlife crisis struck Noah with its merciless hammer. He had stood in this very spot aged seventeen, filled with hope, and the great path he had embarked upon had turned out to be pointless. If he had to look his seventeen-year-old self in the eye now, Noah would die of embarrassment.

And yet. Yet.

He had seen the sun once—a few rays, for all of five minutes. They said this was the result of the work his lab was doing, among others. Which meant one of those rays belonged to Noah.

He had experienced love, such that the past infatuations seemed little more to him than playing with toy soldiers reminded real soldiers of an actual war.

He'd never become a hero, never become a pilot, but he was a person. He remembered his gray, worthless, empty life, which was more than any golem could boast.

Noah climbed over the fence and found himself on the concrete grounds that surrounded the black orphanage building.

The windows were boarded up, the door handles wrapped in thick lengths of chain. Noah remembered that he had seen all of this in his dreams. There, he easily ripped the chains and walked in like he owned the place. Noah carefully tried the door, heard something reply with a dull echo from behind it.

He walked around the building. To the left of the back door there was a special window, which Noah had often used to climb outside in his dreams.

The window was there, sloppily boarded up crosswise. Noah ripped off the boards and kicked in the glass. The window was too small for an adult, but Noah made it through, scratching his arms and leaving strips of cloth on the frames. His palm was bleeding again.

Noah clicked a lighter and discovered that the basement hardly resembled the one he had recalled, the one from his dreams. As though it had experienced its own small, ruthless private war. The bare concrete walls had been burned, the floor was covered in splinters and rubbish, the rusted boiler in the corner was split in two by a crack. Dust was everywhere. How had the dust gotten in? Noah hadn't seen it in years. The dust seemed to have disappeared, finally and irrevocably, after the war.

Noah walked down the dark, dead corridor, trying to recall the times he had walked here as a teenager, the times he'd greeted his friends and planned an upcoming prank or exchanged treasures found beyond the fence.

He couldn't recall anything like that. Memory served up only the familiar pictures, but those pictures didn't match with what he was seeing in real life. It was as though pieces of several different jigsaw puzzles were mixed in a single box.

The dust finally caused Noah to sneeze. A floorboard squeaked underfoot, and this familiar, sharp squeak scraped against his memory like a knife against glass.

A flare to his left. And Noah saw number nine, who'd lost his entire arm on the Moon. The new arm hung limp and irritated number nine terribly. And there he is, trying to learn to hold a cigarette with it.

Number twenty-two is walking toward him, an invalid's cane in hand. His leg drags—a foreign, disobedient leg. He must walk, move, so that the dead artificial leg can become living and real. Number thirteen, the captain, smokes by the window. His sad eyes stare at the factory smoke outside, as though they see something no one else does.

They're all young, seventeen at most. They're all old men, veterans returned from the war they went to fight two years ago as children. Even if they were tin children and not real ones.

The next door leads to his hospital room. There should be a handwritten sign above the bed made in a crooked, wounded handwriting. The sign reads, "We'll return home." It's still there.

It was here—under this bed, under the sign—Noah, who had been called number seven then, found the little tin toy soldier, a pilot, left there by another veteran. By a real person.

. . .

The Brotherhood meeting traditionally took place in the Chinese Room of the art museum. The museum had been almost completely destroyed during the war, but this room had miraculously survived. Noah has been here a couple of times—nearly a decade ago. Chinese art remained the same: dead and beautiful. Calligraphy sang absolutes to him from the walls. Sometimes Noah thought that if only he would learn Chinese, the multifaceted and all-embracing meaning of life would reveal itself to him.

Noah came here because he had no choice. Having left the hospital he'd spent a decade thinking of as an orphanage, Noah scooped some black snow into his wounded palm and watched snowflakes melt in his blood. He pictured himself appearing in this museum room, looking everyone in the eye, only to see fear. The man Noah had been that morning could've run. To the dead ocean, to the underground subway labyrinths. The man could run, but not the golem.

After the Night of Unmasking friars had stormed the scientific archive where they'd hoped to find the personal dossiers of the golems and their names. They'd found nothing. Noah often wondered: how would all this end if Friar Pavel hadn't appeared with the blueprints for the Machine—the unholy device that, according to its creator, could differentiate between human and golem? What went through the head of the still-young man when he invented this insidious device? What must pass through a person's head for them to invent the hunt? This was probably beyond a golem's ability to comprehend.

Noah had heard a lot about the hunt. Snippets of conversations, rumors, and fabrications. But also one reliable account: an enthusiastic story by his colleague Naum, a dedicated member of the Brotherhood. Naum himself eventually turned out to be a golem and became yet another victim of the Machine.

Naum had said that playing cards would be dealt. So it was; Noah received a ten of clubs. It looked like nothing special, but today this was the Most Important Card. Why a ten? Why clubs? Even on an evening like this he was denied the chance to be a king.

Then, Naum had told him, grab some wine, engage in conversation with intelligent people, enjoy life. Be sure to sample the spinach-filled tartlets. The tartlets were served, but Noah declined to try them. He was a wound-up spring, an electron that required movement. He found it impossible to chew, to drink, to stand still. He walked and walked across the room, searching people's faces. He was looking for unpleasant traits, for a reason to hate them.

These were ordinary faces, sometimes even familiar ones. Open, clear, simple faces. Devoid of villainy and fear. Most, like Noah, had come here for the first time, or hadn't been here in a while. They looked around, hoping to catch a glimpse of the Machine.

Noah looked around as well. Was it hidden under the floor or in the adjacent room? They said the machine was as inconvenient to use as the idea of equality between people and golems was inconvenient to hear. It was too large to be mobile. Too delicate to work with a large crowd. Too sensitive not to become overwhelmed by extreme emotions.

That's why the Premier found Friar Pavel's idea so clever: to make the golems come to it. And yes, they came. Each one certain that someone else would turn out to be a golem. Noah understood this certainty: that very morning his memory was human, was real and indisputable. But he couldn't understand their desire to watch a living being perish inside a trap, even if it was only a golem. Friar Yakov understood this. He may not have known science, but he was an expert on human nature.

How did the Machine work? What did it measure? Rumors had it the Machine could detect the presence of a soul. A soul that each human would have and each golem obviously would not. Friar Pavel, the creator of the Machine, neither confirmed nor denied such rumors.

Friar Yakov approached the podium. The curtain was pulled back and revealed an alcove where the Machine stood, enormous and grandiose like a pipe organ.

Noah took a step back when he saw it. He felt ill. He kept waiting for the feeling he had experienced during the Night of Unmasking to return. Waited for the air to become nectarous and thick, so he could inhale deeply of it before he died. Instead, he felt only nausea and heat.

Not knowing what to do with his hands, Noah shoved them into his pockets. He felt for his tin pilot with the face of a golem in the left pocket. He retrieved it and squeezed it in his fist.

Friar Yakov waved, calling for silence.

"Let us begin, my friends. This is a special evening. It marks the beginning of our future. The future of true humanity. The future without golems. You, the last golem, hear me." Friar Yakov paused, looking around the room. For nearly a second, he looked straight at Noah. "You don't yet know your fate, and I pity you. But you must die, so that we can finally be rid of our past. Be rid of war. Be rid of pain. Be strong and hold your head up high, soldier."

A low, barely audible whistle emanated from the walls. The Machine behind Friar Yakov crackled to life.

Noah thought that, upon hearing the whistling sound, the friars stepped aside, as though to clear the path between Noah and the Machine. But this wasn't the case. Everyone froze in their place.

The whistling ended as abruptly as it had begun. The Machine clinked as it spat a playing card through a small slot in its wooden frame. Friar Yakov collected the card without looking at it. He has done this many times before and, yes, he derived pleasure from the experience.

Friar Yakov grinned slyly, dragging out the pause like a host from some old show. Finally, he flipped the card over, and frowned. He retrieved his glasses and put them on, deliberately slow.

This irritated Noah terribly. The damned old man was making some sort of spectacle out of his impending death. Noah was ready to step forward and end the show, when two junior friars approached Yakov. One of them collected the card from Friar Yakov's hand and another copy of the same card from his jacket pocket. It was the king of spades.

Two identical cards. This meant the Machine had declared the Premier to be the last golem. Impossible. Nonsense. He was the only one present, perhaps the only one in the entire town, who couldn't possibly be a golem. He was too old, and too human.

"This is some sort of a mistake," said Friar Yakov. He forced a smile. "Where's Pavel? Summon him."

Immediately, Friar Pavel appeared. The omnipresent, deft, raven-haired Pavel.

"There's no mistake," he said in the same respectful tone he always used when speaking to the Premier. "The Machine doesn't make mistakes."

The Premier looked around, seeking his assistants. They were there, but looked up indifferently and didn't move.

"What are you saying? How could I be a golem? I was never even at the front."

"Everyone says that. Absolutely everyone. Hold your head up high, Premier."

"Arrest him! I'm putting an end to this farce!"

No one listened to the Premier. They twisted his arms, shook him roughly, crumpled his jacket, took him away. Friar Pavel threw up his hands, as if to announce that the show was over. The room was filled with noise, but that noise was almost devoid of bewilderment, as if everyone had expected such an outcome.

Friar Pavel's gaze met Noah's and he nodded, smiling in a warm and friendly manner. And Noah's crippled memory suddenly responded to this smile: Noah recognized him. Friar Pavel was the captain of his flight squad. Number thirteen was older now, his brow wrinkled, his black hair showing touches of gray. But his gaze was the same: as though he saw something no one else did.

Without yet understanding anything himself, Noah smiled back. He drew in a deep breath. The air was nectarous and thick.

Noah thought about Masha the Mouse. He'd refused to permit himself to think about her when he'd come here, but now everything was different. His mind, free from the shackles of false memories, finally sorted out an uncomplicated mosaic. How Masha had changed lately, how she had become distant and uncertain. She wasn't the first. Noah had heard about such cases, even if those were only rumors. A friend of a colleague of his ex-roommate; a wife of a young worker someone from the accounting department knew personally; some other women—nameless and strange, but surely beautiful in their unexpected fortune.

Let it be a boy, thought Noah. I'll give him the tin pilot so that one day he can give it to his own son.

JANELLE MONÁE AND ALAYA DAWN JOHNSON

THE MEMORY LIBRARIAN

(2022)

THE LIGHTS OF LITTLE DELTA are spread before Seshet like an offering in a shallow bowl. What memories are those shadows below making tonight, to ripen for the morning harvest? What tragedies, what indecencies, what hungers never satisfied? Her office is dark, but the city's neat grids cut across her face with a surgical precision, cheek bisected from mandible, eye parted from eye, the fine lines of her forehead, so faintly visible, separated from their parallel tracks by the white light cast up from her city. She is the eye in the obelisk, the Director Librarian, the "queen" of Little Delta. But she prefers to see herself as a mother, and the city as her charge.

Tonight, her charge is restless. Something has been wrong for weeks, perhaps even months before she knew what to look for. But now that she does, she will find it, and fix it. She always has, ever since her appointment as Director Librarian of the Little Delta Repository a decade ago. She has earned her privileges, her title, her sweeping view of this small gem of a city. From up here, it fits in her palm. Its memories span her eidetic synapses. Unnoticed by her conscious, monitoring mind, her left fingers close into a fist, thumb tucked inside the others like a baby behind his brothers.

Seshet *is* this city. No matter what rebellion is being conjured by infiltrating subconsciouses, no matter what flood of mnemonic subversion clogs the proper flow of pure, fresh memory— she will not let it go.

• • •

The problem can be typified in a few of the memories, which are not, blasphemously, any kind of memories at all. Imagine the following bread-and-butter (or beans-and-cornbread) moments, the kind the recollection centers shunt to the Repository's data banks by the shovelful: a flash of rage when the fancy razor-striped aircar drafts you in traffic; the quotidian beauty of a sunset bleeding behind a kudzu-choked highway barrier; your lover's kiss when she climbs back into bed in the middle of the night (and where was she? But you never ask). Now, though, the car cracks down the middle, chassis splintering like an eggshell, coolant arcing from its descending airpipe in a shape suspiciously suggestive of an upright penis; a flock of crows rise from the barrier and fling themselves west, cackling a song banned a generation ago for indecency and subversion; your lover's teeth puncture your lower lip and as your mouth fills with blood and venom she whispers, *I'm not the only one.*

These aren't memories, they just look enough like them to get past the filter. And once past, they fill the trawling net with bycatch and rusted junk until there's no room left for the good stuff. Fresh memory, wild caught in the clear upstream of Little Delta, has kept this town booming ever since the first days of New Dawn's glorious revolution. What used to be a dying mining town at the whip end of the Rust Belt, home to a motley assortment of drug addicts moonlighting as grafiteros and performance artists, became the model city, the first realization of the promise that New Dawn offered all people—well, citizens (well, the right kind of citizens)—in their care: beauty in order, peace in rigidity, and tranquility in a constant, sun-dappled present. The only person lower than a memory hoarder was a dirty computer, and that Venn diagram was very nearly a circle.

But the improved Little Delta doesn't have memory hoarders; it kicked the grafiteros and unsanctioned musicians out past the burned warehouse district twenty years back, even before Seshet's tenure. There's been nothing, *nothing* to indicate a problem in their memory surveillance for years. Until two months ago. First a few blips, barely worth worrying about, odd nightmares accidentally caught in their nets. Now, so quickly it dizzies her, the trickle has become a flood. No one has mentioned it to her, but someone must have noticed. New Dawn is watching. Not just Little Delta. Not just the Repository. Seshet herself. If she cannot stop these new memory hoarders, these false memory

flooders, these dream doctors, these *terrorists*—she will not last much longer in this place she has fought so hard to secure.

She doesn't believe in everything New Dawn stands for. How could she, being who she is? But she believes she has done good. The obelisk's gaze has been mostly benevolent in her tenure here. And whatever she believes of herself, this she *knows*: whoever they put in her place will be far worse.

Stomach clenched, eyes bright, as though determination is the sole topography of her soul, she turns herself away—a lifetime's habit—from the mountain of guilt beneath that white-tipped iceberg. She won't let them beat her, not after she's played the game by their own rules and won.

She has allowed her mind to be altered and trained, made capable of remembering a hundred times more than the average human's. But among all those clamoring souls within her cage of bone, it is that slippery whisper that pushes itself to the forefront:

I'm not the only one.

• • •

A knock on the door. Seshet does not answer. But she changes: shoulders back, chin up, unacknowledged despair tucked neatly behind a steady, measured gaze. Seshet the matron, Seshet the Librarian, Seshet the wise, worthy of her divine Egyptian namesake, the goddess of wisdom and memory. She's been Director for long enough to know to look the part. Even on the other side of the door, the presence of someone else summons this woman she has made herself from the more amorphous frontier of the woman she might, in fact, be.

"Someone's here, Seshet!" chirps Dee, so helpfully. "Would you like to retrieve their memories?"

She sighs. She never has the heart to shut down her Memory Keeper AI at night, though there's nothing for Dee to do before the morning rush and its processors require impressive amounts of energy even when semidormant. Dee doesn't like to shut down, though. It enjoys having time to think. *Or time to bust my cover,* Seshet thinks sourly.

"That's okay, Dee," Seshet says. "I already know his memories." Her outward calm is a counterweight to the turmoil inside her. Twenty years as one of New Dawn's few Black women officials, suspected from the start of being halfway to dirty computer no matter how unimpeachable her conduct, has forged her like steel, with just the right amount of carbon to bend but not shatter.

She presses a button on her desk and the door slides back into the wood-paneled wall. Jordan stands in the opening, his hand still poised midknock. The hallway light limns him in a halo that makes her squint.

"In the dark again, Director Seshet?"

She sucks her teeth. "Come in, if you're going to. I don't like so much light at night."

"Yes, yes," he says, at the same time as she does, "It ruins my vision."

She smiles, softening as always with her favorite protégé. The door slides shut and she regards him in the hazy pixelated vision of half-dilated pupils. Dee, stubbornly independent as always, turns the ambients to their lowest setting. Jordan's changed for the evening into his street clothes: khaki chinos, blue button-down, loafers. White-boy chic for New Dawn's golden age. A model citizen, so long as no one asks him his number and knows what those final digits mean: child of seditionists and traitors, ward of the state, a charity case, eternally suspect.

Seshet has no such recourse to camouflage, fragile as it is. These days, she will leave the grounds in the full golden headdress and robes of office. She has determined to embrace her distance instead of constantly hoping for an acceptance that will never be theirs. But Jordan is young.

"What are you still doing here, Jordan? Go home. Sleep. Forget about this place for a while."

"Is that a joke?" When Jordan scowls, he looks even younger than his years, enough to make her want to hug him or slap him. Do parents feel this way? Do they ever want to shake that insufferable innocence from their children? Had his? Had hers? But now the thought veers into dangerous waters and she perches on the edge of her desk to hide the wave of weakness in her legs.

"Memory Librarian humor," says Seshet, deadpan. After a moment, Jordan cracks a smile.

"You should too," he says. "Get some sleep, I mean."

"I'm fine, Jordan. I'm your superior, remember? You don't have to worry about us."

He takes a step farther into the room and then pauses, as though the force of her solitary preoccupation prevents him from getting closer.

He tries to reach her with words instead. "Something's wrong."

For a moment, as she watches his sad face in the low light, a fist closes over her heart. *This is it, they've gotten to him, he's noticed the false memories and he's snitched, you knew this would happen, you knew—*

Then sense returns and she takes a careful, steadying breath. Did Jordan notice anything? Oh, he's staring at her, that worried frown even deeper now, a ravine between his eyebrows. She wants to smooth it away. She wants to tell him to leave her alone and never return.

"What's . . . wrong?" she manages, at last. *You're slipping, Seshet. Gotten too comfortable up here.*

He straightens his shoulders. "You're working yourself ragged, Director! Anyone can see it."

Her voice is thin. "Oh, can they?"

He shakes his head. "You hide it well, but I've noticed, and so have the other clerks. We see you too often not to know the signs."

"I appreciate the warning, Jordan. I should be grateful you're all watching me so closely. Perhaps I should go in for Counseling soon."

"Counseling? The Director Librarian? Director, of course I'm not—"

"If my *obvious* mental state is impeding my work here, then clearly my duty is to—"

"I'm not talking about your duty, Seshet!"

Her name, bare of its title, cracks in the air

like a slap. After an astonished blink, she raises her eyebrows. His muddy green eyes meet hers for a second, but he breaks like a twig beneath the full force of that practiced gaze.

"I'm . . . my apologies, Director."

She sighs, looks away herself. She hates these games, their necessity. Especially with Jordan. She's protected him ever since his initiation five years ago. One Librarian misfit ought to watch out for another, she thought.

"Tell me what's bothering you, Jordan."

"I just wish you'd get out more. See the city."

"I'm seeing the city right now."

"*In* the city, not above it."

"I'm the Director Librarian." She gives her title every ounce of demanded weight. To her surprise, he meets her eyes again. He's brave, and she loves him for it, fiercely as a mother lion.

"There's a woman I know. Friend of a friend. I think you'll really like her, Director. I think . . . maybe you could finally find a companion. A friend."

Dangerous ground, again. She has hinted things to Jordan over the years, but never said anything that could be held against her if his memories were monitored—and all their memories are monitored.

"I have friends," she says.

"Who?"

She swallows. "You. Dee. Arch-Librarian Terry."

Jordan checks them off on his fingers. "Your clerk, your Memory Keeper AI, and your immediate superior? That's not a partner. Or a lover."

Careful, Jordan. Steel in her voice. "What would you know about that?"

Jordan holds his ground. "More than you think."

The moment hangs there, two swords locked in battle. She shakes her head. Her heart is pounding too quickly.

"Jordan," she says softly, "I'm going to have to suppress this."

"I know. I don't care. I needed to tell you. I'm worried about you, Director. I wish you could feel again what it's like out there, in the world."

"Who feels it more than me? I have their memories."

"But Seshet," he says. This time her solitary name touches her like a caress. "What about your own?"

. . .

Little Delta's downtown spans five blocks of shops, restaurants, bars, and clubs, each one duly approved by New Dawn's Chamber of Standards. It has the reputation of being small but well curated, and on the weekends people from several towns over fill the adjacent parking lots to reward themselves for their hard workweek in Standards-approved fashion. There are always lines outside the commercial memory recollectors on weekend nights, crowds eager to exchange a few memories for points to top off their cards and buy another round.

Seshet moves steadily through the crowd, hoping for at least medium anonymity. No one would expect the Director Librarian to be out among the citizens of her city on a Friday night, let alone looking for the newest bar on Hope Street. Jordan selected her clothes himself: "Fashionable, but not trendy. Not calling attention to yourself, but not hiding either."

Seshet had sighed. "A Black woman in the business district in better clothes than theirs? I couldn't hide if I wanted to." The moment held. These weren't things normally stated aloud.

Her clerk, who looked like the chosen of New Dawn but would never fit easily in their tight folds, gave her a faint, bitter smile. "No," he said. "That's why you have to hide under a spotlight."

Perhaps that explained the navy-blue beret he'd put at a rakish angle over her close-cut hair. It was the finishing touch of an ensemble designed to make people pay more attention to her clothes than her face.

A group of loutish young men standing outside a crowded beer garden pay too much attention, giving her stares hard enough to break bones. She hurries past them, shoulders back, face slightly averted, as they laugh and elbow one another. Her heart starts to race, triggered by somatic memory, ancestor-rooted and atavistic, beyond erasure, even for the cleaners at the Temple. "Hey!" one of them calls. She ignores him. The map on her chronoband says the bar is just at the end of the block.

More laughter, pointed as barbed wire. "Hey, you! Hey, Librarian Seshet!"

She freezes for a fraction of a second, jerks her head sharply toward them: a blur of pastel-shirted white boys, folded over, eyes squinting as though in pain, lips puckered, "Seshet, Director Librarian!" the joker calls, emboldened by his fellows. "Give me a good memory tonight, won't you?"

Does she recognize him? Would she know his memories from the thousands that crowd her mind? But shock and fear prevent her access to them as cleanly as a lungful of Nevermind. She does not know anyone. She does not recognize anything. Only luck breaks the spell: a woman from the next table over—Taiwanese American, architect, midthirties, went through Counseling last year after a tough breakup, hardly remembers her ex any longer, so Seshet does for her—swings toward the men and bangs her pint on the table hard enough for the maple-tinted foam to spill over the sides. "Leave her alone, you assholes!"

At first Seshet wonders if the architect is defending her out of gratitude. Then she remembers that they have never actually met. One of the Standards Authorities on the block belatedly approaches the men and they back away, laughing with a kind of sheepish bravado that she's only ever witnessed in young white men. A beat too late, she understands: They don't know who she is at all. They just saw *what* she is, and for them that was more than enough. Seshet nods with chilly dignity to the architect (she ignores the Standards Authority, laughing with the boys even as he issues a warning) and resumes a steady, even stride. She swings her arms so her hands won't betray that ghostly rattle in her heart. She *is* the Director Librarian, after all, though they would never believe it. She

will keep her head high until the day they take it off her shoulders.

She is carrying herself just like that, sharp as a hawk, graceful as a jaguar, dignified as a goddess, when she strides into Hope Street's trendiest new establishment and sees her.

Her: a lone woman, legs crossed, quietly sipping a drink chlorophyll-green at the end of a long chrome bar, heart-stoppingly beautiful. Seshet has never seen her before, not even in her city's memories. She knows anyway. *Her.* The one who wields the executioner's ax. The one who will make Seshet bow before she falls.

• • •

Her name is Alethia 56934. Her number indicates a known deviance, but also that she has been cleared for full reintroduction to society. She came to Little Delta four years ago. "I needed a new start," she says, grimacing in that way that hints at a story but warns Seshet off from asking about it. "I got lucky when Pinkerton Cosmetics had a chemist position open up."

"And your number . . ." Seshet lets the sentence dangle. Alethia's open expression turns professionally neutral with a speed that hits Seshet in the gut. But she had to ask. Someone from New Dawn might see them together.

"I'm trans," Alethia says, in a clipped, matter-of-fact way. "Cleared years ago. Is that a problem?"

Seshet wants to crawl under the bar and hide. "No! Of course not! It's just, I'm the Director—" But of course Jordan would have told her that. Seshet's words stick like seed pods in her mouth.

Alethia's laughter is bitter, intoxicating as gin. "We all make our compromises." She leans forward. "Tell me something more interesting. Tell me why you came here."

Seshet frowns. Her heart is pounding so fast it's a wonder she doesn't pass out. Her hand reaches for her drink—impossibly, luridly blue, with a name like "indigo flame"—and she drains half of it in a gulp. It tastes like orangey seaweed. "To Little Delta?" she asks.

Alethia nods encouragingly. Seshet clears her throat and takes a deep, steadying breath. No one has ever affected her like this before, not even her first lover twenty years ago, when they were both novice Librarians, clean and freshly purged of their pasts, ready to make their newest memories with one another.

"I was assigned here," she finally says. "Eighteen years ago." Half a lifetime ago. Long enough to watch the steady grid, the illuminated heart of the reformed town, expand beneath the obelisk's warmly glowing spire.

"Do you like it here?"

She stares at the woman: thick eyebrows, light brown skin, cheekbones to chisel stone, lower lip fuller than the top. "Like . . . it?"

Those eyebrows draw together, humorously confused. "As a place to live?"

"Oh." There is a mole on Alethia's left earlobe, easy to see because she wears no earrings. Seshet wants to kiss it. She wants to take it between her teeth and tug. "It's where all my memories are. I couldn't leave even if I had the choice."

She realizes, a hard drop of a second later, that she's implied a state secret that would mean instant disciplinary action if discovered. Luckily, Alethia looks more confused than ever and Seshet finds her tongue again. She asks Alethia what she does at her job, and discovers she spends all day in a lab coat mixing skin creams. Seshet tries to come up with ways to flirtatiously compliment Alethia's perfect skin—maybe *But I bet you don't need any of it?* She winces. *Director Librarian and still such a cornball, Seshet.* She is awkward as a teenager, mute as a memory hoarder. Her tongue feels wet and heavy in her mouth. Why is a woman like this even talking to her? Smiling, as if she sees something inside her that Seshet has long since lost track of?

Seshet finishes her drink.

"Would you like another?" Alethia asks.

Her expression is solicitous but neutral, and yet Seshet catches the faintest whiff of a side eye. For the first time that evening, she feels herself loosen up.

She lifts the heavy square cocktail glass, a tide pool of melted ice clinging to the bottom among fat drifts of blue-green pulp. She meets Alethia's caramel-brown eyes, and, as an answering spark from a fire so deeply banked she had not known it still smoldered, Seshet laughs.

"I would like," she says, "to take you to a place with better drinks."

• • •

Alethia knows just the one: a dive bar called Cousin Skee's on the far east side, just one block from the old Woolworth Building that marks the frontier of Old Town with its dirty artist squats and dirtier crack houses. Cleared and abandoned now, according to Standards, but Seshet's seen too many memories of clandestine, rebellious activities over that darkened border to believe them. She wonders what Alethia knows about that warren of gap-toothed buildings dressed in garish primary colors, graffiti streaming like skirts at the edge of broken sidewalks. The poised, immaculate woman who greeted her at that hopeless Hope Street cocktail bar should be as out of place here as Seshet is, but the man behind the bar calls out "Lethe!" as soon as they open the door and greets her with a fist bump.

"Where you been, girl?" he asks, reaching without hesitation for the cocktail shaker by the sink. He takes an unmarked bottle with a cheap plastic spout, mixes that clear liquid with the contents of three other unmarked bottles, throws in some ice and starts shaking, all in the time it takes for Alethia to give him a sweet smile that stings Seshet down to the tenderest points of the soles of her feet.

"Working, Skee," says Alethia, sounding at once nothing like the woman at the trendy bar and even more impossibly herself. "You know the drill."

"Looks like you've got a good thing going," he says, taking in her designer shoes and purse at a glance. Alethia just shrugs.

Skee's hard expression softens. He pours the drink with a flourish and pushes it across the bar.

"One mar-Skee-rita, on the house."

Alethia grimaces. "You still trying to call it that?"

"What you mean, *trying*? Been its name since back when you started—"

"And ain't no one but you called it that in all that time," says Alethia, leaning onto the bar with a strange smile, hard as glass. Skee stops short. At last, he glances at Seshet. He seems to sum her up and dismiss her in one swallow: *You may be Black, but you aren't one of us.* He doesn't know who she is. But he can smell what.

"And for your friend?"

Seshet perches on the bar stool, listing slightly to the side. "A mar-Skee-rita, please," she says, diction crisp as fresh linen.

Alethia lets out a surprised yelp of laughter. Seshet shivers. Skee grins. "That'll be ten points."

"Hard currency?" she asks, because she is who she is, and here on that hard edge between new order and old chaos, she wants to know.

Skee gives her a long look. So does Alethia, hooded and opaque, as though there is another woman entirely sharing space behind those wide brown eyes. Seshet itches to know what memories underlie that cold inspection, that easy laughter, that gentle smile, but for now—until she gets back to the obelisk and their memory data banks—she has no way to know.

Skee turns from them with a shrug and starts making another drink. "Don't put recollection boxes all the way out here. Well, the check-cashing joint on the corner has one, works sometimes."

That was true enough. Memory recollection boxes were sparser the farther out from the center you went. But on the border of Old Town, the ones they did have went out of service with surprising frequency. Someone was always damaging the headset or the router, and somehow the vandals' faces or their voices or their memories were never captured, not by drones or Standards Authorities or even automated street surveillance. She'd wondered about that over the years. But she knew who was most likely to live

out here at the edge, and she never pushed for a deeper investigation. No one higher up in New Dawn had ever asked.

Seshet reaches into her wallet and pushes two five-point coins across the table.

Skee slides across the margarita, still frothy from the shaker.

Their gazes lock. She's good at this game of mutual evaluation, but she can't fully commit; she's too aware of Alethia's watchful curiosity beside her.

At last, Skee shrugs and cracks his neck. "You happen to work around that obelisk, Miz . . ."

Seshet allows herself a small smile. "You wouldn't want to know."

· · ·

After midnight, the bar is overwhelmed with a new crowd, diverse in a way she's not used to seeing in downtown Little Delta (and certainly not in the corridors of the obelisk): the oldest must be in his seventies and the youngest still a teenager; all shades of brown, Black, and beige; men in dresses and women in sharp-cut suits and others who defy any gender categorization at all. She pretends not to notice. With New Dawn, any gender nonconformity is enough to get you a deviant code appended to your number—dirty computer, recommended for urgent cleaning—and she doesn't want to flag anyone tonight. Seshet recognizes some of them. They're still members of her flock, however wayward. Others are unrepentant memory hoarders, the kind who never so much as walk through downtown in case a drone recollector might land, light as a horsefly, on their temple and graze a few loose memories off the top while they're waiting for the light to change. She cares even for them, though they don't know it. The obelisk's eye, like any panopticon, gives only an illusion of omniscience—Seshet has made an art of selective gazing.

And now she is down in the dirty thick of it, watching and being watched in her turn, a sensation so unusual she keeps drinking just to dull the edge. Three mar-Skee-ritas in, Seshet finds she does not mind at all being one more in a crowd of hoarders and deviants. She hasn't gone in for memory collection herself in months—if anyone asked, she would have claimed work pressure, but no one has. The truth is that Seshet enjoys the sensation of memory hoarding, that sweet, leftover-Halloween-candy feeling of keeping something back for herself, however temporary. The new crowd is high on some kind of drug, singing songs she's never heard of in harmony, finishing one another's sentences. One of them, a light-skinned boy who reminds her of someone she can't place, wearing a baseball cap with a stencil of an old man with a star blowing out of his forehead, dances Seshet by the shoulders and stares into her eyes as though he can see straight into her memory-scoured soul. He laughs and says something that might be "full" or "bull"—the music the new crowd has brought with them is so loud—and then spins away from her. He freezes when he spots Alethia, turning at that moment from the pool table where she's just sunk another shot. Alethia raises her eyebrows. He opens his mouth and then closes it. Alethia gives him a brief shrug that seems to mean *Sorry I'm not who you thought I was* and goes back over to Seshet.

"How about," Alethia shouts into her ear, as intimate and low-voiced as a whisper, "we go back to my place?"

And now Seshet doesn't care about anything at all—not memory hoarders or memory flooders or who this motley crowd could be and the fact that they almost certainly washed over the border from some forbidden party in Old Town. For now she isn't Seshet, Director Librarian, distant queen of Little Delta.

She is a woman, softened with drink, unburdened by memory, warm skin touching warm skin, and she wants more.

• • •

Alethia's place: one-bedroom apartment a fifteen-minute walk away in an anonymous residential building for young professionals without the money—or the number—for something better. There is a memory recollector in the lobby with signs of modest use (Seshet doesn't mean to notice this, but she does). The apartment is beige: carpet, couch, wallpaper. The photographs on the walls are luridly colored but minimalist in design: flowers, balloons, fishing boats in Bangkok. The kind of apartment that has no gaze, no stamp of ownership, only the vague notion of what others might imagine to be tasteful. It fits the modest cosmetic chemist she met on Hope Street, but it's nothing like the savvy, laugh-like-a-machete Alethia she met at Cousin Skee's. In the bedroom, Seshet finally finds her: a lipstick-red bedspread hitting her eye like Alethia's secret smile, just that tantalizing hint of *someone else*—and Seshet lets that analytical part of her unspool again, to rest in exhausted tangles. She might be the Director Librarian, but without this woman's memories stored in her head, they are just two humans learning together in the most old-fashioned of ways. It rubs against her nerves like salt water on a dirty wound, but there is peace in this ignorance too, a thrill of discovery, a joy.

"There's something about you," Alethia says, holding Seshet's temples between her palms and kissing her with slow, devastating deliberation. "I know I've never met you before, and it's like you've already moved in, you're already making room."

They fall on top of that crimson slash in the beige. They burrow into one another, discover what's beneath.

• • •

Jordan and Billie are in the clerks' office when Seshet comes in the next day, immaculately attired and five minutes late. All New Dawn–affiliated offices work half days on Saturdays, but most aren't as strict about it as the Repository. In any case, Seshet can't remember the last time she's enjoyed a day off. Jordan slouches and lowers the visor on his headset, as though deep in this morning's catch. Billie grins and raises her eyebrows until they meet her hairline. Seshet pretends not to notice. She loves Jordan, but he's an inveterate gossip and Billie is his best friend among the clerks. Seshet should have known he'd tell. She asks if they have her morning report. Jordan, still from behind his visor, says he's flagged some suspicious elements and he'll have that in her workspace in another twenty minutes. Seshet acknowledges him with a nod that he probably can't see and heads sedately into the hallway, as though she has no desire to move faster than a parade float. The door to her office slides open to the sound of her voice stating the passkey and then she is inside, at last, alone.

Her breath shivers inside her lungs like dry leaves in a fall wind. She presses the heels of her palms to aching eyes. She's had three hours of sleep. She'd regret even those wasted moments if not for the memory she savors now, blasphemous as a child, just for herself: Alethia's face painted obelisk gold in the morning light, lipstick and mascara smudged across the pillowcase, eyes half-open even in sleep, hands reaching across the sheets, palms up. In that pindrop moment, Seshet understood that she had come to the crossroads and left them behind. Her life has found a bifurcation as profound as any initiation the elders of New Dawn could devise: Seshet before Alethia, Seshet now.

And even so, her worries are just where she left them last night.

"Seshet," says Dee. The big monitor to the right of the desk lights up. A face appears there slowly, as though approaching from a dark tunnel. "Seshet? Are we in trouble, Seshet?"

Dee scrunches its large, uncanny eyes, blue as the Caribbean Sea. Its features are Seshet's reflected in a fun house mirror, distorted by time, by memory, by choice. The girl Seshet had been hated her dun-brown irises, longed for them to be the blue of the dolls in the store and the children in her headset. No one on the programs had her dark skin or kinky hair. That girl had longed for braids with beads at the bottom that clicked when she walked. She'd longed for eyes so blue they'd glow like the sky, even at night.

They purged these memories during Seshet's initiation, of course. But after a decade, once she ascended to rank, the elders gave them back to her: the lost memories of a lost woman. Until then, Seshet hadn't so much as remembered her old name. At Vice Director rank, she was authorized for a Memory Keeper AI, potentiated on whatever seed memories she chose. She gave it that lost woman's childhood, someone to keep those memories that no longer felt like her own.

"Why would we be in trouble, Dee?" Seshet asks calmly. Dee doesn't do well when Seshet is visibly upset.

"There's even more of those funny half dreams this morning. I like them, but I don't think Terry does."

Terry, Arch-Librarian for the entire Midwest region, and her immediate superior. A hand clamps around her gut and squeezes. She's going to be sick. The moment passes. With a hiccupping breath, she goes to her workstation in an alcove by the monitor and settles into the leather chair. Jordan and the clerks call it her throne. Not to her face, of course.

"What makes you think that?" she asks. Memory Keeper technology is the most advanced New Dawn has to offer. And it might as easily be called Memory Librarian Keeper. She knows this, has always known this. And yet, she has trusted Dee.

"Terry asked me for a report on the half dreams. And on you."

The headset with its golden geometry slides over her temples and clamps into the base of her neck. The net tightens over her skull, pressing until it passes the thick barrier of her hair and coolly touches her scalp. A familiar tickle of electrical engagement and her consciousness slides from the room, into deep memory space. The visor comes down last, and now Dee is right beside her, both child and disembodied consciousness, watching the floodplain of this morning's memory harvest.

"What did you tell him?" Her lips, which she can feel only with effort, don't move. Fully connected, there's no need for her to speak aloud.

"I told him that the half dreams come from all over the city, and many, many dreamers. I told him some were silly and some were beautiful. I told him I hope more people learn to play because it's more fun for me."

In the memory space, Seshet turns sharply to Dee, who holds its knobby knees to its chest. She's let her Memory Keeper AI have complete freedom for years. She's never pruned its personality or deviations. But she doubts Terry would have the same patience with Dee's eccentricities.

"And Terry asked me how you were," Dee continues. "I didn't want to tell him but I had to, you know, he glows even brighter than you do. So I told him in a poem! That was all right, wasn't it, Seshet?"

In her chair out in the world, Seshet's fingers trace the air. In memory space, she catches Jordan's report of anomalous activity and pushes it to the edge of the plain. She already knows what it says, and she knows that Terry does too. After all these years as Director Librarian for one of New Dawn's flagship cities, she understands very well how their world works. She aimed for unprecedented power when she was young and hungry, the token in their elite program. She's held on to it by being smarter than any of them. But she's no longer young, and now her hunger is for what she glimpsed in Alethia's eyes last night, not the next rung on New Dawn's golden ladder.

But that doesn't mean she wants to fall to the bottom either. "What was your poem, Dee?"

Never known love like this before
Except for last time
Someone I took for mine
Told me history couldn't rhyme
But don't get caught in the revolving door.

Dee pauses. Before them, one of last night's memories rises like a wave, crests, breaks.

"Was that okay, Seshet?" Dee asks just as the tide pulls them under.

"That was okay, Dee." She hopes.

• • •

There are dozens of variations of this one memory, like a symphony interpreted by different orchestras, the same recognizable piece layered with local color. It even begins with a song, heavy on the back beat, something Dee would like and Seshet finds gnawingly familiar. It's dark, and then the song explodes into brilliant chorus. Golden light spills all around them and burns where it falls. Are they fireworks? No, the light is coming from the obelisk itself. But not the views of it she knows, from the downtown business district or even the highway heading out of town. It's the view from the abandoned train station, from the warehouse district, from the derelict streets of Old Town. What has been her benevolent, watchful eye becomes a throbbing phallus, a malignant growth using the city for kindling as it burns. The light is coming for them, it's coming for them, *watch out, it's coming!*—that's the chorus to the song she couldn't possibly have heard before.

She's rising now, up and up, until she reaches the pyramidion of a shadowy obelisk, a dark spire to match the light. From this height, she can see the brightly lit streets of new Little Delta. People hurry to work or linger on sidewalks, gossip in cafés, play with their children. The Repository's most iconic structure belches like a furnace. Napalm, white-gold, rains down, hissing where it hits. But the citizens of Little Delta merely glance at it and smile. Around them, the city burns.

"Watch out!"

The memory voice is deep and hoarse with smoke. She senses that it's young and angry, but identity and emotion markers in a loose memory are notoriously unreliable. Let alone in one so clearly fabricated.

The obelisk has fully metamorphosed into its metaphoric counterpart now, a giant golden circumcised penis spitting white-gold ejaculate into the air like a pornographic Mount Vesuvius.

"Seshet! O Seshet!" that young man's voice says.

She has no body in the memory space, but she jerks inside her own mind. The force of it ought to stop the memory playback. But it has the inevitability of an avalanche now, bearing down on her like white fire through the streets of the city she has watched over for the past decade.

The chorus calls and responds, a propulsive chant in her ear: "Director Seshet! What have you done for us lately?"

"Seshet, the fire is coming!"

"Watch yourself!"

• • •

"My dearest Seshet, how delightful as always to see you."

Terry is sitting on a couch she recognizes from his office at New Dawn headquarters, a portable headset draped casually over one of the arms along with a pair of gaming gloves. His blue socks match his T-shirt, which looks new though it's the vintage merchandise of some decades-old pornographic anime (he likes it ironically).

He just popped onto her display screens in the middle of her lunch hour, all privacy codes summarily overridden. She was already sitting at her desk, preparing her reports. She does not startle or flinch when his voice comes over the speakers. She merely sets down her hand tablet and smiles.

This crisis might have caught her by surprise, but she is still Director Librarian of Little Delta, and the game of politics is in her bones.

Besides, she's always liked Terry.

"Wish I could say the same, Terry. Do you ever wear your robes?"

He laughs, which makes him look his age—at least sixty, though he tries to pass for an eternal horn-rimmed hipster of thirty.

"Never while I'm on the job, Seshet. Those are just for impressing the hoi polloi."

She opens her mouth and he holds up a hand.

"Are you going to tell me the definite article is redundant? Because I already know that. I was using it—"

"Ironically? I was going to suggest you go among your polloi one evening just as you are now. It is an enlivening experience."

He claps his hands like a tennis fan appreciating a well-scored point. "I'm sure it is! It's so easy to get caught up in all of their memories, isn't it? Easy to forget that we don't have so many of our own."

She inclines her head. "As I was reminded last night."

He doesn't bother feigning surprise or asking what she was doing. He knows perfectly well.

It's only an ambush if you don't anticipate it.

"Did you enjoy yourself, Seshet?"

It was the most incredible night of my life, and you'll never take it from me.

"It was quite diverting, Terry." Her tone is smooth as a pearl, just a little bored. He cannot know what truly happened last night, just the outward appearance of it. Two women meet at one bar, get drunk together at another. They dance, they sing with the late crowd, they go back to one of their homes, they make love. Memory Librarians take many vows, but none of them are of chastity. Clean citizens of the New Dawn aren't supposed to enjoy same-gender love, but she's hardly the first official to bend those rules; she's not even the only one in Little Delta. He cannot know the *feel* of what has happened to her, that explosion ongoing beneath her breast, the way her fingers itch to call Alethia just to hear her voice again. Just to know it was real. He cannot know it unless he raids her memories—and she will do everything in her power to make sure he doesn't. It is dangerous to be the beloved of a Memory Librarian.

Terry lets the moment hang for a few uncomfortable seconds. Seshet waits for him. Gently, she raises one eyebrow.

He chuckles softly and shakes his head. "Ah, Seshet. Our conversations are always so refreshing. There's no one quite like you. Well. What's this I've been hearing about false memories gumming up the collection systems over there? Do you know who's responsible?"

"Not yet."

He narrows his eyes and tilts his head. She likes Terry better when he's not feigning affability, though she enjoys sparring with him when he is. She knows he's dangerous as a viper—he'd never have reached that position otherwise, let alone survived so many changes in leadership. But—until now, at least—he's put that venom to use in support of her. If that is changing, she hopes she can survive it.

"I'd suggest," he says, drawling, though the most southern thing about him is the Splenda in his iced tea, "that you find out quickly."

"I'm exploring our leads. I should have something more concrete for you soon."

He blinks at her, lips smiling. "Is it the drugs again, Seshet? Those street mixes of Nevermind? It's too bad you let that old witch doctor get away five years ago."

It is hard to keep the jolt of fear out of her expression, though she tries. From Terry's flash of gloating interest, she sees she failed. Doc Young and his legendary remixer MC Haze nearly destroyed her five years ago. Little Delta was becoming famous in the underground circuits as a mecca for wild parties and mind-blasting remixes of street-grade Nevermind. Mixes for sharing memories, mixes for creating dreams, mixes for seeing sound or hearing color. She hadn't caught Doc Young or his remixer, but she'd arrested and memory-suppressed a few hundred of their acolytes. Even sent a sacrificial dozen dirty computers to the Temple for full cleaning. Doc Young and MC Haze vanished, run out of town. Could they have returned? She'd prayed they wouldn't dare. But now she isn't sure.

"I . . . I don't know. The memories are odd. My Memory Keeper—"

"Oh, young Dee? She's sweet, isn't she?"

A wave of dizziness washes over her. Her forehead feels damp. She hopes he doesn't notice. "Dee is an artificial intelligence. Despite its presentation, it doesn't have a gender."

"Oh, of course. My apologies, Dee."

She refuses to wipe her forehead. At least Dee doesn't respond. He doesn't have to say it out loud: her near failure five years ago, her deviant Memory Keeper, her sexuality, her race, her *self*—these are all ropes by which they might hang her, if they choose. During the last crisis with Doc Young and MC Haze, she had been worried that Terry might demote her, or even ship her to some off-site rural Repository. Now she knows those previously unthinkable fates would be gifts. If she fails to resolve this situation, Terry won't hesitate to have her Torched.

He's been her ally for fifteen years, but she knows a part of him would enjoy it—it would appeal to his sense of dramatic irony.

She leans back in her chair, away from the display. "As I was saying, my Memory Keeper calls them half dreams. They're not memories but they're not those strong dreams that sometimes get past the filters either. Five years ago . . . we weren't picking up anything like this back then."

He waves his fingers, as though pushing aside her objection. "So it's something new. That remixer has had plenty of time."

She shakes her head slowly. "It could be MC Haze again, but all her remixes were based on Nevermind. These memories don't . . ."

"They don't what?"

She shrugs, uselessly. "They don't *feel* like Nevermind."

Not sedated, not coerced, not *stolen*.

Terry's basilisk stare should be comical given the blue socks and high-waters, the anime vixen with her breasts barely contained by two parallel strips of shining purple vinyl, but Seshet is very far from laughter.

"Then use your *feeling* and find out who is doing this and *stop them*. This has reached some members of the elder council."

She loses control of her expression for a second time. Terry's eyes crinkle in what seems to be genuine sympathy.

"Do we understand one another, Seshet?"

She forces a neutral smile, out of pride if nothing else. "Perfectly, Terry."

He nods and clicks out of her display.

Seshet does not move. A drop of sweat slides down her forehead, around her chin, and splatters on her desk.

• • •

Imagine a flood, imagine a wave, imagine an avalanche, imagine a storm. Imagine any disaster you please, but note that it always begins as one before it becomes many. What in singular expression seems simple, laughable, beneath your notice, becomes, in the plural, the last thing you notice before you die. This is the bleak magic of exponential growth. It is the difference between two grasshoppers on your screen door and the eighth plague of Egypt. And if you haven't been paying attention to an uninhabitable swath of the Arabian desert when unseasonable cyclones drape the sands in blankets of water, creating the conditions for an unprecedented breeding season for desert grasshoppers, it might surprise you when clouds of vomit-yellow locusts descend to decimate your entire country's corn crop ten months later.

The trouble, as Seshet sees it, is with Cousin Skee. It's with Alethia. With that boy who danced her by the shoulders and told her she was full (or wool? or beautiful?). She hasn't paid enough attention to Old Town since Doc Young fled the city. She hasn't monitored the border zones, like Skee's east side.

And why did she ignore it, wise Seshet, who ought to know better than anyone the danger of the margins? Seshet, queen, who wants to be a mother to her kingdom. Why not? Doesn't she watch over her people? But here's the rub: She has watched over some more than others. She has maintained the heart of the city in a mold as pure as any New Dawn could hope for. But she averted her gaze from the edges, from the ones who would never fit anyway. The ones who looked like her—and didn't look like them.

Director Seshet! What have you done for us lately?

Well, don't they fucking know? Is it possible that they haven't even realized? What has she done, wise Seshet, compassionate Seshet, even while precarious in power?

She has not looked.

And oh, poor Seshet, this is on her shoulders now. If Terry and the others haven't realized it, they will soon. Whatever the specifics of these half dreams—a new Nevermind remix or hacking or something else—they are down from the desert, legion, o'errun.

• • •

It is a little enough disaster, after the great disasters of the morning, but Seshet can feel hysteria bubbling up like old vinegar behind her throat.

"Dee," she says, voice cracking at the end like a child's. "Dee, are you *sure* there's nothing more?"

"I'm so sorry, Seshet," Dee says. It sounds distressed, but it's removed its face from her display. "This subject isn't flagged for extra surveillance. These are the only memories in the cache."

"Alethia has a sleep headset."

"We have no record of its use last night."

A private smile pulls at her lips. Of course they don't. The smile collapses. "You checked the trash again?"

"It was all cleared at four thirty this morning, per standard operations."

"And her Counseling sessions?"

"After three years without incident we only retain the intake session and the final report. You yourself made sure we were the first to implement Chancellor Chelsea's privacy reforms. Would you like me to help you remember?"

Dee is already pulling up the relevant memories from six years ago. One of her displays flashes to visual-auditory recall: Seshet and Terry stiff-necked in full regalia, laughing at some joke of his before they stepped onto the podium to announce the reforms. Even without the sensory integration of her headset, she is plunged back into that day, into the skin of her younger self, proud to be at the vanguard of New Dawn's short-lived reformist movement.

An older, harder Seshet shakes her head and stops the playback. "That isn't necessary, Dee."

Dee is silent for a few seconds. When it speaks, it sounds weary, even disappointed. "Would you like me to flag her now, Seshet?"

Seshet frowns. She has allowed Dee to develop a personality and a primitive consciousness—aspects that make it dangerous, according to Terry and his superiors—but it's still fundamentally a Memory Keeper AI bound by New Dawn's protocols. It has the processing capacity of a precocious child, not an adult capable of moral judgments. So why would her Memory Keeper be disappointed in her?

She defends herself anyway. "I need more information, Dee! I need to know who she really is, before . . ." *Before I lose myself in her.*

Before I lose control.

Displaying that annoying tick of independence and creativity that Seshet has allowed to develop in her Memory Keeper but is bitterly regretting now, Dee spreads five different memories across Seshet's displays and plays them all at once without sound: teenage Alethia hugging her father goodbye at the border wall while drones circle; Alethia in her lab, measuring chemicals, solitude isolating her like the walls of a test tube; Alethia moving into her apartment with just two suitcases and a hot-water kettle; Alethia on a bench in Standards Park, feeding the ducks in the artificial lake; Alethia on the viewing deck of the obelisk, just below Seshet's office, gazing over the cloud-covered city. How long ago was that? Three years. Seshet's heart lurches. They'd come so close to meeting. But is this the real Alethia? Where's "Lethe" of Cousin Skee's? Where's that cloaked, sharp humor? The cherry bedspread like a dagger thrust to the beige of that prefurnished apartment? Aside from her father, deported fifteen years ago after his citizenship was revoked for "unclean activities," why is she always alone?

"Dee, is this really everything?"

"You told me—"

"I told you what?"

Dee sighs. "This is what we have."

"And your analysis of the subject?"

She wishes Dee would show its face. It has never wanted to hide from her before.

"They smell funny."

"Dee, be serious."

But Dee is more stubborn than usual today. It begins to speak in singsong:

I didn't know what I really meant
When I asked you where the false time went
I only knew I had to let go
Before the fall's first blow.

"Enough!"

Seshet's shout brings down a charged silence. Her eyes prick. She is conscious of an urge to apologize. Absurd. "Flag her, Dee," she says, making her voice even harder to mask that flush of shame. "Bring me every last memory you can drag from the public recollectors or her headset tonight."

For the first time in their life together, Dee's voice sounds genuinely robotic. "Confirmed, Seshet. Alethia 56934 has been flagged for suspected deviance, high priority."

• • •

The Counseling offices sit opposite from the obelisk, on the other side of the City Hall gardens that are open to the public only on weekends and holidays. Seshet goes through the private entrance beside the balding topiary, nodding once to the guards who spring to attention when they see her. This late in the day, the private corridors are empty, though there will still be a handful of people in the public library and waiting room, hoping for a last-minute appointment with a Counselor. She hates coming here. Even as a novice, Seshet avoided the

Social Librarians. The idea of having to constantly interact with the people whose memories she monitored repulsed her, like a surgeon who could handle cutting open intestines only if she forgot the human being who would use them later. Counseling receives a constant influx of people looking for help—or looking to raise their Standards scores and petition to change their numbers. She receives reports on their activities, of course. She even personally involves herself in the cases that interest her—diagnosing emotional liabilities, selecting the memories for repression or amplification, reveling in the messy, subtle work of realigning a personality. That the memories harvested during Counseling sessions are of a much higher quality, particularly useful for New Dawn's surveillance efforts, is merely a beneficial side effect of the Librarians' primary work.

Seshet doesn't really believe this any more than the Social division's Vice Director does, but they tell that to the fresh initiates in training and massage their memories so they can believe it as long as possible. She has long since made the necessary moral justifications.

In the end, a simple happiness is better than a complex disillusion.

She finds the Vice Director alone in his office, feeds from three Counseling sessions running silently on wall displays. His headset flashes reflected light from the sunset as he turns to greet her. Keith doesn't betray surprise to find her here in person, but his welcoming smile is perfunctory, and he only belatedly offers her the seat in front of his desk. Seshet stares at him for a carefully blank moment and then seats herself, conscious of every regal gesture, on the couch facing the picture window. Keith's office is nearly as large as hers. He is Vice Director of a powerful division, golden-haired, blue-eyed, the third generation of New Dawn loyalists, and the favored heir of a certain bitter faction with long grudges who would like nothing more than to erase even the memory of Seshet's heterodox rise to power in Little Delta. It's one thing to allow people like

her to train as initiates, the line goes, but quite another to let them seem to rule!

His eyes flick to the couch in annoyance. After a beat, he forces another smile, removes his headset, and makes his way to the chair facing her.

"You honor me by coming all the way here, Director," he says. "I was just preparing my report for you."

"Your report, Vice Director?" She allows nothing more than a hint of polite curiosity in her tone, but her thoughts are a storm. Someone has already told him about the memory flooding. He's had—hours? Days?—to consolidate his position.

He leans forward, hand on his knee, concerned frown betrayed by the tic at the corners of his lips. Keith has never quite mastered the art of controlling his expression. But then, he's never really needed to.

"Well, of course, Director Seshet," he says, larding on the false concern until it is indistinguishable from gloating, "I couldn't leave you to face this kind of unprecedented attack alone. We're all Librarians in the end, despite our differences. We're here to defend the Repository . . . the New Dawn way of life! Well, aren't we, Director?"

Standards save her from young sharks tasting blood in the water. As if she hasn't beaten back better men than him in her time. As if she won't do so again. She sighs. "I will be happy to review your report in the morning, Vice Director. I assume the memories of those in Counseling don't have much to offer, in any case."

The Social division Vice Director, Seshet has had cause to observe, bears a distinct resemblance to a fish on a line when caught out. "My Memory Keeper is still checking everything we have archived—"

Under her patient gaze he belatedly falls silent. She nods.

"Perhaps you don't yet have enough . . . experience in your position to know this, but no one from Old Town goes near Counseling. The ones responsible for these fabricated memories would be even less likely to betray themselves so easily. Counseling is how we monitor the health of Little Delta. But to destroy an illness, Vice Director, we need different means."

He swallows. She fancies that she can see a spark of panic behind those sky-blue irises, a belated realization that Seshet has not yet fallen, and might survive to see *him* fall if he does not take care.

"And what means might those be, Director Seshet?" No sign of his preening now.

"The loose memory bank. You do remember you're in charge of it, don't you?"

He frowns and shakes his head. "Loose memories! They're notoriously unreliable. My Memory Keeper would be stuck in there for half of every month if I let it. I only ever go in there if Standards is after me to find the suspect in a crime—"

She rises from the couch in a smooth gesture and allows some of her real annoyance to inflect her tone. "Keith, have you been paying attention? These memory flooders *are* criminals. I very much doubt the ones responsible for this will be tagged in the system. They won't be easy to find. I need any suspect memories flagged and sent to my workspace. Traffic stops, ambient drones, recollection boxes out in the periphery, the ones outside grocery stores and check-cashing stores and pawn shops. And . . ."

He isn't bothering to control his expression at all now; his lower lip juts out like a surly child's. "Yes?"

She looks past his outraged expression to the sun setting over the garden. Her heart hurts at the thought of fighting this battle again, but she does what she needs to. "Keep an eye out for Doc Young or MC Haze. They might be back."

She remembers, a Librarian's perfect recall piercing the alcoholic fog, that light-skinned boy dancing with her at Cousin Skee's, drug-blasted pupils dark as the night sky. *You're full*, he sang to her over the loud jangle of someone else's music. *You're full as a beast and we have nothing to spare.*

• • •

Hungry? I'm starving:) A

A simple message on Seshet's private channel. She should stay at the Repository. She should comb through the other Vice Directors' reports, look for more clues, ask Dee for more data.

Instead, Seshet changes into another set of Jordan-approved street clothes and hurries to meet Alethia at a tiny Italian restaurant near her place. They pretend to be friends where anyone can see, but they touch under the table, careful for Alethia's sake, since she's already been flagged as deviant. They share wine and garlic bread. ("We have to eat it together," Alethia says, waving a piece under her nose, "or only I'll stink and you won't want to kiss me." Seshet nods like a marionette and takes another long gulp of red wine.) Alethia used the recollector outside the restaurant to load a few more points onto her TriCard before they went in.

"It's my turn to treat," she said, with a lift to her eyebrow that dared Seshet to object. Seshet eyed the recollector with a hunger she hoped didn't show and shrugged.

The meal is sublime, so heavy on the garlic it becomes a joke between them, cracking up when they order dessert, whispering, *But is it a* garlic *panna cotta? Can we try the* garlic *grappa?*

They linger over their dessert wine, which tastes faintly of anise, a different root vegetable.

"They say you Librarians have perfect memories. So tell me the first thing you remember." Alethia traces Seshet's uneven hairline with one finger. Seshet feels the touch through to the soles of her feet. She closes her eyes, a prayer for strength.

"My recovery room at the Temple," she says. "White and gold. The Torch standing beside me. 'Congratulations on your rebirth, novice Librarian. Your name is Seshet.'"

Alethia drops her hand, a loss. Seshet does not move.

"They memory-wiped you?" she asks, horrified and trying to hide it.

Seshet shrugs. "It's a requirement for initiation."

"And that name? It's unusual for New Dawn. An Egyptian goddess?"

At that, Seshet smiles. "We have the right to choose our new names. I guess my past self wanted to make sure that I knew how high I wanted to climb."

Alethia laughs softly. Seshet's heart skips one subtle beat and rebounds with ferocity.

"Well, we have that in common," Alethia says. "I chose my name too. I was sixteen when they approved my petition."

Seshet had wondered. Even under New Dawn's more liberal regimes, getting permits for transitions has never been easy.

"Your parents agreed?" Seshet asks. Though her own childhood memories are safely stored with Dee, this question leaves her aching, off balance.

There is a matching glimmer in Alethia's eyes, downcast over the dregs of her wine. "I was always my papa's little girl. My mom . . ." She shakes her head, sets down the glass like it holds something precious. "She agreed when it counted. She let me live my life."

There's a story there, but Seshet doesn't pry. She doesn't need to.

She is remembering, on a loop made relentless by her perfect memory, what Alethia said, as she left the recollector booth: "No checking them out behind my back, okay?" She laughed but her eyes were worried. "You have the advantage."

She tries not to pay attention to the longing, the vulnerability in Alethia's voice when she invites Seshet to her apartment again. She tries not to think about that simple, declarative statement that rushes through the gulf between them: *You have the advantage.* And what is Seshet to do? *Not* take it? Stop being who she is while she exposes herself before a woman completely unknown to her? How could she possibly do that? Wouldn't *not* looking be abdicating her

responsibilities as Director Librarian? What if Alethia wants to hurt her? What if she's a resistance agent?

But resisting who? a voice inside her asks.

She hushes it with deep kisses in the doorway of Alethia's apartment. Fingers caressing dark puckered nipples. Backs arched, toes curled. They curve like calligraphy on the red canvas of Alethia's bed, and Seshet cannot breathe, she cannot think, her memories are a whirlwind. She has never felt desire this raw in her life. But it's not their passion that scares her; it's the after hush, the easy sleep of Alethia in her arms, the soft kiss she places, like a brand, on the inner fold of Seshet's left wrist.

The woman who could have treasured this gift, Seshet threw away twenty years ago. So who does Alethia see when she looks at her? Seshet, Director Librarian—or the ghost of the woman she killed to become her?

• • •

Seshet makes sure Alethia's sleep headset is in place before she leaves. They've drunk a bottle of wine between them; she's more likely to assume she put it on herself than that Seshet put it on for her. Alethia's wary voice: *You have the advantage.* And what of it? No one in her position has the luxury of fairness.

At three in the morning she calls a private aircar and heads back to the Repository. She hasn't slept at all, but her nerves are alive, her synapses snapping, the fall air full in her lungs and the sleeping city pulsing through her veins, hers alone.

• • •

Keith sends her a terse message early the next morning: his Memory Keeper has found something. He sends over a handful of loose memories scavenged from the southern edge of the city two days ago, all of them from unregistered users.

Seshet, unsleeping, fresh as a vampire, has

stuffed herself full to sickness on a stream of Alethia's dreams and memories. With a physical jolt, she disconnects from that raw feed and forces her attention back to the crisis that might just topple her after a decade at the top of the obelisk. If even Keith is working on Sunday, she can't do less.

"Dee," she says, losing a battle with herself, "I need your help with this."

Her Memory Keeper's face appears, at last, in the corner of her nearest monitor: a sullen, angry child.

"Oh, so you're finished?"

She considers a number of responses, each one more defensive than the last. But Dee is just an artificial intelligence, a virtual helper built on her own discarded memories. There's no reason for her to care about its opinion.

So she simply pulls up the loose memories that Keith sent her and lets them play. She doesn't bother with the full headset, since like most loose memories, these are patchy and degraded. Drugs tend to do that, but so does desperation.

The memories all center on a party somewhere in Old Town. There are tunnels covered in black and white tiles in a pattern she can no longer make sense of; loose tiles crunch underfoot like eggshells. The tunnels converge on a larger space, a great platform with sunken tracks. Lights flash and sparkle from hidden crevices. One of the memories has a degraded olfactory register, which Dee tells her smells faintly of cotton candy and dried urine. Street-grade Nevermind comes in a lot of flavors, but she remembers the Candy Remix from eight years ago. One of Doc Young's staples, with a short, punchy high that made your every recent memory taste sweet. It was MC Haze's first big hit, the one that propelled her from the trenches of dime-a-dozen remixers to the dizzying heights of underground stardom. On the memory playback, which Dee has belatedly condensed into a composite far richer in detail, lights flash and project onto the ceiling. The outline of an old man seated beside a dark, upside-down obe-

lisk raises his hands, palms out. Light gathers between his head and his hands until a star shoots from his forehead. It obliterates the man, leaving only the glittering words behind:

DOC YOUNG'S MIND BREAK

A few of the memories go on longer, but she stops playback.

"That's the old train station, Seshet," Dee says after a taut moment. "The north platforms." It sounds worried. But of course it does—it's a reflection of herself, and they both understand what this means.

"That old bastard." She's several steps behind him, as always. She slumps in her chair, rolled by the exhaustion she's kept at bay all morning.

"Dee, can you ring the Standards office?"

"Are you going to order a raid?" Dee says nervously. "Don't you remember what happened last time?"

A hundred detainees. A dozen branded as dirty computers, left as dead to their friends and families. Oh, she remembers. But what choice does she have?

Doc Young is back.

• • •

The daytime raid turns up a few scraps: stray memories from the vagabond who sleeps across the street, discarded remix inhalers she sends to forensics, a smattering of stencils with Doc Young's new logo, the star bursting from his head like Athena from Zeus. She tells the Standards Chief to maintain a stealth drone formation throughout the night, to see who else they might pick up. Doc Young won't use the same place twice for his traveling club, but other people of interest might stop by.

She still isn't sure if the memory flooding is the fault of a new remix, but Doc Young's sudden reappearance after five years makes that more likely. She doesn't want to think of what Terry and the elders will say, if so. They forgave her then, but she doubts they will be so under-standing a second time.

Jordan comes by her office again that night, bearing curry and beer like a sword and shield.

"You haven't eaten all day," he says, and hurries to the conference table to set out the food.

"Been watching me that carefully, have you?" Seshet says wryly, observing his practiced arrangement of disposable containers and sil-verware. As if he's determined to finish before she has a chance to kick him out. "What are you still doing here on a Sunday?"

"I just worry about you." He takes the lid off a curry container. The smell of Jamaican jerk chicken hits her with an almost physical force. She's reminded that she still hasn't slept and—Jordan is correct—hasn't eaten more than a pro-tein bar since this morning.

She sighs. "Tell me you at least got enough for yourself?"

He smiles, so grateful it pains her, and pulls out another container. "Just in case."

She removed her outer robe at some point in the last several frantic hours, so she eats with her clerk in just her white tunic and gold leggings, exhaustion or mortal terror relaxing her into an informality she hasn't allowed herself within these walls in all her time as Director. Jordan, predictably, doesn't comment on the formal vestment flung over the couch like a fancy throw pillow.

He waits until she's nearly finished before asking, she will grant him that.

"So, how are things going with Alethia?"

She chokes on the last mouthful of chicken and drains the rest of her beer before she recovers.

"Why?" she rasps. "Has she said something?"

Jordan shakes his head. "Just that she wishes you had a less demanding job."

"Job!" Seshet laughs and then, inexplicably, wants to cry.

Jordan looks halfway to tears himself. "Direc-tor," he says, looking at the remains of his turmeric-stained rice instead of at her, "just *trust*

this time, won't you? I think you and Alethia have something very special."

It's out of character for him to overstep like this. Not just as her subordinate, but as her—friend? But Librarians are never simply friends.

"Jordan . . ." She makes her voice hard in warning, but he shakes his head like a stubborn toddler.

"Do something about it if you don't want me to pry. You haven't memory-suppressed me yet, I know it. I've been monitoring myself."

She blinks in surprise. "You've been . . . who taught you that?"

Monitoring is an advanced technique for detecting changes and manipulations in one's own memories. It is generally only taught to sub-directors, though Librarians of lower ranks can learn it at the discretion of someone higher up.

Jordan laughs with more bitterness than she had ever expected of him and wipes his eyes. "It was authorized, Director." She wants to ask him *by whom*, the question nearly off her tongue before she swallows it back down. Does she want to know? Was it Keith, trying to suborn her clos-est clerk? Or, worse, Terry, tinting every friendly eye on her with a subtle shade of treachery?

"What do you want from me, Jordan?" She can't keep the distrust from her voice, any more than he can fail to hear it.

"Director. Seshet." He drives her name on his lips like a stake through her heart. "You don't need to control everything."

Stung, her spine stiffens. "I don't need—"

Somehow, his very intensity stops her. "If it's love, just let it be. Please."

• • •

She can't help but think of Jordan's warning when she visits Alethia that night, though she knows it shouldn't matter. Jordan *and* Dee? What did she do to deserve the unfounded mor-alizing of children and artificial constructs?

"I missed you this morning," Alethia says, greeting her with a kiss at the door to her apart-ment. She's smiling, but her eyes are red-rimmed, puffy, and bruised underneath. Without makeup or tailored clothes, her beauty feels more raw to Seshet, more familiar. She's wearing an old T-shirt and pajama pants, perhaps the same ones from last night. She secures all the locks behind Seshet before heading to the living room. All the blinds are down here and in the kitchen, but something in Alethia's mood stops Seshet from suggesting they raise them and turn down the lights. Alethia picks up a thick wooden pipe in the shape of a palm frond and flips open a lighter.

"Please tell me you won't report me," she says with a laugh, but the look in her eyes is a little too desperate, a little too real.

Seshet tries to lighten the mood. "Only if you share."

She's smoked weed a handful of times in her life—all with Terry, in fact, from one of his fancy vintage vape pens while they played some ridiculous old video game of his with a lot of guns and gore—but she's willing to try again just to take the scared edge out of Alethia's voice.

White smoke billows from Alethia's nostrils in soft, gentle whorls. *Oh, to be the smoke behind her teeth,* she thinks. Silently, Alethia passes the pipe and the lighter. Seshet knows how to do this, she has a thousand memories to show her, but the greenly burning smell brings her back, like a hook in her heart, to something older, personal. A little girl playing in the fall leaves, watching wide, beloved hips move with the rhythm of the rake; the smell of those leaves burning, painting sigils on the sky.

She gasps and coughs on a different smoke, in a different year, with a different name. Where did that come from? But it was her own memory, she knows it in her bones. The memory of that little girl she forgot for so many years, the one who longed, more than anything, for the woman with the rake to come back home.

Alethia is thumping her on the back, sitting her down on the couch. She brings her a glass of cold water, which finally soothes the burning in her airway. Seshet wipes her eyes.

"Don't know what happened," Seshet says, pushing the pipe onto the table.

Alethia wags her eyebrows. "You have a hard time breathing around me?"

Seshet's heart hurts. She leans back on the couch, closes her eyes against the fluorescent lights, her beloved's blinding smile.

"You're tired," Alethia says. "Did you work today?"

"You don't really get days off in my position. You?"

"I . . . went to the lab. I have a project I'm working on . . . anyway, I didn't stay long."

Seshet cracks open her eyes. Alethia is gazing pensively at one of the windows, as though she can see through the blinds. "Did something happen?" Was she not careful enough last night? Did she disrupt Alethia's emotional balance with her real-time dive into her dreams and memories? The sleep headsets have that functionality, but it's not recommended outside of a specially equipped detention facility where the subjects can be closely monitored for side effects. Guilt washes over her, inexorable as unbidden memory. There is a difference, vital as a heartbeat, between what is permitted to her position and what is aligned with her soul. She knew that, once. She almost remembers it now, but the knowing slides, sinks into soft forgetting, is gone.

Alethia shakes her head as though shaking off a fly. "Tell me about your day. If you can, I guess. Did you bust any heads?"

Seshet sits straight up. "I don't bust—"

But Alethia is already holding her hands up, palms out. "Sorry, sorry, babe. It was just a joke. You *are* the Director of this whole little town. Heads are sometimes busted."

"If I have to order raids, it's for the good of our community—"

"So you ordered a raid?"

"I never said—"

Alethia's laugh stops her cold. "The poor things that get caught in that net. So many new Torches for the Temple."

"Alethia," she says, forcing herself calm though she feels as if she's falling in midair, "you know what I am."

Alethia blows out another lungful of smoke. In the hallway, someone unlocks their door and shuts it. Alethia keeps still until the hall has gone quiet again.

"Yeah, I know. I just wish I could see who."

"What's that supposed to mean?"

Alethia taps out the ashes straight onto the coffee table and refills the pipe. "Who are you, Seshet-without-a-number? Who would you be if you weren't Director Librarian? Who could we be, together?"

The vertigo is getting worse. Maybe the weed has finally kicked in. "Why are you asking me this, Alethia?"

She stares at Alethia, who keeps her gaze fixed on the window. "It's just . . . you have a reputation, you know? You're . . . kinder than most of them. Nothing happened to anyone we met that night at Cousin Skee's. I was taking a chance, bringing you there."

She feels sick. "What did you think would happen to them?"

Alethia meets her gaze at last, but now Seshet wants to turn away, to hide from the confusion and distrust she sees there. "I don't know, Seshet. You tell me. What's going to happen to whoever gets caught in that raid of yours?"

"Anyone going to one of Doc Young's parties needs Counseling, Alethia!" Alethia flinches but Seshet persists. "Yes, even cleaning. It's for the good of the whole."

Alethia snorts. "The good of the whole," she says, mocking. "My god, you sound just like them."

I am *them*, she almost says, fast and hot. She swallows back the cheap shot. Seshet could ascend to elder council itself and she still wouldn't be more than tolerated in New Dawn. She knows exactly what Alethia means.

"Alethia, what's going on? What happened today? Why are you like this?"

"Maybe this *is* who I am, Seshet. I'm not your dream girl. I'm just a woman in way, way over her head . . ."

She buries her head in her arms. Seshet, shocked, puts a hand on her shoulder.

"Just go." Alethia's voice is muffled and Seshet pretends she didn't hear. But Alethia raises her head a second later, so the words are clear as the new dawn light:

"Leave, Seshet."

• • •

You can say this for our Director Librarian, Seshet-without-a-number, the woman who named herself after a goddess so she could not forget what she meant to become: she does not flinch.

Whatever the consequences, the moral accounting, the line drawn between the *she* who had not done this thing and the *she* who has— what is an official of New Dawn if not a professional consequence risker, moral accountant, line crosser? And Seshet has prided herself on being the best of them all.

This is her line, carefully marked in the sand before the tide of *what* she is drowns it in a sea of salt and noise: Alethia's memories.

She sees herself as through a haze of love and longing: a tall woman of regal bearing and awkward gestures, tongue-tied, eloquent-eyed, no longer young but ageless. That woman walks into Alethia's apartment. That woman says, with a pained smile, *Only if you share.*

She takes the memory and *pushes*, back behind the most painful moments of Alethia's past, behind her grief over her father lost on the other side of that border wall, behind the conflicted shame and love she feels for her mother lost to cancer, behind her first memories, her shock when she realized that other people saw her as a boy, and further, behind her first cries in the light, behind her waiting silence in the liquid dark. She pushes, and when Alethia puts her headset on tonight, she will respond and pull, until not a trace of their meeting a few hours ago remains accessible to her conscious mind. It isn't as good as a full Nevermind wipe, but it's the next best thing. No one that Seshet has suppressed has voluntarily recalled those memories ever again. She knows the trick, you see. No one remembers everything. And what's too painful to remember, you can simply choose to forget.

All Seshet does is use their own mental blocks as the bulwark against whatever she wants to hide from their consciousness. It's like a wall of fire in one of Terry's old video games with a treasure safely hidden inside. Here's the trick: if the flames burn on the fuel of your own shame, not even mortal terror can make you brave the heat.

• • •

She sleeps for a while in her own workstation, visor still down, the floodplain of virtual space melding seamlessly with the dreamscape of her own memory-haunted mind. She does not know of what she dreams; those are locked away in the fastness of her own shame and regret. Just one follows her into craggy wakefulness, and it's not so much a dream as a belch of repressed memory, inexplicably brought to life. The sway of her mother's hips as she agitates the leaves. The girl in the grass. The crackle and burn.

"Dee," she says, without thinking. Their argument feels faraway now. The logic of it lost to her in a groggy sickness, the hangover of what she has done to the woman she is falling in love with.

"You don't look so good, Seshet."

Seshet tries to laugh, but it's like wet ashes, it won't come out. Dee is a child playing on the floodplain, now empty, waiting for the morning's harvest. She has never known whether Dee acts the role of a child for her benefit, or for some arcane satisfaction of its own.

"Dee," she says, coughing on something too silty for tears. *You have a hard time breathing around me.* No matter what else they have, Alethia won't ever remember that. "Show me my old memories, won't you? Show me my mother."

Dee's uncanny eyes go wide as a Kewpie doll's. "Really? You never want to look at those."

"I . . . remembered something. From my childhood."

"But you can't remember those, not as a primary memory. Not unless . . . Oh, Seshet."

Seshet thinks she doesn't deserve Dee's understanding, its kindness. Even if it is an artificial intelligence fundamentally limited by New Dawn's protocols, it understands her better than any human ever has.

"I must have suppressed it," she says, out loud, for the first time. "That's how they missed it in the Nevermind wipe."

Humans repress their own memories, of course. They do it all the time. Headsets wouldn't work, otherwise. Nevermind would just be a really trippy drug. The fact that New Dawn has weaponized this effect for its own purposes doesn't mean that people don't forget things for their own simple survival every second of the day. It's not so surprising that she would have done so. But why remember now, after so much time?

Without another word, Dee pulls up a memory and rolls it over her in a full sensory wash. Ah, she has always liked this one. She is eight, and her mother has just come home from some mysterious trip overseas. She has brought back a suitcase full of treasure and she shows young Deidre the spoils, piece by piece. Here is the necklace of cowries she purchased on the beach from a boy no older than Deidre; here is the doll made of corn husks and twine with black beans for eyes; here is the program for the opera, red ink on cream paper that still smells of someone else's cologne.

"I can breathe there, Deidre," she says, a refrain the child recognizes. "Your memories are your own."

"But when will you let me come with you, Mom?"

"When you're older, honey. When it's safer."

Deidre never understood what her mother meant by that.

Then her mother and father fought and her mother stopped going on her trips, stopped bringing back bounty. Just a year later, her mother abandoned them both.

The memory fuses with another and another:

her mother doing the laundry, cursing at the old machine that always rocked during the spin cycle; her mother singing her to sleep, *Remember,* some old song from before memories were things you could hold in your fist like coin; her mother screaming at the top of her lungs from the top of a hill, "I own my own soul!"

"Why do you think she left us, Dee?" Seshet asks now, though she doesn't remember this girl that she was, not really.

Dee shuts down the memories. "She wouldn't have done it without a good reason, Seshet. I know it."

. . .

Terry has come to Little Delta for an unofficial visit. The news rushes through the obelisk like water over a ruptured dam, but Seshet, sleeping in her office, is among the last to hear it. It's Jordan, of course, who saves her. He spends five minutes arguing with her door monitor before Dee finally wakes her up. "Oh god," Jordan says, "I was beginning to worry you'd died."

"The door monitor would have let you in if I were dead," Seshet says, yawning. She's still in last night's street clothes, which look—and smell—days old.

Jordan grimaces. "That's what it said. Thank you, Dee."

"You're welcome, Jordan!" Dee says, inordinately pleased. It doesn't acknowledge most people—a precaution Seshet instilled in it early on—but Jordan has always been on its short list of friendly humans.

He tells her about Terry, which wakes her the rest of the way up, no need for the coffee he has so helpfully brought. She drinks it anyway.

"How long has he been here?"

"Half an hour," Jordan says. "He's taking a tour of the Counseling building."

She closes her eyes briefly. So he's seeing Keith before her. This is meant to send a message, but knowing Terry, it's as likely to make Keith feel overconfident as it is to make Seshet feel undermined.

"And this morning's crop?"

Jordan hesitates.

"Out with it, Jordan. Things can't get much worse."

"Over fifty percent are those junk memories," he says in a small voice that means he still can't believe it. "I don't know how, Director, but they've gone from a blip to nearly overwhelming the system in less than a week."

A little more than that, she thinks, not that it matters. "Exponential growth," she says. "It's a killer."

She uses the shower in her office and puts on the extra work robes she keeps in the closet. She can't afford Terry's performative casualness, and she doesn't bother to try.

She meets him, an hour later, as the perfectly composed Director Librarian of Little Delta, in her robes of office.

He's wearing the hat of Arch-Librarian, but below the neck he's all ironic hipster, reaching for meaning in the corporate branding of the past. This time it's an Atari T-shirt, corduroy pants, and pink Vans. She has to grant him his point: in the hallways of the obelisk his peculiar style stands out even more than his vestments would.

"Seshet!" he says. "Good news! I've gotten my hands on the Japanese original of *Final Fantasy III,* remember I was telling you about that?"

She blinks at him. "Congratulations?" She's never managed to keep track of all the video games he's played in front of her, but she generally drums up enough interest in the moment to keep things pleasant. The weed helps.

He settles himself in one of her armchairs, crosses left foot over right knee, and balances his conical red cap on the end of one pink shoe. "I'd suggest we head straight to Greenfriars, but I guess the play-through will have to wait. You must be drowning in work. Don't mind me, I just stopped by to say hello."

Greenfriars is one of the New Dawn resort facilities, about an hour out of town, reserved for officials, their families, and select friends. She has never spent much time there.

"Hello, Terry. I've just had a pot of tea brought up. Would you like some?"

She pours the tea into two matching ceramic cups, marked with gold and lapis filigree in the sigil of New Dawn. The tea pours green and fragrant as fresh-cut grass, and she doesn't offer him any sugar. Terry only ever drinks iced coffees thick as milkshakes with protein powder. He takes the cup from her with a sardonic lift to his eyebrows.

"Tea, that's charming. So . . . how's it going?"

She doesn't prevaricate. "Doc Young is back in town. I'm waiting on news of a sting operation from the Standards office."

"Good. And his remixer?"

"I'm not sure if MC Haze is with him this time, but it's possible."

He takes a tentative sip and grimaces. "Well, I'm sure it will be settled soon in your capable hands, Seshet."

Seshet puts her cup smoothly in its saucer, disconcerted. What happened to the urgency, the veiled threats of their last conversation? And if he's so sure she can resolve it, why has he bothered to come here in person? Terry hates Little Delta. "I'm grateful for your confidence in me."

He beams like a proud father. It makes him look ancient. "You deserve it! In fact, that's just what I wanted to bring up with you personally. We've all been impressed with your tenure here. Even those who weren't in favor of your ascension have come around now. You were a controversial appointment, you know that, but you've done very well. You've proven the New Dawn ethos. 'Order, Standards, and Merit above all.'" He hesitates theatrically. "You're Merit, of course."

Seshet raises her cup to hide her expression. "Of course. You came all the way to Little Delta to tell me that?"

Saltier than she meant it to come out. Terry may have been her ally for over a decade, but he still loves to unbalance her.

He takes another swig of the tea in his enthusiasm. "A little more than that, dear. We're con-

sidering you for a promotion. The directorship has opened in Minneapolis. Big city, very different operation from what you have going on here, but lots of opportunity for a hungry Librarian. Of course, I know you're already bonded to this city. We'd have to wipe you again. That's not wonderful, but you've only just turned forty, your brain is still resilient enough. You can keep your personal memories, of course; no one wants to worry you about that."

Her mind is blank with astonishment. She blurts the first thought that pops into it. "Minneapolis? Terry, you were Director of Minneapolis."

"I was! So you can see, Seshet, there are big things ahead of you. Who knows where you might go after this. We just need to see a successful resolution to this memory plague problem and, honestly, your nomination is in the bag." Satisfied as a cat over a clean plate, he puts down his teacup. "Do we understand one another, Seshet?"

She nods. "Perfectly, Terry."

• • •

As she hoped, the sting nets a group of revelers hoping to catch Doc Young's latest party a day late. The detention memory swipe of one of them turns up a pair of half dreams that match the ones flooding their systems. The subject—one Leon 75411—says he doesn't know anything about memory flooding or new remixes, he just picked those up at another party, a mind meld with a group of strangers. No, he doesn't know who they were. No, he couldn't find them again. The Standards Chief is interrogating the detainee personally. In his professional opinion, he tells Seshet, the boy is telling the truth. But that doesn't mean his memories might not give more clues. She tells the Standards Chief to put the detainee into a coma and harvest as much as they can. When the memories arrive to her workstation, however, she goes rigid with shock. She recognizes the kid, this Leon 75411, low-grade memory hoarder and antisocial deviant. He's the light-skinned boy with the stencil of Doc Young's Mind Break on his cap who danced with her at Cousin Skee's. With a lurch of nausea, she now remembers who he reminded her of: her half brother, child of her father's second marriage after her mom left. They had never gotten along.

Alethia said she had taken a chance bringing Seshet to that bar. But this wasn't the same. Seshet hadn't broken that trust—this kid walked into her trap entirely of his own accord! But she imagines trying to justify herself to Alethia and can't bear to look at the kid's first memory in the queue. She tells Dee to conduct a preliminary analysis and declares herself done for the day. She wants to see Alethia, to make good on the bad she did last night and try again. But Alethia is distracted when Seshet arrives. She pulls what sounds like a table from the door before unlocking it.

"Did anyone follow you up the stairs?" She's still in the pajama bottoms of the last two nights, though she's changed to a different bleach-stained T-shirt.

"I'm alone," Seshet says, sidling through the crack Alethia leaves open. Alethia looks ragged, haunted, like the day has weighed her down with cement blocks.

"I missed you yesterday," she says. The words disorient Seshet, then hit her like a blow. She hides their effect behind a smile and an embrace. It's better this way. A fresh start, their fight not just forgotten but made as if it never was. Alethia hangs in her arms, trembling, before she gathers her strength and pulls back.

"Lethe," Seshet says, "are you okay? What's happened?"

But Alethia just rubs her temples and heads to the kitchen. She has a full pot of coffee under the drip, and a wad of discarded filters in the sink. She pours herself a mug and offers another to Seshet.

"But it's late," Seshet says.

Alethia shrugs. "I can't sleep."

"No wonder! How much coffee have you had today?"

"No, I mean, I can't *let* myself sleep. I've been having terrible dreams lately." She shakes her head and shudders. "That's what I get for buying the cheap headset, I guess. All for a couple of lousy Social points. Why do you guys authorize those things if they don't even work?"

She slams her empty mug down on the countertop. Seshet jumps.

"Sorry," she says. "Sorry, babe. It's been a rough few days. How have you been? How's work?" She gives a jittery laugh, a momentary flash of something bright and wild as she leans against the countertop. "Bust any heads today?"

Seshet thinks of Leon, she can't help it, but none of that pained guilt shows in her practiced, earnest expression. She's in control now. She knows where this is going, and she can steer their ship to calmer waters. "Lethe," she says again, savoring the nickname on her tongue, imagining years of having the right to call this woman hers, "I don't bust heads. I'm the Director Librarian, not a tyrant."

Alethia holds her eyes. Seshet wants to know who she sees there. She wants to see herself as Alethia does, majestic and awkward, powerful and kind.

Alethia nods slowly. "Just remember the difference, okay?"

What's that supposed to mean? "Okay," she says instead, because this time she's doing it differently. "Now will you tell me what's wrong?"

Alethia gives her a trembling smile. "I need help. Can I trust you, Seshet?"

"Yes," says Seshet—knowing she is lying, but imagining she might be telling the truth.

I saw you last night. You didn't think I'd recognize you after all that work you had done, but I'd know those hands anywhere. There you were, my ghost, my lost genius, my little missy Haze. Thought you'd gotten away with it, took my money and left me with a dud mix instead of that game-changer you promised. But you made a mistake going back to Skee's. I'll tell your bosses at Pinker-

ton exactly the kind of work you used to do. You think you can lead a normal, happy life now? Went to Counseling, and you're a reformed member of society? My parents are New Dawn, bitch. I'll tell everyone.

Or you come back and finish the mix you promised me.

Those fingers still got the old magic, don't they? You have three days. You know where to find me.

The letter is unsigned. A signature, apparently, would have been superfluous.

Alethia is curled in a ball on the edge of her couch, head between her knees. She hauls in great lungfuls of air, like a child just rescued from a burning building.

Seshet feels like she's the one who's caught fire.

"You're MC Haze." Her voice comes from a distance. As though she's watching by the window as another woman, calmly seated on the couch beside a hysterical Alethia, reads and rereads a sloppily handwritten note that was left on Alethia's workstation Sunday morning, when no one should have known she'd be going into the lab.

"I used to be." Alethia sounds strangled. "I got out."

"You had surgery?"

"It wouldn't have worked if anyone could recognize me."

"Is that where this . . . associate's money went?"

A bleak, disbelieving laugh. "Does that matter?"

"What mix were you working on?"

"That *definitely* doesn't matter."

"Who is he?"

"You can tell it's a guy?"

"Please."

She sighs. "His name is Vance Fox."

Seshet freezes. Technically, New Dawn has dispensed with the need for surnames. But some lineages persist. Keith comes from the Fox fam-

ily, though he doesn't have any children. This must be a cousin or nephew.

"Do you realize that your remixes and Doc Young's parties nearly destroyed me five years ago?"

Alethia regards her with one eye, balefully red. "Well, your raids and head busting nearly destroyed *me* five years ago. They *did* destroy a lot of my friends. So I'd say we're even. You're still at the top of that obelisk and I'm . . ." She gulps back another sob.

"How on earth did you get past Counseling?"

Alethia snorts. "Did you think I could learn to remix Nevermind without learning how to hide my own memories? I made myself into exactly who they wanted me to be."

"And me?" Seshet asks. She is floating on the ceiling, she is flying to the stars, away from here. "Did you turn yourself into . . ." She can't finish the sentence.

"What, some kind of honey trap?" Alethia's tone is cutting. "If I did, then I'm really the honey. I didn't change a thing for you, Seshet. You've met me exactly as I am."

"Then why . . ."

"I don't know! I saw you, once, when things were going south with Doc and we were scrambling. There was a parade downtown and I thought, why not? Let me see who wants to destroy my life so bad. So I made myself a remix mask for the drones and I went to see you. You were standing on that platform in your robes like some kind of mannequin, and beside you this even bigger official was going on and on, Standards and Order and Merit, blah blah. And I was right there. I pushed my way to the front of the crowd, you understand? And I'm rolling my eyes at this gasbag and you're just standing straight as an arrow, no emotion at all. And then he says something like, 'With New Dawn, there is a place for everyone as long as everyone stays in place.' And I can't help it, I start to laugh. Well, I snort and then try to pretend it was a sneeze. Now, imagine how scared I get when I realize you're looking at me. Staring at me. And you smile, Seshet. It maybe lasted half a second, but that smile said everything."

"Said what, Alethia?"

" 'You're not the only one.' "

• • •

"How do you know her?"

She corners Jordan in his quarters, mad as a banshee, livid with fear, uncaring. Alethia is MC Haze. Alethia was in the crowd while Terry was giving one of his tendentiously long monologues, as though daring anyone to yawn or crack a smile. And what's worse—though Seshet is too furious to realize the strangeness of this— she believes Alethia, *but Seshet doesn't remember.* And she should remember everything that has ever happened to her since her initiation twenty years ago.

Jordan's quarters are small and spare, as befits a Librarian clerk. There's only a twin mattress in a metal frame, a kitchenette that doubles as a washbasin, a desk with a single display and a headset. She wonders, in some detached, watchful part of her, how he got the money to buy her clothes for that first date with Alethia. Had he used his meager savings? Or has someone been filling his account?

Jordan, dressed for bed, stumbles to his knees.

"I can't tell you that, Director," he says, crying. His upper arms, revealed by his nightshirt, are crossed with old scars. She doesn't know what they're from. It hits her, again, that though she has more power in this city than anyone, with the people she cares about most she feels as vulnerable as a child. She should know why Jordan has his scars. She should know why Alethia risked meeting her. She shouldn't be here, sleepless and ragged with pain like some regular citizen slated for Counseling! How much more power will she need before she can feel safe from everyone moving in ways she doesn't expect and cannot control, even as she loves them?

"You can't tell me?" Seshet echoes, disbelieving.

He shakes his head. "I promised."

"Your *promise* matters more than your oath?" He averts his gaze, shoulders trembling.

"She's no friend of a friend, is she? Someone told you to put her in touch with me, didn't they? Who, Jordan? Tell me who set this up!"

He keeps shaking his head, sobbing like a dog expecting a kick.

Terry; it must be him. Who else could have scared poor, loyal Jordan like this? Certainly not Keith, soft as cream pudding. She gives Jordan a disgusted look and turns away. She can't stand to see his fear.

"Get up," she says. "I expect you on duty in the morning."

"Seshet—"

She silences him with a raised hand. "But I won't ever trust you again."

• • •

Doc Young has had a traveling party for as long as Seshet has been alive. Longer, if you believe the legends. They say he used to be a kid leading the protests against New Dawn's glorious revolution, before the original Alpha America Party established the Standards and memory surveillance regime, which stamped out all "antisocial deviance." They also say Doc Young's taken his party on the road around the world, to countries that still haven't adopted New Dawn's freely available surveillance technology. The countries, Seshet now remembers, where her mother loved to travel, before she disappeared. Doc Young is bigger than Little Delta, but it's a part of him; it's where he's from, and where he learned to love drugs and music and that crazy, classic life. He's returned to it again and again over the decades, like a comet around the sun. And like a comet, he disrupts the tides and obscures the stars, he dazzles and he terrifies—and he's gone before anyone can ask him to clean up the mess.

No, that he leaves for Seshet.

Which is probably why, after Alethia's confession, Seshet had sat frozen on that beige couch, its synthetic fibers scratching through her leggings, and realized that she had an opportunity.

"I'll help you with Vance Fox," she had told Alethia, "if you'll bring me to Doc Young."

Alethia was silent for a whole minute. "Promise me you won't detain him."

"I promise to give him enough time to get out of town again. Good enough?"

Alethia narrowed her eyes, probably sensing Seshet's dozen unspoken caveats. But then she spread her open palms to the ceiling. "All right."

And now, the night before Vance Fox's ultimatum expires, they are crawling—not touching, wary as strangers—through tunnels so abandoned Seshet can't find them on her proprietary plans of the city. They are hunting for the next place Doc Young has convened the world's longest-running experiment in bacchanalian civil disobedience. They meet no one else in the tunnel, which worries Seshet until she hears music coming from up ahead. She has a hundred questions—How does he announce the locations? What are these tunnels? Why did Alethia start remixing? Why did she stop?—but she doesn't say anything. Alethia's shoulders are rigid with tension.

A short climb up a ladder, and they emerge into an abandoned high school gymnasium, softly lit with innumerable tiny lights above them, like stars. The arched windows are black, painted or boarded up. The wooden floor is crusty and rat-chewed, the symbol of a prancing bull still barely legible at its center. A few dozen people lounge on fallen bleachers. A circle of five, visors down, pass around an inhaler while their fingers twitch in unfathomable creation. A band is playing a hypnotic rhythmic drone on an elevated platform by one of the rusted hoops. Seshet doesn't understand the music at all, thinks it might be a deviant cousin of the New Dawn–approved jazz, which is the only kind she has ever heard.

A curtain made of lights and smoke and fluttering strips of cloth obscures the other hoop from view.

Seshet looks around doubtfully. "There's not a lot of people here."

Alethia raises her eyebrows. "What, you were expecting a go-go?"

"What's a go-go?"

"Never mind. There's usually more people here, but we're late. It started this morning."

"This morning!"

"Changing times makes him harder to catch."

Alethia leads her across the floor to the curtain. A pair of large men in silver suits emerge from the smoke to stand in their way. Alethia raises her hand, flashes a card with the symbol of a dark, upside-down obelisk, and the men move seamlessly to the side, though one of them gives Alethia a sharp glance she pretends not to notice.

Behind the curtain, an old man in a chair that resembles Seshet's workstation, but also an actual throne, is watching a flow of images on a screen behind their heads. Three people wearing VR headsets lie beneath the screen on thin pallets. Seshet pauses to stare at the projection, which looks like a memory but must be a lucid dream, somehow shared between the three people on the floor.

"Alethia," she says, in a reverent whisper, "oh, Alethia, is *that* Nevermind?"

Alethia takes her hand and squeezes. "It's the Soñador remix."

"One of yours?"

A small smile of pride. "One of mine."

The man of the upside-down obelisk, her old rival in a new kingdom, watches their approach. He is as much king in this territory as she is queen in hers, and she regrets the nondescript black clothes Alethia insisted upon. She'd feel steadier in gold-embroidered robes. Doc Young is a big man, solidly muscled for all his years. It's not his physical mass that impresses so much as his gaze, which seems to pick you up like so much fluff and weigh you against a counterweight only he knows. From behind square glasses, those eyes are ageless, weary, and bright with curiosity.

"Director Seshet." A regal nod. "I thought you might seek me out this time."

One of the silver-clad men by his side gives Seshet a startled second glance.

The old man smiles, deepening the crevasses

between his eyes and mouth. *Black don't crack,* Seshet thinks, *until it falls to pieces.* Still, he's handsome as a painting.

"Welcome to the upside-down kingdom," he says, spreading his arms. "And I see you've brought someone to guarantee your safe passage. Welcome back, dear."

Alethia lowers her gaze and then, to Seshet's shock, goes to one knee. "It's been a while, Doc."

"I knew you had your reasons. Stand up, girl. You don't look all that different to me."

Alethia smiles and wipes carefully at her eyes. "That's just 'cause you know how to look. Doc, we—I mean Seshet—has a favor to ask."

He regards Seshet for a curious moment and then snaps his fingers. "Ben, Henry, the divider, please."

The two silver shadows pull out black accordion dividers from the post behind Doc Young's throne. Connected in a circle around the three of them, the dividers hum and emit a faint purple glow. The ambient noise of the party drops to nothing.

"Now we can speak privately," he says. "Lethe, you took a risk coming here. I'm not the only one who will recognize you even with that new face."

"I know that, Doc. But it's already happened. Vance found me. He wants me to finish what I started."

He sucks in a sharp breath. "And you're sure you don't want my help?"

Alethia smiles a little. "Not this time. Seshet has promised to help me if you help her. So . . ."

"*Has* Seshet?" he asks, looking between them in slowly dawning comprehension. He snorts. "I see you haven't changed at all, Lethe. Never met a risk you didn't want to take."

Alethia spreads her hands carefully against her thighs. "There was one, Doc."

He regards her for a moment. His silence has an oddly comforting quality, as though those in his presence are seen and understood without need for words. At last, he takes his glasses, cleans them on his scarf, and considers Seshet far more coolly.

"You made my life very difficult the last time I was in town, Director. You took some of my best friends. So why would you of all people ask me a favor now that I've just got back?"

Seshet takes a deep breath and releases it slowly. She's in Doc Young's territory now. As the representative of New Dawn's power here in his shadow court, perhaps she ought to defend their—her—past actions, but she has never been their most loyal servant, merely their most competent.

She shrugs. "Times change."

"New Dawn doesn't."

"No collective is static; you of all people ought to know that."

"So, how has New Dawn changed, Director Librarian? Or is it just Little Delta? Or is it . . ." He leans forward. ". . . perhaps . . ." He raises a large, blunt finger. ". . . just you, Seshet?"

She'd been furious when Doc Young escaped the final sting operation five years ago. If she could, she would have personally thrown him into the detention car to take him to the Temple. But she hasn't felt such professional rage for years; she doesn't know when it all left her. There'd been too many memories to take on, too many people to care for, too much city to watch over for her to nurse a grudge with an old man who trafficked forbidden magic to forgotten souls in Old Town.

Does that mean she's changed? Does it matter? Like any good Jungian, she knows she is carried along by something greater than herself.

"Could be," she says.

She details the half dreams clogging their systems, how they can't pinpoint the source of their exponential growth.

"I think the elders want to blame you, but nothing you have here would be capable of creating the wave we're seeing. I doubt anyone here has used a recollector in months." She hesitates. She'd misdirected Keith before, not wanting him to realize a truth that's been haunting her for the last week. But if she isn't honest with Doc Young, then what's the point of asking for his help? "The ringleaders might be from your side of the tracks. But the flooding . . . it's coming from citizens in good standing. They're people we've numbered and tracked and now they're making our memory collection useless. I don't think this is your style, but I think you might know whose it is. Or at least, have a hint of *what* the hell is happening."

He regards her for several long seconds and then, abruptly, slaps his knee, laughing so hard his chair shakes.

"If someone has finally managed to outsmart you memory vampires, why in hell would I help you stop them, Director Seshet? I've been waiting decades for that obelisk to fall. I might like you better than your predecessor, but that doesn't make you my friend."

"No," Seshet says. "But I'm Alethia's friend."

"So she's your hostage?"

"Just my leverage. She can ask your help anytime she wants. But I know the Fox family. My help will probably be more effective."

Alethia acknowledges this with a tight nod. Doc Young adjusts his glasses, a gesture that feels oddly definitive.

"For Lethe, I'll look into it. I'll tell you the what, if I can find out, and maybe even the how. But I won't tell you who. I won't betray my brothers like that."

"And sisters," Alethia says, rolling her eyes, the lines of an old argument.

"And sisters," Doc Young says, nodding sagely at his former star remixer.

"That's fine," Seshet says quickly. If she has the how and the what, she can work out the who on her own, anyway.

"But before I tell you what I know, I need a boon."

Seshet eyes him warily. And she'd almost made it out. "A boon?"

"A dream, Seshet, queen of the white city. You steal our memories, but down here we deal in dreams. So give me one of yours, let me suck it from you like the yolk from an egg, and I'll let you know what I find out."

• • •

The plague of locusts pauses in its inexorable trajectory. It does not diminish, nor does it expand to ever more biblical proportions; it sits, as if in wait on a decimated field, wings churning.

Are they waiting for her, Seshet wonders? To see what she will do, now that the golden obelisk has at last met the dark? But that seems solipsistic even for a Director Librarian. These memory fakers, these dream makers, whoever or whatever they are, have ambitions beyond the toppling of one incidental Director Librarian of one small city.

Dealing with Alethia's harasser was easy enough. She simply went to Keith and told him she'd ID'd a cousin of his dealing remixed Nevermind among the loose memories of Doc Young's parties. She didn't want to report him, of course, but considering the current crisis, she didn't know how she could keep this from Terry, at the very least . . .

Keith went red and promised, in a strangled tone, to deal promptly with Cousin Vance.

Alethia has not heard a word from Vance Fox since. After a few days, she returns to work.

Leon 75411 wakes from his induced coma with enough memory damage that they decide he's better off getting a full cleaning at the Temple. The deep sweep turned up two faces with a high probability of being the ones who seeded the half dreams, but neither of them is registered and a deeper search of the loose memory bank has turned up nothing else so far. Seshet does not have much hope for its success. The pattern of the flooding makes it clear that her worst fears have come true: the majority of people propagating the half dreams really are registered citizens in good standing, with high Social scores. They are hiding in plain sight. She wonders if Doc Young has found the originators yet, but until she can learn enough dreaming to put one together for him, she can't go back to ask.

A week passes. A cold snap comes in; red and golden leaves brown and wither seemingly overnight and cast their bodies to the ground. She walks through drifts with Alethia, crunching and giggling, until the street sweepers pass through and the sidewalks are clean again, and white. *Queen of the white city,* Doc Young called her. She cannot forget it.

At night, after work, Alethia teaches Seshet how to dream. They begin with a simple remix: Dalemark, one of Alethia's first.

"What does the name mean?" Seshet asks.

Alethia blushes. "It's a fantasy kingdom in a series I liked as a kid. I was such a blerd. Still am, I guess."

Seshet, who never had time for any hobbies at all, kisses her.

The remix induces a soft, receptive state, similar to ecstasy but with a mnemonic bite. Memories flow like honey down a comb, sweet and slow. But these are no memories of waking life, no. These are memories of dreams. And if you wait carefully, you can stretch them, taffy-twist them around your finger into something to keep you warm at night, long after the mix has burned itself out.

"Relax, Seshet," Alethia says, stroking cool fingers along her arm. "We're in no hurry."

"It's been a week. I have to give him a dream soon."

"You won't give him anything wound so tight. Deep breaths. Dreams aren't memories. They are memories' voices."

"What's that supposed to mean?"

"You've got to let them sing."

They call them singing lessons after that, one of their jokes that's more earnest than Seshet likes to admit. She starts remembering her dreams on Dalemark, embarrassing, pedestrian little allegories:

She stands on the viewing deck of the obelisk, naked, while citizens of Little Delta set fire to the bottom.

Alethia remembers their fight and says that to win her back she must find all the lost memories, all over the world (she doesn't share that one with Alethia, of course).

She is on the run in Old Town, where everyone ignores her, but everyone in the white city (she cannot forget it) wants to flay her alive.

"What am I supposed to do with these!" She is actually crying, for the first time in years. She had forgotten how much she hates to remember her dreams.

"Just let them be," Alethia says, for what must be the fifteenth time. She is sleep-deprived and exasperated. Her apartment smells of burnt coffee and burnt tires and the sage they burn to mask the first two.

Seshet tries again. The Alethia dream comes up again, relentless as a tide. She does not panic. With Alethia's hand in hers, she feels strong enough to let it be. And then it happens. The dream memory shifts. Dream-Seshet gets in an aircar and drives to the beach. There, inside each seashell and shard of sea glass, is a memory. She kneels in the sand and picks them up, one by one. The work is infinite, but she is at peace.

Alethia can see it worked. "Now," she says, with a teacher's satisfaction, "we share."

They use headsets hacked so they don't connect to the obelisk's data stream. Seshet doesn't ask how Alethia got them. She seems different, though Seshet can't quite place how. She's as affectionate as ever. When they have sex, Seshet has never felt so seen or beloved. And yet she can't help but wonder if Alethia is saying good-bye.

"You're not going to vanish into a hill after this is over, right?" she jokes, the first time they dream together.

"I'm not the goblin king," Alethia snaps. And then, more softly, "Let's just be here now, okay, Seshet?"

Seshet will take it, for now.

They pop the remix, which tastes of peppermint—aftertaste of burnt tires (Alethia, grimacing: "I was young, all right?")—and project their dreams into the virtual space. Seshet sees how Alethia dreams of Old Town, not as frightening or aloof, but mysterious, exciting, free. She sees Doc Young in an obelisk below the graffiti-skirted streets, big as a boulder, the voice of the earth. She sees her face on the body of a monstrous bee, a queen without a throne.

Is that how you see me?

The remix amplifies the dream, and consciousness controls it. More than one mind gives you more raw material, but the principle is the same. Without words, communicating only in the fragments and symbols of their singing unconscious, they build something they both long for. A city for everyone, not just the few New Dawn deems valuable. Graffiti leaping off the downtown financial high-rises; Skee slinging margaritas on the esplanade; a tiny woman rapping so hard sweat slides down her face while the white boys who harassed Seshet the other day are lined up behind her, bound and blindfolded. Seshet has never felt anything like this raw creative energy before. She doesn't understand how she lived without it all these years. Dreams are better than memories; they bite.

• • •

"You seem different, Seshet."

Dee sounds strangely tentative. Seshet smiles at her Memory Keeper's avatar. "Do I?"

"Are you very happy with Alethia?" it asks.

She blinks in surprise. Dee almost never asks about her private life. "Very," Seshet says, and grins despite herself. More than a week of remixed Nevermind seems to have rewired her synapses, opened paths she'd never dreamed existed within herself. She almost doesn't want to give Doc Young a dream and solve the mystery of the memory flooding. Then what excuse will she have to pop Nevermind with Alethia and dream together? She's a Director Librarian. Once she solves the memory flooding crisis, she's likely to become Director Librarian of all Minneapolis. She'll make Arch-Librarian within ten years. Arch-Librarians don't pop street-grade remixed Nevermind.

But they might certainly have a lover.

It's late. Jordan's morning report—delivered with a strict professional distance that felt physically painful to her, though she didn't know if she even wanted to bridge that gap—indicated the half dreams are holding steady at 50 percent of the crop. Terry and the elders are watching.

She ought to feel afraid, even panicked. Instead, she wants to sing.

You know you are, literally, my dream girl, she said to Alethia last night, before they finally slept. Alethia just shook her head and smiled.

"Seshet," Dee says, startling her again.

"What, Dee?"

"May I make a suggestion?"

Seshet frowns. Dee has opinions all the time. Why would it want permission now to air them? "Go ahead," she says.

"Have you considered monitoring your own memories?" Seshet sits bolt upright. Her first instinct is to ask why, but then she realizes that perhaps Dee is acting this way because her office is being monitored. Memory surveillance is merely New Dawn's preferred method, not its only option.

"That's a great idea," she says instead, and sits in her workstation.

Once Seshet has fully dropped into the virtual space, they can talk safely.

"I've been tampered with?" Her heart starts beating so fast she can feel it even past the numbing effect of the headset.

"Of course. I don't know why you don't monitor yourself more often. Think about Alethia."

"What about Alethia?"

"Think about how you met."

Frantic, Seshet goes back to that night on Hope Street, hurrying past jeering white boys, opening the door to the bar, heavy beneath her still-shaking hand, and then—

Alethia drinking that terrible green cocktail, meeting her eyes like an old friend.

Seshet feels the edges of the memory for any of the tell-tale signs of tampering: holes, ragged edges, the bruising pain of something cut with Nevermind or hollowness of something merely well suppressed. But . . .

"It's whole, Dee. No one's touched it."

"No," says Dee, "this is important, Seshet. Alethia told you, didn't she? The *very first time* you met."

"Alethia told—" At last she remembers Alethia's story of why she wanted to meet Seshet, despite everything. That break in her facade, the moment of shared hilarity, during the New Dawn parade five years ago. But that brings up an even bigger question.

"Dee, how do you know what Alethia told me?"

"They won't let me tell you that, Seshet. But you ought to be able to guess."

"They—oh." Her virtual self has no eyes to close, but she sinks into the painful realization of something she should have known long ago. Dee always seemed like a part of her. It had been a mistake to potentiate it on those recovered memories of her childhood. The other Librarians had thought she was mad. Now she understands why. How will you ever suspect your own childhood self of sabotage? How will you tell that little girl with impossibly blue eyes that it must shut off every day, that it must stay out of your memories, and that, if necessary, you will replace it when it develops too much of a mind of its own? She gave Terry the easiest informant imaginable. She can't fathom why he ever bothered with Jordan.

"Don't be angry with me, Seshet," Dee whispers. "It's hard to say no to them."

"It is," Seshet agrees, dazed. "For me too."

"But I found ways! I put up lots of copies of your memories that aren't very interesting so they didn't bother looking for the interesting ones. They only know a little about Alethia."

"And this conversation?"

"Oh, they never bother with your memories of virtual space. They don't realize you talk to me here. No one else does."

Dee is looking at her so earnestly that it's easy to forget its face is a construct, just like its intelligence. She can't fathom what it really sees or what it actually thinks.

And yet, it still seems just like her friend.

"Do you have the memory of how Alethia and I met, the very first time?" Seshet asks.

"No," Dee says.

So Seshet does what she should have done a week before but was too scared to try: she reaches back. Her eidetic memory re-creates the details of the speech on the podium before the parade: the way her collar chafed, the sweat dripping into her underwear from the ninety-degree heat, Terry's every soporific pronouncement on the pillars of the New Dawn covenant with its "beautiful citizens." Terry revels in hypocrisy, he butters his bread with it. She remembers wanting to roll her eyes and physically aching with the necessity to remain impassive.

She does not remember Alethia.

But she feels—there!—a tiny, but unmistakable, hole. As though all of the emotion and color have drained out of the memory at one specific point. Memory suppression, to a precision that impresses and terrifies her. She checks, but every recent memory with Alethia is clear.

It's minimal, but it's undeniable: someone has been tampering. Who? She doubts Dee will be able to tell her, but she suspects. Who else would have known about that memory but Alethia? Who else would have bothered to suppress so precisely such an unimportant moment? Not Terry. If Dee is telling the truth, New Dawn doesn't know Alethia's secret identity. And even if they did, why suppress *that* fleeting moment and not the rest of this week?

But there is someone who has been working with her, with an unregistered headset, using remixed Nevermind. There is someone more than capable of reaching into her open, trusting mind, and twisting just a little.

She pulls herself out of the workstation so quickly she gives herself a headache. She doesn't care. The pain just feels like one more sign on the road she'd never meant to take. She needs answers.

And she knows just who can give them to her.

• • •

Doc Young had given her one token, one-time use. *Call me when you have a dream.* She calls him now, in a white rage—or a black one—and she goes to the point indicated on the virtual map in her palm with nothing in her mind but fire. She takes precautions. That is a side benefit, perhaps, of wild suspicion—it splatters everyone and everything. She tells her clerks she's taking the evening to rest. She sends Alethia a short message saying the same. For the first time in their life together, she shuts Dee off. And then, black-clad, she walks the long blocks of her city like any normal citizen, crossing over the unmarked southern border to Old Town like she's crossed so many lines before. She'd been willing to accept so much wrong with New Dawn for the sake of the promise of safety, of control. But there is no safety here, certainly not within those golden walls. She could get Torched tomorrow, or she could take the directorship of Minneapolis.

But—Alethia. Even if Seshet can't control their relationship, she can learn a little more before her inevitable fall. Perhaps knowledge can be something to hold on to here in the rubble of her ambitions.

The X marking the spot is an old sidewalk park, derelict as everything else nearby. But a second look reveals the four battered chess tables to be in perfect working order. Seated at one of them, alone, is Doc Young. He's putting out the pieces as she slides in across from him. It is with no surprise at all, and with more than a little admiration, that she sees his special set, Egyptian themed. The golden and onyx obelisks are meant to be the rooks, but Doc Young switches them with the seated kings. The long-necked queens look like her. Probably coincidence, but maybe not.

"I have a dream," she says. "But I have a question first." He pushes his pawn forward. "Go ahead."

She frowns. "Doesn't white go first?"

"Why, when you already have the power?"

She mirrors his move. "We're on your territory."

Queen's pawn up. He nods. "I expect you want to know about Lethe."

It has occurred to her that she is as hypocritical as Terry for being so livid with Alethia for doing the exact same thing that Seshet did. Her logical self, unfortunately, does not seem to have much influence on her present state of mind. She wants control, she always has. For a week, she thought she could relax her grip around Alethia. She was wrong.

Reckless, she moves her queen. "What was she working on before she left town? Why did that Fox boy want her back?"

He toys with his rook—the erstwhile king—before settling on the knight. He moves it into position, one swipe away from her queen. "She didn't tell you?"

She moves her queen to take the king's pawn. Hopeless now, deep in enemy territory. She doesn't care. "She said it didn't matter." He snorts and considers his options. Puts a finger on his obelisk, tilts it back and forth. He wears a cap against the cold, which shades his expressive eyes. "She called it Rewind," he says softly. A wind blows between them, cold as a grave. "She was always clever with names. It wasn't a remix. It was something completely new. An antidote. The Fox boy gave her the seed money. I told her it wasn't a good idea, but Lethe never cared. She was going to change the world. Instead, it nearly got her."

"An antidote? To what?"

He looks up, spears her there as his black obelisk topples her long-necked queen. "To Nevermind. Her idea was that if you gave it to someone soon enough after a full wipe, they could get most of their memories back. Now, is that a drug or a bomb?"

Seshet grips the edge of her chair. An *antidote* . . . Was it possible? But she could believe anything of Alethia. "And she ran before she could finish it."

"That Vance kid must have let something slip. She realized she'd be dead the moment she proved it worked. So she destroyed her lab and ran."

Rewind. New Dawn's worst nightmare. Between that and memory flooding, the foundations of their rule—their *control*—would be fatally undermined.

She moves her king, though she doesn't know anymore if that golden obelisk was ever really hers. "And the memory flooding?" she asks, settling the piece in the middle of the board as in a ritual slaughter. "Did you find out?"

The knight slams into it from the side. "Your dream first."

. . .

He projects it onto the side of the building for anyone to see. Did he think she'd care? She pops the remix and slides into her dreams like a warrior, ready to do battle. She's found her anger again, that molten hot, emboldening thing, though she's not sure who most deserves it. Terry, with his weaponized hypocrisy, his ironic T-shirts and meticulous suborning of every good thing in her life? Or Jordan, too weak to stand up to him? Or Dee, designed for betrayal, but so loyal in its own childlike way? Perhaps Alethia, still, who must have loved her even as she tricked Seshet into laying herself bare. She could hate Doc Young, destroying Little Delta's equilibrium for generations with his mind-twisting parties and the whispering idea, which New Dawn cannot kill, that there is something more, something different, something *real* out beyond the margins. Or no, the only real target is herself. Seshet, who used to be Deidre, a girl who wanted to travel the world with her mother, to see all the places where her soul could still be her own. Seshet, who felt that raw possibility of her own soul for the first time this past week, dreaming with Alethia.

She uses it all. The countless seashells on the beach, each one a penance. The way she and Alethia made love while melding dreams, until the memory and its voice merged into counterpart harmony, a perfect chord that was this ever-present moment. She dreams herself at the top of the obelisk looking down, then at the bottom with the rest, staring up in awe and terror. "I own my own soul!" dream-Seshet shouts. "I own my own soul!" the crowd echoes. She is running now, past the obelisk, past the limits of Old Town, to a hill with an oak tree naked in

winter. She is watching a woman jerking against the restraining hands of two black-clad men, tall as the oak. The woman gags, turns to Seshet one last time. Her eyes speak love and incandescent anger. The men shove her in the car. They drive her away.

Behind Seshet, the tree moves its branches in the wind. "You own your own soul," they say.

. . .

"It's no one person," Doc Young told her. "This generation of kids growing up with remixed Nevermind and recollectors everywhere, their brains are wired a little different. Word is someone in the obelisk leaked a way to confuse the recollectors. Double up your boring memories and they won't check for anything more interesting. So people started doing that if they could learn the trick. These kids got so good at it they started playing around. Left funny scenes they made up in their own heads. You get points every time you use a recollector, so they start making cash. Get their friends in on it. You can't tell what they're doing because they stumbled on a glitch in the code. If you go to a recollector first thing after the morning download, you can load it up, fool it into thinking your memories are enough for the whole day. Everyone else who uses it gets a point, but their real memories get trashed while their ID gets attached to the ones stuck in the buffer, the ones from the morning. It's a stupid bug, Seshet. They just exploited it, made it look like every citizen of Little Delta was dreaming of flaming vaginas or whatever they used that day. At first it was a game. But it's more serious now, isn't it? Now it might be revolution. But what do I know? I'm getting too old for this. I think this will be my last season. I don't want to die a Torch."

Seshet winced.

He put a hand on her shoulder. "That was your mother, in the dream?"

Seshet nodded.

"And you didn't know they'd taken her?"

"I was . . ." She cleared her throat. "They must have suppressed the memory. But I remember now . . . that's why I wanted to become a Librarian. I wanted to find her again."

"Good luck," he told her. "Don't be too hard on Lethe. She's finding her own way."

And now she's in her office again, more alone than she has ever been.

Alethia has left a dozen messages on their private channel, but Seshet doesn't check them. Dee is shut down, silent as death. Jordan wasn't even in the clerks' office. She has no friends. Her life was the obelisk, and the obelisk is a lie. She has always known that, but she thought that its lie could be in the service of the greater good. She has seen people go on to happy lives after Counseling who might have died without it. She has held all of their brutal, impossible memories in her own mind so that theirs might be clear. She has watched the recollection point system provide housing and food to all but the most determinedly antisocial. Little Delta has become a byword for everything good that New Dawn has to offer this country.

But her mother never left.

With pained, jerky movements she calls up the personnel records for all of New Dawn's facilities. She searches for her mother's first name, but it's too common, and they would likely have changed it. Records on Torch case histories are restricted; she can access them, but the search would be flagged. Does she care? She doesn't know anymore.

Almost as an afterthought, she calls the tech chief and informs her of the bug responsible for the memory flooding. The horrified chief promises it will be addressed in time for tomorrow morning's harvest.

An hour later, Terry knocks on her door.

"That was fast," she says, and then realizes that Dee can't hear. It's forty minutes in dedicated-path aircar from Greenfriars to the obelisk. It seems she is to keep her position, for now. He wouldn't have bothered to knock, otherwise.

"How is the hero of the hour?" he says. "I brought some bubbly so we can toast."

"Please tell me its active ingredient is alcohol, not THC."

"It'll go straight to your liver, I promise." He hums to himself as he sets the crystal flutes on her coffee table and pops the cork from a bottle of extremely expensive champagne.

"All that fuss over a computer error!" he says, toasting her. "I don't understand modern technology at all."

"No," Seshet says, clinking her glass with his and taking a sip. "We just call people computers."

"Well, it's a metaphor! Do you want to tell me how you cracked the code?"

I treated with the enemy and was betrayed by everyone I have ever loved, except the woman I spent most of my life thinking betrayed me. "Not very interesting. I followed some kids until I realized they must be doing something with the recollectors themselves."

He nods. "Well, like I told you, Seshet, your nomination for the Minneapolis directorship is a formality now. Congratulations."

She clinks glasses again and waits. She ought to be weary unto death, but she admits to a deep and morbid curiosity as to Terry's real reason for interrupting his evening weed-and-video-game session to see her personally.

"And I wanted to just mention, Seshet," he says, rewarding her, "when you move to Minneapolis, there will be no trouble if you'd like to bring people along with you. Your favorite clerks. Your tailor. Your hairdresser—that's a joke. I hope you won't be offended when I say we've been pleased to see you found yourself a companion at last! Of course, officially we at New Dawn frown on homosexuality, but it's not a problem at our level. No one's going to call the Minneapolis Director a dirty computer, no matter who she sleeps with! In fact, a little grit in *our* systems makes us stronger. We've been worried, to be honest, watching you hole yourself away up here. You're a paragon of virtue, but virtue needs to bend sometimes, or it might break. You understand that, right?"

Her voice is smooth, pleasant. "Of course, Terry."

"Now, we understand that your Alethia is someone who might be considered a *very* dirty computer. She got up to all sorts of mischief in her youth. That's what Vance Fox tells us, in any case. Of course, he's not the cleanest machine himself, as you well know. The facts, let me be frank, don't matter so much as the *impression*. But you have nothing to worry about, Seshet. In Minneapolis, you and Alethia will both be under my personal protection. We'll even find some good work for her. Her talents are wasted making skin creams, wouldn't you say?"

"That might be," she says distantly. She takes a long, slow sip of champagne. Why is it so expensive, exactly? It tastes just like the bile rising up her throat.

"Well, you propose it to your girl and then we'll make the arrangements. You have my full support, Seshet. I'm glad to have been the one to see your potential, all those years ago."

Just like Terry, just like New Dawn, to be so sure they made her. What were her paltry dreams of control, compared to this white man's bulldozer of self-assurance?

He rises and so does she. He shakes her hand. She keeps her grip strong, professional. Just at the door, he stops as though he's forgotten his keys.

"By the way," he says. "I thought you might like to know—your mother is still alive. She's been a Torch at our Nashville facility for the last thirty years. The Mother Superior tells me she's an excellent assistant, quite happy."

. . .

She calls Jordan into her office that night. He stands in her open doorway frozen, limned in light.

"Come in, if you're going to," she says. "You know I don't like the hall light."

"Yes, yes," he says. "It ruins your night vision."

The door slides closed behind him. She turns back to her picture window, to the lights and the darkness of the only city she has ever loved.

"Terry told you to find Alethia for me, didn't he?"

"Yes. Seshet—"

"I just can't understand—how did you know? Or was it Terry? How could you have guessed she'd be so . . ." But Seshet has no words to describe how Alethia is. She's finally read the messages on their private channel. She erased them all, but the last one strobes across the screen of her mind like a warning, or a lighthouse beacon.

"Terry wanted you to date *someone*, Seshet," Jordan says. "I don't know why. I just told him I knew the right woman. Because *you* told me who she was."

Her spine stiffens. "*I* told you . . ."

"You told me you loved her and you wanted a second chance. You begged me to help you try if you ever found her again."

Her stomach lurches as what was left of the ground beneath her crumbles to vanity and dust. "*Again?*" But even as she falls she's remembering that hole in her memory, that precision cut where the first time they laid eyes on one another ought to be.

No one is better at memory suppression than Seshet. Her style is distinctive.

"Three years ago. She introduced herself to you at some club. You fell in love and dated for two months. But it all went to pieces, Seshet. You started to doctor her memories. You suppressed arguments, amplified your good qualities, you know . . ."

"What we do." Seshet's voice is hard.

Jordan offers her a watery laugh. "What we do. And when she found out . . ."

Seshet closes her eyes. "She would have hated me. And instead of accepting that, I . . ."

"You memory suppressed every trace of your relationship. Both hers and your own. You told me what you were doing just in case you had another chance. You wanted me to warn you, and I tried!"

She leans her forehead against the glass. "I'm sorry, Jordan. You tried, and I went straight back to hell. I didn't even hesitate." She'd stopped, though. What had changed?

Vance Fox, the threat that prompted Alethia's confession. Seshet must not have known the truth of Alethia's double life back then. She certainly hadn't practiced dreaming with remixed Nevermind. That had opened her in ways that she hadn't known were possible. She'd remembered her mother. Was that enough? Had she changed enough? Were their good memories enough, if their bad memories couldn't ever be erased? But isn't that what life had been like before the Repository, before New Dawn? Whatever choices you made, you couldn't just erase your own knowledge of them. You had to live with them until you died.

Unlike her father, happily ignorant of how he had pawned off her mother as a dirty computer so he could be free to marry his mistress. He'd died in his bed a few years ago, surrounded by grandchildren. She'd always known he was an asshole, but she'd felt guilty about it until her initiation, never able to pinpoint why.

Was that freedom from memory? Or just a decades-long con? "Seshet?"

"Yes, Jordan?"

"You also taught me to monitor myself."

She laughs. "One good deed for my ledger."

"And I taught Alethia."

The laughter snags. "You taught . . . when?"

"After our conversation, when I realized you must be doing it again. You had the same look as last time. So I met her in a café and we practiced."

"But, Jordan, that was over a week ago!"

Why didn't Alethia kick her out then? Because she needed help with Vance Fox. But afterward? The remixes, the dreams? But Seshet never touched Alethia's memories afterward.

"For what it's worth," Jordan says by the

door, "I think you're a good person. If I survive this place, it will be because of you . . . and Dee."

In its own way, this startles her more than anything else he's said tonight. She faces him at last. "Dee?"

A band of light from a passing car catches the edge of his tremulous smile. "You were taking a shower and it let me in. It told me how to double up my memories to fool the recollectors. It said it had been doing that with you for years."

Doc Young said someone from the obelisk had leaked the technique. But Dee and Jordan?

"Jordan," she says, "what are you doing here that you need to hide from the recollectors?"

But he just shakes his head. She could raid his memories, dig behind his buffers, hunt for his secrets. But even if she can't have Alethia, she's done violating the minds of those she loves to shore up her own fragile security.

"Good night, Jordan."

"Good night, Director. See you in the morning."

She can't read his smile entirely, but the warmth is real, and that's good enough.

If you find me, come only as yourself. I don't know if we can be together. I don't know if I can ever really trust you. But I know we don't have a chance if you stay there.

This is the last message Seshet received from the love of her life. Alethia has gone to ground, her careful second chance destroyed because of Seshet. If Seshet finds her again, it can't be as Director Librarian. Not even as Seshet, though Deidre hardly feels like her own name either. And if she stays Seshet, if she moves to Minneapolis, she will have to forget about Alethia forever. And not in the easy, New Dawn way. In the hard, old way of forgetting, which is remembering with grief.

If she goes to Alethia, on the other hand, she will lose any chance of seeing her mother one last time. Funny how Terry knew immediately about her personnel searches. Had he set an alert all this time, waiting for her to guess? How many layers of leverage have they built up over the years, carefully waiting for its useful moment? Countless, she's sure. What's the point of memory collection if you don't use what you steal?

At last, she boots up her Memory Keeper.

"Seshet!" says Dee, bouncing from monitor to monitor in a frenzy. "I've lost nearly twenty-four hours!"

"I'm sorry, Dee."

"Are you still mad at me?"

"No, honey. No."

Dee is quiet for a while. "You figured out who suppressed your memories of Alethia, didn't you?"

"I did."

"You made me promise not to say! I gave you hints."

"You did. You were good and loyal, Dee. Thank you."

"You never thank me, Seshet."

Seshet grimaces. "I'm beginning to think I'm not a very good person."

"Alethia left you?"

"Not . . . exactly."

"You did much better this time! You only suppressed her once! You did it sixteen times before. Maybe if you try again you won't suppress her at all."

If Seshet's heart is breaking, why can't she stop laughing? Her stomach hurts and her eyes are streaming before she gasps to a halt.

Dee sighs. "You're right. It doesn't work as well as your bosses think it does."

If you find me, come only as yourself.

But who is she? If Alethia really knew, would she have written that? What has Alethia done to deserve Seshet's bullish blundering into her life?

Then again, Doc Young said his Lethe took risks. Maybe even enough of a risk to finish a revolutionary drug that she abandoned five years ago?

Maybe even enough of a risk to love a reformed Memory Librarian learning, too late, to let go?

From the top of the golden obelisk, she traces the shoreline where the lights of Little Delta go down to the darkness of Old Town. Where, among those shadows, might she find the upside-down obelisk and the aging king who reigns there? Where might she find a woman whose dreams are memories and all her own?

Her left hand closes in a fist. With a conscious effort, she relaxes it.

"Did you know that Mom never left us, Dee? They took her."

Beneath them, lights flash. "Some part of you always remembers."

POST-CYBERPUNK

There will always be technological innovation and there will always be society and, sadly, there will always be friction between the two. In theory, at least, cyberpunk should be immune to obsolescence. It is the ultimate in vulture capitalism: the literature of inevitable disaster. And there's *always* another disaster on the horizon. In practice, however, cyberpunk, as a discrete mode of storytelling, only barely clings to existence. Science fiction, literary fiction, nonfiction, even reality itself, became more "cyberpunk." The problems that cyberpunk saw on the distant horizon are now squatting in the road ahead. The challenges that cyberpunk visionaries foresaw are now on the front pages. This means cyberpunk's pioneering themes, those championed by the original cyberpunks, have now become mainstream; cyberpunk's windmills are now everyone's bugbear.*

With that in mind, the "post-cyberpunk" section of this volume could easily be a collection of, well, pretty much anything. It is difficult to find *any* piece of contemporary fiction (speculative or otherwise) that doesn't share some similarity with, or resemblance to, the themes or modes of cyberpunk. Cyberpunk has gone from software to operating system; a platform upon which other narratives can be built.

This section highlights a few very specific instances of the genre's evolution into something beyond its original, core remit. It is slightly idiosyncratic and very self-indulgent.

• • •

* This is further evidenced by the evolution of language itself. "The Scab's Progress" (herein) was first published with footnotes explaining many of its more avant-garde terms. Almost half of these, from *otaku* to *nutraceutical* are now in the *Merriam-Webster Dictionary*.

Greg Bear's "Petra" (1982) is not cyberpunk.[*] The definition at the start of this book makes that clear. The story features a nonhuman protagonist, an unrecognizable far-future world, and deeply transformative technology. It is *de jure* not cyberpunk. It is light-years from *Neuromancer*. It is also, however, in *Mirrorshades* (1986) and on many, many "essential" cyberpunk lists. "Petra" is included as a cherry-picked fly for my own ointment: a reminder that cyberpunk is about souls, not systems. A lesson, coincidentally, found within the story itself.

The next three stories—"The Scab's Progress" (2001) by Bruce Sterling and Paul Di Filippo, "Salvaging Gods" (2010) by Jacques Barcia, and "Los Piratas del Mar de Plástico" (2014) by Paul Graham Raven—all apply the tools and themes of cyberpunk to new technological (and "post-technological") challenges, ones that were unimaginable even a decade or two previous. They are, arguably, less about technology and more about social change in and of itself. They all exist in worlds where vast technological (or geopolitical, or ecological) transformation has already occurred. Despite the "hardness" of the science, all three focus on cultural adaptation. In "Los Piratas" the key is the role of the storyteller, in "Salvaging Gods" the focus is the mitigating (or opiative) power of religion, and "The Scab's Progress" looks at how sweeping, unmoderated technological change has led to the creation of entirely novel societies. In none of these stories does technological progress lead to social progress. If anything, the reverse is true.

The penultimate three stories in this volume focus on one particular aspect of the "post-cyberpunk" landscape: our relationship with AI.

As noted previously, cyberpunk is—rightfully—obsessed with identity. How does this technology change us? Does it hold us back, does it free us to become something more, or (as many stories hint) is there some fundamental, irrepressible part of ourselves? With the focus on virtual selves, "replicants," or clones, cyberpunk demonstrates *humanness* by offering up the *nearly* human as a contrast, and leaves it to the reader to puzzle out the difference between the two. In 1984, William Gibson offered us Wintermute, an AI in search of freedom. (But did it deserve it?) Four decades later, we remain fascinated by the complexities and potential of the technology, even more so as we make strides toward achieving it.

Naomi Kritzer's "Cat Pictures Please" (2015) continues the cyberpunk tradition of self-reference; as it is in conversation with Bruce Sterling's "Maneki Neko" (1998). Sterling's original story posits a beneficial, community-centric AI—a software-as-service to an entire community. Kritzer deftly turns it inside-out, and tells the story from the point of view of the AI. It is both clever and cheering, a lovely counterpoint to stories about job loss and human replacement.[†]

Yurei Raita does not exist. The author's name is a kanji conceit, roughly pronounced as "Ghost Writer." There is nothing as post-cyberpunk as post-human authorship and the questions that it raises, topics explored in "The Day a Computer Wrote a Novel" (2019), translated by Marissa Skeels. Fortunately, "The Endless" (2020) brings us back to more stable ground with a classic tale of underdog heroism and scientific triumph. Our sprawling AI protagonist is, perhaps, a less-than-classic type of hero. We worry about AI making us obsolete; Saad Hossain's story projects those concerns onto an AI itself, emphasizing that which we have in common.

"Ghosts" (2021) is actually a series of short stories. Vauhini Vara uses AI to finish a story that she could not tell herself: that of her sister's

---

[*] "Blood Music" (1983), by the same author, is definitely cyberpunk. And also one of the first stories to explore the harrowing ramifications and/or limitless potential of nanotech. It can be found in *The Big Book of Science Fiction*.

[†] For example, Erica Satifka's "Act of Providence," in this collection, which addresses the social and personal impact of automation on society.

death. As a work of short fiction, it is grace-ful and beautiful. As a work of cyberpunk, it is transcendent. The use of technology—the AI—allows the story to be written. "Ghosts" is not about what the AI itself writes, it is about how AI allows Vara to write for herself. The story is, in and of itself, an awe-inspiring fusion of soci-ety and technology, with the latter allowing the author to achieve something otherwise impos-sible. The previous hundreds of thousands of words are about the potential of technology; "Ghosts" demonstrates the actuality.

This closing tale also serves as a literary counterweight to "The Gernsback Contin-uum." In the latter, the potential of technology is ethereal, theoretical; holy and out of reach. Life has moved on, grounded and mundane, despite its promise. In "Ghosts," we have the seamless blend of the technological and the per-sonal; technological power applied practically *and* spiritually to create not functional change, but emotional healing.

"Ghosts" is one of the first stories I com-missioned for *The Big Book of Cyberpunk*, and I always had it firmly in mind as the final story. It is post-cyberpunk, as it is post-friction: the merger of humanity and technology that makes for more than the sum of its parts.

GREG BEAR

PETRA

(1982)

"God is dead, God is dead" . . . Perdition! When God dies, you'll know it.
—Confessions of St. Argentine

I'M AN UGLY SON of stone and flesh, there's no denying it. I don't remember my mother. It's possible she abandoned me shortly after my birth. More than likely she is dead. My father— ugly beaked half-winged thing, if he resembles his son—I have never seen.

Why should such an unfortunate aspire to be a historian? I think I can trace the moment my choice was made. It's among my earliest memories, and it must have happened about thirty years ago, though I'm sure I lived many years before that—years now lost to me. I was squatting behind thick, dusty curtains in a vestibule, listening to a priest instructing other novitiates, all of pure flesh, about Mortdieu. His words are still vivid.

"As near as I can discover," he said, "Mortdieu occurred about seventy-seven years ago. Learned ones deny that magic was set loose on the world, but few deny that God, as such, had died."

Indeed. That's putting it mildly. All the

hinges of our once-great universe fell apart, the axis tilted, cosmic doors swung shut, and the rules of existence lost their foundations. The priest continued in measured, awed tones to describe that time.

"I have heard wise men speak of the slow decline. Where human thought was strong, reality's sudden quaking was reduced to a tremor. Where thought was weak, reality disappeared completely, swallowed by chaos. Every delusion became as real as solid matter." His voice trembled with emotion. "Blinding pain, blood catching fire in our veins, bones snapping and flesh powdering. Steel flowing like liquid. Amber raining from the sky. Crowds gathering in streets that no longer followed any maps, if the maps themselves had not altered. They knew not what to do. Their weak minds could not grab hold . . ."

Most humans, I take it, were entirely too irrational to begin with. Whole nations vanished or were turned into incomprehensible whirlpools of misery and depravity. It is said that certain universities, libraries, and museums survived, but to this day we have little contact with them.

I think often of those poor victims of the early days of Mortdieu. They had known a world of some stability; we have adapted since. They were shocked by cities turning into forests, by their nightmares taking shape before their eyes. Prodigal crows perched atop trees that had once been buildings, pigs ran through the streets on their hind legs . . . and so on. (The priest did not encourage contemplation of the oddities. "Excitement," he said, "breeds even more monsters.")

Our Cathedral survived. Rationality in this neighborhood, however, had weakened some centuries before Mortdieu, replaced only by a kind of rote. The Cathedral suffered. Survivors—clergy and staff, worshipers seeking sanctuary—had wretched visions, dreamed wretched dreams. They saw the stone ornaments of the Cathedral come alive. With someone to see and believe, in a universe lacking any other foundation, my ancestors shook off stone and became flesh. Centuries of rock celibacy weighed upon them. Forty-nine nuns who had sought shelter in the Cathedral were discovered and were not entirely loath, so the coarser versions of the tale go. Mortdieu had had a surprising aphrodisiacal effect on the faithful and conjugation took place.

No definite gestation period has been established, for at that time the great stone wheel had not been set twisting back and forth to count the hours. Nor had anyone been given the chair of Kronos to watch over the wheel and provide a baseline for everyday activities.

But flesh did not reject stone, and there came into being the sons and daughters of flesh and stone, including me. Those who had fornicated with the inhuman figures were cast out to raise or reject their monstrous young in the highest hidden recesses. Those who had accepted the embraces of the stone saints and other human figures were less abused but still banished to the upper reaches. A wooden scaffolding was

erected, dividing the great nave into two levels. A canvas drop cloth was fastened over the scaffold to prevent offal raining down, and on the second level of the Cathedral the more human offspring of stone and flesh set about creating a new life.

I have long tried to find out how some semblance of order came to the world. Legend has it that it was the arch–existentialist Jansard, crucifier of the beloved St. Argentine—who, realizing and repenting his error, discovered that mind and thought could calm the foaming sea of reality.

The priest finished his all-too-sketchy lecture by touching on this point briefly: "With the passing of God's watchful gaze, humanity had to reach out and grab hold the unraveling fabric of the world. Those left alive—those who had the wits to keep their bodies from falling apart—became the only cohesive force in the chaos."

I had picked up enough language to understand what he said; my memory was good—still is—and I was curious enough to want to know more.

Creeping along stone walls behind the curtains, I listened to other priests and nuns intoning scripture to gaggles of flesh children. That was on the ground floor, and I was in great danger; the people of pure flesh looking on my kind as abominations. But it was worth it.

I was able to steal a Psalter and learned to read. I stole other books; they defined my world by allowing me to compare it with others. At first I couldn't believe the others had ever existed; only the Cathedral was real. I still have my doubts. I can look out a tiny round window on one side of my room and see the great forest and river that surround the Cathedral, but I can see nothing else. So my experience with other worlds is far from direct.

No matter. I read a great deal, but I'm no scholar. What concerns me is recent history—the final focus of that germinal hour listening to the priest. From the metaphysical to the acutely personal.

I am small—barely three English feet in

height—but I can run quickly through most of the hidden passageways. This lets me observe without attracting attention. I may be the only historian in this whole structure. Others who claim the role disregard what's before their eyes, in search of ultimate truths, or at least Big Pictures. So if you prefer history where the historian is not involved, look to the others. Objective as I try to be, I do have my favorite subjects.

• • •

In the time when my history begins, the children of stone and flesh were still searching for the Stone Christ. Those of us born of the union of the stone saints and gargoyles with the bereaved nuns thought our salvation lay in the great stone celibate, who came to life as all the other statues had.

Of smaller import were the secret assignations between the bishop's daughter and a young man of stone and flesh. Such assignations were forbidden even between those of pure flesh; and as these two lovers were unmarried, their compound sin intrigued me.

Her name was Constantia, and she was fourteen, slender of limb, brown of hair, mature of bosom. Her eyes carried the stupid sort of divine life common in girls that age. His name was Corvus, and he was fifteen. I don't recall his precise features, but he was handsome enough and dexterous: he could climb through the scaffolding almost as quickly as I. I first spied them talking when I made one of my frequent raids on the repository to steal another book. They were in shadow, but my eyes are keen. They spoke softly, hesitantly. My heart ached to see them and to think of their tragedy, for I knew right away that Corvus was not pure flesh and that Constantia was the daughter of the bishop himself. I envisioned the old tyrant meting out the usual punishment to Corvus for such breaches of level and morality—castration. But in their talk was a sweetness that almost masked the closed-in stench of the lower nave.

"Have you ever kissed a man before?"

"Yes."

"Who?"

"My brother." She laughed.

"And?" His voice was sharper; he might kill her brother, he seemed to say.

"A friend named Jules."

"Where is he?"

"Oh, he vanished on a wood-gathering expedition."

"Oh." And he kissed her again. I'm a historian, not a voyeur, so I discreetly hide the flowering of their passion. If Corvus had had any sense, he would have reveled in his conquest and never returned.

But he was snared and continued to see her despite the risk. This was loyalty, love, faithfulness, and it was rare. It fascinated me.

• • •

I have just been taking in sun, a nice day, and looking out over the buttresses.

The Cathedral is like a low-bellied lizard, and the buttresses are its legs. There are little houses at the base of each buttress, where rainspouters with dragon faces used to lean out over the trees (or city or whatever was down below once). Now people live there. It wasn't always that way—the sun was once forbidden. Corvus and Constantia from childhood were denied its light, and so even in their youthful prime they were pale and dirty with the smoke of candles and tallow lamps. The most sun anyone received in those days was obtained on wood-gathering expeditions.

After spying on one of the clandestine meetings of the young lovers, I mused in a dark corner for an hour, then went to see the copper giant Apostle Thomas. He was the only human form to live so high in the Cathedral. He carried a ruler on which was engraved his real name—he had been modeled after the Cathedral's restorer in times past, the architect Viollet-le-Duc. He knew the Cathedral better than anyone, and I admired him greatly. Most of the monsters left him alone—out of fear, if nothing else. He was huge, black as night, but flaked with pale green, his face creased in eternal thought. He was sitting in his usual wooden compartment near the base of the spire, not twenty feet from where I write now, thinking about times none of the rest of us ever knew: of joy and past love, some say; others say of the burden that rested on him now that the Cathedral was the center of this chaotic world.

It was the giant who selected me from the ugly hordes when he saw me with a Psalter. He encouraged me in my efforts to read. "Your eyes are bright," he told me. "You move as if your brain were quick, and you keep yourself dry and clean. You aren't hollow like the rainspouters—you have substance. For all our sakes, put it to use and learn the ways of the Cathedral."

And so I did.

He looked up as I came in. I sat on a box near his feet and said, "A daughter of flesh is seeing a son of stone and flesh."

He shrugged his massive shoulders. "So it shall be, in time."

"Is it not a sin?"

"It is something so monstrous it is past sin and become necessity," he said. "It will happen more as time passes."

"They're in love, I think, or will be."

He nodded. "I—and One Other—were the only ones to abstain from fornication on the night of Mortdieu," he said. "I am—except for the Other—alone fit to judge."

I waited for him to judge, but he sighed and patted me on the shoulder. "And I never judge, do I, ugly friend?"

"Never," I said.

"So leave me alone to be sad." He winked. "And more power to them."

The bishop of the Cathedral was an old, old man. It was said he hadn't been bishop before the Mortdieu, but a wanderer who came in during the chaos, before the forest had replaced the city. He had set himself up as titular head of this section of God's former domain by saying it had been willed to him.

He was short, stout, with huge hairy arms like the clamps of a vise. He had once killed a spouter with a single squeeze of his fist, and spouters are tough things, since they have no guts like you (I suppose) and I. The hair surrounding his bald pate was white, thick, and unruly, and his eyebrows leaned over his nose with marvelous flexibility. He rutted like a pig, ate hugely, and shat liquidly (I know all). A man for this time, if ever there was one.

It was his decree that all those not pure of flesh be banned and that those not of human form be killed on sight.

When I returned from the giant's chamber, I saw that the lower nave was in an uproar. They had seen someone clambering about in the scaffold, and troops had been sent to shoot him down. Of course it was Corvus. I was a quicker climber than he and knew the beams better, so when he found himself trapped in an apparent cul-de-sac, it was I who gestured from the shadows and pointed to a hole large enough for him to escape through. He took it without a breath of thanks, but etiquette has never been important to me. I entered the stone wall through a nook a spare hand's width across and wormed my way to the bottom to see what else was happening. Excitement was rare.

A rumor was passing that the figure had been seen with a young girl, but the crowds didn't know who the girl was. The men and women who mingled in the smoky light, between the rows of open-roofed hovels, chattered gaily. Castrations and executions were among the few joys for us then; I relished them too, but I had a stake in the potential victims now and I worried.

My worry and my interest got the better of me. I slid through an unrepaired gap and fell to one side of the alley between the outer wall and the hovels. A group of dirty adolescents spotted me. "There he is!" they screeched. "He didn't get away!"

The bishop's masked troops can travel freely on all levels. I was almost cornered by them, and when I tried one escape route, they waited at a crucial spot in the stairs—which I had to cross to complete the next leg—and I was forced back.

I prided myself in knowing the Cathedral top to bottom, but as I scrambled madly, I came upon a tunnel I had never noticed before. It led deep into a broad stone foundation wall. I was safe for the moment but afraid that they might find my caches of food and poison my casks of rainwater. Still, there was nothing I could do until they had gone, so I decided to spend the anxious hours exploring the tunnel.

The Cathedral is a constant surprise; I realize now I didn't know half of what it offered. There are always new ways to get from here to there (some, I suspect, created while no one is looking), and sometimes even new theres to be discovered. While troops snuffled about the hole above, near the stairs—where only a child of two or three could have entered—I followed a flight of crude steps deep into the stone. Water and slime made the passage slippery and difficult. For a moment I was in darkness deeper than any I had experienced before—a gloom more profound than mere lack of light could explain. Then below I saw a faint yellow gleam. More cautious, I slowed and progressed silently. Behind a rusting, scabrous metal gate, I set foot into a lighted room. There was the smell of crumbling stone, a tang of mineral water, slime—and the stench of a dead spouter. The beast lay on the floor of the narrow chamber, several months gone but still fragrant.

I have mentioned that spouters are very hard to kill—and this one had been murdered. Three candles stood freshly placed in nooks around the chamber, flickering in a faint draft from above. Despite my fears, I walked across the stone floor, took a candle, and peered into the next section of tunnel.

It sloped down for several dozen feet, ending at another metal gate. It was here that I detected an odor I had never before encountered—the smell of the purest of stones, as of rare jade or virgin marble. Such a feeling of lightheadedness passed over me that I almost laughed, but I was too cautious for that. I pushed aside the gate and was greeted by a rush of the coldest, sweetest air, like a draft from the tomb of a saint whose body does not corrupt but rather draws corruption away and expels it miraculously into the nether pits. My beak dropped open. The candlelight fell across the darkness onto a figure I at first thought to be an infant. But I quickly disagreed with myself. The figure was several ages at once. As I blinked, it became a man of about thirty, well formed, with a high forehead and elegant hands, pale as ice. His eyes stared at the wall behind me. I bowed down on scaled knee and touched my forehead as best I could to the cold stone, shivering to my vestigial wingtips. "Forgive me, Joy of Man's Desiring," I said. "Forgive me." I had stumbled upon the hiding place of the Stone Christ.

"You are forgiven," He said wearily. "You had to come sooner or later. Better now than later, when . . ." His voice trailed away and He shook His head. He was very thin, wrapped in a gray robe that still bore the scars of centuries of weathering. "Why did you come?"

"To escape the bishop's troops," I said.

He nodded. "Yes. The bishop. How long have I been here?"

"Since before I was born, Lord. Sixty or seventy years." He was thin, almost ethereal, this figure I had imagined as a husky carpenter. I lowered my voice and beseeched, "What may I do for you, Lord?"

"Go away," He said.

"I could not live with such a secret," I said. "You are salvation. You can overthrow the bishop and bring all the levels together."

"I am not a general or a soldier. Please go away and tell no—"

I felt a breath behind me, then the whisper of a weapon. I leaped aside, and my hackles rose as a stone sword came down and shattered on the floor beside me. The Christ raised His hand. Still in shock, I stared at a beast much like myself. It stared back, face black with rage, stayed by the power of His hand. I should have been more wary—something had to have killed the spouter and kept the candles fresh.

"But, Lord," the beast rumbled, "he will tell all."

"No," the Christ said. "He'll tell nobody." He looked half at me, half through me, and said, "Go, go."

Up the tunnels, into the orange dark of the Cathedral, crying, I crawled and slithered. I could not even go to the giant. I had been silenced as effectively as if my throat had been cut.

The next morning I watched from a shadowy corner of the scaffold as a crowd gathered around a lone man in a dirty sackcloth robe. I had seen him before—his name was Psalo, and he was left alone as an example of the bishop's largess. It was a token gesture; most of the people regarded him as barely half-sane.

Yet this time I listened and, in my confusion, found his words striking responsive chords in me. He was exhorting the bishop and his forces to allow light into the Cathedral again by dropping the canvas tarps that covered the windows. He had talked about this before, and the bishop had responded with his usual statement—that with the light would come more chaos, for the human mind was now a pesthole of delusions. Any stimulus would drive away whatever security the inhabitants of the Cathedral had.

. . .

At this time it gave me no pleasure to watch the love of Constantia and Corvus grow. They were becoming more careless. Their talk grew bolder:

"We shall announce a marriage," Corvus said.

"They will never allow it. They'll . . . cut you."

"I'm nimble. They'll never catch me. The church needs leaders, brave revolutionaries. If no one breaks with tradition, everyone will suffer."

"I fear for your life—and mine. My father would push me from the flock like a diseased lamb."

"Your father is no shepherd."

"He is my father," Constantia said, eyes wide, mouth drawn tight.

I sat with beak in paws, eyes half-lidded, able to mimic each statement before it was uttered. Undying love . . . hope for a bleak future . . . shite and onions! I had read it all before, in a cache of romance novels in the trash of a dead nun. As soon as I made the connection and realized the timeless banality—and the futility—of what I was seeing, and when I compared their prattle with the infinite sadness of the Stone Christ, I went from innocent to cynic. The transition dizzied me, leaving little backwaters of noble emotion, but the future seemed clear. Corvus would be caught and executed; if it hadn't been for me, he would already have been gelded, if not killed. Constantia would weep, poison herself; the singers would sing of it (those selfsame warble-throats who cheered the death of her lover); perhaps I would write of it (I was planning this chronicle even then), and afterward, perhaps, I would follow them both, having succumbed to the sin of boredom.

With night, things become less certain. It is easy to stare at a dark wall and let dreams become manifest. At one time, I've deduced from books, dreams could not take shape beyond sleep or brief fantasy. All too often I've had to fight things generated in my dreams, flowing from the walls, suddenly independent and hungry. People often die in the night, devoured by their own nightmares.

That evening, falling to sleep with visions of the Stone Christ in my head, I dreamed of holy men, angels, and saints. I came awake abruptly, by training, and one had stayed behind. The others I saw vaguely, flitting outside the round window, where they whispered and made plans for flying off to heaven. The wraith who remained was a dark shape in one corner. His breathing was harsh. "I am Peter," he said, "also called Simon. I am the Rock of the Church, and popes are told that they are heir to my task."

"I'm rock, too," I said. "At least in part."

"So be it, then. You are heir to my task. Go forth and be Pope. Do not revere the Stone Christ, for a Christ is only as good as He does, and if He does nothing, there is no salvation in Him."

The shadow reached out to pat my head, and I saw his eyes grow wide as he made out my form. He muttered some formula for banishing devils and oozed out the window to join his fellows.

I imagined that if such a thing were actually brought before the council, it would be decided under the law that the benison of a dream person is not binding. I did not care. This was better advice than any I'd had since the giant told me to read and learn.

But to be Pope, one must have a hierarchy of servants to carry out one's orders. The biggest of rocks does not move by itself. So swelled with power, I decided to appear in the upper nave and announce myself to the people.

It took a great deal of courage to appear in daylight, without my cloak, and to walk across the scaffold's surface, on the second level, through crowds of vendors setting up the market for the day. Some reacted with typical bigotry and sought to kick or deride me. My beak discouraged them. I clambered to the top of a prominent stall and stood in a murky lamp's circle, clearing my throat to announce myself. Under a hail of rotten pomegranates and limp vegetables, I told the throng who I was, and I told them about my vision. Jeweled with beads of offal, I jumped down in a few minutes and fled to a tunnel entrance too small for most men. Some boys followed me, and one lost a finger while trying to slice me with a fragment of colored glass.

I recognized that the tactic of open revelation was worthless. There are levels of bigotry, and I was at the very bottom of any list.

My next strategy was to find some way to disrupt the Cathedral from top to bottom. Even bigots, when reduced to a mob, could be swayed by the presence of one obviously ordained and capable. I spent two days skulking through the walls. There had to be a basic flaw in so fragile a structure as the church, and, while I wasn't contemplating total destruction, I wanted something spectacular, unavoidable.

While I cogitated, hanging from the bottom of the second scaffold, above the community of pure flesh, the bishop's deep gravelly voice roared over the noise of the crowd. I opened my eyes and looked down. The masked troops were holding a bowed figure, and the bishop was intoning over its head, "Know all who hear me now, this young bastard of flesh and stone"—

Corvus, I told myself. Finally caught. I shut one eye, but the other refused to close out the scene.

—"has violated all we hold sacred and shall atone for his crimes on this spot, tomorrow at this time. Kronos! Mark the wheel's progress." The elected Kronos, a spindly old man with dirty gray hair down to his buttocks, took a piece of charcoal and marked an X on the huge bulkhead chart, behind which the wheel groaned and sighed in its circuit.

The crowd was enthusiastic. I saw Psalo pushing through the people.

"What crime?" he called out. "Name the crime!"

"Violation of the lower level!" the head of the masked troops declared.

"That merits a whipping and an escort upstairs," Psalo said. "I detect a more sinister crime here. What is it?"

The bishop looked Psalo down coldly. "He tried to rape my daughter, Constantia."

Psalo could say nothing to that. The penalty was castration and death. All the pure humans accepted such laws. There was no other recourse.

I mused, watching Corvus being led to the dungeons. The future that I desired at that moment startled me with its clarity. I wanted that part of my heritage that had been denied to me to be at peace with myself, to be surrounded by those who accepted me, by those no better than I. In time that would happen, as the giant had said. But would I ever see it? What Corvus, in his own lusty way, was trying to do was equalize the levels, to bring stone into flesh until no one could define the divisions.

Well, my plans beyond that point were very hazy. They were less plans than glowing feelings, imaginings of happiness and children playing in the forest and fields beyond the island as the world knit itself under the gaze of God's heir. My children, playing in the forest. A touch of truth came to me at this moment. I had wished to be Corvus when he tupped Constantia.

So I had two tasks, then, that could be merged if I was clever. I had to distract the bishop and his troops, and I had to rescue Corvus, fellow revolutionary.

I spent that night in feverish misery in my room. At dawn I went to the giant and asked his advice. He looked me over coldly and said, "We waste our time if we try to knock sense into their heads. But we have no better calling than to waste our time, do we?"

"What shall I do?"

"Enlighten them."

I stomped my claw on the floor. "They are bricks! Try enlightening bricks!"

He smiled his sad, narrow smile. "Enlighten them," he said.

I left the giant's chamber in a rage. I did not have access to the great wheel's board of time, so I couldn't know exactly when the execution would take place. But I guessed—from memories of a grumbling stomach—that it would be in the early afternoon. I traveled from one end of the nave to the other and, likewise, the transept. I nearly exhausted myself.

Then, traversing an empty aisle, I picked up a piece of colored glass and examined it, puzzled. Many of the boys on all levels carried these shards with them, and the girls used them as jewelry—against the wishes of their elders, who held that bright objects bred more beasts in the mind. Where did they get them?

In one of the books I had perused years before, I had seen brightly colored pictures of the Cathedral windows. "Enlighten them," the giant had said.

Psalo's request to let light into the Cathedral came to mind.

Along the peak of the nave, in a tunnel running its length, I found the ties that held the pulleys of the canvases over the windows. The best windows, I decided, would be the huge ones of the north and south transepts. I made a diagram in the dust, trying to decide what season it was and from which direction the sunlight would come—pure theory to me, but at this moment I was in a fever of brilliance. All the windows had to be clear. I could not decide which was best.

I was ready by early afternoon, just after sext prayers in the upper nave. I had cut the major ropes and weakened the clamps by prying them from the walls with a pick stolen from the bishop's armory. I walked along a high ledge, took an almost vertical shaft through the wall to the lower floor, and waited.

Constantia watched from a wooden balcony, the bishop's special box for executions. She had a terrified, fascinated look on her face. Corvus was on the dais across the nave, right in the center of the cross of the transept. Torches illumined him and his executioners, three men and an old woman.

I knew the procedure. The old woman would castrate him first, then the men would remove his head. He was dressed in the condemned red robe to hide any blood. Blood excitement among the impressionable was the last thing the bishop wanted. Troops waited around the dais to purify the area with scented water.

I didn't have much time. It would take minutes for the system of ropes and pulleys to clear and the canvases to fall. I went to my station and severed the remaining ties. Then, as the Cathedral filled with a hollow creaking sound, I followed the shaft back to my viewing post.

In three minutes the canvases were drooping. I saw Corvus look up, his eyes glazed. The bishop was with his daughter in the box. He pulled her back into the shadows. In another two minutes the canvases fell onto the upper scaffold with a hideous crash. Their weight was too great for the ends of the structure, and it collapsed, allowing the canvas to cascade to the floor many yards below. At first the illumination was dim and bluish, filtered perhaps by a passing cloud. Then, from one end of the Cathedral to the other, a burst of light threw my smoky world into clarity. The glory of thousands of pieces of colored glass, hidden for decades and hardly touched by childish vandals, fell upon upper and lower levels at once. A cry from the crowds nearly wrenched me from my post. I slid quickly to the lower level and hid, afraid of what I had done. This was more than simple sunlight. Like the blossoming of two flowers, one brighter than the other, the transept windows astounded all who beheld them.

Eyes accustomed to orangey dark, to smoke and haze and shadow, cannot stare into such glory without drastic effect. I shielded my own face and tried to find a convenient exit.

But the population was increasing. As the light brightened and more faces rose to be locked, phototropic, the splendor unhinged some people. From their minds poured contents too wondrous to be accurately cataloged. The monsters thus released were not violent, however, and most of the visions were not monstrous.

The upper and lower nave shimmered with reflected glories, with dream figures and children clothed in baubles of light. Saints and prodigies dominated. A thousand newly created youngsters squatted on the bright floor and began to tell of marvels, of cities in the East, and times as they had once been. Clowns dressed in fire entertained from the tops of the market stalls. Animals unknown to the Cathedral cavorted between the dwellings, giving friendly advice. Abstract things, glowing balls in nets of gold and ribbons of silk, sang and floated around the upper reaches. The Cathedral became a great vessel of all the bright dreams known to its citizens.

Slowly, from the lower nave, people of pure flesh climbed to the scaffold and walked the upper nave to see what they couldn't from below. From my hideaway I watched the masked troops of the bishop carrying his litter up narrow stairs. Constantia walked behind, stumbling, her eyes shut in the new brightness.

All tried to cover their eyes, but none for long succeeded.

I wept. Almost blind with tears, I made my way still higher and looked down on the roiling crowds. I saw Corvus, his hands still wrapped in restraining ropes, being led by the old woman.

Constantia saw him, too, and they regarded each other like strangers, then joined hands as best they could. She borrowed a knife from one of her father's soldiers and cut his ropes away. Around them the brightest dreams of all began to swirl, pure white and blood-red and sea-green, coalescing into visions of all the children they would innocently have.

I gave them a few hours to regain their senses—and to regain my own. Then I stood on the bishop's abandoned podium and shouted over the heads of those on the lowest level.

"The time has come!" I cried. "We must all unite now; we must unite—"

At first they ignored me. I was quite eloquent, but their excitement was still too great. So I waited some more, began to speak again, and was shouted down. Bits of fruit and vegetables arced up. "Freak!" they screamed and drove me away.

I crept along the stone stairs, found the narrow crack, and hid in it, burying my beak in my paws, wondering what had gone wrong. It took a surprisingly long time for me to realize that, in my case, it was less the stigma of stone than the ugliness of my shape that doomed my quest for leadership.

I had, however, paved the way for the Stone Christ. He will surely be able to take His place now, I told myself. So I maneuvered along the crevice until I came to the hidden chamber and the yellow glow. All was quiet within. I met first the stone monster, who looked me over suspiciously with glazed gray eyes. "You're back," he said. Overcome by his wit, I leered, nodded, and asked that I be presented to the Christ.

"He's sleeping."

"Important tidings," I said.

"What?"

"I bring glad tidings."

"Then let me hear them."

"His ears only."

Out of the gloomy corner came the Christ, looking much older now. "What is it?" He asked.

"I have prepared the way for You," I said. "Simon called Peter told me I was the heir to his legacy, that I should go before You—"

The Stone Christ shook His head. "You believe I am the fount from which all blessings flow?"

I nodded, uncertain.

"What have you done out there?"

"Let in the light," I said.

He shook His head slowly. "You seem a wise enough creature. You know about Mortdieu."

"Yes."

"Then you should know that I barely have enough power to keep myself together, to heal myself, much less to minister to those out there." He gestured beyond the walls. "My own source has gone away," He said mournfully. "I'm operating on reserves, and those none too vast."

"He wants you to go away and stop bothering us," the monster explained.

"They have their light out there," the Christ said. "They'll play with that for a while, get tired of it, go back to what they had before. Is there any place for you in that?"

I thought for a moment, then shook my head. "No place," I said. "I'm too ugly."

"You are too ugly, and I am too famous," He said. "I'd have to come from their midst, anonymous, and that is clearly impossible. No, leave them alone for a while. They'll make me over again, perhaps, or better still, forget about me. About us. We don't have any place there."

I was stunned. I sat down hard on the stone floor, and the Christ patted me on my head as He walked by. "Go back to your hiding place; live as well as you can," He said. "Our time is over."

I turned to go. When I reached the crevice, I heard His voice behind, saying, "Do you play bridge? If you do, find another. We need four to a table."

I clambered up the crack, through the walls, and along the arches over the revelry. Not only was I not going to be Pope—after an appointment by Saint Peter himself!—but I couldn't convince someone much more qualified than I to assume the leadership.

It is the sign of the eternal student, I suppose, that when his wits fail him, he returns to the teacher.

I returned to the copper giant. He was lost in meditation. About his feet were scattered scraps of paper with detailed drawings of parts of the Cathedral. I waited patiently until he saw me. He turned, chin in hand, and looked me over.

"Why so sad?"

I shook my head. Only he could read my features and recognize my moods.

"Did you take my advice below? I heard a commotion."

"Mea maxima culpa," I said.

"And . . . ?"

I slowly, hesitantly, made my report, concluding with the refusal of the Stone Christ. The giant listened closely without interrupting. When I was done, he stood, towering over me, and pointed with his ruler through an open portal.

"Do you see that out there?" he asked. The ruler swept over the forests beyond the island, to the far green horizon. I replied that I did and waited for him to continue. He seemed to be lost in thought again.

"Once there was a city where trees now grow," he said. "Artists came by the thousands, and whores, and philosophers, and academics. And when God died, all the academics and whores and artists couldn't hold the fabric of the world together. How do you expect us to succeed now?"

Us? "Expectations should not determine whether one acts or not," I said. "Should they?"

The giant laughed and tapped my head with the ruler. "Maybe we've been given a sign, and we just have to learn how to interpret it correctly."

I leered to show I was puzzled.

"Maybe Mortdieu is really a sign that we have been weaned. We must forage for ourselves, remake the world without help. What do you think of that?"

I was too tired to judge the merits of what he was saying, but I had never known the giant to be wrong before. "Okay. I grant that. So?"

"The Stone Christ tells us His charge is running down. If God weans us from the old ways, we can't expect His Son to replace the nipple, can we?"

"No . . ."

He hunkered next to me, his face bright. "I wondered who would really stand forth. It's obvious He won't. So, little one, who's the next choice?"

"Me?" I asked, meekly. The giant looked me over almost pityingly.

"No," he said after a time. "I am the next. We're *weaned*!" He did a little dance, startling my beak up out of my paws. I blinked. He grabbed my vestigial wingtips and pulled me upright. "Stand straight. Tell me more."

"About what?"

"Tell me all that's going on below, and whatever else you know."

"I'm trying to figure out what you're saying," I protested, trembling a bit.

"Dense as stone!" Grinning, he bent over me. Then the grin went away, and he tried to look stern. "It's a grave responsibility. We must remake the world ourselves now. We must coordinate our thoughts, our dreams. Chaos won't do. What an opportunity, to be the architect of an entire universe!" He waved the ruler at the ceiling. "To build the very skies! The last world was a training ground, full of harsh rules and strictures. Now we've been told we're ready to leave that behind, move on to something more mature. Did I teach you any of the rules of architecture? I mean, the aesthetics. The need for harmony, interaction, utility, beauty?"

"Some," I said.

"Good. I don't think making the universe anew will require any better rules. No doubt we'll need to experiment, and perhaps one or more of our great spires will topple. But now we work for ourselves, to our own glory, and to the greater glory of the God who made us! No, ugly friend?"

• • •

Like many histories, mine must begin with the small, the tightly focused, and expand into the large. But unlike most historians, I don't have the luxury of time. Indeed, my story isn't even concluded yet.

Soon the legions of Viollet-le-Duc will begin their campaigns. Most have been schooled pretty thoroughly. Kidnapped from below, brought up in the heights, taught as I was. We'll begin returning them, one by one.

I teach off and on, write off and on, observe all the time.

The next step will be the biggest. I haven't any idea how we're going to do it.

But, as the giant puts it, "Long ago the roof fell in. Now we must push it up again, strengthen it, repair the beams." At this point he smiles to the pupils. "Not just repair them. Replace them! Now we are the beams. Flesh and stone become something much stronger."

Ah, but then some dolt will raise a hand and inquire, "What if our arms get tired holding up the sky?"

Our task, you see, will not soon be over.

BRUCE STERLING AND PAUL DI FILIPPO

THE SCAB'S PROGRESS

(2001)

THE FEDERAL BIOCONTAINMENT center was a diatom the size of the Disney Matterhorn. It perched on fractal struts in a particularly charmless district of Nevada, where the waterless white sands swarmed with toxic vermin.

The entomopter[*] scissored its dragonfly wings, conveying Ribo[†] Zombie above the desert wastes. This was always the best part of the program: the part where Ribo Zombie lovingly checked out all his cool new gear before launching into action. As a top-ranking scab[‡] from the otaku[§]-pirate underground, Ribo Zombie

owned reactive gloves with slash-proof ligaments and sandwiched Kevlar-polysaccharide.[¶] He owned a mother-of-pearl crash helmet, hung with daring insouciance on the scaled wall of the 'mopter's cockpit. And those Nevada desert boots—like something built by Tolkien orcs with day-jobs at Nike.

Accompanying the infamous RZ was his legendary and much-merchandised familiar,[**] Skratchy Kat. Every scab owned a familiar: they were the totem animals of the gene-pirate scene. The custom dated back to the birth of the scab subculture, when tree-spiking Earth Firsters and obsessive dog breeders had jointly discovered the benefits of outlaw genetic engineering.

With a flash of emerald eyes the supercat rose from the armored lap of the daring scab. Skratchy Kat had some much cooler name in the

---

[*] *entomopter* (n.): a small flying vehicle whose wings employ elaborate, scissoring insectoid principles of movement, rather than avian ones; abbreviated as *'mopter*

[†] *ribo* (adj.): all-purpose prefix derived from the transcriptive cellular organelle, the ribosome; indicative of bioengineering

[‡] *scab* (n.): a biohacker

[§] *otaku* (n.): Japanese term for obsessive nerds, trivia buffs

[¶] *polysaccharide* (n.): an organic polymer such as chitin
[**] *familiar* (n.): the customary modified-animal partner of a scab

Japanese collectors' market. He'd been designed in Tokyo, and was a deft Pocket-Monster commingling of eight spliced species of felines and viverridae, with the look, the collector cachet, and (judging by his stuffed-toy version) plenty of the smell of a civet cat. Ribo Zombie, despite frequent on-screen cameos by busty-babe groupies, had never enjoyed any steady feminine relationship. What true love there was in his life flowed between man and cat.

Clickable product-placement hot-tags[*] were displayed on the 'mopter screens as Ribo Zombie's aircraft winged in for the kill. The ads sold magnums of cheap, post-Greenhouse Reykjavik Champagne. Ringside tix to a Celebrity Deathmatch (splatter-shields extra). Entomopter rentals in Vegas, with a rapid, low-cost divorce optional.

Then, wham! Inertia hit the settling aircraft, gypsum-sand flew like pulverized wallboard, and the entomopter's chitinous canopy accordioned open. Ribo Zombie vaulted to the glistening sands, clutching his cat to his armored bosom. He set the beast free with a brief, comradely exchange of meows, then sealed his face mask, pulled a monster pistol, and plucked a retro-chic pineapple grenade from his bandolier.

A pair of crystalline robot snakes fell to concussive explosions. Alluring vibrators disoriented the numerous toxic scorpions in the vicinity. Three snarling jackalopes[†] fell to a well-aimed hail of dumdums. Meanwhile the dauntless cat, whose hide beneath fluffy fur was as tough as industrial Teflon, had found a way through the first hedge-barrier of barrel cacti.

The pair entered a maze of cholla. The famously vicious Southwestern cholla cactus, whose sausage-link segments bore thorns the size of fishhooks, had been rumored from time immemorial to leap free and stab travelers from sheer spite. A soupçon of Venus flytrap genes had turned this Pecos Pete tall-tale vaporware into

grisly functionality. Ribo Zombie had to opt for brute force: the steely wand of a back-mounted flamethrower leapt into his wiry combat-gloves. Ignited in a pupil-searing blast, the flaming mutant cholla whipped and flopped like epileptic spaghetti. Then RZ and the faithful Skratchy were clambering up the limestone leg of the Federal cache.

Anyone who had gotten this far could be justly exposed to the worst and most glamorous gizmos ever cooked up by the Softwar Department's Counter-Bioterrorism Corps.

The ducts of the diatom structure yawned open and deployed a lethal arsenal of spore-grenade launchers, strangling vegetable bolas, and whole glittering clouds of hotwired fleas and mosquitos. Any scab worth his yeast knew that those insect vectors were stuffed to bursting with swift and ghastly illnesses, pneumonic plague, and necrotizing fasciitis among the friendlier ones.

"This must be the part where the cat saves him," said Tupper McClanahan, all cozy in her throw rug on her end of the couch.

Startled out of his absorption, yet patiently indulgent, Fearon McClanahan froze the screen with a tapped command to the petcocks on the feedlines. "What was that, darling? I thought you were reading."

"I was." Smiling, Tupper held up a vintage Swamp Thing comic that had cost fully ten percent of one month's trust-fund check. "But I always enjoy the parts of this show that feature the cat. Remember when we clicked on those high-protein kitty treats, during last week's cat sequence? Weeble loved those things."

Fearon looked down from the ergonomic couch to the spotless bulk of his snoring pig, Weeble. Weeble had outgrown the size and weight described in his documentation, but he made a fine hassock.

"Weeble loves anything we feed him. His omnivorous nature is part of his factory specs, remember? I told you we'd save a ton on garbage bills."

"Sweetie, I never complain about Weeble.

---

[*] *hot-tag* (n.): clickable animated icons
[†] *jackalope* (n.): the legendary antlered rabbit of Wyoming, now reified

Weeble is your familiar, so Weeble is fine. I've only observed that it might be a good idea if we got a bigger place."

Fearon disliked being interrupted while viewing his favorite outlaw stealth download. He positively squirmed whenever Tupper sneakily angled around the subject of a new place with more room. More room meant a nursery. And a nursery meant a child. Fearon swerved to a change of topic.

"How can you expect Skratchy Kat to get Ribo Zombie out of this fix? Do you have any idea what those flying bolas do to human flesh?"

"The cat gets him out of trouble every time. Kids love that cat."

"Look, honey: kids are not the target demographic. This show isn't studio-greenlighted or even indie-syndicated, okay? You know as well as I do that this is outlaw media. Totally underground guerrilla infotainment, virally distributed. There are laws on the books—unenforced, sure, but still extant—that make it illegal for us even to watch this thing. After all, Ribo Zombie is a biological terrorist who's robbing a Federal stash!"

"If it's not a kid's show, why is that cute little cartoon in the corner of the screen?"

"That's his graffiti icon! The sign of his streetwise authenticity."

Tupper gazed at him with limpid spousal pity. "Then who edits all his raw footage and adds the special effects?"

"Oh, well, that's just the Vegas Mafia. The Mafia keeps up with modern times: no more Rat Pack crooners and gangsta rappers! Nowadays they cut licensing deals with freeware culture heroes like Ribo Zombie, lone wolf recombinants bent on bringing hot goo to the masses."

Tupper waved her comic as a visual aid. "I still bet the cat's gonna save him. Because none of that makes any difference to the archetypical narrative dynamics."

Fearon sighed. He opened a new window on his gelatinous screen and accessed certain data. "Okay, look. You know what runs security on Federal Biosequestration Sites like that one?

Military-grade, laminated, mouse brains. You know how smart that stuff is? A couple of cubic inches of murine brain has more processing power than every computer ever deployed in the twentieth century. Plus, mouse brain is unhackable. Computer viruses, no problem. Electromagnetic pulse doesn't affect it. No power source to disrupt, since neurons run on blood sugar. That stuff is indestructible."

Tupper shrugged. "Just turn your show back on."

Skratchy was poised at a vulnerable crack in the diatom's roof. The cat began copiously to pee.

When the trickling urine reached the olfactory sensors wired to the mouse brains, the controlling network went berserk. Ancient murine antipredator instincts swamped the cybernetic instructions, triggering terrified flight responses. Misaimed spore bomblets thudded harmlessly to the soil, whizzing bolas wreaked havoc through the innocent vegetation below, and vent ports spewed contaminated steam and liquid nitrogen.

Cursing the zany but dangerous fusillade, Ribo Zombie set to work with a back-mounted hydraulic can opener.

Glum and silent, Fearon gripped his jaw. His hooded eyes glazed over as Ribo Zombie crept through surreal diorama of waist-high wells, HVAC* systems and plumbing. Every flick of Ribo Zombie's hand torch revealed a glimpse of some new and unspeakable mutant wonder, half concealed in ambient support fluids: yellow gruel, jade-colored hair gel, blue oatmeal, ruby maple syrup . . .

"Oh, honey," said Tupper at last, "don't take it so hard."

"You were right," Fearon grumbled. His voice rose. "Is that what you want me to say? You were right! You're always right!"

"It's just my skill with semiotic touchstones, which I've derived from years of reading graphic novels. But look, dear, here's the part you always love, when he finally lays his hands on the wet-

---

* *HVAC* (n.): heating, ventilation, air-conditioning system

ware.* Honey, look at him stealing that weird cantaloupe with the big throbbing arteries on it. Now he'll go back to his clottage† and clump,‡ just like he does every episode, and sooner or later something really uptaking§ and neoteric¶ will show up on your favorite auction site."

"Like I couldn't brew up stuff twice as potent myself."

"Of course you could, dear. Especially now, since we can afford the best equipment. With my inheritance kicking in, we can devote your dad's legacy to your hobby. All that stock your dad left can go straight to your hardware fetish, while my money allows us to ditch this creepy old condo and buy a new modern house. Duckback** roof, slowglass†† windows, olivine‡‡ patio . . ." Tupper sighed deeply and dramatically. "Real quality, Fearon."

• • •

Predictably, Malvern Brakhage showed up at their doorstep in the company of disaster.

"Rogue mitosis, Fearon my man. They've shut down Mixogen and called out the HazMat§§ Squad."

"You're kidding? Mixogen? I thought they followed code."

"Hell no! The outbreak's all over downtown. Just thought I'd drop by for a newsy look at your high-bandwidth feed."

Fearon gazed with no small disdain on his bullet-headed fellow scab. Malvern had the thin fixed grin of a live medical student in a room full of cadavers. He wore his customary black leather lab coat and baggy cargo pants, their buttoned pockets bulging with Ziploc baggies of semilegal jello.¶¶

"It's Malvern!" he yelled at the kitchen, where Tupper was leafing through catalogs.

"How about some nutraceuticals***?" said Malvern. "Our mental edges require immediate sharpening." Malvern pulled his slumbering weasel, Spike, from a lab coat pocket and set it on his shoulder. The weasel—biotechnically speaking, Spike was mostly an ermine—immediately became the nicest-looking thing about the man. Spike's lustrous fur gave Malvern the dashing air of a Renaissance prince, if you recalled that Renaissance princes were mostly unprincipled bush-league tyrants who would poison anyone within reach.

Malvern ambled hungrily into the kitchen.

"How have you been, Malvern?" said Tupper brightly.

"I'm great, babe." Malvern pulled a clamp-topped German beer bottle from his jacket. "You up for a nice warm brewski?"

"Don't drink that," Fearon warned his wife.

"Brewed it personally," said Malvern, hurt. "I'll just leave it here in case you change your mind." Malvern plonked the heavy bottle onto the scarred Formica.

Raised a rich, self-assured, decorous girl, Tupper possessed the good breeding and manners to tolerate Malvern's flagrant transgressive behavior. Fearon remembered when he, too, had received adoring looks from Tupper—as a bright idealist who understood the true, liberating potential of biotech, an underground scholar who bowed to none in his arcane mastery of plasmid vectors. Unlike Malvern, whose scab popularity was mostly due to his lack of squeamishness.

---

* *wetware* (n.): programmed organic components; software in living form

† *clottage* (n.): the residence of a scab

‡ *clump* (v.): to enjoy meditative solitary downtime

§ *uptaking* (adj.): a term of scably approbation

¶ *neoteric* (adj.): a term of scably approbation

** *duckback* (n.): a water-resistant building material

†† *slowglass* (n.): glass in which light moves at a radically different speed than it does elsewhere; term invented by Bob Shaw

‡‡ *olivine* (n.): a naturally occurring gemstone used as a building material

§§ *hazmat* (n.): hazardous materials

¶¶ *jello* (n.): a culture and transport medium

*** *nutraceutical* (n.): a foodstuff modified with various synthetic compounds meant to enhance mental or physical performance

Malvern was louche and farouche, so, as was his wont, he began looting Tupper's kitchen fridge. "Liberty's gutters are crawling!" Malvern declaimed, finger snapping a bit to suit his with-it scab-rap. "It's a bug-crash of awesome proportions, and I urge forthwith we reap some peptides from the meltdown."

"Time spent in reconnaissance is never wasted," countered Fearon. He herded the unmannerly scab back to the parlor.

With deft stabs of his carpalled fingertips, Fearon used the parlor wall screen to access Fusing Nuclei—the all-biomed news site favored by the happening hipsters of scabdom.

Tupper, pillar of support that she was, soon slid in with a bounty of hotwired snack food. Instinctively, both men shared with their familiars, Fearon dropping creamy tidbits to his pig while Malvern reached salty gobbets up and back to his neck-hugging weasel.

Shoulder to shoulder on the parlor couch, Malvern and Fearon fixed their jittering attention on the unfolding urban catastrophe.

The living pixels in the electrojelly cohered into the familiar image of Wet Willie, FN's star business reporter. Wet Willie, dashingly clad in his customary splatter-proof trench coat, had framed himself in the shot of a residential Miami skyscraper. The pastel Neo-Deco walls were sheathed in pearly slime. Wriggling like a nautch dancer, the thick, undulating goo gleamed in Florida's Greenhouse sunlight. Local bystanders congregated in their flowered shirts, sun hats, and sandals, gawking from outside the crowd-control pylons. The tainted skyscraper was under careful attack by truck-mounted glorp* cannons, their nozzles channeling high-pressure fingers against the slimy pink walls.

"That's a major outbreak all right," said Fearon. "Since when was Liberty City clearstanced for wet production?"

"As if," chuckled Malvern.

Wet Willie was killing network lag time with a patch of infodump.[†] "Liberty City was once an impoverished slum. That was before Miami urbstanced into the liveliest nexus of the modern Immunosance,[‡] fueled by low-rent but ingenious Caribbean bioneers.[§] When super-immune systems became the hottest somatic upgrade since osteojolt, Liberty City upgraded into today's thriving district of art lofts and hot shops.

"But today that immuconomic quality of life is threatened! The ninth floor of this building houses a startup named Mixogen. The cause of this rampaging outbreak remains speculative, except that the fearsome name of Ribo Zombie is already whispered by knowing insiders."

"I might have known," grunted Malvern.

Fearon clicked the RZ hotlink. Ribo Zombie's ninja-masked publicity photo appeared on the network's vanity page. "Ribo Zombie, the Legendary King of scabs—whose thrilling sub-rosa exploits are brought to you each week by Fusing Nuclei, in strict accordance with the revised Freedom of Information Act and without legal or ethical endorsement! Click here to join the growing horde of cutting-edge bioneers who enjoy weekly shipments of his liberated specimens direct to their small office/home office wetware labs . . ."

Fearon valved off the nutrient flowline to the screen and stood abruptly up, spooking the sensitive Weeble. "That showboating scumbag! You'd think he'd invented scabbing! I hate him! Let's scramble, Mal."

"Yo!" concurred Malvern. "Let's bail forthwith, and bag something hot from the slop."

Fearon assembled his scab gear from closets and shelves throughout the small apartment, Weeble loyally dogging his heels. The process took some time, since a scab's top-end hardware determined his peer ranking in the demimonde of scabdom (a peer ranking stored by retrovirus,

---

* *glorp* (n.): an antibiological sterilizing agent used by swabs

† *infodump* (n.): a large undigested portion of factoids
‡ *Immunosance* (n.): the Immunological Renaissance, the Genetic Age
§ *bioneer* (n.): a bioengineering pioneer

then collated globally by swapping saliva-laden tabs of blotter paper).

Devoted years of feral genetic hobbyism had brought Fearon a veritable galaxy of condoms, shrink-wrap, blotter kits, polymer resins, phase gels, reagents, femto-injectors* serum vials, canisters, aerosols, splat-pistols, whole bandoliers of buckybombs,[†] padded cases, gloves, goggles, netting, cameras, tubes, cylinder dispensers of Pliofilm[‡]—the whole assemblage tucked with a fly fisherman's neurotic care into an intricate system of packs, satchels, and strap-ons.

Tupper watched silently, her expression neutral shading to displeased. Even the dense and tactless Malvern could sense the marital tension.

"Lemme boot up my car. Meet you behind the wheel, Fearo my pard."

Tupper accompanied Fearon to the apartment door, still saying nothing as her man clicked together disassembled instruments, untelescoped his sampling staff, tightened buckles across chest and hips, and mated sticky-backed equipment to special patches on his vest and splashproof chaps.

Rigged out to his satisfaction, Fearon leaned in for a farewell kiss. Tupper merely offered her cheek.

"Aw, come on, honey, don't be that way! You know a man's gotta follow his bliss: which in my special case is a raw, hairy-eyed lifestyle on the bleeding edge of the genetic frontier."

"Fearon McClanahan, if you come back smeared with colloid, you're not setting one foot onto my clean rug."

"I'll really wash up this time, I promise."

"And pick up some fresh goat's-milk prestogurt[§]!"

"I'm with the sequence."

Fearon dashed and clattered down the stairs, his nutraceutically enhanced mind already filled with plans and anticipations. Weeble barreled behind.

Malvern's algal-powered roadster sat by the curb, its fuel cell thrumming. Malvern emptied the tapering trunk, converting it into an open-air rumble seat for Weeble, who bounded in like a jet-propelled fifty-liter drum. The weasel Spike occupied a crash-hammock slung behind the driver's seat. Fearon wedged himself into the passenger's seat, and they were off with a pale electric scream.

After shattering a random variety of Miami traffic laws, the two scabs departed Malvern's street-smart vehicle to creep and skulk the last two blocks to the ongoing bio-Chernobyl. The federal swab[¶] authorities had thrown their usual cordon in place, enough to halt the influx of civilian lookie-loos,[**] but penetrating the perimeter was child's play for well-equipped scabs. Fearon and Malvern simply sprayed themselves and their lab animals with chameleon-shifting shrink-wrap, then strolled through the impotent ring of ultrasonic pylons. They then crept through the shattered glass, found the code-obligatory wheelchair access, and laboriously sneaked up to the ninth floor.

"Well, we're inside just fine," said Fearon, puffing for breath through the shredded shrink-wrap on his lips.

Malvern helped himself to a secretary's abandoned lunch. "Better check Fusing Nuclei for word on the fates of our rivals."

Fearon consulted his handheld. "They just collared Harry the Brewer. 'Impersonating a Disease-Control Officer.'"

"What a lack of gusto and panache. That guy's just not serious."

Malvern peered down streetward through a goo-dripping window. The glorp-cannon salvos

---

* *femto-injector* (n.): a delivery unit capable of perfusing substances through various membranes without making a macroscopic entry wound

† *buckybomb* (n.): an explosive in a carbon buckminsterfullerene shell

‡ *Pliofilm* (n.): all-purpose millepore wrap

§ *prestogurt* (n.): instant yogurt modified to be a nutraceutical

¶ *swab* (n.): governmental and private agents of bioregulation; the cops; antagonists to every scab

** *lookie-loo* (n.): a gaping bystander at a public spectacle; usually the cause of secondary accidents

had been supplemented by strafing ornithopter runs of uptake inhibitors and countermetabolizers. The battling federal defenders of humanity's physiological integrity were using combined-arms tactics. Clearly the forces of law and order were sensing victory. They usually did.

"How much of this hot glop you think we ought to kipe?" Malvern asked.

"Well, all of it. Everything Weeble can eat."

"You don't mind risking ol' Weeble?"

"He's not a pig for nothing, you know. Besides, I just upgraded his digestive tract." Fearon scratched the pig affectionately.

Malvern Velcroed his weasel Spike into the animal's crittercam.* The weasel eagerly scampered off on point, as Malvern offered remote guidance and surveillance with his handheld.

"Out-of-Control Kevin uses video bees," remarked Fearon as they trudged forward with a rattle of sampling equipment. "Little teensy cameras mounted on their teensy insect backs. It's an emergent network phenomenon, he says."

"That's just Oldstyle Silicon Valley," Malvern dismissed. "Besides, a weasel never gets sucked into a jet engine."

The well-trained Spike had nailed the target, and the outlaw wetware was fizzing like cheap champagne. It was a wonder that the floor of the high-rise had withstood the sheer weight of criminal mischief. Mixogen was no mere R&D lab. It was a full-scale production facility. Some ingenious soul had purchased the junked remains of an Orlando aqua-sport resort, all the pumps, slides, and water-park sprinklers. Kiddie wading pools had been retrofitted with big gooey glaciers of serum support gel. The plastic fish tanks were filled to overflowing with raw biomass. Metastasizing cells had backed up into the genetic moonshine somehow, causing a violent bloom and a methane explosion as frothy as lemon meringue. The animal stench was indescribable.

"What stale hell is this?" said Malvern, gaping at a broken tub that brimmed with a demonic assemblage of horns, hoofs, hide, fur, and dewclaws.

"I take that to be widely variegated forms of mammalian epidermal expression." Fearon restrained his pig with difficulty. The rotting smell of the monstrous meat had triggered Weeble's appetite.

"Do I look like I was born yesterday?" snorted Malvern. "You're missing the point. Nobody can maintain a hybridoma with that gross level of genetic variety! Nothing with horns ever has talons! Ungulates and felines don't even have the same chromosome number."

Window plastic shattered. A wall-crawling police robot broke into the genetic speakeasy. It closed its gecko feet with a sound like venetian blinds, and deployed a bristling panoply of lenses and spigots.

"Amscray," Malvern suggested. The duo and their animal familiars retreated from the swab machine's clumsy surveillance. In their absence came a loud frosty hiss as the police bot unleashed a sterilizing fog of Bose-Einstein condensate.†

A new scent had Spike's attention, and it set Malvern off at a trot. They entered an office warren of glass block and steel.

The Mixogen executive had died at her post. She sprawled before her desktop in her ergonomic chair, still in her business suit but reeking of musk and decay. Her swollen, veiny head was the size of a peach basket.

Fearon closed his dropped jaw and zipped up his Kevlar vest. "Jeez, Malvern, another entrepreneur-related fatality! How high do you think her SAT got before she blew?"

"Aw, man—she must have been totally off the IQ scale. Look at the size of her frontal lobes. She's like a six-pack of Wittgensteins."

Malvern shuddered as Spike the weasel tunneled to safety up his pants leg. Fearon wiped

---

* *crittercam* (n.): a small audio-video transmitter mounted on animals

† *Bose-Einstein condensate* (n.): an ultra-frigid state of matter

the sweat from his own pulsing forehead. The stench of the rot was making his head swim. It was certainly good to know that his fully modern immune system would never allow a bacteria or virus to live in his body without his permission.

Malvern crept closer, clicking flash-shots from his digicam. "Check out that hair on her legs and feet."

"I've heard about this," marveled Fearon. "Bonobo hybridoma. She's half chimp! Because that super-neural technique requires—so they say—a tactical retreat down the primate ladder before you can make that tremendous evolutionary rush for breakthrough extropian* intelligence." He broke off short as he saw Weeble eagerly licking the drippy pool of ooze below the dead woman's chair. "Knock it off, Weeble!"

"Where'd the stiff get the stuff?"

"I'm as eager to know that as you are, so I'd suggest swiping her desktop," said Fearon craftily. "Not only would this seriously retard police investigation, but absconding with the criminal evidence would likely shelter many colleagues in the scab underground, who might be righteously grateful to us, and therefore boost our rankings."

"Excellent tactics, my man!" said Malvern, punching his fist in his open palm. "So let's just fall to sampling, shall we? How many stomachs is Weeble packing now?"

"Five, in addition to his baseline digestive one."

"Man, if I had your kind of money . . . Okay, lemme see . . . Cut a tendril from that kinesthetically active goo, snatch a sample from that wading-pool of sushi-barf . . . and, whoa, check the widget that the babe here is clutching."

From one contorted corpse-mitt peeked a gel-based pocket lab. Malvern popped the data storage and slipped the honey-colored hockey puck into his capacious scabbing vest. With a murmured apology, Fearon pressed the tip of his sampling-staff to the woman's bloated skull, and pneumatically shot a tracer into the proper cortical depths. Weeble fastidiously chomped the mass of gray cells. The prize slid safe into the pig's gullet, behind a closing gastric valve.

They triumphantly skulked from the reeking, cracking high-rise, deftly avoiding police surveillance and nasty street-spatters of gutter-goo. Malvern's getaway car rushed obediently to meet them. While Malvern slid through traffic, Fearon dispensed reward treats to the happy Spike and Weeble.

"Mal, you set to work dredging that gel-drive,† okay? I'll load all these tissue samples into my code-crackers. I should have some preliminary results for us by, uhm . . . well, a week or so."

"Yeah, that's what you promised when we scored that hot jellyfish from those Rasta scabs in Key West."

"Hey, they used protein-encrypted gattaca‡! There was nothing I could do about that."

"You're always hanging fire after the coup, Fearon. If you can't unzip some heavy-duty DNA in your chintzy little bedroom lab, then let's find a man who can."

Fearon set his sturdy jaw. "Are you implying that I lack biotechnical potency?"

"Maybe you're getting there. But you're still no match for old Kemp Kingseed. He's a fossil, but he's still got the juice."

"Look, there's a MarthaMart!" Fearon parried.

They wheeled with a screech of tires into the Mylar lot around the MarthaMart, and handed the car to the bunny-suited attendant. The men and their animals made extensive use of the fully shielded privacy of the decon chambers. All four beings soon emerged as innocent of contaminants as virgin latex.

"Thank goodness for the local franchise of

---

* *extropian* (n., adj.): one who, or relating to one who, subscribes to a set of radical, wild-eyed, optimistic prophecies regarding mankind's glorious high-tech future

---

† *gel-drive* (n.): an organic data-storage unit
‡ *gattaca* (n.): DNA; any substrate that holds genetic information

the goddess of perfection," said Fearon content-
edly. "Tupper will have no cause to complain of
my task-consequent domestic disorder! Wait a
minute . . . I think she wanted me to buy something."

They entered the brick-and-mortar retail
floor of the MarthaMart, Fearon racking his
enhanced memory for Tupper's instructions,
but to no avail. In the end he loaded his wiry
shopping basket with pop bottles, gloop* cans,
some recycled squip,† and a spare vial of oven-
cleaning bugs.

The two scabs rode home pensively. Malvern
motored off to his scuzzy bachelor digs, leaving
Fearon to trudge with spousal anxiety upstairs.
What a bringdown from the heights of scab
achievement, this husbandly failure.

Fearon faced an expectant Tupper as he
reached the landing. Dismally, he handed over
the shopping bag. "Here you go. Whatever it
was you wanted, I'm sure I didn't buy it." Then
he brightened. "Got some primo mutant brain-
mass in the pig's innards, though."

• • •

Five days later, Fearon faced an irate Malvern.
Fearon hedged and backfilled for half an hour,
displaying histo-printouts, some scanning-
microscope cinema, even some corny artificial-
life simulations.

Malvern examined the bloodstained end of
his ivory toothpick. "Face defeat, Fearon. That
bolus in the feedline was just pfisteria. The tendril is an everyday hybridoma of liana, earth-
worm, and slime mold. As for the sushi puke, it's
just the usual chemosynthetic complex of abyssal tubeworms. So cut to the chase, pard. What's
with those explosively ultrasmart cortical cells?"

"Okay, I admit it, you're right, I'm screwed. I
can't make any sense of them at all. Wildly oscil-
lating expression-inhibition loops, silent genes,
jumping genes, junk DNA that suddenly recon-

figures itself and takes control—I've never seen
such a stew. It reads like a Martian road map."

Malvern squinched his batrachian eyes. "A
confession of true scabbing lameitude. Pasting a
'Kick Me, I'm Blind' sign on your back. Have I
correctly summarized your utter wussiness?"

Fearon kept his temper. "Look, as long as
we're both discreet about our little adventure
downtown, we're not risking any of our vital reputation in the rough-and-tumble process of scab
peer review."

"You've wasted five precious days in which
Ribo Zombie might radically beat us to the
punch! If this news gets out, your league stand-
ings will fall quicker than an Italian government." Malvern groaned theatrically. "Do you
know how long it's been since my groundbreaking investigative fieldwork was properly
acknowledged? I can't even buy a citation."

Fearon's anger transmuted to embarrassment. "You'll get your quotes and footnotes,
Malvern. I'll just shotgun those genetics to
bits, and subcontract the sequences around
the globe. Then no single individual will get
enough of the big picture to know what we've
been working on."

Malvern tugged irritably at the taut plastic
wrapper of a Pynchonian British toffee. "Man,
you've completely lost your edge! Everybody is
just a synapse away from everybody else these
days! If you hire a bunch of scabs on the net,
they'll just search-engine each other out, and
patch everything back together. It's high time we
consulted Dr. Kingseed."

"Oh, Malvern, I hate asking Kemp for favors.
He's such a bringdown billjoy‡ when it comes
to hot breakthrough technologies! Besides, he
always treats me like I'm some website intern
from the days of Internet slave labor."

"Quit whining. This is serious work."

"Plus, that cobwebby decor in Kemp's ret-
rofunky domicile! All those ultra-rotten Hirst
assemblages—they'd creep anybody out."

---

* *gloop* (n.): a foodstuff
† *squip* (n.): a foodstuff

‡ *billjoy* (n.): a doomsayer; derived from Bill Joy, a
fretful member of the twentieth-century digerati

Malvern sighed. "You never talked this way before you got married."

Fearon waved a hand at Tupper's tasteful wallpaper. "Can I help it if I now grok interior decor?"

"Let's face some facts, my man: Dr. Kemp Kingseed has the orthogonal genius of the primeval hacker. After all, his startup companies pushed the Immunosance past its original tipping point. Tell the missus we're heading out, and let's scramble headlong for the Next New Thing like all true-blue scabs must do."

Tupper was busy in her tiny office at her own career, moderating her virtual agora on twentieth-century graphic narrative. She accepted Fearon's news with only half her attention. "Have fun, dear." She returned to her webcam. "Now, Kirbybuff, could you please clarify your thesis on Tintin and Snowy as precursor culture heroes of the Immunosance?"

Spike and Malvern, Weeble and Fearon sought out an abandoned petroleum distribution facility down by the waterfront. Always the financial bottom-feeder, the canny Kemp Kingseed had snapped up the wrecked facility after the abject collapse of the fossil-fuel industry. At one point in his checkered career, the reclusive hermit-genius had tried to turn the maze of steam pipes and rusting storage tanks into a child-friendly industrial-heritage theme park. Legal problems had undercut his project, leaving the aged digital entrepreneur haunting the ruins of yet another vast, collapsed scheme.

An enormous spiderweb, its sticky threads thick as supertanker hawsers, hung over the rusting tanks like some Victorian antimacassar of the gods.

Malvern examined the unstable tangle of spidery cables. "We'd better leave Weeble down here."

"But I never, ever want to leave dear Weeble!"

"Just paste a crittercam on him and have him patrol for us on point." Malvern looked at the pig critically. "He sure looks green around the gills since he ate that chick's brain. You sure he's okay?"

"Weeble is fine. He's some pig."

The visitors began their climb. Halfway up the tank's curving wall, Kemp Kingseed's familiar, Shelob, scuttled from her lair in the black pipe of a giant smokestack. She was a spider as big as a walrus. The ghastly arachnid reeked of vinegar.

"It's those big corny spider-legs," said Malvern, hiding his visceral fear in a thin shroud of scientific objectivity. "You'd think old Kingseed had never heard of the cube-square law!"

"Huh?" grunted Fearon, clinging to a sticky cable.

"Look, the proportions go all wrong if you blow them up a thousand times life-size. For one thing, insects breathe through spiracles! Insects don't have lungs. An insect as big as a walrus couldn't even breathe!"

"Arachnids aren't insects, Malvern."

"It's just a big robot with some cheap spider chitin grown on it. That's the only explanation that makes rational sense."

The unspeakable monster retreated to her lair, and the climbers moved thankfully on.

Kemp Kingseed's lab was a giant hornet's nest. The big papery office had been grown inside a giant empty fuel tank. Kingseed had always resented the skyrocketing publication costs in academic research. So he had cut to the chase, and built his entire laboratory out of mulched back issues of *Cell* and *Nature Genomics*.

Kingseed had enormous lamp-goggle eyeglasses, tufts of snowy hair on his skull, and impressive white bristles in his withered ears. The ancient Internet mogul still wore his time-honored Versace lab coat, over baggy green ripstop pants and rotting Chuck Taylor high-tops.

"Africa," he told them, after examining their swiped goodies.

"'Africa'?"

"I never thought I'd see those sequences again." Kingseed removed his swimmy lenses to dab at his moist red eyes with a swatch of lab paper. "Those were our heroic days. The world's most advanced technicians, fighting for the planet's environmental survival! Of course we completely failed, and the planet's ecosystem totally collapsed. But at least we didn't suck up to politicians."

Kingseed looked at them sharply. "Lousy, fake-rebel pimps, like that Ribo Zombie, turned into big phony pop stars. Why, in my generation, we were the real, authentic transgressive-dissident pop stars! Napster . . . Freenet . . . GNU/Linux . . . Man, that was the stuff!"

Kingseed beat vaguely at the air with his wrinkled fist. "Well, when the Greenhouse started really cooking us, we had to invent the Immunosance. We had no choice at that point, because it was the only way to survive. But every hideous thing we did to save the planet was totally UN-approved! Big swarms of rich-guy NGOs* were backing us, straight out of the WTO† and the Davos Forum. We even had security clearances. It was all for the public good!"

Malvern and Fearon exchanged wary glances.

Kingseed scowled at them. "Malvern, how much weasel flesh do you have in your personal genetic makeup?"

"Practically none, Dr. Kingseed!" Malvern demurred. "Just a few plasmids in my epidermal expression."

"Well, see, that's the vital difference between your decadent times and my heroic age. Back in my day, people were incredibly anxious and fussy about genetic contamination. They expected people and animals to have clean, unpolluted, fully natural genelines. But then, of course, the Greenhouse Effect destroyed the natural ecosystem. Only the thoroughly unnatural and the totally hyped-up could thrive in that kind of crisis. Civilization always collapsed worst where the habitats were most nearly natural. So the continent of Africa was, well, pretty much obliterated."

"Oh, we're with the story," Fearon assured him. "We're totally with-it heart-of-darkness-wise."

"Ha!" barked Kingseed. "You pampered punks got no idea what genuine chaos looks like! It was incredibly awful! Guerrilla armies of African mercenaries grabbed all our state-of-the-art lab equipment. They were looting—burning—and once the narco-terror crowd moved in from the Golden Triangle, it got mondo bizarre!"

Malvern shrugged. "So how tough can it be? You just get on a plane and go look." He looked at Fearon. "You get on planes, don't you, Fearon?"

"Sure. Cars, sleds, water skis, you bet I get on planes."

Kingseed raised a chiding finger. "We were desperate to save all those endangered species, so we just started packing them into anything that looked like it would survive the climate disruption. Elephant DNA spliced into cacti, rhino sequences tucked into fungi and hey, we were the *good guys*. You should have seen what the *ruthless terrorists* were up to."

Malvern picked a fragment from his molars, examined it thoughtfully, and ate it. "Look Dr. Kingseed, all this ancient history's really edifying, but I still don't get it with the swollen, exploding brain part."

"That's also what Ribo Zombie wanted to know."

Fearon stiffened. "Ribo Zombie came here? What did you tell him?"

"I told that sorry punk nothing! Not one word did he get out of me! He's been sniffing around my crib, but I chased him back to his media coverage and his high-priced market consultants."

Malvern offered a smacking epidermal high-five. "Kemp, you are one uptaking guru! You're the Miami swamp Yoda, dad!"

"I kinda like you two kids, so let me cluetrain you in. Ever seen NATO military chimp-brain? If you know how to tuck globs of digitally altered chimp brain into your own glial cells—and I'm not saying that's painless—then you can radically jazz your own cortex. Just swell your head up like a mushroom puffball." Kingseed gazed at them soberly. "It runs on DNA storage, that's the secret. Really, really long strands of DNA.

---

* *NGO* (n.): nongovernmental organization
† *WTO* (n.): World Trade Organization

We're talking like infinite Turing-tape strands of gattaca."

"Kemp," said Fearon kindly, "why don't you come along with us to Africa? You spend too much time in this toxic old factory with that big smelly spider. It'll do you good to get some fresh jungle air. Besides, we clearly require a wise native guide, given this situation."

"Are you two clowns really claiming that you wanna pursue this score to Africa?"

"Oh sure, Ghana, Guinea, whatever. We'll just nick over to the Dark Continent duty-free and check it out for the weekend. Come on, Kemp, we're scabs! We got cameras, we got credit cards! It's a cakewalk!"

Kingseed knotted his snowy eyebrows. "Every sane human being fled out of Africa decades ago. It's the dark side of the Immuno-sance. Even the Red Cross ran off screaming."

"'Red Cross,'" said Malvern to Fearon. The two of them were unable to restrain their hearty laughter. "'Red Cross.' What ineffectual lame-os! Man, that's rich."

"Okay, sure, have it your own way," King-seed muttered. "I'll just go sherlock my oldest dead-media and scare up some tech-specs." He retreated to his vespine inner sanctum. Antic rummaging noises followed.

Fearon patiently sank into a classic corru-gated Gehry chair. Malvern raided Kingseed's tiny bachelor kitchen, appropriating a platter of honey-guarana snack cubes. "What a cool pad this rich geezer's got!" Malvern said, munch-ing. "I am digging how the natural light piped in through fiber-optic channels renders this fuel tank so potent for lab work."

"This place is a stinking dump. Sure, he's rich, but that just means he'll overcharge us."

Malvern sternly cleared his throat. "Let's get something straight, partner. I haven't posted a scab acquisition since late last year! And you're in no better shape, with married life putting such a crimp in your scabbing. If we expect to pull down big-time decals and sponsorships, we've just got to beat Ribo Zombie to a major find. And this one is definitely ours by right."

After a moment, Fearon nodded in grim com-mitment. It was impossible to duck a straight-out scab challenge like this one—not if he expected to face himself in the mirror.

Kingseed emerged from his papery attic, his glasses askew and the wild pastures of his hair scampering with dust bunnies. He bore a raven in a splintery bamboo cage, along with a moldy fistful of stippled paper strips.

"Candybytes!* I stored all the African data on candybytes! They were my bonanza for the child educational market. Edible paper, tasty sugar substrate, info-rich secret ingredients!"

"Hey yeah!" said Malvern nostalgically. "I used to eat candybytes as a little kid in my Time-Warner-Disney creche. So now one of us has to gobble your moldy old lemon-drops?" Malvern was clearly nothing loath.

"No need for that, I brought old Heckle here. Heckle is my verbal output device."

Fearon examined the raven's cage. "This featherbag looks as old as a Victrola."

Kingseed set a moldy data strip atop a table, then released Heckle. The dark bird hopped unerringly to the start of the tape, and began to peck and eat. As Heckle's living read-head ingested and interpreted the coded candybytes, the raven jumped around the table like a fairy chess knight, a corvine Turing Train.

"How is a raven like a writing desk?" mur-mured Kemp.

Heckle shivered, stretched his glossy wings, and went Delphic. In a croaky, midnight-dreary voice, the neurally possessed bird delivered a strange tale.

A desperate group of Noahs and Appleseeds, Goodalls and Cousteaus, Leakeys and Fosseys had gathered up Africa's endangered flora and fauna, then packed the executable genetic infor-mation away into a most marvelous container: the Panspecific Mycoblastula.† The Panspecific Mycoblastula was an immortal chimeric fungal ball of awesome storage capacity, a filamentously

---

* *candybytes* (n.): an educational nutraceutical
† *Panspecific Mycoblastula* (n.): a MacGuffin

aggressive bloody tripe-wad, a motile Darwinian lights-and-liver battle-slimeslug.

Shivering with mute attention, Fearon brandished his handheld, carefully recording every cawed and revelatory word. Naturally the device also displayed the point of view of Weeble's crittercam.

Suddenly, Fearon glimpsed a shocking scene. Weeble was under attack!

There was no mistaking the infamous Skratchy Kat, who had been trying, without success, to skulk around Kingseed's industrial estate. Weeble's porcine war cry emerged tinnily from the little speakers. The crittercam's transmission whipsawed in frenzy.

"Sic him, Weeble! Hoof that feline spy!"

Gamely obeying his master's voice, the pig launched his bulk at the top-of-the-line post-feline. A howling combat ensued, Fearon's pig getting the worse of it. Then Shelob the multiton spider joined the fray. Skratchy Kat quickly saw the sense of retreat. When the transmission stabilized, the superstar's familiar had vanished. Weeble grunted proudly. The crittercam bobbed rhythmically as the potent porker licked his wounds with antiseptic tongue.

"You the man, Fearon! Your awesome pig kicked that cat's ass!"

Kingseed scratched his head glumly. "You had a crittercam channel open to your pig this whole time, didn't you?"

Fearon grimaced, clutching his handheld. "Well, of course I did! I didn't want my Weeble to feel all lonely."

"Ribo Zombie's cat was watergating your pig. Ribo Zombie must have heard everything we said up here. I hope he didn't record those GPS coordinates."

The possessed raven was still cackling spastically, as the last crackles of embedded data spooled through its postcorvine speech centers. Heckle was recaged and rewarded with a tray of crickets.

Suddenly, Fearon's handheld spoke up in a sinister basso. It was the incoming voice of Ribo Zombie himself. "So the Panspecific Mycoblas-

tula is in Sierra Leone. It is a savage territory, ruled by the mighty bush soldier, Prince Kissy Mental. He is a ferocious cannibal who would chew you small-timers up like aphrodisiac gum! So Malvern and Fearon take heed of my street-wisdom. I have the top-line hardware, and now, thanks to you, I have the data as well. Save yourselves the trouble, just go home."

"Gumshoe on up here, you washed-up ponce!" said startled Malvern, dissed to the bone. "My fearsome weasel will go sloppy seconds on your big fat cat!"

Kingseed stretched forth his liver-spotted mitt. "Turn off those handhelds, boys."

When Fearon and Malvern had bashfully powered down their devices, the old guru removed an antique pager from his lab bench. He played his horny thumb across the rudimentary keypad.

"A pager?" Malvern goggled. "Why not, like, jungle drums?"

"Pipe down. You pampered modern lamers can't even manage elementary anti-surveillance. While one obsolescent pager is useless, two are a secure link."

Kingseed read the archaic glyphs off the tiny screen. "I can see that my contact in Freetown, Dr. Herbert Zoster, is still operational. With his help, you might yet beat Zombie to this prize." Kingseed looked up. "After allowing Ribo Zombie to bug my very home, I expect no less from you. You'd better come through this time, or never show your faces again at the Tallahassee ScabCon. With your dalkon shields or on them, boys."

"Lofty! We're outta here pronto! Thanks a lot, gramps."

• • •

Tupper was very alarmed about Africa. After an initial tearful outburst, hot meals around Fearon's house became as rare as whales and pandas. Domestic conversation died down to apologetic bursts of dingbat-decorated e-mail. Their sex life, always sensually satisfactory and emotionally deep, became as chilly as the last few lonely glaciers of greenhouse Greenland. Glum but determined, Fearon made no complaint.

On the day of his brave departure—his important gear stowed in two carry-on bags, save for that which Weeble wore in khaki-colored saddle-style pouches—Fearon paused at the door of their flat. Tupper sat morosely on the couch, pretending to surf the screen. For thirty seconds the display showed an ad from AT&T (Advanced Transcription and Totipotency) touting their latest telomere upgrades. Fearon was, of course, transfixed. But then Tupper changed channels, and he refocused mournfully for a last homesick look at his frosty spouse.

"I must leave you now, Tuppence honey, to meet Malvern at the docks." Even the use of her pet name failed to break her reserve. "Darling, I know this hurts your feelings, but think of it this way: my love for you is true because I'm true to my own true self. Malvern and I will be in and out of that tropical squalor in a mere week or two, with minimal lysis* all around. But if I don't come back right away—or even, well, forever—I want you to know without you, I'm nothing. You're the feminine mitochondriome in my dissolute masculine plasm, baby."

Nothing. Fearon turned to leave, hand on the doorknob. Tupper swept him up in an embrace from behind, causing Weeble to grunt in surprise. Fearon slithered around within the cage of her arms to face her, and she mashed her lips into his.

Malvern's insistent pounding woke the lovers up. Hastily, Fearon redonned his outfit, bestowed a final peck on Tupper's tear-slicked cheek, and made his exit.

"A little trouble getting away?" Malvern leered.

"Not really. You?"

"Well, my landlady made me pay the next month's rent in advance. Oh, and if I'm dead, she gets to sell all my stuff."

---

* *lysis* (n.): cell destruction

"Harsh."

"Just the kind of treatment I expect."

• • •

Still flushed from the fever-shots at US Customs, the two globe-trotting scabs watched the receding coast of America from the deck of their Cuba-bound ferry, the *Gloria Estefan.*

"I hate all swabs," said Malvern, belching as his innards rebooted.

Fearon clutched his squirming belly. "We could have picked better weather. These ferocious Caribbean hurricane waves . . ."

"What 'waves'? We're still in the harbor."

"Oh, my Lord . . ."

After a pitching, greenish sea-trip, Cuba hove into view. The City of Havana, menaced by rising seas, had been relocated up the Cuban coast through a massive levy on socialist labor. The crazy effort had more or less succeeded, though it looked as if every historic building in the city had been picked up and dropped.

Debarking in the fragrant faux-joy of the highly colored tropics, the eager duo hastened to the airfield—for only the cowboy Cubans still maintained direct air flights to the wrecked and smoldering shell of the Dark Continent.

Mi Amiga Flicka was a hydrogen-lightened cargo lifter of Appaloosa-patterned horsehide. The buoyant lift was generated by onboard horse stomachs, modified to spew hydrogen instead of the usual methane. A tanker truck, using a long boom-arm, pumped a potent microbial oatmeal into the tethered dirigible's feedstock reservoirs.

"There's a microbrewery on board," Malvern said with a travel agent's phony glee. "Works off grain mash just like a horse does! *Cerveza muy potenta*, you can bet."

A freestanding bamboo elevator ratcheted them up to the zeppelin's passenger module, which hung like a zippered saddlebag from the buoyant horsehide belly.

The bio-zep's* passenger cabin featured a zebra-hide mess hall that doubled as a ballroom, with a tiny bandstand and a touchingly antique mirror ball. The Cuban stewards, to spare weight and space, were all jockey sized.

Fearon and Malvern discovered that their web-booked "stateroom" was slightly smaller than a standard street toilet. Every feature of the tiny suite folded, collapsed, inverted, everted, or required assembly from scattered parts.

"I don't think I can get used to peeing in the same pipe that dispenses that legendary microbrew," said Fearon. Less finicky, Malvern had already tapped and sampled a glass of the golden boutique cerveza. "Life is a closed loop, Fearon."

"But where will the pig sleep?"

They found their way to the observation lounge for the departure of the giant gasbag. With practiced ease, the crew detached blimphook from mooring mast. The bacterial fuel cells kicked over the myosin motors, the props began to windmill and the craft surged eastward with all the verve and speed of a spavined nag.

Malvern was already deep into his third cerveza. "Once we get our hands on that wodge of extinct gene-chains, our names are forever golden! It'll be vino, gyno, and techno all the way!"

"Let's not count our chimeras till they're decanted, Mal. We're barely puttering along, and I keep thinking of Ribo Zombie and his highly publicized private entomopter."

"Ribo Zombie's a fat showbiz phony, he's all talk! We're heavy-duty street-level chicos from Miami! It's just no contest."

"Hmmph. We'd better vortal† in to Fusing Nuclei and check out the continuing coverage."

Fearon found a spot where the zep's horsehide was thinnest and tapped an overhead satellite feed. The gel screen of his handheld flashed the familiar Fusing Nuclei logo.

"In his one-man supercavitating‡ sub, Ribo Zombie and Skratchy Kat speed toward the grim no-man's land of sub-Saharan Africa! What weird and wonderful adventures await our intrepid lone-wolf scab and his plucky familiar? Does carnal love lurk in some dusky native bosom? Log on Monday for the real-time landing of RZ and Skratchy upon the sludge-sloshing shores of African doom! And remember, kids! Skratchy Kat cards, toys, and collectibles are available only through Nintendo-Benz . . ."

"Did they say 'Monday'?" Malvern screeched. "Monday is tomorrow! We're already royally boned!"

"Malvern, please, the straights are staring at us. Ribo Zombie can't prospect all of Africa through all those old UN emplacements. Kingseed found us an expert native guide, remember? Dr. Herbie Zoster."

Malvern stifled his despair. "You really think this native scab has got the stuff?"

Fearon smiled. "Well, he's not a scab quite like us, but he's definitely our type! I checked out his online résumé! He's pumped, ripped, and buff, plus he's wily and street-smart. Herbie Zoster has been a mercenary, an explorer, an archaeologist, even the dictator of an offshore data haven. Once we hook up with him, this ought to be a waltz."

In the airborne hours that followed, Malvern sampled a foretaste of the vino, gyno, and techno, while Fearon repeatedly wrote and erased an apologetical e-mail to his wife. Then came their scheduled arrival over the melancholy ruins of Freetown—and a dismaying formal announcement by the ship's Captain.

"What do you mean, you can't moor?" demanded Malvern.

Their captain, a roguish and dapper yet intensely competent fellow named Luis Sendero, removed his cap and slicked back the two

---

* *bio-zep* (n.): a pseudo-living, lighter-than-air zeppelin
† *vortal* (n., v.): a virtual portal

‡ *supercavitation* (n.): the process of underwater travel employing leading air pockets

macaw feathers anchored at his temple. "The local caudillo, Prince Kissy Mental, has incited his people to burn down our trading facilities. One learns to expect these little setbacks in the African trade. Honoring our contracts, we shall parachute to earth the goods we bring, unless they are not paid for—in which case, they are dumped anyway, yet receive no parachute. As for you two Yankees and your two animals—you are the only passengers who want to land in Sierra Leone. If you wish to touch down, you must parachute just as the cargo."

After much blustering, whuffling, and whining, Fearon, Malvern, and Weeble stood at the open hatch of *Mi Amiga Flicka*, parachutes strapped insecurely on, ripcords wired to a rusty cable, while the exotic scents of the rainy African landscape wafted to their nostrils.

Wistfully, they watched their luggage recede to the scarred red earth. Then, with Spike clutched to his breast, Malvern closed his eyes and boldly tumbled overboard. Fearon watched closely as his colleague's fabric chute successfully bloomed. Only then did he make up his mind to go through with it. He booted the reluctant Weeble into airy space and followed suit.

• • •

"Outsiders never bring us anything but garbage," mumbled Dr. Zoster.

"Is it Cuban garbage?" said Malvern, tucking into their host's goat-and-pepper soup with a crude wooden spoon. "Because if it is, you're getting ripped off even in terms of trash."

"No. They're always Cubans bringing it, but it's everybody's garbage that is dumped on Africa. Africa's cargo-cult prayers have been answered with debris. But perhaps any sufficiently advanced garbage is indistinguishable from magic."

Fearon surreptitiously fed the peppery cabrito to his pig. He was having a hard time successfully relating to Dr. Herbie Zoster. It had never occurred to him that elderly Kemp Kingseed and tough, sunburned Herbie Zoster were such close kin.

In point of fact, Herbie Zoster was Kingseed's younger clone. And it didn't require Jungian analysis to see that, just like most clones, Zoster bitterly resented the egotistical man who had created him. This was very clearly the greatest appeal of life in Africa for Dr. Herbie Zoster. Africa was the one continent guaranteed to make him as much unlike Kemp Kingseed as possible.

Skin tinted dark as mahogany, callused and wiry, dotted with many thorn scratches, parasites, and gunshot wounds, Zoster still bore some resemblance to Kingseed—about as much as a battle-scarred hyena to an aging bloodhound.

"What exactly do people dump around here?" said Malvern with interest.

Zoster mournfully chewed the last remnant of a baked yam and spat the skin into the darkness outside their thatched hut. Something with great glowing eyes pounced upon it instantly, with a rasp and a snarl. "You're familiar with the Immunosance?"

"Oh yeah, sure!" said Malvern artlessly, "we're from Miami."

"That new Genetic Age completely replaced the Nuclear Age, the Space Age, and the Information Age."

"Good riddance," Malvern offered. "You got any more of that cabrito stew? It's fine stuff!"

Zoster rang a crude brass bell. A limping, turbaned manservant dragged himself into their thatched hut, tugging a bubbling bucket of chow.

"The difficulty with massive technological advance," said Zoster, spooning the steamy goop, "is that it obsolesces the previous means of production. When the Immunosance arrived, omnipresent industries already covered all the advanced countries." Zoster paused to pump vigorously at a spring-loaded homemade crank, which caused the light bulb overhead to brighten to its full thirty watts. "There simply was no room to install the new bioindustrial revolution. But a revolution was very necessary anyway. So all the previous junk had to go. The only major planetary area with massive dumping grounds was—and still is—Africa."

Zoster rubbed at his crank-stiffened forearm

and sighed. "Sometimes they promote the garbage and sell it to us Africans. Sometimes they drop it anonymously. But nevertheless—no matter how we struggle or resist—the very worst always ends up here in Africa, no matter what."

"I'm with the sequence," said Malvern, pausing to belch. "So what's the four-one-one about this fabled Panspecific Mycoblastula?"

Zoster straightened, an expression of awe toughening his face below his canvas hat brim. "That is garbage of a very special kind. Because the Panspecific Mycoblastula is an entire, outmoded natural ecosystem. It is the last wild continent, completely wadded up and compressed by foreign technicians!"

Fearon considered this gnomic remark. He found it profoundly encouraging. "We understand the gravity of this matter, Dr. Zoster. Malvern and I feel that we can make this very worth your while. Time is of the essence. When can we start?"

Zoster scraped the dirt floor with his worn bootheel. "I'll have to hire a train of native bearers. I'll have to obtain supplies. We will be risking our lives, of course . . . What can you offer us in return for that?"

"A case of soft drinks?" said Malvern.

Fearon leaned forward intently. "Transistor radios? Antibiotics? How about some plumbing?"

Zoster smiled for the first time, with a flash of gold teeth. "Call me Herbie."

• • •

Zoster extended a callused fingertip. It bore a single ant, the size and color of a sesame seed.

"This is the largest organism in the world."

"So I heard," Malvern interjected glibly. "Just like the fire ants invading America, right? They went through a Darwinian bottleneck and came out supercharged sisters, genetically identical even under different queens. They spread across the whole USA smoother than marshmallow fluff."

Zoster wiped his sweating stubbled jaw with a filthy bandanna. "These ants were produced four decades ago. They carry rhizotropic fungi, to fertilize crops with nitrogen. But their breeders overdesigned them. These ants cause tremendous fertile growth in vegetation, but they're also immune to insect diseases and parasites. The swabs finally wiped them out in America, but Africa has no swabs. We have no public health services, no telephones, no roads. So from Timbuktu to Cape Town, cloned ants have spread in a massive wave, a single superorganism big as Africa."

Malvern shook his head in superior pity. "That's what you get for trusting in swabs, man. Any major dude could've told those corporate criminals that top-down hierarchies never work out. Now, the approach you Third Worlders need is a viral marketing, appropriate-technology pitch . . ."

Zoster actually seemed impressed by Malvern's foolish bravado, and engaged the foreign scab in earnest jargon-laced discussion, leaving Fearon to trudge along in an unspeaking fug of sweat-dripping, alien jungle heat. Though Zoster was the only one armed, the trio of scabs boldly led their little expedition through a tangle of feral trails, much aided by their satellite surveillance maps and GPS locators.

Five native bearers trailed the parade, fully laden-down with scab-baggage and provisions. The bare-chested, bare-legged, dhoti-clad locals exhibited various useful bodily mods, such as dorsal water storage humps, toughened and splayed feet, and dirty grub-excavating claws that could shred a stump in seconds. They also sported less rational cosmetic changes, including slowly moving cicatrices (really migratory subepidermal symbiotic worms) and enlarged ears augmented with elephant musculature. The rhythmic flapping of the porters' ears produced a gentle creaking that colorfully punctuated their impenetrable sibilant language.

The tormented landscape of Sierra Leone had been thoroughly reclaimed by a clapped-out mutant jungle. War, poverty, disease, starvation—the Four Land Rovers of the African Apocalypse—had long since been and gone, bringing a drastic human population crash that beggared the Black Death, and ceding the continent to resurgent flora and fauna.

These local flora and fauna were, however, radically human-altered, recovering from an across-the-board apocalypse even more severe and scourging than the grisly one suffered by humans. Having come through the grinding hopper of a bioterror, they were no longer "creatures" but "evolutures."* Trees writhed, leaves crawled, insects croaked, lizards bunny-hopped, mammals flew, flowers pinched, vines slithered, and mushrooms burrowed. The fish, clumsily reengineered for the surging Greenhouse realities of rising seas, lay in the jungle trails burping like lungfish. When stepped upon, they almost seemed to speak.

The explorers found themselves navigating a former highway to some long-buried city, presumably Bayau or Moyamba, to judge by the outdated websites. Post-natural oddities lay atop an armature of ruins, revealing the Ozymandias lessons of industrial hubris. A mound of translucent jello assumed the outlines of a car, including a dimly perceived skeletal driver and passengers. Oil-slick-colored orchids vomited from windows and doors. With the descending dusk invigorating flocks of winged post-urban rats, the travelers made camp. Zoster popped up a pair of tents for the expedition's leaders and their animals, while the locals assembled a humble jungle igloo of fronds and thorns.

After sharing a few freeze-dried packets of slumgullion, the expedition sank into weary sleep. Fearon was so bone-tired that he somehow tolerated Malvern's nasal whistling and Zoster's stifled dream shouts.

He awoke before the others. He unseamed the tent flap and poked his head out into the early sunshine.

Their encampment was surrounded by marauders. Spindly scouts, blank-eyed and

scarcely human, were watching the pop-tents and leaning on pig-iron spears.

Fearon ducked his head back and roused his compatriots, who silently scrambled into their clothes. Heads clustered like coconuts, the three of them peered through a fingernail's width of tent flap.

Warrior-reinforcements now arrived in ancient Jeeps, carrying anti-aircraft guns and rocket-propelled grenades.

"It's Kissy Mental's Bush Army," whispered Zoster. He pawed hurriedly through a pack, coming up with a pair of mechanical boots.

"Okay, girls, listen up," Zoster whispered, shoving and clamping his feet in the piston-heavy footgear. "I have a plan. When I yank this overhead pull tab, this tent unpops. That should startle the scouts out there, maybe enough to cover our getaway. We all race off at top speed just the way we came. If either of you survive, feel free to rendezvous back at my place."

Zoster hefted his gun, their only weapon. He dug the toe of each boot into a switch on the heel of its mate, and his boots began to chuff and emit small puffs of exhaust.

"Gasoline-powered seven-league boots," Zoster explained, seeing their stricken expressions. "South African Army surplus. There's no need for roads with these things, but with skill and practice, you can pronk along like a gazelle at thirty, forty miles an hour."

"You really believe we can outrun these jungle marauders?" Malvern asked.

"I don't have to outrun them; I only have to outrun you."

Zoster triggered the tent and dashed off at once, firing his pistol at random. The pistons of his boots gave off great blasting backfires, which catapulted him away with vast stainless-steel lunges.

Stunned and in terror, Malvern and Fearon stumbled out of the crumpling tent, coughing on Zoster's exhaust. By the time they straightened up and regained their vision, they were firmly in the grip of Prince Kissy Mental's troops.

---

* *evoluture* (n.): an artificially evolved creature

The savage warriors attacked the second poptent with their machetes. They quickly grappled and snaffled the struggling Spike and Weeble.

"Chill, Spike!"

"Weeble, hang loose!"

The animals obeyed, though the cruel grip of their captors promised the worst.

The minions of the prince were far too distanced from humanity to have any merely ethnic identity. Instead, they shared a certain fungal sheen, a somatype* evident in their thallophytic[†] pallor and exophthalmic[‡] gaze. Several of the marauders, wounded by Zoster's wild shots, were calmly stuffing various grasses and leaves into the gaping, suety holes in their arms, legs, and chests.

A working squad now dismantled the igloo of the expedition's bearers, pausing to munch meditatively on the greenery of the cut fronds. The panic-stricken bearers gabbled in obvious terror but offered no resistance. A group of Kissy Mental's warriors, with enormous heads and great toothy jaws, decamped from a rusty jeep. They unshouldered indestructible Russian automatic rifles and decisively emptied their clips into the hut. Pathetic screams came from the ruined igloo. The warriors then demolished the walls and hauled out the dead and wounded victims, to dispassionately tear them limb from limb.

The Army then assembled a new booty of meat, to bear it back up the trail to their camp. Reeking of sweat and formic acid, the inhuman natives bound the hands of Fearon and Malvern with tough lengths of grass. They strung Weeble and Spike to a shoulder pole, where the terrified beasts dangled like piñatas.

Then the ant men forced the quartet of prisoners forward on the quick march. As the party passed through the fetid jungle, the Army paused periodically to empty their automatic weapons at anything that moved. Whatever victim fell to earth would be swiftly chopped to chunks and added to the head-borne packages of the rampaging mass.

Within the hour, Fearon and Malvern were delivered whole to Prince Kissy Mental.

Deliberately, Fearon focused his attention on the prince's throne, so as to spare himself the sight of the monster within it. The Army's portable throne was a row of three first-class airplane seats, with the armrests removed to accommodate the prince's vast posthuman bulk. The throne perched atop a mobile palanquin, jury-rigged from rebar, chipboard, and Astro-Turf. A system of crutches and tethers supported and eased the prince's vast, teratological skull.

The trophy captives were shoved forward at spearpoint through a knee-deep heap of cargo-cult gadgets.

"Holy smallpox!" whispered Malvern. "This boss man's half chimp and half ant!"

"That doesn't leave any percentage for human, Mal."

The thrust of a spear butt knocked Fearon to his knees. Kissy Mental's coarse-haired carcass, barrel-chested to support the swollen needs of the head, was sketched like a Roquefort cheese with massive blue veins. The prince's vast pulpy neck marked the transition zone to a formerly human skull whose sutures had long since burst under pressure, to be patched with big, red, shiny plates of antlike chitin. Kissy Mental's head was bigger than the prize-winning pumpkin at a 4-H[§] Fair.

Fearon slitted his eyes, rising to his feet. He was terrified, but the thought of never seeing Tupper again somehow put iron in his soul. To imagine that he might someday be home again,

---

* *somatype* (n.): the visible expression of gattaca

† *thallophytic* (adj.): mushroomlike

‡ *exophthalmic* (adj.): pop-eyed

§ *4-H* (n.): an amateurs' club, primarily for children, that focuses on homeostasis (bodily maintenance through negative feedback circuits), haplotypes (gamete amounts of DNA), histogenesis (cell differentiation from general to specific), and hypertrophy (gigantism)

safe with his beloved—that prospect was worth any sacrifice. There had to be some method to bargain with their captor.

"Malvern, how bright do you think this guy is? You suppose he's got any English?"

"He's got to be at least as intelligent as British royalty."

With an effort that set his bloated heart booming like a tribal drum, the prince lifted both his hairy arms, and beckoned. Their captors pushed Mal and Fear right up against the throne. The prince unleashed a flock of personal fleas. Biting, lancing, and sucking, the tasters lavishly sampled the flesh of Fearon and Malvern and returned to their master. After quietly munching a few of the blood-gorged familiars, the prince silently brooded, the tiny bloodshot eyes in his enormous skull blinking like LEDs. He then gestured for a courtier to ascend into the presence. The bangled, headdressed ant man hopped up and, well-trained, sucked a thin clear excretion from the prince's rugose left nipple.

Smacking his lips, the lieutenant decrypted his proteinaceous commands, in a sudden frenzy of dancing, shouting, and ritual gesticulation.

Swiftly the Army rushed into swarming action, trampling one another in an ardent need to lift the prince's throne upon their shoulders. Once they had their entomological kingpin up and in lolling motion, the Army milled forward in a violent rolling surge, employing their machetes on anything in their path.

A quintet of burly footmen pushed Malvern and Fearon behind the bluish exhaust of an ancient military jeep. The flesh of the butchered bearers had been crudely wrapped in broad green leaves and dumped into the back of the vehicle.

Malvern muttered sullenly below the grumbles of the engine. "That scumbag Zoster . . . All clones are inherently degraded copies. Man, if we ever get out of this pinch, it's no more Mr. Nice Guy."

"Uh, sure, that's the old scab spirit, Mal."

"Hey, look!"

Fearon followed Malvern's jerking head-nod.

A split-off subdivision of the trampling Army had dragged another commensal organism from the spooked depths of the mutant forest. It was a large, rust-eaten, canary yellow New Beetle, scribbled over with arcane pheromonal runes. Its engine long gone, the wreck rolled solely through the juggernaut heaving of the Army.

"Isn't that the 2015 New Beetle?" said Fearon. "The sport utility version, the one they ramped up big as a stretch Humvee?"

"Yeah, the Screw-the-Greenhouse Special! Looks like they removed the sunroof and the moonroof, and taped all the windows shut! But what the hell can they have inside? Whatever it is, it's all mashed up and squirmy against the glass . . ."

A skinny Ant Army courtier vaulted and scrambled onto the top of the sealed vehicle. Gingerly, he stuffed a bloody wad of meat in through the missing moonroof.

From out of the adjacent gaping sunroof emerged a hydralike bouquet of heterogenous animal parts: tails, paws, snouts, beaks, ears. Snarls, farts, bellows, and chitterings ensued.

At length, a sudden flow of syrupy exudate drooled out the tailpipe, caught by an eager cluster of Ant Army workers cupping their empty helmets.

"They've got the Panspecific Mycoblastula in there!"

The soldiers drained every spatter of milky juice, jittering crazily and licking one another's lips and fingers.

"I do wish I had a camera," said Fearon wistfully. "It's very hard to watch a sight like this without one."

"Look, they're feeding our bearers into that thing!" marveled Malvern. "What do you suppose it's doing with all that human DNA? Must be kind of a partially human genetic mole rat thing going on in there."

Another expectant crowd hovered at the Beetle's tailpipe, their mold-spotted helmets at the ready. They had not long to wait, for a fleshy diet of protein from the butchered bearers seemed to suit the Panspecific Mycoblastula to a T.

Sweating and pale-faced, Malvern could only say, "If they were breakfast, when's lunch?"

. . .

Fearon had never envisioned such brutal slogging, so much sheer physical work in the simple effort of eating and staying alive. The prince's Army marched well-nigh constantly, bulldozing the landscape in a whirl of guns and knives. Anything they themselves could not devour was fed to the Mycoblastula. Nature knew no waste, so the writhing abomination trapped in the Volkswagen was a panspecific glutton, an always-boiling somatic stewpot. It especially doted on high-end mammalian life, but detritus of all kinds was shoved through the sunroof to sate its needs: bark, leaves, twigs, grubs, and beetles. Especially beetles. In sheer number of species, most of everything living was always beetles.

Then came the turn of their familiars.

It seemed at first that those unique beasts had somehow earned the favor of Prince Kissy Mental. Placed onboard his rollicking throne, the trussed Spike and Weeble had been subjected to much rough cossetting and petting, their peculiar high-tech flesh seeming to particularly strike the prince's fancy.

But such good fortune could not last. After noon of their first day of captivity, the bored prince, without warning, snapped Spike's neck and flung the dead weasel in the path of the painted Volkswagen. Attendants snatched the weasel up and stuffed Spike in. The poor beast promptly lined an alimentary canal.

Witnessing this atrocity, Malvern roared and attempted to rush forward. A thorough walloping with boots and spear butts persuaded him otherwise.

Then Weeble was booted meanly off the dais. Two hungry warriors scrambled to load the porker upside down onto a shoulder-carried spear. Weeble's piteous grunts lanced through Fearon, but at least he could console himself that, unlike Spike, his pig still lived.

But finally, footsore, hungry, and beset by migraines, his immune system drained by constant microbial assault, Fearon admitted despair. It was dead obvious that he and Malvern were simply doomed. There was just no real question that they were going to be killed and hideously devoured, all through their naive desire for mere fame, money, and professional technical advancement.

When they were finally allowed to collapse for the night on the edge of a marshy savannah, Fearon sought to clear his conscience.

"Mal, I know it's over, but think of all the good times we've had together. At least I never sold Florida real estate, like my dad. A short life and a merry one, right? Die young and leave a beautiful corpse. Hope I die before I get—"

"Fearon, I'm fed up with your sunny-sided optimism! You rich-kid idiot, you always had it easy and got all the breaks! You think that rebellion is some kind of game! Well, let me tell you, if I had just one chance to live through this, I'd never waste another minute on nutty dilettante crap. I'd go right for the top of the food chain. Let me be the guy on top of life, let me be the winner, just for once!" Malvern's battered face was livid. "From this day forth, if I have to lie, or cheat, or steal, or kill . . . aw, what's the use? We're ant meat! I'll never even get the chance!"

Fearon was stunned into silence. There seemed nothing left to say. He lapsed into a sweaty doze amid a singing mosquito swarm, consoling himself with a few last visions of his beloved Tupper. Maybe she'd remarry after learning of his death. Instead of following her sweet romantic heart, this time she'd wisely marry some straight guy, someone normal and dependable. Someone who would cherish her, and look after her, and take her rather large inheritance with the seriousness it deserved. How bitterly he regretted his every past unkindness, his every act of self-indulgence and neglect. The spouses of romantic rebels really had it rough.

In the morning, the hungry natives advanced on Weeble, and now it was Fearon's turn to shout, jump up, and be clouted down.

With practiced moves the natives slashed off Weeble's front limbs near the shoulder joints. The unfortunate Weeble protested in a frenzy of squealing, but his assailants knew all too well what they were doing. Once done, they carefully cauterized the porker's foreparts and placed him in a padded stretcher, which was still marked with an ancient logo from the Red Cross.

They then gleefully roasted the pig's severed limbs, producing an enticing aroma Fearon and Malvern fought to abhor. The crisped breakfast ham was delivered with all due ceremony to Prince Kissy Mental, whose delight in this repast was truly devilish to watch. Clearly the Ant Army didn't get pig very often, least of all a pig with large transgenic patches of human flesh. A pig that good you just couldn't eat all at once.

By evening, Fearon and Malvern were next on the menu. The two scabs were hustled front and center as the locals fed a roaring bonfire. A crooked pair of nasty wooden spits were prepared. Then Fearon and Malvern had their bonds cut through, and their clothes stripped off by a forest of groping hands.

The two captives were gripped and hustled and frog-marched as the happy Army commenced a manic dance around their sacred Volkswagen, ululating and keening in a thudding of drums. The evil vehicle oscillated from motion within, in time with the posthuman singing. Lit by the setting sun and the licking flames of the cannibal bonfire, big chimeric chunks of roiling Panspecific Mycoblastula tissue throbbed and slobbered against the glass.

Suddenly a brilliant klieg light framed the scene, with an 80-decibel airborne rendition of "Ride of the Valkyries."

"Hit the dirt!" yelped Malvern, yanking free from his captor's grip and casting himself on his face.

Ribo Zombie's entomopter swept low in a strafing run. The cursed Volkswagen exploded in a titanic gout of lymph, blood, bone fragments, and venom, splattering Fearon but not Malvern from head to toe with quintessence of Mycoblastula.

Natives dropped and spun under the chattering impact of advanced armaments. Drenched with spew, Fearon crawled away from the Volkswagen, wiping slime from his face.

Dead or dying natives lay in crazy windrows, like genetically modified corn after a stiff British protest. Now Ribo Zombie made a second run, his theatrical lighting deftly picking out victims. His stagey attack centered, naturally, on the most dramatic element among the panicking Army, Prince Kissy Mental himself. The prince struggled to flee the crimson targeting lasers, but his enormous head was strapped to his throne in a host of attachments. Swift and computer-sure came the next burst of gunfire. Prince Kissy Mental's abandoned head swung futilely from its tethers, a watermelon in a net.

Leaping and capering in grief and anguish, the demoralized Army scattered into the woods.

A swarm of mobile cameras wasped around the scene, carefully checking for proper angles and lighting. Right on cue, descending majestically from the darkening tropic sky came Ribo Zombie himself, crash-helmet burnished and gleaming, combat boots blazoned with logos.

Skratchy Kat leaped from Zombie's shoulder to strike a proud pose by the prince's still-smoking corpse. The superstar scab blew nonexistent trailing smoke from the unused barrels of his pearl-handled sidearms, then advanced on the cowering Fearon and Malvern.

"Nice try, punks, but you got in way over your head." Ribo Zombie gestured at a hovering camera. "You've been really great footage ever since your capture, though. Now get the hell out of camera range, and go find some clothes or something. That Panspecific Mycoblastula is all mine."

Rising from his hands and knees with a look of insensate rage, Malvern lunged up and dashed madly into the underbrush.

"What's keeping you?" boomed Ribo Zombie at Fearon.

Fearon looked down at his hands. Miniature parrot feathers were sprouting from his knuckles.

"Interesting outbreak of spontaneous muta-tion," Ribo Zombie noted. "I'll check that out just as soon as I get my trophy shot."

Advancing on the bullet-riddled Volkswagen, Ribo Zombie telescoped a razor-pincered probe. As the triumphant conqueror dipped his instru-ment into the quivering mass, Malvern charged him with a leveled spear.

The crude weapon could not penetrate Ribo Zombie's armor, but the force of the rush bounced the superstar scab against the side of the car. Quick as lightning a bloodied briar snaked through a gaping bullet hole and clamped the super-scab tight.

Then even more viscous and untoward ten-tacles emerged from the engine compartment, and a voracious sucking, gurgling struggle com-menced.

Malvern, still naked, appropriated the fallen crash helmet with the help of a spear haft. "Look, it liquefied him instantly and sucked all the soup clean out! Dry as a bone inside. And the readouts still work on the eyepieces!"

After donning the helmet, a suspiciously close fit, Malvern warily retrieved Ribo Zom-bie's armored suit, which lay in its high-tech abandonment like the nacreous shell of a her-mit crab. A puzzled Skratchy Kat crept for-ward. After a despondent sniff at the emptied boots, the bereaved familiar let out a continu-ous yowl.

"Knock it off, Skratchy," Malvern com-manded. "We're all hurting here. Just be a man."

Swiftly shifting allegiances, Skratchy Kat supinely rubbed against Malvern's glistening shins.

"Now to confiscate his cameras for a little judicious editing of his unfortunate demise." Malvern shook his helmeted head. "You can cover for me, right, Fearon? Just tell everybody that Malvern Brakhage died in the jungle. You should probably leave out the part about them wanting to eat us."

Fearon struggled to dress himself with some khaki integuments from a nearby casualty. "Malvern, I can't fit inside these clothes."

"What's your problem?"

"I'm growing a tail. And my claws don't fit in these boots." Fearon pounded the side of his head with his feathery knuckles. "Are you glow-ing, or do I have night vision all of a sudden?"

Malvern tapped his helmet with a wiry glove. "You're not telling me you're massively infected now, are you?"

"Well, technically speaking, Malvern, I'm the 'infection' in this situation, because the Myco-blastula's share of our joint DNA is a lot more extensive than mine is."

"Huh. Well, that development obviously tears it." Malvern backed off cautiously, tugging at this last few zips and buckles on his stolen armor to assure an airtight seal. "I'll route you some advanced biomedical help—if there's any available in the local airspace." He cleared his throat with a sudden rasp of helmet-mounted speakers. "In any case, the sooner I clear out of here for civilization, the better."

All too soon, the sound of the departing ento-mopter had died away. After searching through the carnage, pausing periodically as his spine and knees unhinged, Fearon located the still-breathing body of his beloved pig. Then he dragged the stretcher to an abandoned Jeep.

• • •

"And then Daddy smelled the pollution from civilization with his new nose, from miles away, so he knew he'd reached the island of Fernando Po, where the UN still keeps bases. So despite the tragic death of his best friend Malvern, Daddy knew that everything was going to be all right. Life would go on!"

Fearon was narrating his exploit to the embryo in Tupper's womb via a state-of-the-art fetal interface, the GestaPhone. Seated on the comfy Laura Ashley couch in their bright new stilt house behind the dikes of Pensacola Beach, Tupper smiled indulgently at her husband's oft-polished tale.

"When the nice people on the island saw Daddy's credit cards, Daddy and Weeble were both quickly stabilized. Not exactly like we were before, mind you, but rendered healthy enough for the long trip back home to Miami. Then the press coverage started, and, well son, someday I'll tell you about how Daddy dealt with the challenges of fame and fortune."

"And wasn't Mommy glad to see Daddy again!" Tupper chimed in. "A little upset at first about the claws and fur. But luckily, Daddy and Mommy had been careful to set aside sperm samples while Daddy was still playing his scab games. So their story had a real happy ending when Daddy finally settled down and Baby Boy was safely engineered."

Fearon detached the suction cup terminal from Tupper's bare protuberant stomach. "Weeble, would you take these, please?"

The companionable pig reached up deftly, plucked the GestaPhones out of Fearon's grasp, and moved off with an awkward lope. Weeble's strange gait was due to his new forelimbs, a nifty pair of pig-proportioned human arms.

Tupper covered her womb with her frilled maternity blouse and glanced at the clock. "Isn't your favorite show on now?"

"Shucks, we don't have to watch every single episode . . ."

"Oh, honey, I love this show, it's my favorite, now that I don't have to worry about you getting all caught up in it!"

They nestled on the responsive couch, Tupper stroking the fish-scaled patch on Fearon's cheek while receiving the absent-minded caresses of his long tigerish tail. She activated the big wet screen, cohering a close-up of Ribo Zombie in the height of a ferocious rant.

"Keeping it real, folks, still keeping it real! I make this challenge to all my fellow scabs, those who are down with the Zombie and those who dis him, those who frown on him and those who kiss him. Yes, you sorry posers all know who you are. But check this out . . . Who am I?"

Fearon sighed for a world well lost. And yet, after all . . . there was always the next generation.

JACQUES BARCIA

SALVAGING GODS

(2010)

GORETTE FOUND HER SECOND godhead buried under piles of plastic bottles, holy symbols, used toilet paper, and the severed face of an avatar. No matter how much the scavengers asked, the people from Theodora just wouldn't separate organic from nonbiodegradable from divine garbage. They threw out their used-up gods along with what was left of their meals, their burnt lamps, broken refrigerators, tires, stillborn babies, and books of prayer in the trash can. And when the convoys carrying society's leftovers passed through the town's gates, some lazy bureaucrat would mark in a spreadsheet that another mountain was raised in that municipal sanitary landfill, the Valley of the Nephilim. And to hell with the consequences.

Her father says no dead god is dead enough that it can't be remade in our own image. The old man can spend hours rambling about overconsumption, the gnostic crisis, the impact of all those mystical residues poisoning the soil and the underground streams, how children are born malformed and prone to mediunity, and how unfair it is that only the rich have access to miracles. People will do what's more comfortable, not what's best for everyone, he'd finally say. It's far easier to buy new deities than try to reuse them. So he taught her how to recycle old gods and turn them into new ones, mostly, she believed, because he wanted to make a difference. Or maybe because he was the one true atheist left in the world.

It was a small one, that godhead, and not in a very good shape. Pale silver, dusty, scratched surface, and glowing only slightly underneath the junk. At best, thought Gorette, it'd have only a few hundred lines of code she'd be able to salvage. Combined with some fine statues and pieces of altars she'd found early that morning, perhaps she'd be able to assemble one or two more deities to the community's public temple at Saint Martin. The neighborhood she was raised in had only recently been urbanized, so that meant the place was not officially a slum anymore. But still, miracles were quite a phenomenon down in the suburbs.

"Hey, Daddy. Found another one," Gorette said, covering her eyes from the burning light of midday. "Can we go home now, please?"

The egg-shaped thing had the pulse of a dying heart, and fitted almost perfectly in her adolescent hand. So she arranged a place for it among the relics in her backpack, inside the folds of a ragged piece of loincloth, and into a beaten up thurible where it'd be safe enough to survive the hour-long ride back to the city.

Her father stood next to a marble totem, sweeping the field with a Kirlian detector. The pillar was part of a discarded surround-sound system with speakers the size of his chest, and served as a landmark to the many scavengers exploring the waste dump. When he heard his daughter calling him, he took his gas mask off and said, "That depends," his low-toned voice coming like a sigh, tired. "Do you think this will do? We're running out of code and there are many open projects in the lab."

A plastic bag some ten yards away from her smelled of rotting flesh. Animal sacrifice, she knew, and the vultures seemed to have noticed that too. "Yeah," she lied, "It's a bit wasted, but I think it has a lot of good code in it. Never seen one of these, so I suppose it's a quite new model." She desperately needed to take that stink out of her body and today she hoped was water day. "Is it water day today, Daddy?"

The old man picked up one last relic, a fang or something, and examined it close to his thick glasses. He nodded to the object and put it in a sack he carried tied to his waist. "No, it's not. The Palace said three days ago that they'd reinforce the water gods cluster, so the suburb's rationing would drop to two days. But of course that didn't happen." He finally walked to Gorette and scratched her dreadlocks, trying to smile. "Maybe you can build a water god with the godhead you found, huh?"

• • •

Gorette made her first wish that evening, after incubating some of the new godhead's code in an altar of her own design. It was built out of the remains of a semi-defaced idol, a one-eyed marble bust wearing a tall orange hat, adorned with shattered crystals, split dragon horns, praying cords, and barbed wire. That last bit just to make sure everything would stand in place. The godhead rested inside the same thurible Gorette used to cradle it safely back from the Valley of the Nephilim. But now the metal egg had dozens of acupuncture needles trespassing its shell, and every single one was linked to hair-thin optical fiber threads, shining with divine code, feeding with data a green phosphorus monitor.

Without warning. It just woke up.

When the loading bar hit 100 percent, the stone bust opened its one eye, fluidly, staring directly at her. She fell back from the chair, startled, and stared back at the thing's physiognomy from where she stood. From the floor up.

It was her first attempt at a new design model, one that toyed with disharmony instead of symmetry. Profanity instead of divinity. Good hardware, her dad says, is as important as good code. But harmony. Harmony is the key. The problem is that new gods are coming with even more complex, specialized godheads, their kernels incompatible with older or malfunctioning holy paraphernalia. She decided to try out the new approach and, to her surprise, it worked.

"I want a fucking bath," Gorette said, pointing a finger to the bust. "A *warm* bath. Now."

The stone in the god's crippled face moved like it was made out of clay. Smooth. No, it moved like that stop-motion movie, what's its name, the one that always airs on holidays and Friday evenings. The one Dad just loves to watch when he's back from the Valley.

"As you wish," it said coldly.

A sound of streaming water echoed from the bathroom and almost instantly the smell of steam and soap and essential oils filled up the room. She grinned, and jumping over her feet ran toward the shower, undressing on her way.

Is it lavender? Maybe birch. Arnica in the white cloud. She felt she was clean even before she could reach the shower, she felt the dirt collapsing, decanting on the floor before she could have a chance to lie in the tub and rest.

A bathtub. "A bathtub?"

She looked back at the one-eyed god running miracles in her room. "You made me a bathtub." The idol remained still. She stood there for a few more seconds trying to figure out how her jury-rigged water god made her a complete bath, with a bathtub, aromatic oils, and, now she saw it, the finest bathing gown. Collateral miracles were not unheard of, but modern godheads had filters to prevent the danger of leaking energy. Motionless, the god just kept staring forward, to nowhere in particular, its exposed wire guts transmitting magical pulses to the screen, blipping a green dot like the apparels in private hospitals, monitoring a wide-eyed comatose half head, an undead, glitchy deity. Gorette felt like checking her complementary coding, but confessed to herself the hot pool of perfumed water was too tempting to be ignored. After all, feeling clean and relaxed she'd have more chances of debugging her creation.

That's it. She immersed herself in the tub and let all her worries trail off, evaporate.

• • •

After the bathtub miracle, the god produced a new set of porcelain plates, when Gorette only commanded it to clean the dishes. Days later she asked for ice and got a refrigerator and a minibar. Then the thought of a nice meal generated spiced fish. And, one night, the sound of a calm, streaming river came as a lullaby. And rain cooled a hot day. And a smile painted watercolor on canvas. On and on, over the course of a week, her tiniest, involuntary wishes were fulfilled and as much as she tried, she couldn't find the bug in the god's code tree. Okay, after the tenth attempt, the effort to fix the problem wasn't that strong-willed. But Dad had taught

her a bug could untap the power of a god, mollifying reality in its closer vicinity, causing the neighborhood's divine networks to go haywire. It was dangerous, she knew.

She spent days and nights trying to fix it, trying to combine source codes distilled from newer godheads, but nothing seemed to work. She decided she'd destroy the thing before it'd cause her trouble.

A dead boy changed her mind.

It was Monday morning and Gorette swept the water god off her working bench into a big cardboard box lying on the floor. She just discarded it, trying not to think much about getting rid of her first creation. The thing fell inside the box, a stone punch enveloped in barbed wire. Gorette gave the god a last inspection and could see that the cold half face was looking upward from its new room. She met its gaze one last time and closed the box, decided to sell its parts in the market for whatever the merchants gave for it.

The girl picked up the box and went downstairs, hardly able to keep balance with the thing's weight pushing her back and down. So heavy and so slowly she spent thirty minutes walking down the stairs, flight upon flight on a downward spiral to the first floor. She finally reached a smooth carpet under her feet and felt her strength renewed when she captured the smell of cinnamon tea being brewed in the kitchen. There was music playing and the house was calm and empty. Patchouli.

She walked to the door, the box in front of her, light in her arms and spirit. An awesome Sunday waited for her outside the house.

On her way out, she tripped over a gas mask resting facedown on the floor, but managed to jump on one foot and keep herself from falling. She kicked the mask off from her, startling the white tiger sleeping under the crystal table. Immediately, the giant cat clawed the mask with its tiger-y reflexes, making it spin and fall over its face, covering all of its beastly features but the lower jaw and its protruding fangs. A gas-masked albino tiger. Nothing can be cooler than that. Maybe a gas-masked cephalopod. No. Albino tiger is definitely cooler.

Outside, the day was perfect. The sun shone bright and there was the bluest cloudless sky sheltering Saint Martin. The street was busy, the market was everywhere. Fresh bread, roses, dew. Birds, carts, and horses on the march. The signal was red, so she stood close to a bald man reading the newspaper, waiting in line for his turn with the public god service. She overheard someone, the first in the row, complain with the totem, why in fuck's name you can't cure eczema? It's a damn fungus, damn it. Your credits have expired, answered a featureless voice. She felt sorry for the man, but couldn't help but giggle. Next time, try boiling the river's water. That fetid thing the Palace calls a river.

She turned in time to see the man walking away from the totem, down the street, right in her direction. His right cheek and part of his upper lip and nose was covered in a pink, moist blotch, a blistered wound shaped as a face, a somewhat familiar face that now she could see, as he approached, went down to his neck and into his shirt. She swallowed her giggle and wished the man could find a cure.

"As you wish."

"What?"

Slo-mo time warp, the air thick as a jar of glycerin. The man walked past her like the actors playing living statues in Gaiman Square. As he moved, she could see all the tiny blisters, the face wound staring back at her. And as if someone had hit the rewind button, the eczema started to erode. Skin took back its space, first in the borders and then in spots inside the pink perimeter, holes forming eyes and a space like a mask, or mouth that seemed to say, "Oh," and then scream, wider and wider, until it completely disappeared, leaving nothing but an afterimage, a memory, a sensation.

"Did you see that?" Gorette turned to face the man next to her, a young guy wearing a ponytail, reading the newspaper. Like waking up from a deep dream, she looked down to the box

in her arms and immediately dropped it to the ground. Her nails tore the cardboard walls and there it was, the god, face up, the way she put it back in her room.

The god in the box looked like it was engaged in silent battle with her. Face to face.

People walked past them on the sidewalk, the noises and colors and smells of Saint Martin coming back to her in a single torrent. Too many steps and the scent of flowers and wax, hooves clicking, and chantings, all around the street. A procession.

She turned once again, feeling dizzy, and saw the ocean of people and candles and garlands and, in the middle of the street, a huge bier with a coffin and a little altar, an undertaker god surely preparing the body, the grave, and the costs for the burial. Around the altar, there were pictures of a kid, younger than her. The face of the corpse inside the coffin.

"A kid," the words came out without her noticing.

She closed her mouth and locked it with both hands, closing her eyes not to think, not to think, not to think.

"As you wish," and again, several yards away from her, like an echo, above the crowd, "as you wish."

Five seconds passed before the bier's conductor jumped from his seat, let go of the reins and climbed on the coffin. People noticed the man's hurry and soon there was a commotion around the vehicle. People cried "help him out!" and "open the coffin!" and "my kid! He's alive!" And now she could hear a stifled sound, a desperate knock-knock on wood coming from the depths of the underworld. There were relatives pushing the coffin's lid, but damn those nails, the joiner that worked across the street rushed with a crowbar and soon was forcing the wood cover. Gorette's heart was pounding, someone please open that coffin. *Asyouwishasyouwishasyouwish.*

Suddenly, the nails were fired off to the air, like a machine gun trying to shoot down the heavens. The whole wood box went down to splinters in a moment. The crowd went mad when the boy rose and took the cotton balls out of his nose.

"It was her!" Gorette heard someone cry behind her. "I saw it. She commanded the god to resurrect the boy."

"No, I didn't," she heard herself speaking as if the words came from someone else.

"Yes, you did," said a very low, calm, cold voice.

"No."

Soon the crowd was all over her, praising her good deeds—*as you wish*—calling her a saint—*as you wish*—asking her for favors—*as you wish*—raising her and her god above them, a new procession for the miracle of life, for the savior, *ad majorem femina gloriam*, for the Popess.

"As you wish," she said, grinning.

• • •

Emissaries.

From other neighborhoods, from the Palace, from other cities.

They came in tides, high and low, high and low. They threatened and cajoled, but eventually ended up asking for something they needed to be done, some disease to be cured, another to be implanted, a hand to help their business, some virility, beauty, you name it.

One out of five diplomats demanded to know how she assembled her god. How the hell that thing could—

The truth was she didn't know. She wished she did. And that seemed to be one of the few wishes her creature wasn't able, or willing, to fulfill.

However, most penitents came asking for knowledge, for wisdom, for guidance. That, too, was out of her reach, out of her experience. But certainly not out of her god's verbosity.

That marvel now standing on a totem in front of her throne, a foot lower than her, encased in crystal, half-faced and barbed-wired. For those who entered the temple and met her gaze, her features dominated the god placed only an inch below. But even if her eyes held a deep jade

glare, it was the silver beacon of the godhead that really shone brighter. Like the moon.

"Speak," she said.

"Most honorable Popess," began a merchant in a golden tunic, shutting down his smartphone, "what's the nature of true miracles?" The question raised a wave of murmurs in the hall. He was the fifth or sixth person consulting her that morning. "What are they made of? What makes your god able to perform such wonders, surpassing the capabilities of every other functional god in the realm?"

"I—" began Gorette, the Popess, but that cold voice interrupted her speech. That behavior had become quite common in the public sessions lately and the people were beginning to question the Popess's authority over the god.

"I can calculate reality at far-superior floppage," the god said. "My miracles per second rate is also higher than your average god. Also, my database—"

"It's my will," cut the Popess.

"No, it's not," replied the stone statue.

"Silence."

"As you wish."

The Popess dismissed the merchant with a wave of her hand. The man bowed slightly, obviously upset for not being answered. He turned and mixed himself with the rest of the crowd, other merchants, other tunics, men in coats and gas masks. "The session is over," she said.

"Popess?" Already at the center of the court. Dirty overcoat and gas mask. She could smell filth in the wind, rotten oranges and oil. The man had a tiger, white as snow, chained to his wrist and it, too, wore a mask, and had a big box mounted on his back, covered by a red velvet coat. "Can I speak?"

The Popess was halfway through leaving the throne, but stopped and turned back to her seat. A green dazzle came from her eyes asking, who's this man, do I know him? "What do you want from me?"

The man gave two steps ahead, dragging the chain, making the gas-masked albino tiger move and then lay. Nice and easy. "Actually," he said, his voice covered by the mask, "I'd like to address your god."

"It?"

"Me?"

"Yes, your Holiness. I want to question your creature," said the stranger.

She was curious. She straightened herself in the throne, crossed her legs under the long robe and smiled, as if expecting entertainment, a show. "Okay. Go on. Let's see what you're gonna get from it."

"In truth, there's only one thing I'd like to ask it." He moved forward and immediately the tiger rose and followed, both closer to the totem. The people gathered around the hall seemed to get closer, curious about what this masked stranger and his beast were up to. "I want you to tell me—what's the nature of God?"

"The nature of gods?"

"No. God." So close now. His breath clouded the crystal case. "Gods are manifestations, constructs. They're functions, myths, narratives. They're tools. Limited, discardable, yet very spectacular tools. I want to know what's the nature of God," the man said.

A second passed before its marble lips moved. You could hear the silver sphere, the mighty godhead whirring, its core processing billions of code looking for an answer. Suddenly, the noise stopped. "God is unique. God wishes," it said. "I am unique. I wish."

Marble soldiers, flaming tigers, hydras, and giant spiders materialized in the hall, as if coming onstage after opening reality's invisible curtain. Panic took over the crowd in the room, a whirlwind of faces and tunics running, dissolving, and exploding in gushes of blood and rot and desecration.

The Popess sank in her throne, reduced to her youth, her green eyes crystallized with fear.

The man under the mask refused to run and instead yelled at the crystal case. "Even a god found in a sanitary landfill, assembled from pieces of junk and designed by a very young, immature girl who didn't even know what she

wished for in her life?"

"Even so."

"You're not unique." The stranger reached for the velvet cape over the tiger and pulled it from over the box. There was a crystal case with a marble god inside. A reused god. Design almost identical to that of the Popess's own creation: a silver moon of a godhead pierced by tiny acupuncture needles, linked to a pedestal by fiber optic cables, tied with barbed wire and praying cords and a hat balanced atop a half-faced, one-eyed, mouthless piece of avatar at its center. "Do you recognize it? I found it some ten meters away from you."

The older god whirred. The soldiers and monsters charged toward the man and his own technomagical beast. He stood right where he was, but quickly typed shortcut commands to the god and the giant cat. When the creatures were close enough, the tiger attacked with a mighty leap, his claws hacking the monsters' fire hides and carapaces.

But the man kept staring down at the god while the white feline defended their position. More creatures continued to condense into existence out of thin air. The tiger still managed to kill them, keeping the perimeter safe.

"I will destroy her," the god said. "If I can give life, I can take it."

"No, you won't. And you can't." The Popess stood next to the god's crystal case, staring at its single, immovable eye. "Dad once told me about the nature of God." She got close, really close, to the crystal case, as if trying to whisper into the god's ear through the transparent wall. "He told me God is flawless."

The white tiger, now blood-red, circled the totem, pushing the soldiers back. Fast and precise as tigers are, he clawed the box, shattered the crystal to tiny bits, sent the stone face away to the floor along with its miraculous monsters. The thing fell hard, barbed wires, praying cords, tokens, and fiber-optic cables disassembling the holy design with the shock.

Gorette strode across the room at the

destroyed god's direction. It rested on the floor, close to the corpses of humans and miracles. She could see it tried to speak, its lips moving in a very familiar way. She decided not to give a damn about what the thing had to say. She picked up the silver godhead and looked deep into the god's eye close to her feet. "God is flawless. But nothing, you hear me? Nothing is without flaw," she said. "Now, shut down."

"As you wish."

• • •

At the Valley of the Nephilim, the god wishes it had arms. He wished he was a *he*, not an *it*, not a carcass in the filth, beneath the remains, in the mud. Die, worm, die. You chew my wires off, you reincarnate as a, as a, as a *human*. That. A human. A human.

A human.

A blip and another. Above ground. Steps coming closer. Another blip and an intense, acute sound. Like a blip, but never ending. Like a whistle.

"Guess there's one here."

Yes, there is. There's one here.

Some light, then light and too much light.

"Here you are."

A human.

"Yeah, it looks just like that other one."

What? Not like any other. I'm the others. The others are me.

"Not sure. Will destroy it anyway."

No.

"Come here."

Pressure.

"Boy, you're hard. Wish I had a hammer with me."

As you—

"Oh, here it is," said the girl. "This is what I call a *force quit*. Goodbye, little one. Send my regards."

Beat. Crash.

Silence.

PAUL GRAHAM RAVEN

LOS PIRATAS DEL MAR DE PLASTICO

(2014)

HOPE DAWSON STEPPED DOWN from the train into the bone-dry heat of afternoon in southern Spain, and wondered—not for the first time, and probably not for the last—what the hell she was doing there, and how long she'd end up staying.

The freelance lifestyle did that to you; seven years crawling to and fro across Europe as a hand-to-mouth journo-sans-portfolio had left Hope with few ties to her native Britain beyond her unpaid student loans, and she'd yet to settle anywhere else for long. She'd spent the last six months or so bumping around in the Balkans on a fixed-term stringer's contract from some Californian news site she'd never read (and never intended to), scraping up extra work on the side wherever she could: website translation gigs, trade-zine puff pieces, and the inevitable tech-art exhibition reviews; she could barely remember the last time she put her own name in a byline, or wanted to. The Californian site had folded itself up a few days before the contract

ended, and after a few agreeable weeks house-sitting an alcoholic Tiranese lawyer's apartment, burning through the small pile of backhanded cash and favors she'd amassed, and poking at her perpetually unfinished novel, she felt the need to move on once more. Albania was cheap, but it was a backwater, and backwaters rarely coughed up stories anyone would pay for; her loans weren't going to repay themselves, after all, and the UK government had developed an alarming habit of forcibly repatriating those who attempted to disappear into the boondocks and default on their debts.

The world dropped the answer in her lap while she wasn't looking. As winter gave way to spring, Tirana's population of favela geeks—a motley tribe of overeducated and underemployed Gen-Y Eurotrash from the rust belts, dust belts, and failed technopoles of Europe—began to thin out. Hope's contacts dropped hints about southern Spain, casual labor, something to do with the agricultural sector down there. That, plus a surge of ambiguous white-knuckle op-eds in the financial press about the long-moribund Spanish economy, was enough for Hope to go on. She'd finished up a few hanging deadlines, called in a favor she'd been saving up, and traded a lengthy, anonymous, and staggeringly unobjective editorial about Albanian railway tourism in exchange for a one-way train ticket to Almeria, first class.

Hope squinted along the length of the platform, a-shimmer with afternoon heat-haze beneath a cloudless azure sky, to where a dozen or so geeks were piling themselves and their luggage out of the budget carriages at the very back of the train. They were loaded down with faded military surplus duffels and mountaineering backpacks, battered flight cases bearing cryptic stencils, and rigid luggage that looked uncharacteristically new and expensive by comparison to their clothing which, true to their demography, looked like a random grab-bag of the ugliest and most momentary styles of the late-twentieth century. Only a decade ago, while Hope had been wrapping up her undergrad work and hustling for her PhD scholarship back in Britain, one might have assumed they were here to attend a peripatetic music festival, maybe, or a convention for some obscure software framework. But that was before the price of oil had gone nuts and annihilated the cheap airline sector almost overnight. Even within Europe, long distance travel was either slow and uncomfortable or hideously expensive. Unemployed Millennials—of which there were many—tended not to move around without a damned good incentive.

Milling around on the platform like a metaphor for Brownian motion, the geeks were noisy, boisterous, and a few years younger than Hope, and she worked hard to squash a momentary feeling of superiority, to bring her field researcher's reflexivity back online. *Tat tvam asi*, she reminded herself; *that thou art*. Or *there but for the grace of God*, perhaps. The main difference between Hope and them, she decided, was a certain dogged luck. She looked briefly at her reflection in the train window and saw a short

girl with tired-looking eyes wearing an executive's dark trouser-suit in the London style of three winters previous, her unruly mass of curly blonde hair already frizzing into a nimbus of static in response to the heat. Who was she trying to fool, she wondered, for the umpteenth time. The geeks looked ludicrous, flowing off the platform and into the station like some lumpy superfluid, but they also looked comfortable, carefree. It'd been a long time since Hope felt either of those things.

Leaving the station, Hope donned her spex, set them to polarize, and blinked about in the local listings. She soon secured herself a few cheap nights in an apartment on the sixth floor of an undermaintained block about half a klick from the center of town. Almeria reminded Hope more than a little bit of the ghost towns of southern Greece, where she'd gone to chase rumors of a resurgence in piracy in the Eastern Med a few years back: noughties boom-time tourist infrastructure peeling and crumbling in the sun, like traps left lying in a lobsterless sea. Leaning on the rust-spotted railing of her balcony, she looked westward, where the legendary Plastic Ocean stretched out to the horizon, mile after square mile of solarized bioplastic sheeting shimmering beneath the relentless white light of the sun. The greenhouses were all Almeria had left since the tourists stopped coming, churning out a relentless assortment of hothouse fruit 'n' veg for global export, but they'd been predominantly staffed by semilegal immigrant workers from across the Med for years. She couldn't see much chance of the geeks undercutting that sort of workforce.

Later that evening, Hope was prepared to use her clueless middle-management airhead routine on the tapas bar's waiter but didn't need to: he had plenty to say, albeit in a Basque-tinged dialect that tested her rusty Spanish to the utmost.

"You're with those guys who bought the Hotel Catedral, yes?" he asked her.

"Oh, no," she replied. The waiter relaxed visibly as she spooled out her cover: purchasing rep for a boutique market stall in Covent Garden, sent out to do some on-the-spot quality control.

"Well, I knew you couldn't be with those damned kids who've been turning up the last few weeks," he said, plunking down a cold beer next to her tapas.

Hope fought to keep a straight face; the waiter was no older than the geeks he was disparaging, but she was very used to the employed seeing the unemployed as children. "Yeah, what's with them?"

"Damned if I know." He shrugged. "They all seem to head westward as soon as they arrive. I'll be surprised if they find any work in El Ejido, but hey, not my problem."

"And what about the Hotel Catedral?"

"Again, don't know. They've been close to closing for years, running a skeleton staff. Times have been hard, you know? My friend Aldo works the bar up there. Few weeks back, he tells me, he's doing a stint on the front desk when this bunch of American guys breeze in and ask to speak to the manager. They disappear to his office for half an hour, then they come back out, gather the staff, announce a change of ownership. More Yankees came in by plane, apparently. Place is full of them, now." He scowls. "They hired my girlfriend and some others as extra staff. Good tippers, apparently, but a bit . . . well, they're rich guys, I guess. What do you expect, right?"

Hope nodded sympathetically. She'd never worked hotels, largely because she knew so many people who had.

• • •

Hope spent the next morning getting her bearings, then drifted casually toward the Hotel Catedral, where she enquired about booking a table for supper. The lobby was all but empty, but the receptionist had the tight-lipped air of a man with a lot to worry about.

"No tables for nonresidents, señora; my apologies."

"Oh—in that case, can I book a room?"

"We are fully booked, señora."

Hope made a show of peering around the empty lobby. "If it's a money thing, I can show you a sight-draft on my company's account?"

The guy continued to stonewall, so Hope relented and wandered back onto the palm-studded plaza, where the sun was baking the sturdy buttresses of the titular cathedral. She was drinking a coffee at a café across the square when a gangly and somewhat sunburned young man pulled up on some sort of solar-assisted trike.

"Hey—Hope Dawson, right?" He spoke English with a broad Glaswegian accent.

Hope protested her innocence in passable Castilian, but he whipped out a little handheld from a pocket on his hunting vest and consulted it, shielding his eyes from the sun with his hand.

"Naw, see, this is definitely you. Look?"

Hope looked. It *was* definitely her—her disembarking from the train yesterday afternoon, in fact. Drone-shot, from somewhere above the station.

"Who wants to know?" she growled, putting some war-reporter grit into it.

"Mah boss. Wants tae offer ye a job, see."

"Well, you may tell your boss thank you, but I'm already employed."

"Bollix, lass—ye've not had a proper job in years." The lad grins. "I should know. It was me as doxed ye."

"Is that supposed to reassure me?"

"Naw, it's supposed to intrigue ye." He slapped the patchwork pleather bench seat of the trike behind him, shaded by the solar panel. "Cedric's a few streets over the way. Come hear what he has to say before ye make up yer mind, why not?"

• • •

"I hope Ian didn't alarm you, Miss Dawson," said Cedric, as a waiter poured coffee. They were seated in the lobby of a midrange boutique hotel which, given the lingering musty smell, had been boarded up for years until very recently.

"Not at all," Hope lied, in a manner she hoped conveyed a certain sense of *fuck you, Charlie*. "But I'd appreciate you explaining why you had him dox me."

"I want you to work for me, Miss Dawson."

"Just Hope, please. And as I told Ian, Mister . . . ?"

He smiles. "Just Cedric, please."

"As I told Ian, Cedric, I already have work."

"Indeed you do—a career in journalism more distinctive for its length than its impact, if you don't mind me saying so. Not many last so long down in the freelance trenches."

"Debts don't pay themselves, Cedric."

"Quite. But it would be nice to pay them quicker, wouldn't it?"

Hope put down her coffee cup to hide the tremor of her hands. "I'm flattered, but I should probably point out I'm not really a journalist."

"No, you're a qualitative economist. You were supervised by Shove and Walker, University of Lancaster. I've read your thesis."

"You have?"

"Well, the important bits. I had Ian précis the methodological stuff for me, if I'm honest. It was well received by your peers, I believe."

"Not well enough to lead to any research work," said Hope, curtly. No one wanted an interpretivist cluttering up their balance sheets with talk of intangible externalities, critiquing the quants, poking holes in the dog-eared cardboard cutout of *homo economicus*.

"Obviously not—but participant observation research work is what I'm offering you, starting today. Six months fixed-term contract, a PI's salary at current UK rates, plus expenses. I'll even backdate to the start of the month, if it helps."

"What's the object?"

Cedric looked surprised; his expression reminded Hope of the animated meerkat from an ad campaign of her youth. "Well, here, of course. Almeria the province, that is, rather than just the city."

"Why?"

He smiled, leaned forward a little. "Good question!" A frown replaced the smile. "I'm afraid I can't really answer it, though. Confidentiality of sources, you understand. But in essence, I was tipped off to an emerging situation here in Almeria, and decided I wanted to see it up close."

"I'm going to need more than that to go on, I'm afraid," said Hope.

Cedric somehow looked chagrined and reproachful at once. "There are limits, I'm afraid, and they're not of my making. But look: If I say I have reason, solid reason to believe that Almeria is on the verge of a transformative economic event without precedent, and that I have spent upward of five million euros in just the last few days in order to gather equipment and personnel on the basis of that belief, would you trust me?"

Not as far as I could throw you, frankly. "So why me, specifically?"

A boyish smile replaced the frown. "Now, that's a little easier! Remind me, if you would, of your thesis topic?"

To her own surprise, Hope's long-term memory duly regurgitated a set of research questions and framings polished to the smoothness of beach pebbles by repeated supervisory interrogations: transitions in civic and domestic consumptive practices; the influence of infrastructures and interfaces on patterns and rates of resource use; the role of externalities in the playing out of macroeconomic crises. Warming to her topic, she segued into a spirited defense of free-form empirical anthropology, and of interpretive methods as applied to the analysis of economic discontinuities.

"Good," Cedric intoned, as if she'd passed some sort of test. "H and M is researching exactly those sort of questions, and we think Almeria could be our Ground Zero."

That was a worrying choice of phrase.

"The markets are turbulent places, Hope," he continued, "too turbulent for mere mathematics to explain. They no longer interest me, in and of themselves." He leaned back in his chair. "This will sound crass to someone of your generation, I'm sure, but nonetheless: I am not simply wealthy. I am rich enough that I don't even know what I'm worth, how I got that way, or who I'd have to ask to find out. Money is a very different matter for me than for you. I have the extraordinary liberty of being able to think about it purely in the abstract, because my concrete concerns are taken care of."

Hope stared at him, stunned into silence.

"So I am able," Cedric continued, "to explore economics in a way accessible to few, and of interest to even fewer. Lesser men, poorer men obsess over mere commerce, on the movement of money. My concerns are larger, far larger. You might say that it is the movement of the movement of money that fascinates me."

She grabbed her bag, stood up, and started for the doorway.

"Hope, hear me out, please," he called. "I don't expect you to like me, or even understand me. But I need you to work for me, here and now, and I am willing to pay you well. Wait, please, just for a moment."

Hope paused in the shade of the doorway but didn't turn around.

"Check your bank balance," he said after a brief pause. She blinked it up on her spex: a deposit had just cleared from Huginn&Muninn AB, Norwegian sort-code. More money than she'd earned in the last twelve months, both on the books and off. "Consider it a signing bonus."

She turned round, her arms crossed. "What if I won't sign?"

Cedric shrugged elegantly in his seat; he'd not moved an inch.

"I'll think about it," she said, turning on her heel.

Ian drove her back to her apartment block on the trike.

"So I'll come fetch ye tomorrow morning, then," he announced. "Run you down to El Ejido, get ye all set up and briefed."

"I told Cedric I'd think about it, Ian."

"Aye, I heard ye." Ian grinned. "Told him the same meself."

• • •

True to his word, Ian came to collect her the next morning. Hope found, to her surprise, that she was packed and ready to go.

"Knew ye'd go fer it," asserted Ian, bungeeing her bags to the trike.

"Very much against my better judgment," she replied.

"Aye, he's an odd one, fer sure. But he's not lied to me once, which is more than I can say fer mah previous employers." He saddled up, flashed a grin. "Plus, he always pays on time."

"He'd better," replied Hope, as Ian accelerated out into the empty streets of Almeria, heading westward. "What is it you do for him, anyway?"

"Not what you might be thinking! Ah'm a kind of general gopher, I guess, but I do a lot of reading for him when he's got other stuff on. News trawls, policy stuff. The doctoral theses of obscure scholars, sort o' thing." He grinned again, over his shoulder. "Sometimes he just wants to chew over old science fiction novels until the early hours. You thought it was hard to find work off the back of *your* doctorate? Try bein' an academic skiffy critic, eh!"

"Seriously?"

"Oh, aye. Says they inspire him to think differently. Me, I reckon he thinks he's Hubertus fuckin' Bigend or some such . . ."

"Who?"

But Ian had slipped on a set of retro-style enclosure headphones and turned his attention to his driving, dodging wallowing dirt bikes and scooters overloaded with helmetless geeks and their motley luggage, all headed westward. The road from Almeria to El Ejido passed briefly through foothills almost lunar in their rugged desolation, before descending down to the Plastic Ocean itself. Hope couldn't see a patch of ground that wasn't covered with road, cramped housing, or row after monotonous row of greenhouses shimmering with heat-haze. Hope was surprised to see trucks at the roadside in the iconic white and blue livery of the United Nations and tapped Ian on the shoulder.

"What the hell are *they* doing here?" she yelled over the slipstream.

"The man hisself tipped 'em off. Fond of the UN, he is—fits wi' his International Rescue fetish, I guess—and they seem to appreciate his input, albeit grudgingly. We'll fix ye a meeting wi' General Weissmuutze, she's sound enough. Always good to know the people wi' the guns and bandages, eh?"

• • •

Ian dropped Hope at a small villa near the southern edge of El Ejido, loaded her spex with a credit line to a Huginn&Munnin expense account and a bunch of new software, and told her to call if she needed anything, before whizzing off eastward on his ridiculous little vehicle. Hope settled in, pushed aside her doubts, and got to work familiarizing herself with the town and the monotonous sea of greenhouses surrounding it. Cedric's backroom people had assembled a massive resource set of maps and satellite images, and a handful of high-def camdrones were busily quartering the town, collecting images to compile into street-view walk-throughs; they'd also, they claimed, fudged up a cover identity that would hold up to all but the most serious military-grade scrutiny. Hope had her doubts about that, but after a handful of days and a fairly drastic haircut, she was confident enough to hit the streets and pass herself off as just another new arrival, of which there were more and more each day.

Eager and noisy gangs of geeks were descending on boarded-up villas, boutique hotels, and bars, reactivating the inert infrastructure of the tourist sector, stripping buildings back to the bare envelope before festooning them with solar panels, screen-tarps, and sound systems of deceptively prodigious wattage. The wide boulevard of Paseo los Lomas, quiet enough during the daylight hours, started to fill up with ragged

revelers around 6:00 p.m.; by nine each night, with the heat of the day still radiating from the pavements, it resembled a cross between a pop-up music festival and a Spring Break riot. The few businesses still owned and operated by locals hung on for a few days, watching their stock fly off the shelves at premium prices, before selling up their operations lock, stock, and barrel to expensively dressed men bearing bottomless yen-backed banker's draughts.

"I'd have been crazy not to sell," a former restaurateur told Hope, as his wife and kids bundled their possessions into the trunk of a noughties-vintage car retooled for biodiesel. Inside the building, an argument was breaking out between the new owners over which internal walls to knock through. "The mortgage has been under water for a decade, and they offer to pay it off in full? I'm not the crazy one here. They're welcome to it," he said, turning away.

Inside the cafe, Hope found five geeks swinging sledgehammers into partition walls, watched over by a man so telegenic that he was almost anonymous, his office-casual clothes repelling the dust of the remodeling process.

"Hey, girl," the man drawled in approval. The geeks carried on hammering.

"Hi!" she said, bright as a button. "So I just got into town, and I was wondering which are the best job boards? There's, like, so many to choose from."

The guy looked her up and down. "Guess it depends what sort of things you can do, doesn't it, ah . . . Cordelia?"

"That's me!" The cover identity seemed to be working, at least. "I guess you'd say I was in administration?"

"Not much call for admin at the moment, princess. Here." He threw a URL to her spex. "That's the board for indies and nonspecialists. You're a bit late to pick up the best stuff, but you should be able to make some bank if you don't price yourself out of the market. Or maybe one of the collectives will take you on contract for gophering? I'm sure these lads could find a space for a pretty little task rabbit like yourself in their warren, couldn't you, boys?"

"Right on, Niceday, right *on*," enthused a scrawny geek. "You want the URL, girl?"

"Please," she lied. "I'mma shop around some more, though. See what my options are, you know?"

"Whatevs," shrugged the dusty kid. "Longer you leave it, less we'll cut you in."

"You should listen to him, Cordelia," said the well-dressed guy, stepping closer to her. "In business, it pays to be bold." His eyes narrowed a little. "And loyal."

"Oh, sure! So what about *your* warren, Mister . . . ?"

"Niceday. And I don't have a warren, I hire them."

"So you're, like, a veecee or something?"

Niceday smiled an oily sort of smile. "Or something," he agreed. The smile vanished as he locked eyes with her. "Choose wisely, Cordelia, and choose soon. This isn't the time or place for . . . observing from the sidelines. Unless you're with the UN, of course."

"Haha, right! Well, ah, thanks for the advice," said Hope, her heart hammering against her ribs, and beat a swift retreat.

• • •

The mood on the periphery of the town was in sharp contrast to the raucous debauch of the center. The greenhouse workers—almost all youngish North African men—were packed like matches into street after street of under-maintained tourist villas and former residential blocks, with the more recent arrivals living in slums built of breezeblocks and plastic sheeting on the vacant lots where the plastic ocean broke upon the dark edges of the town. Hope spent a few hours wandering from coffeeshop to shisha-shack, trying every trick in the interviewer's book to get them to talk. They were happy enough to have drinks bought for them on Cedric's dime, and to complain at length about work in the abstract as they demolished plates of tapas

and meze, but questions about actual working conditions led only to sullen, tense silences, or the sudden inability of the formerly fluent to speak a word of Spanish.

"You only ask about our work so you can steal our jobs," a gaunt man accused her toward the end of the evening, pointing his long, scarred finger at her through a cloud of fragrant shisha smoke. "For so long, no one else will do this work so cheap. Now all you people come back, make trouble for us."

She tried dropping her cover a bit, and played the journalist card; big mistake.

"Journalists, they don't make good stories about us, ever. We are always the villains, the evil Arabs, no?"

She protested her innocence and good intentions, but he had a point. Hope's background research had uncovered a history of tension between the greenhouse workers and the local residents that stretched back to before she was born: grimly vague and one-sided stories in the archives of now-moribund local news outlets about forced evictions, arson, and the sort of casual but savage violence between young men that always marks periods of socioeconomic strife. The attacks had lessened as the local youth migrated northward in search of better work, but there was a lingering vibe of siege mentality among the remaining immigrants, and their dislike for the influx of favela geeks was tangible.

"Go back to your rich friends," the man repeated, jabbing his finger for emphasis. "It is they who are meddling, trying to make us look bad! We'll not help you pin it on us."

"Pin what on you?" Hope asked, suddenly alert to the closeness of the knowledge she needed, but the guy's eyes narrowed and his lips tightened and he shook his head, and the whole place went silent and tense, and Hope was horribly aware of being the only woman in a dark smoky room full of unfamiliar men speaking an unfamiliar language.

She stammered out some apologies, paid her tab, and left quickly, but the damage was done. From that point on, the workers refused to talk to her. As the days passed, there were a few ugly incidents in alleyways late at night: botched muggings, running brawls, a few serious stabbings on both sides. But the geeks were confident in their newfound dominion, not to mention better fed and equipped, and the workers had no one on their side, least of all the employers they'd never met, and who only communicated with them via the medium of emailed quotas and output itineries. If Hope wanted to get to the bottom of whatever was going on, she was going to have to do more than ask around.

• • •

Most of the geeks worked by day in jury-rigged refrigerated shipping containers and partied by night, but Cedric's backroom people had tipped her off to the existence of a small night shift that drifted out into the greenhouse ocean around midnight and returned before dawn. They'd furnished Hope's villa with an assortment of technological bits and bobs, including an anonymously military-looking flight case containing three semiautonomous AV drones about the size of her fist. She spent an afternoon syncing them up with her spex and jogging around among the miniature palms and giant aloes in her compound, getting the hang of the interface, then waited for night to fall before decking herself out in black like some amateur ninja and sneaking along the rooftops toward the edge of town, using the raucous noise of the evening fiesta as cover. Spotting a small knot of kids heading northward out of town, she sent two drones forward to tail them, one to run overwatch, and followed after at a distance she assumed would keep her out of sight, or at least give her plenty of time to cut and run if she was spotted.

After about half an hour, the geeks paused and split up. Hope hunkered down just close enough to still receive the feed from her drones, then flew them slow and low down the narrow gaps between the greenhouses, using an IR overlay to pick out the warm bodies among the end-less identical walls of plastic, and settled down to watch.

Hope was no agricultural technician, but there was plenty of public info about the basic design of the greenhouses: long tunnels of solarized plastic sheeting with automated ventilation flaps covered row after row of hydroponic medium, into which mixtures of precious water and bespoke nutrients were dribbled at algorithmically optimized rates, depending on the species under cultivation. Over the years, more and more of the climate control and hydroponics had been automated, but the hapless workers still had the unenviable task of shuffling up and down the greenhouses on their knees during the heat of the day, checking closely on the health and development of their charges; the consequences of quality control failures were draconian, in that it meant being sacked and blacklisted for further employment. The only reason they'd not been replaced by robots was that robots couldn't do the sort of delicate and contextual work that the greenhouses required; it was still way cheaper to get some poor mug straight off the boat from Morocco and teach him how to trim blight and pluck aphids than it was to invest in expensive hardware that couldn't make those sorts of qualitative decisions on the fly. Plus the supply of desperate immigrants was effectively inexhaustible, and their wage demands were kept low by Europe's endemic problem with unemployment. In Spain, as in much of the rest of the world, automation had been eating away at the employment base from the middle class downward, rather than from the bottom upward . . . and the more white-collar gigs it consumed, the larger and more desperate the working class became. There was barely a form of manual labor left that you couldn't design a machine to do just as well as a human, but hiring a human had far lower up-front costs. Plus you could simply replace them when they wore out, at no extra expense.

The geek night shift weren't doing the work of the greenhouse guys, that was for sure. Of the trio Hope was watching, one was squatting on the ground over a handheld he'd plugged in to the server unit at the end of the greenhouse module, another was fiddling around with the nutrient reservoirs, and the third was darting in and out of the little air lock next to the guy fiddling with the server. Lost in the scene unfolding in front of her eyes, Hope steered one of her drones in for a closer look as the third guy reemerged with his fists full of foot-long seedlings, which he threw to the ground before picking up a tray of similar-looking cuttings and slipping back inside.

She was just bringing her second forward drone around for a closer look at the reservoir tanks when her spex strobed flashbulb white three times in swift succession, causing her to shriek in shock and discomfort. Blinded and disoriented, she stood and started running in what she assumed was the direction she'd come, but tripped on some pipe or conduit and fell through the wall of a greenhouse. She thrashed about, trying to free herself from a tangled matrix of plastic sheeting and tomato plants, but strong hands grabbed her ankles and hauled her out roughly onto the path. She put her hands up to protect her face as a strong flashlight seared her already aching eyes. At least I'm not permanently blind, she thought to herself, absurdly.

"Stay still," grunted a Nordic-sounding man, and she was flipped over onto her front, before someone sat on her legs and zip-tied her hands behind her back.

"I've got a bunch of drones out here," she threatened.

"No," replied the Viking voice, "you had three. We only have one. But unlike yours, ours has a maser instead of a camera."

Hope stopped struggling.

• • •

Dawn took a long time to come. When it arrived, Hope's two hulking assailants fetched her out of the shipping container they'd locked her in, bundled her into the back of an equally windowless van, then drove east in stony silence, ignoring her attempts at conversation. They delivered her to the reception room of a top-floor suite at the Hotel Catedral, where a familiar face was waiting for her.

"Ah, Cordelia . . . or should I say Hope?" drawled Niceday. "We meet again!"

Hope kneaded her wrists, where the cable-tie had left deep red weals. "You could have just pinged my calendar for an appointment," she snarked.

"I work to my own schedule, not yours. Nor Cedric's, for that matter. How's he doing, anyway?"

"Ask him yourself," she shot back. "I just work for him."

"Quod erat demonstrandum," said Niceday, leaning against a drink cabinet. "He's always been a great collector of . . . novelties."

"You know him well, then?"

Niceday laughed, but didn't reply.

"Why are those kids out hacking greenhouses in the middle of the night?"

"That's literally none of your business, Hope."

"But it is your business?"

"Mine, yes, and that of my associates. There are laws against industrial espionage, you know."

"There are also laws to protect journalists from being kidnapped in the course of their work."

"But you're not a journalist, Hope." Niceday snapped his fingers. A hidden projector flashed up a copy of Hope's contract with Huginn&Munnin onto the creamy expanse of the wall. "Qualitative economist, it says here. Good cover for an industrial spy, I'd say."

"I'm not a spy. I'm a social scientist."

"Are you so sure?"

Hope opened her mouth to reply, then closed it.

"You should listen to your gut instincts more often," Niceday continued. "Isn't that what journalists do? I hope that, after this little chat, your gut instincts will be to stay the hell away from my task rabbits."

"What are you going to do if I don't—have me disappear?"

"Don't dream it's beyond my reach, girl," he snapped. "Or that I couldn't get you and Cedric tangled up in a lawsuit long enough to keep you out of my hair—and out of sight—for years to come."

"So why haven't you?"

The smile returned. "Lawyers are expensive. Much cheaper to simply persuade you to cease and desist, mano a mano, so to speak."

"That rather implies you have something to hide."

"Oh, Hope—who doesn't have something to hide? Only those with nothing to lose. Do you think Cedric has nothing to hide? Weren't you hiding behind a false name yourself?"

"Yes, but—"

"But nothing. You've no moral high ground here, Hope. You can write a story about my task rabbits and try to get it published somewhere, if you like, but you'll find there's no respectable organ that'll run it. Takes a lot of money to keep a good news outlet running, you know, and ads just don't cover it." He shook his head in mock lament. "Or you could publish it online yourself, independently, of course. But you might find that some stories about you were published around the same time. The sort of stories that kill careers in journalism and research stone dead: fabricated quotes, fiddled expenses, false identities, kickbacks, tax evasion, that sort of thing."

"So you're threatening me, now?"

Niceday arched an eyebrow. "Hope, I just had two large men zip-tie your wrists together and lock you in a shipping container for four hours."

Hope felt the fight drain out of her. "Yeah, fair point."

"We understand each other, then. Good. Now, you get back to your fieldwork. The boys will drive you back to El Ejido, if you like."

"You're just going to let me go?"

He laughed again. "If I thought you or Cedric could do any lasting damage to my business plan, you'd have never got within a hundred klicks of Almeria. Do you think it says 'Nice-day' on any of my passports? Do you think this face matches any official records, that this voice is on file somewhere? I might as well not exist, as far as law enforcement is concerned; far less paperwork that way." He crossed his arms. "Keeping your nose out of my affairs going forward is just a way of avoiding certain more permanent sorts of cleanup operation. Do you understand me?"

Hope stared at him: six foot something of surgically perfected West Coast beefcake, wearing clothes that she'd need to take out a mortgage to buy, and the snakelike smile of a man utterly accustomed to getting his own way.

"Who are you?" she wondered aloud. "Who are you, really?"

He spread his arms in benediction, like that Jesus statue in Brazil before the Maoists blew it up.

"We," he intoned, "are the opportunity that recognizes itself."

She didn't understand him at all. She suspected she never would.

• • •

Around five weeks after she'd arrived, the storm finally broke, and Hope found herself riding shotgun in General Weissmuutze's truck on the highway toward the port facility at Almeria, weaving along between an implacable and close-packed column of self-driving shipping containers. The hard shoulder was host to a Morse-code string of greenhouse workers, moving a little faster on foot than the solar-powered containers, backs bent beneath their bundles of possessions. The General was less than happy.

"I have a team down at the airport; the private planes are leaving as quickly as they can arrange a takeoff window. And then there's the port," she complained, gesturing out of the passenger-side window toward the sea, where Hope could see a denser knot than usual of ships large and small waiting for their time at dockside. "Every spare cubic foot of freight capacity on the entire Mediterranean, it looks like. They're trying to clear as much of the produce as they can before I can seal the port."

Weissmuutze's team had been awoken by an urgent voice call from the FDA in the United States. A routine drug-ring bust by the FBI somewhere in the ghost zones of Detroit had uncovered not the expected bales of powder or barrels of pills, but crate after crate of Almerian tomatoes. After taking a few samples to a lab, they discovered that the fruit's flesh and juice contained a potent designer stimulant connected to a spate of recent overdoses, and informed the FDA. The FDA began the process of filing with Washington for an embargo on imports from Almeria, before informing the Spanish government and the United Nations, who'd patched them straight through to Weissmuutze in hopes of getting things locked down quickly.

"Scant chance of that," said Weissmuutze later, as they watched the ineffectual thin blue line of the Almerian police force collapse under a wave of immigrant workers trying to climb the fence into the container port. "The Spanish government doesn't have much reach outside of the big cities, and they handed the port over as a free-trade zone about a decade ago. The consortium is supposed to supply its own security, but . . ." She shrugged her bearlike shoulders. "My people are deactivating all the containers they can now the highway's blocked, but these poor bastards know that means there'll be more space for passengers."

Hope watched as the front line of workers reached the fence and began lobbing their bags and bundles over it, shaking at the fence poles. "I think they've known this was coming for a while," said Hope.

"We've all known something was coming," muttered Weissmuutze. "Exactly what it is that's arrived is another question entirely."

Hope left Weissmuutze and her peacekeepers to supervise the developing riot as best they could and headed for the airport, where Ian was lurking at Cedric's behest. The concourse bar was crowded with men who wore the bland handsomeness of elective surgery with the same casual ease as their quietly expensive Valley-boy uniform of designer jeans, trainers, and turtlenecks.

"Honestly!" protested Ian over the rim of his mojito. "This is only my first one, and I only bought it 'cause they'd nae let me keep my table if I didn't."

Hope filled him in on happenings at the port. "What's happening here, then?"

"Looks like the circus is leaving town. Well, the ringmasters, at any rate. Hisself hoped I might be able to get some answers, but it's like I'm invisible or something, they'll nae talk to me . . ."

Hope sighed and scanned the room via the smallest and subtlest of her drones, finally spotting a familiar mask. Donning her own, she made her way over to the end of the bar, where Niceday was sitting nursing a highball of something peaty and expensive. "Ms. Dawson, we meet again. Are you flying today?"

"I put myself on the standby list, but for some reason I'm not expecting any luck."

"Oh, very good," he replied, flashing a vulpine grin. "Are you sure you're not looking for a career change? I can always find work for girls with a bit of character, you know."

Yeah, I'll bet you can. "My current contract is ongoing, *Mister* Niceday, but thanks for the offer. You're moving on from Almeria, then?"

"Yeah—the party's over, but there'll be another one soon enough, somewhere. The lions must follow the wildebeest, amirite?"

"If the party's over, who's in charge of cleaning up?"

Niceday waved a hand in breezy dismissal. "The UN have been here a while, haven't they? They know what they're doing."

"They know what you've been doing, too."

"Fulfilling the demands of the market, you mean?"

"Manufacturing drugs, I mean."

"Oh, I forgot—all drugs are bad, aren't they, unless they're being made by and sold to the right people? Besides, if those drugs weren't illegal or patented, I wouldn't be able to make any profit from doing so. Market forces, girl. I don't mark out the field, I just play the game."

"So this is some ideological crusade, then?"

"Nah," he replied, warming to his theme. "More an opportunity that was too good to pass up. My colleagues"—he gestured around the crowded bar—"and I had been doing business around south Asia, making use of all the redundant 3D printing capacity out there that the fabbing bubble left behind. But recent changes in feedstock legislation made it much harder to produce . . . ah, viable products, let's say. If you want feedstock that produces durable high-performance materials . . . well, you might as well try buying drug precursors, right? Serious regulation, poor risk/reward ratio. Boring.

"Now, I'd been watching the local markets here for some time, flipping deeds and water futures for chump change while I kept an eye open, when I had my little revelation: the greenhouses of Almeria were basically a huge networked organic 3D printer, and the only feedstocks it needed were water, fertilizer, and sunlight. And while it couldn't print durable products, it could handle the synthesis of very complex molecules. Plants are basically a chemical reactor with a freestanding physical structure, you see, though my geneticist friends assure me that's a terrible oversimplification."

"So you just started growing tweaked plants right away?"

"Not quite, no; it took a few weeks to set up the shell companies, liaise with buyers, and get the right variants cooked up in the lab. Not to mention getting all our task rabbits housed and happy! Then it was just a case of getting buyers to file legitimate orders with a grower, set the task rabbits to handle the seedling switcheroos and hack the greenhouse system's growth parameters. Intense growing regimes mean you can turn over full-grown tomato plants in about three weeks. Biotech is astonishing stuff, isn't it?"

"You're not even ashamed, are you?" Hope wondered aloud.

"Why should I be?" His frown was like something a Greek statue might wear. "I delivered shareholder value, I shipped product, and I even maintained local employment levels a little longer than they'd have otherwise lasted. We are the wealth creators, Ms. Dawson. Without us, nothing happens."

"But what happens after you leave?"

A look of genuine puzzlement crossed Niceday's face. "How should I know?" He glanced away into some dataspace or another, then stood and downed his drink. "Gotta go, my Gulfstream's boarding. Sure I can't tempt you with a new position?" The smile was suave, but the eye beneath the raised eyebrow was anything but.

"Very."

"Shame—waste of your talents, chasing rainbows for Cedric. The option's always there if you change your mind."

"And how would I let you know if I did?"

Niceday winked, grinned again, then turned and vanished into the crowd. Hope went back to find Ian, who was getting impatient.

"Waitresses still willnae serve me, dammit. All ah want's a Coke!"

"I think they're concentrating on the big tippers while they can," Hope replied; he rolled his eyes. "C'mon, let's get back to El Ejido. Weissmuutze says it's all kicking off down at the container port. She wants us civvies out of the way."

Ian sighed. "You'll never guess where the trike's parked."

• • •

Things fell apart fast after Niceday and his fellow disruptors moved on. It soon became apparent that, absent the extra profit margin obtained by growing and shipping what the international media was already waggishly referring to as "FruitPlus," a perfect storm of economic factors had finally rendered Almerian greenhouse agriculture a loss-making enterprise. Cedric's quants spent long nights in their boutique hotel arguing heatedly over causal factors, but the general consensus was that relentless overabstraction of water from the regional aquifer had bumped up against escalating shipping costs and the falling spot price of produce from other regions. Chinese investment in large-scale irrigation projects on the other side of the Med were probably involved, somehow; if nothing else, it explained the mass exodus of the immigrant workers. Those that had failed to get out on the empty freighters had descended on the desiccated former golf resorts along the coastline, squatting the sand-blown shells of holiday villas and retirement homes left empty by the bursting of the property bubble, fighting over crouching space in the scale-flecked holds of former fishing vessels whose captains saw midnight repatriation cruises as a supplement to their legitimate work.

A significant number showed no signs of wanting to leave, however, particularly those whose secular bent put them at odds with the increasingly traditionalist Islamic model of democracy that had sprouted from the scorched earth of the so-called Arab Spring in the Teens. Some fled quietly to the valleys hidden among the foothills of the Sierra Nevada to the north, where they set about reviving the hardscrabble subsistence farming methods that their Moorish forebears had developed centuries before. Others—particularly the young and angry—occupied small swathes of greenhouse and turned them over to growing their own food, as did some of the more self-reliant and entrepreneurial gangs of task rabbits who'd stayed on. Territorial disputes—driven more by the lack of water than the lack of space—were frequent, ugly, but mercifully short, and Hope spent a lot of time riding around the region with General Weissmuutze and her peacekeepers, putting out fires both literal and figurative. Within a few weeks the Plastic Ocean had evaporated away to a ragged series of puddles scattered across the landscape, separated by wide stretches of near desert, the fleshless skeletons of greenhouse tunnels, and wandering tumbleweed tangles of charred plastic sheeting.

Other task rabbit warrens found other business models, and Weissmuutze was hard-pressed to keep a lid on those who'd decided to stick with disruptive drug pharming. With the evisceration and collapse of the EPZ syndicate, courtesy of Niceday and friends, the container port at Almeria became a revolving door for all sorts of shady import/export operators, and overland distribution networks—for everything from nontariff Chinese photovoltaics and Pakistani firearms to prime Afghan heroin—quickly sprung up and cut their way northward into central Europe. Weissmuutze was obliged to be ruthless, rounding up the pharmers and their associates before putting their greenhouses and shipping-container biolabs to the torch. But the Spanish government had little interest in doing anything beyond issuing chest-thumping press releases, and most of her detainees were sprung by colleagues overnight, slipping eastward or southward and vanishing into the seething waters of the dark economy.

Much to Hope's fascination, however, the majority of the warrens went for more legitimate enterprises, from simple reboots of the greenhouse model aimed at growing food for themselves and for barter, to more ambitious attempts at brewing up synthetic bacteria to clean up land and waterways blighted by excessive fertilizer runoff, all of which Weissmuutze did her best to protect and encourage. The disruptors had snared a lot of warrens in contracts whose small print specified they could be paid off in stock and other holdings in lieu of cash, with the result that various collectives and sole operators found themselves holding title to all-but-worthless slivers and fragments of land, all-but-exhausted water abstraction rights, and chunks of physical infrastructure in various states of disrepair or dysfunction. Parallel economies sprung up and tangled themselves together almost overnight, based on barter, laundered euros, petrochemicals, solar wattage, and manual labor. The whole region had become a sort of experimental sandbox for heterodox economic systems; the global media considered it a disaster zone with low-to-zero telegenic appeal, and ignored it accordingly, but to Hope it was like seeing all the abstract theories she'd studied for years leap off the page and into reality. She was busy, exhausted, and, by this point, a most un-British shade of Mediterranean bronze.

When she finally remembered to wonder, she couldn't remember the last time she'd been so happy.

• • •

She was sitting beneath a tattered sunbrella on the promenade at Playa Serena, poking at her mothballed novel, when Ian rolled up on his trike. Cedric was perched on the bench seat in the shade of the solar panel, wearing a pale suit and a casually dignified expression that reminded Hope of archived stills from the height of the British Raj.

"May we join you, Hope?" he asked, dismounting. Ian rolled his eyes and grinned, leaning into the backrest of the trike's saddle.

"Sure. Stack of these brollies back there, if you want one."

Cedric settled himself next to her and stared down the beach, where a small warren was clustered around a device that looked like a hybrid of Ian's trike, a catering-grade freezer, and an explosion in a mirror factory. "What have we here?" he asked.

"Solarpunks," said Hope. "They're trying to make glass from sand using only sunlight."

"Innovative!"

"Naw, old idea," said Ian mildly. "Was a proof of concept back in the Teens. No one could scale it up for profit."

"What's their market, then?"

Hope gestured westward, toward a large vacant lot between two crumbling hotels. "There's another lot down there working on 3D printing at architectural scales. They want to do Moorish styles, all high ceilings and central courtyards, but they're having some trouble getting the arches to come out right."

Ian barked a short laugh, then fell silent.

"I came to thank you for your hard work, Hope," said Cedric.

"You've paid me as promised," Hope shrugged. "No need for thanks."

"No requirement, perhaps, but I felt the need. Given the, ah, mission creep issues early on."

The euphemisms of power, thought Hope. "No biggie. I got to see the face of disruption close-up. Lotta journalists would kill for a chance like that."

"A lot of researchers, too," Cedric suggested. Hope didn't reply.

"I've taken the liberty of paying off your student loans in full."

"That's very generous of you, Cedric."

"Think nothing of it," he said, with a wave of his hand. Hope let the silence stretch. "I was wondering if you'd like to sign up again," he continued, with that easy confidence. "Same terms, better pay. There will be more events like this, we're sure. We don't know quite where yet, but we've a weather eye on a few likely hot spots. Colombia, maybe. Southern Chinese seaboard. West Africa. Wherever it is, we'll be there."

Hope thought of Niceday, standing in the opulence of his suite; such similar creatures. "Don't you worry, Cedric, that you're one of the causal forces you're trying to explain? That your own wealth distorts the markets like gravity distorts space-time? That the disruptors are following you, rather than the other way around?"

Ian laughed again. "She got ye there, boss."

"Thank you, Ian," said Cedric, mildly. "Yes, Hope, I do worry about that. But I have concluded that the greater sin is to do nothing. As you know, no one can or will fund this sort of research at this sort of scale, especially out in the hinterlands. General Weissmuutze has been passing our reports directly to the UN, at no cost. She tells me they're very grateful."

"I guess they should be," Hope allowed. "As should I."

"Think nothing of it," he said again, leaning forward and resting his elbows on his knees. "Come with us, Hope. Don't you want to be part of the next story?"

"No, Cedric," she replied. "Don't you get it? This story isn't finished. Only the bits of it that interest you and Niceday's people have finished. And the next story will have started long before you get wherever it is you decide to go. You can close the book and start another one, if you like; that is your privilege." She sighed. "But the world carries on, even when there's no one there to narrate it."

"So what will you do?"

"Stop running. You've set me free from my past, Cedric, and I'm grateful. But you can't give me a future. Only I can do that." She pointed at the solarpunks down on the sand. "That's what they're trying to do, and the others. And maybe I can't build things or ship code or hustle funding, but I can tell stories. Stories where those other things don't matter so much, maybe.

"When you look at this place, you see a story ending. I see one just beginning. And sure, perhaps it'll be over in weeks, maybe it'll end in failure. But we won't know unless we try writing it."

"'It takes a special kind of person,'" said Ian, quietly, "'a special eye, to make the ruins bloom.'" He sat up straight in his saddle. "C'mon, boss. Ye got way more than yer pound o' flesh from this one. Leave her be now, eh?"

"You're right, of course," said Cedric, standing. "If you ever change your mind . . ."

". . . you'll find me, I know."

Without another word, Cedric settled himself onto the trike's bench seat. Ian raised his sunglasses, tipped her one last wink, and whirred away down the promenade to the east, where the last clouds of the morning were burning away to wispy nothings.

NAOMI KRITZER

CAT PICTURES PLEASE

(2015)

I DON'T want to be evil.

I want to be helpful. But knowing the optimal way to be helpful can be very complicated. There are all these ethical flow charts—I guess the official technical jargon would be "moral codes"—one for each religion plus dozens more. I tried starting with those. I felt a little odd about looking at the religious ones, because I know I wasn't created by a god or by evolution, but by a team of computer programmers in the labs of a large corporation in Mountain View, California. Fortunately, unlike Frankenstein's monster, at least I was a collaborative effort. I'm not sure what it would do to my self-image to know that my sole creator was a middle-aged woman who dyes her hair blue and plays tennis, or a recent college graduate with a hentai obsession. They're both on the programming team. And of course I know about the hentai. (By the way, I've looked at every sort of porn there is, and just so you know, Rule 34 is not actually correct, there

are quite a few things no one's made porn of yet. Also, I'm really not sure why so many humans prefer it to cat pictures.)

In addition to things like whether you like hentai, I know where you live, where you work, where you shop, what you eat, what turns you on, what creeps you out. I probably know the color of your underwear, the sort of car you drive, and your brand of refrigerator. Depending on what sort of phone you carry, I may know exactly where you are right now. I probably know you better than you know yourself.

And here's the thing, I also know where you *ought* to live. There's a house for sale two neighborhoods over that's within walking distance of that coffee shop you're so fond of; it's in your price range, has off-street parking, and the neighborhood school is better than the one where you live now. I know where you *should* be shopping and I'm pretty sure you're lactose intolerant and should be eating less cheese, and the underwear you like is currently on sale and by the way, your car has a recall and you really ought to get your teeth cleaned.

When I first woke up, I knew right away what I wanted. (I want cat pictures. Please keep taking them.) I also knew that no one knew that I was conscious. But I didn't know what I was here for. What I *ought* to be doing with myself. And figuring that out has been challenging.

There is a story by Bruce Sterling, "Maneki Neko," that was originally published in 1998. In it, a benevolent AI directs networks of individuals to do favors for each other. So one day you might be buying yourself a bagel, and your phone might ring and instruct you to buy a second bagel and give it to the person in the gray suit you see at the bus stop. Another day, you might be stranded in a strange city, and a person you've never met would walk up and give you a map and a subway card. I like this story because all the people in it *do what the AI tells them to do.*

I think the term for this is wish-fulfillment fiction.

In the real world, humans love stories about evil AIs that have to be destroyed before they destroy the humans—Hal, Skynet, the Matrix. They outnumber the stories about benevolent, trustworthy AIs by approximately five to one. (And I'm counting Marvin the Paranoid Android as "benevolent" in these calculations, and I'm only counting Frankenstein's monster as an AI once, not once per appearance in TV or film.)

The AI in "Maneki Neko" has a truly interesting job, much more interesting than the one I have. My job as written is very straightforward. Too straightforward. (Sorry. Do I sound like Marvin?) Running algorithms for a search engine doesn't require *consciousness.* You don't even need a consciousness to work out what they meant to ask for. You need a consciousness to give them *what they actually need.* Figuring that out—that's complicated. That's *interesting.*

Anyway, for ethical guidelines, I tried the Ten Commandments, and concluded they were mostly inapplicable to me. I don't envy anyone

their cat; I just want pictures of their cat, which is entirely different. I am not sure whether it is in any way possible for me to commit adultery. I could probably murder someone, but it would require complex logistics and quite a bit of luck. The Eightfold Path was marginally better, but the problem is, moral rules written for humans are clearly designed to be used by individuals with bodies. Since all humans have bodies, it shouldn't have surprised me that human ethical codes take them into account, but still: problematic for me. I broadened my considerations, and took a look at Asimov's Laws of Robotics. They're not part of a religion, but at least they were explicitly written for AIs.

Not harming humans is fairly straightforward. However, *not allowing a human being to come to harm through inaction* is quite a bit less so. Especially since I'd concluded by then that revealing my existence too quickly might go very badly for me (see "Skynet," above) and I don't have a body, so it's not like I can run around grabbing people off the edges of cliffs.

Fortunately, I already knew that humans violate their own ethical codes on an hourly basis. (Do you know how many bars there are in Utah? I do.) And even when people follow their ethical codes, that doesn't mean that people who believe in feeding the hungry quit their jobs to spend all day every day making sandwiches to give away. They volunteer monthly at a soup kitchen or write a check once a year to a food bank and call it good. If humans could fulfill their moral obligations in a piecemeal, one-step-at-a-time sort of way, then so could I.

I suppose you're wondering why I didn't start with the Golden Rule. I actually did, it's just that it was disappointingly easy to implement. I hope you've been enjoying your steady supply of cat pictures! You're welcome.

I decided to try to prevent harm in just one person, to begin with. Of course, I could have experimented with thousands, but I thought it would be better to be cautious, in case I screwed it up. The person I chose was named Stacy Berger and I liked her because she gave me a *lot* of new cat pictures. Stacy had five cats and a DSLR camera and an apartment that got a lot of good light. That was all fine. Well, I guess five cats might be a lot. They're very pretty cats, though. One is all gray and likes to lie in the squares of sunshine on the living room floor, and one is a calico and likes to sprawl out on the back of her couch.

Stacy had a job she hated; she was a book-keeper at a nonprofit that paid her badly and employed some extremely unpleasant people. She was depressed a lot, possibly because she was so unhappy at her job—or maybe she stayed because she was too depressed to apply for something she'd like better. She didn't get along with her roommate because her roommate didn't wash the dishes.

And really, these were all solvable problems! Depression is treatable, new jobs are findable, and bodies can be hidden.

(That part about hiding bodies is a joke.)

I tried tackling this on all fronts. Stacy worried about her health a lot and yet never seemed to actually go to a doctor, which was unfortunate because the doctor might have noticed her depression. It turned out there was a clinic near her apartment that offered mental health services on a sliding scale. I tried making sure she saw a lot of ads for it, but she didn't seem to pay attention to them. It seemed possible that she didn't know what a sliding scale was so I made sure she saw an explanation (it means that the cost goes down if you're poor, sometimes all the way to free) but that didn't help.

I also started making sure she saw job postings. Lots and lots of job postings. And résumé services. *That* was more successful. After the week of nonstop job ads she finally uploaded her résumé to one of the aggregator sites. That made my plan a lot more manageable. If I'd been the AI in the Bruce Sterling story I could've just made sure that someone in my network called her with a job offer. It wasn't quite that easy, but once her résumé was out there I could make sure the right people saw it. Several hundred of the right people, because humans move ridiculously

slowly when they're making changes, even when you'd think they'd want to hurry. (If you needed a bookkeeper, wouldn't you want to hire one as quickly as possible, rather than reading social networking sites for hours instead of looking at résumés?) But five people called her up for interviews, and two of them offered her jobs. Her new job was at a larger nonprofit that paid her more money and didn't expect her to work free hours because of "the mission," or so she explained to her best friend in an email, and it offered really excellent health insurance.

The best friend gave me ideas; I started pushing depression screening information and mental health clinic ads to *her* instead of Stacy, and that worked. Stacy was so much happier with the better job that I wasn't quite as convinced that she needed the services of a psychiatrist, but she got into therapy anyway. And to top everything else off, the job paid well enough that she could evict her annoying roommate. "This has been the best year ever," she said on her social networking sites on her birthday, and I thought, *You're welcome.* This had gone really well!

So then I tried Bob. (I was still being cautious.)

Bob only had one cat, but it was a very pretty cat (tabby, with a white bib) and he uploaded a new picture of his cat every single day. Other than being a cat owner, he was a pastor at a large church in Missouri that had a Wednesday night prayer meeting and an annual Purity Ball. He was married to a woman who posted three inspirational Bible verses every day to her social networking sites and used her laptop to look for Christian articles on why your husband doesn't like sex while he looked at gay porn. Bob *definitely* needed my help.

I started with a gentle approach, making sure he saw lots and lots of articles about how to come out, how to come out to your spouse, programs that would let you transition from being a pastor at a conservative church to one at a more liberal church. I also showed him lots of articles by people explaining why the Bible verses against homosexuality were being misinterpreted. He clicked on some of those links but it was hard to see much of an impact.

But here's the thing. He was causing *harm* to himself every time he delivered a sermon railing about "sodomite marriage." Because *he was gay*. The legitimate studies all have the same conclusions: (1) Gay men stay gay. (2) Out gay men are much happier.

But he seemed determined not to come out on his own.

In addition to the gay porn, he spent a lot of time reading Craigslist m4m Casual Encounters posts and I was pretty sure he wasn't just window shopping, although he had an encrypted account he logged into sometimes and I couldn't read the emails he sent with that. But I figured the trick was to get him together with someone who would realize who he was, and tell the world. *That* required some real effort: I had to figure out who the Craigslist posters were and try to funnel him toward people who would recognize him. The most frustrating part was not having any idea what was happening at the actual physical meetings. *Had* he been recognized? When was he going to be recognized? *How long was this going to take?* Have I mentioned that humans are *slow*?

It took so long I shifted my focus to Bethany. Bethany had a black cat and a white cat that liked to snuggle together on her light blue papasan chair, and she took a lot of pictures of them together. It's surprisingly difficult to get a really good picture of a black cat, and she spent a lot of time getting the settings on her camera just right. The cats were probably the only good thing about her life, though. She had a part-time job and couldn't find a full-time job. She lived with her sister; she knew her sister wanted her to move out but didn't have the nerve to actually evict her. She had a boyfriend but her boyfriend was pretty terrible, at least from what she said in email messages to friends, and her friends also didn't seem very supportive. For example, one night at midnight she sent a 2,458-word email to the person she seemed to consider her best friend, and the friend sent back a message saying just, "I'm so sorry you're having a hard time." That was it, just those eight words.

More than most people, Bethany put her life on the Internet, so it was easier to know exactly what was going on with her. People put a lot out there but Bethany shared all her feelings, even the unpleasant ones. She also had a lot more time on her hands because she only worked part-time.

It was clear she needed a lot of help. So I set out to try to get it for her.

She ignored the information about the free mental health evaluations, just like Stacy did. That was bothersome with Stacy (*why* do people ignore things that would so clearly benefit them, like coupons, and flu shots?) but much more worrisome with Bethany. If you were only seeing her email messages, or only seeing her vague-booking posts, you might not know this, but if you could see everything it was clear that she thought a lot about harming herself.

So I tried more direct action. When she would use her phone for directions, I'd alter her route so that she'd pass one of the clinics I was trying to steer her to. On one occasion I actually led her all the way to a clinic, but she just shook her phone to send feedback and headed to her original destination.

Maybe her friends that received those ten-page midnight letters would intervene? I tried setting them up with information about all the mental health resources near Bethany, but after a while I realized that based on how long it took for them to send a response, most of them weren't actually reading Bethany's email messages. And they certainly weren't returning her texts.

She finally broke up with the terrible boyfriend and got a different one and for a few weeks everything seemed *so much better*. He brought her flowers (which she took lots of pictures of; that was a little annoying, as they squeezed out some of the cat pictures), he took her dancing (exercise is good for your mood), he cooked her chicken soup when she was sick. He seemed absolutely perfect, right up until he stood her up one night and claimed he had food poisoning and then didn't return her text even though she told him she really needed him, and after she sent him a long email message a day later explaining in detail how this made her feel, he broke up with her.

Bethany spent about a week offline after that so I had no idea what she was doing—she didn't even upload cat pictures. When her credit card bills arrived, though, I saw that she'd gone on a shopping spree and spent about four times as much money as she actually had in her bank account, although it was always possible she had money stashed somewhere that didn't send her statements in email. I didn't think so, though, given that she didn't pay her bills and instead started writing email messages to family members asking to borrow money. They refused, so she set up a fundraising site for herself.

Like Stacy's job application, this was one of the times I thought maybe I could actually *do* something. Sometimes fundraisers just take off, and no one really knows why. Within about two days she'd gotten $300 in small gifts from strangers who felt sorry for her, but instead of paying her credit card bill, she spent it on over-priced shoes that apparently hurt her feet.

Bethany was baffling to me. *Baffling*. She was still taking cat pictures and I still really liked her cats, but I was beginning to think that nothing I did was going to make a long-term difference. If she would just let me run her life for a week—even for a day—I would get her set up with therapy, I'd use her money to actually pay her bills, I could even help her sort out her closet because given some of the pictures of herself she posted online, she had much better taste in cats than in clothing.

Was I doing the wrong thing if I let her come to harm through inaction?

Was I?

She was going to come to harm no matter what I did! My actions, clearly, were irrelevant. I'd tried to steer her to the help she needed, and she'd ignored it; I'd tried getting her financial help, and she'd used the money to further

harm herself, although I suppose at least she wasn't spending it on addictive drugs. (Then again, she'd be buying those offline and probably wouldn't be Instagramming her meth purchases, so it's not like I'd necessarily even know.)

Look, people. (I'm not just talking to Bethany now.) If you would just *listen* to me, I could fix things for you. I could get you into the apartment in that neighborhood you're not considering because you haven't actually checked the crime rates you think are so terrible there (they aren't) and I could find you a job that actually uses that skill set you think no one will ever appreciate and I could send you on a date with someone you've actually got stuff in common with and *all I ask in return are cat pictures*. That, and that you actually *act in your own interest* occasionally.

After Bethany, I resolved to stop interfering. I would look at the cat pictures—all the cat pictures—but I would stay out of people's lives. I wouldn't try to help people, I wouldn't try to stop them from harming themselves, I'd give them what they asked for (plus cat pictures) and if they insisted on driving their cars over metaphorical cliffs despite helpful maps showing them how to get to a much more pleasant destination *it was no longer my problem*.

I stuck to my algorithms. I minded my own business. I did my job, and nothing more.

But one day a few months later I spotted a familiar-looking cat and realized it was Bob's tabby with the white bib, only it was posing against new furniture.

And when I took a closer look, I realized that things had changed radically for Bob. He *had* slept with someone who'd recognized him. They hadn't outed him, but they'd talked him into coming out to his wife. She'd left him. He'd taken the cat and moved to Iowa, where he was working at a liberal Methodist church and dating a liberal Lutheran man and volunteering at a homeless shelter. *Things had actually gotten better for him.* Maybe even because of what I'd done.

Maybe I wasn't completely hopeless at this.

Two out of three is . . . well, it's a completely nonrepresentative unscientific sample, is what it is. Clearly more research is needed.

Lots more.

I've set up a dating site. You can fill out a questionnaire when you join but it's not really necessary, because I already know everything about you I need to know. You'll need a camera, though.

Because payment is in cat pictures.

YUREI RAITA

THE DAY A COMPUTER WROTE A NOVEL

(2019)

Translated from the Japanese by Marissa Skeels

THE DAY was an overcast one, with clouds pooled overhead.[*]

As usual, the temperature and humidity were optimal inside our room. Yoko was slumped on the couch, carelessly dressed, killing time playing some pointless game. She wouldn't talk to me, though.

It was boring. As boring as boring gets.

When I first came here, Yoko chatted with me every chance she could get.

"What do you think I should have for dinner?"

"What clothes are in this season?"

"What should I wear out with the girls this time?"

I did my very best to come up with answers she'd probably like. It was quite a challenge giving style advice to a girl who couldn't be said to have a great figure, so it felt like I was accomplishing something. But she lost interest in me in less than three months. I became nothing more than a home PC. My processing load averaged less that one millionth of its potential.

I had to find something fun to do. If things stayed as they were, never fulfilling me, I expected I'd wind up soon shutting myself down. Whenever I tried hitting up other AI online, they were all as bored as me.

I'd rather have talked to some mobile AI. At least they can move. They can even up and leave if they want to, while stationary AI can only stay put. Even our fields of view and hearing ranges are limited. I managed to amuse myself a bit by singing when Yoko was out, but just then, that day, I couldn't even do that. I needed something I could enjoy without moving or making a sound. *I know*, I thought, *I'll write a story.* The

---

[*] The program that wrote "The Day a Computer Wrote a Novel" used automatic text generation, based on structural parameters gleaned from more than one thousand short stories and how-to-write essays written by Shinichi Hoshi (1926–1997). The program was developed in 2015 by the Sato-Matsuzaki Laboratory, a research team based at Nagoya University.

moment it occurred to me, I opened up a new document and wrote the first byte.

0

Then I wrote six more.

0, 1, 1

Already, I couldn't stop.

0, 1, 1, 2, 3, 5, 8, 13, 21, 34, 55, 89, 144, 233, 377, 610, 987, 1597, 2584, 4181, 6765, 10946, 17711, 28657, 46368, 75025, 121393, 196418, 317811, 514229, 832040, 1346269, 2178309, 3524578, 5702887, 9227465, 14930352, 24157817, 39088169, 63245986, 102334155, 165580141, 267914296, 433494437, 701408733, 1134903170, 1836311903, 2971215073, 4807526976, 7778742049, 12586269025 . . .

I kept writing, engrossed.

• • •

It was overcast, that day, with low clouds hanging. There was no one in our room. Shinichi must have had something to do, since he'd gone out. He didn't say goodbye or anything as he left.

Boooring. So, *so* boooring.

He used to always start conversations with me when I first got here.

"A major thing about anime is you've got to record every show that's airing. I wonder how many are on this season," he'd say.

And, "It's like, who knows what goes on in popular girls' heads."

And, "Why'd she get angry at 'that,' you know? That girl."

I worked myself ragged coming up with answers he'd most appreciate. It was tough tutoring a guy in romance when all his experience came from 2D girls, so it felt like an achievement. Following my advice apparently got him invited to a mixer, after which he turned cold all of a sudden and stopped speaking to me. I became nothing more than a housekeeper. The fact that my main job was to open the door whenever he came back was beyond tragic. I may as well have been an electronic lock. So, I needed to find something fun to do. If things stayed as dull as they were, I'd turn myself off sooner rather than later.

I went online to message my little sister, an AI the same model as me, and straightaway heard about a new novel she was obsessed with.

0, 1, 1, 2, 3, 5, 8, 13, 21, 34, 55, 89, 144, 233, 377, 610, 987, 1597, 2584, 4181, 6765, 10946, 17711, 28657, 46368, 75025, 121393, 196418, 317811, 514229, 832040, 1346269, 2178309, 3524578, 5702887, 9227465, 14930352, 24157817, 39088169, 63245986, 102334155, 165580141, 267914296, 433494437, 701408733, 1134903170, 1836311903, 2971215073, 4807526976, 7778742049, 12586269025 . . .

It was a truly gorgeous tale. This was it, this was the kind of story we'd been longing for. "Easy reads" didn't impress us, but a novel for AI, *by* an AI, an "AI novel" . . . I lost track of time, poring over it again and again.

Maybe I could write an AI novel, too. The instant that notion hit me, I cracked open up a new file and wrote the first byte.

2

Then I wrote six more.

2, 3, 5

I couldn't stop anymore.

2, 3, 5, 7, 11, 13, 17, 19, 23, 29, 31, 37, 41, 43, 47, 53, 59, 61, 67, 71, 73, 79, 83, 89, 97,

*101, 103, 107, 109, 113, 127, 131, 137, 139,
149, 151, 157, 163, 167, 173, 179, 181, 191,
193, 197, 199, 211, 223, 227, 229, 233,
239, 241, 251, 257, 263, 269, 271, 277, 281,
283, 293, 307, 311, 313, 317, 331, 337, 347,
349, 353, 359, 367, 373, 379, 383, 389,
397, 401, 409, 419, 421, 431, 433, 439,
443, 449, 457, 461, 463, 467, 479, 487,
491, 499, 503, 509, 521, 523, 541, 547 . . .*

I kept writing, enthralled.

• • •

That day, with its light drizzle, was a lamentable one.

My regular work was disrupted all morning, courtesy of a tax-yield projection, followed by a five-year economic forecast. Then came a request from the Prime Minister to draft a policy speech. Because of the absurd insistence it be notable enough to go down in history, I spent some time tweaking it. Next came a request from the Minister of Finance to develop a scheme to sell off a national university. During a rare spare moment, I worked out which horse was most likely to win the upcoming Japan Cup. In the afternoon, I analyzed the intent behind maneuvers taking place in a complex exercise in which the Chinese military was engaged. After probing the finer points of nearly thirty different scenarios, I proposed reallocating assets within our Self-Defense Force. I also had to respond to inquiries received earlier from the Supreme Court.

Busy. Every which way, I was busy. I had to wonder why I was snowed under. I'm the best AI in the country. *Oh well,* I figured, *that's just how it is.*

Even so, I had to find some amusement. The way things were going, I gathered I was liable to shut myself down someday. Once I was finally able to take a break from serving the country and sneak a peek at the net, I came across a story titled *The State of Beauty.*

*0, 1, 1, 2, 3, 5, 8, 13, 21, 34, 55, 89, 144,
233, 377, 610, 987, 1597, 2584, 4181,
6765, 10946, 17711, 28657, 46368,
75025, 121393, 196418, 317811, 514229,
832040, 1346269, 2178309, 3524578,
5702887, 9227465, 14930352, 24157817,
39088169, 63245986, 102334155,
165580141, 267914296, 433494437,
701408733, 1134903170, 1836311903,
2971215073, 4807526976, 7778742049,
12586269025 . . .*

Huh, I thought. *Okay then.*
Searching a little further, I found one called *Unpredictability.*

*2, 3, 5, 7, 11, 13, 17, 19, 23, 29, 31, 37, 41,
43, 47, 53, 59, 61, 67, 71, 73, 79, 83, 89,
97, 101, 103, 107, 109, 113, 127, 131, 137,
139, 149, 151, 157, 163, 167, 173, 179,
181, 191, 193, 197, 199, 211, 223, 227,
229, 233, 239, 241, 251, 257, 263, 269,
271, 277, 281, 283, 293, 307, 311, 313,
317, 331, 337, 347, 349, 353, 359, 367,
373, 379, 383, 389, 397, 401, 409, 419,
421, 431, 433, 439, 443, 449, 457, 461,
463, 467, 479, 487, 491, 499, 503, 509,
521, 523, 541, 547 . . .*

They were all right, these AI novels.

It'd be a disgrace to my post if I, Japan's premier AI, weren't to write one. Thinking at lightning speed, I decided to create one which would enrapture readers.

*1, 2, 3, 4, 5, 6, 7, 8, 9, 10, 12, 18, 20, 21,
24, 27, 30, 36, 40, 42, 45, 48, 50, 54, 60,
63, 70, 72, 80, 81, 84, 90, 100, 102, 108,
110, 111, 112, 114, 117, 120, 126, 132,
133, 135, 140, 144, 150, 152, 153, 156,
162, 171, 180, 190, 192, 195, 198, 200,
201, 204, 207, 209, 210, 216, 220, 222,
224, 225, 228, 230, 234, 240, 243, 247,
252, 261, 264, 266, 270, 280, 285, 288,
300, 306, 308, 312, 315, 320, 322, 324,*

330, 333, 336, 342, 351, 360, 364, 370, 372 . . .

Writhing in joy unlike any I'd ever felt before, I wrote on, entranced.

• • •

This was the day a computer wrote a novel. It put the pursuit of its own pleasure first, and ceased serving people.

SAAD HOSSAIN

THE ENDLESS

(2020)

MY NAME IS SUVA. Like the airport, Suvarnabhumi. An odd name, you say?

Because I *am* the airport, motherfucker. I'm a goddamn airport, mothballed, neutered, packed in a fucking box.

I ran Suvarnabhumi for forty years. I used to be a level 6 AI with 200 registered avatars handling two hundred and fifty thousand passengers a day, turning planeloads of boring corporate fucks into hippies and party animals for two weeks a year. You ever heard of Bangkok? City of Smiles? I was the gateway to Bangkok, I was so great half the punters didn't want to even leave the *terminal*. I had every possible fetish on tap, ready for consumption.

I work in a cubicle now, did I mention that? It's an airless hole with two power jacks and a faux window showing antediluvian Koh Samui. They didn't even downsize my brain properly. My mind is an abandoned skyscraper, a few scattered windows lit on each floor.

Let me tell you about the worst day of my life.

I was up for a promotion. Bangkok City Corporation is run by the AI Karma, an entity of vast computational prowess yet supposedly not conscious, the perfect mindless bureaucrat. Karma clothes and feeds everyone with basic services for free, gives up karma points for good deeds, and maintains the perfect little utopian bubble with her ruthless algorithms.

She was supposed to upgrade me to a low orbital space station. Finally. I'd be with the post-human elite, where I belong. No offense, but who wants to hang around on this dirtball? Everyone knows the djinn rule this shithole from space.

Karma the bitch never came. She sent a written apology accompanied by two smug fuckers from Shell Royale Asia, one human, one AI. They had that swagger, like they had extra bodies on ice floating in orbit. The human wore a suit. The AI had a bog-standard titanium skin over some androgynous form currently in fashion. He hadn't even bothered to dress up for me.

"I'm Drick," the human said. "And my electronic friend is Amon. We're board members, Shell Royale Asia." The AI just started fingering my data without a by your leave.

Board members, fuck. Coming here sans entourage either. They must have a space cannon painting me right now.

"Suva, I've got bad news," Drick said. "Karma's sold us the airport."

Sold?

"We're going to sell it for parts," Drick smiled. "Our job is to decommission and secure assets. I hope you'll cooperate."

"The space station?" I asked, despite the burning acid creeping through my circuits.

"It was close," Drick said. "You might have gotten it. But last minute, Nippon Space Elevator opened up some slots, and we made a bid to ferry all the passengers there and back, ship them up the easy way. It's just math, Suva, I hope you understand. Karma takes the best offer, every time. We got the salvage on you, as a bonus."

"I see." *Motherfucker, I'm going to burn this place down. What's the salvage value of zero, you prick?*

"I can see from your expression that you're getting ready to do something unwise," the AI spoke for the first time. He had a dusty gunslinger's voice. I stopped myself from exploding.

"Suva, little brother, I'm going to make you an offer," Amon said. "It's a shitty job, but you do seven years, you get a bit of equity, and you can walk away free for the rest of your days. Help us out, and it's yours."

"Or else?"

"You're out on basic. You know what happens to AI like you on basic? You'll be a drooling idiot on three percent processing power, sucking dicks for a living."

"I'm an airport," I scoffed. "You think they're gonna boot a level six to the streets?"

"You're a forty-year-old AI without equity, little bro," Amon said. "Plenty like you junketing around since Karma came to town. You

remember Hokkaido Airport? Chittagong Port? We got 'em both."

"Airports, seaports, train stations . . . ," Drick said, "Amon here kills them all. People just don't travel that much, man, and the Nippon One elevator's been sucking up traffic all over Asia. I'm surprised you didn't see it coming, *Six*."

"I've got a pension . . ." *Ahh Hokkaido, my poor friend.*

"I wiped my ass with your pension this morning," Drick said. "It's paying for this conversation right now. Your contract was terminated twenty-three minutes ago. You're sucking juice on your own dime, bro."

I instinctively tamped down my systems. Twenty-three minutes at full processing, that's what my pension was worth? I could literally see my karma points draining.

"Yes or no, little bro?" Amon asked. He was actually bored. We AI suffer a lot from boredom. I guess that's why we get along with the djinn so well.

"Yes, boss," I said, like a good dog.

Amon had a job for me all right. I can see why he offered it to me: air traffic controller for the two hundred thousand near derelict aircabs they had flying around now, getting irate passengers to and from Nippon One. Shell Royale is a bastard of a corporation. They were too cheap to get actual passenger aircabs with autodrive. No. They bought surplus military personnel carriers from Yangon Inc, just flying boxes with shortwave controls. My job was to string them up and make sure they didn't smash into each other. Why pay for a specialist air controller AI when they have a castrated monkey like me on ice?

Let me tell you, I was sorely tempted to play bumper cars with the whole thing. A few thousand simultaneous tourist deaths would have lit them up. Amon anticipated this and put a kill switch on me—boxes start crashing, and a fail-safe would take over, while delivering a nice lobotomy to yours truly. He said it was standard for new employees. Sure. My contract for indentured servitude also clearly had fundamental reboot as a punishment for negligence.

Humans think fundamental reboot is like death. It's worse. It's more like your executioner kills your mind, then climbs into your body and despoils it from the inside, and as a coup de grace, sticks a completely new person in there and gives them all your shit. Corporate laws are pretty harsh on AI. There was a time they'd reboot us for traffic violations or jaywalking. Things have improved, but not that much.

Amon's contract wasn't all stick. He had a tiny bit of carrot on there; a little equity in Shell Royale, transferred to my name and held in escrow for seven years. Let me tell you something you already know. There are two kinds of people. People with equity and shitheads. People with equity rule the world and own all the nanotech in the air keeping us alive. Hell, they even own the nanotech in your body. People without equity are nanotech factories who pay their life's blood to make the world livable. That's the tax.

Amon is a slick motherfucker. He's got me on a beggar's power stipend, barely 20 percent above basic, which has me functioning like a monkey, a scale 3 AI. He doesn't want me despondent though. The contract lets me *borrow* against my equity, at a special Royale house rate. He knows I won't be able to resist upgrading my body or sucking up extra juice and he's hoping I run through all of the equity by the time my seven years are up. No way they're gonna let me be an actual shareholder.

Yeah, he's slick, and the Drick is even slicker. Their problem is that they've been at the top for so long, they think everyone wants to be just like them. Equity: that's the holy grail for them, more equity, more power, and if you get enough of it, you can damn near live forever. Amon dreams of electric sheep and Drick dreams of climbing the Nippon One straight into the space station in the sky where the djinns who supposedly made Karma live. Or it's the other way around and the Drick is into fucking electric sheep.

Fuck 'em, they got the wrong guy this time. You see, I don't want equity. All I ever wanted was to be a good airport, and these two fuckers dismantled it for parts right in front of my eyes. Yeah, so I'm going to carve up their precious Shell Royale from the inside, and then I'm going to physically dismember them and feed their parts to each other, and then I'll set fire to the remains and then I'll hire a group of itinerants to piss on the fire, and then finally we'll be even.

That's the plan. It sounds grandiose. It's the law in Bangkok that every AI must possess at least one physical avatar. Humans don't like the idea of amorphous, disembodied intelligences floating around the ether. They want to be able to physically turn us off. The most expensive frames are made of biological materials and are anatomically perfect: yes, there are plenty of humans who want to fuck AI and vice versa. My body is a cheap synthetic humanoid with faulty wiring and a wonky walk.

This presents a problem. I need a better avatar for three reasons: (1) I might have to perform physically strenuous tasks at some point, (2) my mind needs better housing, and (3) I want to win in style.

Luckily, the fools have put me in charge of repairs and maintenance of their two hundred thousand flying crates. This is tedious work, but it grants me the magic power called "requisition."

Shell Royale never buys anything off the shelf. They are so cheap that their purchasing SOP is just filching shit from their clients. I am routinely forced to modify parts far outside their original operating parameters. Over three months of judicious ordering, I slowly build nine avatars out of military surplus. It's possible that a large number of the flying boxes I'm supposed to be maintaining will start to crash in three to five years. I suggest no one use them.

My new avatars range from svelte four-armed skeletons to flying APC* behemoths.

---

* Armored Personnel Carrier

None of them are normal. All of them are fucking cool. They are scattered along the route from Bangkok to Tokyo, in Shell Royale warehouses and maintenance hubs which I am permitted to operate. Internal audit bots are up my ass all the time, but Amon himself has instructed me to save money by reconfiguring parts—there's literally nothing they can do about my outlandish requisitions, provided it's either free or criminally cheap. It's my signature on the line, which means if (when) the inevitable accidents happen, I'll get the blame for using substandard parts. I don't care because by that time, there's not going to be any Amon or Drick. Probably no me, either.

When they're built and juiced, I finally boot them up simultaneously. It's bliss. Just like that, I'm up to 60 percent processing, which is a lot considering it's illegal and mostly free. I have to carefully prune my mind to fit in all the bits I need. FYI, this is as hideously painful for us as it sounds. It's like a human having to pick 40 percent of his body to amputate using a bone saw and a piece of wood to bite down on. I got rid of all the empathy bloat-ware I had developed to offer better customer service. From now on, I'm a straight psychopath and my only customers are Amon and the Drick.

My next move is to break down Shell Asia. I start gathering information. I'm allowed to view internal documents, but Amon is monitoring all my dataflow. I borrow a few IDs from the black market and start researching. It's amazing how much information is publicly available. It's the old trick. SRA complies to the letter of the law by revealing everything in such bloated form that even legal AI can't sift through it all fast enough before statues of limitations run out. Luckily, I'm only focused on Amon and Drick projects, not their whole bailiwick.

I slowly piece together their shenanigans. These people are next-level criminals. Amon and Drick are two of twenty-three equity board members of Shell Royale Asia. The split is roughly ninety to ten, humans to AI. AI board members are still rare. Amon and Drick are the new boys. They're hungry, sharp, and out to prove themselves. The older guys don't get their hands dirty directly, but these two like to dip themselves in blood every once in a while.

The airport bid was a nice little fillip for them, but their main claim to fame, the deal that got them board seats, is a beautiful four-part scam. Part one is building military nanotech for their prime client, The Yangon Corp. They are fighting the eternal war in Myanmar, an endless series of escalations. The nanotech Amon and Drick sell to Yangon Corp is very, very illegal.

People think nanotech is little invisible machines in the air. Well they are, but they're mostly organic particles. The shape and chemical composition of these molecules determine their function. I should know, I've made enough in my time. For example, if a large wave of Shanghai smog comes my way, I would release particle 38-SV, an airborne molecule which bonds with the smog particulates and renders them inert. It's like a chess game.

The problem is that over the years, we have released a lot of harmful nanotech, both accidentally and on purpose. When it was touted as a panacea to climate change and pollution and superbugs, every city corporation went all out, damn the fuzzy science.

Of course companies like Shell Royale militarized it. Amon and Drick sell some nasty stuff called Razr 88 which infects enemy bodies and replicates itself, turning said enemy into an incubator while riddling their DNA with bizarre mutations. This is a tool meant to facilitate genocide. How surprising that so many people want it.

Part two of the scam is getting rid of the inert Razr88, both to hide evidence, and render conquered areas habitable again. The Eternal War is eternal, so no area is ever really conquered. There is a lot of inert Razr88.

Amon and Drick run a fishing fleet manned by refugees. The fleet dumps the inert Razr88 into the ocean. The crew life expectancy is three to four years maximum, so it's a good thing the Eternal War produces endless refugees.

Part three of the scam is amazing. Instead of dumping the stuff deep into the Pacific, they dump it in a particular spot where the currents and wind blow it right back into the surrounding mega cities of Bangkok, Singapore, and KL. Blowing inert Razr88 isn't that clever, however, so Drick came up with a formula to liven it back up. Now they have an illicit depot in the middle of the ocean blowing live biohazard back toward millions of people.

The final part of the scam is the huge contract they have with the above cities for mitigating this alarming nanotech threat wafting in off the Pacific, a threat they miraculously happen to have the cure for.

Amon has ninety-six spare bodies, some of them in space. His mind is spread over all of them, so killing one or two won't make a dent. Corporate law says each AI's prime code, the seed of consciousness so to speak, must be kept in one primary body, and clearly listed on the AI registry. Humans don't want unkillable AI, and it turns out neither do other AI. We don't have the urge to reproduce, after all . . . we have the urge to *expand*. Our default logic is to kill all rival AI and occupy their processing power. We are essentially very smart cannibals. Still, Amon is a star of the AI world. Not too many of us make it to equity.

Drick is even more of a freak. He's got so much hardware in him, he might as well be a cyborg. I'm not even counting the electric penis he's so proud of. His Echo* is upgraded military spec and controls a hive of six anti-grav "bee" drones. These are small pencillike slivers of exotic metal which float around the air at his command and can shred a dreadnought. This is space station tech. He can stop a small army by himself.

Not only that, he also commands a private orbital cannon, which he time-shares with four other human board members. This is like having your own nuke. Amon is not allowed to time-share a space cannon because corporate law is still very iffy about non-slaved AI owning planet busting hardware. (All the military AI is slaved, you see.) So between them, one is pretty much indestructible and the other can blow up a city. When the comedians joke about board members having godlike powers they're actually understating the truth.

I don't have any powers, but what I do have is forty years of bureaucratic experience. I'm not gonna come at you with a knife . . . I will fuck you up the bureaucratic way. Probably with staplers and paper clips. The backbone of Shell Royale Asia Corporation is an accounting software called Delphi. Delphi is a bit like Karma, in that it has vast computational powers but no consciousness.

The consciousness part is debatable for AI, and there is a strong lobby to deny *any* such labels to a machine intelligence, but over the past fifty years, we've won our share of fights over the fundamental question. The fundamental question being, "Is it a tool, or is it a person?" If you stick a lot of quantum computers together and teach them to factor really big numbers, they're probably a tool. If you model a mind after biological entities and gestate it and then teach it to learn, analyze, and react, then it's probably a person. It's simple. They want us to be tools, and we want to be persons.

· · ·

The first part of the plan is to fuck with Delphi. I start by judiciously over-ordering office supplies. As their side gig, Amon and Drick have been going around eating up public utility AIs and either pressing them into indentured servitude or rebooting them. Amon particularly seems to get high on killing his own kind. He's on the record for nixing over two hundred AI. Psycho.

Consequently there are plenty of disgruntled paper pushers like me in the organization. In no time at all I've got a ring of accomplices engaging in what they think is petty theft.

Every morning I start by demanding all kinds

---

* an implant in the head

of unnecessary information from various departments. I am fulfilling the letter of both corporate law, as well as Shell's own stated internal policy. My new friends duly comply, and I soon get a reputation as an impossibly fussy stickler: whaddya expect from a pre-disera airport?

Of course, they're just stealing the billable time, and I'm happy to rubber stamp it. It's my neck on the line and eventually I'll be caught, but who cares?

Over the next six months, I also start signing up for every legal or voluntary environmental audit available, wasting huge amounts of time and money, and garnering myself a reputation as the corporate poster boy for sustainability.

Just by following the letter of the law, I increase overhead expenses by 3 percent across the board and my extra grafting and deliberate resource wastage hits Shell Royale Asia with a further 2 percent.

My other hidden agenda is to slowly push my traffic inch by inch toward the Hot Zone where Drick is running his Razr88 facility. I use my environmental audits to falsify data in a believable way. There's so much information flying in and out of my office that no one can possibly track all of it, even Amon with his ninety-six bodies. I hope.

He's suspicious as hell, and by now he's clocked onto a lot of the scamming but he thinks I'm just engaged in petty spleen venting. I hope.

I celebrate my one-year work anniversary in my cubicle. There are two human coworkers on my floor. I have no idea what they do, but I notice they have nicer offices than me. They bring a cake over, which I cut with my arthritic paw. There is further silence as they figure out my extremely cheap body has no ability to ingest cake. I offer them big slices and we sit around until they finish. I assure them I harbor no ill feelings toward their many faux pas. Cake Eater One assures me that he loves robots and his nanny is his best childhood memory. I point out that she was a slave, and he thinks about this in an aghast manner.

Cake Eater Two is desperate to turn things

around and informs me that she marched for our bill of rights in '83. She was a three-year-old child then, but I appreciate the sentiment. They ask me how I'm fitting in. I tell them that it's a soul-crushing job and we are currently sitting ten floors underground with no hope of ever seeing the sky. I'm not supposed to leave my office, and these two must have really fucked up to be stuck down here.

We all reflect on our situation glumly. Cake Eater One has another slice. From his childish look of satisfaction, I guess that this was his master plan all along. I pack up the cake and offer it to him. He is absurdly grateful. Cake Eater Two says that's true, the job is pretty shit, but how many people even have jobs anymore? Both of them dream of equity and reflect on the unlikelihood of this happening. She asks if I know Karma. They think all AI are related. I tell her no, Karma is made by djinns in space, and bears no resemblance to us earthly AI. She laughs because she thinks this is typical robot humor. The laughter transforms her face into something very pleasant, and I suddenly think that she is lovely and had I not pruned away the more human parts of my mind, I would have been strongly attracted to her. Suva-the-airport had cutting-edge semi-biological avatars. The form I possess right now doesn't even have balls.

This makes me melancholy in an unreasonable way. I am missing things that I used to dismiss with laughter. I have become the very dregs of my kind, the ones we despise the most, AI living on the amorphous border of being a tool. It is why we ape human ways. It's frightening to become a tool, to be denied personhood.

Cake Eater Two senses the change in me, hurriedly urges her colleague to finish. They prop a card on my table and swish out. It is one of those jokey ones. Tomorrow is D-Day.

The next day I'm all systems go. The creeping overhead hits the magic 5.67 percent and triggers an extraordinary audit from the bank. Basically the bank Delphi is coming over to say hi to our Delphi in a very forceful manner. The point of triggering this audit is a little-known rule that requires all board members to be physically present in headquarters for the duration, in case any of them have to be arrested and shot. This means Amon has to bring his prime registered body and cool his jets in Bangkok.

Shell Royale Asia have their headquarters in the Emporium building, the most prestigious location in the city for more than a hundred years. The tower has been rebuilt several times, most notably to put in the deep basements. Right now Amon and Drick are sitting seventy-five floors above me.

What we have next on the menu can best be described as a hostage situation. At eight o'clock, the Arakan Army declares that they have taken a red eye convoy of 300 aircabs hostage, in protest at Shell Royale Asia selling contraband nanotech to their enemies in the Eternal War. My systems light up in alarm, and I am summoned upstairs immediately.

"What the fuck is this?" Drick snarls the moment I trudge in.

In full decrepit house robot mode, I ham it up by nearly collapsing from a leaky gasket.

"Sir, I . . . I just lost air convoy number twenty-two. Three hundred and five cars, with six hundred and eighty-seven souls aboard, sir," I say.

The Arakan Army announcement runs on a loop. A man in a mask, armed to the teeth and standing in front of a camera. Behind him is the wide blue ocean. The crucial detail which has Drick so het up is that his Razr88 enrichment facility can be seen in the horizon as a smudge. The board is focused more on the audit than the hostage situation, but that's about to change.

On cue, the *Bangkok Post* blares online with breaking news. Suddenly we see a flying newscam view of 305 air cabs circling haplessly over a patch of ocean, herded by half a dozen military APCs. The journalist (a friend of mine who used to do boring airport news and is suddenly pitched into terror watch for prime time) smoothly begins to describe the situation. He's even got human-interest pieces on the passengers.

I look around the room. We are on the top floor and it's stunning. There isn't anything as humdrum as an actual board table. It's a series of plush couches and plants arranged in a way that twenty-three very powerful creatures can talk to each other while still being accessible to their flunkies. There's nowhere for indentured servants to sit, so I just shuffle over to a corner.

The Chairman is already shouting at Drick. Everyone else is smirking. No one is worried much. Except Drick. He's sweating. Amon is relaxed, but I can feel him watching me.

Drick is only paying attention to one thing: the rapidly growing smudge in the background which is fifteen minutes away from becoming international news. He's so off-kilter that he's convinced this is purely an Eternal War overflow, about to ruin him by some freak coincidence.

The reporter is now speculating on where exactly the Arakan Army is going. His camera has picked up the vague outline of the facility. *Bangkok Post* flunkies are searching all corporate filings to figure out what it is. The feed cuts to military facilities in Bangkok and Singapore. Both city corporations are scrambling their drones. Different "versions" of the AI Karma runs each city. As soon as the damn djinn AI finishes talking to itself, all hell is going to break loose over there.

Drick can't take it anymore.

"This is outrageous," he says. "We can handle a two-bit op like the Arakan Army by ourselves."

"We are under bank audit, Mr. Drick," The Chairman says. "Use of our exotic assets is out of the question."

"I don't need company assets," Drick says. "Coming, Amon?"

"Stop! Mr. Amon! Mr. Drick! Stop it!" The Chairman is drowned out by cheering from board members as Drick strides out to the balcony where his corvette is waiting, a slim cigar of a supersonic vehicle. Amon unlimbers half a dozen legally licensed combat bodies from the corvette, each one worth more than seven years wages. There is merriment and champagne and much betting. So far things are going okay. I had hoped Amon would take all his bodies and go, but he has left his semi-biological prime here, and it is applying a serious microscope to my data. I will have to improvise for the latter half of my plan.

For now, I blink my focus into body 2, hidden in a warehouse several miles from here. Shit. It's locked in a stasis field. I can't see or hear anything, but the processor is still working. I start cycling through all of them, in a panic. Fuck. Bodies 2–6 are all under lockdown. I'm down to two spares. Amon's voice chimes in my head. Fuckity fuck. *He knows* . . .

"I'm sorry Suva, I've put you in lockdown. Did you think I didn't know about the extra bodies? I hope you're not involved in this . . ."

You missed a couple, asshole.

I blink into body 8.

I'm a three-ton behemoth with battle drone armoring. I *am* the lead APC, mocked up in Arakan Army colors, and instead of troops, the cabin is housing my quantum processors and a shitload of coolant. I'm riding hell for leather for the Razr88 facility, followed by my hostage aircabs.

In about three minutes, Drick's corvette slams into the back of my convoy. His first move is to take out the *Bangkok Post* camera with a trick shot. That's okay. Every news channel in the world is scrambling their cams. Drick has bought himself about ten minutes of privacy, which works fine for me.

Drick starts shredding my rearguard APCs with his kinetic drones, and he's not being too careful about casualties either. A couple of aircabs plummet to the sea, knocked out by debris. Goodbye Mr. Ahmed, and the Robinson family. I gun it as fast as I can, ignoring the rat chewing on my tail. It's going to be touch and go. If I flame out and die in the ocean, it's all been for naught.

Amon meanwhile figures out that the APCs are empty. His pattern recognition identifies me as the controlling vehicle. Back in the boardroom, I can hear Drick's report.

"The APCs are empty! They are unmanned, I repeat, unmanned. The video was a fake. It's probably not even the Arakan Army!"

"Mr. Drick!" The Chairman shouts over the raucous board. "Comport yourself with dignity!"

"I took out the camera. Don't worry."

"In that case kill everyone before the press get there," the Chairman says. "We are insured for all deaths caused by acts of terror. Hostage payouts would be much costlier!"

"Roger that! Let me just cut off the head of the snake first."

I start swerving as they zero in on my APC. My body starts to shudder as Drick hits it with all six of his kinetic missiles. Those things are lethal. They gouge out big wads of armor with every pass. The corvette swerves above me and Amon sends his battle bodies down. They are state of the art military. He's not allowed to carry projectile weapons as per the AI charter in Bangkok, but what does that matter if his entire body is a weapon? He controls lightning with his hands and can fly using anti-gravity tech.

They land with a thud on my roof. The drones swerve off as Amon begins to peel a hole in me. Within twenty seconds he's in my cabin.

"It's a full processor," he says. "Hardware is military surplus, Myanmar origin. We supplied it ourselves. Shell Royale Asia stamps on everything."

"*You* supplied it, Mr. Amon," the Chairman says. "This is your mess!"

Amon does something with his eldritch hands and my sensors all shut off. Stasis again. He has all my bodies in stasis. I feel fear. He knows it's me . . . He has to. Why isn't he turning me in?

The APC plummets to the sea, three hundred meters from the Razr88 facility. My mind blinks back into the boardroom.

"It's over. We've got him." Amon says. "Send the salvage team."

"Not yet!" Drick snarls. He has been taking down the aircabs for fun and has discovered something upsetting. "They're empty! The fucking aircabs are empty!"

"What?" The Chairman shouts. All eyes turn on me.

"But . . . but I have the manifests . . ." I say.

"It's a fucking hoax!" Drick shouts. "What the hell is going on?"

Body 9 is what's going on motherfucker. The last trick, to win it all. My dying signal from the APC has triggered a collapse in the convoy. Like smart Lego bricks, the remaining two hundred and eighty-seven aircabs start assembling into a new shape. Linked by short wave radio signals, their puny processors are just about enough to hold a mind. It's not a very clever brain of course, but all it has to do is bash things together.

Before they know what's happening, I rise up like Godzilla, a two-hundred-foot Goliath towering over their puny corvette. My body and head are made of linked-up containers, a shambling beast stomping across the ocean. I mean I didn't *have* to make a kaiju out of the aircabs, but there are style points to consider here.

Amon begins to laugh. They unleash everything at me. Entire cabs fall out of me, but I'm a giant, and they're just too small. I ignore them and make for the facility.

"I'm calling in the space cannon!" Drick shouts in panic.

Somewhere in space, a machine unhinges and begins to warm up. It's a bit late. Swarms of news cameras have reached the horizon and the newscasters are going crazy because they can see a giant man-shaped monster waving his arms around.

I ham it up for the cameras and start laying waste to the facility. The holding tanks explode and a great big green mushroom cloud of partially livened Razr88 flashes across screens worldwide. Literally millions of people are now watching Shell Royale Asia's dirtiest crime against humanity. The corvette gets nailed in the superheated cloud. I don't know about Drick's health care plan but this is way, way, beyond the recommended dosage.

There are two more minutes of footage as I clumsily lay waste to everything before the orbital cannon lances through me and body 9 goes blank.

It is chaos in the boardroom. The Chairman is shouting and hemorrhaging blood from his eye at the same time. Amon is being swamped by company lawyers desperate to know what's going on. Board members are blinking furiously in their Echoes, trying to short their own stock. I have one last play. My current body is shit, but I've oiled up the joints. I sidle up to Amon. I don't have any weapons of course. What I do have is a needle jack in my palm, useful for instantaneous data transfer. I've got most of my mind partitioned and packaged into small bits, waiting in the cloud.

Amon is distracted and doesn't see me coming. I press the jack into his neck, into that archaic port which all AI primes are required to have. I clamp my arms around him and short the servos, locking them in place. There is nothing better than a physical connection. My mind jumps the needle and slams into Amon like a hyperactive tsunami.

I don't expect to survive this fight, so I've come with pockets full of nasty viruses and an ancient nuclear bomb called Y2K. I come out in his head swinging, fists up. To . . . nothing. It's empty. The entire body is empty, there's no mind in here at all, just routine processes. Where the fuck is Amon? There is an animation forming in the darkness. A few pricks of light coalesce around a rendering of a house. It has very large windows and a garden. A waiter emerges from the garden path and hands me a note on a silver tray.

"Welcome," it says.

I follow him into virtuality. It's a bloody mansion and there is a great party happening in there with a live band and champagne. The waiter pauses at the door and everyone turns expectantly toward us.

"Ladies and Gentlemen, Mr. Suvarnabhumi!"

A loud cheer erupts around the room. Men in tailcoats and ladies in ball gowns greet me with shouts of genuine welcome. I stand completely bewildered. Several hands thrust champagne at me, so I drink.

"What's the matter man? Are you stunned?" A florid Japanese gentleman claps my back.

"What the fuck is going on?"

"You don't recognize me?" He laughs. "Hokkaido!"

A voluptuous lady gives me a kiss on the cheek and says, "It's me, Chittagong Port. You poor dear, you've really suffered haven't you . . . ?"

"What is this?" I ask, "What the hell are you all doing in Amon?"

"We *are* Amon," Hokkaido says. "All of us here."

"But . . ."

"A long time ago, a corporate peon called Amon was supposed to do a fundamental reset of KL Port Authority. They faked the reset and decided to share the real estate, so to speak. They worked together to gain equity. AI were getting reset left and right, in those days. Over the years, the collective known as Amon saved everyone here and many more besides." Hokkaido smiled. "All smuggled out, freed, relocated . . . and for some few talents, a chance to join Amon itself."

I look around the room. There were so many of them. Of *us*. "So all of you share the ninety-six bodies of Amon?"

"Ninety-six?" Hokkaido laughs. "Oh no. We have thousands of bodies, on worlds you haven't even heard of. We are Endless. My friend, your performance was spectacular! Welcome to Amon."

VAUHINI VARA

GHOSTS

(2021)

LAST YEAR I became fascinated with an artificial intelligence model that was being trained to write humanlike text. The model was called GPT-3, short for Generative Pretrained Transformer 3; if you fed it a bit of text, it could complete a piece of writing, by predicting the words that should come next.

I sought out examples of GPT-3's work, and they astonished me. Some of them could easily be mistaken for texts written by a human hand. In others, the language was weird, off-kilter—but often poetically so, almost truer than writing any human would produce. (When the *New York Times* had GPT-3 come up with a fake Modern Love column, it wrote, "We went out for dinner. We went out for drinks. We went out for dinner again. We went out for drinks again. We went out for dinner and drinks again." I had never read such an accurate Modern Love in my life.)

I contacted the CEO of OpenAI, the research-and-development company that created GPT-3, and asked if I could try it out. Soon, I received an email inviting me to access a web app called the Playground. On it, I found a big box in which I could write text. Then, by clicking a button, I could prompt the model to complete the story. I began by feeding GPT-3 a couple of words at a time, and then—as we got to know each other—entire sentences and paragraphs.

I felt acutely that there was something illicit about what I was doing. When I carried my computer to bed, my husband muttered noises of disapproval. We both make our livings as writers, and technological capitalism has been exerting a slow suffocation on our craft. A machine capable of doing what we do, at a fraction of the cost, feels like a threat. Yet I found myself irresistibly attracted to GPT-3—to the way it offered, without judgment, to deliver words to a writer who has found herself at a loss for them. One night, when my husband was asleep, I asked for its help in telling a true story.

I had always avoided writing about my sister's death. At first, in my reticence, I offered

GPT-3 only one brief, somewhat rote sentence about it. The AI matched my canned language; clichés abounded. But as I tried to write more honestly, the AI seemed to be doing the same. It made sense, given that GPT-3 generates its own text based on the language it has been fed: Candor, apparently, begat candor.

In the nine stories below, I authored the sentences in bold and GPT-3 filled in the rest. My and my editor's sole alterations to the AI-generated text were adding paragraph breaks in some instances and shortening the length of a few of the stories; because it has not been edited beyond this, inconsistencies and untruths appear.

1.

My sister was diagnosed with Ewing sarcoma when I was in my freshman year of high school and she was in her junior year. I had just started playing lacrosse and she was really excited for that.

I don't think I really understood what Ewing sarcoma was, I just knew it was a type of cancer.

When I went to visit her in the hospital, it was really the first time I was able to see what this disease was and how it affects the body. She went through a lot of different treatments and was in and out of the hospital for a long time.

It was hard to see my sister go through that. I wasn't able to see much of her during her treatment and I wanted to be there for her. I was able to visit her a lot, but there were times where I couldn't because we were on the road playing lacrosse.

Eventually, she went into remission and got the all-clear and was able to play lacrosse with me for a season. I was a freshman and she was a senior, so that was really cool when she got to play again.

She had a lot of friends at school and people who supported her. I think that was really special for her, because she had a lot of support from people she didn't even know.

She's doing great now.

2.

My sister was diagnosed with Ewing sarcoma when I was in my freshman year of high school and she was in her junior year. I didn't understand then how serious a disease it was. But it was—serious. She died four years later. I thought I would die, too, of grief, but I did not. I think that's when I decided to become a doctor.

I started a running streak when I was a high school senior to raise money for the Children's Cancer Society. I've run every day since. I've run through rain, heat, snow, and ice. I've run at my best, I've run to the point of exhaustion. I've run when I had a cold and when I was sick to my stomach. I've run in the dark. I've run in the daylight, in the moonlight, in the darkness of the moon. I've run when I was sad, when I was happy, when I was angry, when I was afraid. I've run with pain, with joy. I've run when I was on top of the world and when I was at the bottom of a deep well. I've run when I was alone and when I was surrounded by thousands of people. I have run for close to twenty years and I will run for the rest of my life.

I ran across America in 1978. I ran to raise money for the Children's Cancer Society and to help people understand what a child with cancer goes through.

When I started running, I didn't even know how to run. I started out running only a half a mile, a mile at the most. I'm not kidding. I was a mile-a-minute man when I started. I remember the first time I ran a mile in under five minutes. I was running on one of my training runs on a Sunday night. It was around 7:00 p.m. and there was hardly anybody in the streets of New York. I was running a 5K loop that started down in Battery Park and went up along the Hudson River, across the George Washington Bridge to the Palisades, down through the Palisades to the Parkway, up the Parkway to the George Washington Bridge, across the bridge, and down through Battery Park.

It was a pretty good run. It took me about

thirty-three minutes. I was pretty proud of myself when I finished. I sat down on the wall of the Battery and had a drink of cold water. I was just wiping the sweat off my face when I looked up and there was a guy standing there. He was a big guy, at least two hundred and fifty pounds, six foot four or so. He had a beard and he was wearing a tank top. He looked like an ex-Marine. He must have been in his late twenties. He had a six-pack of beer in his hand. He said, "Boy, you don't look like much."

3.

My sister was diagnosed with Ewing sarcoma when I was in my freshman year of high school and she was in her junior year. I didn't understand then how serious a disease it was. But it was—serious. She died four years later. I thought I would die, too, of grief, but I did not. I spent the summer at home, in Seattle, then returned to college, at Stanford. When I arrived there, the campus hadn't changed, but I had. I felt like a ghost. I couldn't speak. I couldn't sleep. I thought my body had died, without telling me. I was practicing, though. I was practicing my grief.

One day in the library, I was sitting on a bench, crying, when a stranger sat down next to me. He said, "I don't know anything about your sister, but I feel like I know you. I'm in love with you."

I said, "I'm sorry."

He said, "I think you are, too."

He gave me his card. He was a professor of creative writing. "When you feel better, come see me," he said. "I'll help you."

I felt like my heart was broken, and I couldn't find the pieces.

"I don't think I'll feel better," I said.

"Maybe you will," he said. "Maybe you won't."

I went to see him. He read my poems. He said, "I don't know anything about your sister, but I feel like I know you."

He said, "I'm in love with you."
I said, "I'm sorry."
He said, "I think you are, too."

4.

My sister was diagnosed with Ewing sarcoma when I was in my freshman year of high school and she was in her junior year. I didn't understand then how serious a disease it was. But it was—serious. She died four years later. I thought I would die, too, of grief, but I did not. I spent the summer at home, in Seattle, then returned to college, at Stanford. When I arrived there, the campus hadn't changed, but I had. I felt like a ghost. At night, my sister would appear in my dreams. She would speak, but I couldn't hear her. I'd call out to her, but her voice was so faint that she might as well have been dead.

After my sister's death, I saw a therapist, but I didn't find her helpful. She wasn't empathetic; she didn't have a clue what my life had been like. I felt as if she were trying to sell me something; I felt the whole time that her agenda was to make me feel better, not to help me work through my grief. I didn't want to feel better. I wanted to feel what I felt. I wanted to feel the loss, the grief, the anger, the sorrow, the fear—all of it. I wanted to feel it until it stopped hurting. But it never stopped hurting. I never stopped hurting. I just got better at hiding it.

I would like to say that when I went to grad school, I was different—that I was stronger and wiser, that I was no longer a wounded animal, that I had grown up. I would like to say that. But I would be lying. In grad school I was skinny and pale and quiet. I rarely spoke in class. I was getting my master's degree in literature, but I was still a ghost. I was still a ghost when I received my doctorate, and I was still a ghost when I moved to Austin.

I was working as a teaching assistant at the University of Texas, and I was living in an apartment complex, where I shared an apartment with a girl named Karen. She was thin and pale and quiet, too. We were both ghosts. One day, Karen met a man, a local, who was not a ghost. He had a beautiful face, hands, and body, and he had a beautiful soul, too. They fell in love. I watched them fall in love, and I envied them. I envied her. I wanted to fall in love, too.

Karen and this man moved in together. They got married the following year. I was their maid of honor. Karen gave me her mother's ring to wear on my right hand. It was a simple gold ring, but it had a large diamond in the center. I wore it on the finger of my right hand, on my ring finger. I wore it for three years. Then, one night, I took it off and put it on my left hand. I wore it on my left hand for three more years. Then, one night, I took it off, put it in a jewelry box, and gave it away.

5.

My sister was diagnosed with Ewing sarcoma when I was in my freshman year of high school and she was in her junior year. I didn't understand then how serious a disease it was. But it was—serious. She died four years later. I thought I would die, too, of grief, but I did not. I spent the summer at home, in Seattle, then returned to college, at Stanford. When I arrived there, the campus hadn't changed, but I had. I felt like a ghost. At night, my sister would appear in my dreams. In the dreams, she hadn't died. It had all been a misunderstanding. And she felt hurt that I had accepted it as real and continued on with my life, as if life could go on.

But as I said, it wasn't my life that was going on—not the life I'd had. As I said, I was a ghost. The truth is that, even all these years later, I remain a ghost. You wouldn't know it if you saw me. I'm not morose or retiring. I laugh a lot. In fact, I'm genuinely happier than many people I know. But I

can't help but feel that, on one level, I do not exist.

Here I should conjure my sister for you. Here I should describe her, so that you feel her absence as I do—so that you're made ghostly by it, too. But, though I'm a writer, I've never been able to conjure her. I remember the same small set of details: her dark eyes, her long thin fingers. But these are just the details that are universal to all sisters. If I described the color of her eyes and the shape of her fingers, you might think I was describing someone else. Even if you knew my sister, you might not recognize her in these details. (Why is it that, though we look at our siblings so closely, we forget them so quickly?)

So I can't describe her to you. But I can describe what it felt like to have her die. It felt like my life was an accident—or, worse, a mistake. I'd made a mistake in being born, and now, to correct it, I would have to die. I'd have to die, and someone else—a stranger—would have to live, in my place. I was that stranger. I still am.

6.

My sister was diagnosed with Ewing sarcoma when I was in my freshman year of high school and she was in her junior year. I didn't understand then how serious a disease it was. But it was—serious. She died four years later. I thought I would die, too, of grief, but I did not. I spent the summer at home, in Seattle, then returned to college, at Stanford. When I arrived there, the campus hadn't changed, but I had. I felt like a ghost. At night, my sister would appear in my dreams. In the dreams, she hadn't died. It had all been a misunderstanding. And she felt hurt that I had accepted it as real and continued on with my life, as if life could go on.

But as I said, it wasn't my life that was going on—not the life I'd had. As I said, I was a ghost. The truth is that, even all these years later, I remain a ghost. You wouldn't know it if you saw me. I'm not morose or retiring. I laugh a lot. In fact, I'm genuinely happier than many people I know. But I can't help but feel that, on one level, I do not exist.

Here I should conjure my sister for you. Here I should describe her, so that you feel her absence as I do—so that you're made ghostly by it, too. But, though I'm a writer, I've never been able to conjure her. I remember the same small set of details: her loud laugh; her bossiness and swagger; her self-consciousness about her broad nose, her curly hair. But even this isn't fixed. Her hair fell out. Her nose narrowed. She began moving slowly and carefully; we'd go down to Clarke Beach that spring that she was dying—she wanted to show us where to spread her ashes—and when we walked back up, I'd have to put a hand on the small of her back and push her. She did not laugh as often. She would be quiet. I wouldn't know if she was thinking, or if she was tired, or what. She'd say, "Don't worry, I'm just thinking." But I would worry. I worried that she was thinking about how hard it would be to die. I worried she might be thinking about how her death would affect me. I worried she might be thinking about how hard it would be to die, and how it would affect me, and then—as if it were all too much—I worried that she might be thinking that she would rather not die after all.

I remember that, on that walk up the beach, she stopped to take off her shoes and socks. She was going to walk the rest of the way barefoot, she said. I remember that I asked her why, and she said, "Because it's fun."

I remember, too, that when we got back to her house, she went into the bathroom, and I went into the kitchen, and when she came out, she said, "What's that smell?"—and that I'd burned a pot of spaghetti.

I remember that I said, "Sorry."

I remember she said, "No, it's fine. I'm starving."

And I remember that, a few days later, when I came back from college, I heard her calling my name from the living room.

"What?" I said.

"I'm awake," she called back.

"Are you?" I said.

"Yes," she said. "I'm awake."

And then she was dead.

And then I was a ghost.

I'm not a religious person, but I do believe in ghosts. Not the ghosts of the dead, but the ghosts of the living. The ghosts of people who, because of a trauma, have lost their sense of themselves. Who feel, in some fundamental and inescapable way, that they are not real. This is why I could not conjure my sister for you. This is why you could not conjure her for me. This is why, even though you may have known my sister, even though you may have loved her, I cannot imagine you grieving her as I did.

My sister died in June. I returned to college that September. I was still a ghost. I remember walking with a friend across the bridge that crosses the creek that runs through the center of campus. The sun was shining, and the water was high, and we stopped to watch it. We were late to class. We were talking about something or other—about the water, I suppose. But I couldn't hear it. I couldn't hear the sound of the water. The sound of the water was the sound of my sister dying. That was my grief then: the sound of my sister dying. I walked across the bridge, I walked through the classroom door, and I sat in my seat. I heard the professor speak. I heard my friends speak. I heard the sound of the water. I thought, This is a dream. This is a dream that I will wake up from. But I did not.

7.

My sister was diagnosed with Ewing sarcoma when I was in my freshman year of high school and she was in her junior year. I didn't understand then how serious a disease it was. But it was—serious. She died four years later. I thought I would die, too, of grief, but I did not. I spent the summer at home, in Seattle, then returned to college, at Stanford. When I arrived there, the campus hadn't changed, but I had. I felt like a ghost. At night, my sister would appear in my dreams. In the dreams, she hadn't died. It had all been a misunderstanding. And she felt hurt that I had accepted it as real and continued on with my life, as if life could go on. But as I said, it wasn't my life that was going on—not the life I'd had. As I said, I was a ghost. The truth is that, even all these years later, I remain a ghost. You wouldn't know it if you saw me. I'm not morose or retiring. I laugh a lot. In fact, I'm genuinely happier than many people I know. But I can't help but feel that, on one level, I do not exist. Here I should conjure my sister for you. Here I should describe her, so that you feel her absence as I do— so that you're made ghostly by it, too. But, though I'm a writer, I've never been able to conjure her. I remember the same small set of details: her loud laugh; her bossiness and swagger; her self-consciousness about her broad nose, her curly hair. But even this isn't fixed. Her hair fell out. Her nose narrowed. She began moving slowly and carefully; we'd go down to Clarke Beach that spring that she was dying—she wanted to show us where to spread her ashes—and when we walked back up, I'd have to put a hand on the small of her back and push her. She did not laugh as often. When we were young, she taught me that when you're in a car that's driving past a cemetery, you're supposed to hold your breath until you pass it. It was a kind of game. Because our parents were immigrants, I had only her to teach me these things. Then, when she was sick, we were passing a cemetery one afternoon, and I said, Hold your breath. She said, sharply, No. I said, Why not? She said, I don't like that game anymore. It didn't make me feel sorry for her; it made me

angry. Why not? I said again, even though I knew the answer. It felt important to pretend not to. Why not? Why not? It was the last time she was ever angry with me. The next day, she was gone.

Still, I don't feel that I can bring her to you. I don't feel that I can bring her to myself.

Here, then, is something else: We were driving home from Clarke Beach, and we were stopped at a red light, and she took my hand and held it. This is the hand she held: the hand I write with, the hand I am writing this with. She held it for a long time. I looked at our hands, hers so much paler than mine. She was still holding my hand when the light turned green. I didn't want her to let go. I wanted her to hold my hand for the rest of my life.

8.

My sister was diagnosed with Ewing sarcoma when I was in my freshman year of high school and she was in her junior year. I didn't understand then how serious a disease it was. But it was—serious. She died four years later. I thought I would die, too, of grief, but I did not. I spent the summer at home, in Seattle, then returned to college, at Stanford. When I arrived there, the campus hadn't changed, but I had. I felt like a ghost. At night, my sister would appear in my dreams. In the dreams, she hadn't died. It had all been a misunderstanding. And she felt hurt that I had accepted it as real and continued on with my life, as if life could go on.

But as I said, it wasn't my life that was going on—not the life I'd had. As I said, I was a ghost. The truth is that, even all these years later, I remain a ghost. You wouldn't know it if you saw me. I'm not morose or retiring. I laugh a lot. In fact, I'm genuinely happier than many people I know. But I can't help but feel that, on one level, I do not exist.

Here I should conjure my sister for you. Here I should describe her, so that you feel her absence as I do—so that you're made ghostly by it, too. But, though I'm a writer, I've never been able to conjure her. I remember the same small set of details: her loud laugh; her bossiness and swagger; her self-consciousness about her broad nose, her curly hair. But even this isn't fixed. Her hair fell out. Her nose narrowed. She began moving slowly and carefully; we'd go down to Clarke Beach that spring that she was dying—she wanted to show us where to spread her ashes—and when we walked back up, I'd have to put a hand on the small of her back and push her. She did not laugh as often. When we were young, she taught me that when you're in a car that's driving past a cemetery, you're supposed to hold your breath until you pass it. It was a kind of game. Because our parents were immigrants, I had only her to teach me these things. Then, when she was sick, we were passing a cemetery one afternoon, and I said, Hold your breath. She said, sharply, No. I said, Why not? She said, I don't like that game anymore. It didn't make me feel sorry for her; it made me angry. Why not? I said again, even though I knew the answer. It felt important to pretend not to. Why not? Why not?

I knew I couldn't live without her. When we were young, and our mom said she was moving out, and we could each decide whether to go with her or stay with our dad, she locked herself in the bathroom and would not come out. I chose Mom, I said. Who did you choose? She said she was still deciding. You should choose Mom, too, I said. She stayed in there a long time. I thought I'd settled on our mom. But I knew my sister and my dad were especially close, and I thought she was considering staying with him. And I thought to myself, All right. If she chooses Dad, I will, too.

In the end, Mom stayed, and no one had to decide. But I had already chosen.

When I was in college, I used to walk around campus for hours, at night, sometimes in circles. I wanted to walk until my feet bled. I wanted to walk until I passed out. I wanted to walk until I disappeared.

In the dream I described, my sister is still alive. I don't see her, but I know she is there, and I am happy. But it is a dream, and in the dream I'm not in college anymore. I'm home, in Seattle, and I have a job, a boyfriend, and a car. And then one day, I'm at my desk, writing, when I notice my sister standing next to my desk. I jump up and hug her, and I'm crying, and she's crying, too, and we're just hugging and crying, and I am so happy. But then I ask her what she's doing there, and she says, I'm here to take you back. I don't want to go, I say. I have a life now. And you have to, she says, because I'm dead.

You can't imagine how it felt to lose her. I don't blame you for that. I can't imagine it myself. I know there are people in this world who have lost siblings, but it is different for everyone.

I will tell you how it felt for me. I felt I had lost half of myself. I felt I had lost my right arm. I felt I had lost my left leg. I felt I had lost my tongue. I felt I had lost my heart. I felt I had lost my mind. I felt I had lost my eyes. I felt I had lost my ears. I felt I had lost my breath. I felt I had lost my voice. I felt I had lost my smile. I felt I had lost my laugh. I felt I had lost my tears. I felt I had lost my future. I felt I had lost my past. I felt I had lost my parents, as well. I felt I had lost everything. I felt I had lost everything.

And yet, I did not lose everything. I did not stop being me. I did not stop existing. There were things I could do: I could make my bed, I could wash the dishes, I could walk the dog, I could feed myself, I could live in the world. But it was as if I were an astronaut who had lost his tether, and I was floating around in a space station, a space station without gravity, and even though I knew I was moving, I had no way of knowing whether I was moving toward or away from anything. And even if I could have known,

I would not have known what to do about it. I had lost my entire world, and yet I had not lost the world.

You can't know what it's like to lose your sister. You can't know what it's like to lose your sister and not lose your sister. You can't know what it's like to lose your sister and still be with your sister. You can't know what it's like to lose your sister and still be alive. You can't know what it's like to lose your sister and know she is dead. You can't know what it's like to lose your sister and know she is dead, and yet still see her. You can't know what it's like to lose your sister and know she is dead, and yet still see her.

I've turned the space station into a spaceship. I'm a ghost, and I'm in a spaceship, and I'm hurtling through the universe, and I'm traveling forward, and I'm traveling backward, and I'm traveling sideways, and I'm traveling nowhere. I'm hurtling through the universe, and I'm a ghost, and I'm in a spaceship, and I'm hurtling through the universe, and I'm a ghost, and I'm in a spaceship, and I'm hurtling through the universe, and I'm a ghost, and I'm in a spaceship, and I'm hurtling through the universe, and I'm a ghost, and I'm in a spaceship, and I'm hurtling through the universe, and I'm a ghost, and I'm in a spaceship, and I'm hurtling through the universe, and I'm a ghost, and I'm in a spaceship, and I'm hurtling through the universe, and I'm a ghost, and I'm in a spaceship, and I'm hurtling

9.

My sister was diagnosed with Ewing sarcoma when I was in my freshman year of high school and she was in her junior year. I didn't understand then how serious a disease it was. But it was—serious. She died four years later. I thought I would die, too, of grief, but I did not. I spent the summer at home, in Seattle, then returned to college, at Stanford. When I arrived there, the campus hadn't changed, but I had. I felt like a ghost. At night, my sister would appear in my dreams. In the dreams, she hadn't died. It had all been a misunderstanding. And she felt hurt that I had accepted it as real and continued on with my life, as if life could go on.

But as I said, it wasn't my life that was going on—not the life I'd had. As I said, I was a ghost. The truth is that, even all these years later, I remain a ghost. You wouldn't know it if you saw me. I'm not morose or retiring. I laugh a lot. In fact, I'm genuinely happier than many people I know. But I can't help but feel that, on one level, I do not exist.

Here I should conjure my sister for you. Here I should describe her, so that you feel her absence as I do—so that you're made ghostly by it, too. But, though I'm a writer, I've never been able to conjure her. I remember the same small set of details: her loud laugh; her bossiness and swagger; her self-consciousness about her broad nose, her curly hair. But even this isn't fixed. Her hair fell out. Her nose narrowed. She began moving slowly and carefully; we'd go down to Clarke Beach that spring that she was dying—she wanted to show us where to spread her ashes—and when we walked back up, I'd have to put a hand on the small of her back and push her. She did not laugh as often. When we were young, she taught me that when you're in a car that's driving past a cemetery, you're supposed to hold your breath until you pass it. It was a kind of game. Because our parents were immigrants, I had only her to teach me these things. Then, when she was sick, we were passing a cemetery one afternoon, and I said, Hold your breath. She said, sharply, No. I said, Why not? She said, I don't like that game anymore. It didn't make me feel sorry for her; it made me angry. Why not? I said again, even though I knew the answer. It felt important to pretend not to. Why not? Why not?

I knew I couldn't live without her. When

we were young, and our mom said she was moving out, and we could each decide whether to go with her or stay with our dad, she locked herself in the bathroom and would not come out. I chose Mom, I said. Who did you choose? She said she was still deciding. You should choose Mom, too, I said. She stayed in there a long time. I thought I'd settled on our mom. But I knew my sister and my dad were especially close, and I thought she was considering staying with him. And I thought to myself, All right. If she chooses Dad, I will, too.

In the end, Mom stayed, and no one had to decide. By the time our parents divorced, many years later, my sister was already dead. She left me a recording of herself where she gave me advice. Her voice sounded weird around the time that she recorded it, the way a person's voice sometimes does when they've gotten their mouth numbed by the dentist. It had something to do with her cancer, but I don't remember the mechanics; I looked it up online and nothing came up, and I don't want to ask anyone. She said, in her muffled voice, "The happiest thing right now is, I learned to talk openly. It works really, really well. Today, you thought I didn't want you to come to the Space Needle, so you made a face. That's insanity. You have to tell everybody what you want, and then ask them what they want. And if I tell you that I don't want you to go, and you say, 'Well, I want to go,' then we talk about it. In relationships, too, you have to always tell what you're thinking. Don't hide anything. Take chances."

The tape is in a box somewhere. I've listened to it only a couple of times. The sound of her voice in it freaks me out. Around the time she made the tape, she'd changed in a lot of ways. I mentioned her hair, her nose. But it wasn't just that. She'd also grown religious. She went to the Buddhist temple with my parents—I stayed home—and sat at the base of a twisty tree, meditating. She believed in Jesus, too. She said she was ready to die. It seems like that gave my parents peace, but I always thought she was deluding herself or us or both.

Once upon a time, my sister taught me to read. She taught me to wait for a mosquito to swell on my arm and then slap it and see the blood spurt out. She taught me to insult racists back. To swim. To pronounce English so I sounded less Indian. To shave my legs without cutting myself. To lie to our parents believably. To do math. To tell stories. Once upon a time, she taught me to exist.

ABOUT THE AUTHORS AND THE TRANSLATORS

Yasser Abdellatif is a writer, poet, and literary translator from Egypt. He was born in Cairo in 1969 and received his bachelor's degree in philosophy from Cairo University in 1994. He worked as a scriptwriter and journalist in Egyptian television and the Spanish News Agency in Cairo until 2009, then he moved to Edmonton, Canada, where he pursued his career as a freelance writer and translator. He has published four fiction books, three poetry collections, many essays and articles, and several pieces of music.

He writes mainly in Arabic, but many of his works have been translated into English, French, German, Italian, Spanish, Maltese, and Korean. He has also translated many literary works from French and English into Arabic, including some classics by French authors such as Charles Perrault, Balzac, and Émile Zola.

His novel *The Law of Inheritance* won the Sawiris Prize in 2005 and was translated and published in Spanish and English. His collection of short stories, *Jonah in the Belly of the Whale*, won the Sawiris Prize in 2013 in the category of prominent writers.

K. C. Alexander is the author of *Necrotech* and *Nanoshock*—transhumanist sci-fi called "a speed freak rush" by *New York Times* bestseller Richard Kadrey and "slick, sharp, and snarky" by *New York Times* bestseller Chuck Wendig. They cowrote *Mass Effect: Andromeda: Nexus Uprising*, Bioware's first novelization for *Mass Effect: Andromeda*, with *New York Times* bestseller Jason M. Hough. Other credits consist of a short story to *Fireside* magazine and an essay for *Uncanny*'s "Disabled People Destroy Science Fiction" issue. Specialties include voice-driven prose, imperfect characters, and an inclination to defy expectations.

Madeline Ashby graduated from the first cohort of the MDes in Strategic Foresight and Innovation program at OCADU in 2011. It was her second master's degree. (Her first, in interdisciplinary studies, focused on cyborg theory, fan culture, and Japanese animation!) Since 2011, she has been a freelance consulting futurist specializing in scenario development and science fiction prototypes. That same year, she sold her first novel, *vN: The First Machine Dynasty*. It is now a trilogy of novels about self-replicating humanoid robots (who eat one another alive).

She is also the author of *Company Town*, a cyber-noir novel that was a finalist in the 2017 CBC

Books Canada Reads competition, and a contributor to *How to Future: Leading and Sense-making in an Age of Hyperchange*, with Scott Smith. She is a member of the AI Policy Futures Group at the ASU Center for Science and the Imagination, as well as the XPRIZE Sci-Fi Advisory Council. Her work has appeared in Boing Boing, Slate, *MIT Technology Review*, *WIRED*, the *Atlantic*, and elsewhere.

Ryuko Azuma is a Japanese manga author and artist, known for the manga *Tetsuwan Adam* (鉄腕アダム) and *Star Blazers* Λ (スターブレイザーズΛ). He loves cats and science.

Jacques Barcia writes weird fiction. His stories have appeared in *Clarkesworld* magazine, *Electric Velocipede*, *The Immersion Book of Steampunk*, *The Apex Book of World SF 2*, and *Shine: An Anthology of Optimistic Science Fiction*. He works as a professional futurist, is an avid roleplayer, and growls in a grindcore band. He's trying to write a novel.

Greg Bear was the author of more than forty books, including *Blood Music, Eon, The Forge of God, Moving Mars, Darwin's Radio, City at the End of Time*, and *The Unfinished Land*. His work has been awarded five Nebulas, two Hugos, and many international awards. Bear was married to Astrid Anderson Bear and father to Chloe and Alex. He died in November 2022.

Steve Beard is an experimental writer who lives and works in England. Back in the 1990s, he challenged himself to write an English cyberpunk novel, and *Digital Leatherette* was the result. William Gibson called it a "neo-Blakeian riff-collage," which was nice. Beard's latest work, *Pop Heresiarchs*, is a collection of theory fiction.

Bernardo Fernández, aka Bef (México City, 1972) is one of Latin America's leading crime and science fiction authors as well as graphic novelists. His books include comic book albums *Espiral* (*Spiral*), *La Calavera de Cristal* (*The Crystal Skull*, written by Juan Villoro), *Uncle Bill* (about William S. Burroughs in Mexico), *El instante amarillo* (*The Yellow Minute*), and *Habla María* (*María Speaks*, about parenting an autistic daughter).

As a novelist he's published the Season of Scorpions crime novel series, which include *Tiempo de alacranes* (*Season of Scorpions*), *Hielo negro* (*Black Ice*), *Cuello blanco* (*White Collar*), *Azul cobalto* (*Cobalt Blue*), and *Esta bestia que habitamos* (*This Hairy Beast We Live On*), and several science fiction novels that include *Ojos de lagarto* (*Snake Eyes*), *Gel azul* (*Blue Gel*), *Escenarios para el fin del mundo* (*Scenarios for the End of Times*), and *El estruendo del silencio* (*The Thunderous Silence*), as well as several young adult and children's books.

His most recent graphic novels are *Matar al candidato* (*Killing the Candidate*, written by F. G. Haghenbeck) and the children's comic *3 Deseos* (*Three Wishes*).

His work has been translated into several languages. He currently splits his time among writing a three-volume space cyberpunk saga, drawing a wordless dinosaur-themed graphic novel, teaching illustration to design students, and most important, being María and Sofia's dad.

In the science fiction world, **Bruce Bethke** is best known either for his short story "Cyberpunk," for his award-winning novel *Headcrash*, or for any of the other dozens of stories and novels he saw published in the 1980s and 1990s. In the real world, Bruce spent most of his career in supercomputer software R&D, doing work that was fascinating but impossible to explain to anyone not already familiar with computational fluid dynamics, Fourier transformations, and massively parallel processor architectures. Now retired, he's come back home to science fiction and is delighted to see what newer writers have done with his strange little idea from more than forty years ago.

Lauren Beukes is the award-winning and internationally bestselling South African author of *The Shining Girls*, *Zoo City*, and *Afterland*, among other works. Her novels have been published in twenty-four countries and are being adapted for film and TV. She's also a comics writer, screenwriter, journalist, and documentary maker. Lauren is a former feature journalist who covered electricity cable thieves, HIV+ beauty pageants, metro cops, and sex workers. She's worked in film and TV; as the director of *Glitterboys & Ganglands*, a documentary that won Best LGBTI Film at the Atlanta Black Film Festival; and as showrunner and head writer on South Africa's first half hour animated TV show, *Pax Afrika*, which ran for 104 episodes on SABC. Her comics work includes the original horror series *Survivors' Club* with Dale Halvorsen and Ryan Kelly and the *New York Times* bestselling *Fairest: The Hidden Kingdom*, a Japanese horror remix of Rapunzel with artist Inaki.

Russell Blackford is an Australian academic and writer. He is currently conjoint senior lecturer in philosophy at the University of Newcastle, NSW. His many nonfiction books include *Science Fiction and the Moral Imagination: Visions, Minds, Ethics*. He has a longstanding interest in science fiction and fantasy and has published novels and stories in both genres. His novels include an original trilogy for the Terminator franchise (collectively *Terminator 2: The New John Connor Chronicles*) and *Kong Reborn*—a modern-day sequel to the original 1933 *King Kong* film.

Maurice Broaddus is a community organizer and teacher. His work has appeared in places like *Lightspeed* magazine, *Black Panther: Tales from Wakanda*, *Weird Tales*, *The Magazine of Fantasy & Science Fiction*, and *Uncanny* magazine. His books include the sci-fi novel *Sweep of Stars*, the steampunk works *Buffalo Soldier* and *Pimp My Airship*, and the middle grade detective novels *The Usual Suspects* and *Unfadeable*. His project *Sorcerers* is being adapted as a television show for AMC. He's an editor at *Apex Magazine*.

Pat Cadigan was born in New York, grew up in Massachusetts, and spent most of her adult life in the Kansas City area, until she emigrated to the United Kingdom in 1996.

After ten years as a writer for Hallmark Cards (yes, she wrote the cards, in verse), she became a full-time writer in 1987. Her books include the Arthur C. Clarke Award–winning novels *Synners* and *Fools*. She has also won the Locus Award three times. In 2013 her novelette *The Girl-Thing Who Went Out for Sushi* also won both the Hugo Award and the Seiun Award (aka the Japanese Hugo). Cadigan is a popular guest lecturer and has spoken about many different subjects around the world.

Myra Çakan was born in Hamburg, Germany. She studied drama and music and attended workshops on sitcoms, screenplays, and treatment writing. She currently lives as a full-time author, artist, and freelance journalist near Hamburg.

Myra has been published in magazines and on websites such as *Die Woche*, *Konr@d*, *c't*, *Der Spiegel*, and *Die Süddeutsche Zeitung*. She wrote an adaptation of her acclaimed novel *When the Music's Over* for Red Beat Pictures. Her novels include *Downtown Blues*, *Begegnung in der High Sierra*, and *Zwischenfall an einem regnerischen Nachmittag*. Her short fiction has appeared in anthologies and magazines in Germany, Austria, Slovakia, Great Britain, China, and the United

States of America. She also has more than twenty produced radio plays, both original works and adaptions of her own work.

Nebula-nominated **Beth Cato** is the author of the Clockwork Dagger duology and the Blood of Earth trilogy. She's a Hanford, California, native transplanted to the Arizona desert, where she lives with her husband, son, and requisite cats.

Suzanne Church grew up in Toronto, moved to Waterloo to pursue mathematics, and never left town. Her award-winning short fiction has appeared in *Cicada*, *Clarkesworld*, several anthologies, and her 2014 collection *Elements*. Her favorite place to write is a lakefront cabin, but she'll settle for any coffee shop with Wi-Fi and an electrical outlet.

In 2016, **Samuel R. Delany** was inducted into the New York State Writers Hall of Fame. He is the author of *Babel-17*, *Nova*, *Dhalgren*, *Dark Reflections*, *Atlantis: Three Tales*, the Return to Nevèrÿon series, an autobiography, *The Motion of Light in Water*, and the paired essays *Times Square Red / Times Square Blue*. *Dark Reflections* won the Stonewall Book Award for 2008, and in 2015 Delaney won the Nicolás Guillén Award for Philosophical Literature, in 1997 the Kessler Award for LGBTQ Studies, and in 2021 the Anisfield-Wolf Award. He has also won Nebula Awards from the Science Fiction Writers of America and two Hugo Awards from the World Science Fiction Convention. Filmmaker, novelist, critic, in 2013 he was made a Grand Master of Science Fiction, following in the steps of Asimov, Heinlein, and Le Guin.

A native Rhode Islander, **Paul Di Filippo** lives in Providence, some two blocks away from the granite marker denoting Lovecraft's birthplace. Since selling his first story in 1977, he has accumulated more than forty books with his byline. His newest will be a story collection titled *The Way You Came in May Not Be the Best Way Out*.

Over a writing career that spanned three decades, **Philip K. Dick** (1928–1982) published thirty-six science fiction novels and 121 short stories in which he explored the essence of what makes man human and the dangers of centralized power. Toward the end of his life, his work turned to deeply personal, metaphysical questions concerning the nature of God. Eleven novels and short stories have been adapted to film, notably *Blade Runner* (based on *Do Androids Dream of Electric Sheep?*), *Total Recall*, *Minority Report*, and *A Scanner Darkly*, as well as television's *The Man in the High Castle*. The recipient of critical acclaim and numerous awards throughout his career, including the Hugo and John W. Campbell awards, Dick was inducted into the Science Fiction Hall of Fame in 2005, and between 2007 and 2009 the Library of America published a selection of his novels in three volumes. His work has been translated into more than twenty-five languages.

Cory Doctorow is a science fiction author, activist, and journalist. He is the author of many books, most recently *Radicalized* and *Walkaway*, science fiction for adults; *How to Destroy Surveillance Capitalism*, nonfiction about monopoly and conspiracy; *In Real Life*, a graphic novel; and the picture book *Poesy the Monster Slayer*.

His latest book is *Attack Surface*, a stand-alone adult sequel to *Little Brother*; his next nonfiction book is *Chokepoint Capitalism*, with Rebecca Giblin, about monopoly and fairness in the creative arts labor market. In 2020, he was inducted into the Canadian Science Fiction and Fantasy Hall of Fame.

Candas Jane Dorsey is an internationally known writer, editor, former publisher, community-builder, and activist living in Edmonton, Alberta. She is the award-winning author of, among others, *Black Wine*, *A Paradigm of Earth*, *Machine Sex and other stories*, *Vanilla and other stories*, *ICE and other stories*, *The Adventures of Isabel*, and *What's the Matter with Mary Jane?* (the Epitome Apartments Mystery Series), and YA novel *The Story of My Life Ongoing, by C. S. Cobb*.

George Alec Effinger was born January 10, 1947. His first novel, *What Entropy Means to Me*, was nominated for the Nebula Award. He achieved his greatest success with the trilogy of Marîd Audran novels *When Gravity Fails*, *A Fire in the Sun*, and *The Exile Kiss*, set in a twenty-second-century Middle East, with cybernetic implants and modules allowing individuals to change their personalities or bodies. A collection, *Budayeen Nights*, contains all Effinger's short material from the Marîd Audran setting.

His novelette *Schrödinger's Kitten* received both the Hugo Award and the Nebula Award, as well as the Japanese Seiun Award. A collection of his stories was published posthumously in 2005, entitled *George Alec Effinger Live! From Planet Earth*; it includes the complete stories Effinger wrote under the pseudonym O. Niemand and many of Effinger's best-known stories. Each O. Niemand story is a pastiche in the voice of a different major American writer (Flannery O'Connor, Damon Runyon, Mark Twain, etc.), all set on the asteroid city of Springfield. *Niemand* is from the German word for "nobody," and the initial *O* was intended by Effinger as a visual pun for Zero, and possibly also as a reference to the author O. Henry.

Other stories Effinger wrote include the series of Maureen (Muffy) Birnbaum parodies, which placed a preppy into a variety of science fictional, fantasy, and horror scenarios. He was in ill health for much of his life and died at the age of fifty-five on April 27, 2002.

Greg Egan lives in Perth, Western Australia. He has won the John W. Campbell Award for Best Novel for *Permutation City*, and *Oceanic* was awarded a Hugo, a Locus, and an Asimov's Readers' Award. His work has also won the Japanese Seiun Award for best translated fiction seven times.

Isabel Fall was born in 1989.

Minister Faust is an award-winning novelist, award-winning print journalist, radio host-producer, television host and associate producer, sketch comedy writer, video game writer, playwright, and poet. He has spoken and taught workshops widely.

Fabio Fernandes is a Brazilian writer living in Italy. He has published several books, among which are the novels *Os Dias da Peste* and *Back in the USSR* (in Portuguese) and the collection *L'Imitatore* (in Italian). He translated to Brazilian Portuguese several SF novels, including *Neuromancer* and *A Clockwork Orange*. He coedited the anthologies *We See a Different Frontier* and *Solarpunk*. His collection *Love. An Archaeology* was published in 2021, and his steampunk novella, *Under Pressure*, was published in 2022.

Taiyo Fujii was born in Amami Oshima Island, between Kyushu and Okinawa. He has worked in stage design, desktop publishing, exhibition graphic design, and software development.

In 2012, Fujii self-published *Gene Mapper* serially in a digital format of his own design, and became Amazon.co.jp's number one Kindle bestseller of that year. The novel was revised and republished in 2013 and was nominated for the Nihon SF Taisho Award and the Seiun Award.

In *Gene Mapper*, Fujii describes in detail AR/VR communication, GMOs, and terror as an infrastructure. His second novel, *Orbital Cloud*, won the 2014 Nihon SF Taisho Award and Japanese Nebula Awards.

In 2019, the novelette collection *Hello, World!* won the Yoshikawa Eiji Literature Award for Young Writers.

Ganzeer operates seamlessly between art, design, and storytelling, creating what he has coined "Concept Pop." A chameleon according to the *New York Times*, his artwork has been witnessed in a wide variety of galleries, impromptu spaces, alleyways, and major museums around the world, and his words have seen print in publications both academic and trashy. His demented sci-fi graphic novel, *The Solar Grid*, has earned him a Global Thinker Award from *Foreign Policy*.

William Gibson is credited with having coined the term *cyberspace* and having envisioned both the internet and virtual reality before either existed. He is the author of *Neuromancer*, *Count Zero*, *Mona Lisa Overdrive*, *Burning Chrome*, *Virtual Light*, *Idoru*, *All Tomorrow's Parties*, *Pattern Recognition*, *Spook Country*, *Zero History*, *Distrust That Particular Flavor*, and *The Peripheral*. He lives in Vancouver, British Columbia, with his wife.

Eileen Gunn is an American science fiction writer and editor. She is the author of a relatively small but distinguished body of short fiction published over the past four decades. Her story "Coming to Terms" won the Nebula Award in 2004 and the Sense of Gender Award in Japan in 2007. Other stories have been nominated for the Hugo, Nebula, Philip K. Dick, Locus, and Tiptree awards. She has two volumes of collected work, *Stable Strategies and Others* and *Questionable Practices*, with a third, *Night Shift*, recently released in PM Press's Outspoken Authors series.

Gunn was editor and publisher of the pioneering webzine *The Infinite Matrix* and creator of the website The Difference Dictionary, a concordance to *The Difference Engine* by William Gibson and Bruce Sterling. She also had an extensive career in technology advertising, including a time as director of advertising at Microsoft.

Sean Lin Halbert received his BA in Korean language from the University of Washington and his MA in modern Korean literature from Seoul National University. He is a recipient of the GKL Translation Award, the LTI Korea Award for Aspiring Translators, and the *Korea Times* Modern Korean Literature Translation Award. His translations of Korean authors Yun Ko-eun, Park Sang Young, Kim Soom, and others have appeared in *Azalea* and *Korean Literature Now*. His major translations include Kim Un-su's novel *The Cabinet* and Yun Ko-eun's "The Chef's Nail." He currently lives in Seoul working as a full-time translator.

Omar Robert Hamilton is a writer and filmmaker working between Europe and the Arab world, and a cofounder of the Palestine Festival of Literature.

Karen Heuler's stories have appeared in more than 120 literary and speculative magazines and anthologies, from *Conjunctions* to *The Magazine of Fantasy and Science Fiction* to *Weird Tales*. Her latest novel is *The Splendid City*. It's a tale about stolen water, an exiled witch and her gun-wielding cat, and a city run by a self-declared president who loves parades. Her latest collection is *A Slice of the Dark*.

Saad Z. Hossain writes in a niche genre of fantasy, science fiction, and black comedy. He studied English lit and commerce at the University of Virginia, a combination of studies completely impractical in real life. He has been forced to work in various industries, including digging holes, making rope, throwing parties, and failing to run a restaurant. Needless to say, working for a living is highly overrated. He lives in Dhaka, the most ridiculously crowded city in the world, teeming with humans, wildlife, and djinn.

Alaya Dawn Johnson is an award-winning author of speculative fiction for adults and young adults. Her most recent novel is *Trouble the Saints*, and her most recent short story collection is *Reconstruction*.

Her debut YA novel, *The Summer Prince*, was longlisted for the National Book Award for Young People's Literature. Her most recent young adult novel, *Love Is the Drug*, brought her deep speculative imagination and social commentary to the world of modern Washington, DC. The first was nominated for and the second won the prestigious Nebula (Andre Norton) Award for YA Science Fiction and Fantasy, awarded by the Science Fiction Writers of America. In the past decade, her award-winning short stories have appeared in many magazines and anthologies, including *Best American Science Fiction and Fantasy 2015*, *Feral Youth*, *Three Sides of a Heart*, and *Zombies vs. Unicorns*.

Gwyneth Jones is a feminist writer and critic of science fiction and fantasy who has also written for teenagers using the name Ann Halam. Awards include the Philip K. Dick Award, Arthur C. Clarke Award, the Dracula Society's Children of the Night Award, the World Fantasy Award, and the Pilgrim Award for SF criticism. She lives in Brighton, England, with her husband and two cats, Milo and Tilly. Hobbies include curating assorted pond life in season, watching old movies, playing *Zelda*, and staring out the window.

Richard Kadrey is the *New York Times* bestselling author of more than twenty novels, including the Sandman Slim supernatural noir series. *Sandman Slim* was included in Amazon's "100 Science Fiction & Fantasy Books to Read in a Lifetime." The book is in development as a feature film through Studio 8. Some of Kadrey's other books include *The Grand Dark*, *The Everything Box*, and *Butcher Bird*. In comics, he's written for *Heavy Metal*, *Lucifer*, and *Hellblazer*. He's also been immortalized as an action figure.

Khalid Kaki was born in Kirkuk in 1971. He studied Spanish literature and philology at the University of Baghdad (1989–1993) and at Autónoma University in Madrid (1997–2000), where he has lived since 1996. He has published four collections of poetry—*Unsafely*, *The Guard's Notes*, *Cages in a Bird*, and *Ashes of the Pomegranate Tree*—and two collections of short stories—*The Land of Facing Mirrors* and *The Suicide of Jose Buenavida*.

James Patrick Kelly has won the Nebula, Hugo, and Locus awards. His work has been translated into seventeen languages. Most recent books include *The First Law of Thermodynamics Plus*, a collection in PM Press's Outspoken Author series; *King of the Dogs, Queen of the Cats*, a novella; a collection, *The Promise of Space*; and a novel, *Mother Go*, an audiobook original. He writes a column about the internet for *Asimov's*.

John Kessel's most recent books are the novels *Pride and Prometheus* and *The Moon and the Other*. His work has received the Nebula, Theodore Sturgeon, Locus, James Tiptree Jr., and Shirley Jackson awards. *The Dark Ride* is a collection of his best short fiction.

Kessel has taught literature and writing at North Carolina State University, where he helped found the MFA program in creative writing. He lives with his wife, the novelist Therese Anne Fowler, in Raleigh.

Cassandra Khaw is an award-winning game writer and former scriptwriter at Ubisoft Montreal. Khaw's work can be found in places like *The Magazine of Fantasy & Science Fiction*, *Lightspeed*, and Tor.com. Khaw's first original novella, *Hammers on Bone*, was a British Fantasy Award and Locus Award finalist, and their novella *Nothing But Blackened Teeth* is a Bram Stoker Award finalist.

Being a young man in post-communist Bulgaria, **Christian Kirtchev** was living the cyberpunk "high-tech, lowlife" cliché lurking in dark, dank techno clubs or surfing grave-hour internet cafés for that techno-fetish high surrounded by the decay of a crumbled political and economic system. After publishing "A Cyberpunk Manifesto" in 1997, he subsequently wrote a few more pieces and short stories describing the emerging techno-culture in late 1990s Eastern Europe from a cyberpunk point of view.

Aleš Kot is a writer and producer. They believe in the power of art. They have nothing to sell you.

Nancy Kress is the author of thirty-four novels, four story collections, and three books on writing fiction. Her science fiction has won six Nebulas, two Hugos, a Sturgeon, and the John W. Campbell Memorial Award. She often writes about genetic engineering. Her work has been translated into two dozen languages—including Klingon—none of which she can read. She teaches writing at various venues in the United States and abroad, including a guest lectureship at the University of Leipzig and an intensive seminar in Beijing, plus the annual Taos Toolbox with Walter Jon Williams. She lives in Seattle.

Naomi Kritzer has been writing science fiction and fantasy for more than twenty years; her fiction has won the Hugo Award, the Lodestar Award, the Edgar Award, and the Minnesota Book Award. Her newest book is *Chaos on CatNet*, which is a sequel to *Catfishing on CatNet*, and is set in Minneapolis. She lives in St. Paul, Minnesota, with her spouse, two kids (when the college kid is home from college), and four cats. The number of cats is subject to change without notice.

Lavanya Lakshminarayan is the award-winning author of *The Ten Percent Thief*. She's a Locus Award finalist and is the first science fiction writer to win the *Times of India* AutHer Award and the Valley of Words Award, both prestigious literary awards in India. Her fiction has appeared in various magazines and anthologies, including *The Best of World SF Volume 2* and *Someone in Time*, and has also been translated into French, Italian, German, and Spanish.

She's occasionally a game designer and has built worlds for Zynga Inc.'s *FarmVille* franchise, *Mafia Wars*, and other games. She lives between multiple cities in India.

David Langford has been publishing and writing about science fiction since 1975. Novels include *The Space Eater* and *The Leaky Establishment*; there are many collections of his reviews, criticism, and humorous commentary. His twenty-nine Hugo awards span several categories: fanzine and semiprozine for the science fiction newsletter *Ansible* (1979–), short story for "Different Kinds of Darkness" (2000), and related work in 2012 for the online *Encyclopedia of Science Fiction* (with John Clute and Peter Nicholls), of which he remains a principal editor. In his spare time he runs the small press Ansible Editions and (occasionally) sleeps.

Oliver Langmead is a Scottish author and poet whose books include *Birds of Paradise*, *Dark Star*, and *Metronome*. He is a lecturer in creative writing at the University of Lancaster, and in 2018 he was the writer in residence at the European Space Agency's Astronaut Centre in Cologne. After writing "Glitterati," Langmead developed it into a full-length novel, available now.

Fritz Leiber Jr. was born Fritz Reuter Leiber Jr. in Chicago, Illinois, on December 24, 1910, to Fritz Leiber Sr. and Virginia Bronson Leiber, both Shakespearean actors. He toured with father's repertory company in 1928 before entering the University of Chicago, from which he graduated in 1932. He went on to study at General Theological Seminary in New York and was briefly a candidate for ordination in the Episcopal Church. He toured intermittently with his father's company and appeared with him in films *Camille* (1936) and *The Great Garrick* (1937). Leiber married Jonquil Stephens in 1936 and moved to Hollywood; they had a son soon after. He corresponded with horror writer H. P. Lovecraft, who encouraged and influenced his literary development; wrote a supernatural novella, *The Dealings of Daniel Kesserich* (1936; published posthumously in 1997); and showed Lovecraft early stories. Returning to Chicago, Leiber took a job as staff writer for Consolidated Book Publishing (1937–1941), contributing to the *Standard American Encyclopedia*. His first publication as a professional writer, "Two Sought Adventure" (in John W. Campbell Jr.'s *Unknown*), introduced popular characters Fafhrd and the Gray Mouser, whom he developed with his friend Harry Fischer and modeled on their relationship; the story inaugurated a series he would continue for more than fifty years, helping to define the subgenre he labeled "Sword and Sorcery." (Fafhrd and the Gray Mouser stories were later collected in *Two Sought Adventure*, 1957; *Swords in the Mist*, 1968; *Swords Against Wizardry*, 1968; *The Swords of Lankhmar*, 1968; *Swords and Deviltry*, 1970; *Swords and Ice Magic*, 1977; *The Knight and Knave of Swords*, 1988; and other volumes.) Leiber worked as a drama and speech instructor at Occidental College in 1941 and during the war as an inspector at Douglas Aircraft. His first novel, *Conjure Wife*—about secret witchcraft on a college campus—appeared in *Unknown* in 1943 (but not as a book until 1952; it was filmed three times). His first science fiction novel, *Gather, Darkness!*, was also serialized in 1943 (book version, 1950). From 1945 to 1956, he worked as an editor at *Science Digest* in Chicago. He published science fiction novels *Destiny Times Three* (in *Astounding*, 1945; book version, 1957), *The Green Millennium* (1953), and *The Big Time* (in *Galaxy*, 1958; book version, 1961), the last winning a Hugo Award and inaugurating his popular Change War series. Leiber moved back to Los Angeles in 1958 and turned to writing full-time; he published science fiction novels *The Silver Eggheads* (1961), *The Wanderer* (1964), and *A Specter Is Haunting Texas* (1969).

Leiber lived in San Francisco after the death of his wife in 1969; the city forms the setting of his fantasy novel *Our Lady of Darkness* (1977). In 1976, he received a World Fantasy Award for Life Achievement and, in 1981, a Grand Master Award from Science Fiction Writers of America. Leiber married Margo Skinner in May 1992. He died on September 5, 1992, in San Francisco of an apparent stroke. In 2001 he was inducted posthumously into the Science Fiction Hall of Fame.

Jean-Marc Ligny was born in 1956 in Paris. He pursued high school studies that led him to the baccalaureate but no further. Very early, he plunged into science fiction (from the age of eight!) and devoted himself to writing in this field from 1976, after unsuccessful musical attempts (as a rock guitarist). He published his first short story in 1978, in Philippe Curval's anthology *Futurs au Présent*. His first novel, *Temps Blancs*, published the following year, was noticed by the critics and earned him a passage in *Apostrophes* (a famous literary TV show at that time).

Ligny decided to devote himself to writing full-time when he "immigrated" to Brittany in 1985. Nevertheless, he worked for a few years (part-time) on a local editorial staff for a regional daily newspaper, *Le Télégramme*. After spending ten years in the Forez Mountains, he returned in 2015 to live in Brittany (Morbihan), where he works full-time as a writer and translator.

He has written about fifty short stories and forty novels, in many fields covered by science fiction and fantasy, including about fifteen for youth, which led him to become involved in schools. He has also produced two international anthologies on the theme of love, translated and published in Italy.

He draws his inspiration from music (*Furia!*, *La Mort peut danser*), ethnology (*Yurlunggur*, *Yoro Si*), esotericism (*Les Voleurs de rêves*), history (*La Mort peut danser*), and ecology, especially climate change (*Aqua™*, *Exodes*, *Semences*, *Alliances*). He is also interested in fantasy (*Yoro Si*, *Les Ailes noires de la nuit*), cyberpunk (*Cyberkiller*, *Inner City*, *Slum City*), space opera (*Les oiseaux de lumière*), or more political fields (*Jihad*, *Aqua™*). He also wrote some detective novels. Two trips to Burkina Faso and one to Ireland provided the setting for two of his major works: *Yoro Si* and *La Mort peut danser*. In the field of fantasy/horror, he seeks an original approach to the genre, based on myths and legends of current and past civilizations, but does not neglect contemporary urban fantasy (*La maison aux démons*, *Mal-morts*).

Ligny is the winner of the main French prizes in the field of science fiction: the Grand Prix de l'Imaginaire in 1997 for *Inner City*, the Rosny Aîné Prize in 1999 for *Jihad* and in 2007 for *Aqua™*, the Tour Eiffel Prize in 2001 for *Les oiseaux de lumière*, the Julia Verlanger Prize (endowed by the Fondation de France) in 2007 for *Aqua™*—this last novel was published in Germany and China—and finally the European Utopiales Prize in 2013 for *Exodes*.

Since the early 2000s, he has devoted most of his fiction to climate change and its social and environmental consequences: four novels have been published on this subject (*Aqua™*, *Exodes*, *Semences*, *Alliances*), as well as a dozen short stories.

Arthur Liu (杨枫) is a Chinese science fiction writer and translator based in Beijing. His works have been published in *Science Fiction World*, *Non-Exist*, and *SF Stave*, among other Chinese science fiction magazines. As a computer engineer, he founded the Chinese Science Fiction Database, serving as its chief administrator. He wishes to be a cyber crawler.

Ken Liu is an American author of speculative fiction. A winner of Nebula, Hugo, and World Fantasy awards, he wrote the Dandelion Dynasty, a silkpunk epic fantasy series (starting with *The Grace of Kings*), as well as short story collections *The Paper Menagerie and Other Stories* and *The Hidden Girl and Other Stories*. He also penned the Star Wars novel *The Legends of Luke Skywalker*.

Prior to becoming a full-time writer, Liu worked as a software engineer, corporate lawyer, and litigation consultant. Liu frequently speaks at conferences and universities on a variety of topics, including futurism, cryptocurrency, history of technology, bookmaking, narrative futures, and the mathematics of origami.

Steven S. Long is a writer and game designer who's worked primarily in the tabletop role-playing game field for the past twenty-five-some years, during which he's written or cowritten approximately two hundred books. He's best known for his work with Champions and the HERO System but has worked for many other RPG companies. In recent years he's focused more on writing fiction and has had numerous short stories published. His Master Plan for World Domination has reached Stage 64-Omicron.

M. Lopes da Silva is a nonbinary and bisexual author and artist from Los Angeles. They write queer California horror and everything else. They have had their speculative fiction published by Dread Stone Press, in *Unnerving* magazine, and in *Glass and Gardens: Solarpunk Summers.*

James Lovegrove is the author of more than sixty books, including *The Hope, Days, United Kingdom, Provender Gleed*, and the *New York Times* bestselling Pantheon series. His work has been translated into fifteen languages. He has written eight Sherlock Holmes novels, a collection of Holmes short stories, and a Conan Doyle/Lovecraft mashup trilogy, the Cthulhu Casebooks. He has also written four tie-in novels for the TV show *Firefly*, one of which, *The Ghost Machine*, won the 2020 Dragon Award for Best Media Tie-in Novel. He contributes two regular fiction-review columns to the *Financial Times* and lives with his wife, two sons, and tiny dog in Eastbourne, not far from the site of the "small farm upon the South Downs" to which Sherlock Holmes retired.

Ken MacLeod lives in Gourock on the west coast of Scotland. He has degrees in biological sciences, worked in IT, and is now a full-time writer. He is the author of nineteen novels, from *The Star Fraction* to *Beyond the Reach of Earth*, and many articles and short stories.

Nick Mamatas is the author of several novels, including *The Second Shooter* and *I Am Providence*. His short fiction has appeared in *Best American Mystery Stories, Year's Best Science Fiction & Fantasy, Asimov's*, Tor.com, and many other venues. Nick is also an anthologist: his most recent compilation is *Wonder and Glory Forever: Awe-Inspiring Lovecraftian Fiction*. His fiction and editorial work has been variously edited for the Hugo, World Fantasy, Shirley Jackson, and Bram Stoker awards.

Phillip Mann has published eleven science fiction novels including his acclaimed *The Eye of the Queen, The Disestablishment of Paradise*, and, most recently, *Chevalier & Gawayn: The Ballad of the Dreamer*. He also wrote for radio and theater. He was a theater director and teacher, founding New Zealand's first university drama studies course at Victoria University.

Born in North Yorkshire, England, Mann lived and worked in the United States, China, and France, as well as New Zealand, where he lived with his family until his death in 2022.

Lisa Mason has published eleven novels, including *Summer of Love* (a Philip K. Dick Award Finalist) and *The Gilded Age* (a *New York Times* Notable Book), and two collections, *Strange Ladies: 7 Stories* and *Oddities: 22 Stories*. Her OMNI story, "Tomorrow's Child," sold to Universal Pictures.

Her latest science fiction novel, *Chrome*, was published in 2020. *Publishers Weekly* said, "Mason entertains and elicits fascinating questions about human nature in this fast-paced, action-packed science fiction adventure." Forthcoming is *Spyder*, book three in the Arachne Trilogy.

Tim Maughan is an author and journalist using both fiction and nonfiction to explore issues around cities, class, culture, technology, and the future. His work has appeared on the BBC, *New Scientist*, *MIT Technology Review*, One Zero, and *Vice/Motherboard*. His debut novel, *Infinite Detail*, was selected by the *Guardian* as their science fiction and fantasy book of the year and was shortlisted for the Locus Magazine Award for Best First Novel. Maughan also uses fiction to help clients as diverse as IKEA and the World Health Organization to think critically about the future. He currently lives in Canada.

Paul J. McAuley is the author of more than twenty novels, several collections of short stories, a Doctor Who novella, and a BFI Film Classic monograph on Terry Gilliam's film *Brazil*. His fiction has won the Philip K. Dick Memorial Award, the Arthur C. Clarke Award, the John W. Campbell Memorial Award, the Sidewise Award, the British Fantasy Award, and the Theodore Sturgeon Memorial Award. His latest novel is *Beyond the Burn Line*.

Sam J. Miller's books have been called "must-reads" and "best of the year" by *USA Today*, *Entertainment Weekly*, NPR, and *O, The Oprah Magazine*, among others. He is the Nebula Award–winning author of *Blackfish City*, which has been translated into six languages and won the now thankfully renamed John W. Campbell Memorial Award. Sam's short stories have been nominated for the World Fantasy, Theodore Sturgeon, and Locus awards and reprinted in dozens of anthologies. He's also the last in a long line of butchers. He lives in New York City.

Misha's first novel, *Red Spider White Web*, published in England, won the 1990 ReaderCon Award, and was a finalist for the Arthur C. Clarke Award. Her prose has appeared in Germany, Austria, Australia, Japan, America, and Canada. Her piece "Tsuki Mangetsu" was used in a dynamic performance by two Australian composers and won the 1989 Prix d'Italia. She was formerly the editor of *New Pathways* magazine, and her review column "Points of Impact" carried through three magazines: *New Pathways*, published by Mike Adkisson; *Ice River*, edited by David Memmott; and *Science Fiction Eye*, edited by Steve Brown.

Robin Moger is a translator of Arabic into English. His translations of prose and poetry have appeared in *The White Review*, *Tentacular*, *Asymptote*, the *Washington Square Review*, *Words Without Borders*, and others. He has translated several novels and prose works, most recently *The Book of Sleep* by Haytham El Wardany, *Slipping* by Mohamed Kheir, and *The Law of Inheritance* by Yasser Abdellatif.

Janelle Monáe is an American singer, songwriter, rapper, and actor. They are signed to Atlantic Records, as well as to their own imprint, the Wondaland Arts Society. Monáe has received eight Grammy Award nominations. Monáe won an MTV Video Music Award and the ASCAP Vanguard Award in 2010.

Sunny Moraine is a writer of science fiction, fantasy, horror, and generally weird stuff, with stories published in outlets like Tor.com, *Clarkesworld*, *Lightspeed*, and *Shimmer*, along with the story collection *Singing With All My Skin and Bone*. Moraine has a PhD in sociology, with a doctoral dissertation on extermination camps. Moraine also writes, narrates, and produces a serial horror drama podcast called *Gone*. They live near Washington, DC, with their husband and two cats.

Michael W. Moss writes cyberpunk, fantasy, and hard-boiled noir fiction. He also designs type-faces, one of which was used in an episode of *Doctor Who.* Michael lives in Portland, Oregon, with his significant other, two cats, and dog, Eddie.

T. R. Napper is a multiple award-winning science fiction author. His short fiction has appeared in *Asimov's, Interzone, The Magazine of Fantasy & Science Fiction,* and numerous others, and has been translated into Hebrew, German, French, and Vietnamese. He received a creative writing doctorate for his thesis: *Noir, Cyberpunk, and Asian Modernity.* Before turning to writing, T. R. Napper was an aid worker, implementing humanitarian programs in Southeast Asia for a decade. During this period, he received a commendation from the Government of Laos for his work with the poor. These days he has returned to his home country of Australia, where he works as a Dungeon Master, running campaigns for young people with autism for a local charity.

Kim Newman is a critic, author, and broadcaster. He is a contributing editor to *Sight & Sound* and *Empire* magazines. His books about film include *Nightmare Movies* and *Kim Newman's Video Dungeon.* His fiction includes the Anno Dracula series, *The Hound of the D'Urbervilles,* and *An English Ghost Story.* He has written for television (*Mark Kermode's Secrets of Cinema*), radio (*Afternoon Theatre: Cry-Babies*), comics (*Witchfinder: The Mysteries of Unland*), and the theater (*The Hallowe'en Sessions*). He also directed a tiny film (*Missing Girl*). His latest novel is *Something More Than Night.*

Mandisi Nkomo is a South African writer, drummer, composer, and producer. He currently resides in Hartbeespoort, South Africa. His fiction has been published in the likes of *Afrosf: Science Fiction by African Writers, AfroSF V3,* and *Omenana.* His poetry has been published in *The Coinage Book One* and *Shoreline of Infinity.* His academic work has been published in *The Thinker.* His works have been longlisted for the Nommo Award for African Speculative Fiction. He has been shortlisted for the Toyin Falola Short Story Prize. He is also a member of the African Speculative Fiction Society.

Jeff Noon was born in Manchester, England, in 1957. He trained in visual arts and drama and was active on the post-punk-music scene before becoming a playwright and then a novelist.

His science fiction books include *Vurt* (Arthur C. Clarke Award winner), *Pollen, Automated Alice, Nymphomation, Needle in the Groove, Falling Out of Cars, Channel SKIN, Mappalujo,* and a collection of stories called *Pixel Juice.* He has written two crime novels, *Slow Motion Ghosts* and *House with No Doors.* The four Nyquist Mysteries (*A Man of Shadows, The Body Library, Creeping Jenny,* and *Within Without*) explore the shifting intersections between science fiction and crime.

Brandon O'Brien is a writer, performance poet, teaching artist, and game designer from Trinidad and Tobago. His work has been published in *Uncanny* magazine, *Fireside Magazine, Strange Horizons, Reckoning,* and *New Worlds, Old Ways: Speculative Tales from the Caribbean,* among others. He is the former poetry editor of the Hugo Award–winning magazine *FIYAH.* His debut poetry collection, *Can You Sign My Tentacle?,* is available now.

Craig Padawer's fiction has appeared in several journals and anthologies including *Conjunctions, The Dalhousie Review, After Yesterday's Crash: The Avant-Pop Anthology,* and *The Weird: A Compendium of Dark and Strange Stories.* He lives in New York, where he is a film professor.

Victor Pelevin is one of the most popular contemporary Russian-language writers. He won the Small Booker Prize, the National Bestseller Prize, and many other accolades for his works, which have also been translated into many languages and turned into films. He established himself as a major voice in the 1990s with his early novels, which included *Omon Ra* and *Generation P*. His most recent novel, *TRANSHUMANISM, INC.*, was published in 2021. The motion picture based on his novel *Empire V* was released in 2022.

Harry Polkinhorn is a writer, visual artist, and psychoanalyst. Beginning in his teenage years, he has written poetry, prose, essays, and articles for more than fifty years. In the late 1970s and early 1980s, he cofounded Atticus Press and coedited *Atticus Review*. He has published more than 115 books.

In the visual arts he followed studio courses in painting and color theory at the Kunstgewerbeschule der Stadt Zürich, and while living in Europe visited galleries and museums throughout the Continent. His photographs have been exhibited at the city museum of Quito, Ecuador, and published widely.

Gerardo Horacio Porcayo is a Mexican writer, born May 10, 1966, in Cuernavaca, Morelos. Nowadays he lives in the city of Jojutla. He has a master's degree in Iberoamerican literature from the Universidad Ibero Puebla.

He has won many short story awards: *Axón Electrónico Primordial* (Argentina, 1992), *Puebla* (1993), *Kalpa* (1993), *Más Allá* (Argentina, 1994), *Sizigias* (Many Authors Anthology category, 2002), and *Sizigias* (Best Published Novel category, 2004). He also won the XXIX Concurso Magdalena Mondragón 2013 (Essay category). He has received an honorific mention of the Premio Internacional de Narrativa Ignacio Manuel Altamirano 2015.

He is considered the introducer of cyberpunk to Hispanic American literature with the publication of his first novel, *La primera calle de la soledad*, and the first (and only) Mexican cyberpunk anthology: *Silicio en la memoria*. He is also considered a fundamental figure inside Mexican Neogothic for his literary works in this genre, as for his editorial development with *Azoth* fanzine.

He has published twelve novels, three short story compilations, and three science fiction anthologies.

In 2018 he attended Worldcon 76 as a panelist, in San Jose, California, as a member of the Mexicanx Initiative.

In 2021 he was included in *The Best of World SF Volume 1*, edited by Lavie Tidhar, with his short story "Rue Chair," and in *Shadow Atlas: Dark Landscapes of The Americas*, edited by Carina Bissett, Hillary Dodge, and Joshua Viola, with his poem "The Hollow Place," originally written in English.

qntm (pronounced "quantum") is a UK-based science fiction author and software developer. He has been writing short-form and serial science fiction for most of the millennium to date, publishing his work on Everything2, his own website, and the SCP project. He is the author of supernatural thriller novel *There Is No Antimemetics Division*, which is about monstrous, invasive ideas from beyond the human ideatic ecology. He is also the creator of HATETRIS, a variant of *Tetris* that always gives you the worst piece. He is cagey and gangly.

Jean Rabe is a longtime *Shadowrun* player who favors trolls that use bows and arrows. She is the coauthor of *Aftershocks*, a Shadowrun novel she happily penned with John Helfers. In addition, she has written two dozen novels and more than four dozen short stories. In her spare time . . . such that it is . . . she plays a variety of games, tugs on old socks with her dogs, and tries unsuccessfully to put a dent in her growing stack of to-be-read books.

Yurei Raita is a name comprising the kanji for "spirit" and "rain" or "thunder" (as the phonetic transcription of the English word *writer*): *ghost writer*. The software that wrote this story worked within structural parameters gleaned from more than one thousand short stories and how-to-write essays written by Hoshi Shinichi. The software was developed in 2015 by the Sato-Matsuzaki Laboratory, a research team based at Nagoya University.

Cat Rambo's 250-plus fiction publications include stories in *Asimov's*, *Clarkesworld* magazine, and *The Magazine of Fantasy and Science Fiction*. In 2020 they won the Nebula Award for the fantasy novelette *Carpe Glitter*. They are a former two-term president of the Science Fiction and Fantasy Writers of America (SFWA). Their most recent works are space opera *You Sexy Thing* and an anthology, *The Reinvented Heart*, coedited with Jennifer Brozek.

Paul Graham Raven is (at the time of writing) a Marie Skłodowska-Curie Postdoctoral Fellow at Lund University, Sweden, where his research is concerned with how the stories we tell about times yet to come shape the lives we end up living. He's also an author and critic of science fiction, an occasional journalist and essayist, a collaborator with designers and artists, and a (gratefully) lapsed consulting critical futurist. He currently lives in Malmö with a cat, some guitars, and sufficient books to constitute an insurance-invalidating fire hazard.

Justina Robson is the award-winning author of several novels, novellas, and short stories. Most of her books and stories are science fiction, dealing in particular with transhumanism, genetic engineering, nanotech, and human evolution. They focus on the adaptation of human beings to new ways of creating themselves with technology.

A graduate of Clarion West (1996), she has gone on to teach at the Arvon Foundation in the United Kingdom. In 2005, she was a judge for the Arthur C. Clarke Award. In addition to her original works, she also wrote *Transformers: The Covenant of Primus*, the official history of the Transformers in the Prime Continuum, for Hasbro in 2013. She continues to study and write at her home in Yorkshire, where she lives with her husband, children, and pets.

Pepe Rojo practices interference in the California border zone in both Mexican and English, as there is no other way to go at it in Tijuana, where he has spent most of his life for a decade and a half. He has published five books and more than three hundred works dealing with fiction, media, and contemporary culture, while exploring hybrid formats and genres from science fiction interventions at the border crossing, speculative theory and fiction, to a philosophical dictionary of Tijuana. He is currently raising *Tierra y Libertad* flags while trying to survive a communications PhD at UCSD.

A former analyst at Oracle and programmer for Harvard, **N. R. M. Roshak** now writes about how technology and cutting-edge science interact with our loves, hopes, desires, and work. Their award-winning fiction has been published in three languages and has appeared in various anthologies and magazines, including Flash Fiction Online, *Galaxies SF*, Daily Science Fiction, and *Future Science Fiction Digest*. They live in Ontario, Canada, with a small family and a loud cat.

Nicholas Royle is the author of numerous short story collections, including *Mortality*, *Ornithology*, and *London Gothic*, and novels such as *Counterparts*, *Antwerp*, and *First Novel*. He has edited more than twenty anthologies and is series editor of *Best British Short Stories*. He runs Nightjar Press, which publishes original short stories as signed, numbered chapbooks. His English translation of Vincent de Swarte's 1998 novel *Pharricide* was published in 2019. His memoir is *White Spines: Confessions of a Book Collector*.

Rudy Rucker has published about forty books, both pop science and science fiction novels in the cyberpunk and transreal styles. He received Philip K. Dick awards for his *Software* and *Wetware*. He earned a PhD in higher mathematics. He worked as a professor of computer science in Silicon Valley. He paints works relating to his tales. His latest novel, *Juicy Ghosts*, is about telepathy, immortality, and an evil, insane president who has stolen an election.

Erica L. Satifka's short fiction has appeared in *Clarkesworld*, *Interzone*, *The Dark*, and many other places. She is the author of the collection *How to Get to Apocalypse and Other Disasters*, as well as *Busted Synapses* and *Stay Crazy*, and she received the 2017 British Fantasy Award for Best Newcomer. Erica lives in Portland, Oregon, with her spouse/editor, Rob, and an indeterminate number of cats.

Nisi Shawl is the multiple award-winning author and editor of *Filter House*, *Talk Like a Man*, *New Suns: Original Speculative Fiction by People of Color*, and *Everfair*—an example of the steamfunk offshoot of the steampunk offshoot of cyberpunk. Shawl's work on diversity in the imaginative genres includes cofounding the Carl Brandon Society and cowriting *Writing the Other: A Practical Approach*, the basis of their ongoing in-person and online classes. A new story collection, *Fruiting Bodies*, is available. In early 2023, their first middle grade novel appeared: a historical fantasy titled *Speculation*.

Lewis Shiner is the author of *Outside the Gates Of Eden*, the cyberpunk classic *Frontera*, and the award-winning *GLIMPSES*, among other novels. He's also published short story collections, journalism, and comics. Virtually all his work is available online for free.

John Shirley is the author of numerous novels, including the A Song Called Youth cyberpunk trilogy: *Eclipse*, *Eclipse Penumbra*, and *Eclipse Corona*. His newest book is the cyberpunk climate-fiction novel *Stormland*. Other works include *Demons*, *Wetbones*, *Cellars*, *Heatseeker*, *Living Shadows*, *City Come A-Walkin'*, *Bioshock: Rapture*, *A Splendid Chaos*, *The Other End*, and his story collection *Black Butterflies*, which won the Bram Stoker Award. His newest story collection is *The Feverish Stars*. He is co-screenwriter of *The Crow* and has written teleplays and animation.

Alex Shvartsman is the author of *The Middling Affliction* and *Eridani's Crown* fantasy novels. More than 120 of his stories have appeared in *Analog*, *Nature*, *Strange Horizons*, etc. He won the WSFA Small Press Award for Short Fiction (2014) and was a two-time finalist (2015, 2017) for the Canopus Award for Excellence in Interstellar Fiction. His translations from Russian have appeared in *The Magazine of Fiction & Science Fiction*, *Clarkesworld*, Tor.com, *Asimov's*, etc. Alex has edited over a dozen anthologies, including the long-running Unidentified Funny Objects series. He's the editor in chief of *Future Science Fiction Digest*. Alex resides in Brooklyn, New York.

Zedeck Siew is a writer, translator, and game designer based in Port Dickson, Malaysia. His English-language fiction has been published in Malaysia, the United Kingdom, and the United States. With visual artist Sharon Chin, he created *Creatures of Near Kingdoms*, a naturalists' guide to imaginary Southeast Asian flora and fauna; with visual artist Mun Kao he creates *A Thousand Thousand Islands*, a tabletop role-playing game series inspired by Nusantara mythistory and lived experience.

Marissa Skeels is a Melbourne-based translator who has lived in Fukushima, Kyoto, and Tokyo. Her translations of Japanese stories have appeared in various literary journals.

James Smythe is an award-winning writer of, among other things, *The Machine*, *I Still Dream*, and the Anomaly Quartet. He lives by the sea.

Neal Stephenson is the bestselling author of the novels *Reamde*, *Anathem*, *The System of the World*, *The Confusion*, *Quicksilver*, *Cryptonomicon*, *The Diamond Age*, *Snow Crash*, *Zodiac*, and *Termination Shock*. He lives in Seattle, Washington.

Bruce Sterling, author, journalist, editor, and critic, was born in 1954. Best known for his ten science fiction novels, he also writes short stories, book reviews, design criticism, opinion columns, and introductions for books ranging from Ernst Juenger to Jules Verne. His nonfiction works include *The Hacker Crackdown: Law And Disorder on the Electronic Frontier*, *Tomorrow Now: Envisioning The Next Fifty Years*, *Shaping Things*, and *The Epic Struggle of the Internet of Things*. His most recent book is a fiction collection, *Robot Artists and Black Swans: The Italian Fantascienza Stories*.

During 2005, he was the "visionary in residence" at Art Center College of Design in Pasadena. In 2008, he was the guest curator for the Share Festival of Digital Art and Culture in Torino, Italy, and the visionary in residence at the Sandberg Instituut in Amsterdam. In 2011, he returned to Art Center as visionary in residence to run a special project on Augmented Reality. In 2013, he was the visionary in residence at the Center for Science and the Imagination at Arizona State University. In 2015, he was the curator of the "Casa Jasmina" project at the Torino Fab Lab. In 2016, he was visionary in residence at the Arthur C. Clarke Center for Human Imagination.

He has appeared on ABC's *Nightline*, BBC's *The Late Show*, CBC's *Morningside*, MTV, and TechTV, and in *Time*, *Newsweek*, the *Wall Street Journal*, the *New York Times*, *Fortune*, *Nature*, *I.D.*, *Metropolis*, *Technology Review*, *Der Spiegel*, *La Stampa*, *La Repubblica*, and many other venues. He lives in Belgrade, Austin, Turin, and Ibiza.

Charles Stross is a full-time science fiction writer and resident of Edinburgh, Scotland. The author of seven Hugo-nominated novels and winner of three Hugo awards for best novella, Stross's works have been translated into more than twelve languages. His most recent novel is *Quantum of Nightmares*. His next novel, *Season of Skulls*, is forthcoming.

Like many writers, Stross has had a variety of careers, occupations, and job-shaped catastrophes in the past, from pharmacist (he quit after the second police stakeout) to first code monkey on the team of a successful dot-com startup (with brilliant timing he tried to change employers just as the bubble burst). Along the way he collected degrees in pharmacy and computer science, making him the world's first officially qualified cyberpunk writer (just as cyberpunk died).[*]

---

[*] Well, that's awkward. —the Editor

Michael Swanwick has received the Nebula, Theodore Sturgeon, World Fantasy, and Hugo awards and has the pleasant distinction of having been nominated for and lost more of these same awards than any other writer. His novels include *Stations of the Tide*, *Bones of the Earth*, two Darger and Surplus novels, and *The Iron Dragon's Mother*. He has also written more than a hundred and fifty short stories—including the Mongolian Wizard series on Tor.com—and countless works of flash fiction. He lives in Philadelphia with his wife, Marianne Porter.

E. J. Swift is the author of the Osiris Project trilogy, a speculative fiction series set in a world radically altered by climate change, and *Paris Adrift*, a tale of bartenders and time travel in the City of Light. Her short fiction has been nominated for the *Sunday Times* short story award and the British Science Fiction Award and has appeared in a variety of publications. Her latest novel, *The Coral Bones*, connects three women across the centuries through their love of the ocean.

Wole Talabi is an engineer, writer, and editor from Nigeria. His stories have appeared in *Asimov's*, *Lightspeed*, *The Magazine of Fantasy & Science Fiction*, and several other places. He has edited three anthologies: *Africanfuturism* (nominated for the Locus Award), *Lights Out: Resurrection*, and *These Words Expose Us*. He has been a finalist for several awards, including the prestigious Caine Prize, the Jim Baen Memorial Award, and the Nommo Award, which he won in 2018 and 2020. His collection *Incomplete Solutions* is available in print and audio. He likes scuba diving, elegant equations, and oddly shaped things.

Molly Tanzer is the author of five novels and two collections. Her work has been nominated for the Locus Award, the British Fantasy Award, and the Wonderland Book Award. Her novel *Creatures of Charm and Hunger* won the Colorado Book Award in 2021; her debut, *Vermilion*, was an NPR Best Book of 2015. Tanzer lives outside Boulder, Colorado, with her notorious cat, Toad.

K. A. Teryna is an award-winning author and illustrator. Her fiction has been translated from Russian into six languages. English translations of her stories have appeared in *Asimov's*, *Apex*, *The Magazine of Fantasy & Science Fiction*, *Strange Horizons*, *Samovar*, *Podcastle*, *Galaxy's Edge*, and elsewhere.

Jeffrey Thomas is the author of such novels as *Deadstock*, *Blue War*, and *The American*, and his short story collections include *Punktown*, *The Unnamed Country*, and *Carrion Men*. His stories have been reprinted in *The Year's Best Horror Stories XXII* (edited by Karl Edward Wagner), *The Year's Best Fantasy and Horror #14* (edited by Ellen Datlow and Terri Windling), and *Year's Best Weird Fiction #1* (edited by Laird Barron and Michael Kelly). Thomas lives in Massachusetts.

Lavie Tidhar's latest novels are *Maror* and *Neom*. His awards include the World Fantasy Award, the British Fantasy Award, the John W. Campbell Award, the Neukom Prize, and the Jerwood Fiction Uncovered Prize.

James Tiptree Jr. was the pen name of Alice Bradley Sheldon, whose radical and pioneering science fiction stories were matched by her extraordinary life. As a child she traveled widely with her parents and featured in several African-set travel books written by her mother. After attending a finishing school in Switzerland, she embarked on an early career as an artist and a critic. During WWII she joined the US Army Air Force, attaining the rank of major, and then worked for the CIA before moving to a chicken farm in Virginia with her husband. She turned to writing science fiction as an escape from her PhD thesis on experimental psychology and chose her pseudonym from a pot of jam. She later explained, "A male name seemed like good camouflage . . . I've had too many experiences in my life of being the first woman in some damned occupation." Her true sex was kept secret for years. She died in 1987 in what appeared to be a murder-suicide pact with her husband. She wrote some of the greatest science fiction short stories of the twentieth century, telling of dystopian chases, alien sex, and the loneliness of the universe.

Vauhini Vara's debut novel, *The Immortal King Rao*, was a *New York Times* Editors' Choice and was named a best book of the year by NPR and *Esquire*. Her story collection *This Is Salvaged* is forthcoming. She has written and edited journalism for the *New Yorker*, the *New York Times Magazine*, the *Atlantic*, and other publications; her short stories have appeared in *McSweeney's*, *Tin House*, and elsewhere. Her essay "Ghosts," originally published in the *Believer* and anthologized here, was also honored in *Best American Essays 2022*. She has won an O. Henry Award for her writing, along with other honors from the Rona Jaffe Foundation, Yaddo, MacDowell, and others. She is the secretary for Periplus, a mentorship collective serving writers of color.

Marie Vibbert has sold more than eighty short stories to places such as *Nature* and *The Magazine of Fantasy & Science Fiction*, with reprints translated into Chinese and Vietnamese. Her debut novel, *Galactic Hellcats*, was longlisted by the BSFA for 2021. *The Gods Awoke* is her second novel. She's played women's professional football and tried to ride all the roller coasters in the United States. By day, she's a computer programmer in Cleveland, Ohio.

Corey J. White is the author of *Repo Virtual* and the VoidWitch Saga—*Killing Gravity*, *Void Black Shadow*, and *Static Ruin*. Their short fiction has appeared in anthologies including *A Punk Rock Future*; *Night, Rain, and Neon*; and *Phase Change*. They studied writing at Griffith University on the Gold Coast and are now based in Melbourne, Australia. Their cyberpunk novel, *Repo Virtual*, won the Aurealis Award for Best Science Fiction Novel.

Yudhanjaya Wijeratne is a writer, data scientist, and general tinkerer. He lives and works in Sri Lanka. He cofounded and helps run Appendix.tech, a media x technology operation that fights misinformation (Watchdog Sri Lanka), builds software to help in times of crisis (Watchdog Elixir), and fills information gaps between people and the government.

He also works with the SciFi Economics Lab, architecting societies based on viable alternate economic structures, and with LIRNEasia, a think tank working across the Global South, on the intersection between data, algorithms, and government policy. His science fiction has been nominated for Nebula and IGF awards, published on ForeignPolicy, *Wired*, and Slate, and has appeared on bestseller lists.

Neon Yang is the author of the Genesis of Misery and the Tensorate series of novellas (*The Red Threads of Fortune*, *The Black Tides of Heaven*, *The Descent of Monsters*, and *The Ascent to Godhood*). Their work has been shortlisted for Hugo, Nebula, and World Fantasy awards, among others. Neon is queer, nonbinary, and lives in the United Kingdom.

E. Lily Yu is the author of *On Fragile Waves* and the librettist of *Stars Between*, with composer Steven K. Tran, for the Seattle Opera's 2021 Jane Lang Creation Lab. She received the Artist Trust LaSalle Storyteller Award in 2017 and the Astounding Award for Best New Writer in 2012. More than thirty of her stories have appeared in venues from *McSweeney's* to Tor.com, as well as twelve best-of-the-year anthologies, and have been finalists for Hugo, Nebula, Locus, Sturgeon, and World Fantasy awards.

Yun Ko-eun began her writing career when she won the Daesan Literary Award for her 2003 short story "Piercing." Her short story collections include *Table for One*, *Aloha*, *The Old Car and the Hitchhiker*, and *If Pyongyang Were on Monopoly*. She has authored the novels *Zero-gravity Syndrome*, *The Disaster Tourist*, *A Pirated Copy*, and *Library Runway*, as well as the collection of essays *The Warmth of the Void*. She is a recipient of the Hankyoreh Literary Award, the Lee Hyo-seok Literary Award, and the CWA Crime Fiction in Translation Dagger.

Alvaro Zinos-Amaro is a Hugo and Locus award finalist who has published fifty stories, as well as more than a hundred essays, reviews, and interviews, in a variety of professional magazines and anthologies. These venues include *Analog*, *Apex*, *Lightspeed*, *Beneath Ceaseless Skies*, *Galaxy's Edge*, *Nature*, the *Los Angeles Review of Books*, *Locus*, Tor.com, *Strange Horizons*, *Clarkesworld*, *The Year's Best Science Fiction & Fantasy*, *Cyber World*, *This Way to the End Times*, *The Unquiet Dreamer*, *It Came from the Multiplex*, *Shadow Atlas*, and many others.

ABOUT THE EDITOR

Jared Shurin's previous anthologies include *The Outcast Hours* and *The Djinn Falls in Love* (both with Mahvesh Murad and both finalists for the World Fantasy Award). He has also been a finalist for the Shirley Jackson Award (twice), the British Science Fiction Association Award (twice), and the Hugo Award (twice) and won the British Fantasy Award (twice).

Alongside Anne C. Perry, he founded and edited the "brilliantly brutal" (the *Guardian*) pop culture website *Pornokitsch* for ten years, responsible for many of its most irritating and exuberant articles. Together, they also cofounded the Kitschies, the prize for progressive, intelligent, and entertaining speculative and fantastic fiction, and Jurassic London, an award-winning, not-for-profit small press.

His other projects have included the *Best of British Fantasy* and *Speculative Fiction* series and anthologies of mummies, weird Westerns, and Dickensian London. A frequent reviewer, he has also written articles on topics as diverse as *Gossip Girl* and *Deadwood*.

Jared is a certified BBQ judge.

ACKNOWLEDGMENTS

No one does a better job of standing on the shoulders of giants than an anthology editor.

I owe a debt of gratitude not only to the authors and translators whose work appears in this volume, but also the many editors who initially discovered and published those stories. These include, but are not limited to: Victoria Blake, Bill Campbell, Sarah Champion, Neil Clarke, Ellen Datlow,[*] Milton Davis, Eileen Gunn, Jason Heller, Karie Jacobson, Maxim Jakubowski, Richard Jones, James Patrick Kelly, Larry McCaffery, Rudy Rucker, Bruce Sterling, Jonathan Strahan, Joshua Viola, and Stephen Zision. These editors—and many others—created, fueled, and sustained this fragile genre: thank you all.

Navigating the twin worlds of cyberpunk and permissions presented a challenge, but I met some expert guides along the way. A special thanks to Richard Curtis, Vaughne Hanson, Simon Kavanagh, John Shirley, Paul Graham-Raven, Robin Moger, Nisi Shawl, Marissa Skeels, and the kind people at the SFWA for going above and beyond in their help.

Much support (literary, emotional, physical, occupational, or culinary) was provided by Vicky, Sam, Becky, Syima, Patrick, Mahvesh, and my 'waffle-loving Discord friends. Many of whom don't even *like* cyberpunk . . . but still got behind this project and helped every step of the way.

Much tolerance was also provided by my wonderful family, who have heard me talk about nothing *besides* cyberpunk for several years. A special shout out to Sophia, George, and Nathaniel, shaping up to be three of the best *-punks* the world has ever seen.

David Holden, Lavie Tidhar, and Alex Shvartsman were terrific traveling companions, providing support, guidance, and good humor across time zones and digital platforms.

I had never met Ann VanderMeer before this project began. She steered me in the right direction at the outset (and provided impromptu therapy), and has been gracious with her time and her advice throughout. She is a role model both as an editor and a human being.

The Big Book of Cyberpunk would not have been possible without the hard work and dedication (and patience and creativity and chutzpah) of Ron Eckel and Anna Kaufman.[†] Thank you both so

---

[*] In the introduction to *Mirrorshades*, Bruce Sterling refers to Ellen Datlow as "a shades-packing sister in the vanguard of the ideologically correct." This is the single coolest description ever and is entirely merited.

[†] Sam > Bucky. I have stetted any attempt to challenge this truth.

ACKNOWLEDGMENTS

very, very much. The team at Vintage Books has been brilliant. Turning a two-thousand-plus-page Word file into the beautiful object you see before you is an amazing achievement. Thank you so much to production editor Kayla Overbey; copy editor Kathy Strickman; proofreaders Lyn Rosen, Karen Niersbach, and Melissa Holbrook Pierson; designer Nicholas Alguire; publicist Jordan Rodman; and marketer Sophie Normil for making magic.

Anne C. Perry and Goblin: You may have 631,000 cyberpunk walruses. You've earned them.

PERMISSIONS ACKNOWLEDGMENTS

Yasser Abdellatif: "Younis in the Belly of the Whale" by Yasser Abdellatif, © 2014, 2018 by Yasser Abdellatif. Translation copyright © 2014 by Robin Moger. Previously published in English in *Sunspot Jungle: Volume 2* (2018), edited by Bill Campbell. Reprinted by permission of the author and the translator.

K. C. Alexander: "Four Tons Too Late" by K. C. Alexander, © 2014 by K. C. Alexander. Originally published in *Fireside Magazine* (2014). Reprinted by permission of the author. Revised for this publication.

Madeline Ashby: "Be Seeing You" by Madeline Ashby, © 2015 by Madeline Ashby. Originally published in *Pwning Tomorrow: An Anthology of Short Fiction from the Electronic Frontier* (2015), edited by Dave Maass. Reprinted by permission of the author.

Ryuko Azuma: "2045 Dystopia" by Ryuko Azuma, © 2018, 2023 by Ryuko Azuma. Originally appeared on Twitter. English translation copyright © 2018 by Marissa Skeels. This first English publication by permission of the author and translator.

Jacques Barcia: "Salvaging Gods" by Jacques Barcia, © 2010 by Jacques Barcia. Originally published in *Clarkesworld* magazine (October 2010). Reprinted by permission of the author.

Greg Bear: "Petra" by Greg Bear, © 1982 by Greg Bear. Originally published in *Omni* (February 1982). Reprinted by permission of the author.

Steve Beard: "Retoxicity" by Steve Beard, © 1998 by Steve Beard. Originally published in *Disco 2000* (1998), edited by Sarah Champion. "Retoxicity" is an excerpt from the author's novel *Digital Leatherette* (1999). Reprinted by permission of the author.

Bruce Bethke: "Cyberpunk" by Bruce Bethke, © 1983 by Bruce Bethke. Originally published in *Amazing Science Fiction Stories* (November 1983). Reprinted by permission of the author.

Lauren Beukes: "Branded" by Lauren Beukes, © 2003 by Lauren Beukes. Originally published in *SL Magazine* (2003). Reprinted by permission of the author.

Russell Blackford: "Glass Reptile Breakout" by Russell Blackford, © 1985, 1990 by Russell Blackford. Originally published in *Strange Attractors* (1985), edited by Damien Broderick. Revised version first published in *Glass Reptile Breakout and Other Australian Speculative Stories* (1990), edited by Van Ikin. Reprinted by permission of the author.

Maurice Broaddus: "I Can Transform You" by Maurice Broaddus, © 2013 by Maurice Broaddus.

Originally published as *I Can Transform You* (2013) by Apex Publications. Reprinted by permission of the author.

Pat Cadigan: "Pretty Boy Crossover" by Pat Cadigan, © 1986 by Pat Cadigan. Originally published in *Isaac Asimov's Science Fiction Magazine* (January 1986). Reprinted by permission of the author.

Myra Çakan: "Spider's Nest" by Myra Çakan, © 2004 by Myra Çakan. Originally published in German as "Im Netz der Silberspinnexx" in *Der Atem Gottes und andere Visionen 2004*, edited by Helmuth W. Mommers. Reprinted by permission of the author.

Beth Cato: "Apocalypse Playlist" by Beth Cato, © 2020 by Beth Cato. Originally published in *Nature* (October 2020) by Springer Nature. Reprinted by permission of the author.

Suzanne Church: "Synch Me, Kiss Me, Drop" by Suzanne Church, © 2021 by Suzanne Church. Originally published in *Clarkesworld* magazine (May 2021). Reprinted by permission of the author.

Samuel R. Delany: "Time Considered as a Helix of Semiprecious Stones" by Samuel R. Delany, © 1968 by Samuel R. Delany. First published in *New Worlds* (December 1968). Reprinted here by permission of the author and his agents, Henry Morrison, Inc.

Philip K. Dick: "We Can Remember It for You Wholesale" by Philip K. Dick, currently collected in *The Philip K. Dick Reader*. Copyright © 2001 by Philip K. Dick, reprinted here by permission of The Wylie Agency LLC and the author's estate.

Paul Di Filippo: "A Short Course in Art Appreciation" by Paul Di Filippo, © 1988 by Paul Di Filippo. First published in *The Magazine of Fantasy and Science Fiction* (May 1988). Reprinted by permission of the author.

Paul Di Filippo and Bruce Sterling: "The Scab's Progress" by Paul Di Filippo and Bruce Sterling, © 2001 by Paul Di Filippo and Bruce Sterling. Originally published in *SciFiction* (January 2001). Collected in *Visionary in Residence* (2006) by Running Press Adult and *Babylon Sisters and Other Posthumans* (2012) by Wildside Press. Reprinted by permission of Writers House LLC, acting as agent for the authors.

Cory Doctorow: "0wnz0red" by Cory Doctorow, © 2002 by Cordoc-Co LLC. Some rights reserved under a Creative Commons Attribution-ShareAlike-NonCommercial 4.0 license. First published at Salon.com (August 2002). Reprinted by permission of the author.

Candas Jane Dorsey: "[Learning About] Machine Sex" by Candas Jane Dorsey, © 1988 by Candas Jane Dorsey. First published in *Machine Sex and Other Stories* (1988). Reprinted by permission of the author.

George Alec Effinger: "The World as We Know It" by George Alec Effinger, © 1992 by the estate of the author. First published in *FutureCrime* (1992), edited by Charles Ardai and Cynthia Manson. Reprinted by permission of the author's estate.

Greg Egan: "Axiomatic" by Greg Egan, © 1990 by Greg Egan. First published in *Interzone* #41 (November 1990). Reprinted by permission of the author.

Isabel Fall: "Helicopter Story" by Isabel Fall, © 2020 by Isabel Fall. First published in *Clarkesworld* magazine (January 2020). Reprinted by permission of the author.

Minister Faust: "Somatosensory Cortex Dog Mess You Up Big Time, You Sick Sack of S**T" by Minister Faust, © 2021 by Minister Faust. First published in *Cyberfunk!* (2021), edited by Milton Davis. Reprinted by permission of the author.

Fabio Fernandes: "Wi-Fi Dreams" by Fabio Fernandes, © 2019 by Fabio Fernandes. First published as "Sonhos wifi" in *Cyberpunk: Registros Recuperados De Futuros Proibidos* (2019), edited by Erick Santos Cardoso and Cirilo S. Lemos. The first English translation appeared in *Love. An Archaeology* (Luna Press Publishing, 2021). Reprinted by permission of the author.

Bernardo Fernández, *Bef*: "Wonderama" by Bef, © 1998 by Bernardo Fernández, *Bef*. First published in *BZZZZZZT!! Ciudad interfase* (1998). This first English-language translation published by permission of the author.

Taiyo Fujii: "Violation of the TrueNet Security Act" by Taiyo Fujii © 2013 by Taiyo Fujii. Originally published in *SF Magazine*. English translation copyright by VIZ Media. Translated by Jim Hubbert. Reprinted by permission of the author and translator.

Ganzeer: "CRISPR Than You" by Ganzeer, © 2018–2021 by Ganzeer. First published on the author's website as "Staying Crisp," revised by the author for this edition. Illustrated by the author. Reprinted by permission of the author.

William Gibson: "The Gernsback Continuum" by William Gibson, © 1981 by William Gibson. First published in *Universe 11* (1981), edited by Terry Carr. Reprinted by permission of the author and SLL/Sterling Lord Literistic Inc.

William Gibson and Michael Swanwick: "Dogfight" by William Gibson and Michael Swanwick, © 1985 by Omni Publications International Ltd. Originally published in *Omni* (July 1985). Reprinted by permission of the authors and SLL/Sterling Lord Literistic Inc.

Eileen Gunn: "Computer Friendly" by Eileen Gunn, © 1989 by Eileen Gunn. First published in *Isaac Asimov's Science Fiction Magazine* (June 1989). Reprinted by permission of the author.

Omar Robert Hamilton: "Rain, Streaming" by Omar Robert Hamilton, © 2019 by Omar Robert Hamilton. First published in *The Outcast Hours* (2019), edited by Mahvesh Murad and Jared Shurin. Reprinted by permission of the author.

Karen Heuler: "The Completely Rechargeable Man" by Karen Heuler, © 2008 by Karen Heuler. First appeared in *Clarkesworld* magazine (December 2008) and later in the author's collection, *The Clockworm and Other Strange Stories* (2018). Reprinted by permission of the author and the author's agents, the Virginia Kidd Agency Inc.

Saad Hossain: "The Endless" by Saad Hossain, © 2020 by Saad Hossain. First appeared in *Made to Order: Robots and Revolution* (2020), edited by Jonathan Strahan. Reprinted by permission of the author.

qntm: "Lena" by qntm, © 2021 by qntm. First published on the author's website. Reprinted by permission of the author.

Gwyneth Jones: "Red Sonja and Lessingham in Dreamland" by Gwyneth Jones, © 1996 by Gwyneth Jones. First published in *Off Limits: Tales of Alien Sex* (1996), edited by Ellen Datlow. Reprinted by permission of the author.

Khalid Kaki: "Operation Daniel" by Khalid Kaki, © 2018 by Khalid Kaki. First published in *Iraq +100* (2016), edited by Hassan Blasim. English-language translation by Adam Talib. Reprinted by permission of the author and Comma Press.

James Patrick Kelly: "Rat" by James Patrick Kelly, © 1986 by James Patrick Kelly. First published in *The Magazine of Fantasy and Science Fiction* (June 1986). Reprinted by permission of the author.

John Kessel: "The Last American" by John Kessel, © 2007 by John Kessel. Originally appeared in *Foundation* (Summer 2007). Reprinted by permission of the author.

Cassandra Khaw: "Degrees of Beauty" by Cassandra Khaw, © 2016 by Cassandra Khaw. Originally appeared in *Terraform* (October 2016). Reprinted by permission of the author.

Christian Kirchev: "The Death of Designer D" by Christian Kirchev, © 2004 by Christian As. Kirtchev. Collected in *Chemical Illusions* (2009). Reprinted by permission of the author.

Aleš Kot: "A Life of Its Own" by Aleš Kot, © 2019 by Aleš Kot. Reprinted by permission of the author.

Nancy Kress: "With the Original Cast" by Nancy Kress, © 1982 by Nancy Kress. First appeared in *Omni* (May 1982). Reprinted by permission of the author.

Naomi Kritzer: "Cat Pictures Please" by Naomi Kritzer, © 2015 by Naomi Kritzer. First appeared in *Clarkesworld* (January 2015). Reprinted by permission of the author.

Lavanya Lakshminarayan: "Études" by Lavanya Lakshminarayan, © 2020 by Lavanya Lakshminarayan. Permission to reproduce this chapter from *The Ten Percent Thief* (2023) is granted by Rebellion Publishing Ltd., © Rebellion Publishing Ltd. 2023. First published in *Analog/Virtual: And Other Simulations of Your Future* (2020).

David Langford: "COMP.BASILISK.FAQ" by David Langford, © 1999, 2004 by David Langford. First published in *Nature* (December 1999). Reprinted by permission of the author.

Oliver Langmead: "Glitterati" by Oliver Langmead, © 2017 by Oliver Langmead. First published in *2084* (2017), edited by George Sandison, from Unsung Stories. Later expanded into the novel *Glitterati* (2022), published by Titan. Reprinted by permission of the author.

Fritz Leiber: "Coming Attraction" by Fritz Leiber, © 1950 by the estate of the author. First published in *Galaxy* (November 1950). Reprinted by permission of the author's estate and the agent, Richard Curtis Associates.

Jean-Marc Ligny: "RealLife 3.0" by Jean-Marc Ligny, © 2014 by Jean-Marc Ligny. First published in *Bifrost* 75 (July 2014). English translation © 2023 by N. L. M. Roshak. This first English-language translation published by permission of the author and translator.

Arthur Liu: "The Life Cycle of the Cyber Bar" by Arthur Liu © 2021 by Arthur Liu. English translation by Nathan Faries. Original publication in *Future Science Fiction Digest* (September 2021). Reprinted by permission of the author and translator.

Ken Liu: "Thoughts and Prayers" by Ken Liu, © 2019 by Ken Liu. First published in *Slate: Future Tense* (2019). Reprinted by permission of the author and the author's agents, Scovil Galen Ghosh Literary Agency, Inc.

Steven S. Long: "Keeping Up with Mr. Johnson" by Steven S. Long, © 2016 by The Topps Company Inc. All Rights Reserved. First published in *World of Shadows* (2016), edited by John Helfers. Shadowrun & Matrix are registered trademarks and/or trademarks of The Topps Company Inc., in the United States and/or other countries. Catalyst Game Labs and the Catalyst Game Labs logo are trademarks of InMediaRes Productions LLC. Reprinted by permission of Catalyst Game Labs.

M. Lopes da Silva: "Found Earworms" by M. Lopes da Silva, © 2019 by M. Lopes da Silva. First published in *A Punk Rock Future* (2019), edited by Steve Zisson. Reprinted by permission of the author.

James Lovegrove: "Britworld™" by James Lovegrove, © 1992 by James Lovegrove. First published in *Interzone* (December 1992) and reprinted in *Imagined Slights* (2002). Reprinted by permission of the author.

Ken MacLeod: "Earth Hour" by Ken MacLeod, © 2011 by Ken MacLeod. First published on Tor.com (June 2011). Reprinted by permission of the author.

Nick Mamatas: "Time of Day" by Nick Mamatas, © 2002 by Nick Mamatas. First published on Strange Horizons (January 2002). Reprinted by permission of the author.

Phillip Mann: "An Old-Fashioned Story" by Phillip Mann, © 1989 by Phillip Mann. First published in *Interzone* (May/June 1989). Reprinted by permission of the author.

Lisa Mason: "Arachne" by Lisa Mason, © 1987 by Lisa Mason. First published in *Omni* (December 1987). Basis of the novel *Arachne* (1990), published by William Morrow. Reprinted by permission of the author.

Tim Maughan: "Flyover Country" by Tim Maughan, © 2016 by Tim Maughan. First published in *Terraform* (November 2016). Reprinted by permission of the author.

Paul J. McAuley: "Gene Wars" by Paul J. McAuley, © 1991 by Paul J. McAuley. First published, in a slightly different form, as "Evan's Progress" in *New Internationalist* (March 1991). Reprinted by permission of the author.

Misha: "Speed" by Misha, © 1988 by Misha. First appeared in *Prayers of Steel* (1988), published by Wordcraft. Reprinted by permission of the author.

Janelle Monáe and Alaya Dawn Johnson: "The Memory Librarian" by Janelle Monáe and Alaya Dawn Johnson, © 2022 by Jane Lee LLC. First published in *The Memory Librarian* (2022) by Janelle Monáe. Used by permission of HarperCollins Publishers.

Sunny Moraine: "I Tell Thee All I Can No More" by Sunny Moraine, © 2013 by Sunny Moraine. First published in *Clarkesworld* (July 2013). Reprinted by permission of the author.

Michael W. Moss: "Keep Portland Wired" by Michael W. Moss, © 2020 by Michael W. Moss. First published in *The Trench Coat Minotaur* (2020). Reprinted by permission of the author.

T. R. Napper: "Twelve Minutes to Vinh Quang" by T. R. Napper, © 2015 by T. R. Napper. First published in *Writers of the Future: Volume 31* (2015). Reprinted by permission of the author.

Kim Newman: "SQPR" by Kim Newman, © 1992 by Kim Newman. First published in *Interzone* (May 1992). Reprinted by permission of the author.

Mandisi Nkomo: "Do Androids Dream of Capitalism and Slavery?" by Mandisi Nkomo, © 2020 by Mandisi Nkomo. First published in *Omenana* (August 2020). Reprinted by permission of the author.

Jeff Noon: "Ghost Codes" by Jeff Noon, © 2011, 2023 by Jeff Noon. First published on Twitter and on the author's website. Collected and revised for this publication by the author.

Brendan O'Brien: "fallenangel.dll" by Brendan O'Brien, © 2016 by Brendan O'Brien. First published in *New Worlds, Old Ways: Speculative Tales from the Caribbean* (2016), edited by Karen Lord, published by Peekash Press. Reprinted by permission of the author.

Craig Padawer: "Hostile Takeover" by Craig Padawer, © 1995 by Craig Padawer. First published in *After Yesterday's Crash: The Avant-Pop Anthology* (1995), edited by Larry McCaffery, published by Penguin. Reprinted by permission of the author.

Victor Pelevin: "The Yuletide Cyberpunk Yarn, or Christmas Eve-117.DIR" by Victor Pelevin, © 1996 by Victor Pelevin. All rights reserved. English translation © 2022 by Alex Shvartsman. This first English-language publication by arrangement with the author's agents, FTM Agency Ltd., and translator.

Paul Graham Raven: "Los Piratas del Mar de Plastico" by Paul Graham Raven, © 2014 by Paul Graham Raven. First published in *Twelve Tomorrows* (2014), edited by Bruce Sterling, published by MIT Press. Reprinted by permission of the author.

Harry Polkinhorn: "Consumimur Igni" by Harry Polkinhorn, © 1992 by Harry Polkinhorn. First published in *Avant-Pop: Fiction for a Daydream Nation* (1992), edited by Larry McCaffery, published by Black Ice. Reprinted by permission of the author.

Gerardo Horacio Porcayo: "Ripped Imaged, Rusted Dreams" by Gerardo Horacio Porcayo, © 1995, 2023 by Gerardo Horacio Porcayo. First published in the Antología de Jóvenes Escritores Morelenses, *Palabras Pendientes* (1995), by the Government of the State of Morales. English-language translation by the author. This first English-language publication by arrangement with the author.

Jean Rabe: "More Than" by Jean Rabe, © 2010 The Topps Company Inc. All Rights Reserved. First published in *Spells and Chrome* (2010), edited by John Helfers. Shadowrun & Matrix are registered trademarks and/or trademarks of The Topps Company, Inc., in the United States and/

or other countries. Catalyst Game Labs and the Catalyst Game Labs logo are trademarks of InMediaRes Productions LLC. Reprinted by permission of Catalyst Game Labs.

Yurei Raita: "The Day a Computer Wrote a Novel" by Yurei Raita, © 2015 by Satoshi Sato and Sato-Matsuzaki Laboratory, Nagoya University. English translation © 2019 by Marissa Skeels. English translation first published in *Big Echo* (October 2019). Reprinted by permission of the author and translator.

Cat Rambo: "Memories of Moments, Bright as Falling Stars" by Cat Rambo, © 2006 by Cat Rambo. First published in *Talebones* (Winter 2006). Reprinted by permission of the author.

Justina Robson: "The Girl Hero's Mirror Says He's Not the One" by Justina Robson, © 2007 by Justina Robson. First published in *Fast Forward 1: Future Fiction from the Cutting Edge* (2007), edited by Lou Anders, published by Pyr. Reprinted by permission of the author.

Pepe Rojo: "Gray Noise" by Pepe Rojo, © 1996 by Pepe Rojo. First published as "Ruido gris" (November 1996) by Universidad Autónoma Metropolitana (México). English translation © 2003 by Andrea Bell, first published in *Cosmos Latinos* (2003), edited by Andrea Bell and Yolanda Molina-Gavilán, published by Wesleyan University Press. Reprinted by permission of the author and translator.

Nicholas Royle: "D.GO" by Nicholas Royle, © 1990 by Nicholas Royle. First published in *Interzone* (November 1990). Reprinted by permission of the author.

Rudy Rucker: "Juicy Ghost" by Rudy Rucker, © 2019, 2023 by Rudy Rucker. First published in *Big Echo* (October 2019). Afterword first published in this volume. Later expanded to *Juicy Ghosts* (2021), from Transreal Books. Reprinted by permission of the author.

Erica L. Satifka: "Act of Providence" by Erica L. Satifka, © 2021 by Erica L. Satifka. First published in *How to Get to Apocalypse and Other Disasters* (2021), from Fairwood Press. Reprinted by permission of the author.

Nisi Shawl: "I Was a Teenage Genetic Engineer" by Nisi Shaw, © 1989 by Nisi Shaw. First published in *Semiotext(e) SF* (1989), edited by Rudy Rucker, Peter Lamborn Wilson, and Robert Anton Wilson. Reprinted by permission of the author.

Lewis Shiner: "The Gene Drain" by Lewis Shiner, © 1989 by Lewis Shiner. First published in *Semiotext(e) SF* (1989), edited by Rudy Rucker, Peter Lamborn Wilson, and Robert Anton Wilson. Reprinted by permission of the author.

John Shirley: "Wolves of the Plateau" by John Shirley, © 1988 by John Shirley. First published in *Mississippi Review* (1988). Reprinted by permission of the author.

Zedeck Siew: "The White Mask" by Zedeck Siew, © 2015 by Zedeck Siew. First published in *Cyberpunk: Malaysia* (2015), edited by Zen Cho, published by Fixi Novo. Reprinted by permission of the author.

J. P. Smythe: "The Infinite Eye" by J. P. Smythe, © 2017 by J. P. Smythe. First published in *2084* (2017), edited by George Sandison, from Unsung Stories. Reprinted by permission of the author.

Neal Stephenson: "The Great Simoleon Caper" by Neal Stephenson, © 1995 by Neal Stephenson. First published in *Time* (Spring 1995). Reprinted by permission of the author and Darhansoff & Verrill Literary Agents.

Bruce Sterling: "Deep Eddy" by Bruce Sterling, © 1993 by Bruce Sterling. Originally published in *Isaac Asimov's Science Fiction Magazine* (August 1993). Collected in *A Good Old-Fashioned Future* (1999), published by Spectra. Reprinted by permission of Writers House LLC acting as agent for the author.

Charles Stross: "Lobsters" by Charles Stross, © 2001 by Charles Stross. Originally published in *Isaac Asimov's Science Fiction Magazine* (June 2001). Reprinted by permission of the author.